Archie
1000 PAGE COMICS JOY

Archie® 1000 PAGE COMICS JOY

Publisher / Co-CEO: Jon Goldwater
Co-President / Editor-In-Chief: Victor Gorelick
Co-President: Mike Pellerito
Co-President: Alex Segura
Chief Creative Officer: Roberto Aguirre-Sacasa
Chief Operating Officer: William Mooar
Chief Financial Officer: Robert Wintle
Director of Book Sales & Operations: Jonathan Betancourt
Art Director: Vincent Lovallo
Production Manager: Stephen Oswald
Lead Designer: Kari McLachlan
Associate Editor: Carlos Antunes
Editor/Proofreader: Jamie Lee Rotante
Co-CEO: Nancy Silberkleit

Published by Archie Comic Publications, Inc.
629 Fifth Avenue, Suite 100, Pelham, NY 10803-1242

First Printing. Printed in U.S.A. ISBN: 978-1-64576-975-0

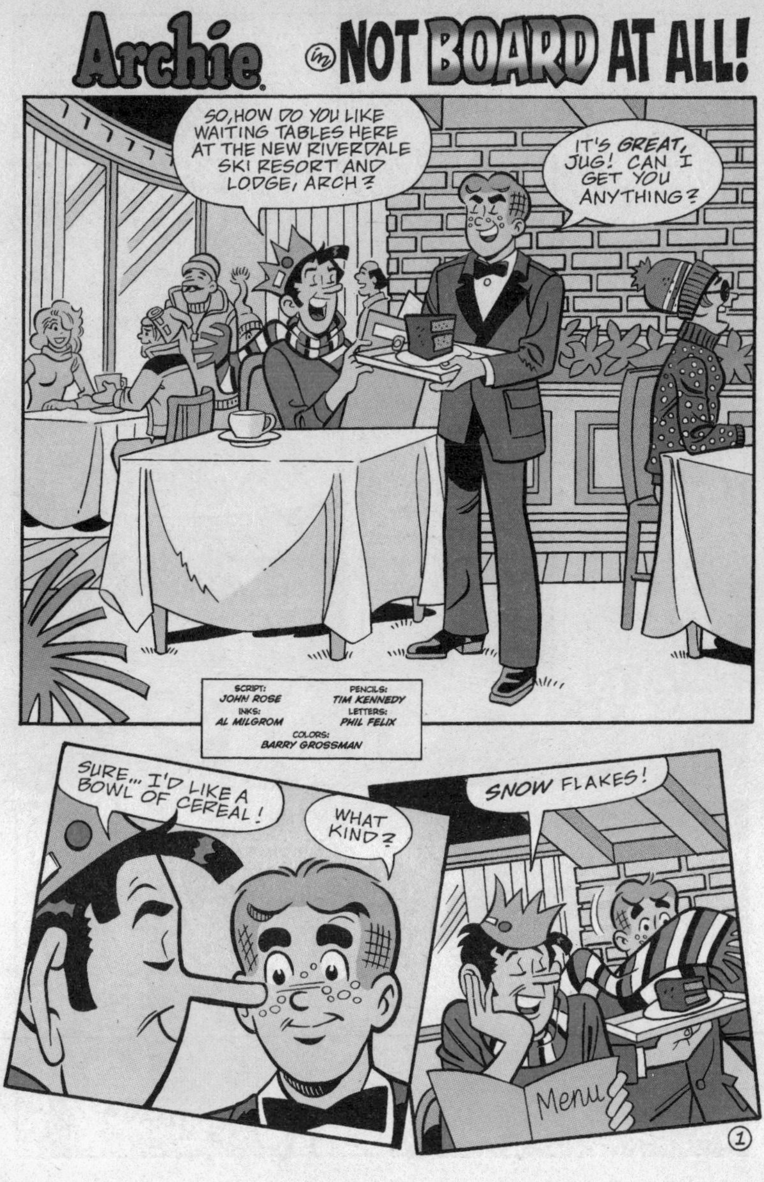
Archie in NOT BOARD AT ALL!
SO, HOW DO YOU LIKE WAITING TABLES HERE AT THE NEW RIVERDALE SKI RESORT AND LODGE, ARCH?
IT'S GREAT, JUG! CAN I GET YOU ANYTHING?
SCRIPT: JOHN ROSE PENCILS: TIM KENNEDY INKS: AL MILGROM LETTERS: PHIL FELIX COLORS: BARRY GROSSMAN
SURE... I'D LIKE A BOWL OF CEREAL!
WHAT KIND?
SNOW FLAKES!
Menu
1

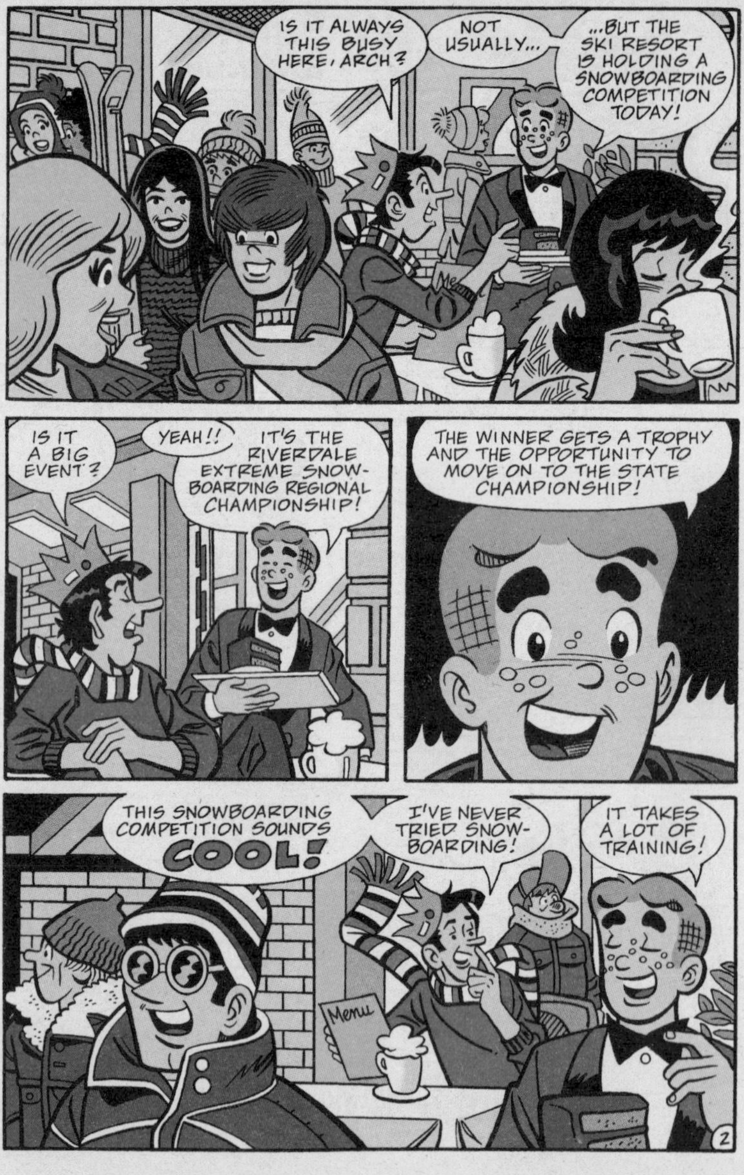

IS IT ALWAYS THIS BUSY HERE, ARCH?
NOT USUALLY...
...BUT THE SKI RESORT IS HOLDING A SNOWBOARDING COMPETITION TODAY!
IS IT A BIG EVENT?
YEAH!!
IT'S THE RIVERDALE EXTREME SNOW-BOARDING REGIONAL CHAMPIONSHIP!
THE WINNER GETS A TROPHY AND THE OPPORTUNITY TO MOVE ON TO THE STATE CHAMPIONSHIP!
THIS SNOWBOARDING COMPETITION SOUNDS COOL!
I'VE NEVER TRIED SNOW-BOARDING!
IT TAKES A LOT OF TRAINING!
Menu
2

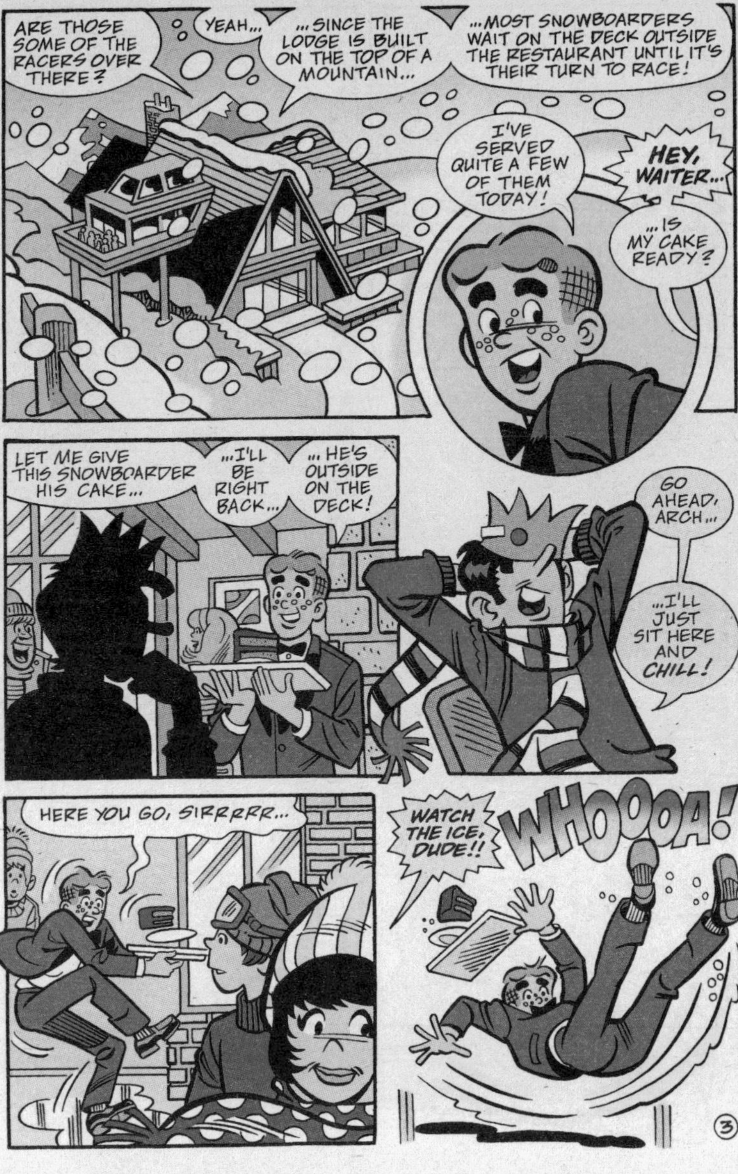
ARE THOSE SOME OF THE RACERS OVER THERE?
YEAH...
...SINCE THE LODGE IS BUILT ON THE TOP OF A MOUNTAIN...
...MOST SNOWBOARDERS WAIT ON THE DECK OUTSIDE THE RESTAURANT UNTIL IT'S THEIR TURN TO RACE!
I'VE SERVED QUITE A FEW OF THEM TODAY!
HEY, WAITER...
...IS MY CAKE READY?
LET ME GIVE THIS SNOWBOARDER HIS CAKE...
...I'LL BE RIGHT BACK...
...HE'S OUTSIDE ON THE DECK!
GO AHEAD, ARCH...
...I'LL JUST SIT HERE AND CHILL!
HERE YOU GO, SIRRRRR...
WATCH THE ICE, DUDE!!
WHOOOA!

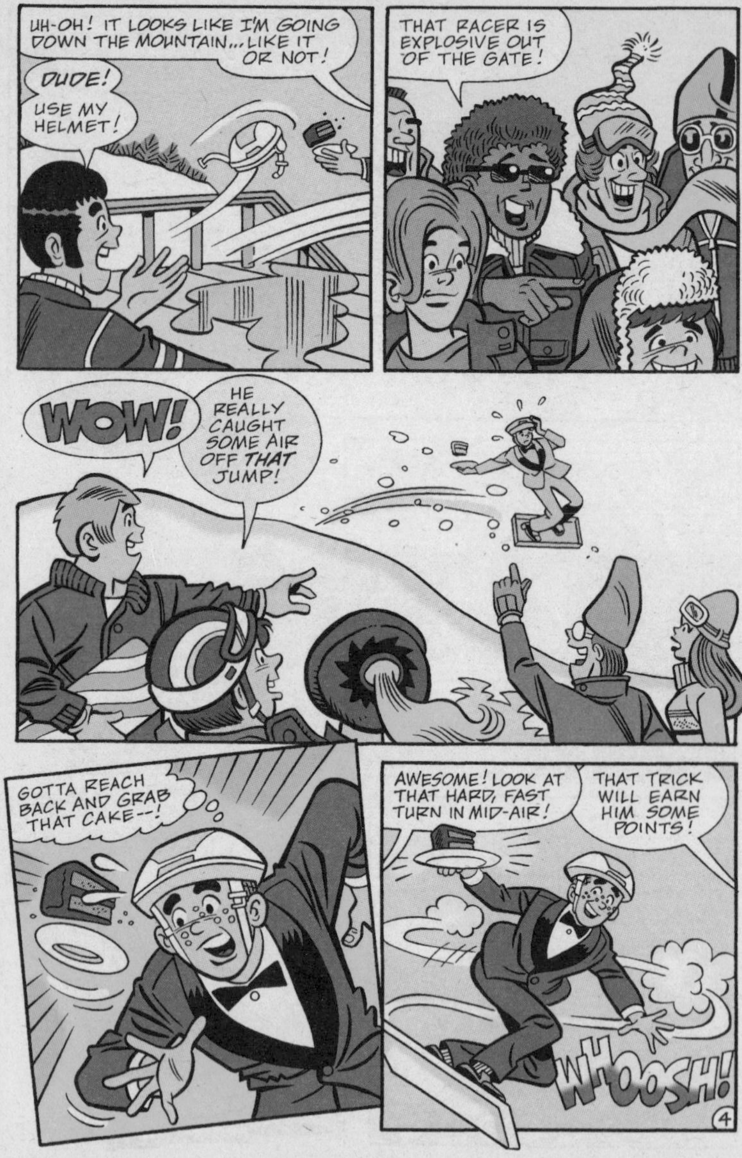
UH-OH! IT LOOKS LIKE I'M GOING DOWN THE MOUNTAIN... LIKE IT OR NOT!
DUDE!
USE MY HELMET!
THAT RACER IS EXPLOSIVE OUT OF THE GATE!
WOW!
HE REALLY CAUGHT SOME AIR OFF THAT JUMP!
GOTTA REACH BACK AND GRAB THAT CAKE--!
AWESOME! LOOK AT THAT HARD, FAST TURN IN MID-AIR!
THAT TRICK WILL EARN HIM SOME POINTS!
WHOOSH!
4

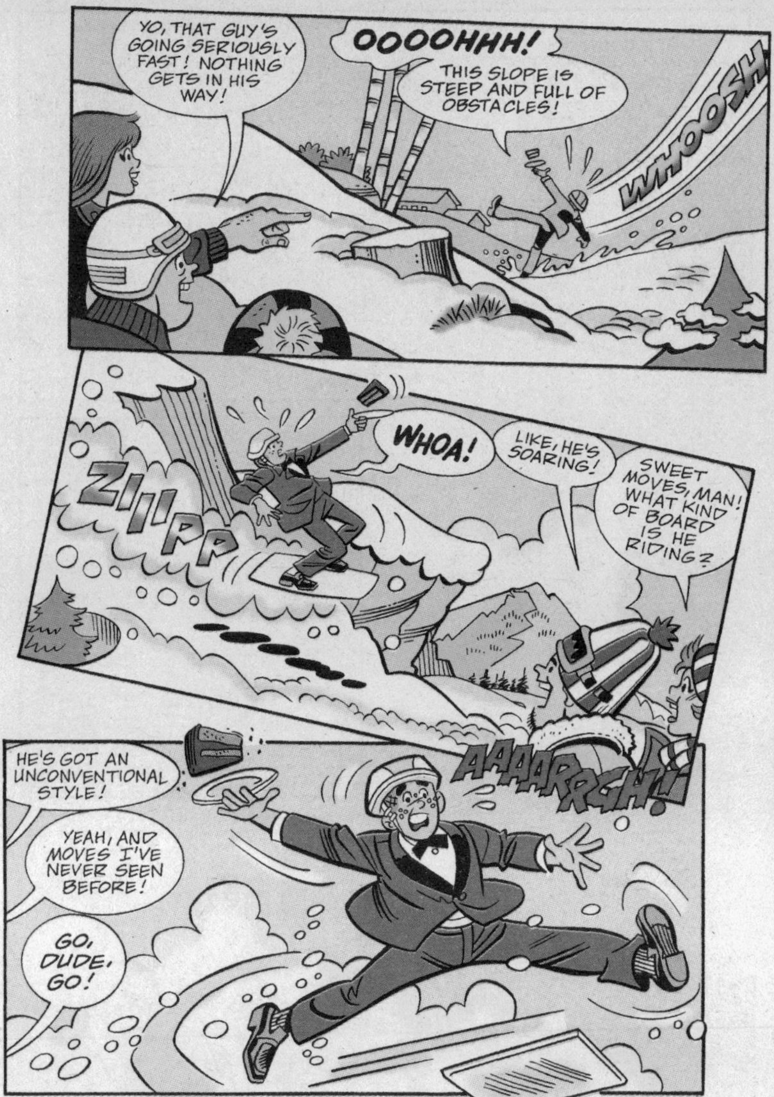
YO, THAT GUY'S GOING SERIOUSLY FAST! NOTHING GETS IN HIS WAY!
OOOOHHH!
THIS SLOPE IS STEEP AND FULL OF OBSTACLES!
WHOOSH
WHOA!
LIKE, HE'S SOARING!
SWEET MOVES, MAN! WHAT KIND OF BOARD IS HE RIDING?
ZIIIPP
HE'S GOT AN UNCONVENTIONAL STYLE!
AAAARRGH!!
YEAH, AND MOVES I'VE NEVER SEEN BEFORE!
GO, DUDE, GO!

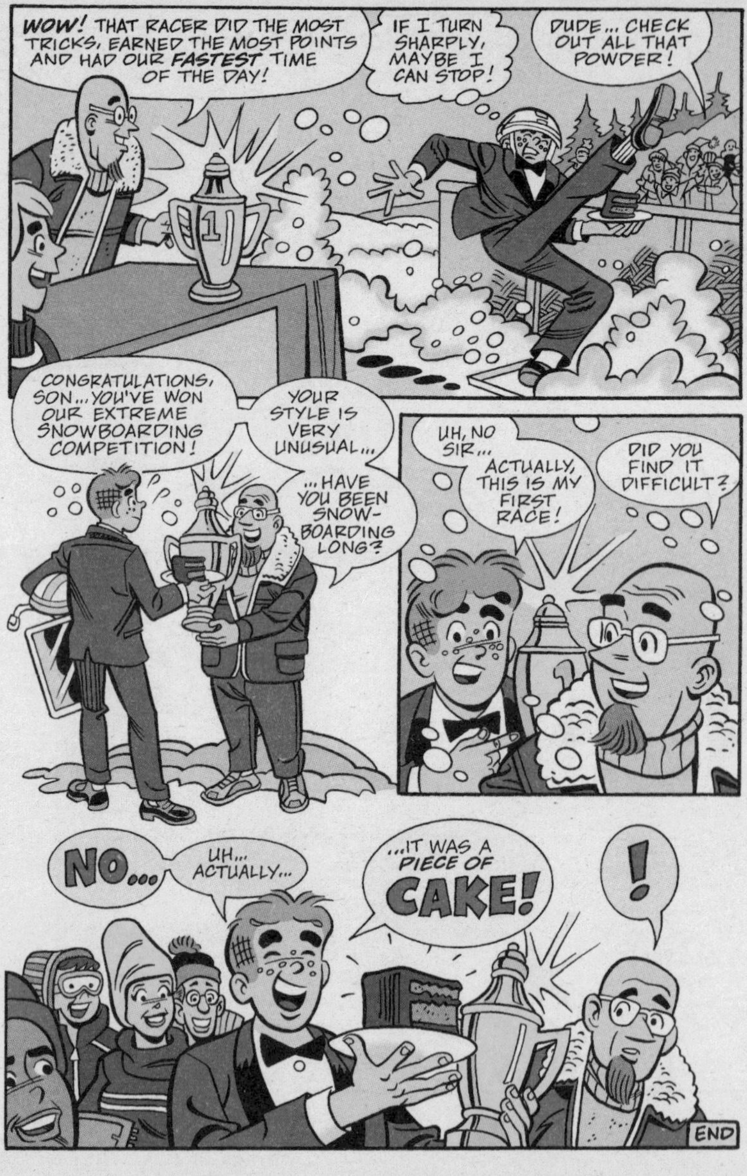
WOW! THAT RACER DID THE MOST TRICKS, EARNED THE MOST POINTS AND HAD OUR FASTEST TIME OF THE DAY!
IF I TURN SHARPLY, MAYBE I CAN STOP!
DUDE... CHECK OUT ALL THAT POWDER!
CONGRATULATIONS, SON... YOU'VE WON OUR EXTREME SNOWBOARDING COMPETITION!
YOUR STYLE IS VERY UNUSUAL...
...HAVE YOU BEEN SNOW-BOARDING LONG?
UH, NO SIR...
ACTUALLY, THIS IS MY FIRST RACE!
DID YOU FIND IT DIFFICULT?
NO...
UH... ACTUALLY...
...IT WAS A PIECE OF CAKE!
!
END

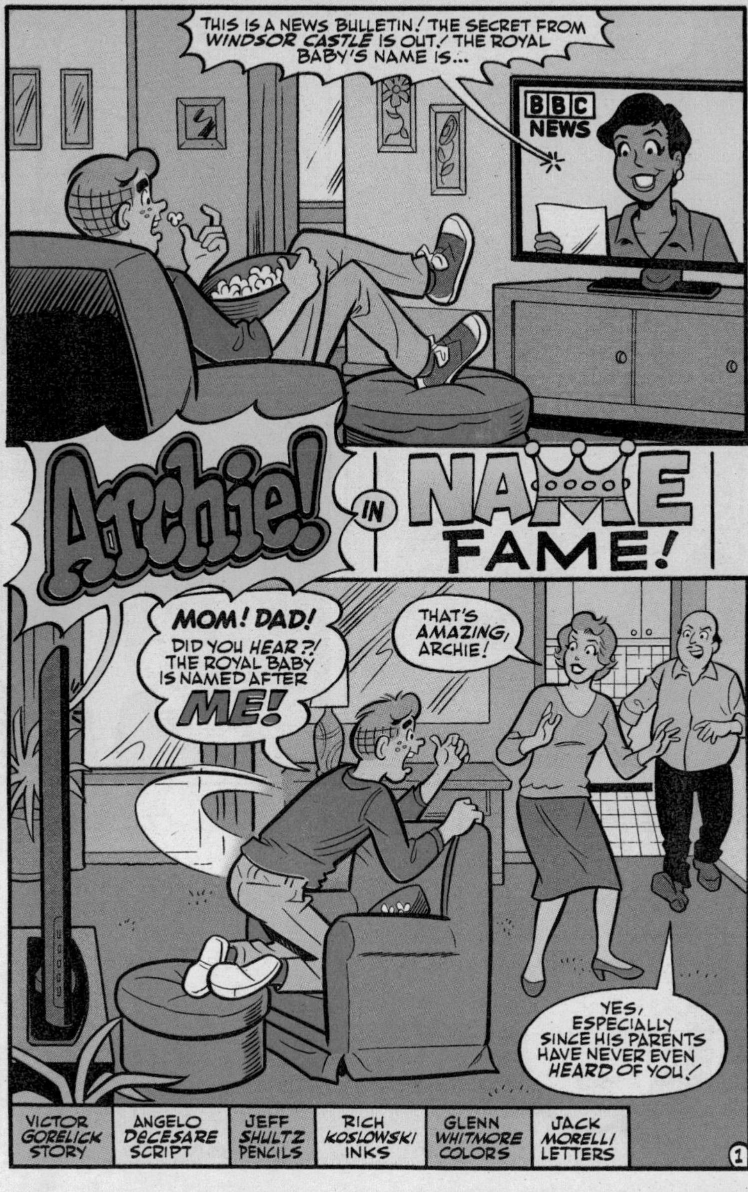
THIS IS A NEWS BULLETIN! THE SECRET FROM WINDSOR CASTLE IS OUT! THE ROYAL BABY'S NAME IS...
BBC NEWS
ARCHIE! IN NAME FAME!
MOM! DAD! DID YOU HEAR?! THE ROYAL BABY IS NAMED AFTER ME!
THAT'S AMAZING, ARCHIE!
YES, ESPECIALLY SINCE HIS PARENTS HAVE NEVER EVEN HEARD OF YOU!
VICTOR GORELICK STORY
ANGELO DECESARE SCRIPT
JEFF SHULTZ PENCILS
RICH KOSLOWSKI INKS
GLENN WHITMORE COLORS
JACK MORELLI LETTERS

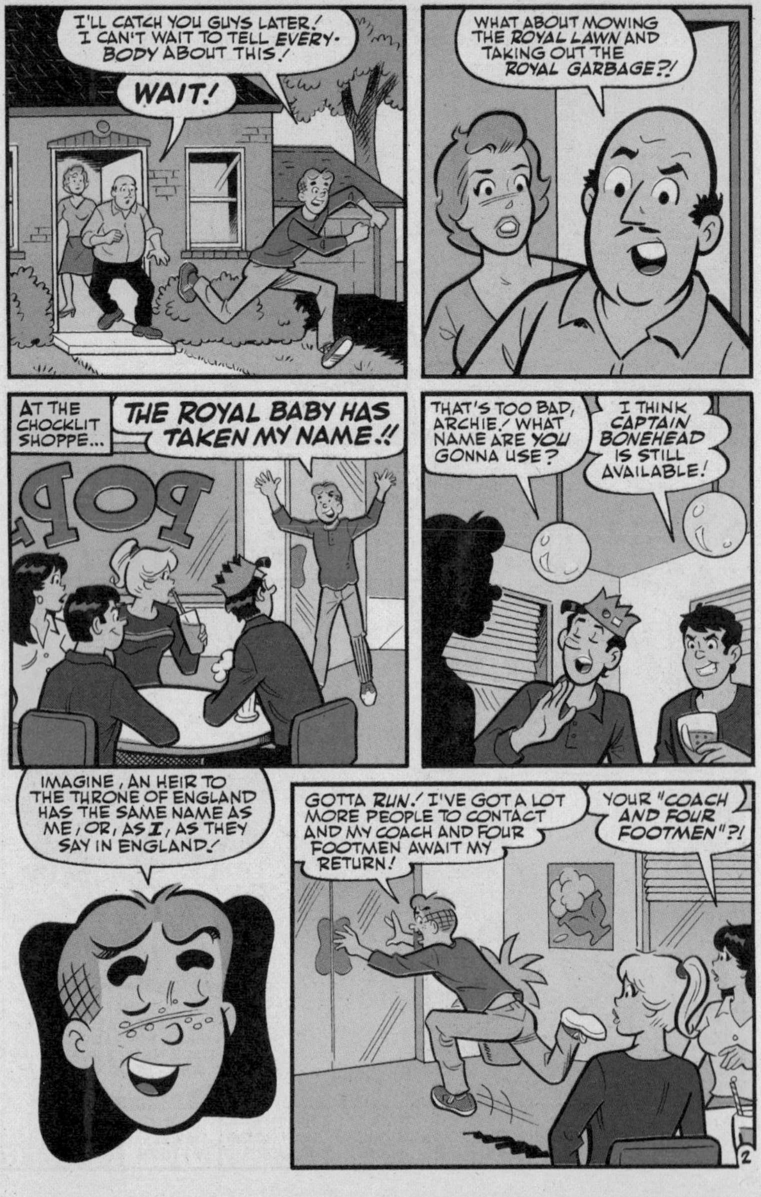
I'LL CATCH YOU GUYS LATER! I CAN'T WAIT TO TELL EVERY-BODY ABOUT THIS!
WAIT!
WHAT ABOUT MOWING THE ROYAL LAWN AND TAKING OUT THE ROYAL GARBAGE?!
AT THE CHOCKLIT SHOPPE...
THE ROYAL BABY HAS TAKEN MY NAME!!
POP
THAT'S TOO BAD, ARCHIE! WHAT NAME ARE YOU GONNA USE?
I THINK CAPTAIN BONEHEAD IS STILL AVAILABLE!
IMAGINE, AN HEIR TO THE THRONE OF ENGLAND HAS THE SAME NAME AS ME, OR, AS I, AS THEY SAY IN ENGLAND!
GOTTA RUN! I'VE GOT A LOT MORE PEOPLE TO CONTACT AND MY COACH AND FOUR FOOTMEN AWAIT MY RETURN!
YOUR "COACH AND FOUR FOOTMEN"?!
2

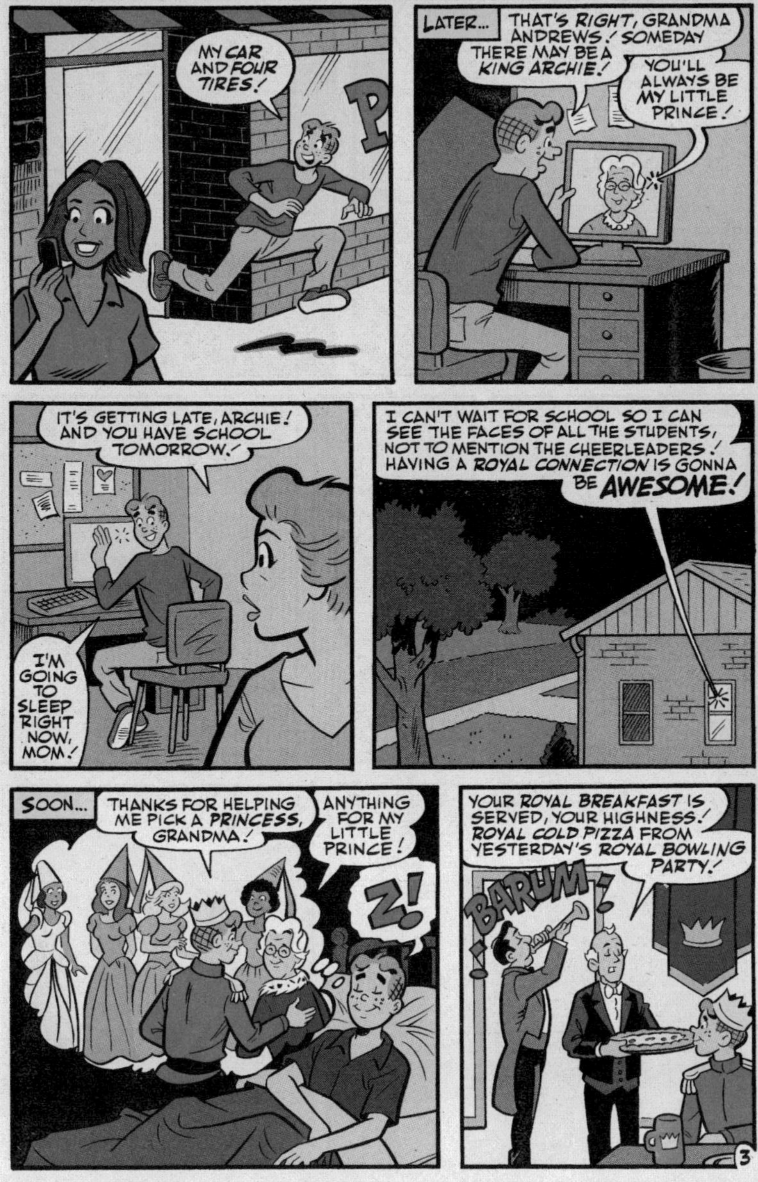
MY CAR AND FOUR TIRES!
LATER...
THAT'S RIGHT, GRANDMA ANDREWS! SOMEDAY THERE MAY BE A KING ARCHIE!
YOU'LL ALWAYS BE MY LITTLE PRINCE!
IT'S GETTING LATE, ARCHIE! AND YOU HAVE SCHOOL TOMORROW!
I'M GOING TO SLEEP RIGHT NOW, MOM!
I CAN'T WAIT FOR SCHOOL SO I CAN SEE THE FACES OF ALL THE STUDENTS, NOT TO MENTION THE CHEERLEADERS! HAVING A ROYAL CONNECTION IS GONNA BE AWESOME!
SOON...
THANKS FOR HELPING ME PICK A PRINCESS, GRANDMA!
ANYTHING FOR MY LITTLE PRINCE!
Z!
YOUR ROYAL BREAKFAST IS SERVED, YOUR HIGHNESS! ROYAL COLD PIZZA FROM YESTERDAY'S ROYAL BOWLING PARTY!
BARUM!
3

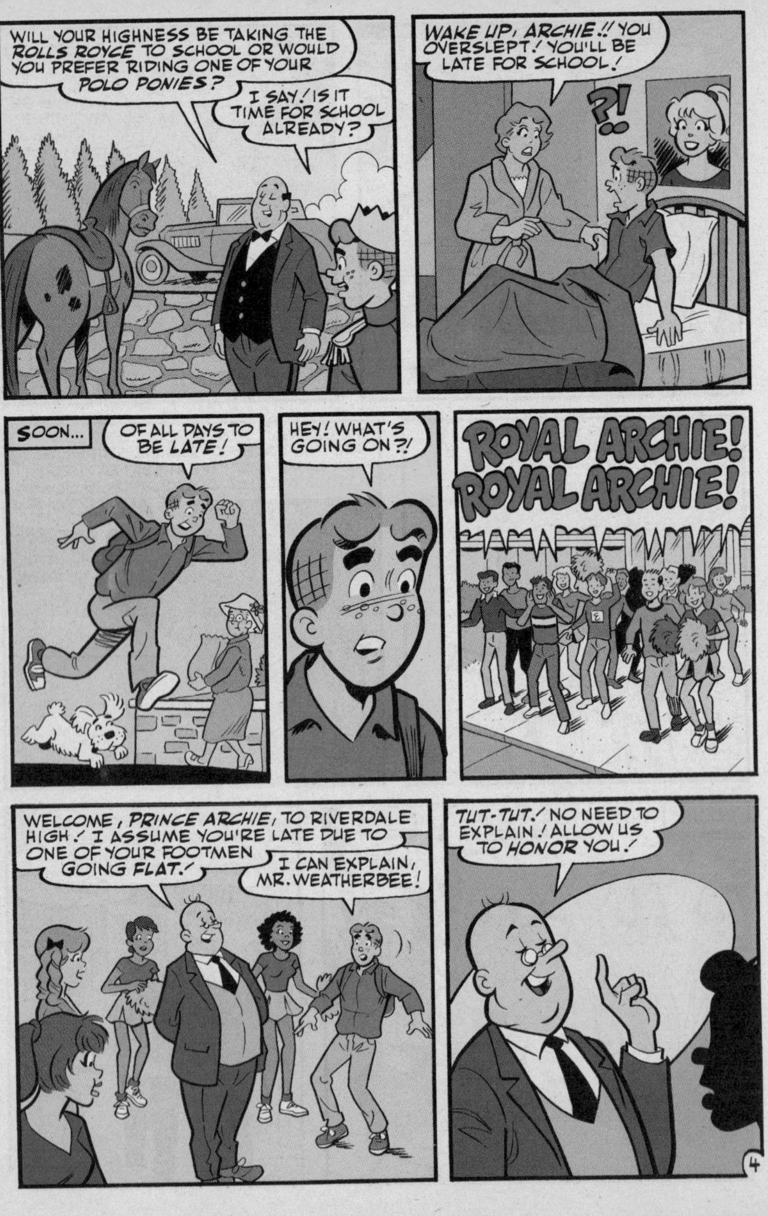
WILL YOUR HIGHNESS BE TAKING THE ROLLS ROYCE TO SCHOOL OR WOULD YOU PREFER RIDING ONE OF YOUR POLO PONIES?
I SAY! IS IT TIME FOR SCHOOL ALREADY?
WAKE UP, ARCHIE!! YOU OVERSLEPT! YOU'LL BE LATE FOR SCHOOL!
?!
SOON...
OF ALL DAYS TO BE LATE!
HEY! WHAT'S GOING ON?!
ROYAL ARCHIE! ROYAL ARCHIE!
WELCOME, PRINCE ARCHIE, TO RIVERDALE HIGH! I ASSUME YOU'RE LATE DUE TO ONE OF YOUR FOOTMEN GOING FLAT!
I CAN EXPLAIN, MR. WEATHERBEE!
TUT-TUT! NO NEED TO EXPLAIN! ALLOW US TO HONOR YOU!
4

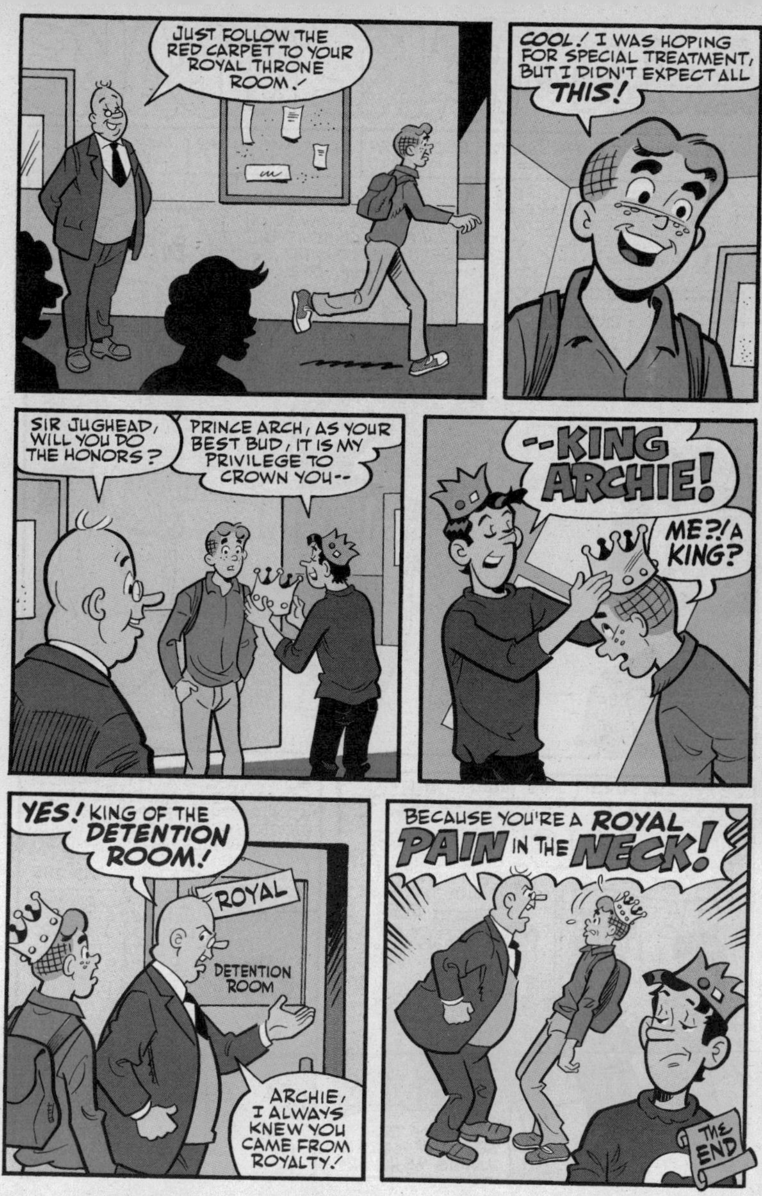
JUST FOLLOW THE RED CARPET TO YOUR ROYAL THRONE ROOM.!
COOL! I WAS HOPING FOR SPECIAL TREATMENT, BUT I DIDN'T EXPECT ALL THIS!
SIR JUGHEAD, WILL YOU DO THE HONORS?
PRINCE ARCH, AS YOUR BEST BUD, IT IS MY PRIVILEGE TO CROWN YOU--
--KING ARCHIE!
ME?! A KING?
YES! KING OF THE DETENTION ROOM!
ROYAL
DETENTION ROOM
ARCHIE, I ALWAYS KNEW YOU CAME FROM ROYALTY!
BECAUSE YOU'RE A ROYAL PAIN IN THE NECK!
THE END

Archie in FAKE 'N' BAKE

FRANCIS BONNET
STORY

JEFF SHULTZ
PENCILS

BOB SMITH
INKS

GLENN WHITMORE
COLORS

JACK MORELLI
LETTERS

CHECK IT OUT! THERE'S GOING TO BE A *BAKE-OFF* CONTEST TOMORROW AT THE RIVERDALE FALL FESTIVAL!

OH! I SHOULD ENTER MY APPLE PIE! I REMEMBER HOW MUCH ARCHIE ENJOYED IT THE LAST TIME I BAKED ONE!

I SURE *DID!!*

RIVERDALE ~FALL~ BAKE OFF FESTIVAL

BETTY, I'M SURE YOUR RECIPE IS FANTASTIC, BUT YOU HAVEN'T HAD MY PUMPKIN PIE! IT'S OUT OF THIS WORLD!

I'VE TRIED IT, AND IT'S DEFINITELY WAY BETTER THAN ANY PIE BETTY CAN BAKE!

NO OFFENSE TO RONNIE, BUT BETTY'S APPLE PIE IS THE BEST *EVER!*

RIVERDALE ~FALL~ BAKE OFF FES

ALL THIS TALK ABOUT DESSERT IS MAKING ME HUNGRY!

SO HOW ABOUT A LITTLE FRIENDLY COMPETITION? SINCE ARCHIE IS SO SURE THAT BETTY'S PIE IS BETTER, HE CAN HELP HER BAKE IT. MEANWHILE, RONNIE AND I WILL BAKE HER PUMPKIN PIE. THEN WE'LL SEE WHO WINS THE CONTEST!

I DON'T CARE WHO WINS JUST AS LONG AS I GET TO EAT BOTH PIES!

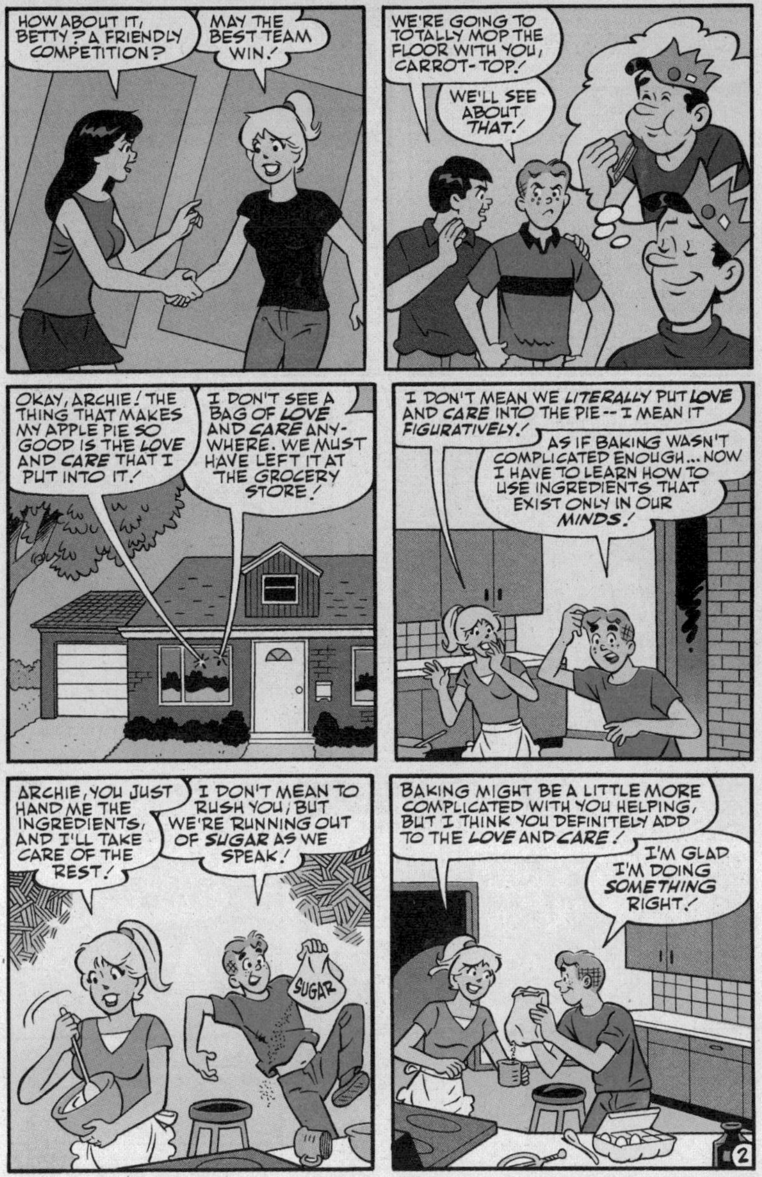

HOW ABOUT IT, BETTY? A FRIENDLY COMPETITION?
MAY THE BEST TEAM WIN!
WE'RE GOING TO TOTALLY MOP THE FLOOR WITH YOU, CARROT-TOP!
WE'LL SEE ABOUT THAT!
OKAY, ARCHIE! THE THING THAT MAKES MY APPLE PIE SO GOOD IS THE LOVE AND CARE THAT I PUT INTO IT!
I DON'T SEE A BAG OF LOVE AND CARE ANYWHERE. WE MUST HAVE LEFT IT AT THE GROCERY STORE!
I DON'T MEAN WE LITERALLY PUT LOVE AND CARE INTO THE PIE -- I MEAN IT FIGURATIVELY!
AS IF BAKING WASN'T COMPLICATED ENOUGH... NOW I HAVE TO LEARN HOW TO USE INGREDIENTS THAT EXIST ONLY IN OUR MINDS!
ARCHIE, YOU JUST HAND ME THE INGREDIENTS, AND I'LL TAKE CARE OF THE REST!
I DON'T MEAN TO RUSH YOU, BUT WE'RE RUNNING OUT OF SUGAR AS WE SPEAK!
SUGAR
BAKING MIGHT BE A LITTLE MORE COMPLICATED WITH YOU HELPING, BUT I THINK YOU DEFINITELY ADD TO THE LOVE AND CARE!
I'M GLAD I'M DOING SOMETHING RIGHT!
2

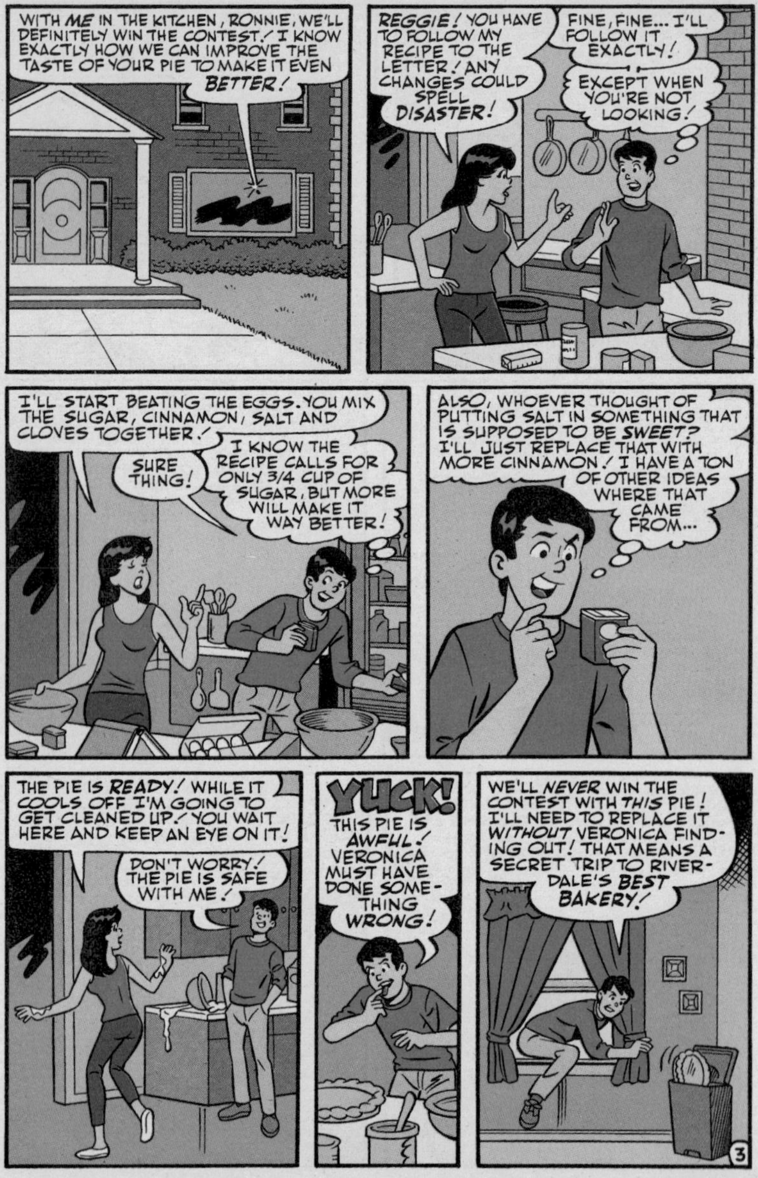
WITH ME IN THE KITCHEN, RONNIE, WE'LL DEFINITELY WIN THE CONTEST! I KNOW EXACTLY HOW WE CAN IMPROVE THE TASTE OF YOUR PIE TO MAKE IT EVEN BETTER!
REGGIE! YOU HAVE TO FOLLOW MY RECIPE TO THE LETTER! ANY CHANGES COULD SPELL DISASTER!
FINE, FINE... I'LL FOLLOW IT EXACTLY!
EXCEPT WHEN YOU'RE NOT LOOKING!
I'LL START BEATING THE EGGS. YOU MIX THE SUGAR, CINNAMON, SALT AND CLOVES TOGETHER!
SURE THING!
I KNOW THE RECIPE CALLS FOR ONLY 3/4 CUP OF SUGAR, BUT MORE WILL MAKE IT WAY BETTER!
ALSO, WHOEVER THOUGHT OF PUTTING SALT IN SOMETHING THAT IS SUPPOSED TO BE SWEET? I'LL JUST REPLACE THAT WITH MORE CINNAMON! I HAVE A TON OF OTHER IDEAS WHERE THAT CAME FROM...
THE PIE IS READY! WHILE IT COOLS OFF I'M GOING TO GET CLEANED UP! YOU WAIT HERE AND KEEP AN EYE ON IT!
DON'T WORRY! THE PIE IS SAFE WITH ME!
YUCK!
THIS PIE IS AWFUL! VERONICA MUST HAVE DONE SOMETHING WRONG!
WE'LL NEVER WIN THE CONTEST WITH THIS PIE! I'LL NEED TO REPLACE IT WITHOUT VERONICA FINDING OUT! THAT MEANS A SECRET TRIP TO RIVERDALE'S BEST BAKERY!
3

Archie: THAT APPLE PIE SMELLS *GREAT*, BETTY!

Betty: WELL, IT WAS A *TEAM EFFORT!* EVEN THOUGH YOU ALMOST BURNED MY HOUSE DOWN THREE AND A HALF TIMES!

Archie: I LEARNED THAT A *FIRE EXTINGUISHER* IS BETTER AT PUTTING OUT FIRES THAN *LOVE* AND *CARE!*

Betty: LET'S WAIT FOR THE PIE TO *COOL* AND HEAD OVER TO THE *FALL FESTIVAL!*

Reggie: THIS SHOULD GUARANTEE OUR WIN FOR SURE!

Veronica: REGGIE! THE PIE SHOULD BE *COOL* BY NOW. ARE YOU READY TO LEAVE FOR THE *FALL FESTIVAL?*

Reggie: I'M *READY!* I'VE BEEN WAITING HERE PATIENTLY THE ENTIRE TIME!

Veronica: *GREAT!* LET'S HEAD OUT!

RIVERDALE BAKERY

Reggie: HERE COME THE CONTEST *LOSERS* NOW!

BAKE-OFF CONTEST

Veronica: C'MON, REGGIE!

Betty: THIS IS SUPPOSED TO BE A *FRIENDLY* COMPETITION!

Reggie: ARCHIE KNOWS I'M ONLY KIDDING, RIGHT, ARCH?

4

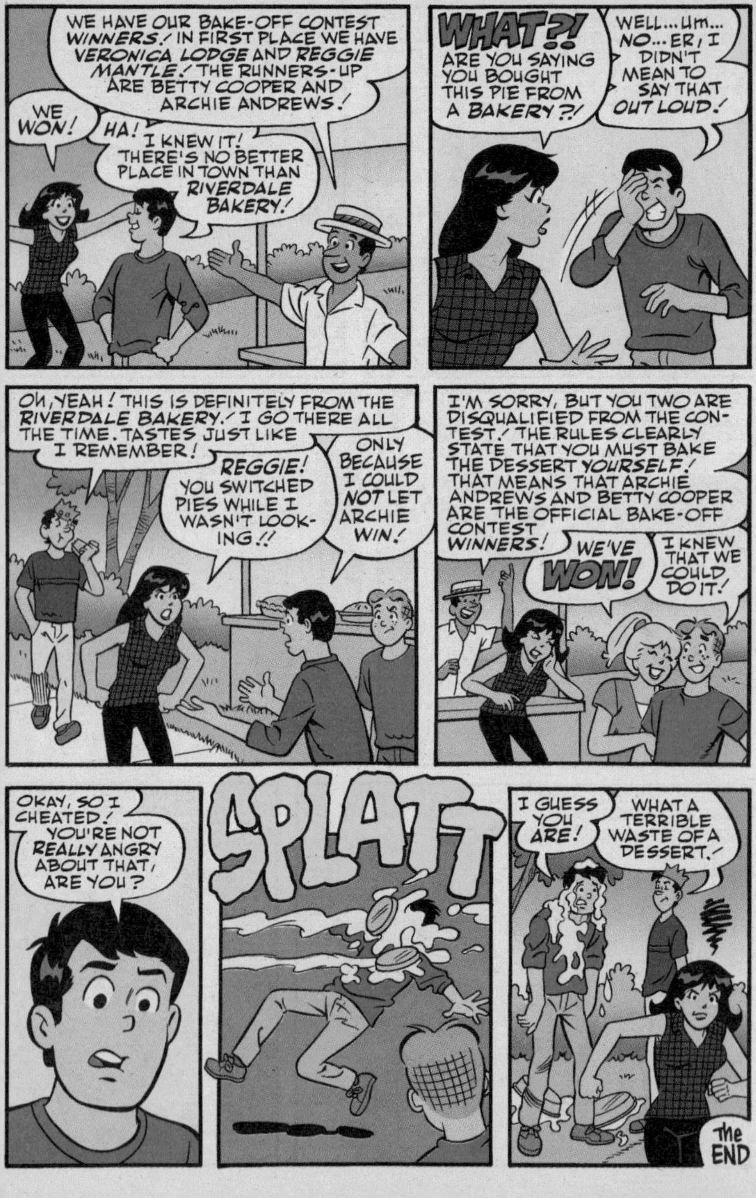
WE HAVE OUR BAKE-OFF CONTEST WINNERS! IN FIRST PLACE WE HAVE VERONICA LODGE AND REGGIE MANTLE! THE RUNNERS-UP ARE BETTY COOPER AND ARCHIE ANDREWS!
WE WON!
HA! I KNEW IT! THERE'S NO BETTER PLACE IN TOWN THAN RIVERDALE BAKERY!
WHAT?!
ARE YOU SAYING YOU BOUGHT THIS PIE FROM A BAKERY?!
WELL...UM... NO...ER, I DIDN'T MEAN TO SAY THAT OUT LOUD!
OH, YEAH! THIS IS DEFINITELY FROM THE RIVERDALE BAKERY! I GO THERE ALL THE TIME. TASTES JUST LIKE I REMEMBER!
REGGIE! YOU SWITCHED PIES WHILE I WASN'T LOOKING!!
ONLY BECAUSE I COULD NOT LET ARCHIE WIN!
I'M SORRY, BUT YOU TWO ARE DISQUALIFIED FROM THE CONTEST! THE RULES CLEARLY STATE THAT YOU MUST BAKE THE DESSERT YOURSELF! THAT MEANS THAT ARCHIE ANDREWS AND BETTY COOPER ARE THE OFFICIAL BAKE-OFF CONTEST WINNERS!
WE'VE WON!
I KNEW THAT WE COULD DO IT!
OKAY, SO I CHEATED! YOU'RE NOT REALLY ANGRY ABOUT THAT, ARE YOU?
SPLATT
I GUESS YOU ARE!
WHAT A TERRIBLE WASTE OF A DESSERT!
THE END

Archie in BOOK MARK

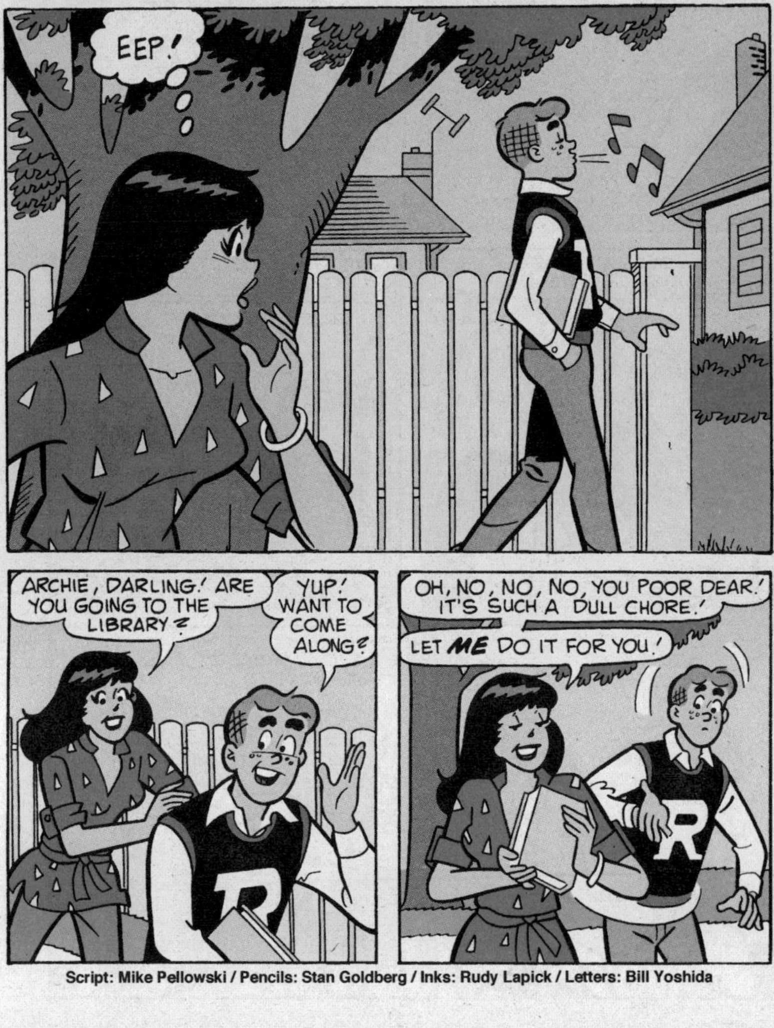
EEP!
ARCHIE, DARLING! ARE YOU GOING TO THE LIBRARY?
YUP! WANT TO COME ALONG?
OH, NO, NO, NO, YOU POOR DEAR! IT'S SUCH A DULL CHORE!
LET ME DO IT FOR YOU!

Script: Mike Pellowski / Pencils: Stan Goldberg / Inks: Rudy Lapick / Letters: Bill Yoshida

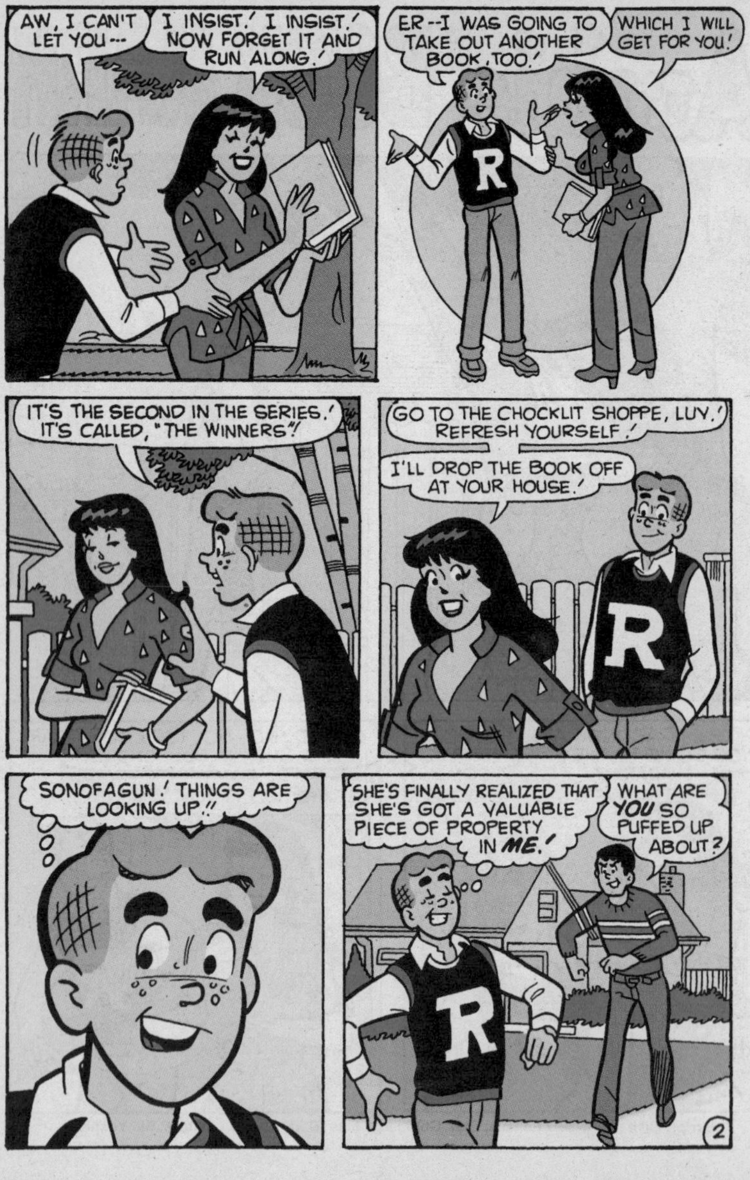
AW, I CAN'T LET YOU---
I INSIST! I INSIST! NOW FORGET IT AND RUN ALONG!
ER--I WAS GOING TO TAKE OUT ANOTHER BOOK, TOO!
WHICH I WILL GET FOR YOU!
IT'S THE SECOND IN THE SERIES! IT'S CALLED, "THE WINNERS"!
GO TO THE CHOCKLIT SHOPPE, LUV! REFRESH YOURSELF!
I'LL DROP THE BOOK OFF AT YOUR HOUSE!
SONOFAGUN! THINGS ARE LOOKING UP!!
SHE'S FINALLY REALIZED THAT SHE'S GOT A VALUABLE PIECE OF PROPERTY IN ME!
WHAT ARE YOU SO PUFFED UP ABOUT?
2

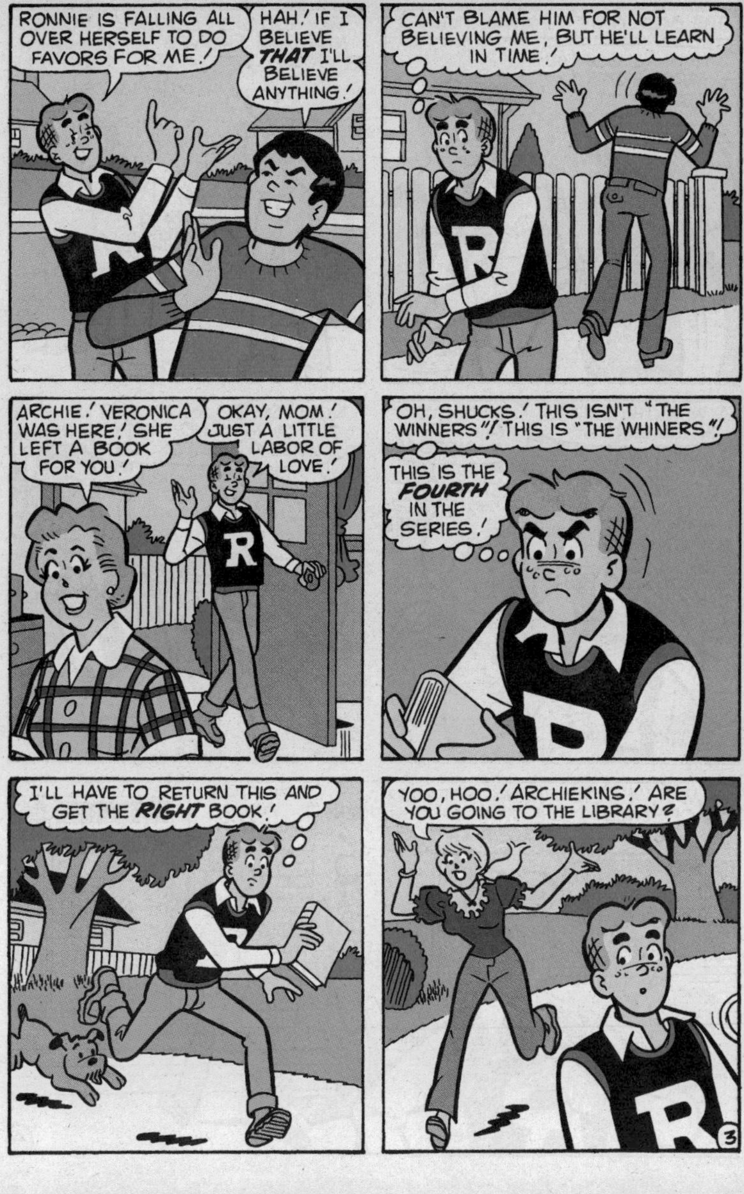
RONNIE IS FALLING ALL OVER HERSELF TO DO FAVORS FOR ME!
HAH! IF I BELIEVE THAT I'LL BELIEVE ANYTHING!
CAN'T BLAME HIM FOR NOT BELIEVING ME, BUT HE'LL LEARN IN TIME!
ARCHIE! VERONICA WAS HERE! SHE LEFT A BOOK FOR YOU!
OKAY, MOM! JUST A LITTLE LABOR OF LOVE!
OH, SHUCKS! THIS ISN'T "THE WINNERS"! THIS IS "THE WHINERS"!
THIS IS THE FOURTH IN THE SERIES!
I'LL HAVE TO RETURN THIS AND GET THE RIGHT BOOK!
YOO, HOO! ARCHIEKINS! ARE YOU GOING TO THE LIBRARY?
3

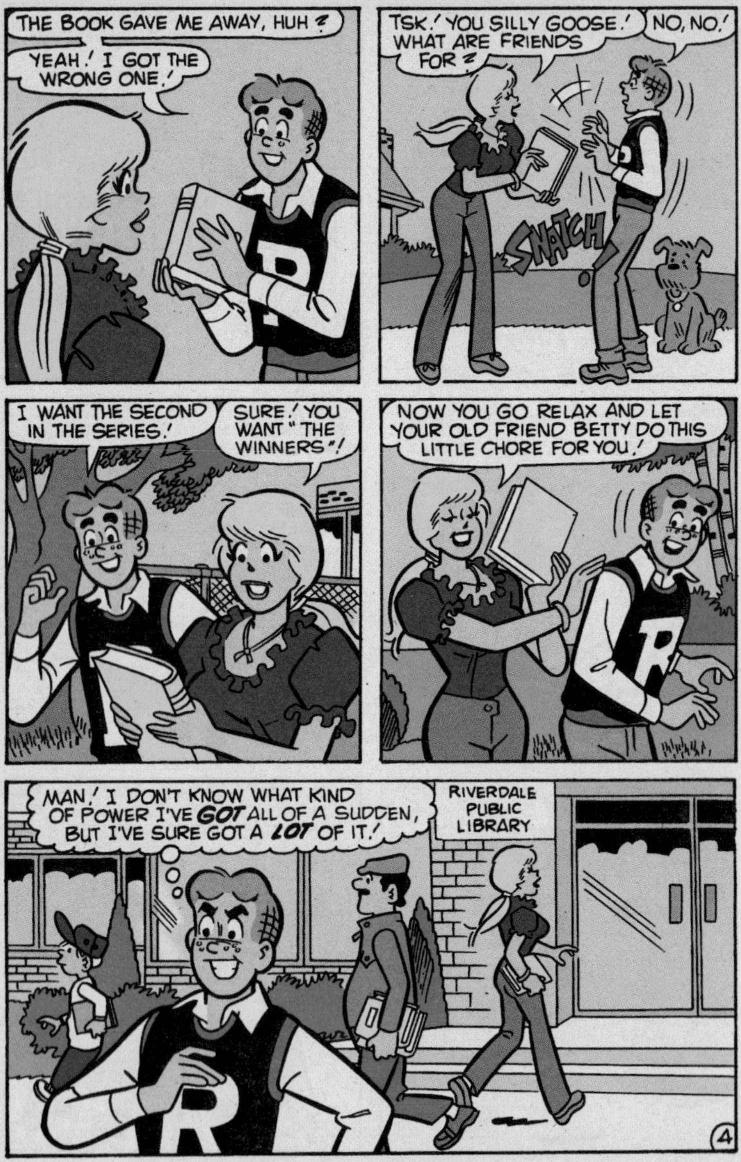
THE BOOK GAVE ME AWAY, HUH?
YEAH! I GOT THE WRONG ONE!
TSK! YOU SILLY GOOSE! WHAT ARE FRIENDS FOR?
NO, NO!
SNATCH
I WANT THE SECOND IN THE SERIES!
SURE! YOU WANT "THE WINNERS"!
NOW YOU GO RELAX AND LET YOUR OLD FRIEND BETTY DO THIS LITTLE CHORE FOR YOU!
MAN! I DON'T KNOW WHAT KIND OF POWER I'VE GOT ALL OF A SUDDEN, BUT I'VE SURE GOT A LOT OF IT!
RIVERDALE PUBLIC LIBRARY
4

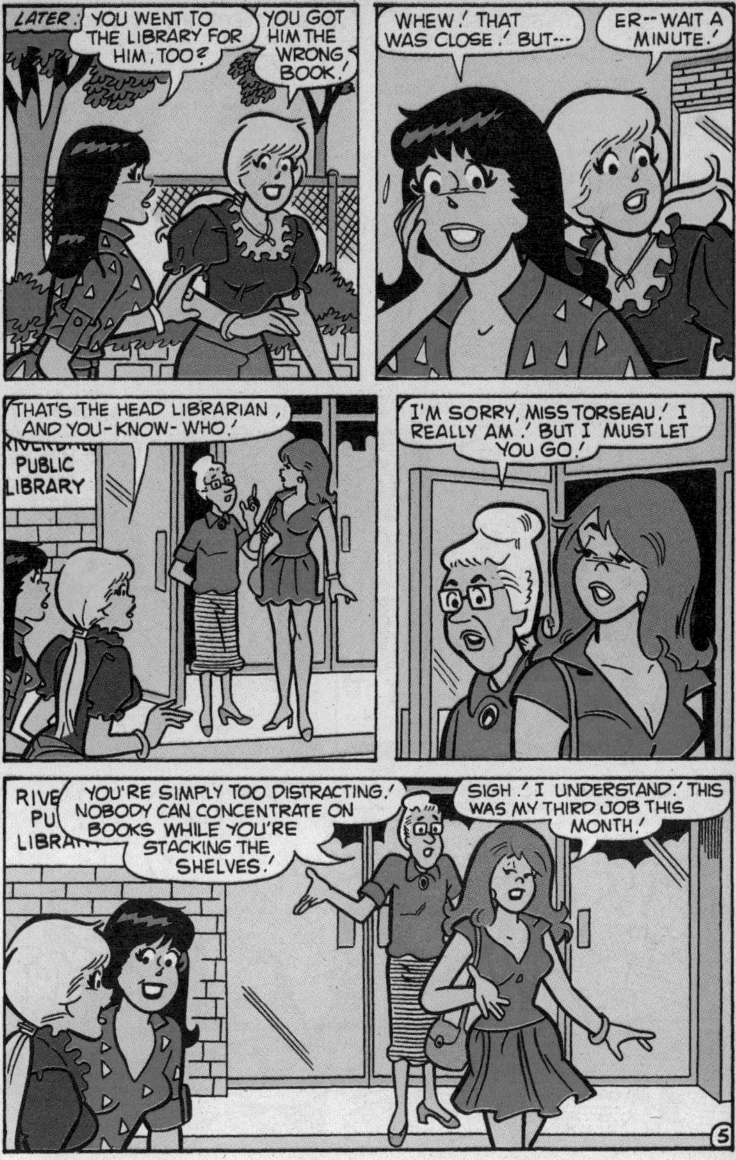
LATER:
YOU WENT TO THE LIBRARY FOR HIM, TOO?
YOU GOT HIM THE WRONG BOOK!
WHEW! THAT WAS CLOSE! BUT---
ER--WAIT A MINUTE!
THAT'S THE HEAD LIBRARIAN, AND YOU-KNOW-WHO!
PUBLIC LIBRARY
I'M SORRY, MISS TORSEAU! I REALLY AM! BUT I MUST LET YOU GO!
YOU'RE SIMPLY TOO DISTRACTING! NOBODY CAN CONCENTRATE ON BOOKS WHILE YOU'RE STACKING THE SHELVES!
SIGH! I UNDERSTAND! THIS WAS MY THIRD JOB THIS MONTH!
5

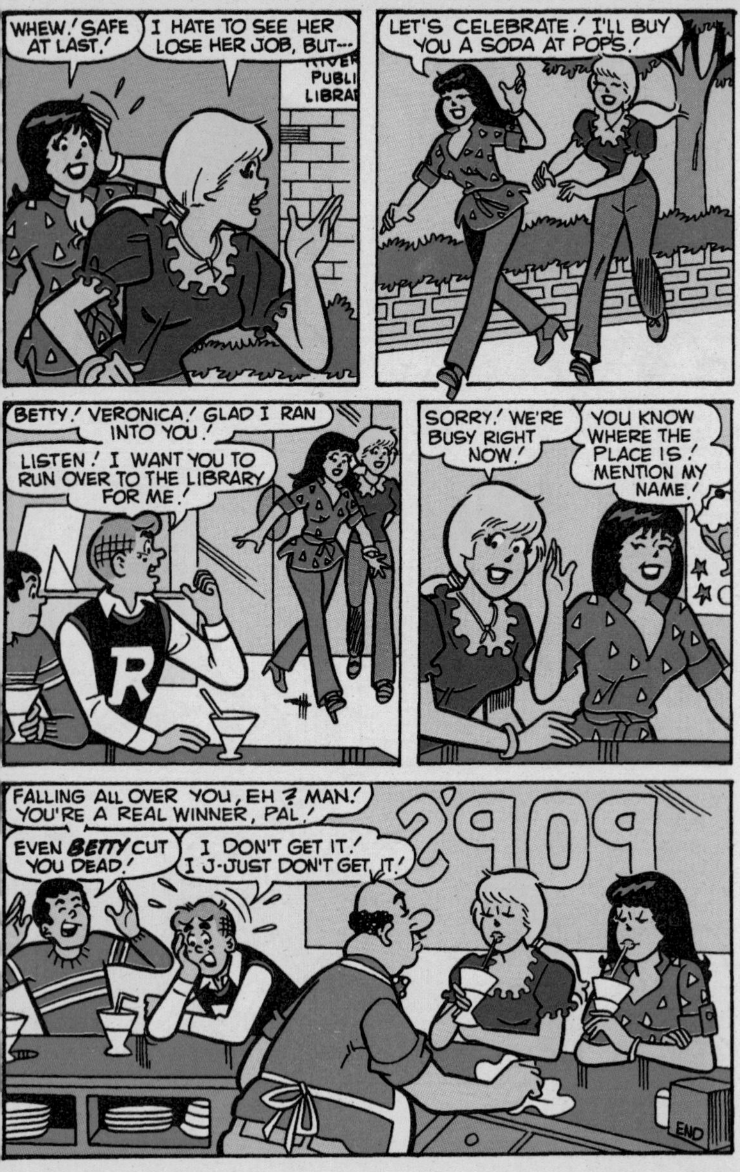
WHEW! SAFE AT LAST!
I HATE TO SEE HER LOSE HER JOB, BUT---
LET'S CELEBRATE! I'LL BUY YOU A SODA AT POP'S!
BETTY! VERONICA! GLAD I RAN INTO YOU!
LISTEN! I WANT YOU TO RUN OVER TO THE LIBRARY FOR ME!
SORRY! WE'RE BUSY RIGHT NOW!
YOU KNOW WHERE THE PLACE IS! MENTION MY NAME!
FALLING ALL OVER YOU, EH? MAN! YOU'RE A REAL WINNER, PAL!
EVEN BETTY CUT YOU DEAD!
I DON'T GET IT! I J-JUST DON'T GET IT!
POP'S
END

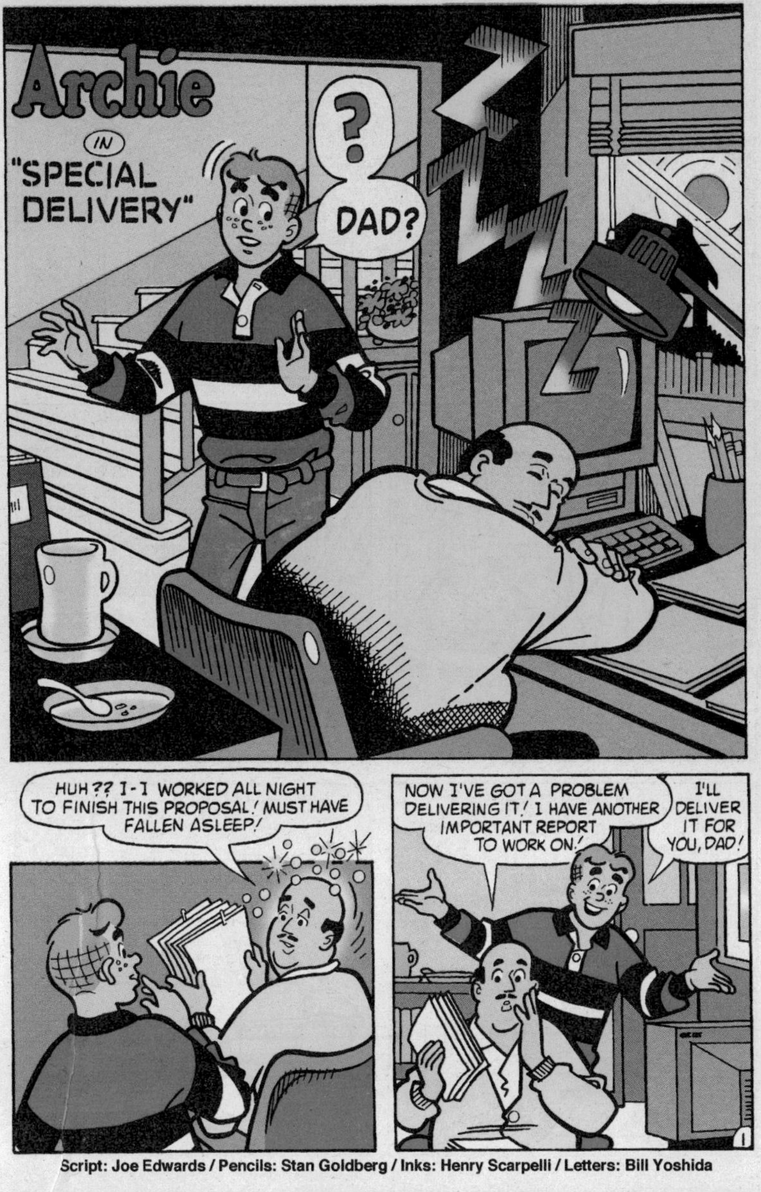
Archie
IN
"SPECIAL DELIVERY"
?
DAD?
Z
Z
Z
HUH?? I-I WORKED ALL NIGHT TO FINISH THIS PROPOSAL! MUST HAVE FALLEN ASLEEP!
NOW I'VE GOT A PROBLEM DELIVERING IT! I HAVE ANOTHER IMPORTANT REPORT TO WORK ON!
I'LL DELIVER IT FOR YOU, DAD!
1

Script: Joe Edwards / Pencils: Stan Goldberg / Inks: Henry Scarpelli / Letters: Bill Yoshida

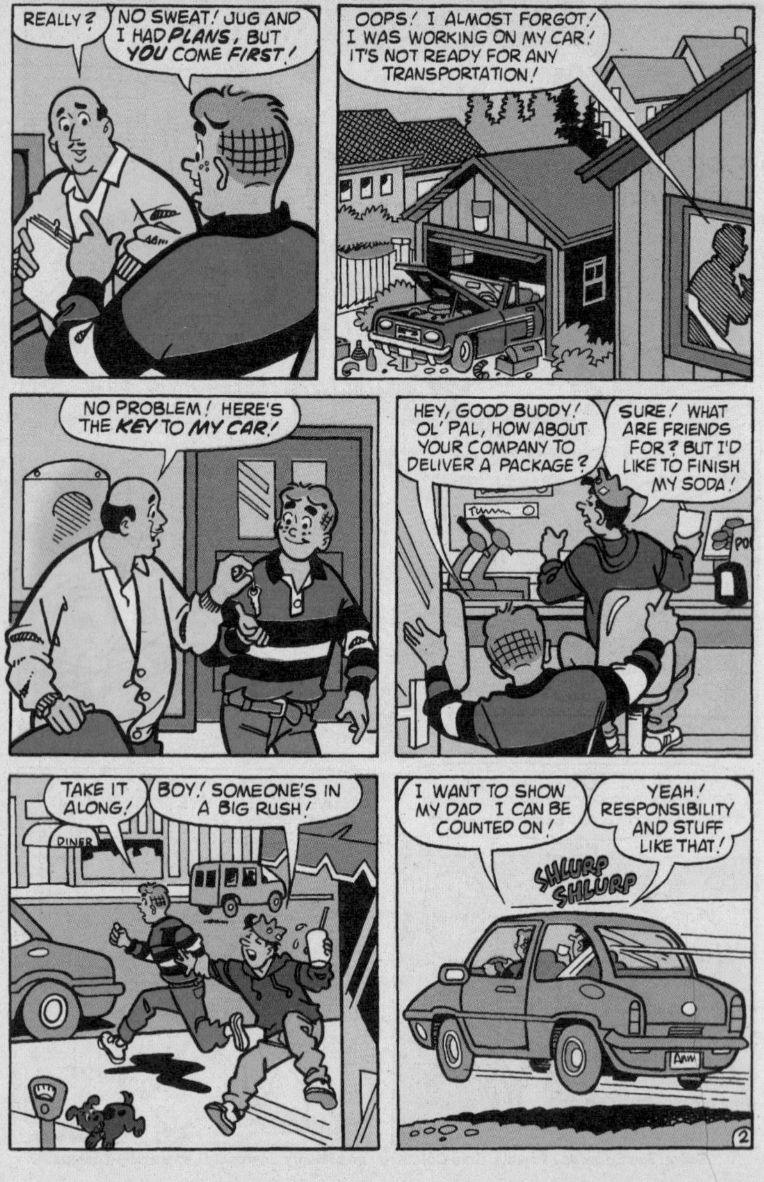
REALLY?
NO SWEAT! JUG AND I HAD PLANS, BUT YOU COME FIRST!
OOPS! I ALMOST FORGOT! I WAS WORKING ON MY CAR! IT'S NOT READY FOR ANY TRANSPORTATION!
NO PROBLEM! HERE'S THE KEY TO MY CAR!
HEY, GOOD BUDDY! OL' PAL, HOW ABOUT YOUR COMPANY TO DELIVER A PACKAGE?
SURE! WHAT ARE FRIENDS FOR? BUT I'D LIKE TO FINISH MY SODA!
TAKE IT ALONG!
BOY! SOMEONE'S IN A BIG RUSH!
DINER
I WANT TO SHOW MY DAD I CAN BE COUNTED ON!
YEAH! RESPONSIBILITY AND STUFF LIKE THAT!
SHLURP SHLURP
2

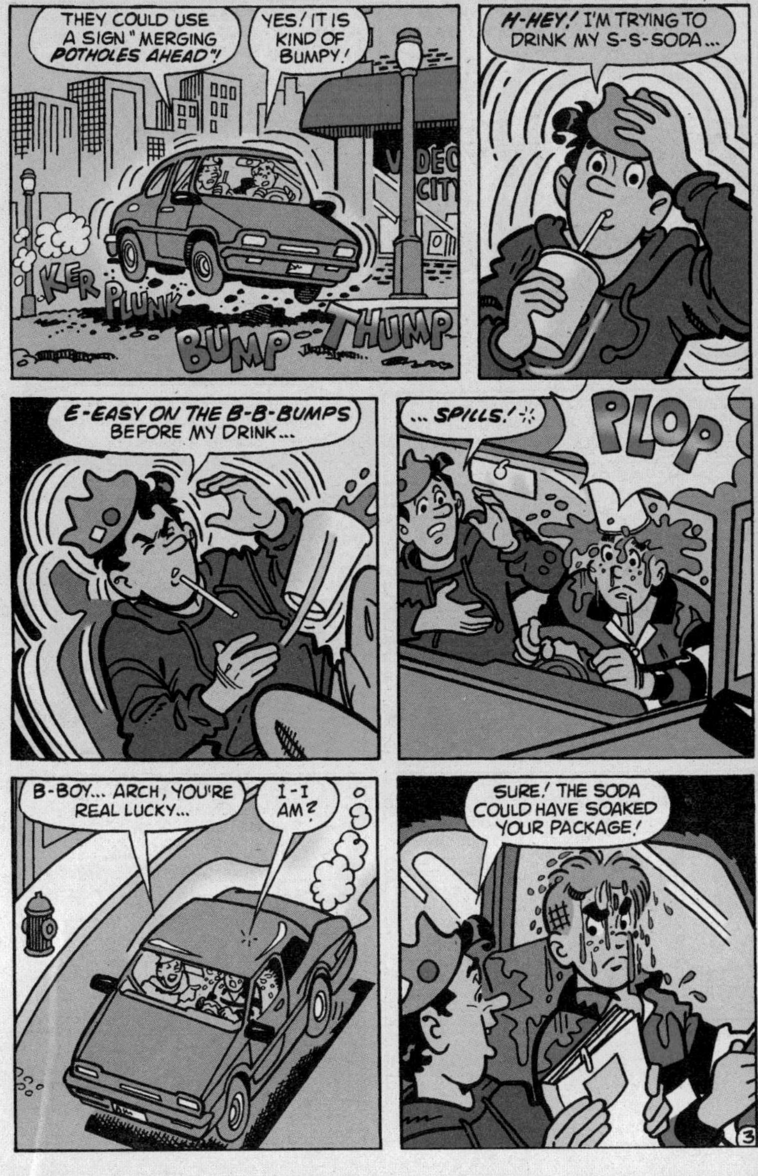
THEY COULD USE A SIGN "MERGING POTHOLES AHEAD"!
YES! IT IS KIND OF BUMPY!
VIDEO CITY
KER PLUNK
BUMP
THUMP
H-HEY! I'M TRYING TO DRINK MY S-S-SODA...
E-EASY ON THE B-B-BUMPS BEFORE MY DRINK...
... SPILLS!
PLOP
B-BOY... ARCH, YOU'RE REAL LUCKY...
I-I AM?
SURE! THE SODA COULD HAVE SOAKED YOUR PACKAGE!
3

WOW, ARCH! YOU ARE *LUCKY!*

HUH? WHY AM I *LUCKY... AGAIN?*

I HAVEN'T BEEN ABLE TO FIND A PARKING SPOT!

THERE!! A CAR IS *PULLING* OUT OF THE *METERED* PARKING SPOT! YOU *LUCKY* DEVIL!

GUESS I'M *LUCKY...* THERE'S A FEW MINUTES MORE ON THE METER! HERE'S A QUARTER *JUST IN CASE!!*

TIC TIC TIC TIC TIC TIC TIC TIC TIC TIC

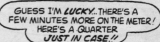

I HAVE TO PERSONALLY HAND IT TO MR. MAPLE!

HAVE A SEAT! HE'S ON AN OVERSEAS PHONE CALL!

MR. MAPLE PRIVATE

GULP! IT'S TAKING ARCH A LONG TIME AND THE METER IS ALMOST EXPIRED...

4

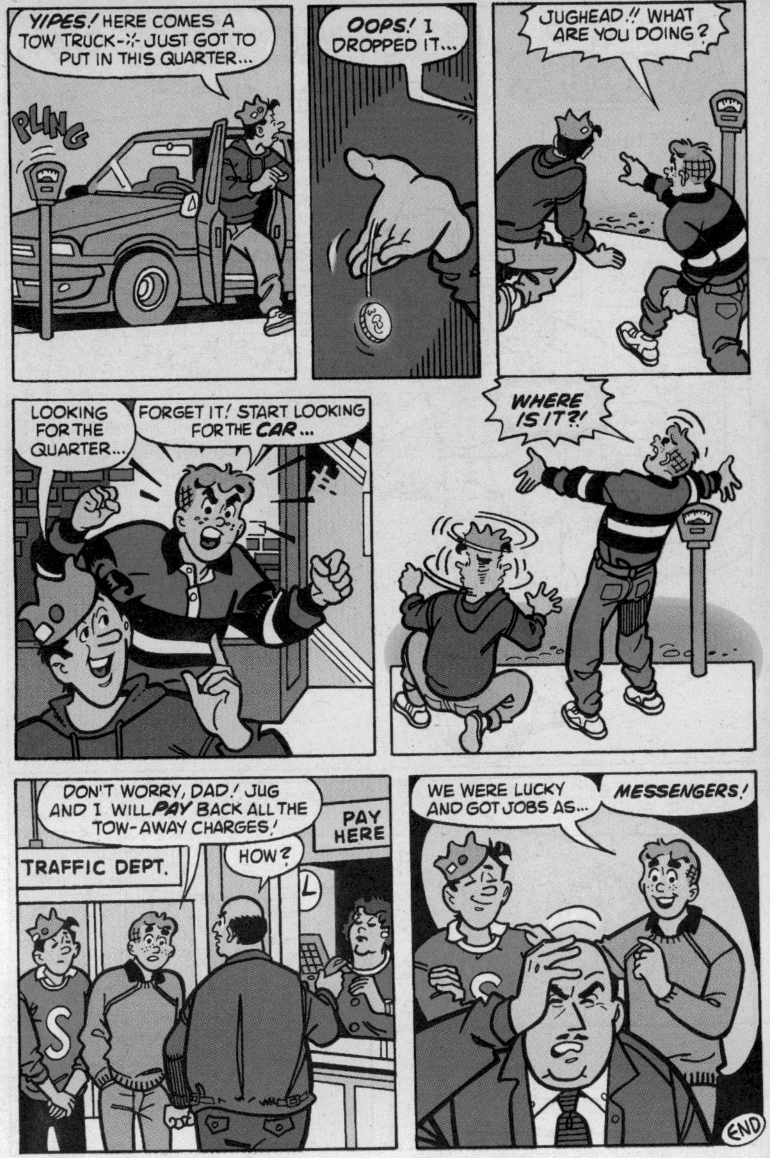

YIPES! HERE COMES A TOW TRUCK-·/·- JUST GOT TO PUT IN THIS QUARTER...
PLING
OOPS! I DROPPED IT...
JUGHEAD!! WHAT ARE YOU DOING?
LOOKING FOR THE QUARTER...
FORGET IT! START LOOKING FOR THE CAR...
WHERE IS IT?!
DON'T WORRY, DAD! JUG AND I WILL PAY BACK ALL THE TOW-AWAY CHARGES!
TRAFFIC DEPT.
PAY HERE
HOW?
WE WERE LUCKY AND GOT JOBS AS...
MESSENGERS!
END

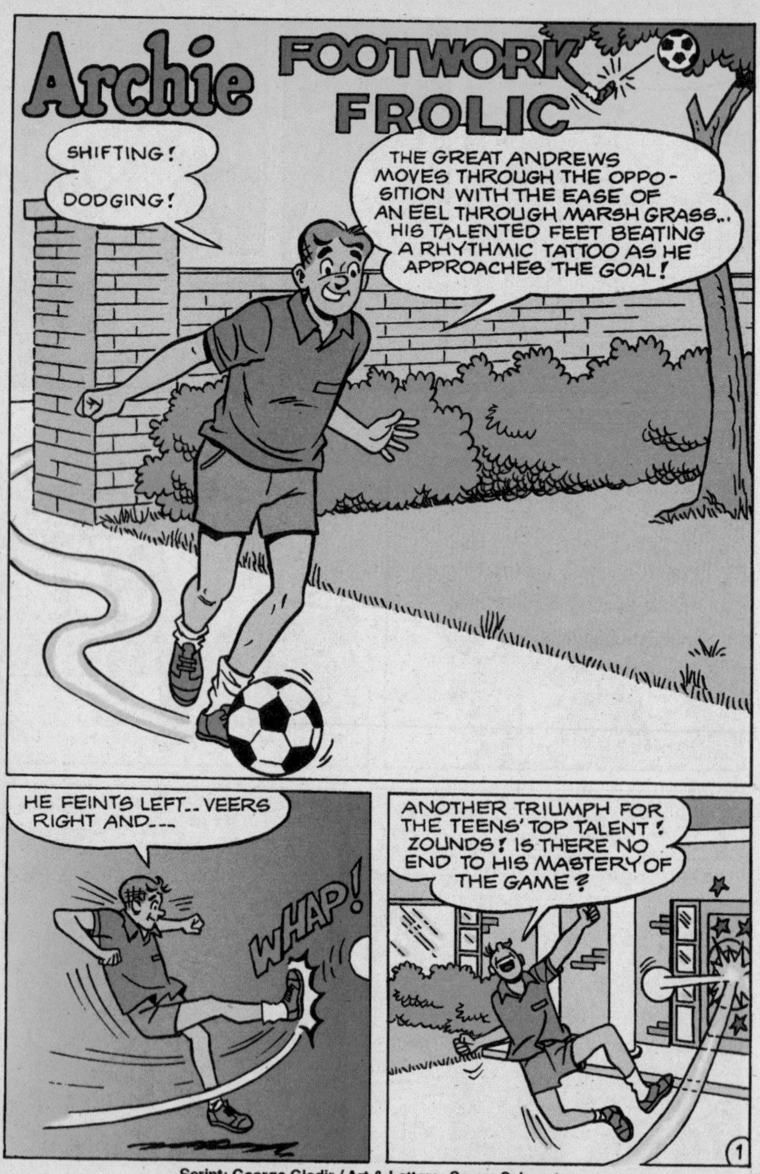
Archie
FOOTWORK FROLIC
SHIFTING! DODGING!
THE GREAT ANDREWS MOVES THROUGH THE OPPO-SITION WITH THE EASE OF AN EEL THROUGH MARSH GRASS.. HIS TALENTED FEET BEATING A RHYTHMIC TATTOO AS HE APPROACHES THE GOAL!
HE FEINTS LEFT.. VEERS RIGHT AND---
WHAP!
ANOTHER TRIUMPH FOR THE TEENS' TOP TALENT! ZOUNDS! IS THERE NO END TO HIS MASTERY OF THE GAME?
1

Script: George Gladir / Art & Letters: Samm Schwartz

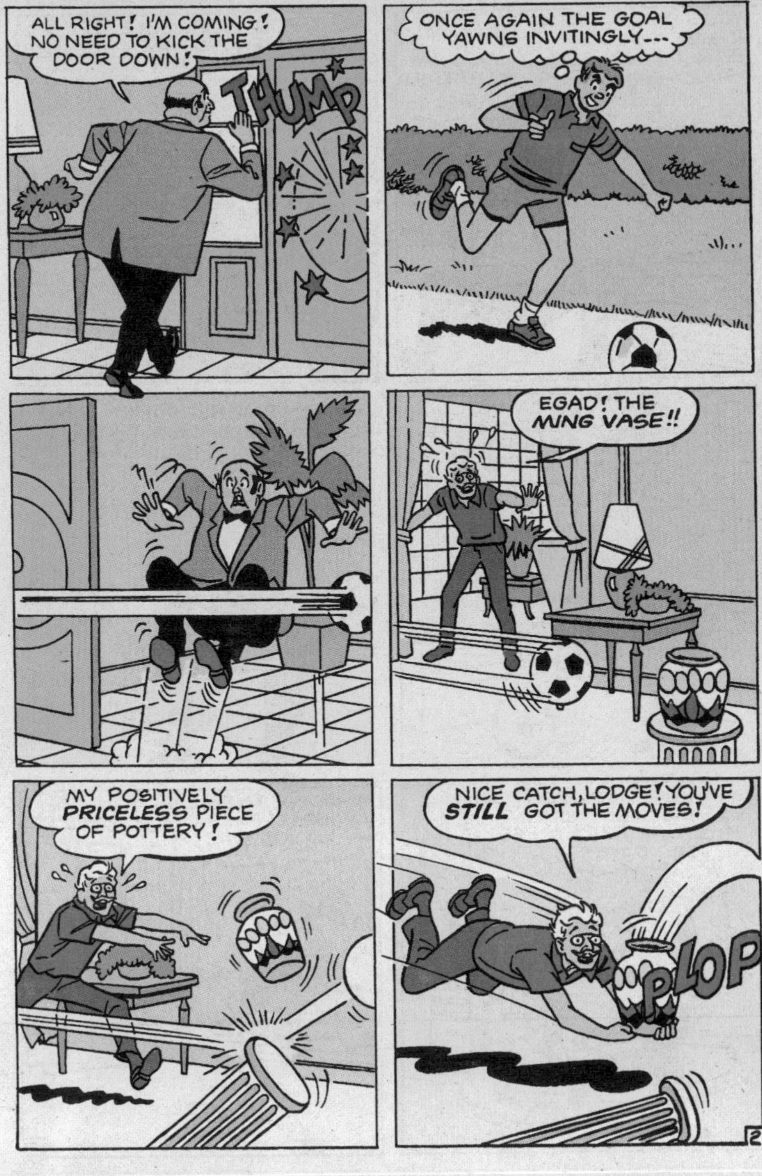
ALL RIGHT! I'M COMING! NO NEED TO KICK THE DOOR DOWN!
THUMP
ONCE AGAIN THE GOAL YAWNS INVITINGLY---
EGAD! THE MING VASE!!
MY POSITIVELY PRICELESS PIECE OF POTTERY!
NICE CATCH, LODGE! YOU'VE STILL GOT THE MOVES!
PLOP
2

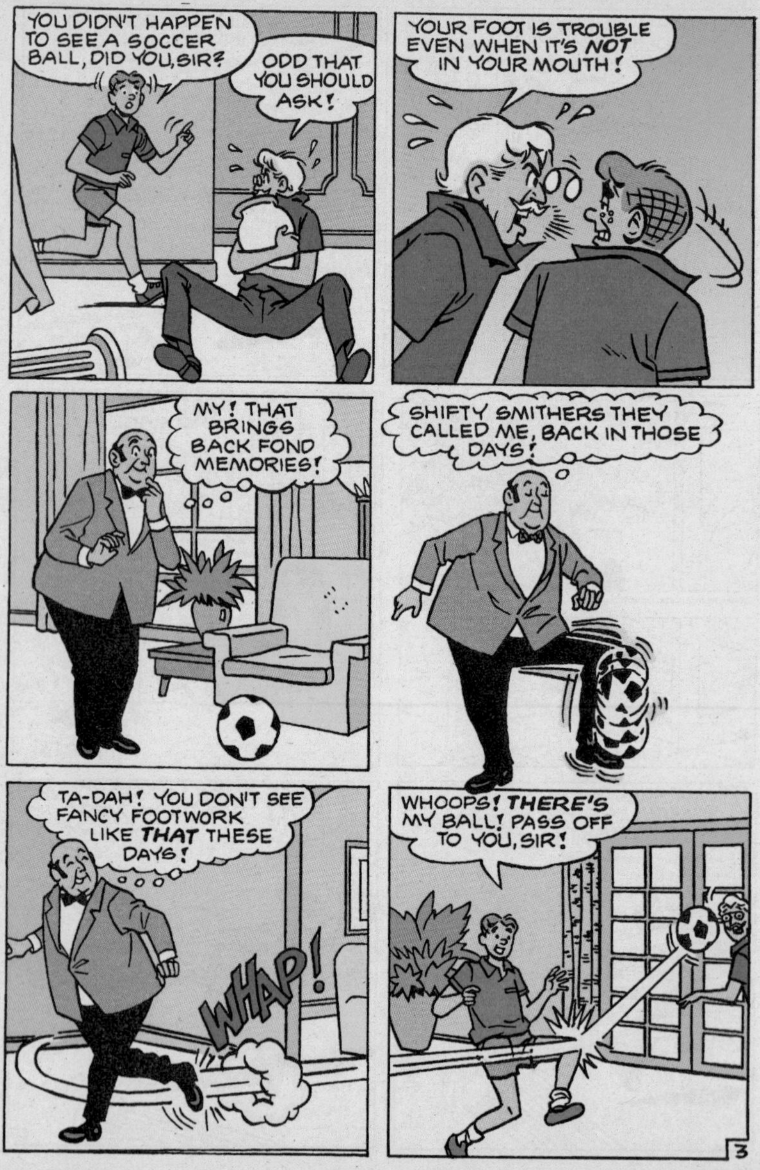
YOU DIDN'T HAPPEN TO SEE A SOCCER BALL, DID YOU, SIR?
ODD THAT YOU SHOULD ASK!
YOUR FOOT IS TROUBLE EVEN WHEN IT'S NOT IN YOUR MOUTH!
MY! THAT BRINGS BACK FOND MEMORIES!
SHIFTY SMITHERS THEY CALLED ME, BACK IN THOSE DAYS!
TA-DAH! YOU DON'T SEE FANCY FOOTWORK LIKE THAT THESE DAYS!
WHAP!
WHOOPS! THERE'S MY BALL! PASS OFF TO YOU, SIR!
3

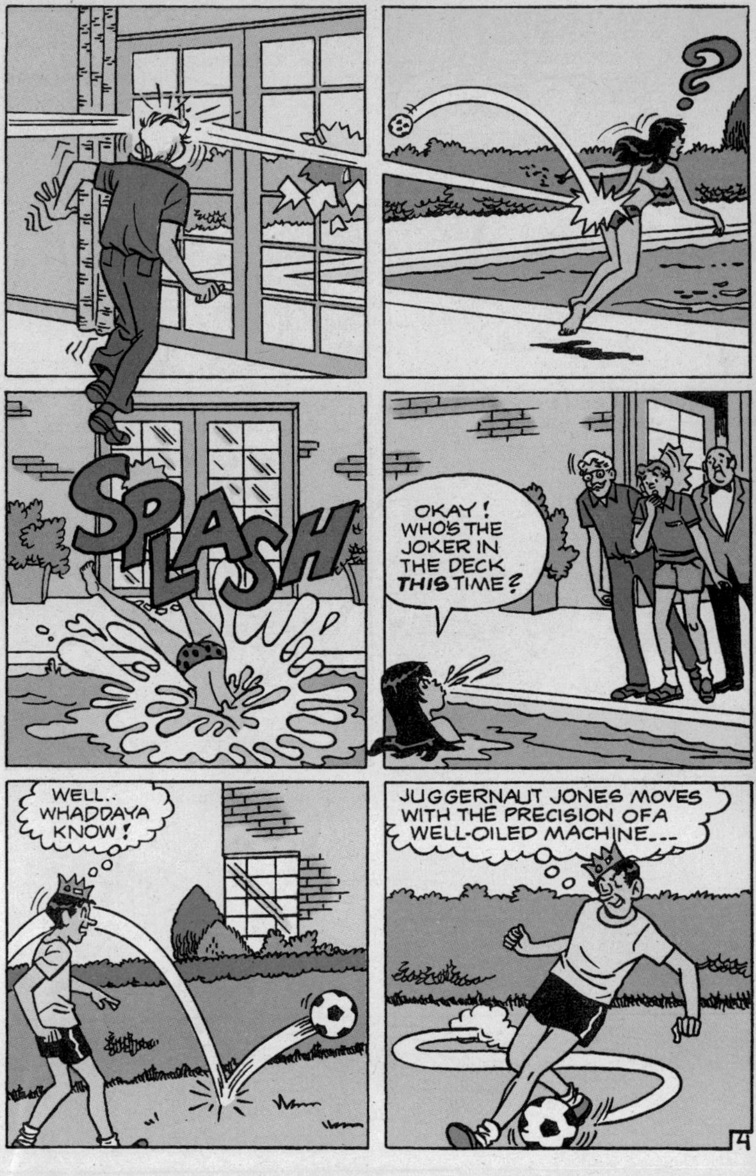
SPLASH
OKAY! WHO'S THE JOKER IN THE DECK **THIS** TIME?
WELL.. WHADDAYA KNOW!
JUGGERNAUT JONES MOVES WITH THE PRECISION OF A WELL-OILED MACHINE---
4

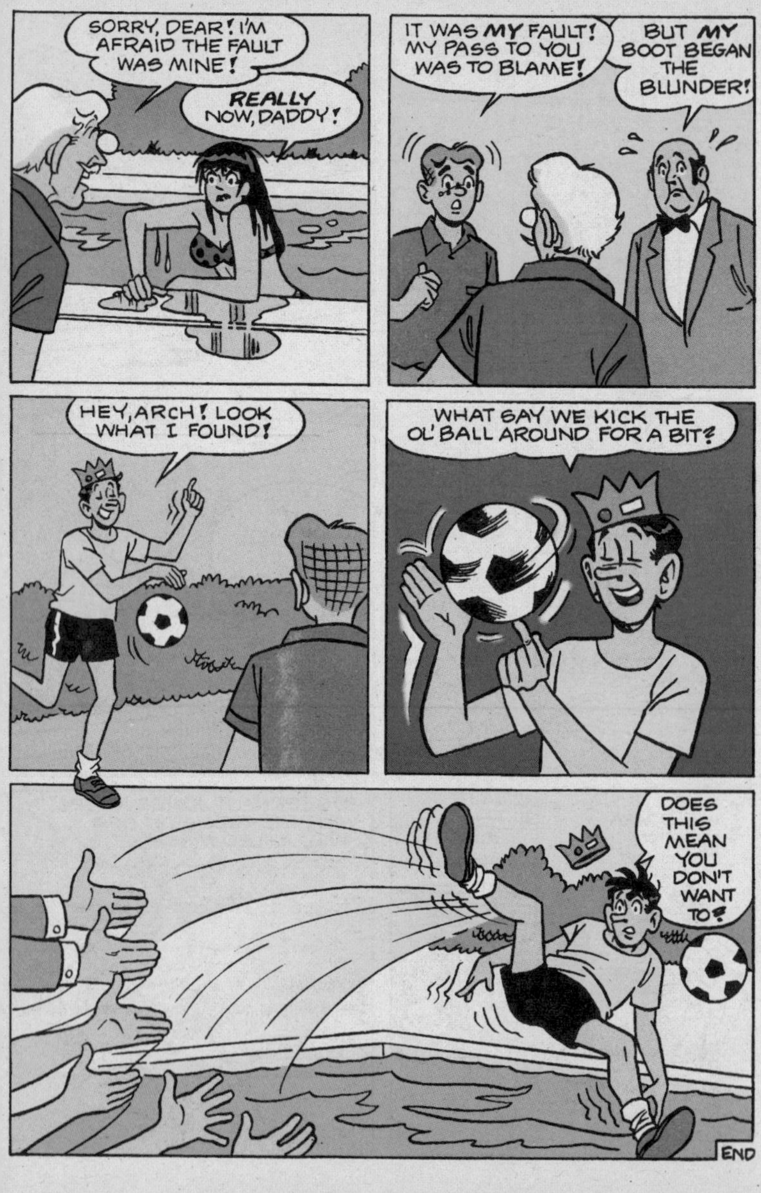
SORRY, DEAR! I'M AFRAID THE FAULT WAS MINE!
REALLY NOW, DADDY!
IT WAS MY FAULT! MY PASS TO YOU WAS TO BLAME!
BUT MY BOOT BEGAN THE BLUNDER!
HEY, ARCH! LOOK WHAT I FOUND!
WHAT SAY WE KICK THE OL' BALL AROUND FOR A BIT?
DOES THIS MEAN YOU DON'T WANT TO?
END

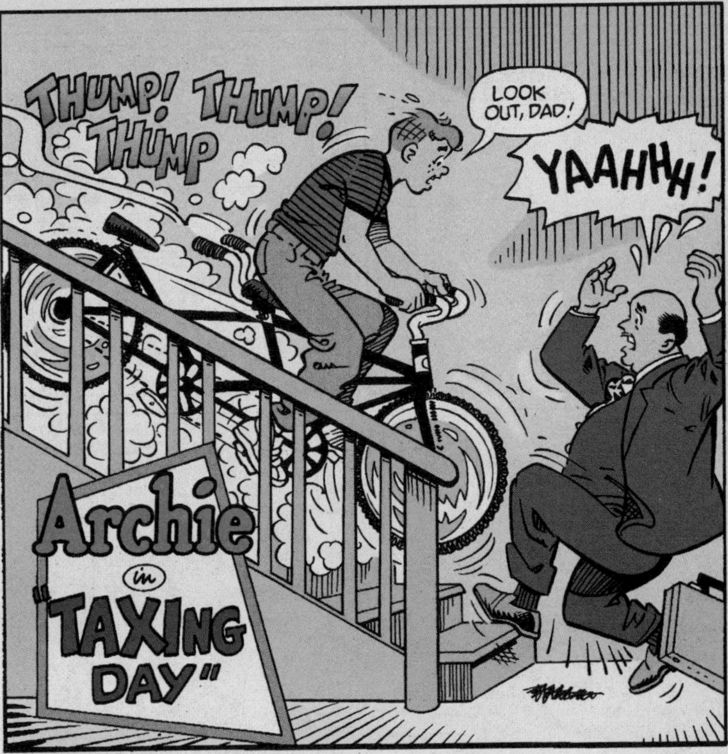
THUMP! THUMP! THUMP
LOOK OUT, DAD!
YAAHHH!
Archie in "TAXING DAY"

Script: Angelo DeCesare / Pencils: Stan Goldberg / Inks: Bob Smith / Letters: Bill Yoshida

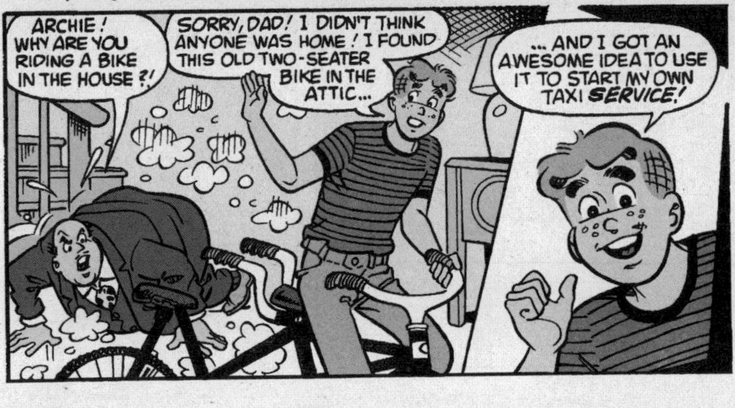
ARCHIE! WHY ARE YOU RIDING A BIKE IN THE HOUSE?!
SORRY, DAD! I DIDN'T THINK ANYONE WAS HOME! I FOUND THIS OLD TWO-SEATER BIKE IN THE ATTIC...
... AND I GOT AN AWESOME IDEA TO USE IT TO START MY OWN TAXI SERVICE!

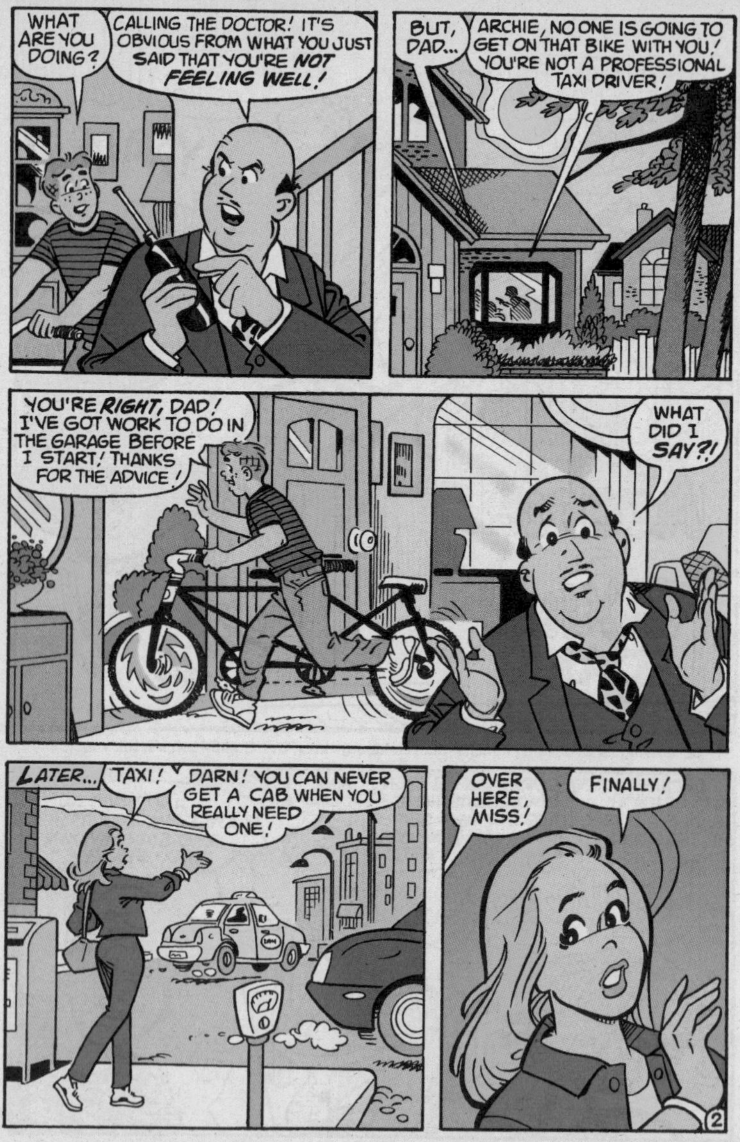
WHAT ARE YOU DOING?
CALLING THE DOCTOR! IT'S OBVIOUS FROM WHAT YOU JUST SAID THAT YOU'RE NOT FEELING WELL!
BUT, DAD...
ARCHIE, NO ONE IS GOING TO GET ON THAT BIKE WITH YOU! YOU'RE NOT A PROFESSIONAL TAXI DRIVER!
YOU'RE RIGHT, DAD! I'VE GOT WORK TO DO IN THE GARAGE BEFORE I START! THANKS FOR THE ADVICE!
WHAT DID I SAY?!
LATER...
TAXI!
DARN! YOU CAN NEVER GET A CAB WHEN YOU REALLY NEED ONE!
OVER HERE, MISS!
FINALLY!
2

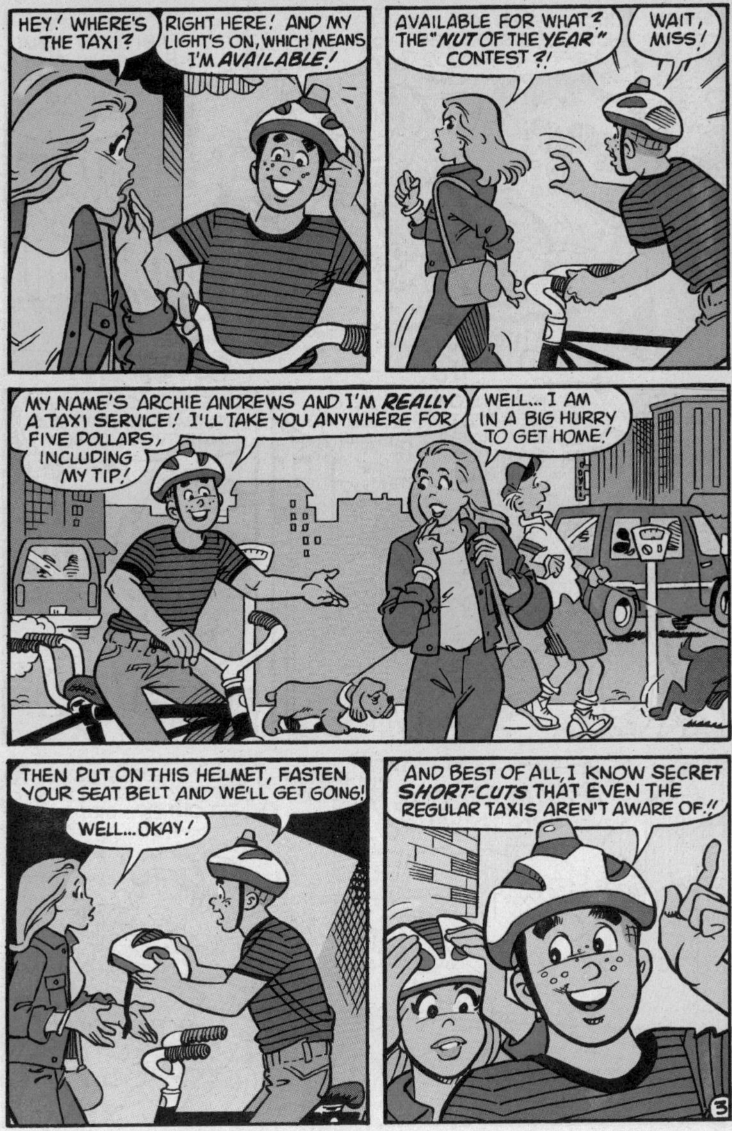
HEY! WHERE'S THE TAXI?
RIGHT HERE! AND MY LIGHT'S ON, WHICH MEANS I'M AVAILABLE!
AVAILABLE FOR WHAT? THE "NUT OF THE YEAR" CONTEST?!
WAIT, MISS!
MY NAME'S ARCHIE ANDREWS AND I'M REALLY A TAXI SERVICE! I'LL TAKE YOU ANYWHERE FOR FIVE DOLLARS, INCLUDING MY TIP!
WELL... I AM IN A BIG HURRY TO GET HOME!
THEN PUT ON THIS HELMET, FASTEN YOUR SEAT BELT AND WE'LL GET GOING!
WELL...OKAY!
AND BEST OF ALL, I KNOW SECRET SHORT-CUTS THAT EVEN THE REGULAR TAXIS AREN'T AWARE OF!!
3

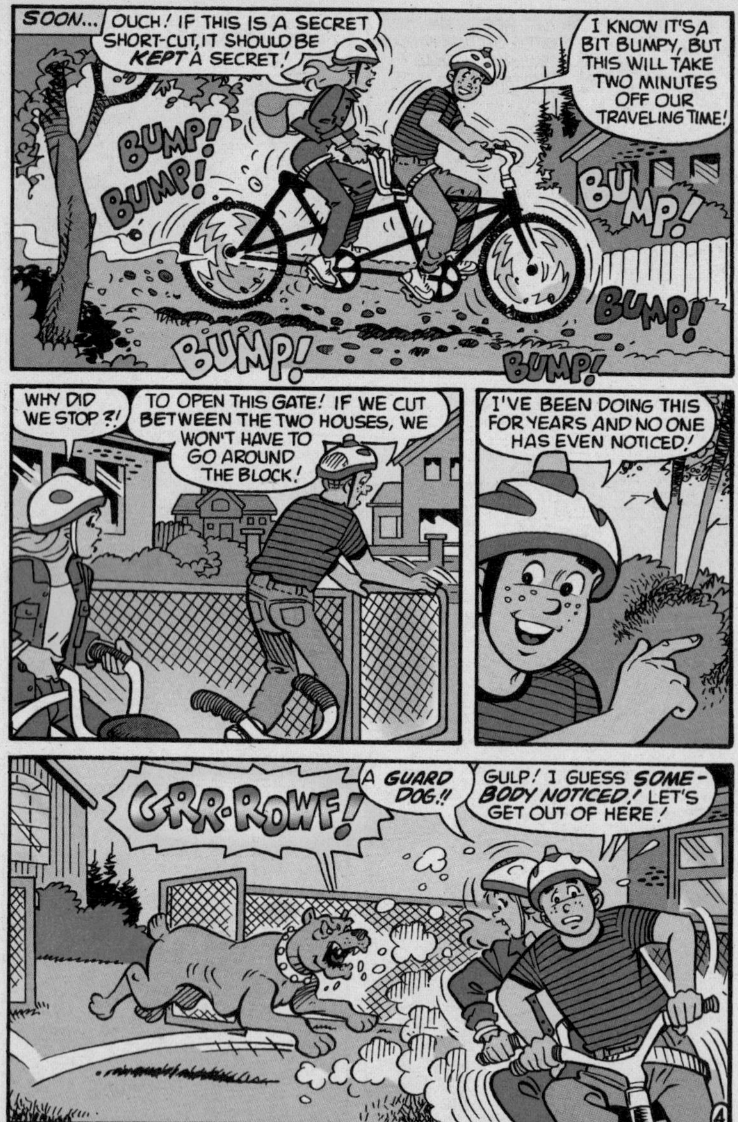
SOON...
OUCH! IF THIS IS A SECRET SHORT-CUT, IT SHOULD BE KEPT A SECRET!
I KNOW IT'S A BIT BUMPY, BUT THIS WILL TAKE TWO MINUTES OFF OUR TRAVELING TIME!
BUMP! BUMP!
BUMP!
BUMP!
BUMP!
BUMP!
WHY DID WE STOP ?!
TO OPEN THIS GATE! IF WE CUT BETWEEN THE TWO HOUSES, WE WON'T HAVE TO GO AROUND THE BLOCK!
I'VE BEEN DOING THIS FOR YEARS AND NO ONE HAS EVEN NOTICED!
GRR-ROWF!
A GUARD DOG!!
GULP! I GUESS SOMEBODY NOTICED! LET'S GET OUT OF HERE!
4

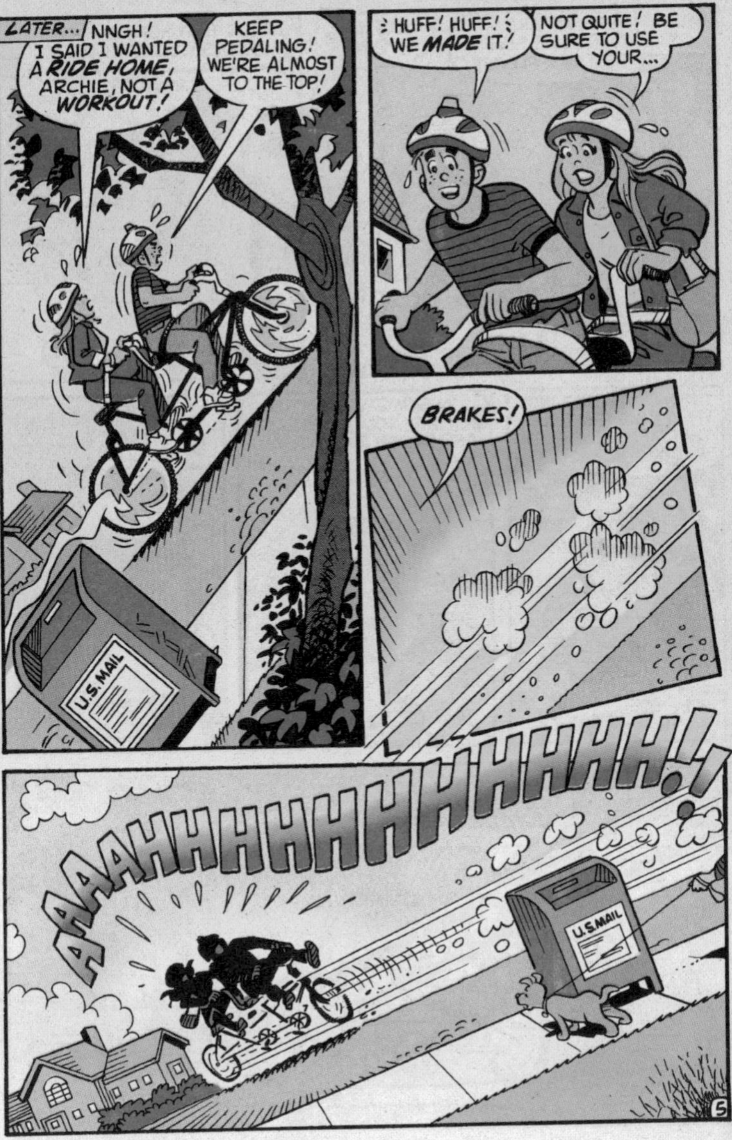
LATER...
NNGH! I SAID I WANTED A RIDE HOME, ARCHIE, NOT A WORKOUT!
KEEP PEDALING! WE'RE ALMOST TO THE TOP!
U.S. MAIL
HUFF! HUFF! WE MADE IT!
NOT QUITE! BE SURE TO USE YOUR...
BRAKES!
AAAAHHHHHHHHHHHHH!!
U.S. MAIL
5

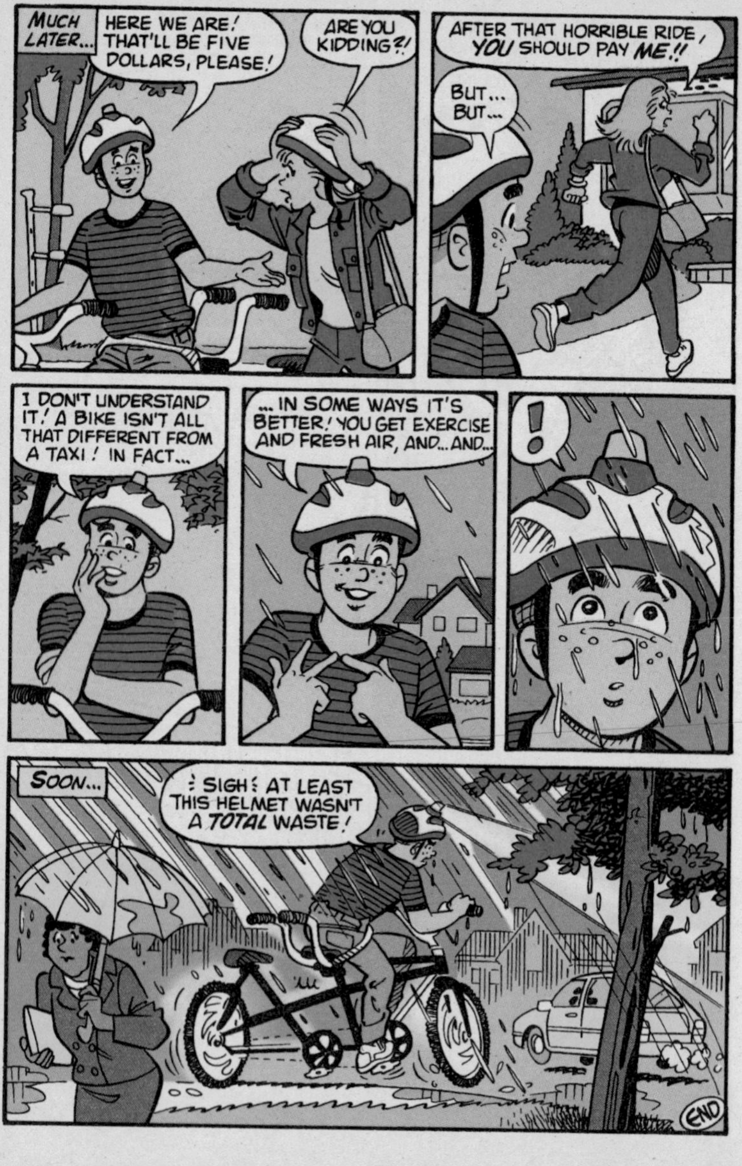
MUCH LATER...
HERE WE ARE! THAT'LL BE FIVE DOLLARS, PLEASE!
ARE YOU KIDDING?!
AFTER THAT HORRIBLE RIDE, YOU SHOULD PAY ME!!
BUT... BUT...
I DON'T UNDERSTAND IT! A BIKE ISN'T ALL THAT DIFFERENT FROM A TAXI! IN FACT...
...IN SOME WAYS IT'S BETTER! YOU GET EXERCISE AND FRESH AIR, AND...AND...
!
SOON...
SIGH AT LEAST THIS HELMET WASN'T A TOTAL WASTE!
END

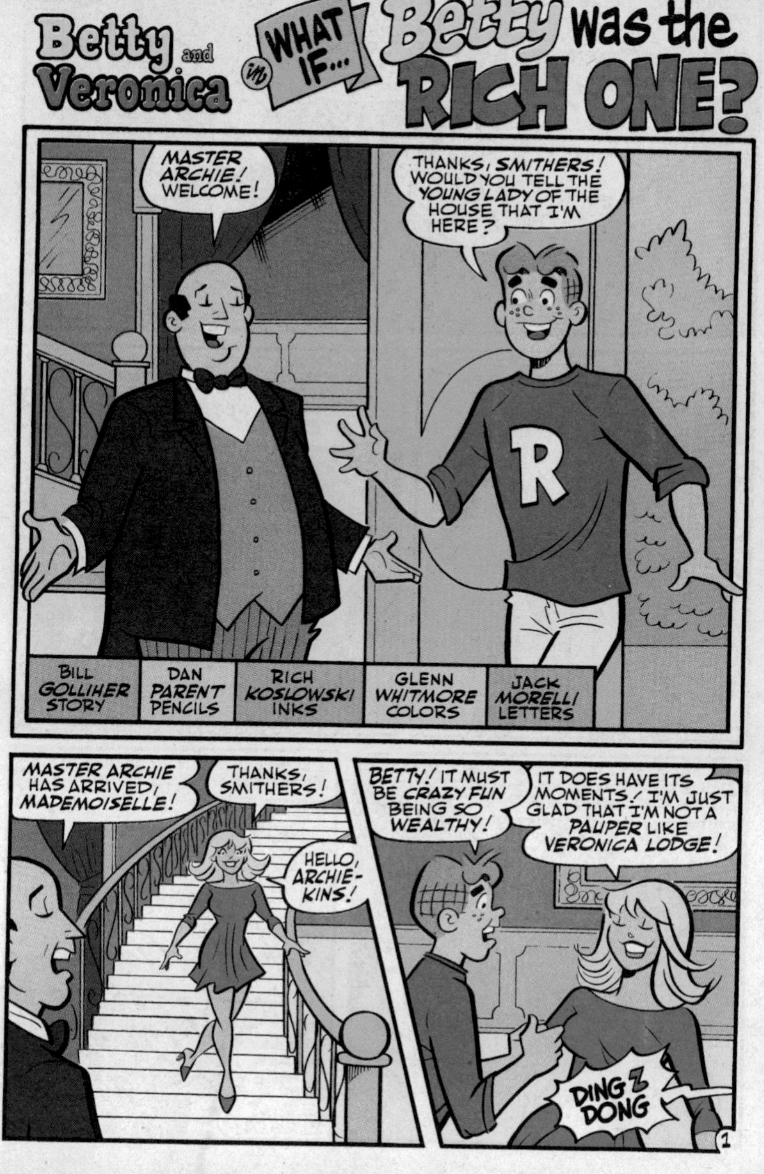
Betty and Veronica in WHAT IF... Betty was the RICH ONE?
MASTER ARCHIE! WELCOME!
THANKS, SMITHERS! WOULD YOU TELL THE YOUNG LADY OF THE HOUSE THAT I'M HERE?
BILL GOLLIHER STORY
DAN PARENT PENCILS
RICH KOSLOWSKI INKS
GLENN WHITMORE COLORS
JACK MORELLI LETTERS
MASTER ARCHIE HAS ARRIVED, MADEMOISELLE!
THANKS, SMITHERS!
HELLO, ARCHIE-KINS!
BETTY! IT MUST BE CRAZY FUN BEING SO WEALTHY!
IT DOES HAVE ITS MOMENTS! I'M JUST GLAD THAT I'M NOT A PAUPER LIKE VERONICA LODGE!
DING DONG
1

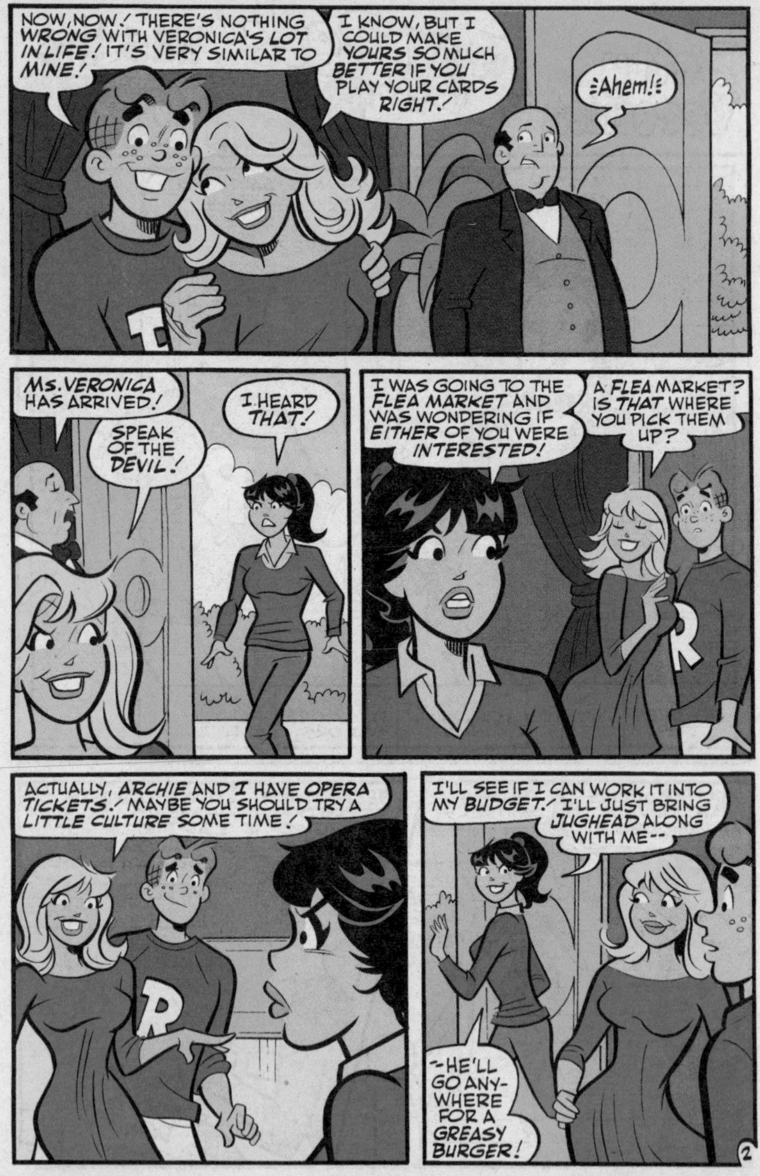
NOW, NOW! THERE'S NOTHING WRONG WITH VERONICA'S LOT IN LIFE! IT'S VERY SIMILAR TO MINE!
I KNOW, BUT I COULD MAKE YOURS SO MUCH BETTER IF YOU PLAY YOUR CARDS RIGHT!
Ahem!
MS. VERONICA HAS ARRIVED!
SPEAK OF THE DEVIL!
I HEARD THAT!
I WAS GOING TO THE FLEA MARKET AND WAS WONDERING IF EITHER OF YOU WERE INTERESTED!
A FLEA MARKET? IS THAT WHERE YOU PICK THEM UP?
ACTUALLY, ARCHIE AND I HAVE OPERA TICKETS! MAYBE YOU SHOULD TRY A LITTLE CULTURE SOME TIME!
I'LL SEE IF I CAN WORK IT INTO MY BUDGET! I'LL JUST BRING JUGHEAD ALONG WITH ME--
--HE'LL GO ANYWHERE FOR A GREASY BURGER!
2

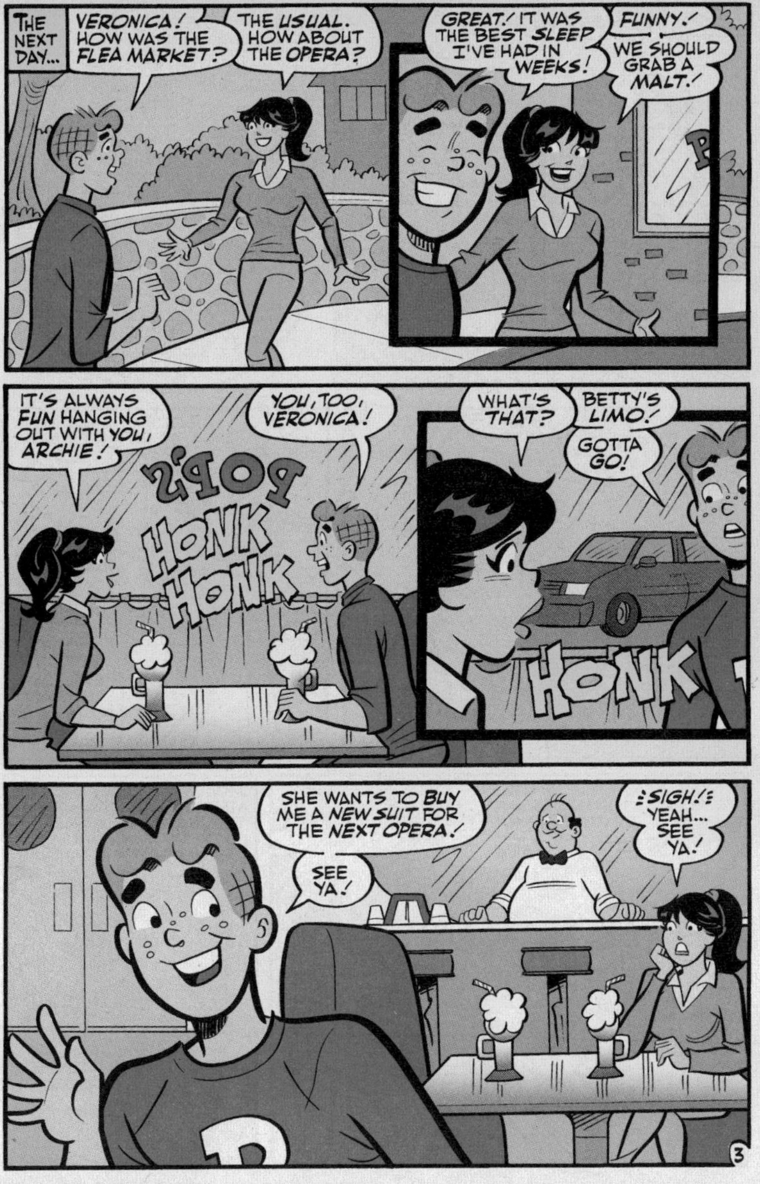
THE NEXT DAY...
VERONICA! HOW WAS THE FLEA MARKET?
THE USUAL. HOW ABOUT THE OPERA?
GREAT! IT WAS THE BEST SLEEP I'VE HAD IN WEEKS!
FUNNY!
WE SHOULD GRAB A MALT!
IT'S ALWAYS FUN HANGING OUT WITH YOU, ARCHIE!
YOU, TOO, VERONICA!
POP'S
HONK HONK
WHAT'S THAT?
BETTY'S LIMO!
GOTTA GO!
HONK
SHE WANTS TO BUY ME A NEW SUIT FOR THE NEXT OPERA!
SEE YA!
SIGH! YEAH... SEE YA!
3

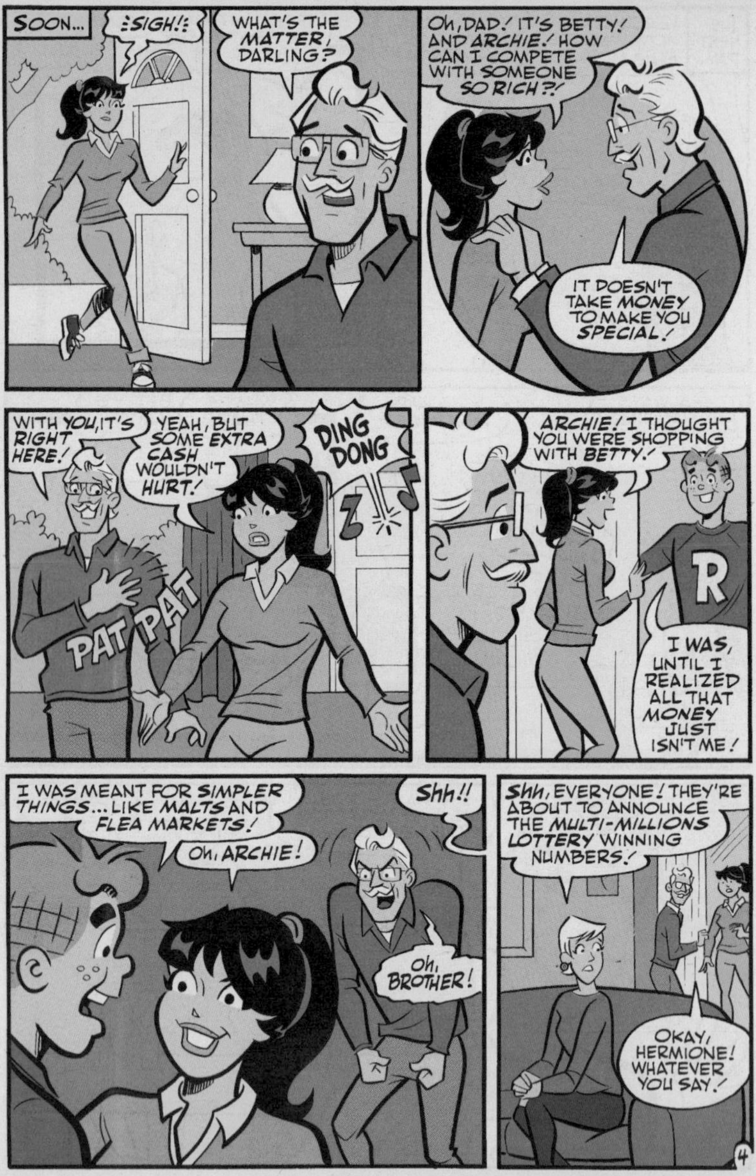
SOON...
:SIGH!:
WHAT'S THE MATTER, DARLING?
OH, DAD! IT'S BETTY! AND ARCHIE! HOW CAN I COMPETE WITH SOMEONE SO RICH?!
IT DOESN'T TAKE MONEY TO MAKE YOU SPECIAL!
WITH YOU, IT'S RIGHT HERE!
PAT PAT
YEAH, BUT SOME EXTRA CASH WOULDN'T HURT!
DING DONG
ARCHIE! I THOUGHT YOU WERE SHOPPING WITH BETTY!
I WAS, UNTIL I REALIZED ALL THAT MONEY JUST ISN'T ME!
I WAS MEANT FOR SIMPLER THINGS... LIKE MALTS AND FLEA MARKETS!
OH, ARCHIE!
SHH!!
OH, BROTHER!
SHH, EVERYONE! THEY'RE ABOUT TO ANNOUNCE THE MULTI-MILLIONS LOTTERY WINNING NUMBERS!
OKAY, HERMIONE! WHATEVER YOU SAY!
4

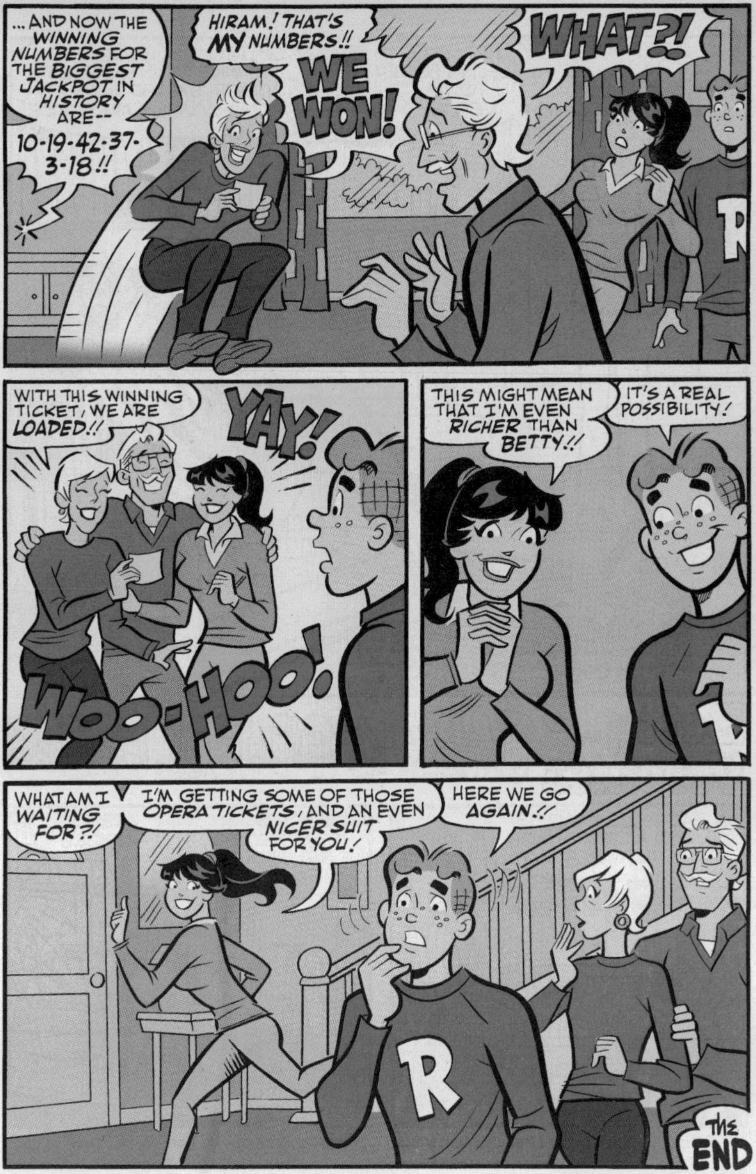

...AND NOW THE WINNING NUMBERS FOR THE BIGGEST JACKPOT IN HISTORY ARE-- 10-19-42-37-3-18!!
HIRAM! THAT'S MY NUMBERS!!
WE WON!
WHAT?!
WITH THIS WINNING TICKET, WE ARE LOADED!!
YAY!
WOO-HOO!
THIS MIGHT MEAN THAT I'M EVEN RICHER THAN BETTY!!
IT'S A REAL POSSIBILITY!
WHAT AM I WAITING FOR?!
I'M GETTING SOME OF THOSE OPERA TICKETS, AND AN EVEN NICER SUIT FOR YOU!
HERE WE GO AGAIN!!
THE END

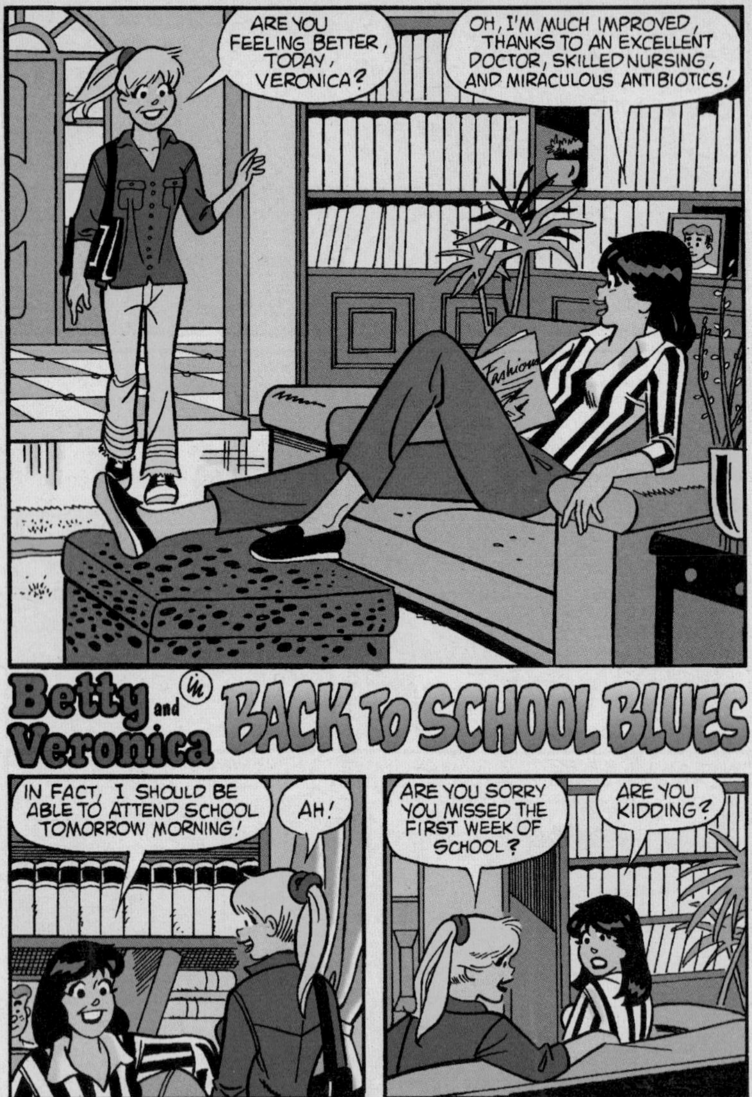
ARE YOU FEELING BETTER, TODAY, VERONICA?
OH, I'M MUCH IMPROVED, THANKS TO AN EXCELLENT DOCTOR, SKILLED NURSING, AND MIRACULOUS ANTIBIOTICS!
Fashions
Betty and Veronica in
BACK TO SCHOOL BLUES
IN FACT, I SHOULD BE ABLE TO ATTEND SCHOOL TOMORROW MORNING!
AH!
ARE YOU SORRY YOU MISSED THE FIRST WEEK OF SCHOOL?
ARE YOU KIDDING?

Script: Kathleen Webb / Pencils: Dan DeCarlo / Inks: Henry Scarpelli / Letters: Bill Yoshida

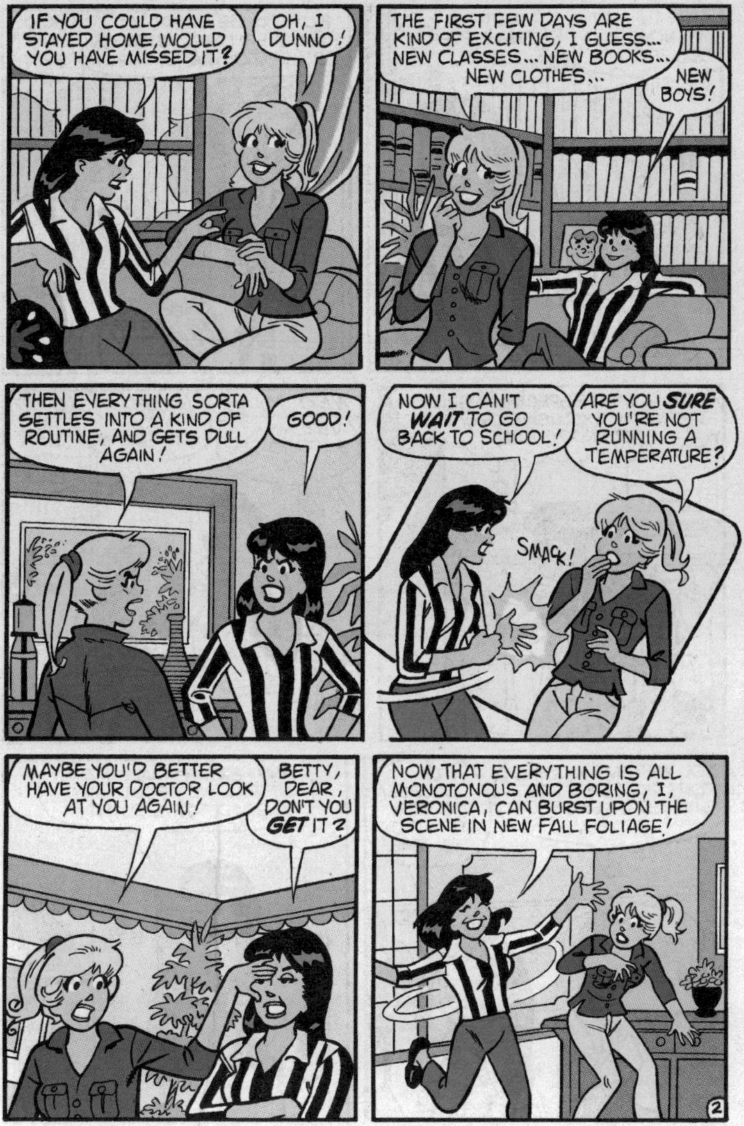
IF YOU COULD HAVE STAYED HOME, WOULD YOU HAVE MISSED IT?
OH, I DUNNO!
THE FIRST FEW DAYS ARE KIND OF EXCITING, I GUESS... NEW CLASSES... NEW BOOKS... NEW CLOTHES...
NEW BOYS!
THEN EVERYTHING SORTA SETTLES INTO A KIND OF ROUTINE, AND GETS DULL AGAIN!
GOOD!
NOW I CAN'T WAIT TO GO BACK TO SCHOOL!
ARE YOU SURE YOU'RE NOT RUNNING A TEMPERATURE?
SMACK!
MAYBE YOU'D BETTER HAVE YOUR DOCTOR LOOK AT YOU AGAIN!
BETTY, DEAR, DON'T YOU GET IT?
NOW THAT EVERYTHING IS ALL MONOTONOUS AND BORING, I, VERONICA, CAN BURST UPON THE SCENE IN NEW FALL FOLIAGE!
2

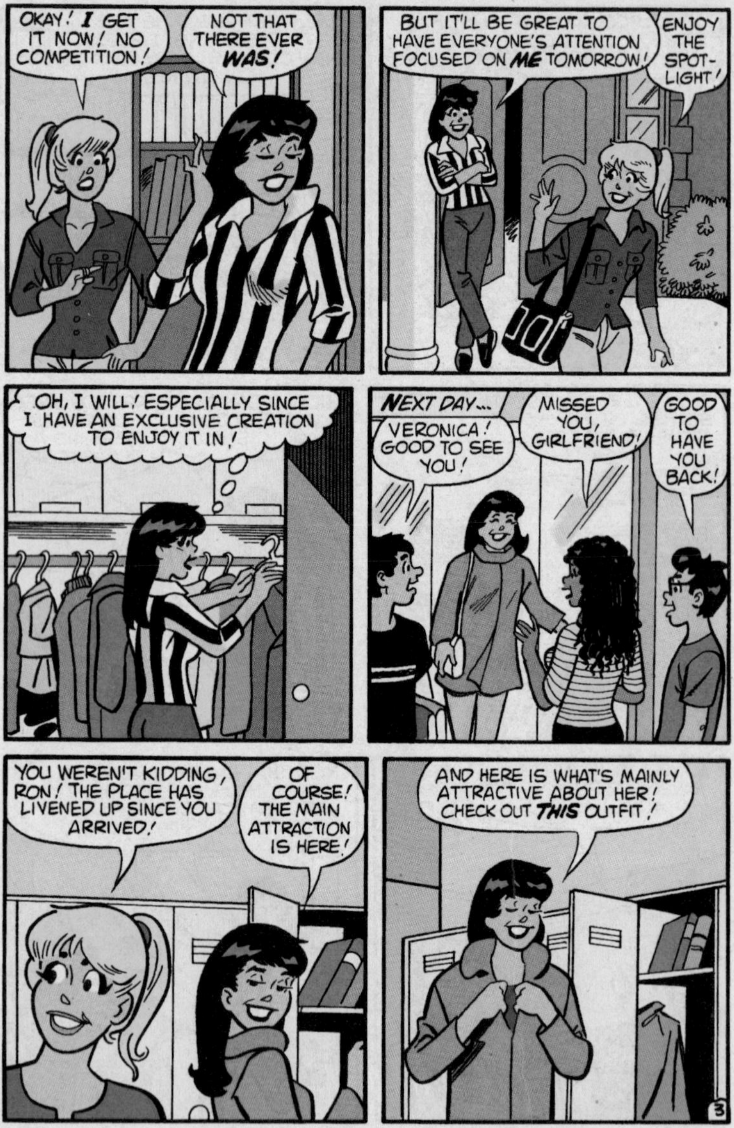

OKAY! I GET IT NOW! NO COMPETITION!
NOT THAT THERE EVER WAS!
BUT IT'LL BE GREAT TO HAVE EVERYONE'S ATTENTION FOCUSED ON ME TOMORROW!
ENJOY THE SPOT-LIGHT!
OH, I WILL! ESPECIALLY SINCE I HAVE AN EXCLUSIVE CREATION TO ENJOY IT IN!
NEXT DAY...
VERONICA! GOOD TO SEE YOU!
MISSED YOU, GIRLFRIEND!
GOOD TO HAVE YOU BACK!
YOU WEREN'T KIDDING, RON! THE PLACE HAS LIVENED UP SINCE YOU ARRIVED!
OF COURSE! THE MAIN ATTRACTION IS HERE!
AND HERE IS WHAT'S MAINLY ATTRACTIVE ABOUT HER! CHECK OUT THIS OUTFIT!
3

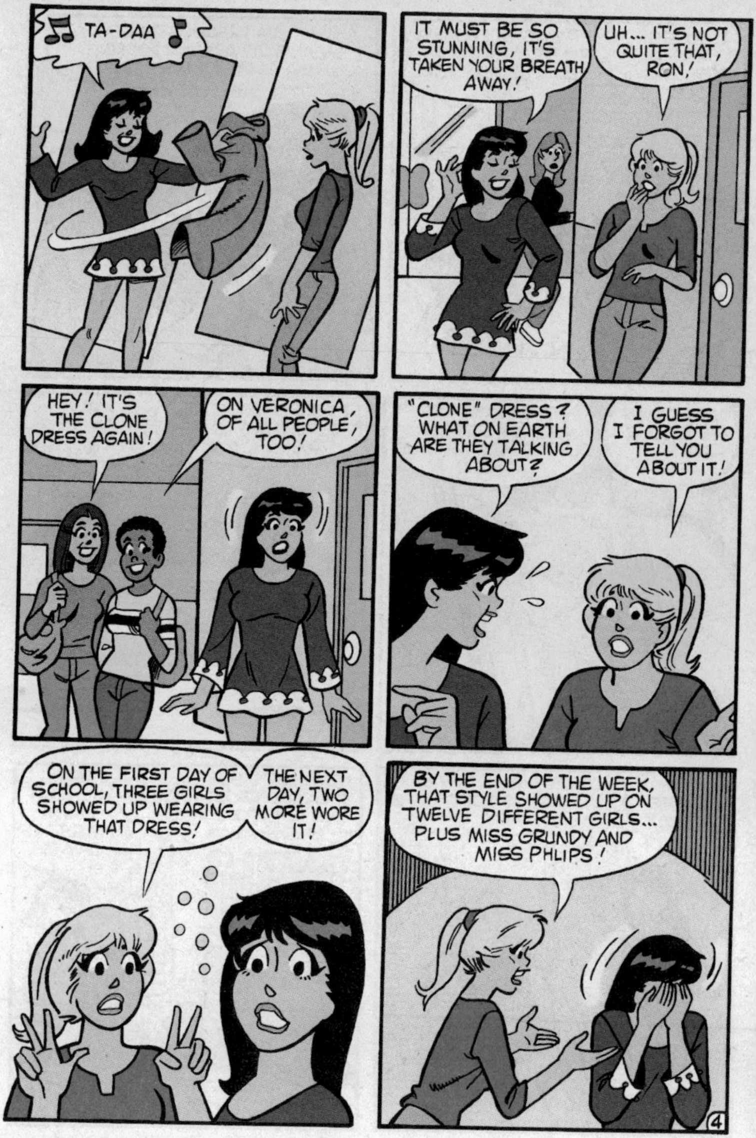
TA-DAA
IT MUST BE SO STUNNING, IT'S TAKEN YOUR BREATH AWAY!
UH... IT'S NOT QUITE THAT, RON!
HEY! IT'S THE CLONE DRESS AGAIN!
ON VERONICA, OF ALL PEOPLE, TOO!
"CLONE" DRESS? WHAT ON EARTH ARE THEY TALKING ABOUT?
I GUESS I FORGOT TO TELL YOU ABOUT IT!
ON THE FIRST DAY OF SCHOOL, THREE GIRLS SHOWED UP WEARING THAT DRESS!
THE NEXT DAY, TWO MORE WORE IT!
BY THE END OF THE WEEK, THAT STYLE SHOWED UP ON TWELVE DIFFERENT GIRLS... PLUS MISS GRUNDY AND MISS PHLIPS!
4

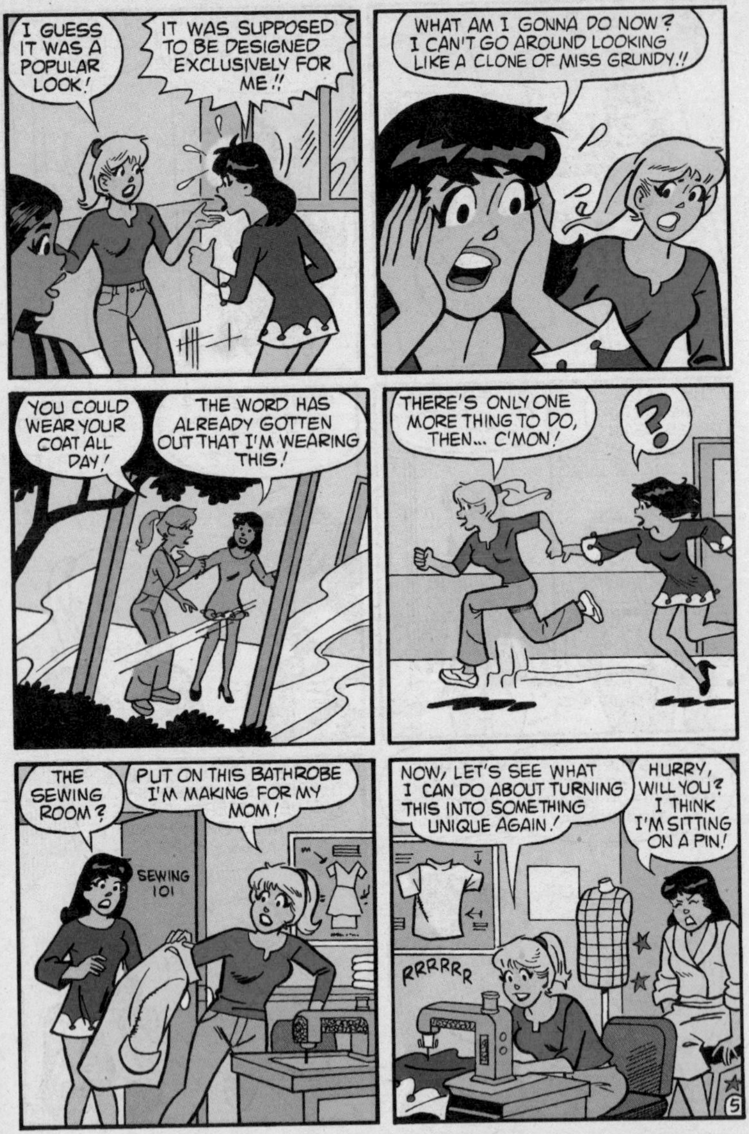
I GUESS IT WAS A POPULAR LOOK!
IT WAS SUPPOSED TO BE DESIGNED EXCLUSIVELY FOR ME!!
WHAT AM I GONNA DO NOW? I CAN'T GO AROUND LOOKING LIKE A CLONE OF MISS GRUNDY!!
YOU COULD WEAR YOUR COAT ALL DAY!
THE WORD HAS ALREADY GOTTEN OUT THAT I'M WEARING THIS!
THERE'S ONLY ONE MORE THING TO DO, THEN... C'MON!
?
THE SEWING ROOM?
PUT ON THIS BATHROBE I'M MAKING FOR MY MOM!
SEWING 101
NOW, LET'S SEE WHAT I CAN DO ABOUT TURNING THIS INTO SOMETHING UNIQUE AGAIN!
HURRY, WILL YOU? I THINK I'M SITTING ON A PIN!
RRRRRR
5

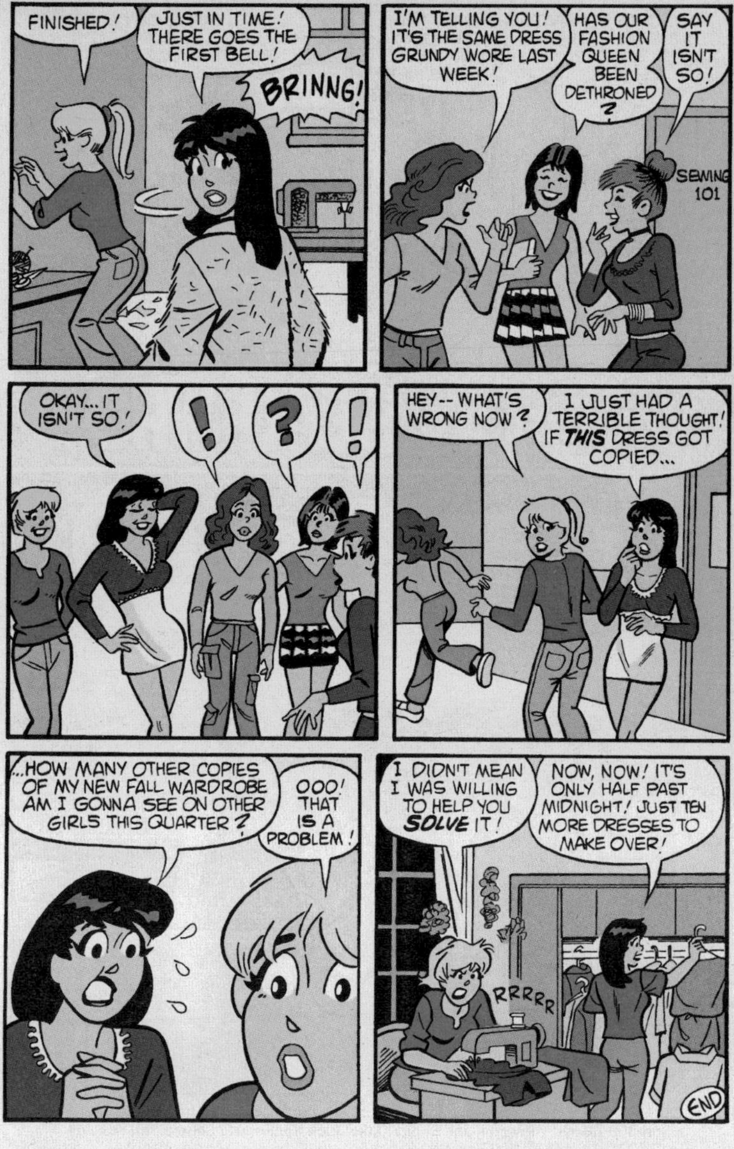
FINISHED!
JUST IN TIME! THERE GOES THE FIRST BELL!
BRINNG!
I'M TELLING YOU! IT'S THE SAME DRESS GRUNDY WORE LAST WEEK!
HAS OUR FASHION QUEEN BEEN DETHRONED?
SAY IT ISN'T SO!
SEWING 101
OKAY... IT ISN'T SO!
!
?
!
HEY-- WHAT'S WRONG NOW?
I JUST HAD A TERRIBLE THOUGHT! IF THIS DRESS GOT COPIED...
...HOW MANY OTHER COPIES OF MY NEW FALL WARDROBE AM I GONNA SEE ON OTHER GIRLS THIS QUARTER?
OOO! THAT IS A PROBLEM!
I DIDN'T MEAN I WAS WILLING TO HELP YOU SOLVE IT!
NOW, NOW! IT'S ONLY HALF PAST MIDNIGHT! JUST TEN MORE DRESSES TO MAKE OVER!
RRRRR
END

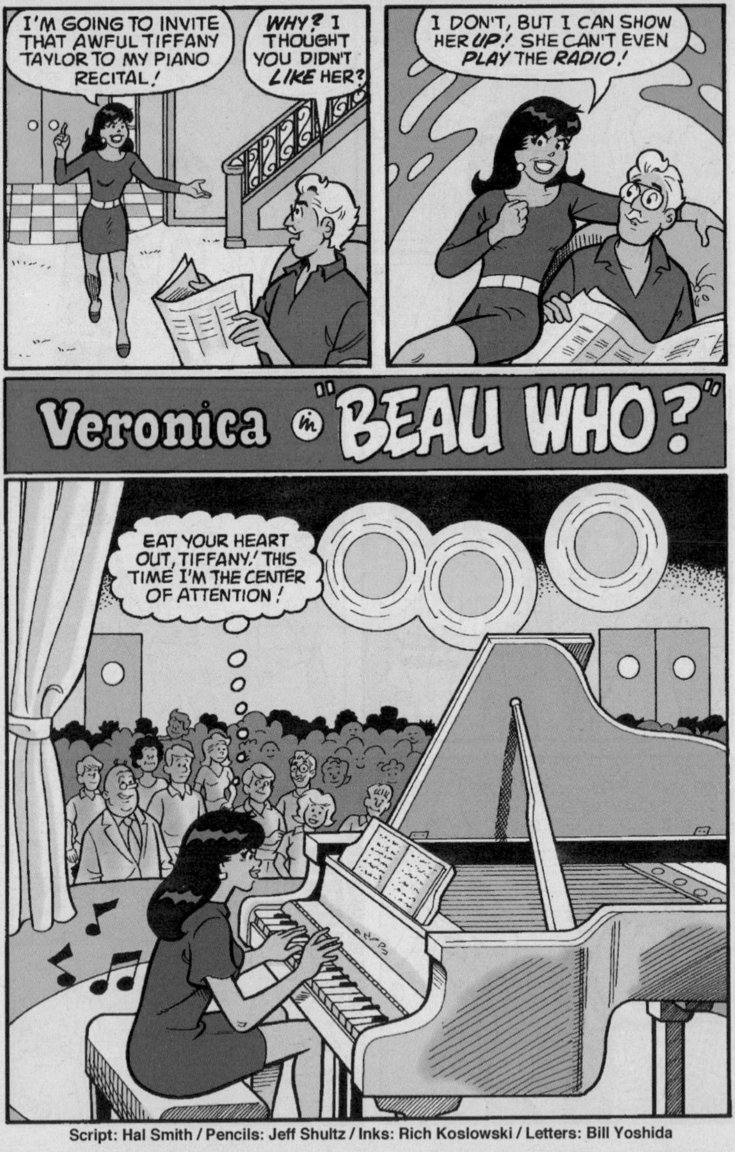
I'M GOING TO INVITE THAT AWFUL TIFFANY TAYLOR TO MY PIANO RECITAL!
WHY? I THOUGHT YOU DIDN'T LIKE HER?
I DON'T, BUT I CAN SHOW HER UP! SHE CAN'T EVEN PLAY THE RADIO!
Veronica in "BEAU WHO?"
EAT YOUR HEART OUT, TIFFANY! THIS TIME I'M THE CENTER OF ATTENTION!

Script: Hal Smith / Pencils: Jeff Shultz / Inks: Rich Koslowski / Letters: Bill Yoshida

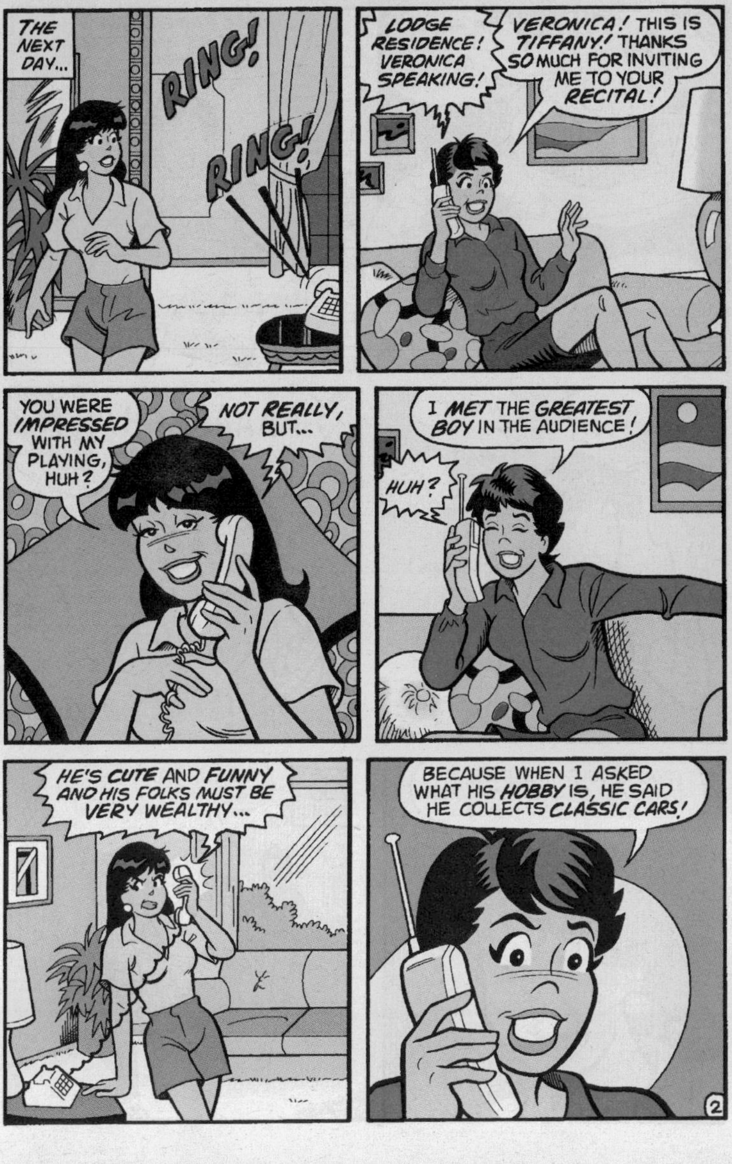
THE NEXT DAY...
RING!
RING!
LODGE RESIDENCE! VERONICA SPEAKING!
VERONICA! THIS IS TIFFANY! THANKS SO MUCH FOR INVITING ME TO YOUR RECITAL!
YOU WERE IMPRESSED WITH MY PLAYING, HUH?
NOT REALLY, BUT...
I MET THE GREATEST BOY IN THE AUDIENCE!
HUH?
HE'S CUTE AND FUNNY AND HIS FOLKS MUST BE VERY WEALTHY...
BECAUSE WHEN I ASKED WHAT HIS HOBBY IS, HE SAID HE COLLECTS CLASSIC CARS!
2

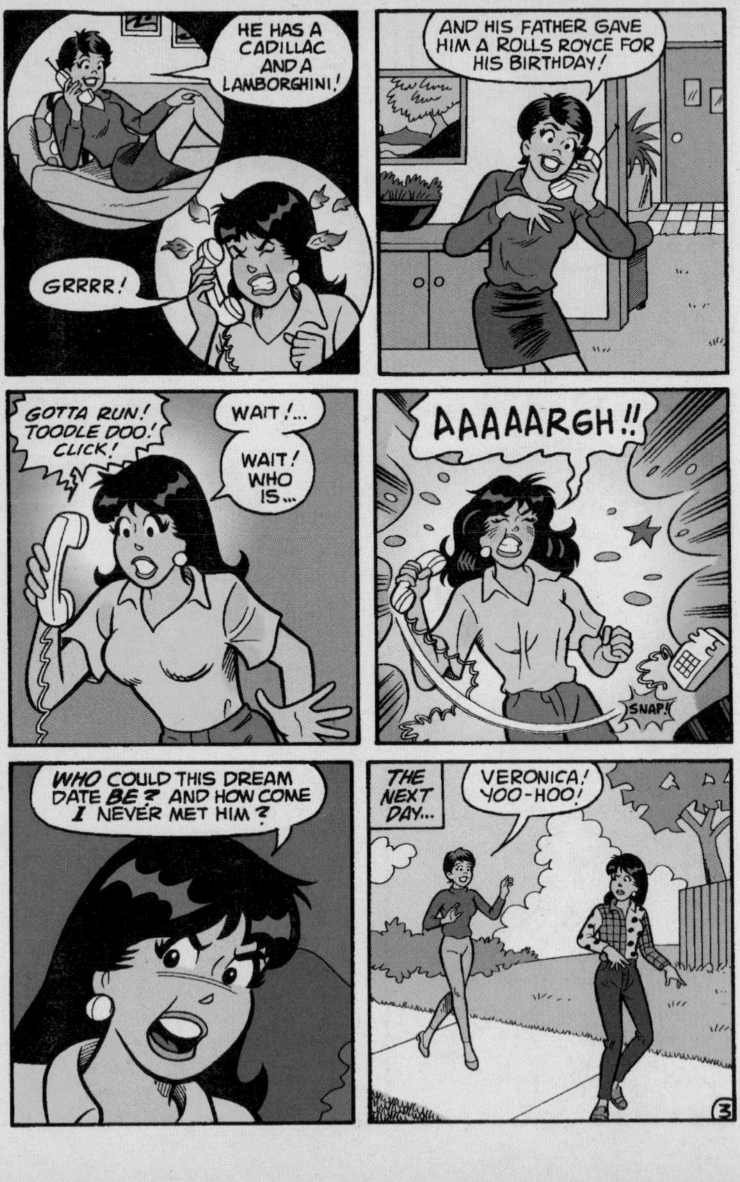
HE HAS A CADILLAC AND A LAMBORGHINI!
GRRRR!
AND HIS FATHER GAVE HIM A ROLLS ROYCE FOR HIS BIRTHDAY!
GOTTA RUN! TOODLE DOO! CLICK!
WAIT!...
WAIT! WHO IS...
AAAAARGH!!
SNAP!
WHO COULD THIS DREAM DATE BE? AND HOW COME I NEVER MET HIM?
THE NEXT DAY...
VERONICA! YOO-HOO!
3

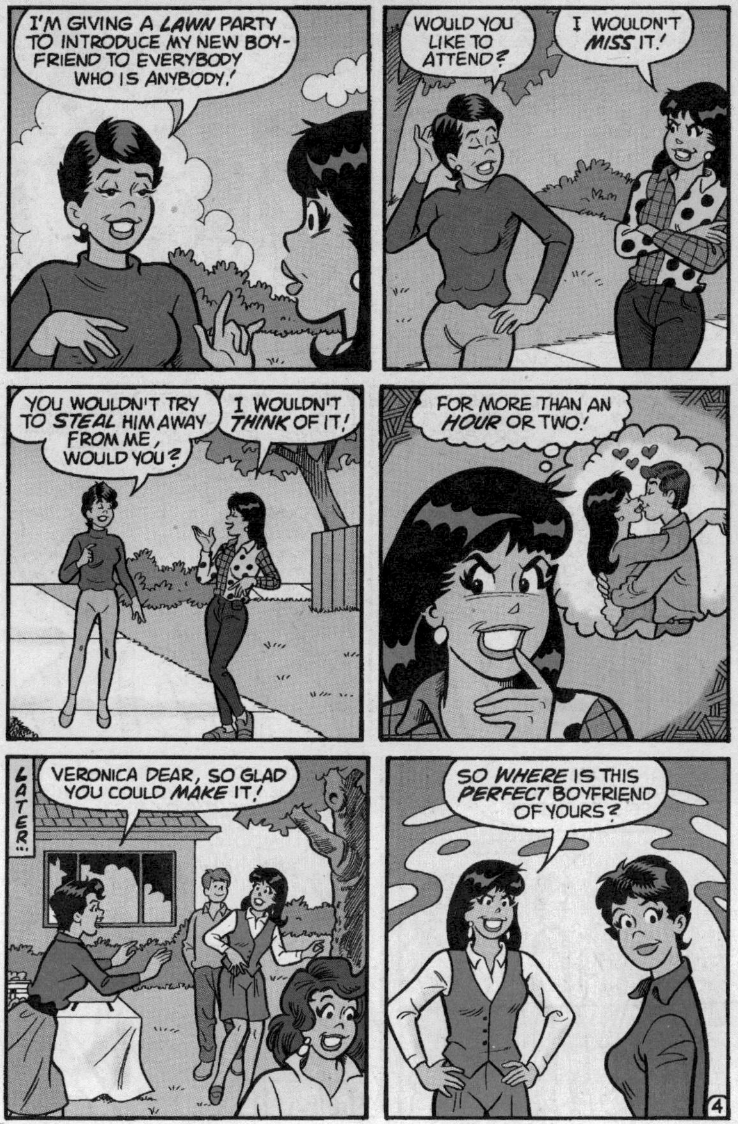

I'M GIVING A LAWN PARTY TO INTRODUCE MY NEW BOY-FRIEND TO EVERYBODY WHO IS ANYBODY!
WOULD YOU LIKE TO ATTEND?
I WOULDN'T MISS IT!
YOU WOULDN'T TRY TO STEAL HIM AWAY FROM ME, WOULD YOU?
I WOULDN'T THINK OF IT!
FOR MORE THAN AN HOUR OR TWO!
LATER...
VERONICA DEAR, SO GLAD YOU COULD MAKE IT!
SO WHERE IS THIS PERFECT BOYFRIEND OF YOURS?
4

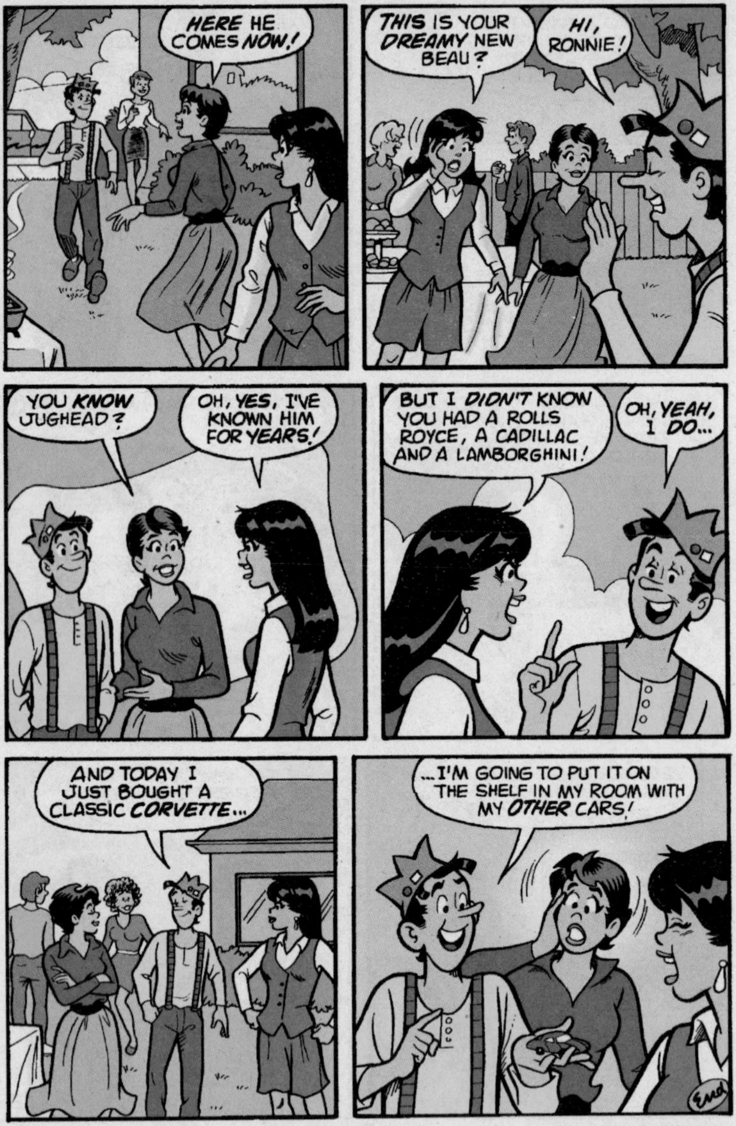
HERE HE COMES NOW!
THIS IS YOUR DREAMY NEW BEAU?
HI, RONNIE!
YOU KNOW JUGHEAD?
OH, YES, I'VE KNOWN HIM FOR YEARS!
BUT I DIDN'T KNOW YOU HAD A ROLLS ROYCE, A CADILLAC AND A LAMBORGHINI!
OH, YEAH, I DO...
AND TODAY I JUST BOUGHT A CLASSIC CORVETTE...
...I'M GOING TO PUT IT ON THE SHELF IN MY ROOM WITH MY OTHER CARS!
End

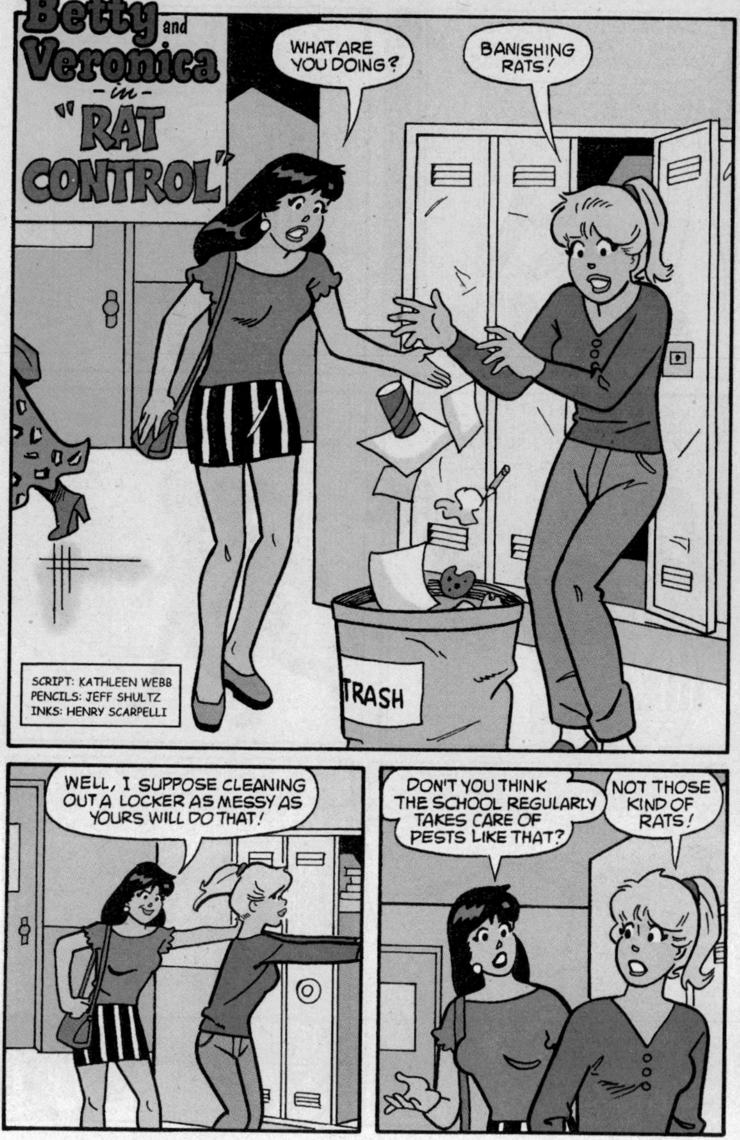
Betty and Veronica
-in-
"RAT CONTROL"
WHAT ARE YOU DOING?
BANISHING RATS!
SCRIPT: KATHLEEN WEBB
PENCILS: JEFF SHULTZ
INKS: HENRY SCARPELLI
TRASH
WELL, I SUPPOSE CLEANING OUT A LOCKER AS MESSY AS YOURS WILL DO THAT!
DON'T YOU THINK THE SCHOOL REGULARLY TAKES CARE OF PESTS LIKE THAT?
NOT THOSE KIND OF RATS!

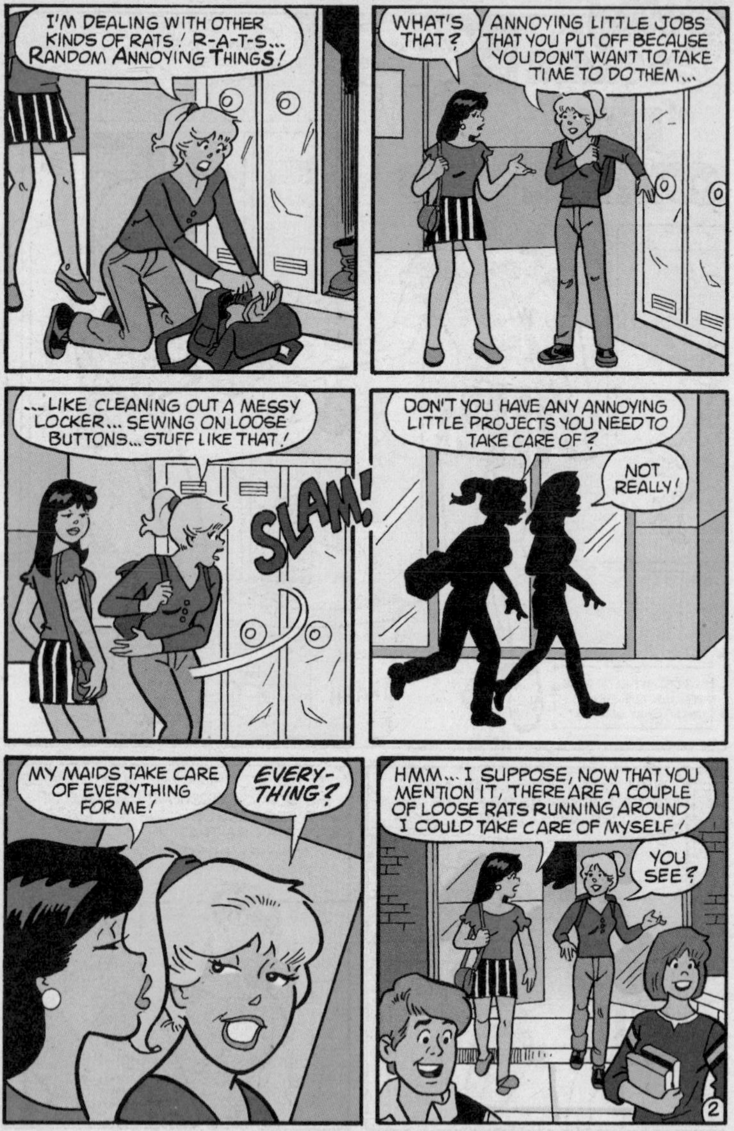

I'M DEALING WITH OTHER KINDS OF RATS! R-A-T-S... RANDOM ANNOYING THINGS!
WHAT'S THAT?
ANNOYING LITTLE JOBS THAT YOU PUT OFF BECAUSE YOU DON'T WANT TO TAKE TIME TO DO THEM...
...LIKE CLEANING OUT A MESSY LOCKER... SEWING ON LOOSE BUTTONS... STUFF LIKE THAT!
SLAM!
DON'T YOU HAVE ANY ANNOYING LITTLE PROJECTS YOU NEED TO TAKE CARE OF?
NOT REALLY!
MY MAIDS TAKE CARE OF EVERYTHING FOR ME!
EVERY-THING?
HMM... I SUPPOSE, NOW THAT YOU MENTION IT, THERE ARE A COUPLE OF LOOSE RATS RUNNING AROUND I COULD TAKE CARE OF MYSELF!
YOU SEE?
2

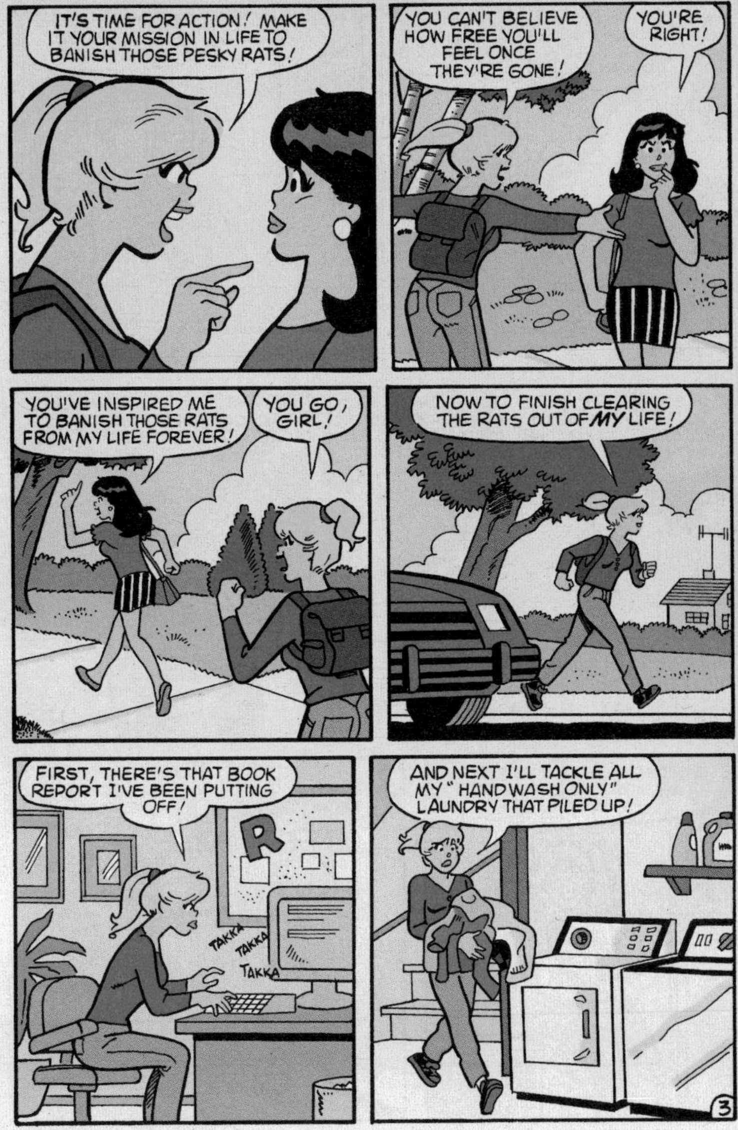
IT'S TIME FOR ACTION! MAKE IT YOUR MISSION IN LIFE TO BANISH THOSE PESKY RATS!
YOU CAN'T BELIEVE HOW FREE YOU'LL FEEL ONCE THEY'RE GONE!
YOU'RE RIGHT!
YOU'VE INSPIRED ME TO BANISH THOSE RATS FROM MY LIFE FOREVER!
YOU GO, GIRL!
NOW TO FINISH CLEARING THE RATS OUT OF MY LIFE!
FIRST, THERE'S THAT BOOK REPORT I'VE BEEN PUTTING OFF!
R
TAKKA
TAKKA
TAKKA
AND NEXT I'LL TACKLE ALL MY "HANDWASH ONLY" LAUNDRY THAT PILED UP!
3

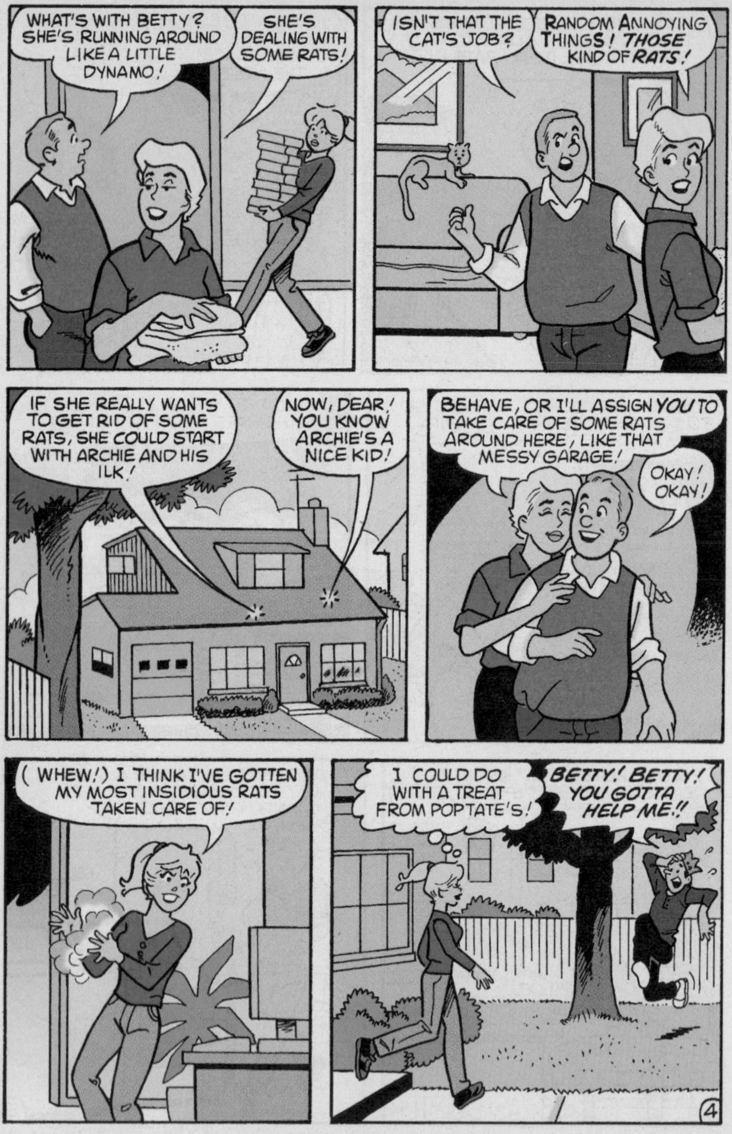
WHAT'S WITH BETTY? SHE'S RUNNING AROUND LIKE A LITTLE DYNAMO!
SHE'S DEALING WITH SOME RATS!
ISN'T THAT THE CAT'S JOB?
RANDOM ANNOYING THINGS! THOSE KIND OF RATS!
IF SHE REALLY WANTS TO GET RID OF SOME RATS, SHE COULD START WITH ARCHIE AND HIS ILK!
NOW, DEAR! YOU KNOW ARCHIE'S A NICE KID!
BEHAVE, OR I'LL ASSIGN YOU TO TAKE CARE OF SOME RATS AROUND HERE, LIKE THAT MESSY GARAGE!
OKAY! OKAY!
(WHEW!) I THINK I'VE GOTTEN MY MOST INSIDIOUS RATS TAKEN CARE OF!
I COULD DO WITH A TREAT FROM POPTATE'S!
BETTY! BETTY! YOU GOTTA HELP ME!!
4

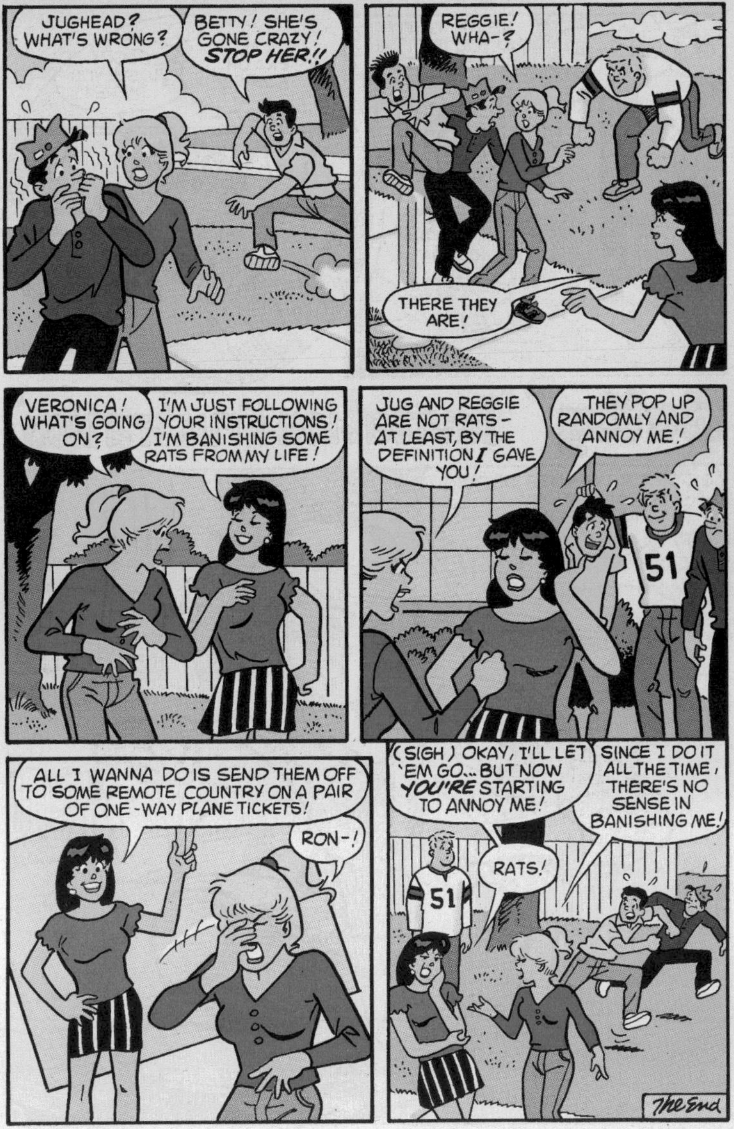
JUGHEAD? WHAT'S WRONG?
BETTY! SHE'S GONE CRAZY! STOP HER!!
REGGIE! WHA-?
THERE THEY ARE!
VERONICA! WHAT'S GOING ON?
I'M JUST FOLLOWING YOUR INSTRUCTIONS! I'M BANISHING SOME RATS FROM MY LIFE!
JUG AND REGGIE ARE NOT RATS - AT LEAST, BY THE DEFINITION I GAVE YOU!
THEY POP UP RANDOMLY AND ANNOY ME!
ALL I WANNA DO IS SEND THEM OFF TO SOME REMOTE COUNTRY ON A PAIR OF ONE-WAY PLANE TICKETS!
RON-!
(SIGH) OKAY, I'LL LET 'EM GO... BUT NOW YOU'RE STARTING TO ANNOY ME!
SINCE I DO IT ALL THE TIME, THERE'S NO SENSE IN BANISHING ME!
RATS!
The End

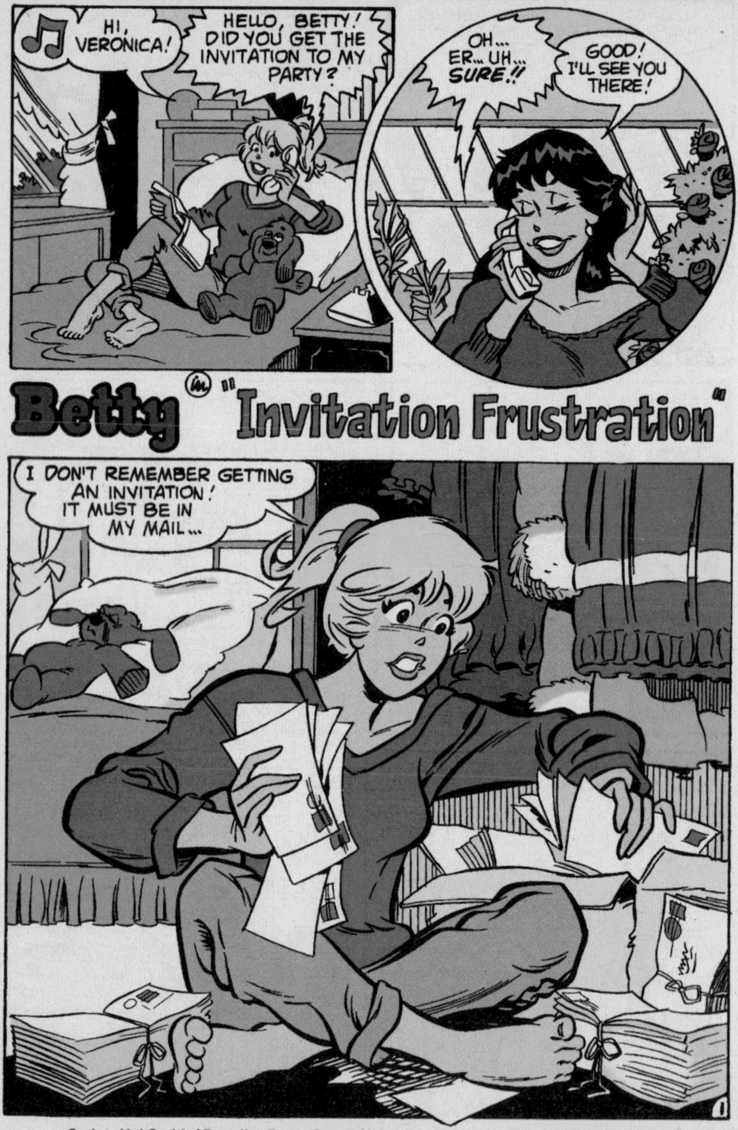
HI, VERONICA!
HELLO, BETTY! DID YOU GET THE INVITATION TO MY PARTY?
OH... ER... UH... SURE!!
GOOD! I'LL SEE YOU THERE!
Betty in "Invitation Frustration"
I DON'T REMEMBER GETTING AN INVITATION! IT MUST BE IN MY MAIL...
1

Script: Hal Smith / Pencils: Doug Crane / Inks: Pat Kennedy / Letters: Bill Yoshida

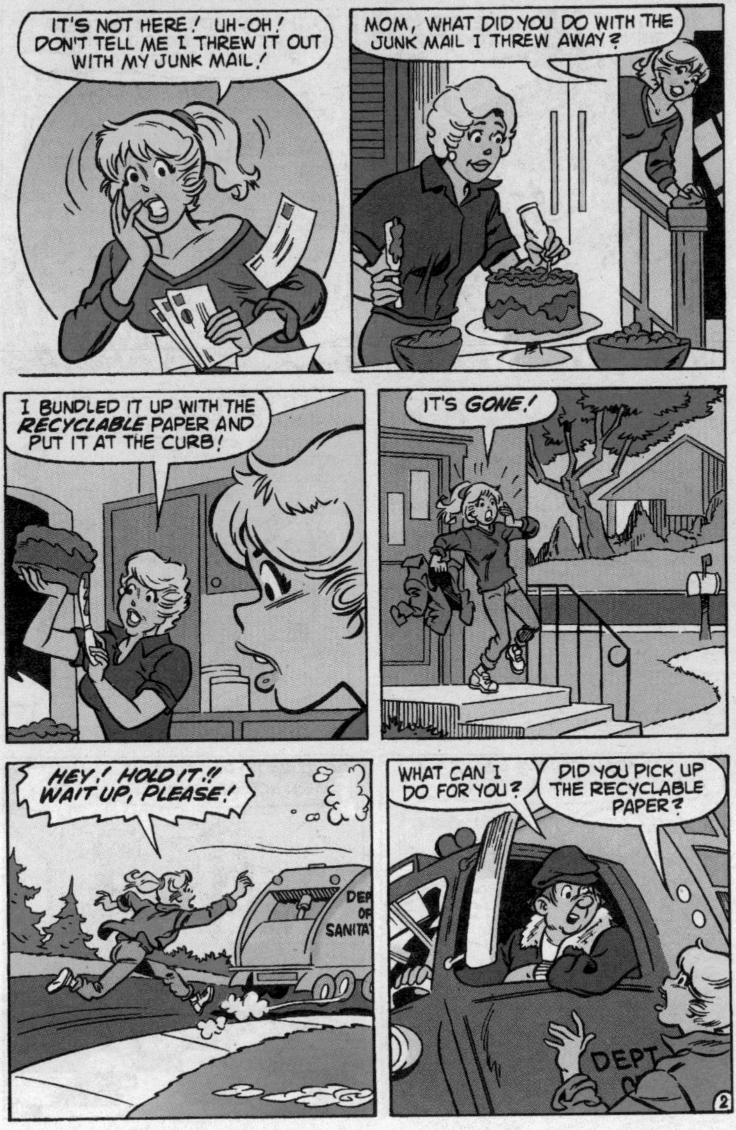
IT'S NOT HERE! UH-OH! DON'T TELL ME I THREW IT OUT WITH MY JUNK MAIL!
MOM, WHAT DID YOU DO WITH THE JUNK MAIL I THREW AWAY?
I BUNDLED IT UP WITH THE RECYCLABLE PAPER AND PUT IT AT THE CURB!
IT'S GONE!
HEY! HOLD IT!! WAIT UP, PLEASE!
DEPT OF SANITA
WHAT CAN I DO FOR YOU?
DID YOU PICK UP THE RECYCLABLE PAPER?
DEPT
2

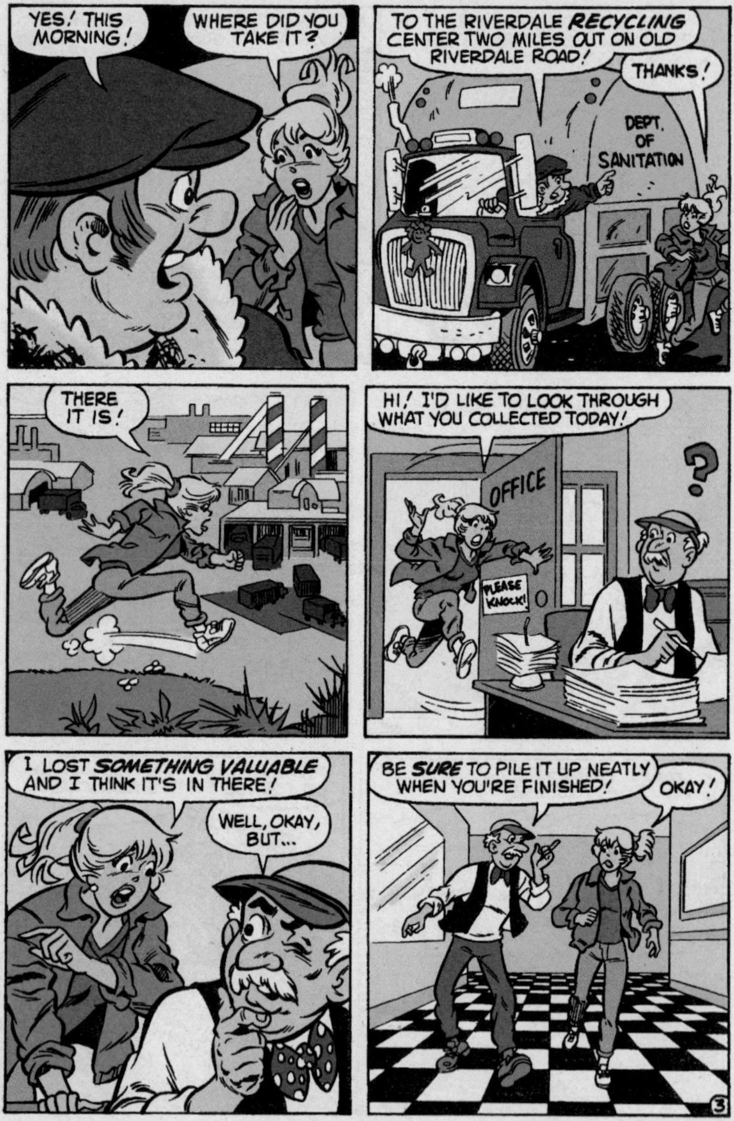
YES! THIS MORNING!
WHERE DID YOU TAKE IT?
TO THE RIVERDALE RECYCLING CENTER TWO MILES OUT ON OLD RIVERDALE ROAD!
THANKS!
DEPT. OF SANITATION
THERE IT IS!
HI! I'D LIKE TO LOOK THROUGH WHAT YOU COLLECTED TODAY!
OFFICE
PLEASE KNOCK!
?
I LOST SOMETHING VALUABLE AND I THINK IT'S IN THERE!
WELL, OKAY, BUT...
BE SURE TO PILE IT UP NEATLY WHEN YOU'RE FINISHED!
OKAY!

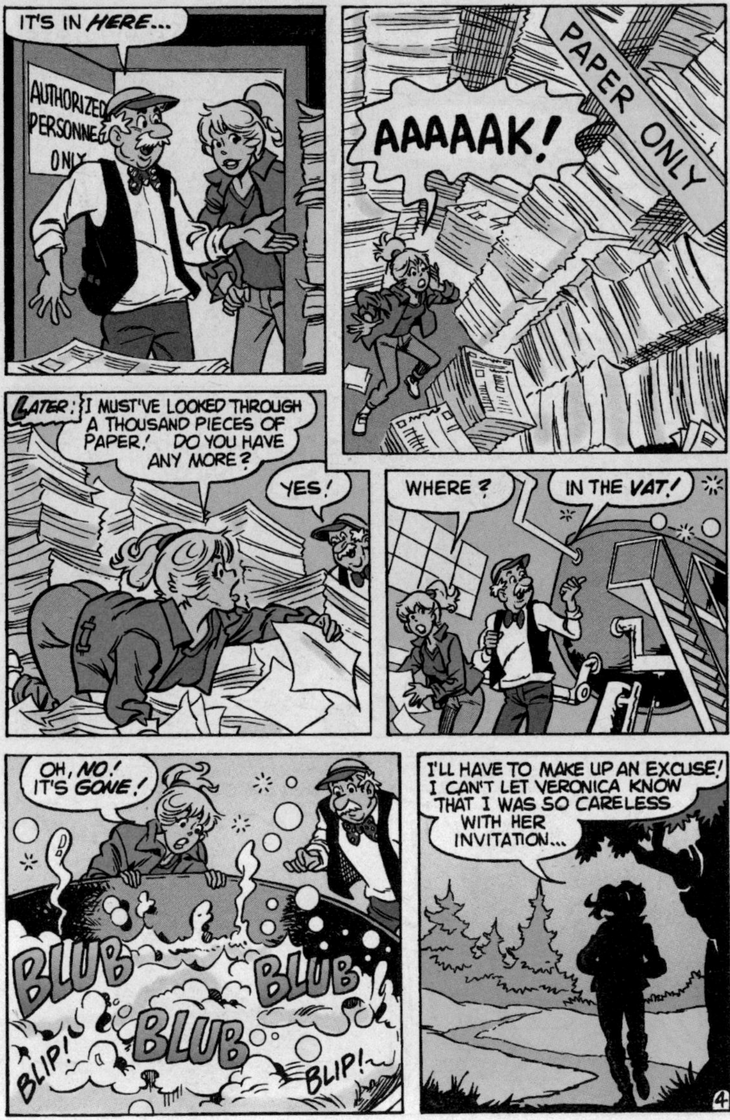
IT'S IN *HERE*...
AUTHORIZED PERSONNEL ONLY
PAPER ONLY
AAAAK!
LATER:
I MUST'VE LOOKED THROUGH A THOUSAND PIECES OF PAPER! DO YOU HAVE ANY MORE?
YES!
WHERE?
IN THE *VAT*!
OH, *NO*! IT'S *GONE*!
BLUB
BLUB
BLUB
BLIP!
BLIP!
I'LL HAVE TO MAKE UP AN EXCUSE! I CAN'T LET VERONICA KNOW THAT I WAS SO CARELESS WITH HER INVITATION...
4

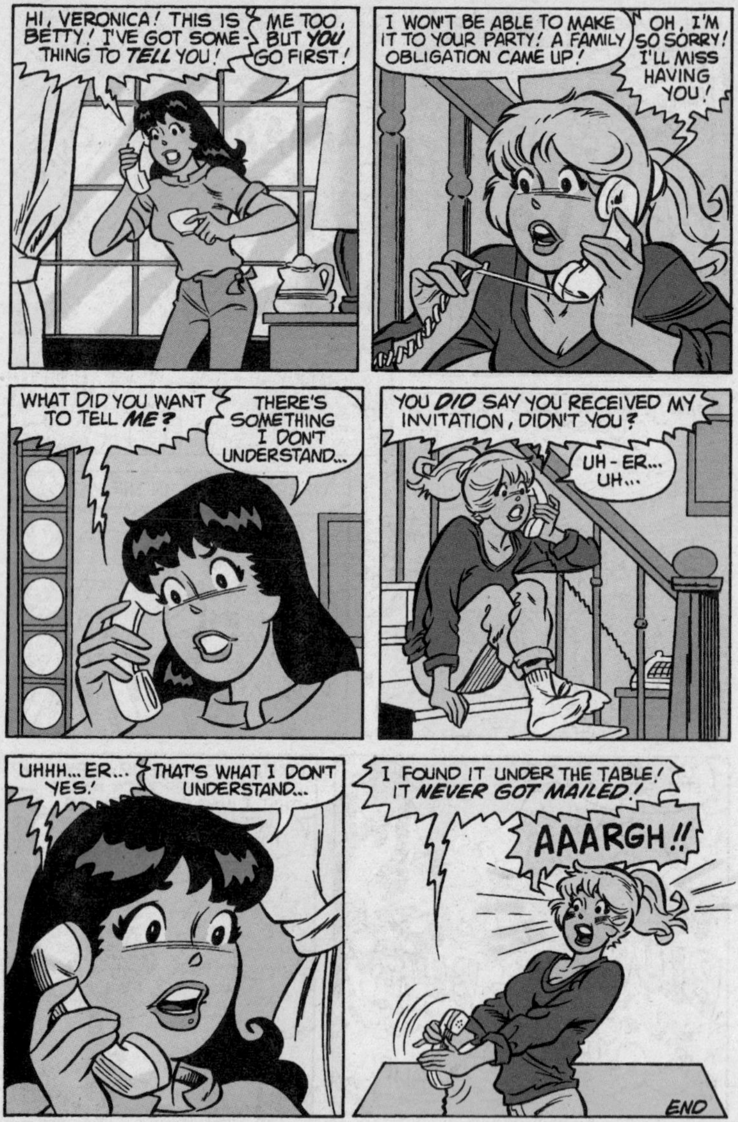
HI, VERONICA! THIS IS BETTY! I'VE GOT SOMETHING TO TELL YOU!
ME TOO, BUT YOU GO FIRST!
I WON'T BE ABLE TO MAKE IT TO YOUR PARTY! A FAMILY OBLIGATION CAME UP!
OH, I'M SO SORRY! I'LL MISS HAVING YOU!
WHAT DID YOU WANT TO TELL ME?
THERE'S SOMETHING I DON'T UNDERSTAND...
YOU DID SAY YOU RECEIVED MY INVITATION, DIDN'T YOU?
UH-ER... UH...
UHHH... ER... YES!
THAT'S WHAT I DON'T UNDERSTAND...
I FOUND IT UNDER THE TABLE! IT NEVER GOT MAILED!
AAARGH!!
END

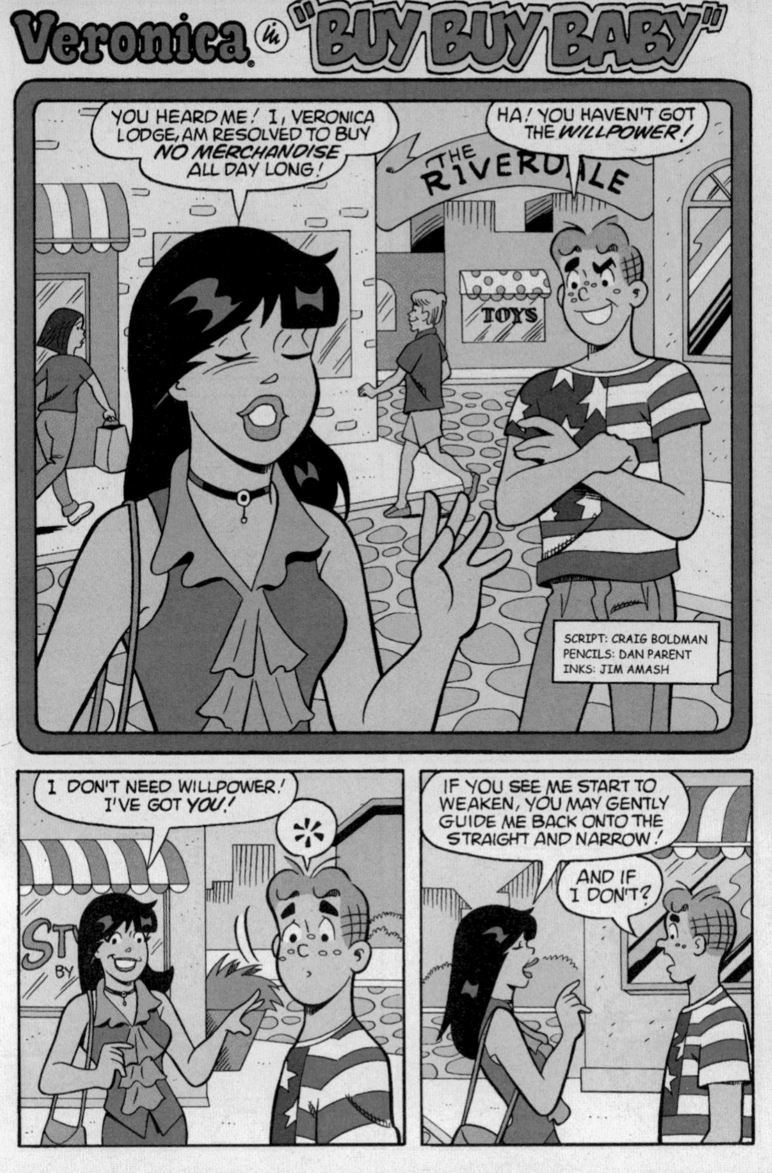

Veronica in "BUY BUY BABY"
YOU HEARD ME! I, VERONICA LODGE, AM RESOLVED TO BUY NO MERCHANDISE ALL DAY LONG!
HA! YOU HAVEN'T GOT THE WILLPOWER!
THE RIVERDALE
TOYS
SCRIPT: CRAIG BOLDMAN
PENCILS: DAN PARENT
INKS: JIM AMASH
I DON'T NEED WILLPOWER! I'VE GOT YOU!
IF YOU SEE ME START TO WEAKEN, YOU MAY GENTLY GUIDE ME BACK ONTO THE STRAIGHT AND NARROW!
AND IF I DON'T?

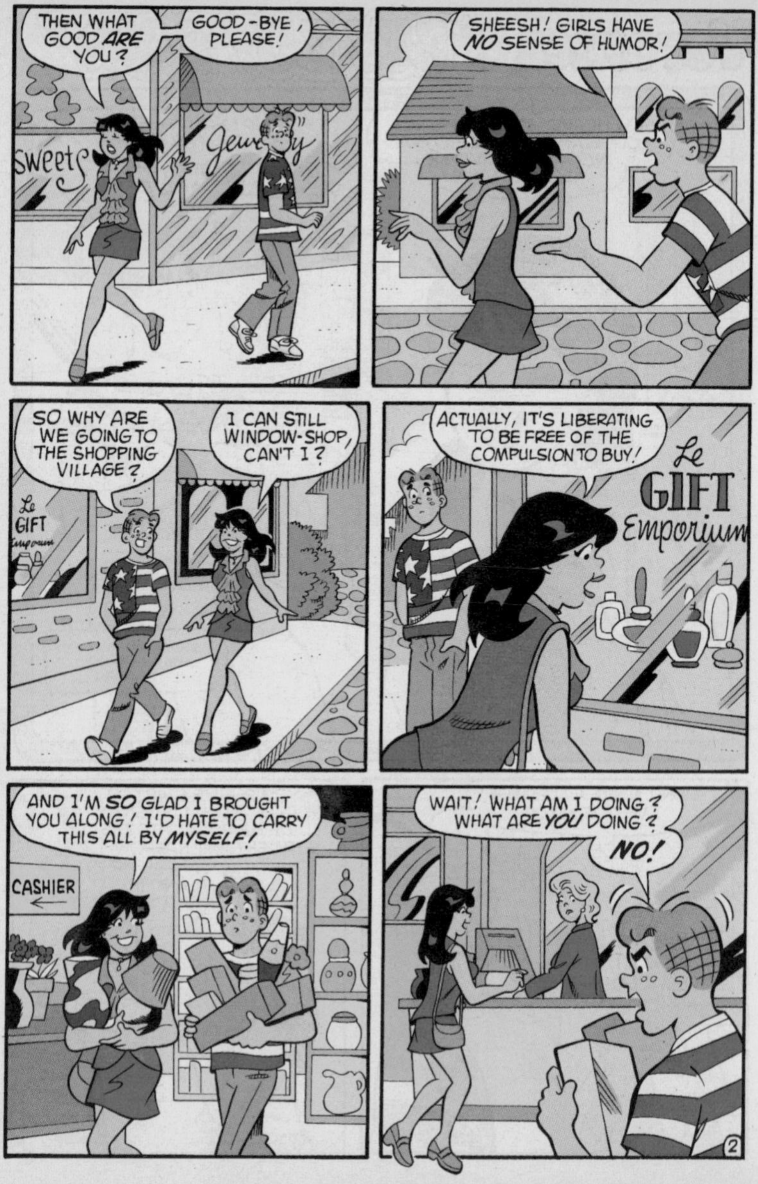
THEN WHAT GOOD ARE YOU?
GOOD-BYE, PLEASE!
Sweets
Jewelry
SHEESH! GIRLS HAVE NO SENSE OF HUMOR!
SO WHY ARE WE GOING TO THE SHOPPING VILLAGE?
I CAN STILL WINDOW-SHOP, CAN'T I?
Le GIFT
ACTUALLY, IT'S LIBERATING TO BE FREE OF THE COMPULSION TO BUY!
Le GIFT Emporium
AND I'M SO GLAD I BROUGHT YOU ALONG! I'D HATE TO CARRY THIS ALL BY MYSELF!
CASHIER
WAIT! WHAT AM I DOING? WHAT ARE YOU DOING?
NO!

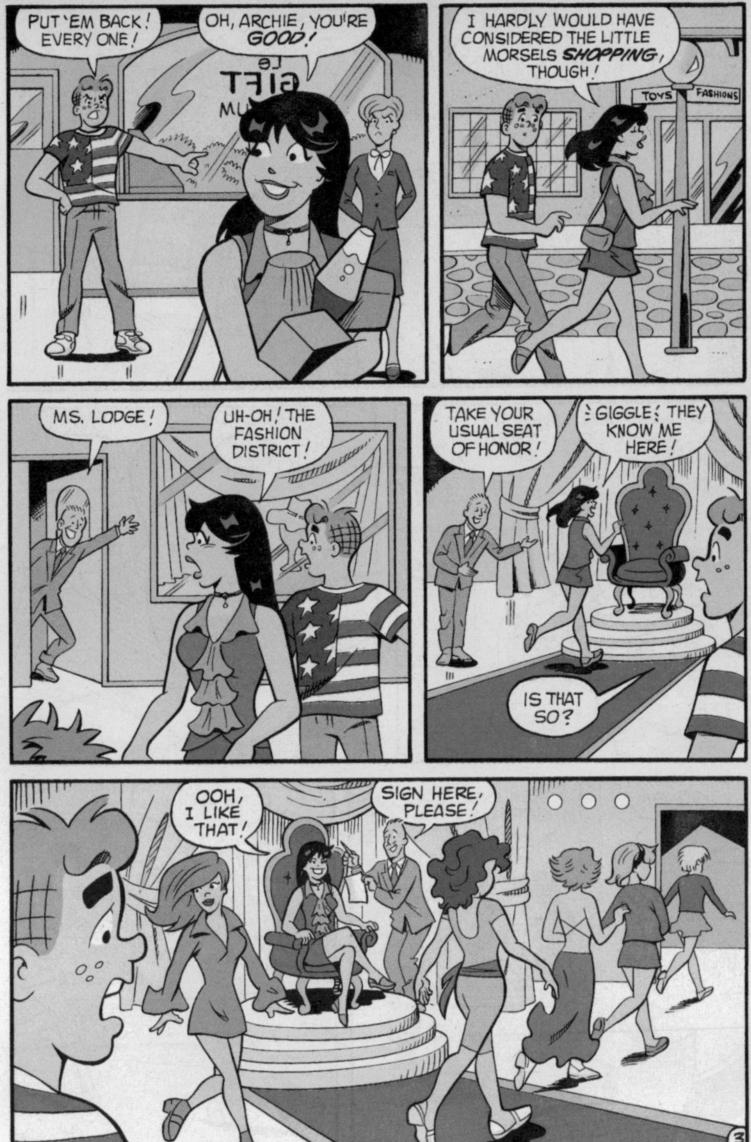

PUT 'EM BACK! EVERY ONE!
OH, ARCHIE, YOU'RE GOOD!
I HARDLY WOULD HAVE CONSIDERED THE LITTLE MORSELS SHOPPING, THOUGH!
TOYS
FASHIONS
MS. LODGE!
UH-OH! THE FASHION DISTRICT!
TAKE YOUR USUAL SEAT OF HONOR!
GIGGLE! THEY KNOW ME HERE!
IS THAT SO?
OOH, I LIKE THAT!
SIGN HERE, PLEASE!

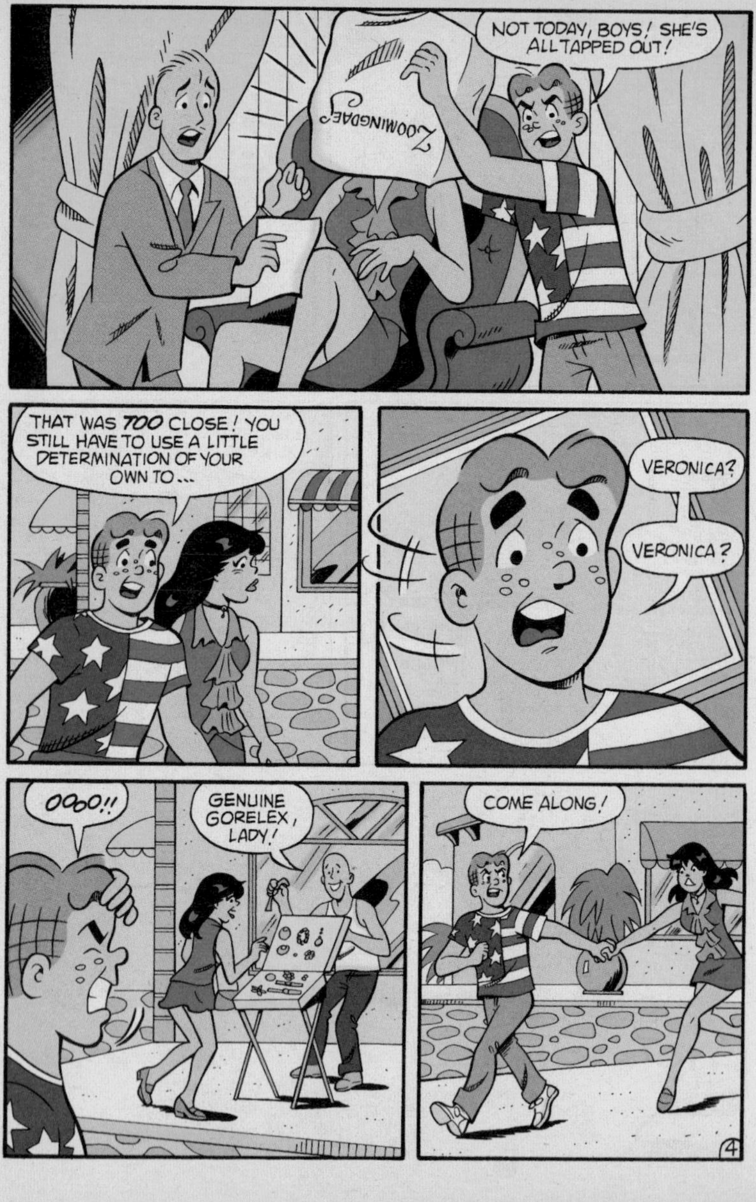
NOT TODAY, BOYS! SHE'S ALL TAPPED OUT!
THAT WAS TOO CLOSE! YOU STILL HAVE TO USE A LITTLE DETERMINATION OF YOUR OWN TO...
VERONICA?
VERONICA?
OOOO!!
GENUINE GORELEX, LADY!
COME ALONG!

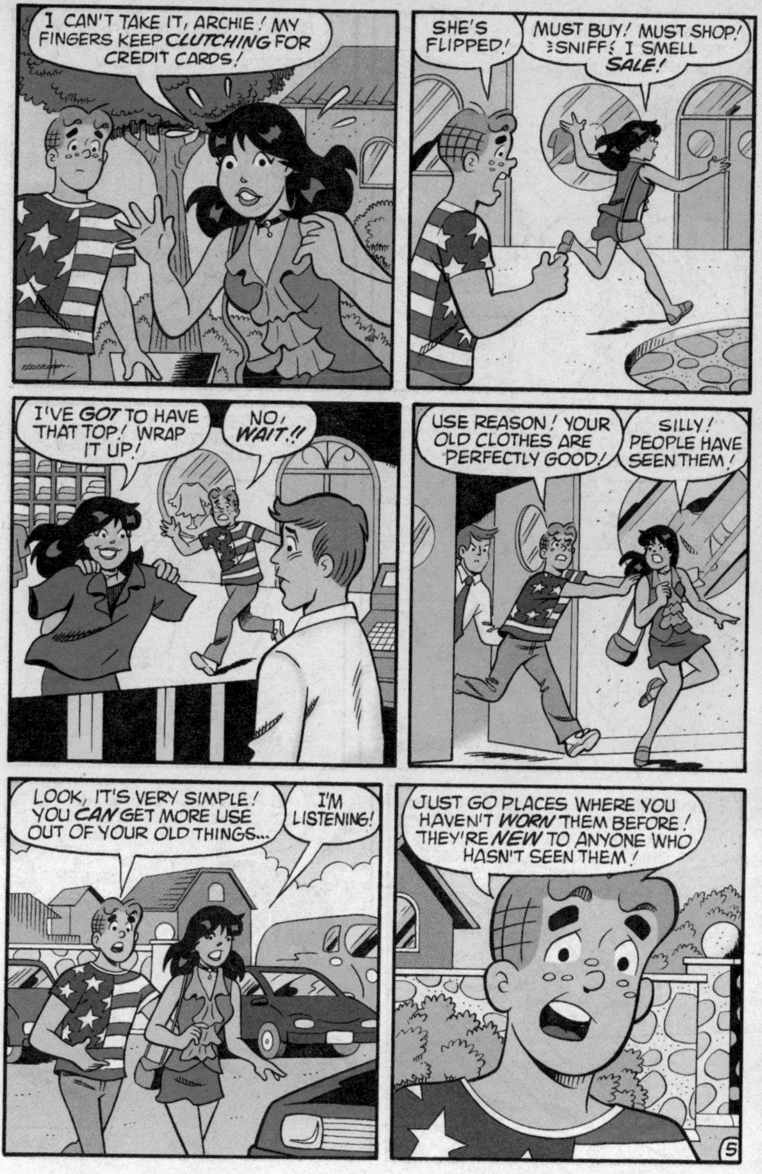

I CAN'T TAKE IT, ARCHIE! MY FINGERS KEEP CLUTCHING FOR CREDIT CARDS!
SHE'S FLIPPED!
MUST BUY! MUST SHOP! SNIFF! I SMELL SALE!
I'VE GOT TO HAVE THAT TOP! WRAP IT UP!
NO, WAIT!!
USE REASON! YOUR OLD CLOTHES ARE PERFECTLY GOOD!
SILLY! PEOPLE HAVE SEEN THEM!
LOOK, IT'S VERY SIMPLE! YOU CAN GET MORE USE OUT OF YOUR OLD THINGS...
I'M LISTENING!
JUST GO PLACES WHERE YOU HAVEN'T WORN THEM BEFORE! THEY'RE NEW TO ANYONE WHO HASN'T SEEN THEM!
5

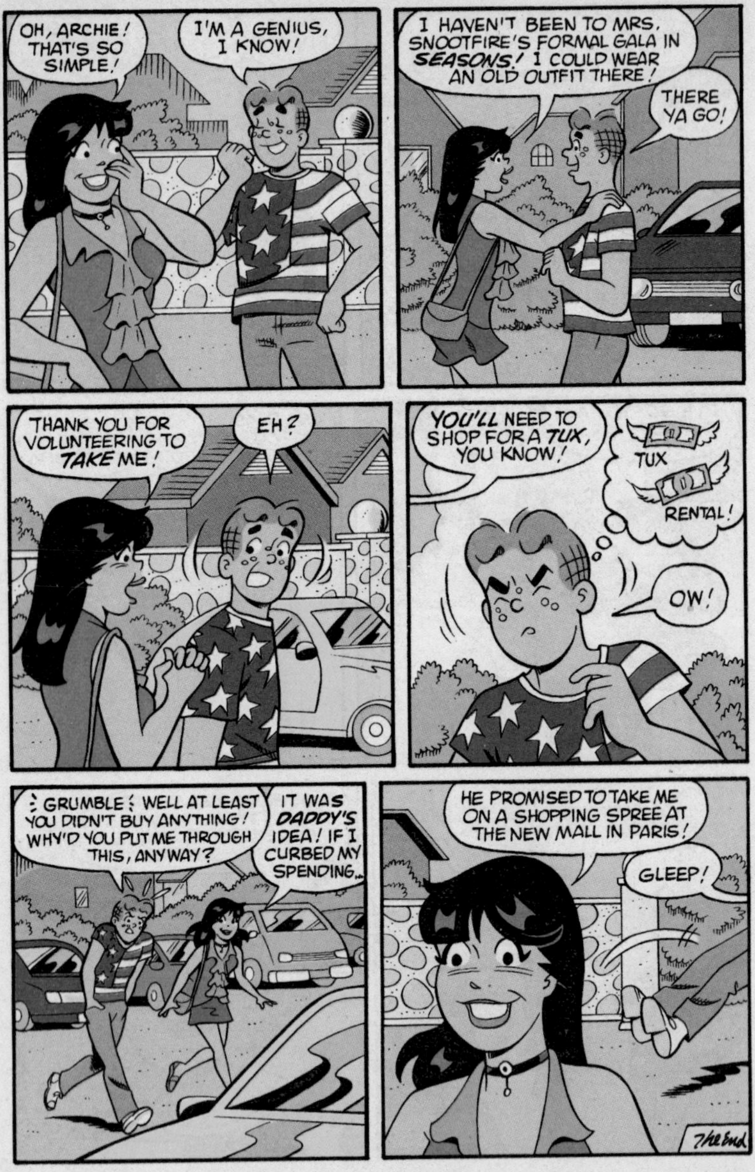
OH, ARCHIE! THAT'S SO SIMPLE!
I'M A GENIUS, I KNOW!
I HAVEN'T BEEN TO MRS. SNOOTFIRE'S FORMAL GALA IN SEASONS! I COULD WEAR AN OLD OUTFIT THERE!
THERE YA GO!
THANK YOU FOR VOLUNTEERING TO TAKE ME!
EH?
YOU'LL NEED TO SHOP FOR A TUX, YOU KNOW!
TUX
RENTAL!
OW!
:GRUMBLE: WELL AT LEAST YOU DIDN'T BUY ANYTHING! WHY'D YOU PUT ME THROUGH THIS, ANYWAY?
IT WAS DADDY'S IDEA! IF I CURBED MY SPENDING...
HE PROMISED TO TAKE ME ON A SHOPPING SPREE AT THE NEW MALL IN PARIS!
GLEEP!
The End

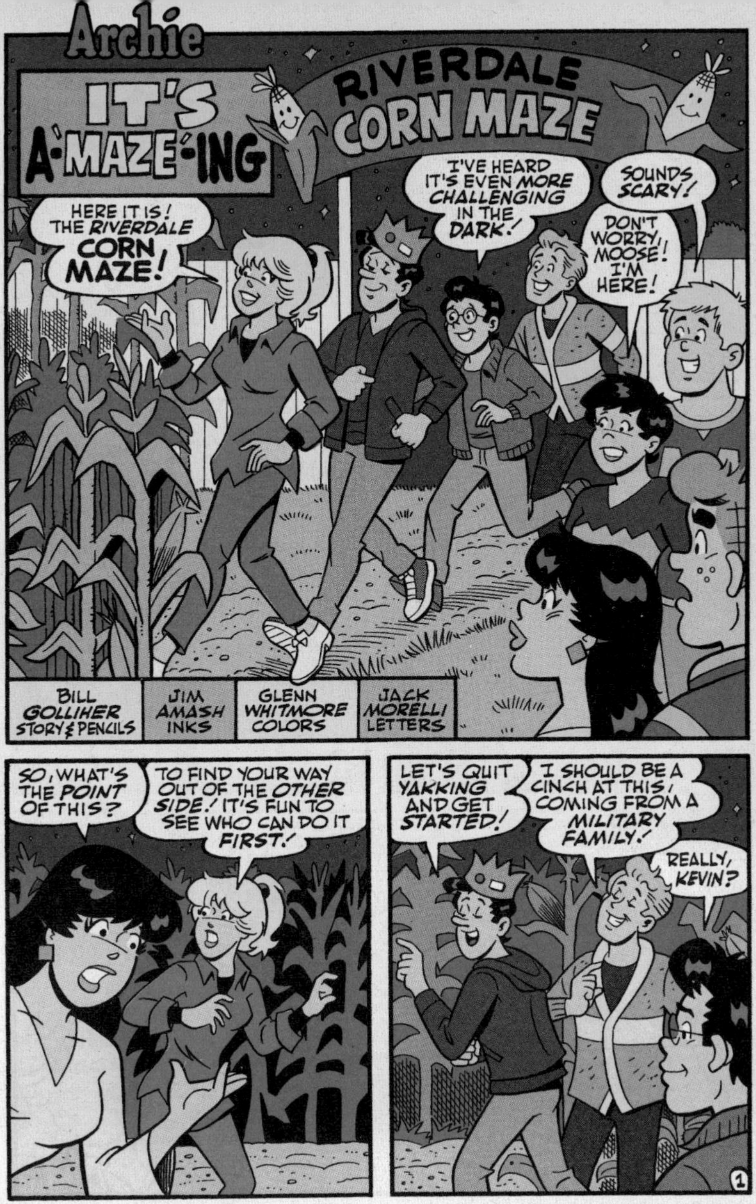
Archie
IT'S A-MAZE-ING
RIVERDALE CORN MAZE
HERE IT IS! THE RIVERDALE CORN MAZE!
I'VE HEARD IT'S EVEN MORE CHALLENGING IN THE DARK!
SOUNDS SCARY!
DON'T WORRY, MOOSE! I'M HERE!
BILL GOLLIHER STORY & PENCILS
JIM AMASH INKS
GLENN WHITMORE COLORS
JACK MORELLI LETTERS
SO, WHAT'S THE POINT OF THIS?
TO FIND YOUR WAY OUT OF THE OTHER SIDE! IT'S FUN TO SEE WHO CAN DO IT FIRST!
LET'S QUIT YAKKING AND GET STARTED!
I SHOULD BE A CINCH AT THIS, COMING FROM A MILITARY FAMILY!
REALLY, KEVIN?

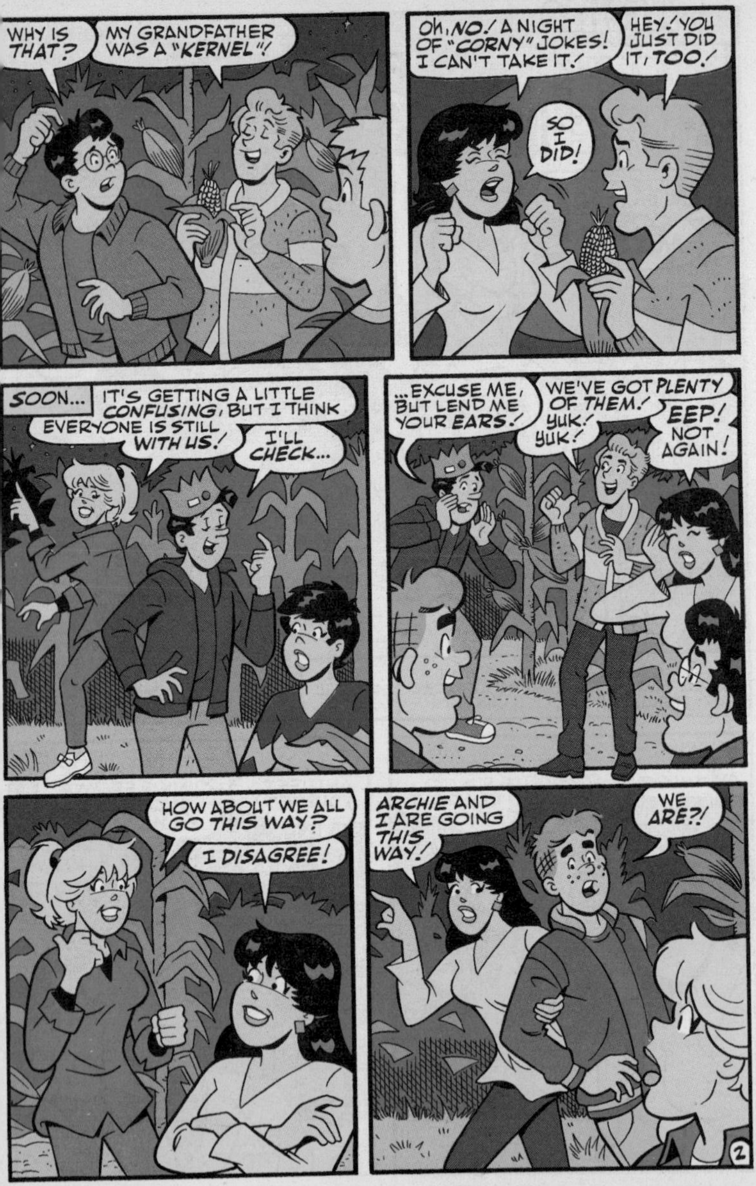
WHY IS THAT?
MY GRANDFATHER WAS A "KERNEL"!
OH, NO! A NIGHT OF "CORNY" JOKES! I CAN'T TAKE IT!
HEY! YOU JUST DID IT, TOO!
SO I DID!
SOON...
IT'S GETTING A LITTLE CONFUSING, BUT I THINK EVERYONE IS STILL WITH US!
I'LL CHECK...
...EXCUSE ME, BUT LEND ME YOUR EARS!
WE'VE GOT PLENTY OF THEM! YUK! YUK!
EEP! NOT AGAIN!
HOW ABOUT WE ALL GO THIS WAY?
I DISAGREE!
ARCHIE AND I ARE GOING THIS WAY!
WE ARE?!

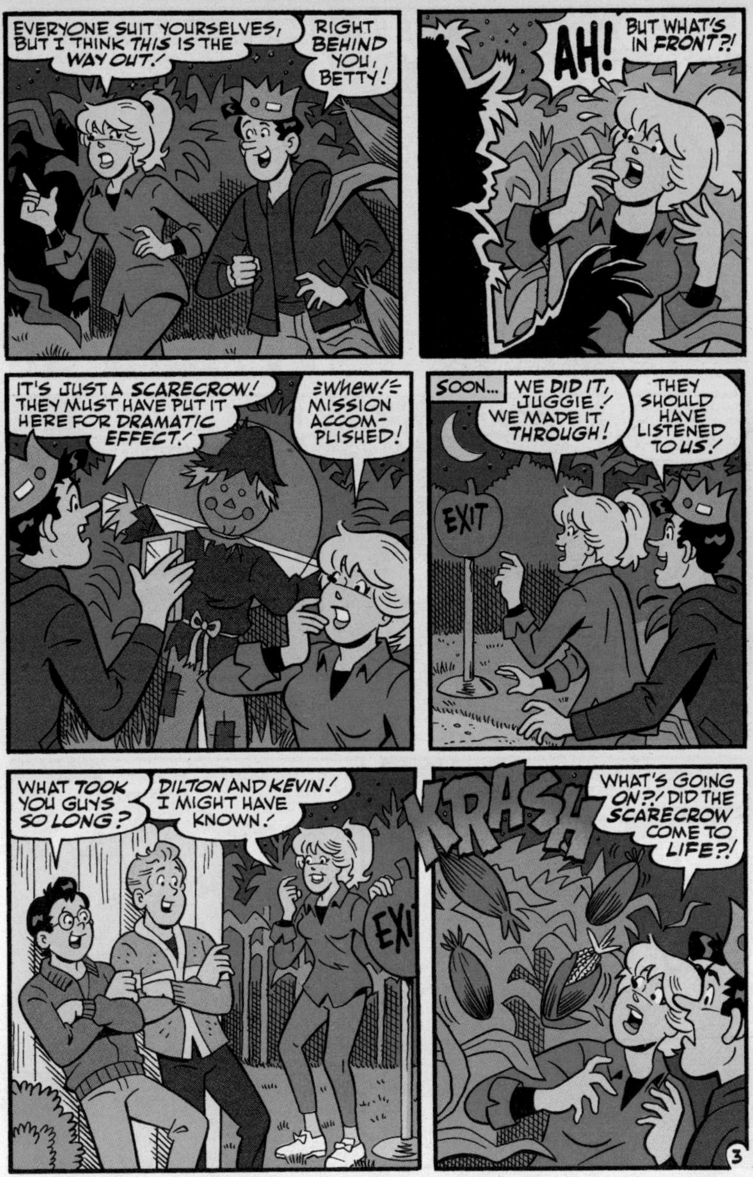

EVERYONE SUIT YOURSELVES, BUT I THINK THIS IS THE WAY OUT!
RIGHT BEHIND YOU, BETTY!
AH!
BUT WHAT'S IN FRONT?!
IT'S JUST A SCARECROW! THEY MUST HAVE PUT IT HERE FOR DRAMATIC EFFECT!
WHEW! MISSION ACCOMPLISHED!
SOON...
WE DID IT, JUGGIE! WE MADE IT THROUGH!
THEY SHOULD HAVE LISTENED TO US!
EXIT
WHAT TOOK YOU GUYS SO LONG?
DILTON AND KEVIN! I MIGHT HAVE KNOWN!
KRASH
WHAT'S GOING ON?! DID THE SCARECROW COME TO LIFE?!

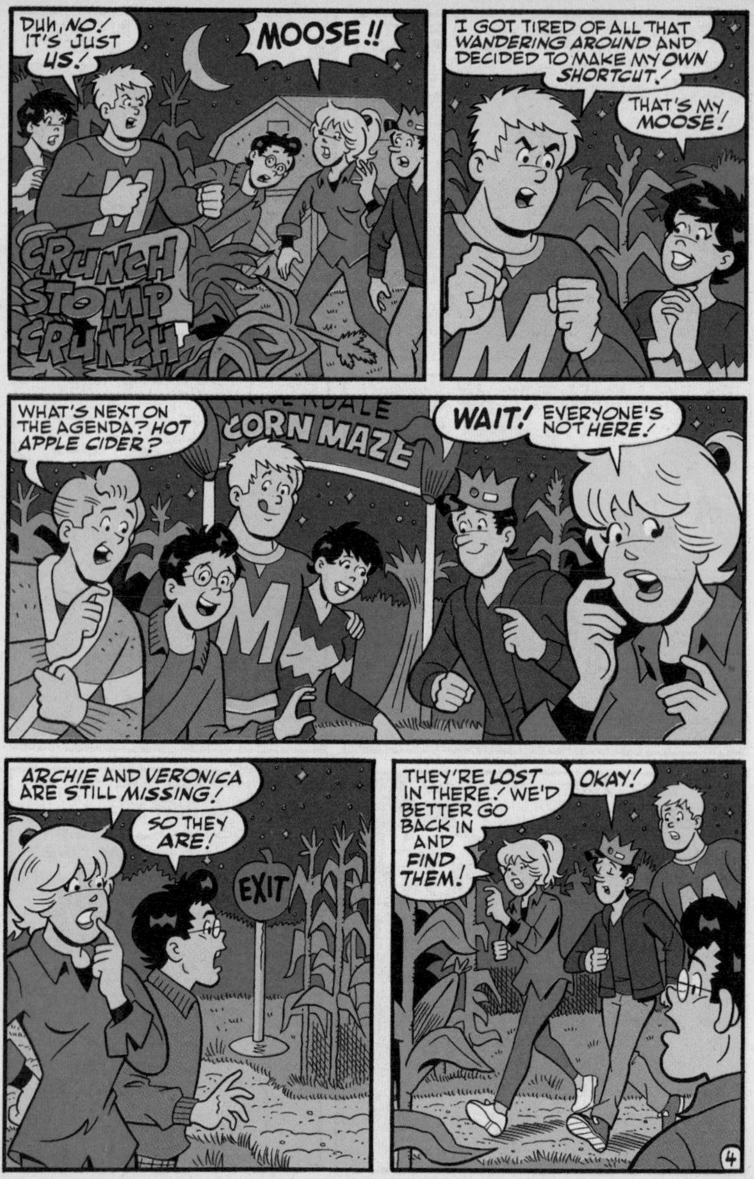
Duh, NO! IT'S JUST US!
MOOSE!!
CRUNCH STOMP CRUNCH
I GOT TIRED OF ALL THAT WANDERING AROUND AND DECIDED TO MAKE MY OWN SHORTCUT!
THAT'S MY MOOSE!
WHAT'S NEXT ON THE AGENDA? HOT APPLE CIDER?
CORN MAZE
WAIT! EVERYONE'S NOT HERE!
ARCHIE AND VERONICA ARE STILL MISSING!
SO THEY ARE!
EXIT
THEY'RE LOST IN THERE! WE'D BETTER GO BACK IN AND FIND THEM!
OKAY!
4

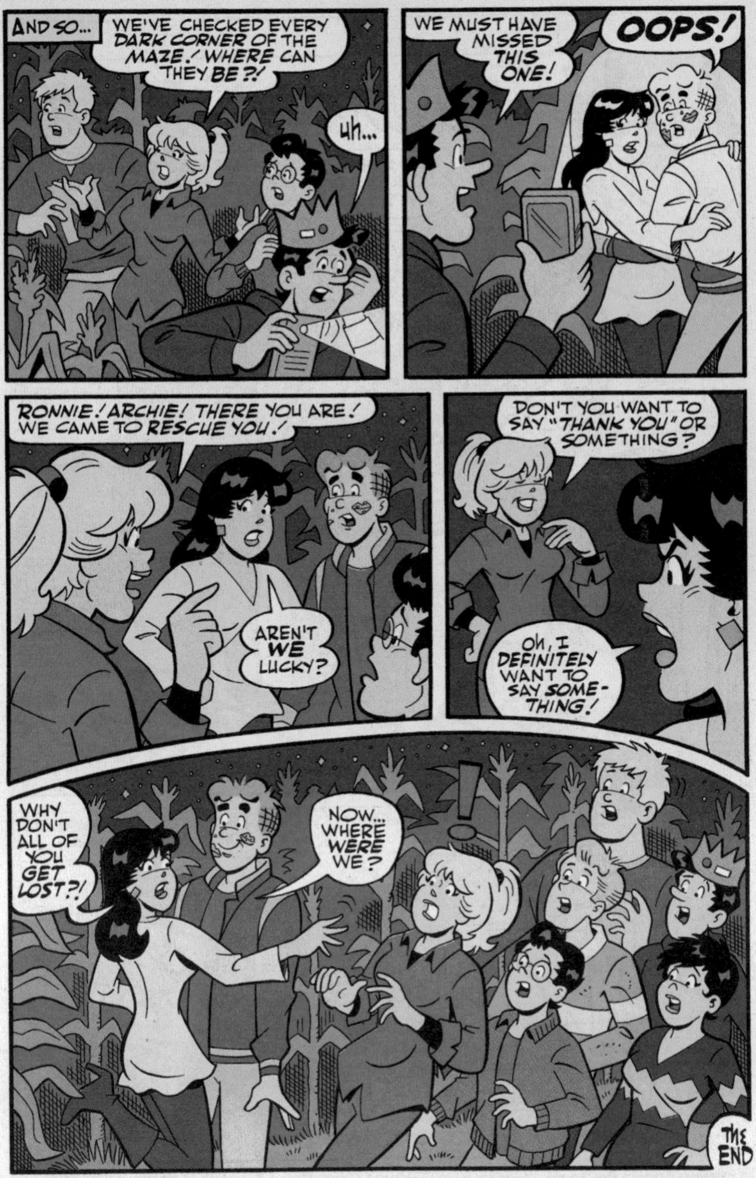

AND SO...
WE'VE CHECKED EVERY DARK CORNER OF THE MAZE! WHERE CAN THEY BE?!
uh...
WE MUST HAVE MISSED THIS ONE!
OOPS!
RONNIE! ARCHIE! THERE YOU ARE! WE CAME TO RESCUE YOU!
AREN'T WE LUCKY?
DON'T YOU WANT TO SAY "THANK YOU" OR SOMETHING?
Oh, I DEFINITELY WANT TO SAY SOME-THING!
WHY DON'T ALL OF YOU GET LOST?!
NOW... WHERE WERE WE?
!
THE END

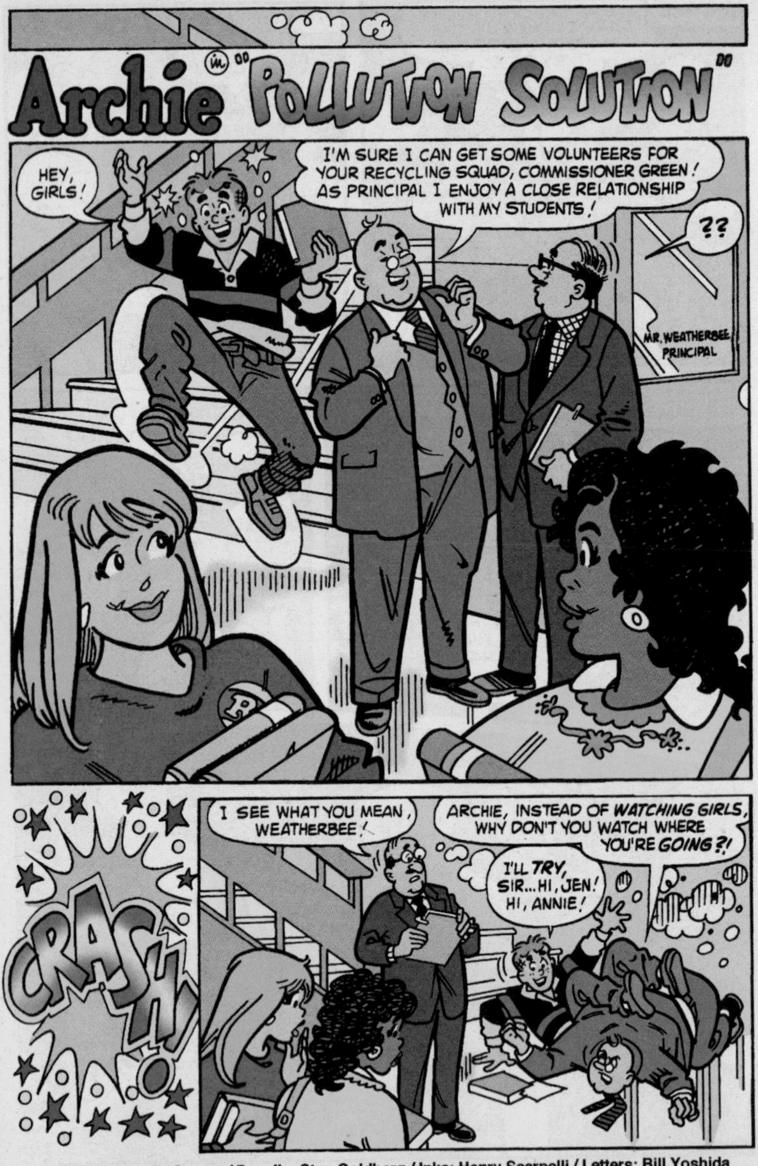
Archie in "POLLUTION SOLUTION"
HEY, GIRLS!
I'M SURE I CAN GET SOME VOLUNTEERS FOR YOUR RECYCLING SQUAD, COMMISSIONER GREEN! AS PRINCIPAL I ENJOY A CLOSE RELATIONSHIP WITH MY STUDENTS!
??
MR. WEATHERBEE PRINCIPAL
CRASH!
I SEE WHAT YOU MEAN, WEATHERBEE!
ARCHIE, INSTEAD OF WATCHING GIRLS, WHY DON'T YOU WATCH WHERE YOU'RE GOING?!
I'LL TRY, SIR...HI, JEN! HI, ANNIE!

Script: Angelo DeCesare / Pencils: Stan Goldberg / Inks: Henry Scarpelli / Letters: Bill Yoshida

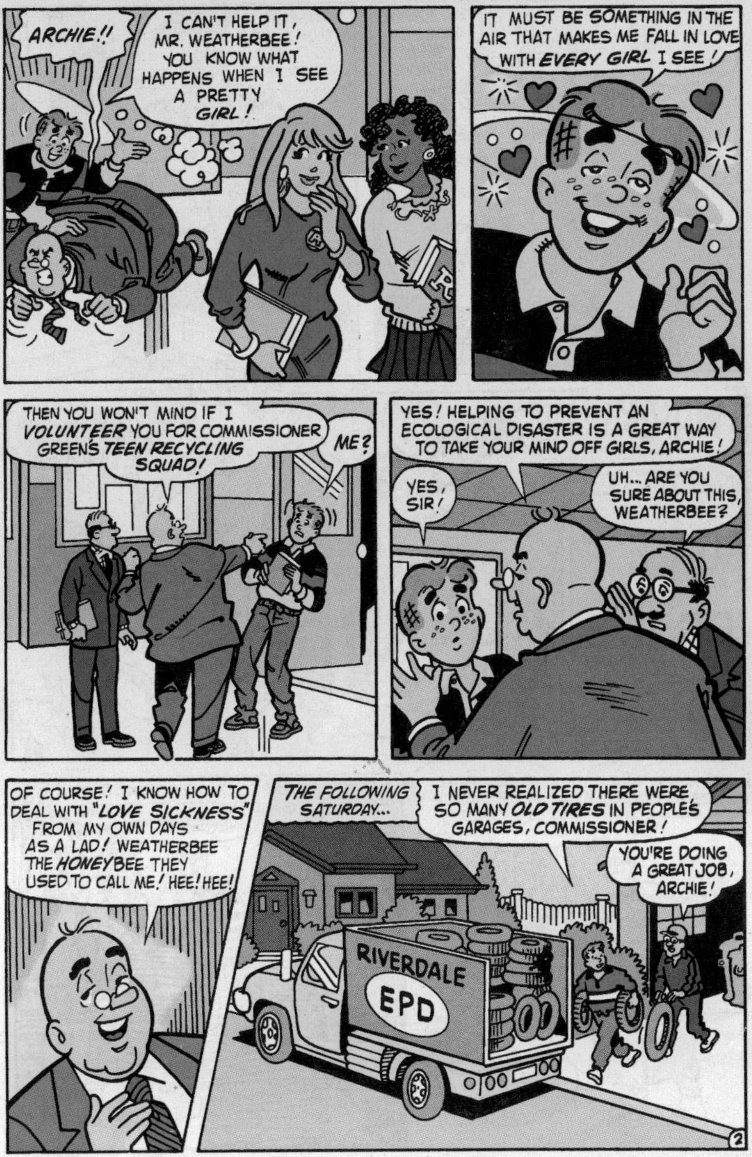
ARCHIE!!
I CAN'T HELP IT, MR. WEATHERBEE! YOU KNOW WHAT HAPPENS WHEN I SEE A PRETTY GIRL!
IT MUST BE SOMETHING IN THE AIR THAT MAKES ME FALL IN LOVE WITH EVERY GIRL I SEE!
THEN YOU WON'T MIND IF I VOLUNTEER YOU FOR COMMISSIONER GREEN'S TEEN RECYCLING SQUAD!
ME?
YES! HELPING TO PREVENT AN ECOLOGICAL DISASTER IS A GREAT WAY TO TAKE YOUR MIND OFF GIRLS, ARCHIE!
YES, SIR!
UH... ARE YOU SURE ABOUT THIS, WEATHERBEE?
OF COURSE! I KNOW HOW TO DEAL WITH "LOVE SICKNESS" FROM MY OWN DAYS AS A LAD! WEATHERBEE THE HONEYBEE THEY USED TO CALL ME! HEE! HEE!
THE FOLLOWING SATURDAY...
I NEVER REALIZED THERE WERE SO MANY OLD TIRES IN PEOPLE'S GARAGES, COMMISSIONER!
YOU'RE DOING A GREAT JOB, ARCHIE!
RIVERDALE
EPD
2

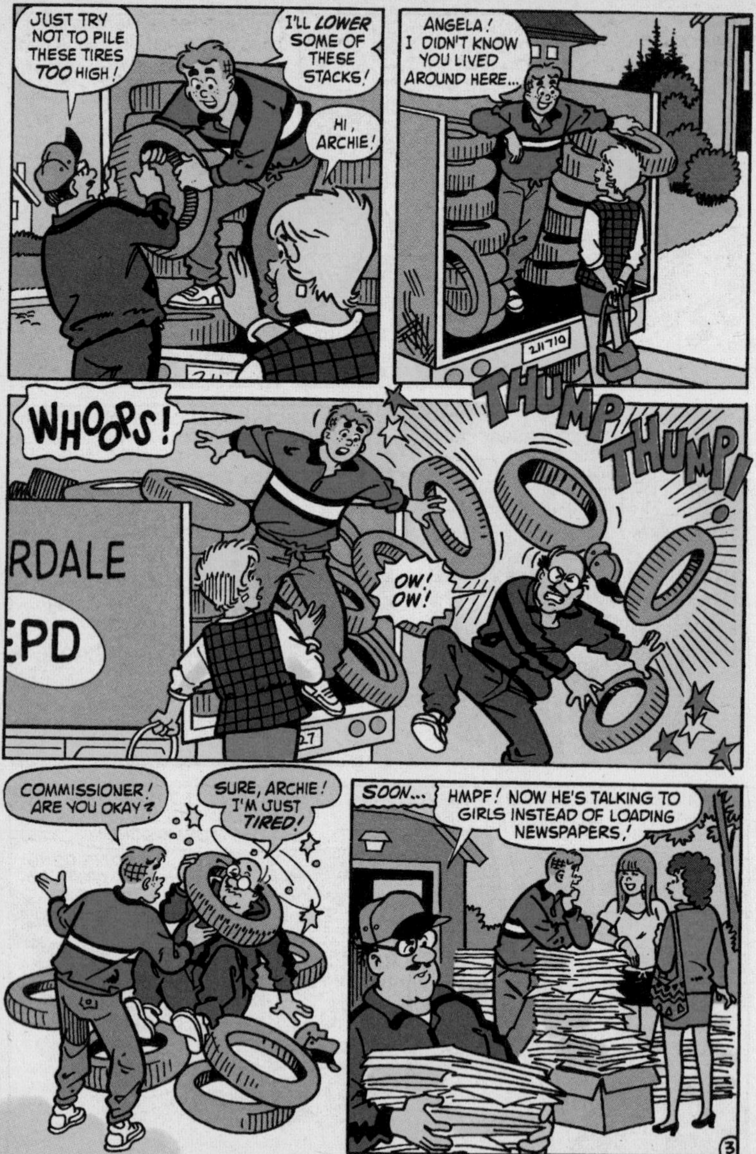
JUST TRY NOT TO PILE THESE TIRES TOO HIGH!
I'LL LOWER SOME OF THESE STACKS!
HI, ARCHIE!
ANGELA! I DIDN'T KNOW YOU LIVED AROUND HERE...
WHOOPS!
THUMP THUMP!
OW! OW!
RDALE
EPD
COMMISSIONER! ARE YOU OKAY?
SURE, ARCHIE! I'M JUST TIRED!
SOON...
HMPF! NOW HE'S TALKING TO GIRLS INSTEAD OF LOADING NEWSPAPERS!
3

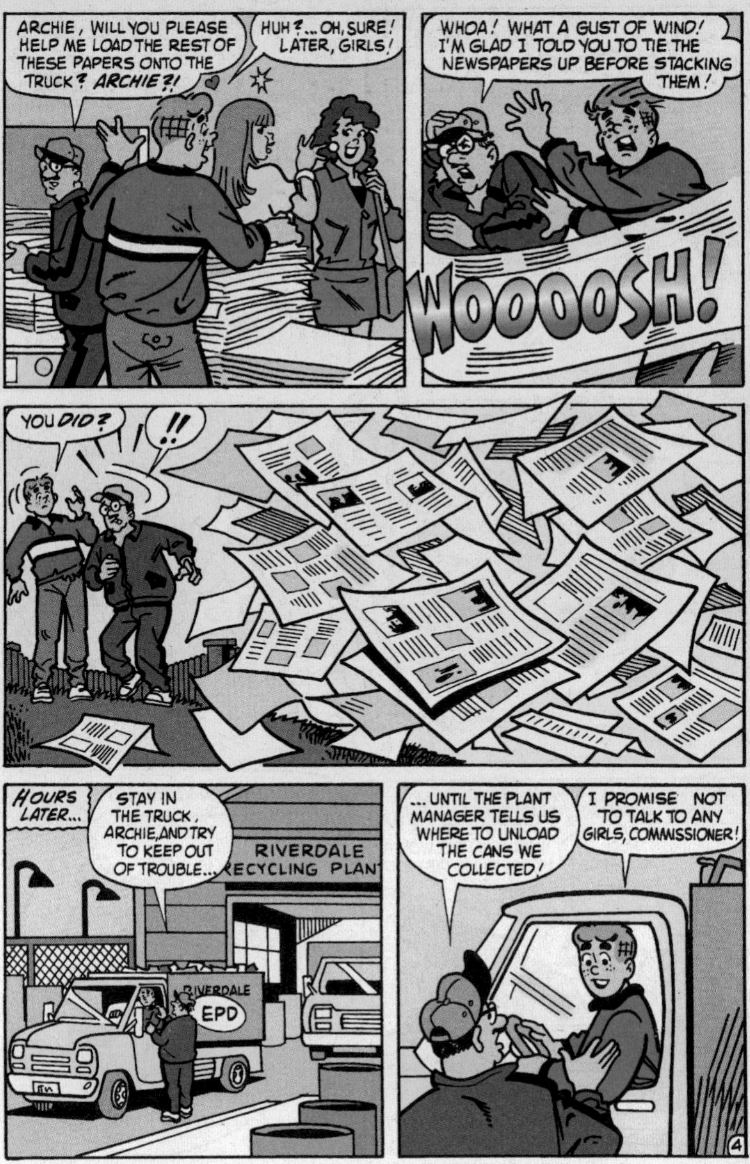
ARCHIE, WILL YOU PLEASE HELP ME LOAD THE REST OF THESE PAPERS ONTO THE TRUCK? ARCHIE?!
HUH?... OH, SURE! LATER, GIRLS!
WHOA! WHAT A GUST OF WIND! I'M GLAD I TOLD YOU TO TIE THE NEWSPAPERS UP BEFORE STACKING THEM!
WOOOOSH!
YOU DID?
!!
HOURS LATER...
STAY IN THE TRUCK, ARCHIE, AND TRY TO KEEP OUT OF TROUBLE...
RIVERDALE RECYCLING PLANT
RIVERDALE
EPD
... UNTIL THE PLANT MANAGER TELLS US WHERE TO UNLOAD THE CANS WE COLLECTED!
I PROMISE NOT TO TALK TO ANY GIRLS, COMMISSIONER!
4

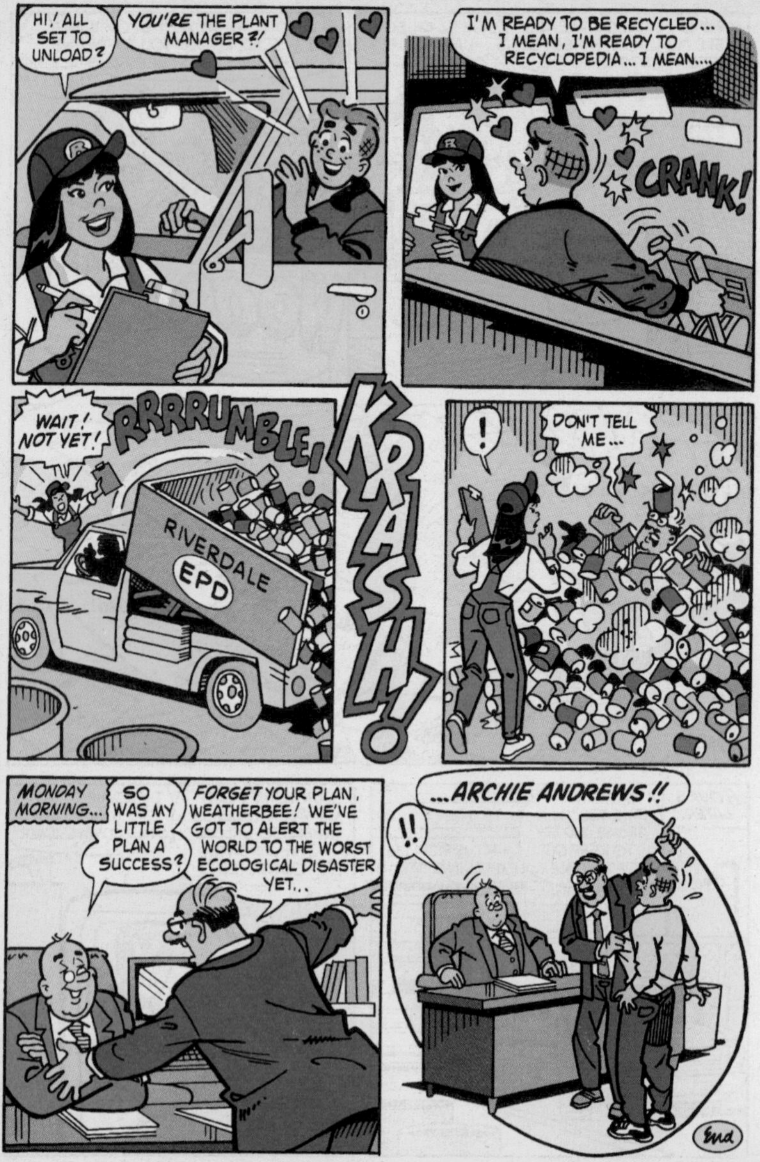

HI! ALL SET TO UNLOAD?
YOU'RE THE PLANT MANAGER?!
I'M READY TO BE RECYCLED... I MEAN, I'M READY TO RECYCLOPEDIA... I MEAN....
CRANK!
WAIT! NOT YET!
RRRRUMBLE!
RIVERDALE
EPD
KRASH!
!
DON'T TELL ME...
MONDAY MORNING...
SO WAS MY LITTLE PLAN A SUCCESS?
FORGET YOUR PLAN, WEATHERBEE! WE'VE GOT TO ALERT THE WORLD TO THE WORST ECOLOGICAL DISASTER YET...
...ARCHIE ANDREWS!!
!!
End

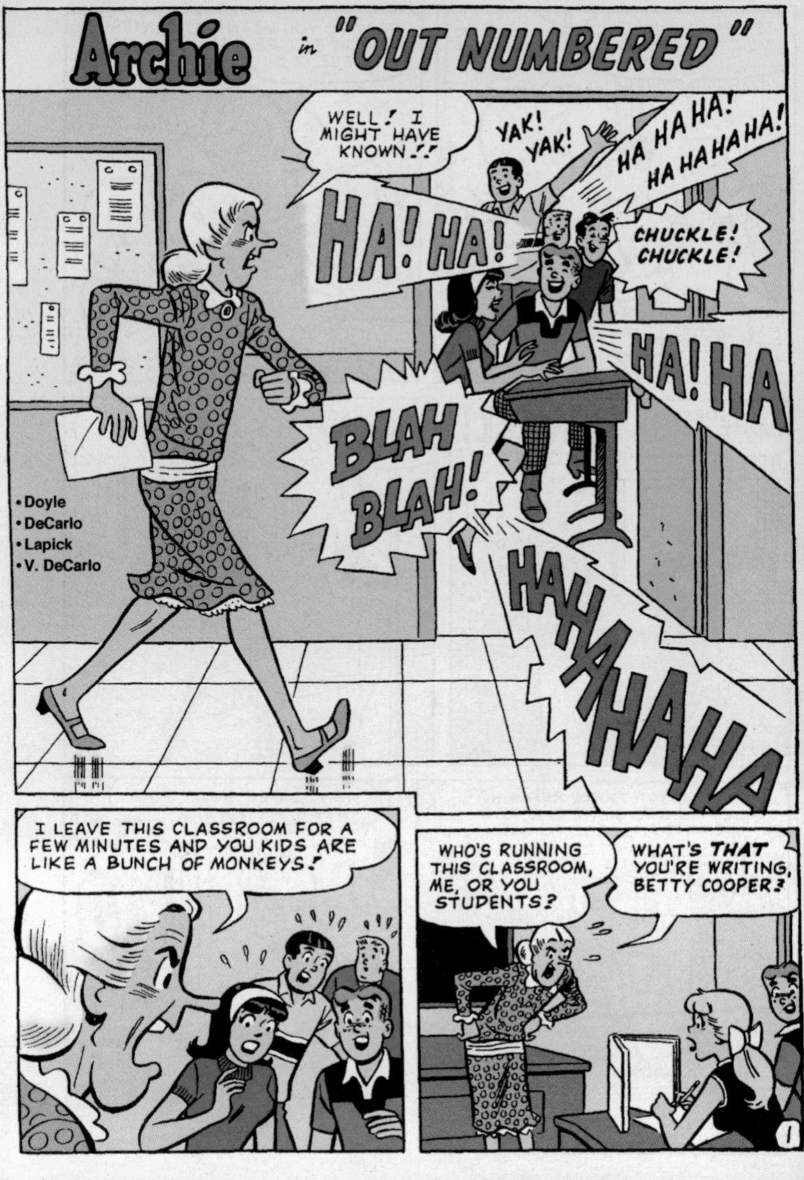
Archie in "OUT NUMBERED"
WELL! I MIGHT HAVE KNOWN!!
YAK! YAK!
HA HA HA! HA HA HA HA HA!
HA! HA!
CHUCKLE! CHUCKLE!
HA! HA
BLAH BLAH!
HAHAHAHAHAHA
•Doyle
•DeCarlo
•Lapick
•V. DeCarlo
I LEAVE THIS CLASSROOM FOR A FEW MINUTES AND YOU KIDS ARE LIKE A BUNCH OF MONKEYS!
WHO'S RUNNING THIS CLASSROOM, ME, OR YOU STUDENTS?
WHAT'S THAT YOU'RE WRITING, BETTY COOPER?
1

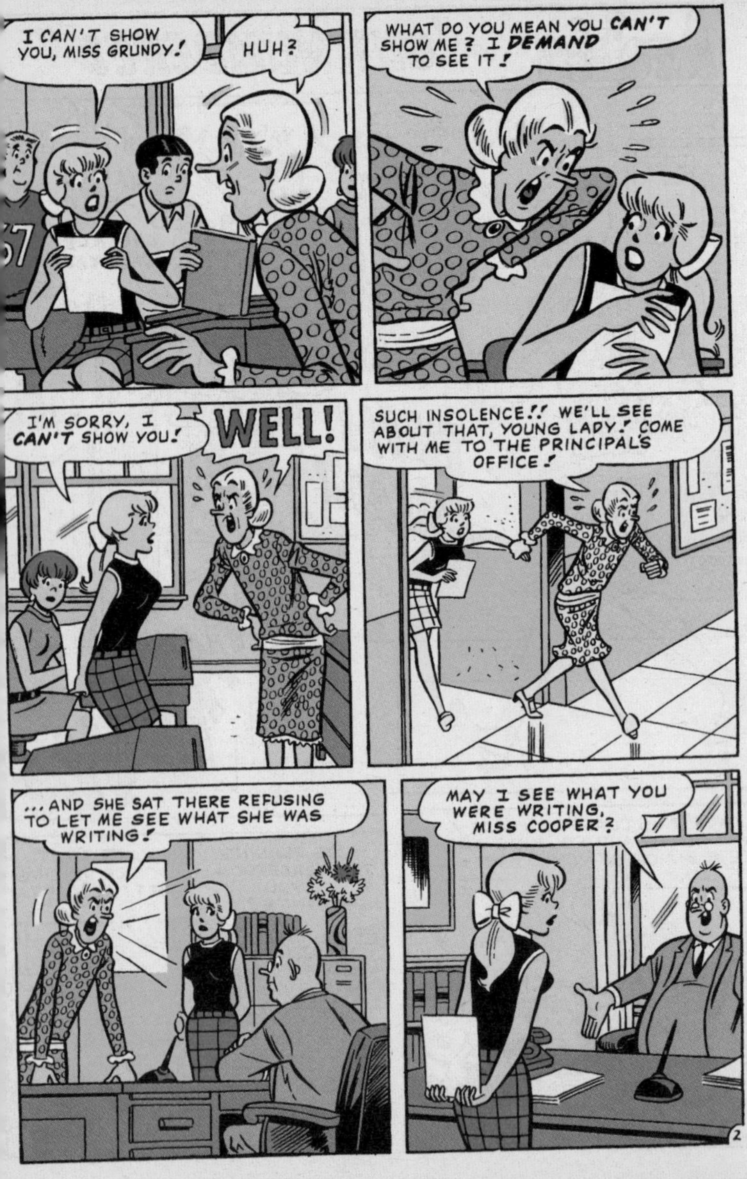
I CAN'T SHOW YOU, MISS GRUNDY!
HUH?
WHAT DO YOU MEAN YOU CAN'T SHOW ME? I DEMAND TO SEE IT!
I'M SORRY, I CAN'T SHOW YOU!
WELL!
SUCH INSOLENCE!! WE'LL SEE ABOUT THAT, YOUNG LADY! COME WITH ME TO THE PRINCIPAL'S OFFICE!
...AND SHE SAT THERE REFUSING TO LET ME SEE WHAT SHE WAS WRITING!
MAY I SEE WHAT YOU WERE WRITING, MISS COOPER?
2

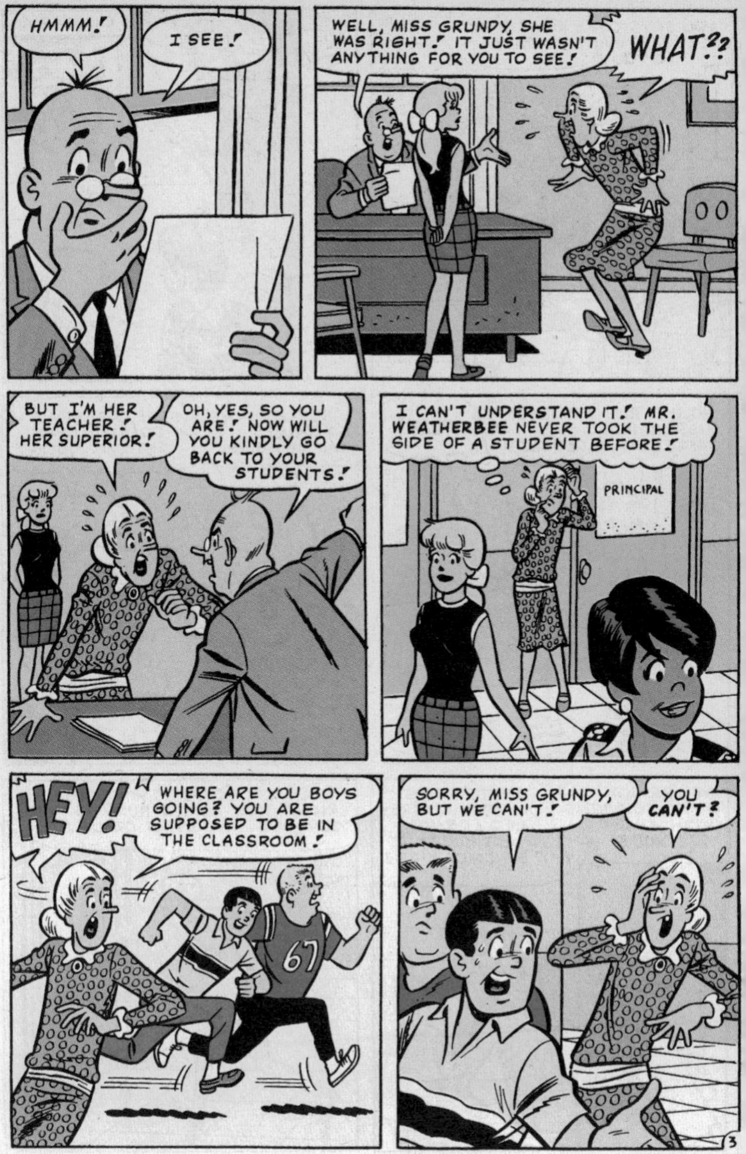

HMMM!
I SEE!
WELL, MISS GRUNDY, SHE WAS RIGHT! IT JUST WASN'T ANYTHING FOR YOU TO SEE!
WHAT??
BUT I'M HER TEACHER! HER SUPERIOR!
OH, YES, SO YOU ARE! NOW WILL YOU KINDLY GO BACK TO YOUR STUDENTS!
I CAN'T UNDERSTAND IT! MR. WEATHERBEE NEVER TOOK THE SIDE OF A STUDENT BEFORE!
PRINCIPAL
HEY!
WHERE ARE YOU BOYS GOING? YOU ARE SUPPOSED TO BE IN THE CLASSROOM!
67
SORRY, MISS GRUNDY, BUT WE CAN'T!
YOU CAN'T?
3

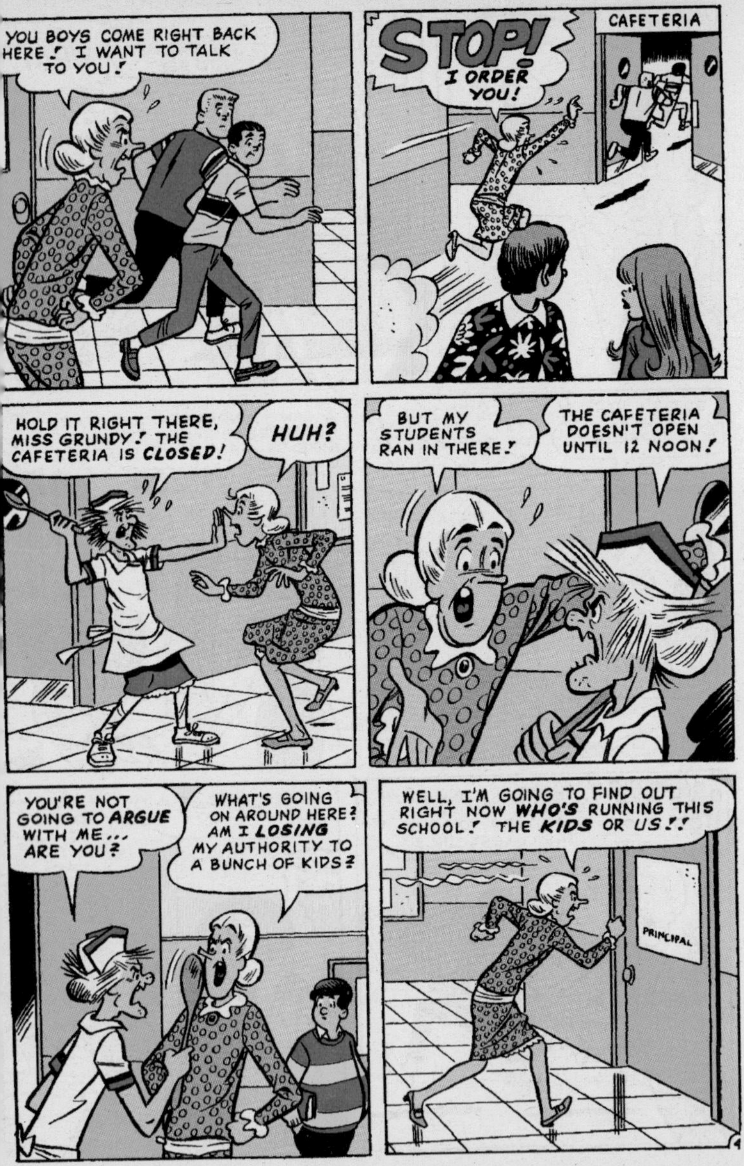

YOU BOYS COME RIGHT BACK HERE! I WANT TO TALK TO YOU!
CAFETERIA
STOP! I ORDER YOU!
HOLD IT RIGHT THERE, MISS GRUNDY! THE CAFETERIA IS CLOSED!
HUH?
BUT MY STUDENTS RAN IN THERE!
THE CAFETERIA DOESN'T OPEN UNTIL 12 NOON!
YOU'RE NOT GOING TO ARGUE WITH ME... ARE YOU?
WHAT'S GOING ON AROUND HERE? AM I LOSING MY AUTHORITY TO A BUNCH OF KIDS?
WELL, I'M GOING TO FIND OUT RIGHT NOW WHO'S RUNNING THIS SCHOOL! THE KIDS OR US!!
PRINCIPAL
4

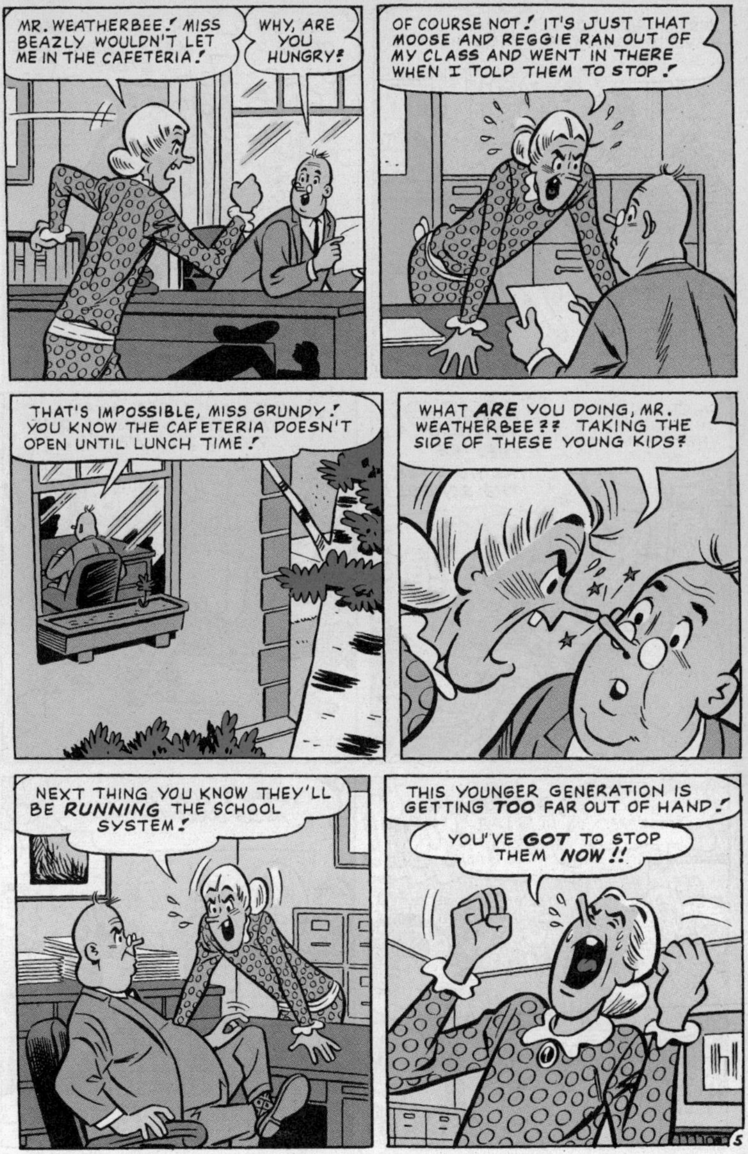
MR. WEATHERBEE! MISS BEAZLY WOULDN'T LET ME IN THE CAFETERIA!
WHY, ARE YOU HUNGRY?
OF COURSE NOT! IT'S JUST THAT MOOSE AND REGGIE RAN OUT OF MY CLASS AND WENT IN THERE WHEN I TOLD THEM TO STOP!
THAT'S IMPOSSIBLE, MISS GRUNDY! YOU KNOW THE CAFETERIA DOESN'T OPEN UNTIL LUNCH TIME!
WHAT ARE YOU DOING, MR. WEATHERBEE?? TAKING THE SIDE OF THESE YOUNG KIDS?
NEXT THING YOU KNOW THEY'LL BE RUNNING THE SCHOOL SYSTEM!
THIS YOUNGER GENERATION IS GETTING TOO FAR OUT OF HAND!
YOU'VE GOT TO STOP THEM NOW!!

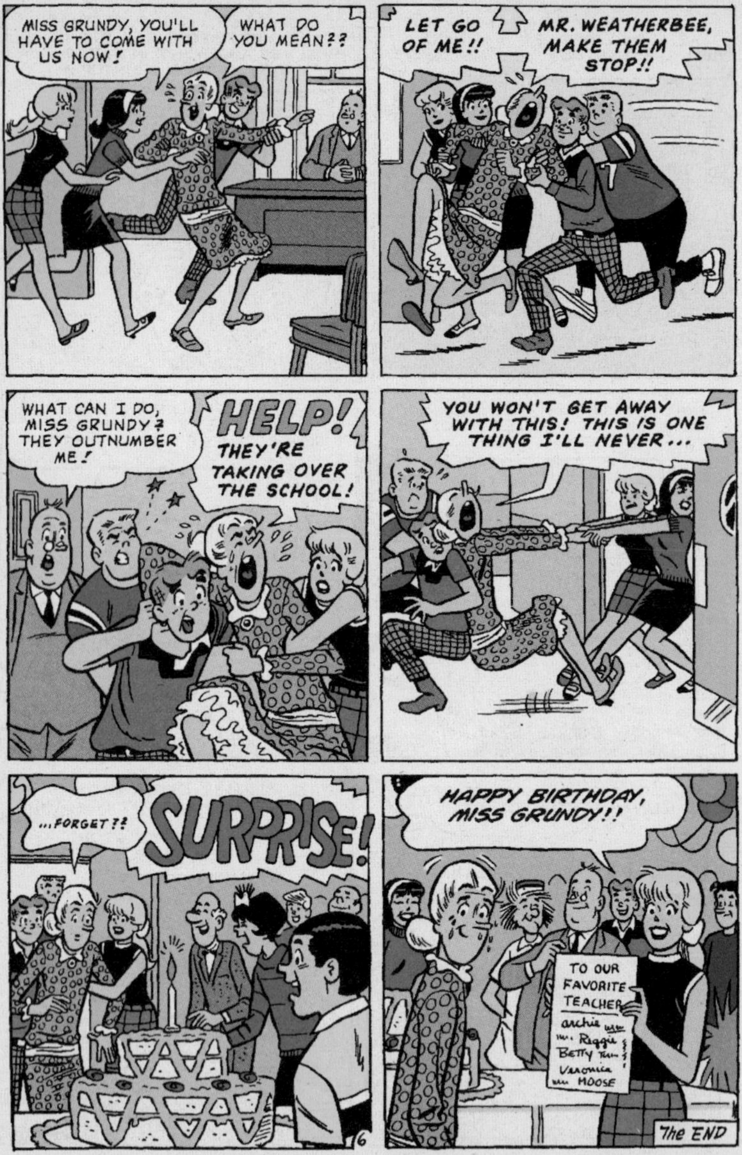
MISS GRUNDY, YOU'LL HAVE TO COME WITH US NOW!
WHAT DO YOU MEAN??
LET GO OF ME!!
MR. WEATHERBEE, MAKE THEM STOP!!
WHAT CAN I DO, MISS GRUNDY? THEY OUTNUMBER ME!
HELP! THEY'RE TAKING OVER THE SCHOOL!
YOU WON'T GET AWAY WITH THIS! THIS IS ONE THING I'LL NEVER...
...FORGET??
SURPRISE!
HAPPY BIRTHDAY, MISS GRUNDY!!
TO OUR FAVORITE TEACHER
archie
Reggie
Betty
Veronica
MOOSE
6
The END

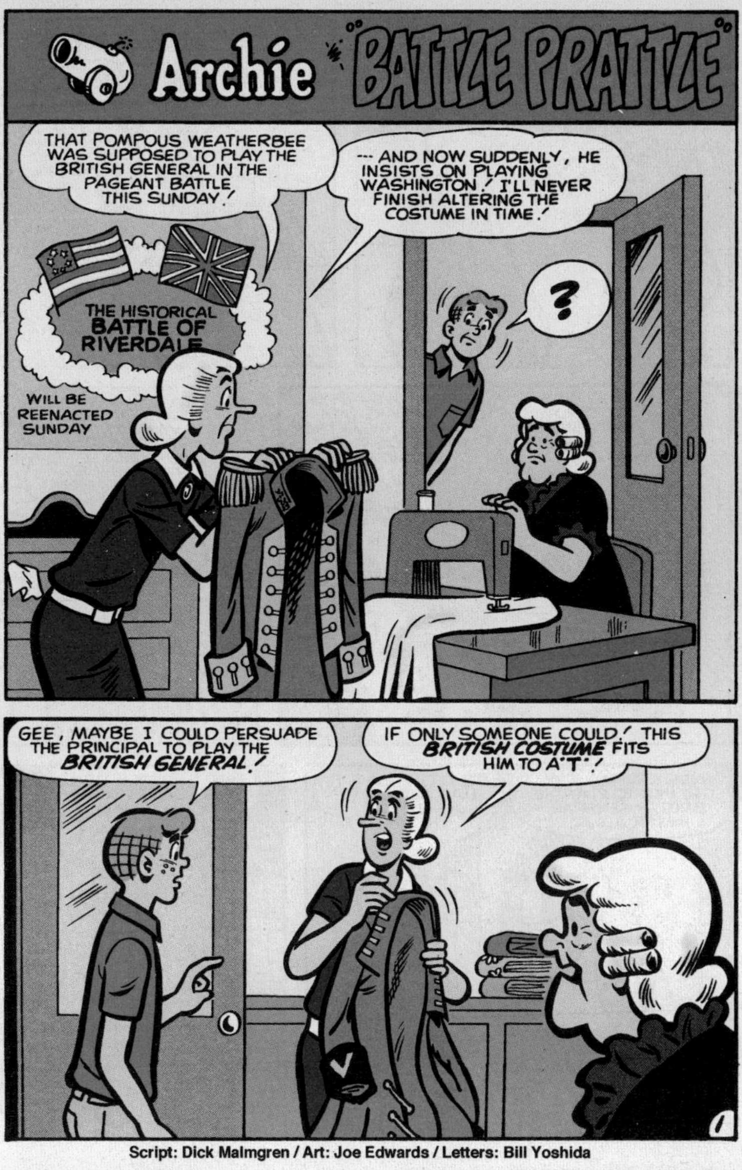
Archie
BATTLE PRATTLE
THAT POMPOUS WEATHERBEE WAS SUPPOSED TO PLAY THE BRITISH GENERAL IN THE PAGEANT BATTLE THIS SUNDAY!
--- AND NOW SUDDENLY, HE INSISTS ON PLAYING WASHINGTON! I'LL NEVER FINISH ALTERING THE COSTUME IN TIME!
THE HISTORICAL BATTLE OF RIVERDALE WILL BE REENACTED SUNDAY
?
GEE, MAYBE I COULD PERSUADE THE PRINCIPAL TO PLAY THE *BRITISH GENERAL*!
IF ONLY SOMEONE COULD! THIS *BRITISH COSTUME* FITS HIM TO A "T"!
1

Script: Dick Malmgren / Art: Joe Edwards / Letters: Bill Yoshida

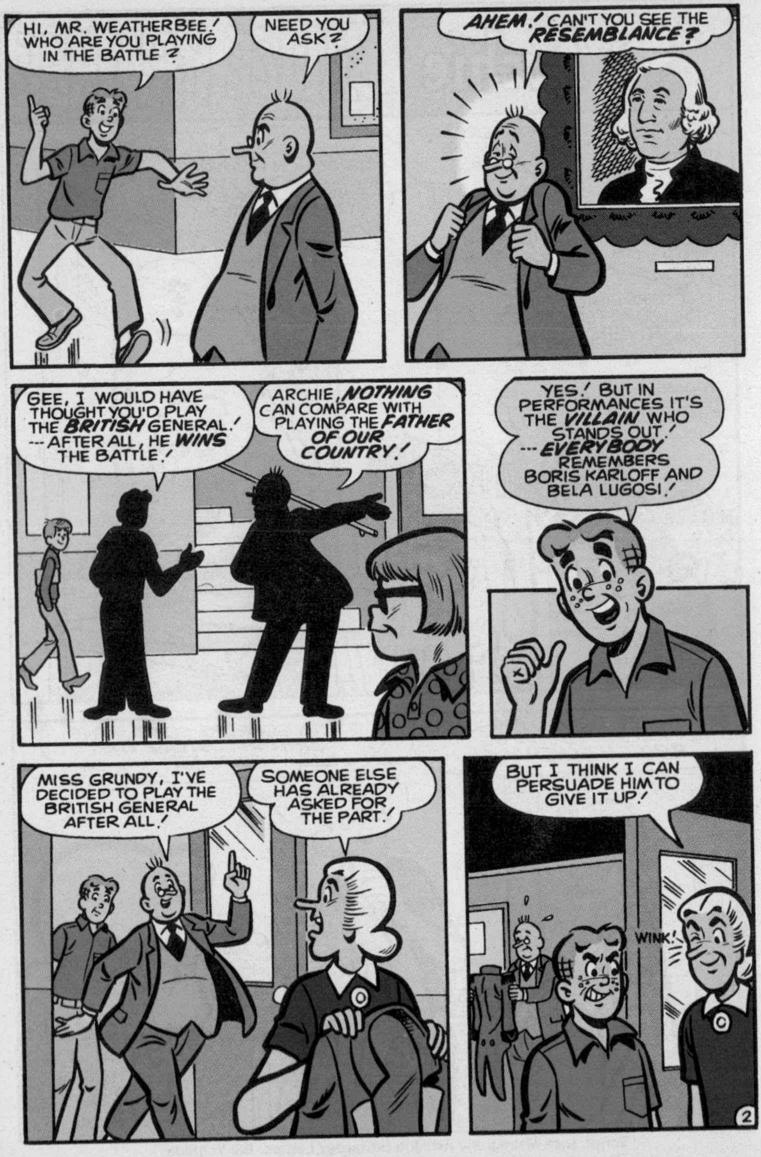

HI, MR. WEATHERBEE! WHO ARE YOU PLAYING IN THE BATTLE?
NEED YOU ASK?
AHEM! CAN'T YOU SEE THE RESEMBLANCE?
GEE, I WOULD HAVE THOUGHT YOU'D PLAY THE BRITISH GENERAL! --- AFTER ALL, HE WINS THE BATTLE!
ARCHIE, NOTHING CAN COMPARE WITH PLAYING THE FATHER OF OUR COUNTRY!
YES! BUT IN PERFORMANCES IT'S THE VILLAIN WHO STANDS OUT! --- EVERYBODY REMEMBERS BORIS KARLOFF AND BELA LUGOSI!
MISS GRUNDY, I'VE DECIDED TO PLAY THE BRITISH GENERAL AFTER ALL!
SOMEONE ELSE HAS ALREADY ASKED FOR THE PART!
BUT I THINK I CAN PERSUADE HIM TO GIVE IT UP!
WINK!
2

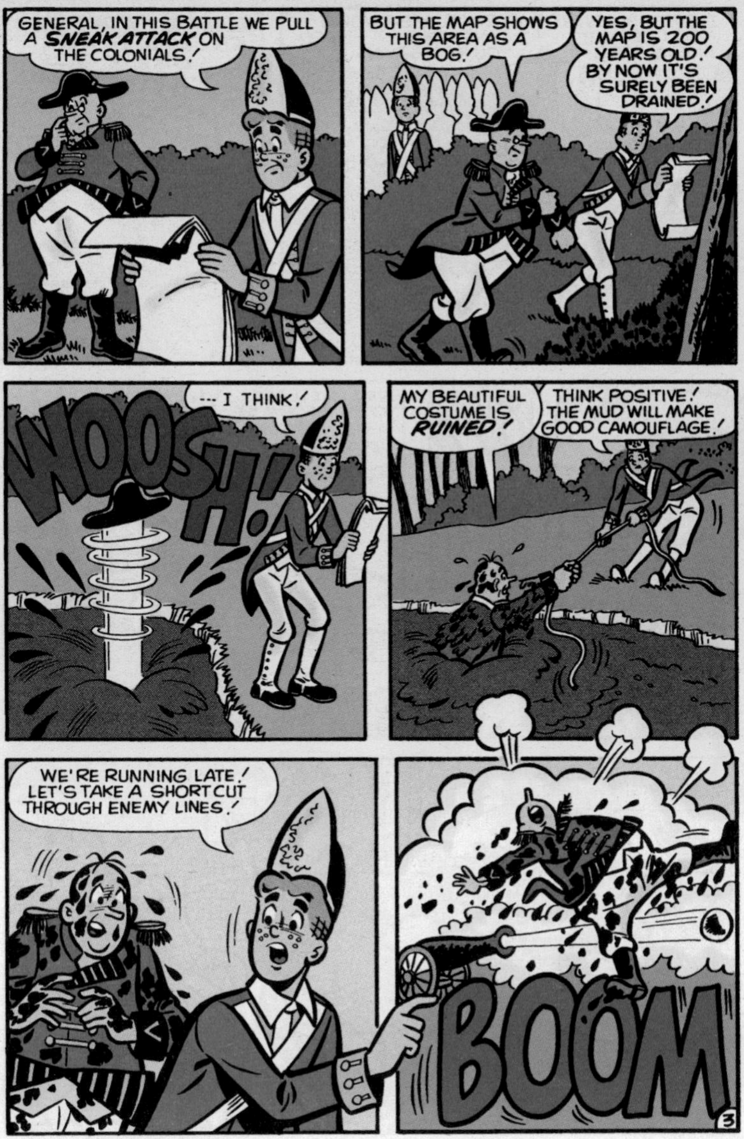
GENERAL, IN THIS BATTLE WE PULL A SNEAK ATTACK ON THE COLONIALS!
BUT THE MAP SHOWS THIS AREA AS A BOG!
YES, BUT THE MAP IS 200 YEARS OLD! BY NOW IT'S SURELY BEEN DRAINED!
WOOSH!
--- I THINK!
MY BEAUTIFUL COSTUME IS RUINED!
THINK POSITIVE! THE MUD WILL MAKE GOOD CAMOUFLAGE!
WE'RE RUNNING LATE! LET'S TAKE A SHORTCUT THROUGH ENEMY LINES!
BOOM
3

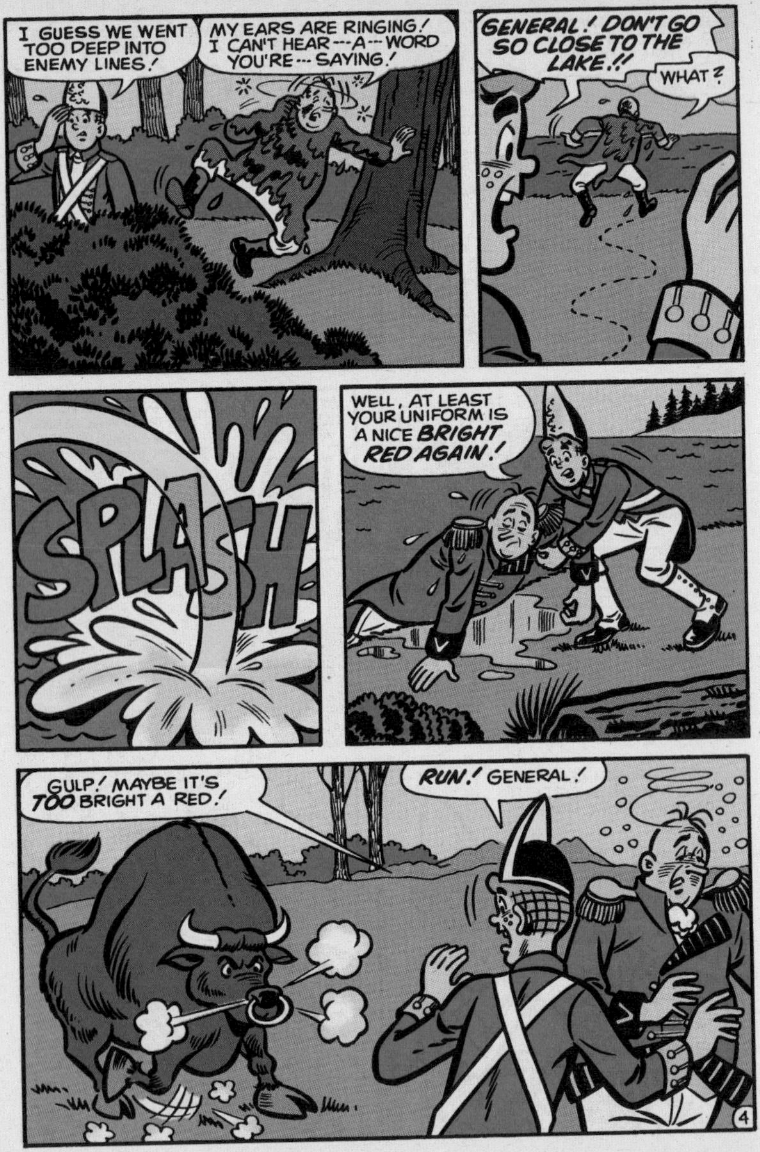
I GUESS WE WENT TOO DEEP INTO ENEMY LINES!
MY EARS ARE RINGING! I CAN'T HEAR---A---WORD YOU'RE---SAYING!
GENERAL! DON'T GO SO CLOSE TO THE LAKE!!
WHAT?
SPLASH
WELL, AT LEAST YOUR UNIFORM IS A NICE BRIGHT RED AGAIN!
GULP! MAYBE IT'S TOO BRIGHT A RED!
RUN! GENERAL!
4

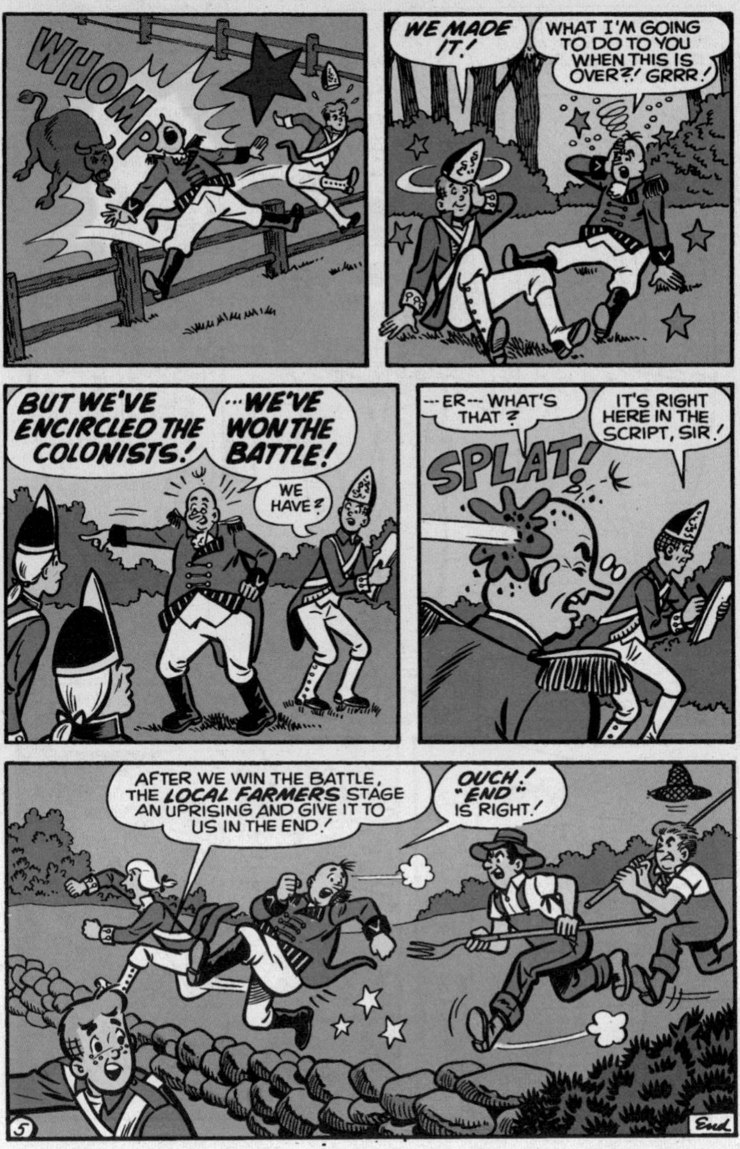
WHOMP
WE MADE IT!
WHAT I'M GOING TO DO TO YOU WHEN THIS IS OVER?! GRRR!
BUT WE'VE ENCIRCLED THE COLONISTS!
...WE'VE WON THE BATTLE!
WE HAVE?
---ER--- WHAT'S THAT?
IT'S RIGHT HERE IN THE SCRIPT, SIR!
SPLAT!
AFTER WE WIN THE BATTLE, THE LOCAL FARMERS STAGE AN UPRISING AND GIVE IT TO US IN THE END!
OUCH! "END" IS RIGHT!
5
End

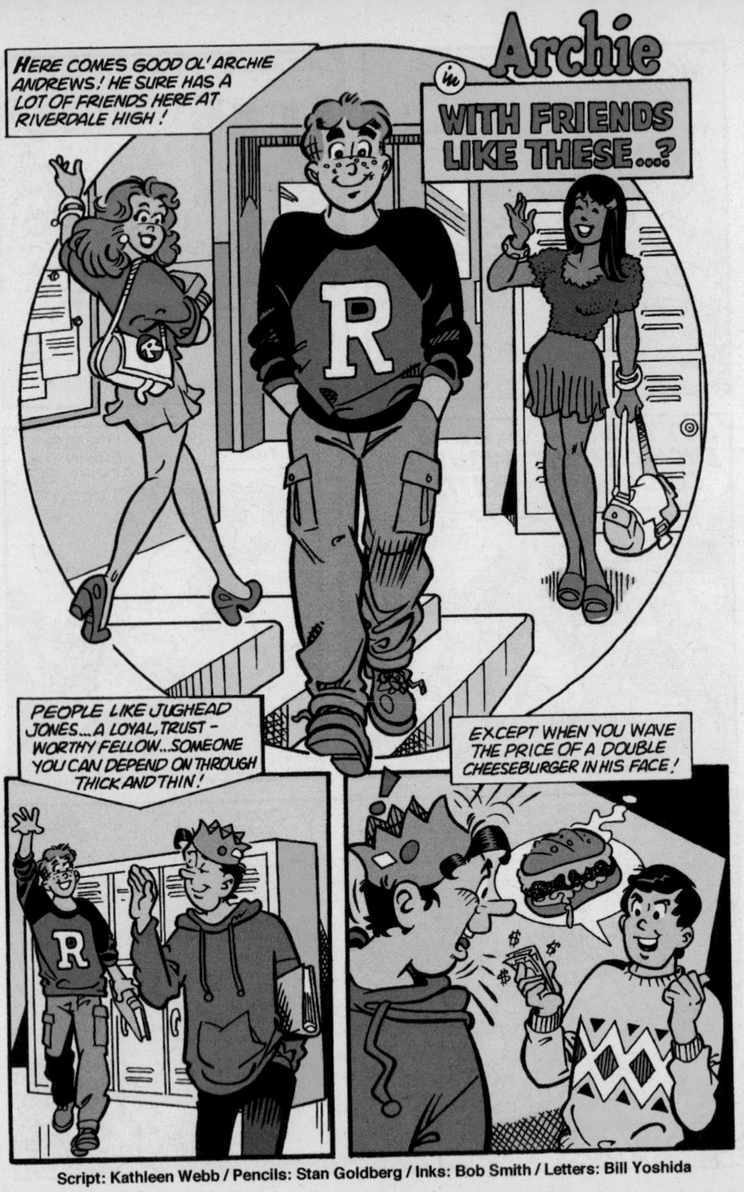
Archie
in
WITH FRIENDS LIKE THESE...?
HERE COMES GOOD OL' ARCHIE ANDREWS! HE SURE HAS A LOT OF FRIENDS HERE AT RIVERDALE HIGH!
PEOPLE LIKE JUGHEAD JONES... A LOYAL, TRUST-WORTHY FELLOW... SOMEONE YOU CAN DEPEND ON THROUGH THICK AND THIN!
EXCEPT WHEN YOU WAVE THE PRICE OF A DOUBLE CHEESEBURGER IN HIS FACE!

Script: Kathleen Webb / Pencils: Stan Goldberg / Inks: Bob Smith / Letters: Bill Yoshida

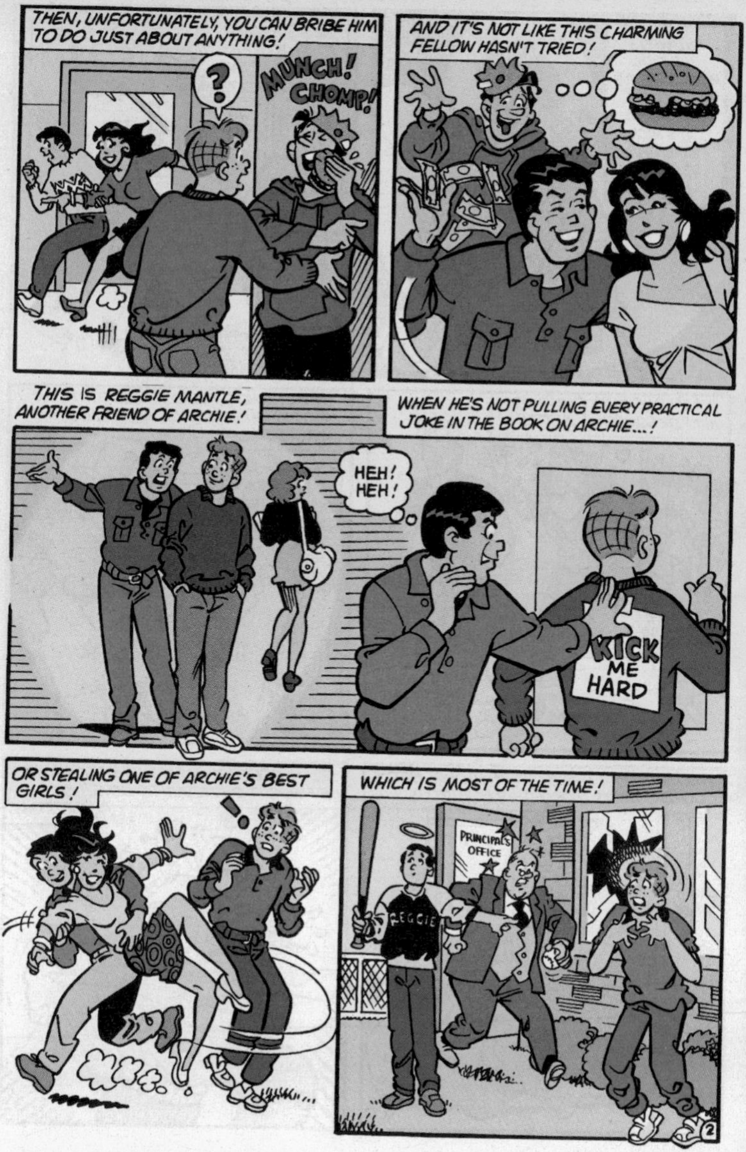
THEN, UNFORTUNATELY, YOU CAN BRIBE HIM TO DO JUST ABOUT ANYTHING!
?
MUNCH! CHOMP!
AND IT'S NOT LIKE THIS CHARMING FELLOW HASN'T TRIED!
THIS IS REGGIE MANTLE, ANOTHER FRIEND OF ARCHIE!
WHEN HE'S NOT PULLING EVERY PRACTICAL JOKE IN THE BOOK ON ARCHIE...!
HEH! HEH!
KICK ME HARD
OR STEALING ONE OF ARCHIE'S BEST GIRLS!
!
WHICH IS MOST OF THE TIME!
PRINCIPAL'S OFFICE
REGGIE
2

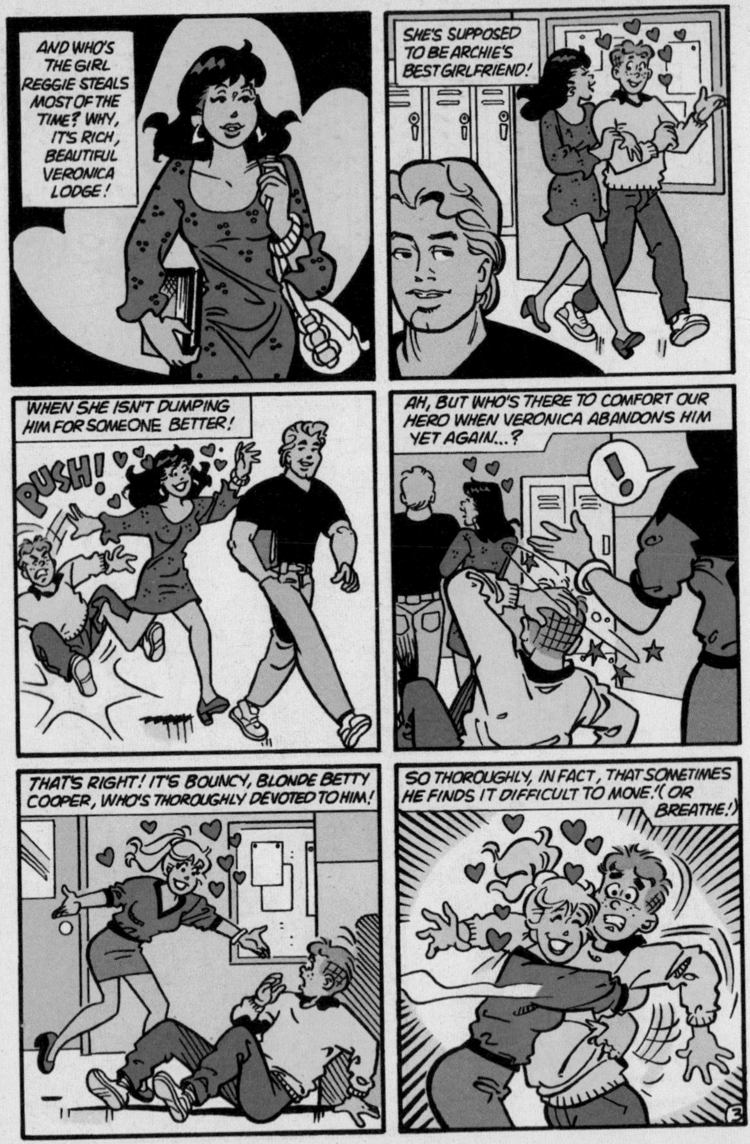
AND WHO'S THE GIRL REGGIE STEALS MOST OF THE TIME? WHY, IT'S RICH, BEAUTIFUL VERONICA LODGE!
SHE'S SUPPOSED TO BE ARCHIE'S BEST GIRLFRIEND!
WHEN SHE ISN'T DUMPING HIM FOR SOMEONE BETTER!
PUSH!
AH, BUT WHO'S THERE TO COMFORT OUR HERO WHEN VERONICA ABANDONS HIM YET AGAIN...?
!
THAT'S RIGHT! IT'S BOUNCY, BLONDE BETTY COOPER, WHO'S THOROUGHLY DEVOTED TO HIM!
SO THOROUGHLY, IN FACT, THAT SOMETIMES HE FINDS IT DIFFICULT TO MOVE! (OR BREATHE!)
3

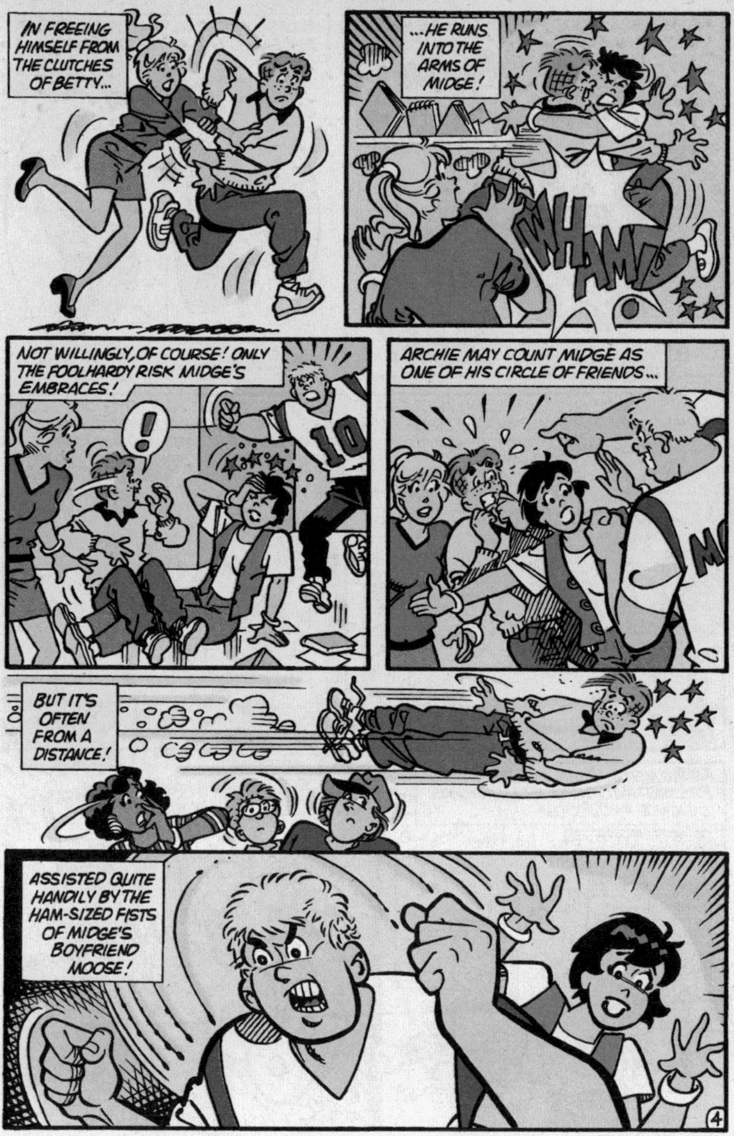

IN FREEING HIMSELF FROM THE CLUTCHES OF BETTY...
...HE RUNS INTO THE ARMS OF MIDGE!
WHAM!
NOT WILLINGLY, OF COURSE! ONLY THE FOOLHARDY RISK MIDGE'S EMBRACES!
!
10
ARCHIE MAY COUNT MIDGE AS ONE OF HIS CIRCLE OF FRIENDS...
BUT IT'S OFTEN FROM A DISTANCE!
ASSISTED QUITE HANDILY BY THE HAM-SIZED FISTS OF MIDGE'S BOYFRIEND MOOSE!
4

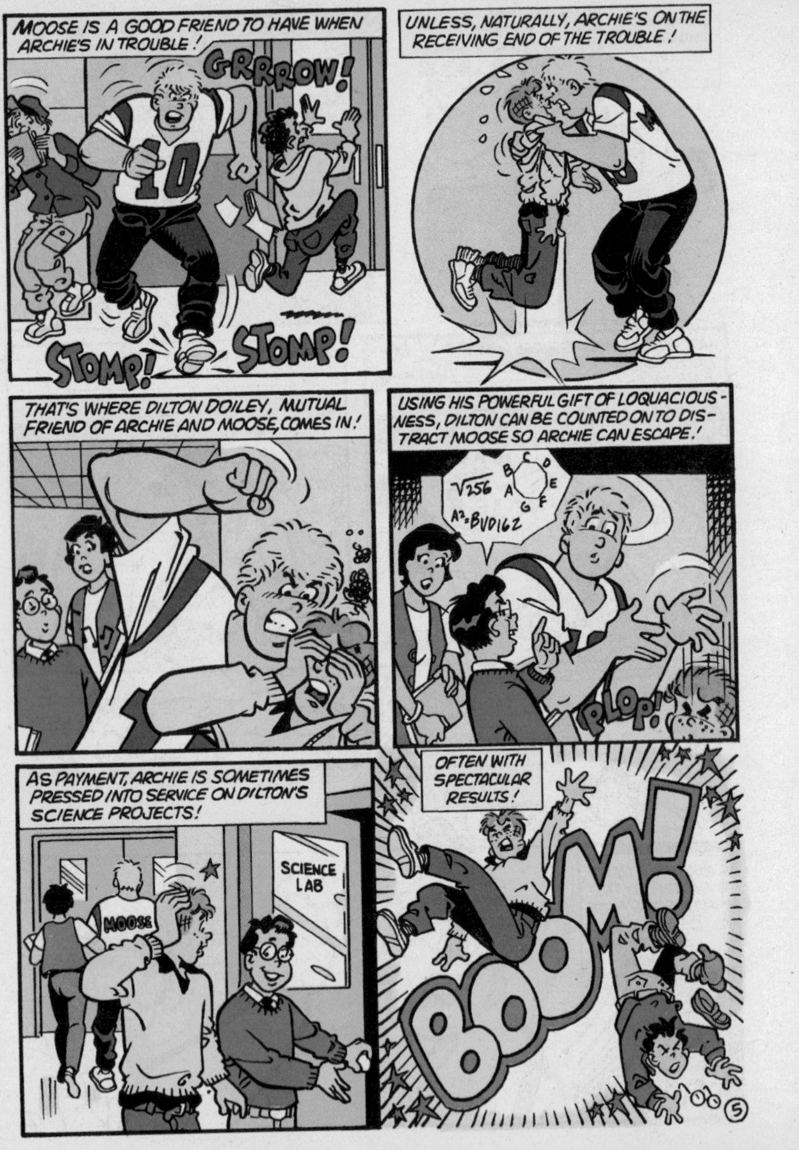
MOOSE IS A GOOD FRIEND TO HAVE WHEN ARCHIE'S IN TROUBLE!
GRRROW!
STOMP!
STOMP!
UNLESS, NATURALLY, ARCHIE'S ON THE RECEIVING END OF THE TROUBLE!
THAT'S WHERE DILTON DOILEY, MUTUAL FRIEND OF ARCHIE AND MOOSE, COMES IN!
USING HIS POWERFUL GIFT OF LOQUACIOUS-NESS, DILTON CAN BE COUNTED ON TO DIS-TRACT MOOSE SO ARCHIE CAN ESCAPE!
√256
A B C D E F G
A²=BVD162
PLOP!
AS PAYMENT, ARCHIE IS SOMETIMES PRESSED INTO SERVICE ON DILTON'S SCIENCE PROJECTS!
SCIENCE LAB
MOOSE
OFTEN WITH SPECTACULAR RESULTS!
BOOOM!
5

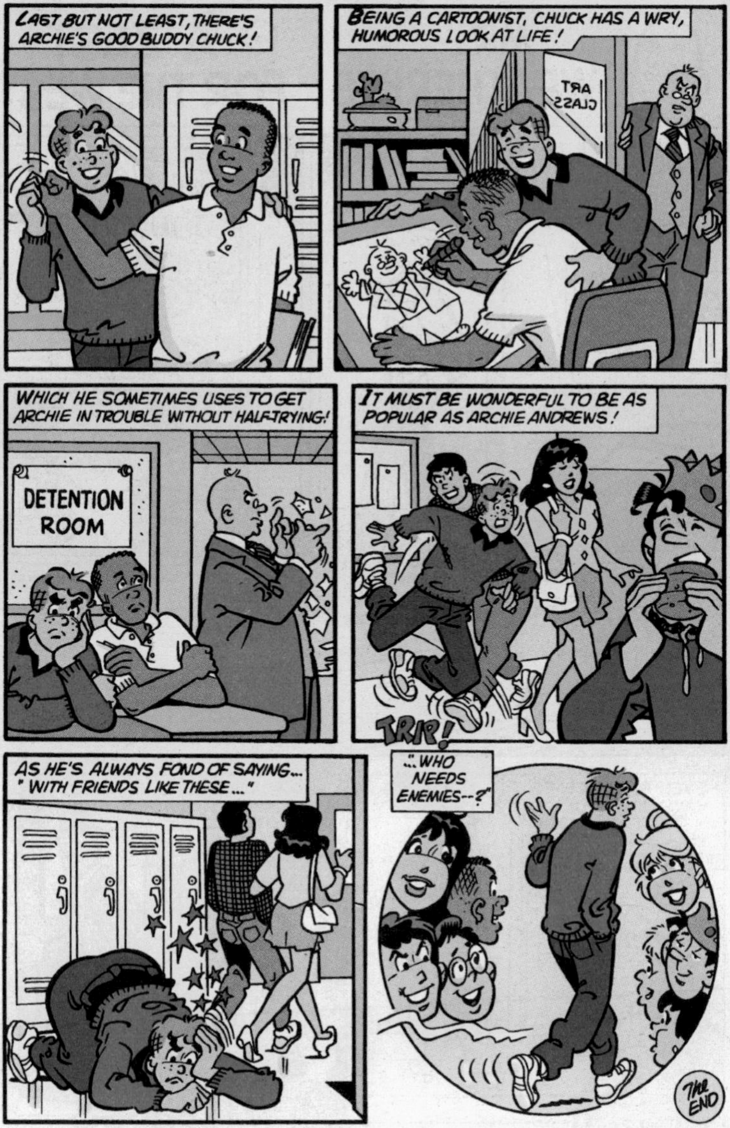
LAST BUT NOT LEAST, THERE'S ARCHIE'S GOOD BUDDY CHUCK!
BEING A CARTOONIST, CHUCK HAS A WRY, HUMOROUS LOOK AT LIFE!
ART CLASS
WHICH HE SOMETIMES USES TO GET ARCHIE IN TROUBLE WITHOUT HALF-TRYING!
DETENTION ROOM
IT MUST BE WONDERFUL TO BE AS POPULAR AS ARCHIE ANDREWS!
TRIP!
AS HE'S ALWAYS FOND OF SAYING... " WITH FRIENDS LIKE THESE..."
"...WHO NEEDS ENEMIES--?"
THE END

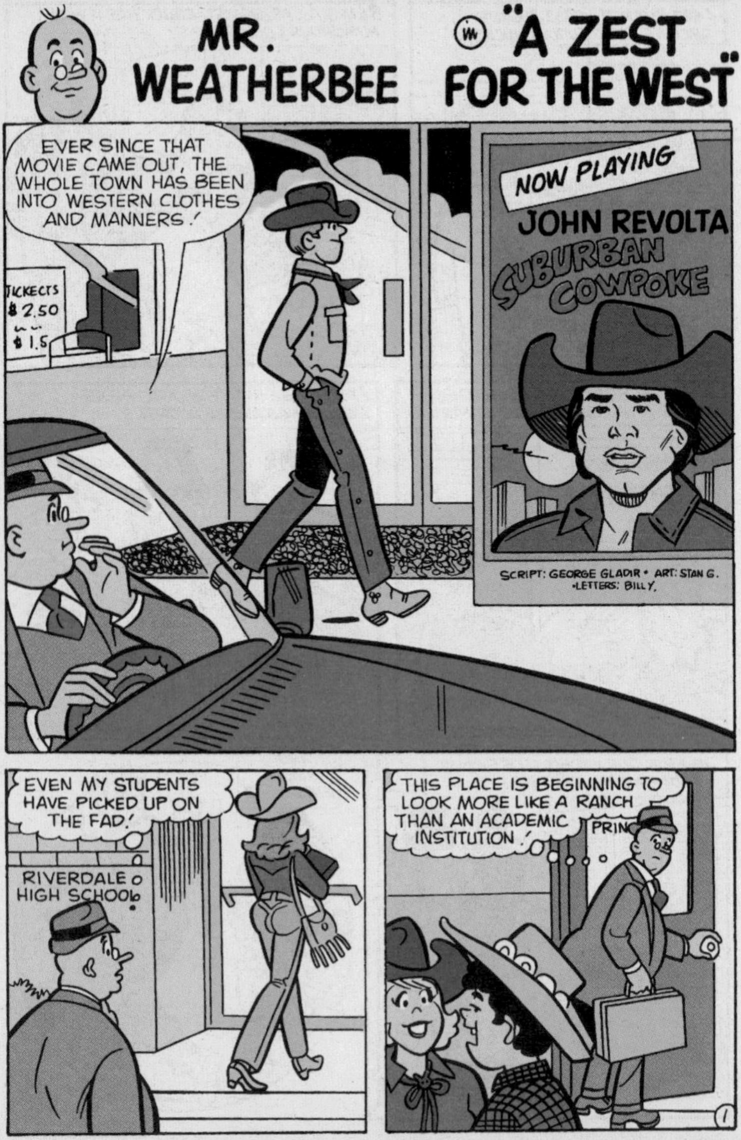
MR. WEATHERBEE
in "A ZEST FOR THE WEST"
EVER SINCE THAT MOVIE CAME OUT, THE WHOLE TOWN HAS BEEN INTO WESTERN CLOTHES AND MANNERS!
TICKECTS
$2.50
$1.5
NOW PLAYING
JOHN REVOLTA
SUBURBAN COWPOKE
SCRIPT: GEORGE GLADIR • ART: STAN G. • LETTERS: BILLY.
EVEN MY STUDENTS HAVE PICKED UP ON THE FAD!
RIVERDALE HIGH SCHOOL
THIS PLACE IS BEGINNING TO LOOK MORE LIKE A RANCH THAN AN ACADEMIC INSTITUTION!
PRIN
1

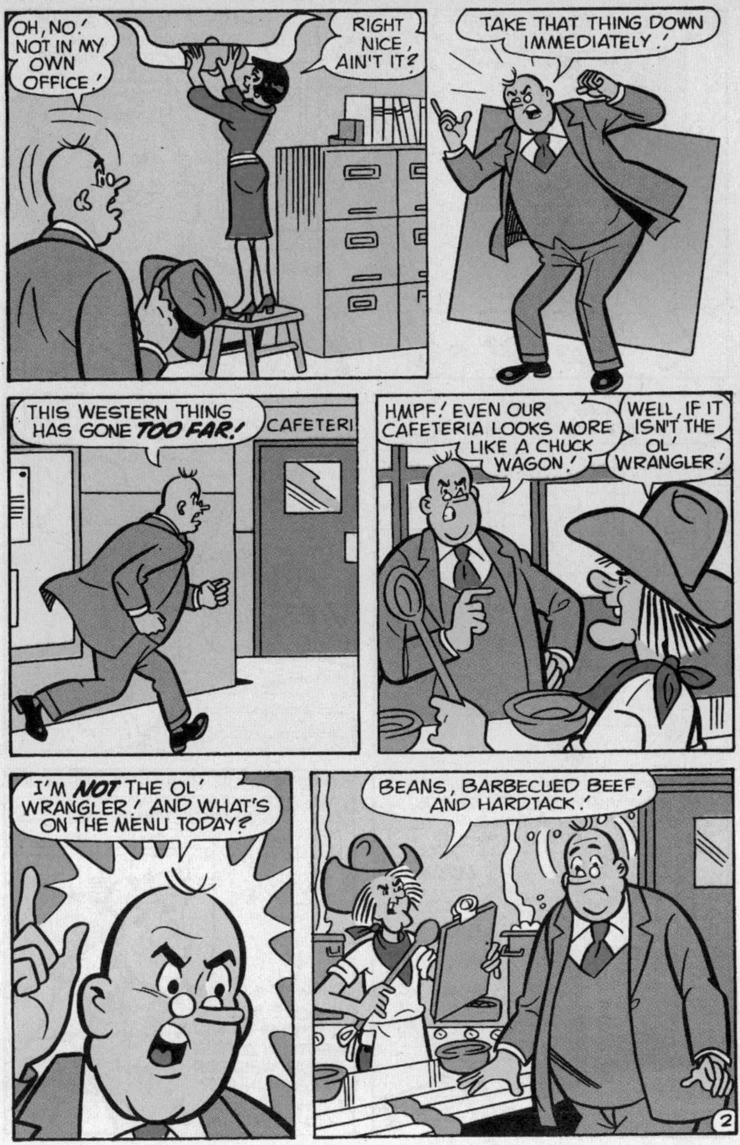
OH, NO! NOT IN MY OWN OFFICE!
RIGHT NICE, AIN'T IT?
TAKE THAT THING DOWN IMMEDIATELY!
THIS WESTERN THING HAS GONE TOO FAR!
CAFETERI
HMPF! EVEN OUR CAFETERIA LOOKS MORE LIKE A CHUCK WAGON!
WELL, IF IT ISN'T THE OL' WRANGLER!
I'M NOT THE OL' WRANGLER! AND WHAT'S ON THE MENU TODAY?
BEANS, BARBECUED BEEF, AND HARDTACK!
2

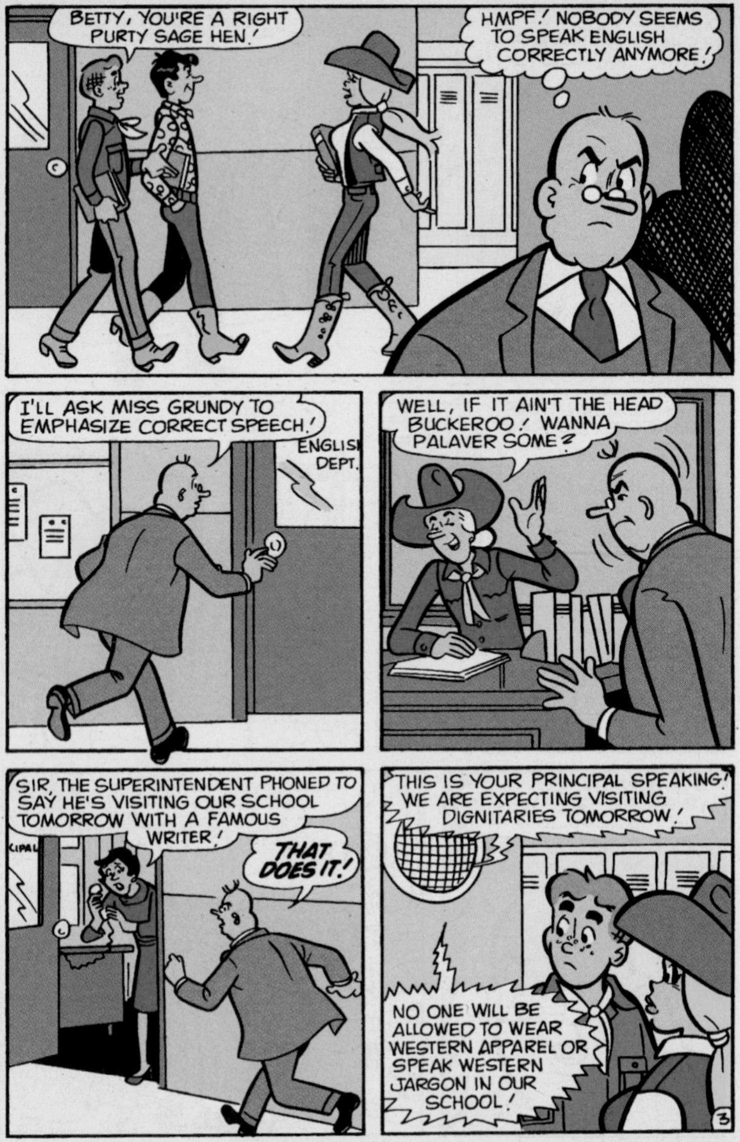
BETTY, YOU'RE A RIGHT PURTY SAGE HEN!
HMPF! NOBODY SEEMS TO SPEAK ENGLISH CORRECTLY ANYMORE!
I'LL ASK MISS GRUNDY TO EMPHASIZE CORRECT SPEECH!
ENGLISH DEPT.
WELL, IF IT AIN'T THE HEAD BUCKEROO! WANNA PALAVER SOME?
SIR, THE SUPERINTENDENT PHONED TO SAY HE'S VISITING OUR SCHOOL TOMORROW WITH A FAMOUS WRITER!
THAT DOES IT!
THIS IS YOUR PRINCIPAL SPEAKING! WE ARE EXPECTING VISITING DIGNITARIES TOMORROW!
NO ONE WILL BE ALLOWED TO WEAR WESTERN APPAREL OR SPEAK WESTERN JARGON IN OUR SCHOOL!
3

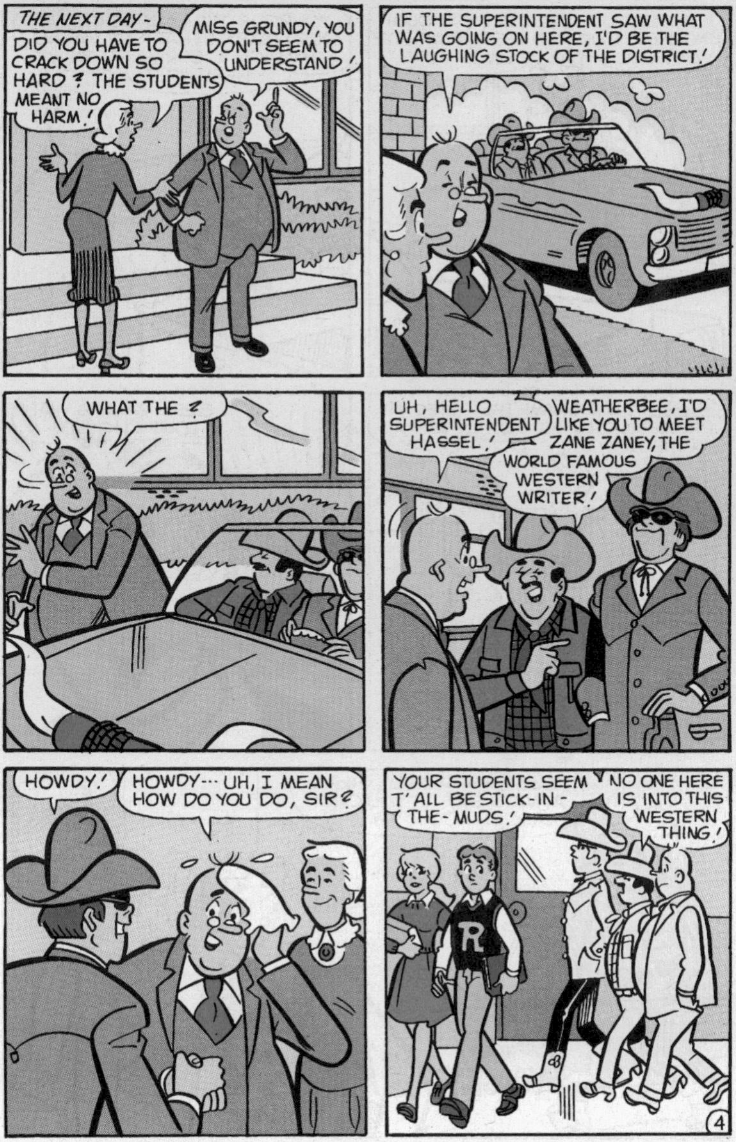
THE NEXT DAY-
DID YOU HAVE TO CRACK DOWN SO HARD? THE STUDENTS MEANT NO HARM!
MISS GRUNDY, YOU DON'T SEEM TO UNDERSTAND!
IF THE SUPERINTENDENT SAW WHAT WAS GOING ON HERE, I'D BE THE LAUGHING STOCK OF THE DISTRICT!
WHAT THE ?
UH, HELLO SUPERINTENDENT HASSEL!
WEATHERBEE, I'D LIKE YOU TO MEET ZANE ZANEY, THE WORLD FAMOUS WESTERN WRITER!
HOWDY!
HOWDY... UH, I MEAN HOW DO YOU DO, SIR?
YOUR STUDENTS SEEM T' ALL BE STICK-IN-THE-MUDS!
NO ONE HERE IS INTO THIS WESTERN THING!

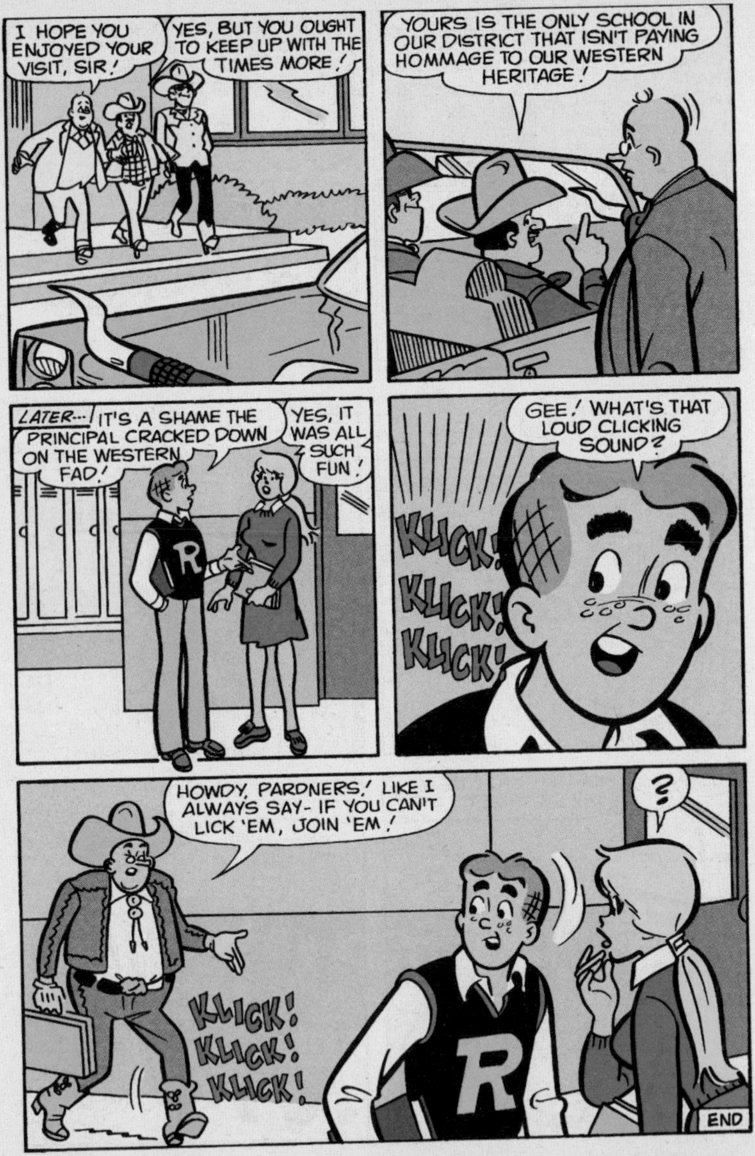
I HOPE YOU ENJOYED YOUR VISIT, SIR!
YES, BUT YOU OUGHT TO KEEP UP WITH THE TIMES MORE!
YOURS IS THE ONLY SCHOOL IN OUR DISTRICT THAT ISN'T PAYING HOMMAGE TO OUR WESTERN HERITAGE!
LATER...
IT'S A SHAME THE PRINCIPAL CRACKED DOWN ON THE WESTERN FAD!
YES, IT WAS ALL SUCH FUN!
GEE! WHAT'S THAT LOUD CLICKING SOUND?
KLICK! KLICK! KLICK!
HOWDY, PARDNERS! LIKE I ALWAYS SAY- IF YOU CAN'T LICK 'EM, JOIN 'EM!
?
KLICK! KLICK! KLICK!
END

Betty and Veronica in WHAT IF... Archie HAD AN IDENTICAL TWIN?

ARCHIE: BART! COME ON, WE'VE GOT TO HURRY, LITTLE BROTHER!

BART: LITTLE BROTHER?! I'M ONLY FIVE MINUTES YOUNGER THAN YOU, ARCHIE!

BILL GOLLIHER STORY	DAN PARENT PENCILS	RICH KOSLOWSKI INKS	GLENN WHITMORE COLORS	JACK MORELLI LETTERS

ARCHIE: WE'VE GOT TO GET TO POP'S! THE GIRLS ARE DROPPING BY!

BART: NOT THAT IT MATTERS TO ME! IT'S YOU THEY'RE ALWAYS AFTER!

BETTY: HI, ARCHIE!

BART: HI, BETTY! DID YOU SEE BART?

1

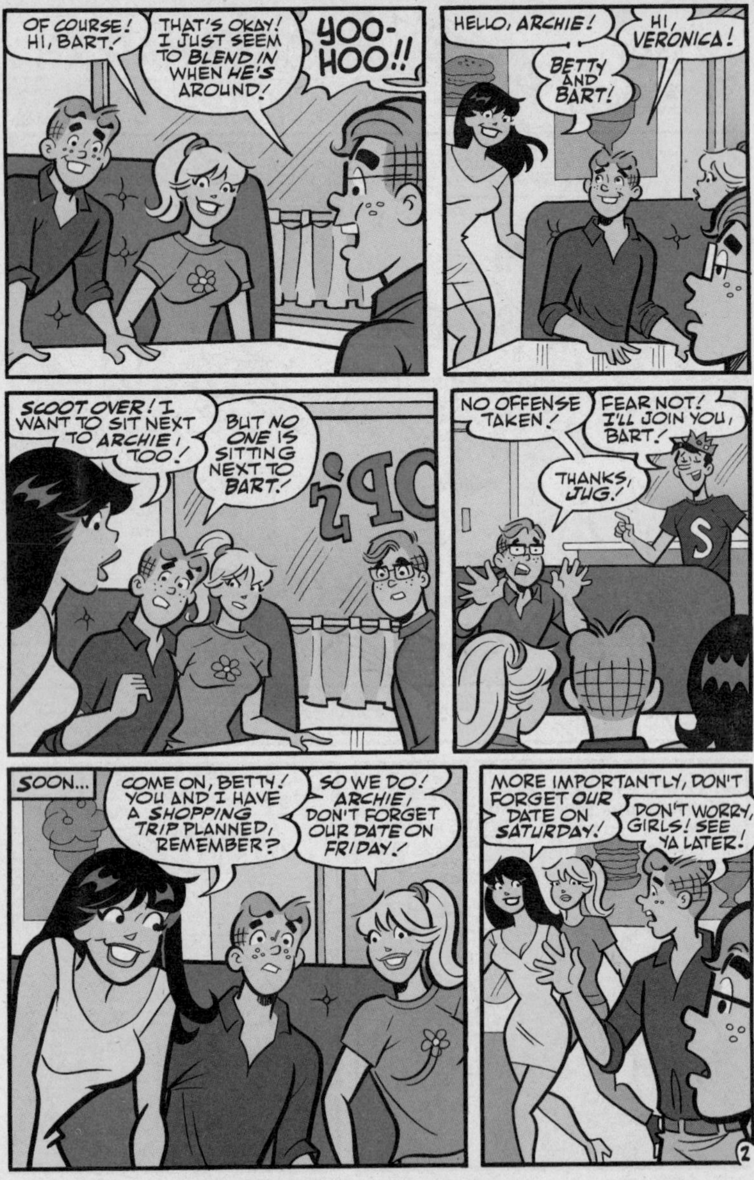

OF COURSE! HI, BART!
THAT'S OKAY! I JUST SEEM TO BLEND IN WHEN HE'S AROUND!
YOO-HOO!!
HELLO, ARCHIE!
BETTY AND BART!
HI, VERONICA!
SCOOT OVER! I WANT TO SIT NEXT TO ARCHIE, TOO!
BUT NO ONE IS SITTING NEXT TO BART!
OP'S
NO OFFENSE TAKEN!
FEAR NOT! I'LL JOIN YOU, BART!
THANKS, JUG!
SOON...
COME ON, BETTY! YOU AND I HAVE A SHOPPING TRIP PLANNED, REMEMBER?
SO WE DO! ARCHIE, DON'T FORGET OUR DATE ON FRIDAY!
MORE IMPORTANTLY, DON'T FORGET OUR DATE ON SATURDAY!
DON'T WORRY, GIRLS! SEE YA LATER!
2

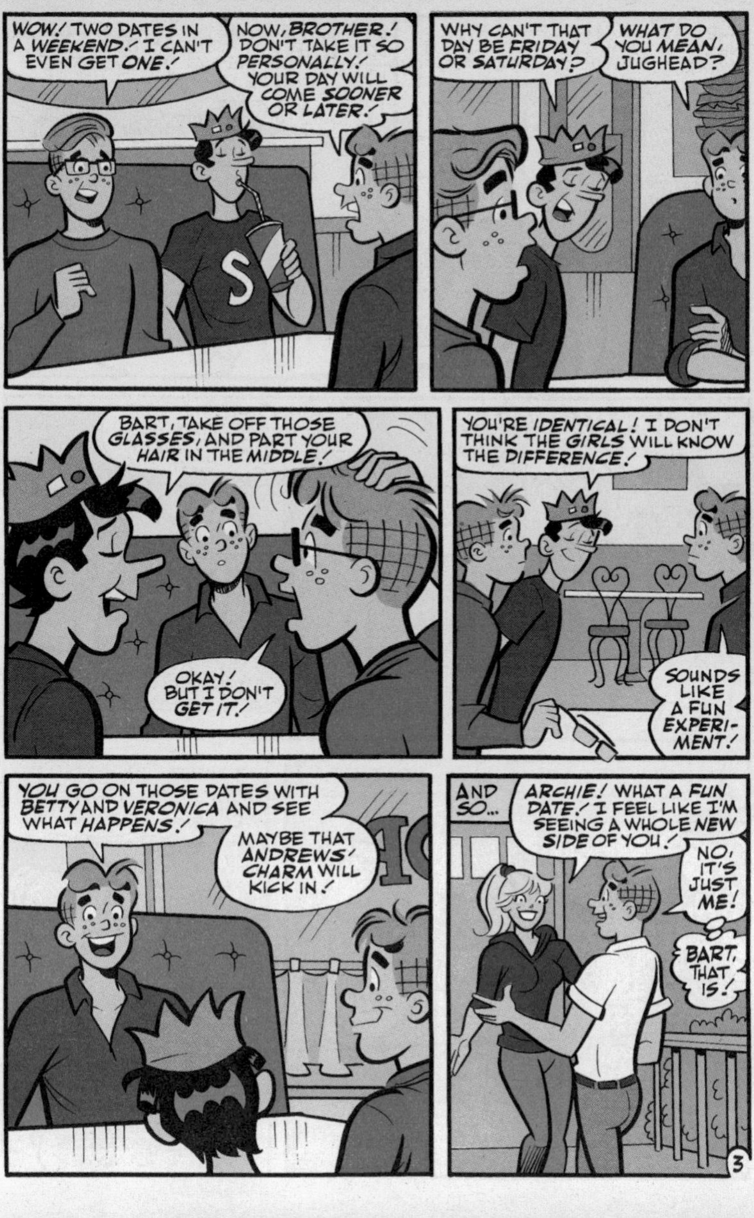

WOW! TWO DATES IN A WEEKEND! I CAN'T EVEN GET ONE!
NOW, BROTHER! DON'T TAKE IT SO PERSONALLY! YOUR DAY WILL COME SOONER OR LATER!
WHY CAN'T THAT DAY BE FRIDAY OR SATURDAY?
WHAT DO YOU MEAN, JUGHEAD?
BART, TAKE OFF THOSE GLASSES, AND PART YOUR HAIR IN THE MIDDLE!
OKAY! BUT I DON'T GET IT!
YOU'RE IDENTICAL! I DON'T THINK THE GIRLS WILL KNOW THE DIFFERENCE!
SOUNDS LIKE A FUN EXPERIMENT!
YOU GO ON THOSE DATES WITH BETTY AND VERONICA AND SEE WHAT HAPPENS!
MAYBE THAT ANDREWS' CHARM WILL KICK IN!
AND SO...
ARCHIE! WHAT A FUN DATE! I FEEL LIKE I'M SEEING A WHOLE NEW SIDE OF YOU!
NO, IT'S JUST ME!
BART, THAT IS!
3

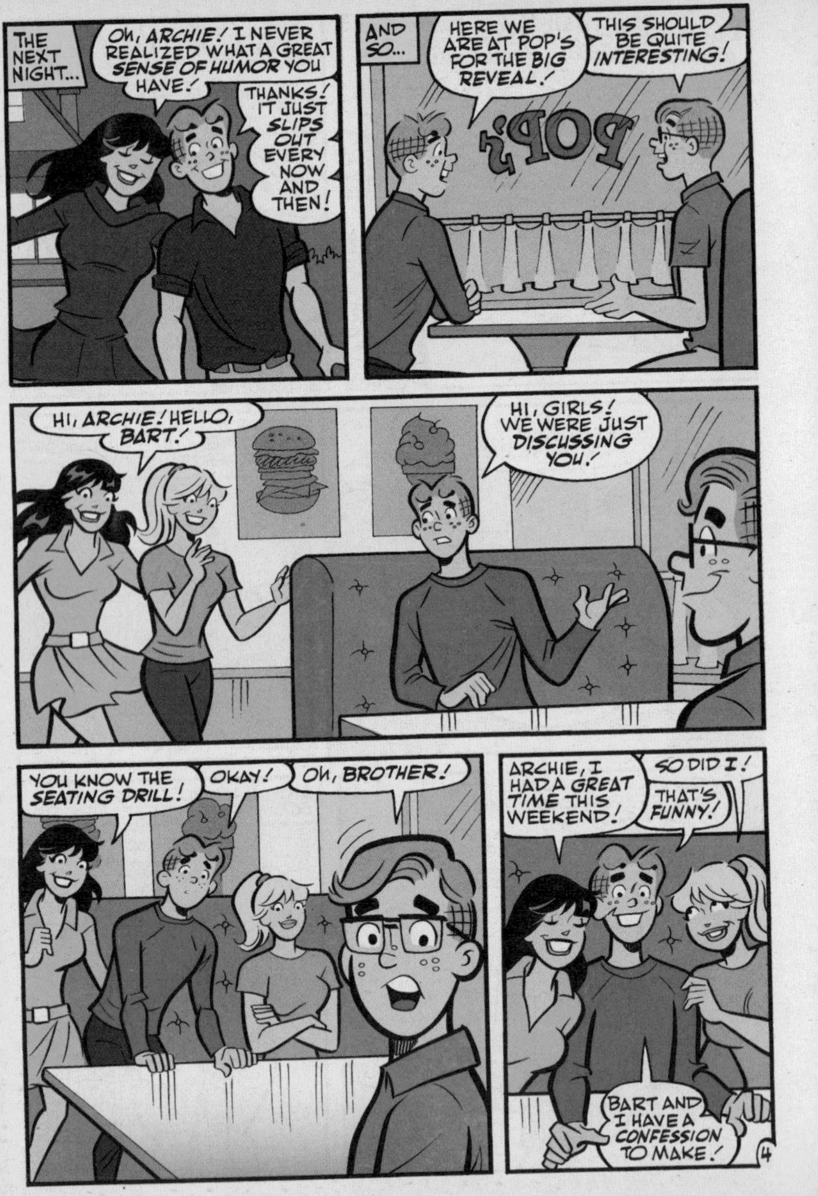

THE NEXT NIGHT...
OH, ARCHIE! I NEVER REALIZED WHAT A GREAT SENSE OF HUMOR YOU HAVE!
THANKS! IT JUST SLIPS OUT EVERY NOW AND THEN!
AND SO...
HERE WE ARE AT POP'S FOR THE BIG REVEAL!
THIS SHOULD BE QUITE INTERESTING!
POP'S
HI, ARCHIE! HELLO, BART!
HI, GIRLS! WE WERE JUST DISCUSSING YOU!
YOU KNOW THE SEATING DRILL!
OKAY!
OH, BROTHER!
ARCHIE, I HAD A GREAT TIME THIS WEEKEND!
SO DID I!
THAT'S FUNNY!
BART AND I HAVE A CONFESSION TO MAKE!
4

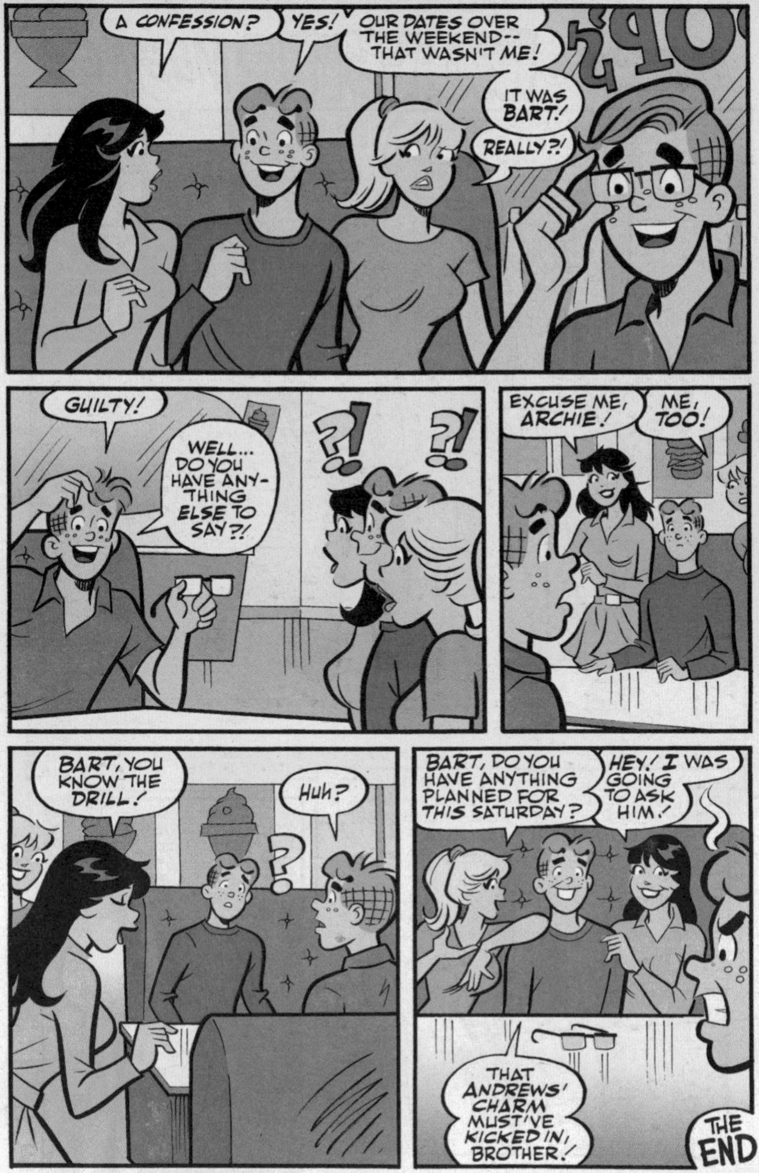
A CONFESSION?
YES!
OUR DATES OVER THE WEEKEND-- THAT WASN'T ME!
IT WAS BART!
REALLY?!
GUILTY!
WELL... DO YOU HAVE ANYTHING ELSE TO SAY?!
?!
?!
EXCUSE ME, ARCHIE!
ME, TOO!
BART, YOU KNOW THE DRILL!
Huh?
?
BART, DO YOU HAVE ANYTHING PLANNED FOR THIS SATURDAY?
HEY! I WAS GOING TO ASK HIM!
THAT ANDREWS' CHARM MUST'VE KICKED IN, BROTHER!
THE END

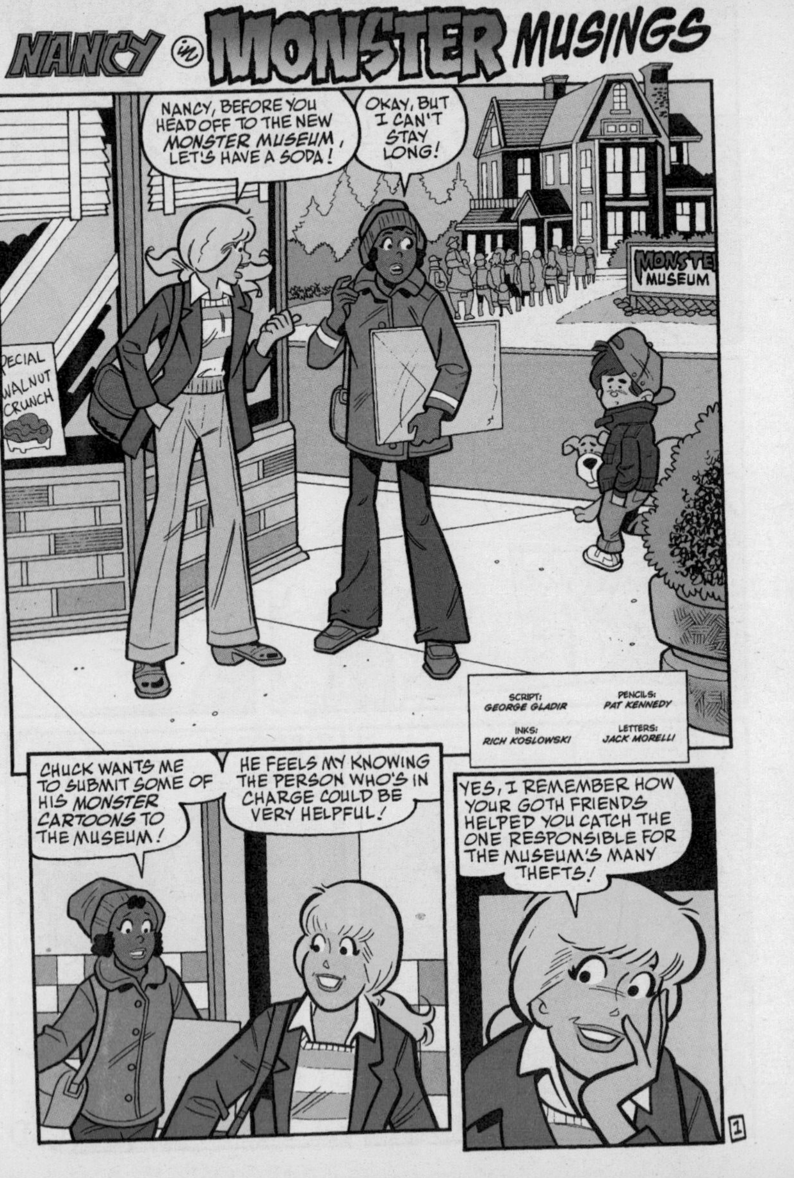
NANCY in MONSTER MUSINGS
NANCY, BEFORE YOU HEAD OFF TO THE NEW MONSTER MUSEUM, LET'S HAVE A SODA!
OKAY, BUT I CAN'T STAY LONG!
MONSTER MUSEUM
PECIAL WALNUT CRUNCH
SCRIPT: GEORGE GLADIR
PENCILS: PAT KENNEDY
INKS: RICH KOSLOWSKI
LETTERS: JACK MORELLI
CHUCK WANTS ME TO SUBMIT SOME OF HIS MONSTER CARTOONS TO THE MUSEUM!
HE FEELS MY KNOWING THE PERSON WHO'S IN CHARGE COULD BE VERY HELPFUL!
YES, I REMEMBER HOW YOUR GOTH FRIENDS HELPED YOU CATCH THE ONE RESPONSIBLE FOR THE MUSEUM'S MANY THEFTS!
1

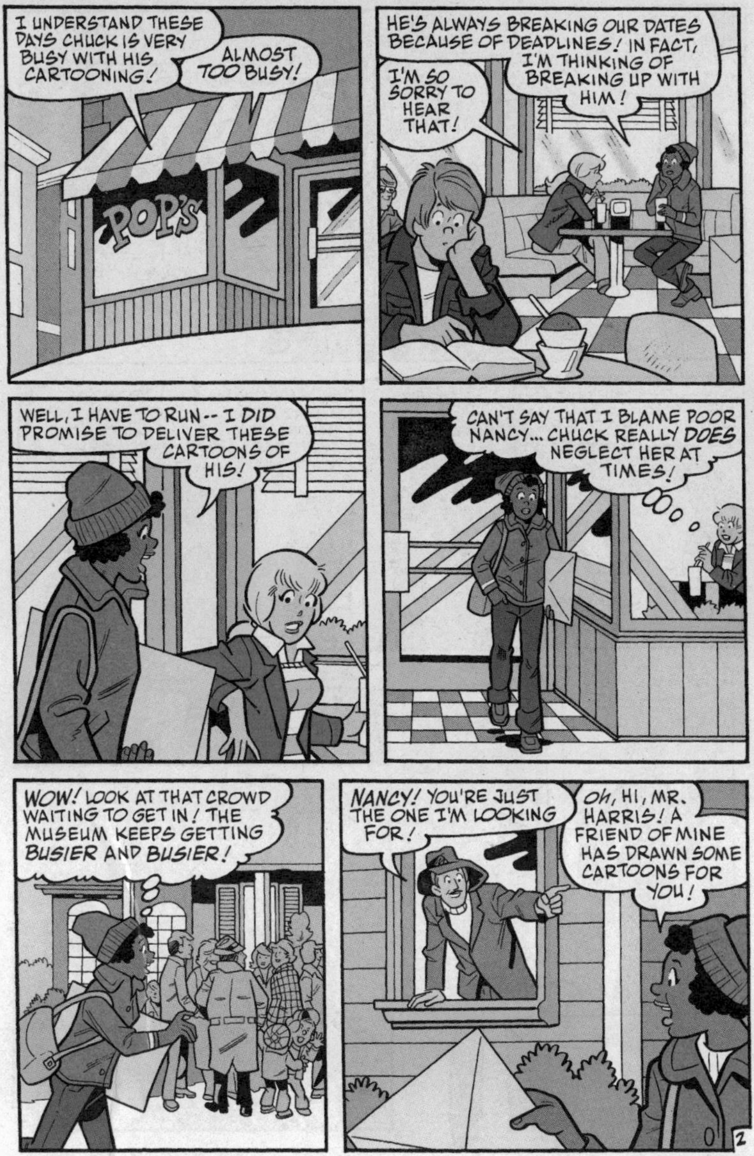
I UNDERSTAND THESE DAYS CHUCK IS VERY BUSY WITH HIS CARTOONING!
ALMOST TOO BUSY!
POP'S
HE'S ALWAYS BREAKING OUR DATES BECAUSE OF DEADLINES! IN FACT, I'M THINKING OF BREAKING UP WITH HIM!
I'M SO SORRY TO HEAR THAT!
WELL, I HAVE TO RUN -- I DID PROMISE TO DELIVER THESE CARTOONS OF HIS!
CAN'T SAY THAT I BLAME POOR NANCY... CHUCK REALLY DOES NEGLECT HER AT TIMES!
WOW! LOOK AT THAT CROWD WAITING TO GET IN! THE MUSEUM KEEPS GETTING BUSIER AND BUSIER!
NANCY! YOU'RE JUST THE ONE I'M LOOKING FOR!
Oh, HI, MR. HARRIS! A FRIEND OF MINE HAS DRAWN SOME CARTOONS FOR YOU!
2

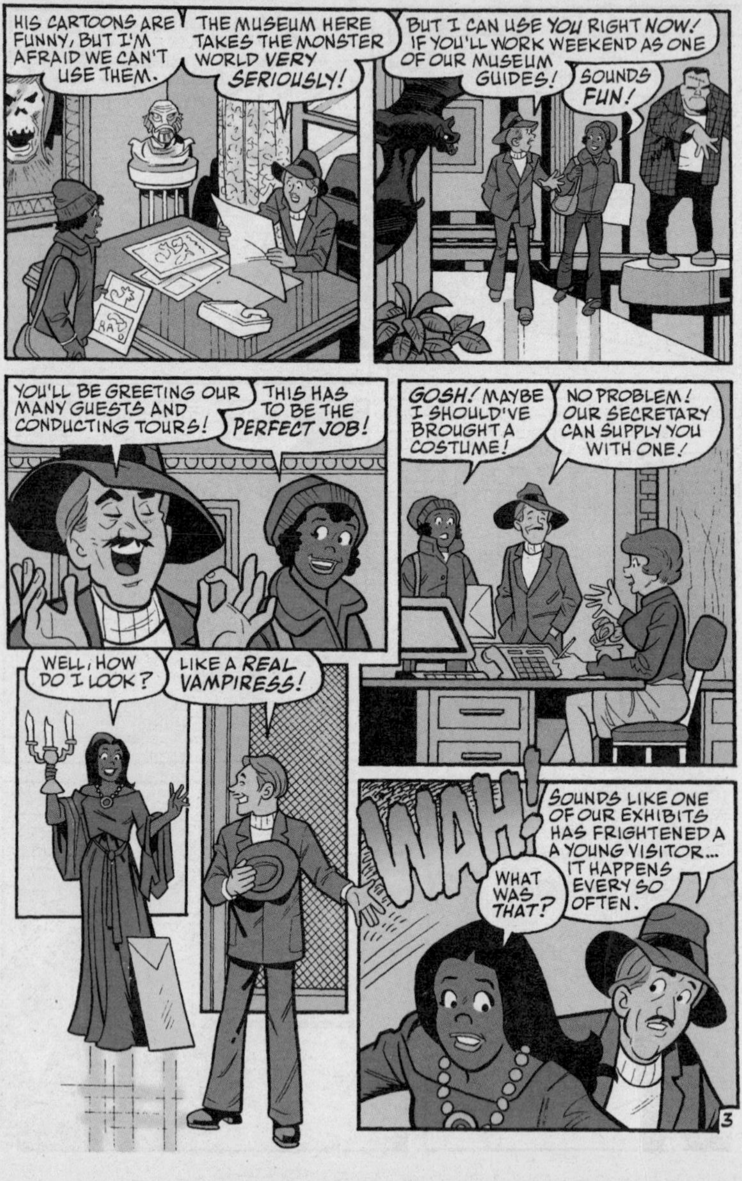

HIS CARTOONS ARE FUNNY, BUT I'M AFRAID WE CAN'T USE THEM.
THE MUSEUM HERE TAKES THE MONSTER WORLD VERY SERIOUSLY!
BUT I CAN USE YOU RIGHT NOW! IF YOU'LL WORK WEEKEND AS ONE OF OUR MUSEUM GUIDES!
SOUNDS FUN!
YOU'LL BE GREETING OUR MANY GUESTS AND CONDUCTING TOURS!
THIS HAS TO BE THE PERFECT JOB!
GOSH! MAYBE I SHOULD'VE BROUGHT A COSTUME!
NO PROBLEM! OUR SECRETARY CAN SUPPLY YOU WITH ONE!
WELL, HOW DO I LOOK?
LIKE A REAL VAMPIRESS!
WAH!
SOUNDS LIKE ONE OF OUR EXHIBITS HAS FRIGHTENED A A YOUNG VISITOR... IT HAPPENS EVERY SO OFTEN.
WHAT WAS THAT?

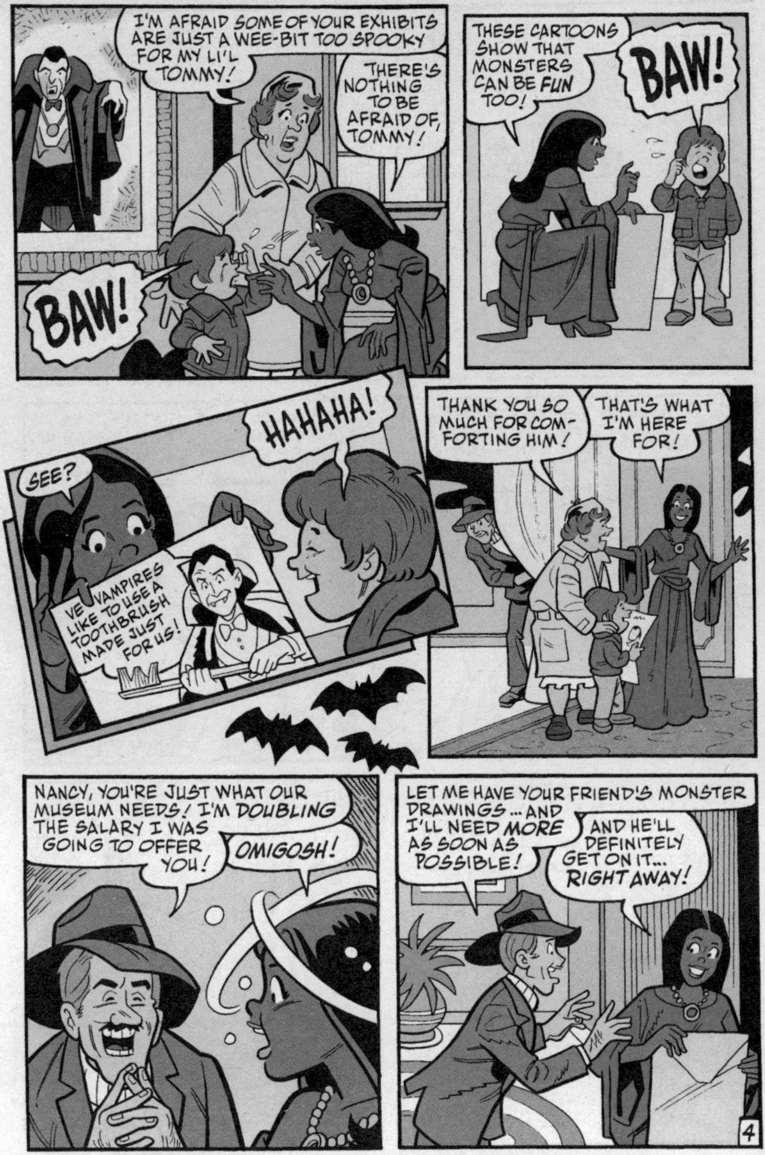
I'M AFRAID SOME OF YOUR EXHIBITS ARE JUST A WEE-BIT TOO SPOOKY FOR MY LI'L TOMMY!
THERE'S NOTHING TO BE AFRAID OF, TOMMY!
BAW!
THESE CARTOONS SHOW THAT MONSTERS CAN BE FUN TOO!
BAW!
HAHAHA!
SEE?
VE VAMPIRES LIKE TO USE A TOOTHBRUSH MADE JUST FOR US!
THANK YOU SO MUCH FOR COMFORTING HIM!
THAT'S WHAT I'M HERE FOR!
NANCY, YOU'RE JUST WHAT OUR MUSEUM NEEDS! I'M DOUBLING THE SALARY I WAS GOING TO OFFER YOU!
OMIGOSH!
LET ME HAVE YOUR FRIEND'S MONSTER DRAWINGS ... AND I'LL NEED MORE AS SOON AS POSSIBLE!
AND HE'LL DEFINITELY GET ON IT... RIGHT AWAY!

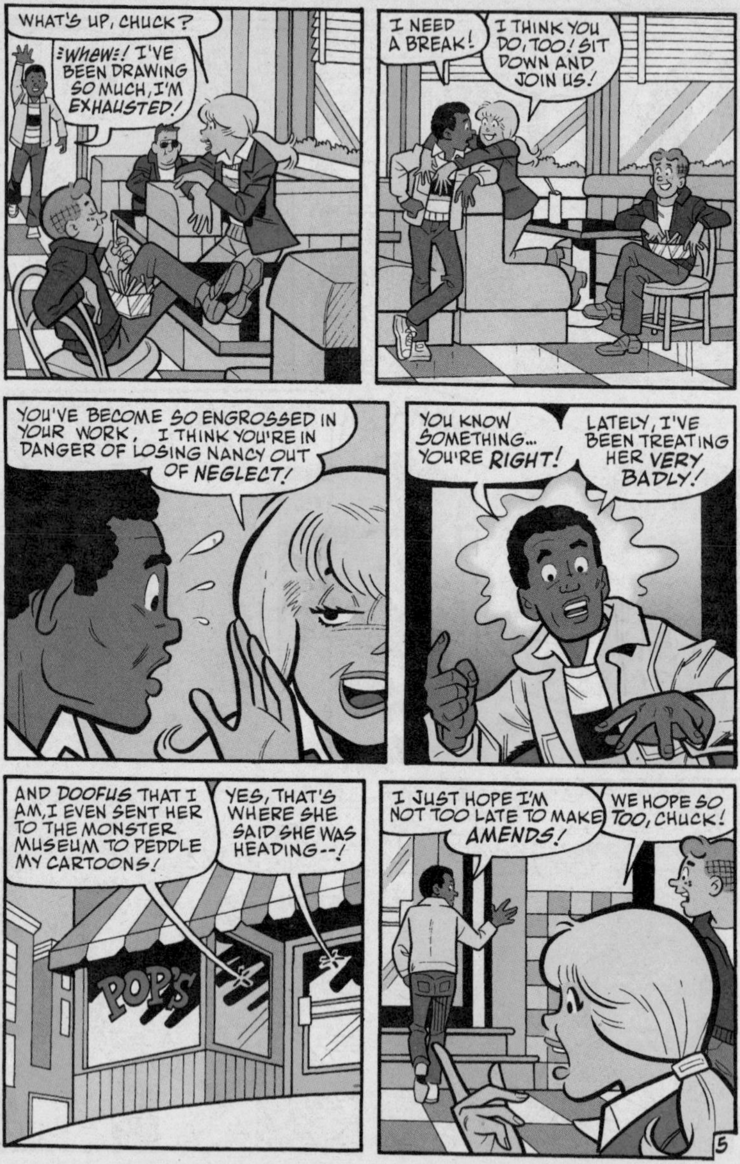
WHAT'S UP, CHUCK?
WHEW! I'VE BEEN DRAWING SO MUCH, I'M EXHAUSTED!
I NEED A BREAK!
I THINK YOU DO, TOO! SIT DOWN AND JOIN US!
YOU'VE BECOME SO ENGROSSED IN YOUR WORK, I THINK YOU'RE IN DANGER OF LOSING NANCY OUT OF NEGLECT!
YOU KNOW SOMETHING... YOU'RE RIGHT!
LATELY, I'VE BEEN TREATING HER VERY BADLY!
AND DOOFUS THAT I AM, I EVEN SENT HER TO THE MONSTER MUSEUM TO PEDDLE MY CARTOONS!
YES, THAT'S WHERE SHE SAID SHE WAS HEADING--!
POP'S
I JUST HOPE I'M NOT TOO LATE TO MAKE AMENDS!
WE HOPE SO TOO, CHUCK!

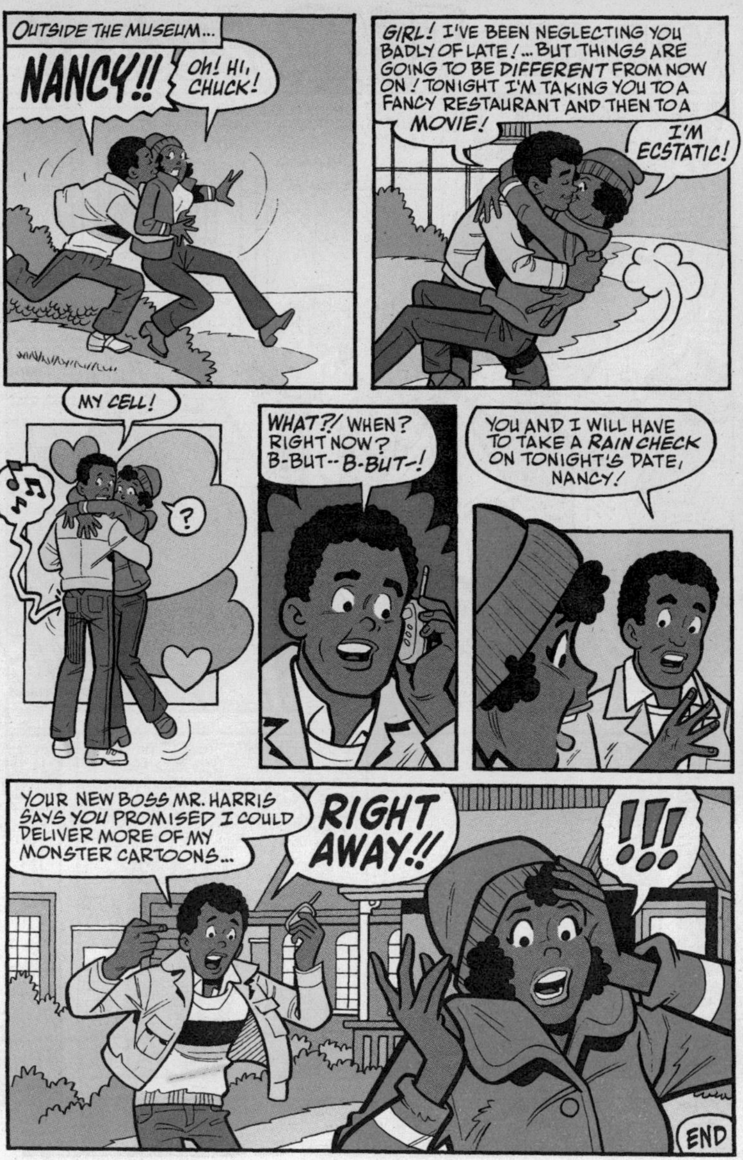
OUTSIDE THE MUSEUM...
NANCY!!
OH! HI, CHUCK!
GIRL! I'VE BEEN NEGLECTING YOU BADLY OF LATE! ...BUT THINGS ARE GOING TO BE DIFFERENT FROM NOW ON! TONIGHT I'M TAKING YOU TO A FANCY RESTAURANT AND THEN TO A MOVIE!
I'M ECSTATIC!
MY CELL!
?
WHAT?! WHEN? RIGHT NOW? B-BUT-- B-BUT-!
YOU AND I WILL HAVE TO TAKE A RAIN CHECK ON TONIGHT'S DATE, NANCY!
YOUR NEW BOSS MR. HARRIS SAYS YOU PROMISED I COULD DELIVER MORE OF MY MONSTER CARTOONS...
RIGHT AWAY!!
!!!
END

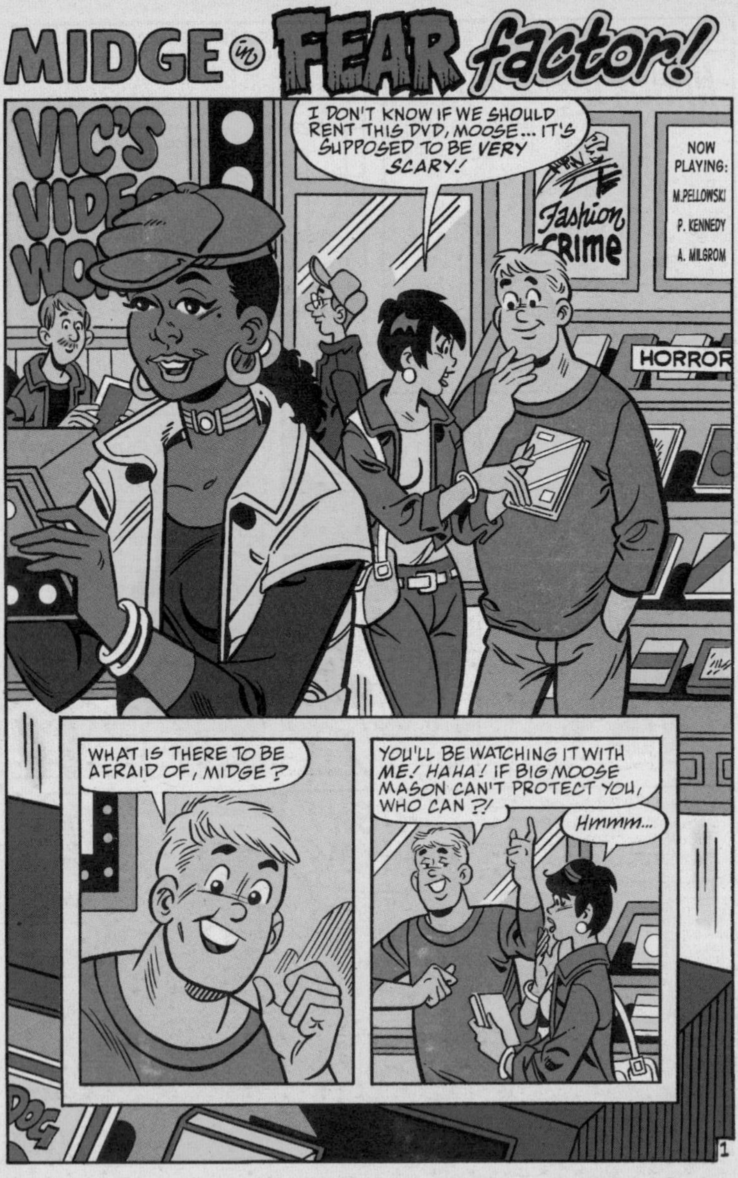
MIDGE in FEAR factor!
VIC'S VIDE WO
I DON'T KNOW IF WE SHOULD RENT THIS DVD, MOOSE... IT'S SUPPOSED TO BE VERY SCARY!
Fashion Crime
NOW PLAYING: M.PELLOWSKI P. KENNEDY A. MILGROM
HORROR
WHAT IS THERE TO BE AFRAID OF, MIDGE?
YOU'LL BE WATCHING IT WITH ME! HAHA! IF BIG MOOSE MASON CAN'T PROTECT YOU, WHO CAN?!
Hmmm...
DOG

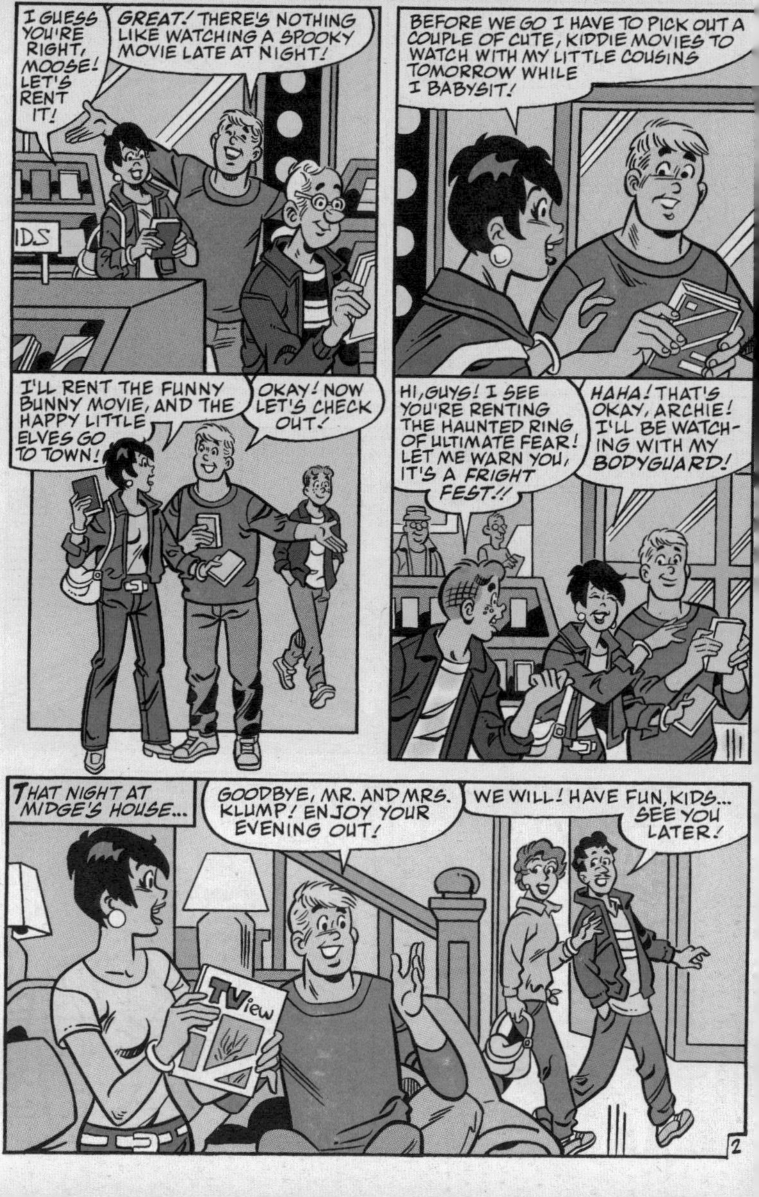
I GUESS YOU'RE RIGHT, MOOSE! LET'S RENT IT!
GREAT! THERE'S NOTHING LIKE WATCHING A SPOOKY MOVIE LATE AT NIGHT!
BEFORE WE GO I HAVE TO PICK OUT A COUPLE OF CUTE, KIDDIE MOVIES TO WATCH WITH MY LITTLE COUSINS TOMORROW WHILE I BABYSIT!
I'LL RENT THE FUNNY BUNNY MOVIE, AND THE HAPPY LITTLE ELVES GO TO TOWN!
OKAY! NOW LET'S CHECK OUT!
HI, GUYS! I SEE YOU'RE RENTING THE HAUNTED RING OF ULTIMATE FEAR! LET ME WARN YOU, IT'S A FRIGHT FEST!!
HAHA! THAT'S OKAY, ARCHIE! I'LL BE WATCHING WITH MY BODYGUARD!
THAT NIGHT AT MIDGE'S HOUSE...
GOODBYE, MR. AND MRS. KLUMP! ENJOY YOUR EVENING OUT!
WE WILL! HAVE FUN, KIDS... SEE YOU LATER!
TView
2

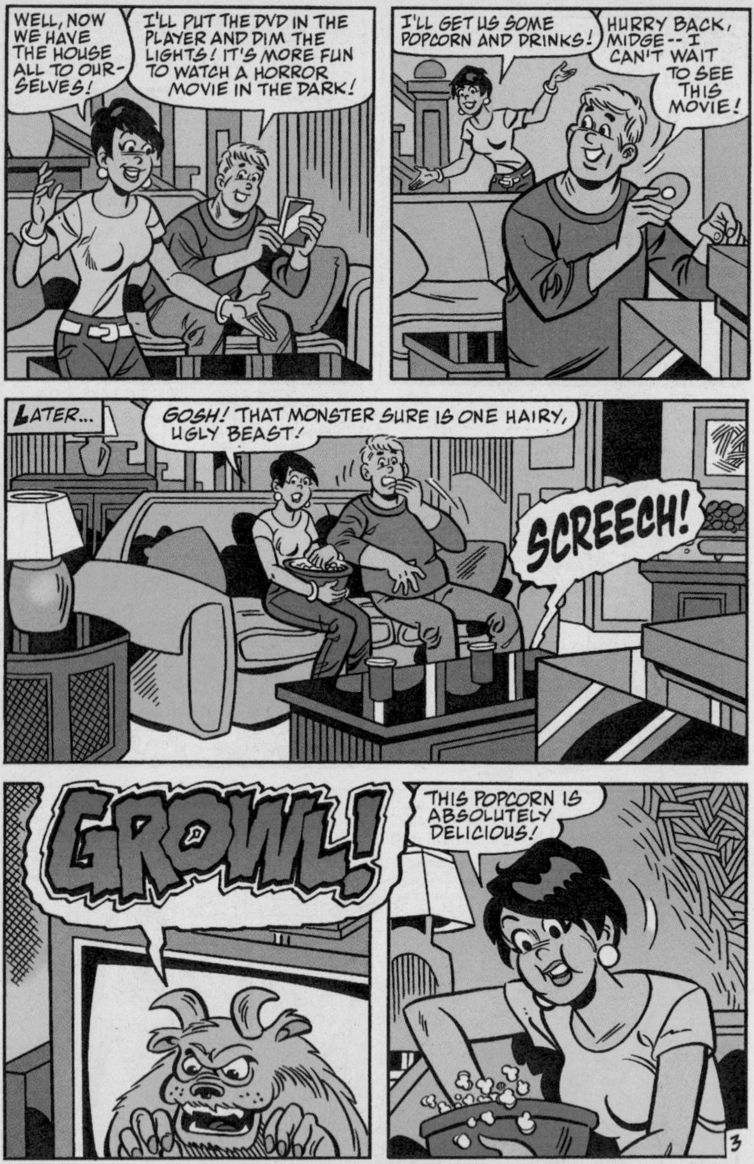
WELL, NOW WE HAVE THE HOUSE ALL TO OUR-SELVES!
I'LL PUT THE DVD IN THE PLAYER AND DIM THE LIGHTS! IT'S MORE FUN TO WATCH A HORROR MOVIE IN THE DARK!
I'LL GET US SOME POPCORN AND DRINKS!
HURRY BACK, MIDGE-- I CAN'T WAIT TO SEE THIS MOVIE!
LATER...
GOSH! THAT MONSTER SURE IS ONE HAIRY, UGLY BEAST!
SCREECH!
GROWL!
THIS POPCORN IS ABSOLUTELY DELICIOUS!
3

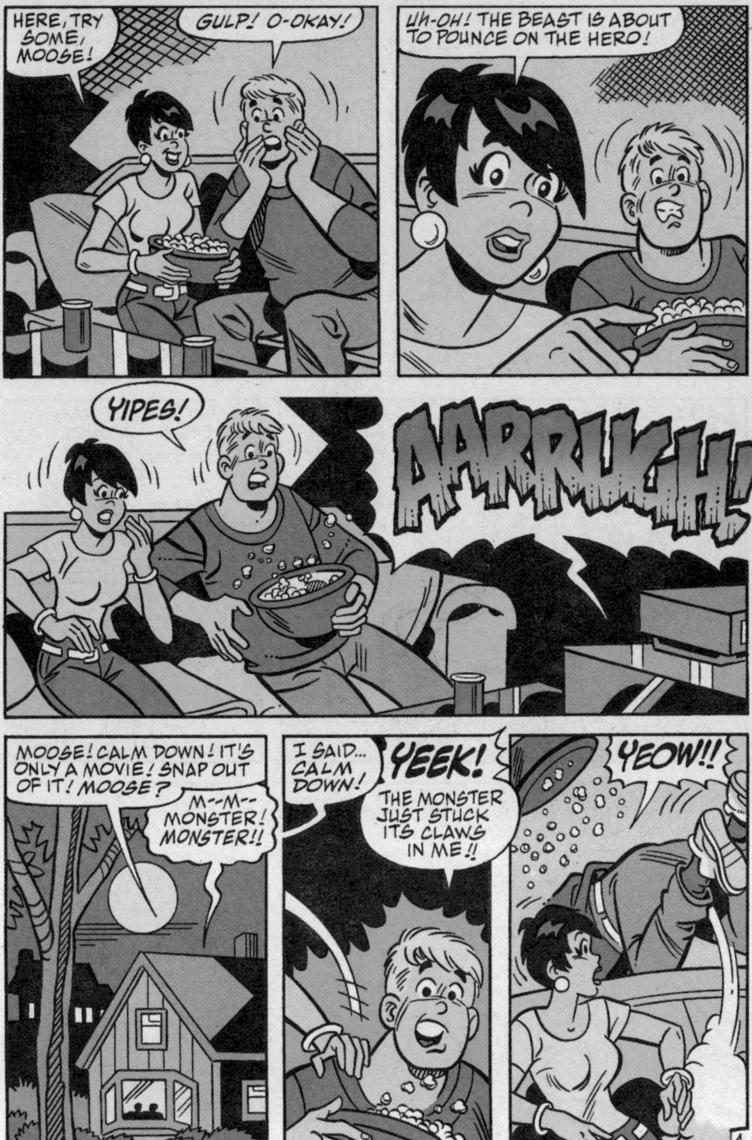
HERE, TRY SOME, MOOSE!
GULP! O-OKAY!
UH-OH! THE BEAST IS ABOUT TO POUNCE ON THE HERO!
YIPES!
AARRUGH!
MOOSE! CALM DOWN! IT'S ONLY A MOVIE! SNAP OUT OF IT! MOOSE?
M--M-- MONSTER! MONSTER!!
I SAID... CALM DOWN!
YEEK!
THE MONSTER JUST STUCK ITS CLAWS IN ME!!
YEOW!!
4

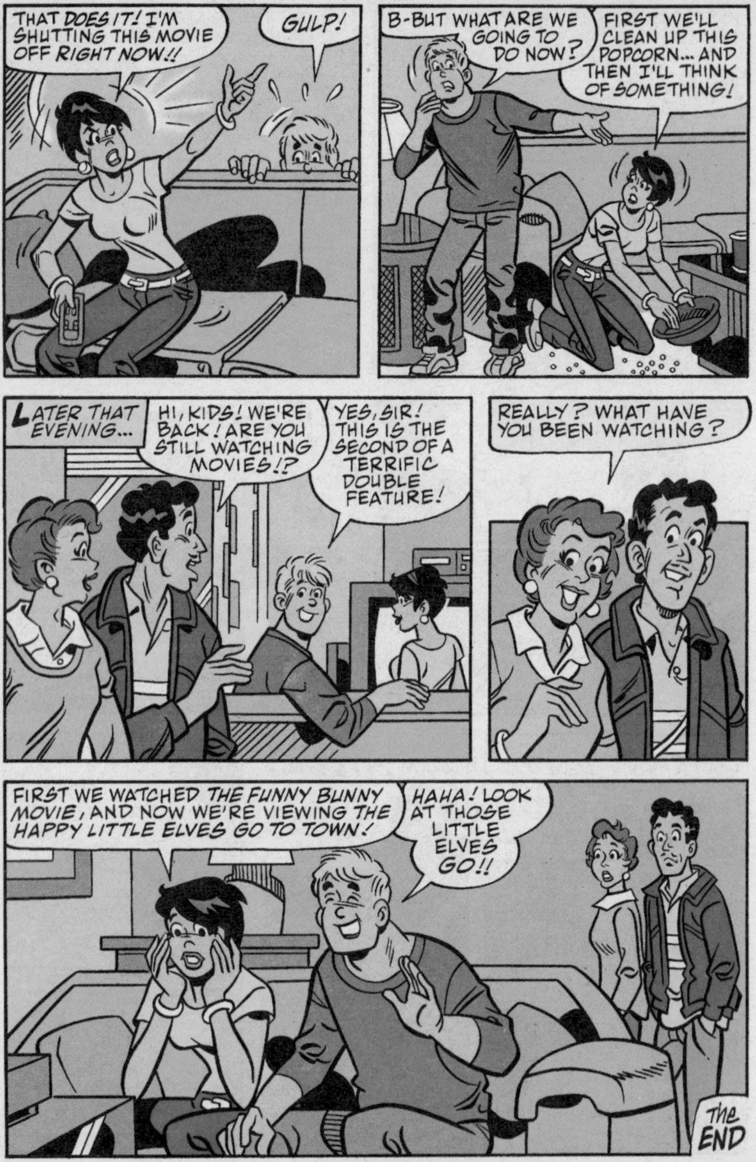
THAT DOES IT! I'M SHUTTING THIS MOVIE OFF RIGHT NOW!!
GULP!
B-BUT WHAT ARE WE GOING TO DO NOW?
FIRST WE'LL CLEAN UP THIS POPCORN... AND THEN I'LL THINK OF SOMETHING!
LATER THAT EVENING...
HI, KIDS! WE'RE BACK! ARE YOU STILL WATCHING MOVIES!?
YES, SIR! THIS IS THE SECOND OF A TERRIFIC DOUBLE FEATURE!
REALLY? WHAT HAVE YOU BEEN WATCHING?
FIRST WE WATCHED THE FUNNY BUNNY MOVIE, AND NOW WE'RE VIEWING THE HAPPY LITTLE ELVES GO TO TOWN!
HAHA! LOOK AT THOSE LITTLE ELVES GO!!
The END

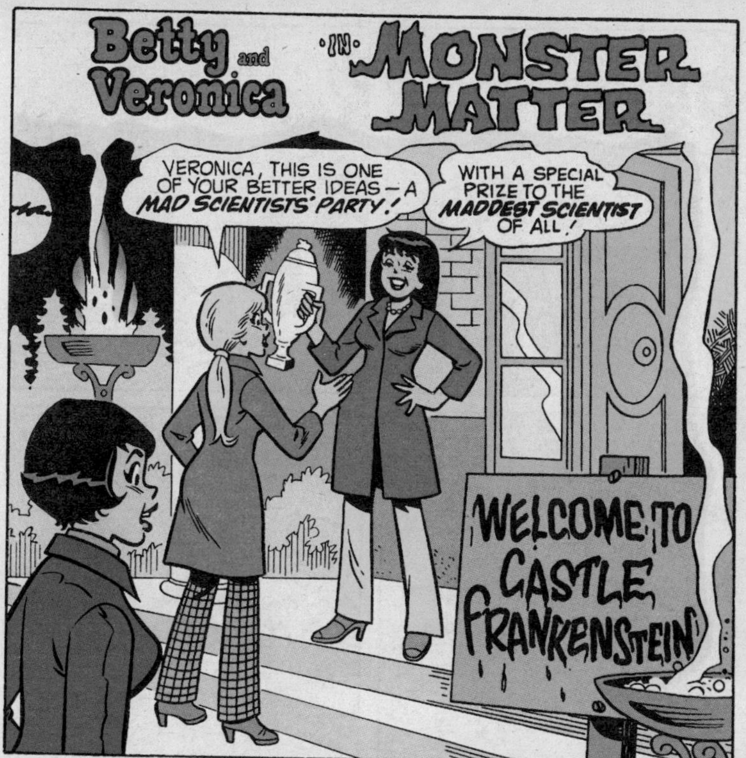
Betty and Veronica
·IN·
MONSTER MATTER
VERONICA, THIS IS ONE OF YOUR BETTER IDEAS — A MAD SCIENTISTS' PARTY!
WITH A SPECIAL PRIZE TO THE MADDEST SCIENTIST OF ALL!
WELCOME TO CASTLE FRANKENSTEIN

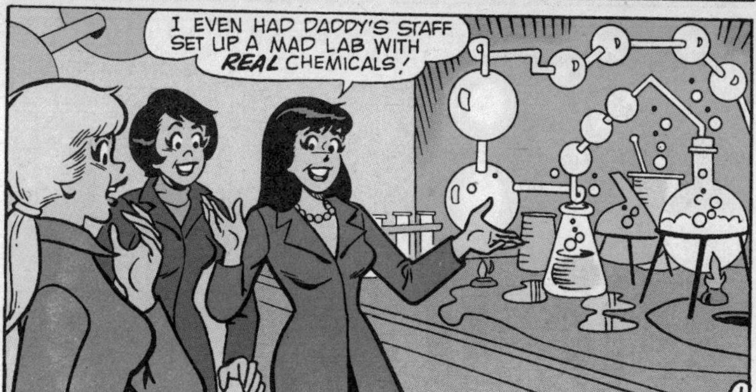
I EVEN HAD DADDY'S STAFF SET UP A MAD LAB WITH REAL CHEMICALS!
1

Script: George Gladir / Pencils: Stan Goldberg / Inks: Jon D'Agostino / Letters: Bill Yoshida

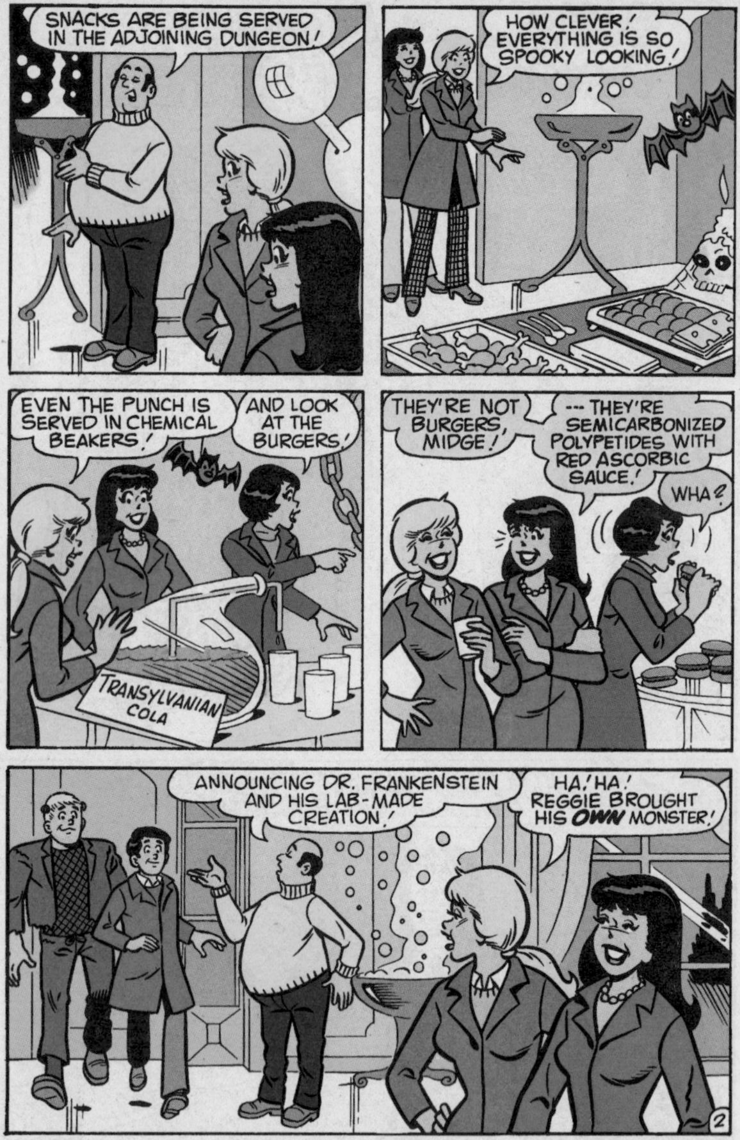
SNACKS ARE BEING SERVED IN THE ADJOINING DUNGEON!
HOW CLEVER! EVERYTHING IS SO SPOOKY LOOKING!
EVEN THE PUNCH IS SERVED IN CHEMICAL BEAKERS!
AND LOOK AT THE BURGERS!
TRANSYLVANIAN COLA
THEY'RE NOT BURGERS, MIDGE!
--- THEY'RE SEMICARBONIZED POLYPETIDES WITH RED ASCORBIC SAUCE!
WHA?
ANNOUNCING DR. FRANKENSTEIN AND HIS LAB-MADE CREATION!
HA! HA! REGGIE BROUGHT HIS OWN MONSTER!
2

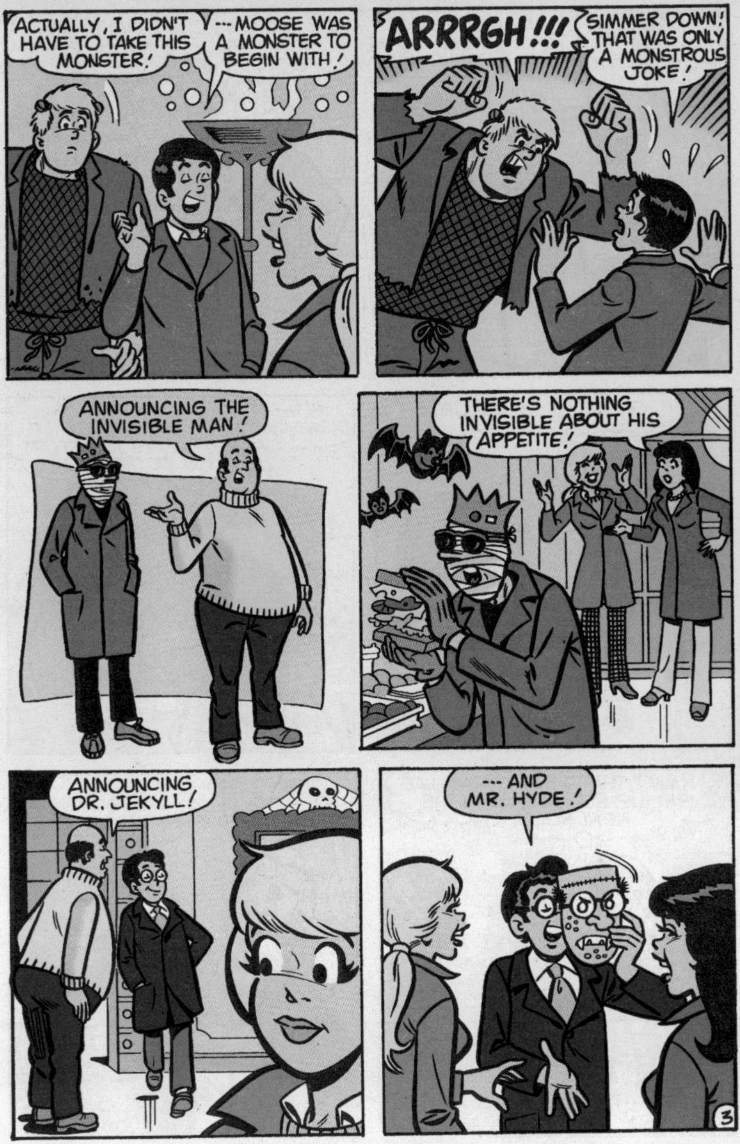
ACTUALLY, I DIDN'T HAVE TO TAKE THIS MONSTER!
---MOOSE WAS A MONSTER TO BEGIN WITH!
ARRRGH!!!
SIMMER DOWN! THAT WAS ONLY A MONSTROUS JOKE!
ANNOUNCING THE INVISIBLE MAN!
THERE'S NOTHING INVISIBLE ABOUT HIS APPETITE!
ANNOUNCING DR. JEKYLL!
--- AND MR. HYDE!
3

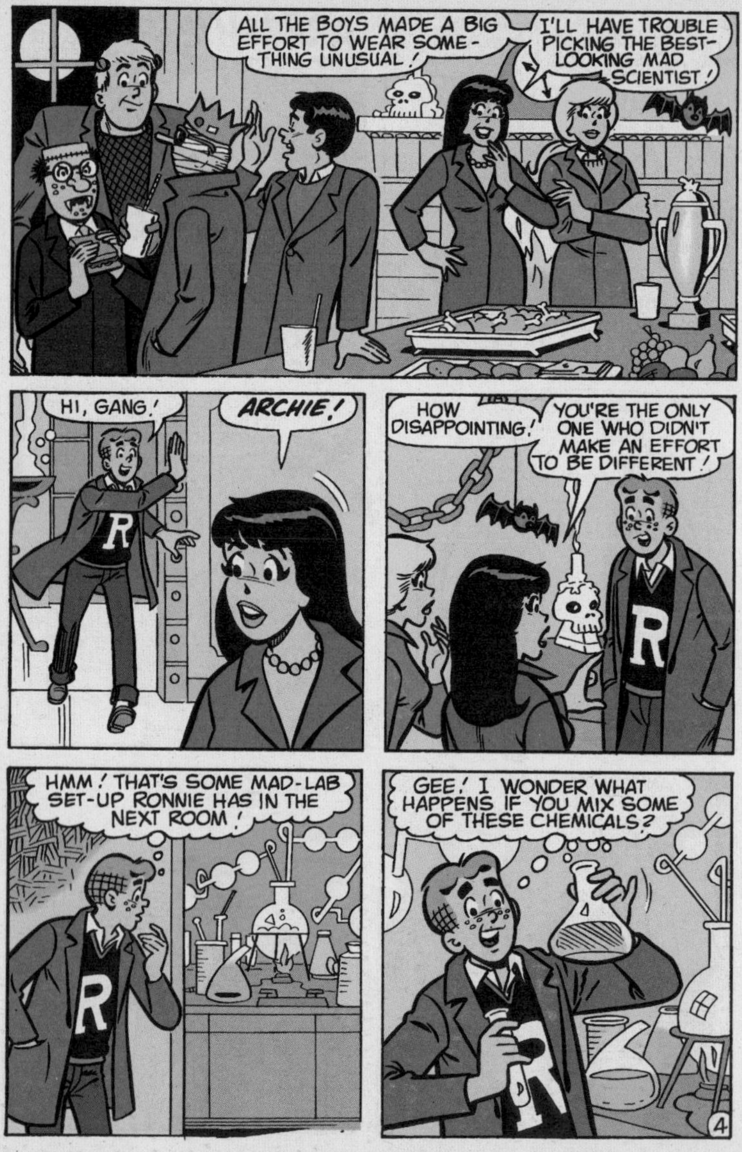
ALL THE BOYS MADE A BIG EFFORT TO WEAR SOME-THING UNUSUAL!
I'LL HAVE TROUBLE PICKING THE BEST-LOOKING MAD SCIENTIST!
HI, GANG!
ARCHIE!
HOW DISAPPOINTING!
YOU'RE THE ONLY ONE WHO DIDN'T MAKE AN EFFORT TO BE DIFFERENT!
HMM! THAT'S SOME MAD-LAB SET-UP RONNIE HAS IN THE NEXT ROOM!
GEE! I WONDER WHAT HAPPENS IF YOU MIX SOME OF THESE CHEMICALS?
4

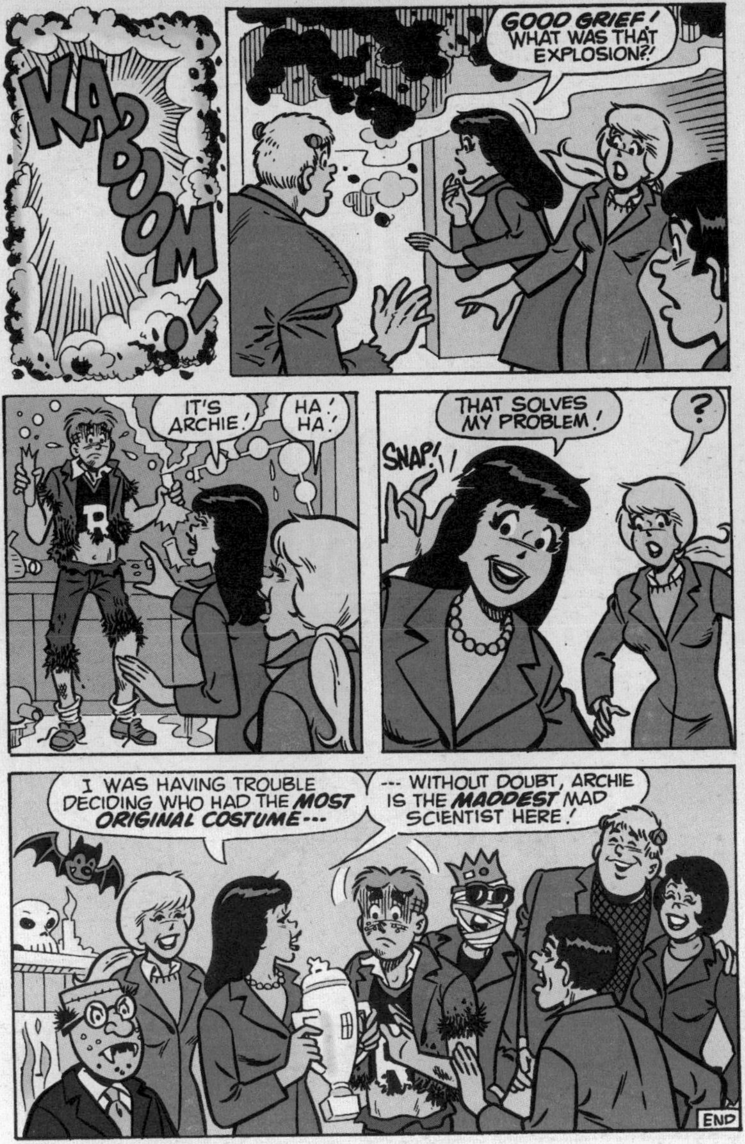
KA-BOOM!
GOOD GRIEF! WHAT WAS THAT EXPLOSION?!
IT'S ARCHIE!
HA! HA!
SNAP!
THAT SOLVES MY PROBLEM!
?
I WAS HAVING TROUBLE DECIDING WHO HAD THE MOST ORIGINAL COSTUME---
--- WITHOUT DOUBT, ARCHIE IS THE MADDEST MAD SCIENTIST HERE!
END

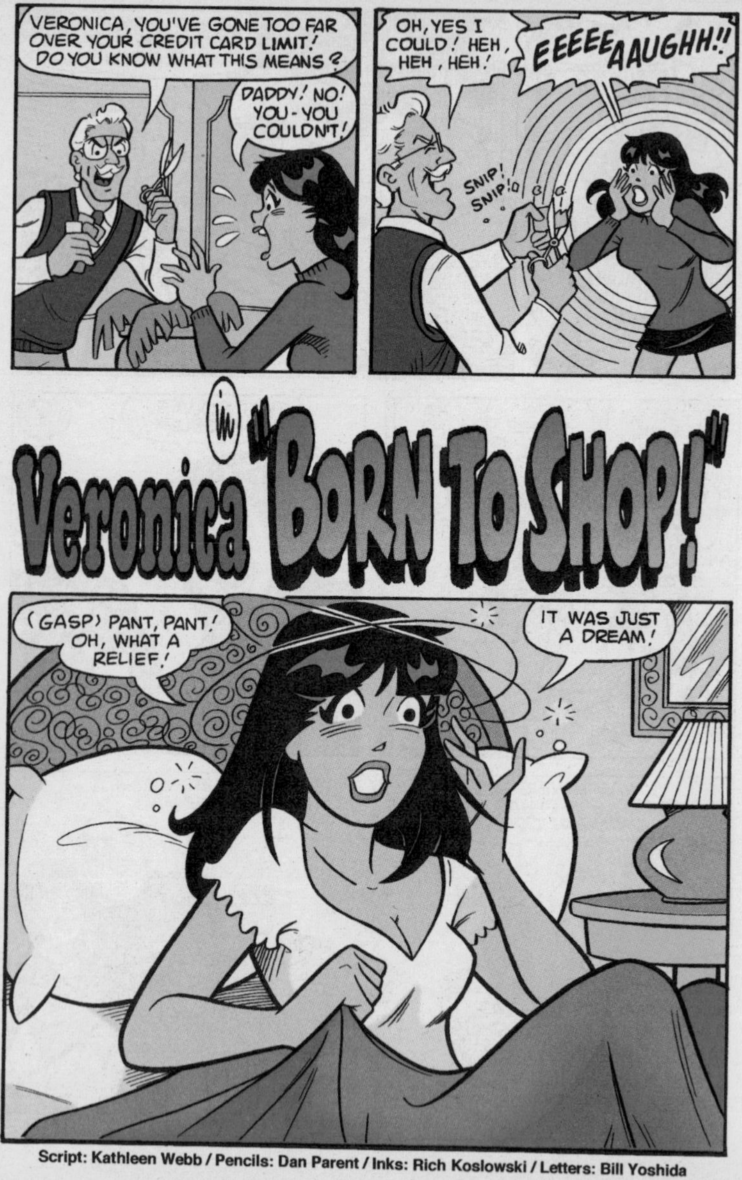
VERONICA, YOU'VE GONE TOO FAR OVER YOUR CREDIT CARD LIMIT! DO YOU KNOW WHAT THIS MEANS?
DADDY! NO! YOU-YOU COULDN'T!
OH, YES I COULD! HEH, HEH, HEH!
EEEEEAAUGHH!!
SNIP! SNIP!
Veronica
in
"BORN TO SHOP!"
(GASP) PANT, PANT! OH, WHAT A RELIEF!
IT WAS JUST A DREAM!

Script: Kathleen Webb / Pencils: Dan Parent / Inks: Rich Koslowski / Letters: Bill Yoshida

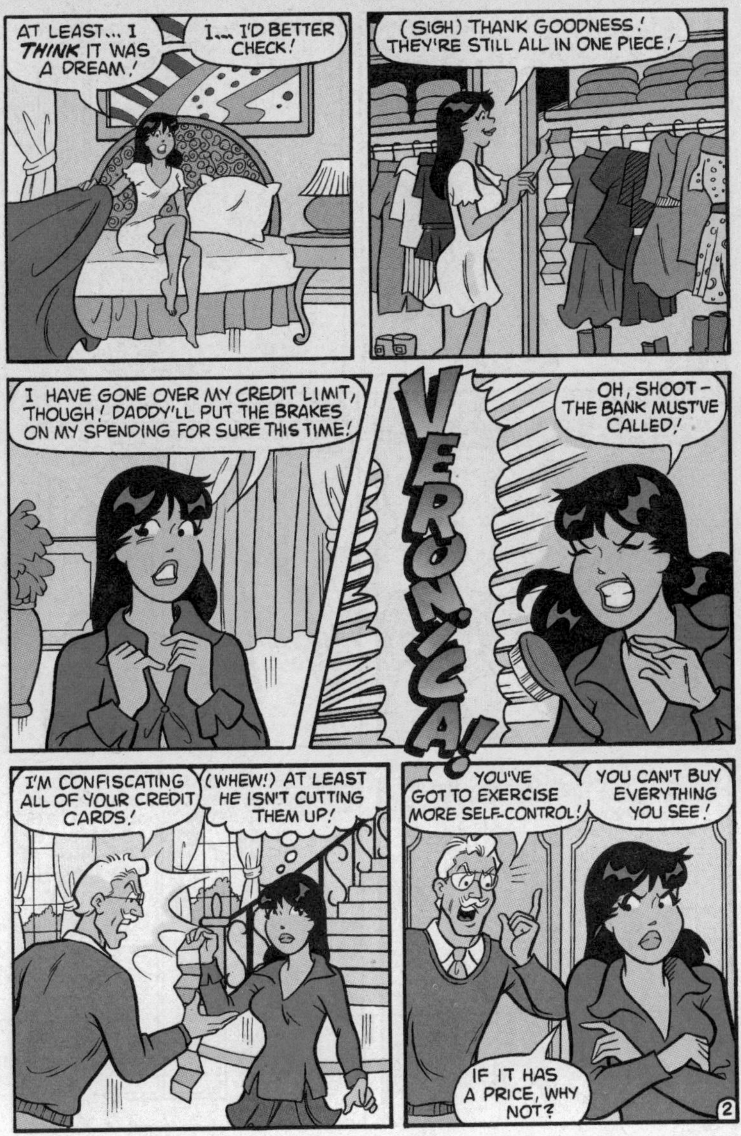
AT LEAST... I THINK IT WAS A DREAM!
I... I'D BETTER CHECK!
(SIGH) THANK GOODNESS! THEY'RE STILL ALL IN ONE PIECE!
I HAVE GONE OVER MY CREDIT LIMIT, THOUGH! DADDY'LL PUT THE BRAKES ON MY SPENDING FOR SURE THIS TIME!
VERONICA!
OH, SHOOT - THE BANK MUST'VE CALLED!
I'M CONFISCATING ALL OF YOUR CREDIT CARDS!
(WHEW!) AT LEAST HE ISN'T CUTTING THEM UP!
YOU'VE GOT TO EXERCISE MORE SELF-CONTROL!
YOU CAN'T BUY EVERYTHING YOU SEE!
IF IT HAS A PRICE, WHY NOT?
2

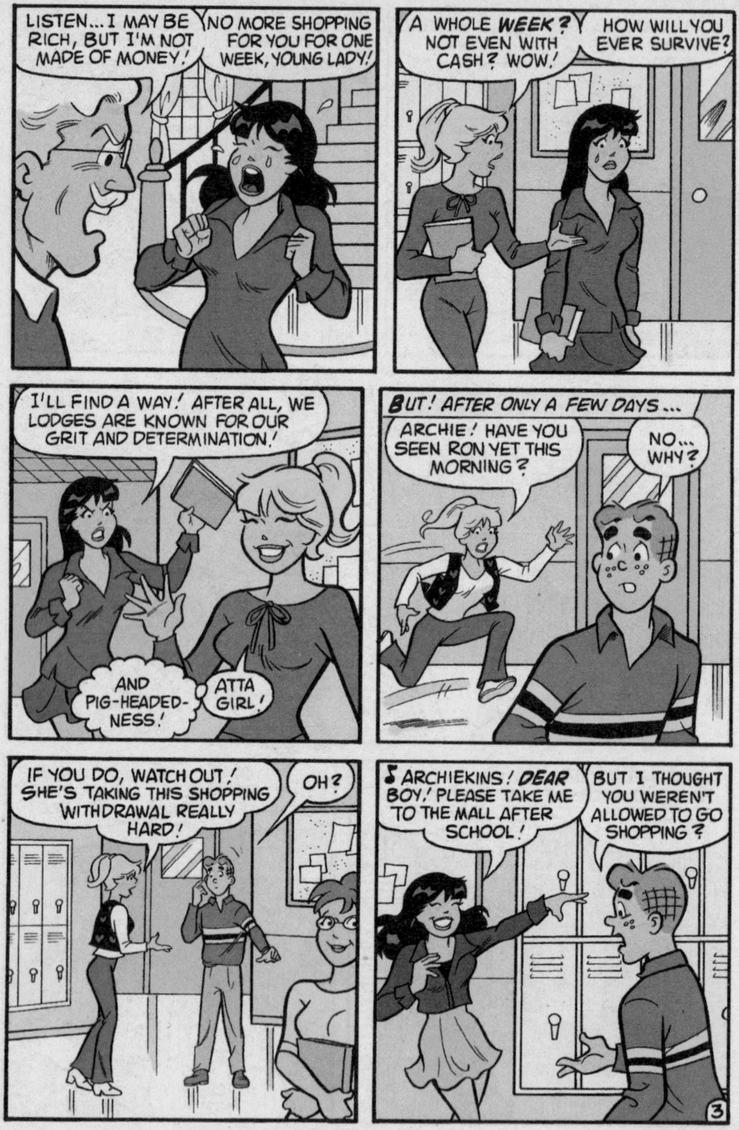
LISTEN... I MAY BE RICH, BUT I'M NOT MADE OF MONEY!
NO MORE SHOPPING FOR YOU FOR ONE WEEK, YOUNG LADY!
A WHOLE WEEK? NOT EVEN WITH CASH? WOW!
HOW WILL YOU EVER SURVIVE?
I'LL FIND A WAY! AFTER ALL, WE LODGES ARE KNOWN FOR OUR GRIT AND DETERMINATION!
AND PIG-HEADED-NESS!
ATTA GIRL!
BUT! AFTER ONLY A FEW DAYS...
ARCHIE! HAVE YOU SEEN RON YET THIS MORNING?
NO... WHY?
IF YOU DO, WATCH OUT! SHE'S TAKING THIS SHOPPING WITHDRAWAL REALLY HARD!
OH?
ARCHIEKINS! DEAR BOY! PLEASE TAKE ME TO THE MALL AFTER SCHOOL!
BUT I THOUGHT YOU WEREN'T ALLOWED TO GO SHOPPING?
3

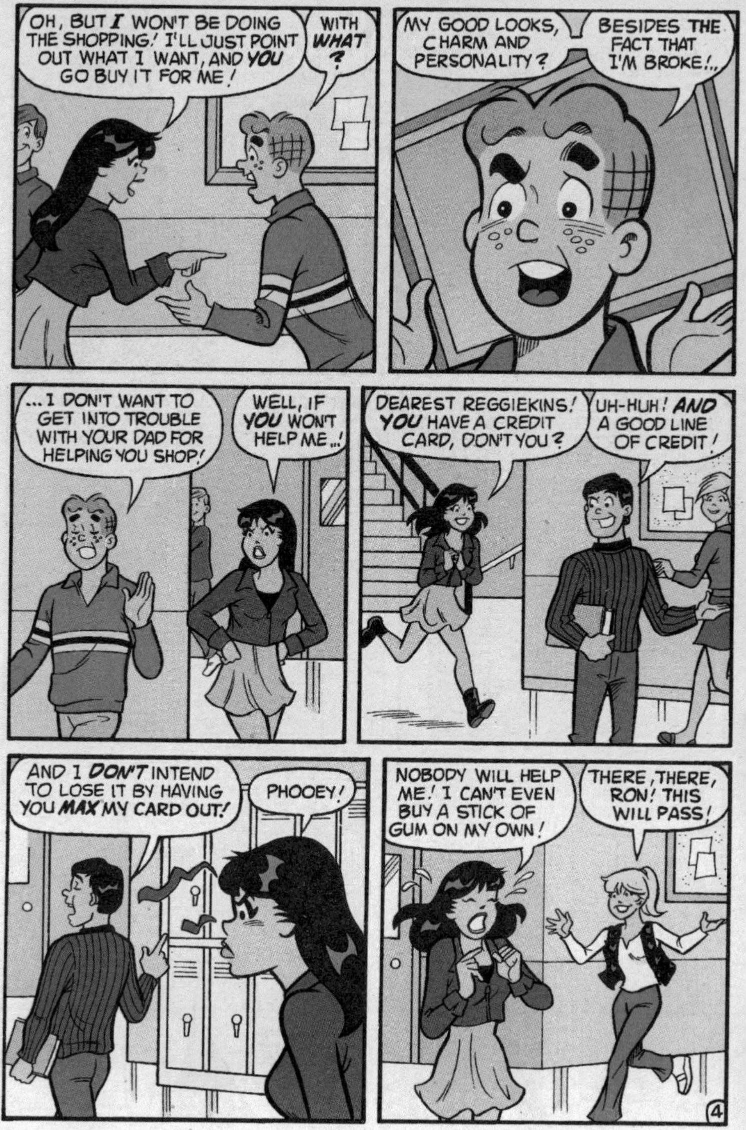
OH, BUT I WON'T BE DOING THE SHOPPING! I'LL JUST POINT OUT WHAT I WANT, AND YOU GO BUY IT FOR ME!
WITH WHAT ?
MY GOOD LOOKS, CHARM AND PERSONALITY?
BESIDES THE FACT THAT I'M BROKE!..
...I DON'T WANT TO GET INTO TROUBLE WITH YOUR DAD FOR HELPING YOU SHOP!
WELL, IF YOU WON'T HELP ME...!
DEAREST REGGIEKINS! YOU HAVE A CREDIT CARD, DON'T YOU?
UH-HUH! AND A GOOD LINE OF CREDIT!
AND I DON'T INTEND TO LOSE IT BY HAVING YOU MAX MY CARD OUT!
PHOOEY!
NOBODY WILL HELP ME! I CAN'T EVEN BUY A STICK OF GUM ON MY OWN!
THERE, THERE, RON! THIS WILL PASS!
4

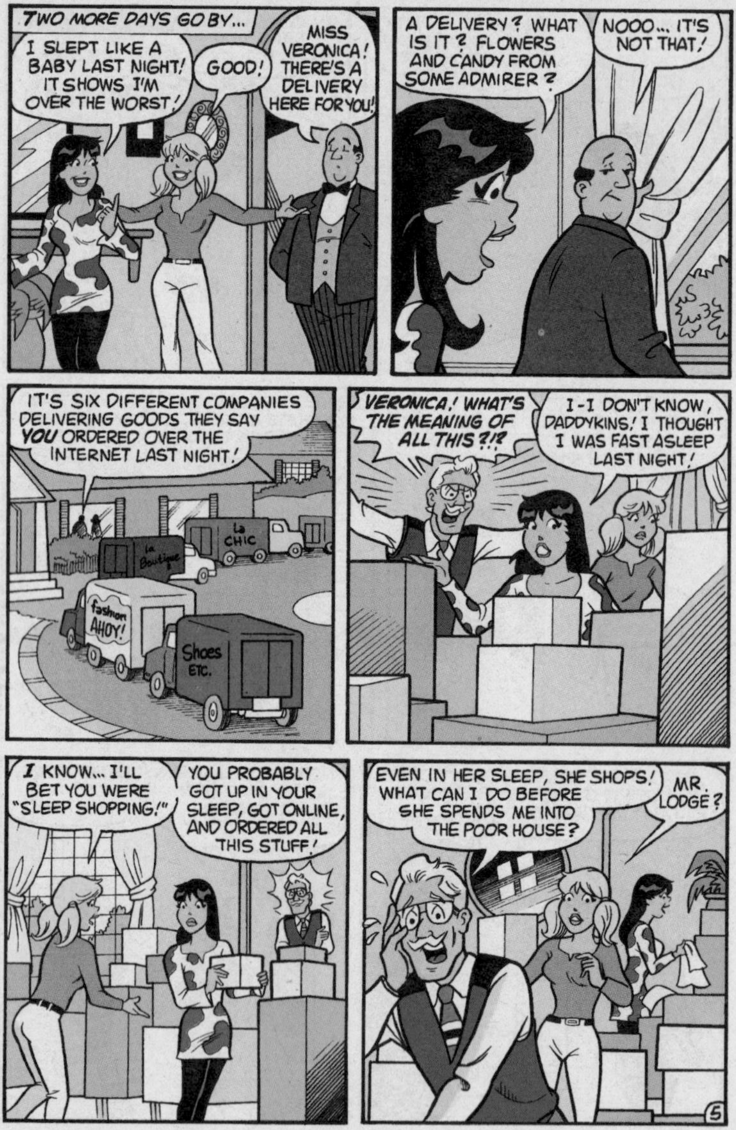
TWO MORE DAYS GO BY...
I SLEPT LIKE A BABY LAST NIGHT! IT SHOWS I'M OVER THE WORST!
GOOD!
MISS VERONICA! THERE'S A DELIVERY HERE FOR YOU!
A DELIVERY? WHAT IS IT? FLOWERS AND CANDY FROM SOME ADMIRER?
NOOO... IT'S NOT THAT!
IT'S SIX DIFFERENT COMPANIES DELIVERING GOODS THEY SAY YOU ORDERED OVER THE INTERNET LAST NIGHT!
La CHIC
La Boutique
fashion AHOY!
Shoes ETC.
VERONICA! WHAT'S THE MEANING OF ALL THIS?!?
I-I DON'T KNOW, DADDYKINS! I THOUGHT I WAS FAST ASLEEP LAST NIGHT!
I KNOW... I'LL BET YOU WERE "SLEEP SHOPPING!"
YOU PROBABLY GOT UP IN YOUR SLEEP, GOT ONLINE, AND ORDERED ALL THIS STUFF!
EVEN IN HER SLEEP, SHE SHOPS! WHAT CAN I DO BEFORE SHE SPENDS ME INTO THE POOR HOUSE?
MR. LODGE?
5

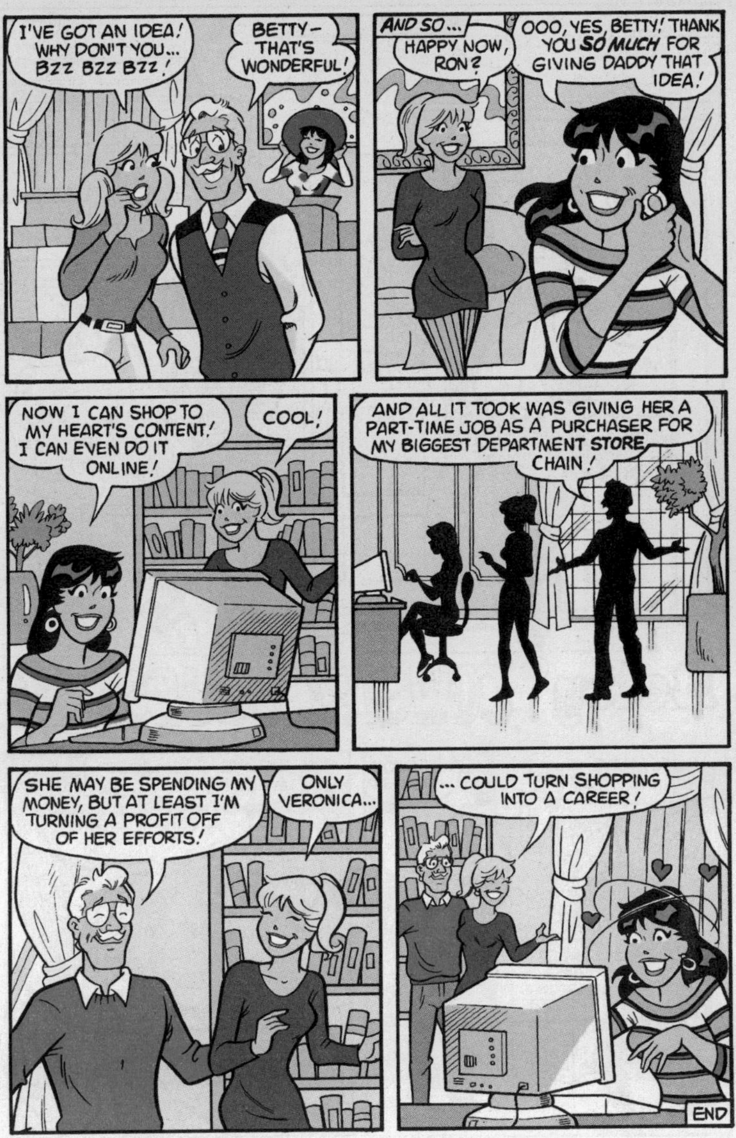
I'VE GOT AN IDEA! WHY DON'T YOU... BZZ BZZ BZZ!
BETTY– THAT'S WONDERFUL!
AND SO...
HAPPY NOW, RON?
OOO, YES, BETTY! THANK YOU SO MUCH FOR GIVING DADDY THAT IDEA!
NOW I CAN SHOP TO MY HEART'S CONTENT! I CAN EVEN DO IT ONLINE!
COOL!
AND ALL IT TOOK WAS GIVING HER A PART-TIME JOB AS A PURCHASER FOR MY BIGGEST DEPARTMENT STORE CHAIN!
SHE MAY BE SPENDING MY MONEY, BUT AT LEAST I'M TURNING A PROFIT OFF OF HER EFFORTS!
ONLY VERONICA...
... COULD TURN SHOPPING INTO A CAREER!
END

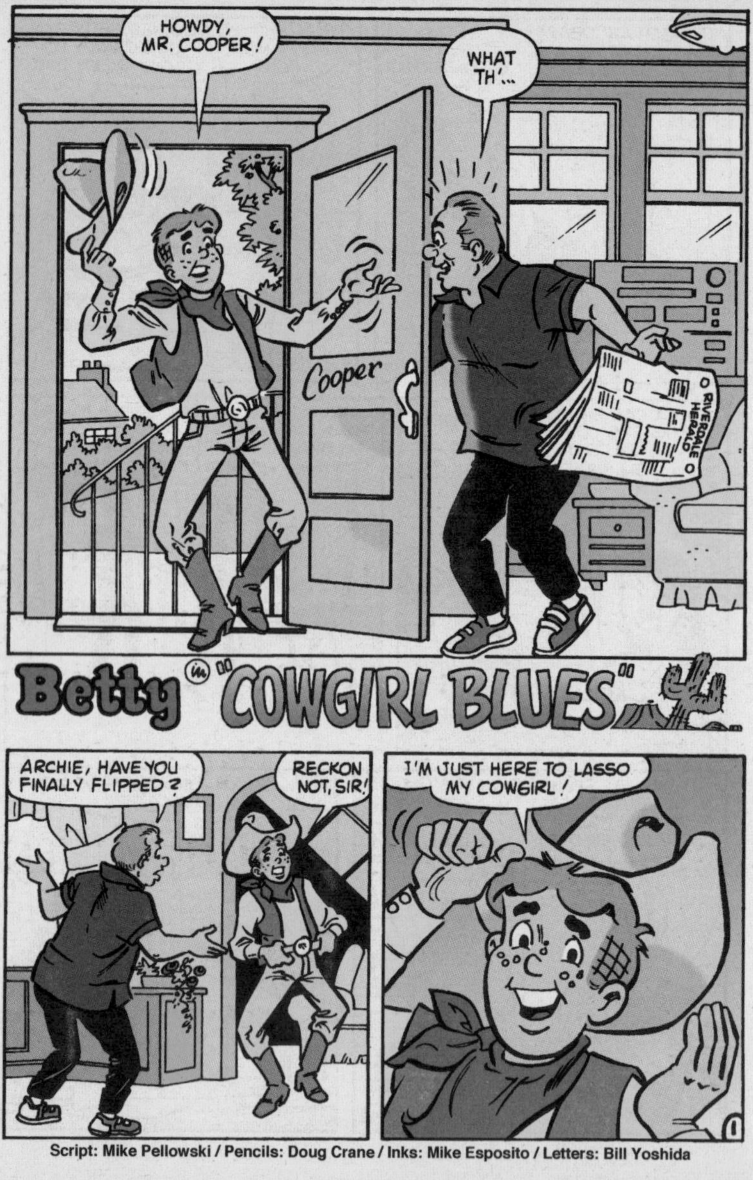
HOWDY, MR. COOPER!
WHAT TH'...
Cooper
RIVERDALE HERALD
Betty in "COWGIRL BLUES"
ARCHIE, HAVE YOU FINALLY FLIPPED?
RECKON NOT, SIR!
I'M JUST HERE TO LASSO MY COWGIRL!
1

Script: Mike Pellowski / Pencils: Doug Crane / Inks: Mike Esposito / Letters: Bill Yoshida

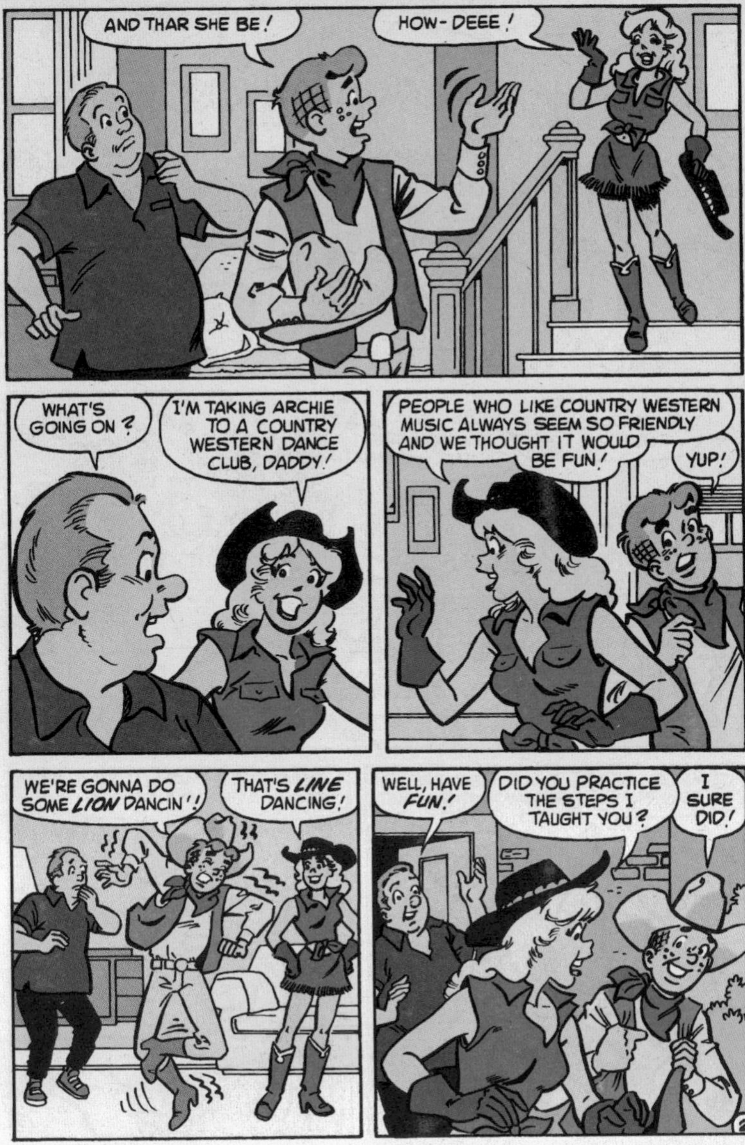
AND THAR SHE BE!
HOW-DEEE!
WHAT'S GOING ON?
I'M TAKING ARCHIE TO A COUNTRY WESTERN DANCE CLUB, DADDY!
PEOPLE WHO LIKE COUNTRY WESTERN MUSIC ALWAYS SEEM SO FRIENDLY AND WE THOUGHT IT WOULD BE FUN!
YUP!
WE'RE GONNA DO SOME *LION* DANCIN'!
THAT'S *LINE* DANCING!
WELL, HAVE *FUN!*
DID YOU PRACTICE THE STEPS I TAUGHT YOU?
I SURE DID!
2

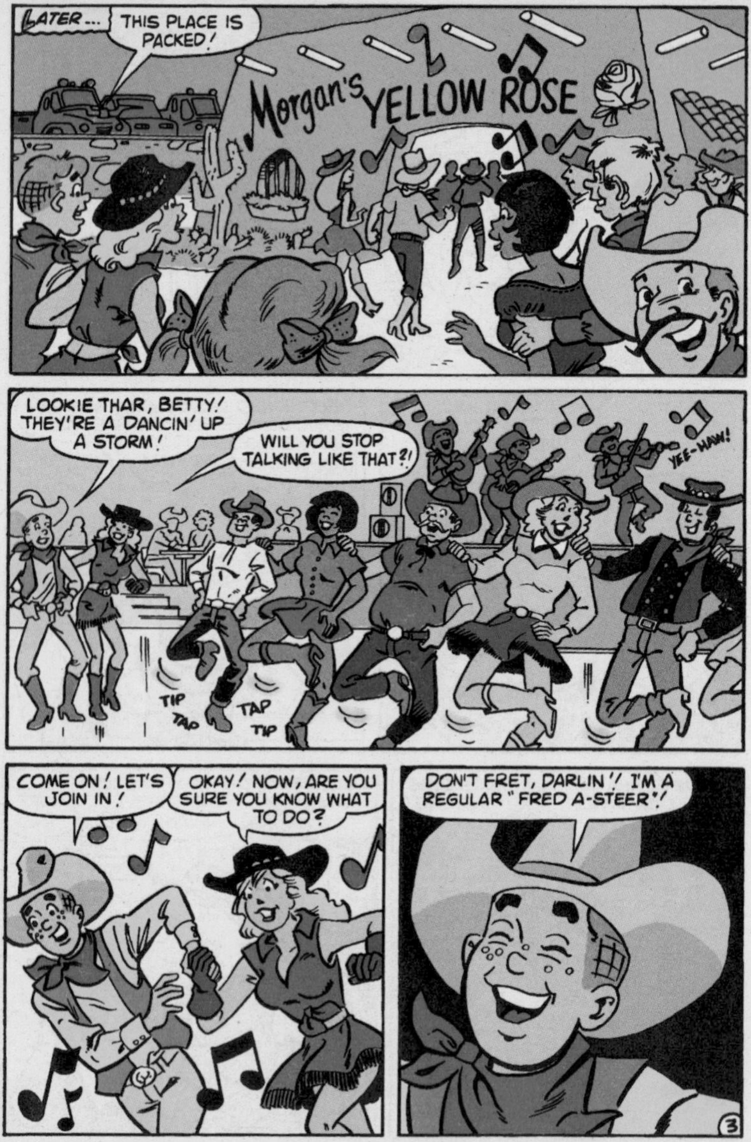
LATER...
THIS PLACE IS PACKED!
Morgan's YELLOW ROSE
LOOKIE THAR, BETTY! THEY'RE A DANCIN' UP A STORM!
WILL YOU STOP TALKING LIKE THAT?!
YEE-HAW!
TIP
TAP
TAP
TIP
COME ON! LET'S JOIN IN!
OKAY! NOW, ARE YOU SURE YOU KNOW WHAT TO DO?
DON'T FRET, DARLIN'! I'M A REGULAR "FRED A-STEER"!
3

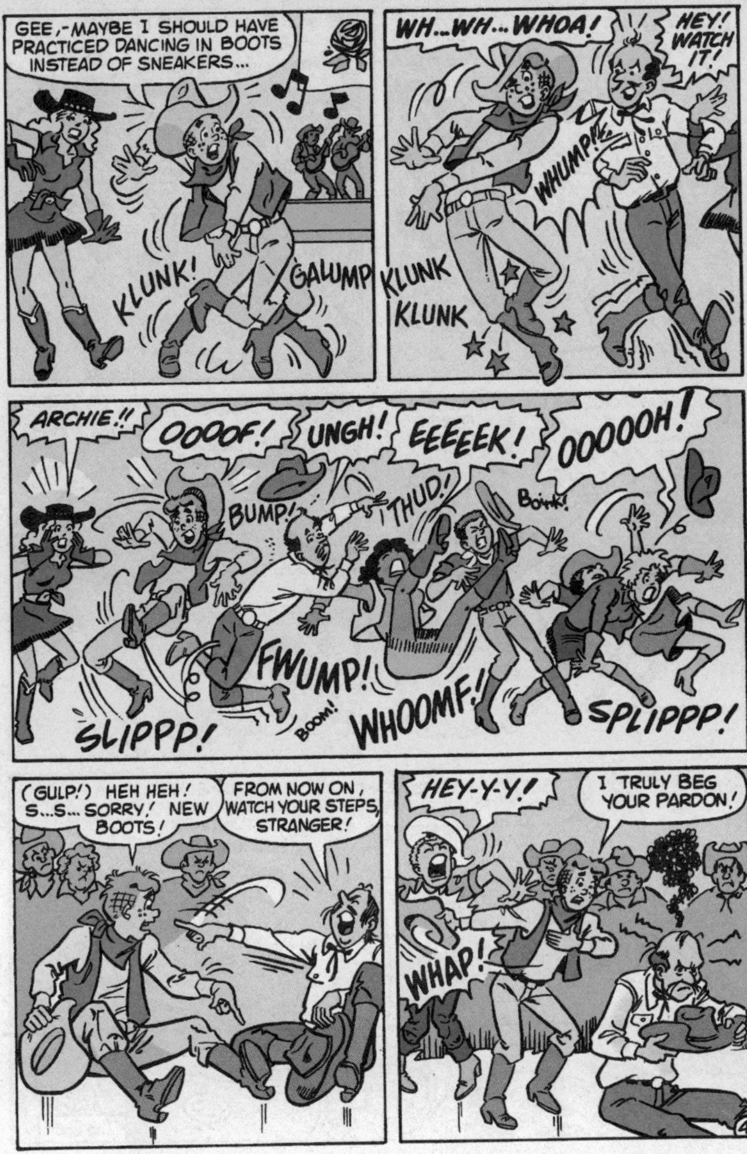
GEE,-MAYBE I SHOULD HAVE PRACTICED DANCING IN BOOTS INSTEAD OF SNEAKERS...
KLUNK!
GALUMP
WH...WH...WHOA!
HEY! WATCH IT!
WHUMP!!
KLUNK
KLUNK
ARCHIE!!
OOOOF!
UNGH!
EEEEEK!
OOOOOOH!
BUMP!
THUD!
Boink!
FWUMP!
WHOOMF!
SPLIPPP!
SLIPPP!
BOOM!
(GULP!) HEH HEH! S...S... SORRY! NEW BOOTS!
FROM NOW ON, WATCH YOUR STEPS, STRANGER!
HEY-Y-Y!
I TRULY BEG YOUR PARDON!
WHAP!
4

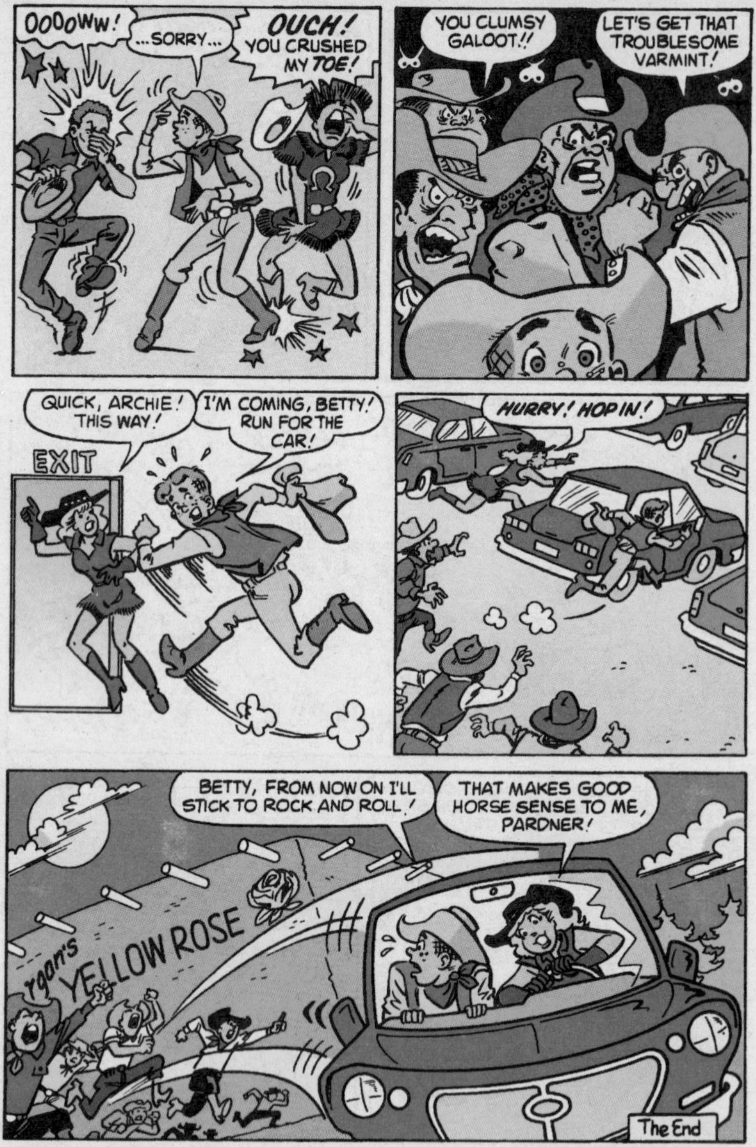
OOOOWW!
...SORRY...
OUCH! YOU CRUSHED MY TOE!
YOU CLUMSY GALOOT!!
LET'S GET THAT TROUBLESOME VARMINT!
QUICK, ARCHIE! THIS WAY!
I'M COMING, BETTY! RUN FOR THE CAR!
EXIT
HURRY! HOP IN!
BETTY, FROM NOW ON I'LL STICK TO ROCK AND ROLL!
THAT MAKES GOOD HORSE SENSE TO ME, PARDNER!
YELLOW ROSE
The End

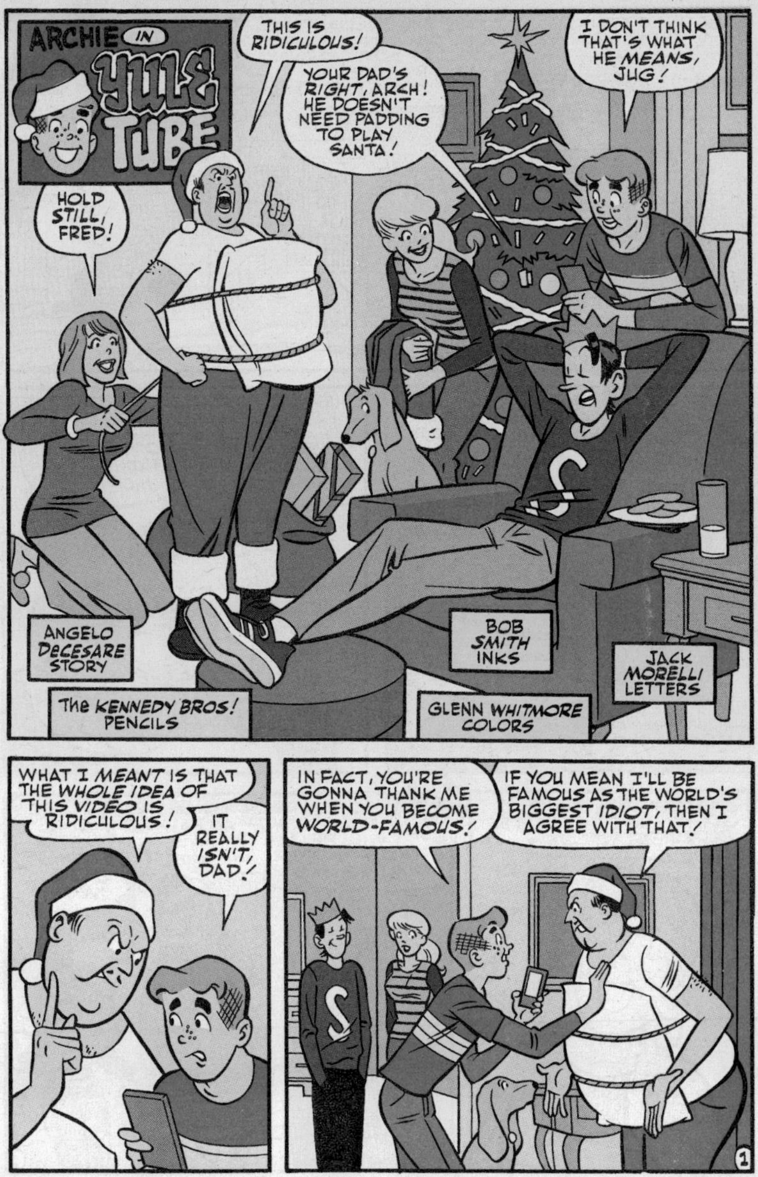
ARCHIE IN YULE TUBE
THIS IS RIDICULOUS!
YOUR DAD'S RIGHT, ARCH! HE DOESN'T NEED PADDING TO PLAY SANTA!
I DON'T THINK THAT'S WHAT HE MEANS, JUG!
HOLD STILL, FRED!
ANGELO DECESARE STORY
The KENNEDY BROS! PENCILS
BOB SMITH INKS
GLENN WHITMORE COLORS
JACK MORELLI LETTERS
WHAT I MEANT IS THAT THE WHOLE IDEA OF THIS VIDEO IS RIDICULOUS!
IT REALLY ISN'T, DAD!
IN FACT, YOU'RE GONNA THANK ME WHEN YOU BECOME WORLD-FAMOUS!
IF YOU MEAN I'LL BE FAMOUS AS THE WORLD'S BIGGEST IDIOT, THEN I AGREE WITH THAT!

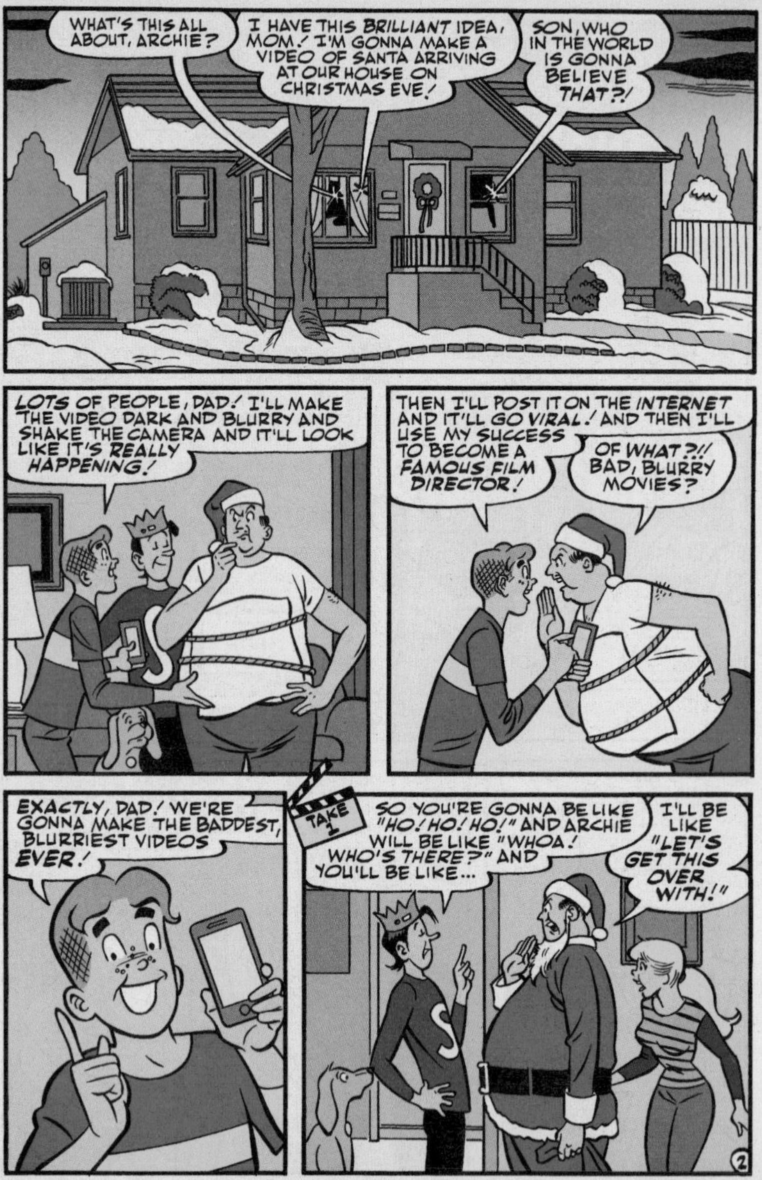
WHAT'S THIS ALL ABOUT, ARCHIE?
I HAVE THIS BRILLIANT IDEA, MOM! I'M GONNA MAKE A VIDEO OF SANTA ARRIVING AT OUR HOUSE ON CHRISTMAS EVE!
SON, WHO IN THE WORLD IS GONNA BELIEVE THAT?!
LOTS OF PEOPLE, DAD! I'LL MAKE THE VIDEO DARK AND BLURRY AND SHAKE THE CAMERA AND IT'LL LOOK LIKE IT'S REALLY HAPPENING!
THEN I'LL POST IT ON THE INTERNET AND IT'LL GO VIRAL! AND THEN I'LL USE MY SUCCESS TO BECOME A FAMOUS FILM DIRECTOR!
OF WHAT?!! BAD, BLURRY MOVIES?
EXACTLY, DAD! WE'RE GONNA MAKE THE BADDEST, BLURRIEST VIDEOS EVER!
TAKE 1
SO YOU'RE GONNA BE LIKE "HO! HO! HO!" AND ARCHIE WILL BE LIKE "WHOA! WHO'S THERE?" AND YOU'LL BE LIKE...
I'LL BE LIKE "LET'S GET THIS OVER WITH!"

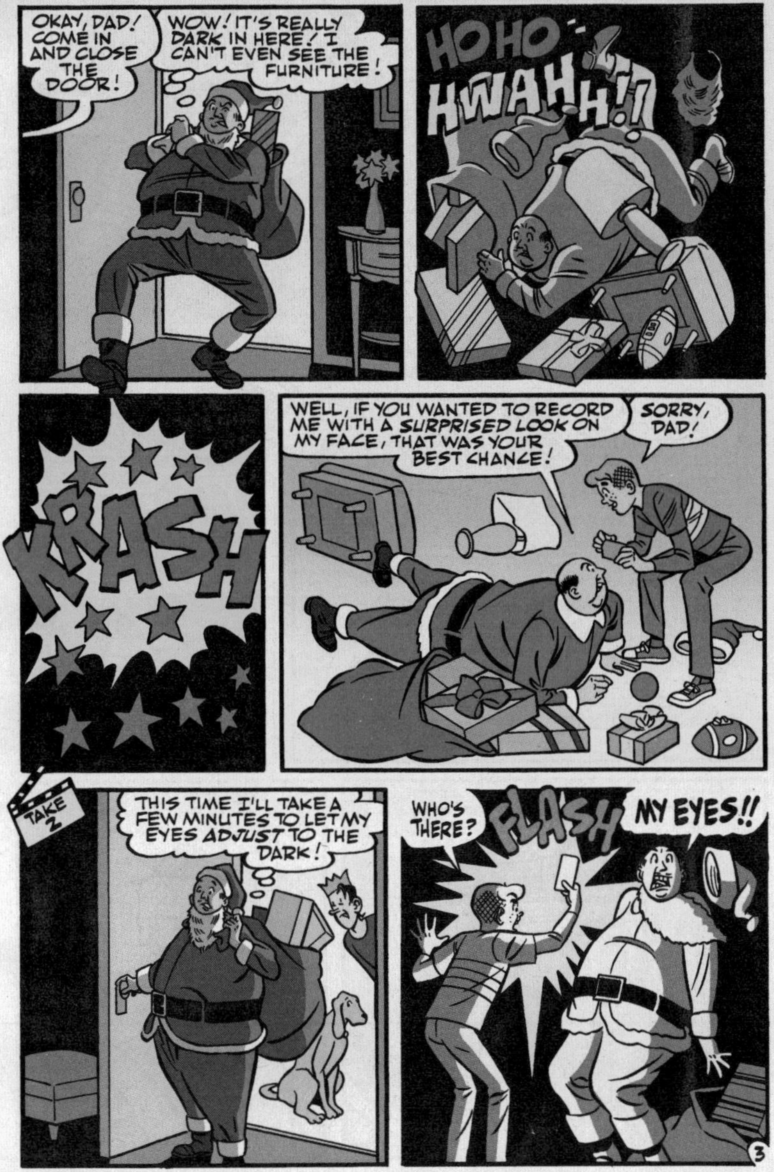
OKAY, DAD! COME IN AND CLOSE THE DOOR!
WOW! IT'S REALLY DARK IN HERE! I CAN'T EVEN SEE THE FURNITURE!
HO HO-
HWAHH!!
KRASH
WELL, IF YOU WANTED TO RECORD ME WITH A SURPRISED LOOK ON MY FACE, THAT WAS YOUR BEST CHANCE!
SORRY, DAD!
TAKE 2
THIS TIME I'LL TAKE A FEW MINUTES TO LET MY EYES ADJUST TO THE DARK!
WHO'S THERE?
FLASH
MY EYES!!
3

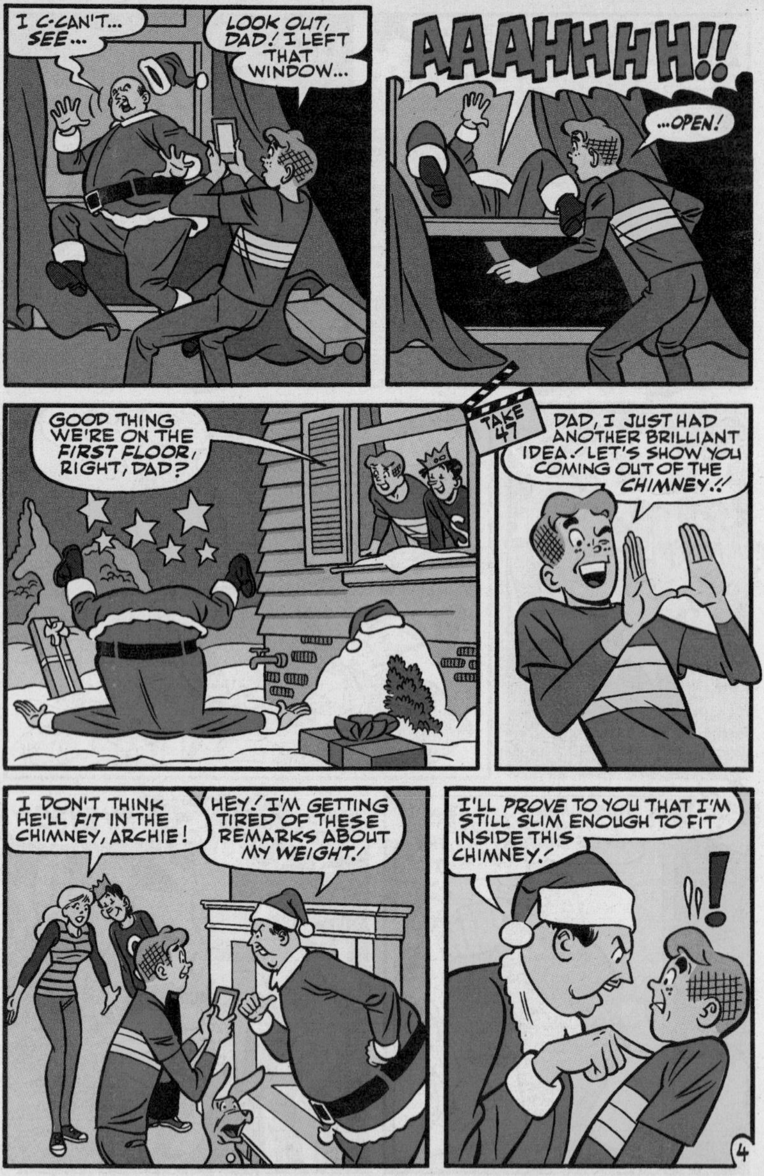
I C-CAN'T... SEE...
LOOK OUT, DAD! I LEFT THAT WINDOW...
AAAHHHH!!
...OPEN!
TAKE 47
GOOD THING WE'RE ON THE FIRST FLOOR, RIGHT, DAD?
DAD, I JUST HAD ANOTHER BRILLIANT IDEA! LET'S SHOW YOU COMING OUT OF THE CHIMNEY!!
I DON'T THINK HE'LL FIT IN THE CHIMNEY, ARCHIE!
HEY! I'M GETTING TIRED OF THESE REMARKS ABOUT MY WEIGHT!
I'LL PROVE TO YOU THAT I'M STILL SLIM ENOUGH TO FIT INSIDE THIS CHIMNEY!
!!
4

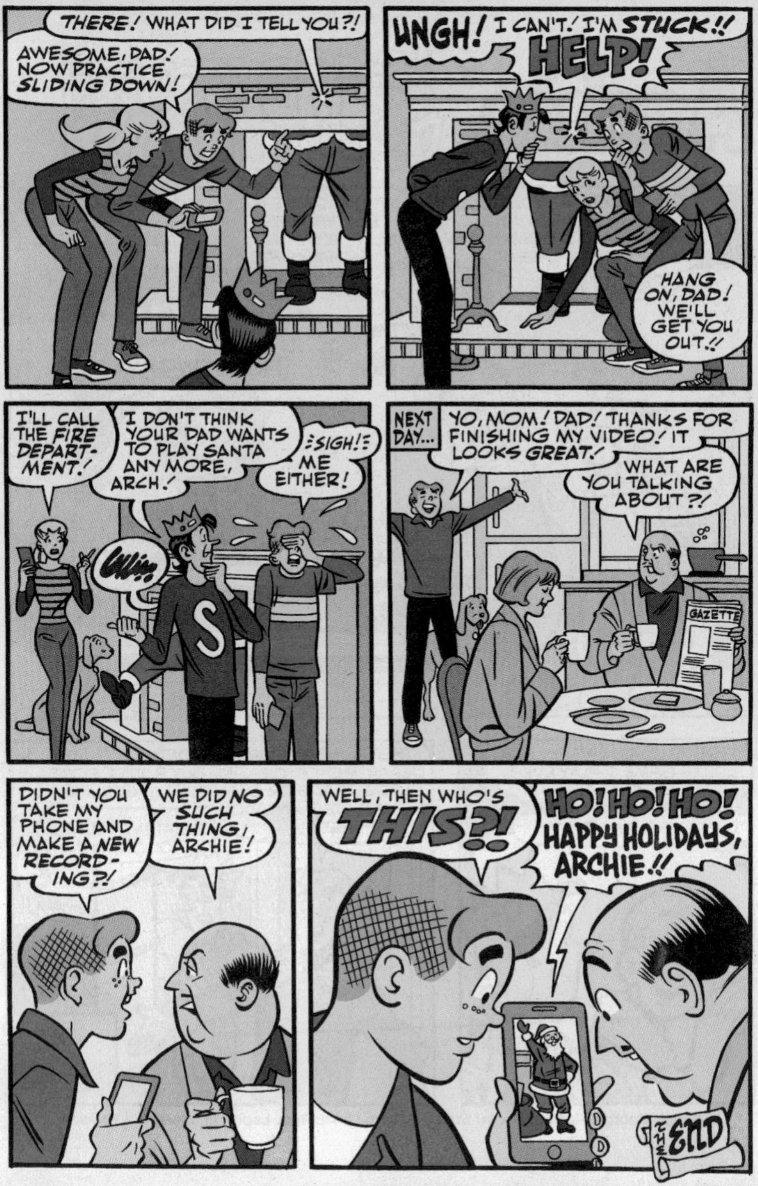
THERE! WHAT DID I TELL YOU?!
AWESOME, DAD! NOW PRACTICE SLIDING DOWN!
UNGH! I CAN'T! I'M STUCK!! HELP!
HANG ON, DAD! WE'LL GET YOU OUT!!
I'LL CALL THE FIRE DEPART-MENT!
I DON'T THINK YOUR DAD WANTS TO PLAY SANTA ANY MORE, ARCH!
SIGH! ME EITHER!
NEXT DAY...
YO, MOM! DAD! THANKS FOR FINISHING MY VIDEO! IT LOOKS GREAT!
WHAT ARE YOU TALKING ABOUT?!
GAZETTE
DIDN'T YOU TAKE MY PHONE AND MAKE A NEW RECORD-ING?!
WE DID NO SUCH THING, ARCHIE!
WELL, THEN WHO'S THIS?!
HO! HO! HO! HAPPY HOLIDAYS, ARCHIE!!
THE END

Archie -in- "SHOPWORN"

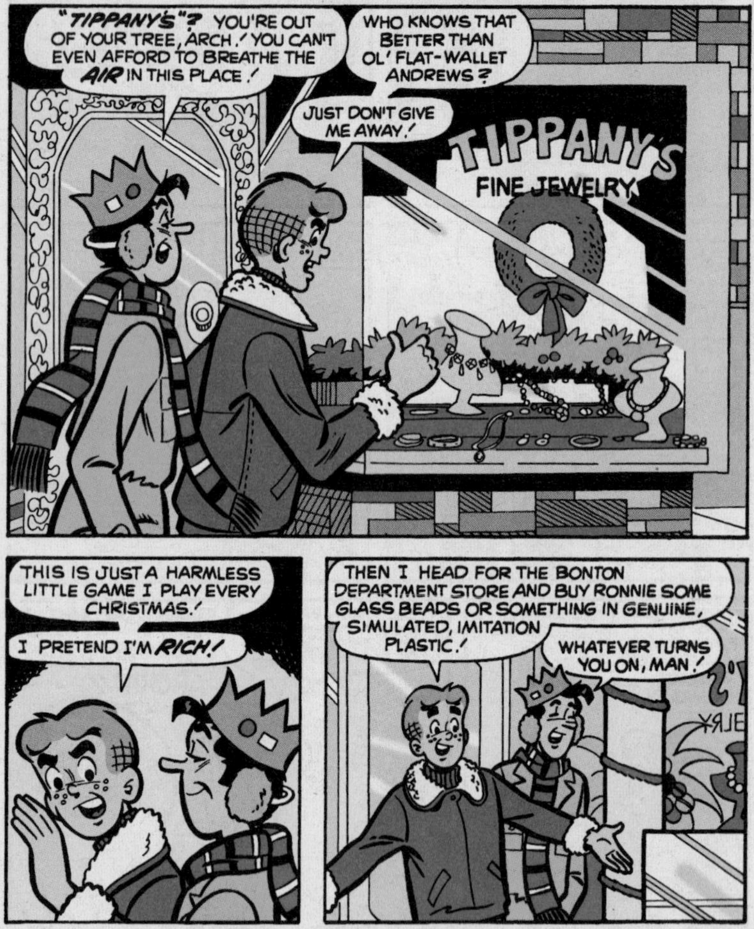
"TIPPANY'S"? YOU'RE OUT OF YOUR TREE, ARCH! YOU CAN'T EVEN AFFORD TO BREATHE THE AIR IN THIS PLACE!
WHO KNOWS THAT BETTER THAN OL' FLAT-WALLET ANDREWS?
JUST DON'T GIVE ME AWAY!
TIPPANY'S
FINE JEWELRY
THIS IS JUST A HARMLESS LITTLE GAME I PLAY EVERY CHRISTMAS!
I PRETEND I'M RICH!
THEN I HEAD FOR THE BONTON DEPARTMENT STORE AND BUY RONNIE SOME GLASS BEADS OR SOMETHING IN GENUINE, SIMULATED, IMITATION PLASTIC!
WHATEVER TURNS YOU ON, MAN!

Script: George Gladir / Pencils: Stan Goldberg / Inks: Rudy Lapick / Letters: Bill Yoshida

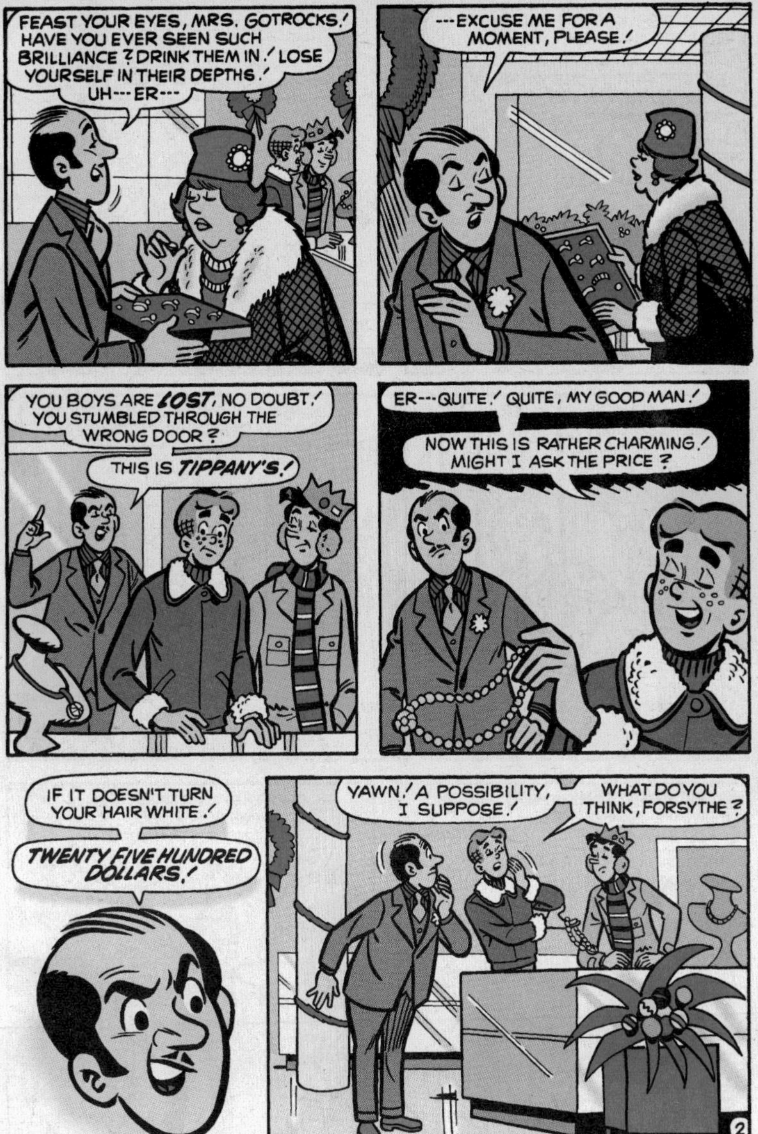
FEAST YOUR EYES, MRS. GOTROCKS! HAVE YOU EVER SEEN SUCH BRILLIANCE? DRINK THEM IN! LOSE YOURSELF IN THEIR DEPTHS!
UH--- ER---
---EXCUSE ME FOR A MOMENT, PLEASE!
YOU BOYS ARE LOST, NO DOUBT! YOU STUMBLED THROUGH THE WRONG DOOR?
THIS IS TIPPANY'S!
ER---QUITE! QUITE, MY GOOD MAN!
NOW THIS IS RATHER CHARMING! MIGHT I ASK THE PRICE?
IF IT DOESN'T TURN YOUR HAIR WHITE!
TWENTY FIVE HUNDRED DOLLARS!
YAWN! A POSSIBILITY, I SUPPOSE!
WHAT DO YOU THINK, FORSYTHE?
2

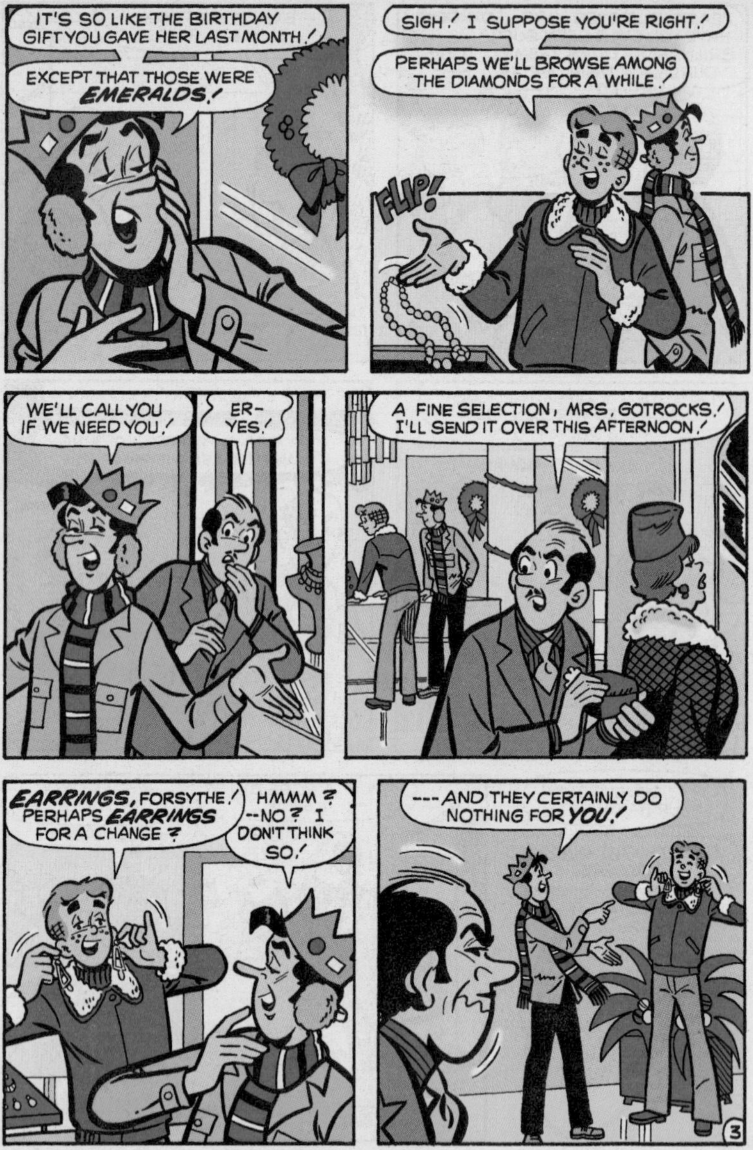
IT'S SO LIKE THE BIRTHDAY GIFT YOU GAVE HER LAST MONTH!
EXCEPT THAT THOSE WERE EMERALDS!
SIGH! I SUPPOSE YOU'RE RIGHT!
PERHAPS WE'LL BROWSE AMONG THE DIAMONDS FOR A WHILE!
FLIP!
WE'LL CALL YOU IF WE NEED YOU!
ER-YES!
A FINE SELECTION, MRS. GOTROCKS! I'LL SEND IT OVER THIS AFTERNOON!
EARRINGS, FORSYTHE! PERHAPS EARRINGS FOR A CHANGE?
HMMM? --NO? I DON'T THINK SO!
---AND THEY CERTAINLY DO NOTHING FOR YOU!
3

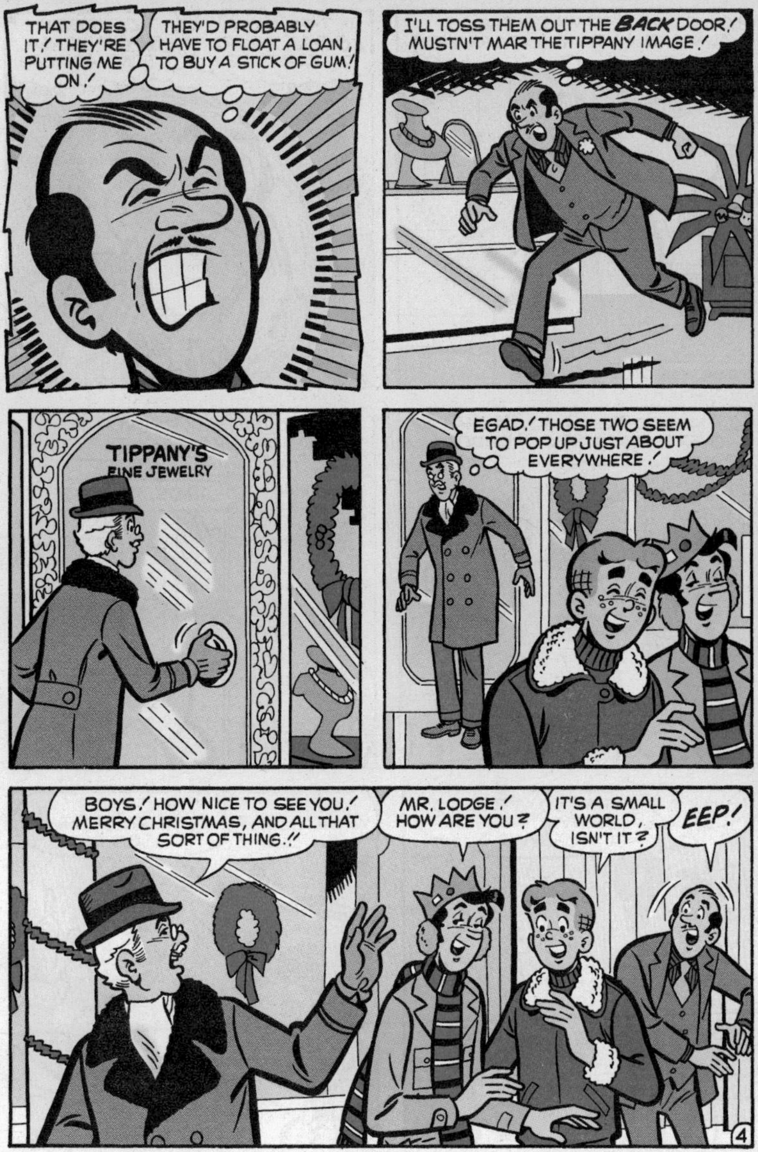
THAT DOES IT! THEY'RE PUTTING ME ON!
THEY'D PROBABLY HAVE TO FLOAT A LOAN, TO BUY A STICK OF GUM!
I'LL TOSS THEM OUT THE BACK DOOR! MUSTN'T MAR THE TIPPANY IMAGE!
TIPPANY'S FINE JEWELRY
EGAD! THOSE TWO SEEM TO POP UP JUST ABOUT EVERYWHERE!
BOYS! HOW NICE TO SEE YOU! MERRY CHRISTMAS, AND ALL THAT SORT OF THING!!
MR. LODGE! HOW ARE YOU?
IT'S A SMALL WORLD, ISN'T IT?
EEP!
4

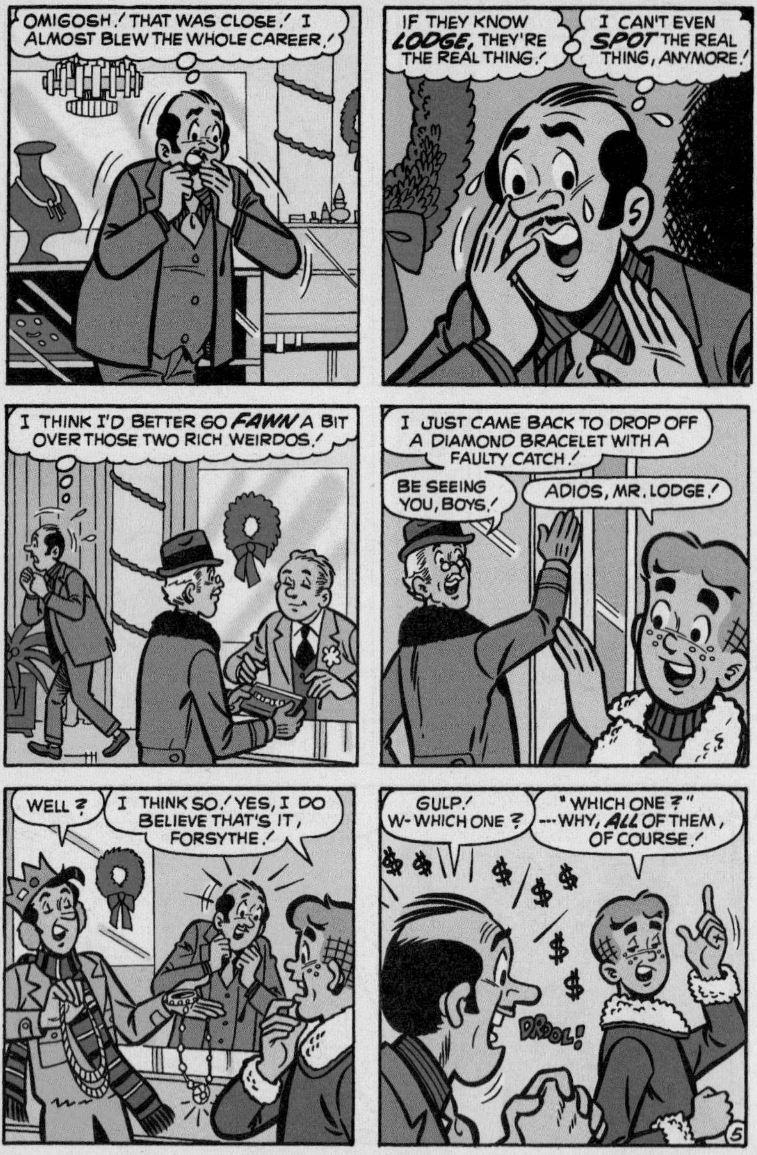

OMIGOSH! THAT WAS CLOSE! I ALMOST BLEW THE WHOLE CAREER!
IF THEY KNOW LODGE, THEY'RE THE REAL THING!
I CAN'T EVEN SPOT THE REAL THING, ANYMORE!
I THINK I'D BETTER GO FAWN A BIT OVER THOSE TWO RICH WEIRDOS!
I JUST CAME BACK TO DROP OFF A DIAMOND BRACELET WITH A FAULTY CATCH!
BE SEEING YOU, BOYS!
ADIOS, MR. LODGE!
WELL?
I THINK SO! YES, I DO BELIEVE THAT'S IT, FORSYTHE!
GULP! W-WHICH ONE?
"WHICH ONE?" ---WHY, ALL OF THEM, OF COURSE!
DROOL!
5

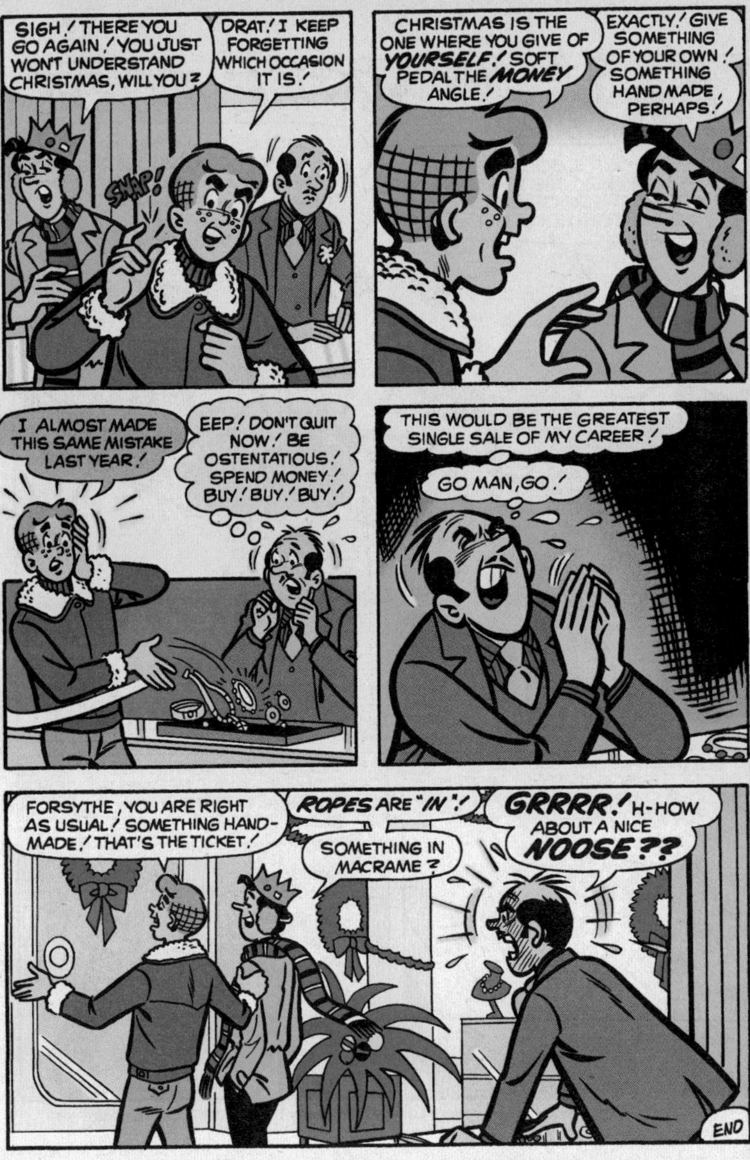
SIGH! THERE YOU GO AGAIN! YOU JUST WON'T UNDERSTAND CHRISTMAS, WILL YOU?
DRAT! I KEEP FORGETTING WHICH OCCASION IT IS!
SNAP!
CHRISTMAS IS THE ONE WHERE YOU GIVE OF YOURSELF! SOFT PEDAL THE MONEY ANGLE!
EXACTLY! GIVE SOMETHING OF YOUR OWN! SOMETHING HAND MADE, PERHAPS!
I ALMOST MADE THIS SAME MISTAKE LAST YEAR!
EEP! DON'T QUIT NOW! BE OSTENTATIOUS! SPEND MONEY! BUY! BUY! BUY!
THIS WOULD BE THE GREATEST SINGLE SALE OF MY CAREER!
GO MAN, GO!
FORSYTHE, YOU ARE RIGHT AS USUAL! SOMETHING HAND-MADE! THAT'S THE TICKET!
ROPES ARE "IN"!
SOMETHING IN MACRAME?
GRRRR! H-HOW ABOUT A NICE NOOSE??
END

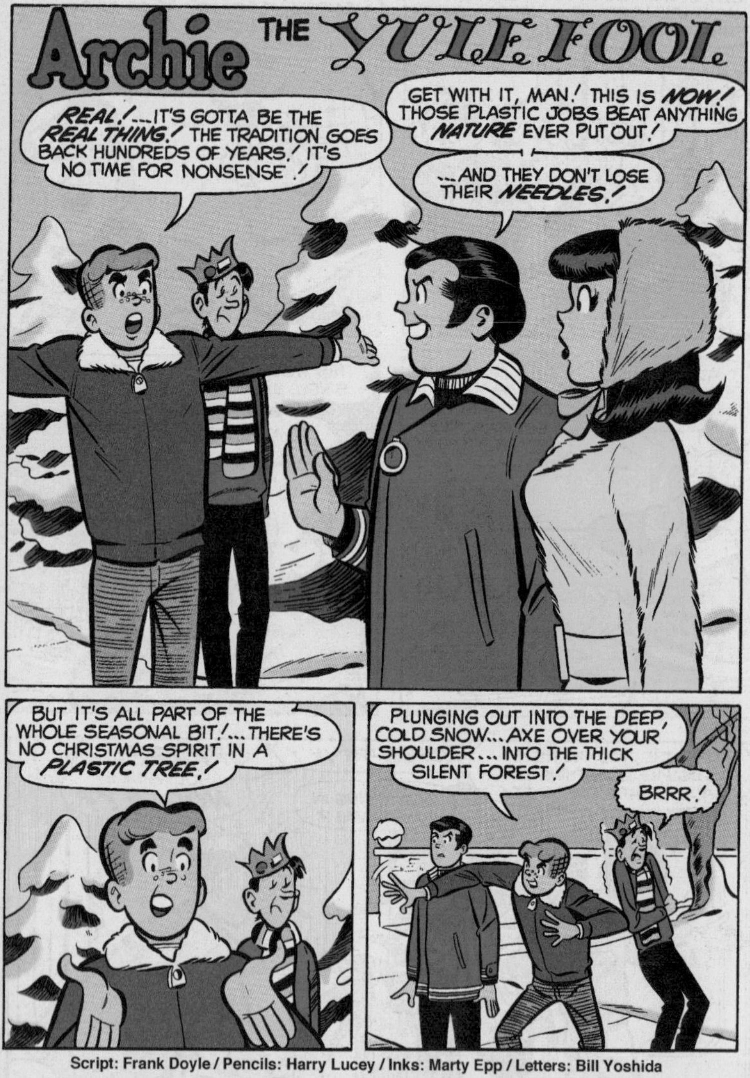
Archie THE YULE FOOL
REAL!...IT'S GOTTA BE THE REAL THING! THE TRADITION GOES BACK HUNDREDS OF YEARS! IT'S NO TIME FOR NONSENSE!
GET WITH IT, MAN! THIS IS NOW! THOSE PLASTIC JOBS BEAT ANYTHING NATURE EVER PUT OUT!
...AND THEY DON'T LOSE THEIR NEEDLES!
BUT IT'S ALL PART OF THE WHOLE SEASONAL BIT!...THERE'S NO CHRISTMAS SPIRIT IN A PLASTIC TREE!
PLUNGING OUT INTO THE DEEP, COLD SNOW...AXE OVER YOUR SHOULDER...INTO THE THICK SILENT FOREST!
BRRR!

Script: Frank Doyle / Pencils: Harry Lucey / Inks: Marty Epp / Letters: Bill Yoshida

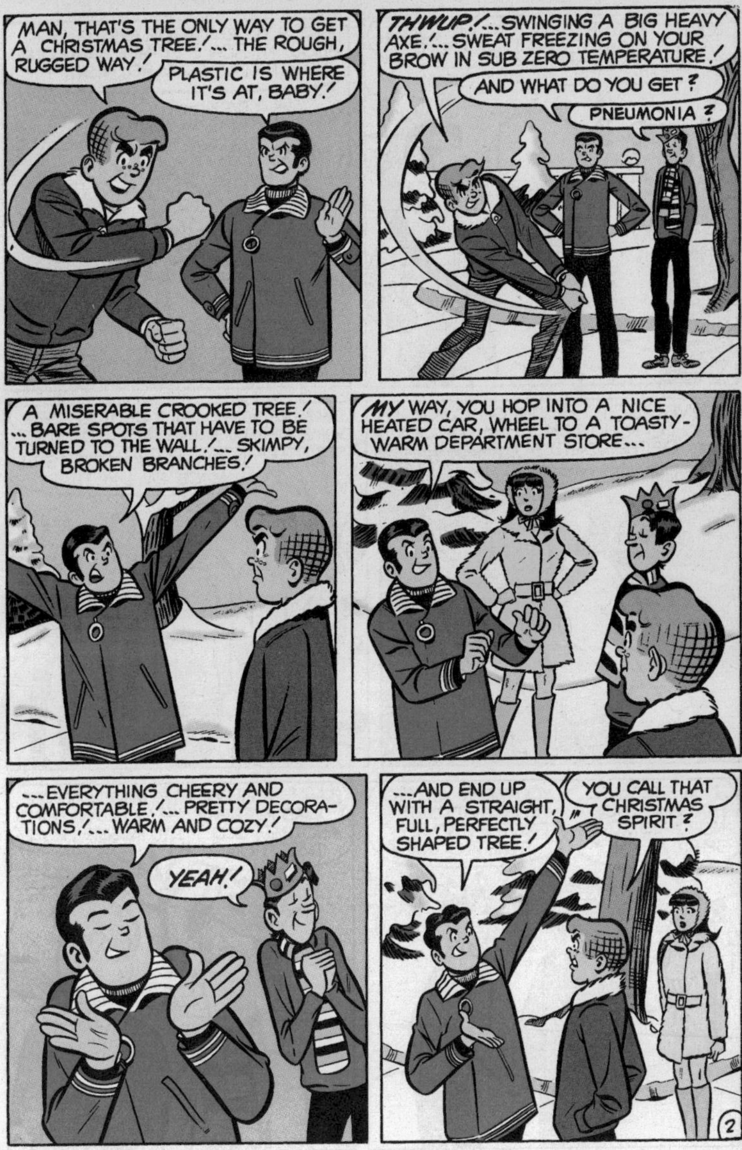
MAN, THAT'S THE ONLY WAY TO GET A CHRISTMAS TREE!... THE ROUGH, RUGGED WAY!
PLASTIC IS WHERE IT'S AT, BABY!
THWUP!... SWINGING A BIG HEAVY AXE!... SWEAT FREEZING ON YOUR BROW IN SUB ZERO TEMPERATURE!
AND WHAT DO YOU GET?
PNEUMONIA?
A MISERABLE CROOKED TREE!... BARE SPOTS THAT HAVE TO BE TURNED TO THE WALL!... SKIMPY, BROKEN BRANCHES!
MY WAY, YOU HOP INTO A NICE HEATED CAR, WHEEL TO A TOASTY-WARM DEPARTMENT STORE...
...EVERYTHING CHEERY AND COMFORTABLE!... PRETTY DECORATIONS!... WARM AND COZY!
YEAH!
...AND END UP WITH A STRAIGHT, FULL, PERFECTLY SHAPED TREE!
YOU CALL THAT CHRISTMAS SPIRIT?
2

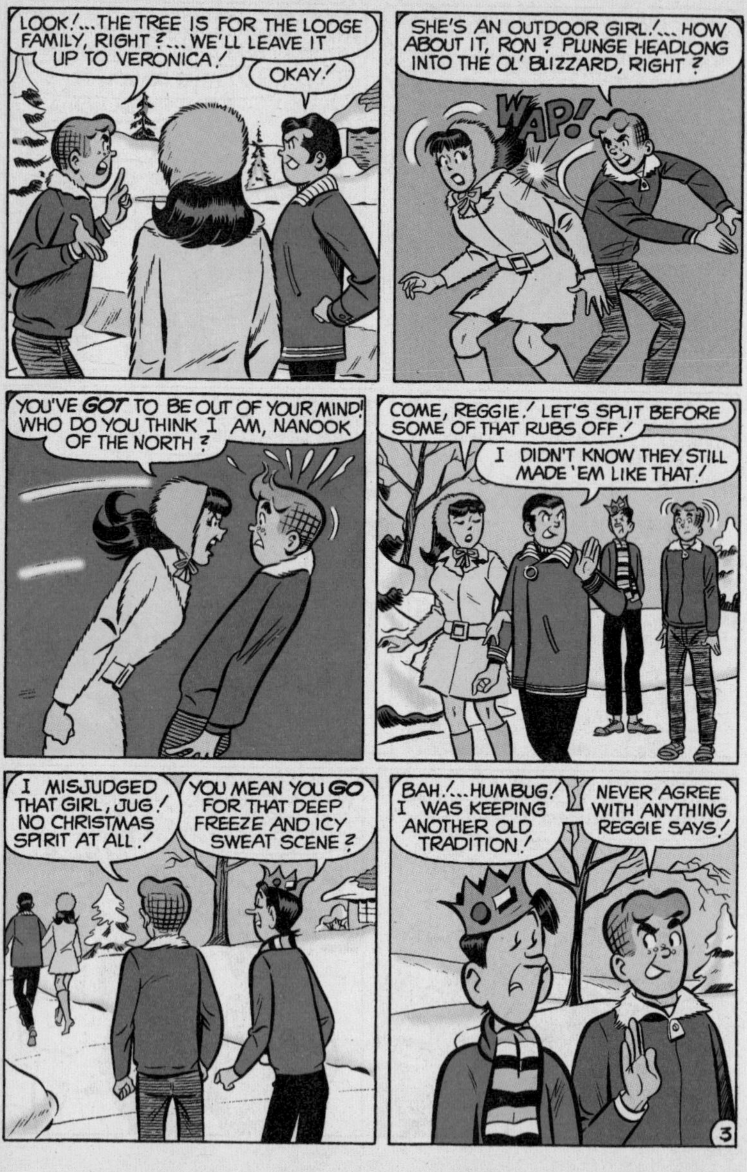
LOOK!...THE TREE IS FOR THE LODGE FAMILY, RIGHT?... WE'LL LEAVE IT UP TO VERONICA!
OKAY!
SHE'S AN OUTDOOR GIRL!... HOW ABOUT IT, RON? PLUNGE HEADLONG INTO THE OL' BLIZZARD, RIGHT?
WAP!
YOU'VE GOT TO BE OUT OF YOUR MIND! WHO DO YOU THINK I AM, NANOOK OF THE NORTH?
COME, REGGIE! LET'S SPLIT BEFORE SOME OF THAT RUBS OFF!
I DIDN'T KNOW THEY STILL MADE 'EM LIKE THAT!
I MISJUDGED THAT GIRL, JUG! NO CHRISTMAS SPIRIT AT ALL!
YOU MEAN YOU GO FOR THAT DEEP FREEZE AND ICY SWEAT SCENE?
BAH!...HUMBUG! I WAS KEEPING ANOTHER OLD TRADITION!
NEVER AGREE WITH ANYTHING REGGIE SAYS!
3

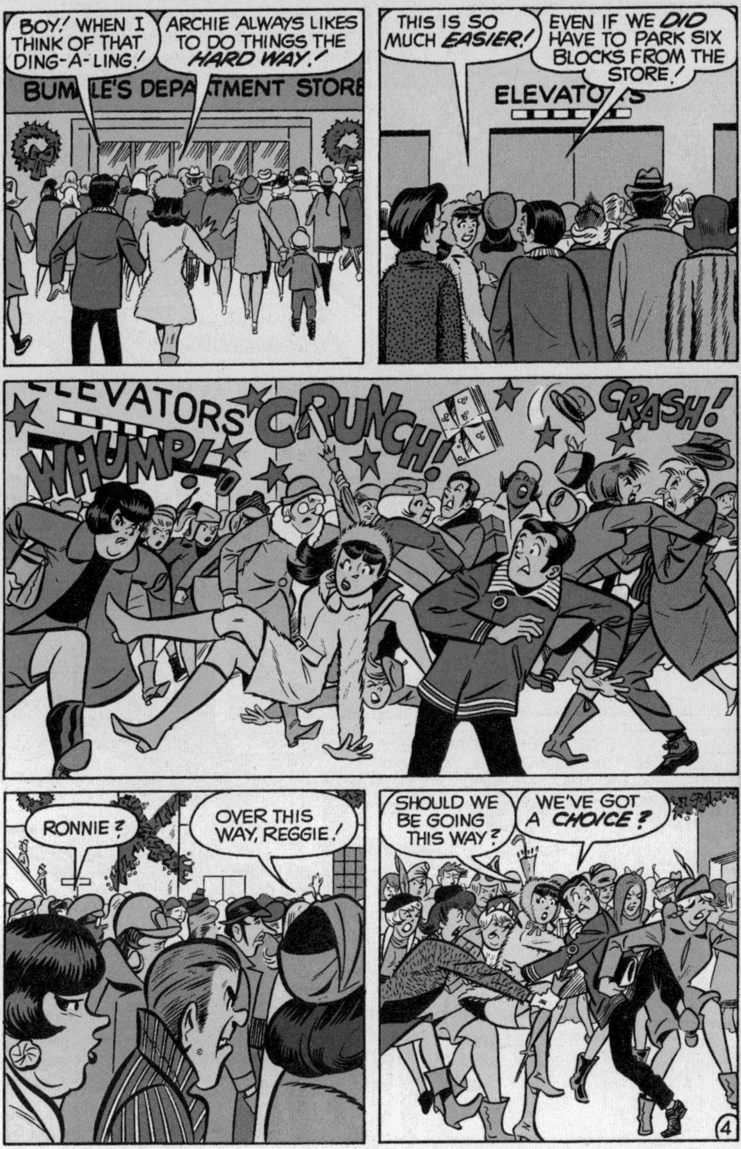
BOY! WHEN I THINK OF THAT DING-A-LING!
ARCHIE ALWAYS LIKES TO DO THINGS THE HARD WAY!
BUMBLE'S DEPARTMENT STORE
THIS IS SO MUCH EASIER!
EVEN IF WE DID HAVE TO PARK SIX BLOCKS FROM THE STORE!
ELEVATORS
ELEVATORS
WHUMP!
CRUNCH!
CRASH!
RONNIE?
OVER THIS WAY, REGGIE!
SHOULD WE BE GOING THIS WAY?
WE'VE GOT A CHOICE?
4

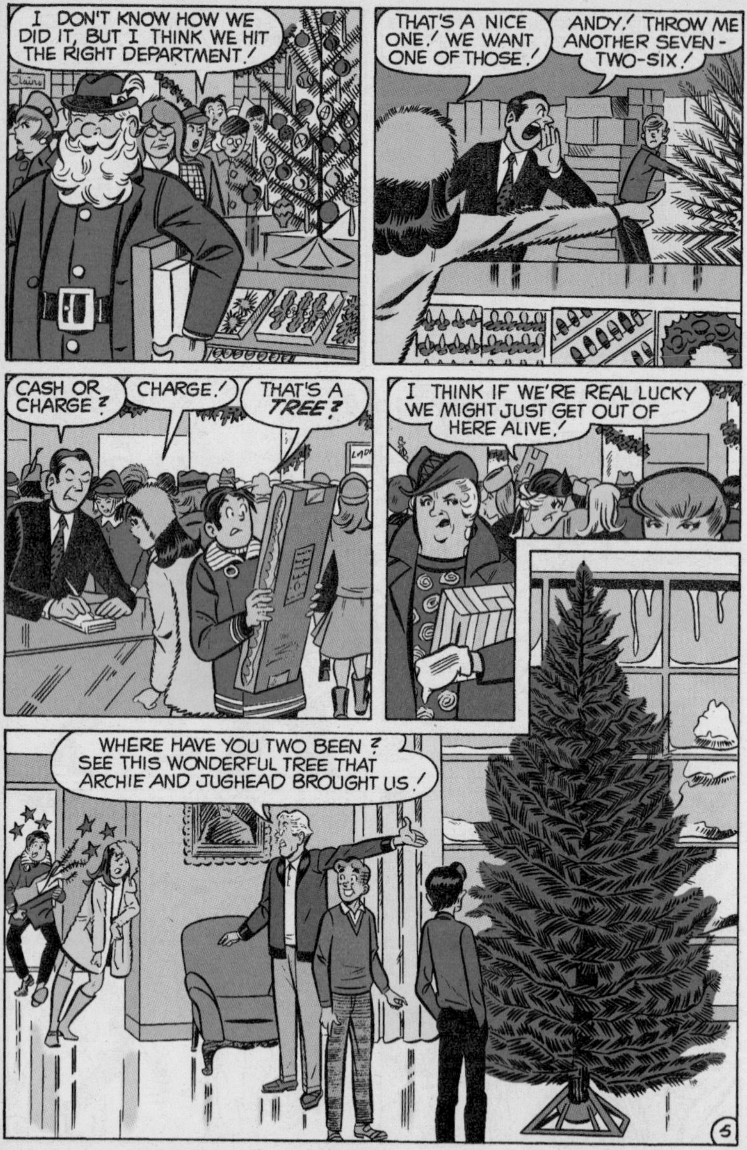

I DON'T KNOW HOW WE DID IT, BUT I THINK WE HIT THE RIGHT DEPARTMENT!
THAT'S A NICE ONE! WE WANT ONE OF THOSE!
ANDY! THROW ME ANOTHER SEVEN-TWO-SIX!
CASH OR CHARGE?
CHARGE!
THAT'S A *TREE?*
I THINK IF WE'RE REAL LUCKY WE MIGHT JUST GET OUT OF HERE ALIVE!
WHERE HAVE YOU TWO BEEN? SEE THIS WONDERFUL TREE THAT ARCHIE AND JUGHEAD BROUGHT US!
5

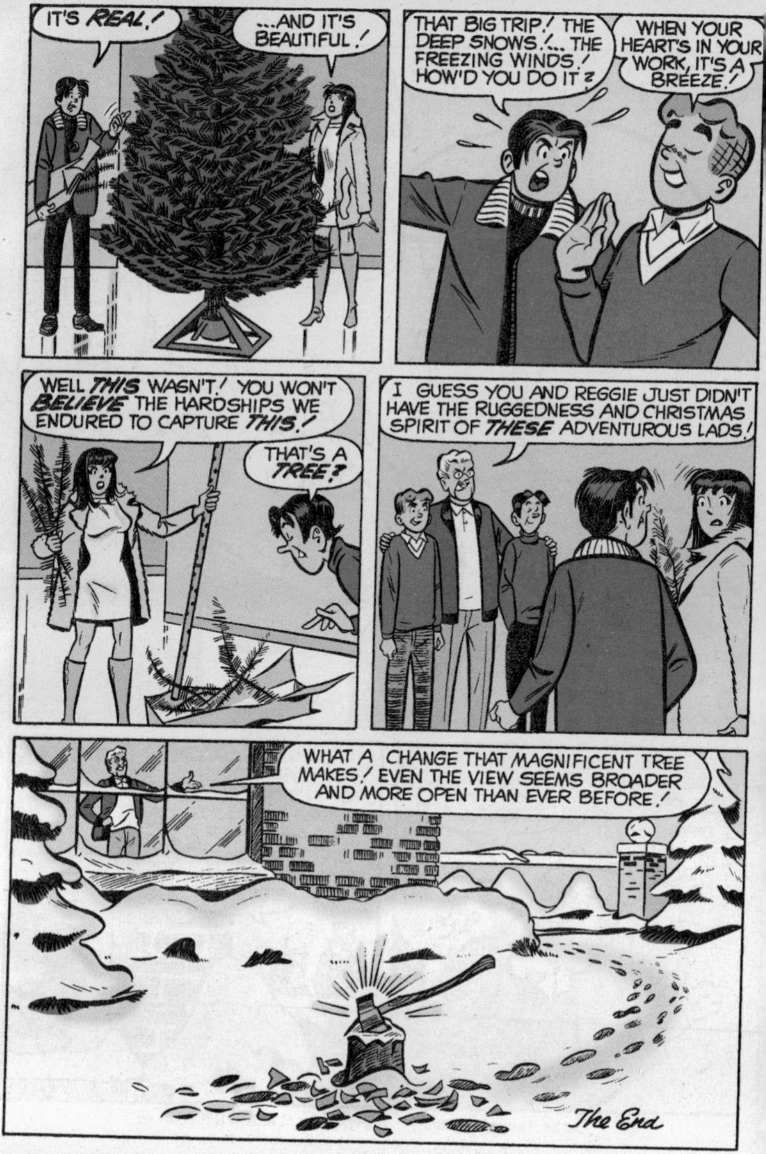
IT'S REAL!
...AND IT'S BEAUTIFUL!
THAT BIG TRIP! THE DEEP SNOWS!... THE FREEZING WINDS! HOW'D YOU DO IT?
WHEN YOUR HEART'S IN YOUR WORK, IT'S A BREEZE!
WELL THIS WASN'T! YOU WON'T BELIEVE THE HARDSHIPS WE ENDURED TO CAPTURE THIS!
THAT'S A TREE?
I GUESS YOU AND REGGIE JUST DIDN'T HAVE THE RUGGEDNESS AND CHRISTMAS SPIRIT OF THESE ADVENTUROUS LADS!
WHAT A CHANGE THAT MAGNIFICENT TREE MAKES! EVEN THE VIEW SEEMS BROADER AND MORE OPEN THAN EVER BEFORE!
The End

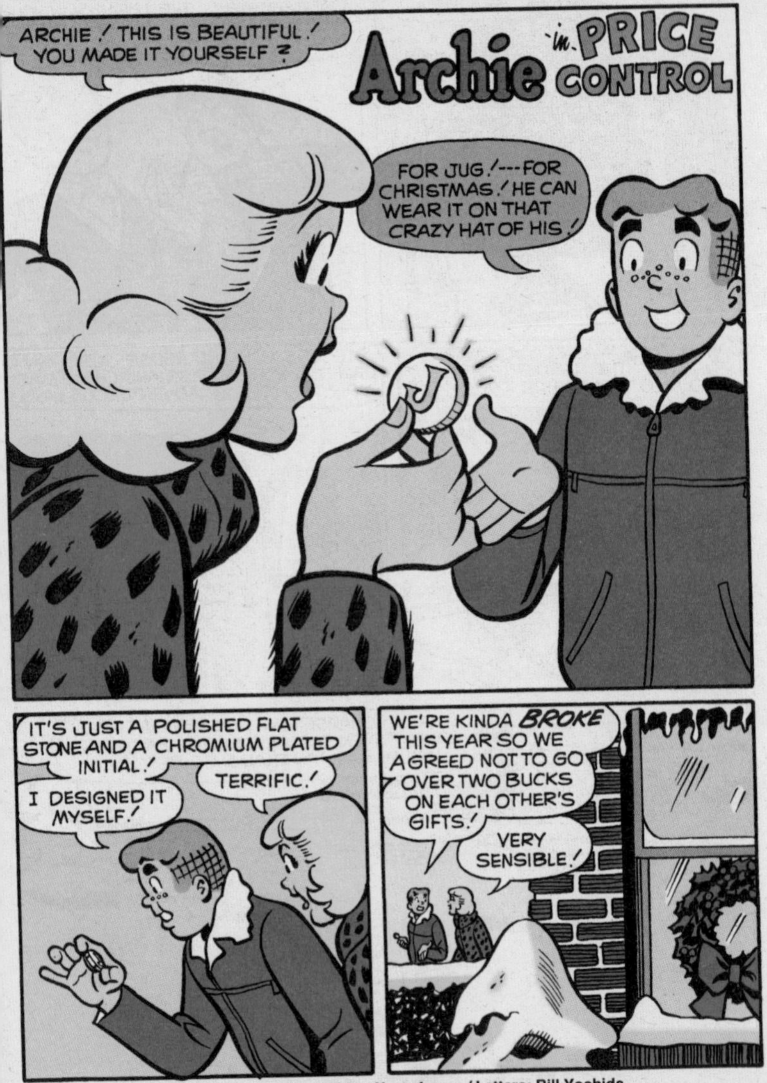
ARCHIE! THIS IS BEAUTIFUL! YOU MADE IT YOURSELF?
Archie in PRICE CONTROL
FOR JUG!---FOR CHRISTMAS! HE CAN WEAR IT ON THAT CRAZY HAT OF HIS!
IT'S JUST A POLISHED FLAT STONE AND A CHROMIUM PLATED INITIAL!
I DESIGNED IT MYSELF!
TERRIFIC!
WE'RE KINDA BROKE THIS YEAR SO WE AGREED NOT TO GO OVER TWO BUCKS ON EACH OTHER'S GIFTS!
VERY SENSIBLE!

Script: George Gladir / Art: Harry Lucey / Letters: Bill Yoshida

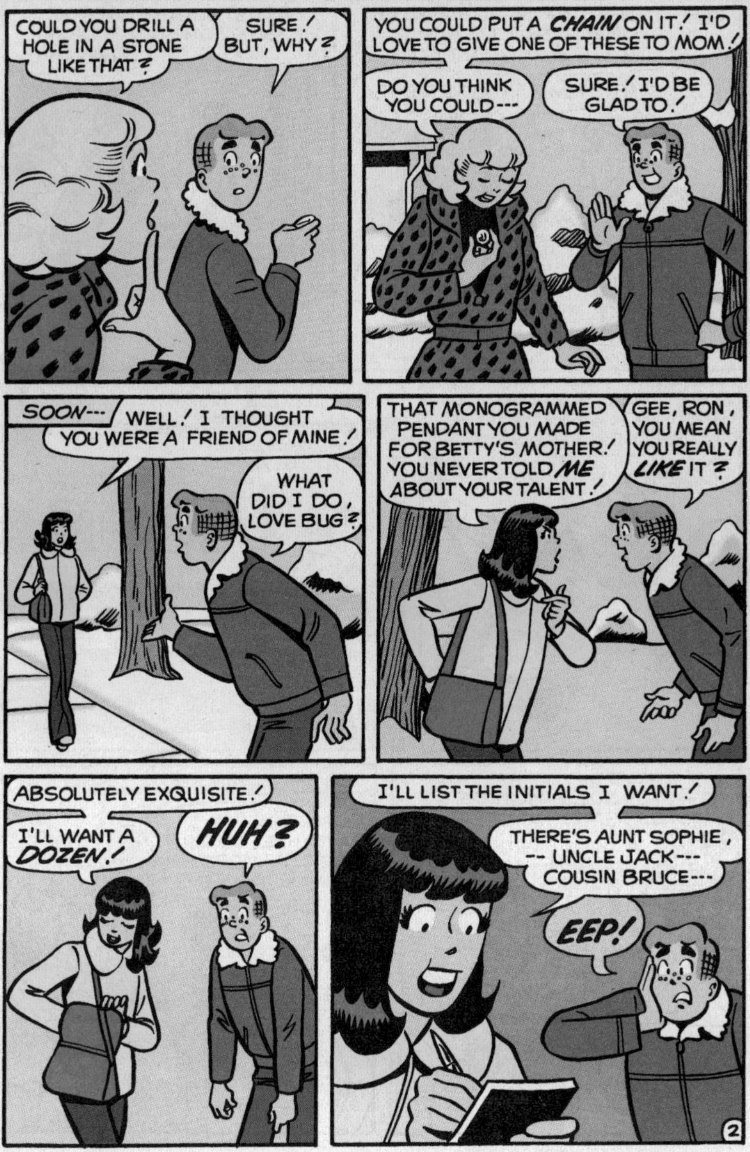

COULD YOU DRILL A HOLE IN A STONE LIKE THAT ?
SURE ! BUT, WHY ?
YOU COULD PUT A CHAIN ON IT ! I'D LOVE TO GIVE ONE OF THESE TO MOM !
DO YOU THINK YOU COULD---
SURE ! I'D BE GLAD TO !
SOON---
WELL ! I THOUGHT YOU WERE A FRIEND OF MINE !
WHAT DID I DO, LOVE BUG ?
THAT MONOGRAMMED PENDANT YOU MADE FOR BETTY'S MOTHER ! YOU NEVER TOLD ME ABOUT YOUR TALENT !
GEE, RON, YOU MEAN YOU REALLY LIKE IT ?
ABSOLUTELY EXQUISITE !
I'LL WANT A DOZEN !
HUH ?
I'LL LIST THE INITIALS I WANT !
THERE'S AUNT SOPHIE, -- UNCLE JACK--- COUSIN BRUCE---
EEP!
2

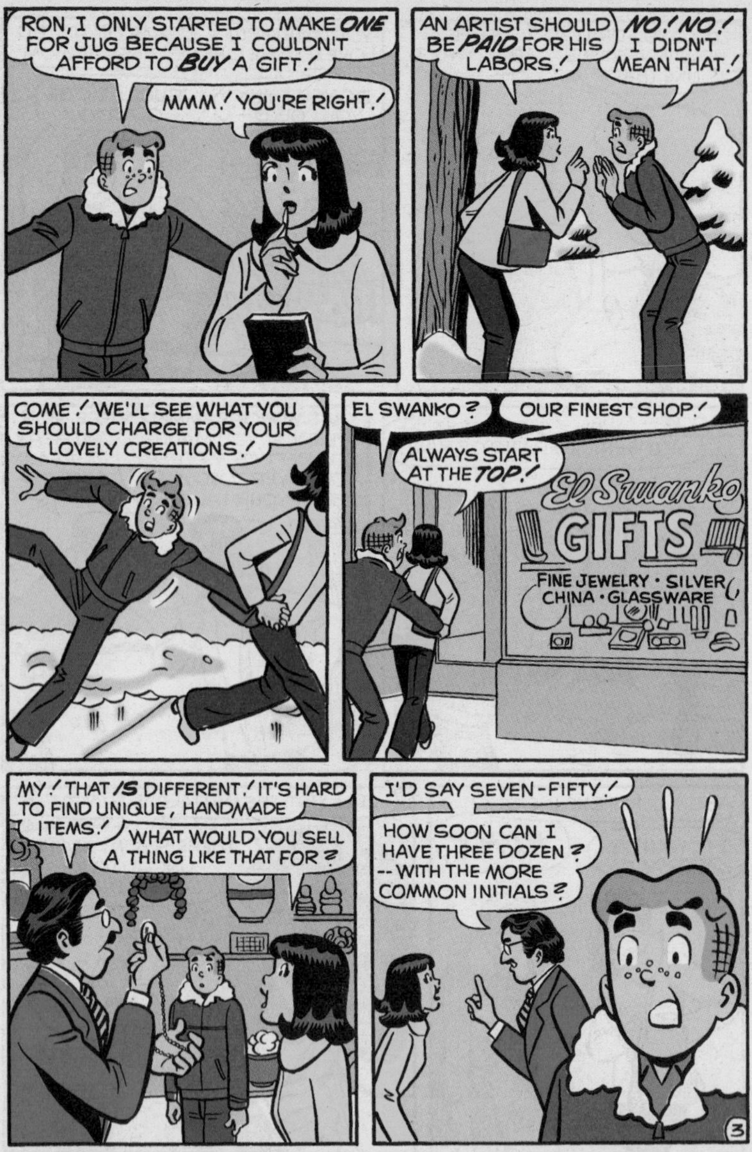
RON, I ONLY STARTED TO MAKE ONE FOR JUG BECAUSE I COULDN'T AFFORD TO BUY A GIFT!
MMM! YOU'RE RIGHT!
AN ARTIST SHOULD BE PAID FOR HIS LABORS!
NO! NO! I DIDN'T MEAN THAT!
COME! WE'LL SEE WHAT YOU SHOULD CHARGE FOR YOUR LOVELY CREATIONS!
EL SWANKO?
OUR FINEST SHOP!
ALWAYS START AT THE TOP!
El Swanko
GIFTS
FINE JEWELRY · SILVER
CHINA · GLASSWARE
MY! THAT IS DIFFERENT! IT'S HARD TO FIND UNIQUE, HANDMADE ITEMS!
WHAT WOULD YOU SELL A THING LIKE THAT FOR?
I'D SAY SEVEN-FIFTY!
HOW SOON CAN I HAVE THREE DOZEN? -- WITH THE MORE COMMON INITIALS?
3

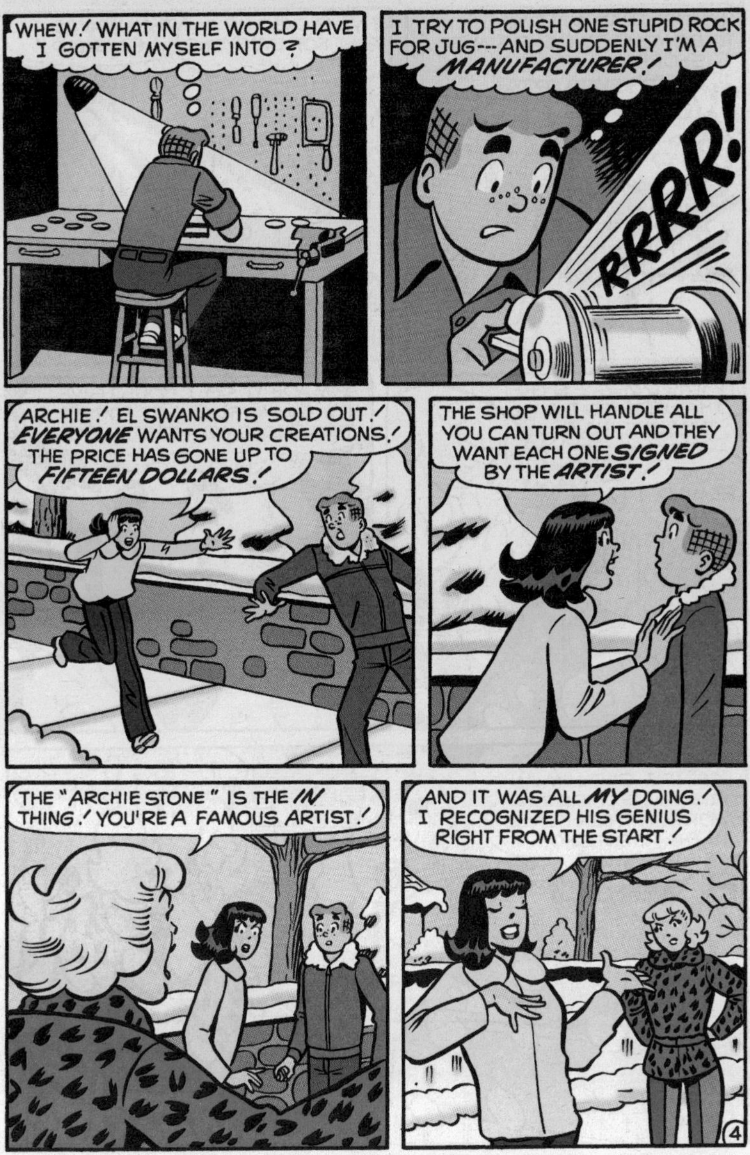
WHEW! WHAT IN THE WORLD HAVE I GOTTEN MYSELF INTO?
I TRY TO POLISH ONE STUPID ROCK FOR JUG---AND SUDDENLY I'M A MANUFACTURER!
RRRR!
ARCHIE! EL SWANKO IS SOLD OUT! EVERYONE WANTS YOUR CREATIONS! THE PRICE HAS GONE UP TO FIFTEEN DOLLARS!
THE SHOP WILL HANDLE ALL YOU CAN TURN OUT AND THEY WANT EACH ONE SIGNED BY THE ARTIST!
THE "ARCHIE STONE" IS THE IN THING! YOU'RE A FAMOUS ARTIST!
AND IT WAS ALL MY DOING! I RECOGNIZED HIS GENIUS RIGHT FROM THE START!
4

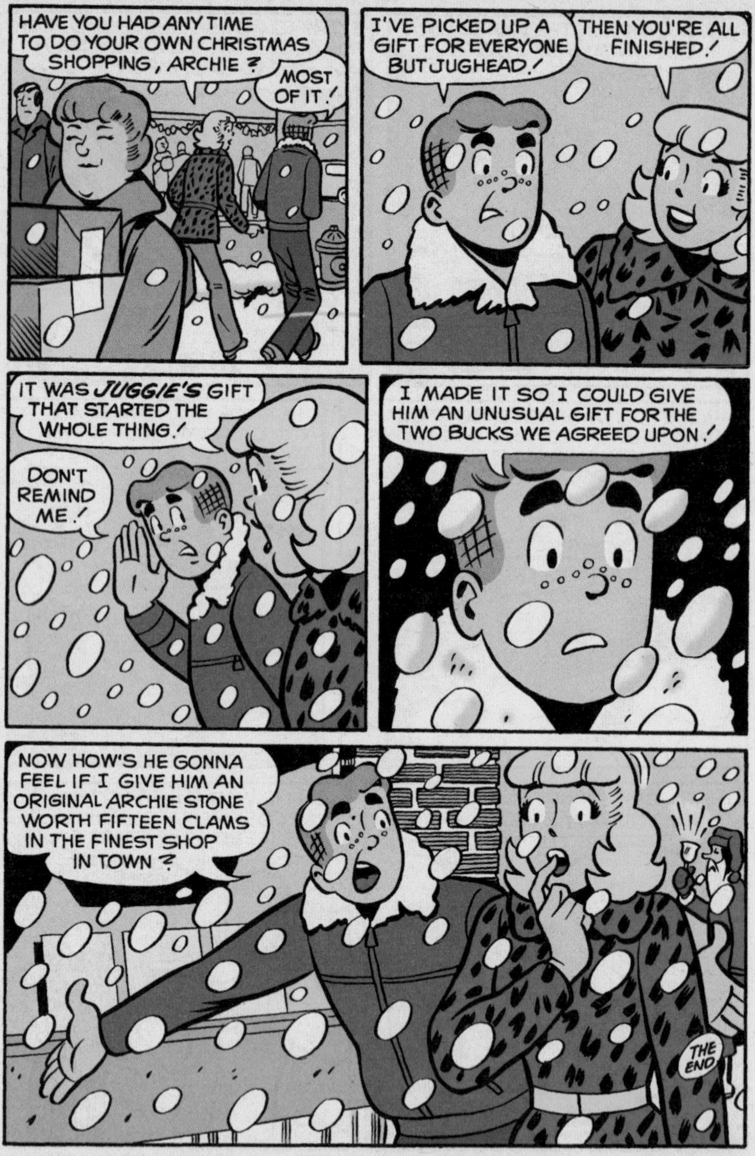
HAVE YOU HAD ANY TIME TO DO YOUR OWN CHRISTMAS SHOPPING, ARCHIE ?
MOST OF IT!
I'VE PICKED UP A GIFT FOR EVERYONE BUT JUGHEAD!
THEN YOU'RE ALL FINISHED!
IT WAS JUGGIE'S GIFT THAT STARTED THE WHOLE THING!
DON'T REMIND ME!
I MADE IT SO I COULD GIVE HIM AN UNUSUAL GIFT FOR THE TWO BUCKS WE AGREED UPON!
NOW HOW'S HE GONNA FEEL IF I GIVE HIM AN ORIGINAL ARCHIE STONE WORTH FIFTEEN CLAMS IN THE FINEST SHOP IN TOWN ?
THE END

Archie's Christmas Stocking

"A Bird in the Hand"

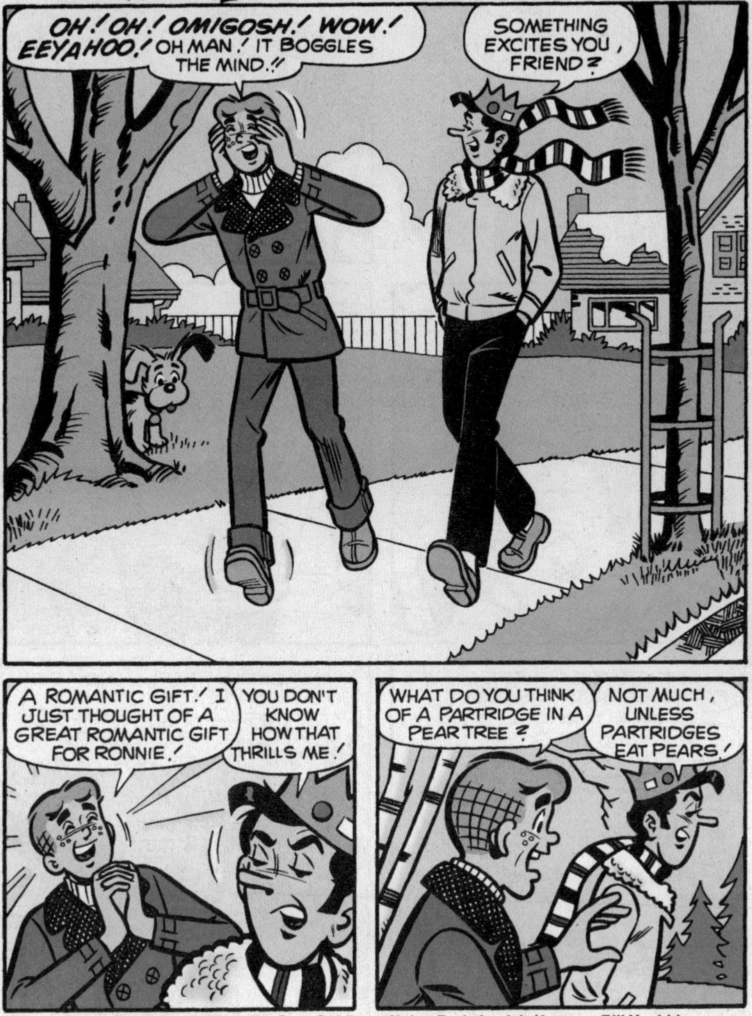
OH! OH! OMIGOSH! WOW! EEYAHOO! OH MAN! IT BOGGLES THE MIND!!
SOMETHING EXCITES YOU, FRIEND?
A ROMANTIC GIFT! I JUST THOUGHT OF A GREAT ROMANTIC GIFT FOR RONNIE!
YOU DON'T KNOW HOW THAT THRILLS ME!
WHAT DO YOU THINK OF A PARTRIDGE IN A PEAR TREE?
NOT MUCH, UNLESS PARTRIDGES EAT PEARS!

Script: Frank Doyle / Pencils: Stan Goldberg / Inks: Rudy Lapick / Letters: Bill Yoshida

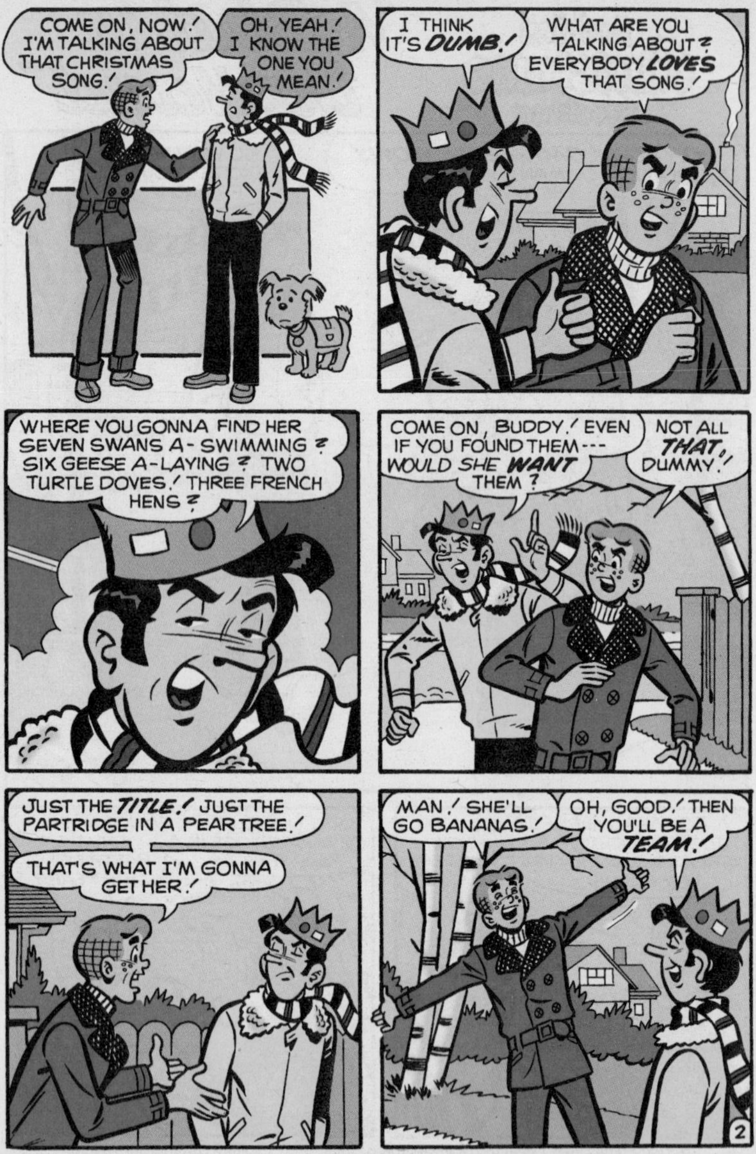
COME ON, NOW! I'M TALKING ABOUT THAT CHRISTMAS SONG!
OH, YEAH! I KNOW THE ONE YOU MEAN!
I THINK IT'S DUMB!
WHAT ARE YOU TALKING ABOUT? EVERYBODY LOVES THAT SONG!
WHERE YOU GONNA FIND HER SEVEN SWANS A-SWIMMING? SIX GEESE A-LAYING? TWO TURTLE DOVES! THREE FRENCH HENS?
COME ON, BUDDY! EVEN IF YOU FOUND THEM--- WOULD SHE WANT THEM?
NOT ALL THAT, DUMMY!
JUST THE TITLE! JUST THE PARTRIDGE IN A PEAR TREE!
THAT'S WHAT I'M GONNA GET HER!
MAN! SHE'LL GO BANANAS!
OH, GOOD! THEN YOU'LL BE A TEAM!
2

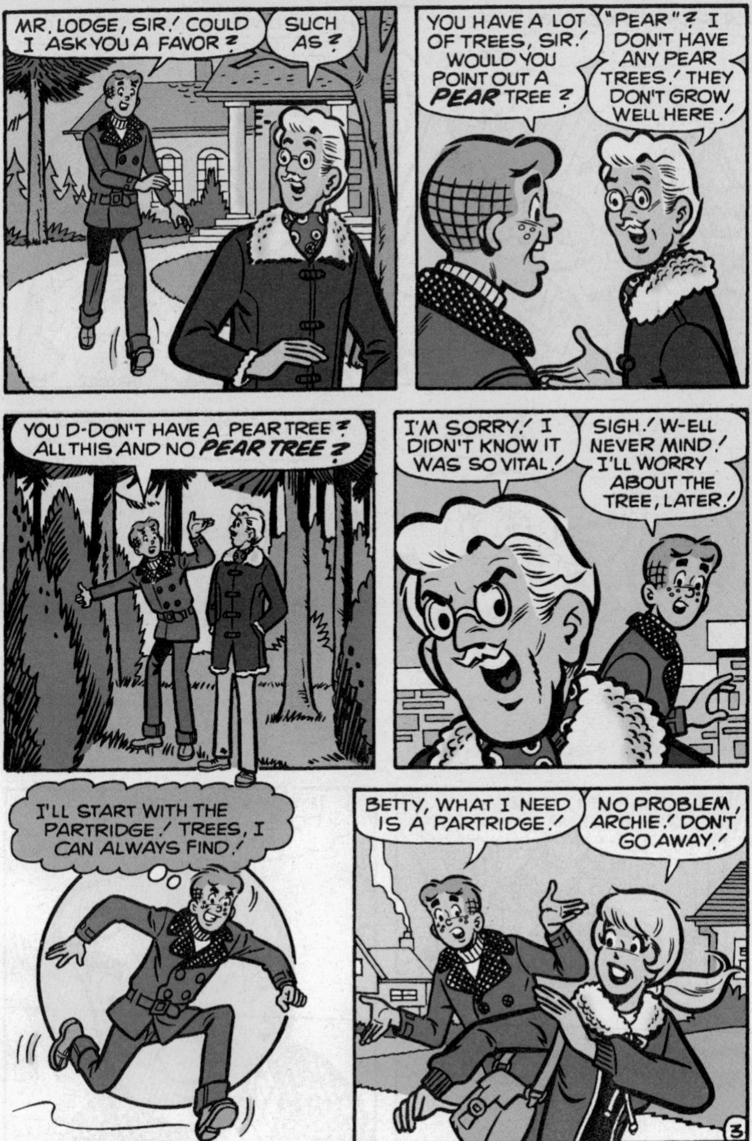

MR. LODGE, SIR! COULD I ASK YOU A FAVOR?
SUCH AS?
YOU HAVE A LOT OF TREES, SIR! WOULD YOU POINT OUT A PEAR TREE?
"PEAR"? I DON'T HAVE ANY PEAR TREES! THEY DON'T GROW WELL HERE!
YOU D-DON'T HAVE A PEAR TREE? ALL THIS AND NO PEAR TREE?
I'M SORRY! I DIDN'T KNOW IT WAS SO VITAL!
SIGH! W-ELL NEVER MIND! I'LL WORRY ABOUT THE TREE, LATER!
I'LL START WITH THE PARTRIDGE! TREES, I CAN ALWAYS FIND!
BETTY, WHAT I NEED IS A PARTRIDGE!
NO PROBLEM, ARCHIE! DON'T GO AWAY!
3

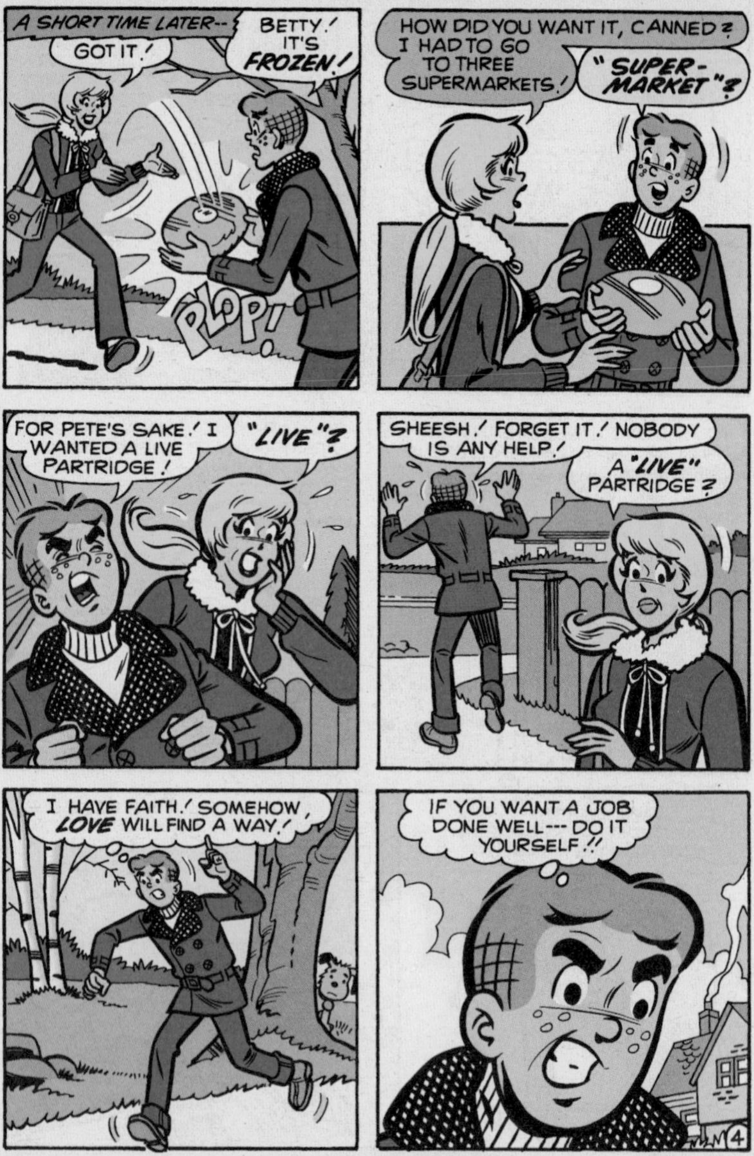
A SHORT TIME LATER--
GOT IT!
BETTY! IT'S FROZEN!
PLOP!
HOW DID YOU WANT IT, CANNED? I HAD TO GO TO THREE SUPERMARKETS!
"SUPER-MARKET"?
FOR PETE'S SAKE! I WANTED A LIVE PARTRIDGE!
"LIVE"?
SHEESH! FORGET IT! NOBODY IS ANY HELP!
A "LIVE" PARTRIDGE?
I HAVE FAITH! SOMEHOW, LOVE WILL FIND A WAY!
IF YOU WANT A JOB DONE WELL--- DO IT YOURSELF!!
4

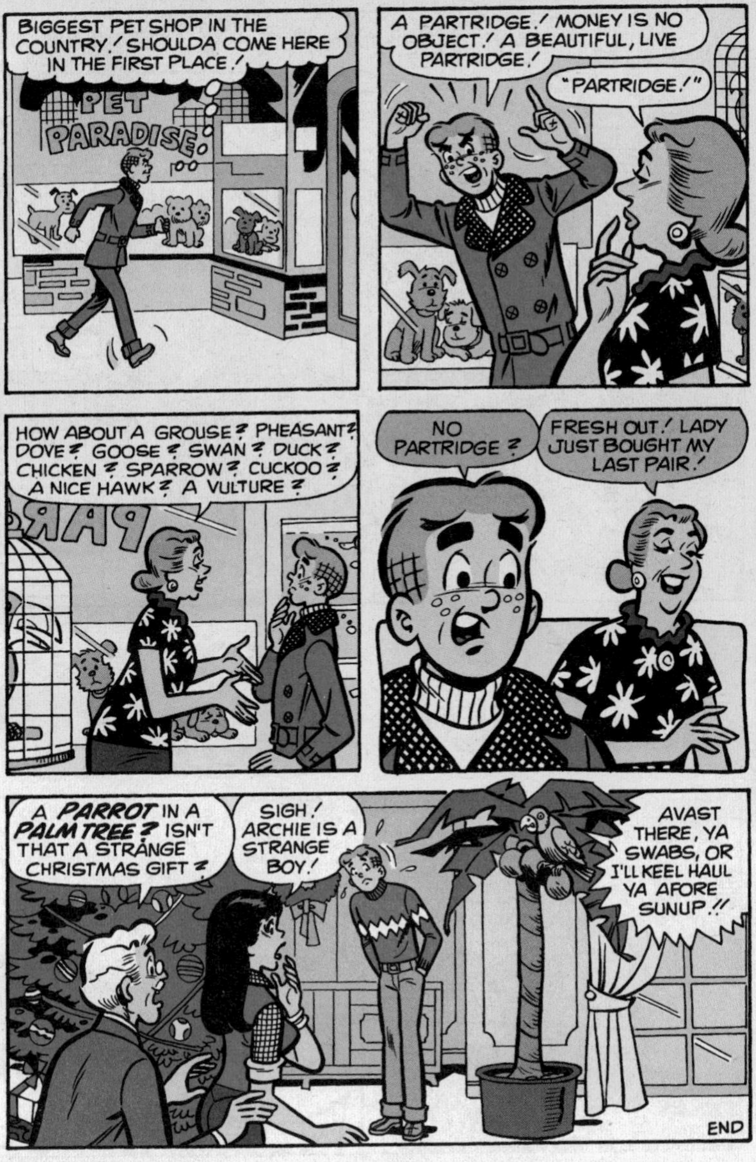
BIGGEST PET SHOP IN THE COUNTRY! SHOULDA COME HERE IN THE FIRST PLACE!
PET PARADISE
A PARTRIDGE! MONEY IS NO OBJECT! A BEAUTIFUL, LIVE PARTRIDGE!
"PARTRIDGE!"
HOW ABOUT A GROUSE? PHEASANT? DOVE? GOOSE? SWAN? DUCK? CHICKEN? SPARROW? CUCKOO? A NICE HAWK? A VULTURE?
NO PARTRIDGE?
FRESH OUT! LADY JUST BOUGHT MY LAST PAIR!
A PARROT IN A PALM TREE? ISN'T THAT A STRANGE CHRISTMAS GIFT?
SIGH! ARCHIE IS A STRANGE BOY!
AVAST THERE, YA SWABS, OR I'LL KEEL HAUL YA AFORE SUNUP!!
END

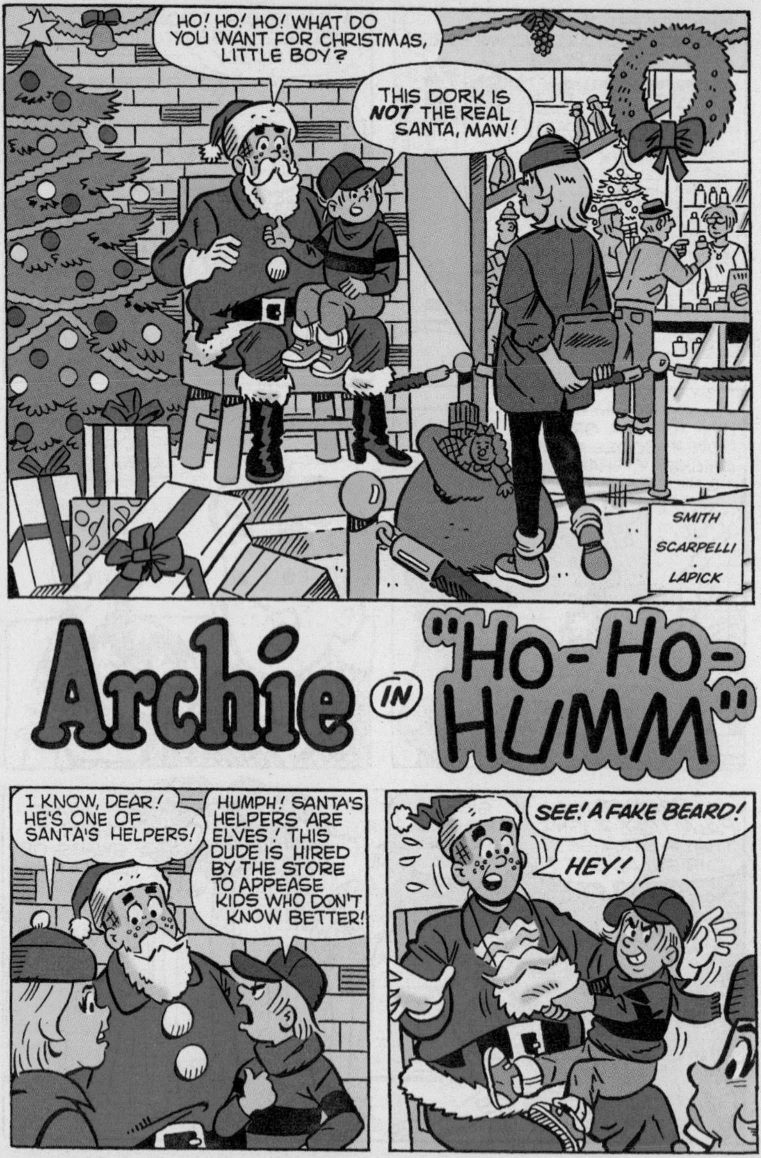
HO! HO! HO! WHAT DO YOU WANT FOR CHRISTMAS, LITTLE BOY?
THIS DORK IS *NOT* THE REAL SANTA, MAW!
SMITH
SCARPELLI
LAPICK
Archie IN "HO-HO-HUMM"
I KNOW, DEAR! HE'S ONE OF SANTA'S HELPERS!
HUMPH! SANTA'S HELPERS ARE ELVES! THIS DUDE IS HIRED BY THE STORE TO APPEASE KIDS WHO DON'T KNOW BETTER!
SEE! A FAKE BEARD!
HEY!

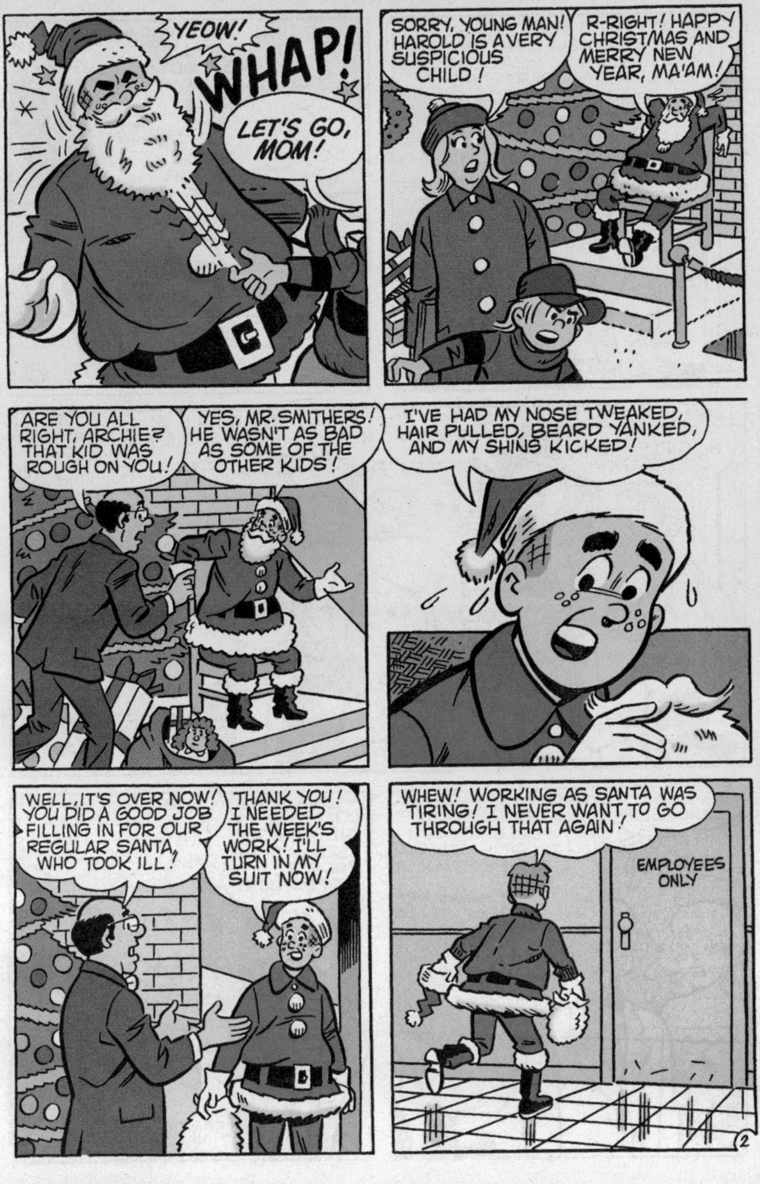
YEOW!
WHAP!
LET'S GO, MOM!
SORRY, YOUNG MAN! HAROLD IS A VERY SUSPICIOUS CHILD!
R-RIGHT! HAPPY CHRISTMAS AND MERRY NEW YEAR, MA'AM!
ARE YOU ALL RIGHT, ARCHIE? THAT KID WAS ROUGH ON YOU!
YES, MR. SMITHERS! HE WASN'T AS BAD AS SOME OF THE OTHER KIDS!
I'VE HAD MY NOSE TWEAKED, HAIR PULLED, BEARD YANKED, AND MY SHINS KICKED!
WELL, IT'S OVER NOW! YOU DID A GOOD JOB FILLING IN FOR OUR REGULAR SANTA, WHO TOOK ILL!
THANK YOU! I NEEDED THE WEEK'S WORK! I'LL TURN IN MY SUIT NOW!
WHEW! WORKING AS SANTA WAS TIRING! I NEVER WANT TO GO THROUGH THAT AGAIN!
EMPLOYEES ONLY

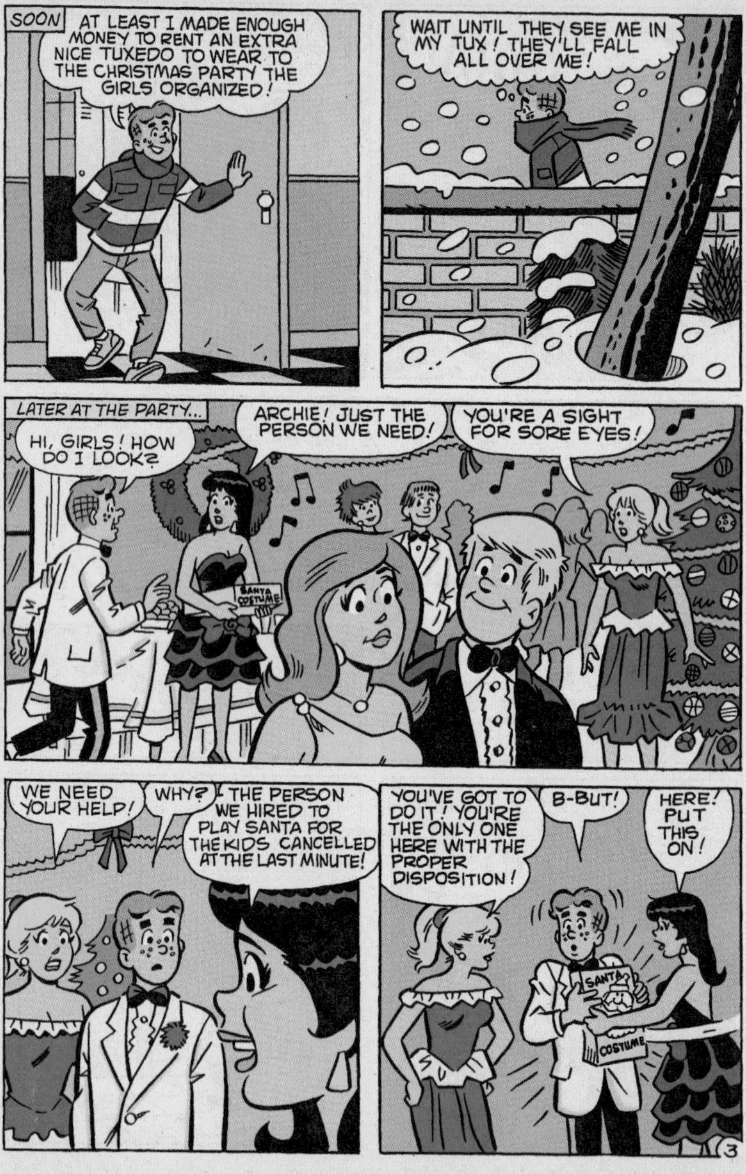
SOON
AT LEAST I MADE ENOUGH MONEY TO RENT AN EXTRA NICE TUXEDO TO WEAR TO THE CHRISTMAS PARTY THE GIRLS ORGANIZED!
WAIT UNTIL THEY SEE ME IN MY TUX! THEY'LL FALL ALL OVER ME!
LATER AT THE PARTY...
HI, GIRLS! HOW DO I LOOK?
ARCHIE! JUST THE PERSON WE NEED!
YOU'RE A SIGHT FOR SORE EYES!
SANTA COSTUME
WE NEED YOUR HELP!
WHY?
THE PERSON WE HIRED TO PLAY SANTA FOR THE KIDS CANCELLED AT THE LAST MINUTE!
YOU'VE GOT TO DO IT! YOU'RE THE ONLY ONE HERE WITH THE PROPER DISPOSITION!
B-BUT!
HERE! PUT THIS ON!
SANTA
COSTUME

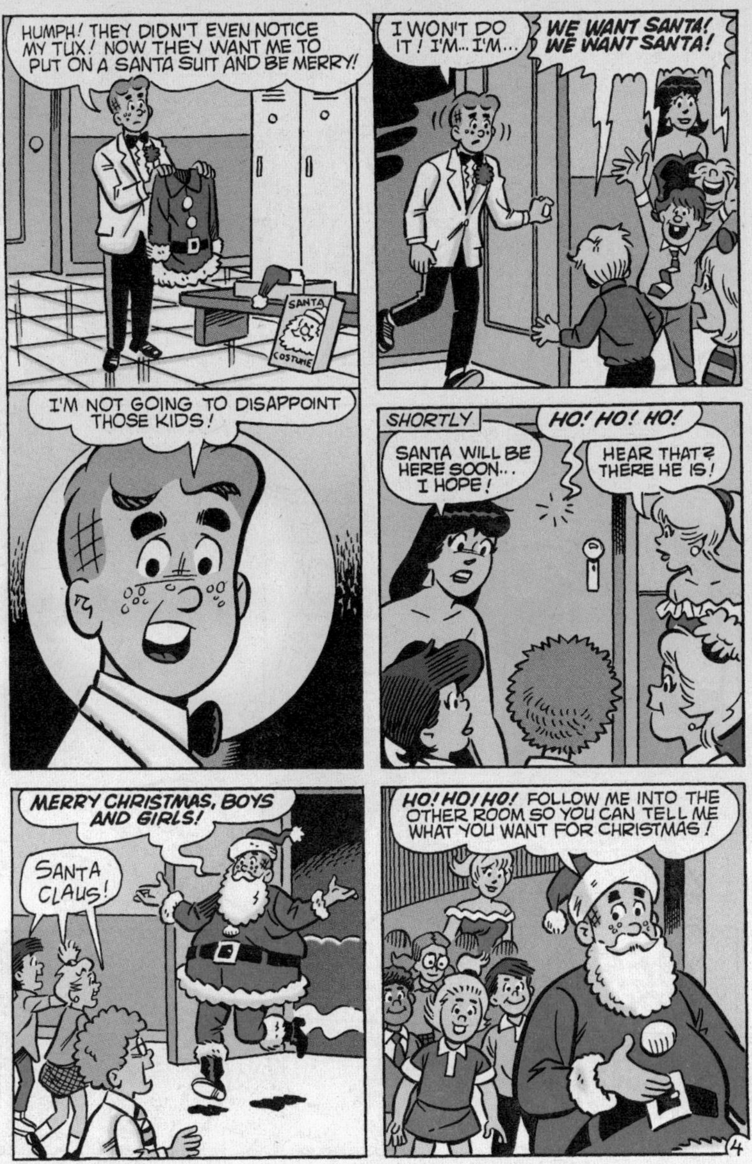
HUMPH! THEY DIDN'T EVEN NOTICE MY TUX! NOW THEY WANT ME TO PUT ON A SANTA SUIT AND BE MERRY!
SANTA COSTUME
I WON'T DO IT! I'M... I'M...
WE WANT SANTA! WE WANT SANTA!
I'M NOT GOING TO DISAPPOINT THOSE KIDS!
SHORTLY
SANTA WILL BE HERE SOON... I HOPE!
HO! HO! HO!
HEAR THAT? THERE HE IS!
MERRY CHRISTMAS, BOYS AND GIRLS!
SANTA CLAUS!
HO! HO! HO! FOLLOW ME INTO THE OTHER ROOM SO YOU CAN TELL ME WHAT YOU WANT FOR CHRISTMAS!
4

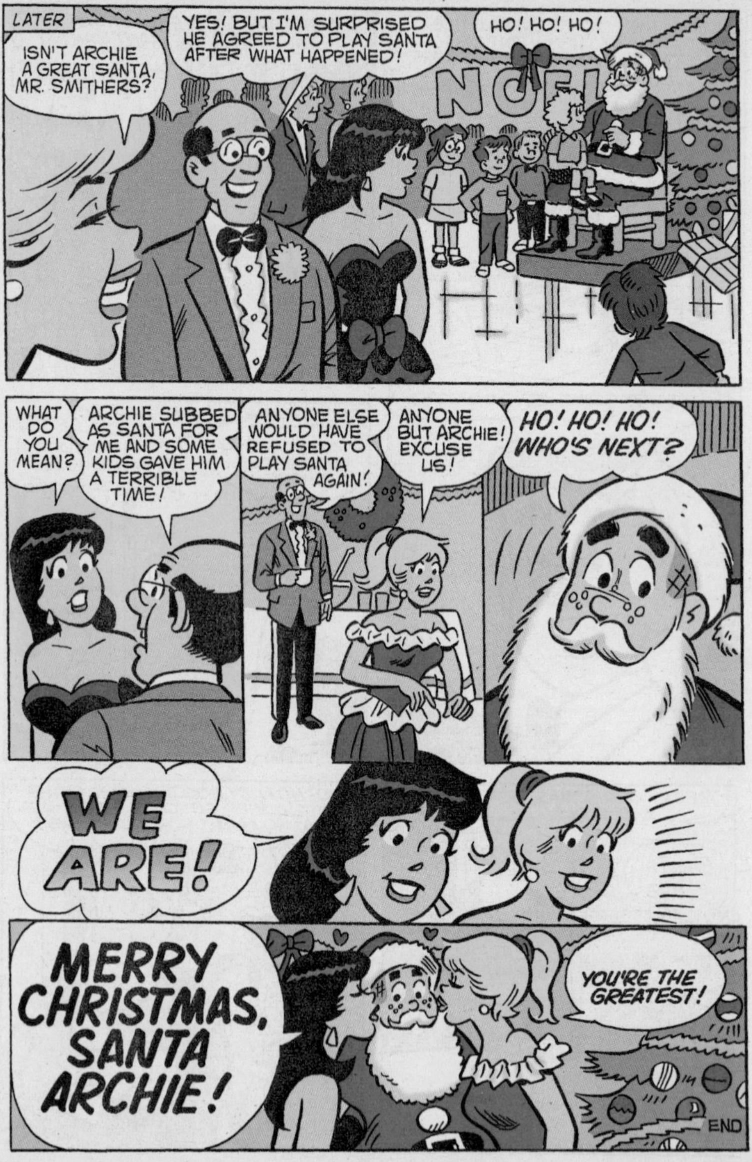
LATER
ISN'T ARCHIE A GREAT SANTA, MR. SMITHERS?
YES! BUT I'M SURPRISED HE AGREED TO PLAY SANTA AFTER WHAT HAPPENED!
HO! HO! HO!
NOEL
WHAT DO YOU MEAN?
ARCHIE SUBBED AS SANTA FOR ME AND SOME KIDS GAVE HIM A TERRIBLE TIME!
ANYONE ELSE WOULD HAVE REFUSED TO PLAY SANTA AGAIN!
ANYONE BUT ARCHIE! EXCUSE US!
HO! HO! HO! WHO'S NEXT?
WE ARE!
MERRY CHRISTMAS, SANTA ARCHIE!
YOU'RE THE GREATEST!
END

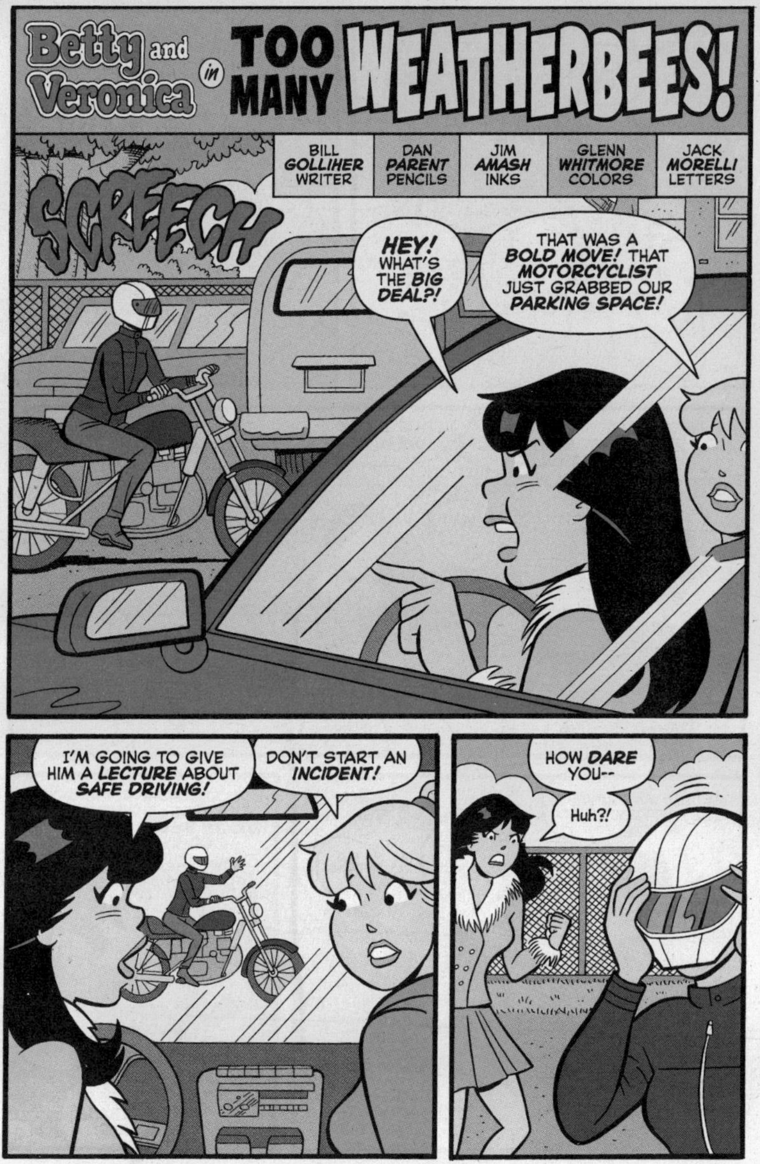
Betty and Veronica in
TOO MANY WEATHERBEES!
BILL GOLLIHER WRITER
DAN PARENT PENCILS
JIM AMASH INKS
GLENN WHITMORE COLORS
JACK MORELLI LETTERS
SCREECH
HEY! WHAT'S THE BIG DEAL?!
THAT WAS A BOLD MOVE! THAT MOTORCYCLIST JUST GRABBED OUR PARKING SPACE!
I'M GOING TO GIVE HIM A LECTURE ABOUT SAFE DRIVING!
DON'T START AN INCIDENT!
HOW DARE YOU--
Huh?!

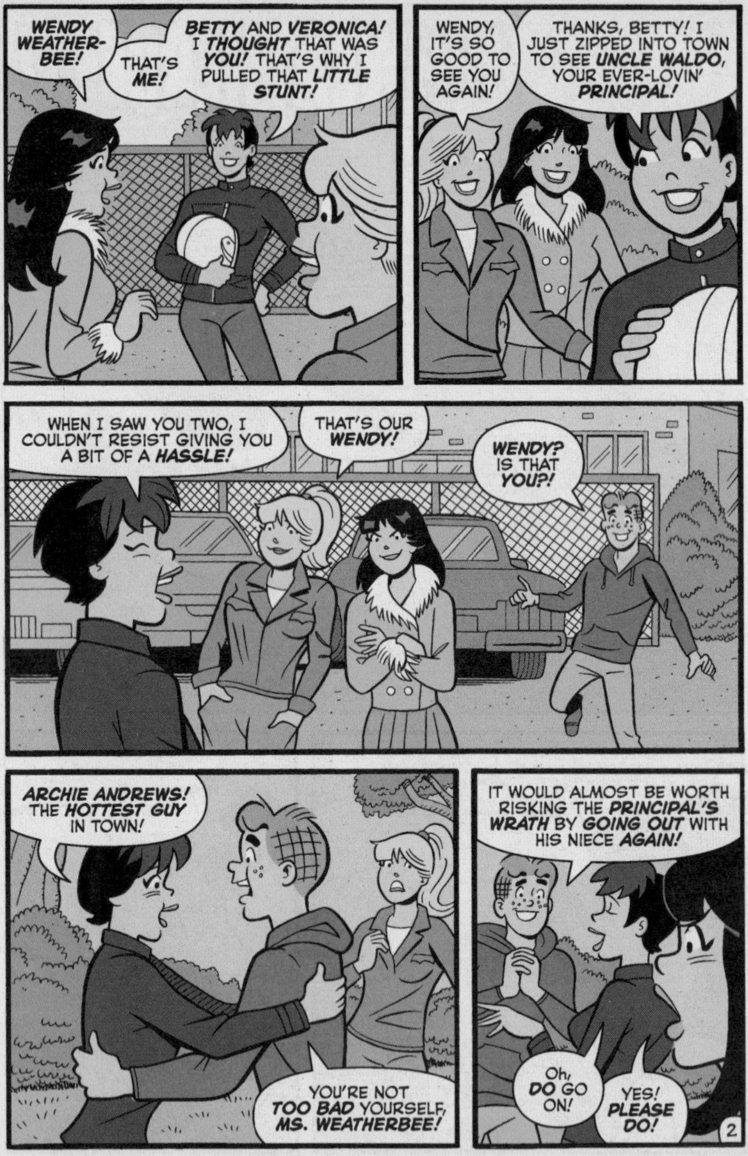
WENDY WEATHER-BEE!
THAT'S ME!
BETTY AND VERONICA! I THOUGHT THAT WAS YOU! THAT'S WHY I PULLED THAT LITTLE STUNT!
WENDY, IT'S SO GOOD TO SEE YOU AGAIN!
THANKS, BETTY! I JUST ZIPPED INTO TOWN TO SEE UNCLE WALDO, YOUR EVER-LOVIN' PRINCIPAL!
WHEN I SAW YOU TWO, I COULDN'T RESIST GIVING YOU A BIT OF A HASSLE!
THAT'S OUR WENDY!
WENDY? IS THAT YOU?!
ARCHIE ANDREWS! THE HOTTEST GUY IN TOWN!
YOU'RE NOT TOO BAD YOURSELF, MS. WEATHERBEE!
IT WOULD ALMOST BE WORTH RISKING THE PRINCIPAL'S WRATH BY GOING OUT WITH HIS NIECE AGAIN!
Oh, DO GO ON!
YES! PLEASE DO!
2

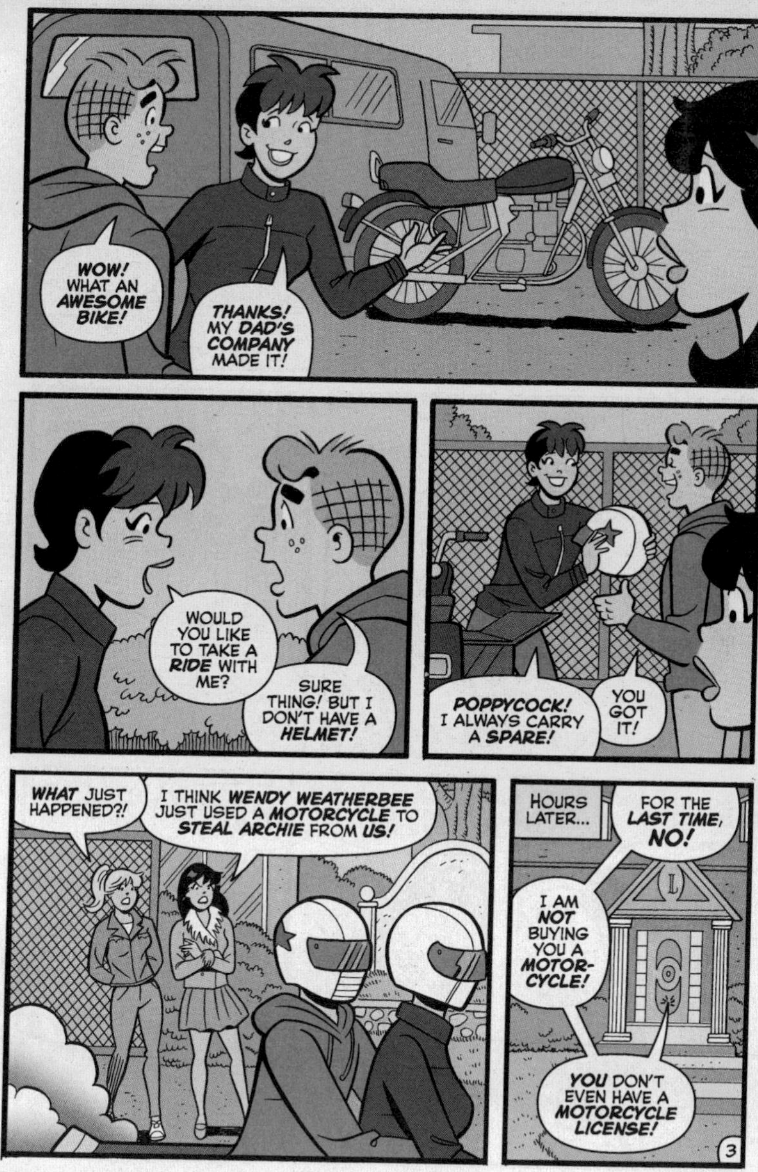

WOW! WHAT AN AWESOME BIKE!
THANKS! MY DAD'S COMPANY MADE IT!
WOULD YOU LIKE TO TAKE A RIDE WITH ME?
SURE THING! BUT I DON'T HAVE A HELMET!
POPPYCOCK! I ALWAYS CARRY A SPARE!
YOU GOT IT!
WHAT JUST HAPPENED?!
I THINK WENDY WEATHERBEE JUST USED A MOTORCYCLE TO STEAL ARCHIE FROM US!
HOURS LATER...
FOR THE LAST TIME, NO!
I AM NOT BUYING YOU A MOTOR-CYCLE!
YOU DON'T EVEN HAVE A MOTORCYCLE LICENSE!

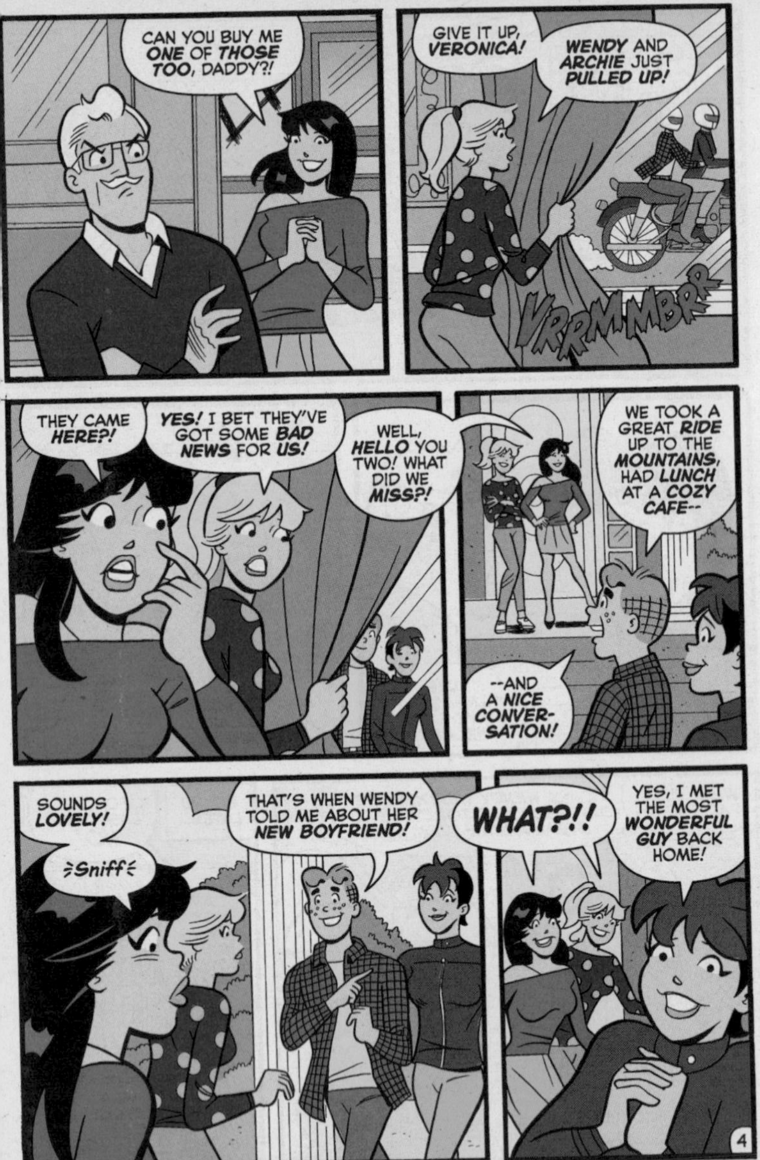
CAN YOU BUY ME ONE OF THOSE TOO, DADDY?!
GIVE IT UP, VERONICA!
WENDY AND ARCHIE JUST PULLED UP!
VRRMMMBRR
THEY CAME HERE?!
YES! I BET THEY'VE GOT SOME BAD NEWS FOR US!
WELL, HELLO YOU TWO! WHAT DID WE MISS?!
WE TOOK A GREAT RIDE UP TO THE MOUNTAINS, HAD LUNCH AT A COZY CAFE--
--AND A NICE CONVER-SATION!
SOUNDS LOVELY!
Sniff
THAT'S WHEN WENDY TOLD ME ABOUT HER NEW BOYFRIEND!
WHAT?!!
YES, I MET THE MOST WONDERFUL GUY BACK HOME!
4

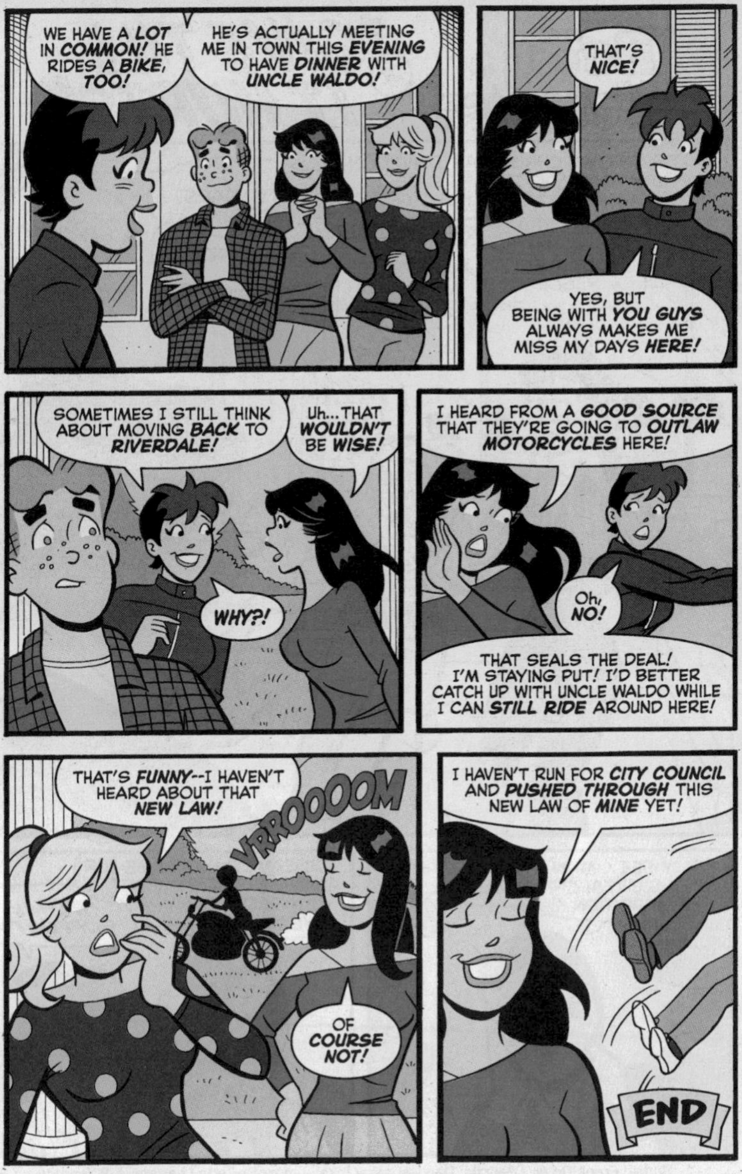
WE HAVE A LOT IN COMMON! HE RIDES A BIKE, TOO!
HE'S ACTUALLY MEETING ME IN TOWN THIS EVENING TO HAVE DINNER WITH UNCLE WALDO!
THAT'S NICE!
YES, BUT BEING WITH YOU GUYS ALWAYS MAKES ME MISS MY DAYS HERE!
SOMETIMES I STILL THINK ABOUT MOVING BACK TO RIVERDALE!
Uh...THAT WOULDN'T BE WISE!
WHY?!
I HEARD FROM A GOOD SOURCE THAT THEY'RE GOING TO OUTLAW MOTORCYCLES HERE!
Oh, NO!
THAT SEALS THE DEAL! I'M STAYING PUT! I'D BETTER CATCH UP WITH UNCLE WALDO WHILE I CAN STILL RIDE AROUND HERE!
THAT'S FUNNY--I HAVEN'T HEARD ABOUT THAT NEW LAW!
VRROOOOM
OF COURSE NOT!
I HAVEN'T RUN FOR CITY COUNCIL AND PUSHED THROUGH THIS NEW LAW OF MINE YET!
END

Betty and Veronica in "GIVE TILL IT HURTS"

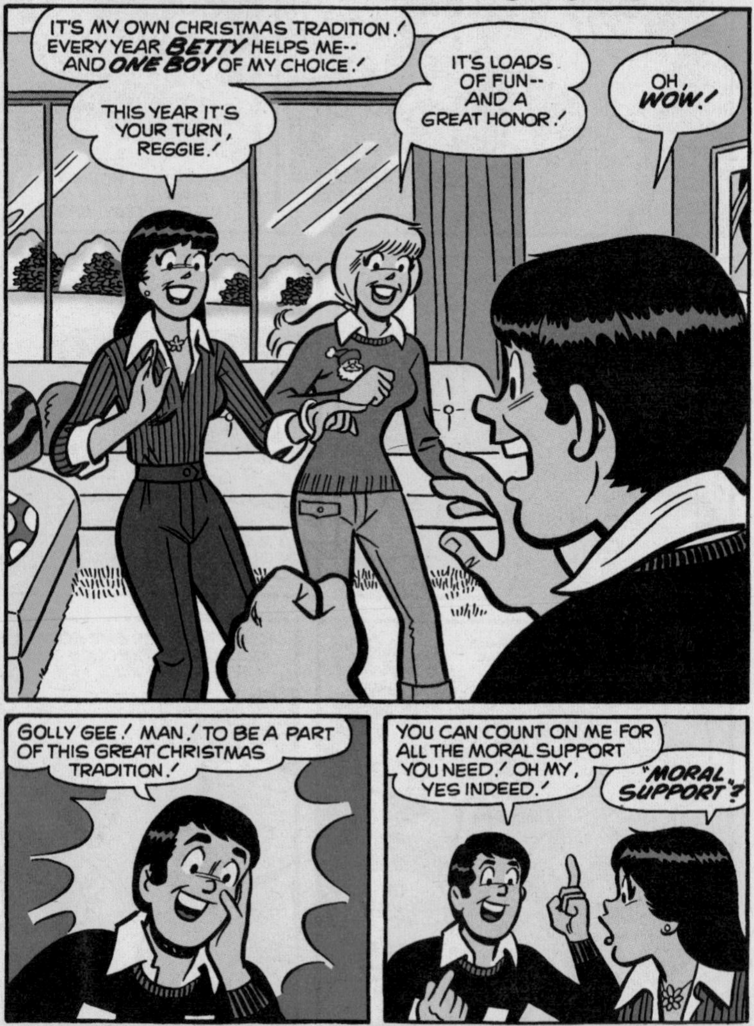
IT'S MY OWN CHRISTMAS TRADITION! EVERY YEAR BETTY HELPS ME-- AND ONE BOY OF MY CHOICE!
THIS YEAR IT'S YOUR TURN, REGGIE!
IT'S LOADS OF FUN-- AND A GREAT HONOR!
OH, WOW!
GOLLY GEE! MAN! TO BE A PART OF THIS GREAT CHRISTMAS TRADITION!
YOU CAN COUNT ON ME FOR ALL THE MORAL SUPPORT YOU NEED! OH MY, YES INDEED!
"MORAL SUPPORT"?

Script: Frank Doyle / Pencils: Dan DeCarlo / Inks: Jimmy DeCarlo / Letters: Bill Yoshida

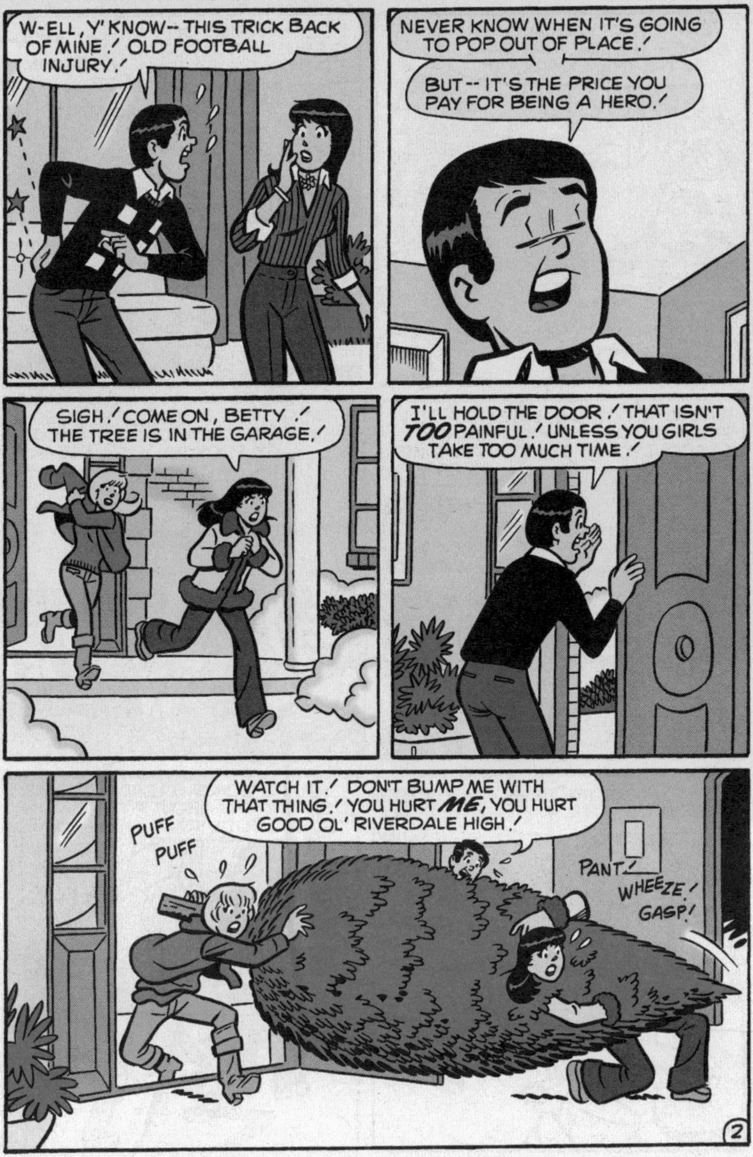
W-ELL, Y' KNOW-- THIS TRICK BACK OF MINE! OLD FOOTBALL INJURY!
NEVER KNOW WHEN IT'S GOING TO POP OUT OF PLACE!
BUT -- IT'S THE PRICE YOU PAY FOR BEING A HERO!
SIGH! COME ON, BETTY! THE TREE IS IN THE GARAGE!
I'LL HOLD THE DOOR! THAT ISN'T TOO PAINFUL! UNLESS YOU GIRLS TAKE TOO MUCH TIME!
PUFF
PUFF
WATCH IT! DON'T BUMP ME WITH THAT THING! YOU HURT ME, YOU HURT GOOD OL' RIVERDALE HIGH!
PANT!
WHEEZE!
GASP!
2

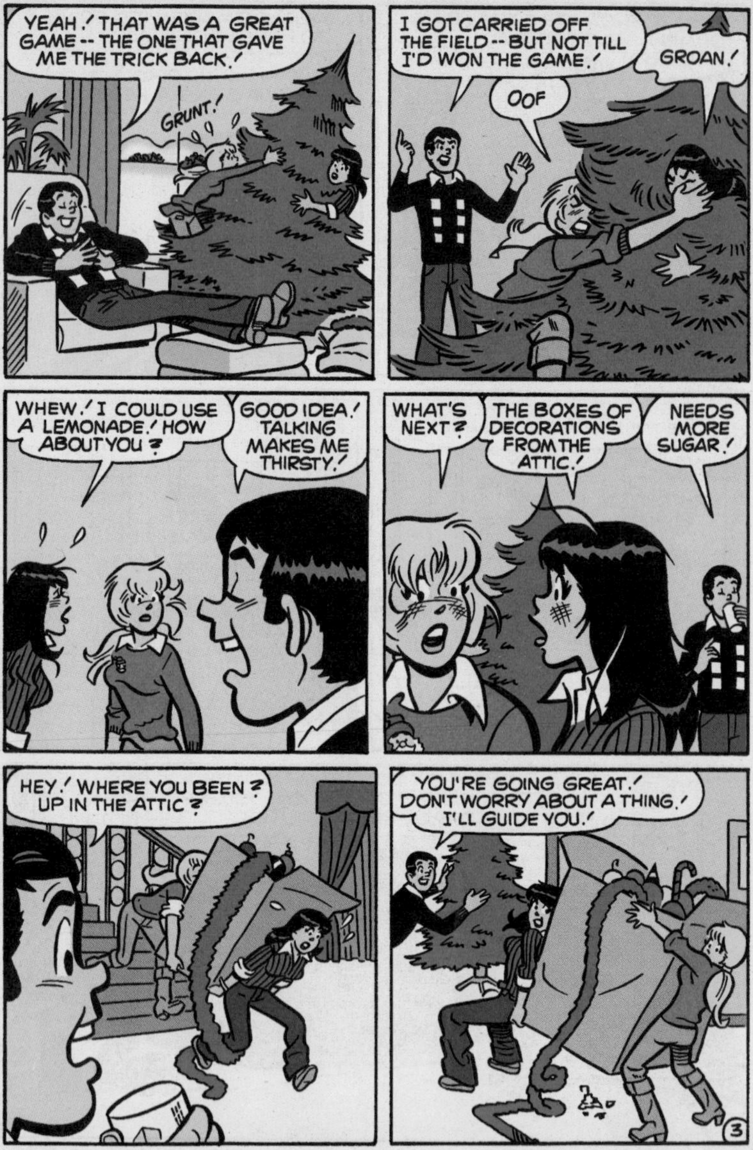
YEAH! THAT WAS A GREAT GAME -- THE ONE THAT GAVE ME THE TRICK BACK!
GRUNT!
I GOT CARRIED OFF THE FIELD -- BUT NOT TILL I'D WON THE GAME!
OOF
GROAN!
WHEW! I COULD USE A LEMONADE! HOW ABOUT YOU?
GOOD IDEA! TALKING MAKES ME THIRSTY!
WHAT'S NEXT?
THE BOXES OF DECORATIONS FROM THE ATTIC!
NEEDS MORE SUGAR!
HEY! WHERE YOU BEEN? UP IN THE ATTIC?
YOU'RE GOING GREAT! DON'T WORRY ABOUT A THING! I'LL GUIDE YOU!
3

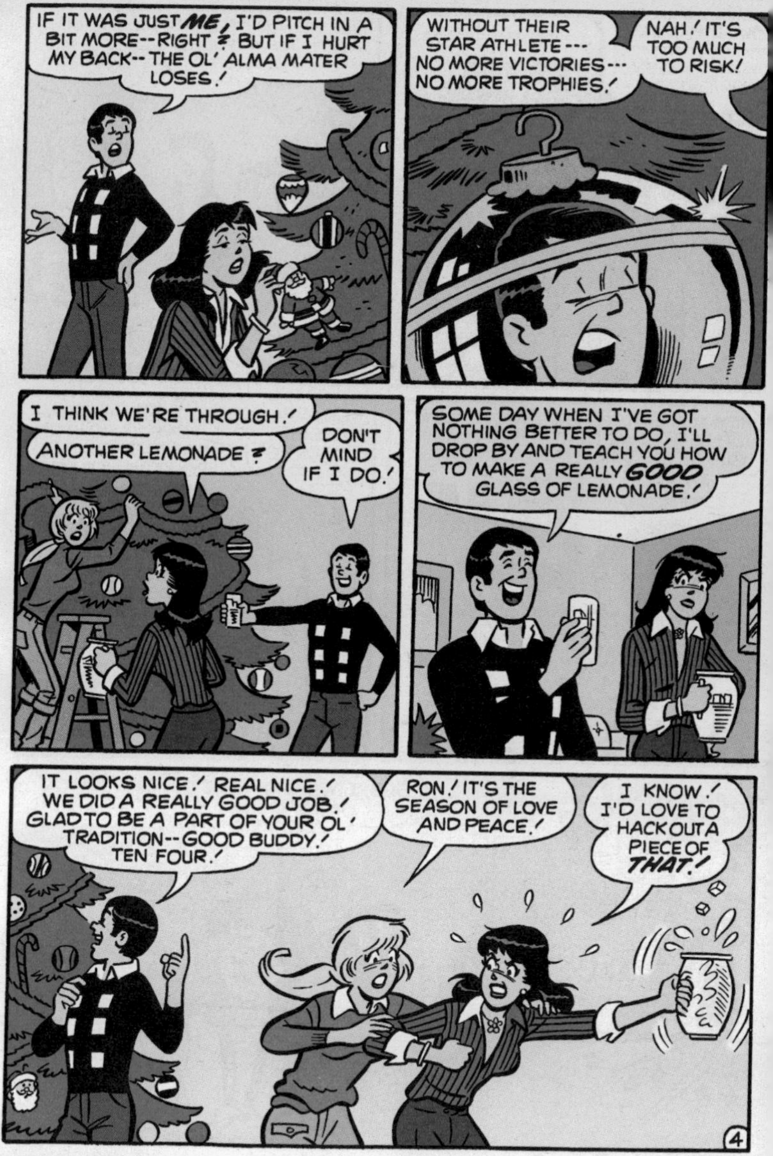
IF IT WAS JUST ME, I'D PITCH IN A BIT MORE--RIGHT? BUT IF I HURT MY BACK-- THE OL' ALMA MATER LOSES!
WITHOUT THEIR STAR ATHLETE--- NO MORE VICTORIES--- NO MORE TROPHIES!
NAH! IT'S TOO MUCH TO RISK!
I THINK WE'RE THROUGH!
ANOTHER LEMONADE?
DON'T MIND IF I DO!
SOME DAY WHEN I'VE GOT NOTHING BETTER TO DO, I'LL DROP BY AND TEACH YOU HOW TO MAKE A REALLY GOOD GLASS OF LEMONADE!
IT LOOKS NICE! REAL NICE! WE DID A REALLY GOOD JOB! GLAD TO BE A PART OF YOUR OL' TRADITION--GOOD BUDDY! TEN FOUR!
RON! IT'S THE SEASON OF LOVE AND PEACE!
I KNOW! I'D LOVE TO HACK OUT A PIECE OF THAT!
4

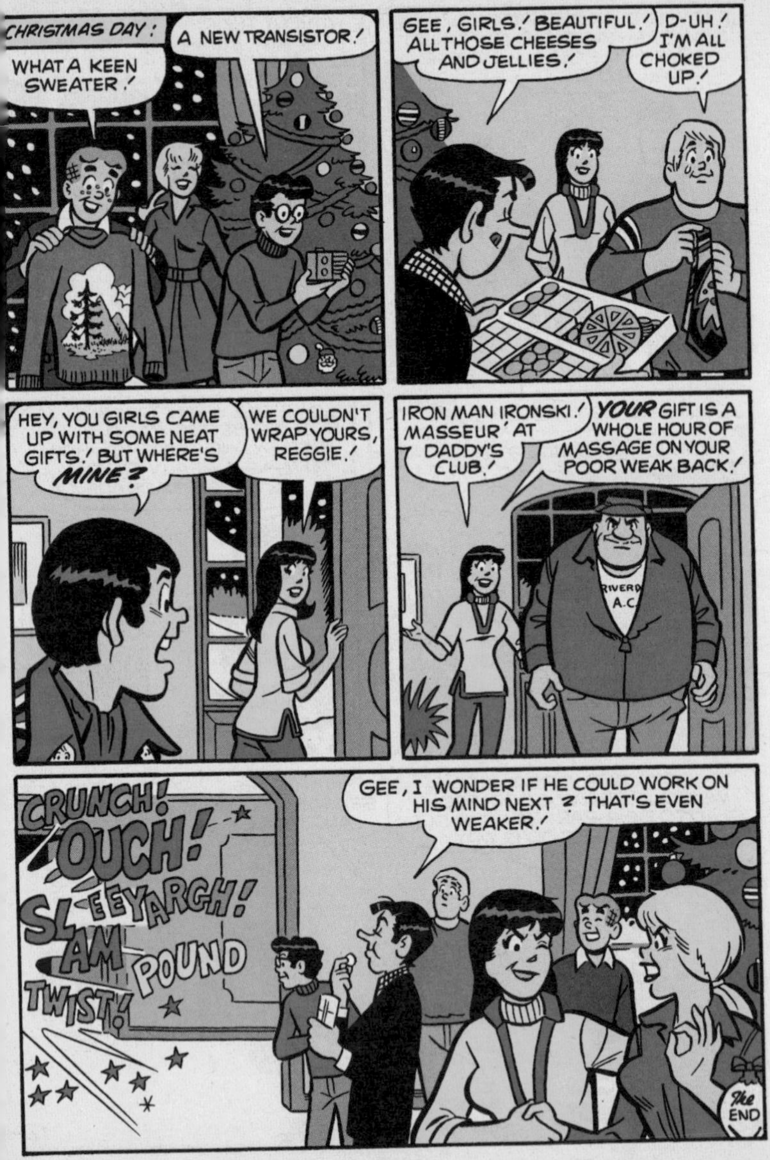
CHRISTMAS DAY:
WHAT A KEEN SWEATER!
A NEW TRANSISTOR!
GEE, GIRLS! BEAUTIFUL! ALL THOSE CHEESES AND JELLIES!
D-UH! I'M ALL CHOKED UP!
HEY, YOU GIRLS CAME UP WITH SOME NEAT GIFTS! BUT WHERE'S MINE?
WE COULDN'T WRAP YOURS, REGGIE!
IRON MAN IRONSKI! MASSEUR AT DADDY'S CLUB!
YOUR GIFT IS A WHOLE HOUR OF MASSAGE ON YOUR POOR WEAK BACK!
RIVERD A.C.
CRUNCH!
OUCH!
EEYARGH!
SLAM
POUND
TWIST!
GEE, I WONDER IF HE COULD WORK ON HIS MIND NEXT? THAT'S EVEN WEAKER!
The END

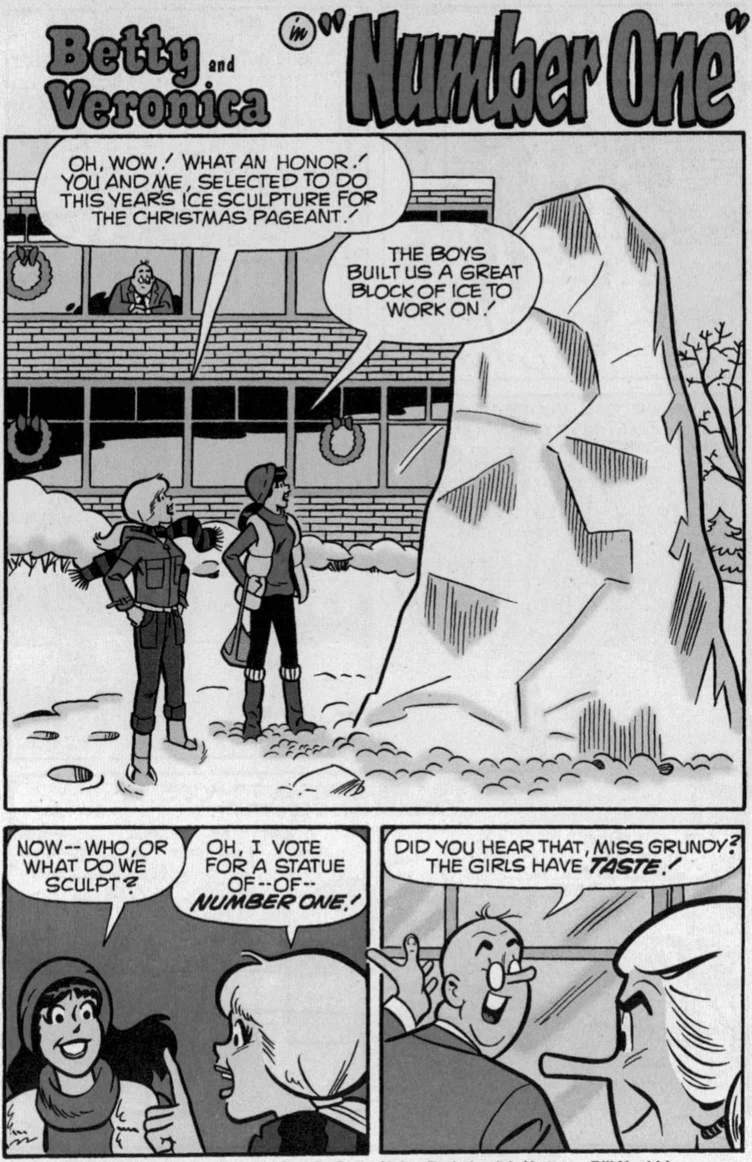
Betty and Veronica in "Number One"
OH, WOW! WHAT AN HONOR! YOU AND ME, SELECTED TO DO THIS YEAR'S ICE SCULPTURE FOR THE CHRISTMAS PAGEANT!
THE BOYS BUILT US A GREAT BLOCK OF ICE TO WORK ON!
NOW--WHO, OR WHAT DO WE SCULPT?
OH, I VOTE FOR A STATUE OF--OF-- NUMBER ONE!
DID YOU HEAR THAT, MISS GRUNDY? THE GIRLS HAVE TASTE!

Script: Frank Doyle / Pencils: Dan DeCarlo / Inks: Rudy Lapick / Letters: Bill Yoshida

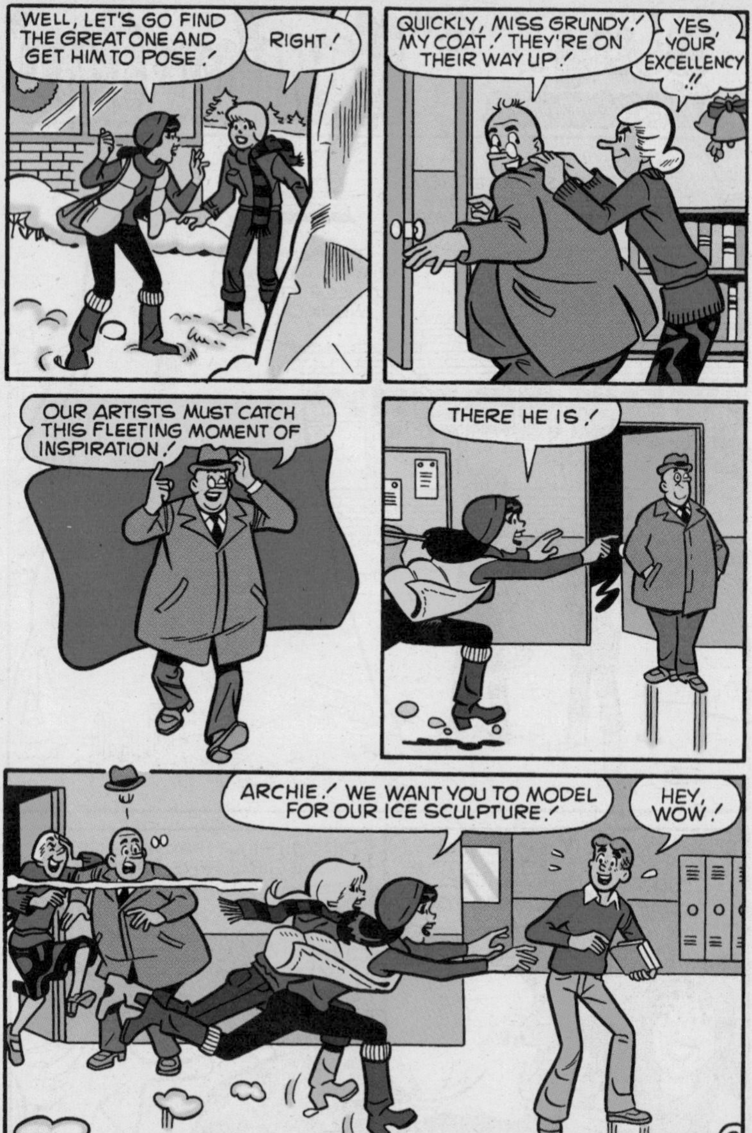
WELL, LET'S GO FIND THE GREAT ONE AND GET HIM TO POSE!
RIGHT!
QUICKLY, MISS GRUNDY! MY COAT! THEY'RE ON THEIR WAY UP!
YES, YOUR EXCELLENCY!!
OUR ARTISTS MUST CATCH THIS FLEETING MOMENT OF INSPIRATION!
THERE HE IS!
ARCHIE! WE WANT YOU TO MODEL FOR OUR ICE SCULPTURE!
HEY, WOW!
2

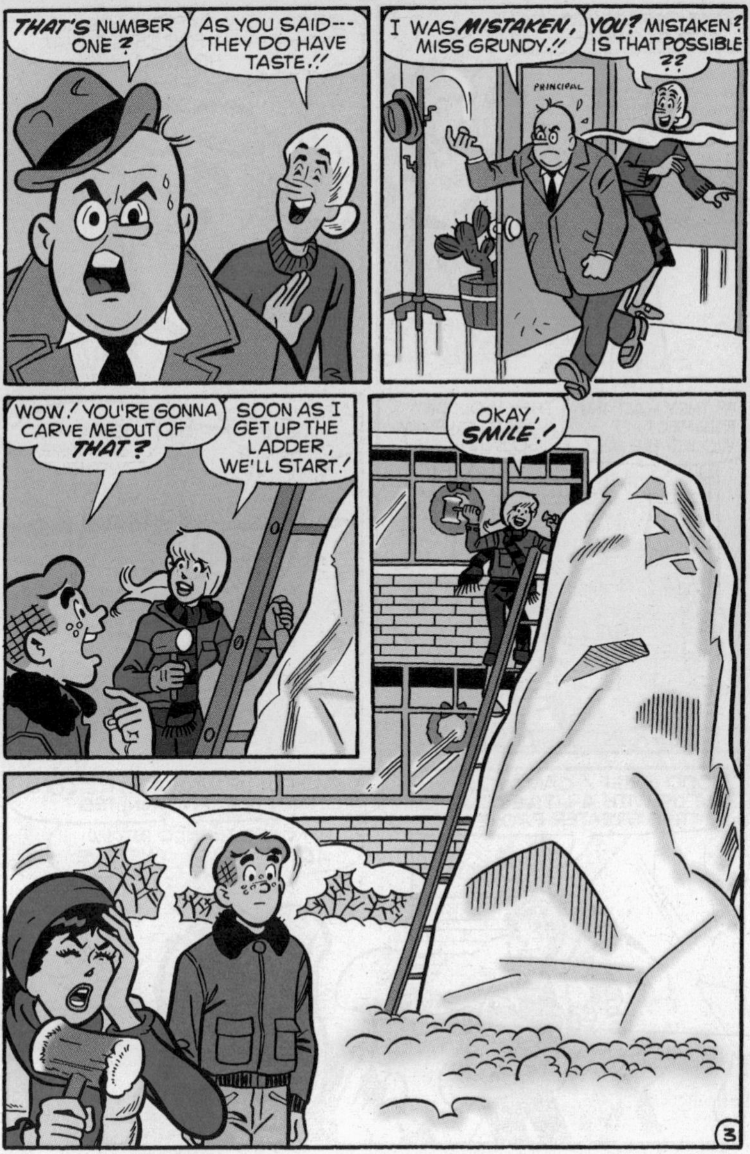
THAT'S NUMBER ONE ?
AS YOU SAID--- THEY DO HAVE TASTE.!!
I WAS MISTAKEN, MISS GRUNDY.!!
YOU? MISTAKEN? IS THAT POSSIBLE ??
PRINCIPAL
WOW! YOU'RE GONNA CARVE ME OUT OF THAT ?
SOON AS I GET UP THE LADDER, WE'LL START!
OKAY, SMILE!
3

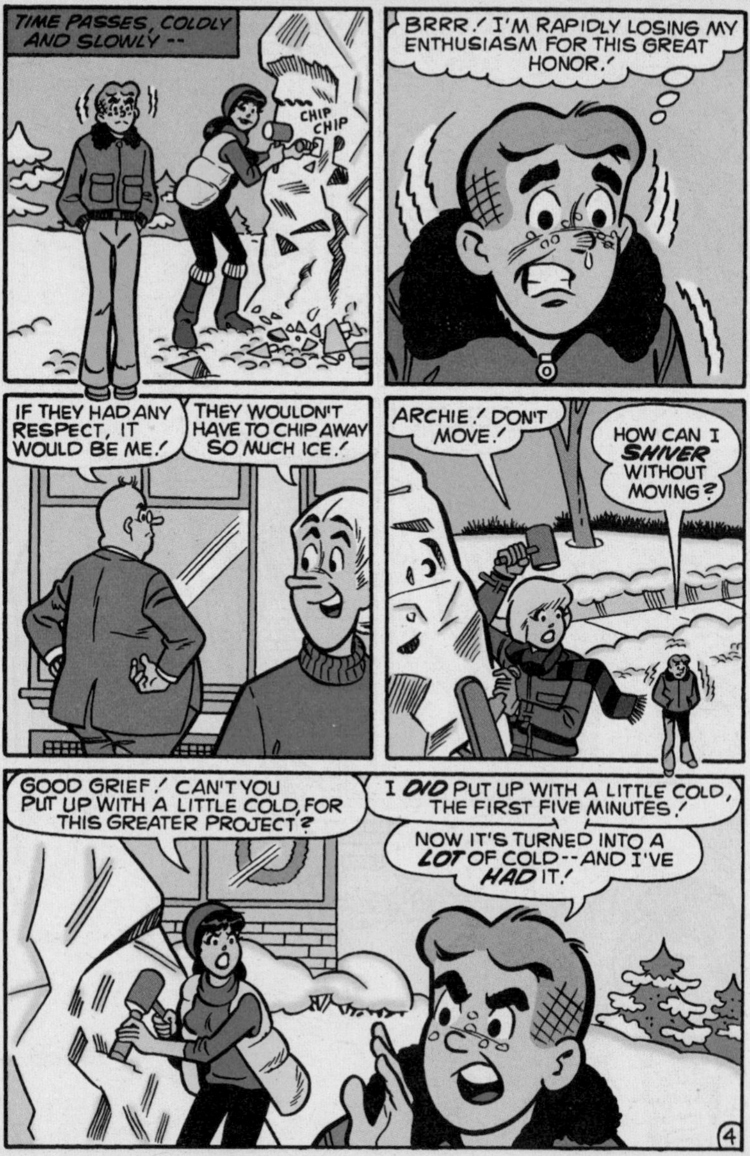

TIME PASSES, COLDLY AND SLOWLY --
CHIP CHIP
BRRR! I'M RAPIDLY LOSING MY ENTHUSIASM FOR THIS GREAT HONOR!
IF THEY HAD ANY RESPECT, IT WOULD BE ME!
THEY WOULDN'T HAVE TO CHIP AWAY SO MUCH ICE!
ARCHIE! DON'T MOVE!
HOW CAN I SHIVER WITHOUT MOVING?
GOOD GRIEF! CAN'T YOU PUT UP WITH A LITTLE COLD, FOR THIS GREATER PROJECT?
I DID PUT UP WITH A LITTLE COLD, THE FIRST FIVE MINUTES!
NOW IT'S TURNED INTO A LOT OF COLD -- AND I'VE HAD IT!
4

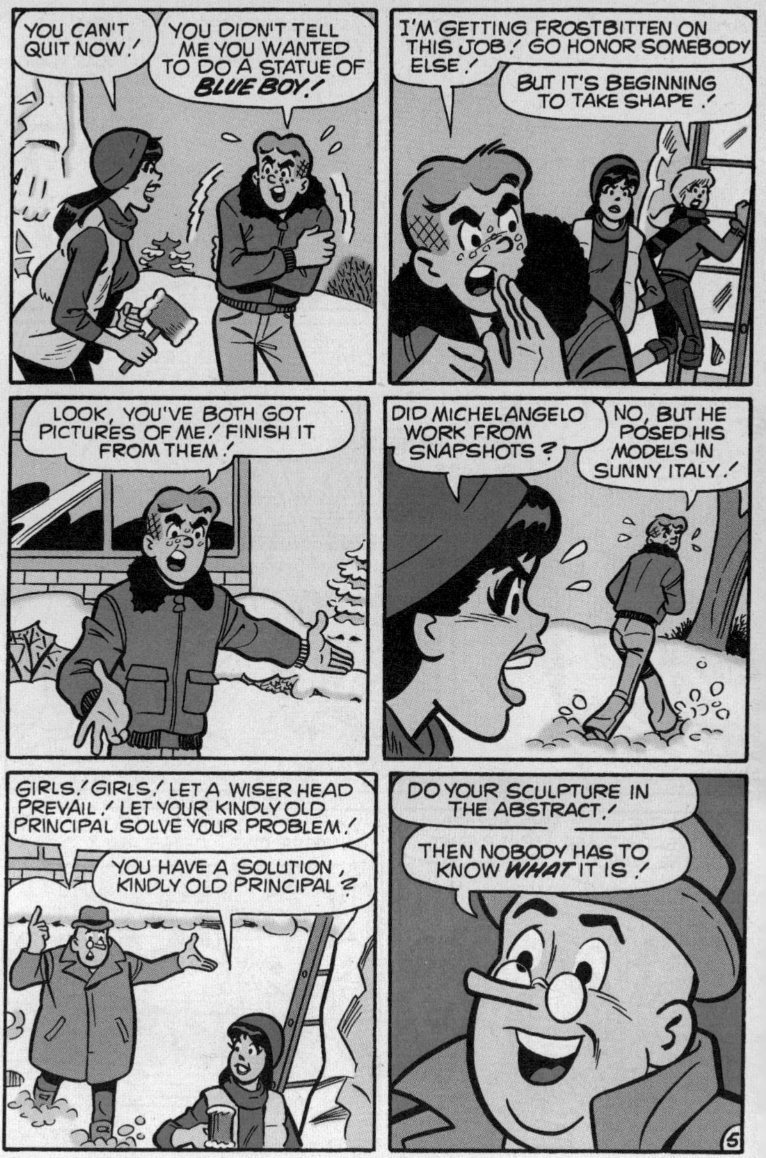
YOU CAN'T QUIT NOW.!
YOU DIDN'T TELL ME YOU WANTED TO DO A STATUE OF BLUE BOY.!
I'M GETTING FROSTBITTEN ON THIS JOB.! GO HONOR SOMEBODY ELSE.!
BUT IT'S BEGINNING TO TAKE SHAPE.!
LOOK, YOU'VE BOTH GOT PICTURES OF ME.! FINISH IT FROM THEM.!
DID MICHELANGELO WORK FROM SNAPSHOTS?
NO, BUT HE POSED HIS MODELS IN SUNNY ITALY.!
GIRLS.! GIRLS.! LET A WISER HEAD PREVAIL.! LET YOUR KINDLY OLD PRINCIPAL SOLVE YOUR PROBLEM.!
YOU HAVE A SOLUTION, KINDLY OLD PRINCIPAL?
DO YOUR SCULPTURE IN THE ABSTRACT.!
THEN NOBODY HAS TO KNOW WHAT IT IS.!
5

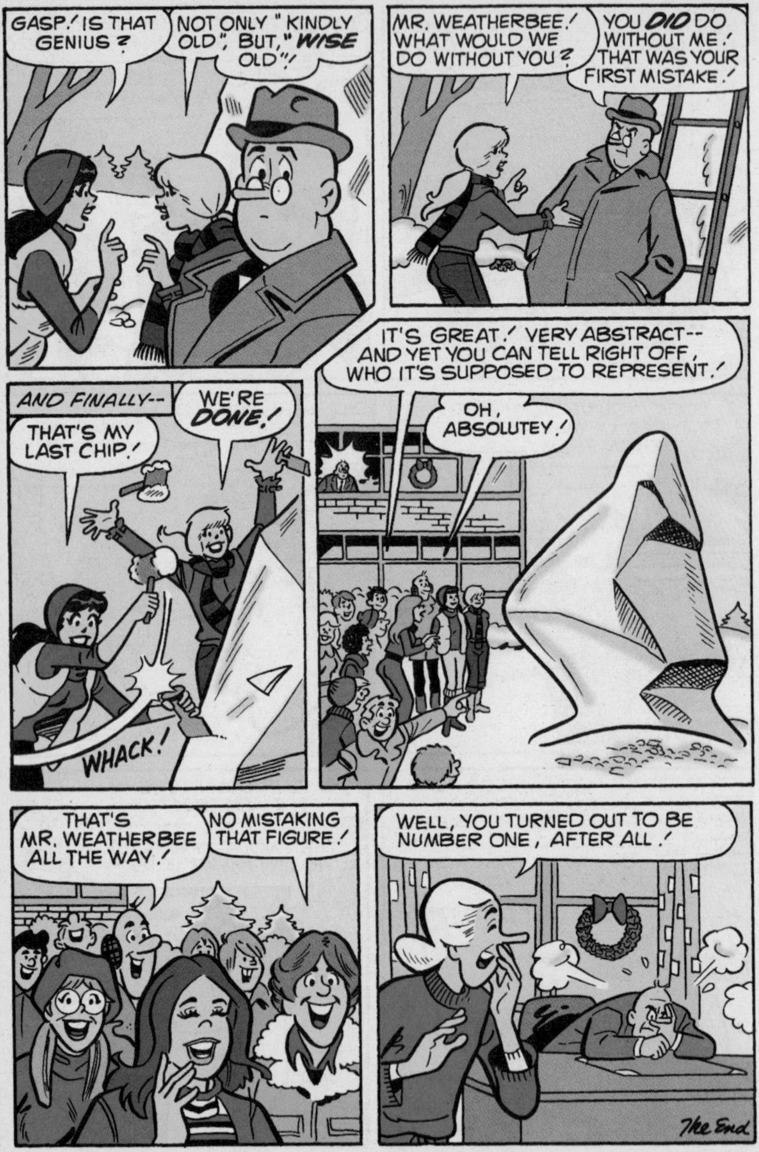
GASP! IS THAT GENIUS?
NOT ONLY "KINDLY OLD", BUT, "WISE OLD"!
MR. WEATHERBEE! WHAT WOULD WE DO WITHOUT YOU?
YOU DID DO WITHOUT ME! THAT WAS YOUR FIRST MISTAKE!
AND FINALLY--
THAT'S MY LAST CHIP!
WE'RE DONE!
WHACK!
IT'S GREAT! VERY ABSTRACT-- AND YET YOU CAN TELL RIGHT OFF, WHO IT'S SUPPOSED TO REPRESENT!
OH, ABSOLUTEY!
THAT'S MR. WEATHERBEE ALL THE WAY!
NO MISTAKING THAT FIGURE!
WELL, YOU TURNED OUT TO BE NUMBER ONE, AFTER ALL!
The End

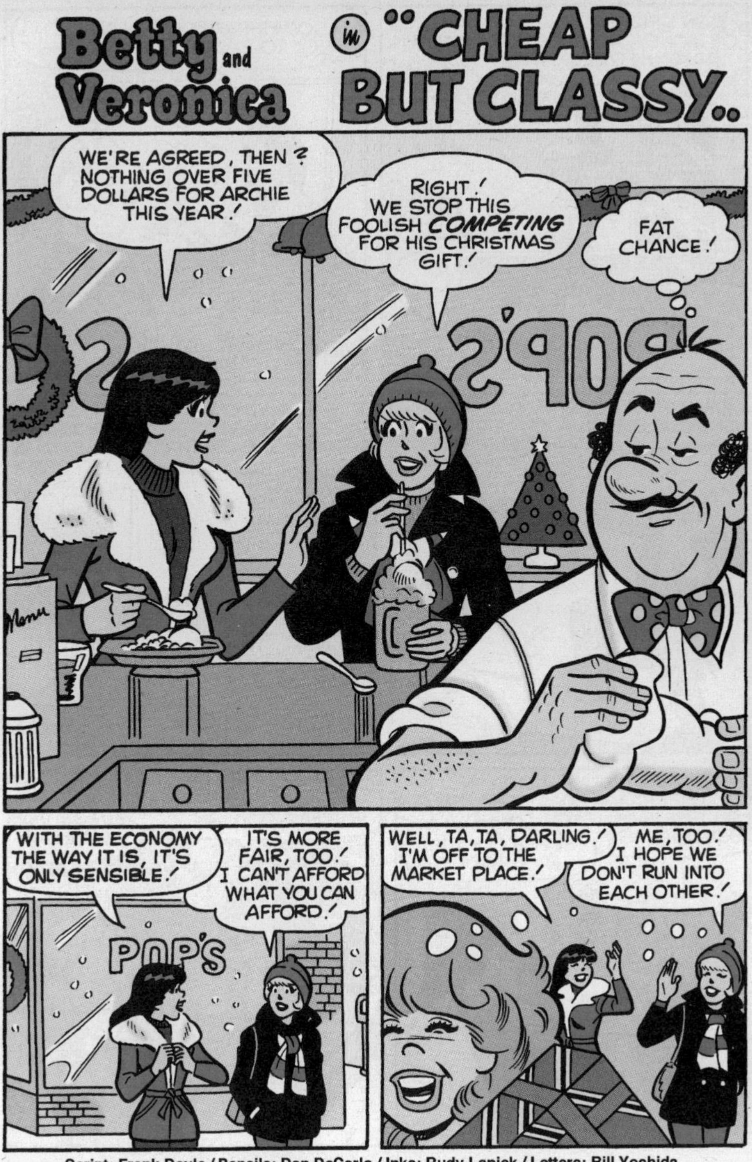
Betty and Veronica in "CHEAP BUT CLASSY.."
WE'RE AGREED, THEN? NOTHING OVER FIVE DOLLARS FOR ARCHIE THIS YEAR!
RIGHT! WE STOP THIS FOOLISH COMPETING FOR HIS CHRISTMAS GIFT!
FAT CHANCE!
POP'S
Menu
WITH THE ECONOMY THE WAY IT IS, IT'S ONLY SENSIBLE!
IT'S MORE FAIR, TOO! I CAN'T AFFORD WHAT YOU CAN AFFORD!
POP'S
WELL, TA, TA, DARLING! I'M OFF TO THE MARKET PLACE!
ME, TOO! I HOPE WE DON'T RUN INTO EACH OTHER!

Script: Frank Doyle / Pencils: Dan DeCarlo / Inks: Rudy Lapick / Letters: Bill Yoshida

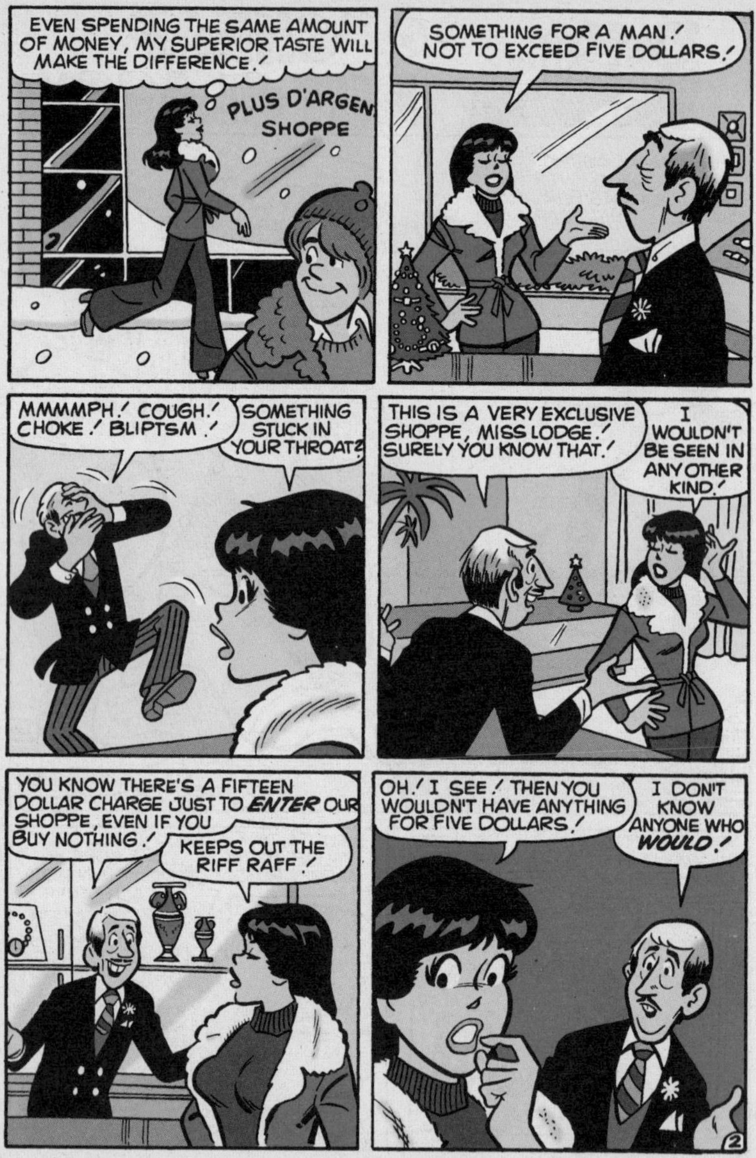

EVEN SPENDING THE SAME AMOUNT OF MONEY, MY SUPERIOR TASTE WILL MAKE THE DIFFERENCE!
PLUS D'ARGENT
SHOPPE
SOMETHING FOR A MAN! NOT TO EXCEED FIVE DOLLARS!
MMMMPH! COUGH! CHOKE! BLIPTSM!
SOMETHING STUCK IN YOUR THROAT?
THIS IS A VERY EXCLUSIVE SHOPPE, MISS LODGE! SURELY YOU KNOW THAT!
I WOULDN'T BE SEEN IN ANY OTHER KIND!
YOU KNOW THERE'S A FIFTEEN DOLLAR CHARGE JUST TO *ENTER* OUR SHOPPE, EVEN IF YOU BUY NOTHING!
KEEPS OUT THE RIFF RAFF!
OH! I SEE! THEN YOU WOULDN'T HAVE ANYTHING FOR FIVE DOLLARS!
I DON'T KNOW ANYONE WHO *WOULD*!
2

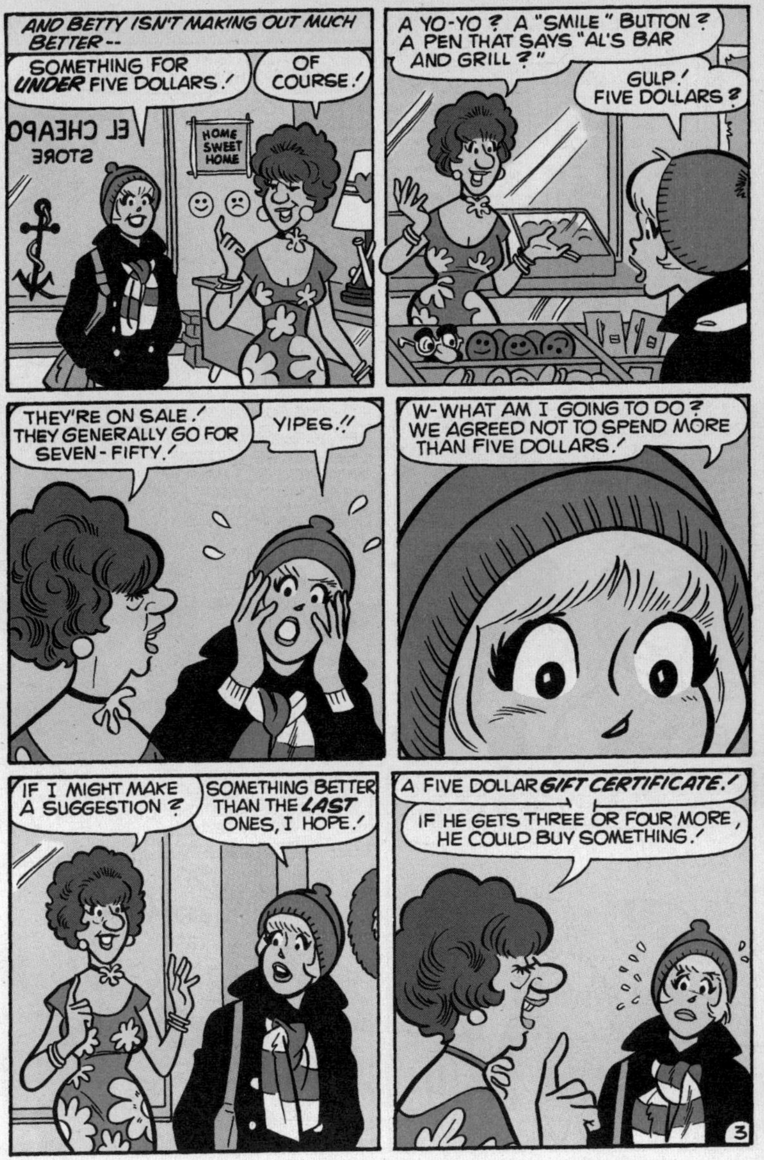
AND BETTY ISN'T MAKING OUT MUCH BETTER--
SOMETHING FOR UNDER FIVE DOLLARS!
OF COURSE!
EL CHEAPO STORE
HOME SWEET HOME
A YO-YO? A "SMILE" BUTTON? A PEN THAT SAYS "AL'S BAR AND GRILL?"
GULP! FIVE DOLLARS?
THEY'RE ON SALE! THEY GENERALLY GO FOR SEVEN-FIFTY!
YIPES!!
W-WHAT AM I GOING TO DO? WE AGREED NOT TO SPEND MORE THAN FIVE DOLLARS!
IF I MIGHT MAKE A SUGGESTION?
SOMETHING BETTER THAN THE LAST ONES, I HOPE!
A FIVE DOLLAR GIFT CERTIFICATE!
IF HE GETS THREE OR FOUR MORE, HE COULD BUY SOMETHING!
3

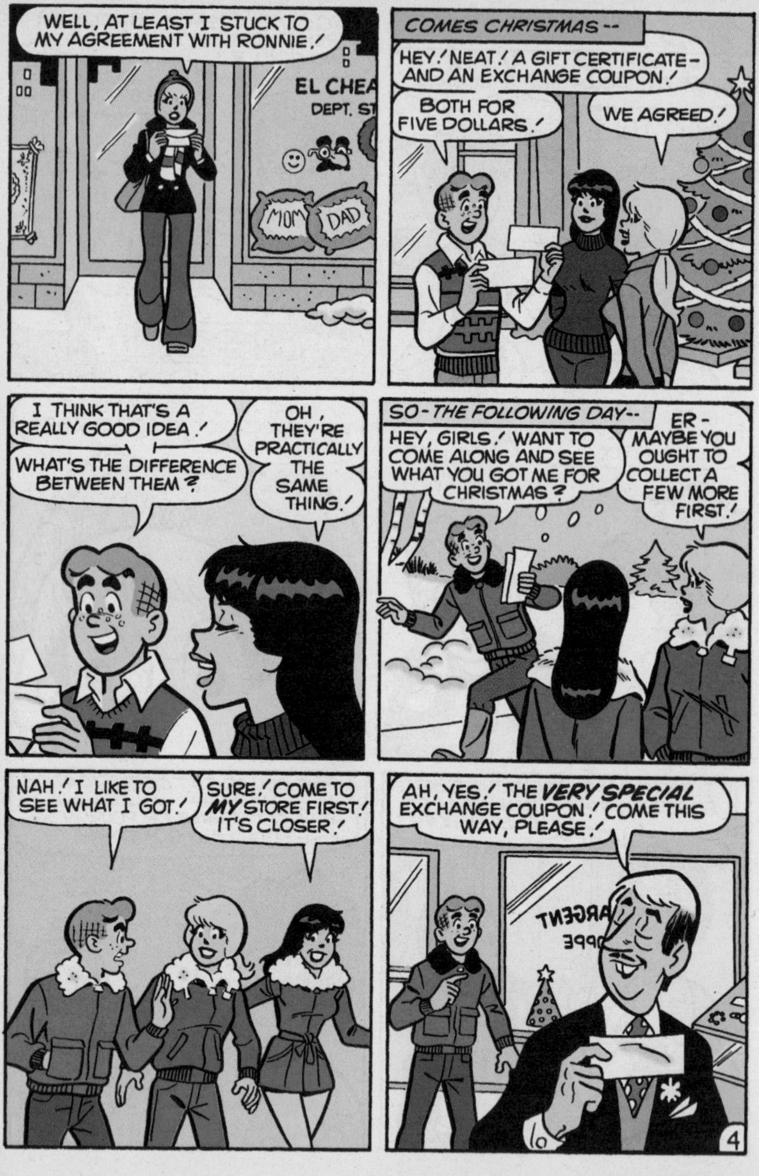
WELL, AT LEAST I STUCK TO MY AGREEMENT WITH RONNIE!
EL CHEA
DEPT. ST
MOM
DAD
COMES CHRISTMAS --
HEY! NEAT! A GIFT CERTIFICATE - AND AN EXCHANGE COUPON!
BOTH FOR FIVE DOLLARS!
WE AGREED!
I THINK THAT'S A REALLY GOOD IDEA!
WHAT'S THE DIFFERENCE BETWEEN THEM?
OH, THEY'RE PRACTICALLY THE SAME THING!
SO- THE FOLLOWING DAY--
HEY, GIRLS! WANT TO COME ALONG AND SEE WHAT YOU GOT ME FOR CHRISTMAS?
ER - MAYBE YOU OUGHT TO COLLECT A FEW MORE FIRST!
NAH! I LIKE TO SEE WHAT I GOT!
SURE! COME TO MY STORE FIRST! IT'S CLOSER!
AH, YES! THE VERY SPECIAL EXCHANGE COUPON! COME THIS WAY, PLEASE!
4

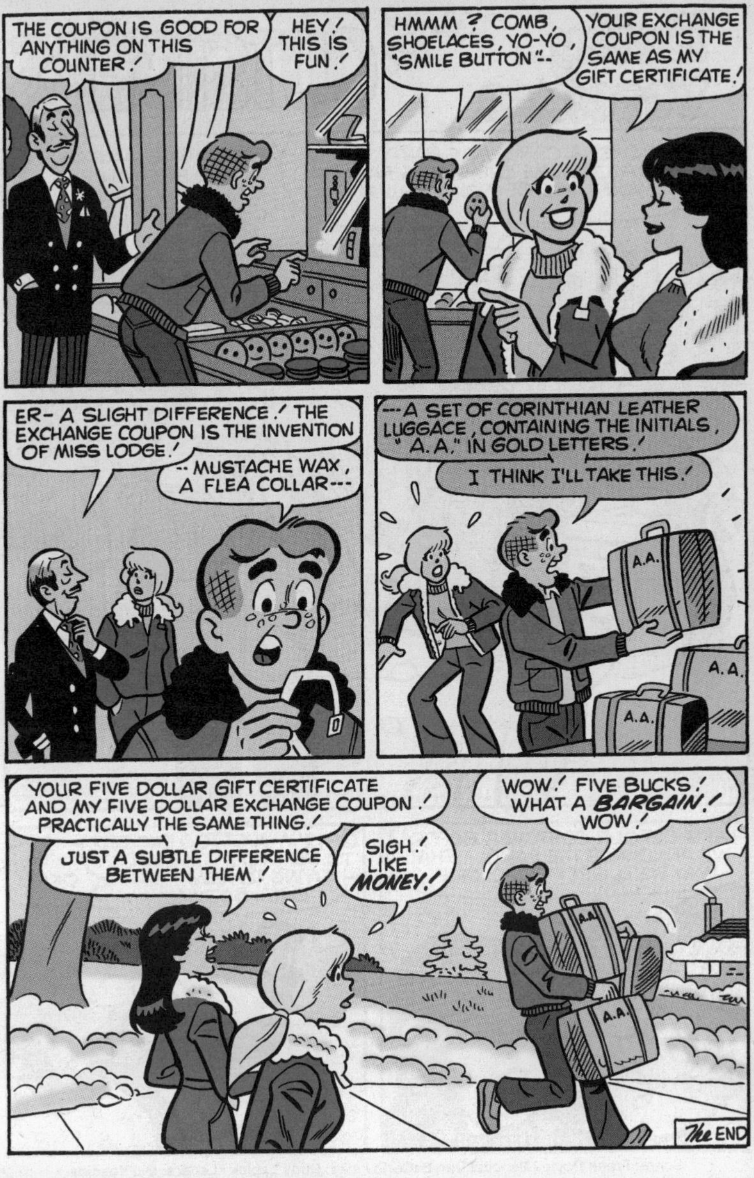

THE COUPON IS GOOD FOR ANYTHING ON THIS COUNTER.!
HEY! THIS IS FUN.!
HMMM? COMB, SHOELACES, YO-YO, "SMILE BUTTON"--
YOUR EXCHANGE COUPON IS THE SAME AS MY GIFT CERTIFICATE!
ER- A SLIGHT DIFFERENCE! THE EXCHANGE COUPON IS THE INVENTION OF MISS LODGE!
-- MUSTACHE WAX, A FLEA COLLAR---
---A SET OF CORINTHIAN LEATHER LUGGAGE, CONTAINING THE INITIALS, "A. A." IN GOLD LETTERS!
I THINK I'LL TAKE THIS!
A.A.
A.A.
A.A.
YOUR FIVE DOLLAR GIFT CERTIFICATE AND MY FIVE DOLLAR EXCHANGE COUPON! PRACTICALLY THE SAME THING!
JUST A SUBTLE DIFFERENCE BETWEEN THEM!
SIGH! LIKE MONEY!
WOW! FIVE BUCKS! WHAT A BARGAIN! WOW!
A.A.
A.A.
The END

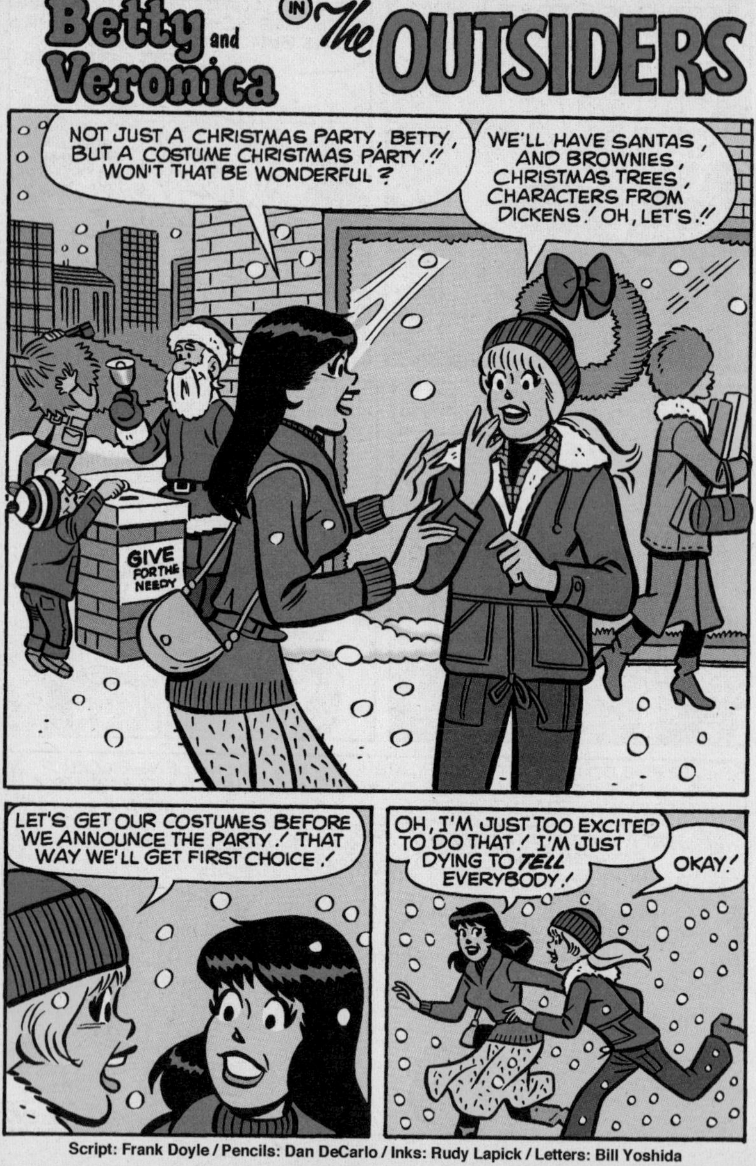
Betty and Veronica
IN The OUTSIDERS
NOT JUST A CHRISTMAS PARTY, BETTY, BUT A COSTUME CHRISTMAS PARTY.!! WON'T THAT BE WONDERFUL?
WE'LL HAVE SANTAS, AND BROWNIES, CHRISTMAS TREES, CHARACTERS FROM DICKENS.! OH, LET'S.!!
GIVE FOR THE NEEDY
LET'S GET OUR COSTUMES BEFORE WE ANNOUNCE THE PARTY.! THAT WAY WE'LL GET FIRST CHOICE.!
OH, I'M JUST TOO EXCITED TO DO THAT.! I'M JUST DYING TO TELL EVERYBODY.!
OKAY!

Script: Frank Doyle / Pencils: Dan DeCarlo / Inks: Rudy Lapick / Letters: Bill Yoshida

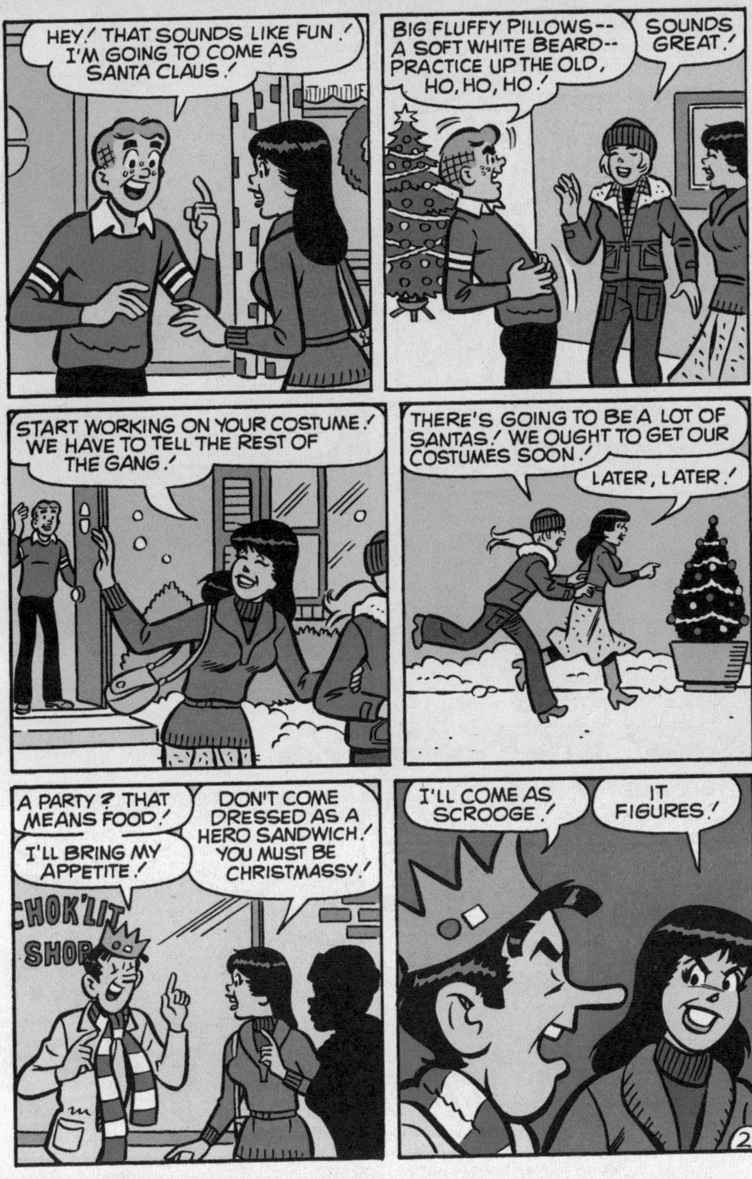
HEY! THAT SOUNDS LIKE FUN! I'M GOING TO COME AS SANTA CLAUS!
BIG FLUFFY PILLOWS-- A SOFT WHITE BEARD-- PRACTICE UP THE OLD, HO, HO, HO!
SOUNDS GREAT!
START WORKING ON YOUR COSTUME! WE HAVE TO TELL THE REST OF THE GANG!
THERE'S GOING TO BE A LOT OF SANTAS! WE OUGHT TO GET OUR COSTUMES SOON!
LATER, LATER!
A PARTY? THAT MEANS FOOD!
I'LL BRING MY APPETITE!
DON'T COME DRESSED AS A HERO SANDWICH! YOU MUST BE CHRISTMASSY!
CHOK'LIT SHOP
I'LL COME AS SCROOGE!
IT FIGURES!
2

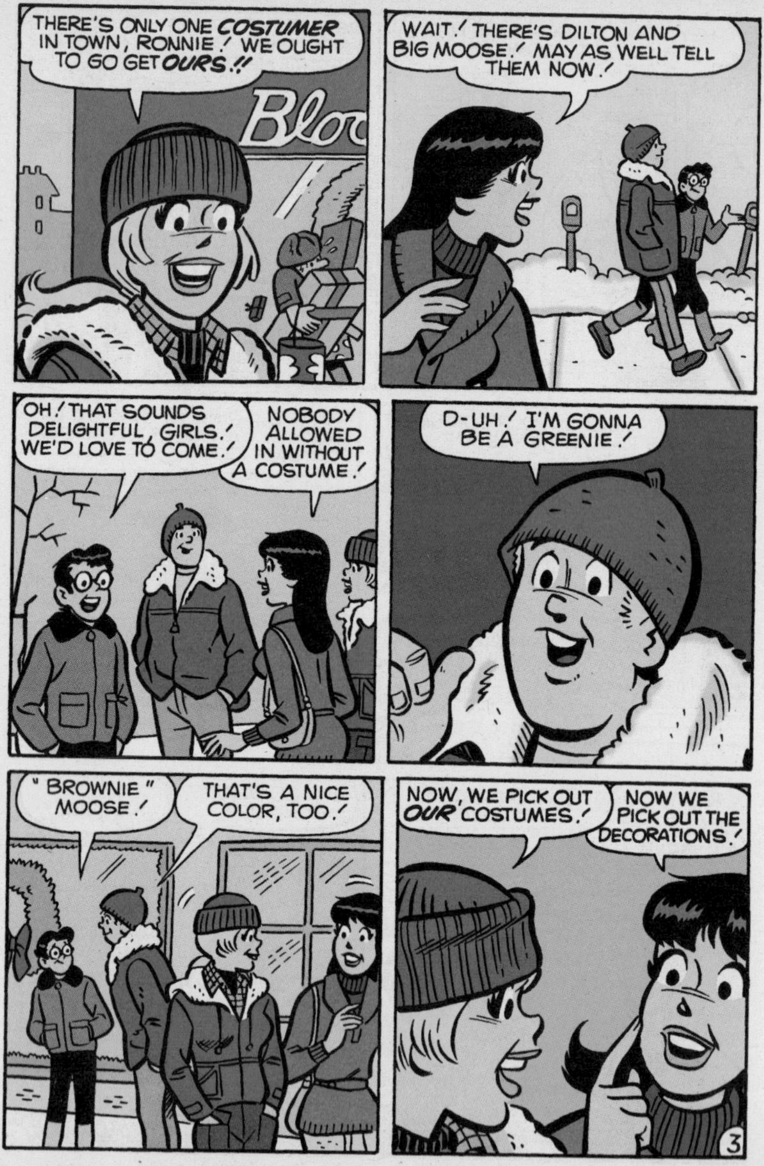
THERE'S ONLY ONE COSTUMER IN TOWN, RONNIE! WE OUGHT TO GO GET OURS!!
Blo
WAIT! THERE'S DILTON AND BIG MOOSE! MAY AS WELL TELL THEM NOW!
OH! THAT SOUNDS DELIGHTFUL, GIRLS! WE'D LOVE TO COME!
NOBODY ALLOWED IN WITHOUT A COSTUME!
D-UH! I'M GONNA BE A GREENIE!
"BROWNIE" MOOSE!
THAT'S A NICE COLOR, TOO!
NOW, WE PICK OUT OUR COSTUMES!
NOW WE PICK OUT THE DECORATIONS!
3

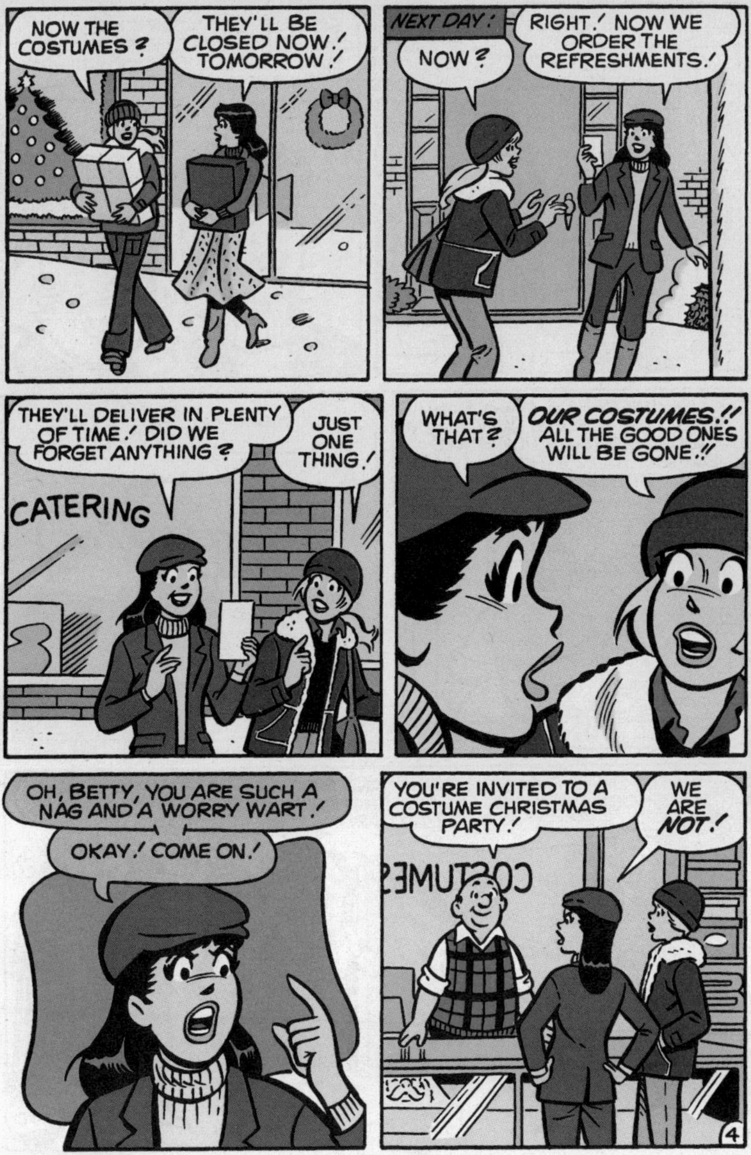
NOW THE COSTUMES ?
THEY'LL BE CLOSED NOW.! TOMORROW.!
NEXT DAY:
NOW ?
RIGHT.! NOW WE ORDER THE REFRESHMENTS.!
THEY'LL DELIVER IN PLENTY OF TIME.! DID WE FORGET ANYTHING ?
JUST ONE THING.!
CATERING
WHAT'S THAT ?
OUR COSTUMES.!! ALL THE GOOD ONES WILL BE GONE.!!
OH, BETTY, YOU ARE SUCH A NAG AND A WORRY WART.!
OKAY.! COME ON.!
YOU'RE INVITED TO A COSTUME CHRISTMAS PARTY.!
WE ARE NOT.!
COSTUMES
4

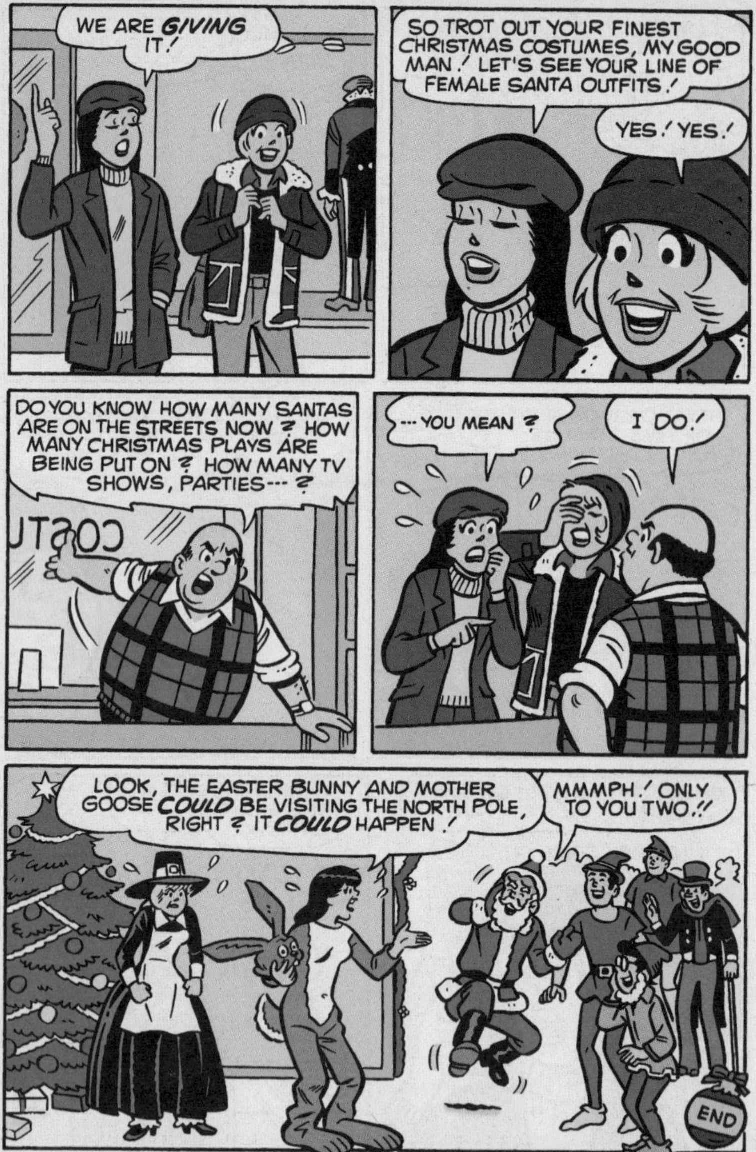

WE ARE GIVING IT.!
SO TROT OUT YOUR FINEST CHRISTMAS COSTUMES, MY GOOD MAN.! LET'S SEE YOUR LINE OF FEMALE SANTA OUTFITS.!
YES.! YES.!
DO YOU KNOW HOW MANY SANTAS ARE ON THE STREETS NOW? HOW MANY CHRISTMAS PLAYS ARE BEING PUT ON? HOW MANY TV SHOWS, PARTIES---?
COSTU
---YOU MEAN?
I DO.!
LOOK, THE EASTER BUNNY AND MOTHER GOOSE COULD BE VISITING THE NORTH POLE, RIGHT? IT COULD HAPPEN.!
MMMPH.! ONLY TO YOU TWO.!!
END

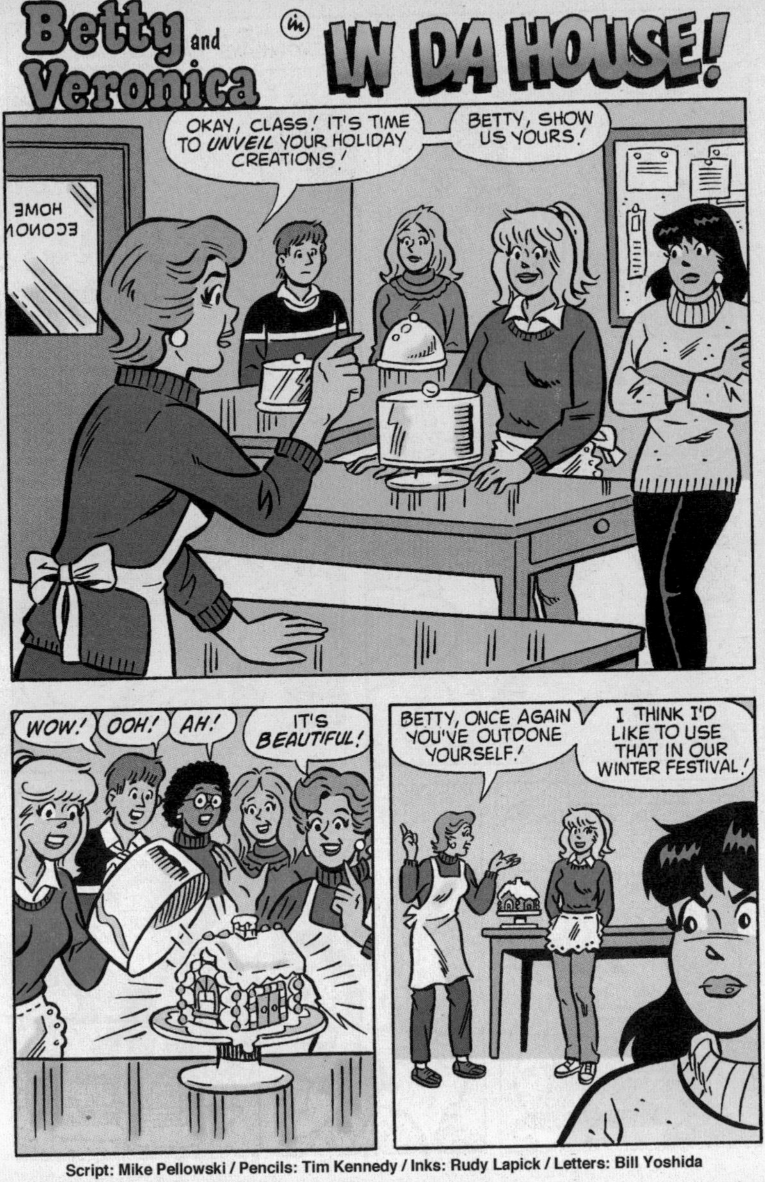
Betty and Veronica in
IN DA HOUSE!
OKAY, CLASS! IT'S TIME TO UNVEIL YOUR HOLIDAY CREATIONS!
BETTY, SHOW US YOURS!
HOME ECONO
WOW!
OOH!
AH!
IT'S BEAUTIFUL!
BETTY, ONCE AGAIN YOU'VE OUTDONE YOURSELF!
I THINK I'D LIKE TO USE THAT IN OUR WINTER FESTIVAL!

Script: Mike Pellowski / Pencils: Tim Kennedy / Inks: Rudy Lapick / Letters: Bill Yoshida

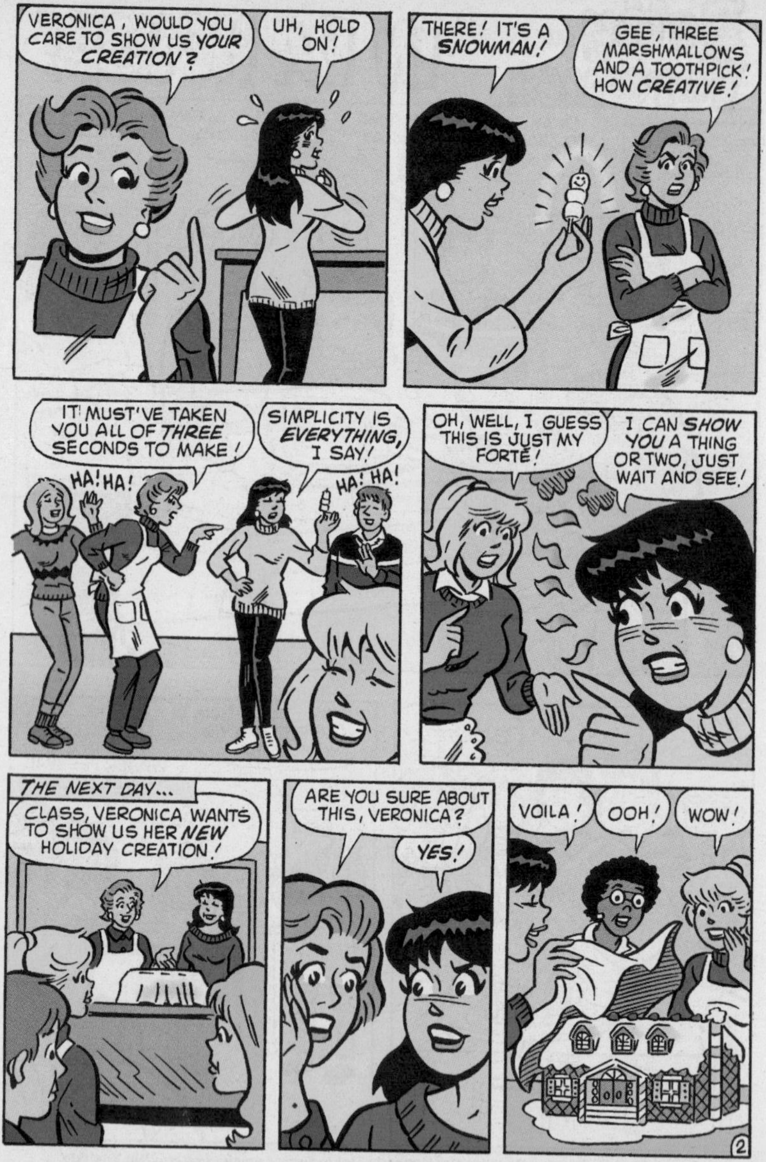
VERONICA, WOULD YOU CARE TO SHOW US YOUR CREATION?
UH, HOLD ON!
THERE! IT'S A SNOWMAN!
GEE, THREE MARSHMALLOWS AND A TOOTHPICK! HOW CREATIVE!
IT MUST'VE TAKEN YOU ALL OF THREE SECONDS TO MAKE!
HA! HA!
SIMPLICITY IS EVERYTHING, I SAY!
HA! HA!
OH, WELL, I GUESS THIS IS JUST MY FORTÉ!
I CAN SHOW YOU A THING OR TWO, JUST WAIT AND SEE!
THE NEXT DAY...
CLASS, VERONICA WANTS TO SHOW US HER NEW HOLIDAY CREATION!
ARE YOU SURE ABOUT THIS, VERONICA?
YES!
VOILA!
OOH!
WOW!
2

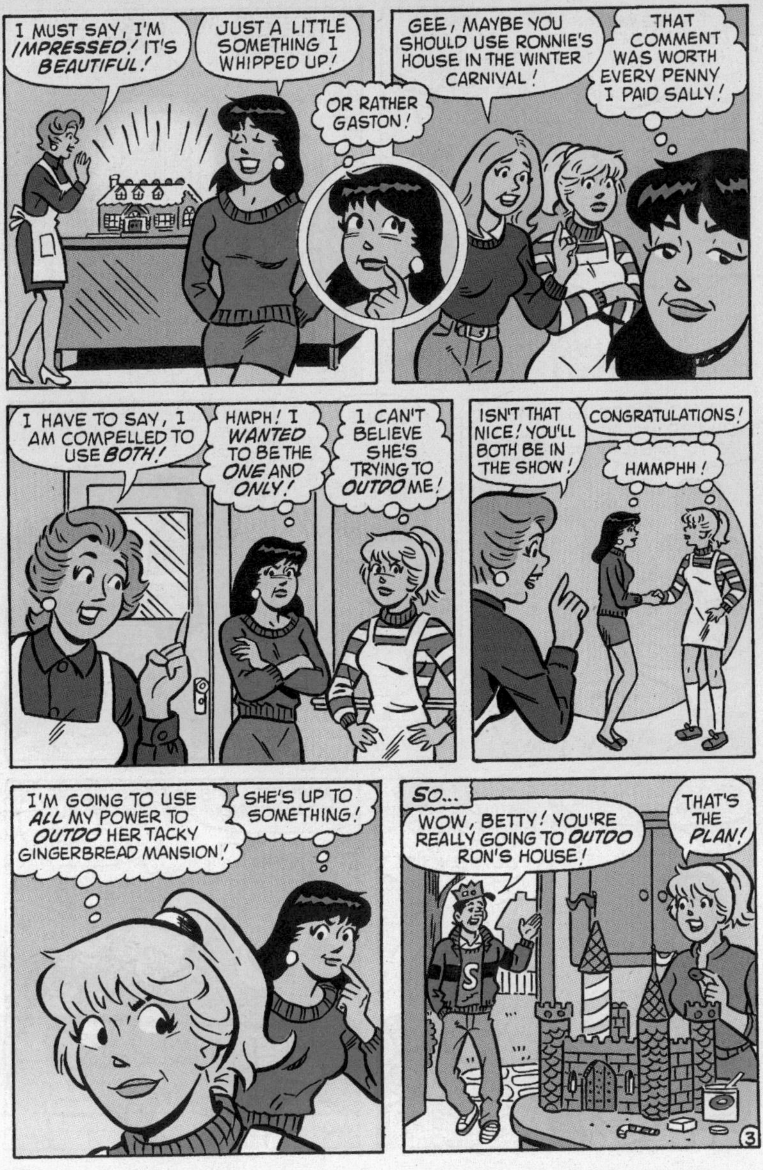
I MUST SAY, I'M IMPRESSED! IT'S BEAUTIFUL!
JUST A LITTLE SOMETHING I WHIPPED UP!
OR RATHER GASTON!
GEE, MAYBE YOU SHOULD USE RONNIE'S HOUSE IN THE WINTER CARNIVAL!
THAT COMMENT WAS WORTH EVERY PENNY I PAID SALLY!
I HAVE TO SAY, I AM COMPELLED TO USE BOTH!
HMPH! I WANTED TO BE THE ONE AND ONLY!
I CAN'T BELIEVE SHE'S TRYING TO OUTDO ME!
ISN'T THAT NICE! YOU'LL BOTH BE IN THE SHOW!
CONGRATULATIONS!
HMMPHH!
I'M GOING TO USE ALL MY POWER TO OUTDO HER TACKY GINGERBREAD MANSION!
SHE'S UP TO SOMETHING!
SO...
WOW, BETTY! YOU'RE REALLY GOING TO OUTDO RON'S HOUSE!
THAT'S THE PLAN!
3

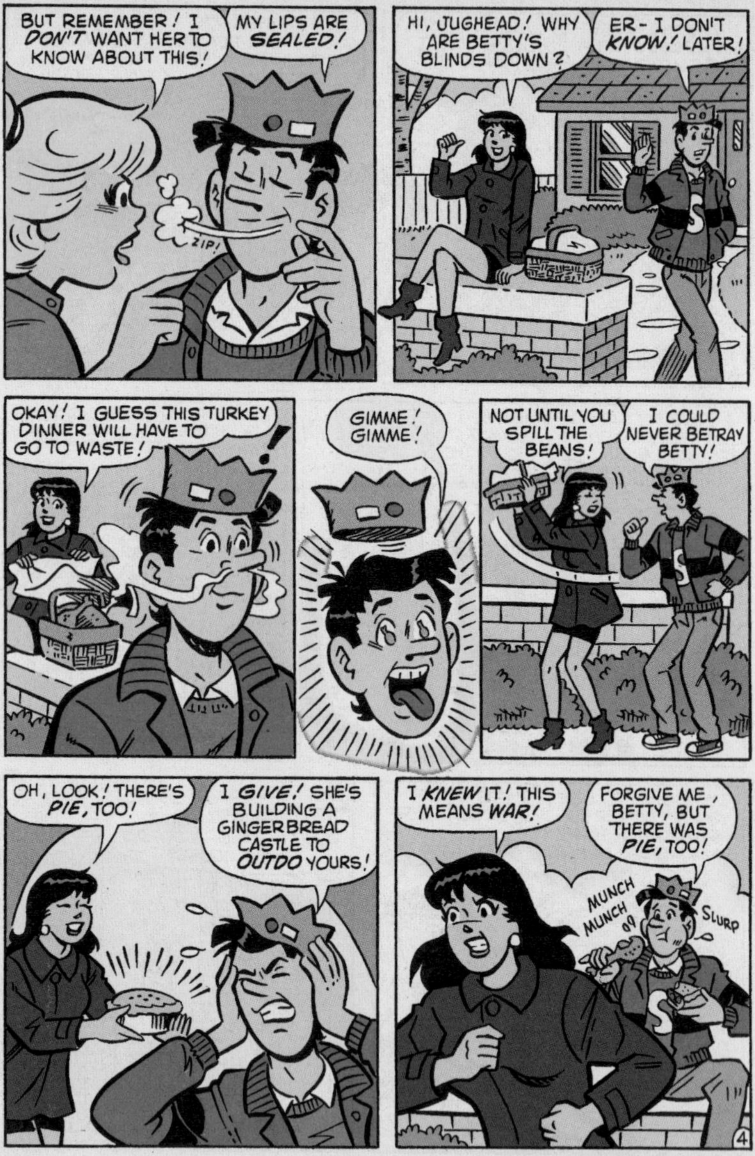
BUT REMEMBER! I DON'T WANT HER TO KNOW ABOUT THIS!
MY LIPS ARE SEALED!
ZIP!
HI, JUGHEAD! WHY ARE BETTY'S BLINDS DOWN?
ER - I DON'T KNOW! LATER!
OKAY! I GUESS THIS TURKEY DINNER WILL HAVE TO GO TO WASTE!
GIMME! GIMME!
NOT UNTIL YOU SPILL THE BEANS!
I COULD NEVER BETRAY BETTY!
OH, LOOK! THERE'S PIE, TOO!
I GIVE! SHE'S BUILDING A GINGERBREAD CASTLE TO OUTDO YOURS!
I KNEW IT! THIS MEANS WAR!
FORGIVE ME, BETTY, BUT THERE WAS PIE, TOO!
MUNCH MUNCH
SLURP
4

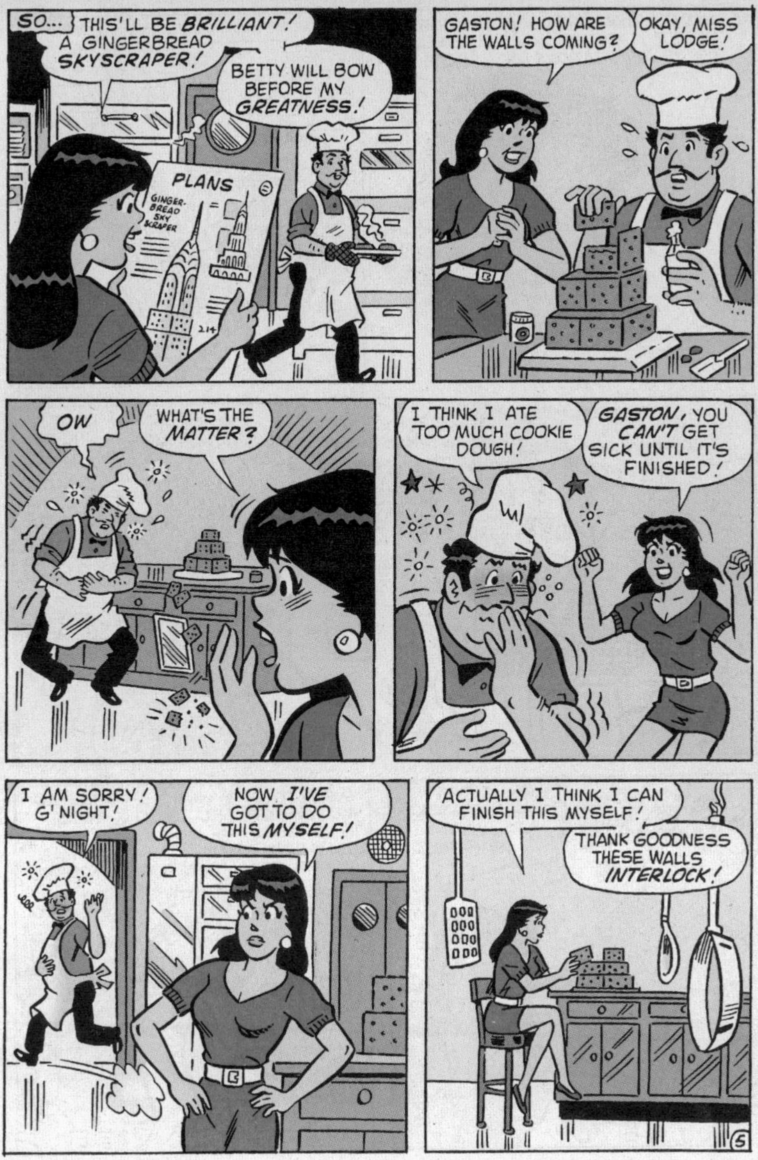
SO... THIS'LL BE BRILLIANT! A GINGERBREAD SKYSCRAPER!
BETTY WILL BOW BEFORE MY GREATNESS!
PLANS
GINGER-BREAD SKY SCRAPER
GASTON! HOW ARE THE WALLS COMING?
OKAY, MISS LODGE!
OW
WHAT'S THE MATTER?
I THINK I ATE TOO MUCH COOKIE DOUGH!
GASTON, YOU CAN'T GET SICK UNTIL IT'S FINISHED!
I AM SORRY! G' NIGHT!
NOW I'VE GOT TO DO THIS MYSELF!
ACTUALLY I THINK I CAN FINISH THIS MYSELF!
THANK GOODNESS THESE WALLS INTERLOCK!
5

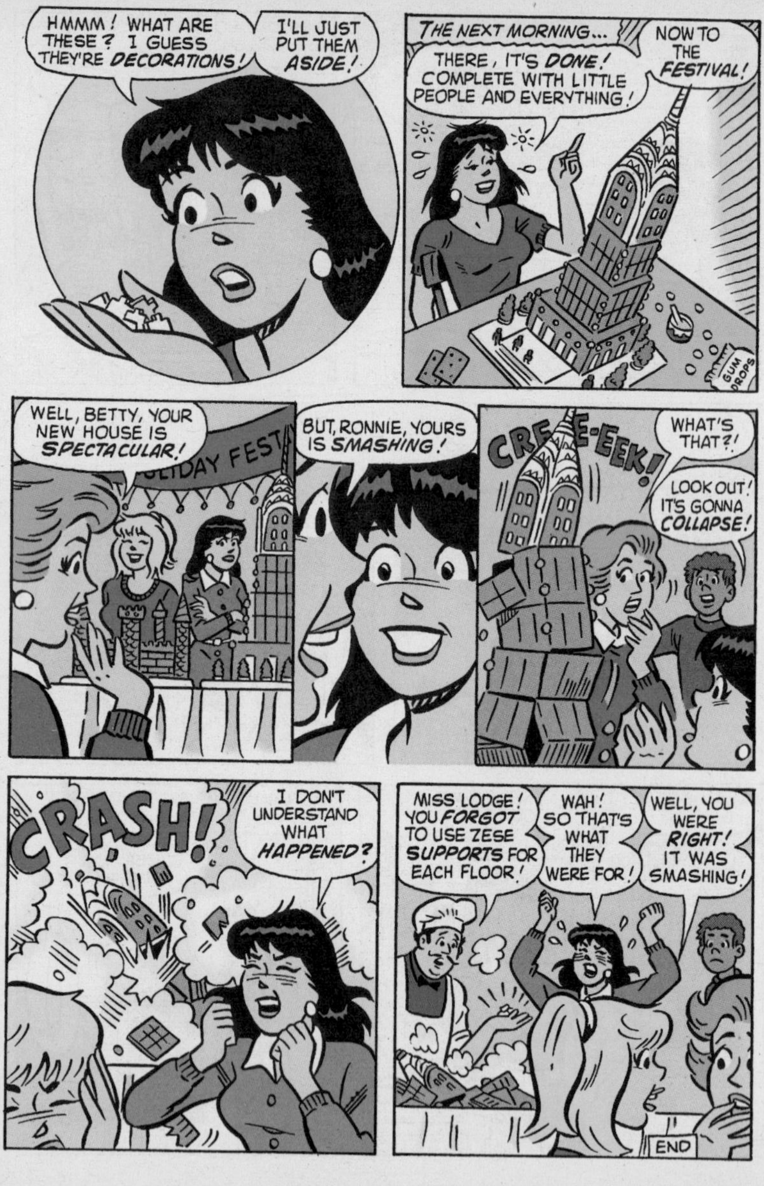
HMMM! WHAT ARE THESE? I GUESS THEY'RE DECORATIONS!
I'LL JUST PUT THEM ASIDE!
THE NEXT MORNING...
THERE, IT'S DONE! COMPLETE WITH LITTLE PEOPLE AND EVERYTHING!
NOW TO THE FESTIVAL!
GUM DROPS
WELL, BETTY, YOUR NEW HOUSE IS SPECTACULAR!
BUT, RONNIE, YOURS IS SMASHING!
CRE-E-EEK!
WHAT'S THAT?!
LOOK OUT! IT'S GONNA COLLAPSE!
CRASH!
I DON'T UNDERSTAND WHAT HAPPENED?
MISS LODGE! YOU FORGOT TO USE ZESE SUPPORTS FOR EACH FLOOR!
WAH! SO THAT'S WHAT THEY WERE FOR!
WELL, YOU WERE RIGHT! IT WAS SMASHING!
END

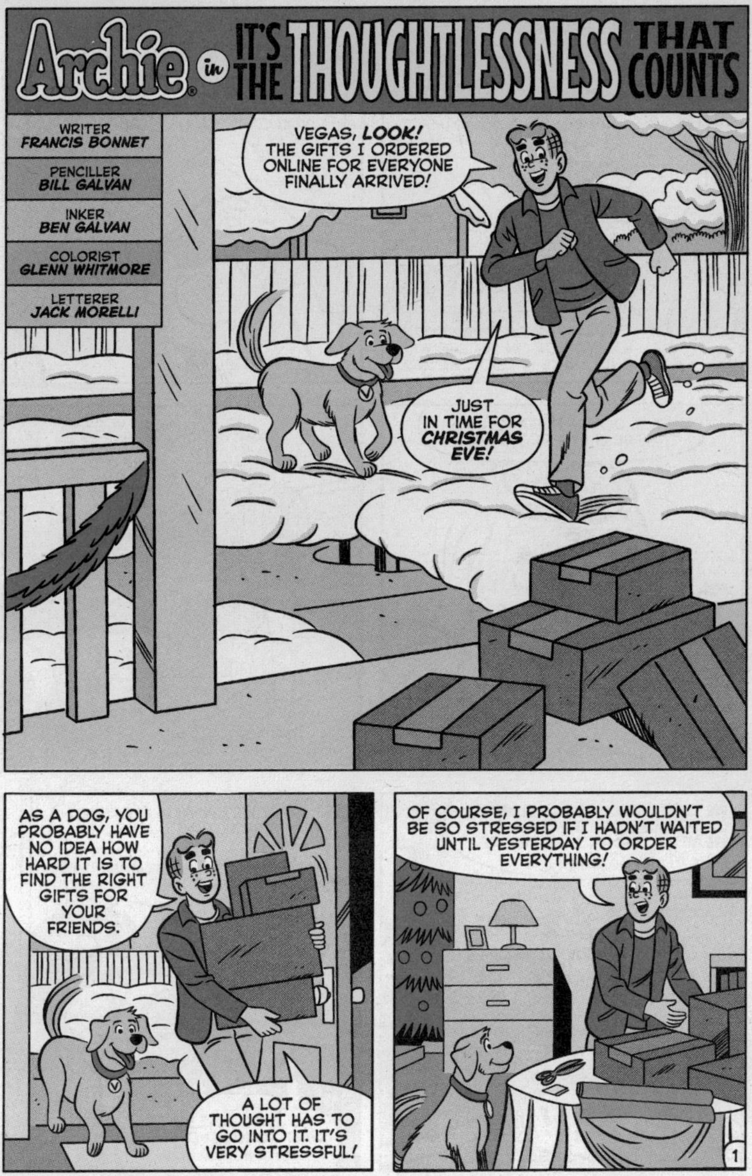

Archie in IT'S THE THOUGHTLESSNESS THAT COUNTS
WRITER FRANCIS BONNET
PENCILLER BILL GALVAN
INKER BEN GALVAN
COLORIST GLENN WHITMORE
LETTERER JACK MORELLI
VEGAS, LOOK! THE GIFTS I ORDERED ONLINE FOR EVERYONE FINALLY ARRIVED!
JUST IN TIME FOR CHRISTMAS EVE!
AS A DOG, YOU PROBABLY HAVE NO IDEA HOW HARD IT IS TO FIND THE RIGHT GIFTS FOR YOUR FRIENDS.
A LOT OF THOUGHT HAS TO GO INTO IT. IT'S VERY STRESSFUL!
OF COURSE, I PROBABLY WOULDN'T BE SO STRESSED IF I HADN'T WAITED UNTIL YESTERDAY TO ORDER EVERYTHING!
1

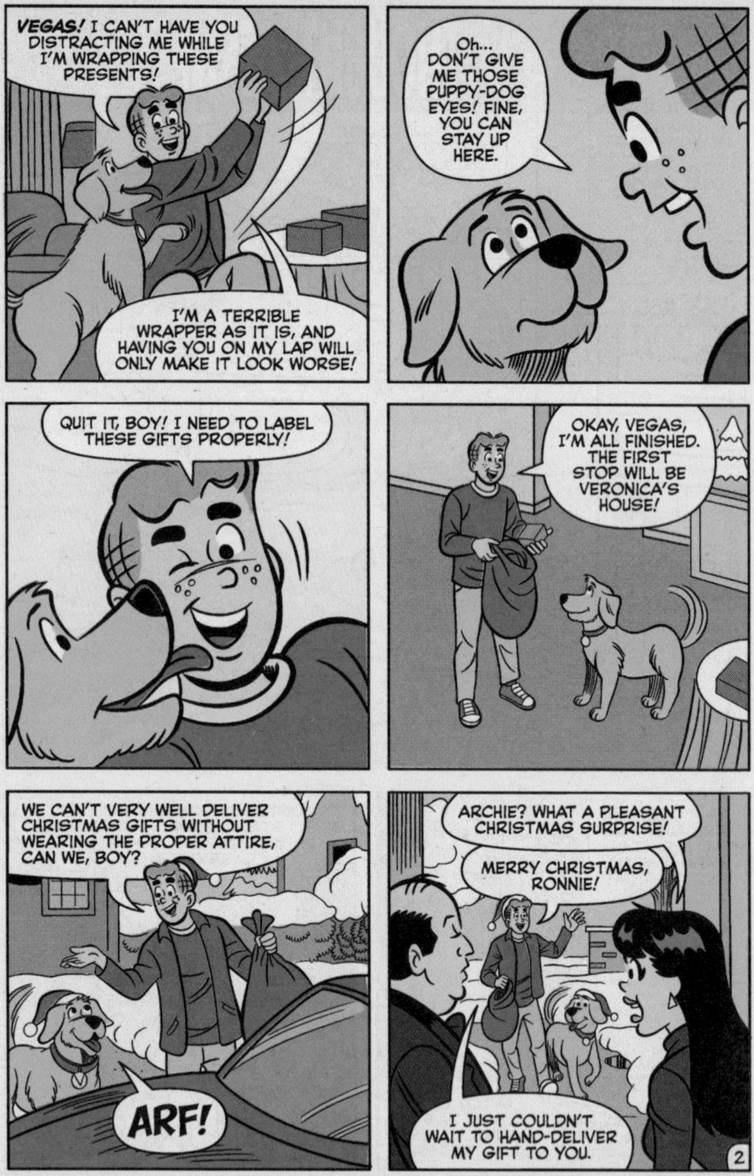

VEGAS! I CAN'T HAVE YOU DISTRACTING ME WHILE I'M WRAPPING THESE PRESENTS!
I'M A TERRIBLE WRAPPER AS IT IS, AND HAVING YOU ON MY LAP WILL ONLY MAKE IT LOOK WORSE!
Oh... DON'T GIVE ME THOSE PUPPY-DOG EYES! FINE, YOU CAN STAY UP HERE.
QUIT IT, BOY! I NEED TO LABEL THESE GIFTS PROPERLY!
OKAY, VEGAS, I'M ALL FINISHED. THE FIRST STOP WILL BE VERONICA'S HOUSE!
WE CAN'T VERY WELL DELIVER CHRISTMAS GIFTS WITHOUT WEARING THE PROPER ATTIRE, CAN WE, BOY?
ARF!
ARCHIE? WHAT A PLEASANT CHRISTMAS SURPRISE!
MERRY CHRISTMAS, RONNIE!
I JUST COULDN'T WAIT TO HAND-DELIVER MY GIFT TO YOU.
2

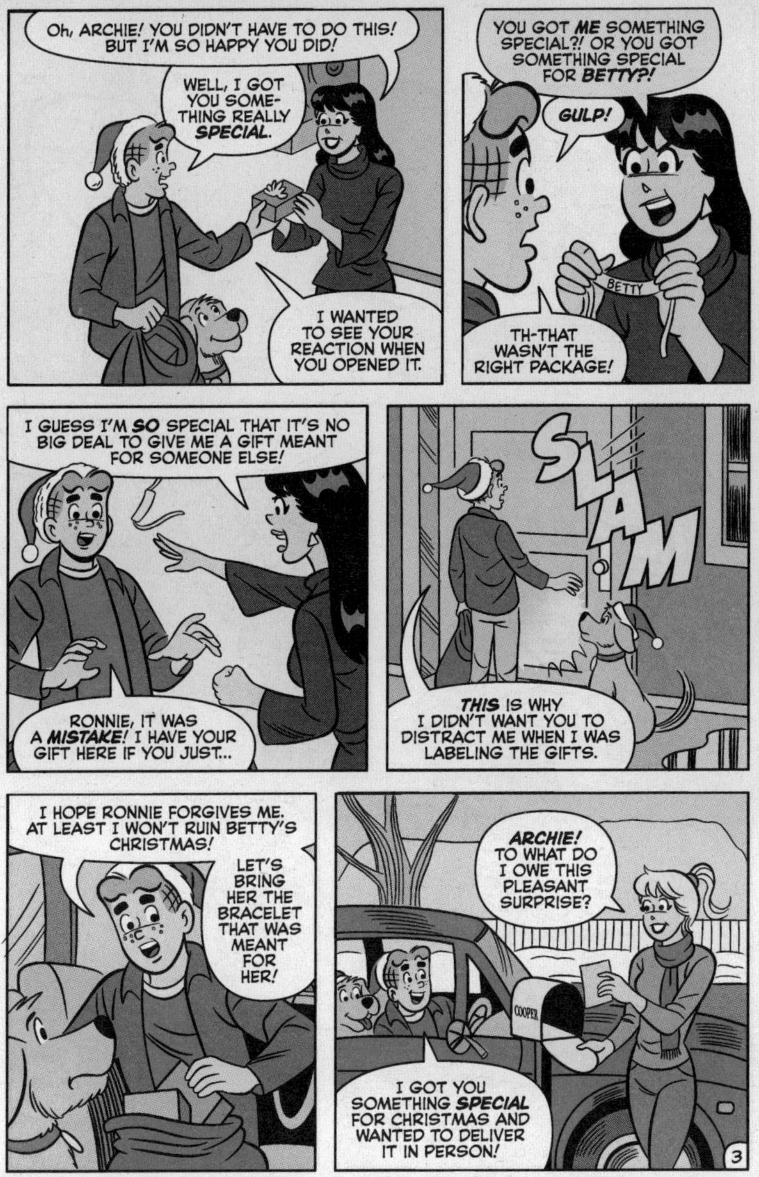

Oh, ARCHIE! YOU DIDN'T HAVE TO DO THIS! BUT I'M SO HAPPY YOU DID!
WELL, I GOT YOU SOME-THING REALLY SPECIAL.
I WANTED TO SEE YOUR REACTION WHEN YOU OPENED IT.
YOU GOT ME SOMETHING SPECIAL?! OR YOU GOT SOMETHING SPECIAL FOR BETTY?!
GULP!
BETTY
TH-THAT WASN'T THE RIGHT PACKAGE!
I GUESS I'M SO SPECIAL THAT IT'S NO BIG DEAL TO GIVE ME A GIFT MEANT FOR SOMEONE ELSE!
RONNIE, IT WAS A MISTAKE! I HAVE YOUR GIFT HERE IF YOU JUST...
SLAM
THIS IS WHY I DIDN'T WANT YOU TO DISTRACT ME WHEN I WAS LABELING THE GIFTS.
I HOPE RONNIE FORGIVES ME. AT LEAST I WON'T RUIN BETTY'S CHRISTMAS!
LET'S BRING HER THE BRACELET THAT WAS MEANT FOR HER!
ARCHIE! TO WHAT DO I OWE THIS PLEASANT SURPRISE?
COOPER
I GOT YOU SOMETHING SPECIAL FOR CHRISTMAS AND WANTED TO DELIVER IT IN PERSON!

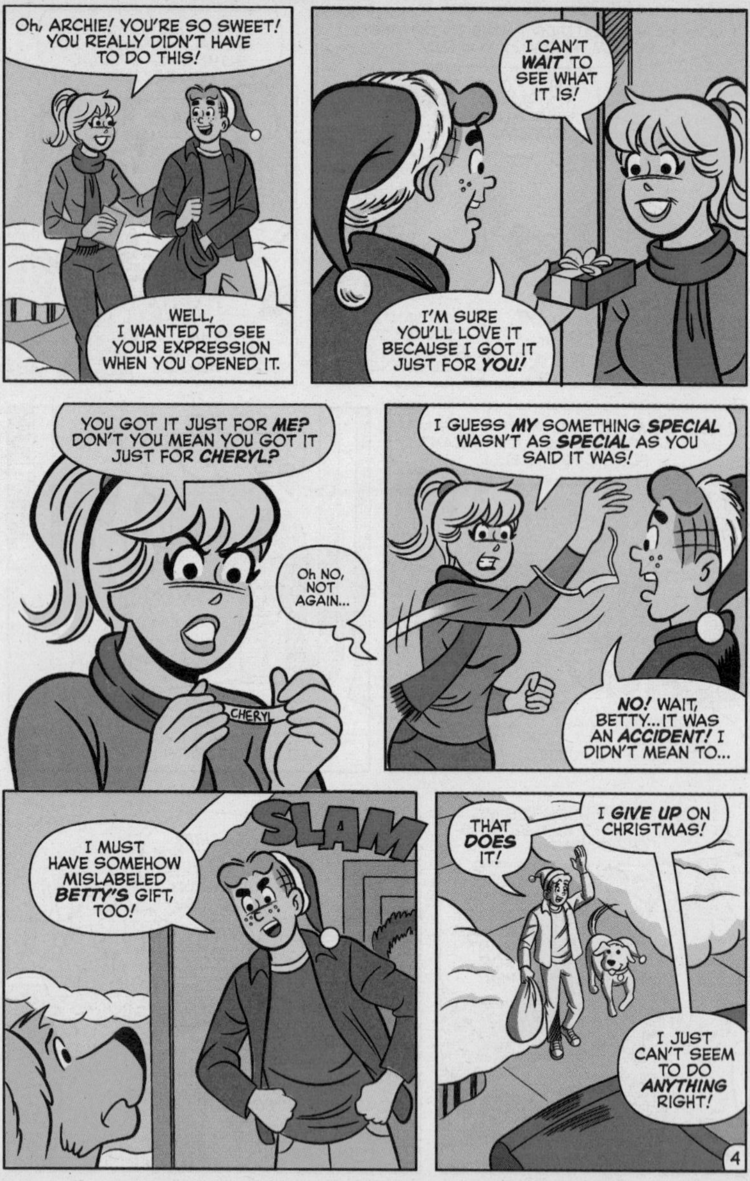

Oh, ARCHIE! YOU'RE SO SWEET! YOU REALLY DIDN'T HAVE TO DO THIS!
WELL, I WANTED TO SEE YOUR EXPRESSION WHEN YOU OPENED IT.
I CAN'T WAIT TO SEE WHAT IT IS!
I'M SURE YOU'LL LOVE IT BECAUSE I GOT IT JUST FOR YOU!
YOU GOT IT JUST FOR ME? DON'T YOU MEAN YOU GOT IT JUST FOR CHERYL?
Oh NO, NOT AGAIN...
CHERYL
I GUESS MY SOMETHING SPECIAL WASN'T AS SPECIAL AS YOU SAID IT WAS!
NO! WAIT, BETTY...IT WAS AN ACCIDENT! I DIDN'T MEAN TO...
SLAM
I MUST HAVE SOMEHOW MISLABELED BETTY'S GIFT, TOO!
THAT DOES IT!
I GIVE UP ON CHRISTMAS!
I JUST CAN'T SEEM TO DO ANYTHING RIGHT!

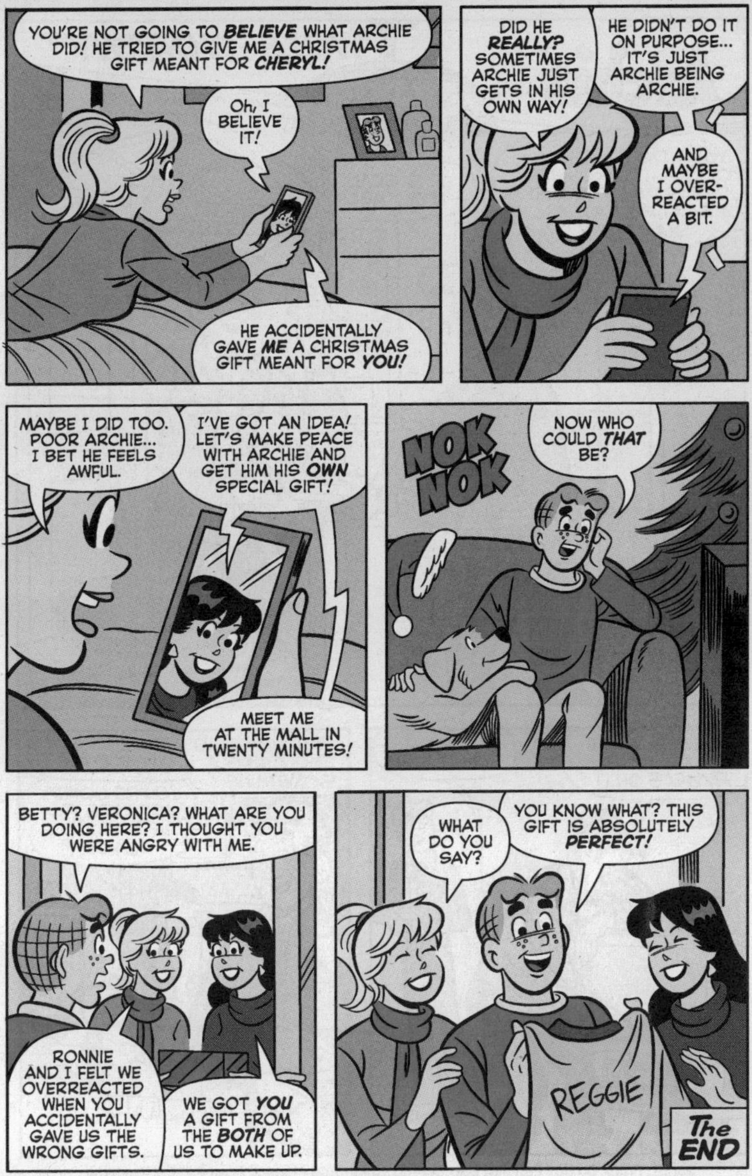
YOU'RE NOT GOING TO BELIEVE WHAT ARCHIE DID! HE TRIED TO GIVE ME A CHRISTMAS GIFT MEANT FOR CHERYL!
Oh, I BELIEVE IT!
HE ACCIDENTALLY GAVE ME A CHRISTMAS GIFT MEANT FOR YOU!
DID HE REALLY? SOMETIMES ARCHIE JUST GETS IN HIS OWN WAY!
HE DIDN'T DO IT ON PURPOSE... IT'S JUST ARCHIE BEING ARCHIE.
AND MAYBE I OVER-REACTED A BIT.
MAYBE I DID TOO. POOR ARCHIE... I BET HE FEELS AWFUL.
I'VE GOT AN IDEA! LET'S MAKE PEACE WITH ARCHIE AND GET HIM HIS OWN SPECIAL GIFT!
MEET ME AT THE MALL IN TWENTY MINUTES!
NOK NOK
NOW WHO COULD THAT BE?
BETTY? VERONICA? WHAT ARE YOU DOING HERE? I THOUGHT YOU WERE ANGRY WITH ME.
RONNIE AND I FELT WE OVERREACTED WHEN YOU ACCIDENTALLY GAVE US THE WRONG GIFTS.
WE GOT YOU A GIFT FROM THE BOTH OF US TO MAKE UP.
WHAT DO YOU SAY?
YOU KNOW WHAT? THIS GIFT IS ABSOLUTELY PERFECT!
REGGIE
The END

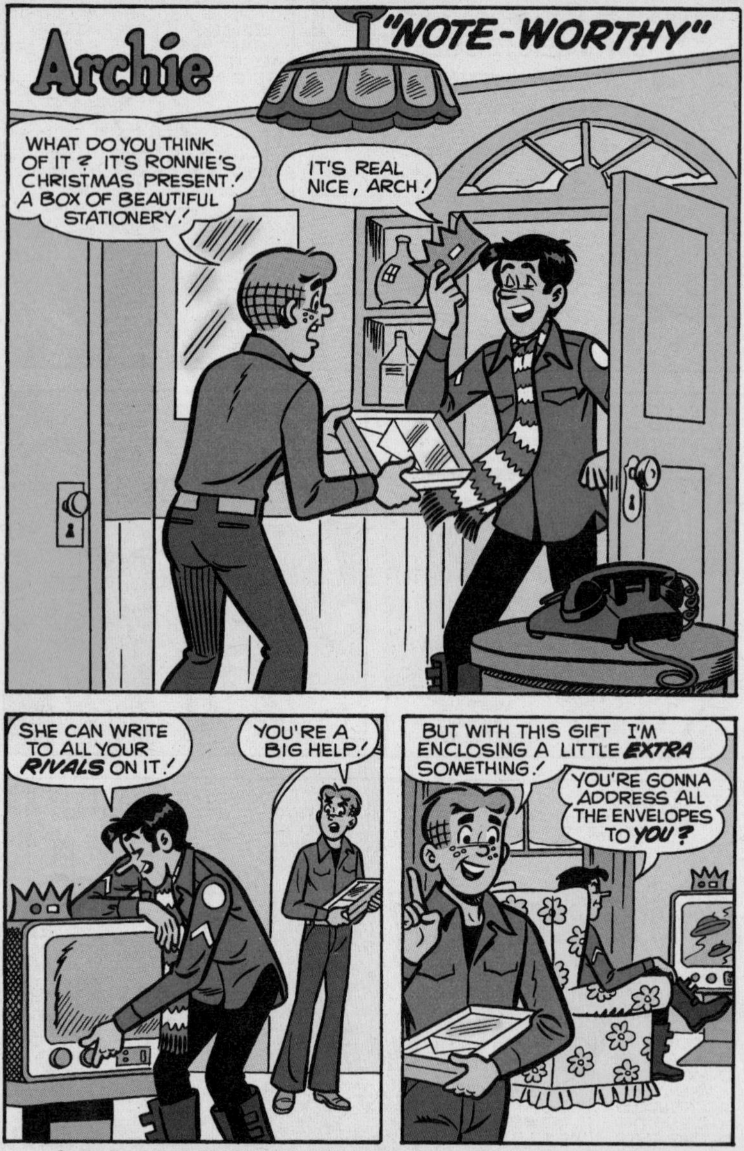
Archie
"NOTE-WORTHY"
WHAT DO YOU THINK OF IT? IT'S RONNIE'S CHRISTMAS PRESENT! A BOX OF BEAUTIFUL STATIONERY!
IT'S REAL NICE, ARCH!
SHE CAN WRITE TO ALL YOUR RIVALS ON IT!
YOU'RE A BIG HELP!
BUT WITH THIS GIFT I'M ENCLOSING A LITTLE EXTRA SOMETHING!
YOU'RE GONNA ADDRESS ALL THE ENVELOPES TO YOU?

Script: Frank Doyle / Pencils: Bob Bolling / Inks: Rudy Lapick / Letters: Bill Yoshida

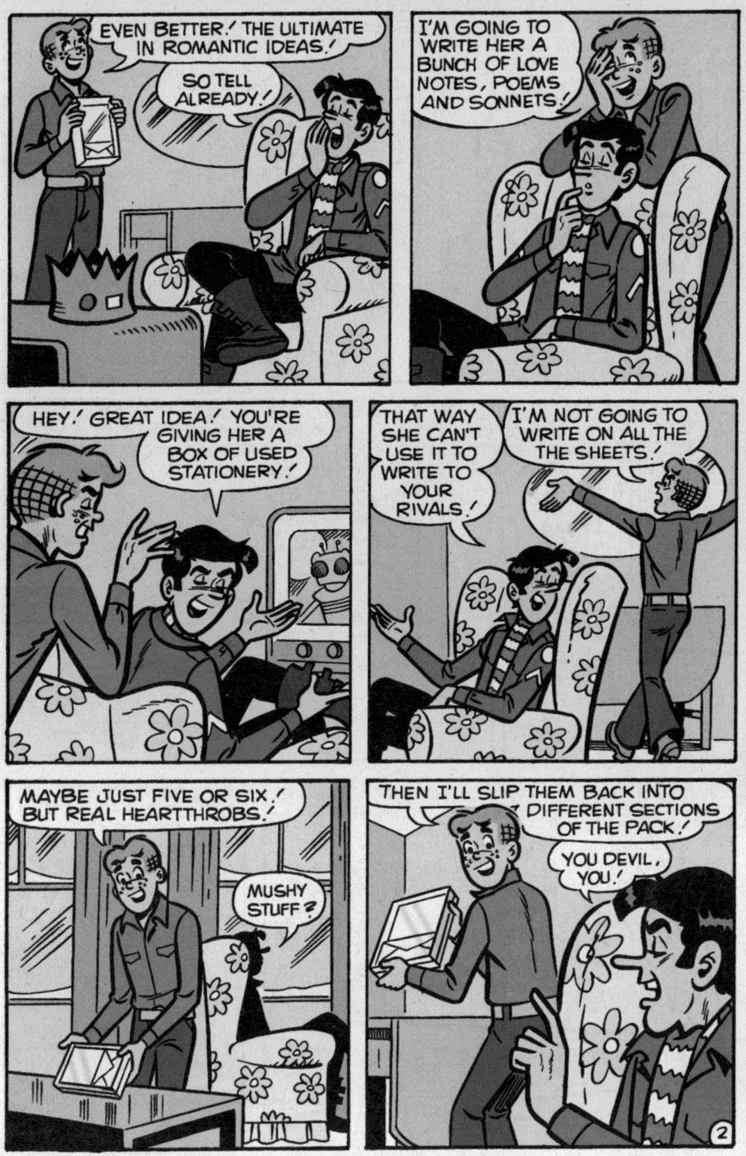
EVEN BETTER! THE ULTIMATE IN ROMANTIC IDEAS!
SO TELL ALREADY!
I'M GOING TO WRITE HER A BUNCH OF LOVE NOTES, POEMS AND SONNETS!
HEY! GREAT IDEA! YOU'RE GIVING HER A BOX OF USED STATIONERY!
I'M NOT GOING TO WRITE ON ALL THE THE SHEETS!
THAT WAY SHE CAN'T USE IT TO WRITE TO YOUR RIVALS!
MAYBE JUST FIVE OR SIX! BUT REAL HEARTTHROBS!
MUSHY STUFF?
THEN I'LL SLIP THEM BACK INTO DIFFERENT SECTIONS OF THE PACK!
YOU DEVIL, YOU!
2

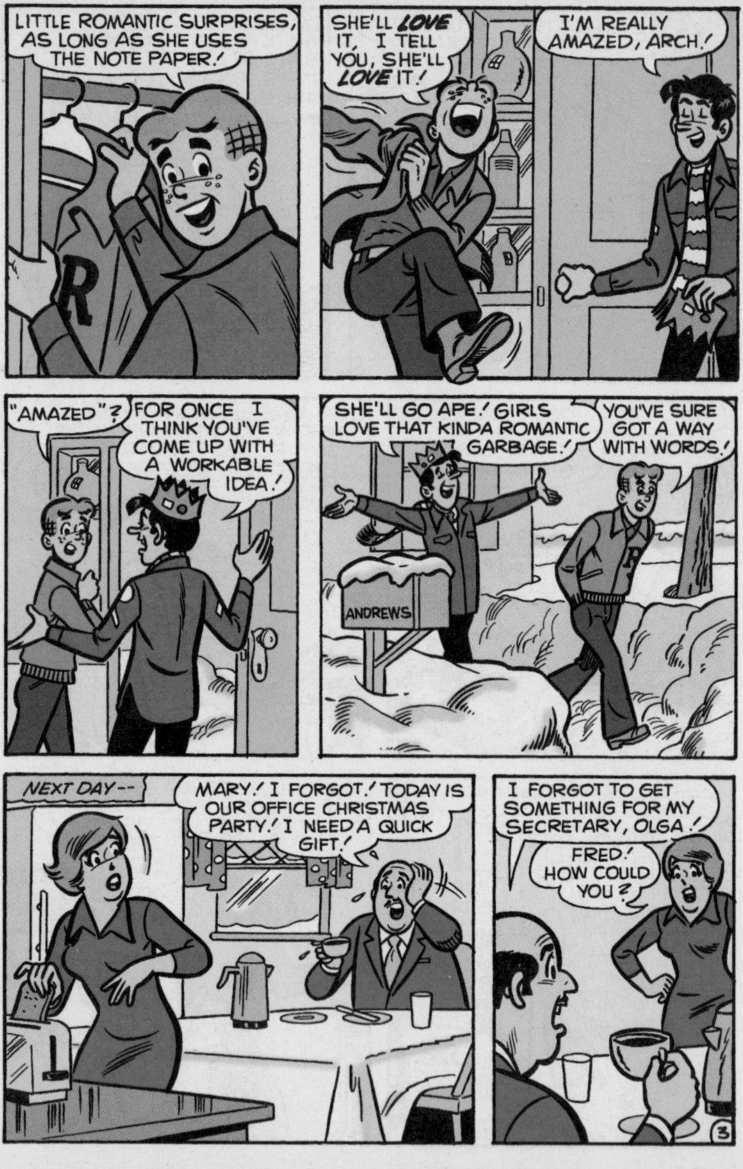
LITTLE ROMANTIC SURPRISES, AS LONG AS SHE USES THE NOTE PAPER!
SHE'LL LOVE IT, I TELL YOU, SHE'LL LOVE IT!
I'M REALLY AMAZED, ARCH!
"AMAZED"?
FOR ONCE I THINK YOU'VE COME UP WITH A WORKABLE IDEA!
SHE'LL GO APE! GIRLS LOVE THAT KINDA ROMANTIC GARBAGE!
YOU'VE SURE GOT A WAY WITH WORDS!
ANDREWS
NEXT DAY--
MARY! I FORGOT! TODAY IS OUR OFFICE CHRISTMAS PARTY! I NEED A QUICK GIFT!
I FORGOT TO GET SOMETHING FOR MY SECRETARY, OLGA!
FRED! HOW COULD YOU?
3

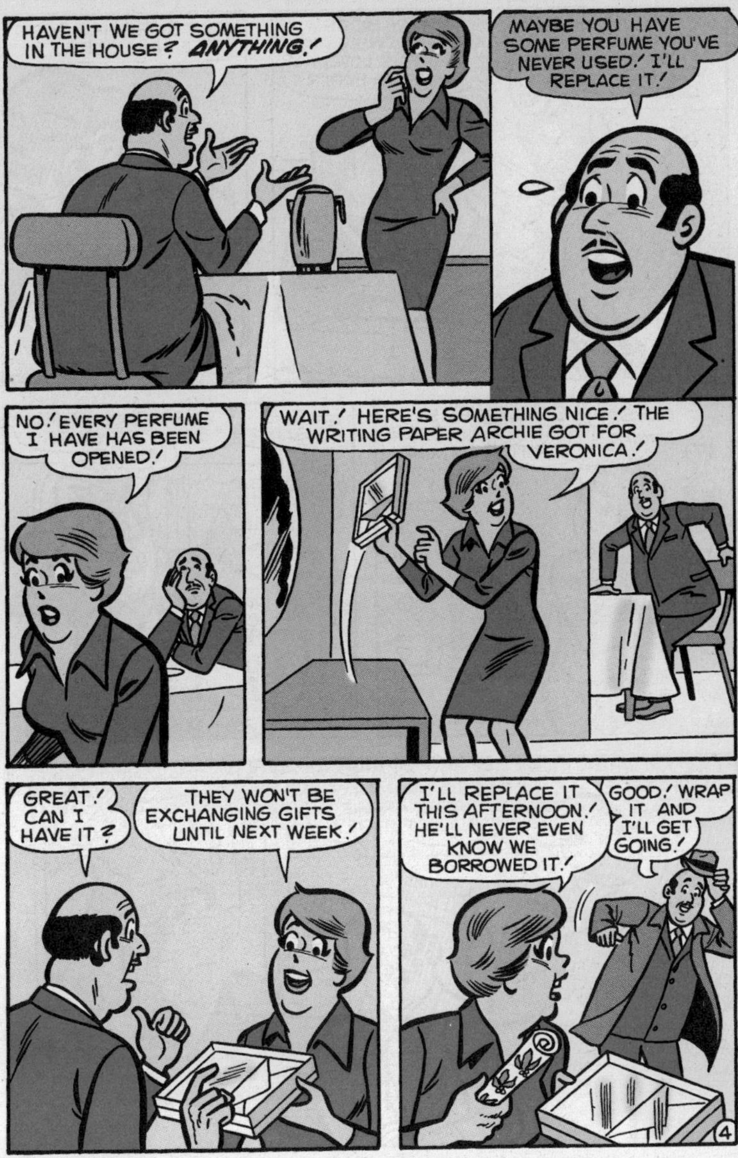
HAVEN'T WE GOT SOMETHING IN THE HOUSE? ANYTHING!
MAYBE YOU HAVE SOME PERFUME YOU'VE NEVER USED! I'LL REPLACE IT!
NO! EVERY PERFUME I HAVE HAS BEEN OPENED!
WAIT! HERE'S SOMETHING NICE! THE WRITING PAPER ARCHIE GOT FOR VERONICA!
GREAT! CAN I HAVE IT?
THEY WON'T BE EXCHANGING GIFTS UNTIL NEXT WEEK!
I'LL REPLACE IT THIS AFTERNOON! HE'LL NEVER EVEN KNOW WE BORROWED IT!
GOOD! WRAP IT AND I'LL GET GOING!
4

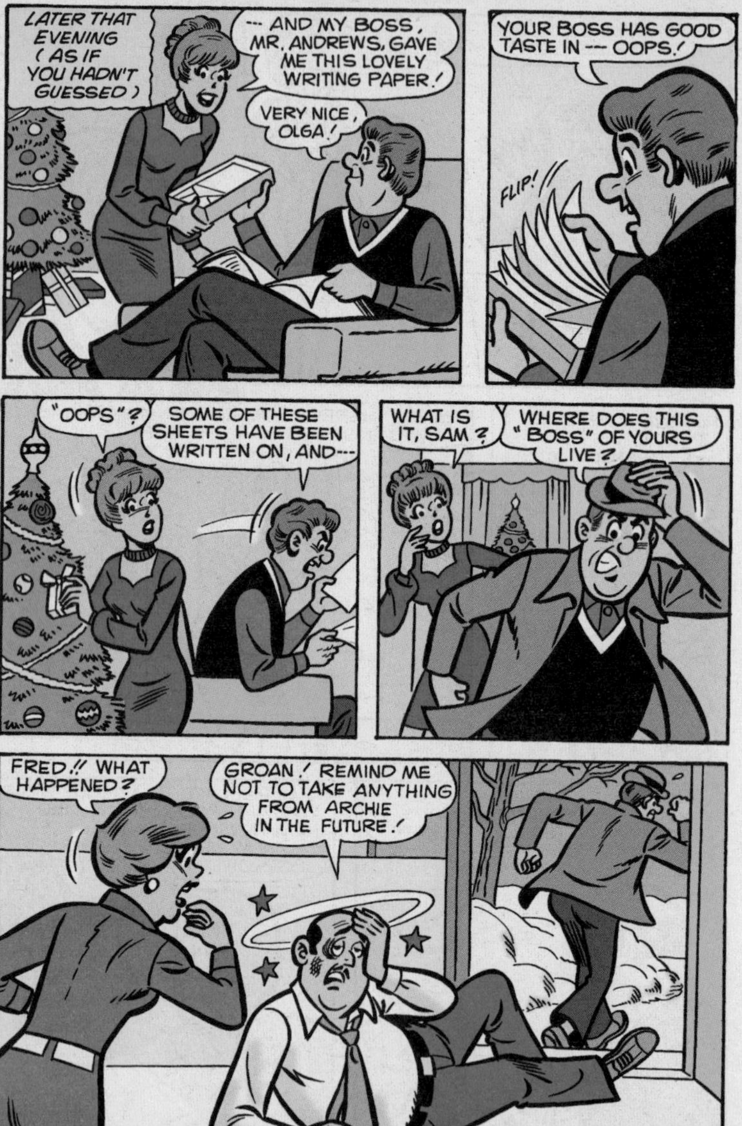
LATER THAT EVENING (AS IF YOU HADN'T GUESSED)
--- AND MY BOSS, MR. ANDREWS, GAVE ME THIS LOVELY WRITING PAPER!
VERY NICE, OLGA!
YOUR BOSS HAS GOOD TASTE IN --- OOPS!
FLIP!
"OOPS"?
SOME OF THESE SHEETS HAVE BEEN WRITTEN ON, AND---
WHAT IS IT, SAM?
WHERE DOES THIS "BOSS" OF YOURS LIVE?
FRED!! WHAT HAPPENED?
GROAN! REMIND ME NOT TO TAKE ANYTHING FROM ARCHIE IN THE FUTURE!
END

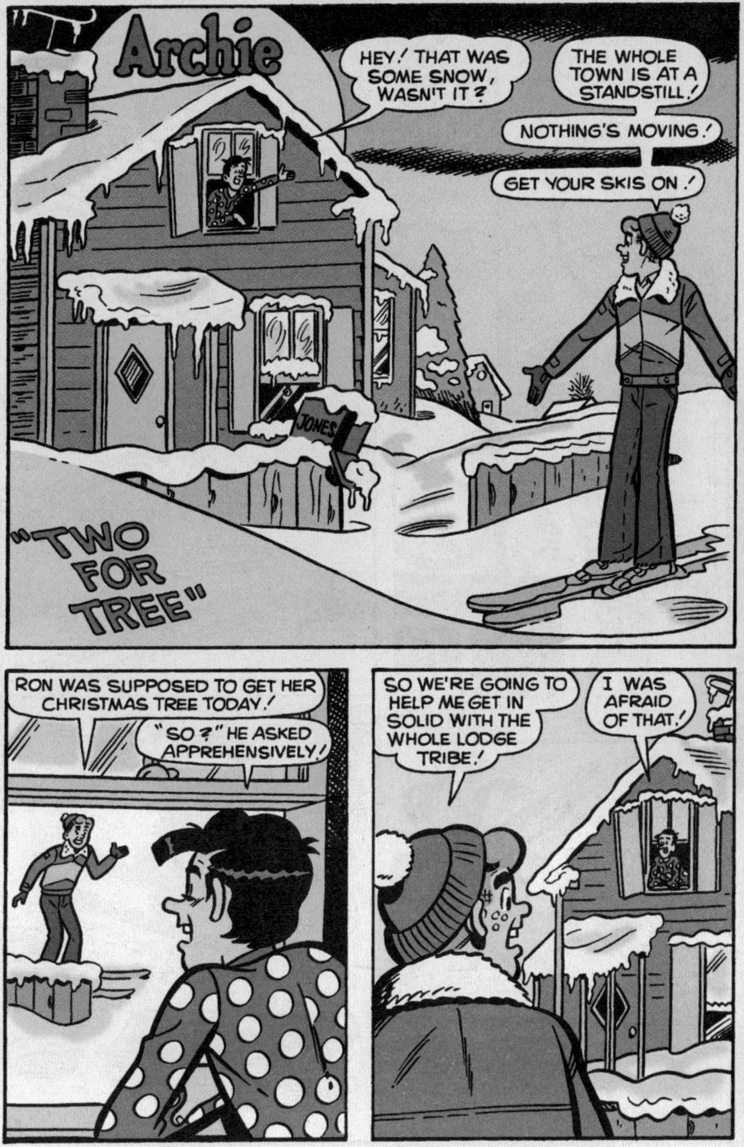
Archie
HEY! THAT WAS SOME SNOW, WASN'T IT?
THE WHOLE TOWN IS AT A STANDSTILL!
NOTHING'S MOVING!
GET YOUR SKIS ON!
JONES
"TWO FOR TREE"
RON WAS SUPPOSED TO GET HER CHRISTMAS TREE TODAY!
"SO?" HE ASKED APPREHENSIVELY!
SO WE'RE GOING TO HELP ME GET IN SOLID WITH THE WHOLE LODGE TRIBE!
I WAS AFRAID OF THAT!

Script: George Gladir / Pencils: Bob Bolling / Inks: Rudy Lapick / Letters: Bill Yoshida

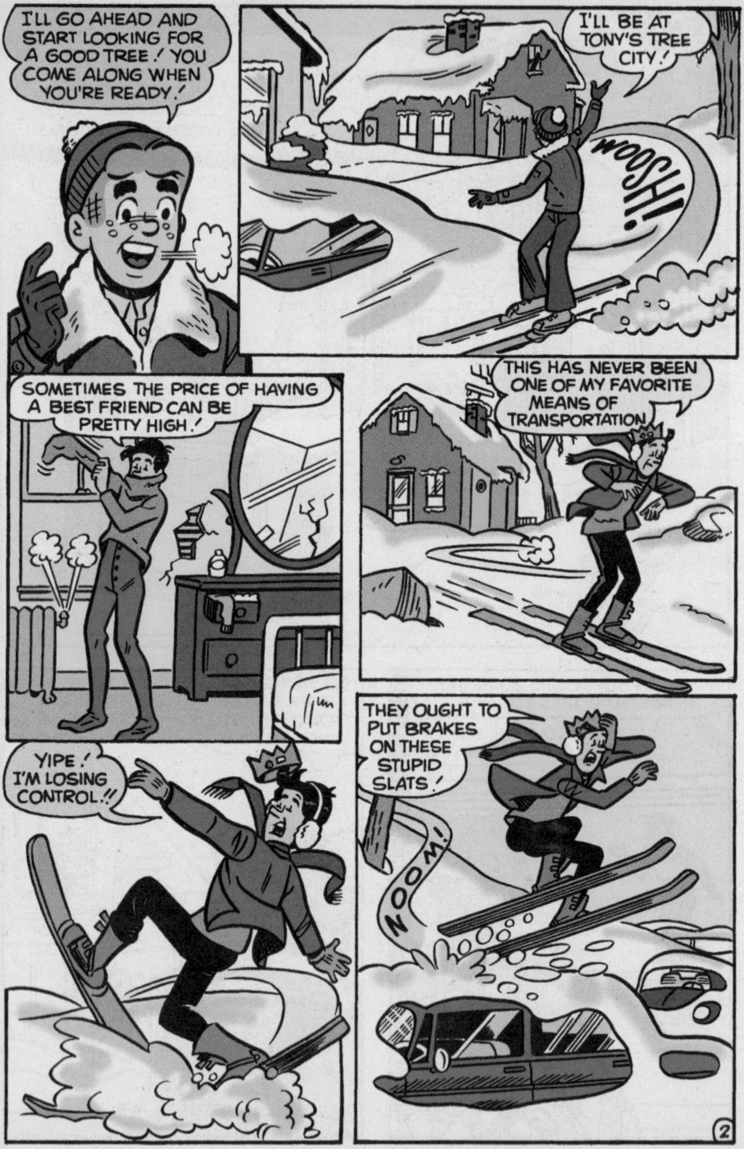
I'LL GO AHEAD AND START LOOKING FOR A GOOD TREE! YOU COME ALONG WHEN YOU'RE READY!
I'LL BE AT TONY'S TREE CITY!
WOOSH!
SOMETIMES THE PRICE OF HAVING A BEST FRIEND CAN BE PRETTY HIGH!
THIS HAS NEVER BEEN ONE OF MY FAVORITE MEANS OF TRANSPORTATION!
YIPE! I'M LOSING CONTROL!!
THEY OUGHT TO PUT BRAKES ON THESE STUPID SLATS!
ZOOOM!
2

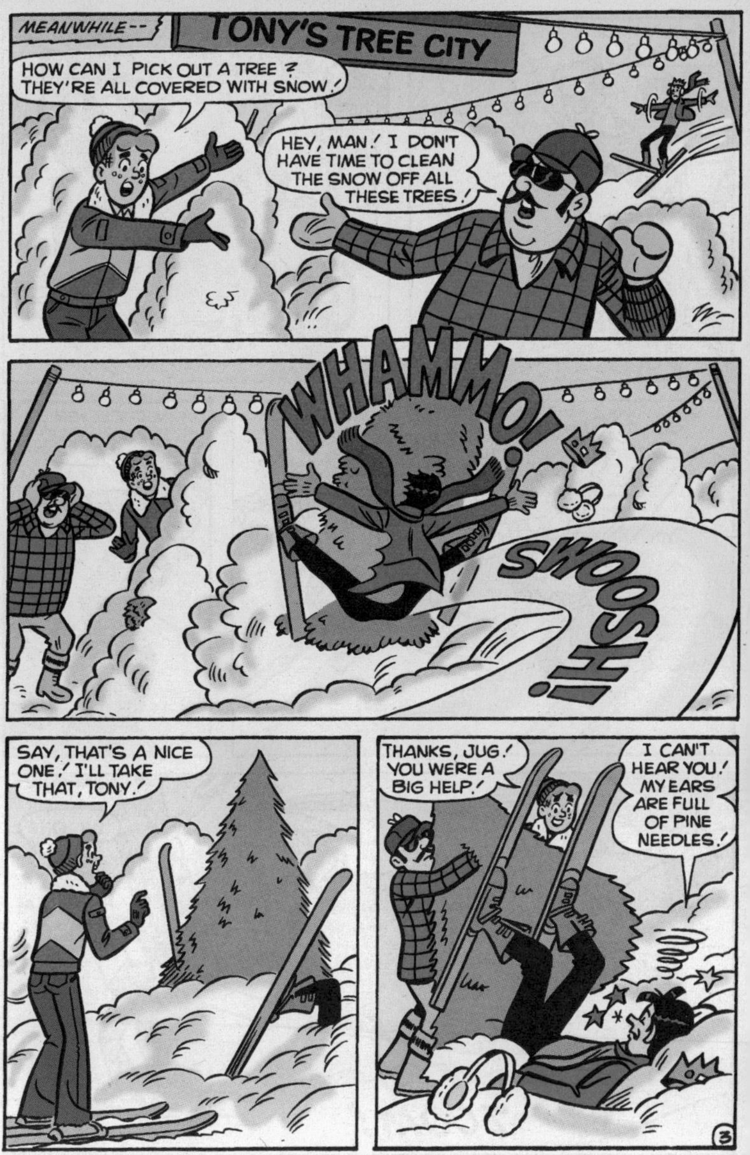
MEANWHILE--
TONY'S TREE CITY
HOW CAN I PICK OUT A TREE? THEY'RE ALL COVERED WITH SNOW!
HEY, MAN! I DON'T HAVE TIME TO CLEAN THE SNOW OFF ALL THESE TREES!
WHAMMO!
SWOOSH!!
SAY, THAT'S A NICE ONE! I'LL TAKE THAT, TONY!
THANKS, JUG! YOU WERE A BIG HELP!
I CAN'T HEAR YOU! MY EARS ARE FULL OF PINE NEEDLES!
3

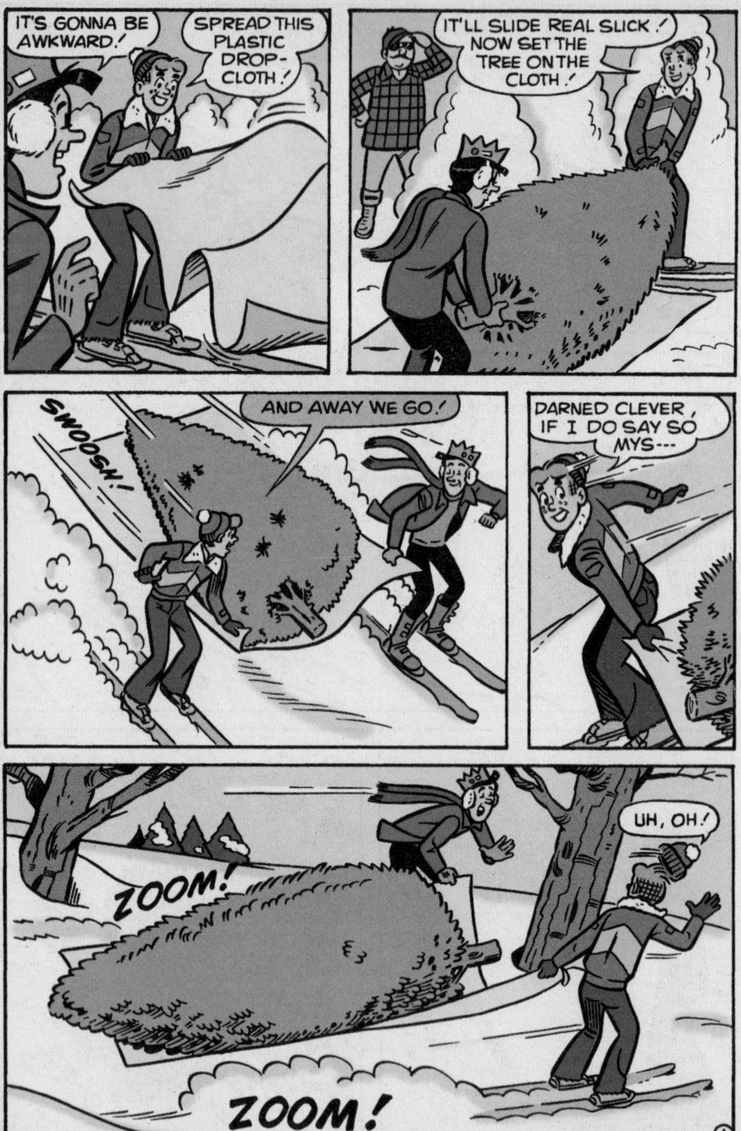
IT'S GONNA BE AWKWARD!
SPREAD THIS PLASTIC DROP-CLOTH!
IT'LL SLIDE REAL SLICK! NOW SET THE TREE ON THE CLOTH!
SWOOSH!
AND AWAY WE GO!
DARNED CLEVER, IF I DO SAY SO MYS---
ZOOM!
UH, OH!
ZOOM!
4

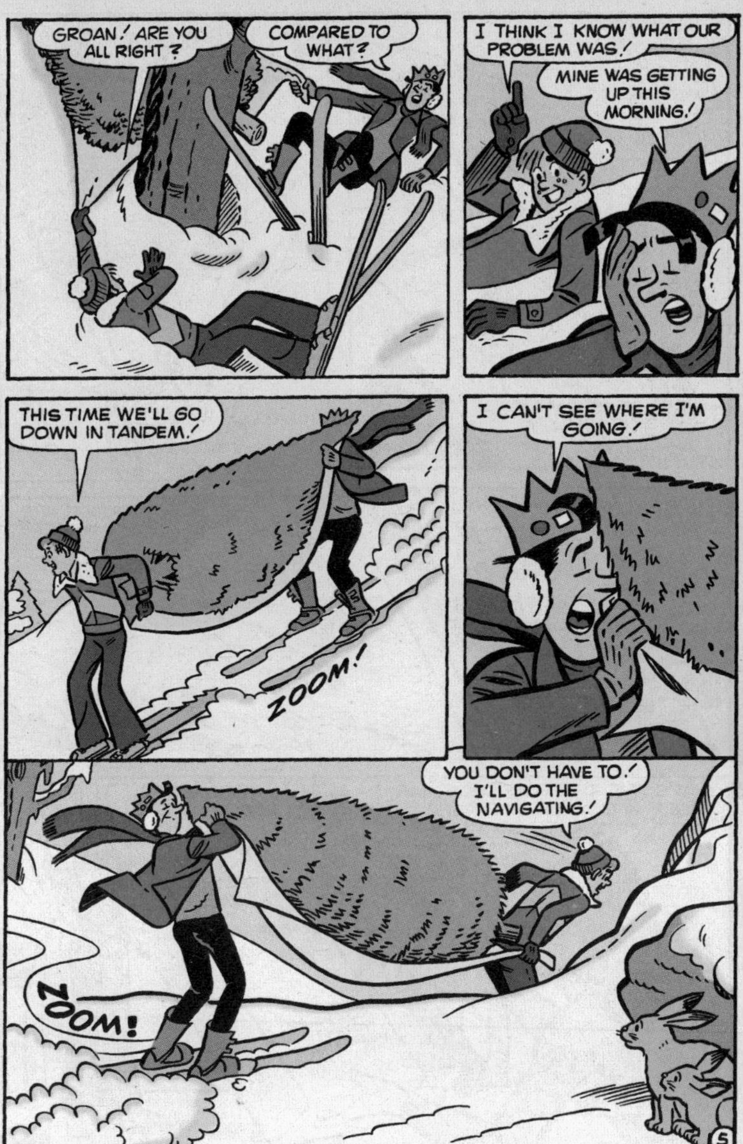
GROAN! ARE YOU ALL RIGHT?
COMPARED TO WHAT?
I THINK I KNOW WHAT OUR PROBLEM WAS!
MINE WAS GETTING UP THIS MORNING!
THIS TIME WE'LL GO DOWN IN TANDEM!
ZOOM!
I CAN'T SEE WHERE I'M GOING!
YOU DON'T HAVE TO! I'LL DO THE NAVIGATING!
ZOOM!
5

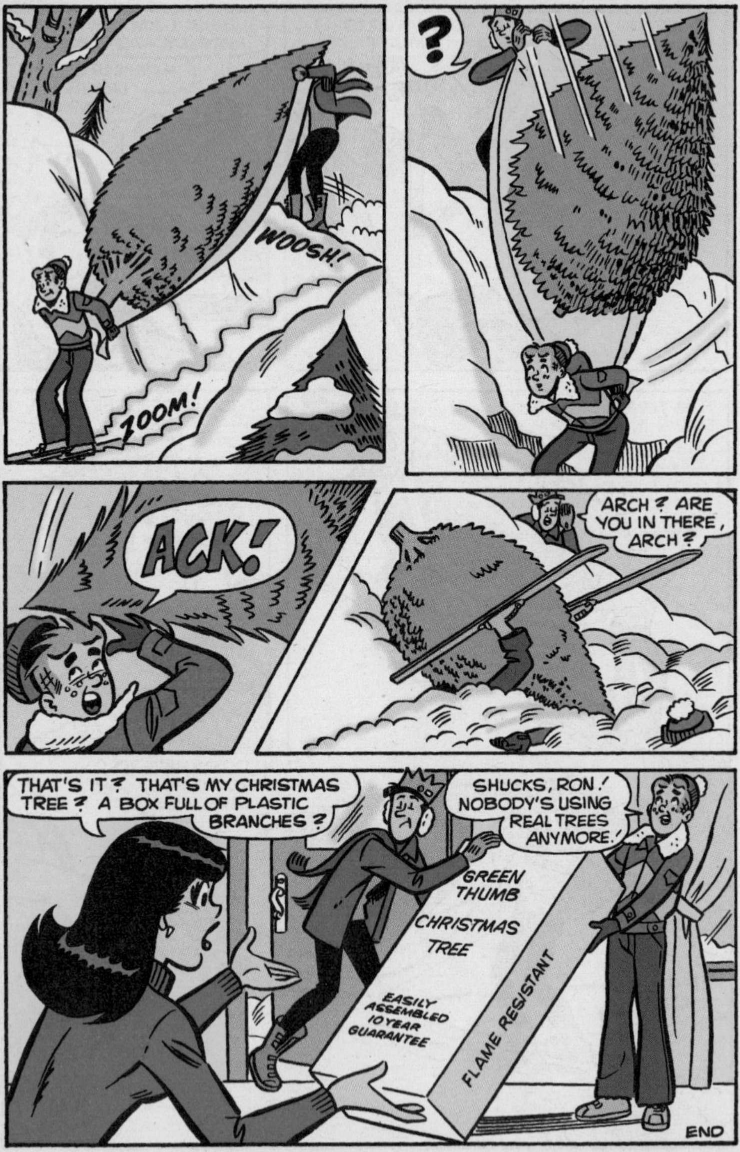
WOOSH!
ZOOM!
?
ACK!
ARCH? ARE YOU IN THERE, ARCH?
THAT'S IT? THAT'S MY CHRISTMAS TREE? A BOX FULL OF PLASTIC BRANCHES?
SHUCKS, RON! NOBODY'S USING REAL TREES ANYMORE!
GREEN THUMB
CHRISTMAS TREE
EASILY ASSEMBLED 10 YEAR GUARANTEE
FLAME RESISTANT
END

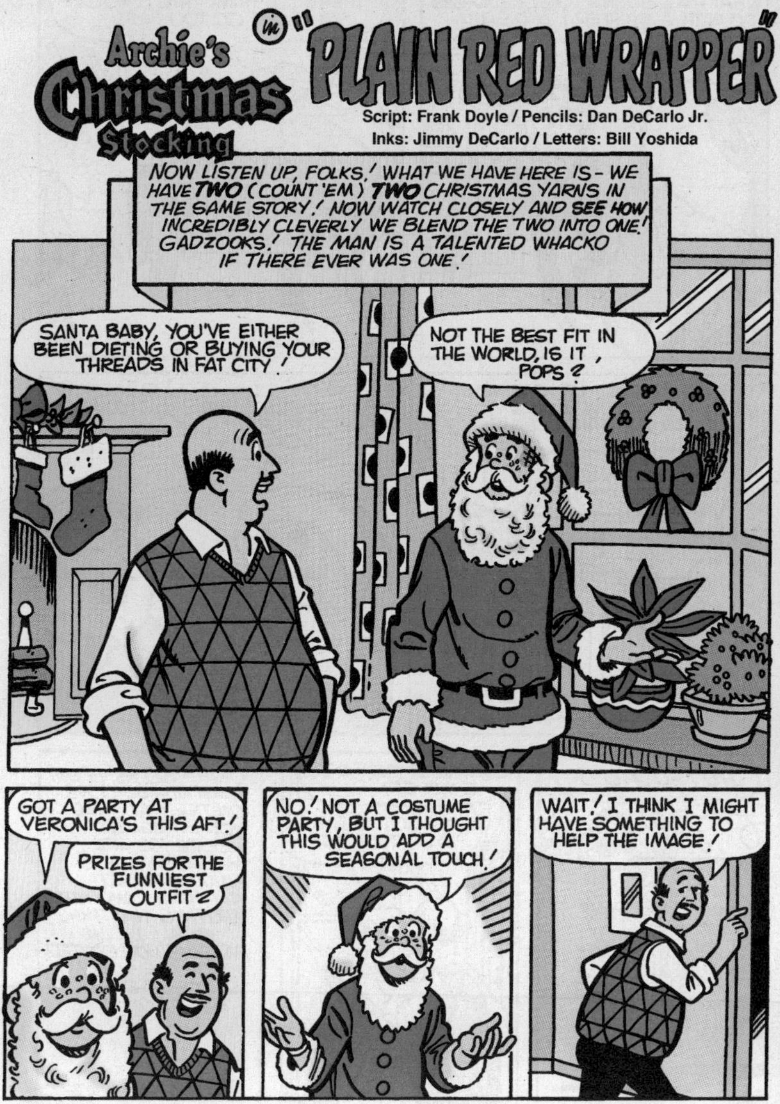
Archie's Christmas Stocking
in "PLAIN RED WRAPPER"
Script: Frank Doyle / Pencils: Dan DeCarlo Jr.
Inks: Jimmy DeCarlo / Letters: Bill Yoshida
NOW LISTEN UP, FOLKS! WHAT WE HAVE HERE IS - WE HAVE TWO (COUNT 'EM) TWO CHRISTMAS YARNS IN THE SAME STORY! NOW WATCH CLOSELY AND SEE HOW INCREDIBLY CLEVERLY WE BLEND THE TWO INTO ONE! GADZOOKS! THE MAN IS A TALENTED WHACKO IF THERE EVER WAS ONE!
SANTA BABY, YOU'VE EITHER BEEN DIETING OR BUYING YOUR THREADS IN FAT CITY!
NOT THE BEST FIT IN THE WORLD, IS IT, POPS?
GOT A PARTY AT VERONICA'S THIS AFT!
PRIZES FOR THE FUNNIEST OUTFIT?
NO! NOT A COSTUME PARTY, BUT I THOUGHT THIS WOULD ADD A SEASONAL TOUCH!
WAIT! I THINK I MIGHT HAVE SOMETHING TO HELP THE IMAGE!

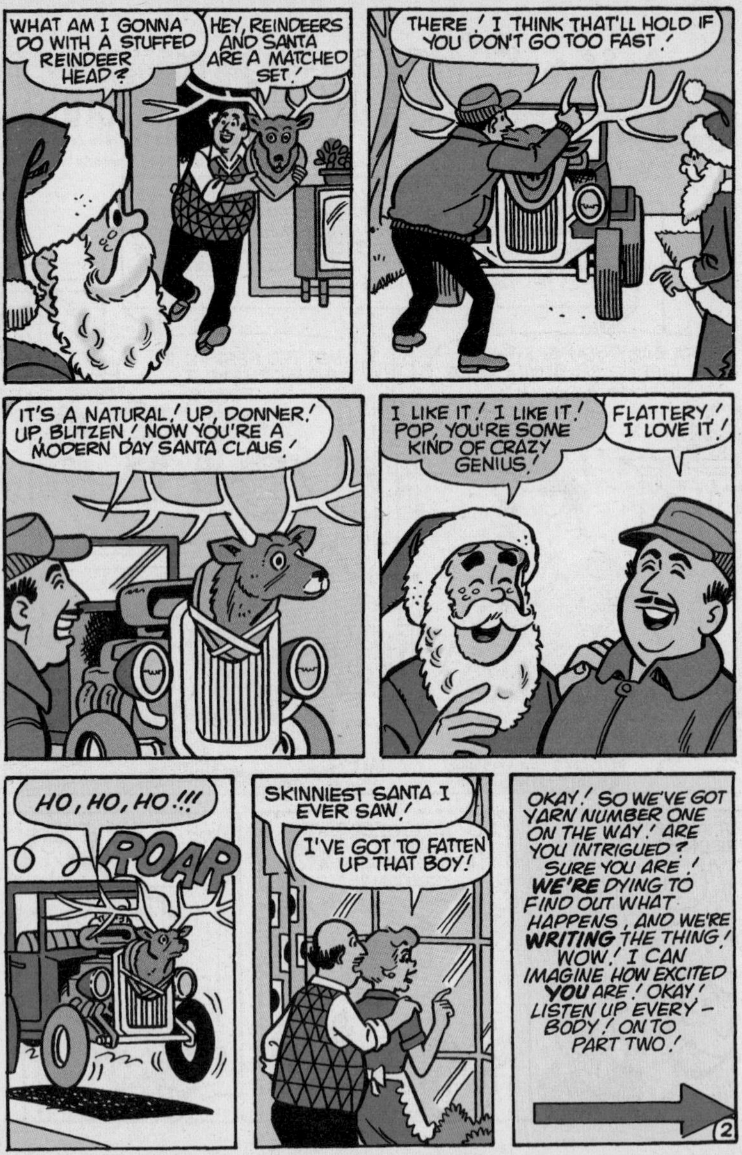
WHAT AM I GONNA DO WITH A STUFFED REINDEER HEAD?
HEY, REINDEERS AND SANTA ARE A MATCHED SET!
THERE! I THINK THAT'LL HOLD IF YOU DON'T GO TOO FAST!
IT'S A NATURAL! UP, DONNER! UP, BLITZEN! NOW YOU'RE A MODERN DAY SANTA CLAUS!
I LIKE IT! I LIKE IT! POP, YOU'RE SOME KIND OF CRAZY GENIUS!
FLATTERY! I LOVE IT!
HO, HO, HO!!!
ROAR
SKINNIEST SANTA I EVER SAW!
I'VE GOT TO FATTEN UP THAT BOY!
OKAY! SO WE'VE GOT YARN NUMBER ONE ON THE WAY! ARE YOU INTRIGUED? SURE YOU ARE! WE'RE DYING TO FIND OUT WHAT HAPPENS, AND WE'RE WRITING THE THING! WOW! I CAN IMAGINE HOW EXCITED YOU ARE! OKAY! LISTEN UP EVERY-BODY! ON TO PART TWO!
2

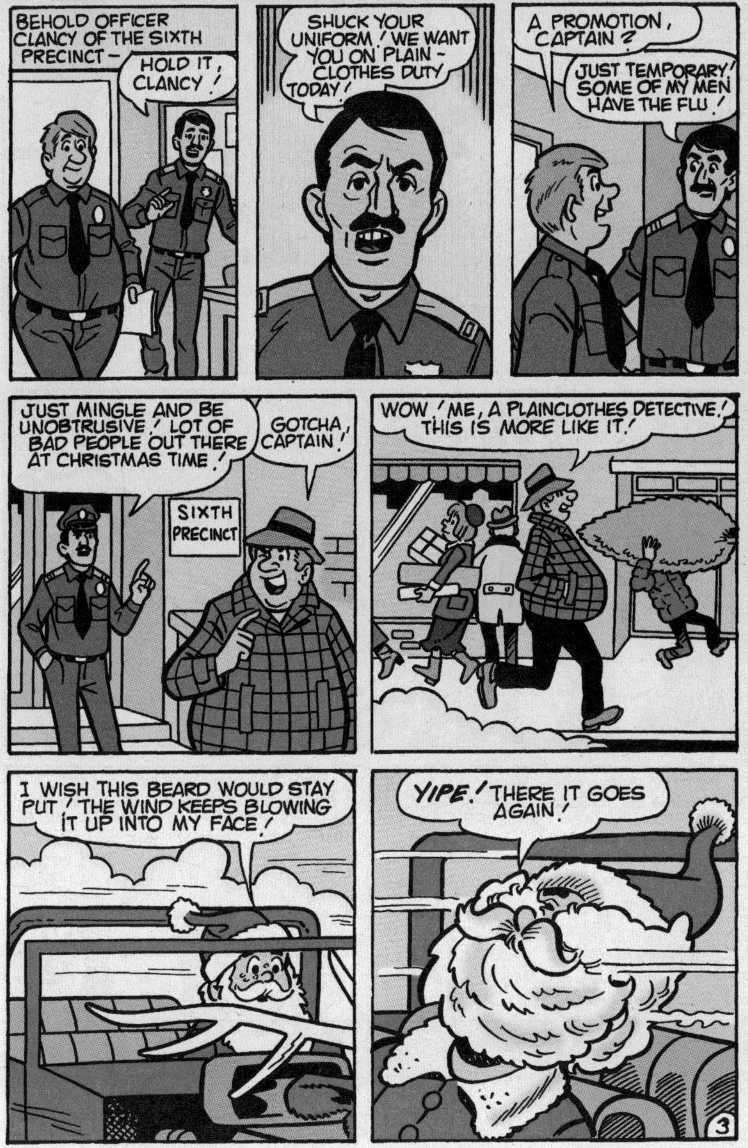
BEHOLD OFFICER CLANCY OF THE SIXTH PRECINCT —
HOLD IT, CLANCY!
SHUCK YOUR UNIFORM! WE WANT YOU ON PLAIN-CLOTHES DUTY TODAY!
A PROMOTION, CAPTAIN?
JUST TEMPORARY! SOME OF MY MEN HAVE THE FLU!
JUST MINGLE AND BE UNOBTRUSIVE! LOT OF BAD PEOPLE OUT THERE AT CHRISTMAS TIME!
GOTCHA, CAPTAIN!
SIXTH PRECINCT
WOW! ME, A PLAINCLOTHES DETECTIVE! THIS IS MORE LIKE IT!
I WISH THIS BEARD WOULD STAY PUT! THE WIND KEEPS BLOWING IT UP INTO MY FACE!
YIPE! THERE IT GOES AGAIN!
3

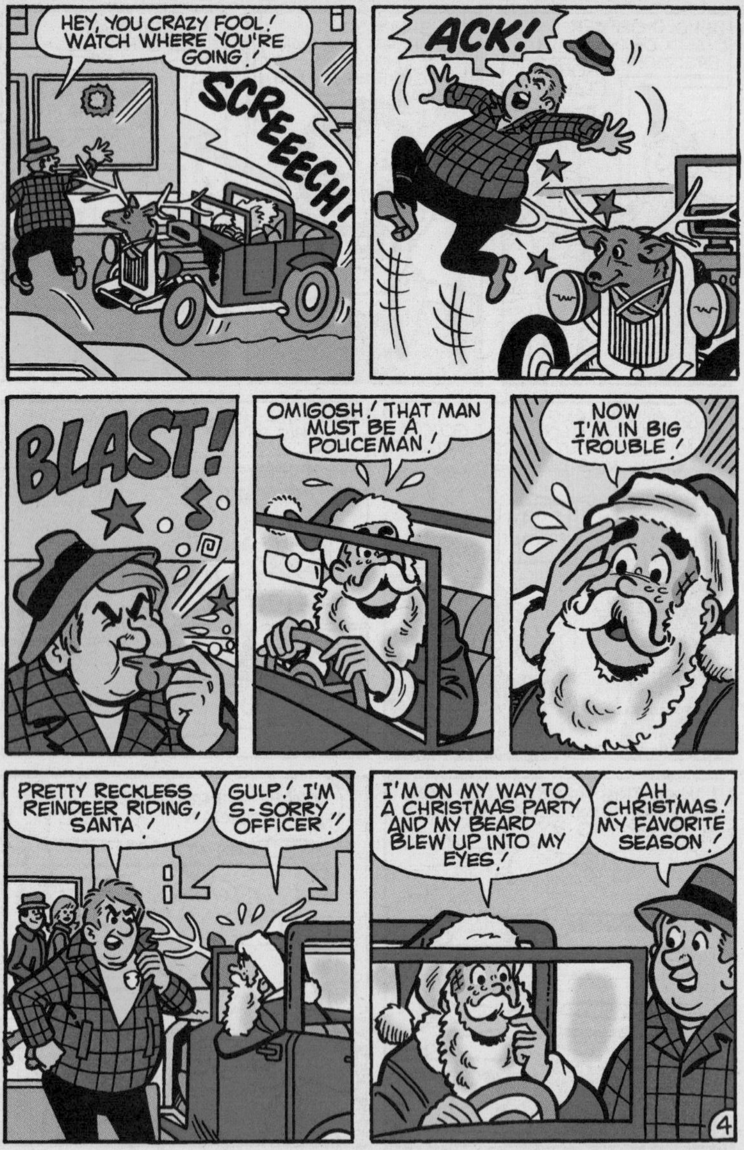
HEY, YOU CRAZY FOOL! WATCH WHERE YOU'RE GOING!
SCREEECH!
ACK!
BLAST!
OMIGOSH! THAT MAN MUST BE A POLICEMAN!
NOW I'M IN BIG TROUBLE!
PRETTY RECKLESS REINDEER RIDING, SANTA!
GULP! I'M S-SORRY OFFICER!
I'M ON MY WAY TO A CHRISTMAS PARTY AND MY BEARD BLEW UP INTO MY EYES!
AH, CHRISTMAS! MY FAVORITE SEASON!
4

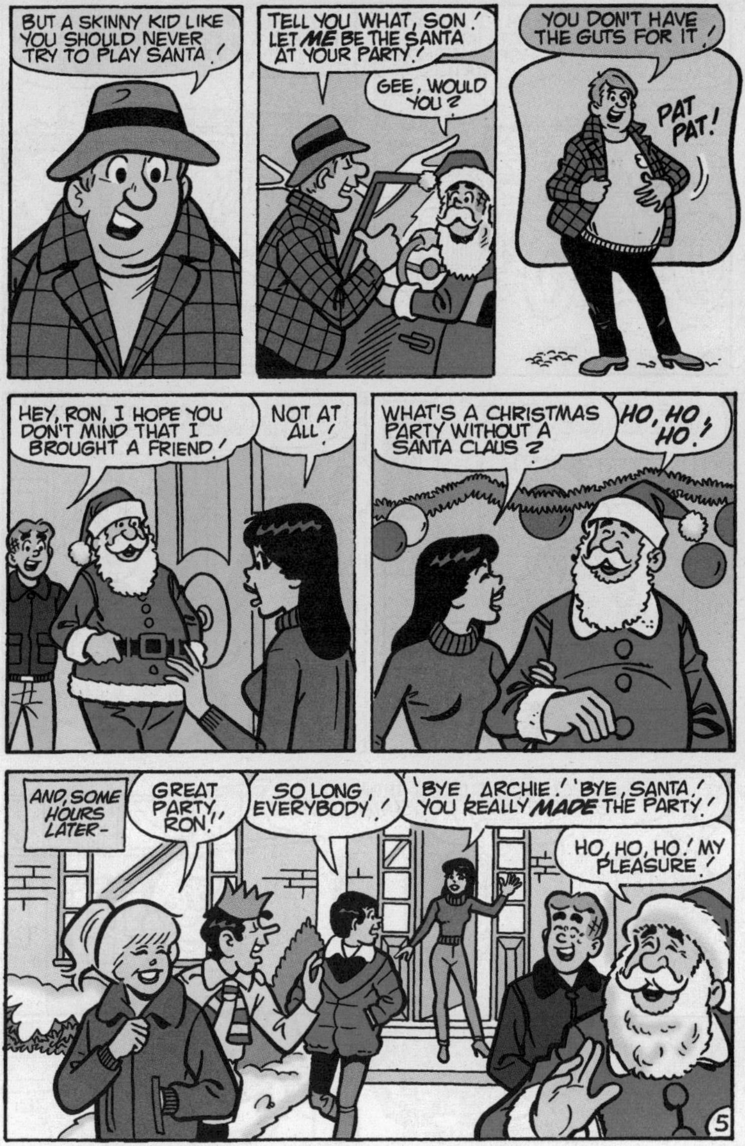
BUT A SKINNY KID LIKE YOU SHOULD NEVER TRY TO PLAY SANTA!
TELL YOU WHAT, SON! LET ME BE THE SANTA AT YOUR PARTY!
GEE, WOULD YOU?
YOU DON'T HAVE THE GUTS FOR IT!
PAT PAT!
HEY, RON, I HOPE YOU DON'T MIND THAT I BROUGHT A FRIEND!
NOT AT ALL!
WHAT'S A CHRISTMAS PARTY WITHOUT A SANTA CLAUS?
HO, HO, HO!
AND, SOME HOURS LATER-
GREAT PARTY, RON!
SO LONG, EVERYBODY!
'BYE ARCHIE! 'BYE, SANTA! YOU REALLY MADE THE PARTY!
HO, HO, HO! MY PLEASURE!
5

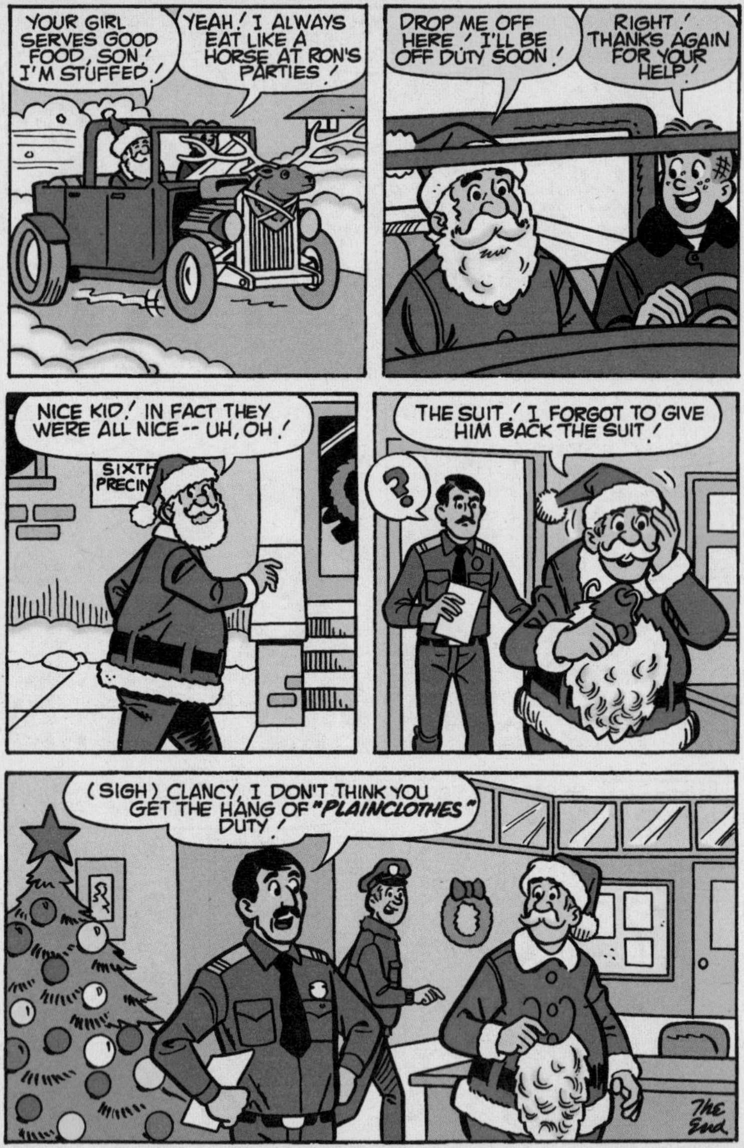
YOUR GIRL SERVES GOOD FOOD, SON! I'M STUFFED!
YEAH! I ALWAYS EAT LIKE A HORSE AT RON'S PARTIES!
DROP ME OFF HERE! I'LL BE OFF DUTY SOON!
RIGHT! THANKS AGAIN FOR YOUR HELP!
NICE KID! IN FACT THEY WERE ALL NICE -- UH, OH!
SIXTH PRECIN
?
THE SUIT! I FORGOT TO GIVE HIM BACK THE SUIT!
(SIGH) CLANCY, I DON'T THINK YOU GET THE HANG OF "PLAINCLOTHES" DUTY!
THE End

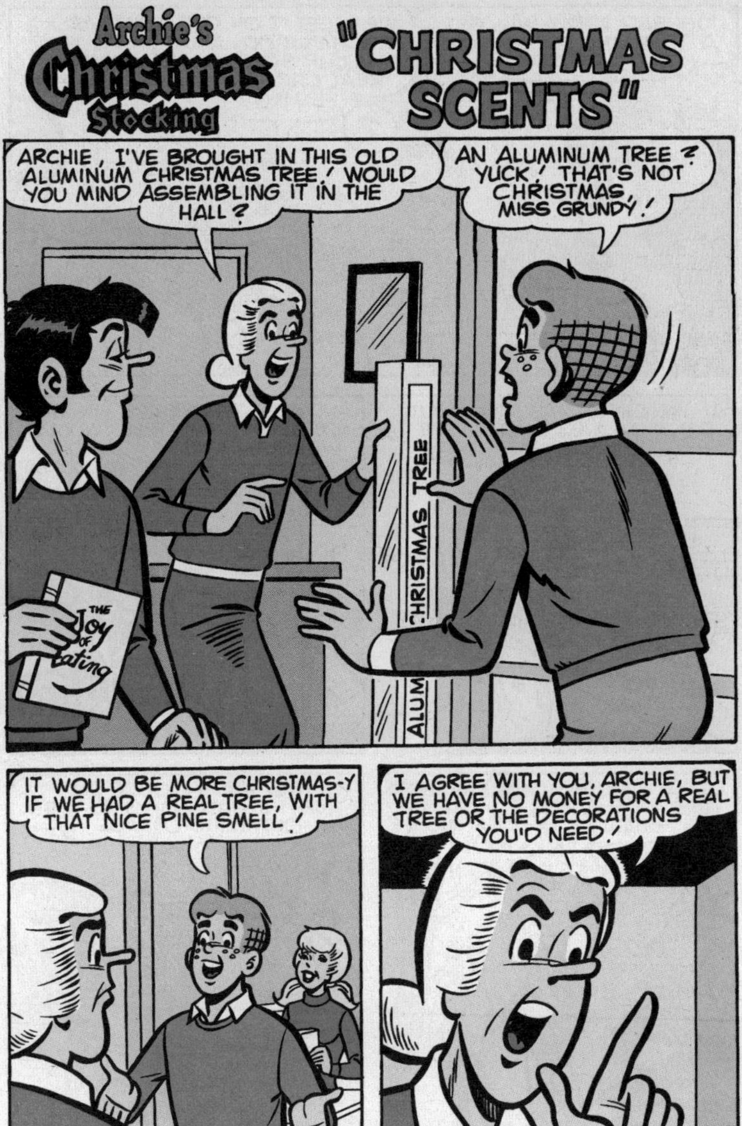
Archie's Christmas Stocking
"CHRISTMAS SCENTS"
ARCHIE, I'VE BROUGHT IN THIS OLD ALUMINUM CHRISTMAS TREE! WOULD YOU MIND ASSEMBLING IT IN THE HALL?
AN ALUMINUM TREE? YUCK! THAT'S NOT CHRISTMAS, MISS GRUNDY!
ALUM CHRISTMAS TREE
THE Joy OF Eating
IT WOULD BE MORE CHRISTMAS-Y IF WE HAD A REAL TREE, WITH THAT NICE PINE SMELL!
I AGREE WITH YOU, ARCHIE, BUT WE HAVE NO MONEY FOR A REAL TREE OR THE DECORATIONS YOU'D NEED!

Script & Pencils: Dick Malmgren / Inks: Jon D'Agostino / Letters: Bill Yoshida

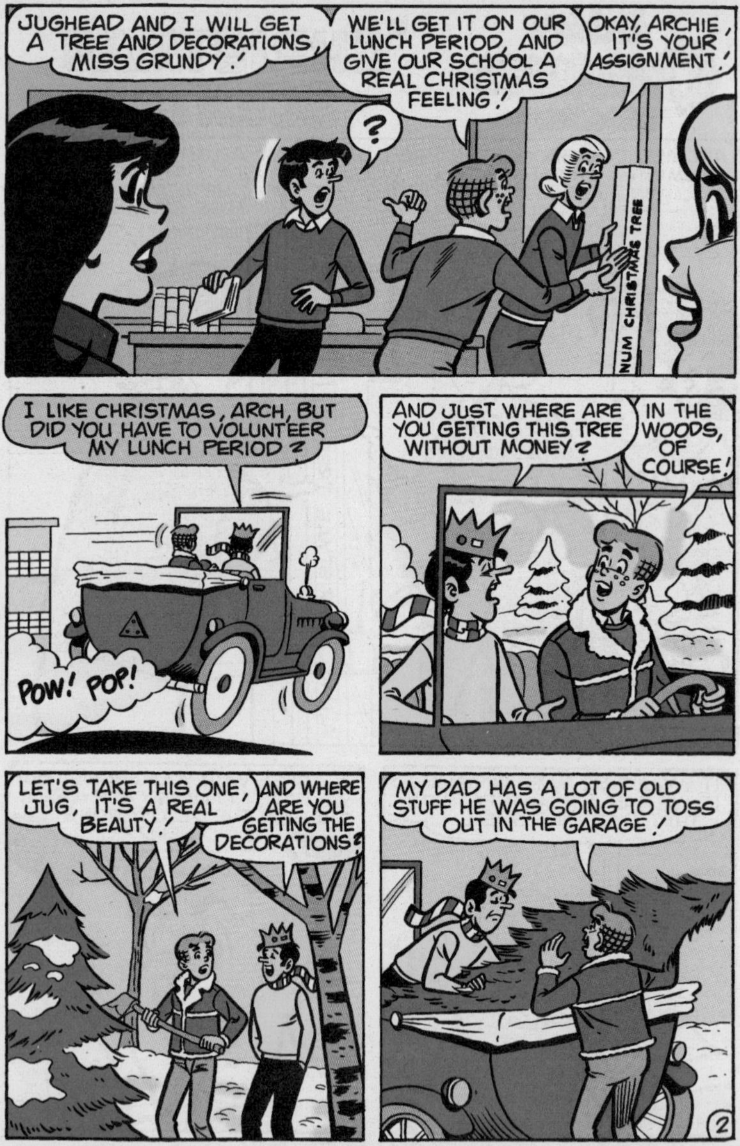
JUGHEAD AND I WILL GET A TREE AND DECORATIONS, MISS GRUNDY!
WE'LL GET IT ON OUR LUNCH PERIOD, AND GIVE OUR SCHOOL A REAL CHRISTMAS FEELING!
OKAY, ARCHIE, IT'S YOUR ASSIGNMENT!
?
NUM CHRISTMAS TREE
I LIKE CHRISTMAS, ARCH, BUT DID YOU HAVE TO VOLUNTEER MY LUNCH PERIOD?
POW! POP!
AND JUST WHERE ARE YOU GETTING THIS TREE WITHOUT MONEY?
IN THE WOODS, OF COURSE!
LET'S TAKE THIS ONE, JUG, IT'S A REAL BEAUTY!
AND WHERE ARE YOU GETTING THE DECORATIONS?
MY DAD HAS A LOT OF OLD STUFF HE WAS GOING TO TOSS OUT IN THE GARAGE!
2

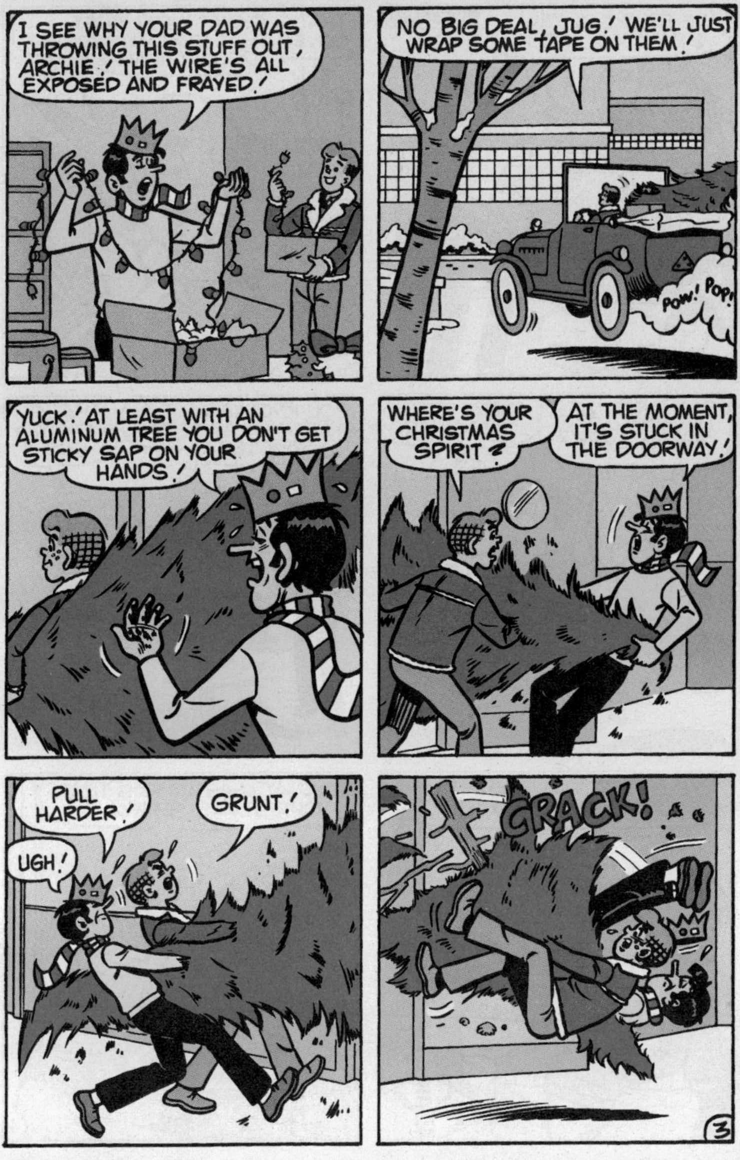
I SEE WHY YOUR DAD WAS THROWING THIS STUFF OUT, ARCHIE! THE WIRE'S ALL EXPOSED AND FRAYED!
NO BIG DEAL, JUG! WE'LL JUST WRAP SOME TAPE ON THEM!
POW! POP!
YUCK! AT LEAST WITH AN ALUMINUM TREE YOU DON'T GET STICKY SAP ON YOUR HANDS!
WHERE'S YOUR CHRISTMAS SPIRIT?
AT THE MOMENT, IT'S STUCK IN THE DOORWAY!
PULL HARDER!
GRUNT!
UGH!
CRACK!
3

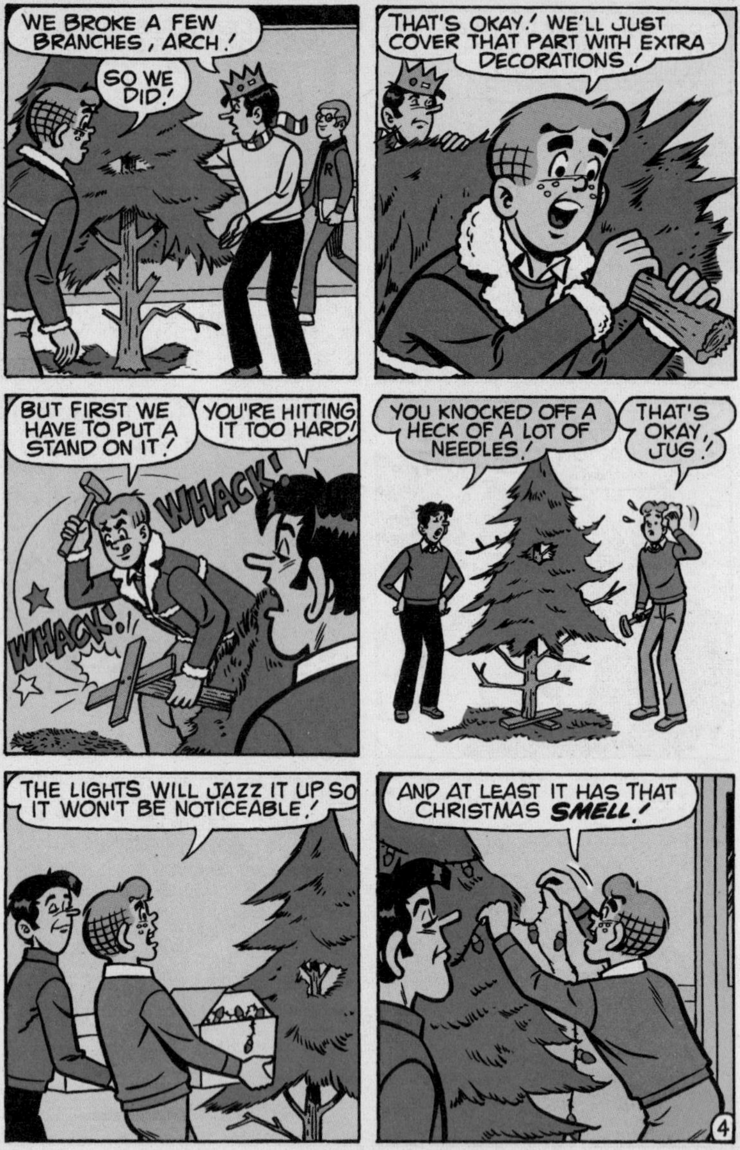
WE BROKE A FEW BRANCHES, ARCH!
SO WE DID!
THAT'S OKAY! WE'LL JUST COVER THAT PART WITH EXTRA DECORATIONS!
BUT FIRST WE HAVE TO PUT A STAND ON IT!
YOU'RE HITTING IT TOO HARD!
WHACK!
WHACK!
YOU KNOCKED OFF A HECK OF A LOT OF NEEDLES!
THAT'S OKAY, JUG!
THE LIGHTS WILL JAZZ IT UP SO IT WON'T BE NOTICEABLE!
AND AT LEAST IT HAS THAT CHRISTMAS **SMELL**!
4

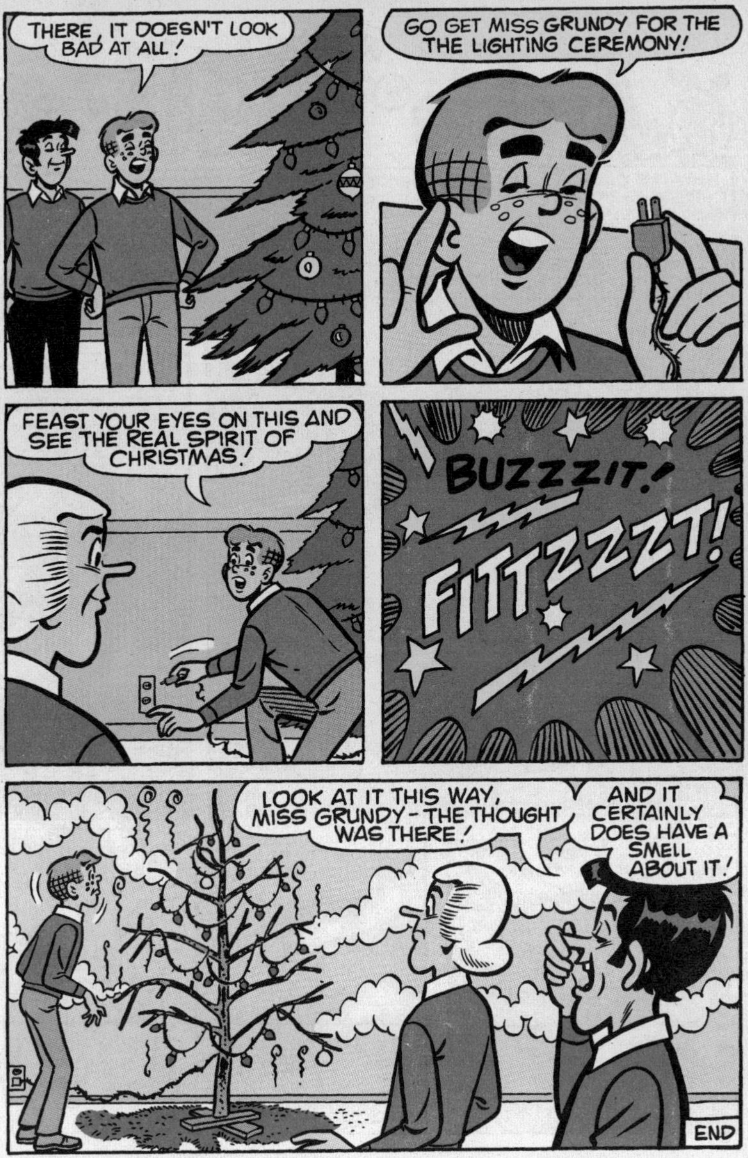
THERE, IT DOESN'T LOOK BAD AT ALL!
GO GET MISS GRUNDY FOR THE THE LIGHTING CEREMONY!
FEAST YOUR EYES ON THIS AND SEE THE REAL SPIRIT OF CHRISTMAS!
BUZZZIT!
FITTZZZZT!
LOOK AT IT THIS WAY, MISS GRUNDY - THE THOUGHT WAS THERE!
AND IT CERTAINLY DOES HAVE A SMELL ABOUT IT!
END

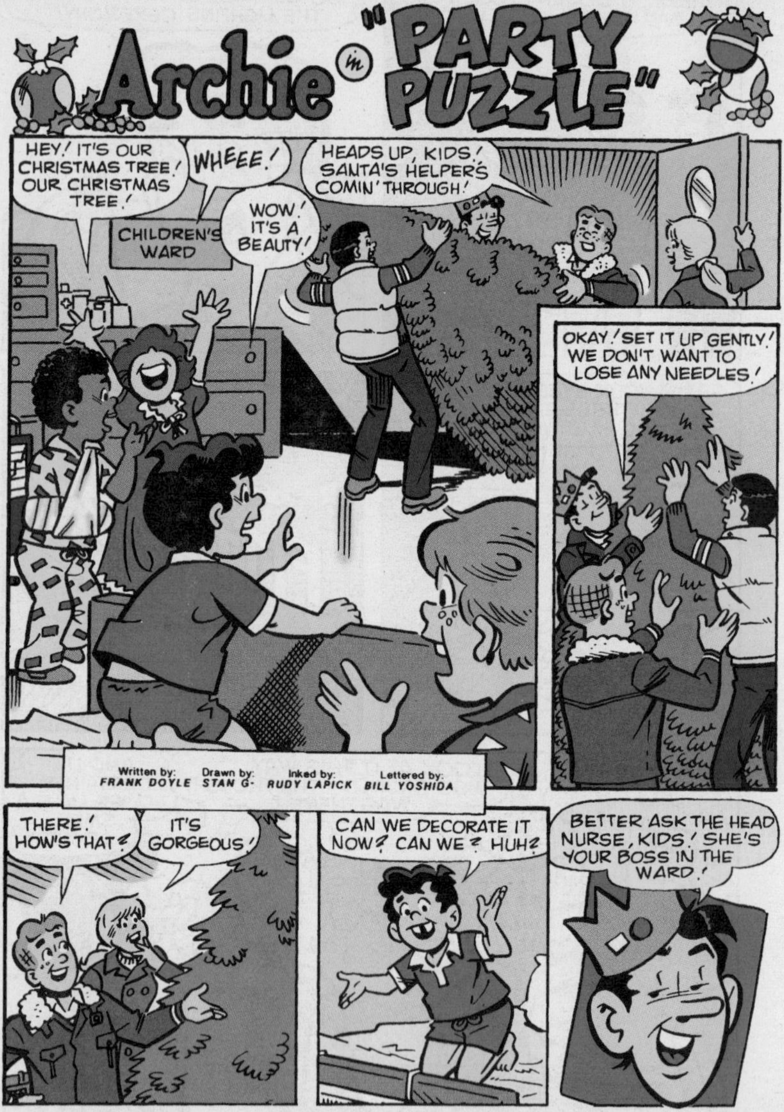
Archie in "PARTY PUZZLE"
HEY! IT'S OUR CHRISTMAS TREE! OUR CHRISTMAS TREE!
WHEEE!
HEADS UP, KIDS! SANTA'S HELPERS COMIN' THROUGH!
CHILDREN'S WARD
WOW! IT'S A BEAUTY!
OKAY! SET IT UP GENTLY! WE DON'T WANT TO LOSE ANY NEEDLES!
Written by: FRANK DOYLE
Drawn by: STAN G-
Inked by: RUDY LAPICK
Lettered by: BILL YOSHIDA
THERE! HOW'S THAT?
IT'S GORGEOUS!
CAN WE DECORATE IT NOW? CAN WE? HUH?
BETTER ASK THE HEAD NURSE, KIDS! SHE'S YOUR BOSS IN THE WARD!

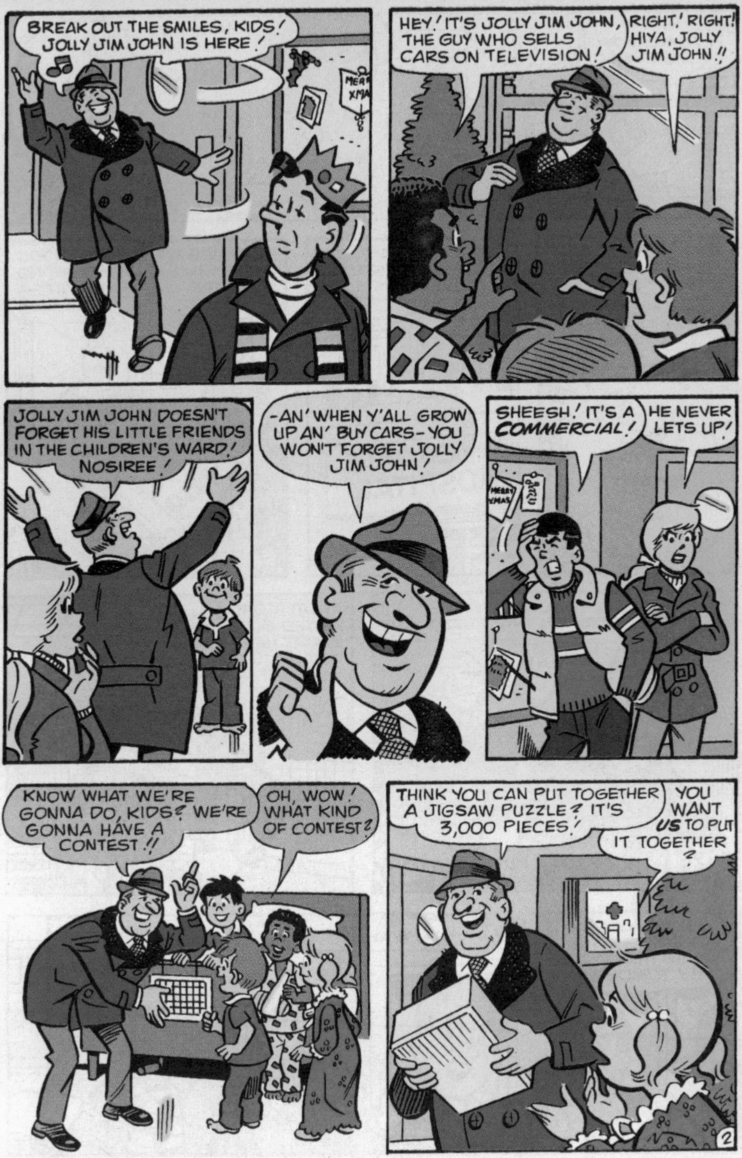
BREAK OUT THE SMILES, KIDS! JOLLY JIM JOHN IS HERE!
MERRY XMAS
HEY! IT'S JOLLY JIM JOHN, THE GUY WHO SELLS CARS ON TELEVISION!
RIGHT! RIGHT! HIYA, JOLLY JIM JOHN!!
JOLLY JIM JOHN DOESN'T FORGET HIS LITTLE FRIENDS IN THE CHILDREN'S WARD! NOSIREE!
-AN' WHEN Y'ALL GROW UP AN' BUY CARS- YOU WON'T FORGET JOLLY JIM JOHN!
SHEESH! IT'S A COMMERCIAL!
HE NEVER LETS UP!
MERRY XMAS
KNOW WHAT WE'RE GONNA DO, KIDS? WE'RE GONNA HAVE A CONTEST!!
OH, WOW! WHAT KIND OF CONTEST?
THINK YOU CAN PUT TOGETHER A JIGSAW PUZZLE? IT'S 3,000 PIECES!
YOU WANT US TO PUT IT TOGETHER?
2

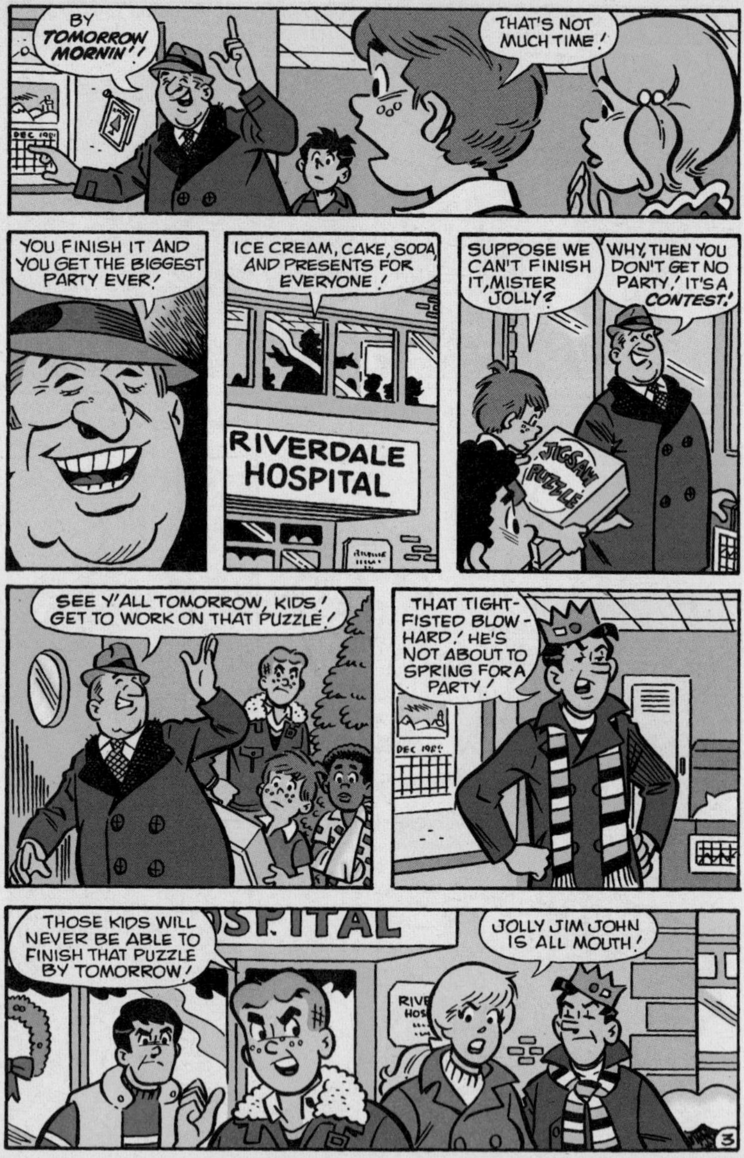
BY TOMORROW MORNIN'!
THAT'S NOT MUCH TIME!
YOU FINISH IT AND YOU GET THE BIGGEST PARTY EVER!
ICE CREAM, CAKE, SODA, AND PRESENTS FOR EVERYONE!
RIVERDALE HOSPITAL
SUPPOSE WE CAN'T FINISH IT, MISTER JOLLY?
WHY, THEN YOU DON'T GET NO PARTY! IT'S A CONTEST!
JIGSAW PUZZLE
SEE Y'ALL TOMORROW, KIDS! GET TO WORK ON THAT PUZZLE!
THAT TIGHT-FISTED BLOW-HARD! HE'S NOT ABOUT TO SPRING FOR A PARTY!
THOSE KIDS WILL NEVER BE ABLE TO FINISH THAT PUZZLE BY TOMORROW!
JOLLY JIM JOHN IS ALL MOUTH!
3

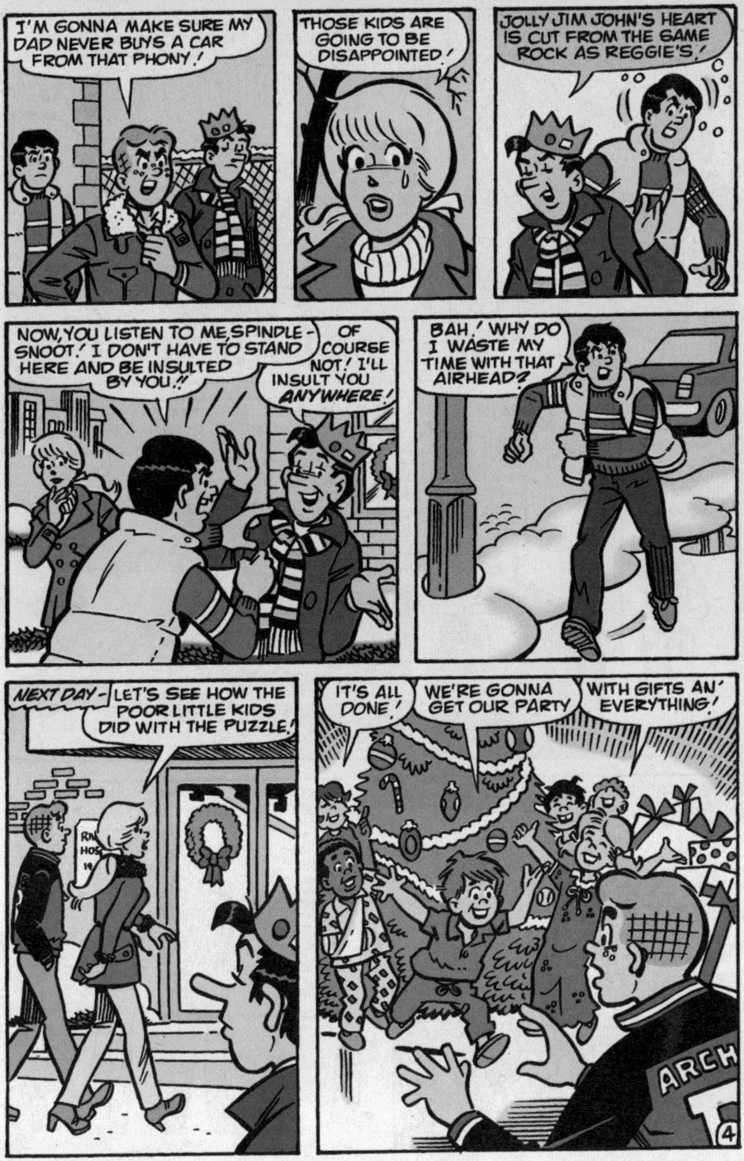
I'M GONNA MAKE SURE MY DAD NEVER BUYS A CAR FROM THAT PHONY!
THOSE KIDS ARE GOING TO BE DISAPPOINTED!
JOLLY JIM JOHN'S HEART IS CUT FROM THE SAME ROCK AS REGGIE'S!
NOW, YOU LISTEN TO ME, SPINDLE-SNOOT! I DON'T HAVE TO STAND HERE AND BE INSULTED BY YOU!!
OF COURSE NOT! I'LL INSULT YOU ANYWHERE!
BAH! WHY DO I WASTE MY TIME WITH THAT AIRHEAD?
NEXT DAY-
LET'S SEE HOW THE POOR LITTLE KIDS DID WITH THE PUZZLE!
IT'S ALL DONE!
WE'RE GONNA GET OUR PARTY
WITH GIFTS AN' EVERYTHING!
ARCH
4

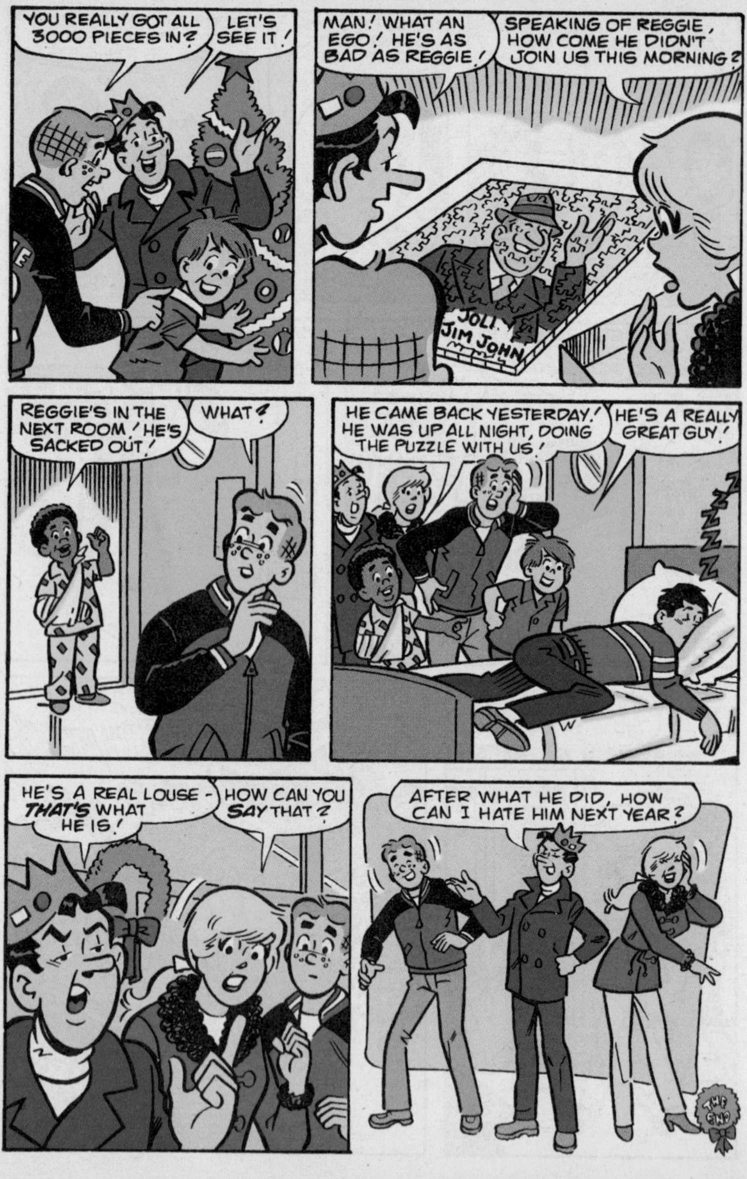
YOU REALLY GOT ALL 3000 PIECES IN?
LET'S SEE IT!
MAN! WHAT AN EGO! HE'S AS BAD AS REGGIE!
SPEAKING OF REGGIE, HOW COME HE DIDN'T JOIN US THIS MORNING?
JOLI. JIM JOHN
REGGIE'S IN THE NEXT ROOM! HE'S SACKED OUT!
WHAT?
HE CAME BACK YESTERDAY! HE WAS UP ALL NIGHT, DOING THE PUZZLE WITH US!
HE'S A REALLY GREAT GUY!
HE'S A REAL LOUSE - *THAT'S* WHAT HE IS!
HOW CAN YOU *SAY* THAT?
AFTER WHAT HE DID, HOW CAN I HATE HIM NEXT YEAR?
THE END

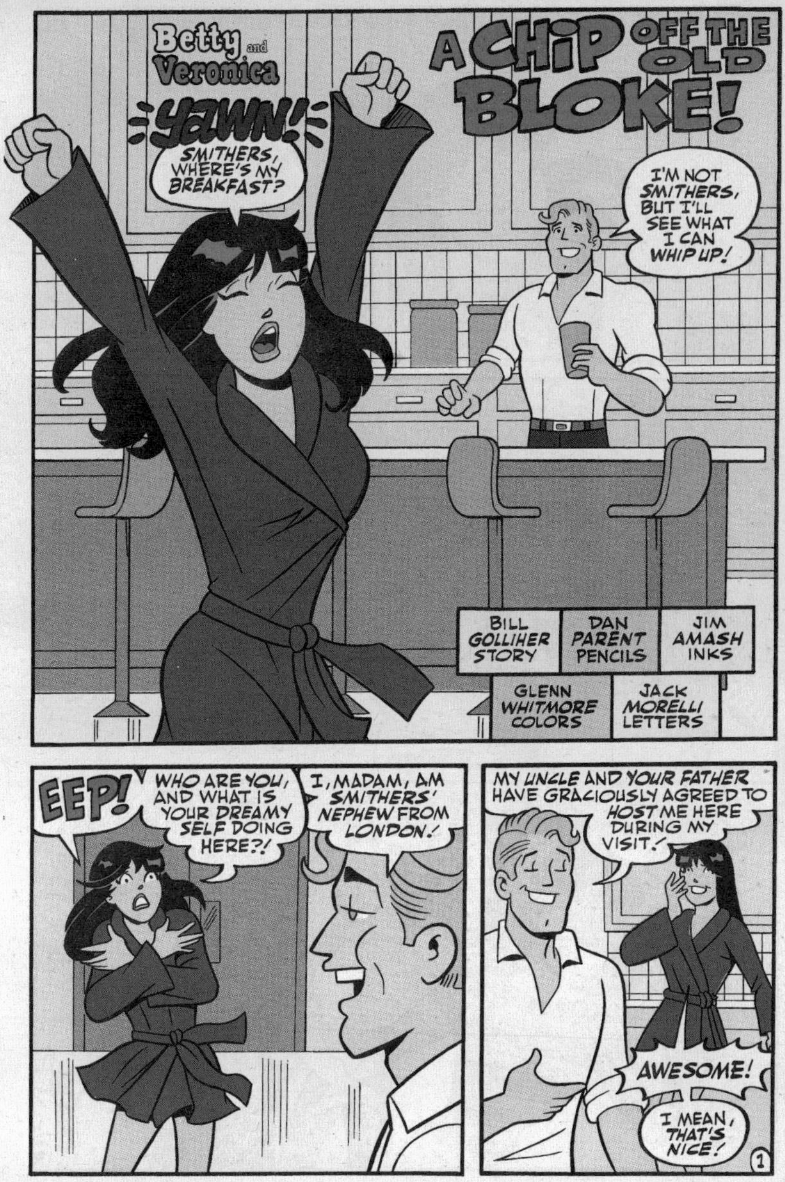
Betty and Veronica
A CHIP OFF THE OLD BLOKE!
YAWN!
SMITHERS, WHERE'S MY BREAKFAST?
I'M NOT SMITHERS, BUT I'LL SEE WHAT I CAN WHIP UP!
BILL GOLLIHER STORY
DAN PARENT PENCILS
JIM AMASH INKS
GLENN WHITMORE COLORS
JACK MORELLI LETTERS
EEP!
WHO ARE YOU, AND WHAT IS YOUR DREAMY SELF DOING HERE?!
I, MADAM, AM SMITHERS' NEPHEW FROM LONDON!
MY UNCLE AND YOUR FATHER HAVE GRACIOUSLY AGREED TO HOST ME HERE DURING MY VISIT!
AWESOME!
I MEAN, THAT'S NICE!
1

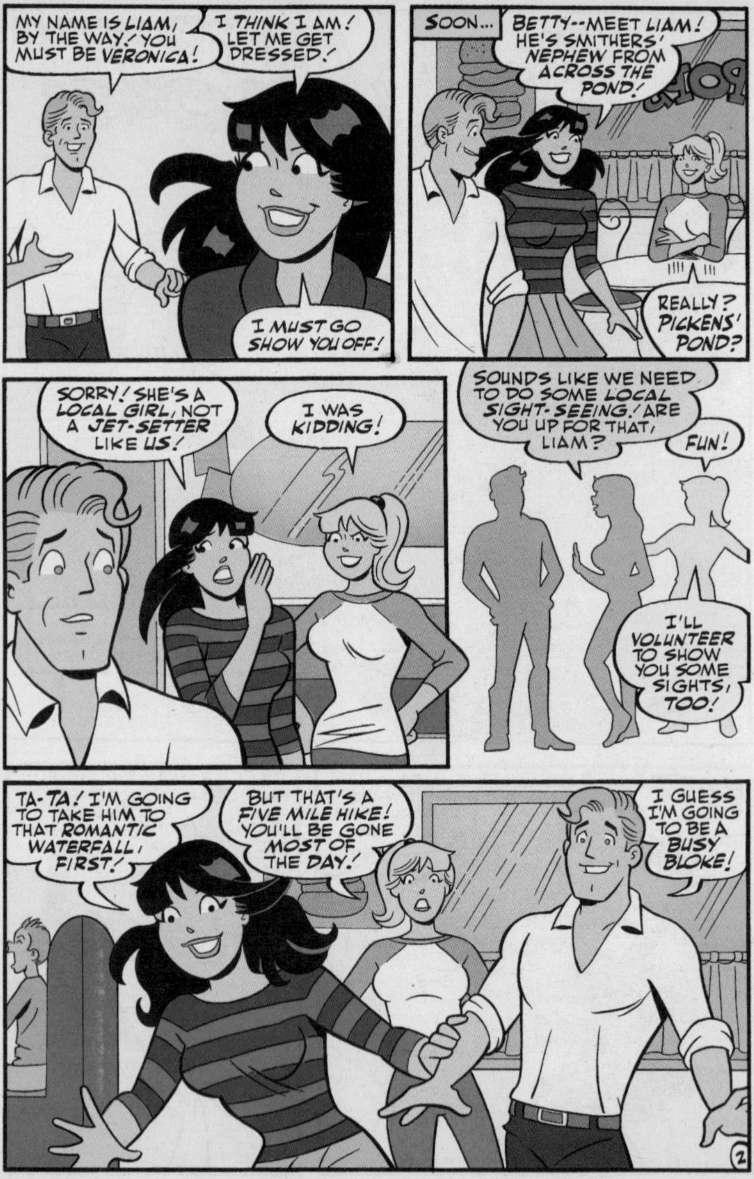
MY NAME IS LIAM, BY THE WAY! YOU MUST BE VERONICA!
I THINK I AM! LET ME GET DRESSED!
I MUST GO SHOW YOU OFF!
SOON...
BETTY--MEET LIAM! HE'S SMITHERS' NEPHEW FROM ACROSS THE POND!
REALLY? PICKENS' POND?
SORRY! SHE'S A LOCAL GIRL, NOT A JET-SETTER LIKE US!
I WAS KIDDING!
SOUNDS LIKE WE NEED TO DO SOME LOCAL SIGHT-SEEING! ARE YOU UP FOR THAT, LIAM?
FUN!
I'LL VOLUNTEER TO SHOW YOU SOME SIGHTS, TOO!
TA-TA! I'M GOING TO TAKE HIM TO THAT ROMANTIC WATERFALL, FIRST!
BUT THAT'S A FIVE MILE HIKE! YOU'LL BE GONE MOST OF THE DAY!
I GUESS I'M GOING TO BE A BUSY BLOKE!
2

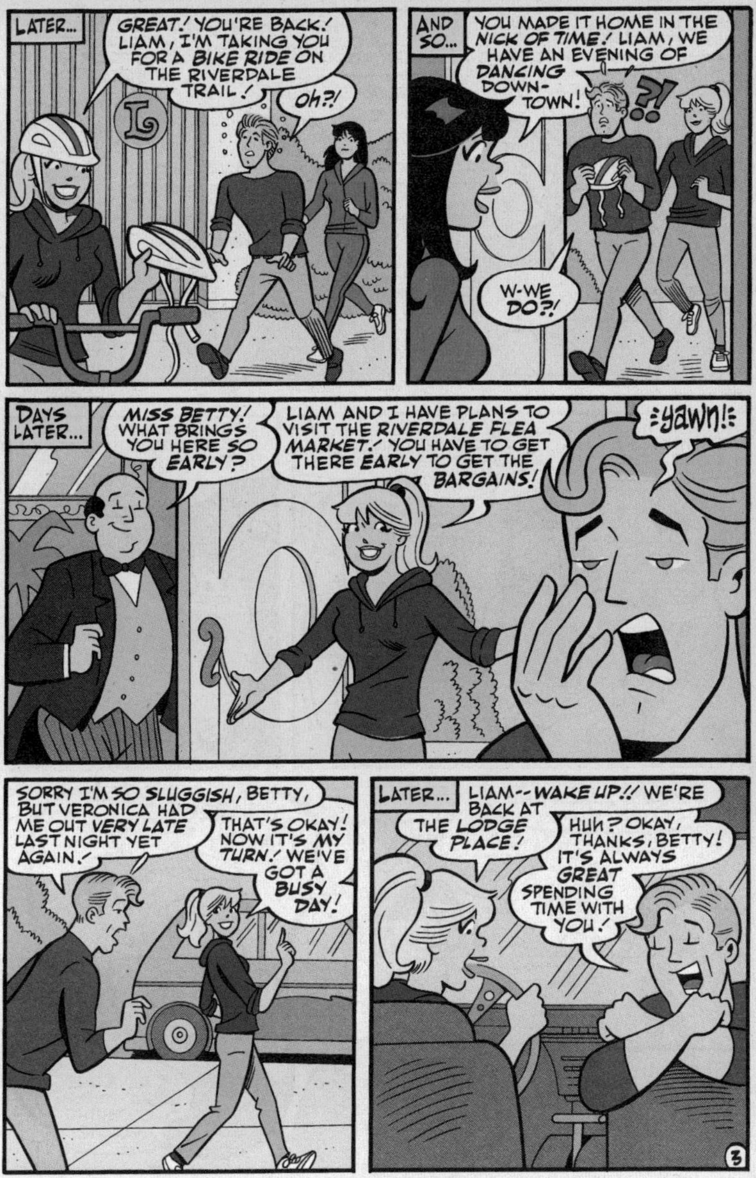
LATER...
GREAT! YOU'RE BACK! LIAM, I'M TAKING YOU FOR A BIKE RIDE ON THE RIVERDALE TRAIL!
Oh?!
AND SO...
YOU MADE IT HOME IN THE NICK OF TIME! LIAM, WE HAVE AN EVENING OF DANCING DOWN-TOWN!
?!
W-WE DO?!
DAYS LATER...
MISS BETTY! WHAT BRINGS YOU HERE SO EARLY?
LIAM AND I HAVE PLANS TO VISIT THE RIVERDALE FLEA MARKET! YOU HAVE TO GET THERE EARLY TO GET THE BARGAINS!
YAWN!
SORRY I'M SO SLUGGISH, BETTY, BUT VERONICA HAD ME OUT VERY LATE LAST NIGHT YET AGAIN!
THAT'S OKAY! NOW IT'S MY TURN! WE'VE GOT A BUSY DAY!
LATER...
LIAM--WAKE UP!! WE'RE BACK AT THE LODGE PLACE!
HUH? OKAY, THANKS, BETTY! IT'S ALWAYS GREAT SPENDING TIME WITH YOU!
3

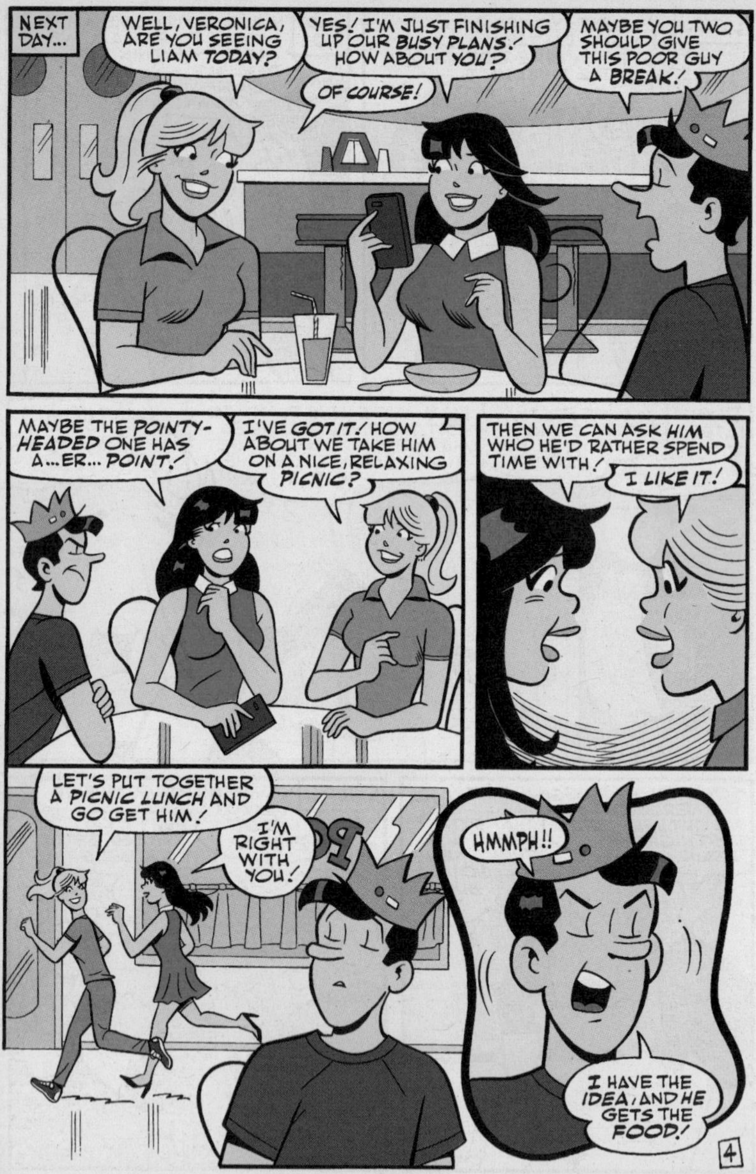
NEXT DAY...
WELL, VERONICA, ARE YOU SEEING LIAM TODAY?
YES! I'M JUST FINISHING UP OUR BUSY PLANS! HOW ABOUT YOU?
OF COURSE!
MAYBE YOU TWO SHOULD GIVE THIS POOR GUY A BREAK!
MAYBE THE POINTY-HEADED ONE HAS A...ER... POINT!
I'VE GOT IT! HOW ABOUT WE TAKE HIM ON A NICE, RELAXING PICNIC?
THEN WE CAN ASK HIM WHO HE'D RATHER SPEND TIME WITH!
I LIKE IT!
LET'S PUT TOGETHER A PICNIC LUNCH AND GO GET HIM!
I'M RIGHT WITH YOU!
HMMPH!!
I HAVE THE IDEA, AND HE GETS THE FOOD!
4

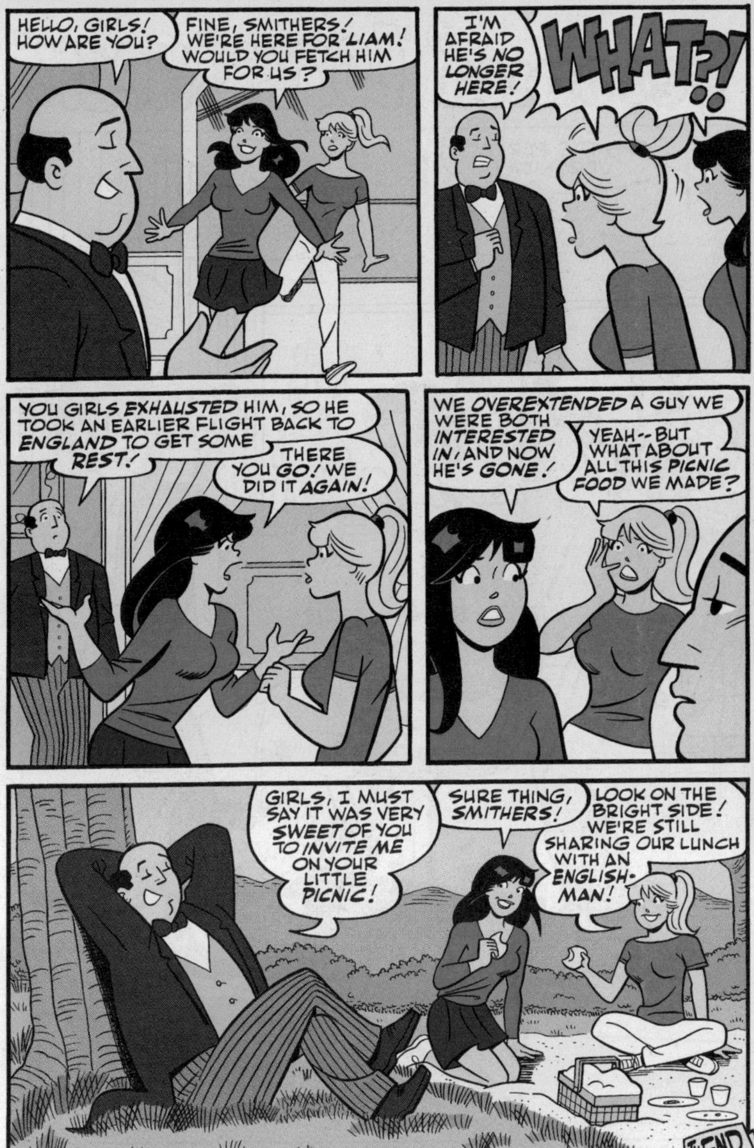
HELLO, GIRLS! HOW ARE YOU?
FINE, SMITHERS! WE'RE HERE FOR LIAM! WOULD YOU FETCH HIM FOR US?
I'M AFRAID HE'S NO LONGER HERE!
WHAT?!
YOU GIRLS EXHAUSTED HIM, SO HE TOOK AN EARLIER FLIGHT BACK TO ENGLAND TO GET SOME REST!
THERE YOU GO! WE DID IT AGAIN!
WE OVEREXTENDED A GUY WE WERE BOTH INTERESTED IN, AND NOW HE'S GONE!
YEAH--BUT WHAT ABOUT ALL THIS PICNIC FOOD WE MADE?
GIRLS, I MUST SAY IT WAS VERY SWEET OF YOU TO INVITE ME ON YOUR LITTLE PICNIC!
SURE THING, SMITHERS!
LOOK ON THE BRIGHT SIDE! WE'RE STILL SHARING OUR LUNCH WITH AN ENGLISH-MAN!
THE END

Veronica in "Lock Shock"

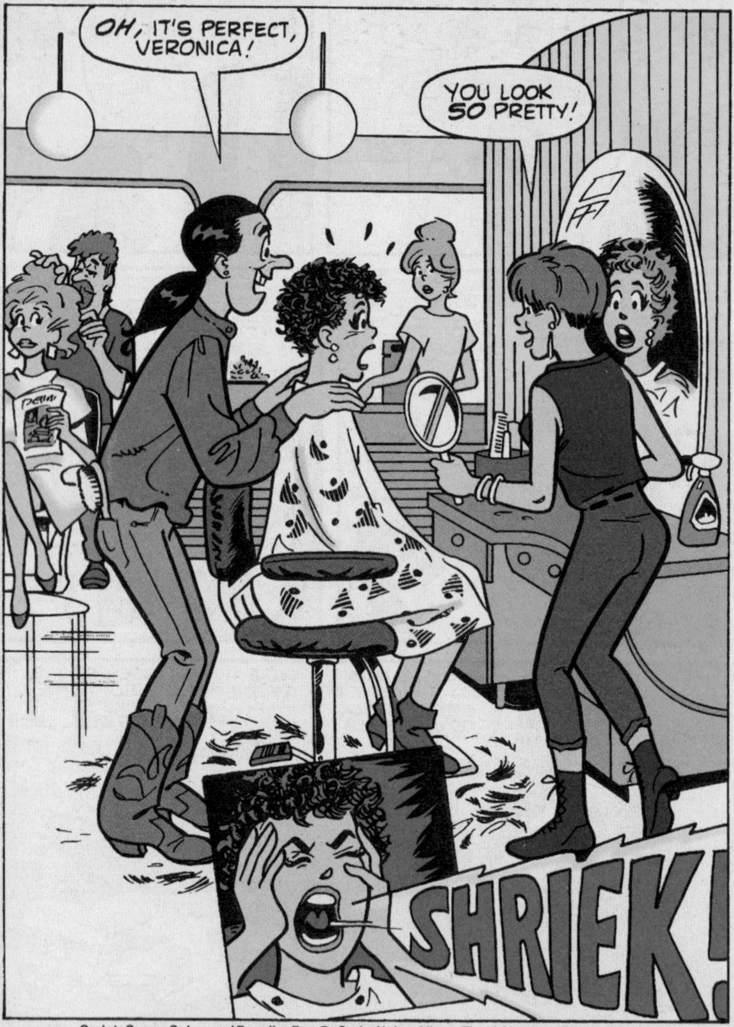

OH, IT'S PERFECT, VERONICA!
YOU LOOK SO PRETTY!
SHRIEK!

Script: Susan Solomon / Pencils: Dan DeCarlo / Inks: Alison Flood / Letters: Bill Yoshida

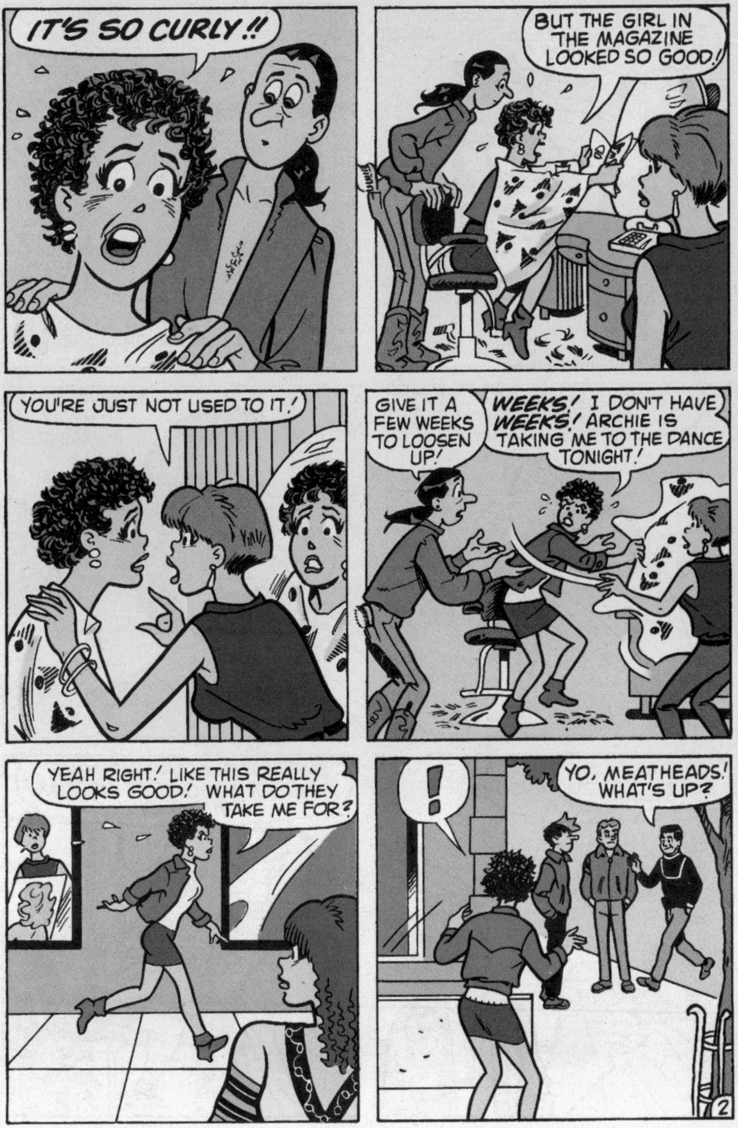
IT'S SO CURLY!!
BUT THE GIRL IN THE MAGAZINE LOOKED SO GOOD!
YOU'RE JUST NOT USED TO IT!
GIVE IT A FEW WEEKS TO LOOSEN UP!
WEEKS! I DON'T HAVE WEEKS! ARCHIE IS TAKING ME TO THE DANCE TONIGHT!
YEAH RIGHT! LIKE THIS REALLY LOOKS GOOD! WHAT DO THEY TAKE ME FOR?
!
YO, MEATHEADS! WHAT'S UP?
2

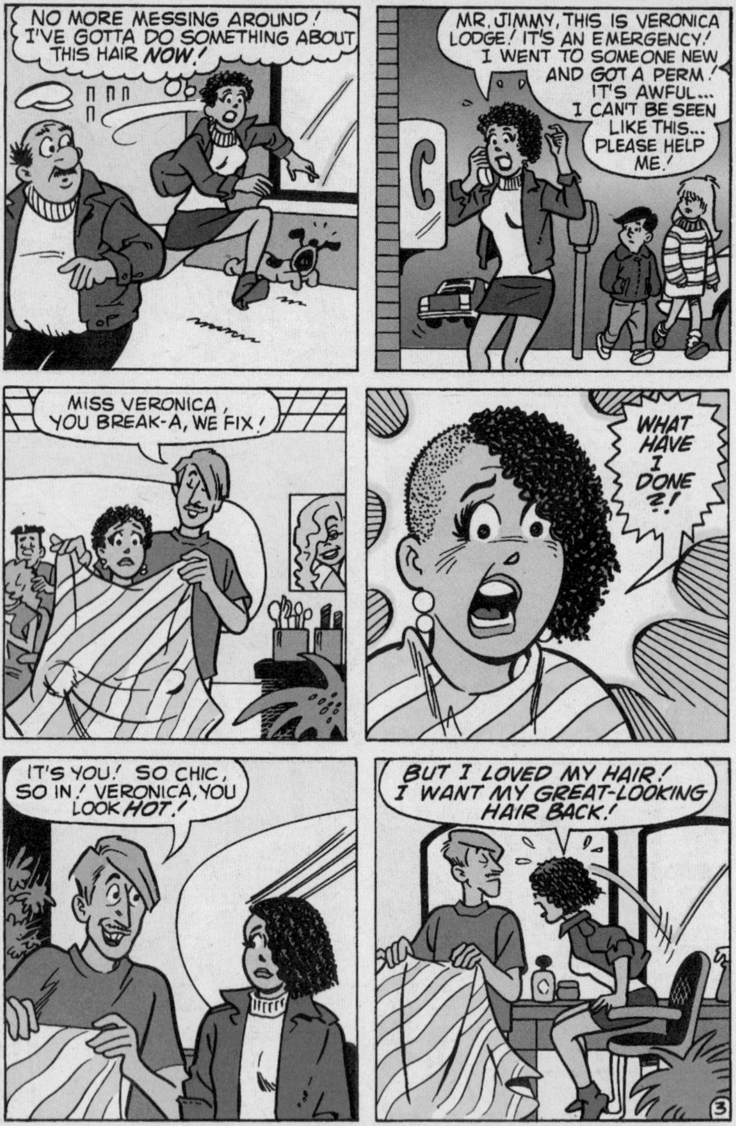
NO MORE MESSING AROUND! I'VE GOTTA DO SOMETHING ABOUT THIS HAIR NOW!
MR. JIMMY, THIS IS VERONICA LODGE! IT'S AN EMERGENCY! I WENT TO SOMEONE NEW AND GOT A PERM! IT'S AWFUL... I CAN'T BE SEEN LIKE THIS... PLEASE HELP ME!
MISS VERONICA, YOU BREAK-A, WE FIX!
WHAT HAVE I DONE ?!
IT'S YOU! SO CHIC, SO IN! VERONICA, YOU LOOK HOT!
BUT I LOVED MY HAIR! I WANT MY GREAT-LOOKING HAIR BACK!
3

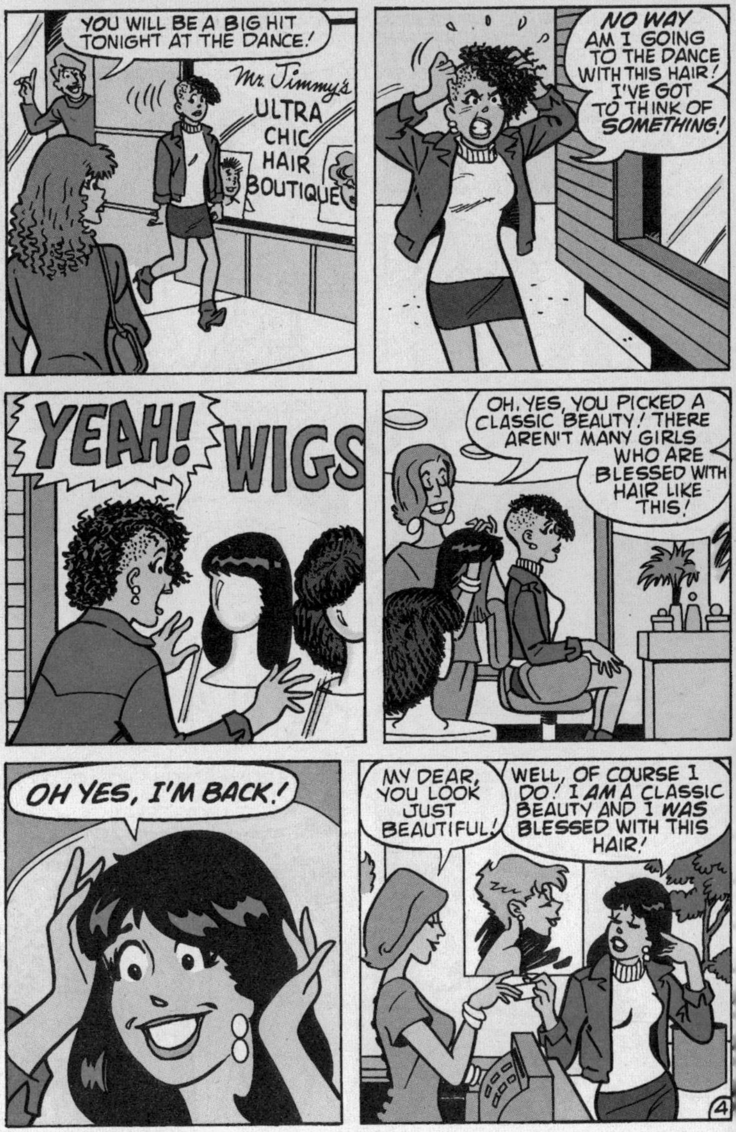
YOU WILL BE A BIG HIT TONIGHT AT THE DANCE!
Mr. Jimmy's ULTRA CHIC HAIR BOUTIQUE
NO WAY AM I GOING TO THE DANCE WITH THIS HAIR! I'VE GOT TO THINK OF SOMETHING!
YEAH!
WIGS
OH, YES, YOU PICKED A CLASSIC BEAUTY! THERE AREN'T MANY GIRLS WHO ARE BLESSED WITH HAIR LIKE THIS!
OH YES, I'M BACK!
MY DEAR, YOU LOOK JUST BEAUTIFUL!
WELL, OF COURSE I DO! I AM A CLASSIC BEAUTY AND I WAS BLESSED WITH THIS HAIR!
4

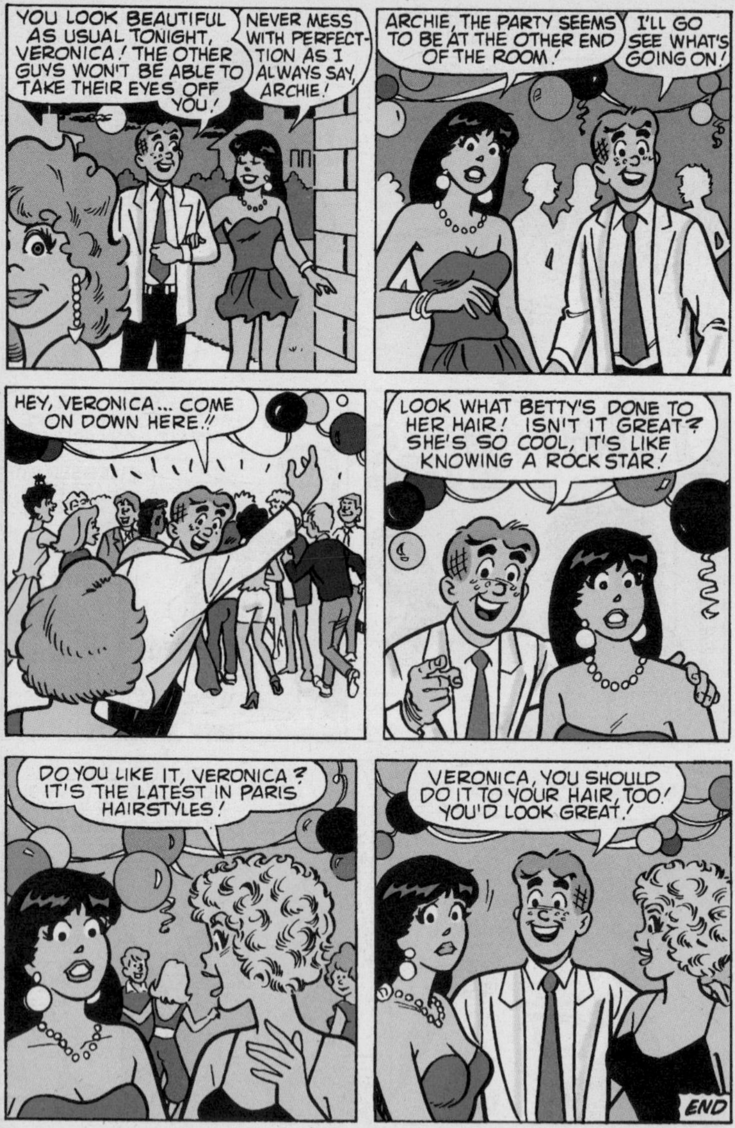
YOU LOOK BEAUTIFUL AS USUAL TONIGHT, VERONICA! THE OTHER GUYS WON'T BE ABLE TO TAKE THEIR EYES OFF YOU!
NEVER MESS WITH PERFECTION AS I ALWAYS SAY, ARCHIE!
ARCHIE, THE PARTY SEEMS TO BE AT THE OTHER END OF THE ROOM!
I'LL GO SEE WHAT'S GOING ON!
HEY, VERONICA... COME ON DOWN HERE!!
LOOK WHAT BETTY'S DONE TO HER HAIR! ISN'T IT GREAT? SHE'S SO COOL, IT'S LIKE KNOWING A ROCK STAR!
DO YOU LIKE IT, VERONICA? IT'S THE LATEST IN PARIS HAIRSTYLES!
VERONICA, YOU SHOULD DO IT TO YOUR HAIR, TOO! YOU'D LOOK GREAT!
END

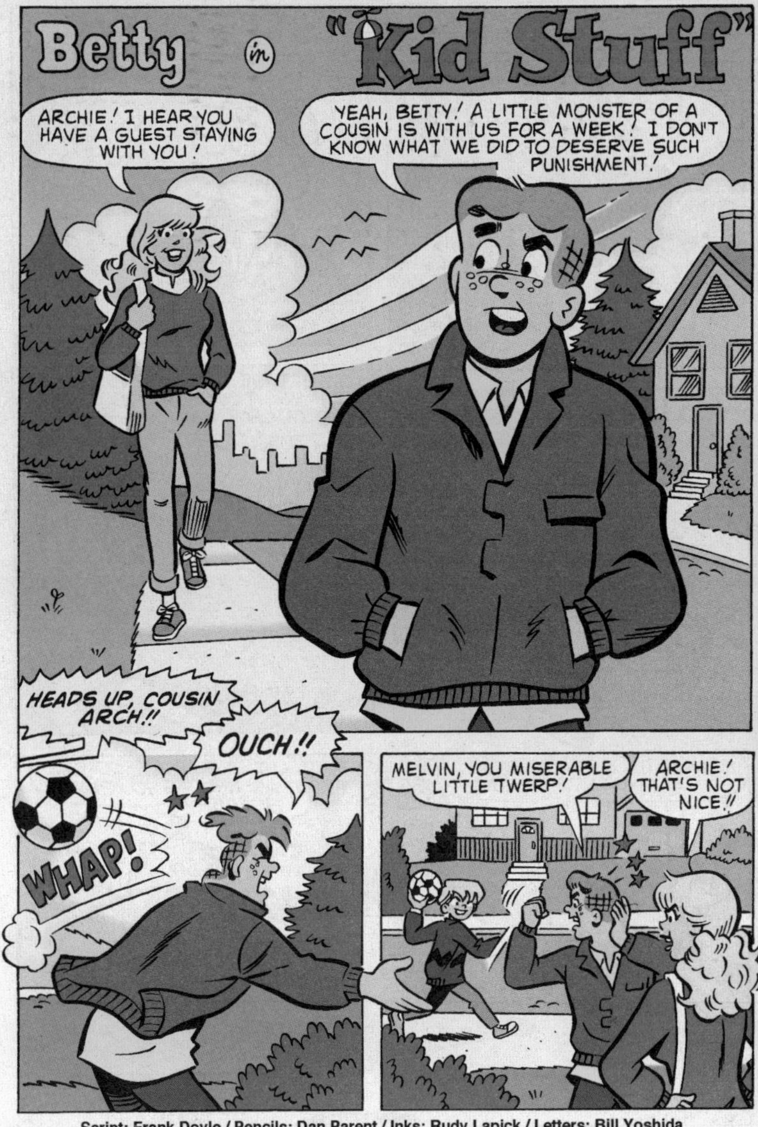
Betty in "Kid Stuff"
ARCHIE! I HEAR YOU HAVE A GUEST STAYING WITH YOU!
YEAH, BETTY! A LITTLE MONSTER OF A COUSIN IS WITH US FOR A WEEK! I DON'T KNOW WHAT WE DID TO DESERVE SUCH PUNISHMENT!
HEADS UP, COUSIN ARCH!!
OUCH!!
WHAP!
MELVIN, YOU MISERABLE LITTLE TWERP!
ARCHIE! THAT'S NOT NICE!!

Script: Frank Doyle / Pencils: Dan Parent / Inks: Rudy Lapick / Letters: Bill Yoshida

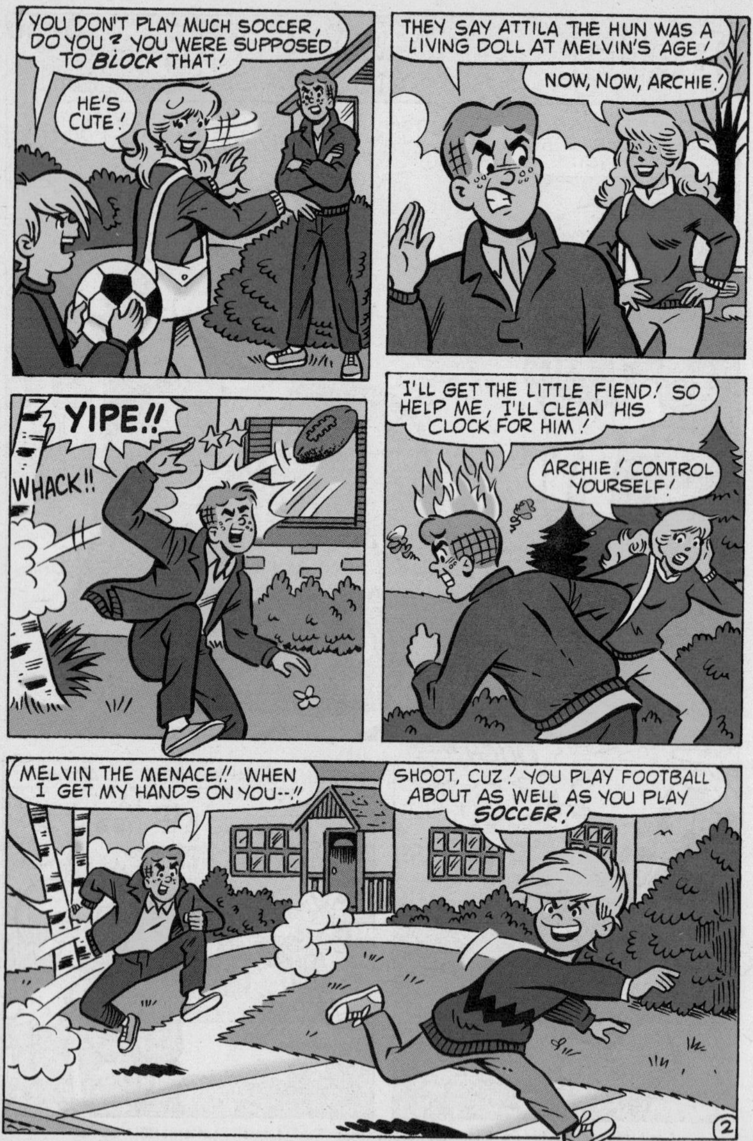
YOU DON'T PLAY MUCH SOCCER, DO YOU? YOU WERE SUPPOSED TO BLOCK THAT!
HE'S CUTE!
THEY SAY ATTILA THE HUN WAS A LIVING DOLL AT MELVIN'S AGE!
NOW, NOW, ARCHIE!
YIPE!!
WHACK!!
I'LL GET THE LITTLE FIEND! SO HELP ME, I'LL CLEAN HIS CLOCK FOR HIM!
ARCHIE! CONTROL YOURSELF!
MELVIN THE MENACE!! WHEN I GET MY HANDS ON YOU--!!
SHOOT, CUZ! YOU PLAY FOOTBALL ABOUT AS WELL AS YOU PLAY SOCCER!
2

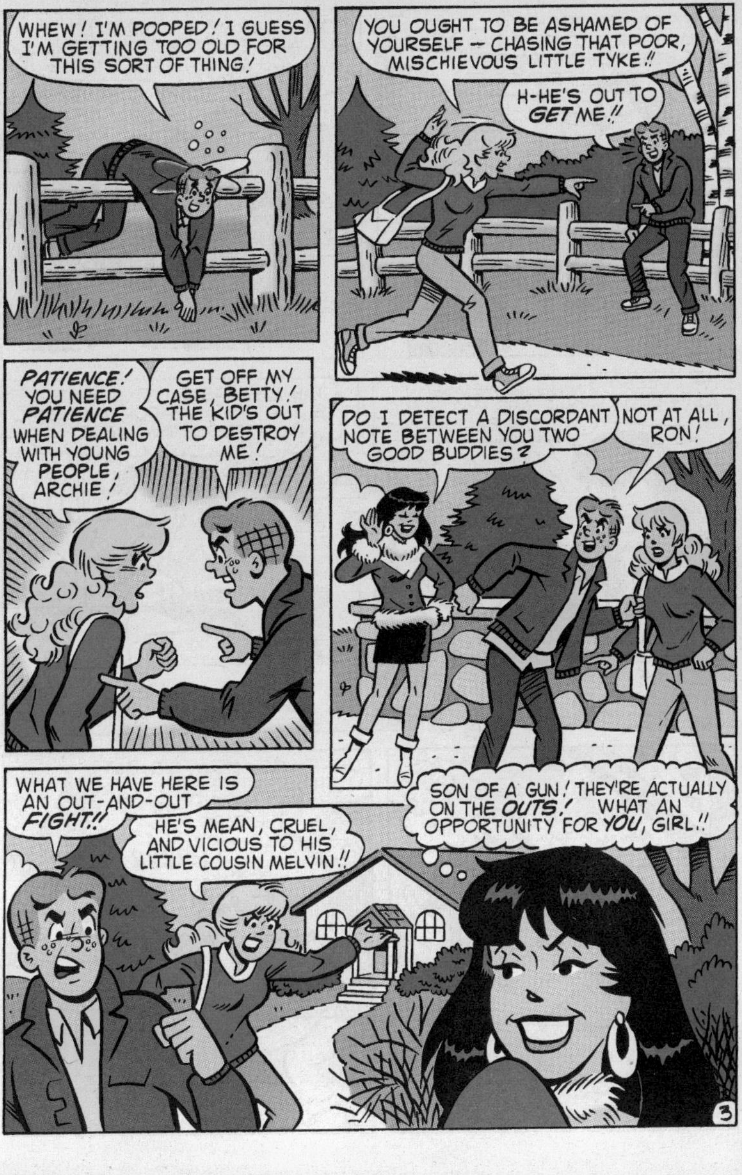
WHEW! I'M POOPED! I GUESS I'M GETTING TOO OLD FOR THIS SORT OF THING!
YOU OUGHT TO BE ASHAMED OF YOURSELF -- CHASING THAT POOR, MISCHIEVOUS LITTLE TYKE!!
H-HE'S OUT TO GET ME!!
PATIENCE! YOU NEED PATIENCE WHEN DEALING WITH YOUNG PEOPLE, ARCHIE!
GET OFF MY CASE, BETTY! THE KID'S OUT TO DESTROY ME!
DO I DETECT A DISCORDANT NOTE BETWEEN YOU TWO GOOD BUDDIES?
NOT AT ALL, RON!
WHAT WE HAVE HERE IS AN OUT-AND-OUT FIGHT!!
HE'S MEAN, CRUEL, AND VICIOUS TO HIS LITTLE COUSIN MELVIN!!
SON OF A GUN! THEY'RE ACTUALLY ON THE OUTS! WHAT AN OPPORTUNITY FOR YOU, GIRL!!
3

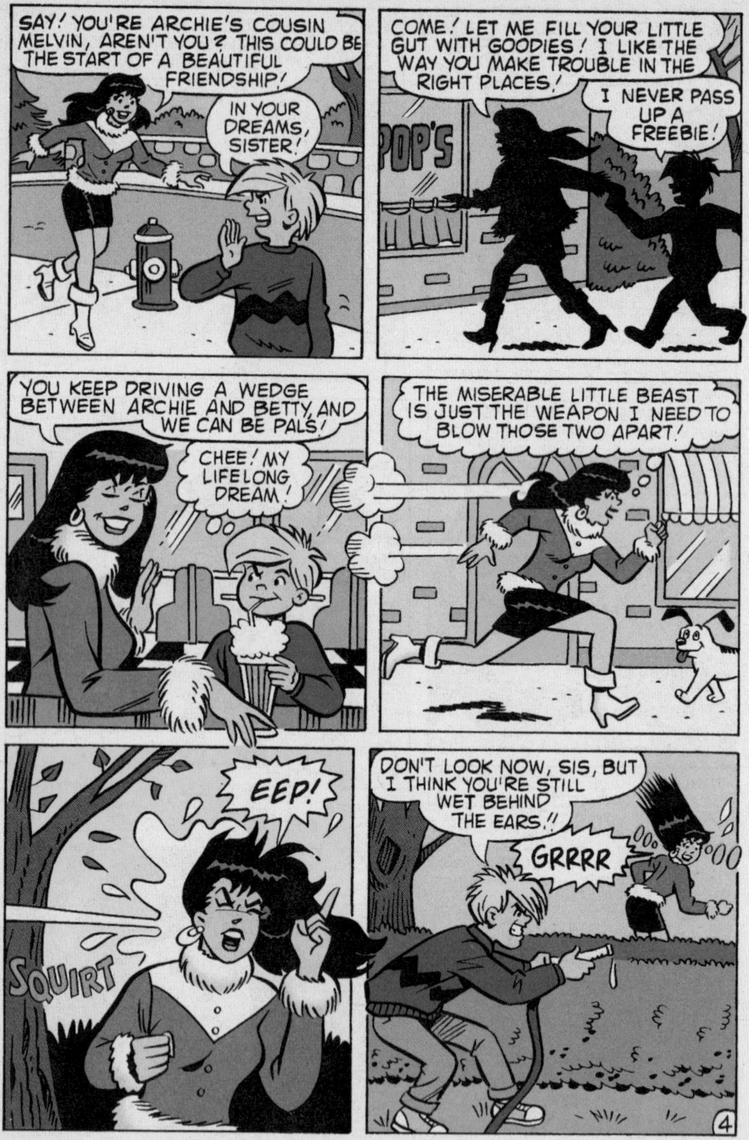
SAY! YOU'RE ARCHIE'S COUSIN MELVIN, AREN'T YOU? THIS COULD BE THE START OF A BEAUTIFUL FRIENDSHIP!
IN YOUR DREAMS, SISTER!
COME! LET ME FILL YOUR LITTLE GUT WITH GOODIES! I LIKE THE WAY YOU MAKE TROUBLE IN THE RIGHT PLACES!
I NEVER PASS UP A FREEBIE!
POP'S
YOU KEEP DRIVING A WEDGE BETWEEN ARCHIE AND BETTY, AND WE CAN BE PALS!
CHEE! MY LIFELONG DREAM!
THE MISERABLE LITTLE BEAST IS JUST THE WEAPON I NEED TO BLOW THOSE TWO APART!
EEP!
SQUIRT
DON'T LOOK NOW, SIS, BUT I THINK YOU'RE STILL WET BEHIND THE EARS!!
GRRRR
4

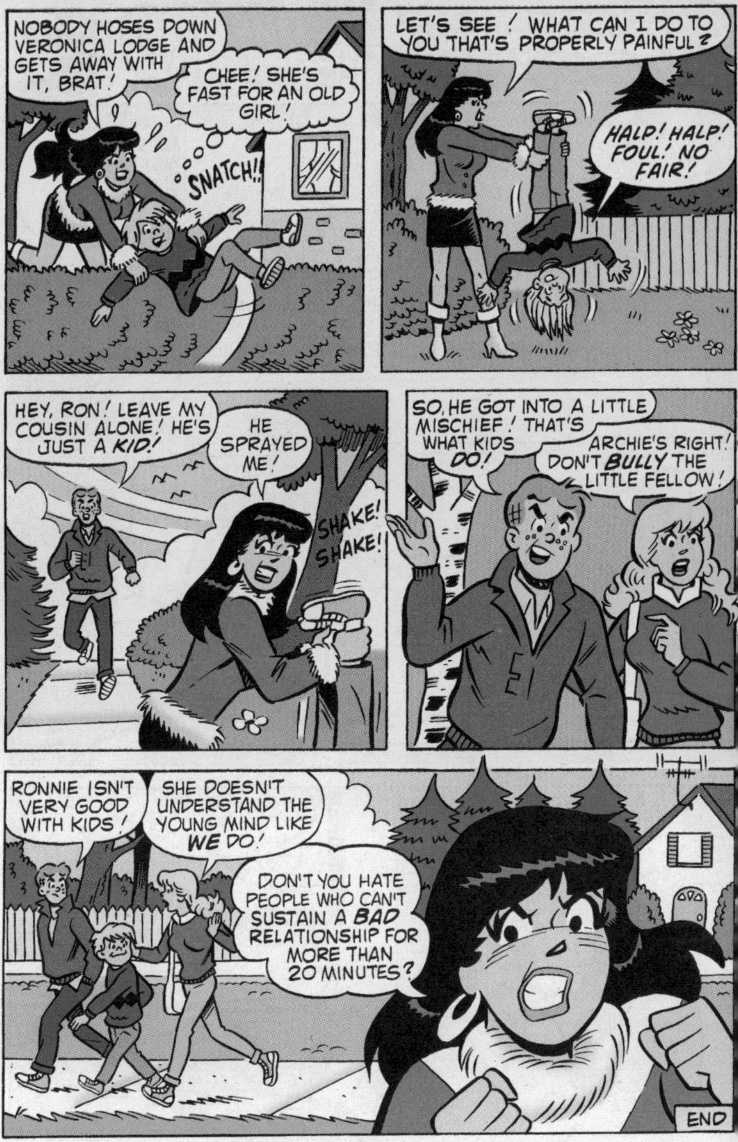

NOBODY HOSES DOWN VERONICA LODGE AND GETS AWAY WITH IT, BRAT!
CHEE! SHE'S FAST FOR AN OLD GIRL!
SNATCH!!
LET'S SEE! WHAT CAN I DO TO YOU THAT'S PROPERLY PAINFUL?
HALP! HALP! FOUL! NO FAIR!
HEY, RON! LEAVE MY COUSIN ALONE! HE'S JUST A KID!
HE SPRAYED ME!
SHAKE! SHAKE!
SO, HE GOT INTO A LITTLE MISCHIEF! THAT'S WHAT KIDS DO!
ARCHIE'S RIGHT! DON'T BULLY THE LITTLE FELLOW!
RONNIE ISN'T VERY GOOD WITH KIDS!
SHE DOESN'T UNDERSTAND THE YOUNG MIND LIKE WE DO!
DON'T YOU HATE PEOPLE WHO CAN'T SUSTAIN A BAD RELATIONSHIP FOR MORE THAN 20 MINUTES?
END

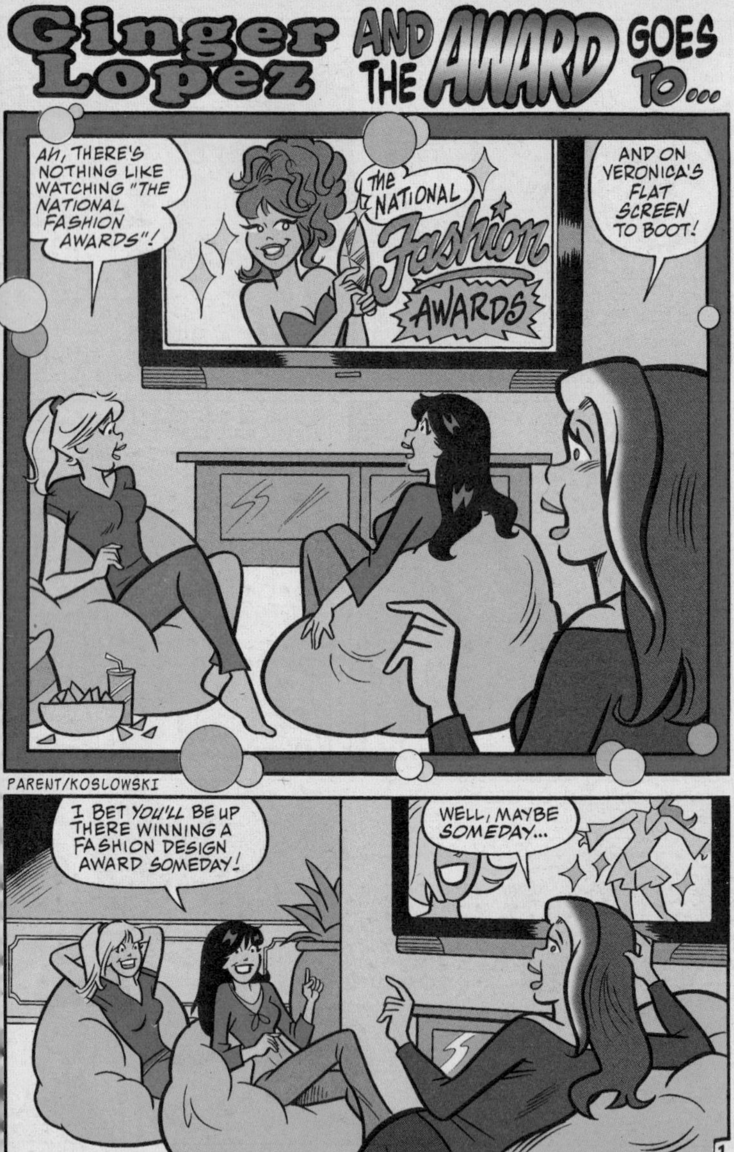
Ginger Lopez
AND THE AWARD GOES TO...
AH, THERE'S NOTHING LIKE WATCHING "THE NATIONAL FASHION AWARDS"!
The NATIONAL Fashion AWARDS
AND ON VERONICA'S FLAT SCREEN TO BOOT!
PARENT/KOSLOWSKI
I BET YOU'LL BE UP THERE WINNING A FASHION DESIGN AWARD SOMEDAY!
WELL, MAYBE SOMEDAY...
1

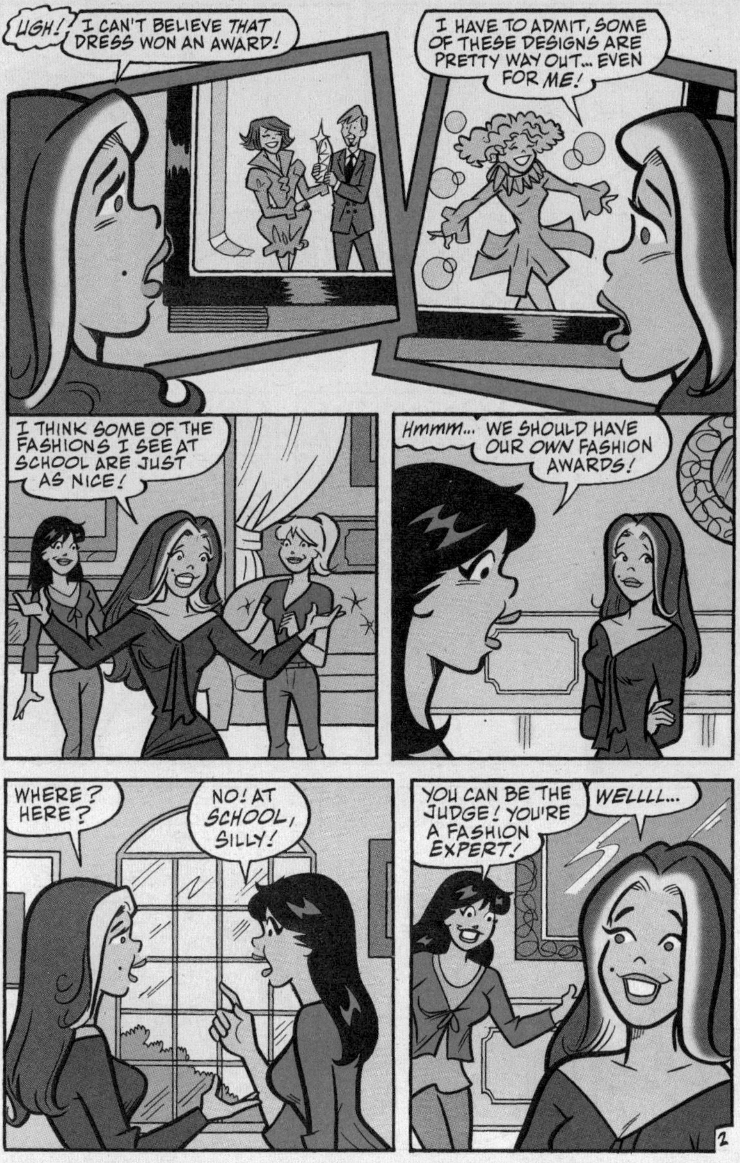
UGH!
I CAN'T BELIEVE THAT DRESS WON AN AWARD!
I HAVE TO ADMIT, SOME OF THESE DESIGNS ARE PRETTY WAY OUT... EVEN FOR ME!
I THINK SOME OF THE FASHIONS I SEE AT SCHOOL ARE JUST AS NICE!
Hmmm...
WE SHOULD HAVE OUR OWN FASHION AWARDS!
WHERE? HERE?
NO! AT SCHOOL, SILLY!
YOU CAN BE THE JUDGE! YOU'RE A FASHION EXPERT!
WELLLL...
2

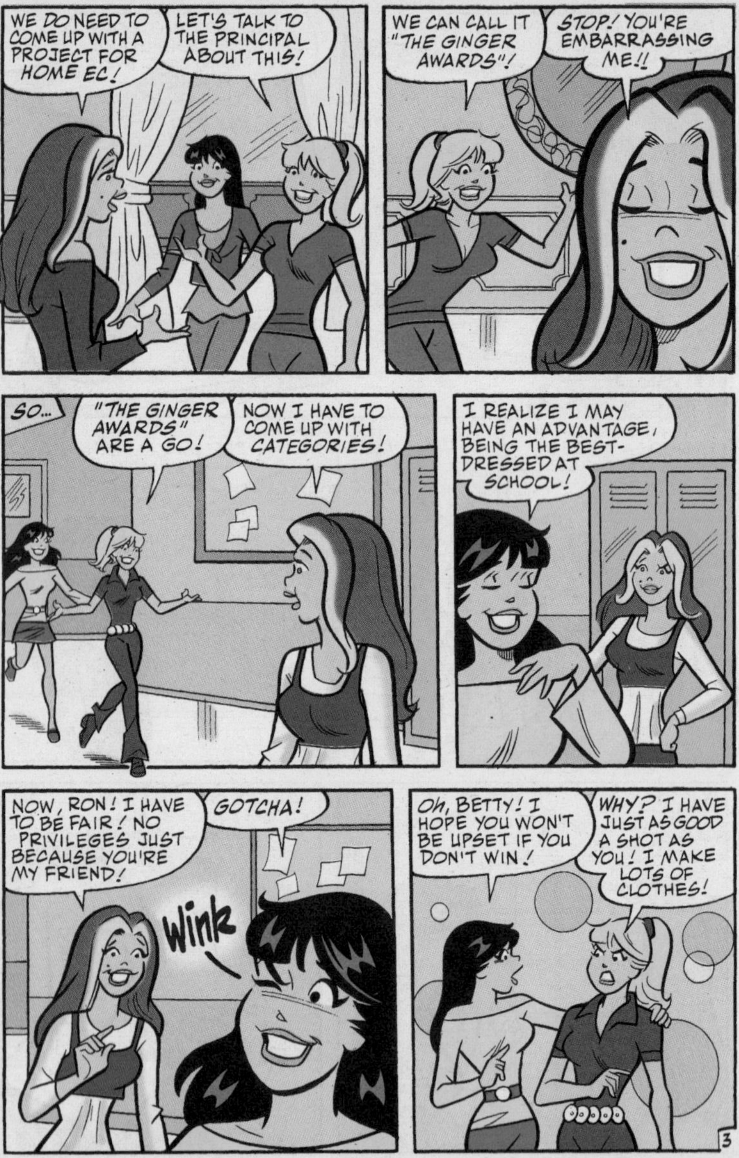
WE DO NEED TO COME UP WITH A PROJECT FOR HOME EC!
LET'S TALK TO THE PRINCIPAL ABOUT THIS!
WE CAN CALL IT "THE GINGER AWARDS"!
STOP! YOU'RE EMBARRASSING ME!!
SO...
"THE GINGER AWARDS" ARE A GO!
NOW I HAVE TO COME UP WITH CATEGORIES!
I REALIZE I MAY HAVE AN ADVANTAGE, BEING THE BEST-DRESSED AT SCHOOL!
NOW, RON! I HAVE TO BE FAIR! NO PRIVILEGES JUST BECAUSE YOU'RE MY FRIEND!
GOTCHA!
Wink
Oh, BETTY! I HOPE YOU WON'T BE UPSET IF YOU DON'T WIN!
WHY? I HAVE JUST AS GOOD A SHOT AS YOU! I MAKE LOTS OF CLOTHES!
3

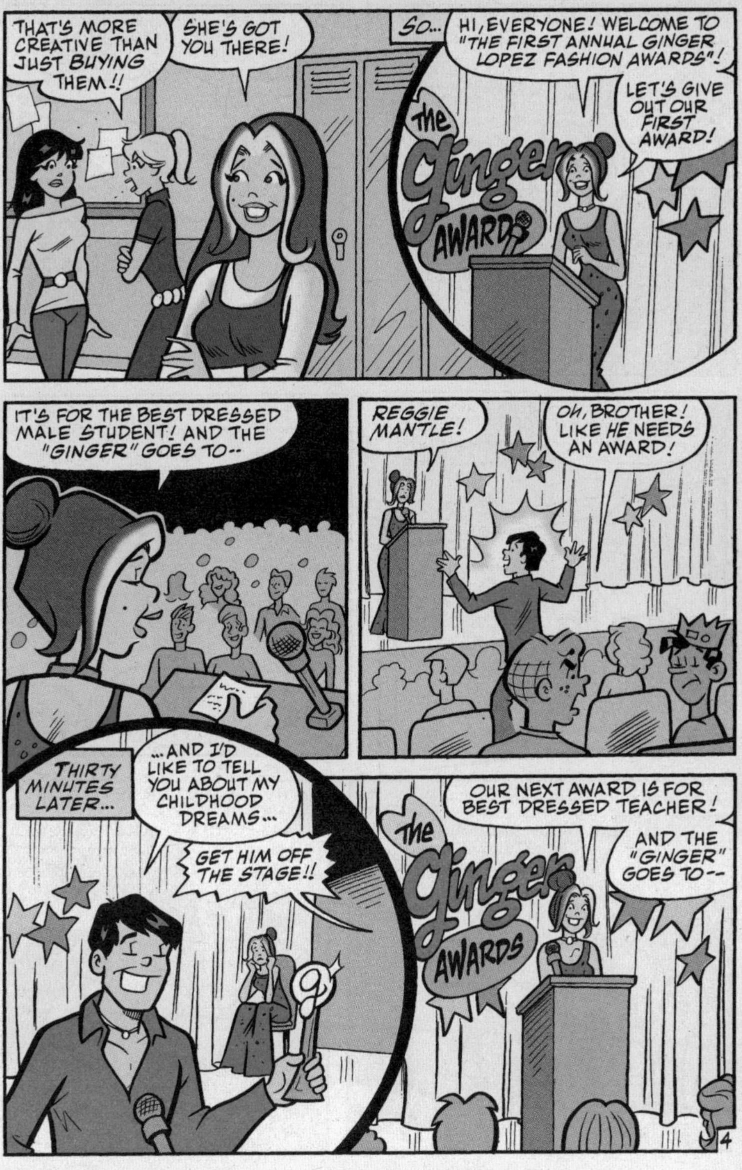
THAT'S MORE CREATIVE THAN JUST BUYING THEM!!
SHE'S GOT YOU THERE!
SO...
HI, EVERYONE! WELCOME TO "THE FIRST ANNUAL GINGER LOPEZ FASHION AWARDS"!
LET'S GIVE OUT OUR FIRST AWARD!
The Ginger AWARDS
IT'S FOR THE BEST DRESSED MALE STUDENT! AND THE "GINGER" GOES TO--
REGGIE MANTLE!
OH, BROTHER! LIKE HE NEEDS AN AWARD!
THIRTY MINUTES LATER...
...AND I'D LIKE TO TELL YOU ABOUT MY CHILDHOOD DREAMS...
GET HIM OFF THE STAGE!!
OUR NEXT AWARD IS FOR BEST DRESSED TEACHER!
AND THE "GINGER" GOES TO--
The Ginger AWARDS
4

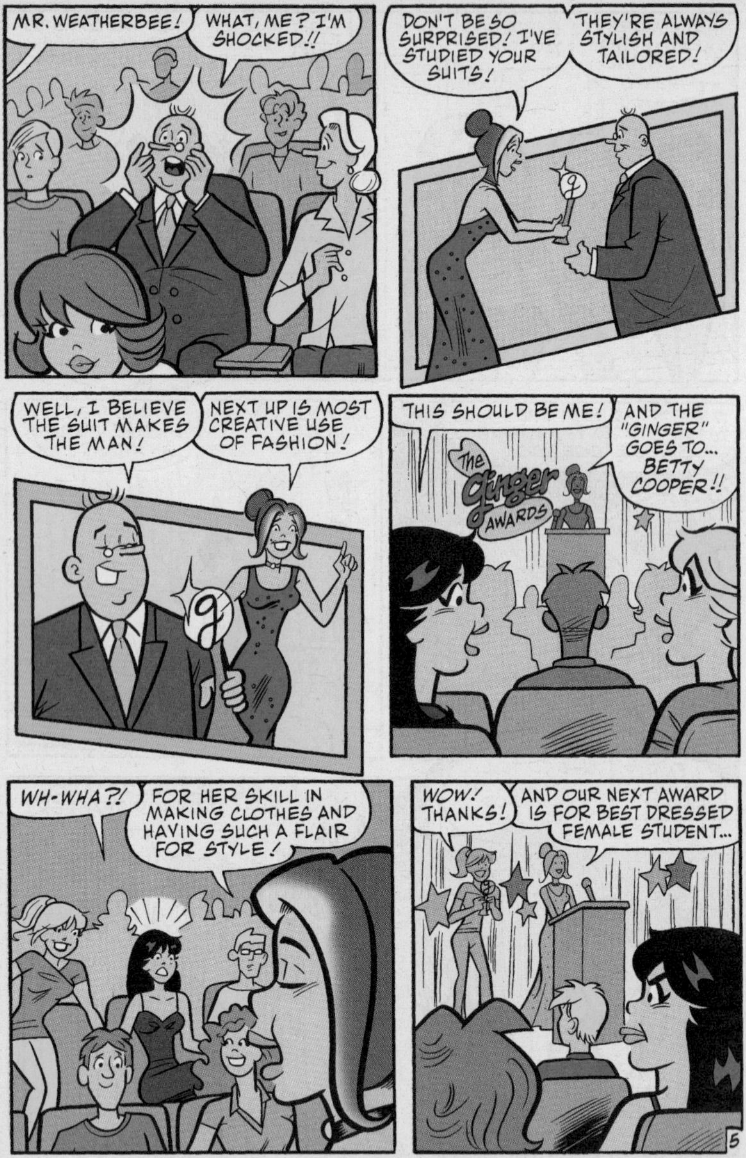
MR. WEATHERBEE!
WHAT, ME? I'M SHOCKED!!
DON'T BE SO SURPRISED! I'VE STUDIED YOUR SUITS!
THEY'RE ALWAYS STYLISH AND TAILORED!
WELL, I BELIEVE THE SUIT MAKES THE MAN!
NEXT UP IS MOST CREATIVE USE OF FASHION!
THIS SHOULD BE ME!
AND THE "GINGER" GOES TO... BETTY COOPER!!
The Ginger AWARDS
WH-WHA?!
FOR HER SKILL IN MAKING CLOTHES AND HAVING SUCH A FLAIR FOR STYLE!
WOW! THANKS!
AND OUR NEXT AWARD IS FOR BEST DRESSED FEMALE STUDENT...
5

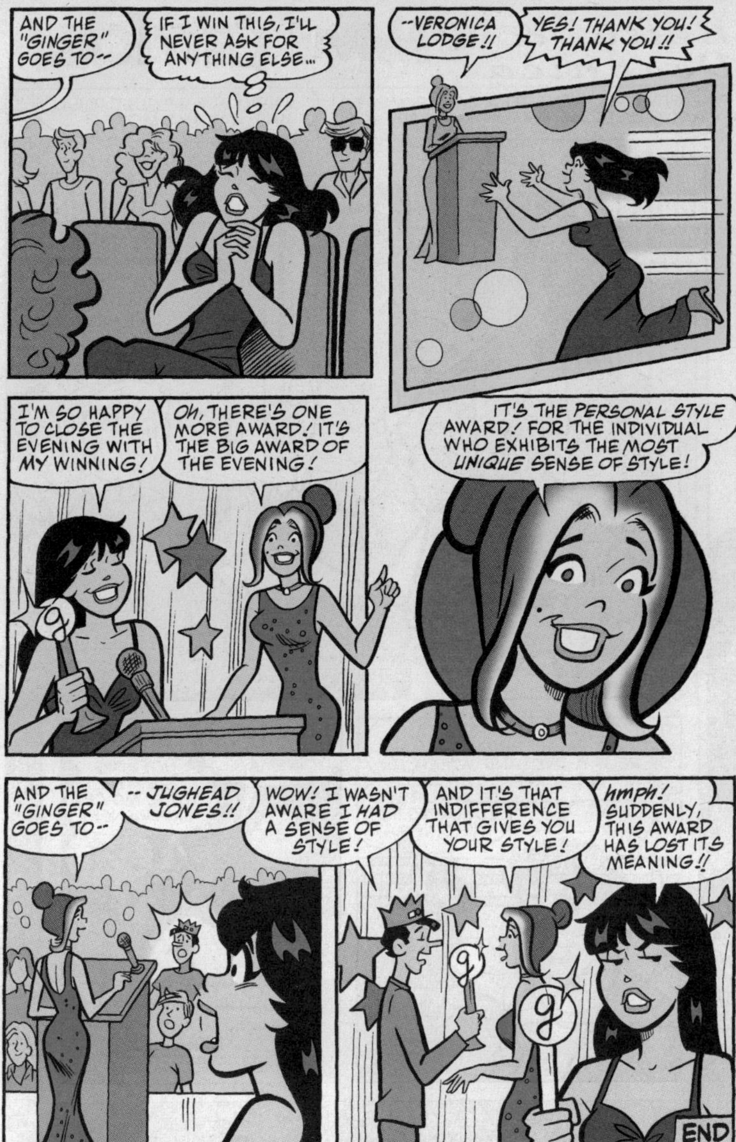

AND THE "GINGER" GOES TO--
IF I WIN THIS, I'LL NEVER ASK FOR ANYTHING ELSE...
--VERONICA LODGE!!
YES! THANK YOU! THANK YOU!!
I'M SO HAPPY TO CLOSE THE EVENING WITH MY WINNING!
Oh, THERE'S ONE MORE AWARD! IT'S THE BIG AWARD OF THE EVENING!
IT'S THE PERSONAL STYLE AWARD! FOR THE INDIVIDUAL WHO EXHIBITS THE MOST UNIQUE SENSE OF STYLE!
AND THE "GINGER" GOES TO--
--JUGHEAD JONES!!
WOW! I WASN'T AWARE I HAD A SENSE OF STYLE!
AND IT'S THAT INDIFFERENCE THAT GIVES YOU YOUR STYLE!
hmph! SUDDENLY, THIS AWARD HAS LOST ITS MEANING!!
END

Betty & Veronica in MOVIE CRITICAL!

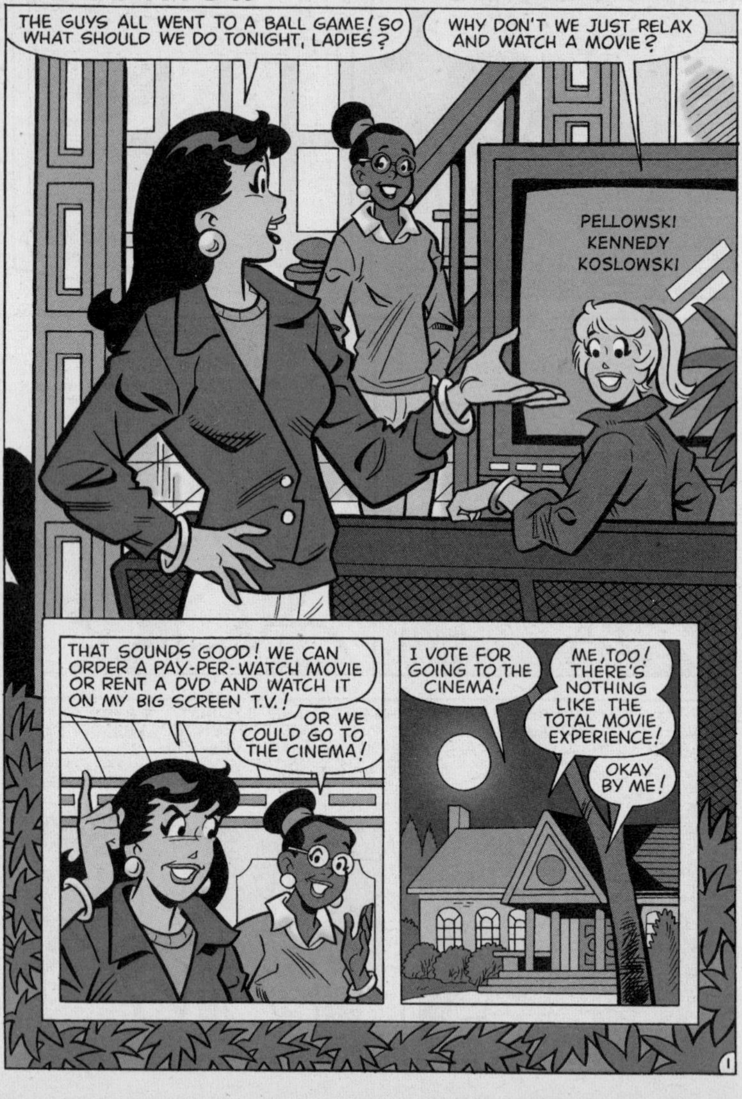
THE GUYS ALL WENT TO A BALL GAME! SO WHAT SHOULD WE DO TONIGHT, LADIES?
WHY DON'T WE JUST RELAX AND WATCH A MOVIE?
PELLOWSKI KENNEDY KOSLOWSKI
THAT SOUNDS GOOD! WE CAN ORDER A PAY-PER-WATCH MOVIE OR RENT A DVD AND WATCH IT ON MY BIG SCREEN T.V.!
OR WE COULD GO TO THE CINEMA!
I VOTE FOR GOING TO THE CINEMA!
ME, TOO! THERE'S NOTHING LIKE THE TOTAL MOVIE EXPERIENCE!
OKAY BY ME!

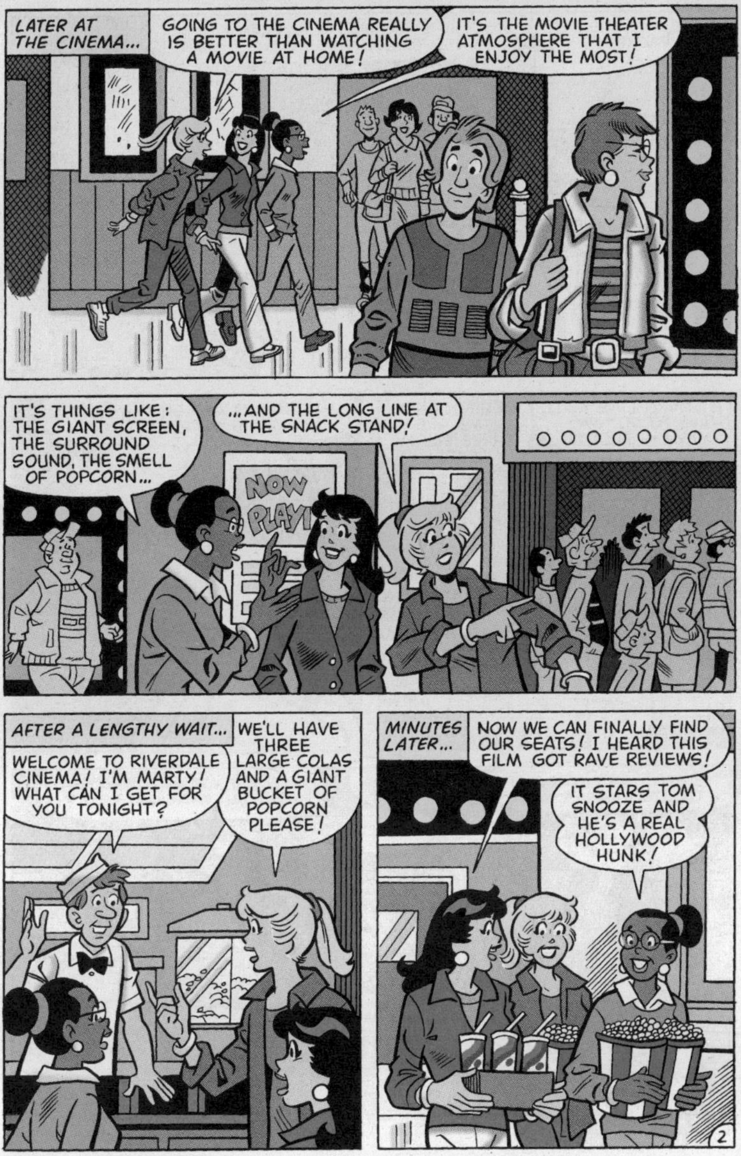
LATER AT THE CINEMA...
GOING TO THE CINEMA REALLY IS BETTER THAN WATCHING A MOVIE AT HOME!
IT'S THE MOVIE THEATER ATMOSPHERE THAT I ENJOY THE MOST!
IT'S THINGS LIKE: THE GIANT SCREEN, THE SURROUND SOUND, THE SMELL OF POPCORN...
...AND THE LONG LINE AT THE SNACK STAND!
NOW PLAYI
AFTER A LENGTHY WAIT...
WELCOME TO RIVERDALE CINEMA! I'M MARTY! WHAT CAN I GET FOR YOU TONIGHT?
WE'LL HAVE THREE LARGE COLAS AND A GIANT BUCKET OF POPCORN PLEASE!
MINUTES LATER...
NOW WE CAN FINALLY FIND OUR SEATS! I HEARD THIS FILM GOT RAVE REVIEWS!
IT STARS TOM SNOOZE AND HE'S A REAL HOLLYWOOD HUNK!
2

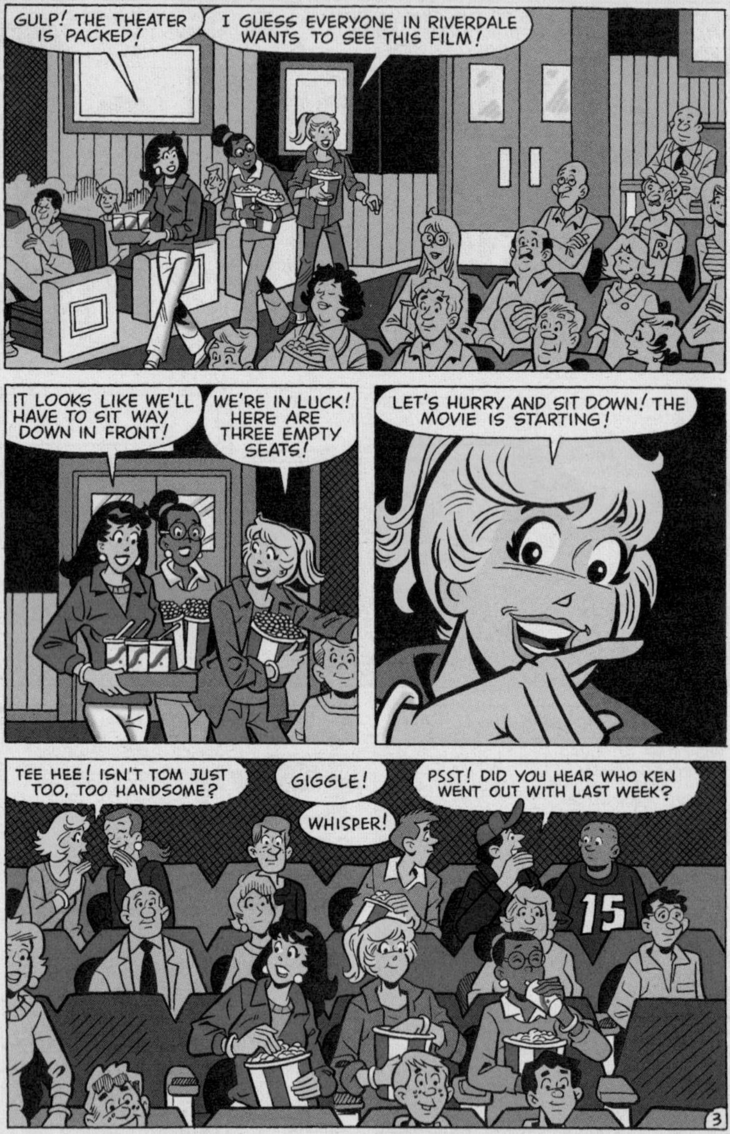
GULP! THE THEATER IS PACKED!
I GUESS EVERYONE IN RIVERDALE WANTS TO SEE THIS FILM!
IT LOOKS LIKE WE'LL HAVE TO SIT WAY DOWN IN FRONT!
WE'RE IN LUCK! HERE ARE THREE EMPTY SEATS!
LET'S HURRY AND SIT DOWN! THE MOVIE IS STARTING!
TEE HEE! ISN'T TOM JUST TOO, TOO HANDSOME?
GIGGLE!
WHISPER!
PSST! DID YOU HEAR WHO KEN WENT OUT WITH LAST WEEK?
15

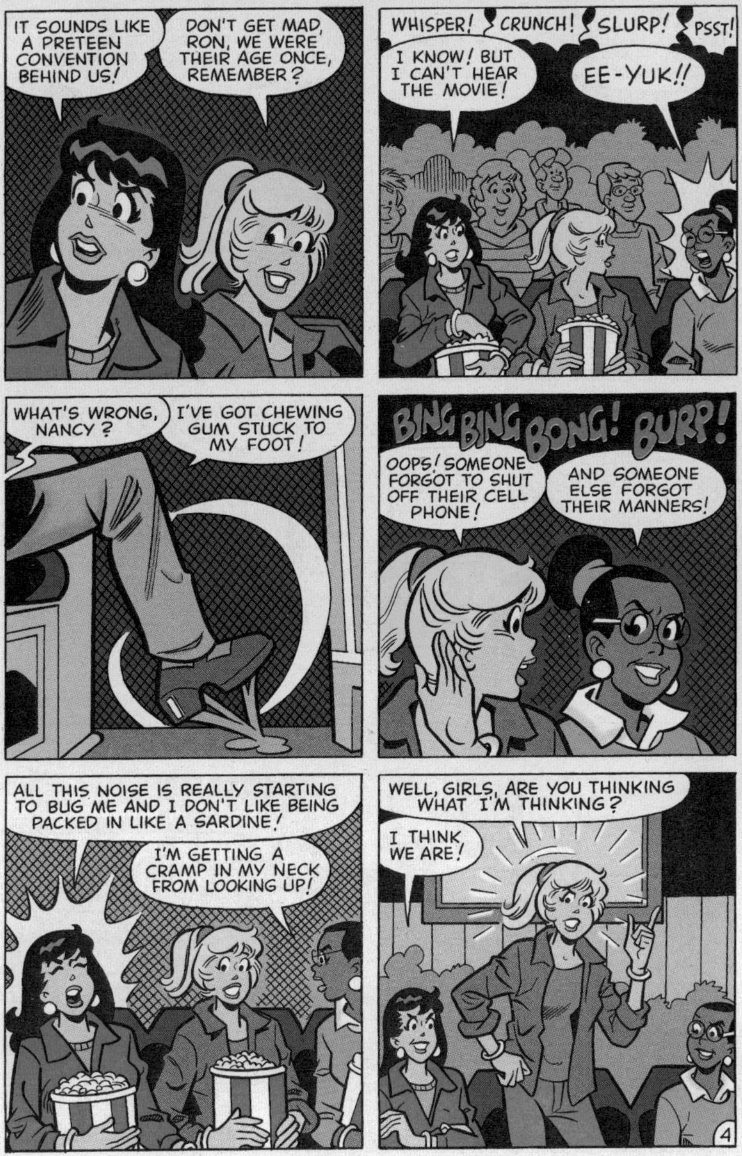
IT SOUNDS LIKE A PRETEEN CONVENTION BEHIND US!
DON'T GET MAD, RON, WE WERE THEIR AGE ONCE, REMEMBER?
WHISPER!
CRUNCH!
SLURP!
PSST!
I KNOW! BUT I CAN'T HEAR THE MOVIE!
EE-YUK!!
WHAT'S WRONG, NANCY?
I'VE GOT CHEWING GUM STUCK TO MY FOOT!
BING BING BONG! BURP!
OOPS! SOMEONE FORGOT TO SHUT OFF THEIR CELL PHONE!
AND SOMEONE ELSE FORGOT THEIR MANNERS!
ALL THIS NOISE IS REALLY STARTING TO BUG ME AND I DON'T LIKE BEING PACKED IN LIKE A SARDINE!
I'M GETTING A CRAMP IN MY NECK FROM LOOKING UP!
WELL, GIRLS, ARE YOU THINKING WHAT I'M THINKING?
I THINK WE ARE!
4

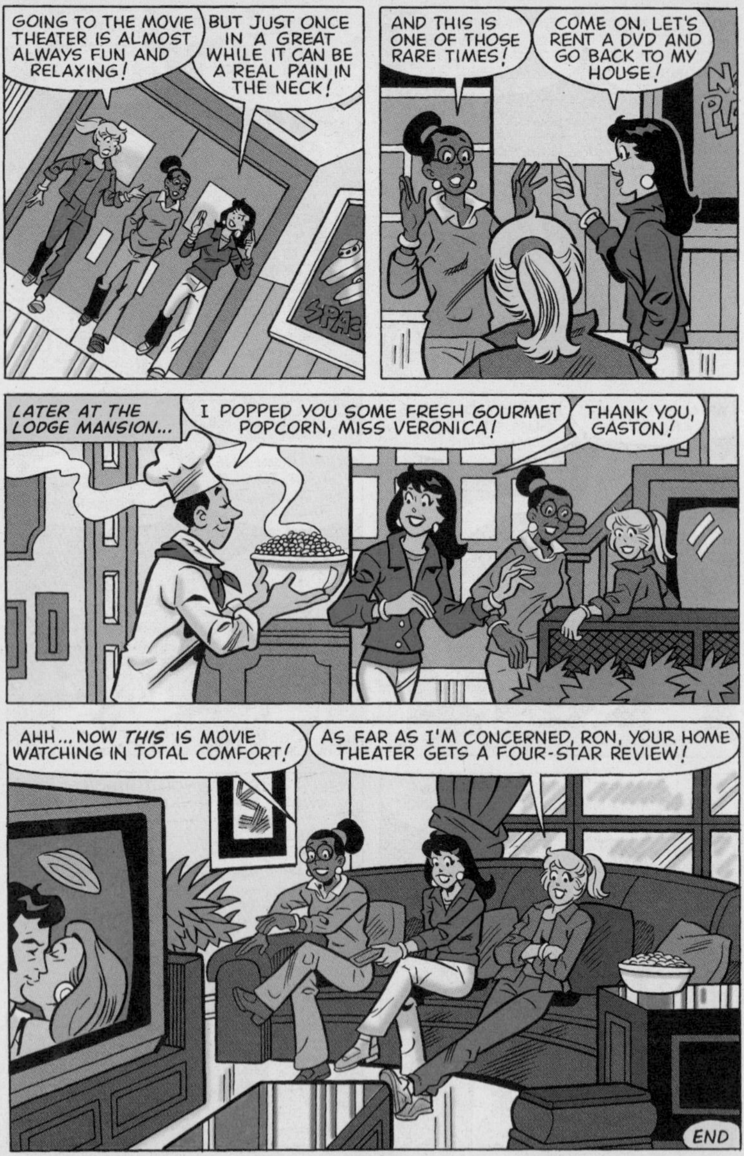
GOING TO THE MOVIE THEATER IS ALMOST ALWAYS FUN AND RELAXING!
BUT JUST ONCE IN A GREAT WHILE IT CAN BE A REAL PAIN IN THE NECK!
AND THIS IS ONE OF THOSE RARE TIMES!
COME ON, LET'S RENT A DVD AND GO BACK TO MY HOUSE!
LATER AT THE LODGE MANSION...
I POPPED YOU SOME FRESH GOURMET POPCORN, MISS VERONICA!
THANK YOU, GASTON!
AHH... NOW *THIS* IS MOVIE WATCHING IN TOTAL COMFORT!
AS FAR AS I'M CONCERNED, RON, YOUR HOME THEATER GETS A FOUR-STAR REVIEW!
END

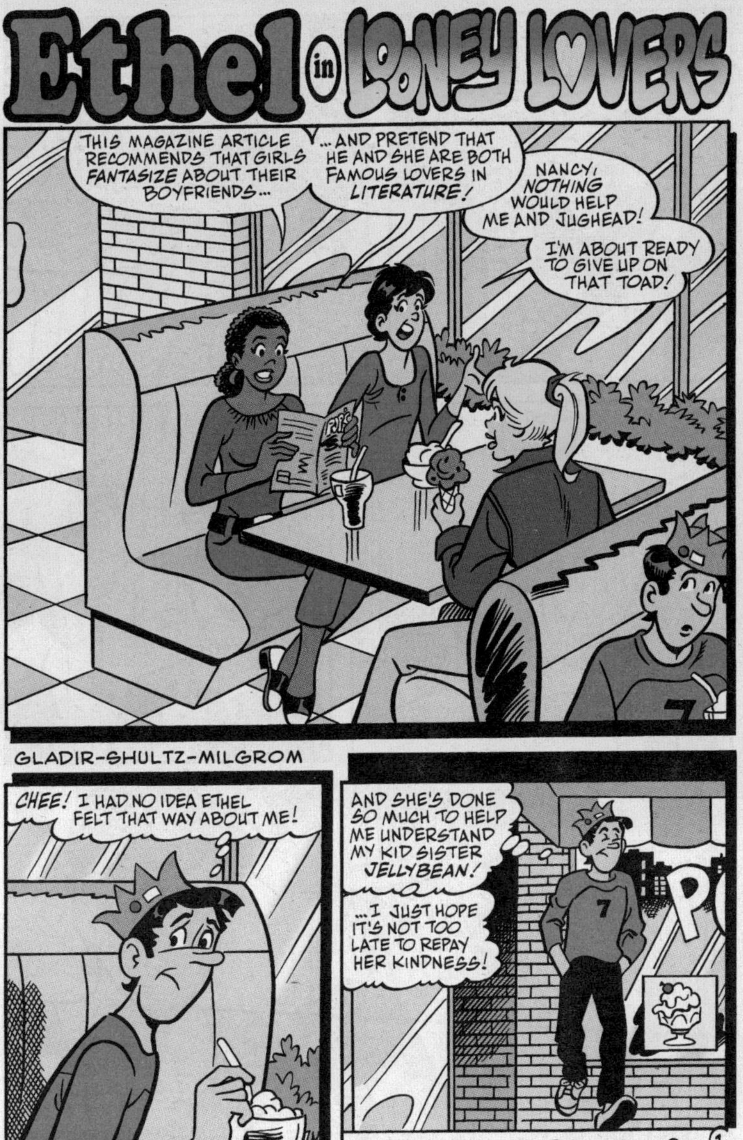
Ethel in LOONEY LOVERS
THIS MAGAZINE ARTICLE RECOMMENDS THAT GIRLS FANTASIZE ABOUT THEIR BOYFRIENDS...
...AND PRETEND THAT HE AND SHE ARE BOTH FAMOUS LOVERS IN LITERATURE!
NANCY, NOTHING WOULD HELP ME AND JUGHEAD!
I'M ABOUT READY TO GIVE UP ON THAT TOAD!
GLADIR-SHULTZ-MILGROM
CHEE! I HAD NO IDEA ETHEL FELT THAT WAY ABOUT ME!
AND SHE'S DONE SO MUCH TO HELP ME UNDERSTAND MY KID SISTER JELLYBEAN!
...I JUST HOPE IT'S NOT TOO LATE TO REPAY HER KINDNESS!
1

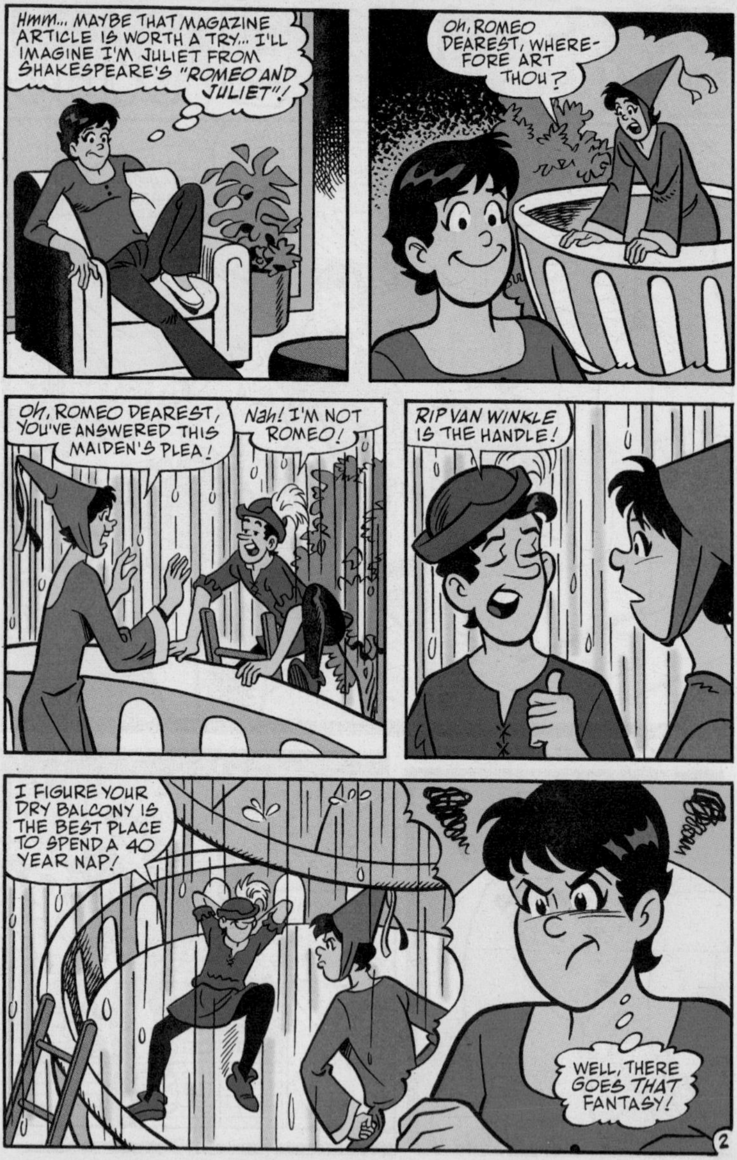
HMM... MAYBE THAT MAGAZINE ARTICLE IS WORTH A TRY... I'LL IMAGINE I'M JULIET FROM SHAKESPEARE'S "ROMEO AND JULIET"!
OH, ROMEO DEAREST, WHEREFORE ART THOU?
OH, ROMEO DEAREST, YOU'VE ANSWERED THIS MAIDEN'S PLEA!
NAH! I'M NOT ROMEO!
RIP VAN WINKLE IS THE HANDLE!
I FIGURE YOUR DRY BALCONY IS THE BEST PLACE TO SPEND A 40 YEAR NAP!
WELL, THERE GOES THAT FANTASY!
2

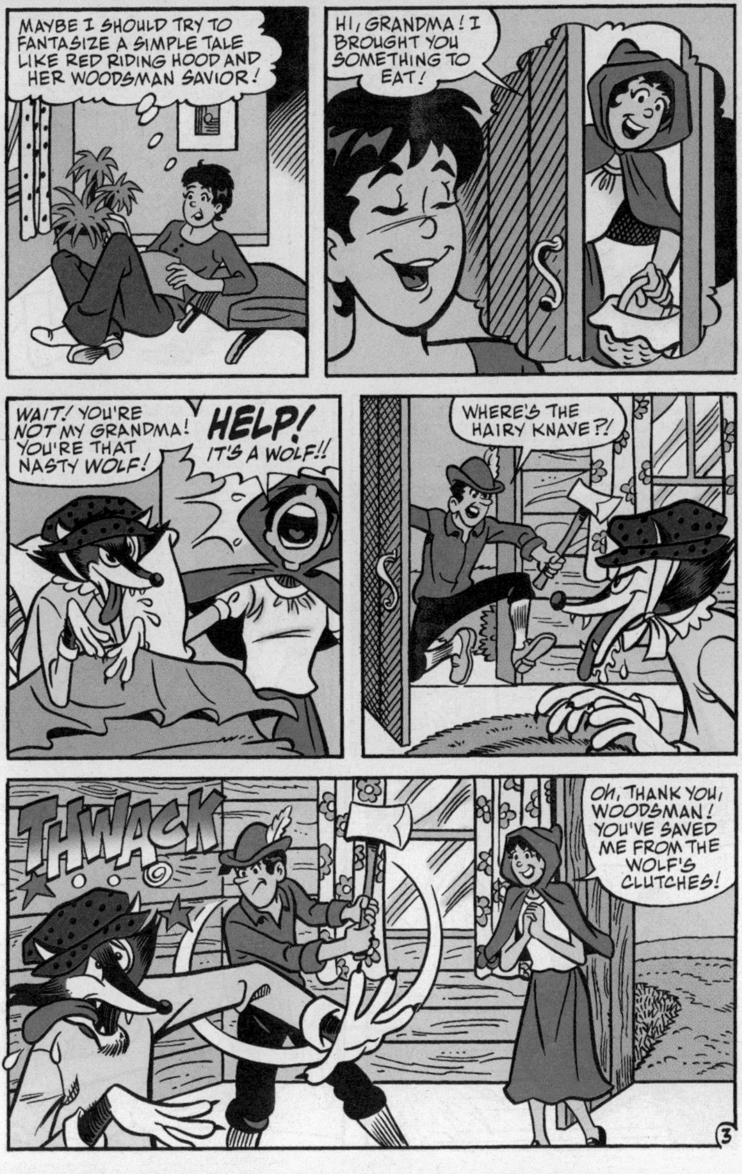
MAYBE I SHOULD TRY TO FANTASIZE A SIMPLE TALE LIKE RED RIDING HOOD AND HER WOODSMAN SAVIOR!
HI, GRANDMA! I BROUGHT YOU SOMETHING TO EAT!
WAIT! YOU'RE NOT MY GRANDMA! YOU'RE THAT NASTY WOLF!
HELP! IT'S A WOLF!!
WHERE'S THE HAIRY KNAVE?!
THWACK
OH, THANK YOU, WOODSMAN! YOU'VE SAVED ME FROM THE WOLF'S CLUTCHES!
3

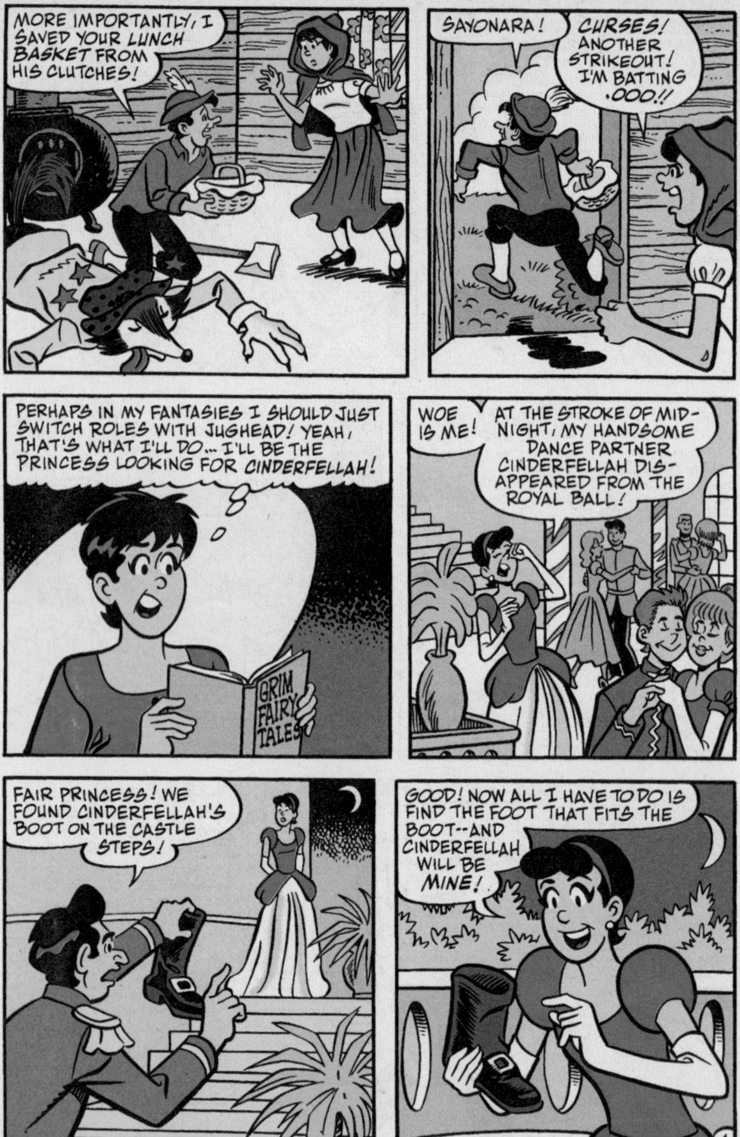

MORE IMPORTANTLY, I SAVED YOUR LUNCH BASKET FROM HIS CLUTCHES!
SAYONARA!
CURSES! ANOTHER STRIKEOUT! I'M BATTING .000!!
PERHAPS IN MY FANTASIES I SHOULD JUST SWITCH ROLES WITH JUGHEAD! YEAH, THAT'S WHAT I'LL DO... I'LL BE THE PRINCESS LOOKING FOR CINDERFELLAH!
GRIM FAIRY TALES
WOE IS ME!
AT THE STROKE OF MID-NIGHT, MY HANDSOME DANCE PARTNER CINDERFELLAH DIS-APPEARED FROM THE ROYAL BALL!
FAIR PRINCESS! WE FOUND CINDERFELLAH'S BOOT ON THE CASTLE STEPS!
GOOD! NOW ALL I HAVE TO DO IS FIND THE FOOT THAT FITS THE BOOT--AND CINDERFELLAH WILL BE MINE!
4

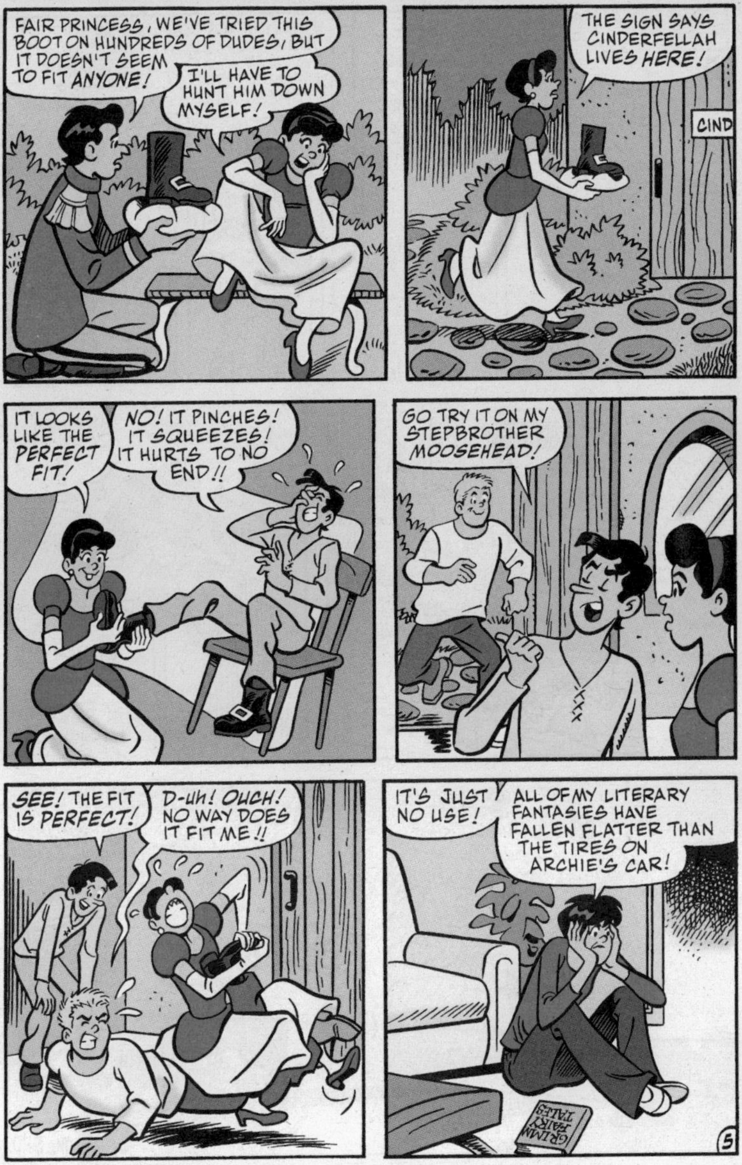
FAIR PRINCESS, WE'VE TRIED THIS BOOT ON HUNDREDS OF DUDES, BUT IT DOESN'T SEEM TO FIT ANYONE!
I'LL HAVE TO HUNT HIM DOWN MYSELF!
THE SIGN SAYS CINDERFELLAH LIVES HERE!
CIND
IT LOOKS LIKE THE PERFECT FIT!
NO! IT PINCHES! IT SQUEEZES! IT HURTS TO NO END!!
GO TRY IT ON MY STEPBROTHER MOOSEHEAD!
SEE! THE FIT IS PERFECT!
D-uh! OUCH! NO WAY DOES IT FIT ME!!
IT'S JUST NO USE!
ALL OF MY LITERARY FANTASIES HAVE FALLEN FLATTER THAN THE TIRES ON ARCHIE'S CAR!
GRIMM FAIRY TALES
5

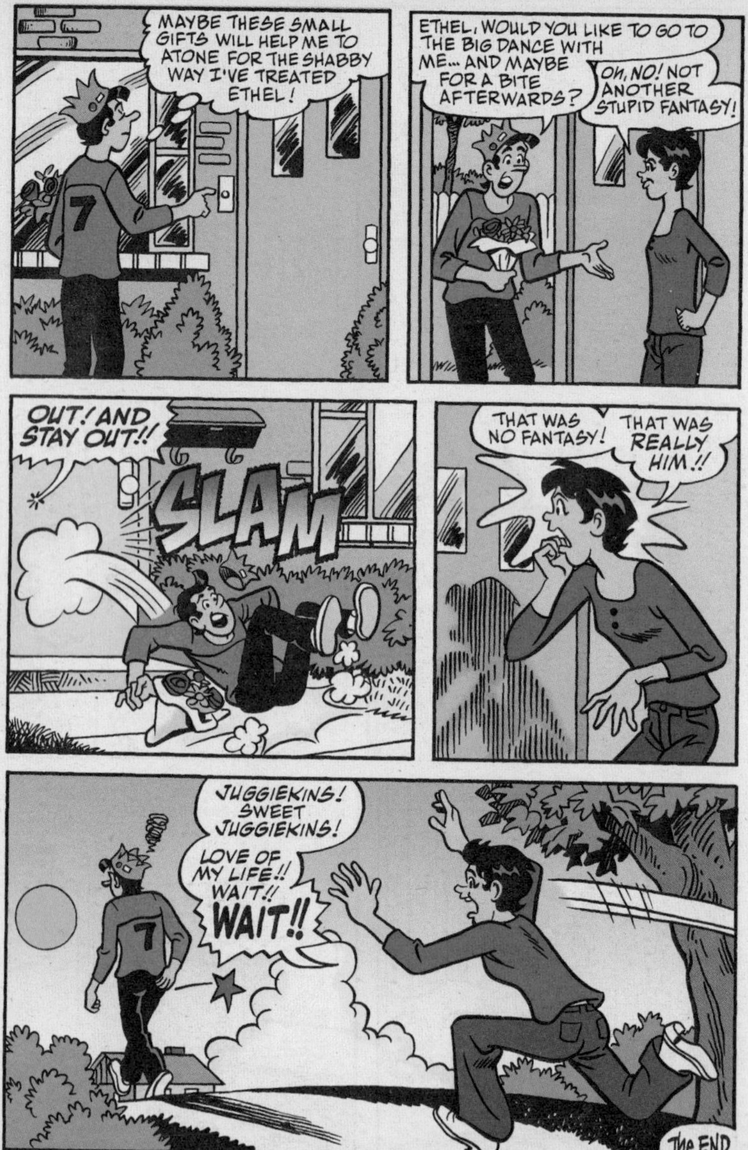
MAYBE THESE SMALL GIFTS WILL HELP ME TO ATONE FOR THE SHABBY WAY I'VE TREATED ETHEL!
ETHEL, WOULD YOU LIKE TO GO TO THE BIG DANCE WITH ME... AND MAYBE FOR A BITE AFTERWARDS?
OH, NO! NOT ANOTHER STUPID FANTASY!
OUT! AND STAY OUT!!
SLAM
THAT WAS NO FANTASY!
THAT WAS REALLY HIM!!
JUGGIEKINS! SWEET JUGGIEKINS!
LOVE OF MY LIFE!! WAIT!! WAIT!!
The END

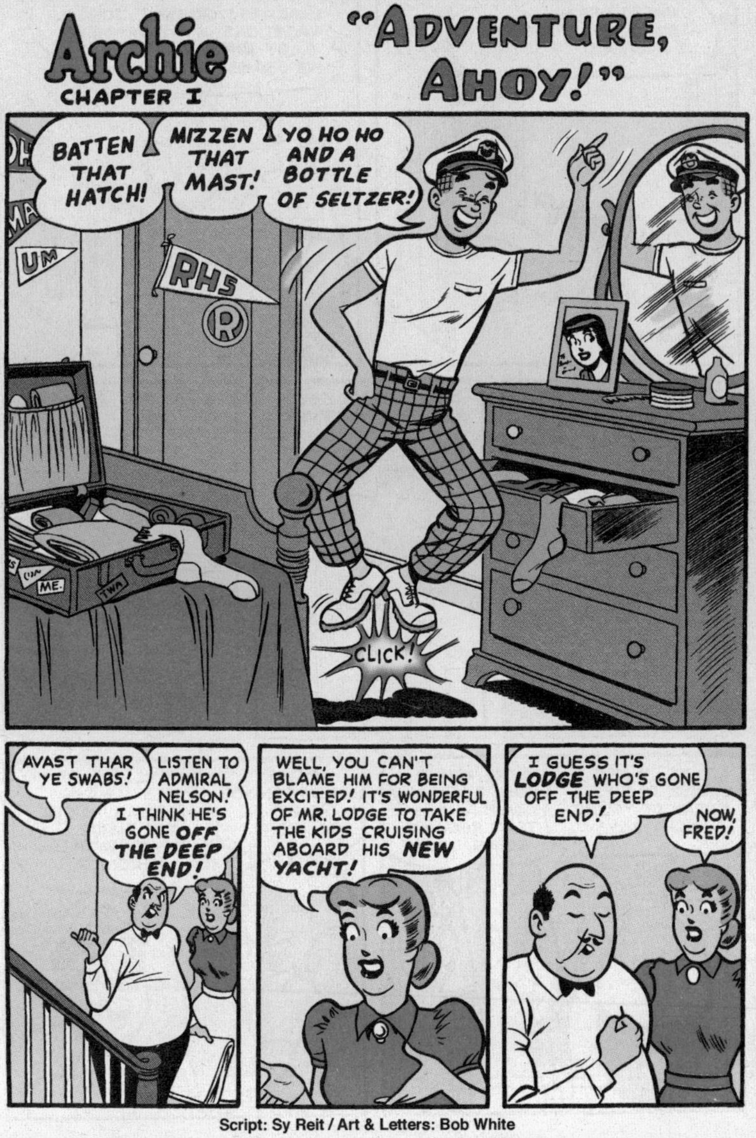
Archie
CHAPTER I
"ADVENTURE, AHOY!"
BATTEN THAT HATCH!
MIZZEN THAT MAST!
YO HO HO AND A BOTTLE OF SELTZER!
RHS
UM
CLICK!
AVAST THAR YE SWABS!
LISTEN TO ADMIRAL NELSON! I THINK HE'S GONE OFF THE DEEP END!
WELL, YOU CAN'T BLAME HIM FOR BEING EXCITED! IT'S WONDERFUL OF MR. LODGE TO TAKE THE KIDS CRUISING ABOARD HIS NEW YACHT!
I GUESS IT'S LODGE WHO'S GONE OFF THE DEEP END!
NOW, FRED!

Script: Sy Reit / Art & Letters: Bob White

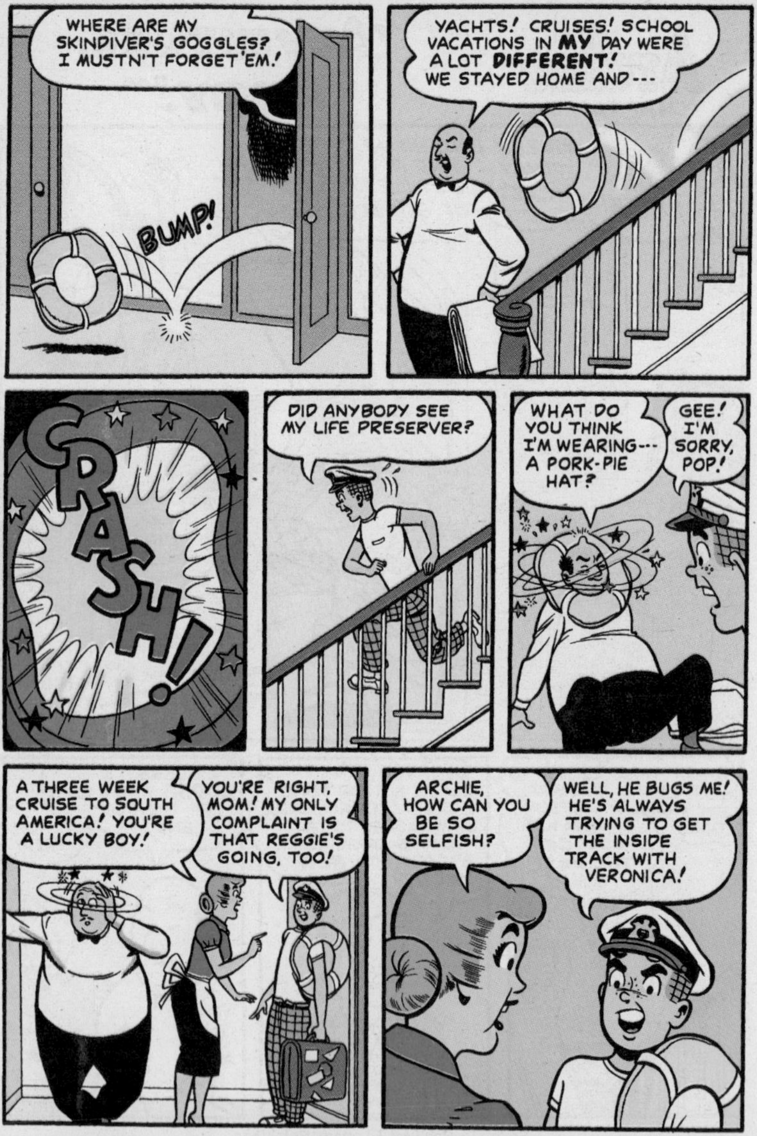
WHERE ARE MY SKINDIVER'S GOGGLES? I MUSTN'T FORGET 'EM!
BUMP!
YACHTS! CRUISES! SCHOOL VACATIONS IN MY DAY WERE A LOT DIFFERENT! WE STAYED HOME AND ---
CRASH!
DID ANYBODY SEE MY LIFE PRESERVER?
WHAT DO YOU THINK I'M WEARING--- A PORK-PIE HAT?
GEE! I'M SORRY, POP!
A THREE WEEK CRUISE TO SOUTH AMERICA! YOU'RE A LUCKY BOY!
YOU'RE RIGHT, MOM! MY ONLY COMPLAINT IS THAT REGGIE'S GOING, TOO!
ARCHIE, HOW CAN YOU BE SO SELFISH?
WELL, HE BUGS ME! HE'S ALWAYS TRYING TO GET THE INSIDE TRACK WITH VERONICA!

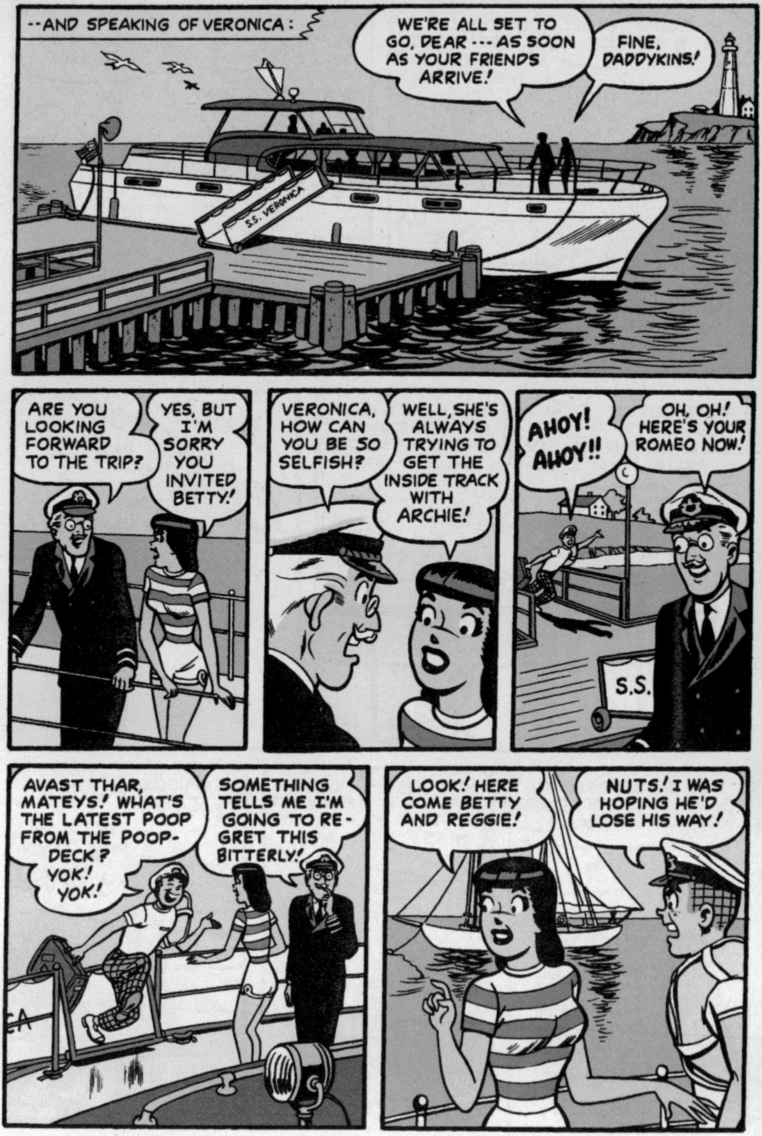
--AND SPEAKING OF VERONICA:
WE'RE ALL SET TO GO, DEAR --- AS SOON AS YOUR FRIENDS ARRIVE!
FINE, DADDYKINS!
S.S. VERONICA
ARE YOU LOOKING FORWARD TO THE TRIP?
YES, BUT I'M SORRY YOU INVITED BETTY!
VERONICA, HOW CAN YOU BE SO SELFISH?
WELL, SHE'S ALWAYS TRYING TO GET THE INSIDE TRACK WITH ARCHIE!
AHOY! AHOY!!
OH, OH! HERE'S YOUR ROMEO NOW!
S.S.
AVAST THAR, MATEYS! WHAT'S THE LATEST POOP FROM THE POOP-DECK? YOK! YOK!
SOMETHING TELLS ME I'M GOING TO RE-GRET THIS BITTERLY!
LOOK! HERE COME BETTY AND REGGIE!
NUTS! I WAS HOPING HE'D LOSE HIS WAY!

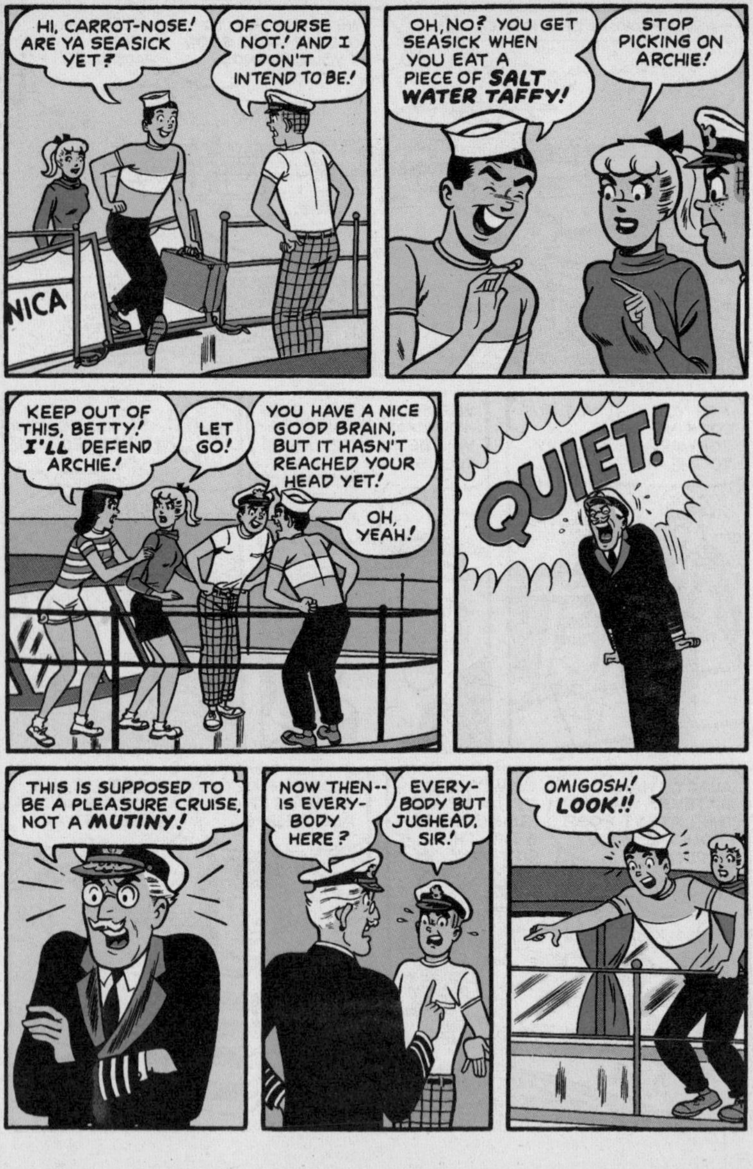
HI, CARROT-NOSE! ARE YA SEASICK YET?
OF COURSE NOT! AND I DON'T INTEND TO BE!
NICA
OH, NO? YOU GET SEASICK WHEN YOU EAT A PIECE OF SALT WATER TAFFY!
STOP PICKING ON ARCHIE!
KEEP OUT OF THIS, BETTY! I'LL DEFEND ARCHIE!
LET GO!
YOU HAVE A NICE GOOD BRAIN, BUT IT HASN'T REACHED YOUR HEAD YET!
OH, YEAH!
QUIET!
THIS IS SUPPOSED TO BE A PLEASURE CRUISE, NOT A MUTINY!
NOW THEN-- IS EVERYBODY HERE?
EVERYBODY BUT JUGHEAD, SIR!
OMIGOSH! LOOK!!

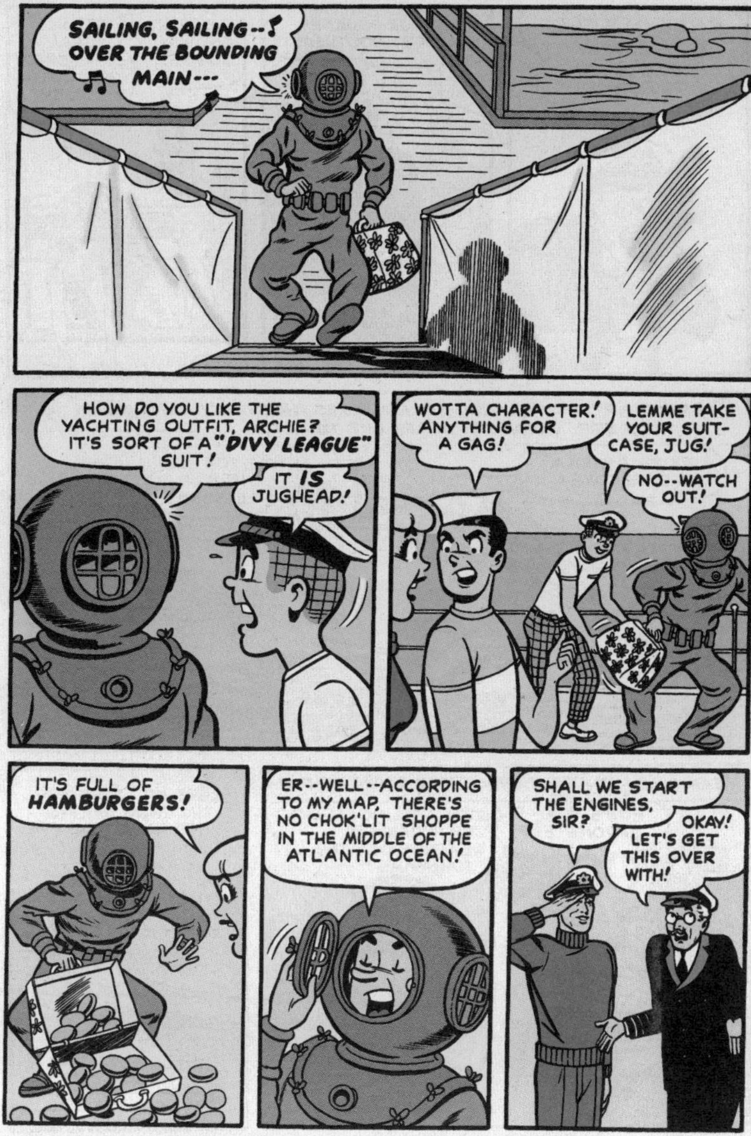
SAILING, SAILING--! OVER THE BOUNDING MAIN---
HOW DO YOU LIKE THE YACHTING OUTFIT, ARCHIE? IT'S SORT OF A "DIVY LEAGUE" SUIT!
IT IS JUGHEAD!
WOTTA CHARACTER! ANYTHING FOR A GAG!
LEMME TAKE YOUR SUIT-CASE, JUG!
NO--WATCH OUT!
IT'S FULL OF HAMBURGERS!
ER--WELL--ACCORDING TO MY MAP, THERE'S NO CHOK'LIT SHOPPE IN THE MIDDLE OF THE ATLANTIC OCEAN!
SHALL WE START THE ENGINES, SIR?
OKAY! LET'S GET THIS OVER WITH!

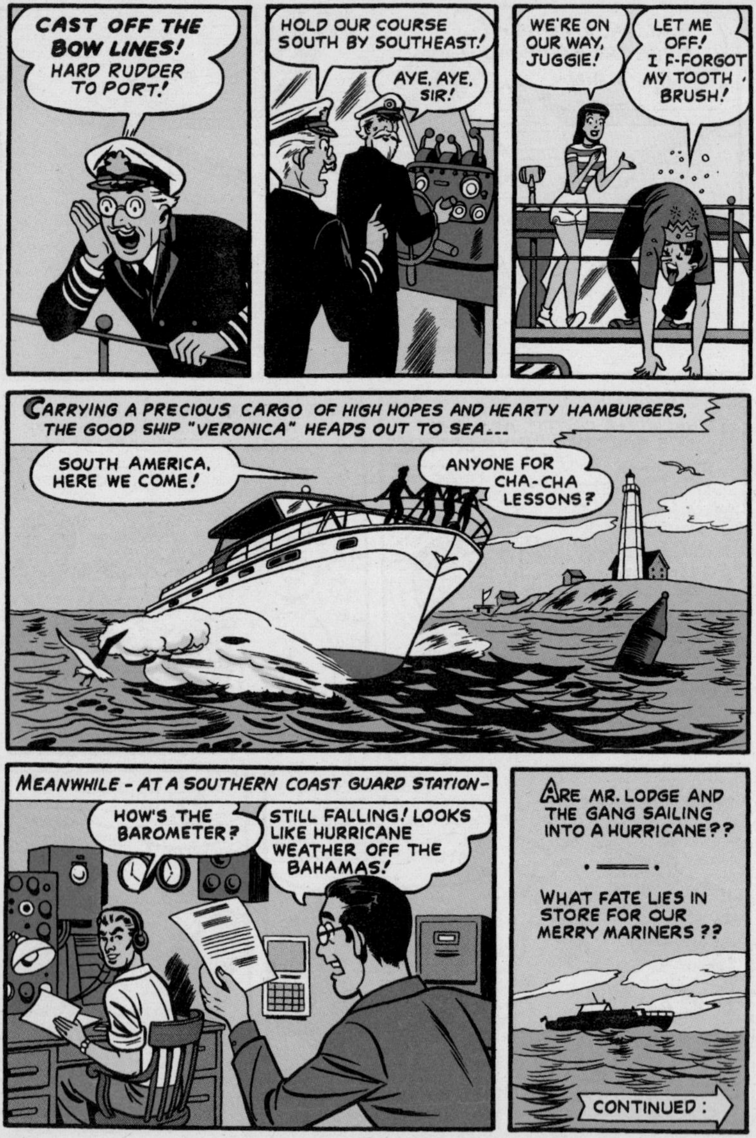
CAST OFF THE BOW LINES! HARD RUDDER TO PORT!
HOLD OUR COURSE SOUTH BY SOUTHEAST!
AYE, AYE, SIR!
WE'RE ON OUR WAY, JUGGIE!
LET ME OFF! I F-FORGOT MY TOOTH BRUSH!
CARRYING A PRECIOUS CARGO OF HIGH HOPES AND HEARTY HAMBURGERS, THE GOOD SHIP "VERONICA" HEADS OUT TO SEA...
SOUTH AMERICA, HERE WE COME!
ANYONE FOR CHA-CHA LESSONS?
MEANWHILE - AT A SOUTHERN COAST GUARD STATION-
HOW'S THE BAROMETER?
STILL FALLING! LOOKS LIKE HURRICANE WEATHER OFF THE BAHAMAS!
ARE MR. LODGE AND THE GANG SAILING INTO A HURRICANE??
WHAT FATE LIES IN STORE FOR OUR MERRY MARINERS??
CONTINUED :

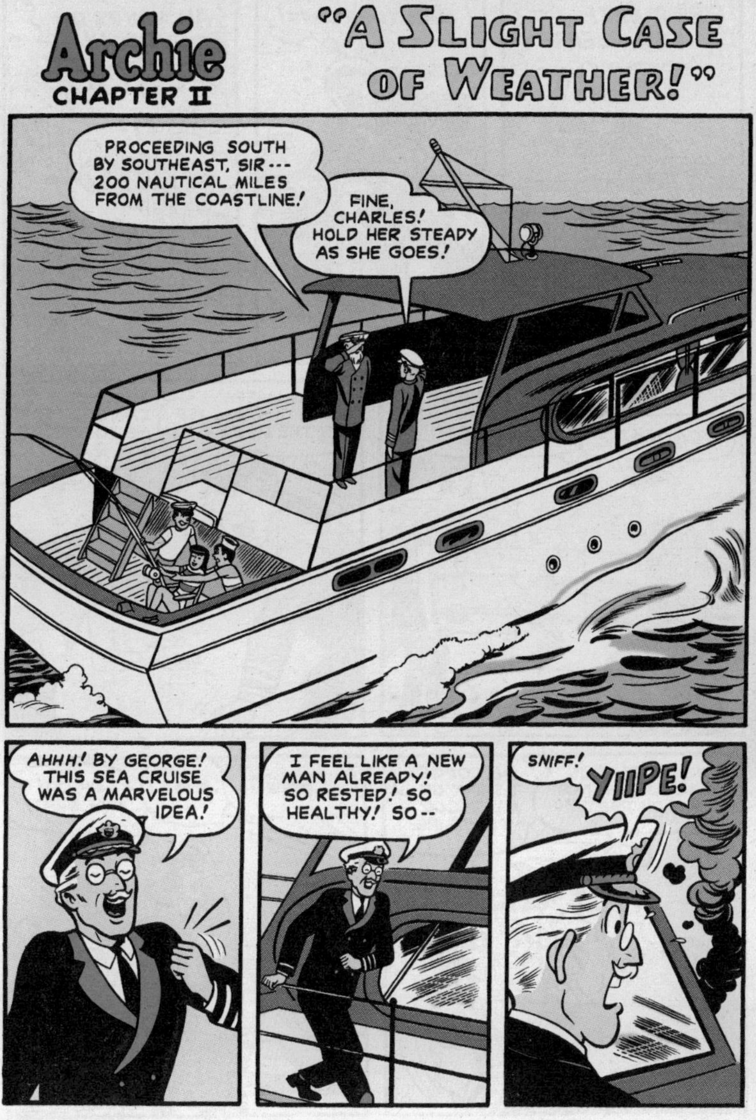
Archie
CHAPTER II
"A SLIGHT CASE OF WEATHER!"
PROCEEDING SOUTH BY SOUTHEAST, SIR--- 200 NAUTICAL MILES FROM THE COASTLINE!
FINE, CHARLES! HOLD HER STEADY AS SHE GOES!
AHHH! BY GEORGE! THIS SEA CRUISE WAS A MARVELOUS IDEA!
I FEEL LIKE A NEW MAN ALREADY! SO RESTED! SO HEALTHY! SO--
SNIFF!
YIIPE!

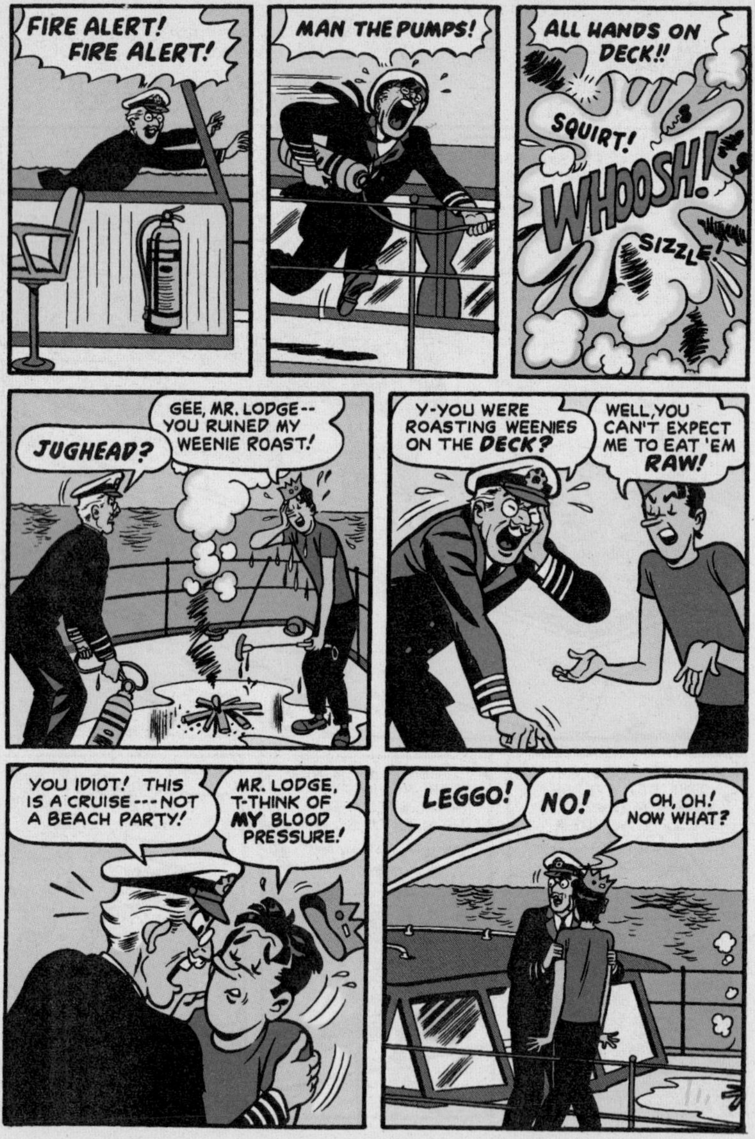
FIRE ALERT! FIRE ALERT!
MAN THE PUMPS!
ALL HANDS ON DECK!!
SQUIRT!
WHOOSH!
SIZZLE!
JUGHEAD?
GEE, MR. LODGE-- YOU RUINED MY WEENIE ROAST!
Y-YOU WERE ROASTING WEENIES ON THE DECK?
WELL, YOU CAN'T EXPECT ME TO EAT 'EM RAW!
YOU IDIOT! THIS IS A CRUISE---NOT A BEACH PARTY!
MR. LODGE, T-THINK OF MY BLOOD PRESSURE!
LEGGO!
NO!
OH, OH! NOW WHAT?

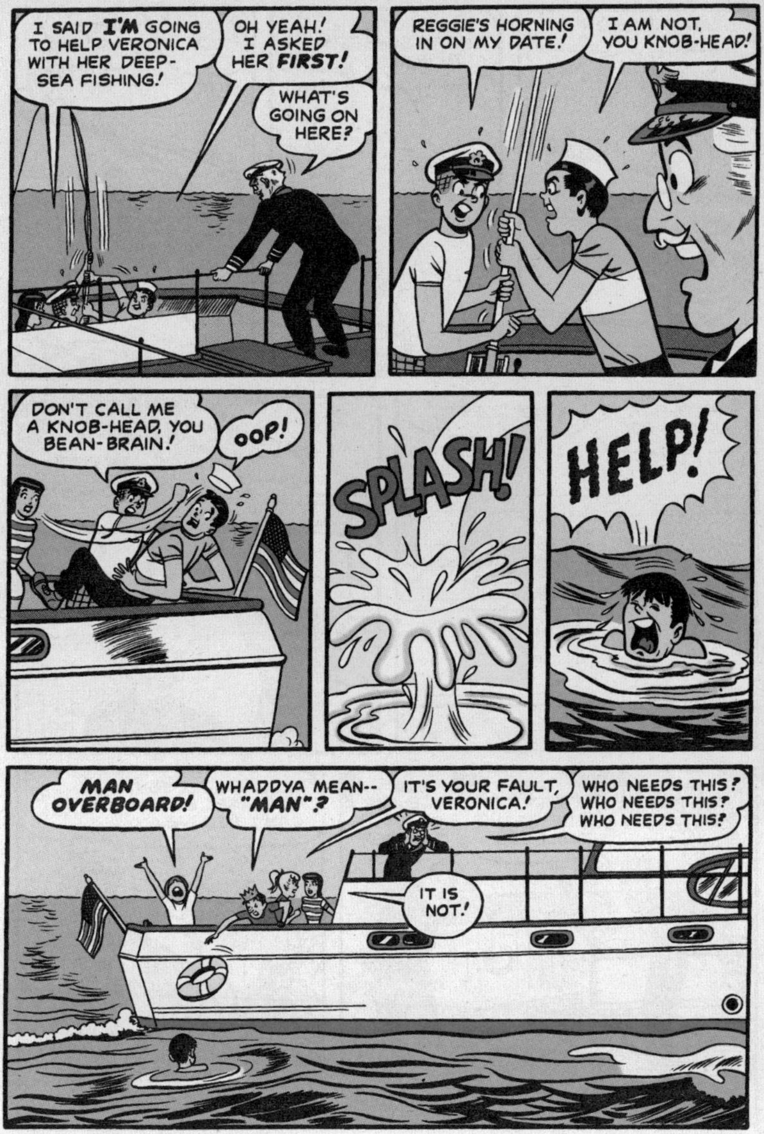
I SAID I'M GOING TO HELP VERONICA WITH HER DEEP-SEA FISHING!
OH YEAH! I ASKED HER FIRST!
WHAT'S GOING ON HERE?
REGGIE'S HORNING IN ON MY DATE!
I AM NOT, YOU KNOB-HEAD!
DON'T CALL ME A KNOB-HEAD, YOU BEAN-BRAIN!
OOP!
SPLASH!
HELP!
MAN OVERBOARD!
WHADDYA MEAN-- "MAN"?
IT'S YOUR FAULT, VERONICA!
IT IS NOT!
WHO NEEDS THIS? WHO NEEDS THIS? WHO NEEDS THIS?

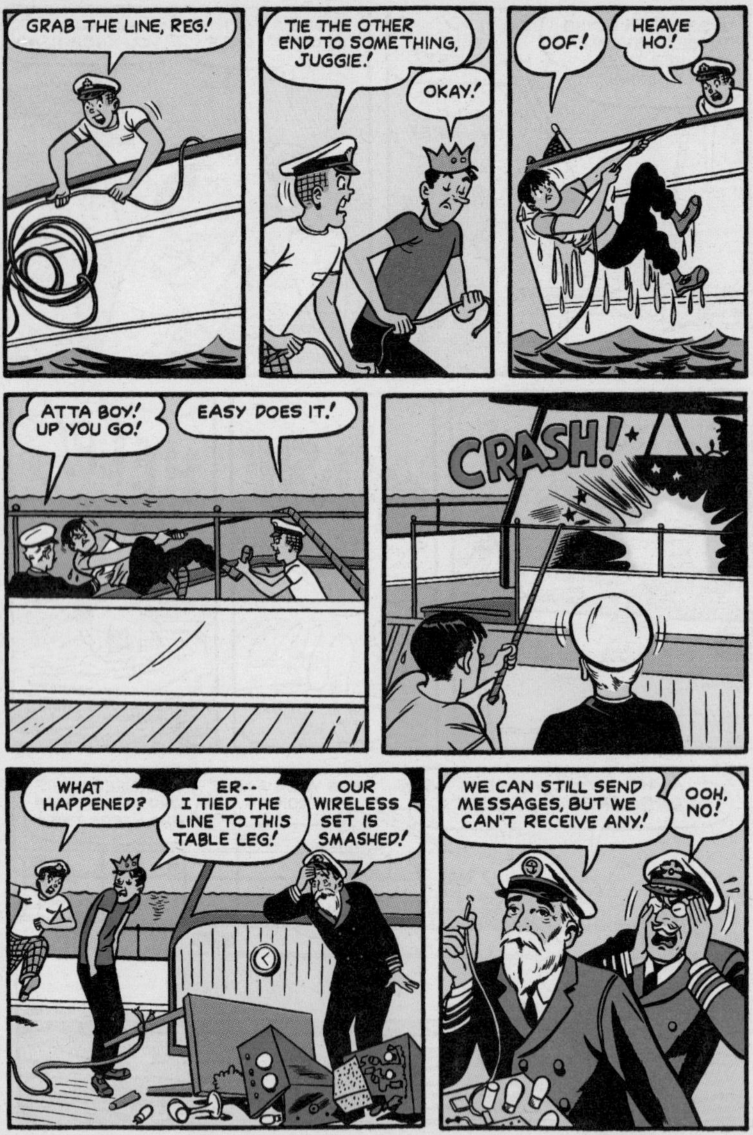
GRAB THE LINE, REG!
TIE THE OTHER END TO SOMETHING, JUGGIE!
OKAY!
OOF!
HEAVE HO!
ATTA BOY! UP YOU GO!
EASY DOES IT!
CRASH!
WHAT HAPPENED?
ER-- I TIED THE LINE TO THIS TABLE LEG!
OUR WIRELESS SET IS SMASHED!
WE CAN STILL SEND MESSAGES, BUT WE CAN'T RECEIVE ANY!
OOH, NO!

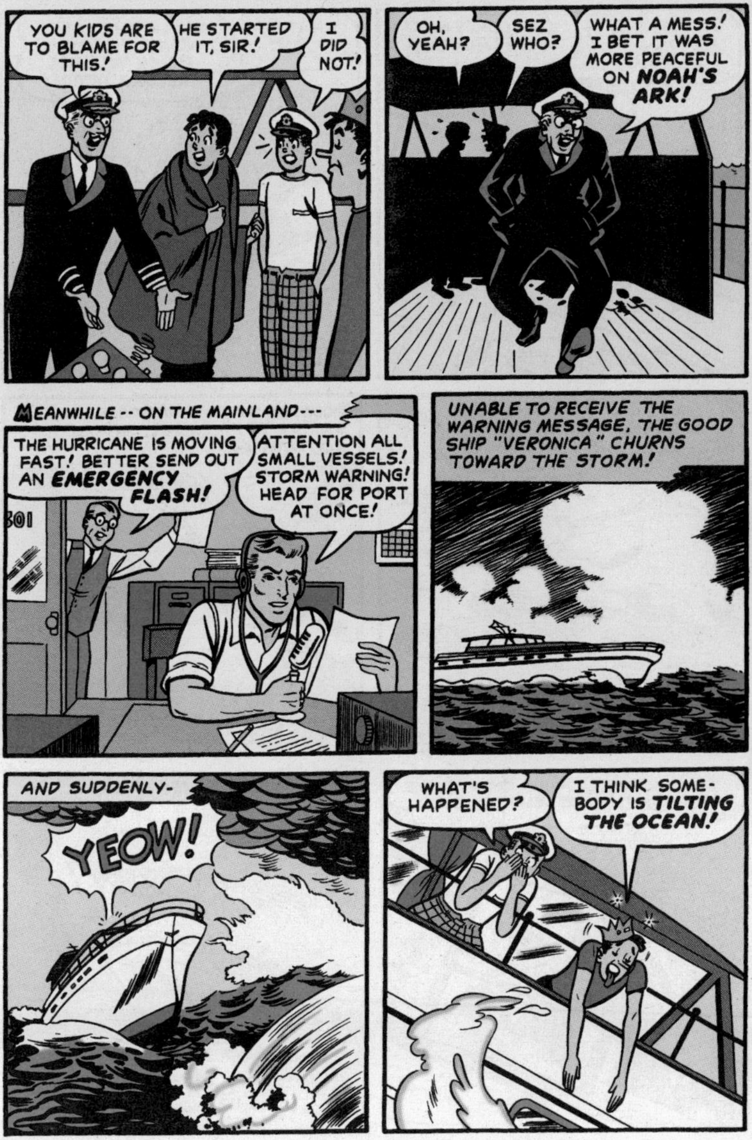
YOU KIDS ARE TO BLAME FOR THIS!
HE STARTED IT, SIR!
I DID NOT!
OH, YEAH?
SEZ WHO?
WHAT A MESS! I BET IT WAS MORE PEACEFUL ON NOAH'S ARK!
MEANWHILE -- ON THE MAINLAND---
THE HURRICANE IS MOVING FAST! BETTER SEND OUT AN EMERGENCY FLASH!
ATTENTION ALL SMALL VESSELS! STORM WARNING! HEAD FOR PORT AT ONCE!
UNABLE TO RECEIVE THE WARNING MESSAGE, THE GOOD SHIP "VERONICA" CHURNS TOWARD THE STORM!
AND SUDDENLY-
YEOW!
WHAT'S HAPPENED?
I THINK SOME-BODY IS TILTING THE OCEAN!

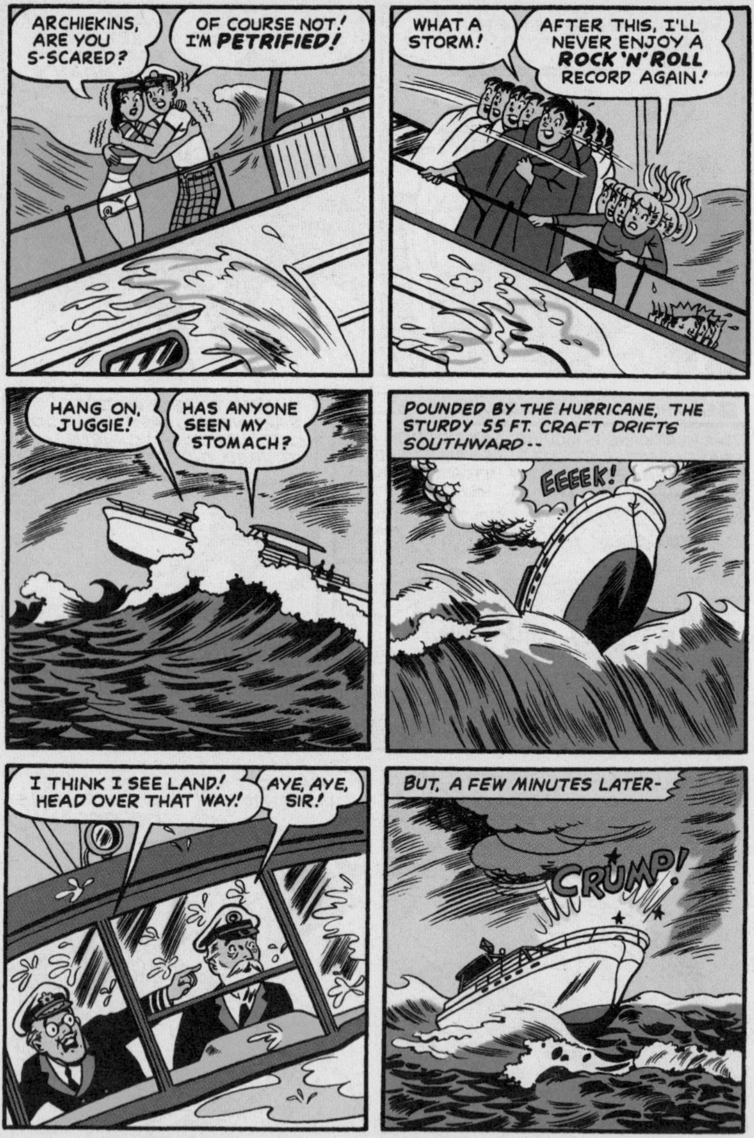
ARCHIEKINS, ARE YOU S-SCARED?
OF COURSE NOT! I'M PETRIFIED!
WHAT A STORM!
AFTER THIS, I'LL NEVER ENJOY A ROCK 'N' ROLL RECORD AGAIN!
HANG ON, JUGGIE!
HAS ANYONE SEEN MY STOMACH?
POUNDED BY THE HURRICANE, THE STURDY 55 FT. CRAFT DRIFTS SOUTHWARD--
EEEEK!
I THINK I SEE LAND! HEAD OVER THAT WAY!
AYE, AYE, SIR!
BUT, A FEW MINUTES LATER-
CRUMP!

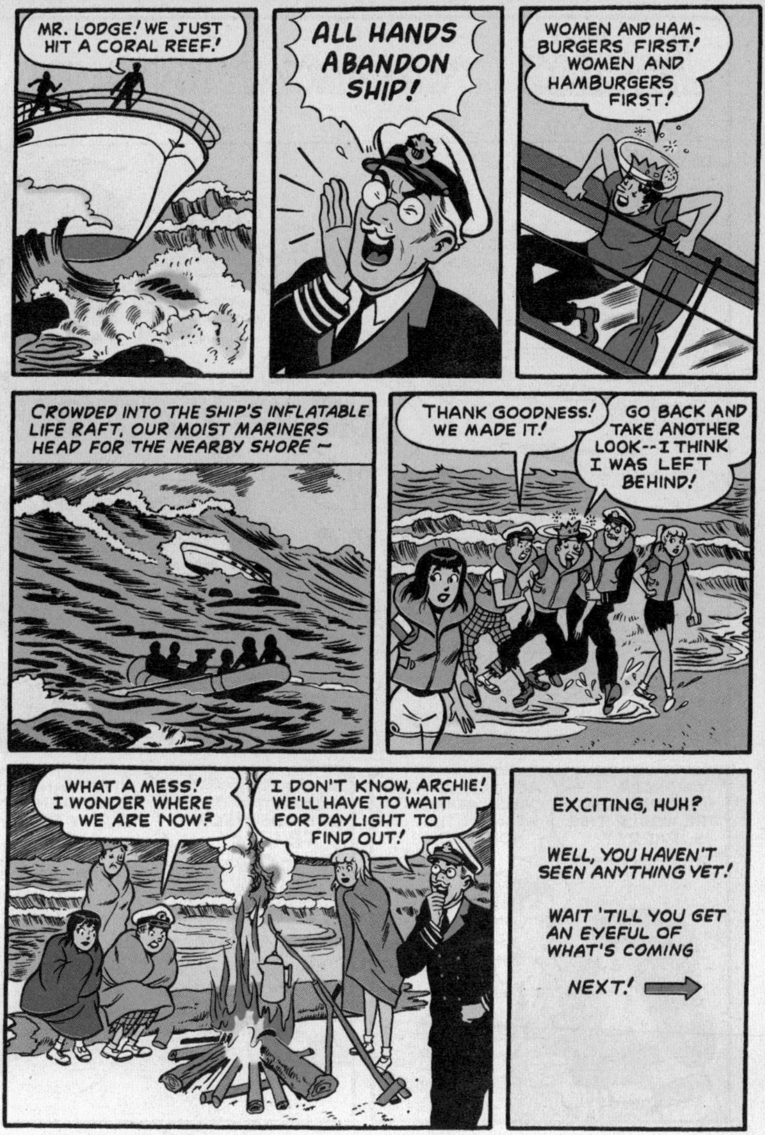
MR. LODGE! WE JUST HIT A CORAL REEF!
ALL HANDS ABANDON SHIP!
WOMEN AND HAMBURGERS FIRST! WOMEN AND HAMBURGERS FIRST!
CROWDED INTO THE SHIP'S INFLATABLE LIFE RAFT, OUR MOIST MARINERS HEAD FOR THE NEARBY SHORE ~
THANK GOODNESS! WE MADE IT!
GO BACK AND TAKE ANOTHER LOOK--I THINK I WAS LEFT BEHIND!
WHAT A MESS! I WONDER WHERE WE ARE NOW?
I DON'T KNOW, ARCHIE! WE'LL HAVE TO WAIT FOR DAYLIGHT TO FIND OUT!
EXCITING, HUH?
WELL, YOU HAVEN'T SEEN ANYTHING YET!
WAIT 'TILL YOU GET AN EYEFUL OF WHAT'S COMING
NEXT!

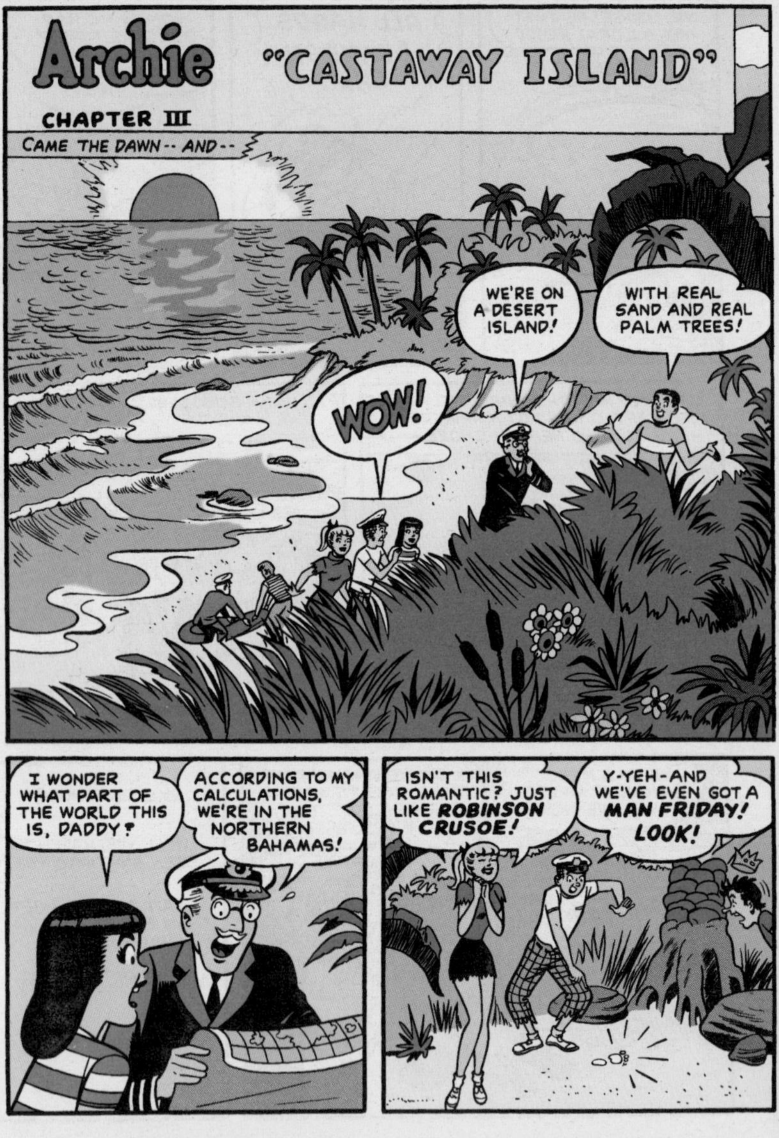
Archie
"CASTAWAY ISLAND"
CHAPTER III
CAME THE DAWN -- AND --
WOW!
WE'RE ON A DESERT ISLAND!
WITH REAL SAND AND REAL PALM TREES!
I WONDER WHAT PART OF THE WORLD THIS IS, DADDY?
ACCORDING TO MY CALCULATIONS, WE'RE IN THE NORTHERN BAHAMAS!
ISN'T THIS ROMANTIC? JUST LIKE ROBINSON CRUSOE!
Y-YEH-AND WE'VE EVEN GOT A MAN FRIDAY! LOOK!

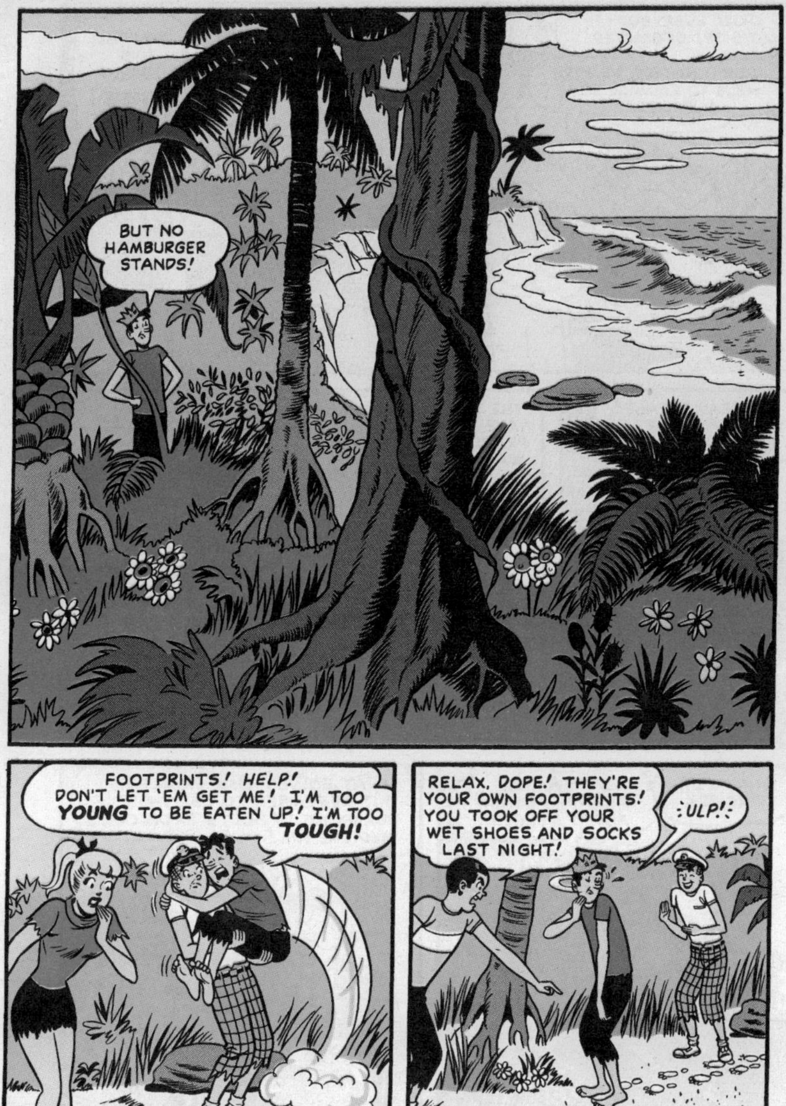

BUT NO HAMBURGER STANDS!
FOOTPRINTS! HELP! DON'T LET 'EM GET ME! I'M TOO YOUNG TO BE EATEN UP! I'M TOO TOUGH!
RELAX, DOPE! THEY'RE YOUR OWN FOOTPRINTS! YOU TOOK OFF YOUR WET SHOES AND SOCKS LAST NIGHT!
ULP!

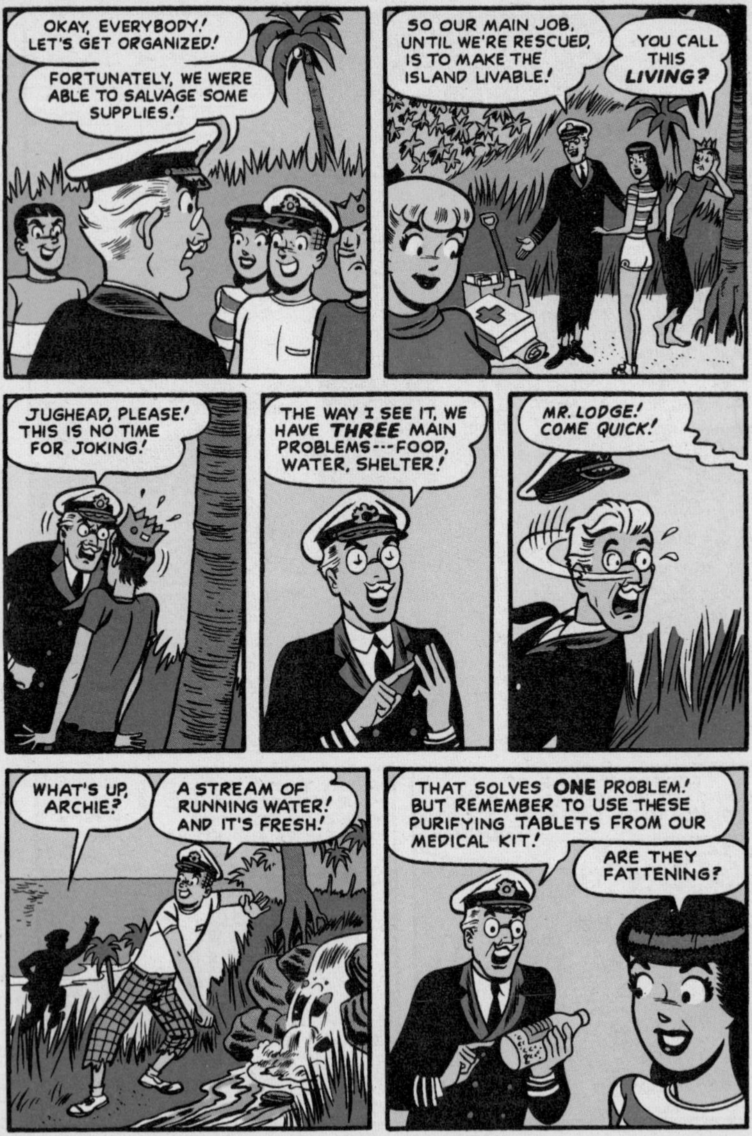
OKAY, EVERYBODY! LET'S GET ORGANIZED!
FORTUNATELY, WE WERE ABLE TO SALVAGE SOME SUPPLIES!
SO OUR MAIN JOB, UNTIL WE'RE RESCUED, IS TO MAKE THE ISLAND LIVABLE!
YOU CALL THIS LIVING?
JUGHEAD, PLEASE! THIS IS NO TIME FOR JOKING!
THE WAY I SEE IT, WE HAVE THREE MAIN PROBLEMS---FOOD, WATER, SHELTER!
MR. LODGE! COME QUICK!
WHAT'S UP, ARCHIE?
A STREAM OF RUNNING WATER! AND IT'S FRESH!
THAT SOLVES ONE PROBLEM! BUT REMEMBER TO USE THESE PURIFYING TABLETS FROM OUR MEDICAL KIT!
ARE THEY FATTENING?

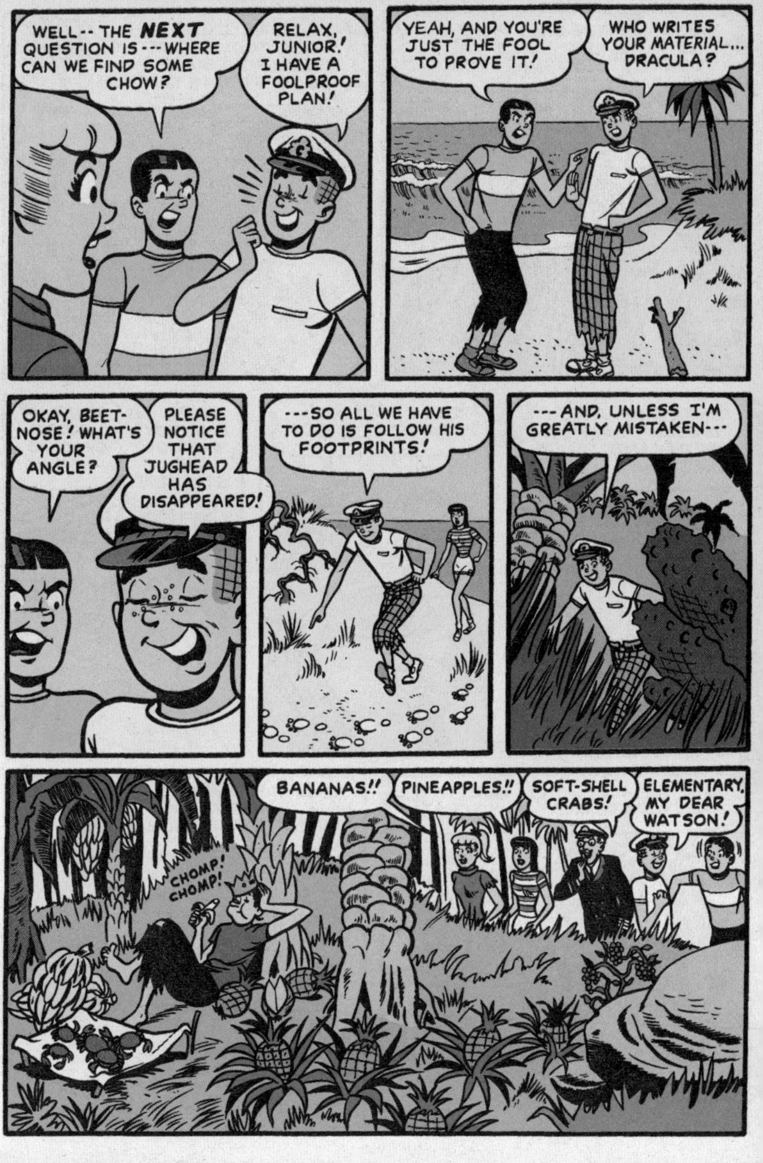

WELL-- THE **NEXT** QUESTION IS---WHERE CAN WE FIND SOME CHOW?
RELAX, JUNIOR! I HAVE A FOOLPROOF PLAN!
YEAH, AND YOU'RE JUST THE FOOL TO PROVE IT!
WHO WRITES YOUR MATERIAL... DRACULA?
OKAY, BEET-NOSE! WHAT'S YOUR ANGLE?
PLEASE NOTICE THAT JUGHEAD HAS DISAPPEARED!
---SO ALL WE HAVE TO DO IS FOLLOW HIS FOOTPRINTS!
---AND, UNLESS I'M GREATLY MISTAKEN---
BANANAS!!
PINEAPPLES!!
SOFT-SHELL CRABS!
ELEMENTARY, MY DEAR WATSON!
CHOMP! CHOMP!

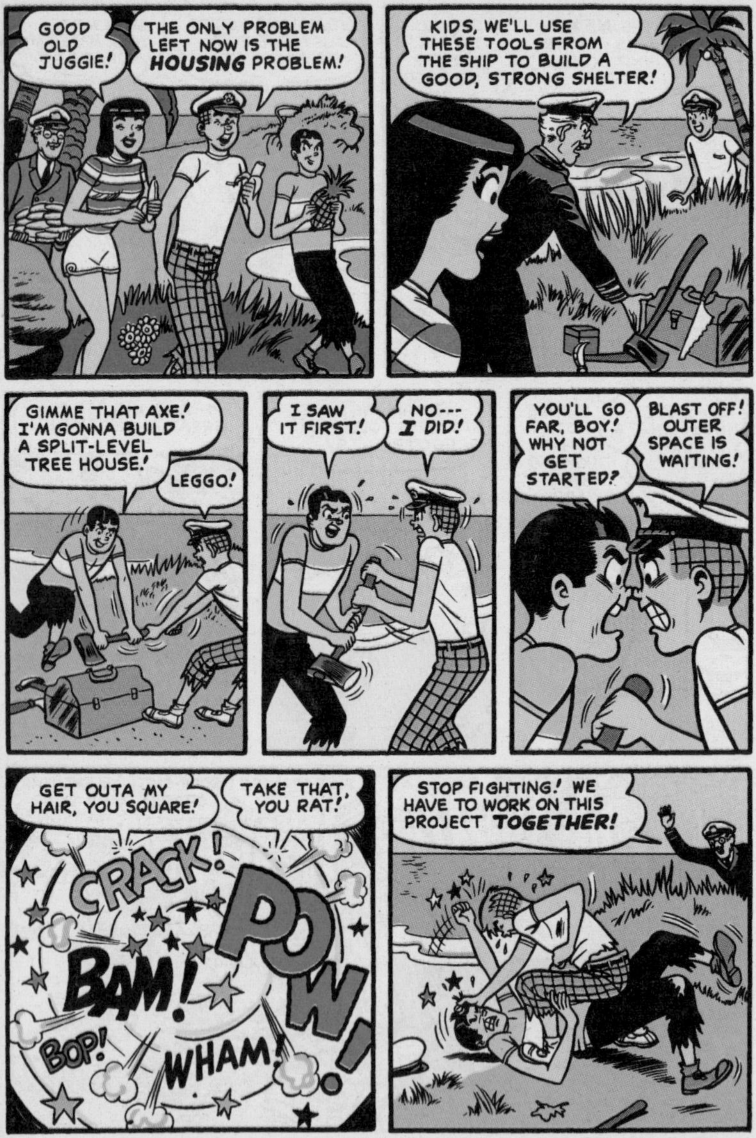
GOOD OLD JUGGIE!
THE ONLY PROBLEM LEFT NOW IS THE **HOUSING** PROBLEM!
KIDS, WE'LL USE THESE TOOLS FROM THE SHIP TO BUILD A GOOD, STRONG SHELTER!
GIMME THAT AXE! I'M GONNA BUILD A SPLIT-LEVEL TREE HOUSE!
LEGGO!
I SAW IT FIRST!
NO--- **I** DID!
YOU'LL GO FAR, BOY! WHY NOT GET STARTED?
BLAST OFF! OUTER SPACE IS WAITING!
GET OUTA MY HAIR, YOU SQUARE!
TAKE THAT, YOU RAT!
CRACK!
POW!
BAM!
BOP!
WHAM!
STOP FIGHTING! WE HAVE TO WORK ON THIS PROJECT **TOGETHER!**

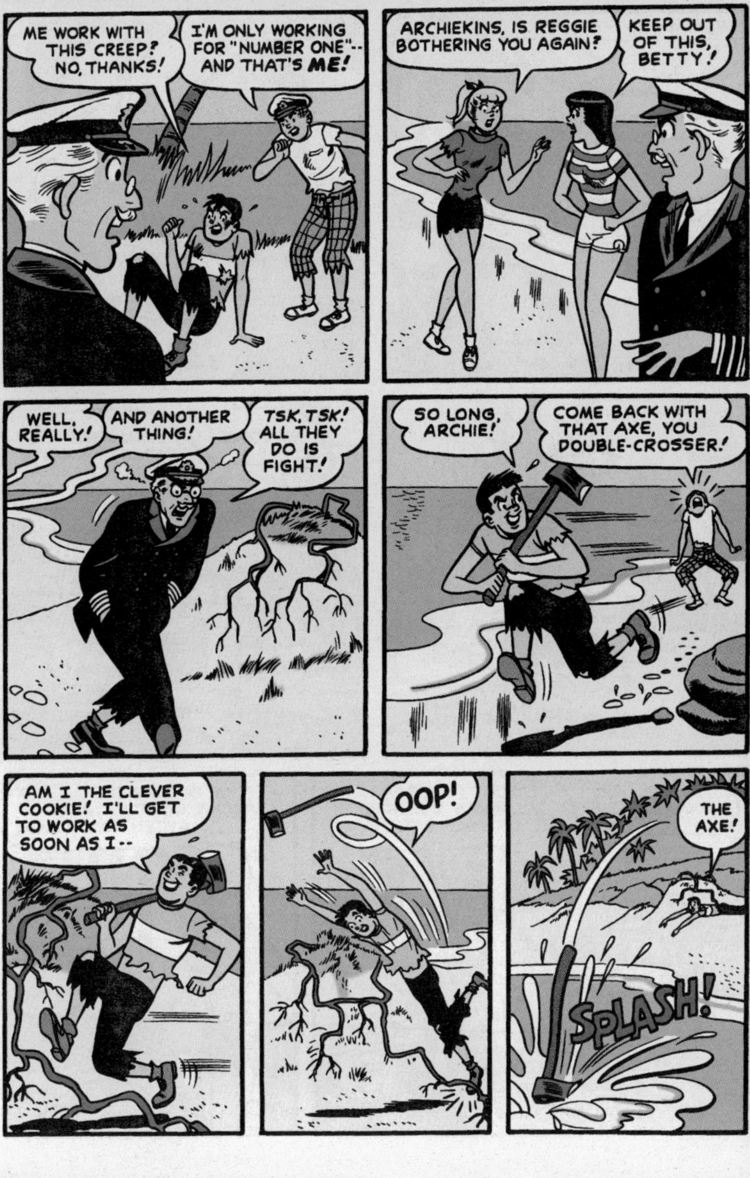

ME WORK WITH THIS CREEP? NO, THANKS!
I'M ONLY WORKING FOR "NUMBER ONE"-- AND THAT'S ME!
ARCHIEKINS, IS REGGIE BOTHERING YOU AGAIN?
KEEP OUT OF THIS, BETTY!
WELL, REALLY!
AND ANOTHER THING!
TSK, TSK! ALL THEY DO IS FIGHT!
SO LONG, ARCHIE!
COME BACK WITH THAT AXE, YOU DOUBLE-CROSSER!
AM I THE CLEVER COOKIE! I'LL GET TO WORK AS SOON AS I--
OOP!
THE AXE!
SPLASH!

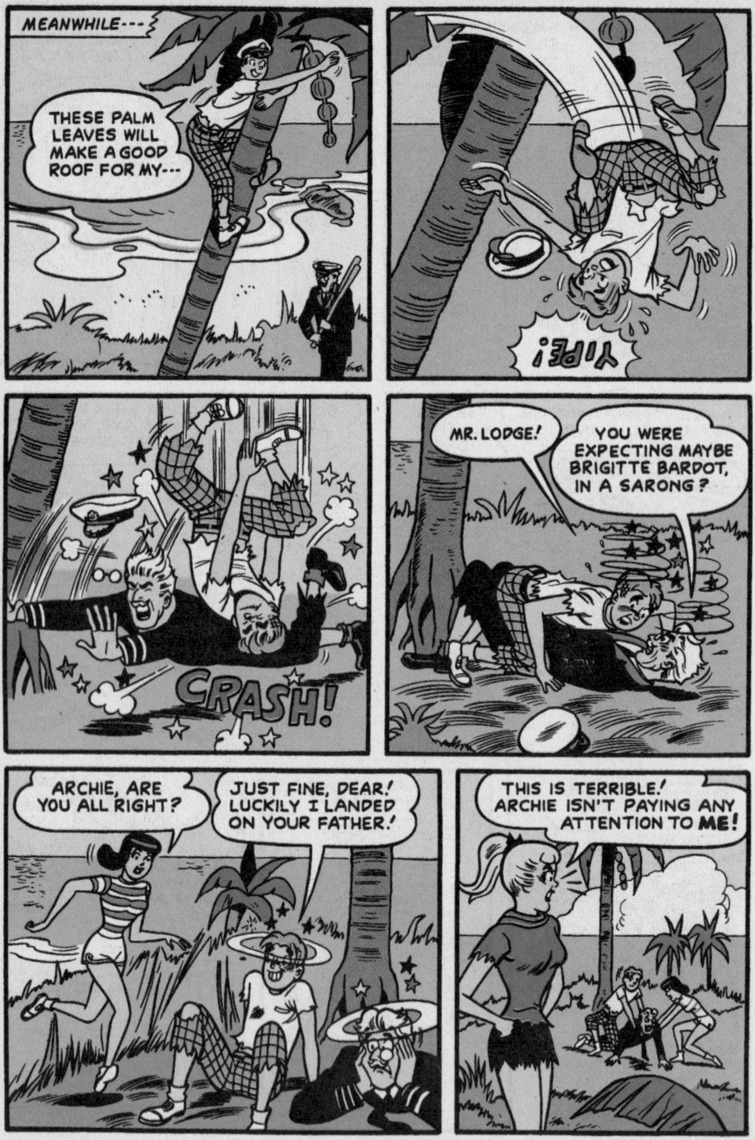
MEANWHILE---
THESE PALM LEAVES WILL MAKE A GOOD ROOF FOR MY---
YIPE!
CRASH!
MR. LODGE!
YOU WERE EXPECTING MAYBE BRIGITTE BARDOT, IN A SARONG?
ARCHIE, ARE YOU ALL RIGHT?
JUST FINE, DEAR! LUCKILY I LANDED ON YOUR FATHER!
THIS IS TERRIBLE! ARCHIE ISN'T PAYING ANY ATTENTION TO ME!

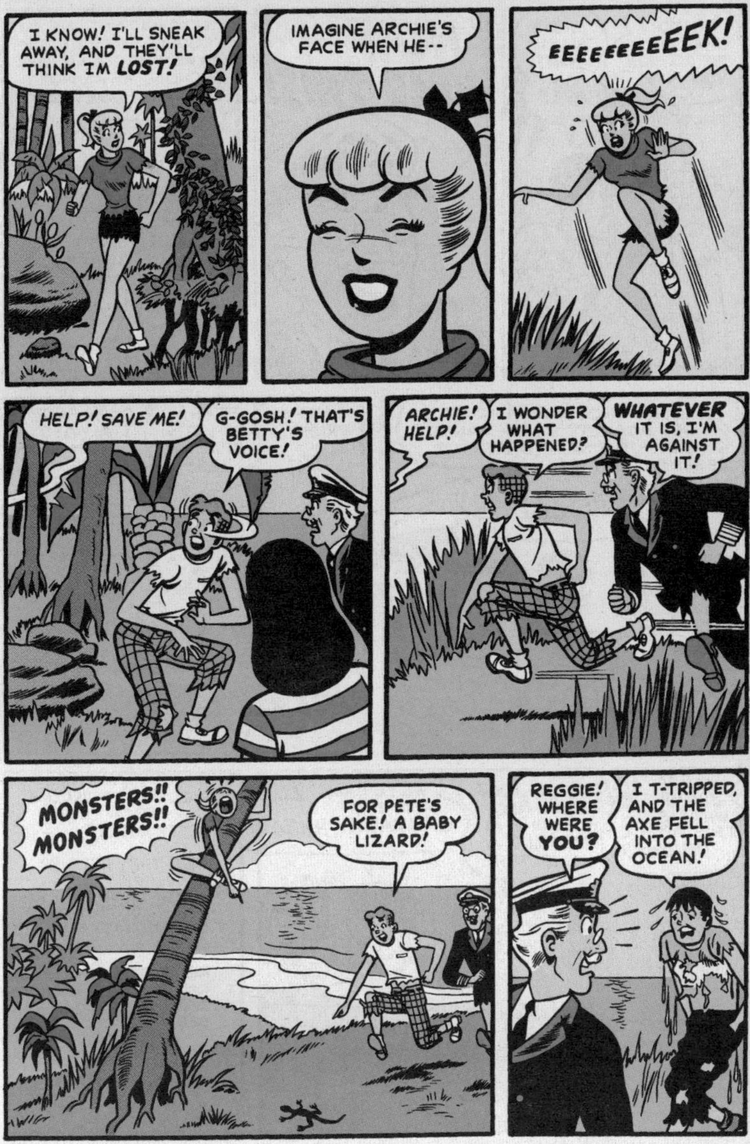
I KNOW! I'LL SNEAK AWAY, AND THEY'LL THINK IM LOST!
IMAGINE ARCHIE'S FACE WHEN HE--
EEEEEEEEEEEK!
HELP! SAVE ME!
G-GOSH! THAT'S BETTY'S VOICE!
ARCHIE! HELP!
I WONDER WHAT HAPPENED?
WHATEVER IT IS, I'M AGAINST IT!
MONSTERS!! MONSTERS!!
FOR PETE'S SAKE! A BABY LIZARD!
REGGIE! WHERE WERE YOU?
I T-TRIPPED, AND THE AXE FELL INTO THE OCEAN!

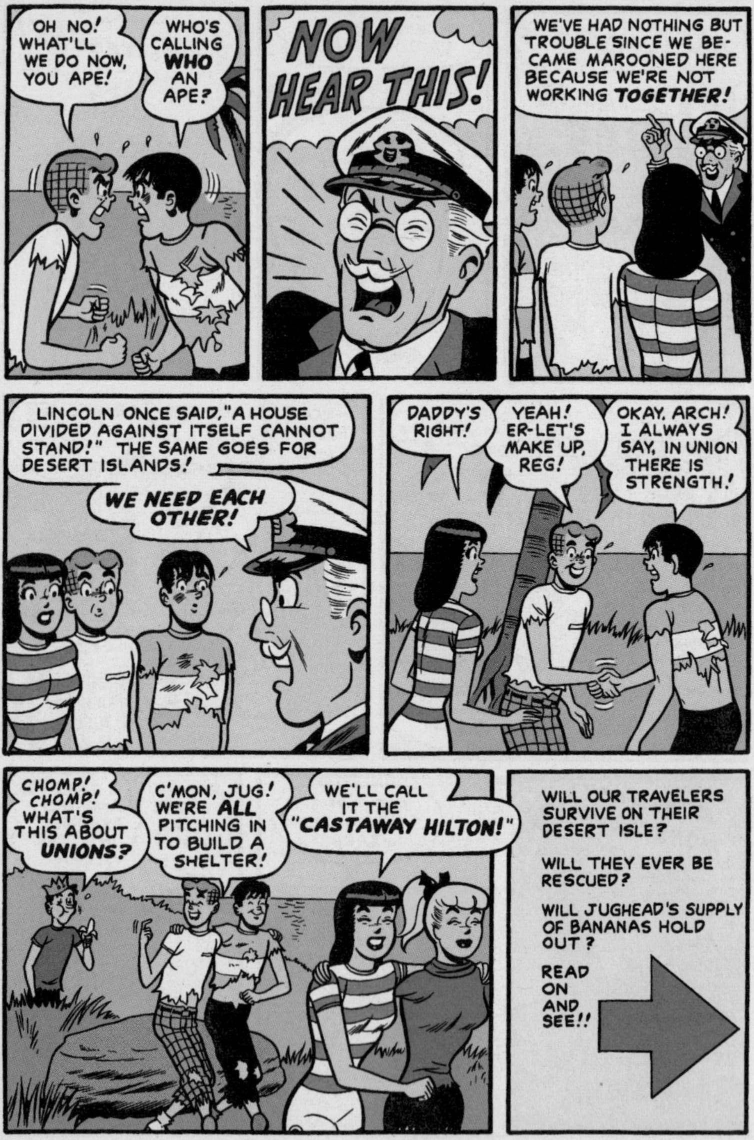
OH NO! WHAT'LL WE DO NOW, YOU APE!
WHO'S CALLING **WHO** AN APE?
NOW HEAR THIS!
WE'VE HAD NOTHING BUT TROUBLE SINCE WE BECAME MAROONED HERE BECAUSE WE'RE NOT WORKING **TOGETHER!**
LINCOLN ONCE SAID, "A HOUSE DIVIDED AGAINST ITSELF CANNOT STAND!" THE SAME GOES FOR DESERT ISLANDS!
WE NEED EACH OTHER!
DADDY'S RIGHT!
YEAH! ER-LET'S MAKE UP, REG!
OKAY, ARCH! I ALWAYS SAY, IN UNION THERE IS STRENGTH!
CHOMP! CHOMP! WHAT'S THIS ABOUT **UNIONS?**
C'MON, JUG! WE'RE **ALL** PITCHING IN TO BUILD A SHELTER!
WE'LL CALL IT THE **"CASTAWAY HILTON!"**
WILL OUR TRAVELERS SURVIVE ON THEIR DESERT ISLE?
WILL THEY EVER BE RESCUED?
WILL JUGHEAD'S SUPPLY OF BANANAS HOLD OUT?
READ ON AND SEE!!

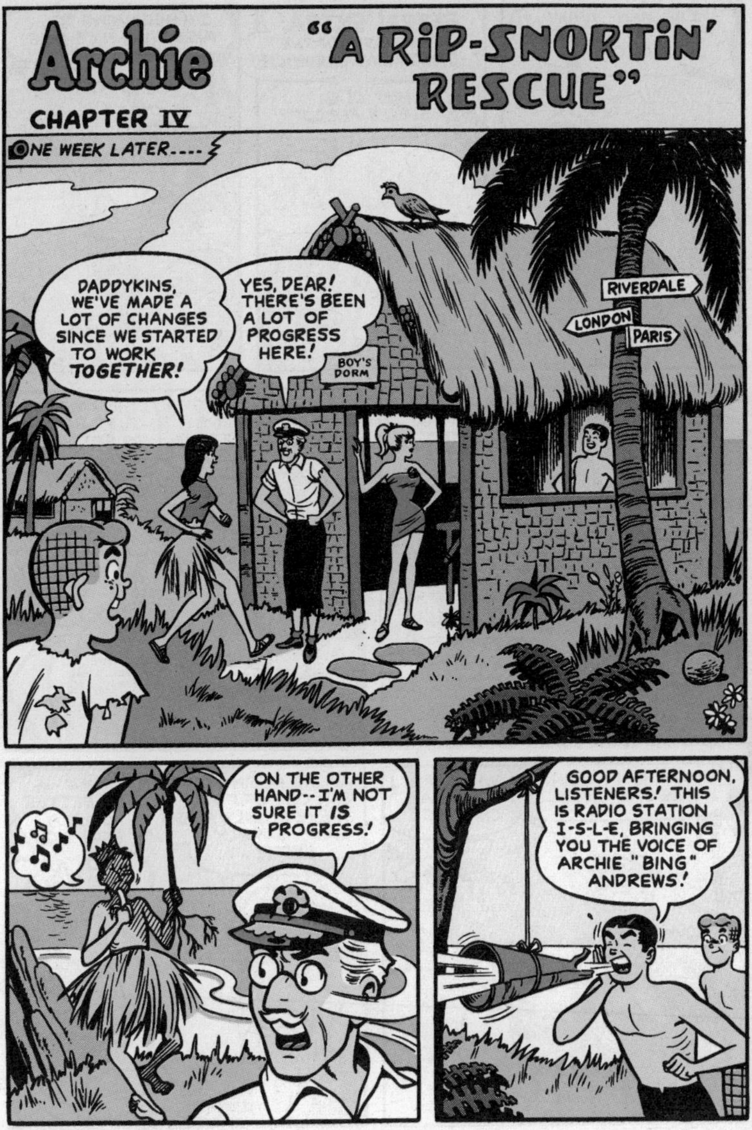
Archie
"A RiP-SNORTiN' RESCUE"
CHAPTER IV
ONE WEEK LATER....
DADDYKINS, WE'VE MADE A LOT OF CHANGES SINCE WE STARTED TO WORK TOGETHER!
YES, DEAR! THERE'S BEEN A LOT OF PROGRESS HERE!
BOY'S DORM
RIVERDALE
LONDON
PARIS
ON THE OTHER HAND-- I'M NOT SURE IT IS PROGRESS!
GOOD AFTERNOON, LISTENERS! THIS IS RADIO STATION I-S-L-E, BRINGING YOU THE VOICE OF ARCHIE "BING" ANDREWS!

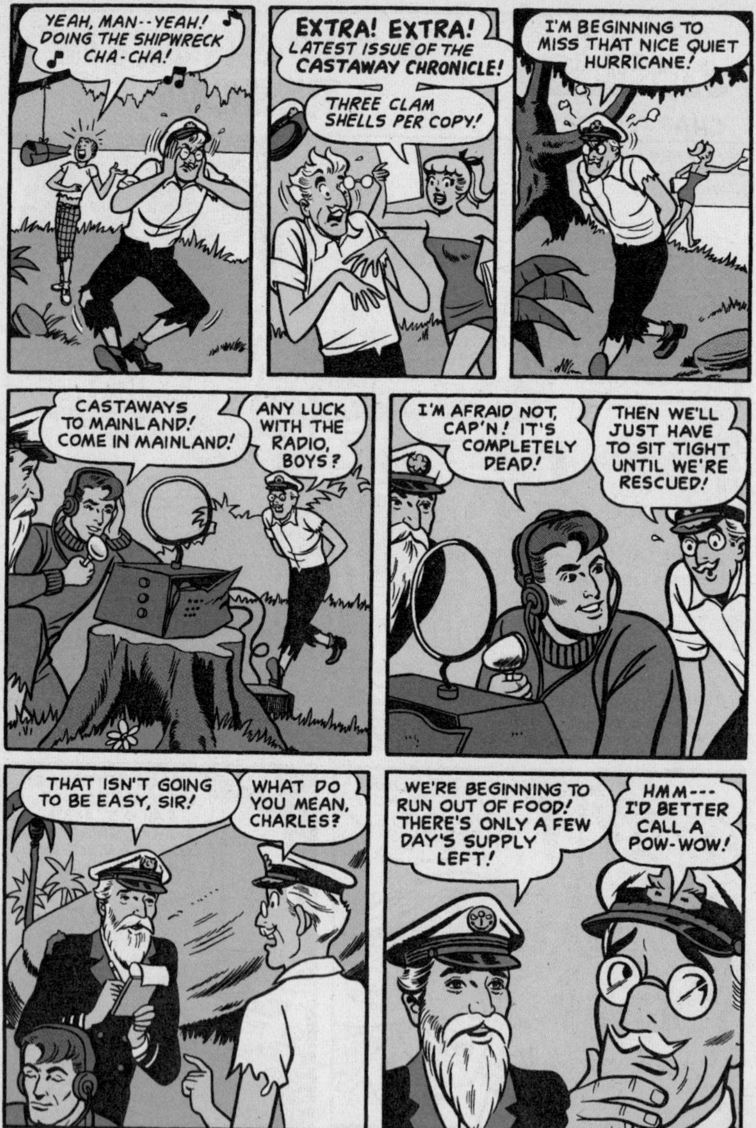
YEAH, MAN--YEAH! DOING THE SHIPWRECK CHA-CHA!
EXTRA! EXTRA! LATEST ISSUE OF THE CASTAWAY CHRONICLE!
THREE CLAM SHELLS PER COPY!
I'M BEGINNING TO MISS THAT NICE QUIET HURRICANE!
CASTAWAYS TO MAINLAND! COME IN MAINLAND!
ANY LUCK WITH THE RADIO, BOYS?
I'M AFRAID NOT, CAP'N! IT'S COMPLETELY DEAD!
THEN WE'LL JUST HAVE TO SIT TIGHT UNTIL WE'RE RESCUED!
THAT ISN'T GOING TO BE EASY, SIR!
WHAT DO YOU MEAN, CHARLES?
WE'RE BEGINNING TO RUN OUT OF FOOD! THERE'S ONLY A FEW DAY'S SUPPLY LEFT!
HMM--- I'D BETTER CALL A POW-WOW!

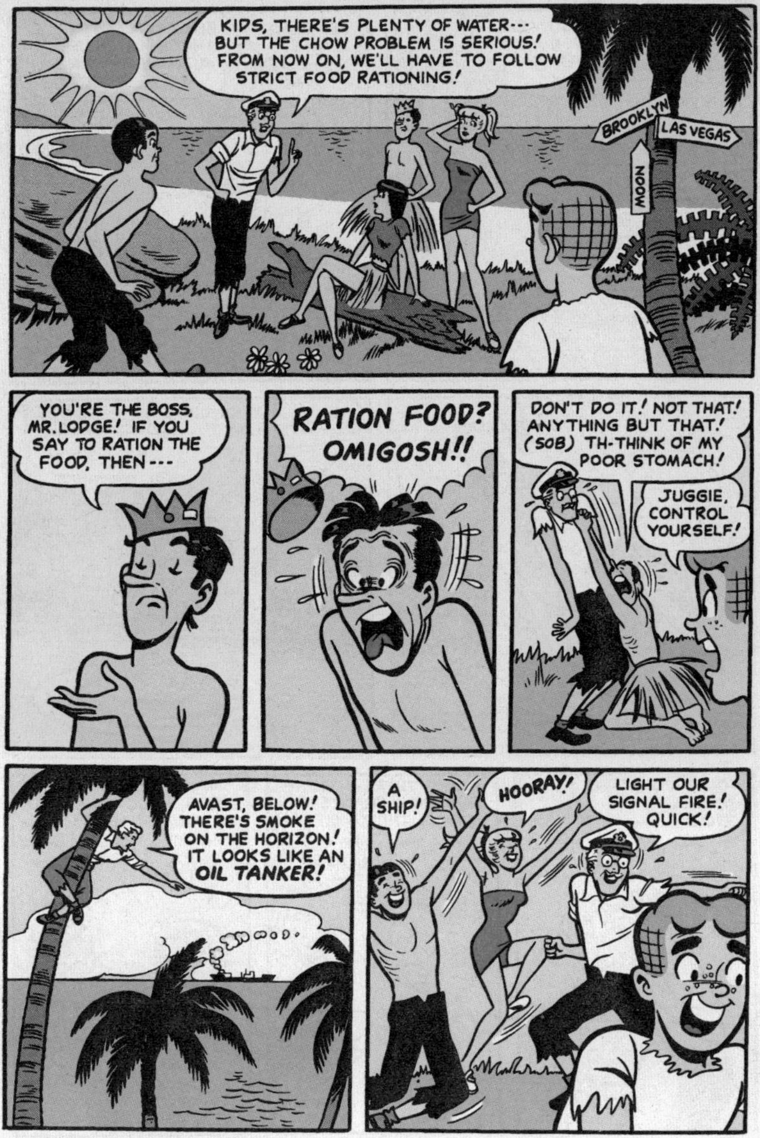
KIDS, THERE'S PLENTY OF WATER--- BUT THE CHOW PROBLEM IS SERIOUS! FROM NOW ON, WE'LL HAVE TO FOLLOW STRICT FOOD RATIONING!
BROOKLYN
LAS VEGAS
MOON
YOU'RE THE BOSS, MR. LODGE! IF YOU SAY TO RATION THE FOOD, THEN---
RATION FOOD? OMIGOSH!!
DON'T DO IT! NOT THAT! ANYTHING BUT THAT! (SOB) TH-THINK OF MY POOR STOMACH!
JUGGIE, CONTROL YOURSELF!
AVAST, BELOW! THERE'S SMOKE ON THE HORIZON! IT LOOKS LIKE AN OIL TANKER!
A SHIP!
HOORAY!
LIGHT OUR SIGNAL FIRE! QUICK!

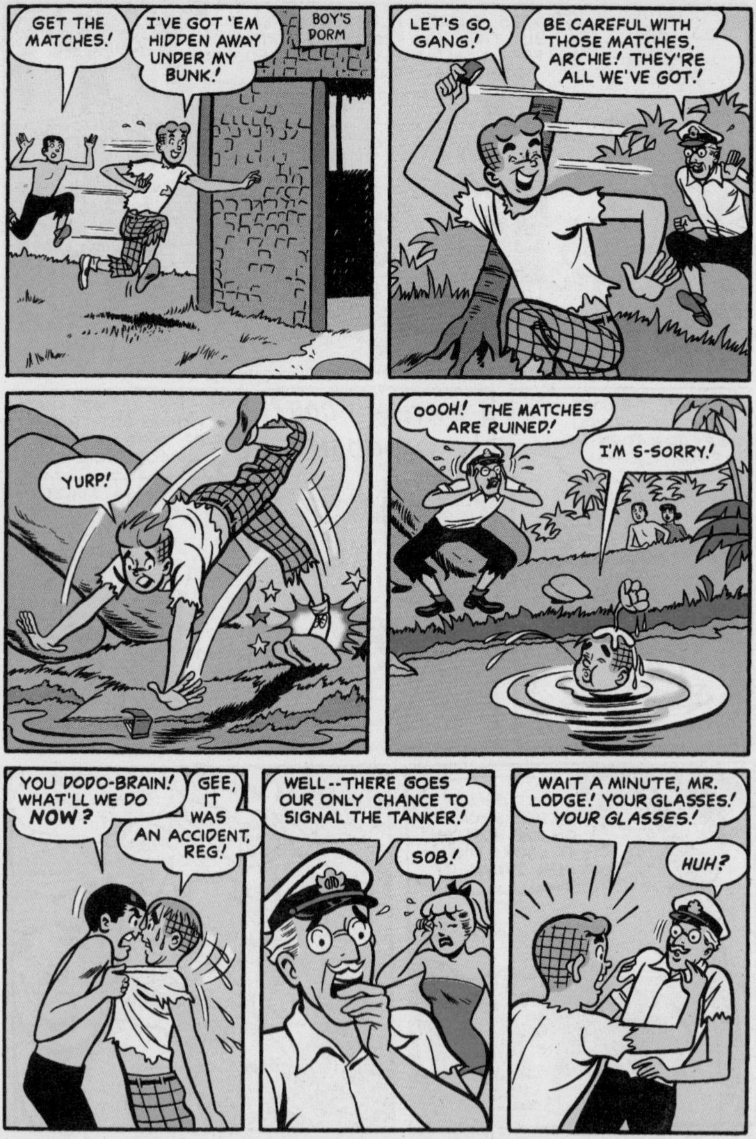
GET THE MATCHES!
I'VE GOT 'EM HIDDEN AWAY UNDER MY BUNK!
BOY'S DORM
LET'S GO, GANG!
BE CAREFUL WITH THOSE MATCHES, ARCHIE! THEY'RE ALL WE'VE GOT!
YURP!
OOOH! THE MATCHES ARE RUINED!
I'M S-SORRY!
YOU DODO-BRAIN! WHAT'LL WE DO NOW?
GEE, IT WAS AN ACCIDENT, REG!
WELL--THERE GOES OUR ONLY CHANCE TO SIGNAL THE TANKER!
SOB!
WAIT A MINUTE, MR. LODGE! YOUR GLASSES! YOUR GLASSES!
HUH?

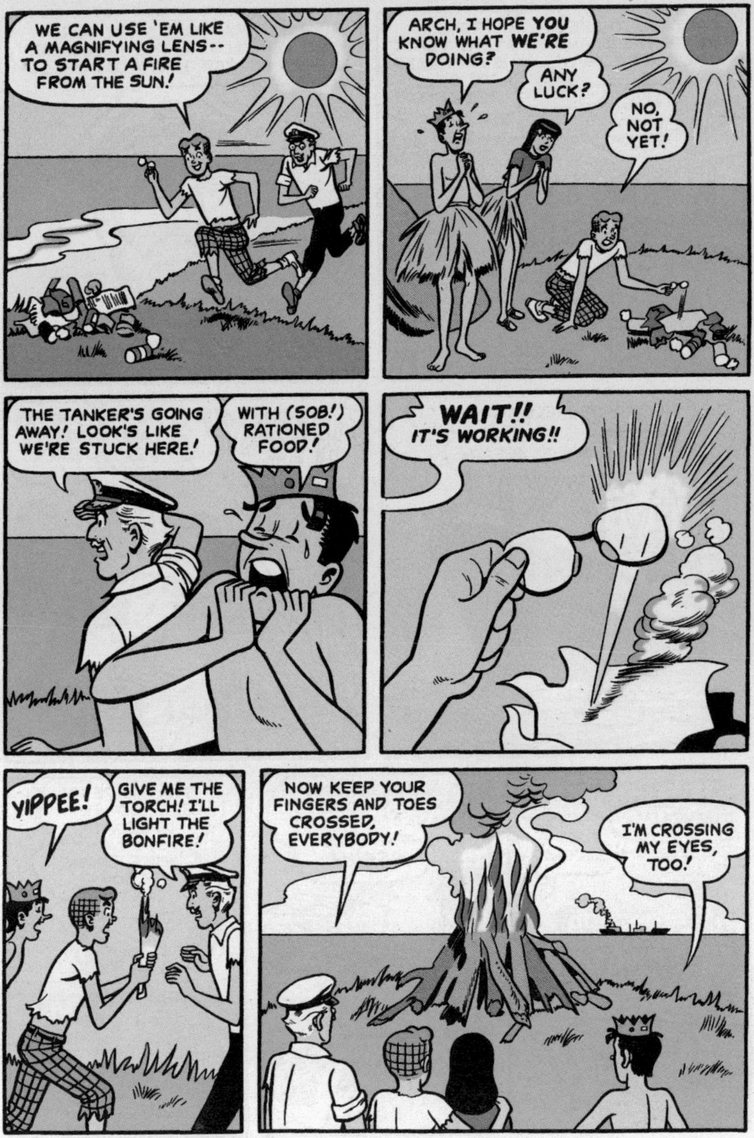
WE CAN USE 'EM LIKE A MAGNIFYING LENS-- TO START A FIRE FROM THE SUN!
ARCH, I HOPE YOU KNOW WHAT WE'RE DOING?
ANY LUCK?
NO, NOT YET!
THE TANKER'S GOING AWAY! LOOK'S LIKE WE'RE STUCK HERE!
WITH (SOB!) RATIONED FOOD!
WAIT!! IT'S WORKING!!
YIPPEE!
GIVE ME THE TORCH! I'LL LIGHT THE BONFIRE!
NOW KEEP YOUR FINGERS AND TOES CROSSED, EVERYBODY!
I'M CROSSING MY EYES, TOO!

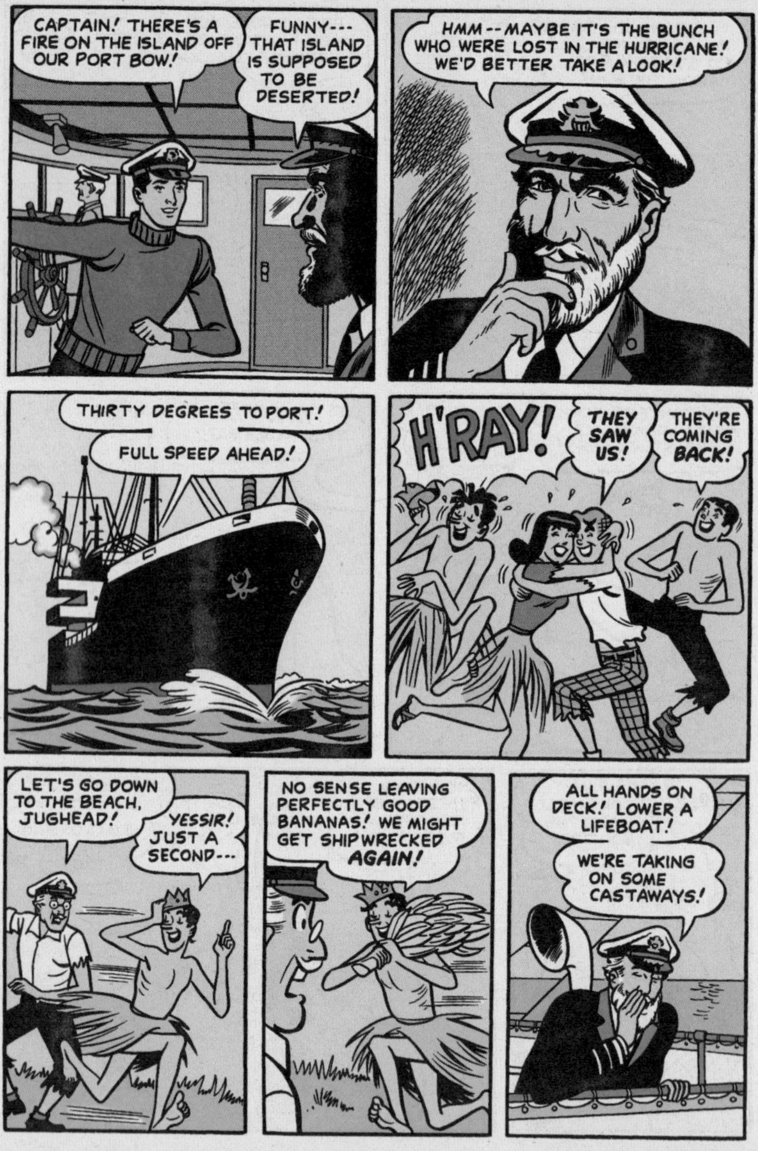
CAPTAIN! THERE'S A FIRE ON THE ISLAND OFF OUR PORT BOW!
FUNNY--- THAT ISLAND IS SUPPOSED TO BE DESERTED!
HMM -- MAYBE IT'S THE BUNCH WHO WERE LOST IN THE HURRICANE! WE'D BETTER TAKE A LOOK!
THIRTY DEGREES TO PORT!
FULL SPEED AHEAD!
H'RAY!
THEY SAW US!
THEY'RE COMING BACK!
LET'S GO DOWN TO THE BEACH, JUGHEAD!
YESSIR! JUST A SECOND---
NO SENSE LEAVING PERFECTLY GOOD BANANAS! WE MIGHT GET SHIPWRECKED AGAIN!
ALL HANDS ON DECK! LOWER A LIFEBOAT!
WE'RE TAKING ON SOME CASTAWAYS!

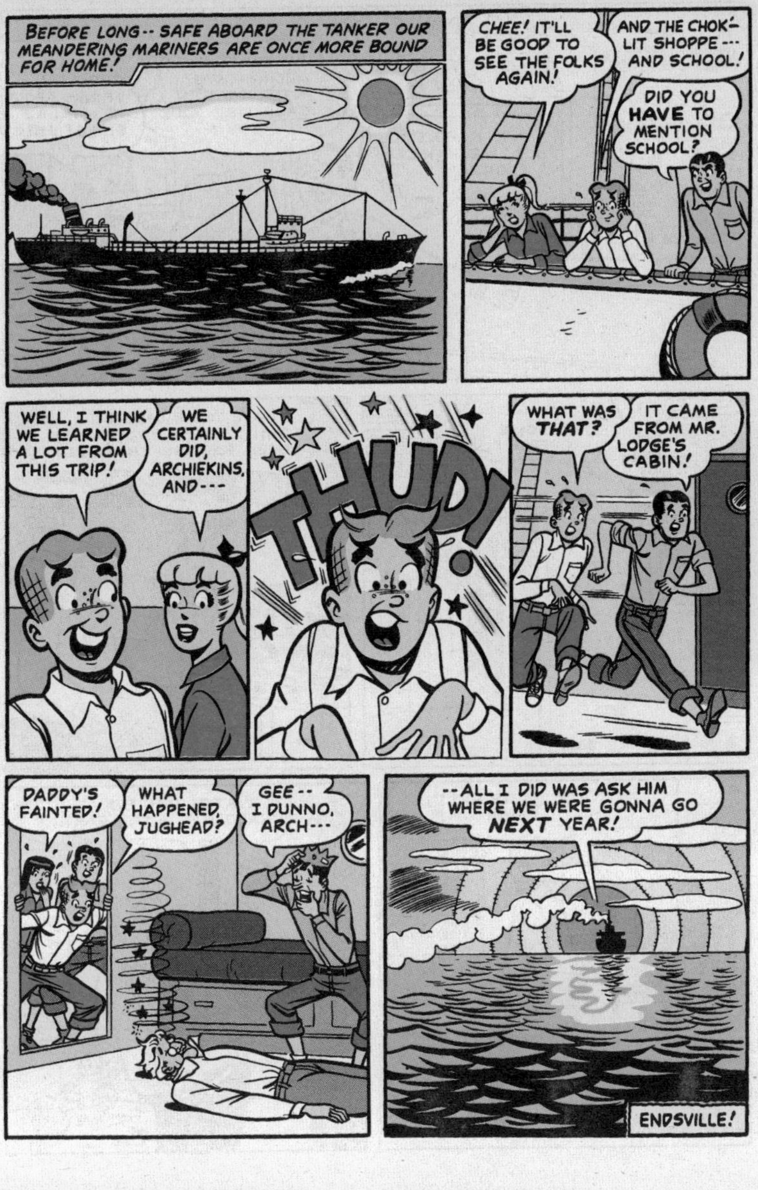
BEFORE LONG-- SAFE ABOARD THE TANKER OUR MEANDERING MARINERS ARE ONCE MORE BOUND FOR HOME!
CHEE! IT'LL BE GOOD TO SEE THE FOLKS AGAIN!
AND THE CHOK'-LIT SHOPPE --- AND SCHOOL!
DID YOU HAVE TO MENTION SCHOOL?
WELL, I THINK WE LEARNED A LOT FROM THIS TRIP!
WE CERTAINLY DID, ARCHIEKINS, AND---
THUD!
WHAT WAS THAT?
IT CAME FROM MR. LODGE'S CABIN!
DADDY'S FAINTED!
WHAT HAPPENED, JUGHEAD?
GEE -- I DUNNO, ARCH---
--ALL I DID WAS ASK HIM WHERE WE WERE GONNA GO NEXT YEAR!
ENDSVILLE!

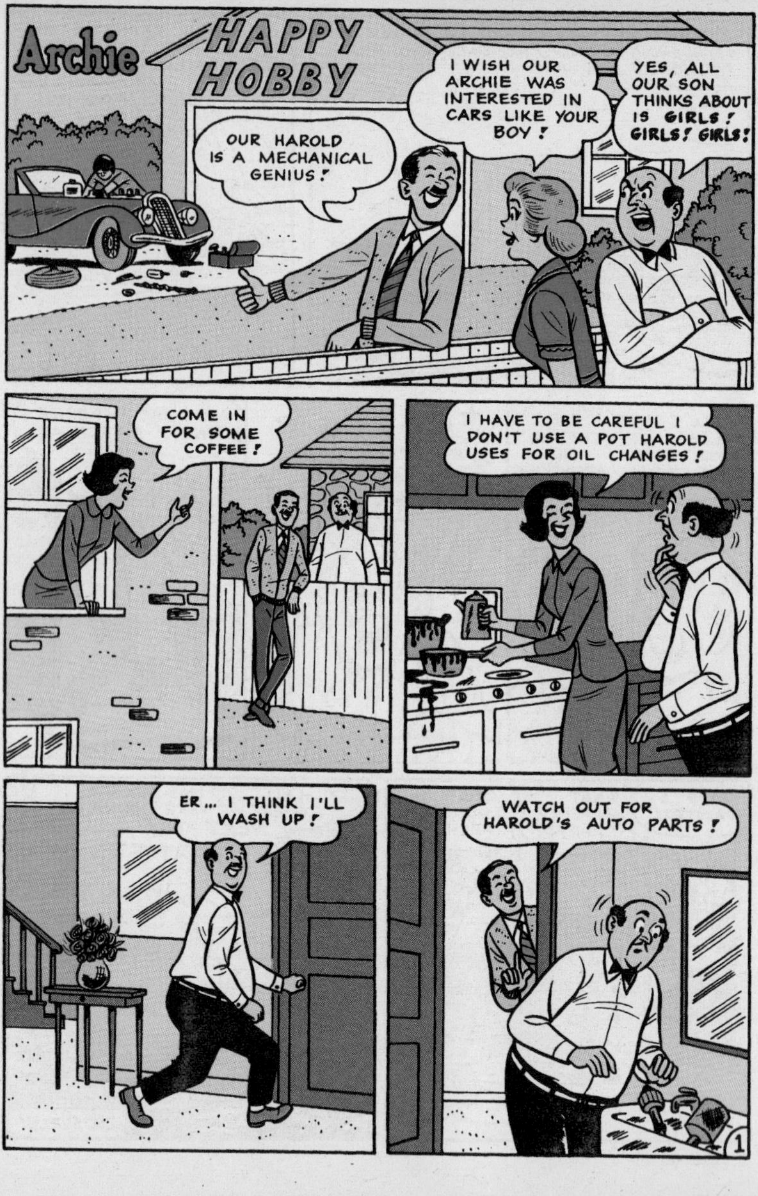
Archie
HAPPY HOBBY
OUR HAROLD IS A MECHANICAL GENIUS!
I WISH OUR ARCHIE WAS INTERESTED IN CARS LIKE YOUR BOY!
YES, ALL OUR SON THINKS ABOUT IS GIRLS! GIRLS! GIRLS!
COME IN FOR SOME COFFEE!
I HAVE TO BE CAREFUL I DON'T USE A POT HAROLD USES FOR OIL CHANGES!
ER... I THINK I'LL WASH UP!
WATCH OUT FOR HAROLD'S AUTO PARTS!
1

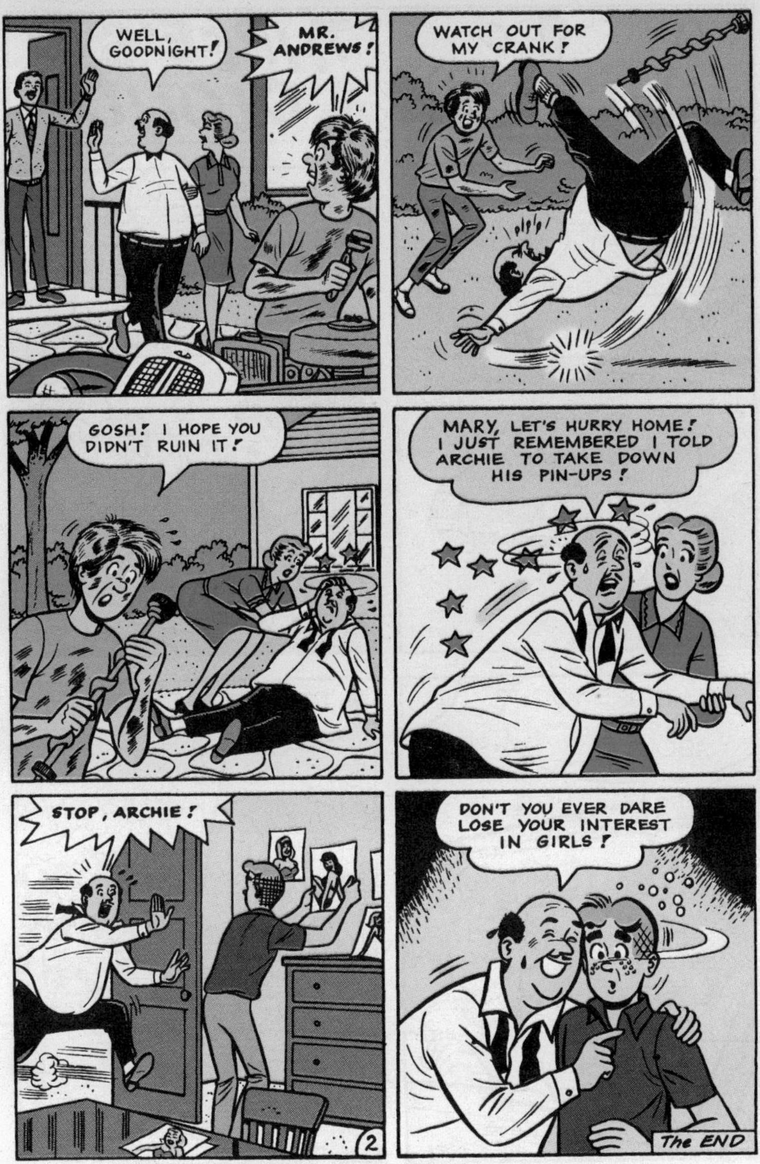
WELL, GOODNIGHT!
MR. ANDREWS!
WATCH OUT FOR MY CRANK!
GOSH! I HOPE YOU DIDN'T RUIN IT!
MARY, LET'S HURRY HOME! I JUST REMEMBERED I TOLD ARCHIE TO TAKE DOWN HIS PIN-UPS!
STOP, ARCHIE!
2
DON'T YOU EVER DARE LOSE YOUR INTEREST IN GIRLS!
The END

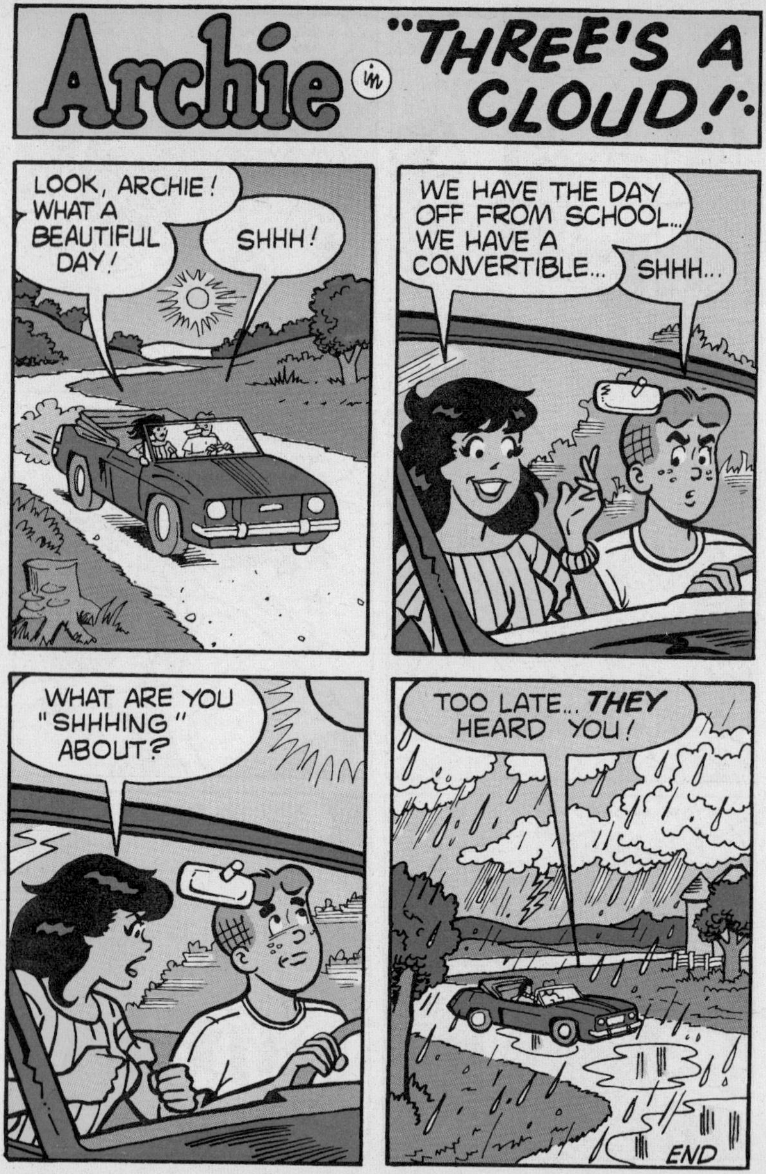
Archie in "THREE'S A CLOUD!"
LOOK, ARCHIE! WHAT A BEAUTIFUL DAY!
SHHH!
WE HAVE THE DAY OFF FROM SCHOOL... WE HAVE A CONVERTIBLE...
SHHH...
WHAT ARE YOU "SHHHING" ABOUT?
TOO LATE... THEY HEARD YOU!
END

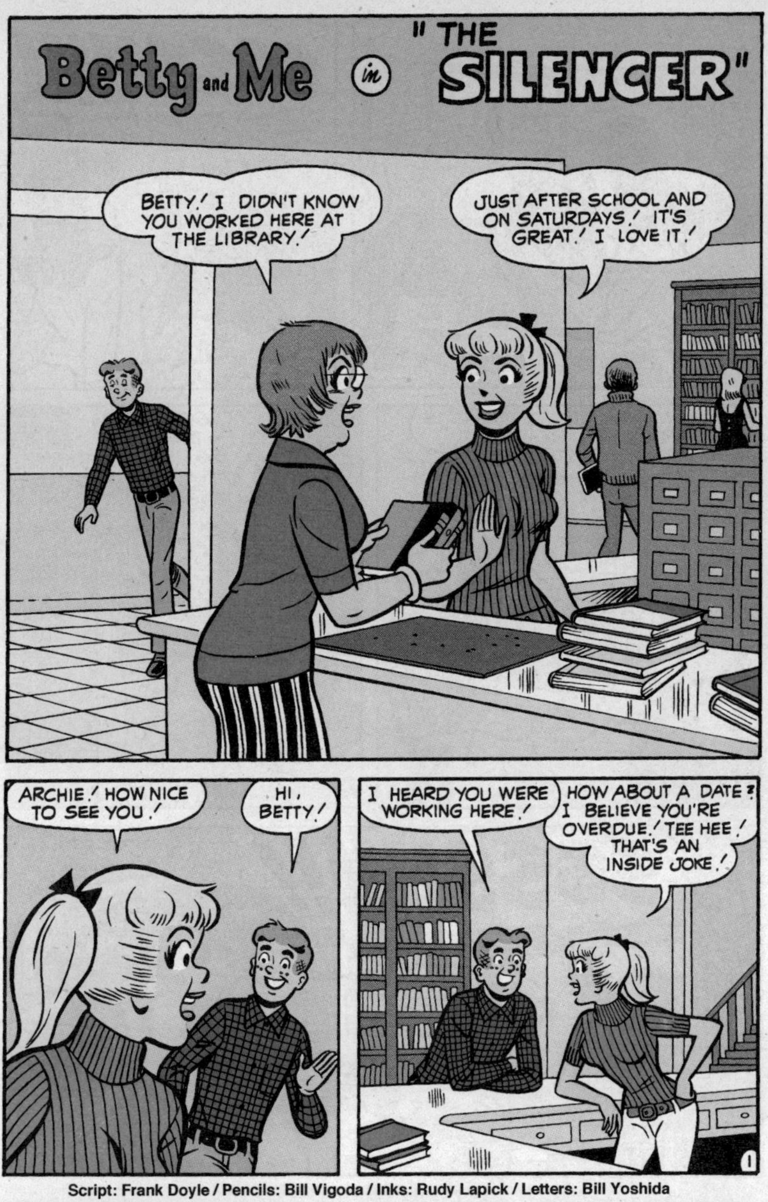
Betty and Me
in
"THE SILENCER"
BETTY! I DIDN'T KNOW YOU WORKED HERE AT THE LIBRARY!
JUST AFTER SCHOOL AND ON SATURDAYS! IT'S GREAT! I LOVE IT!
ARCHIE! HOW NICE TO SEE YOU!
HI, BETTY!
I HEARD YOU WERE WORKING HERE!
HOW ABOUT A DATE? I BELIEVE YOU'RE OVERDUE! TEE HEE! THAT'S AN INSIDE JOKE!
1
Script: Frank Doyle / Pencils: Bill Vigoda / Inks: Rudy Lapick / Letters: Bill Yoshida

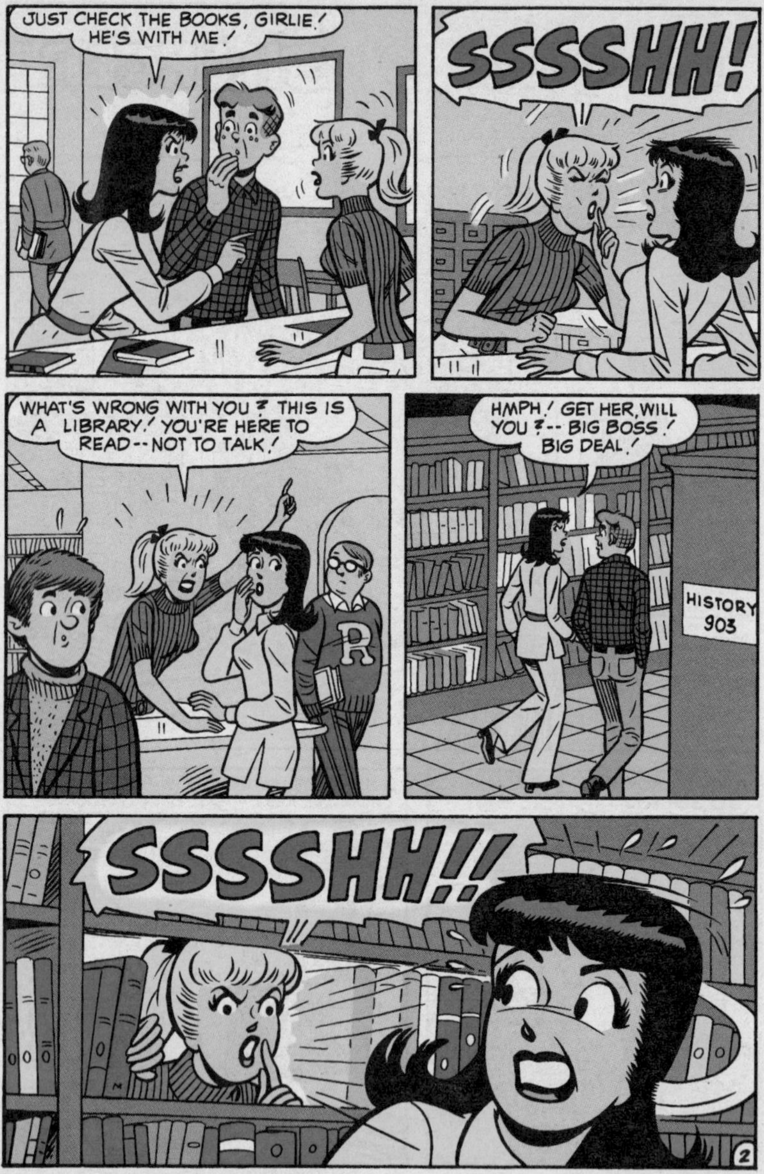

JUST CHECK THE BOOKS, GIRLIE! HE'S WITH ME!
SSSSHH!
WHAT'S WRONG WITH YOU? THIS IS A LIBRARY! YOU'RE HERE TO READ--NOT TO TALK!
HMPH! GET HER, WILL YOU?-- BIG BOSS! BIG DEAL!
HISTORY 903
SSSSHH!!
2

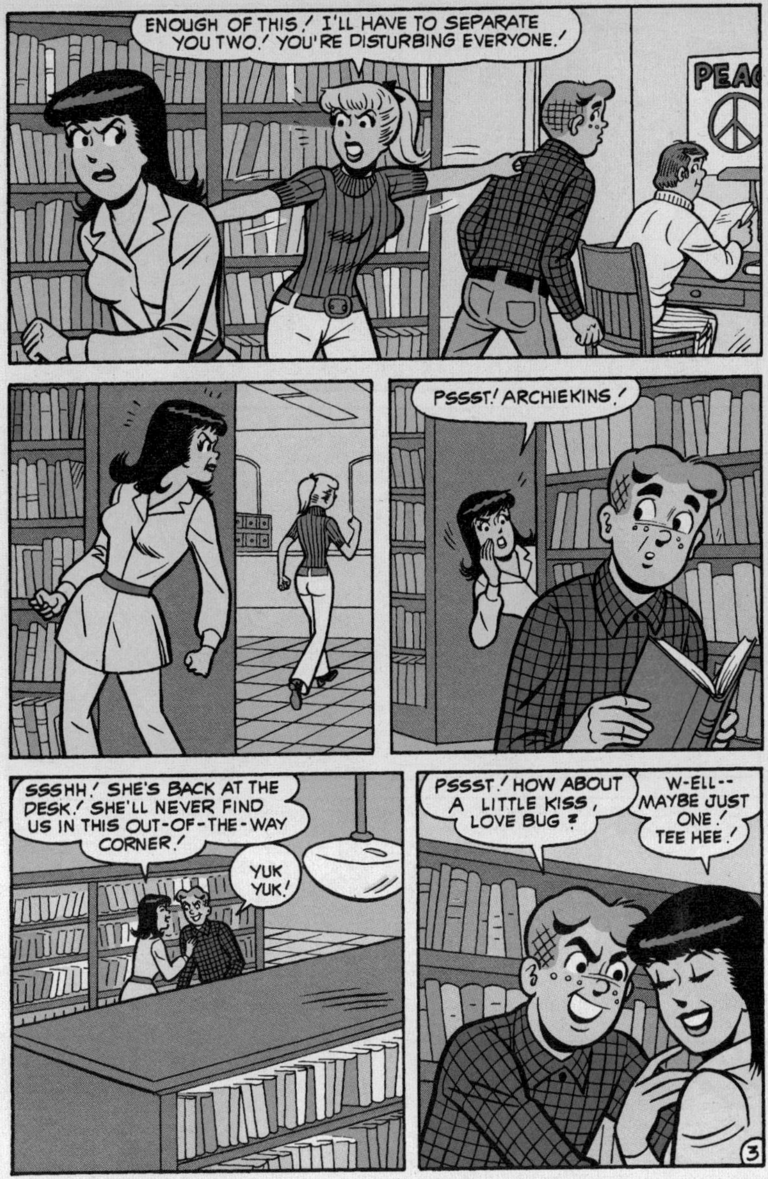
ENOUGH OF THIS! I'LL HAVE TO SEPARATE YOU TWO! YOU'RE DISTURBING EVERYONE!
PEAC
PSSST! ARCHIEKINS!
SSSHH! SHE'S BACK AT THE DESK! SHE'LL NEVER FIND US IN THIS OUT-OF-THE-WAY CORNER!
YUK YUK!
PSSST! HOW ABOUT A LITTLE KISS, LOVE BUG?
W-ELL-- MAYBE JUST ONE! TEE HEE!
3

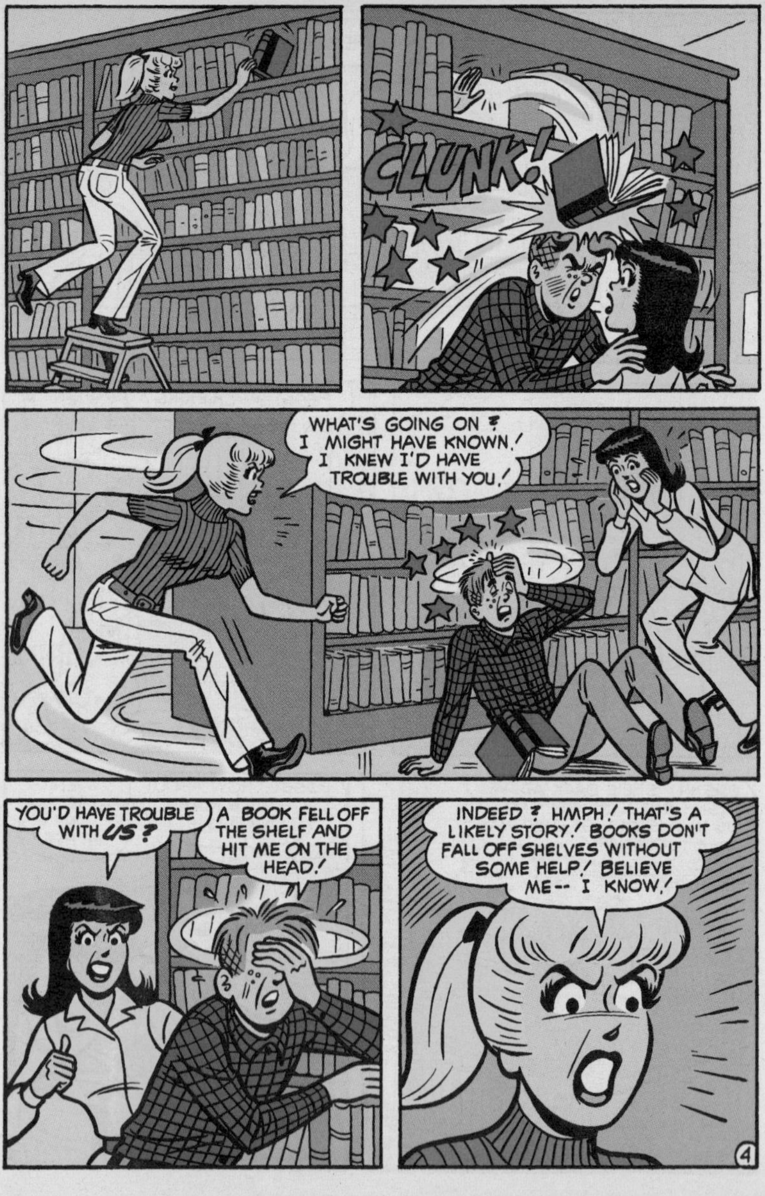
CLUNK!
WHAT'S GOING ON ? I MIGHT HAVE KNOWN! I KNEW I'D HAVE TROUBLE WITH YOU!
YOU'D HAVE TROUBLE WITH US ?
A BOOK FELL OFF THE SHELF AND HIT ME ON THE HEAD!
INDEED ? HMPH! THAT'S A LIKELY STORY! BOOKS DON'T FALL OFF SHELVES WITHOUT SOME HELP! BELIEVE ME-- I KNOW!
4

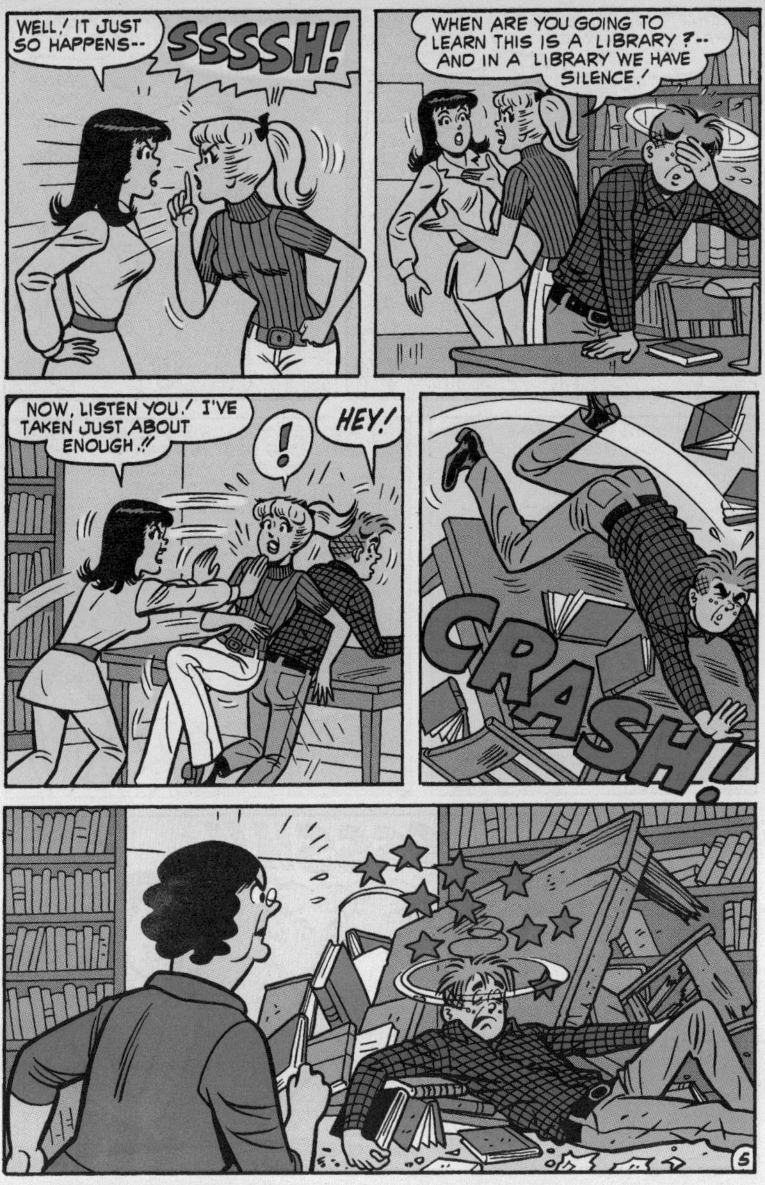

WELL! IT JUST SO HAPPENS--
SSSSH!
WHEN ARE YOU GOING TO LEARN THIS IS A LIBRARY ?-- AND IN A LIBRARY WE HAVE SILENCE!
NOW, LISTEN YOU! I'VE TAKEN JUST ABOUT ENOUGH!!
!
HEY!
CRASH!
5

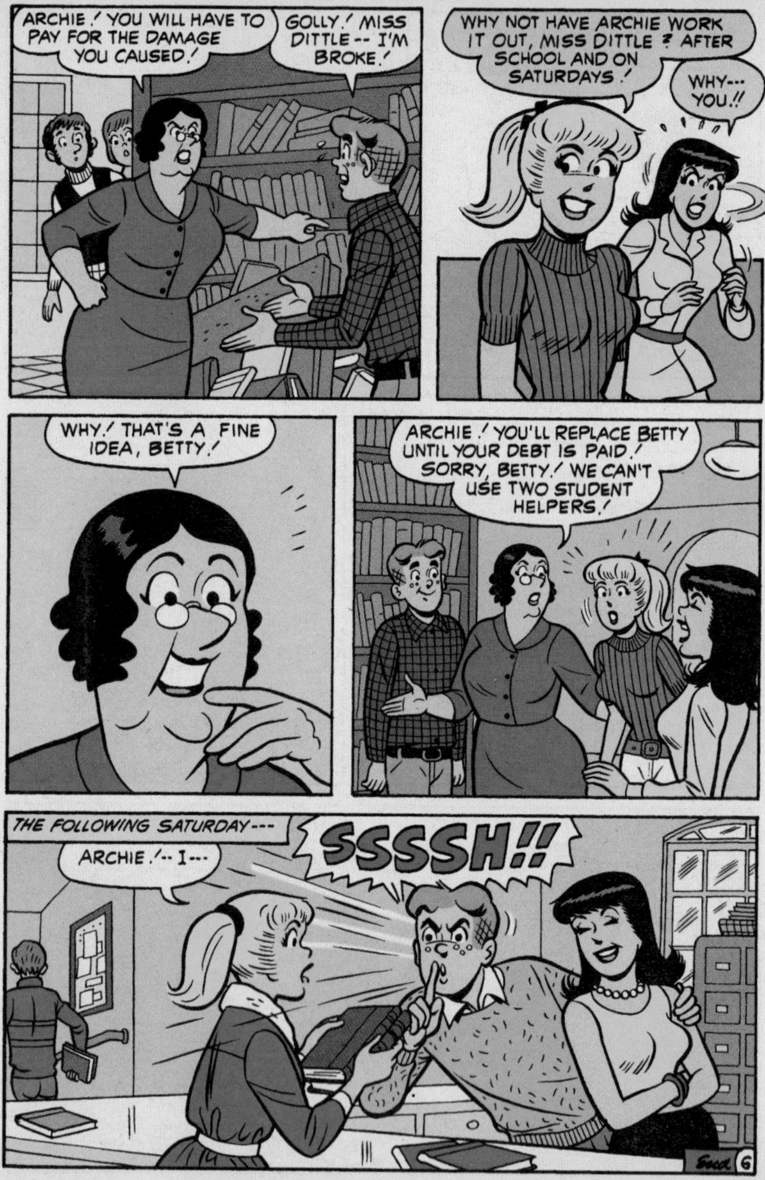
ARCHIE! YOU WILL HAVE TO PAY FOR THE DAMAGE YOU CAUSED!
GOLLY! MISS DITTLE -- I'M BROKE!
WHY NOT HAVE ARCHIE WORK IT OUT, MISS DITTLE? AFTER SCHOOL AND ON SATURDAYS!
WHY--- YOU!!
WHY! THAT'S A FINE IDEA, BETTY!
ARCHIE! YOU'LL REPLACE BETTY UNTIL YOUR DEBT IS PAID! SORRY, BETTY! WE CAN'T USE TWO STUDENT HELPERS!
THE FOLLOWING SATURDAY---
ARCHIE!-- I---
SSSSH!!
6

Betty and Me in "Small Medium"

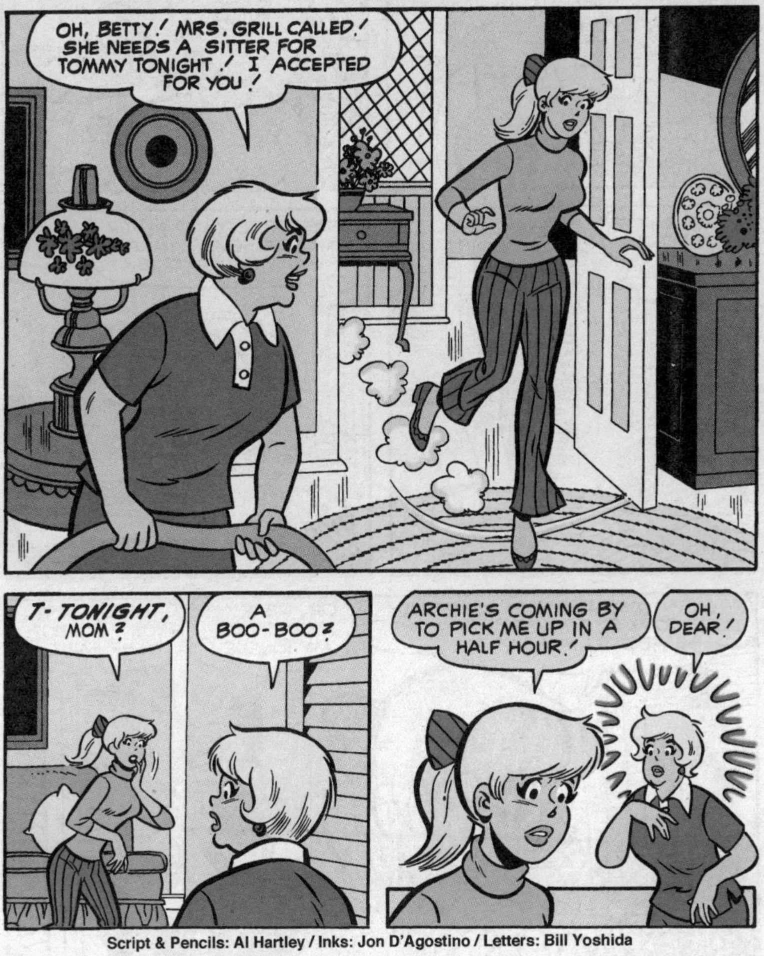

OH, BETTY! MRS. GRILL CALLED! SHE NEEDS A SITTER FOR TOMMY TONIGHT! I ACCEPTED FOR YOU!
T-TONIGHT, MOM?
A BOO-BOO?
ARCHIE'S COMING BY TO PICK ME UP IN A HALF HOUR!
OH, DEAR!

Script & Pencils: Al Hartley / Inks: Jon D'Agostino / Letters: Bill Yoshida

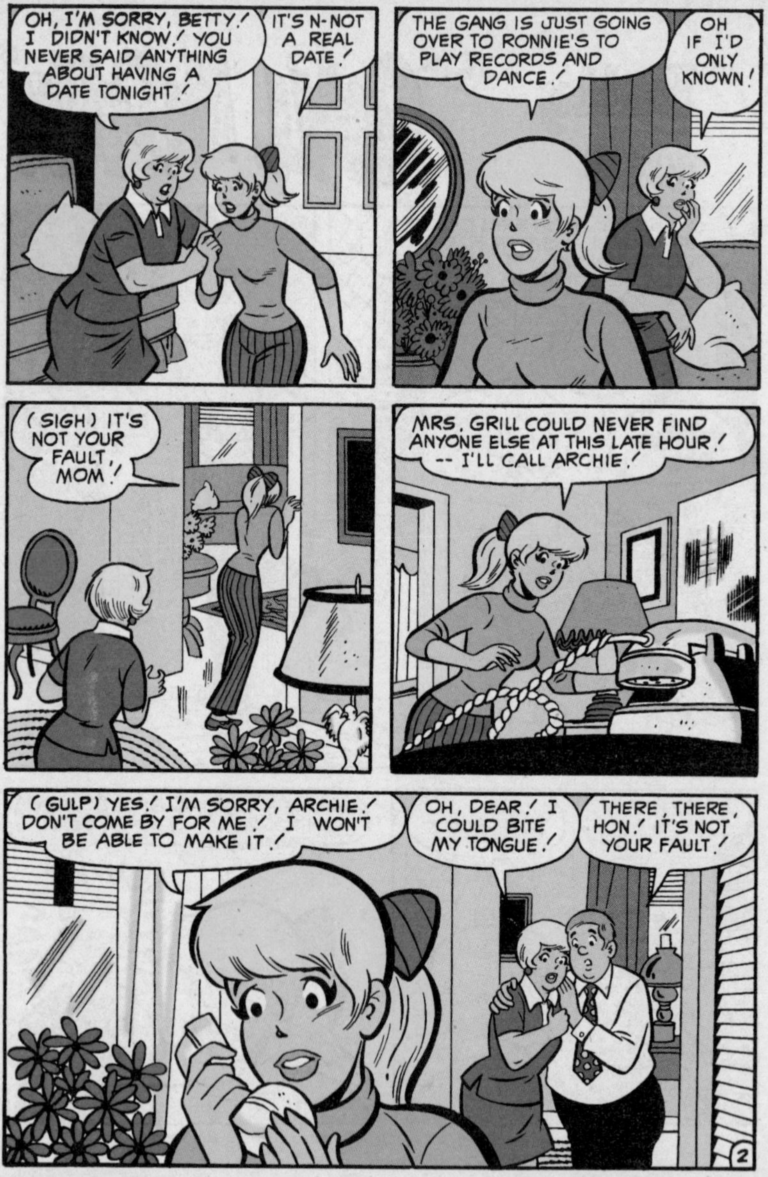
OH, I'M SORRY, BETTY! I DIDN'T KNOW! YOU NEVER SAID ANYTHING ABOUT HAVING A DATE TONIGHT!
IT'S N-NOT A REAL DATE!
THE GANG IS JUST GOING OVER TO RONNIE'S TO PLAY RECORDS AND DANCE!
OH IF I'D ONLY KNOWN!
(SIGH) IT'S NOT YOUR FAULT, MOM!
MRS. GRILL COULD NEVER FIND ANYONE ELSE AT THIS LATE HOUR! -- I'LL CALL ARCHIE!
(GULP) YES! I'M SORRY, ARCHIE! DON'T COME BY FOR ME! I WON'T BE ABLE TO MAKE IT!
OH, DEAR! I COULD BITE MY TONGUE!
THERE, THERE, HON! IT'S NOT YOUR FAULT!
2

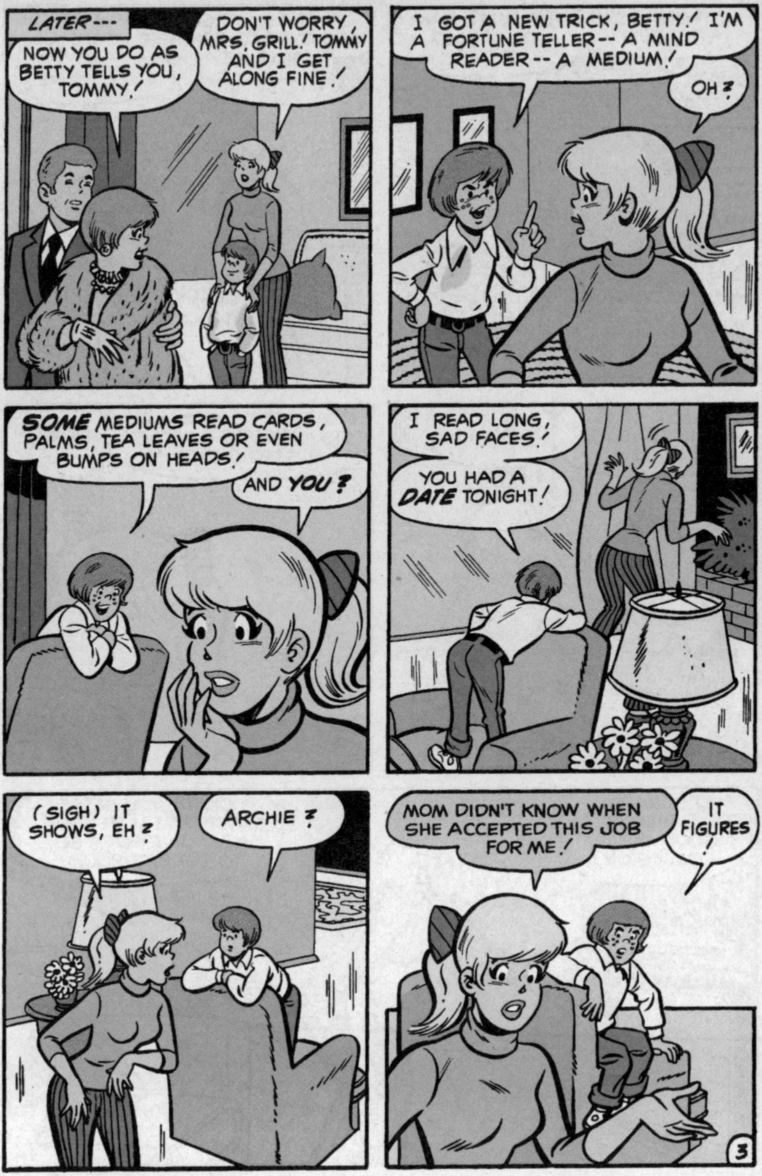

LATER---
NOW YOU DO AS BETTY TELLS YOU, TOMMY!
DON'T WORRY, MRS. GRILL! TOMMY AND I GET ALONG FINE!
I GOT A NEW TRICK, BETTY! I'M A FORTUNE TELLER-- A MIND READER-- A MEDIUM!
OH?
SOME MEDIUMS READ CARDS, PALMS, TEA LEAVES OR EVEN BUMPS ON HEADS!
AND YOU?
I READ LONG, SAD FACES!
YOU HAD A DATE TONIGHT!
(SIGH) IT SHOWS, EH?
ARCHIE?
MOM DIDN'T KNOW WHEN SHE ACCEPTED THIS JOB FOR ME!
IT FIGURES!
3

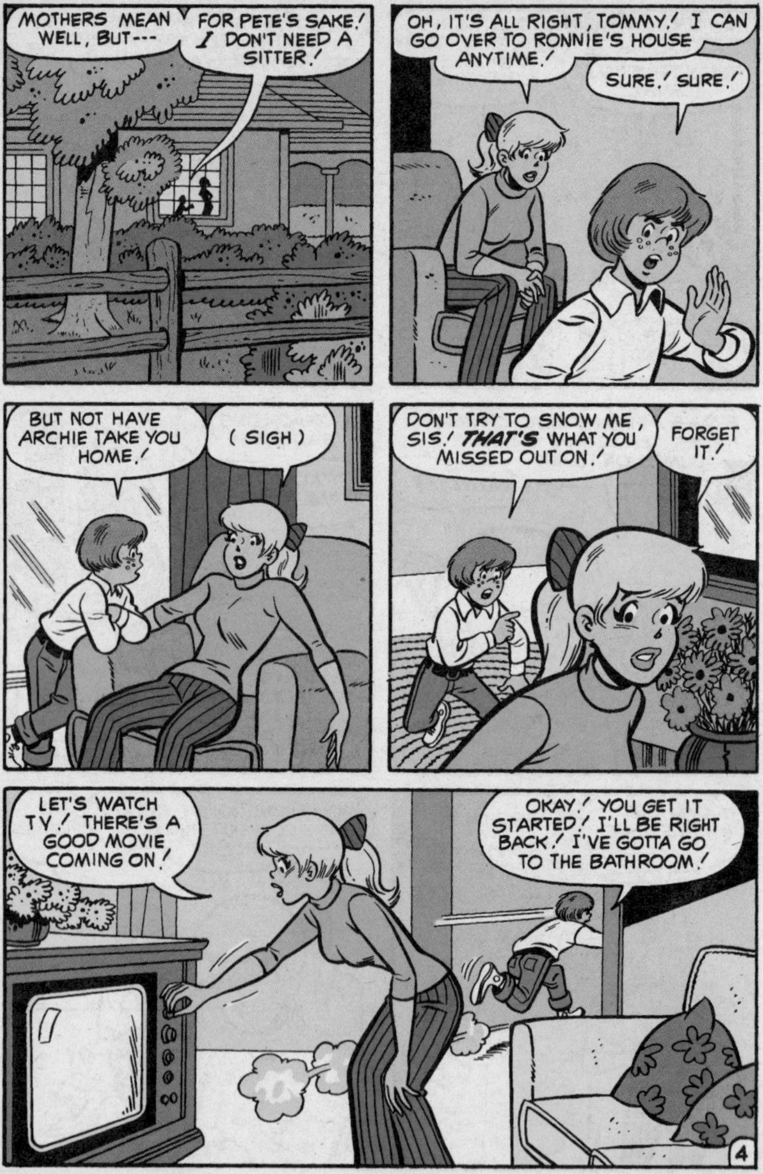
MOTHERS MEAN WELL, BUT---
FOR PETE'S SAKE! *I* DON'T NEED A SITTER!
OH, IT'S ALL RIGHT, TOMMY! I CAN GO OVER TO RONNIE'S HOUSE ANYTIME!
SURE! SURE!
BUT NOT HAVE ARCHIE TAKE YOU HOME!
(SIGH)
DON'T TRY TO SNOW ME, SIS! ***THAT'S*** WHAT YOU MISSED OUT ON!
FORGET IT!
LET'S WATCH TV! THERE'S A GOOD MOVIE COMING ON!
OKAY! YOU GET IT STARTED! I'LL BE RIGHT BACK! I'VE GOTTA GO TO THE BATHROOM!
4

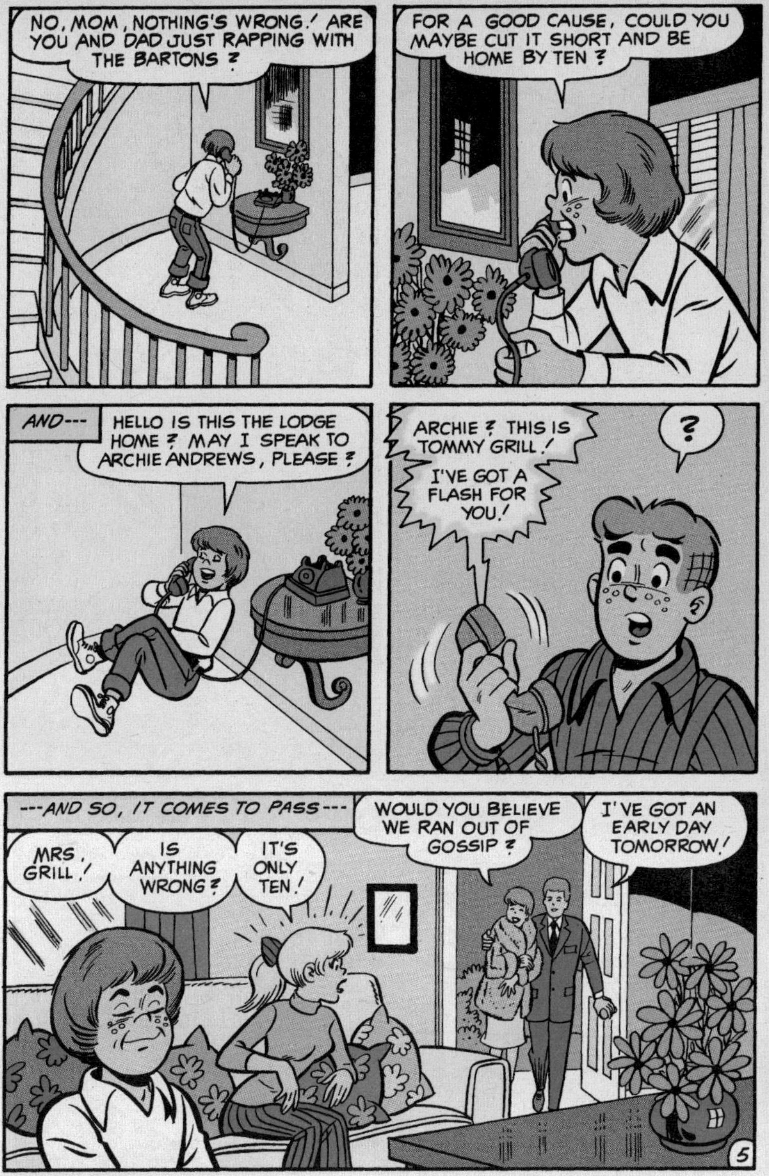
NO, MOM, NOTHING'S WRONG! ARE YOU AND DAD JUST RAPPING WITH THE BARTONS?
FOR A GOOD CAUSE, COULD YOU MAYBE CUT IT SHORT AND BE HOME BY TEN?
AND---
HELLO IS THIS THE LODGE HOME? MAY I SPEAK TO ARCHIE ANDREWS, PLEASE?
ARCHIE? THIS IS TOMMY GRILL!
I'VE GOT A FLASH FOR YOU!
?
---AND SO, IT COMES TO PASS---
MRS. GRILL!
IS ANYTHING WRONG?
IT'S ONLY TEN!
WOULD YOU BELIEVE WE RAN OUT OF GOSSIP?
I'VE GOT AN EARLY DAY TOMORROW!
5

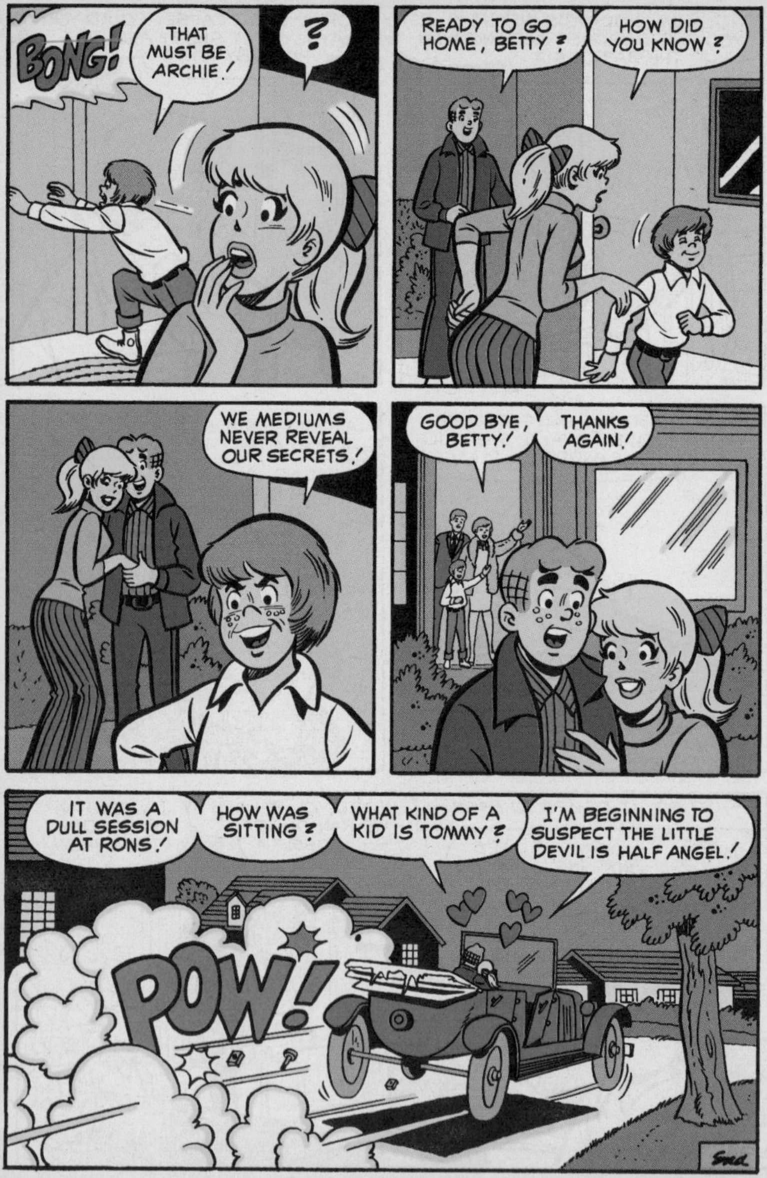
BONG!
THAT MUST BE ARCHIE!
?
READY TO GO HOME, BETTY?
HOW DID YOU KNOW?
WE MEDIUMS NEVER REVEAL OUR SECRETS!
GOOD BYE, BETTY!
THANKS AGAIN!
IT WAS A DULL SESSION AT RONS!
HOW WAS SITTING?
WHAT KIND OF A KID IS TOMMY?
I'M BEGINNING TO SUSPECT THE LITTLE DEVIL IS HALF ANGEL!
POW!

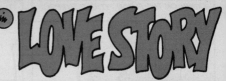

Betty and Me in LOVE STORY

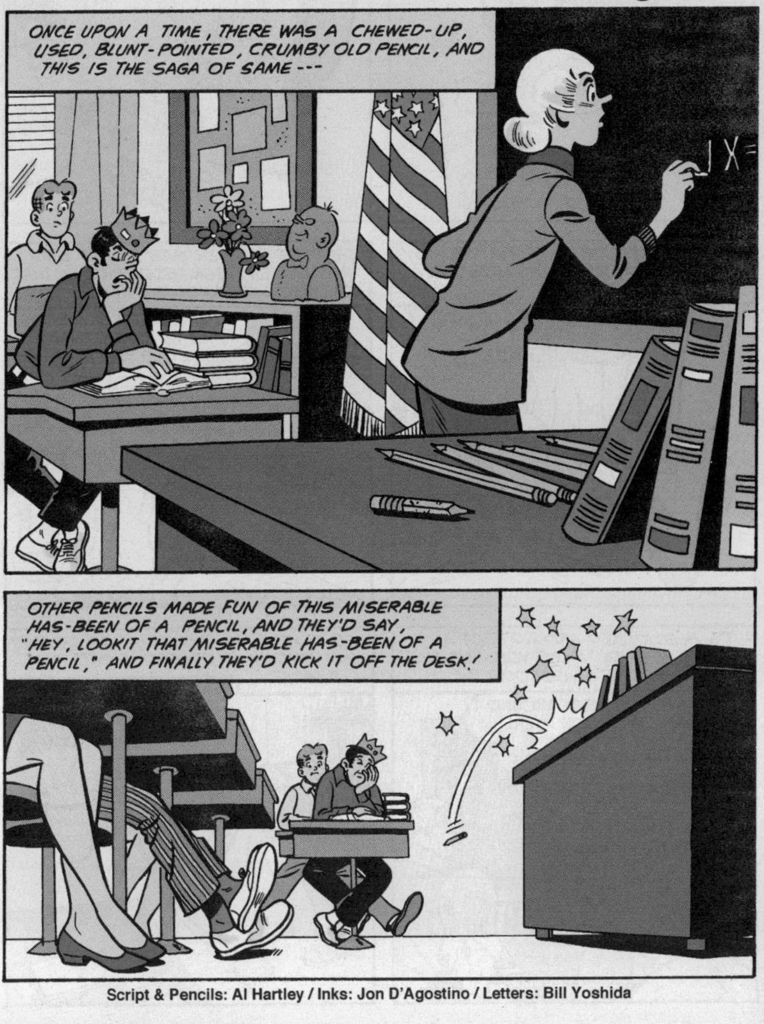
ONCE UPON A TIME, THERE WAS A CHEWED-UP, USED, BLUNT-POINTED, CRUMBY OLD PENCIL, AND THIS IS THE SAGA OF SAME ---
OTHER PENCILS MADE FUN OF THIS MISERABLE HAS-BEEN OF A PENCIL, AND THEY'D SAY, "HEY, LOOKIT THAT MISERABLE HAS-BEEN OF A PENCIL," AND FINALLY THEY'D KICK IT OFF THE DESK!

Script & Pencils: Al Hartley / Inks: Jon D'Agostino / Letters: Bill Yoshida

DOWN ON THE FLOOR, IT GOT STEPPED ON---
CRUNCH!
IT WAS KICKED ABOUT AND GENERALLY MISTREATED---
WHOP!
POK!
BUNK!
KICK
IT SAID TO ITSELF, "I AM A CRUMBY, USED UP OLD PENCIL AND IT IS ONLY TO BE EXPECTED"!
THEN THE TEACHER SAW IT AND SAID, "WHY DOESN'T SOMEBODY PICK UP THAT CRUMBY OLD PENCIL?"
WHY DOESN'T SOMBODY PICK UP THAT CRUMBY OLD PENCIL?
"IT'S BEEN KICKED AROUND HERE ALL DAY", SHE SAID, "DON'T YOU HAVE ANY PRIDE IN YOUR CLASSROOM?"
IT'S BEEN KICKED AROUND HERE ALL DAY! DON'T YOU HAVE ANY PRIDE IN YOUR CLASSROOM?
SO SOMEBODY PICKED UP THE CRUMBY OLD PENCIL AND TOSSED IT INTO THE BASKET!
PLUNK
2

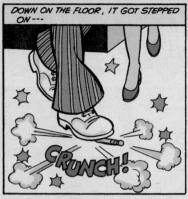

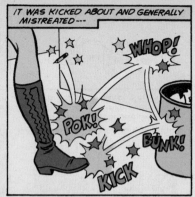

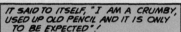

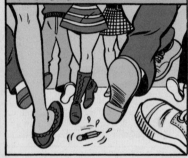

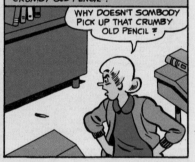

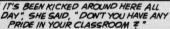

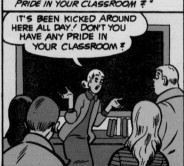

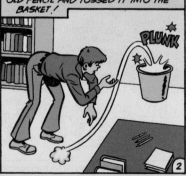

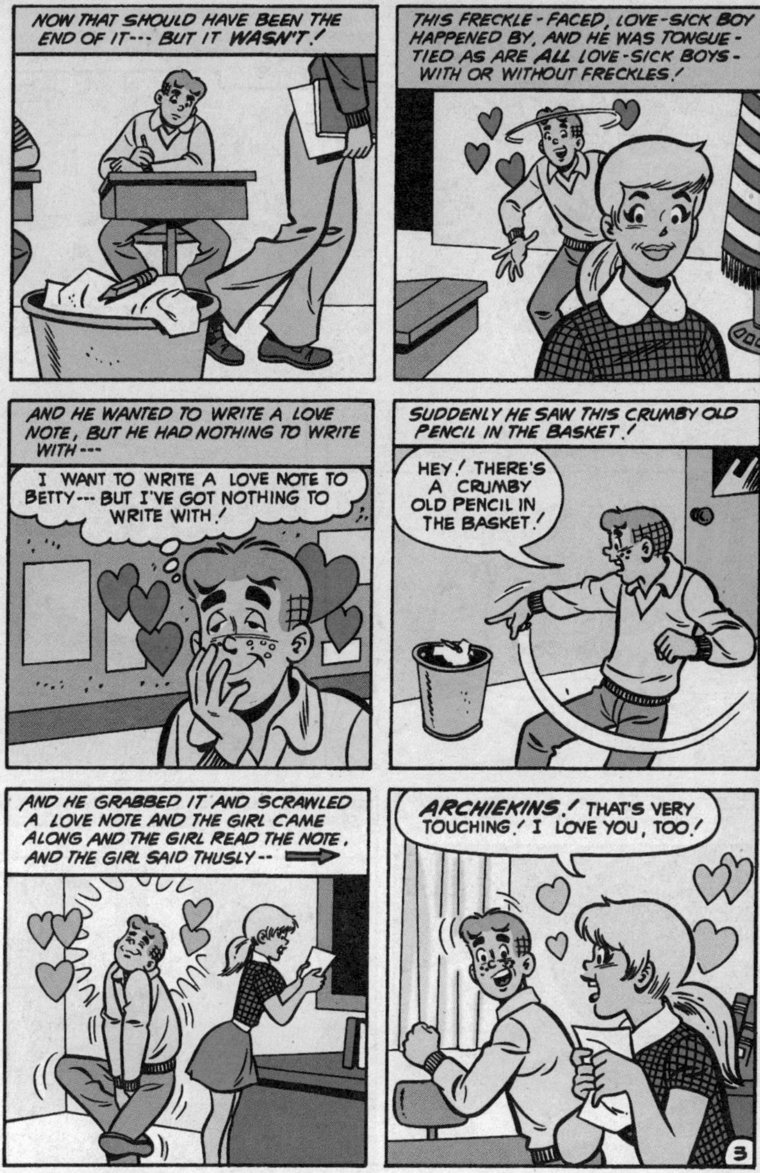

NOW THAT SHOULD HAVE BEEN THE END OF IT--- BUT IT WASN'T!
THIS FRECKLE-FACED, LOVE-SICK BOY HAPPENED BY, AND HE WAS TONGUE-TIED AS ARE ALL LOVE-SICK BOYS-WITH OR WITHOUT FRECKLES!
AND HE WANTED TO WRITE A LOVE NOTE, BUT HE HAD NOTHING TO WRITE WITH---
I WANT TO WRITE A LOVE NOTE TO BETTY--- BUT I'VE GOT NOTHING TO WRITE WITH!
SUDDENLY HE SAW THIS CRUMBY OLD PENCIL IN THE BASKET!
HEY! THERE'S A CRUMBY OLD PENCIL IN THE BASKET!
AND HE GRABBED IT AND SCRAWLED A LOVE NOTE AND THE GIRL CAME ALONG AND THE GIRL READ THE NOTE. AND THE GIRL SAID THUSLY--
ARCHIEKINS! THAT'S VERY TOUCHING! I LOVE YOU, TOO!
3

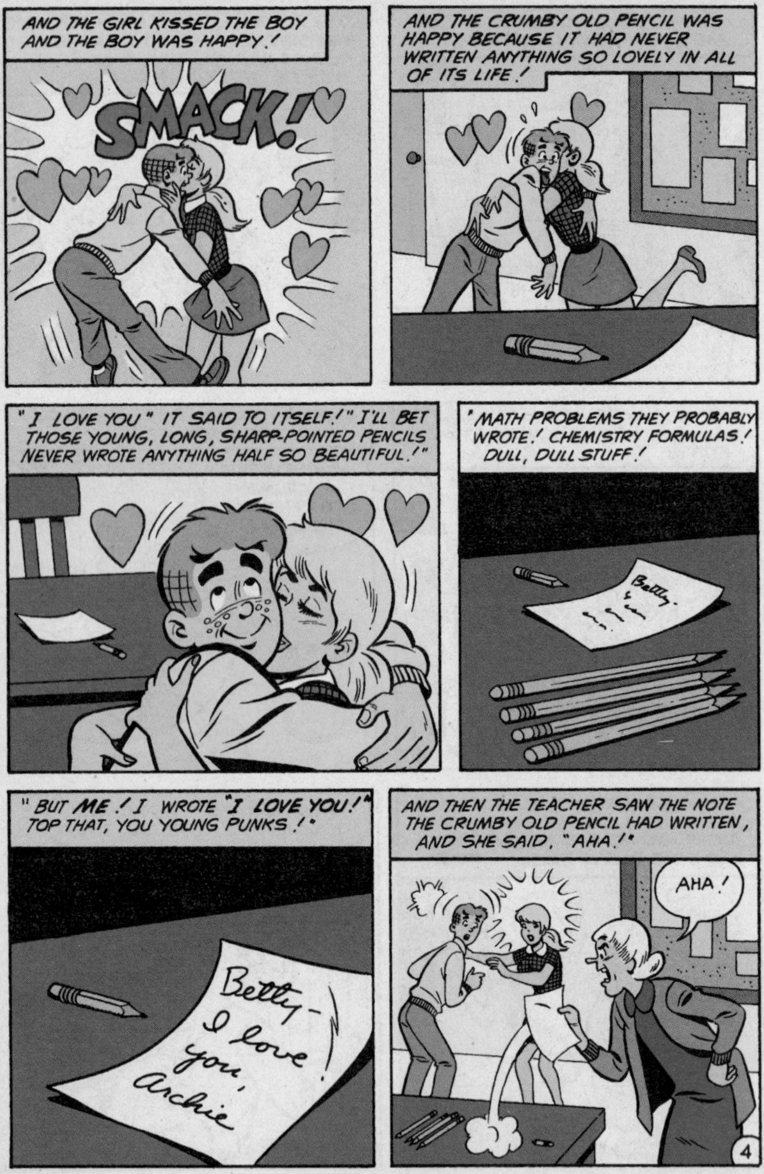
AND THE GIRL KISSED THE BOY AND THE BOY WAS HAPPY!
SMACK!
AND THE CRUMBY OLD PENCIL WAS HAPPY BECAUSE IT HAD NEVER WRITTEN ANYTHING SO LOVELY IN ALL OF ITS LIFE!
"I LOVE YOU" IT SAID TO ITSELF! "I'LL BET THOSE YOUNG, LONG, SHARP-POINTED PENCILS NEVER WROTE ANYTHING HALF SO BEAUTIFUL!"
"MATH PROBLEMS THEY PROBABLY WROTE! CHEMISTRY FORMULAS! DULL, DULL STUFF!
"BUT ME! I WROTE "I LOVE YOU!" TOP THAT, YOU YOUNG PUNKS!"
Betty- I love you, Archie
AND THEN THE TEACHER SAW THE NOTE THE CRUMBY OLD PENCIL HAD WRITTEN, AND SHE SAID, "AHA!"
AHA!
4

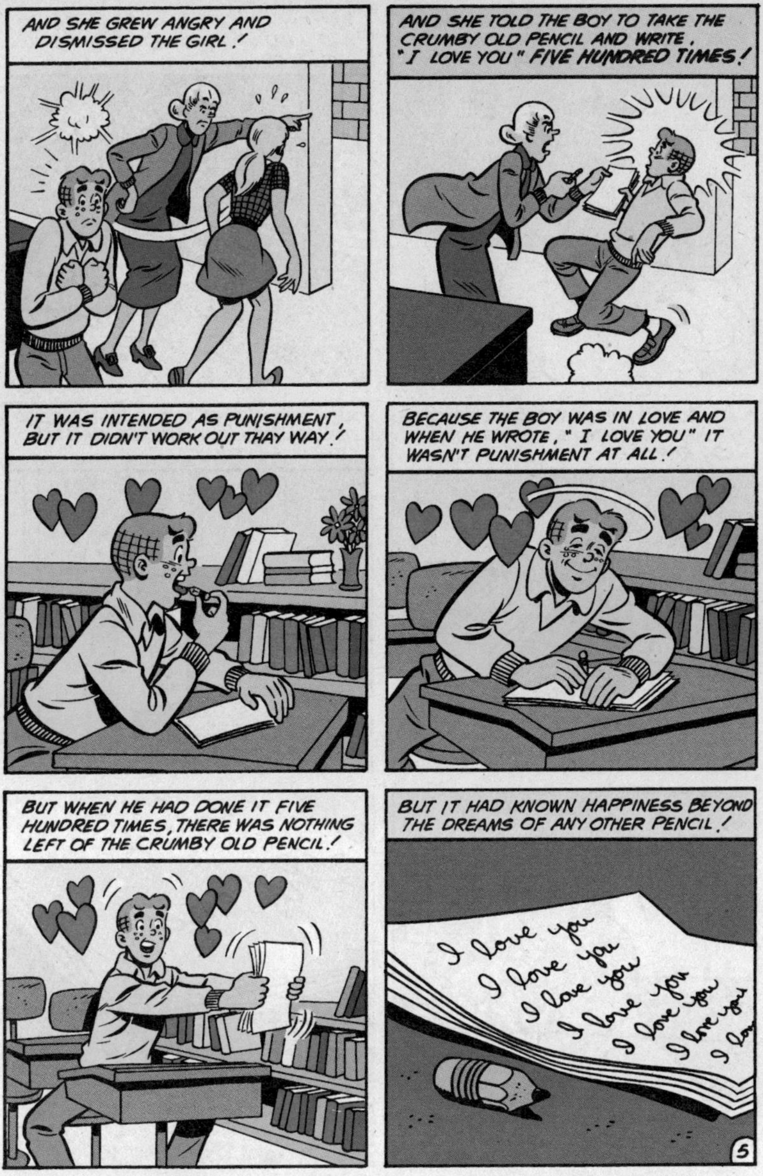
AND SHE GREW ANGRY AND DISMISSED THE GIRL!
AND SHE TOLD THE BOY TO TAKE THE CRUMBY OLD PENCIL AND WRITE, "I LOVE YOU" FIVE HUNDRED TIMES!
IT WAS INTENDED AS PUNISHMENT, BUT IT DIDN'T WORK OUT THAY WAY!
BECAUSE THE BOY WAS IN LOVE AND WHEN HE WROTE, "I LOVE YOU" IT WASN'T PUNISHMENT AT ALL!
BUT WHEN HE HAD DONE IT FIVE HUNDRED TIMES, THERE WAS NOTHING LEFT OF THE CRUMBY OLD PENCIL!
BUT IT HAD KNOWN HAPPINESS BEYOND THE DREAMS OF ANY OTHER PENCIL!
I love you
I love you
I love you
I love you
I love you
I love you
5

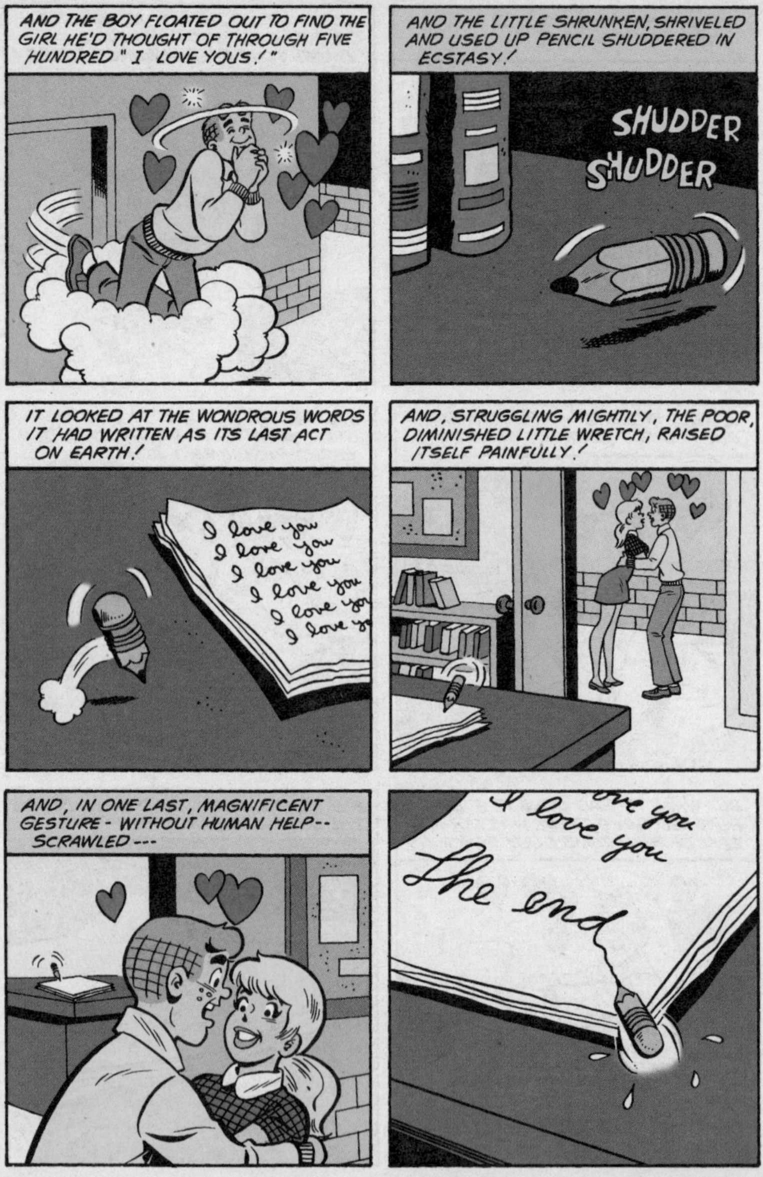
AND THE BOY FLOATED OUT TO FIND THE GIRL HE'D THOUGHT OF THROUGH FIVE HUNDRED "I LOVE YOUS!"
AND THE LITTLE SHRUNKEN, SHRIVELED AND USED UP PENCIL SHUDDERED IN ECSTASY!
SHUDDER
SHUDDER
IT LOOKED AT THE WONDROUS WORDS IT HAD WRITTEN AS ITS LAST ACT ON EARTH!
I love you
I love you
I love you
I love you
AND, STRUGGLING MIGHTILY, THE POOR, DIMINISHED LITTLE WRETCH, RAISED ITSELF PAINFULLY!
AND, IN ONE LAST, MAGNIFICENT GESTURE - WITHOUT HUMAN HELP-- SCRAWLED---
love you
The end

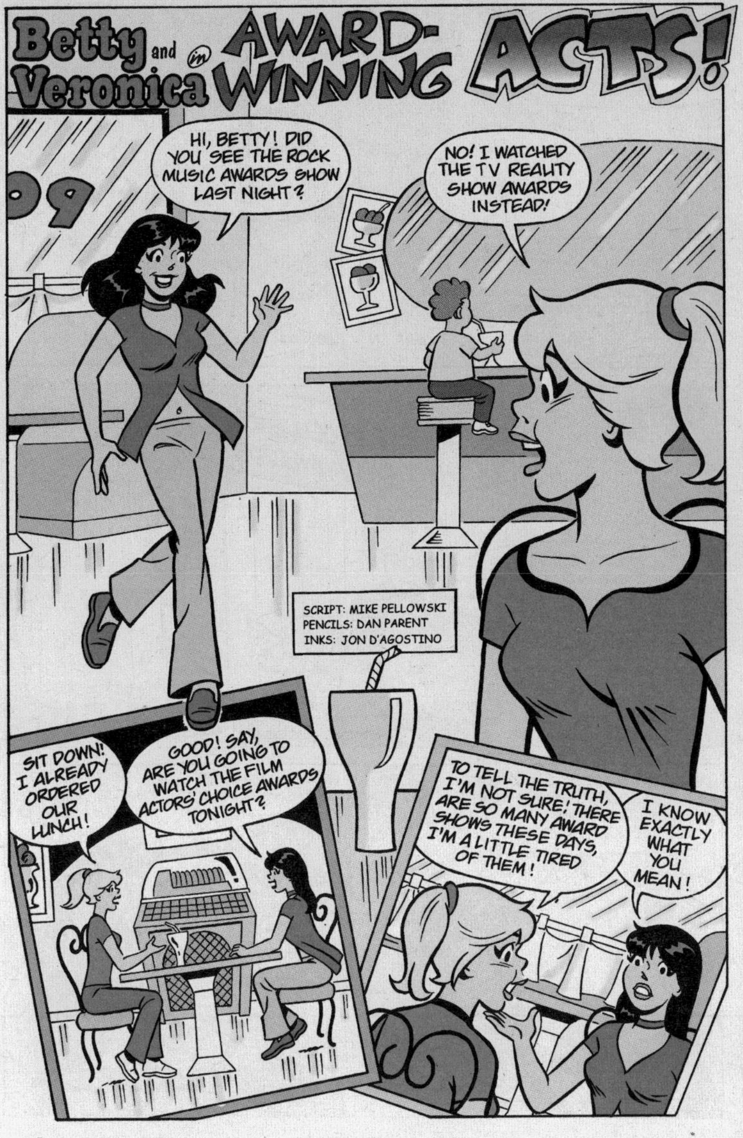
Betty and Veronica in AWARD-WINNING ACTS!
HI, BETTY! DID YOU SEE THE ROCK MUSIC AWARDS SHOW LAST NIGHT?
NO! I WATCHED THE TV REALITY SHOW AWARDS INSTEAD!
SCRIPT: MIKE PELLOWSKI
PENCILS: DAN PARENT
INKS: JON D'AGOSTINO
SIT DOWN! I ALREADY ORDERED OUR LUNCH!
GOOD! SAY, ARE YOU GOING TO WATCH THE FILM ACTORS' CHOICE AWARDS TONIGHT?
TO TELL THE TRUTH, I'M NOT SURE! THERE ARE SO MANY AWARD SHOWS THESE DAYS, I'M A LITTLE TIRED OF THEM!
I KNOW EXACTLY WHAT YOU MEAN!

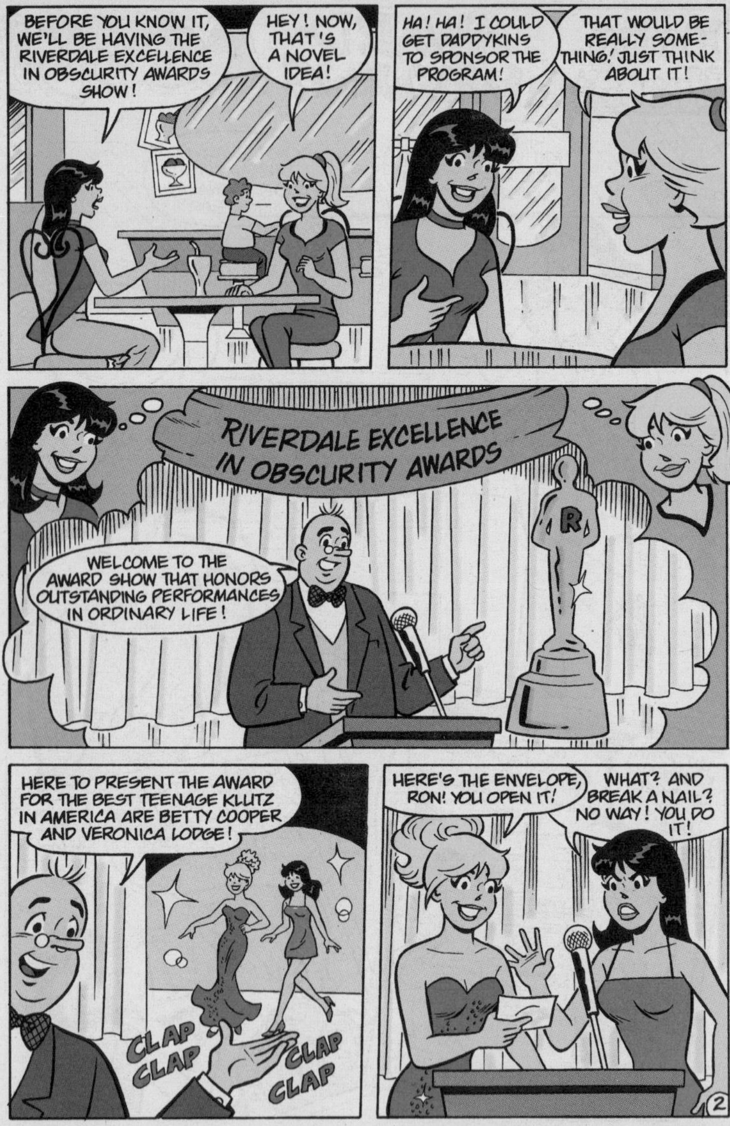
BEFORE YOU KNOW IT, WE'LL BE HAVING THE RIVERDALE EXCELLENCE IN OBSCURITY AWARDS SHOW!
HEY! NOW, THAT'S A NOVEL IDEA!
HA! HA! I COULD GET DADDYKINS TO SPONSOR THE PROGRAM!
THAT WOULD BE REALLY SOME-THING! JUST THINK ABOUT IT!
RIVERDALE EXCELLENCE IN OBSCURITY AWARDS
WELCOME TO THE AWARD SHOW THAT HONORS OUTSTANDING PERFORMANCES IN ORDINARY LIFE!
R
HERE TO PRESENT THE AWARD FOR THE BEST TEENAGE KLUTZ IN AMERICA ARE BETTY COOPER AND VERONICA LODGE!
CLAP CLAP
CLAP CLAP
HERE'S THE ENVELOPE, RON! YOU OPEN IT!
WHAT? AND BREAK A NAIL? NO WAY! YOU DO IT!
2

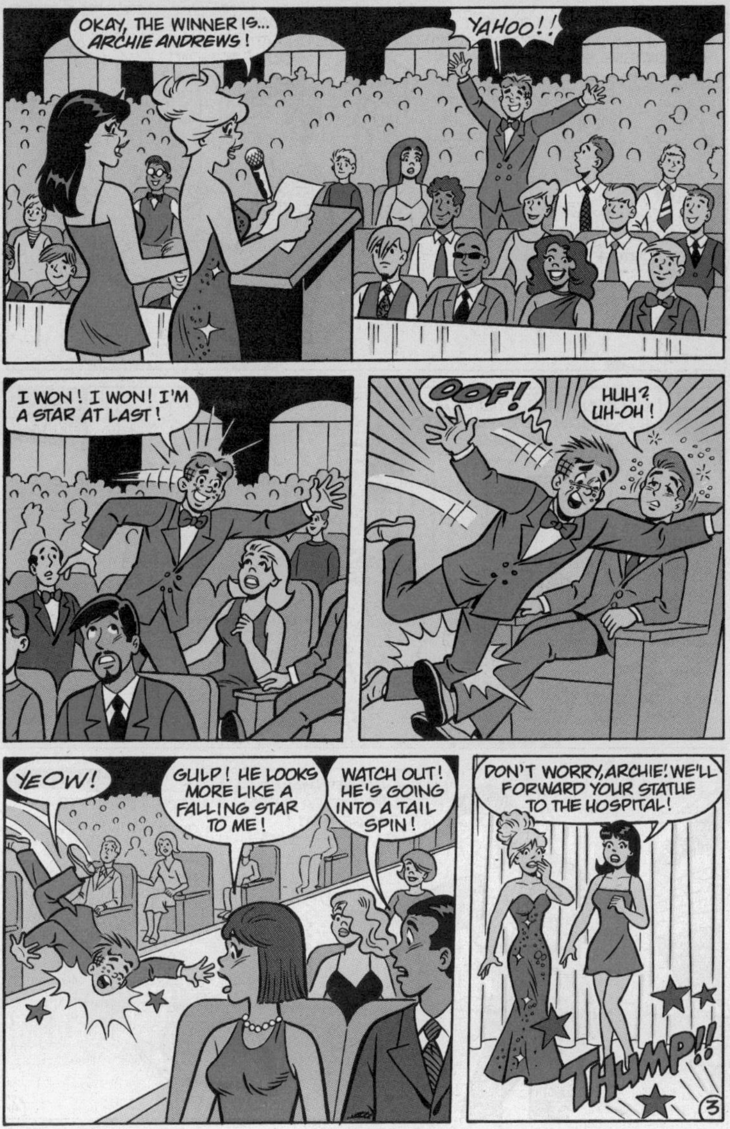

OKAY, THE WINNER IS... ARCHIE ANDREWS!
YAHOO!!
I WON! I WON! I'M A STAR AT LAST!
OOF!
HUH? UH-OH!
YEOW!
GULP! HE LOOKS MORE LIKE A FALLING STAR TO ME!
WATCH OUT! HE'S GOING INTO A TAIL SPIN!
DON'T WORRY, ARCHIE! WE'LL FORWARD YOUR STATUE TO THE HOSPITAL!
THUMP!!
3

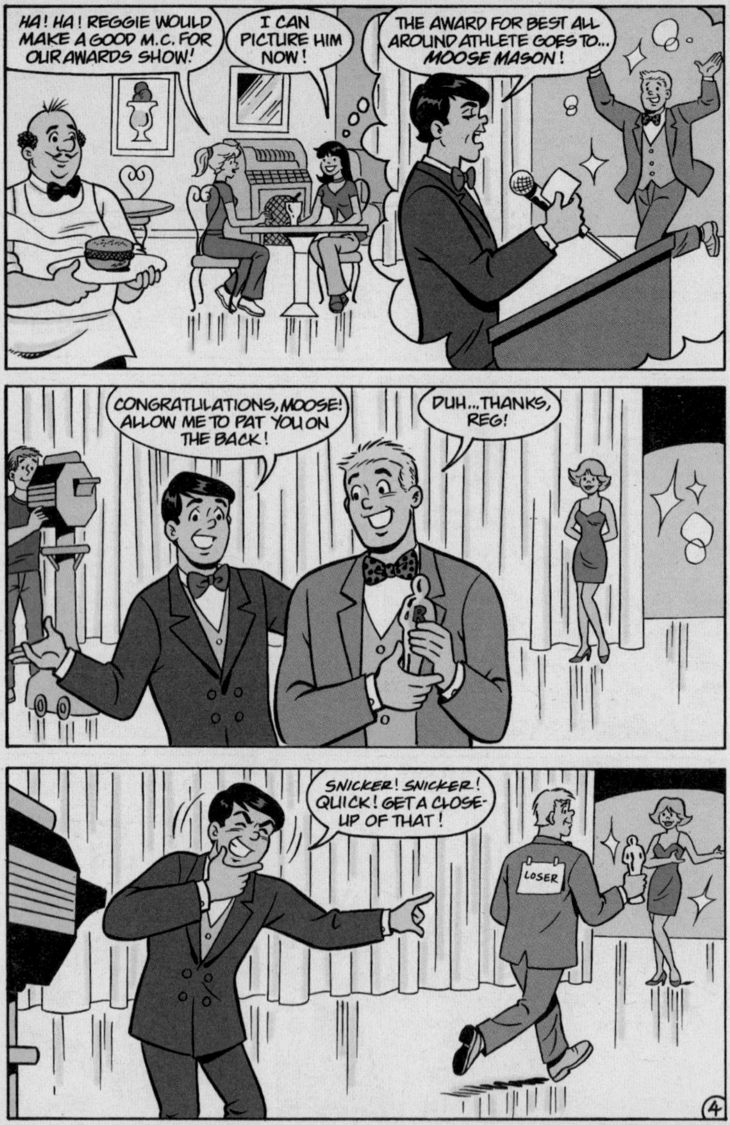
HA! HA! REGGIE WOULD MAKE A GOOD M.C. FOR OUR AWARDS SHOW!
I CAN PICTURE HIM NOW!
THE AWARD FOR BEST ALL AROUND ATHLETE GOES TO... MOOSE MASON!
CONGRATULATIONS, MOOSE! ALLOW ME TO PAT YOU ON THE BACK!
DUH... THANKS, REG!
SNICKER! SNICKER! QUICK! GET A CLOSE-UP OF THAT!
LOSER
4

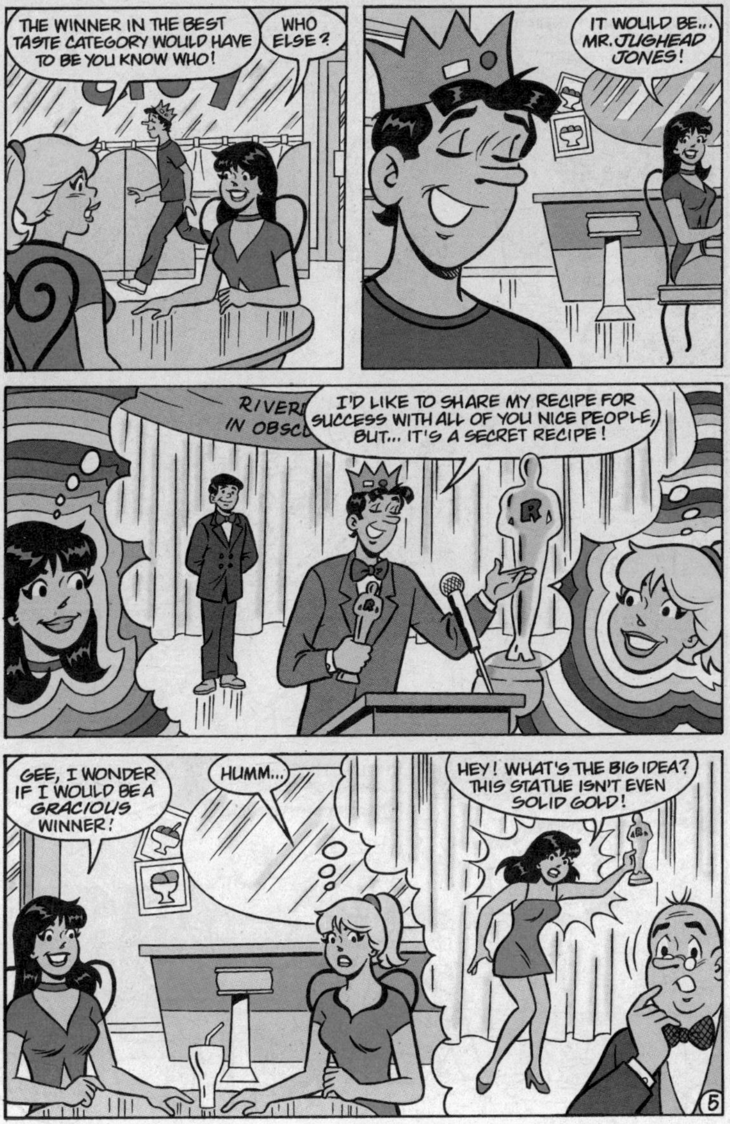
THE WINNER IN THE BEST TASTE CATEGORY WOULD HAVE TO BE YOU KNOW WHO!
WHO ELSE?
IT WOULD BE... MR. JUGHEAD JONES!
I'D LIKE TO SHARE MY RECIPE FOR SUCCESS WITH ALL OF YOU NICE PEOPLE, BUT... IT'S A SECRET RECIPE!
GEE, I WONDER IF I WOULD BE A GRACIOUS WINNER!
HUMM...
HEY! WHAT'S THE BIG IDEA? THIS STATUE ISN'T EVEN SOLID GOLD!

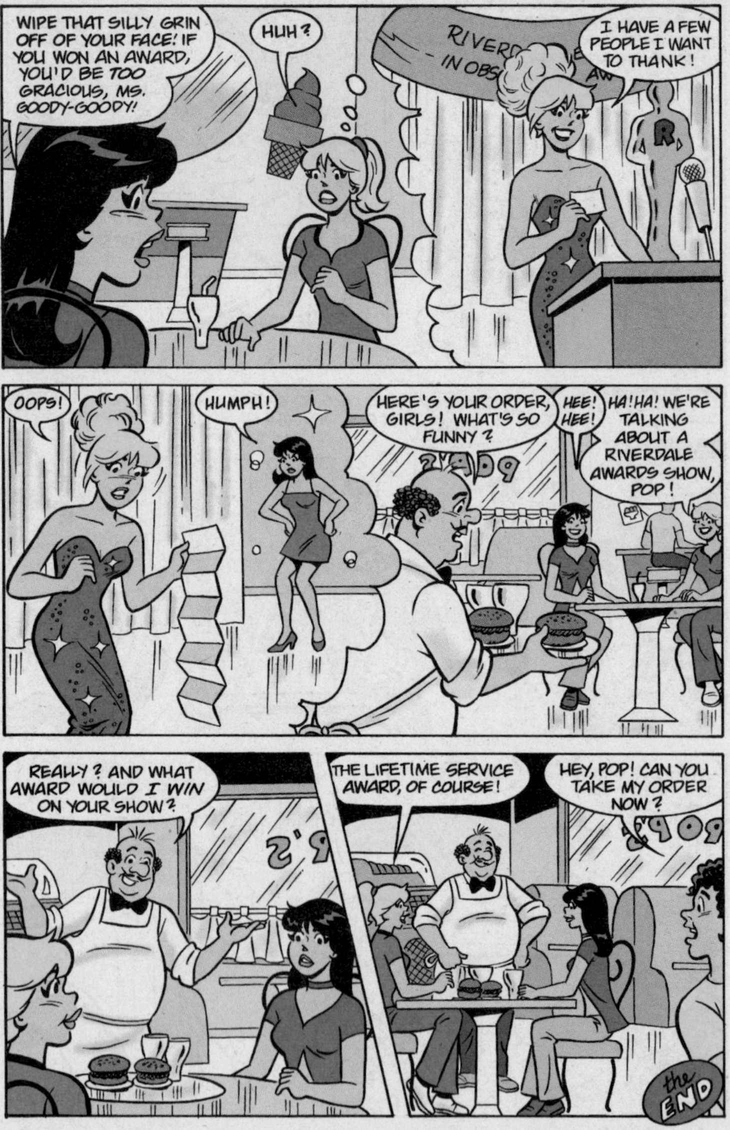
WIPE THAT SILLY GRIN OFF OF YOUR FACE! IF YOU WON AN AWARD, YOU'D BE TOO GRACIOUS, MS. GOODY-GOODY!
HUH?
I HAVE A FEW PEOPLE I WANT TO THANK!
OOPS!
HUMPH!
HERE'S YOUR ORDER, GIRLS! WHAT'S SO FUNNY?
HEE! HEE!
HA! HA! WE'RE TALKING ABOUT A RIVERDALE AWARDS SHOW, POP!
REALLY? AND WHAT AWARD WOULD I WIN ON YOUR SHOW?
THE LIFETIME SERVICE AWARD, OF COURSE!
HEY, POP! CAN YOU TAKE MY ORDER NOW?
the END

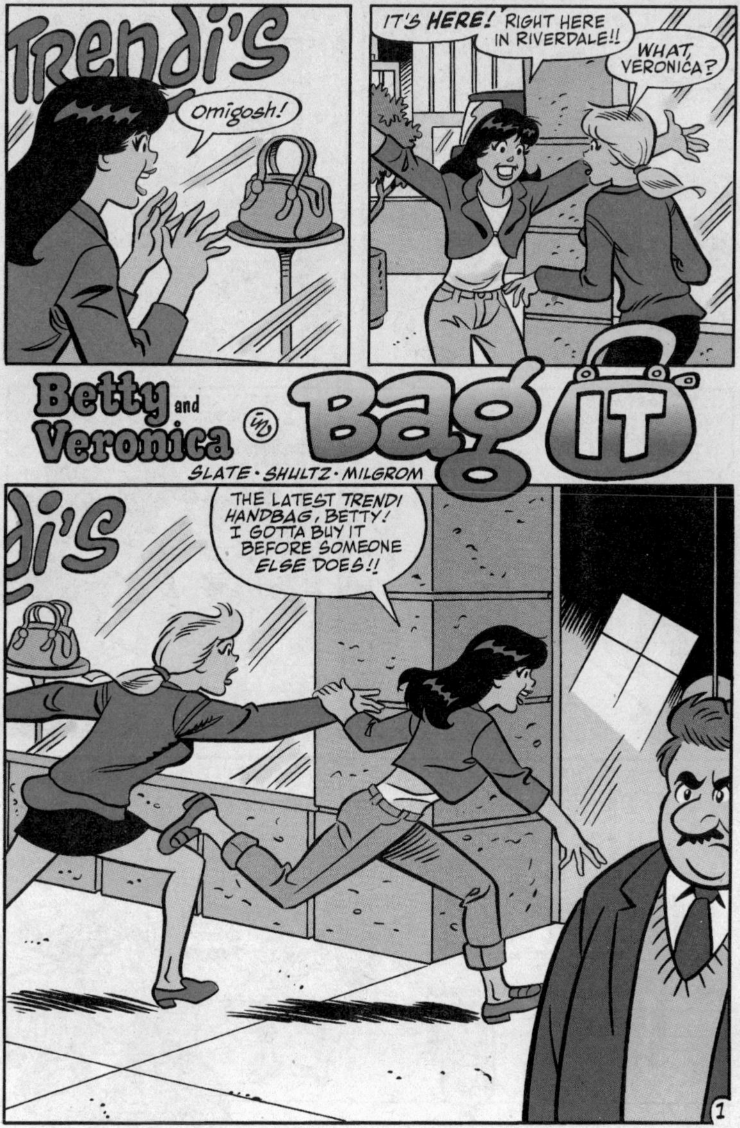
Trendi's
Omigosh!
IT'S HERE! RIGHT HERE IN RIVERDALE!!
WHAT, VERONICA?
Betty and Veronica in Bag IT
SLATE · SHULTZ · MILGROM
THE LATEST TRENDI HANDBAG, BETTY! I GOTTA BUY IT BEFORE SOMEONE ELSE DOES!!
1

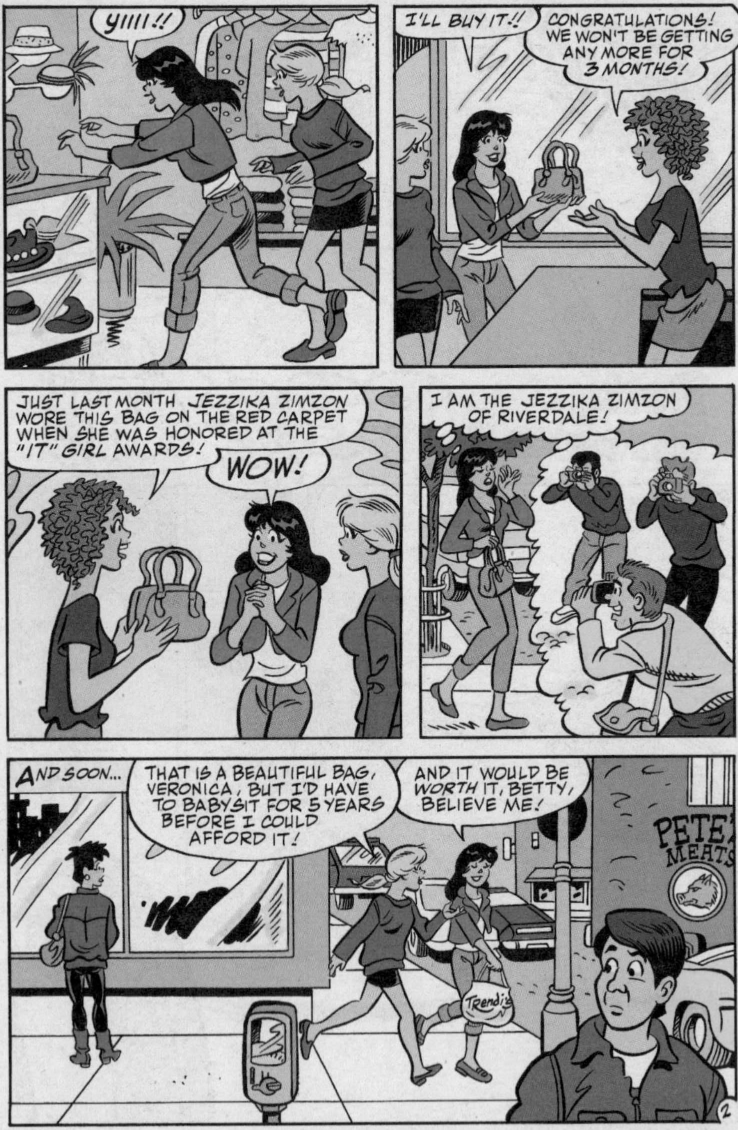
YIIII!!
I'LL BUY IT!!
CONGRATULATIONS! WE WON'T BE GETTING ANY MORE FOR 3 MONTHS!
JUST LAST MONTH JEZZIKA ZIMZON WORE THIS BAG ON THE RED CARPET WHEN SHE WAS HONORED AT THE "IT" GIRL AWARDS!
WOW!
I AM THE JEZZIKA ZIMZON OF RIVERDALE!
AND SOON...
THAT IS A BEAUTIFUL BAG, VERONICA, BUT I'D HAVE TO BABYSIT FOR 5 YEARS BEFORE I COULD AFFORD IT!
AND IT WOULD BE WORTH IT, BETTY, BELIEVE ME!
PETE'S MEATS
Trendi's
2

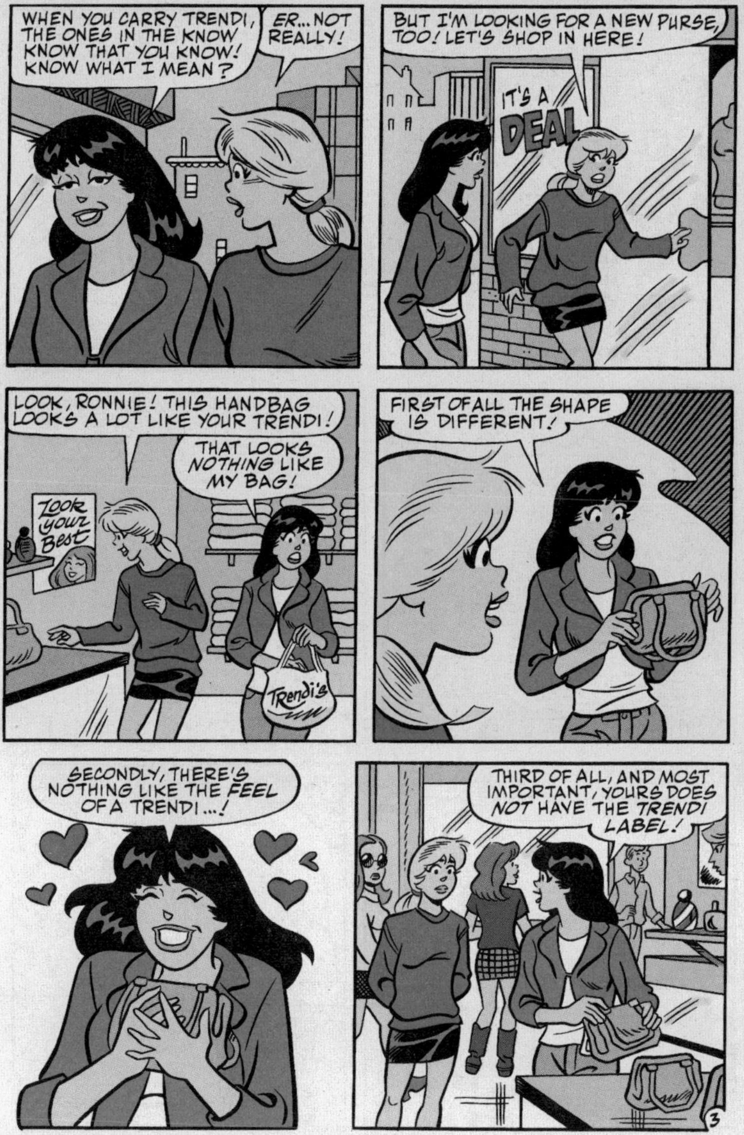
WHEN YOU CARRY TRENDI, THE ONES IN THE KNOW KNOW THAT YOU KNOW! KNOW WHAT I MEAN?
ER...NOT REALLY!
BUT I'M LOOKING FOR A NEW PURSE, TOO! LET'S SHOP IN HERE!
IT'S A DEAL
LOOK, RONNIE! THIS HANDBAG LOOKS A LOT LIKE YOUR TRENDI!
THAT LOOKS NOTHING LIKE MY BAG!
Look your Best
Trendi's
FIRST OF ALL THE SHAPE IS DIFFERENT!
SECONDLY, THERE'S NOTHING LIKE THE FEEL OF A TRENDI...!
THIRD OF ALL, AND MOST IMPORTANT, YOURS DOES NOT HAVE THE TRENDI LABEL!
3

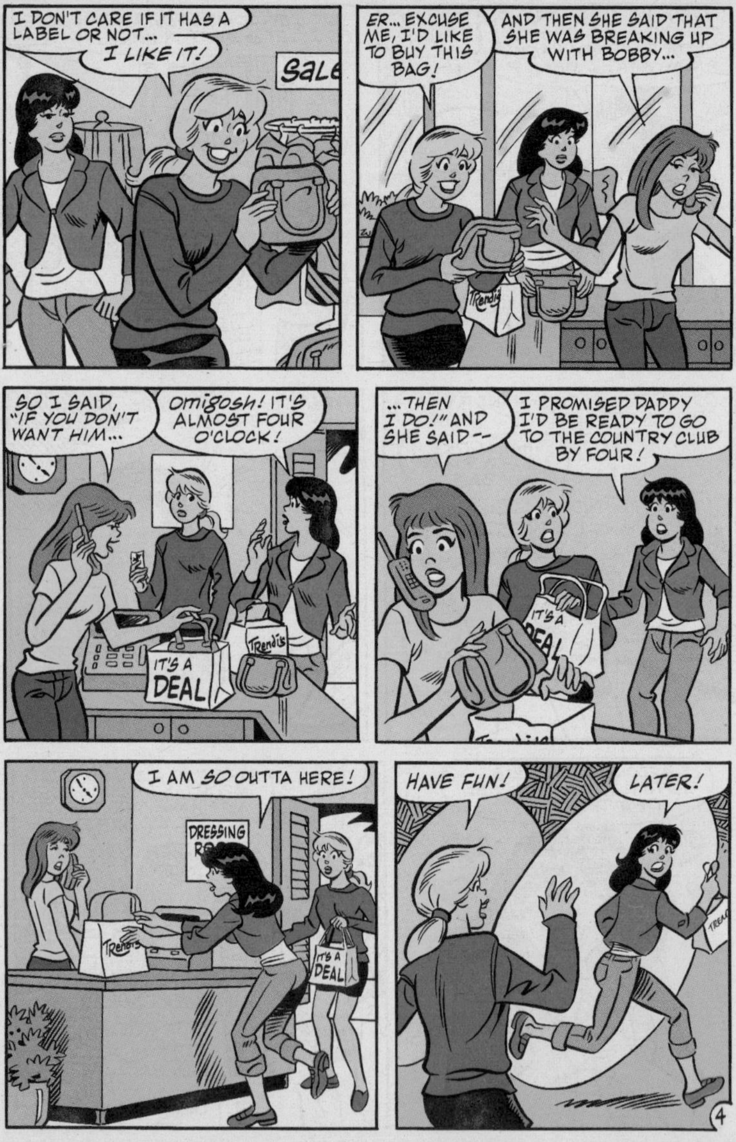
I DON'T CARE IF IT HAS A LABEL OR NOT...
I LIKE IT!
SALE
ER... EXCUSE ME, I'D LIKE TO BUY THIS BAG!
AND THEN SHE SAID THAT SHE WAS BREAKING UP WITH BOBBY...
SO I SAID, "IF YOU DON'T WANT HIM...
OMIGOSH! IT'S ALMOST FOUR O'CLOCK!
IT'S A DEAL
...THEN I DO!" AND SHE SAID --
I PROMISED DADDY I'D BE READY TO GO TO THE COUNTRY CLUB BY FOUR!
IT'S A DEAL
I AM SO OUTTA HERE!
DRESSING
IT'S A DEAL
HAVE FUN!
LATER!
4

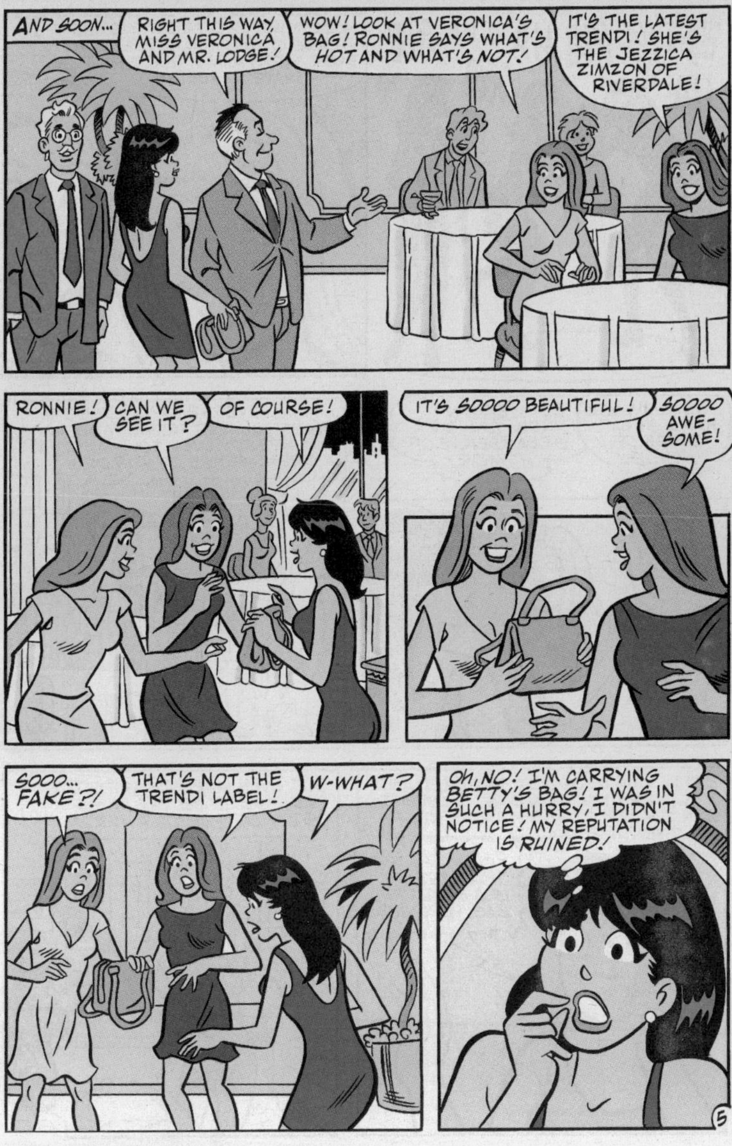
AND SOON...
RIGHT THIS WAY, MISS VERONICA AND MR. LODGE!
WOW! LOOK AT VERONICA'S BAG! RONNIE SAYS WHAT'S HOT AND WHAT'S NOT!
IT'S THE LATEST TRENDI! SHE'S THE JEZZICA ZIMZON OF RIVERDALE!
RONNIE!
CAN WE SEE IT?
OF COURSE!
IT'S SOOOO BEAUTIFUL!
SOOOO AWE-SOME!
SOOO... FAKE?!
THAT'S NOT THE TRENDI LABEL!
W-WHAT?
OH, NO! I'M CARRYING BETTY'S BAG! I WAS IN SUCH A HURRY, I DIDN'T NOTICE! MY REPUTATION IS RUINED!

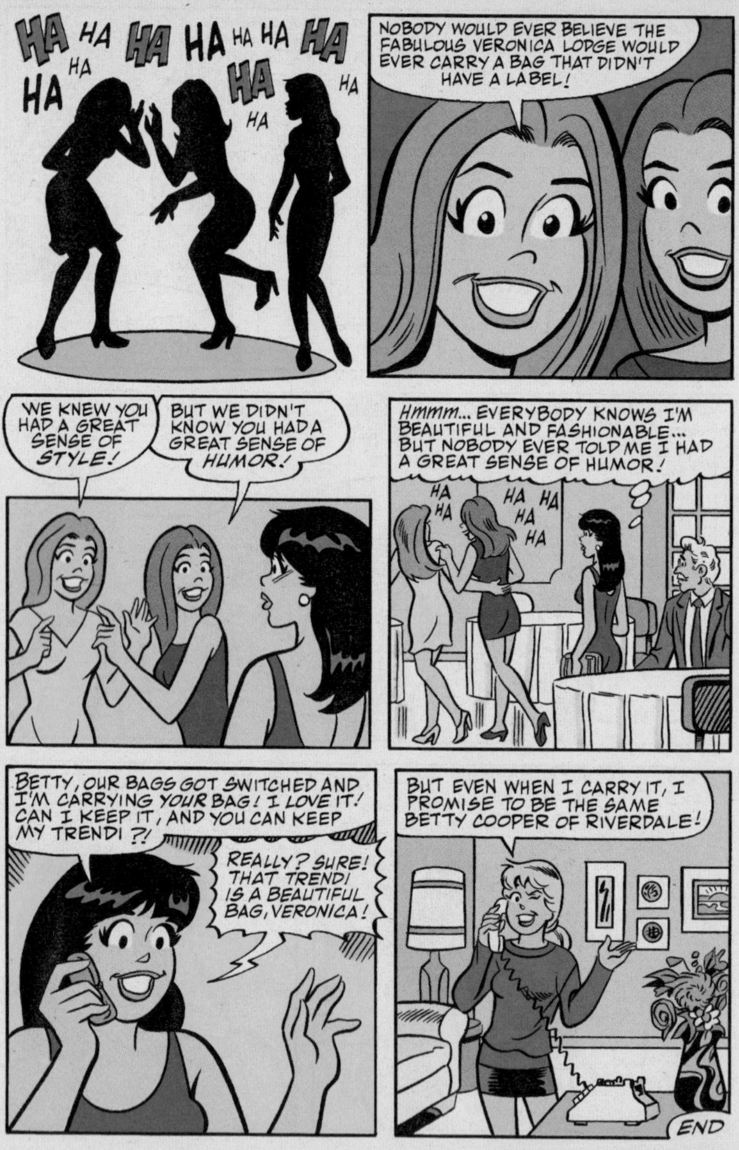
HA HA HA HA HA HA HA HA HA HA HA HA HA
NOBODY WOULD EVER BELIEVE THE FABULOUS VERONICA LODGE WOULD EVER CARRY A BAG THAT DIDN'T HAVE A LABEL!
WE KNEW YOU HAD A GREAT SENSE OF STYLE!
BUT WE DIDN'T KNOW YOU HAD A GREAT SENSE OF HUMOR!
Hmmm... EVERYBODY KNOWS I'M BEAUTIFUL AND FASHIONABLE... BUT NOBODY EVER TOLD ME I HAD A GREAT SENSE OF HUMOR!
HA HA HA HA HA HA
BETTY, OUR BAGS GOT SWITCHED AND I'M CARRYING YOUR BAG! I LOVE IT! CAN I KEEP IT, AND YOU CAN KEEP MY TRENDI ?!
REALLY? SURE! THAT TRENDI IS A BEAUTIFUL BAG, VERONICA!
BUT EVEN WHEN I CARRY IT, I PROMISE TO BE THE SAME BETTY COOPER OF RIVERDALE!
END

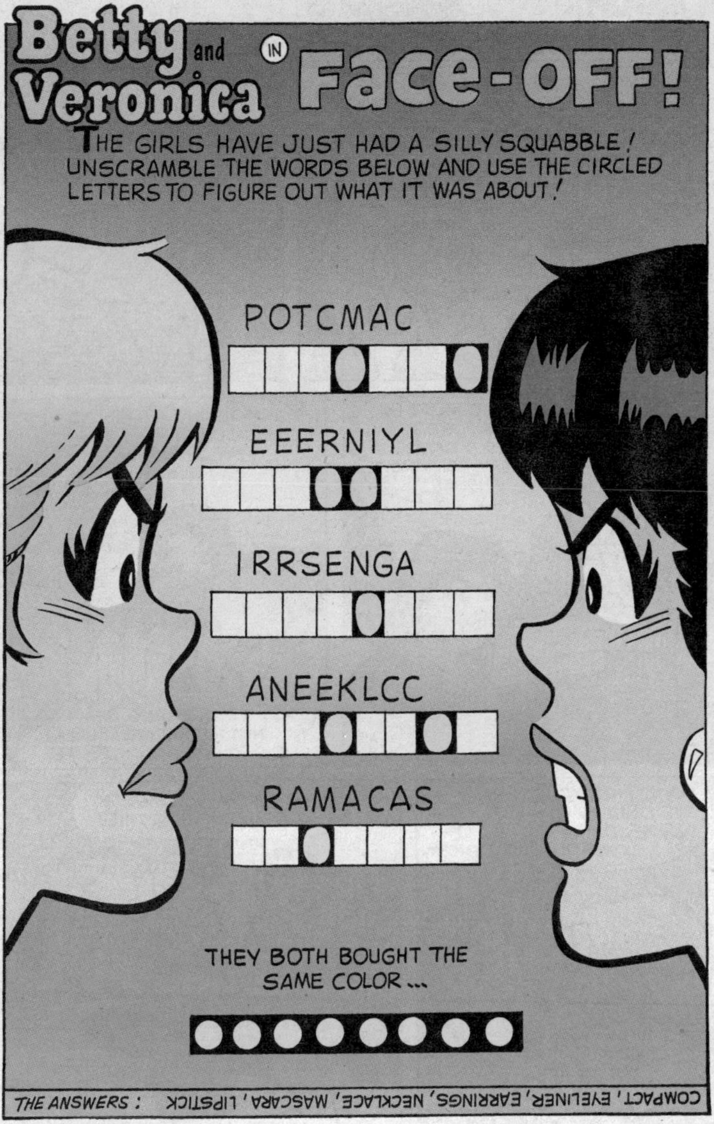
Betty and Veronica IN Face-OFF!
THE GIRLS HAVE JUST HAD A SILLY SQUABBLE! UNSCRAMBLE THE WORDS BELOW AND USE THE CIRCLED LETTERS TO FIGURE OUT WHAT IT WAS ABOUT!
POTCMAC
EEERNIYL
IRRSENGA
ANEEKLCC
RAMACAS
THEY BOTH BOUGHT THE SAME COLOR...
THE ANSWERS : COMPACT, EYELINER, EARRINGS, NECKLACE, MASCARA, LIPSTICK

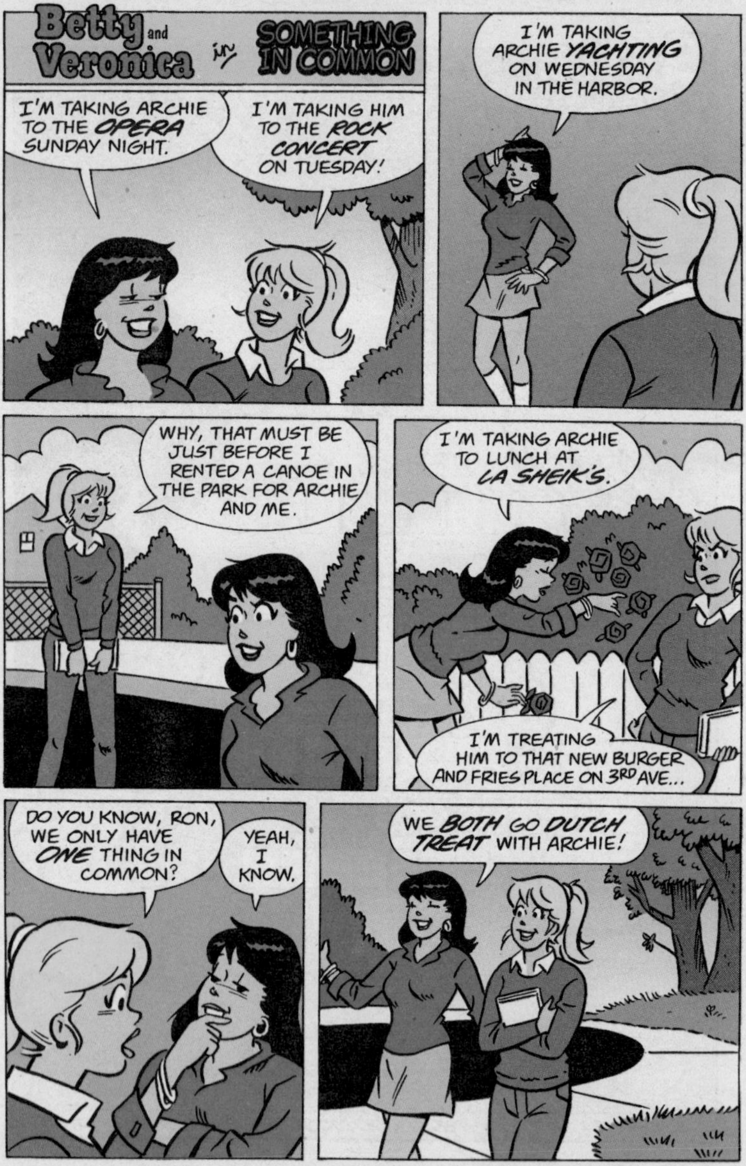
Betty and Veronica in SOMETHING IN COMMON
I'M TAKING ARCHIE TO THE OPERA SUNDAY NIGHT.
I'M TAKING HIM TO THE ROCK CONCERT ON TUESDAY!
I'M TAKING ARCHIE YACHTING ON WEDNESDAY IN THE HARBOR.
WHY, THAT MUST BE JUST BEFORE I RENTED A CANOE IN THE PARK FOR ARCHIE AND ME.
I'M TAKING ARCHIE TO LUNCH AT LA SHEIK'S.
I'M TREATING HIM TO THAT NEW BURGER AND FRIES PLACE ON 3RD AVE...
DO YOU KNOW, RON, WE ONLY HAVE ONE THING IN COMMON?
YEAH, I KNOW.
WE BOTH GO DUTCH TREAT WITH ARCHIE!

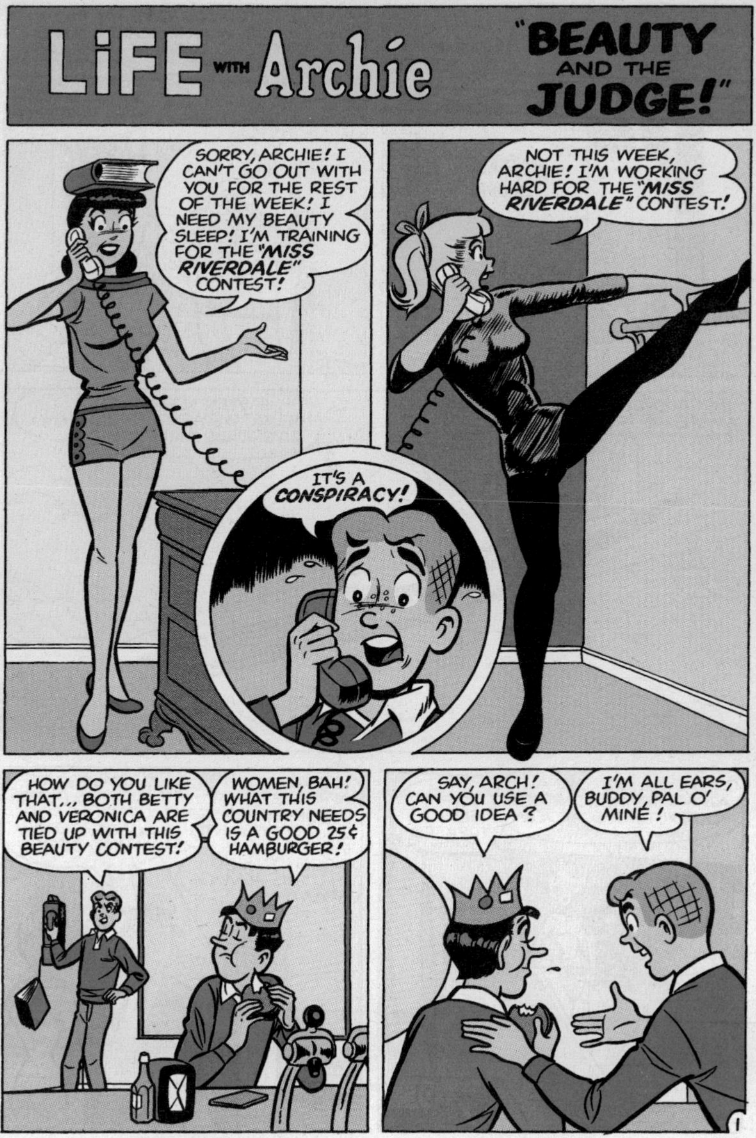
LiFE WITH Archie
"BEAUTY AND THE JUDGE!"
SORRY, ARCHIE! I CAN'T GO OUT WITH YOU FOR THE REST OF THE WEEK! I NEED MY BEAUTY SLEEP! I'M TRAINING FOR THE "MISS RIVERDALE" CONTEST!
NOT THIS WEEK, ARCHIE! I'M WORKING HARD FOR THE "MISS RIVERDALE" CONTEST!
IT'S A CONSPIRACY!
HOW DO YOU LIKE THAT... BOTH BETTY AND VERONICA ARE TIED UP WITH THIS BEAUTY CONTEST!
WOMEN, BAH! WHAT THIS COUNTRY NEEDS IS A GOOD 25¢ HAMBURGER!
SAY, ARCH! CAN YOU USE A GOOD IDEA?
I'M ALL EARS, BUDDY, PAL O' MINE!
1

Script: Sy Reit / Pencils: Bob White / Inks & Letters: Marty Epp

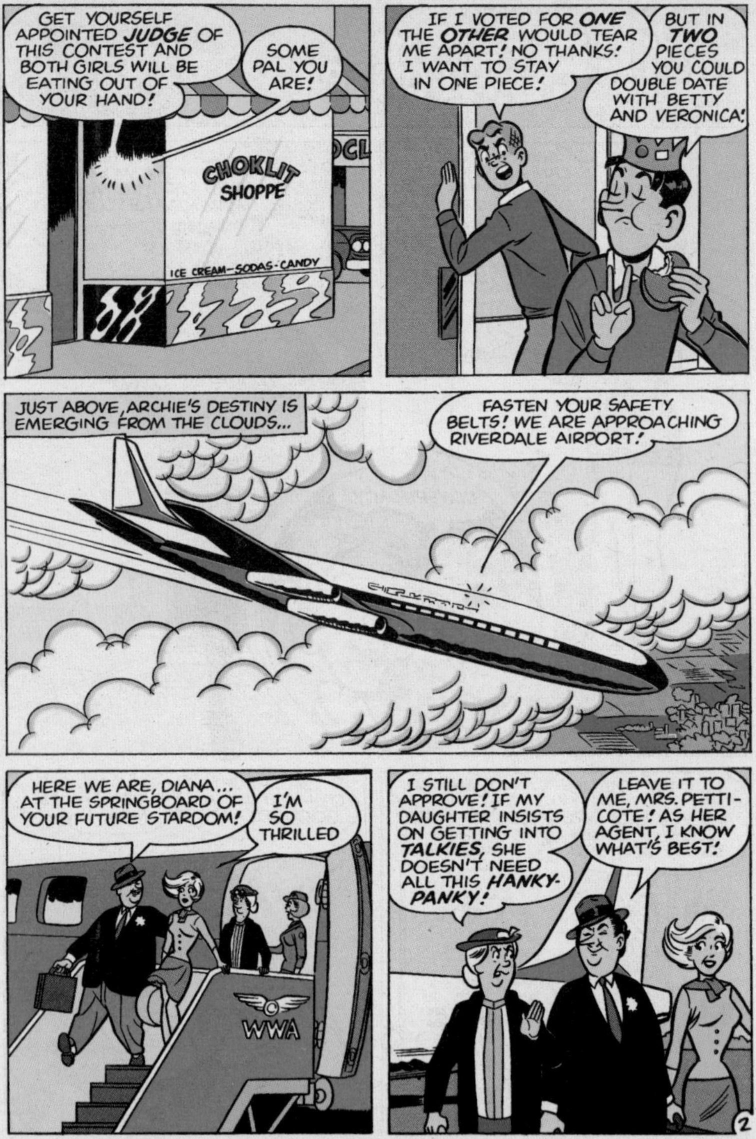
GET YOURSELF APPOINTED JUDGE OF THIS CONTEST AND BOTH GIRLS WILL BE EATING OUT OF YOUR HAND!
SOME PAL YOU ARE!
CHOKLIT SHOPPE
ICE CREAM-SODAS-CANDY
IF I VOTED FOR ONE THE OTHER WOULD TEAR ME APART! NO THANKS! I WANT TO STAY IN ONE PIECE!
BUT IN TWO PIECES YOU COULD DOUBLE DATE WITH BETTY AND VERONICA!
JUST ABOVE, ARCHIE'S DESTINY IS EMERGING FROM THE CLOUDS...
FASTEN YOUR SAFETY BELTS! WE ARE APPROACHING RIVERDALE AIRPORT!
HERE WE ARE, DIANA... AT THE SPRINGBOARD OF YOUR FUTURE STARDOM!
I'M SO THRILLED
WWA
I STILL DON'T APPROVE! IF MY DAUGHTER INSISTS ON GETTING INTO TALKIES, SHE DOESN'T NEED ALL THIS HANKY-PANKY!
LEAVE IT TO ME, MRS. PETTICOTE! AS HER AGENT, I KNOW WHAT'S BEST!
2

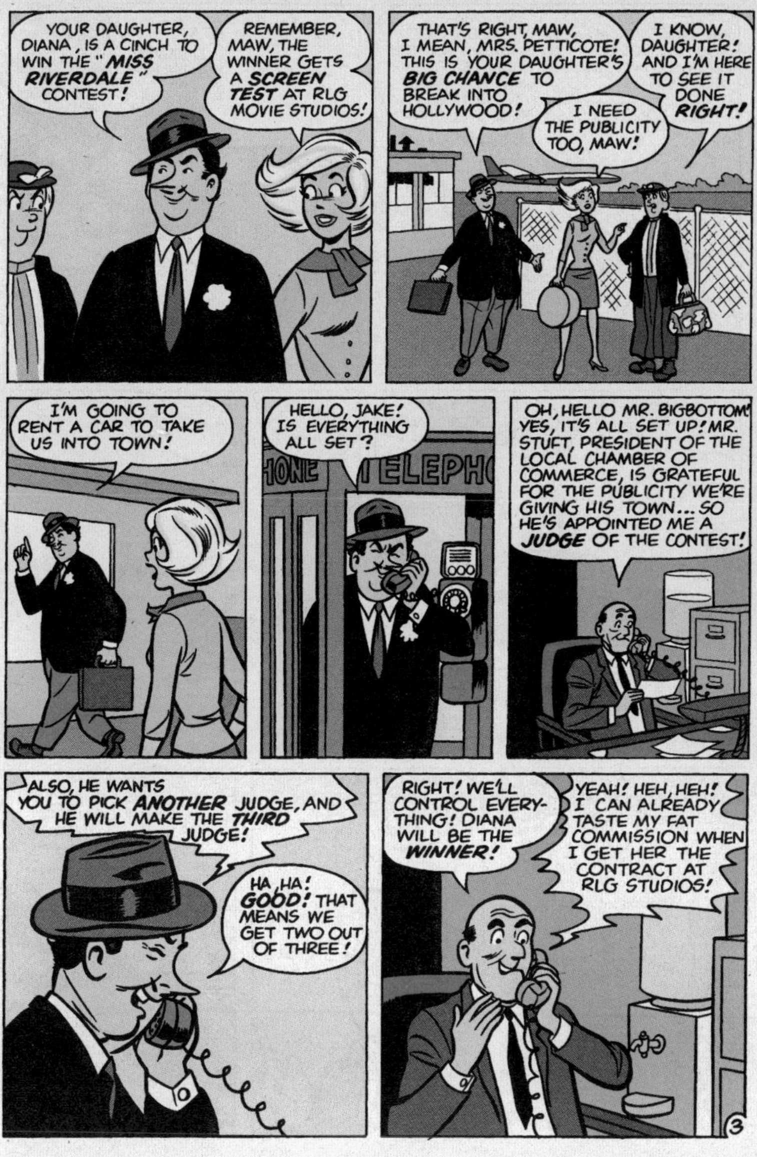
YOUR DAUGHTER, DIANA, IS A CINCH TO WIN THE "MISS RIVERDALE" CONTEST!
REMEMBER, MAW, THE WINNER GETS A SCREEN TEST AT RLG MOVIE STUDIOS!
THAT'S RIGHT, MAW, I MEAN, MRS. PETTICOTE! THIS IS YOUR DAUGHTER'S BIG CHANCE TO BREAK INTO HOLLYWOOD!
I NEED THE PUBLICITY TOO, MAW!
I KNOW, DAUGHTER! AND I'M HERE TO SEE IT DONE RIGHT!
I'M GOING TO RENT A CAR TO TAKE US INTO TOWN!
HELLO, JAKE! IS EVERYTHING ALL SET?
HONE TELEPH
OH, HELLO MR. BIGBOTTOM! YES, IT'S ALL SET UP! MR. STUFT, PRESIDENT OF THE LOCAL CHAMBER OF COMMERCE, IS GRATEFUL FOR THE PUBLICITY WE'RE GIVING HIS TOWN... SO HE'S APPOINTED ME A JUDGE OF THE CONTEST!
ALSO, HE WANTS YOU TO PICK ANOTHER JUDGE, AND HE WILL MAKE THE THIRD JUDGE!
HA HA! GOOD! THAT MEANS WE GET TWO OUT OF THREE!
RIGHT! WE'LL CONTROL EVERY-THING! DIANA WILL BE THE WINNER!
YEAH! HEH, HEH! I CAN ALREADY TASTE MY FAT COMMISSION WHEN I GET HER THE CONTRACT AT RLG STUDIOS!

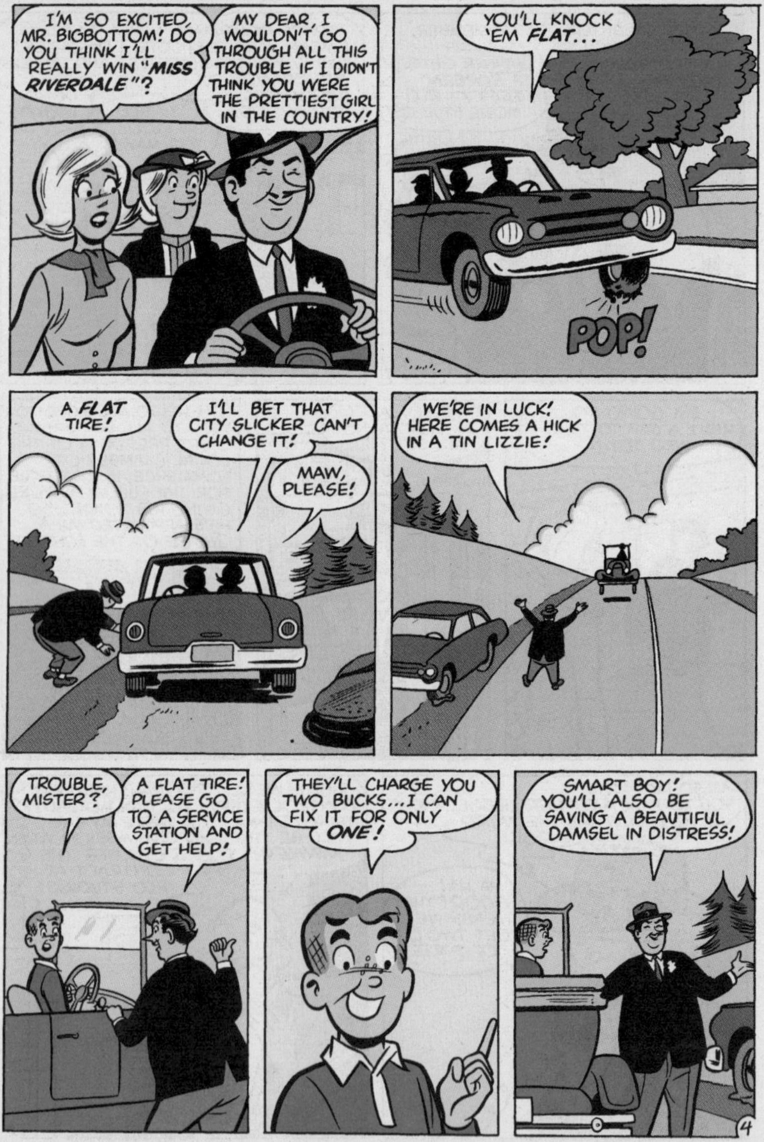
I'M SO EXCITED, MR. BIGBOTTOM! DO YOU THINK I'LL REALLY WIN "MISS RIVERDALE"?
MY DEAR, I WOULDN'T GO THROUGH ALL THIS TROUBLE IF I DIDN'T THINK YOU WERE THE PRETTIEST GIRL IN THE COUNTRY!
YOU'LL KNOCK 'EM FLAT...
POP!
A FLAT TIRE!
I'LL BET THAT CITY SLICKER CAN'T CHANGE IT!
MAW, PLEASE!
WE'RE IN LUCK! HERE COMES A HICK IN A TIN LIZZIE!
TROUBLE, MISTER?
A FLAT TIRE! PLEASE GO TO A SERVICE STATION AND GET HELP!
THEY'LL CHARGE YOU TWO BUCKS...I CAN FIX IT FOR ONLY ONE!
SMART BOY! YOU'LL ALSO BE SAVING A BEAUTIFUL DAMSEL IN DISTRESS!
4

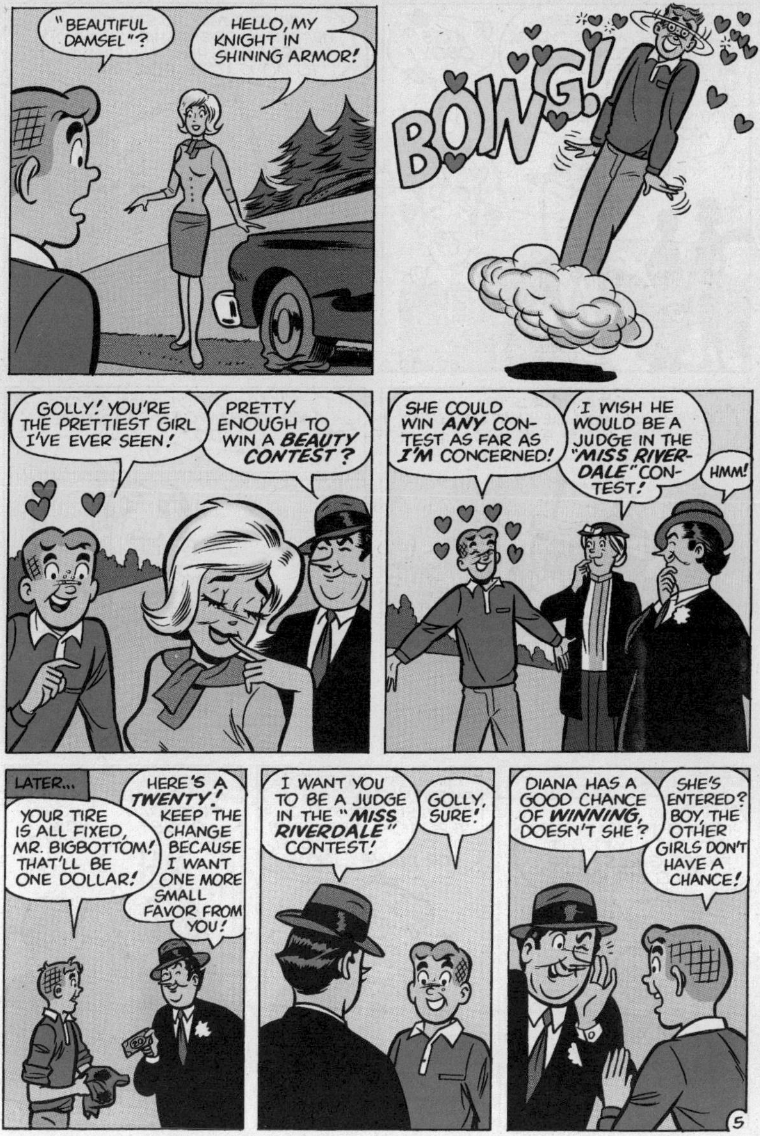
"BEAUTIFUL DAMSEL"?
HELLO, MY KNIGHT IN SHINING ARMOR!
BOING!
GOLLY! YOU'RE THE PRETTIEST GIRL I'VE EVER SEEN!
PRETTY ENOUGH TO WIN A BEAUTY CONTEST?
SHE COULD WIN ANY CONTEST AS FAR AS I'M CONCERNED!
I WISH HE WOULD BE A JUDGE IN THE "MISS RIVERDALE" CONTEST!
HMM!
LATER...
YOUR TIRE IS ALL FIXED, MR. BIGBOTTOM! THAT'LL BE ONE DOLLAR!
HERE'S A TWENTY! KEEP THE CHANGE BECAUSE I WANT ONE MORE SMALL FAVOR FROM YOU!
I WANT YOU TO BE A JUDGE IN THE "MISS RIVERDALE" CONTEST!
GOLLY, SURE!
DIANA HAS A GOOD CHANCE OF WINNING, DOESN'T SHE?
SHE'S ENTERED? BOY, THE OTHER GIRLS DON'T HAVE A CHANCE!
5

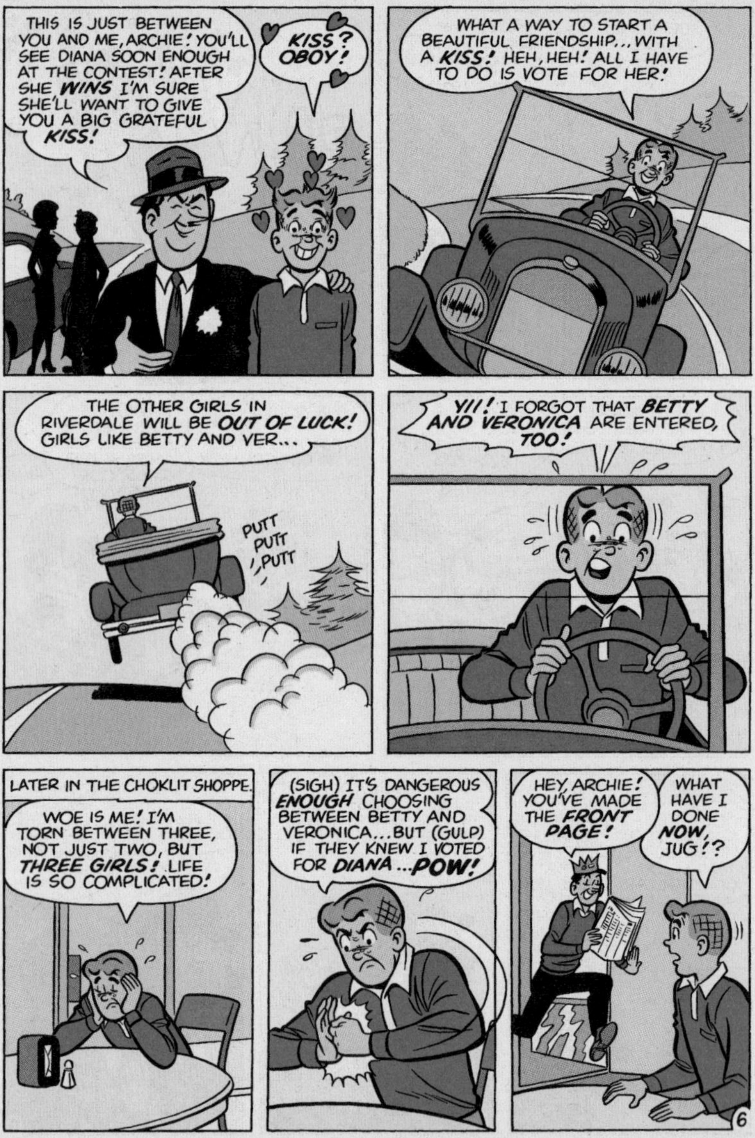

THIS IS JUST BETWEEN YOU AND ME, ARCHIE! YOU'LL SEE DIANA SOON ENOUGH AT THE CONTEST! AFTER SHE WINS I'M SURE SHE'LL WANT TO GIVE YOU A BIG GRATEFUL KISS!
KISS? OBOY!
WHAT A WAY TO START A BEAUTIFUL FRIENDSHIP... WITH A KISS! HEH, HEH! ALL I HAVE TO DO IS VOTE FOR HER!
THE OTHER GIRLS IN RIVERDALE WILL BE OUT OF LUCK! GIRLS LIKE BETTY AND VER...
PUTT PUTT PUTT
YII! I FORGOT THAT BETTY AND VERONICA ARE ENTERED, TOO!
LATER IN THE CHOKLIT SHOPPE.
WOE IS ME! I'M TORN BETWEEN THREE, NOT JUST TWO, BUT THREE GIRLS! LIFE IS SO COMPLICATED!
(SIGH) IT'S DANGEROUS ENOUGH CHOOSING BETWEEN BETTY AND VERONICA... BUT (GULP) IF THEY KNEW I VOTED FOR DIANA... POW!
HEY, ARCHIE! YOU'VE MADE THE FRONT PAGE!
WHAT HAVE I DONE NOW, JUG!?
6

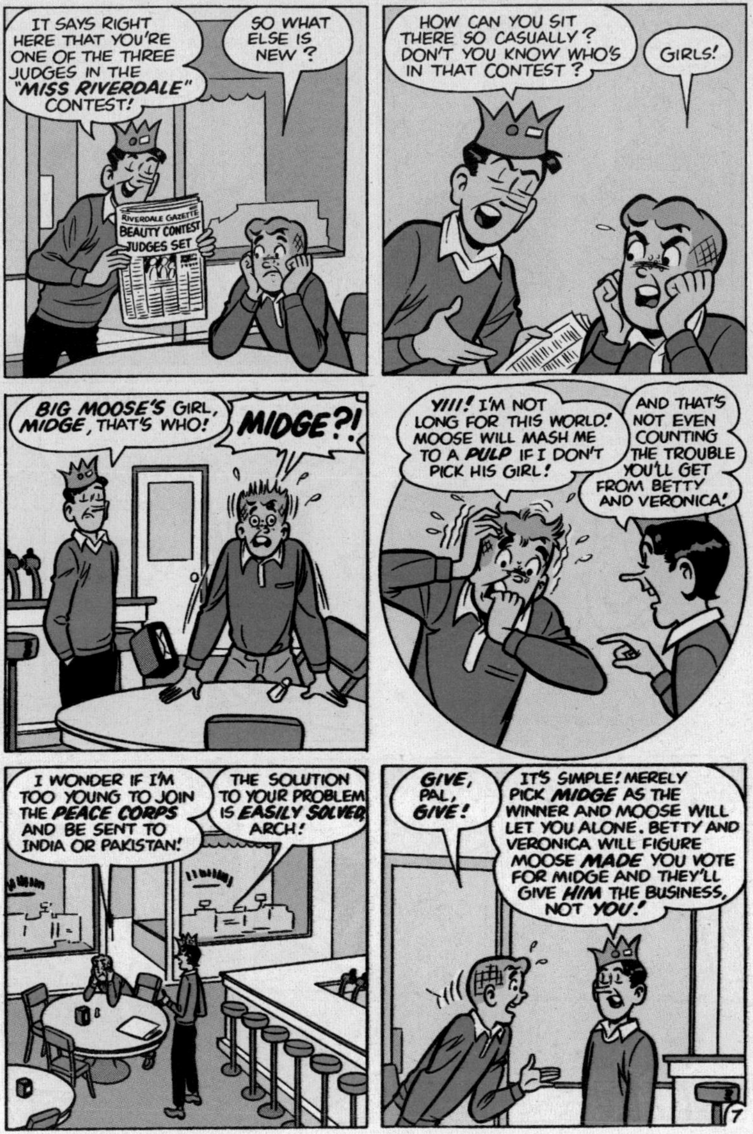

IT SAYS RIGHT HERE THAT YOU'RE ONE OF THE THREE JUDGES IN THE "MISS RIVERDALE" CONTEST!
RIVERDALE GAZETTE
BEAUTY CONTEST JUDGES SET
SO WHAT ELSE IS NEW?
HOW CAN YOU SIT THERE SO CASUALLY? DON'T YOU KNOW WHO'S IN THAT CONTEST?
GIRLS!
BIG MOOSE'S GIRL, MIDGE, THAT'S WHO!
MIDGE?!
YIII! I'M NOT LONG FOR THIS WORLD! MOOSE WILL MASH ME TO A PULP IF I DON'T PICK HIS GIRL!
AND THAT'S NOT EVEN COUNTING THE TROUBLE YOU'LL GET FROM BETTY AND VERONICA!
I WONDER IF I'M TOO YOUNG TO JOIN THE PEACE CORPS AND BE SENT TO INDIA OR PAKISTAN!
THE SOLUTION TO YOUR PROBLEM IS EASILY SOLVED, ARCH!
GIVE, PAL, GIVE!
IT'S SIMPLE! MERELY PICK MIDGE AS THE WINNER AND MOOSE WILL LET YOU ALONE. BETTY AND VERONICA WILL FIGURE MOOSE MADE YOU VOTE FOR MIDGE AND THEY'LL GIVE HIM THE BUSINESS, NOT YOU!

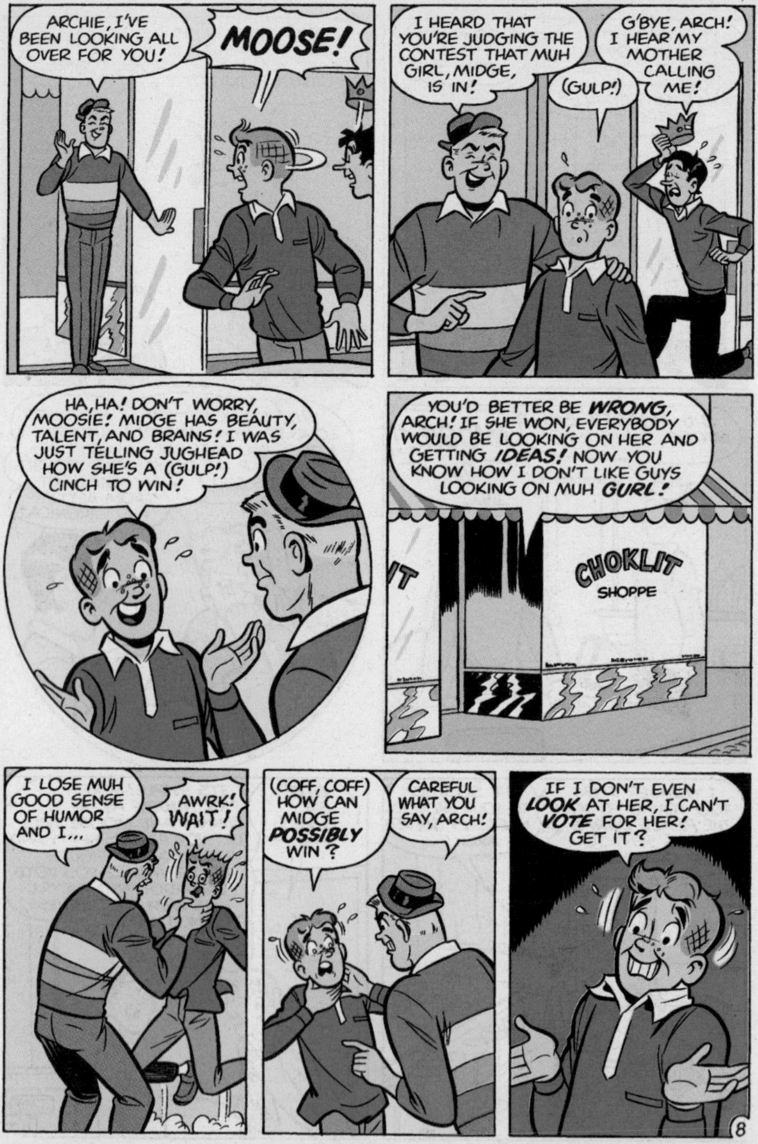

ARCHIE, I'VE BEEN LOOKING ALL OVER FOR YOU!
MOOSE!
I HEARD THAT YOU'RE JUDGING THE CONTEST THAT MUH GIRL, MIDGE, IS IN!
(GULP!)
G'BYE, ARCH! I HEAR MY MOTHER CALLING ME!
HA, HA! DON'T WORRY, MOOSIE! MIDGE HAS BEAUTY, TALENT, AND BRAINS! I WAS JUST TELLING JUGHEAD HOW SHE'S A (GULP!) CINCH TO WIN!
YOU'D BETTER BE WRONG, ARCH! IF SHE WON, EVERYBODY WOULD BE LOOKING ON HER AND GETTING IDEAS! NOW YOU KNOW HOW I DON'T LIKE GUYS LOOKING ON MUH GURL!
CHOKLIT
SHOPPE
I LOSE MUH GOOD SENSE OF HUMOR AND I,...
AWRK! WAIT!
(COFF, COFF) HOW CAN MIDGE POSSIBLY WIN?
CAREFUL WHAT YOU SAY, ARCH!
IF I DON'T EVEN LOOK AT HER, I CAN'T VOTE FOR HER! GET IT?

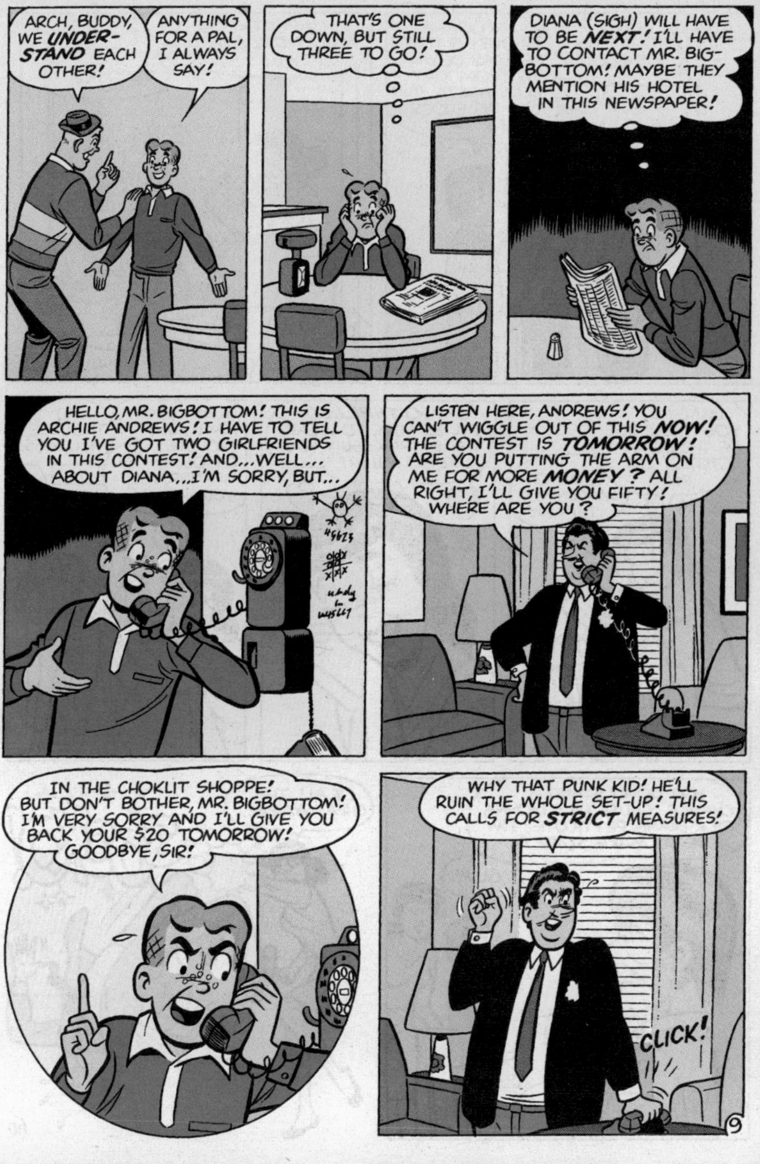
ARCH, BUDDY, WE UNDERSTAND EACH OTHER!
ANYTHING FOR A PAL, I ALWAYS SAY!
THAT'S ONE DOWN, BUT STILL THREE TO GO!
DIANA (SIGH) WILL HAVE TO BE NEXT! I'LL HAVE TO CONTACT MR. BIGBOTTOM! MAYBE THEY MENTION HIS HOTEL IN THIS NEWSPAPER!
HELLO, MR. BIGBOTTOM! THIS IS ARCHIE ANDREWS! I HAVE TO TELL YOU I'VE GOT TWO GIRLFRIENDS IN THIS CONTEST! AND... WELL... ABOUT DIANA... I'M SORRY, BUT...
LISTEN HERE, ANDREWS! YOU CAN'T WIGGLE OUT OF THIS NOW! THE CONTEST IS TOMORROW! ARE YOU PUTTING THE ARM ON ME FOR MORE MONEY? ALL RIGHT, I'LL GIVE YOU FIFTY! WHERE ARE YOU?
IN THE CHOKLIT SHOPPE! BUT DON'T BOTHER, MR. BIGBOTTOM! I'M VERY SORRY AND I'LL GIVE YOU BACK YOUR $20 TOMORROW! GOODBYE, SIR!
WHY THAT PUNK KID! HE'LL RUIN THE WHOLE SET-UP! THIS CALLS FOR STRICT MEASURES!
CLICK!

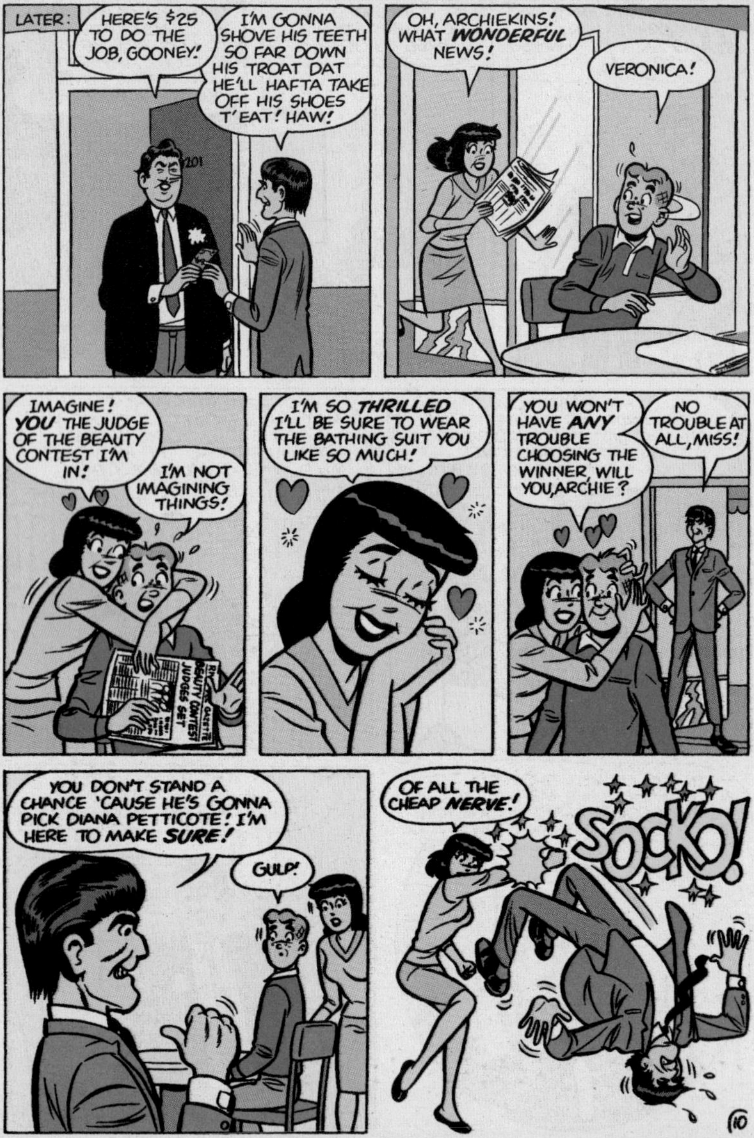

LATER:
HERE'S $25 TO DO THE JOB, GOONEY!
I'M GONNA SHOVE HIS TEETH SO FAR DOWN HIS TROAT DAT HE'LL HAFTA TAKE OFF HIS SHOES T'EAT! HAW!
201
OH, ARCHIEKINS! WHAT WONDERFUL NEWS!
VERONICA!
IMAGINE! YOU THE JUDGE OF THE BEAUTY CONTEST I'M IN!
I'M NOT IMAGINING THINGS!
RIVERDALE GAZETTE
BEAUTY CONTEST JUDGES SET
I'M SO THRILLED I'LL BE SURE TO WEAR THE BATHING SUIT YOU LIKE SO MUCH!
YOU WON'T HAVE ANY TROUBLE CHOOSING THE WINNER, WILL YOU, ARCHIE?
NO TROUBLE AT ALL, MISS!
YOU DON'T STAND A CHANCE 'CAUSE HE'S GONNA PICK DIANA PETTICOTE! I'M HERE TO MAKE SURE!
GULP!
OF ALL THE CHEAP NERVE!
SOCKO!

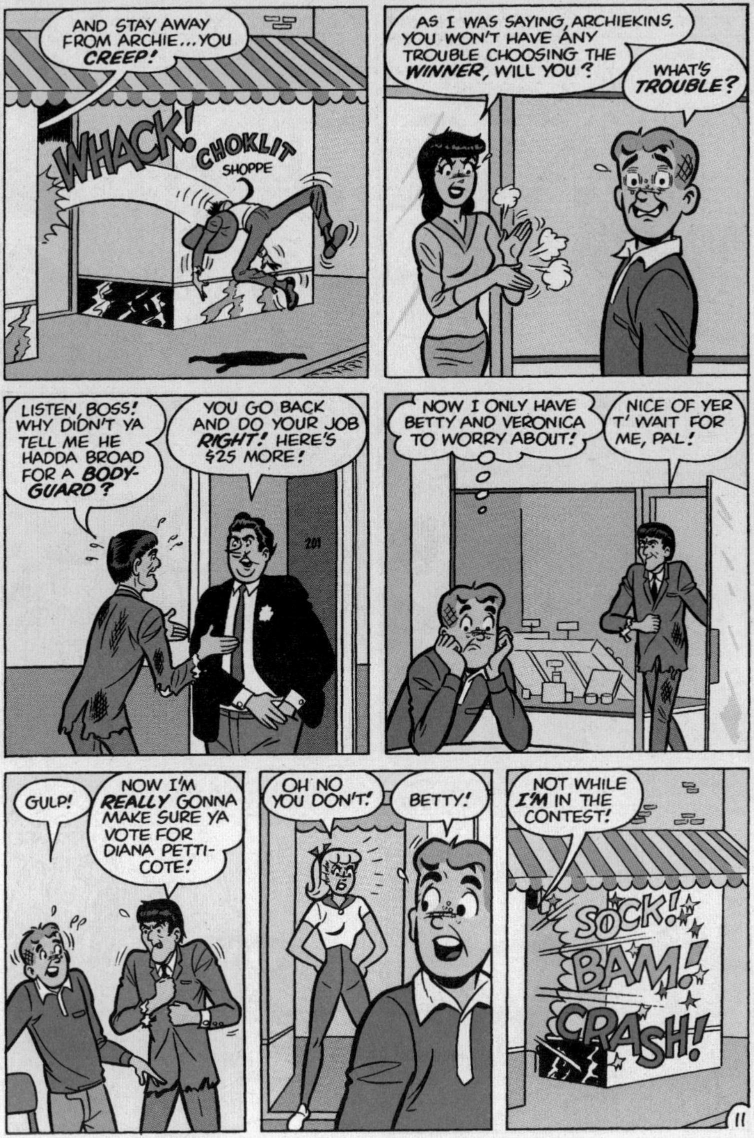
AND STAY AWAY FROM ARCHIE...YOU CREEP!
WHACK!
CHOKLIT SHOPPE
AS I WAS SAYING, ARCHIEKINS, YOU WON'T HAVE ANY TROUBLE CHOOSING THE WINNER, WILL YOU?
WHAT'S TROUBLE?
LISTEN, BOSS! WHY DIDN'T YA TELL ME HE HADDA BROAD FOR A BODY-GUARD?
YOU GO BACK AND DO YOUR JOB RIGHT! HERE'S $25 MORE!
201
NOW I ONLY HAVE BETTY AND VERONICA TO WORRY ABOUT!
NICE OF YER T' WAIT FOR ME, PAL!
GULP!
NOW I'M REALLY GONNA MAKE SURE YA VOTE FOR DIANA PETTI-COTE!
OH NO YOU DON'T!
BETTY!
NOT WHILE I'M IN THE CONTEST!
SOCK!
BAM!
CRASH!

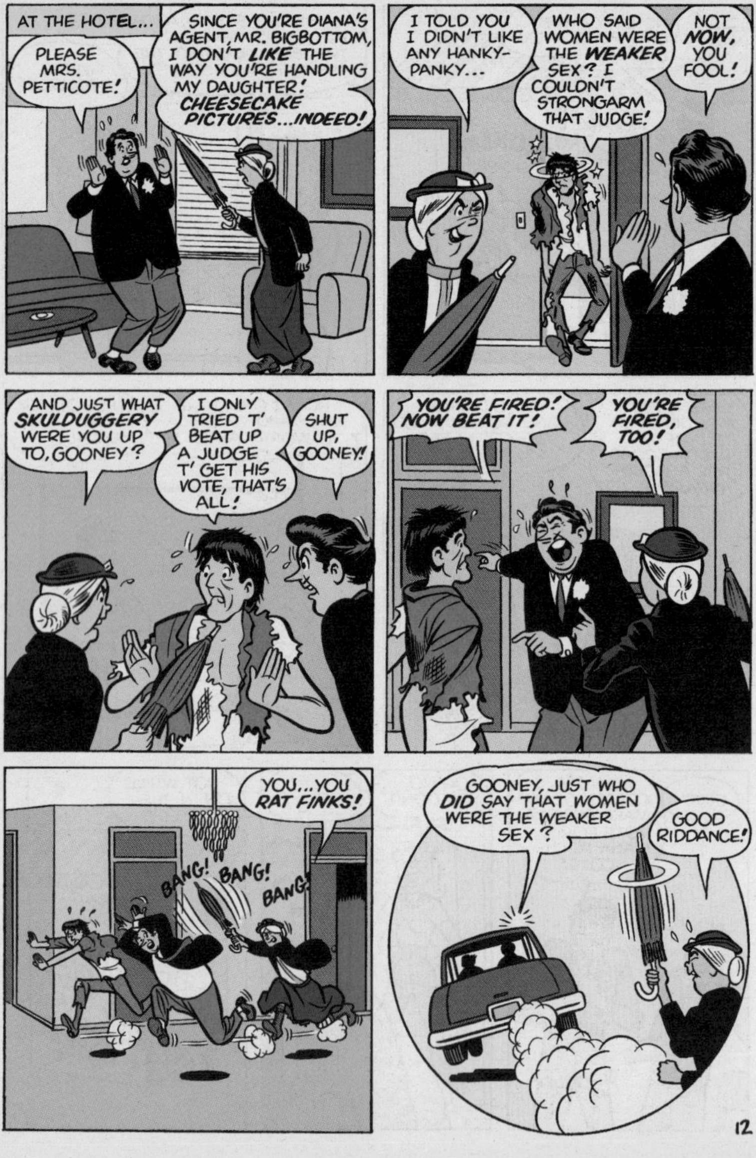
AT THE HOTEL...
PLEASE MRS. PETTICOTE!
SINCE YOU'RE DIANA'S AGENT, MR. BIGBOTTOM, I DON'T LIKE THE WAY YOU'RE HANDLING MY DAUGHTER! CHEESECAKE PICTURES...INDEED!
I TOLD YOU I DIDN'T LIKE ANY HANKY-PANKY...
WHO SAID WOMEN WERE THE WEAKER SEX? I COULDN'T STRONGARM THAT JUDGE!
NOT NOW, YOU FOOL!
AND JUST WHAT SKULDUGGERY WERE YOU UP TO, GOONEY?
I ONLY TRIED T' BEAT UP A JUDGE T' GET HIS VOTE, THAT'S ALL!
SHUT UP, GOONEY!
YOU'RE FIRED! NOW BEAT IT!
YOU'RE FIRED, TOO!
YOU...YOU RAT FINKS!
BANG! BANG! BANG!
GOONEY, JUST WHO DID SAY THAT WOMEN WERE THE WEAKER SEX?
GOOD RIDDANCE!

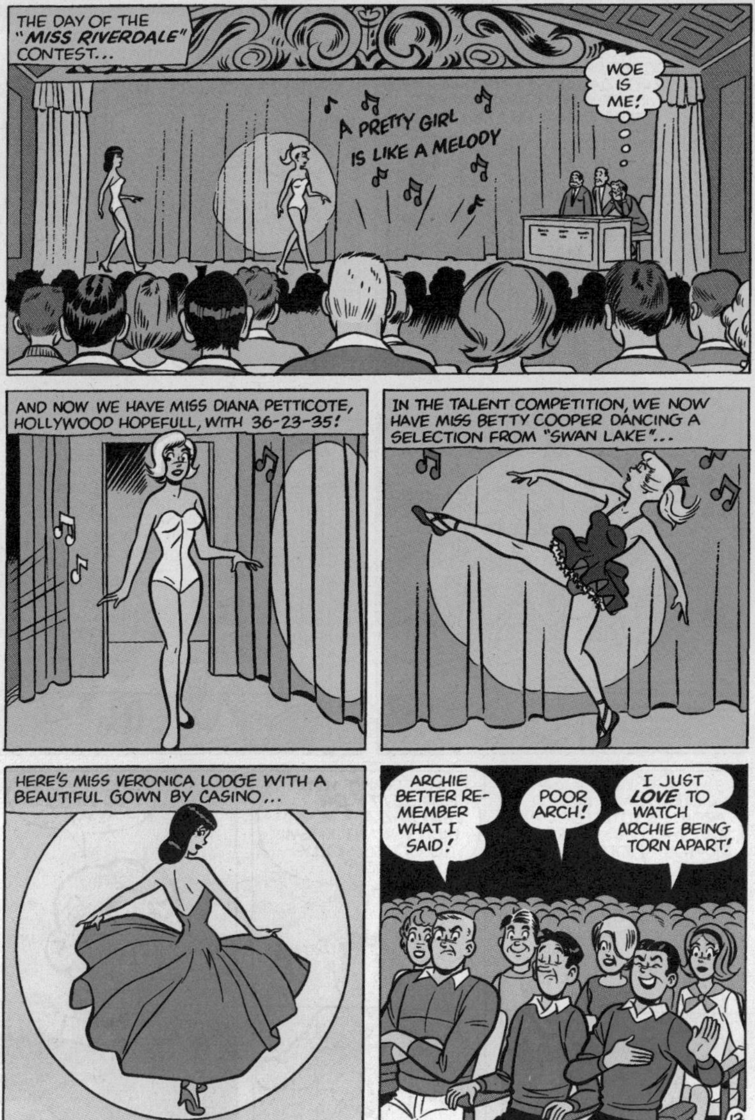
THE DAY OF THE "MISS RIVERDALE" CONTEST...
A PRETTY GIRL IS LIKE A MELODY
WOE IS ME!
AND NOW WE HAVE MISS DIANA PETTICOTE, HOLLYWOOD HOPEFULL, WITH 36-23-35!
IN THE TALENT COMPETITION, WE NOW HAVE MISS BETTY COOPER DANCING A SELECTION FROM "SWAN LAKE"...
HERE'S MISS VERONICA LODGE WITH A BEAUTIFUL GOWN BY CASINO...
ARCHIE BETTER RE-MEMBER WHAT I SAID!
POOR ARCH!
I JUST LOVE TO WATCH ARCHIE BEING TORN APART!
13

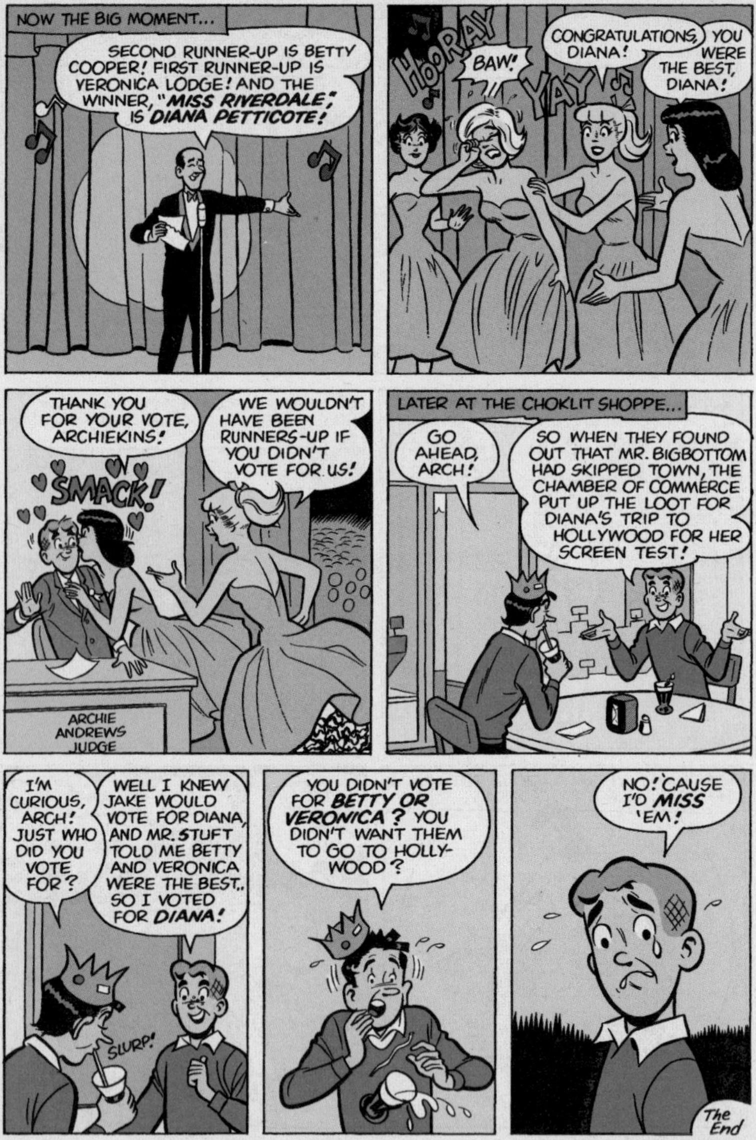
NOW THE BIG MOMENT...
SECOND RUNNER-UP IS BETTY COOPER! FIRST RUNNER-UP IS VERONICA LODGE! AND THE WINNER, "MISS RIVERDALE," IS DIANA PETTICOTE!
HOORAY
BAW!
YAY
CONGRATULATIONS, DIANA!
YOU WERE THE BEST, DIANA!
THANK YOU FOR YOUR VOTE, ARCHIEKINS!
SMACK!
WE WOULDN'T HAVE BEEN RUNNERS-UP IF YOU DIDN'T VOTE FOR US!
ARCHIE ANDREWS JUDGE
LATER AT THE CHOKLIT SHOPPE...
GO AHEAD, ARCH!
SO WHEN THEY FOUND OUT THAT MR. BIGBOTTOM HAD SKIPPED TOWN, THE CHAMBER OF COMMERCE PUT UP THE LOOT FOR DIANA'S TRIP TO HOLLYWOOD FOR HER SCREEN TEST!
I'M CURIOUS, ARCH! JUST WHO DID YOU VOTE FOR?
WELL I KNEW JAKE WOULD VOTE FOR DIANA, AND MR. STUFT TOLD ME BETTY AND VERONICA WERE THE BEST.. SO I VOTED FOR DIANA!
SLURP!
YOU DIDN'T VOTE FOR BETTY OR VERONICA? YOU DIDN'T WANT THEM TO GO TO HOLLY-WOOD?
NO! 'CAUSE I'D MISS 'EM!
The End

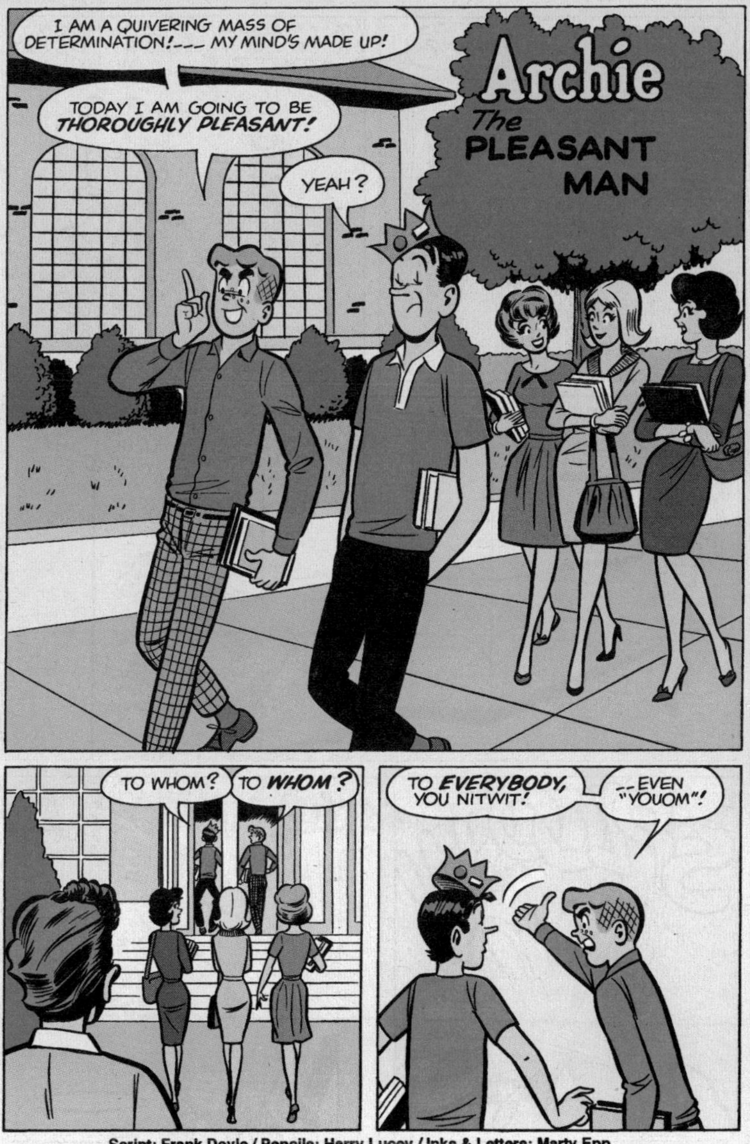
Archie
The PLEASANT MAN
I AM A QUIVERING MASS OF DETERMINATION!--- MY MIND'S MADE UP!
TODAY I AM GOING TO BE THOROUGHLY PLEASANT!
YEAH?
TO WHOM?
TO WHOM?
TO EVERYBODY, YOU NITWIT!
--EVEN "YOUOM"!

Script: Frank Doyle / Pencils: Harry Lucey / Inks & Letters: Marty Epp

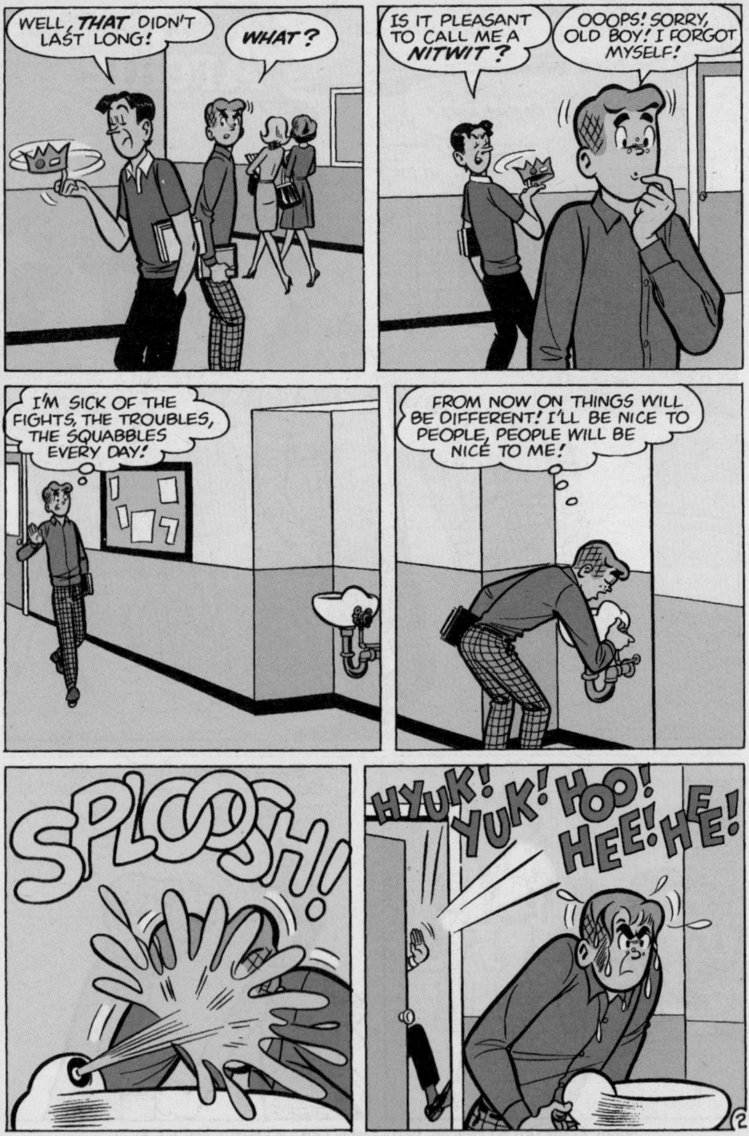

WELL, THAT DIDN'T LAST LONG!
WHAT?
IS IT PLEASANT TO CALL ME A NITWIT?
OOOPS! SORRY, OLD BOY! I FORGOT MYSELF!
I'M SICK OF THE FIGHTS, THE TROUBLES, THE SQUABBLES EVERY DAY!
FROM NOW ON THINGS WILL BE DIFFERENT! I'LL BE NICE TO PEOPLE, PEOPLE WILL BE NICE TO ME!
SPLOOSH!
HYUK! YUK! HOO! HEE! HEE!
2

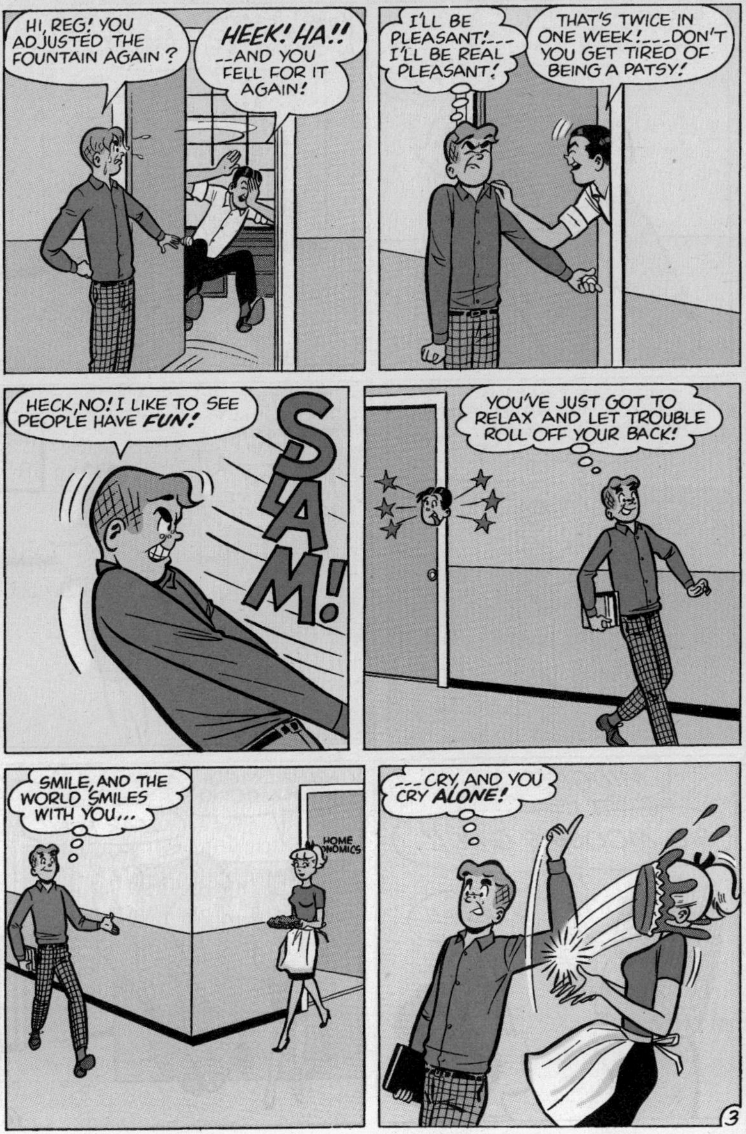
HI, REG! YOU ADJUSTED THE FOUNTAIN AGAIN?
HEEK! HA!! --AND YOU FELL FOR IT AGAIN!
I'LL BE PLEASANT!--- I'LL BE REAL PLEASANT!
THAT'S TWICE IN ONE WEEK!---DON'T YOU GET TIRED OF BEING A PATSY!
HECK, NO! I LIKE TO SEE PEOPLE HAVE FUN!
SLAM!
YOU'VE JUST GOT TO RELAX AND LET TROUBLE ROLL OFF YOUR BACK!
SMILE, AND THE WORLD SMILES WITH YOU...
HOME ONOMICS
---CRY, AND YOU CRY ALONE!
3

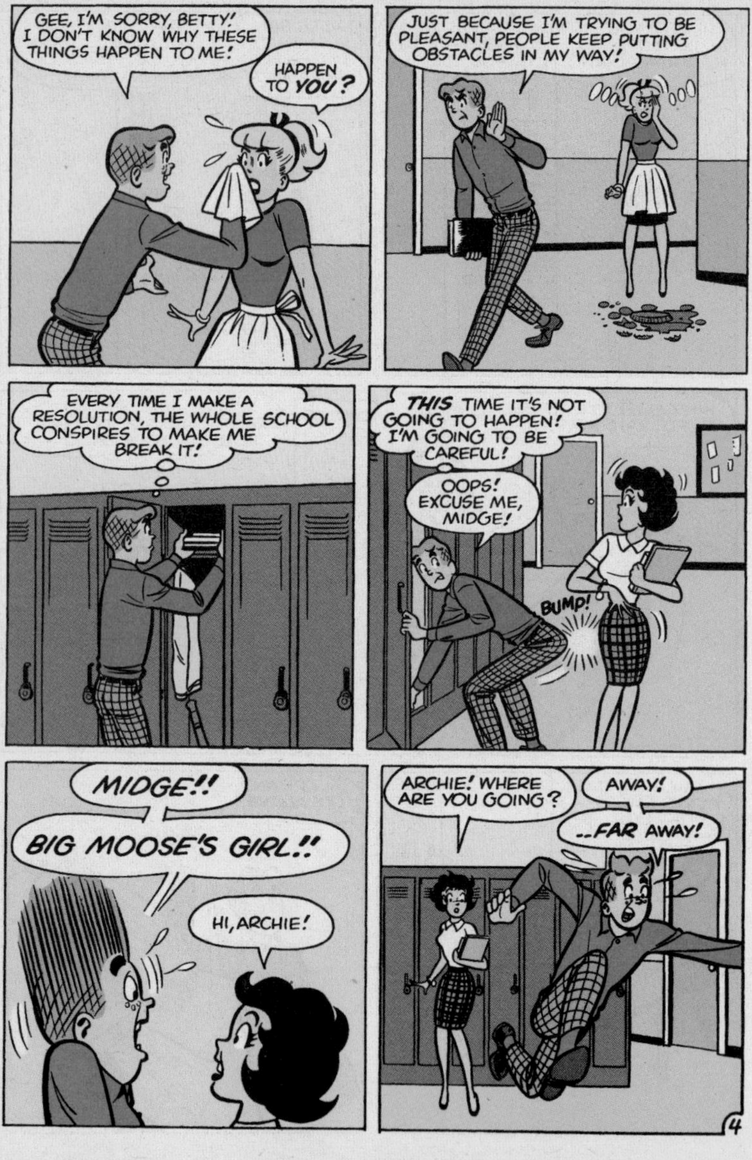
GEE, I'M SORRY, BETTY! I DON'T KNOW WHY THESE THINGS HAPPEN TO ME!
HAPPEN TO YOU?
JUST BECAUSE I'M TRYING TO BE PLEASANT, PEOPLE KEEP PUTTING OBSTACLES IN MY WAY!
EVERY TIME I MAKE A RESOLUTION, THE WHOLE SCHOOL CONSPIRES TO MAKE ME BREAK IT!
THIS TIME IT'S NOT GOING TO HAPPEN! I'M GOING TO BE CAREFUL!
OOPS! EXCUSE ME, MIDGE!
BUMP!
MIDGE!!
BIG MOOSE'S GIRL!!
HI, ARCHIE!
ARCHIE! WHERE ARE YOU GOING?
AWAY!
..FAR AWAY!
4

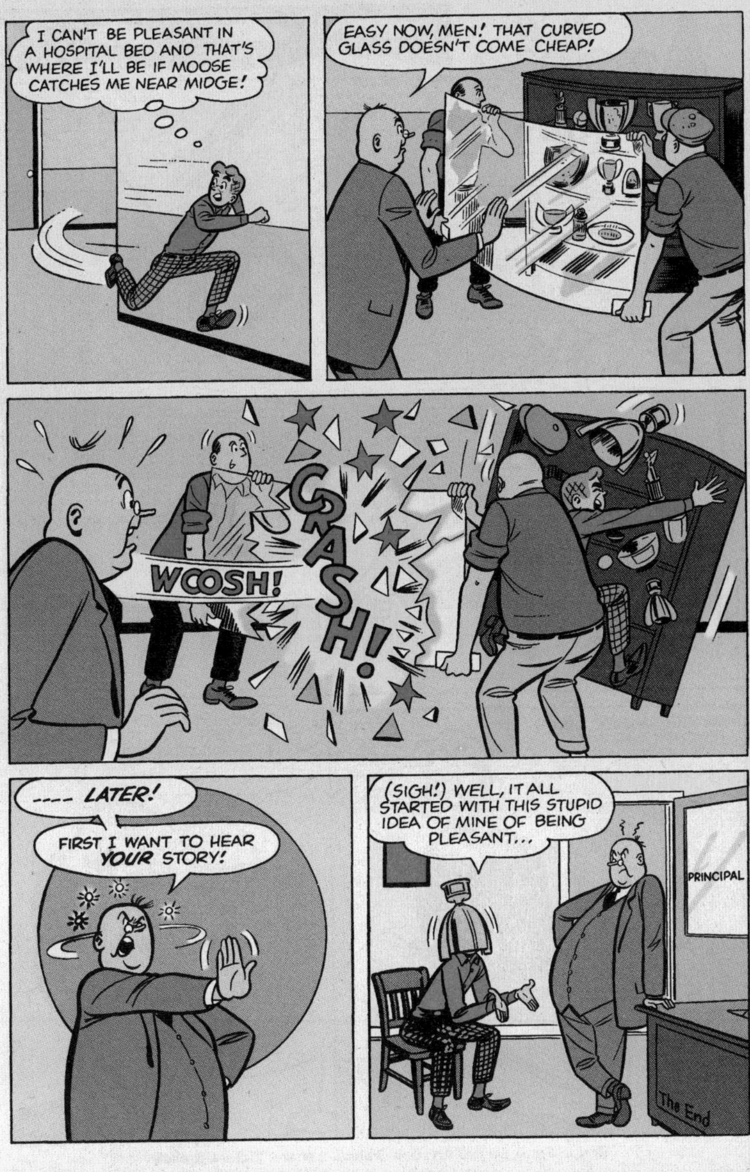

I CAN'T BE PLEASANT IN A HOSPITAL BED AND THAT'S WHERE I'LL BE IF MOOSE CATCHES ME NEAR MIDGE!
EASY NOW, MEN! THAT CURVED GLASS DOESN'T COME CHEAP!
WOOSH!
CRASH!
---- LATER!
FIRST I WANT TO HEAR YOUR STORY!
(SIGH!) WELL, IT ALL STARTED WITH THIS STUPID IDEA OF MINE OF BEING PLEASANT...
PRINCIPAL
The End

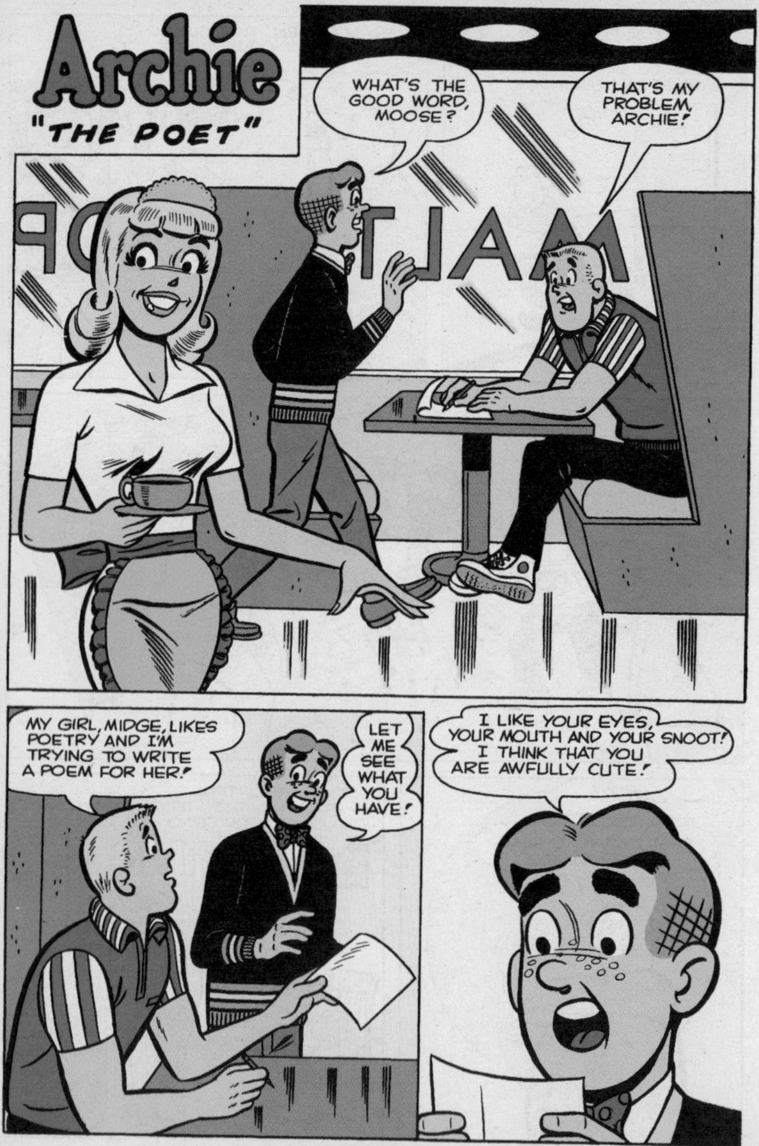
Archie
"THE POET"
WHAT'S THE GOOD WORD, MOOSE?
THAT'S MY PROBLEM, ARCHIE!
MALT
MY GIRL, MIDGE, LIKES POETRY AND I'M TRYING TO WRITE A POEM FOR HER!
LET ME SEE WHAT YOU HAVE!
I LIKE YOUR EYES, YOUR MOUTH AND YOUR SNOOT! I THINK THAT YOU ARE AWFULLY CUTE!

Script: Frank Doyle / Art: Bob Bolling / Letters: Victor Gorelick

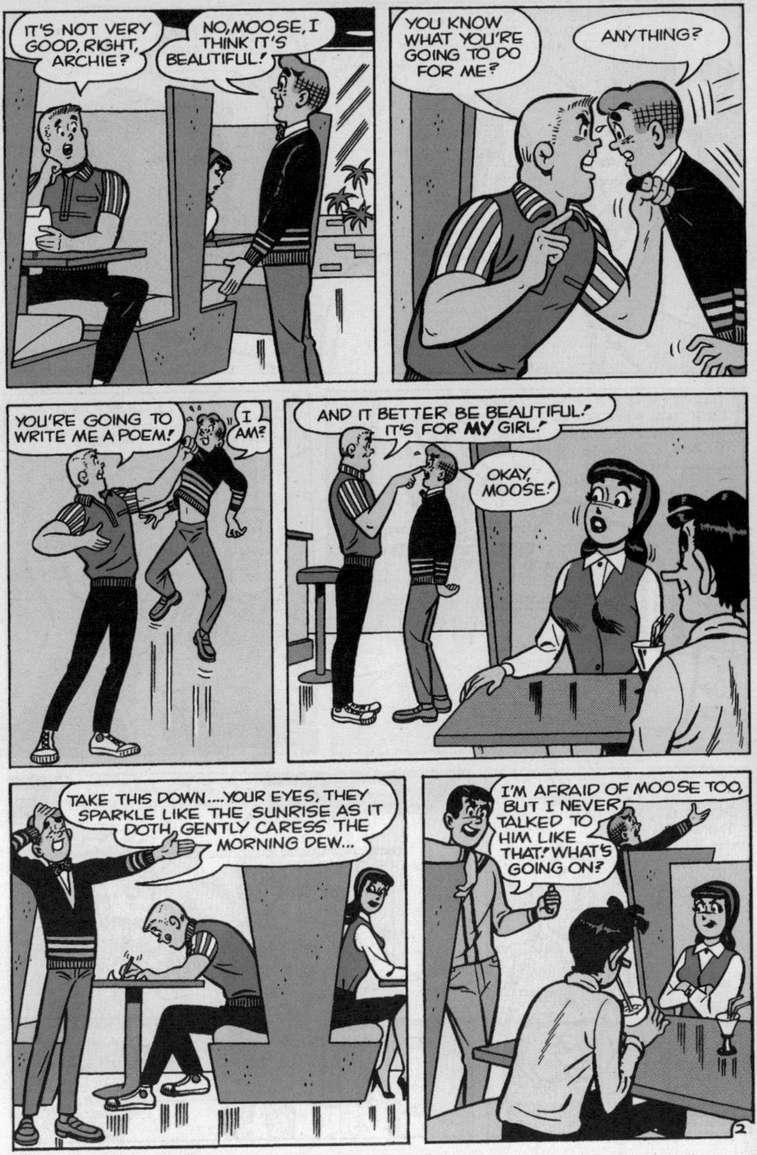
IT'S NOT VERY GOOD, RIGHT, ARCHIE?
NO, MOOSE, I THINK IT'S BEAUTIFUL!
YOU KNOW WHAT YOU'RE GOING TO DO FOR ME?
ANYTHING?
YOU'RE GOING TO WRITE ME A POEM!
I AM?
AND IT BETTER BE BEAUTIFUL! IT'S FOR MY GIRL!
OKAY, MOOSE!
TAKE THIS DOWN....YOUR EYES, THEY SPARKLE LIKE THE SUNRISE AS IT DOTH, GENTLY CARESS THE MORNING DEW...
I'M AFRAID OF MOOSE TOO, BUT I NEVER TALKED TO HIM LIKE THAT! WHAT'S GOING ON?
2

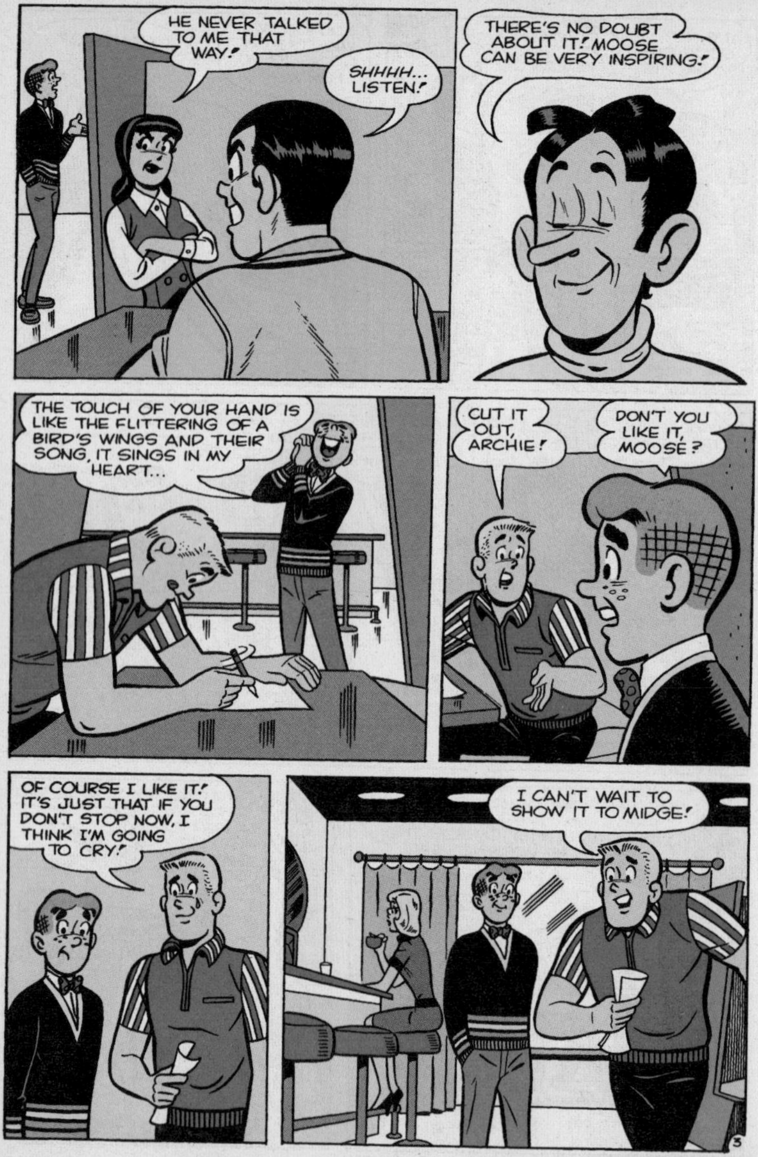
HE NEVER TALKED TO ME THAT WAY!
SHHHH... LISTEN!
THERE'S NO DOUBT ABOUT IT! MOOSE CAN BE VERY INSPIRING!
THE TOUCH OF YOUR HAND IS LIKE THE FLITTERING OF A BIRD'S WINGS AND THEIR SONG, IT SINGS IN MY HEART...
CUT IT OUT, ARCHIE!
DON'T YOU LIKE IT, MOOSE?
OF COURSE I LIKE IT! IT'S JUST THAT IF YOU DON'T STOP NOW, I THINK I'M GOING TO CRY!
I CAN'T WAIT TO SHOW IT TO MIDGE!
3

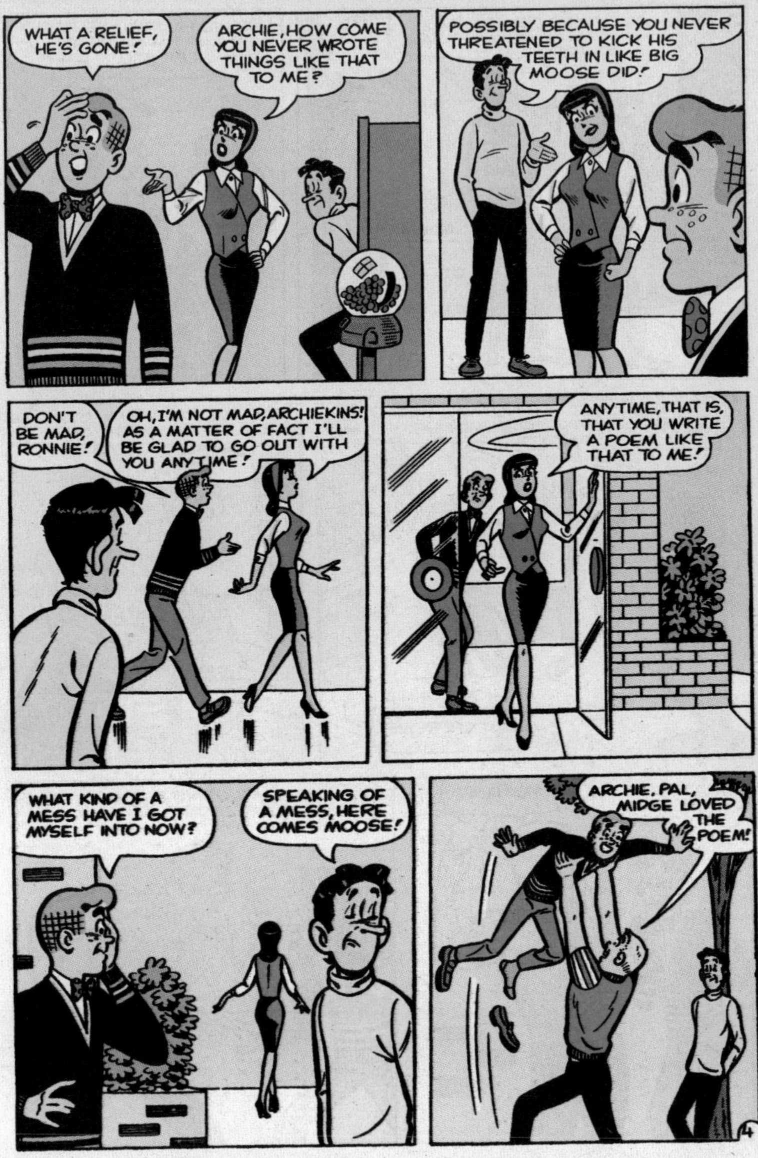
WHAT A RELIEF, HE'S GONE!
ARCHIE, HOW COME YOU NEVER WROTE THINGS LIKE THAT TO ME?
POSSIBLY BECAUSE YOU NEVER THREATENED TO KICK HIS TEETH IN LIKE BIG MOOSE DID!
DON'T BE MAD, RONNIE!
OH, I'M NOT MAD, ARCHIEKINS! AS A MATTER OF FACT I'LL BE GLAD TO GO OUT WITH YOU ANYTIME!
ANYTIME, THAT IS, THAT YOU WRITE A POEM LIKE THAT TO ME!
WHAT KIND OF A MESS HAVE I GOT MYSELF INTO NOW?
SPEAKING OF A MESS, HERE COMES MOOSE!
ARCHIE, PAL, MIDGE LOVED THE POEM!
4

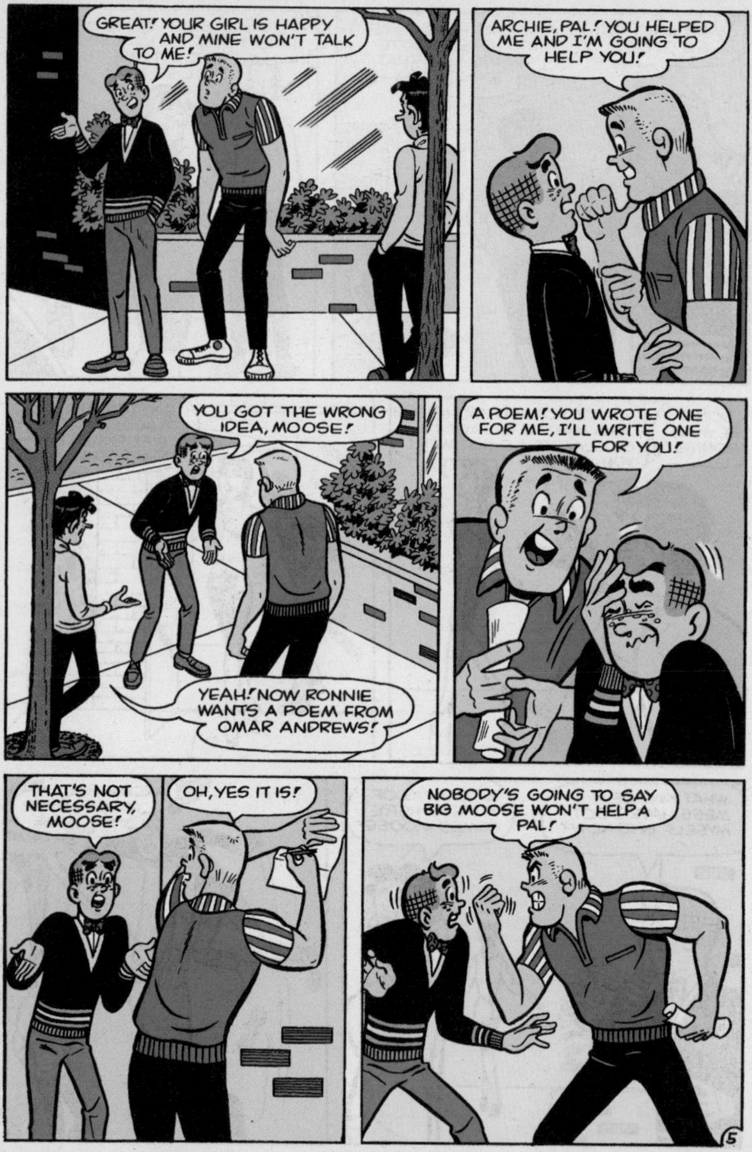
GREAT! YOUR GIRL IS HAPPY AND MINE WON'T TALK TO ME!
ARCHIE, PAL! YOU HELPED ME AND I'M GOING TO HELP YOU!
YOU GOT THE WRONG IDEA, MOOSE!
YEAH! NOW RONNIE WANTS A POEM FROM OMAR ANDREWS!
A POEM! YOU WROTE ONE FOR ME, I'LL WRITE ONE FOR YOU!
THAT'S NOT NECESSARY, MOOSE!
OH, YES IT IS!
NOBODY'S GOING TO SAY BIG MOOSE WON'T HELP A PAL!

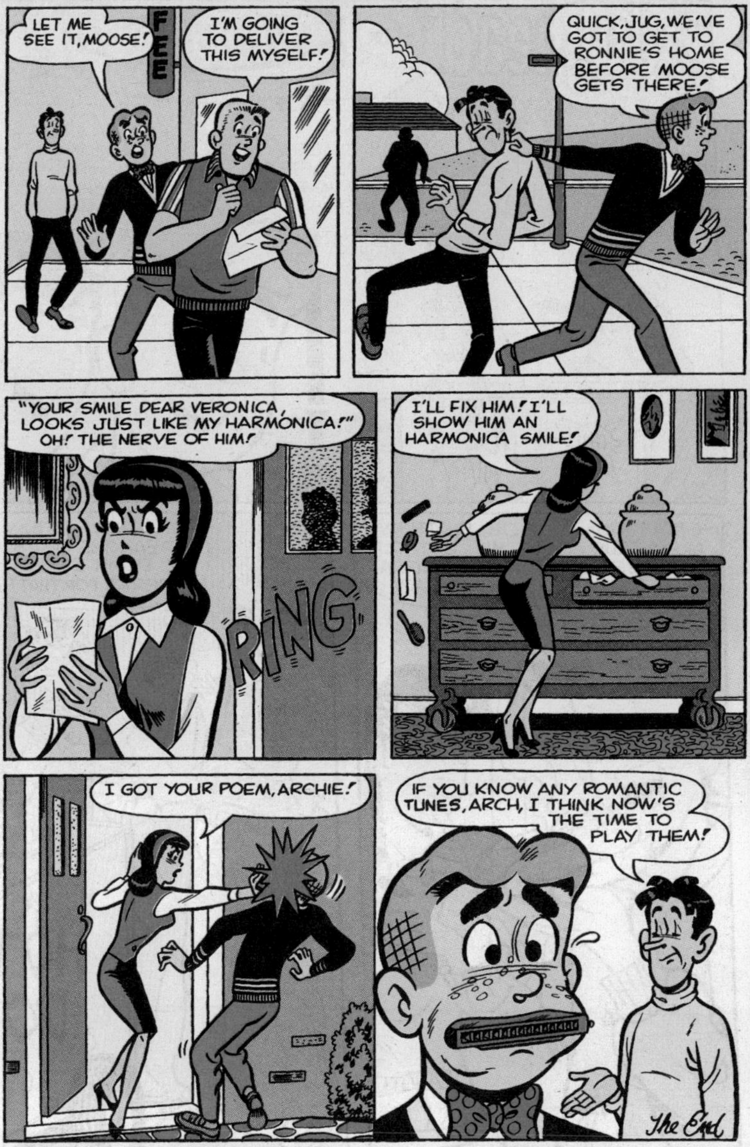
LET ME SEE IT, MOOSE!
FEE
I'M GOING TO DELIVER THIS MYSELF!
QUICK, JUG, WE'VE GOT TO GET TO RONNIE'S HOME BEFORE MOOSE GETS THERE!
"YOUR SMILE DEAR VERONICA, LOOKS JUST LIKE MY HARMONICA!" OH! THE NERVE OF HIM!
RING
I'LL FIX HIM! I'LL SHOW HIM AN HARMONICA SMILE!
I GOT YOUR POEM, ARCHIE!
IF YOU KNOW ANY ROMANTIC TUNES, ARCH, I THINK NOW'S THE TIME TO PLAY THEM!
The End

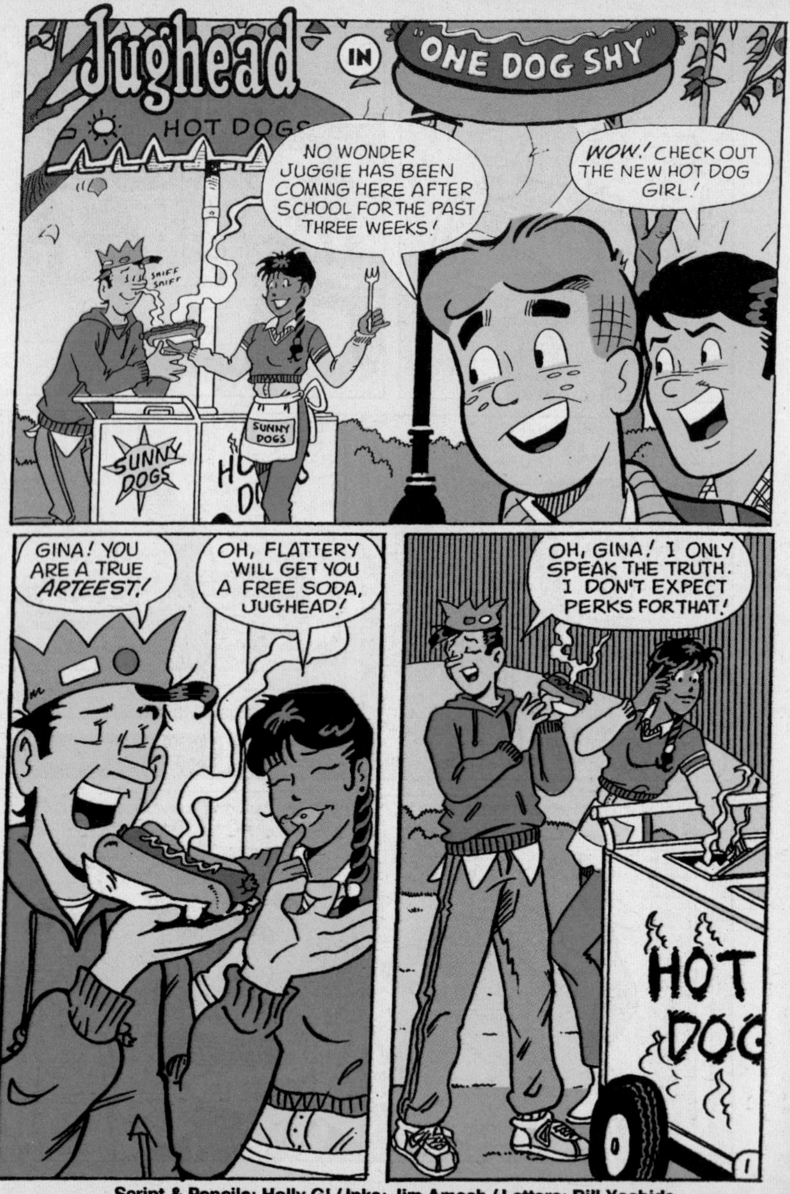
Jughead
IN
"ONE DOG SHY"
HOT DOGS
NO WONDER JUGGIE HAS BEEN COMING HERE AFTER SCHOOL FOR THE PAST THREE WEEKS!
WOW! CHECK OUT THE NEW HOT DOG GIRL!
SNIFF SNIFF
SUNNY DOGS
SUNNY DOGS
GINA! YOU ARE A TRUE ARTEEST!
OH, FLATTERY WILL GET YOU A FREE SODA, JUGHEAD!
OH, GINA! I ONLY SPEAK THE TRUTH. I DON'T EXPECT PERKS FOR THAT!
HOT DOG
1

Script & Pencils: Holly G! / Inks: Jim Amash / Letters: Bill Yoshida

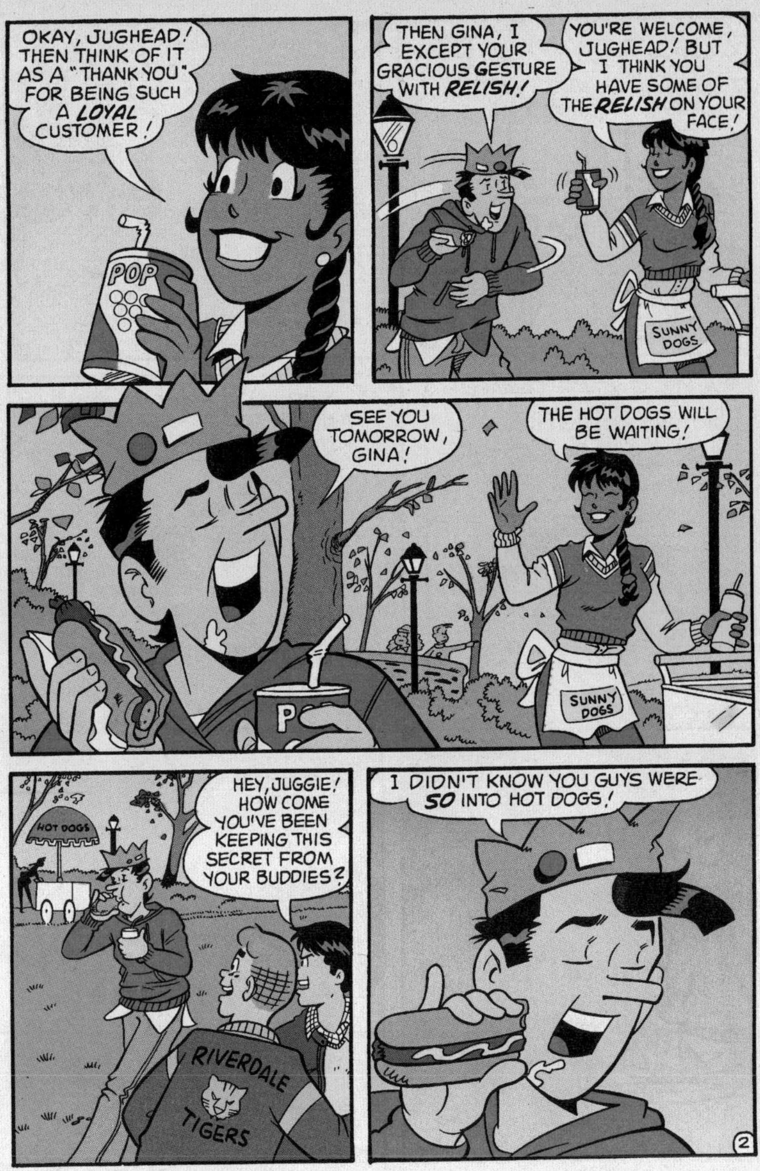

OKAY, JUGHEAD! THEN THINK OF IT AS A "THANK YOU" FOR BEING SUCH A LOYAL CUSTOMER!
POP
THEN GINA, I EXCEPT YOUR GRACIOUS GESTURE WITH RELISH!
YOU'RE WELCOME, JUGHEAD! BUT I THINK YOU HAVE SOME OF THE RELISH ON YOUR FACE!
SUNNY DOGS
SEE YOU TOMORROW, GINA!
THE HOT DOGS WILL BE WAITING!
SUNNY DOGS
HOT DOGS
HEY, JUGGIE! HOW COME YOU'VE BEEN KEEPING THIS SECRET FROM YOUR BUDDIES?
RIVERDALE TIGERS
I DIDN'T KNOW YOU GUYS WERE SO INTO HOT DOGS!
2

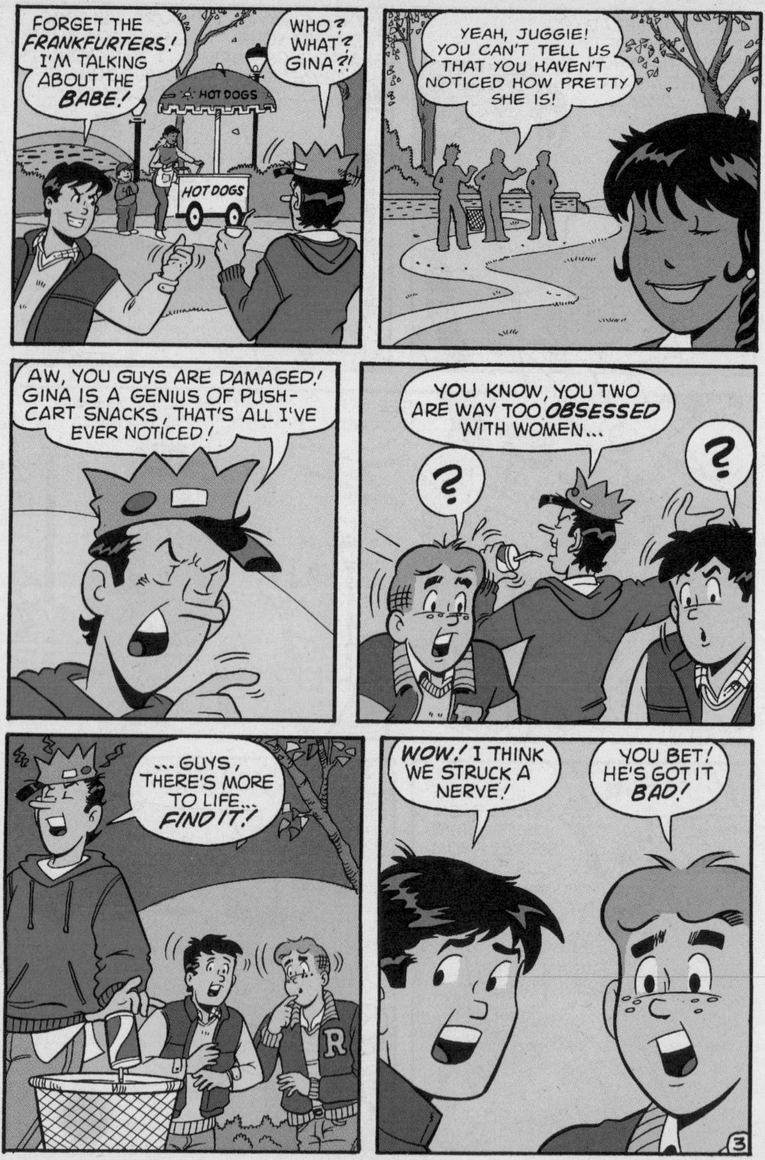
FORGET THE FRANKFURTERS! I'M TALKING ABOUT THE BABE!
WHO? WHAT? GINA?!
HOT DOGS
HOT DOGS
YEAH, JUGGIE! YOU CAN'T TELL US THAT YOU HAVEN'T NOTICED HOW PRETTY SHE IS!
AW, YOU GUYS ARE DAMAGED! GINA IS A GENIUS OF PUSH-CART SNACKS, THAT'S ALL I'VE EVER NOTICED!
YOU KNOW, YOU TWO ARE WAY TOO OBSESSED WITH WOMEN...
?
?
...GUYS, THERE'S MORE TO LIFE... FIND IT!
R
WOW! I THINK WE STRUCK A NERVE!
YOU BET! HE'S GOT IT BAD!
3

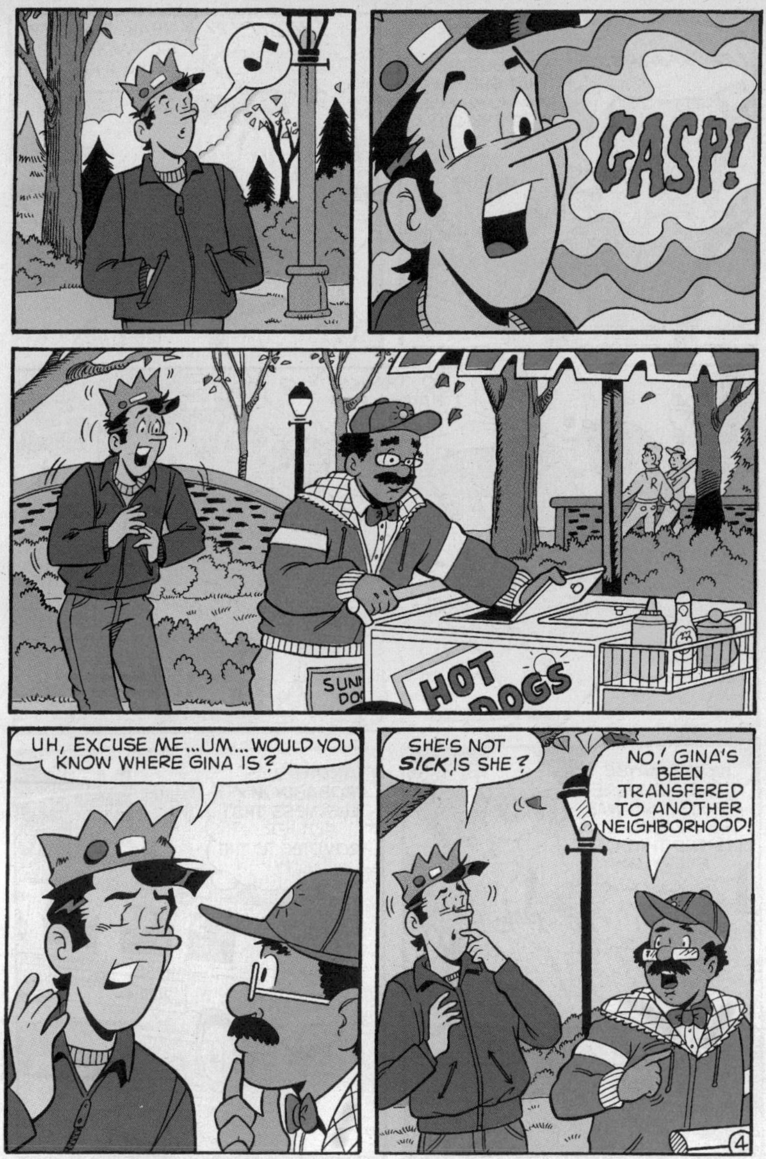
GASP!
HOT DOGS
UH, EXCUSE ME...UM...WOULD YOU KNOW WHERE GINA IS?
SHE'S NOT SICK, IS SHE?
NO! GINA'S BEEN TRANSFERED TO ANOTHER NEIGHBORHOOD!
4

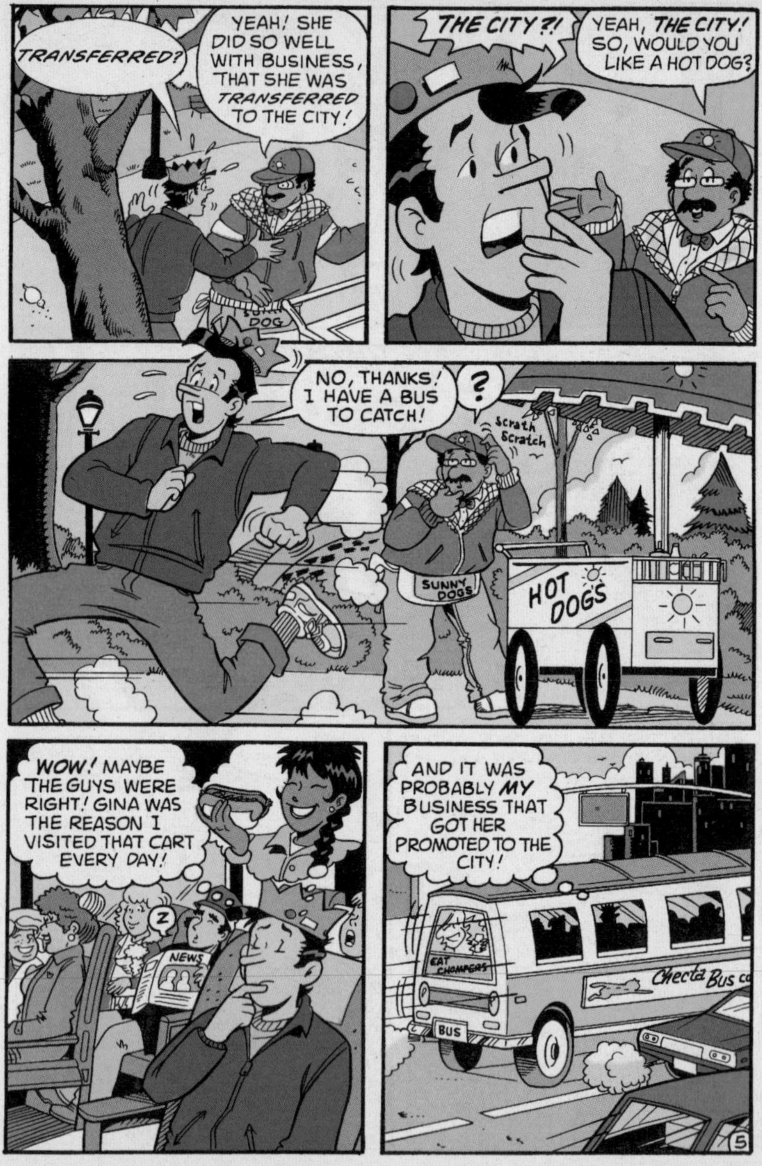

TRANSFERRED?
YEAH! SHE DID SO WELL WITH BUSINESS, THAT SHE WAS TRANSFERRED TO THE CITY!
THE CITY?!
YEAH, THE CITY! SO, WOULD YOU LIKE A HOT DOG?
NO, THANKS! I HAVE A BUS TO CATCH!
?
Scrath Scratch
SUNNY DOGS
HOT DOGS
WOW! MAYBE THE GUYS WERE RIGHT! GINA WAS THE REASON I VISITED THAT CART EVERY DAY!
Z
NEWS
AND IT WAS PROBABLY MY BUSINESS THAT GOT HER PROMOTED TO THE CITY!
EAT CHOMPERS
Checta Bus co
BUS
5

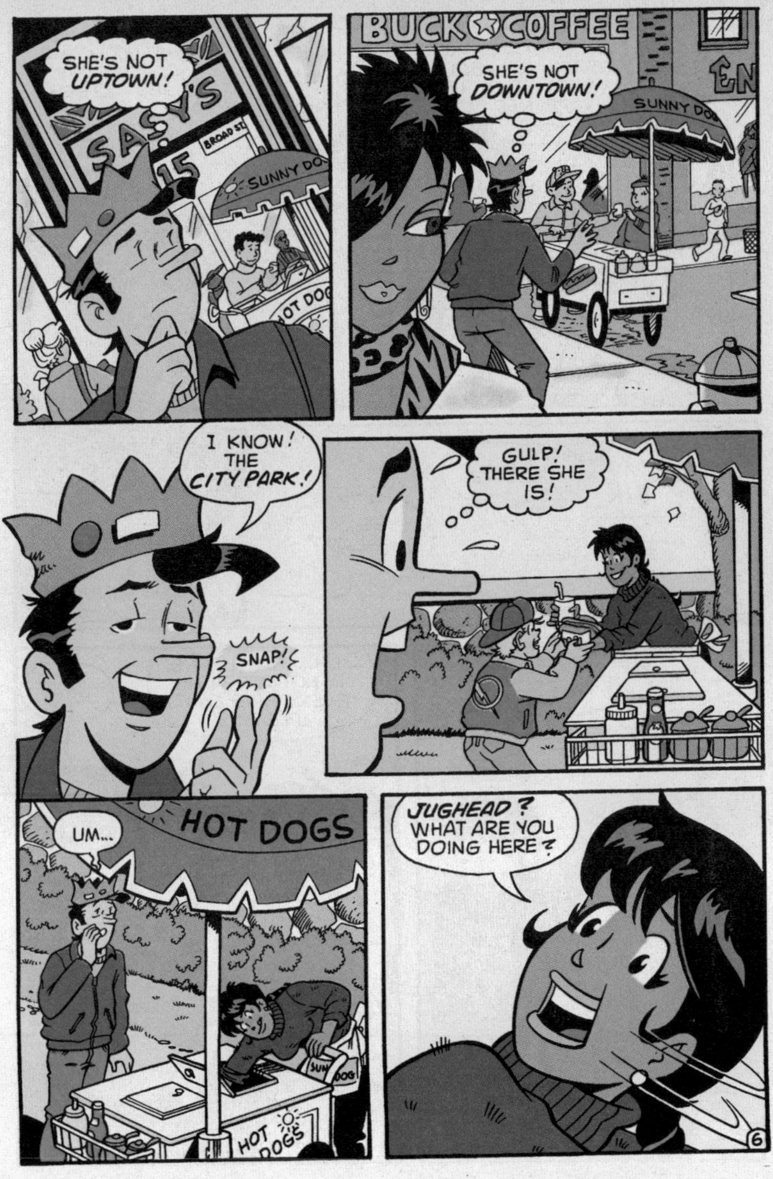
SHE'S NOT *UPTOWN!*
SASSY'S
15
BROAD ST.
SUNNY DO
HOT DOG
BUCK COFFEE
SHE'S NOT *DOWNTOWN!*
SUNNY DO
I KNOW! THE *CITY PARK!*
SNAP!
GULP! THERE SHE IS!
UM...
HOT DOGS
JUGHEAD? WHAT ARE YOU DOING HERE?
HOT DOGS
6

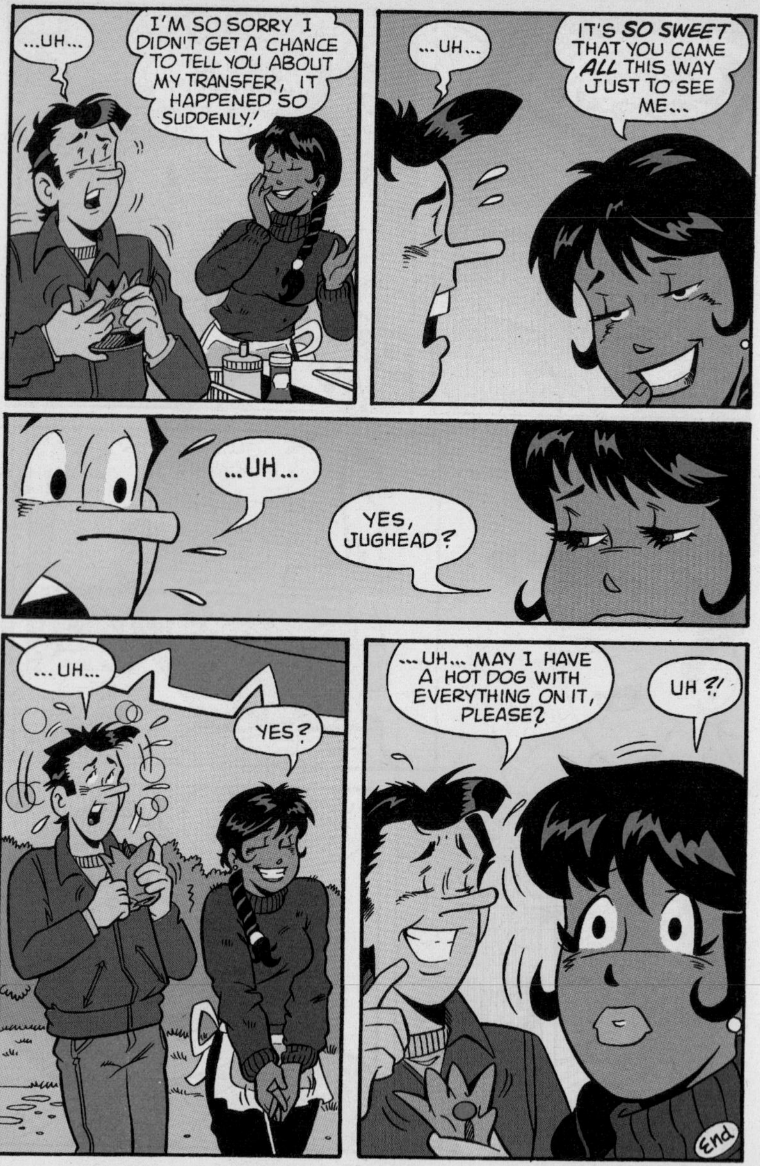
...UH...
I'M SO SORRY I DIDN'T GET A CHANCE TO TELL YOU ABOUT MY TRANSFER, IT HAPPENED SO SUDDENLY!
...UH...
IT'S SO SWEET THAT YOU CAME ALL THIS WAY JUST TO SEE ME...
...UH...
YES, JUGHEAD?
...UH...
YES?
...UH... MAY I HAVE A HOT DOG WITH EVERYTHING ON IT, PLEASE?
UH ?!
End

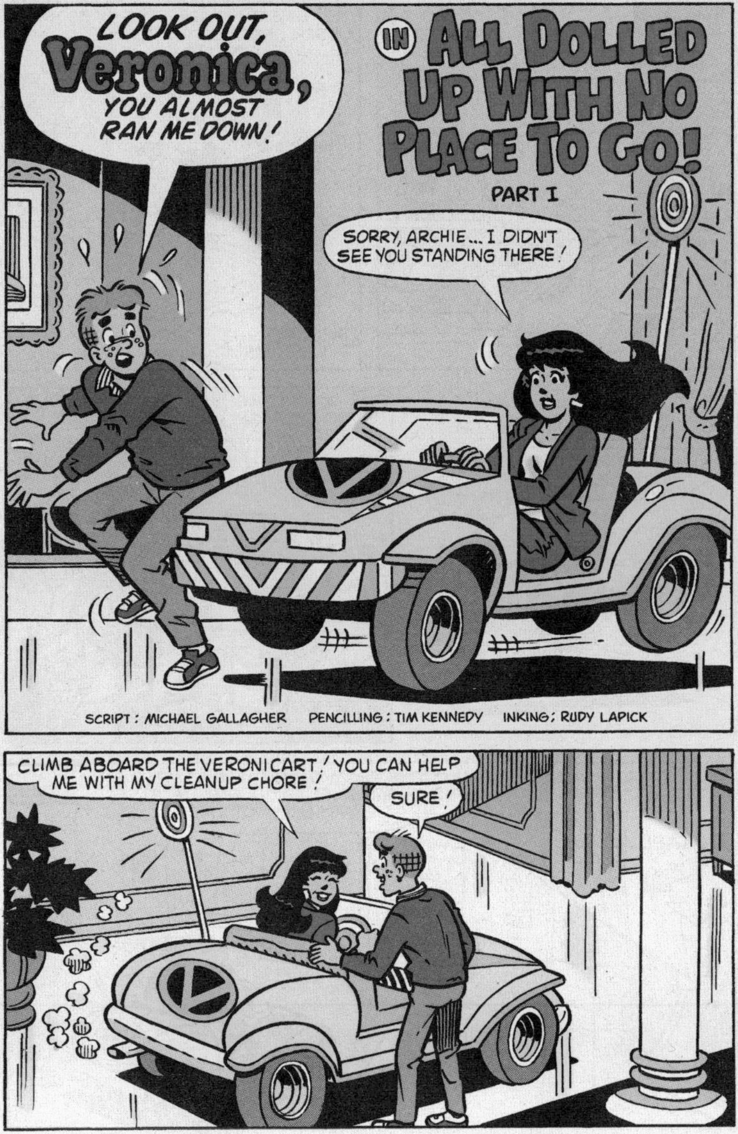
LOOK OUT, Veronica, YOU ALMOST RAN ME DOWN!
IN ALL DOLLED UP WITH NO PLACE TO GO!
PART I
SORRY, ARCHIE... I DIDN'T SEE YOU STANDING THERE!
SCRIPT: MICHAEL GALLAGHER PENCILLING: TIM KENNEDY INKING: RUDY LAPICK
CLIMB ABOARD THE VERONICART! YOU CAN HELP ME WITH MY CLEANUP CHORE!
SURE!

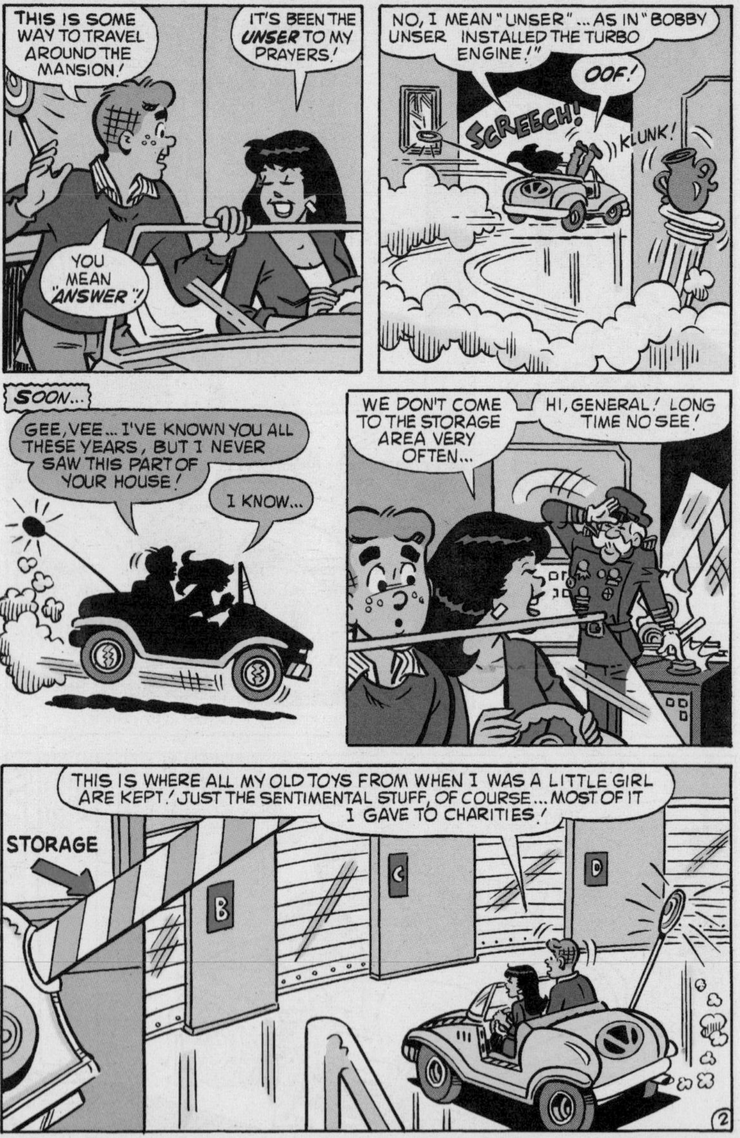
THIS IS SOME WAY TO TRAVEL AROUND THE MANSION!
IT'S BEEN THE UNSER TO MY PRAYERS!
YOU MEAN "ANSWER"?!
NO, I MEAN "UNSER"... AS IN "BOBBY UNSER INSTALLED THE TURBO ENGINE!"
OOF!
SCREECH!
KLUNK!
SOON...
GEE, VEE... I'VE KNOWN YOU ALL THESE YEARS, BUT I NEVER SAW THIS PART OF YOUR HOUSE!
I KNOW...
WE DON'T COME TO THE STORAGE AREA VERY OFTEN...
HI, GENERAL! LONG TIME NO SEE!
THIS IS WHERE ALL MY OLD TOYS FROM WHEN I WAS A LITTLE GIRL ARE KEPT! JUST THE SENTIMENTAL STUFF, OF COURSE... MOST OF IT I GAVE TO CHARITIES!
STORAGE
B
C
D
2

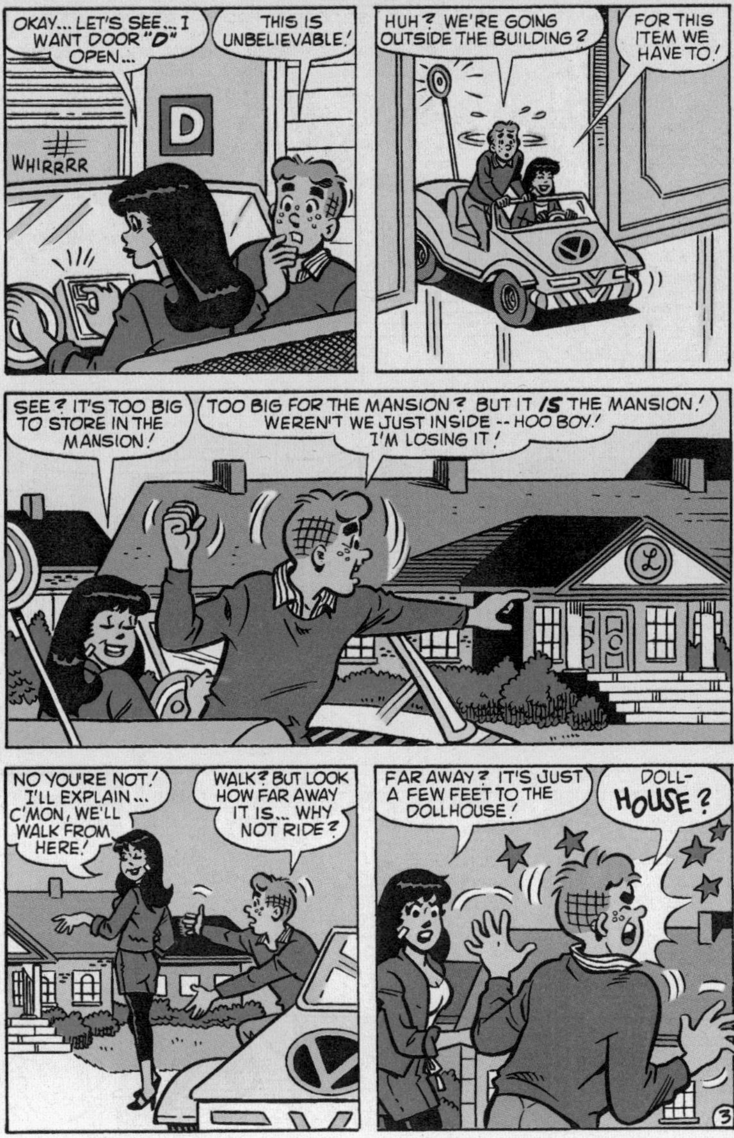
OKAY... LET'S SEE... I WANT DOOR "D" OPEN...
THIS IS UNBELIEVABLE!
D
WHIRRRR
HUH? WE'RE GOING OUTSIDE THE BUILDING?
FOR THIS ITEM WE HAVE TO!
SEE? IT'S TOO BIG TO STORE IN THE MANSION!
TOO BIG FOR THE MANSION? BUT IT IS THE MANSION! WEREN'T WE JUST INSIDE -- HOO BOY! I'M LOSING IT!
NO YOU'RE NOT! I'LL EXPLAIN... C'MON, WE'LL WALK FROM HERE!
WALK? BUT LOOK HOW FAR AWAY IT IS... WHY NOT RIDE?
FAR AWAY? IT'S JUST A FEW FEET TO THE DOLLHOUSE!
DOLL-HOUSE?
3

Panel 1:
THIS IS A MINIATURE!

OF COURSE! DADDY HAD THIS REPLICA OF THE HOUSE BUILT FOR ME YEARS AGO! I HAD THE BEST TIMES IN IT!

Panel 2:
IN IT? YOU CAN GO INSIDE?

CERTAINLY! A MASTER CARPENTER DESIGNED IT... COME ON IN!

Panel 3:
AMAZING! LOOK AT THE DETAIL!

EVERY ROOM IS TO SCALE AND FULLY FURNISHED... ONLY THE HALLS ARE BIG TO ALLOW MOVEMENT!

Panel 4:
- AND SPEAKING OF MOVEMENT, I JUST SAW SOME!

OH, WOW! LOOK AT THE LIBRARY!

ZOOM!

④

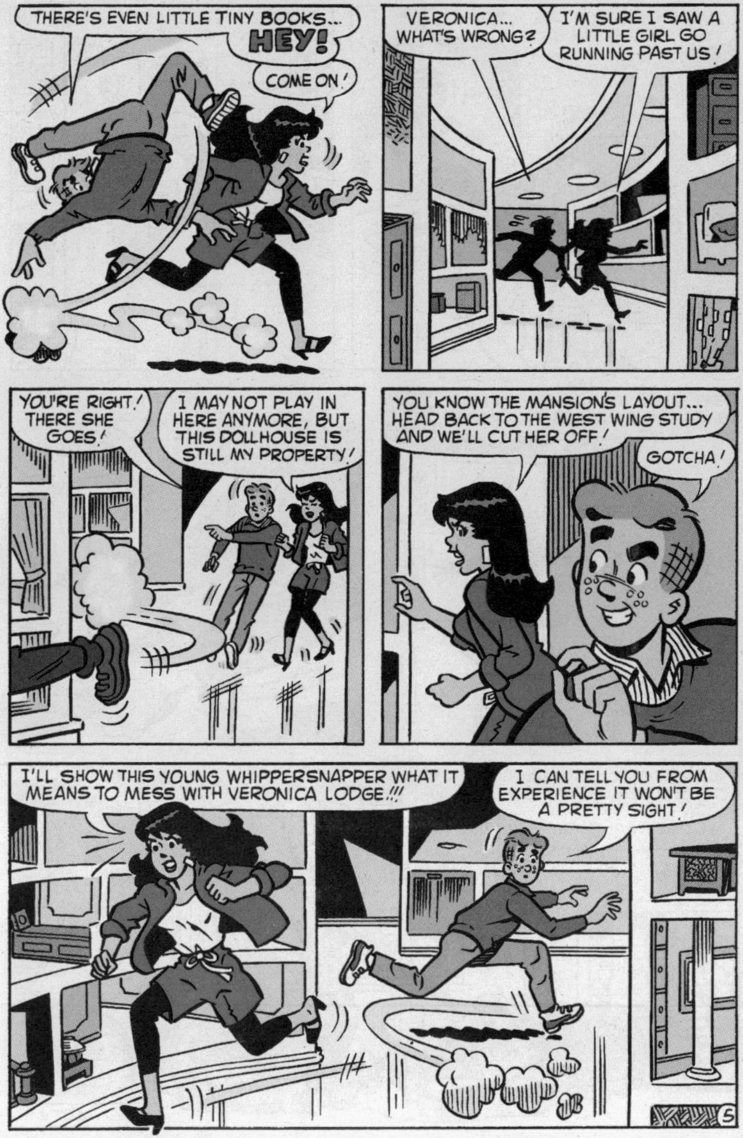

THERE'S EVEN LITTLE TINY BOOKS... HEY!
COME ON!
VERONICA... WHAT'S WRONG?
I'M SURE I SAW A LITTLE GIRL GO RUNNING PAST US!
YOU'RE RIGHT! THERE SHE GOES!
I MAY NOT PLAY IN HERE ANYMORE, BUT THIS DOLLHOUSE IS STILL MY PROPERTY!
YOU KNOW THE MANSION'S LAYOUT... HEAD BACK TO THE WEST WING STUDY AND WE'LL CUT HER OFF!
GOTCHA!
I'LL SHOW THIS YOUNG WHIPPERSNAPPER WHAT IT MEANS TO MESS WITH VERONICA LODGE!!!
I CAN TELL YOU FROM EXPERIENCE IT WON'T BE A PRETTY SIGHT!
5

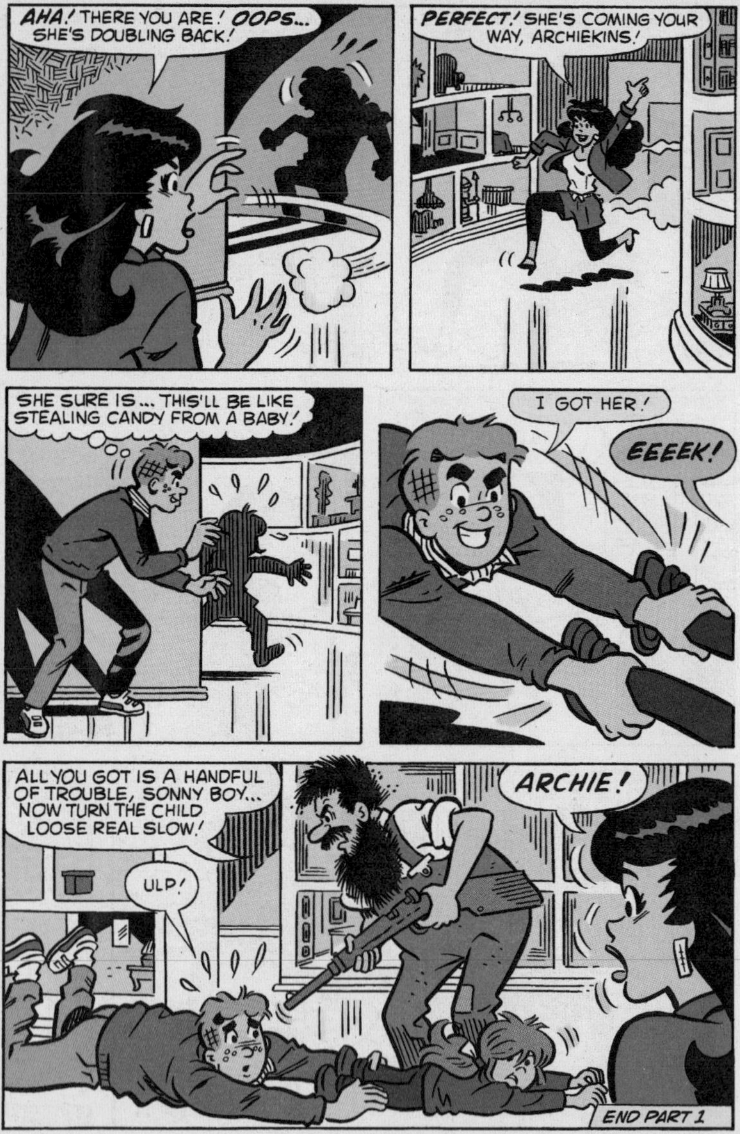
AHA! THERE YOU ARE! OOPS... SHE'S DOUBLING BACK!
PERFECT! SHE'S COMING YOUR WAY, ARCHIEKINS!
SHE SURE IS... THIS'LL BE LIKE STEALING CANDY FROM A BABY!
I GOT HER!
EEEEK!
ALL YOU GOT IS A HANDFUL OF TROUBLE, SONNY BOY... NOW TURN THE CHILD LOOSE REAL SLOW!
ARCHIE!
ULP!
END PART 1

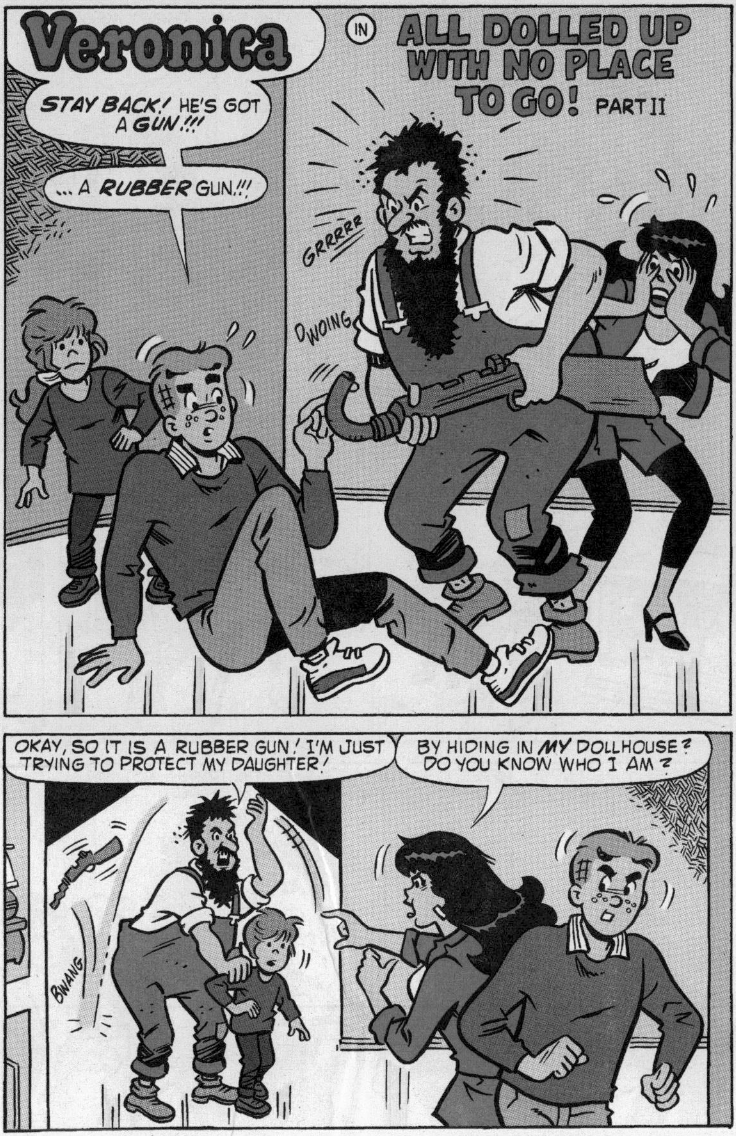

Veronica
IN
ALL DOLLED UP WITH NO PLACE TO GO! PART II
STAY BACK! HE'S GOT A GUN!!!
...A RUBBER GUN!!!
GRRRRR
DWOING
OKAY, SO IT IS A RUBBER GUN! I'M JUST TRYING TO PROTECT MY DAUGHTER!
BY HIDING IN MY DOLLHOUSE? DO YOU KNOW WHO I AM?
BWANG

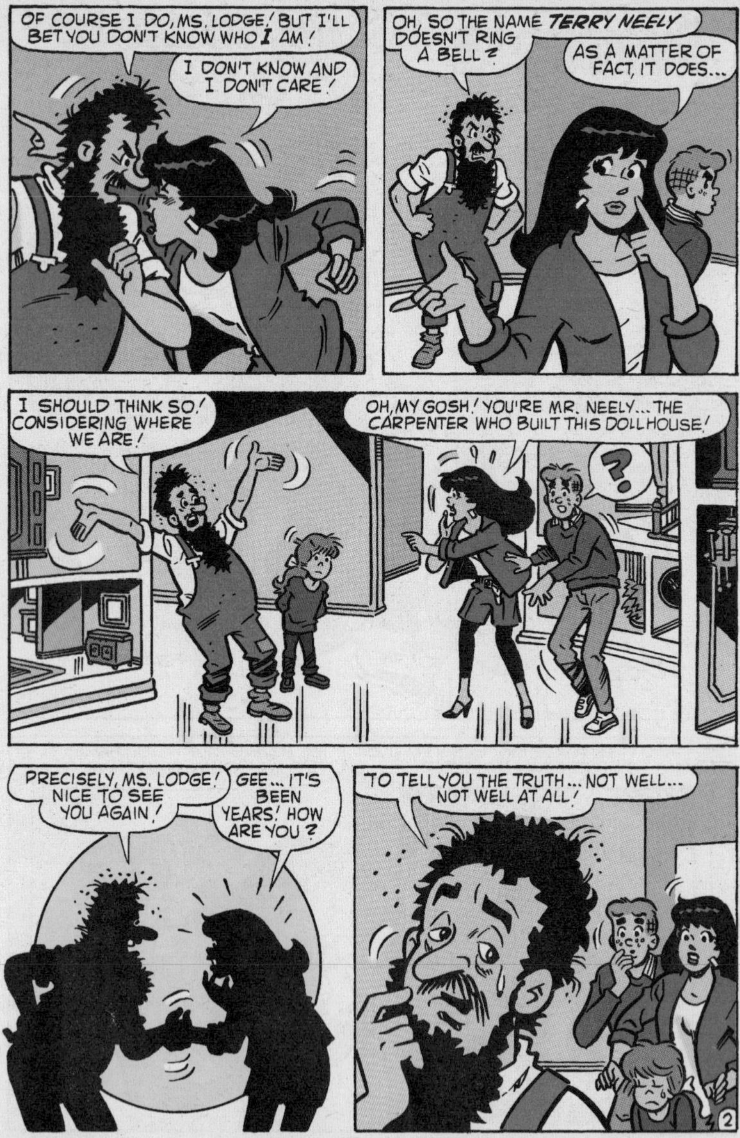
OF COURSE I DO, MS. LODGE! BUT I'LL BET YOU DON'T KNOW WHO I AM!
I DON'T KNOW AND I DON'T CARE!
OH, SO THE NAME TERRY NEELY DOESN'T RING A BELL?
AS A MATTER OF FACT, IT DOES...
I SHOULD THINK SO! CONSIDERING WHERE WE ARE!
OH, MY GOSH! YOU'RE MR. NEELY... THE CARPENTER WHO BUILT THIS DOLLHOUSE!
?
PRECISELY, MS. LODGE! NICE TO SEE YOU AGAIN!
GEE... IT'S BEEN YEARS! HOW ARE YOU?
TO TELL YOU THE TRUTH... NOT WELL... NOT WELL AT ALL!
2

YEARS AGO, WHEN I DID JOBS LIKE THIS DOLLHOUSE, BUSINESS WAS GOOD!

AS MY REPUTATION GREW, I STARTED MY OWN COMPANY! LATER, I GOT MARRIED AND EVENTUALLY STARTED A FAMILY...

BUT THEN THE ECONOMY WENT SOUR! I'D EXPANDED TOO FAST AND COULDN'T KEEP UP! BEFORE I KNEW IT, I WAS BANKRUPT!

BAD NEWS!

PAST DUE!

CONSTRUCTION INDUSTRY IN SLUMP

PAY UP!

I.O.U.

MY WIFE AND I TRIED TO COPE, BUT THINGS WENT FROM BAD TO WORSE... EVENTUALLY, SHE LEFT US!

FOR SALE

WE BECAME HOMELESS! THEN I PASSED THE LODGE STORAGE YARDS AND SAW THE OLD DOLLHOUSE! AN IDEA STRUCK ME!

LODGE MANSION NO TRESPASSING

WE SNUCK IN AND TOOK UP RESIDENCE! I'M SORRY, MS. LODGE... I DID IT FOR MY DAUGHTER'S SAKE!

GOLLY!

CAN'T YOU HELP THEM, RON?

3

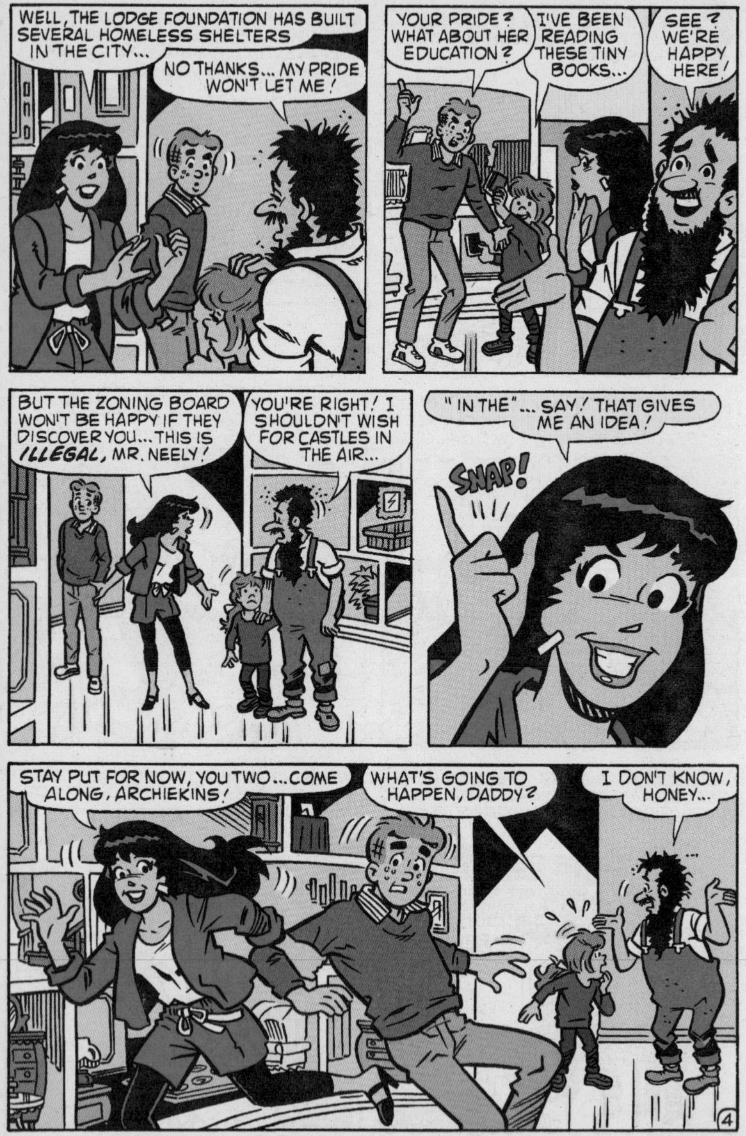
WELL, THE LODGE FOUNDATION HAS BUILT SEVERAL HOMELESS SHELTERS IN THE CITY...
NO THANKS... MY PRIDE WON'T LET ME!
YOUR PRIDE? WHAT ABOUT HER EDUCATION?
I'VE BEEN READING THESE TINY BOOKS...
SEE? WE'RE HAPPY HERE!
BUT THE ZONING BOARD WON'T BE HAPPY IF THEY DISCOVER YOU... THIS IS ILLEGAL, MR. NEELY!
YOU'RE RIGHT! I SHOULDN'T WISH FOR CASTLES IN THE AIR...
"IN THE"... SAY! THAT GIVES ME AN IDEA!
SNAP!
STAY PUT FOR NOW, YOU TWO...COME ALONG, ARCHIEKINS!
WHAT'S GOING TO HAPPEN, DADDY?
I DON'T KNOW, HONEY...
4

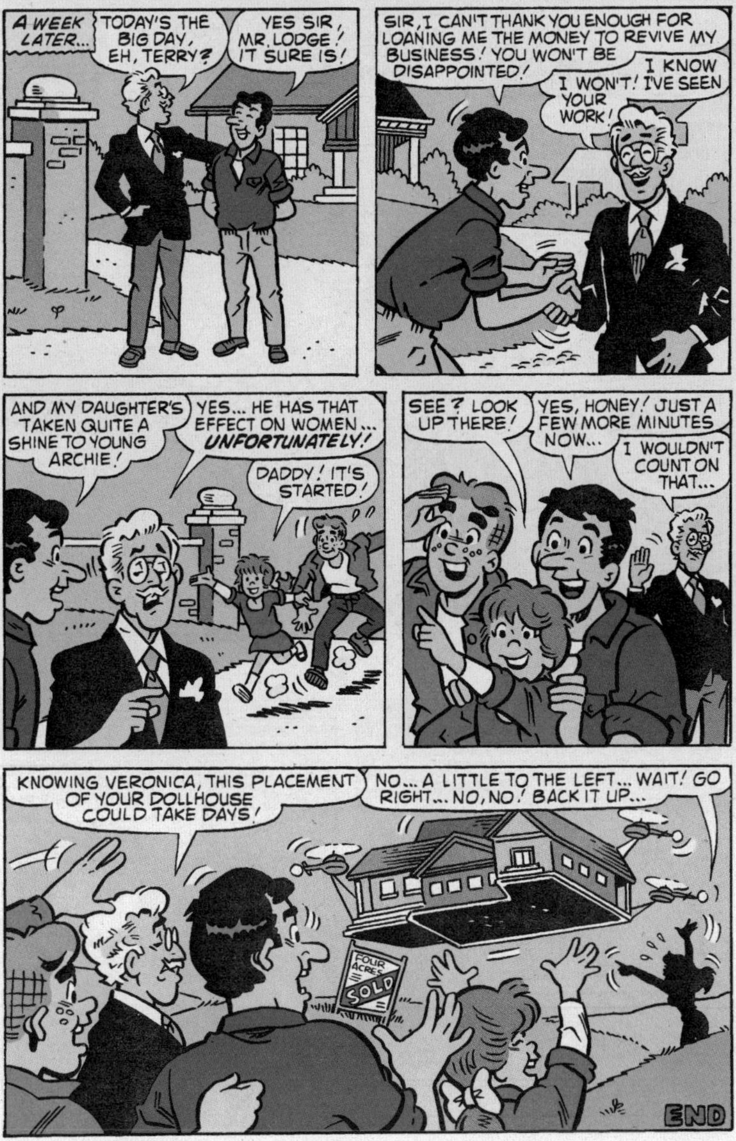
A WEEK LATER...
TODAY'S THE BIG DAY, EH, TERRY?
YES SIR, MR. LODGE! IT SURE IS!
SIR, I CAN'T THANK YOU ENOUGH FOR LOANING ME THE MONEY TO REVIVE MY BUSINESS! YOU WON'T BE DISAPPOINTED!
I KNOW I WON'T! I'VE SEEN YOUR WORK!
AND MY DAUGHTER'S TAKEN QUITE A SHINE TO YOUNG ARCHIE!
YES... HE HAS THAT EFFECT ON WOMEN... UNFORTUNATELY!
DADDY! IT'S STARTED!
SEE? LOOK UP THERE!
YES, HONEY! JUST A FEW MORE MINUTES NOW...
I WOULDN'T COUNT ON THAT...
KNOWING VERONICA, THIS PLACEMENT OF YOUR DOLLHOUSE COULD TAKE DAYS!
NO... A LITTLE TO THE LEFT... WAIT! GO RIGHT... NO, NO! BACK IT UP...
FOUR ACRES
SOLD
END

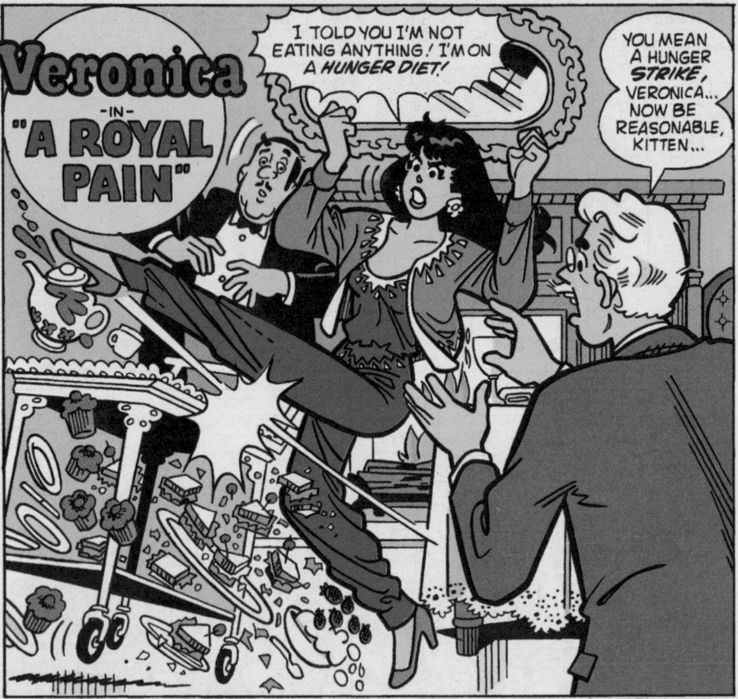
Veronica
-IN-
"A ROYAL PAIN"
I TOLD YOU I'M NOT EATING ANYTHING! I'M ON A HUNGER DIET!
YOU MEAN A HUNGER STRIKE, VERONICA... NOW BE REASONABLE, KITTEN...

SCRIPT: ANGELO DECESARE PENCILLING: STAN GOLDBERG INKING: HENRY SCARPELLI

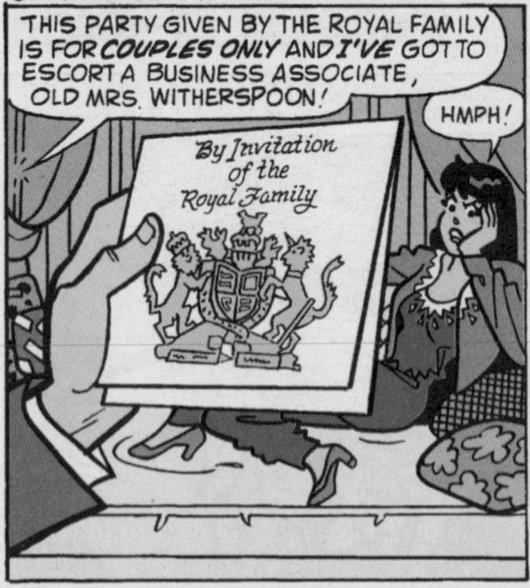
THIS PARTY GIVEN BY THE ROYAL FAMILY IS FOR COUPLES ONLY AND I'VE GOT TO ESCORT A BUSINESS ASSOCIATE, OLD MRS. WITHERSPOON!
HMPH!
By Invitation of the Royal Family

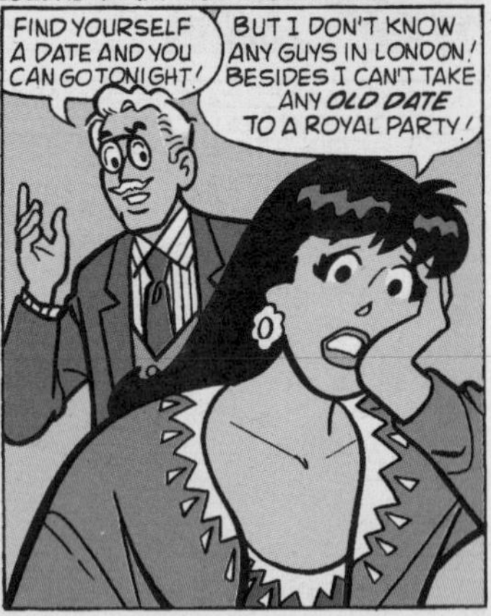
FIND YOURSELF A DATE AND YOU CAN GO TONIGHT!
BUT I DON'T KNOW ANY GUYS IN LONDON! BESIDES I CAN'T TAKE ANY OLD DATE TO A ROYAL PARTY!

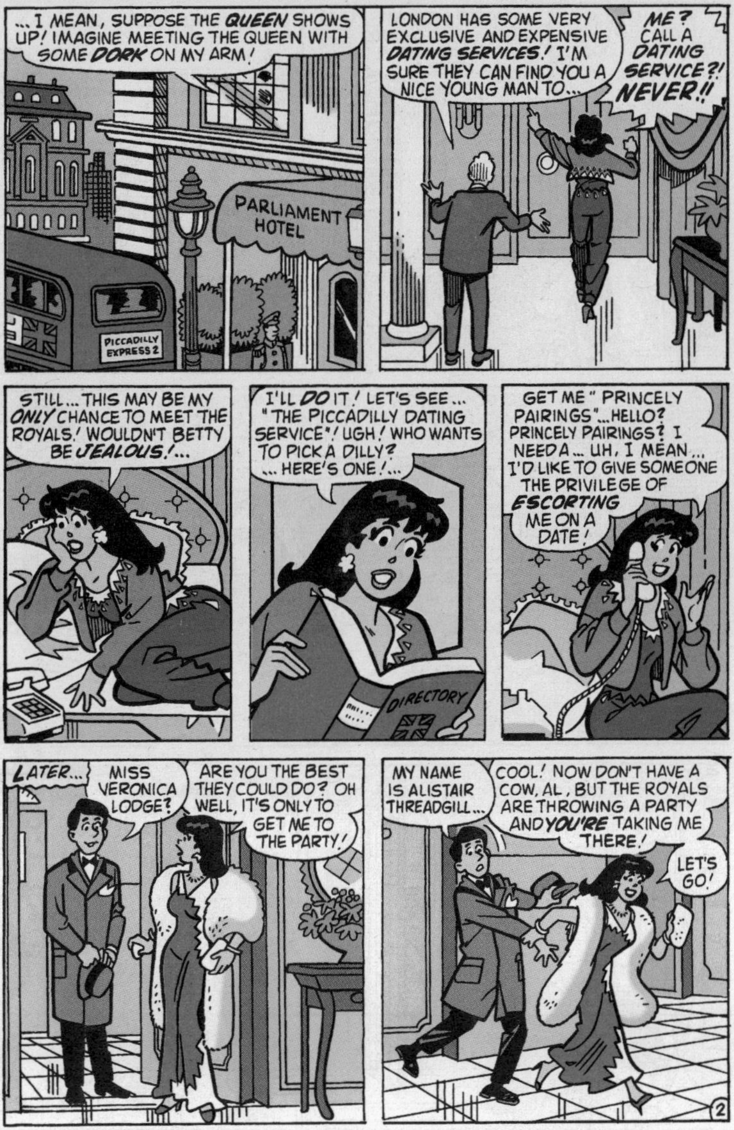
...I MEAN, SUPPOSE THE QUEEN SHOWS UP! IMAGINE MEETING THE QUEEN WITH SOME DORK ON MY ARM!
PARLIAMENT HOTEL
PICCADILLY EXPRESS 2
LONDON HAS SOME VERY EXCLUSIVE AND EXPENSIVE DATING SERVICES! I'M SURE THEY CAN FIND YOU A NICE YOUNG MAN TO...
ME? CALL A DATING SERVICE?! NEVER!!
STILL... THIS MAY BE MY ONLY CHANCE TO MEET THE ROYALS! WOULDN'T BETTY BE JEALOUS!...
I'LL DO IT! LET'S SEE... "THE PICCADILLY DATING SERVICE"! UGH! WHO WANTS TO PICK A DILLY? ...HERE'S ONE!...
DIRECTORY
GET ME "PRINCELY PAIRINGS"...HELLO? PRINCELY PAIRINGS? I NEED A... UH, I MEAN... I'D LIKE TO GIVE SOMEONE THE PRIVILEGE OF ESCORTING ME ON A DATE!
LATER...
MISS VERONICA LODGE?
ARE YOU THE BEST THEY COULD DO? OH WELL, IT'S ONLY TO GET ME TO THE PARTY!
MY NAME IS ALISTAIR THREADGILL...
COOL! NOW DON'T HAVE A COW, AL, BUT THE ROYALS ARE THROWING A PARTY AND YOU'RE TAKING ME THERE!
LET'S GO!
2

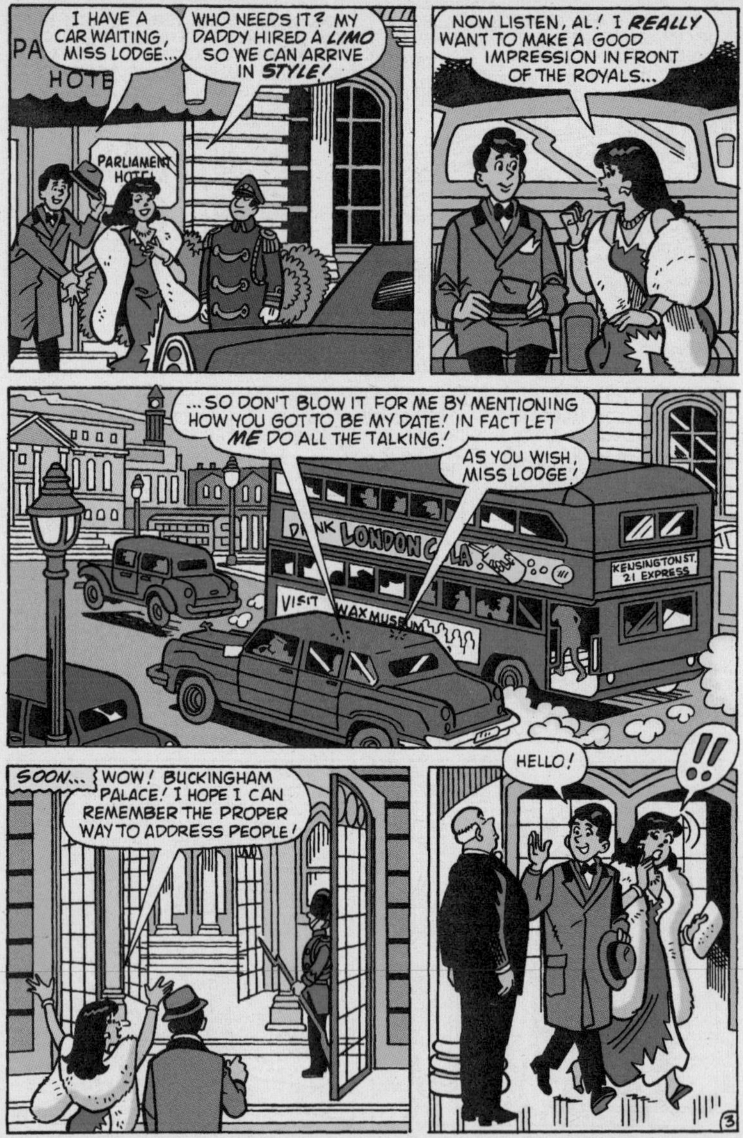

PARLIAMENT HOTEL
I HAVE A CAR WAITING, MISS LODGE...
WHO NEEDS IT? MY DADDY HIRED A LIMO SO WE CAN ARRIVE IN STYLE!
NOW LISTEN, AL! I REALLY WANT TO MAKE A GOOD IMPRESSION IN FRONT OF THE ROYALS...
...SO DON'T BLOW IT FOR ME BY MENTIONING HOW YOU GOT TO BE MY DATE! IN FACT LET ME DO ALL THE TALKING!
AS YOU WISH, MISS LODGE!
DRINK LONDON COLA
KENSINGTON ST. 21 EXPRESS
VISIT WAX MUSEUM
SOON...
WOW! BUCKINGHAM PALACE! I HOPE I CAN REMEMBER THE PROPER WAY TO ADDRESS PEOPLE!
HELLO!
!!
3

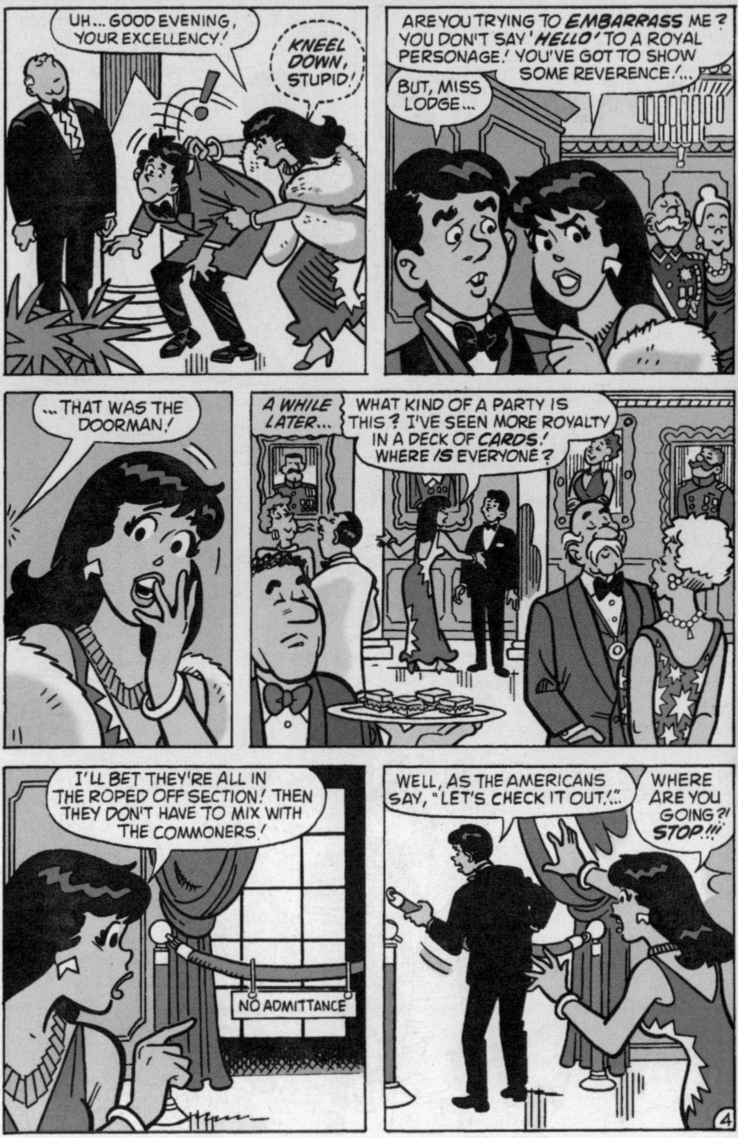
UH... GOOD EVENING, YOUR EXCELLENCY!
KNEEL DOWN, STUPID!
ARE YOU TRYING TO EMBARRASS ME? YOU DON'T SAY 'HELLO' TO A ROYAL PERSONAGE! YOU'VE GOT TO SHOW SOME REVERENCE!...
BUT, MISS LODGE...
...THAT WAS THE DOORMAN!
A WHILE LATER...
WHAT KIND OF A PARTY IS THIS? I'VE SEEN MORE ROYALTY IN A DECK OF CARDS! WHERE IS EVERYONE?
I'LL BET THEY'RE ALL IN THE ROPED OFF SECTION! THEN THEY DON'T HAVE TO MIX WITH THE COMMONERS!
NO ADMITTANCE
WELL, AS THE AMERICANS SAY, "LET'S CHECK IT OUT!"...
WHERE ARE YOU GOING?! STOP!!!
4

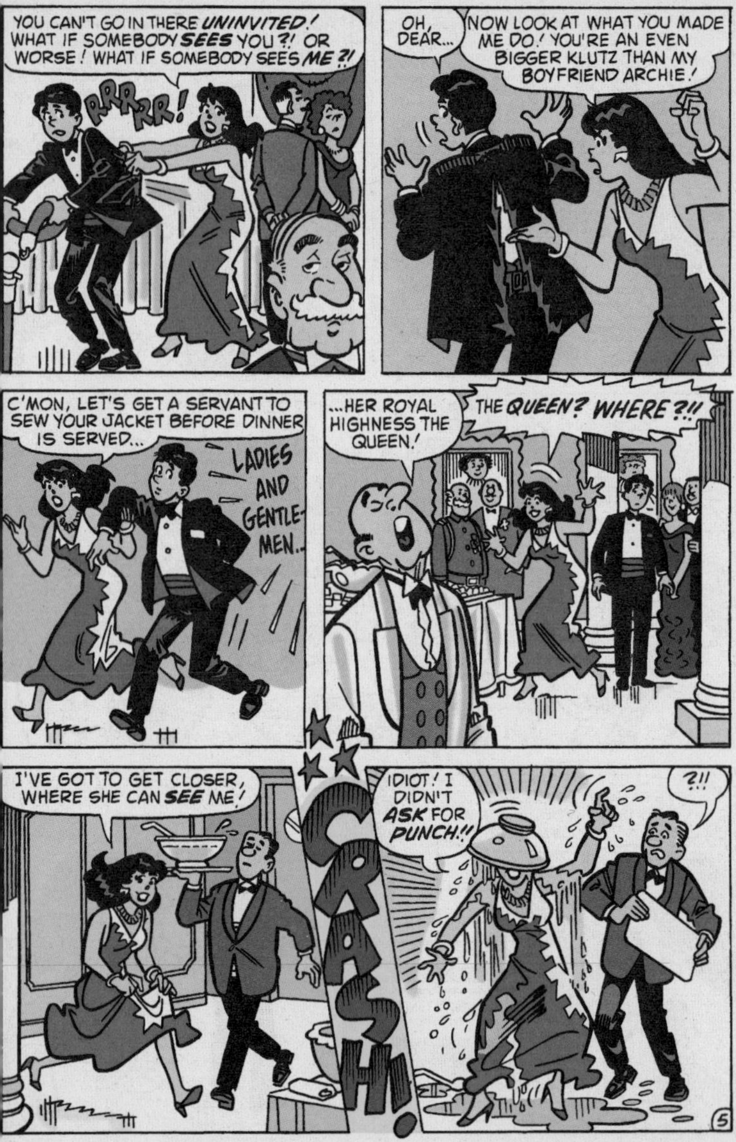
YOU CAN'T GO IN THERE UNINVITED! WHAT IF SOMEBODY SEES YOU?! OR WORSE! WHAT IF SOMEBODY SEES ME?!
RRRRR!
OH, DEAR...
NOW LOOK AT WHAT YOU MADE ME DO! YOU'RE AN EVEN BIGGER KLUTZ THAN MY BOYFRIEND ARCHIE!
C'MON, LET'S GET A SERVANT TO SEW YOUR JACKET BEFORE DINNER IS SERVED...
LADIES AND GENTLE-MEN...
...HER ROYAL HIGHNESS THE QUEEN!
THE QUEEN? WHERE?!!
I'VE GOT TO GET CLOSER, WHERE SHE CAN SEE ME!
CRASH!
IDIOT! I DIDN'T ASK FOR PUNCH!!
?!!
5

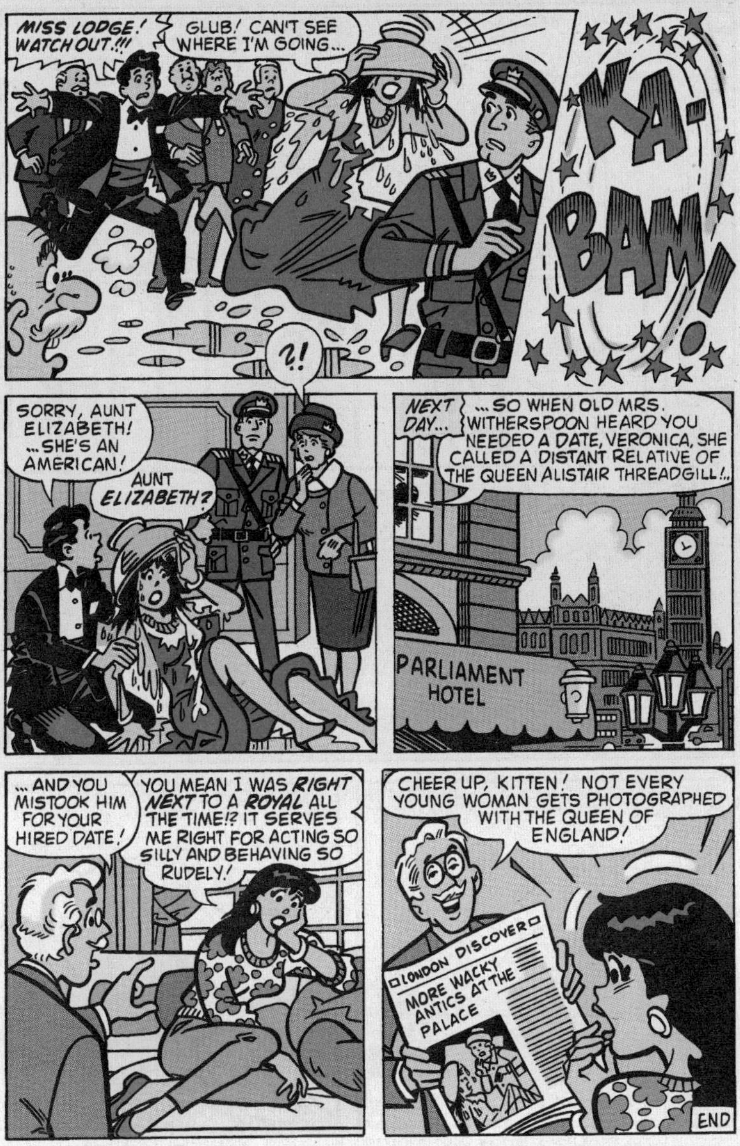
MISS LODGE! WATCH OUT!!!
GLUB! CAN'T SEE WHERE I'M GOING...
KA-BAM!
?!
SORRY, AUNT ELIZABETH! ...SHE'S AN AMERICAN!
AUNT ELIZABETH?
NEXT DAY...
...SO WHEN OLD MRS. WITHERSPOON HEARD YOU NEEDED A DATE, VERONICA, SHE CALLED A DISTANT RELATIVE OF THE QUEEN ALISTAIR THREADGILL!..
PARLIAMENT HOTEL
...AND YOU MISTOOK HIM FOR YOUR HIRED DATE!
YOU MEAN I WAS RIGHT NEXT TO A ROYAL ALL THE TIME!? IT SERVES ME RIGHT FOR ACTING SO SILLY AND BEHAVING SO RUDELY!
CHEER UP, KITTEN! NOT EVERY YOUNG WOMAN GETS PHOTOGRAPHED WITH THE QUEEN OF ENGLAND!
LONDON DISCOVER
MORE WACKY ANTICS AT THE PALACE
END

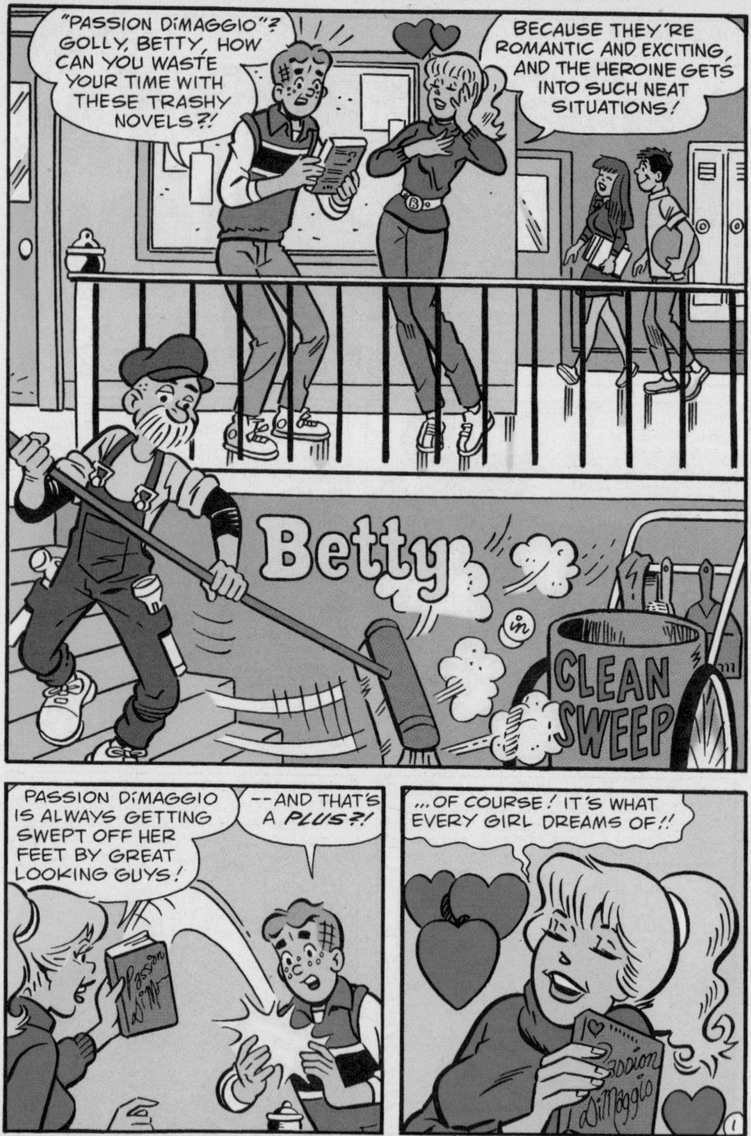
"PASSION DiMAGGIO"? GOLLY, BETTY, HOW CAN YOU WASTE YOUR TIME WITH THESE TRASHY NOVELS?!
BECAUSE THEY'RE ROMANTIC AND EXCITING, AND THE HEROINE GETS INTO SUCH NEAT SITUATIONS!
Betty
in
CLEAN SWEEP
PASSION DiMAGGIO IS ALWAYS GETTING SWEPT OFF HER FEET BY GREAT LOOKING GUYS!
--AND THAT'S A PLUS?!
...OF COURSE! IT'S WHAT EVERY GIRL DREAMS OF!!
1

Script: Frank Doyle / Pencils: Doug Crane / Inks: Rudy Lapick / Letters: Rod Ollerenshaw

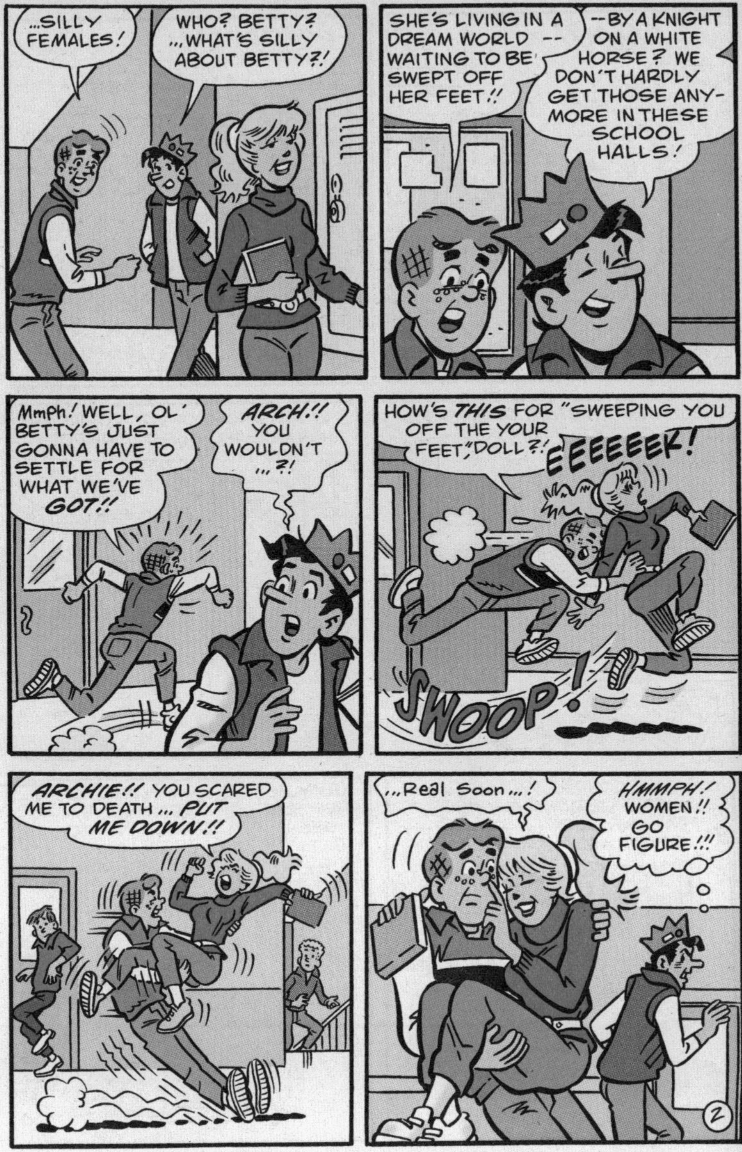
...SILLY FEMALES!
WHO? BETTY? ...WHAT'S SILLY ABOUT BETTY?!
SHE'S LIVING IN A DREAM WORLD -- WAITING TO BE SWEPT OFF HER FEET!!
--BY A KNIGHT ON A WHITE HORSE? WE DON'T HARDLY GET THOSE ANYMORE IN THESE SCHOOL HALLS!
Mmph! WELL, OL' BETTY'S JUST GONNA HAVE TO SETTLE FOR WHAT WE'VE GOT!!
ARCH!! YOU WOULDN'T ...?!
HOW'S THIS FOR "SWEEPING YOU OFF THE YOUR FEET," DOLL?!
EEEEEEK!
SWOOP!
ARCHIE!! YOU SCARED ME TO DEATH ... PUT ME DOWN!!
...Real Soon...!
HMMPH! WOMEN!! GO FIGURE!!!
2

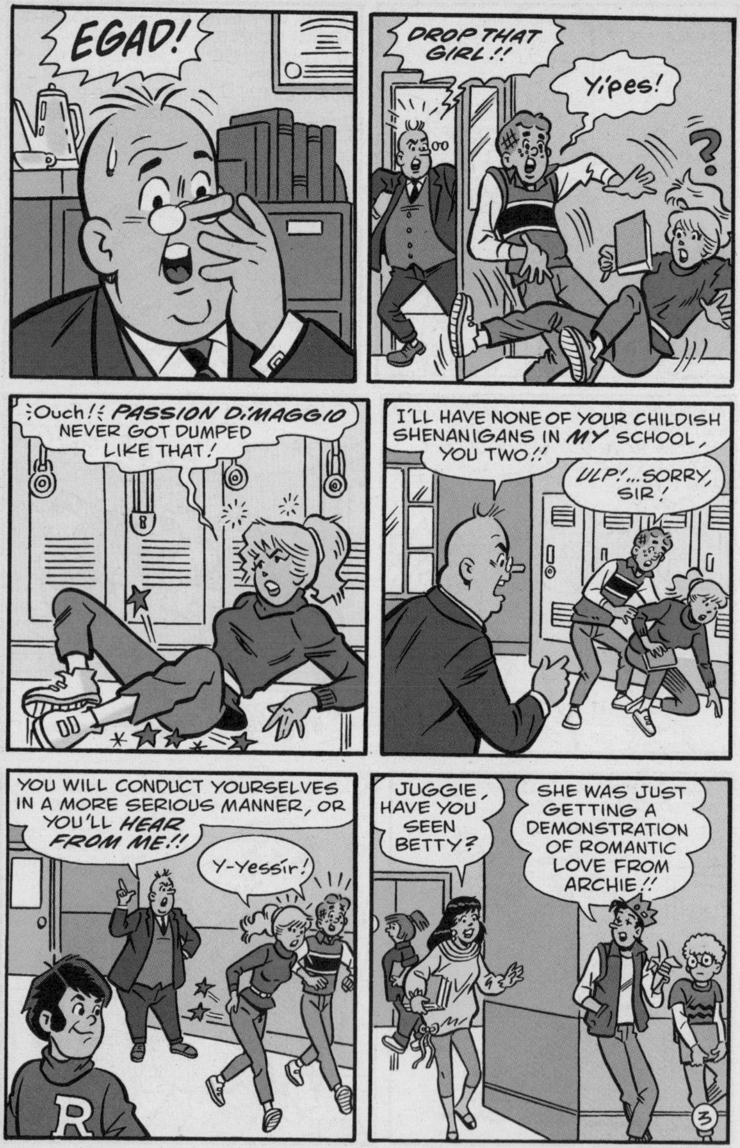
EGAD!
DROP THAT GIRL!!
Yipes!
?
Ouch!! PASSION DiMAGGIO NEVER GOT DUMPED LIKE THAT!
I'LL HAVE NONE OF YOUR CHILDISH SHENANIGANS IN MY SCHOOL, YOU TWO!!
ULP!...SORRY, SIR!
YOU WILL CONDUCT YOURSELVES IN A MORE SERIOUS MANNER, OR YOU'LL HEAR FROM ME!!
Y-Yessir!
JUGGIE, HAVE YOU SEEN BETTY?
SHE WAS JUST GETTING A DEMONSTRATION OF ROMANTIC LOVE FROM ARCHIE!!
3

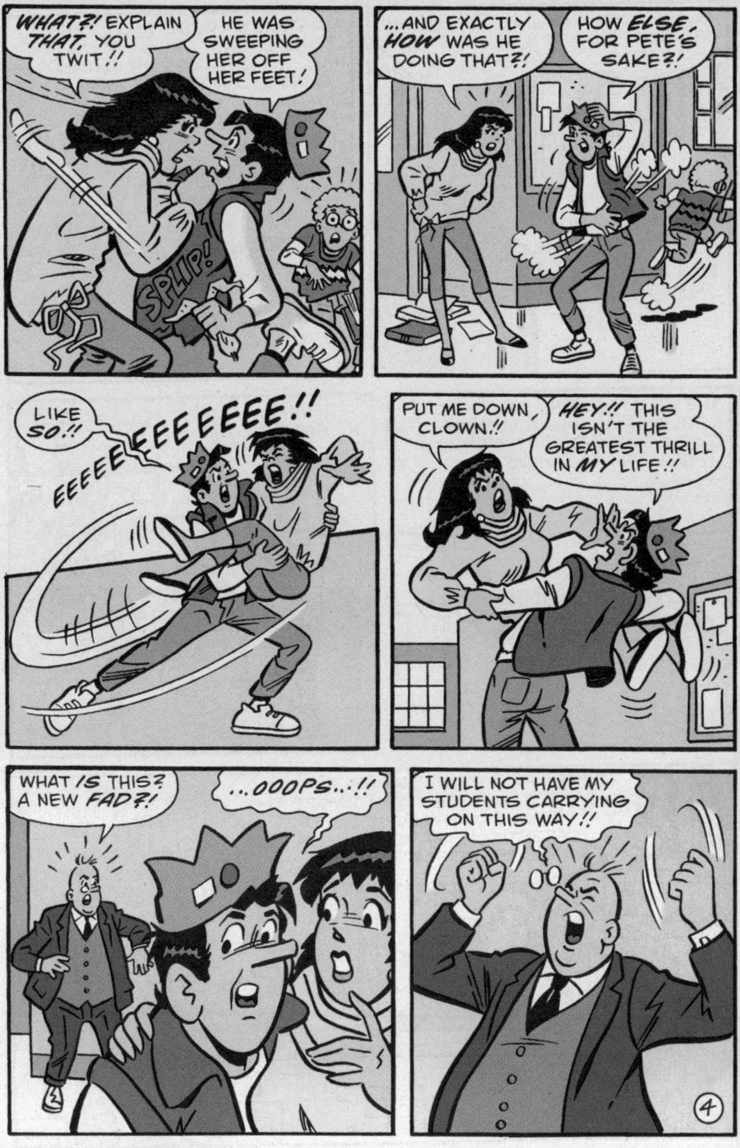
WHAT?! EXPLAIN THAT, YOU TWIT!!
HE WAS SWEEPING HER OFF HER FEET!
SPLIP!
...AND EXACTLY HOW WAS HE DOING THAT?!
HOW ELSE, FOR PETE'S SAKE?!
LIKE SO!!
EEEEEEEEEEEEE!!
PUT ME DOWN, CLOWN!!
HEY!! THIS ISN'T THE GREATEST THRILL IN MY LIFE!!
WHAT IS THIS? A NEW FAD?!
...OOOPS...!!
I WILL NOT HAVE MY STUDENTS CARRYING ON THIS WAY!!
4

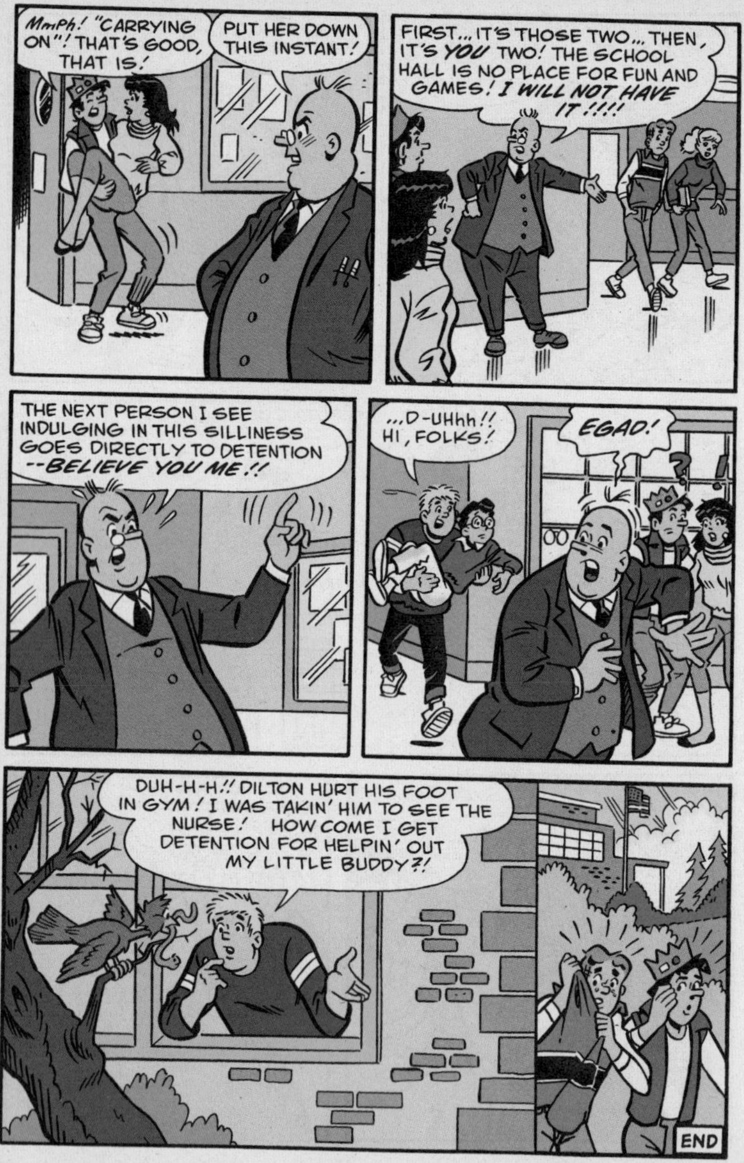
Mmph! "CARRYING ON"! THAT'S GOOD, THAT IS!
PUT HER DOWN THIS INSTANT!
FIRST... IT'S THOSE TWO... THEN, IT'S YOU TWO! THE SCHOOL HALL IS NO PLACE FOR FUN AND GAMES! I WILL NOT HAVE IT!!!!
THE NEXT PERSON I SEE INDULGING IN THIS SILLINESS GOES DIRECTLY TO DETENTION --BELIEVE YOU ME!!
...D-UHhh!! HI, FOLKS!
EGAD!
DUH-H-H!! DILTON HURT HIS FOOT IN GYM! I WAS TAKIN' HIM TO SEE THE NURSE! HOW COME I GET DETENTION FOR HELPIN' OUT MY LITTLE BUDDY?!
END

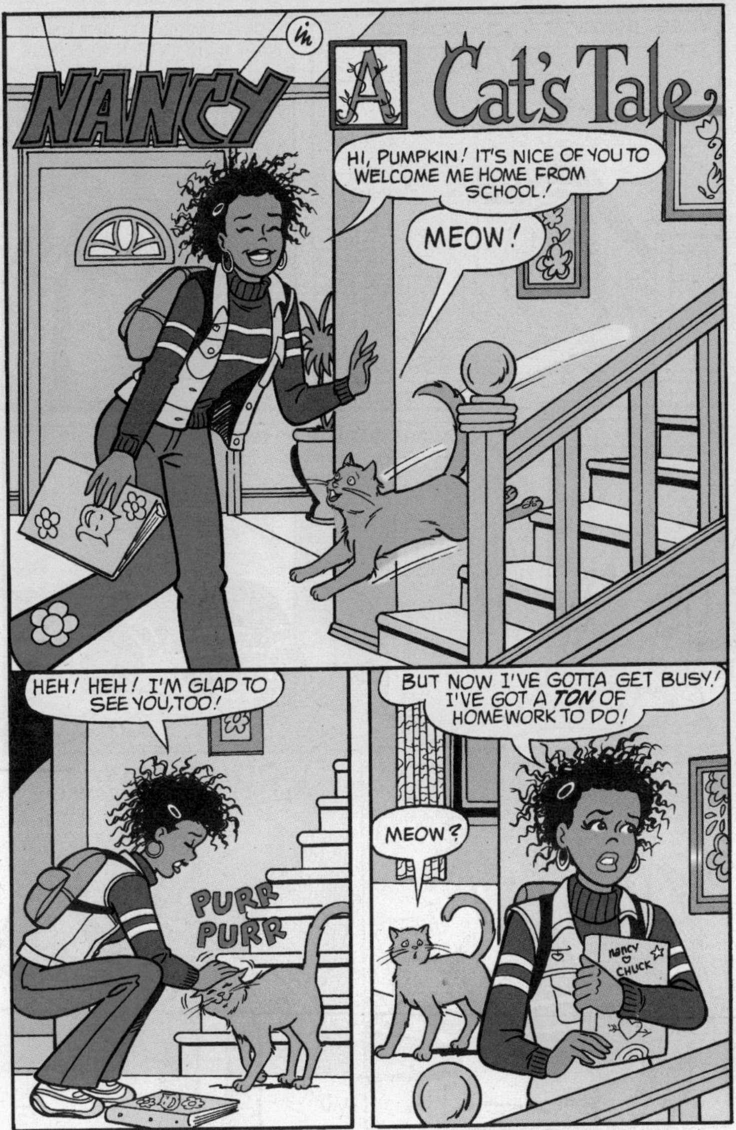
NANCY
in
A Cat's Tale
HI, PUMPKIN! IT'S NICE OF YOU TO WELCOME ME HOME FROM SCHOOL!
MEOW!
HEH! HEH! I'M GLAD TO SEE YOU, TOO!
PURR PURR
BUT NOW I'VE GOTTA GET BUSY! I'VE GOT A TON OF HOMEWORK TO DO!
MEOW?
NANCY ♡ CHUCK

Script: Mike Pellowski / Pencils: Holly G! / Inks: John Costanza / Letters: Bill Yoshida

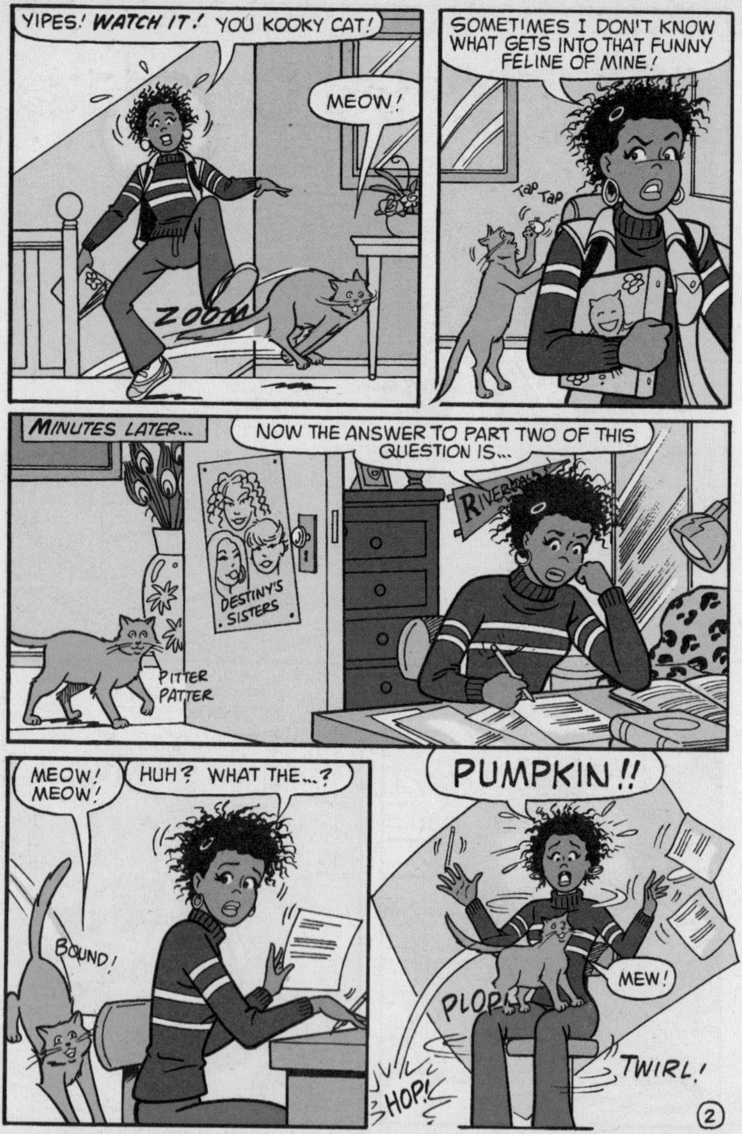
YIPES! WATCH IT! YOU KOOKY CAT!
MEOW!
ZOOM
SOMETIMES I DON'T KNOW WHAT GETS INTO THAT FUNNY FELINE OF MINE!
TAP TAP
MINUTES LATER...
NOW THE ANSWER TO PART TWO OF THIS QUESTION IS...
DESTINY'S SISTERS
PITTER PATTER
MEOW! MEOW!
HUH? WHAT THE...?
BOUND!
PUMPKIN!!
MEW!
PLOP!
TWIRL!
HOP!

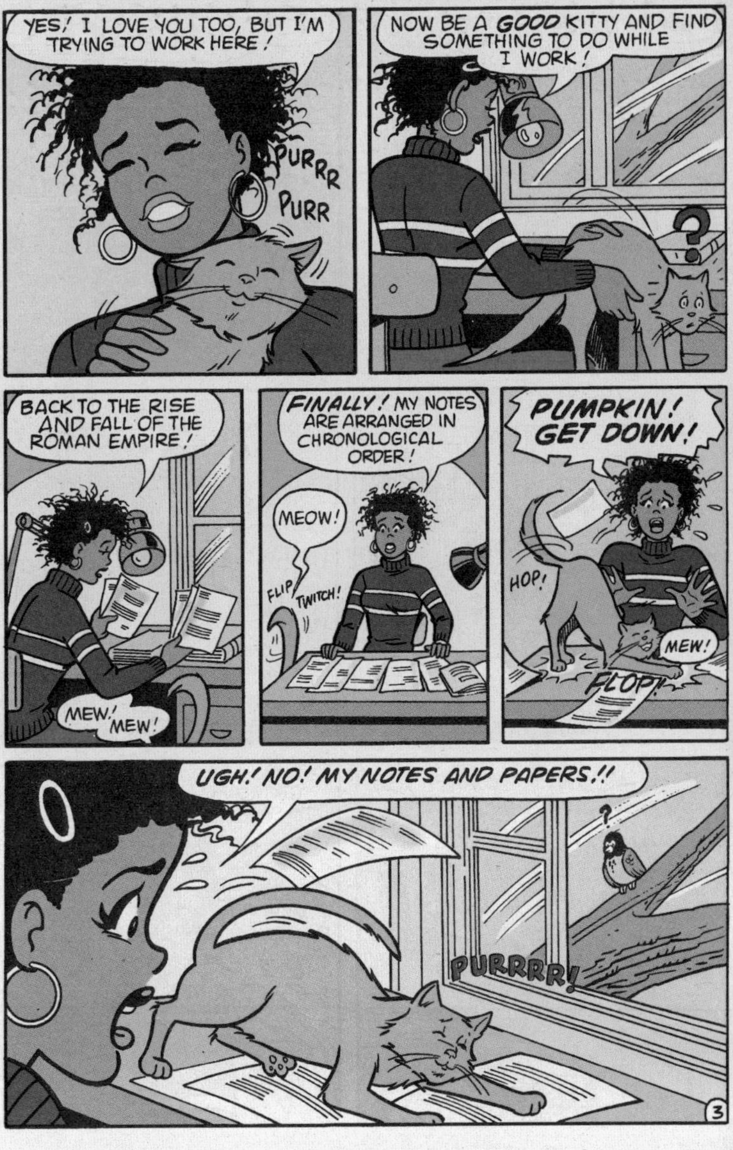
YES! I LOVE YOU TOO, BUT I'M TRYING TO WORK HERE!
PURRRR
PURR
NOW BE A GOOD KITTY AND FIND SOMETHING TO DO WHILE I WORK!
?
BACK TO THE RISE AND FALL OF THE ROMAN EMPIRE!
MEW! MEW!
FINALLY! MY NOTES ARE ARRANGED IN CHRONOLOGICAL ORDER!
MEOW!
FLIP
TWITCH!
PUMPKIN! GET DOWN!
HOP!
MEW!
FLOP!
UGH! NO! MY NOTES AND PAPERS!!
?
PURRRRR!
3

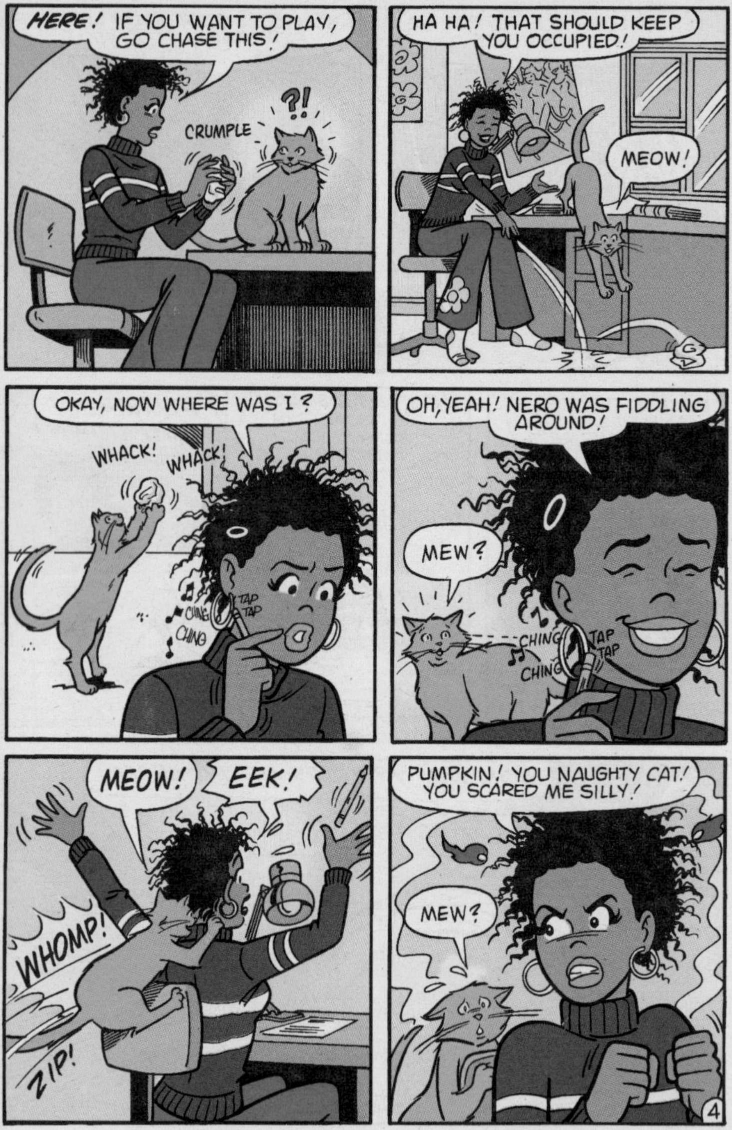
HERE! IF YOU WANT TO PLAY, GO CHASE THIS!
?!
CRUMPLE
HA HA! THAT SHOULD KEEP YOU OCCUPIED!
MEOW!
OKAY, NOW WHERE WAS I?
WHACK!
WHACK!
CHING
CHING
TAP TAP
OH, YEAH! NERO WAS FIDDLING AROUND!
MEW?
CHING
CHING
TAP TAP
MEOW!
EEK!
WHOMP!
ZIP!
PUMPKIN! YOU NAUGHTY CAT! YOU SCARED ME SILLY!
MEW?
4

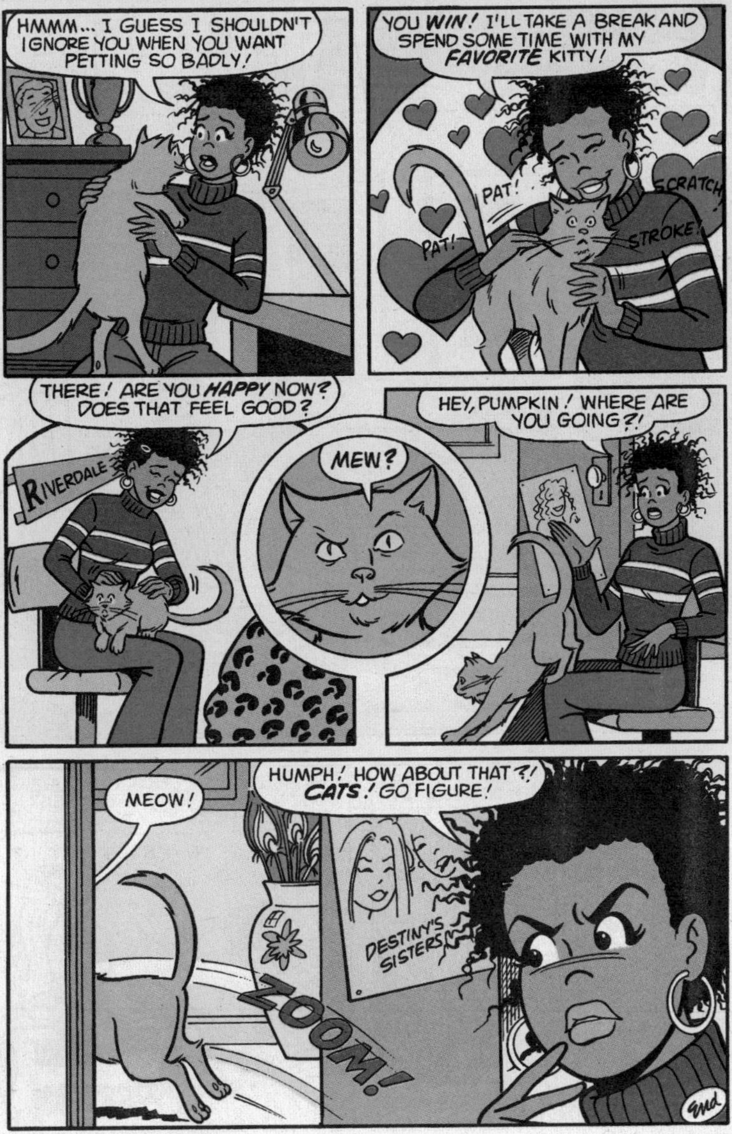
HMMM... I GUESS I SHOULDN'T IGNORE YOU WHEN YOU WANT PETTING SO BADLY!
YOU WIN! I'LL TAKE A BREAK AND SPEND SOME TIME WITH MY FAVORITE KITTY!
PAT!
PAT!
SCRATCH
STROKE!
THERE! ARE YOU HAPPY NOW? DOES THAT FEEL GOOD?
RIVERDALE
MEW?
HEY, PUMPKIN! WHERE ARE YOU GOING?!
MEOW!
HUMPH! HOW ABOUT THAT?! CATS! GO FIGURE!
DESTINY'S SISTERS
ZOOM!
END

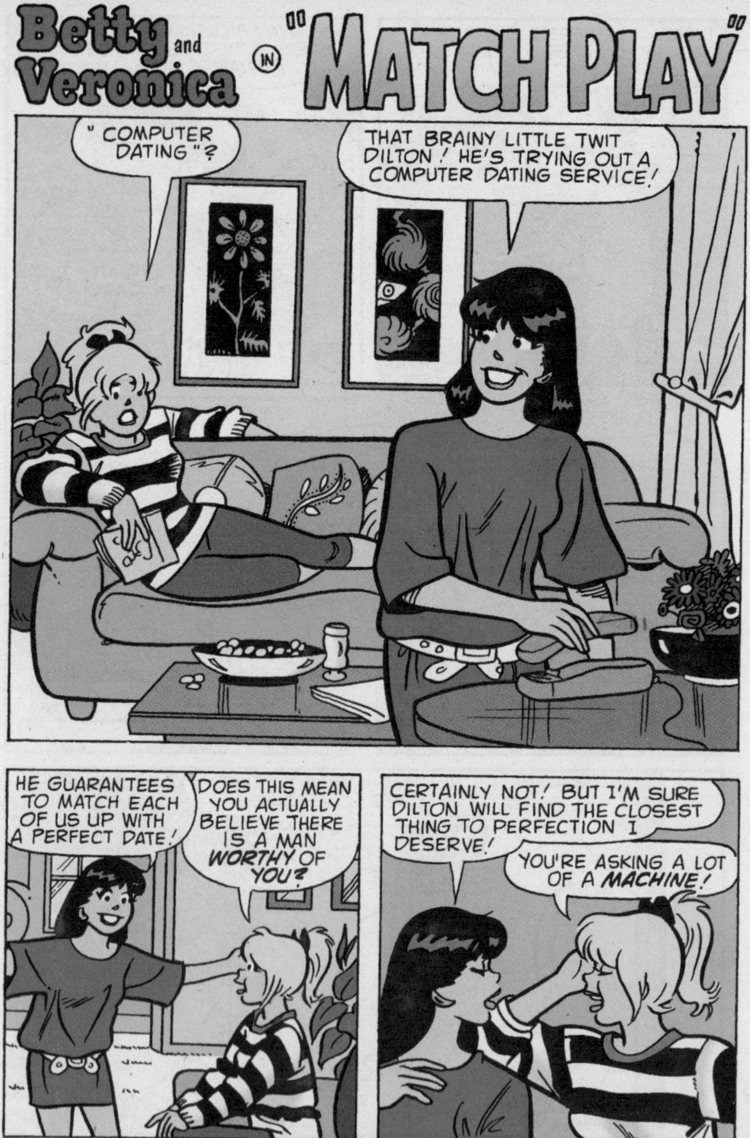
Betty and Veronica
IN
"MATCH PLAY"
" COMPUTER DATING "?
THAT BRAINY LITTLE TWIT DILTON! HE'S TRYING OUT A COMPUTER DATING SERVICE!
HE GUARANTEES TO MATCH EACH OF US UP WITH A PERFECT DATE!
DOES THIS MEAN YOU ACTUALLY BELIEVE THERE IS A MAN WORTHY OF YOU?
CERTAINLY NOT! BUT I'M SURE DILTON WILL FIND THE CLOSEST THING TO PERFECTION I DESERVE!
YOU'RE ASKING A LOT OF A MACHINE!

Script: Frank Doyle / Art: Dan DeCarlo / Letters: Bill Yoshida

HE'S DOING A FREE WORK-UP OF HIS FRIENDS!

W-ELL, THE PRICE IS RIGHT!

IF IT WORKS OUT, HE'LL PROBABLY GO INTO THE BUSINESS AND MAKE HIS FORTUNE!

EXACTLY HOW DOES HE WORK IT?

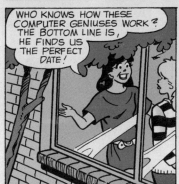

WHO KNOWS HOW THESE COMPUTER GENIUSES WORK? THE BOTTOM LINE IS, HE FINDS US THE PERFECT DATE!

HE CONTACTS THESE HUNKS AND THEY SHOW UP ON OUR DOOR-STEP!

I THINK DILTON'S PORCH LIGHT IS GETTING A BIT DIM!

THAT MIGHT BE THE GRAND PRIZE WINNER NOW!

BONG BONG

FERDIE VON PELF TO SEE MISS VERONICA LODGE! ANNOUNCE ME IMMEDIATELY, MY GOOD MAN! IMMEDIATELY!

SNAP SNAP

②

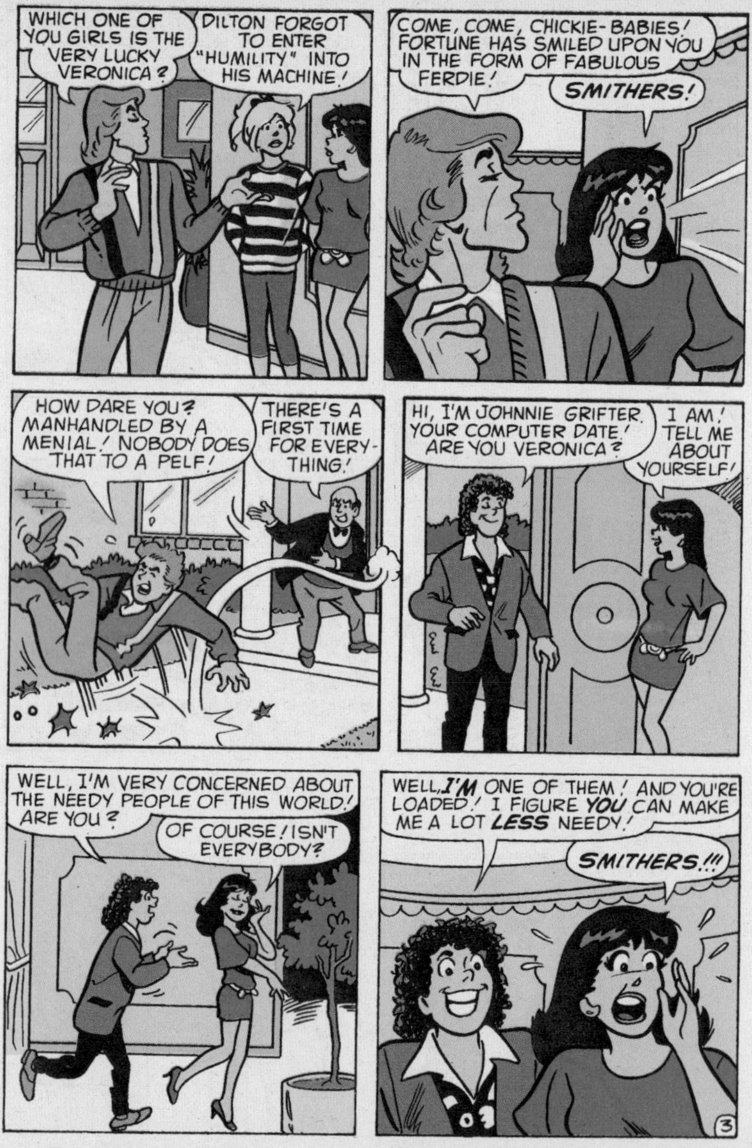
WHICH ONE OF YOU GIRLS IS THE VERY LUCKY VERONICA?
DILTON FORGOT TO ENTER "HUMILITY" INTO HIS MACHINE!
COME, COME, CHICKIE-BABIES! FORTUNE HAS SMILED UPON YOU IN THE FORM OF FABULOUS FERDIE!
SMITHERS!
HOW DARE YOU? MANHANDLED BY A MENIAL! NOBODY DOES THAT TO A PELF!
THERE'S A FIRST TIME FOR EVERY-THING!
HI, I'M JOHNNIE GRIFTER. YOUR COMPUTER DATE! ARE YOU VERONICA?
I AM! TELL ME ABOUT YOURSELF!
WELL, I'M VERY CONCERNED ABOUT THE NEEDY PEOPLE OF THIS WORLD! ARE YOU?
OF COURSE! ISN'T EVERYBODY?
WELL, I'M ONE OF THEM! AND YOU'RE LOADED! I FIGURE YOU CAN MAKE ME A LOT LESS NEEDY!
SMITHERS!!!
3

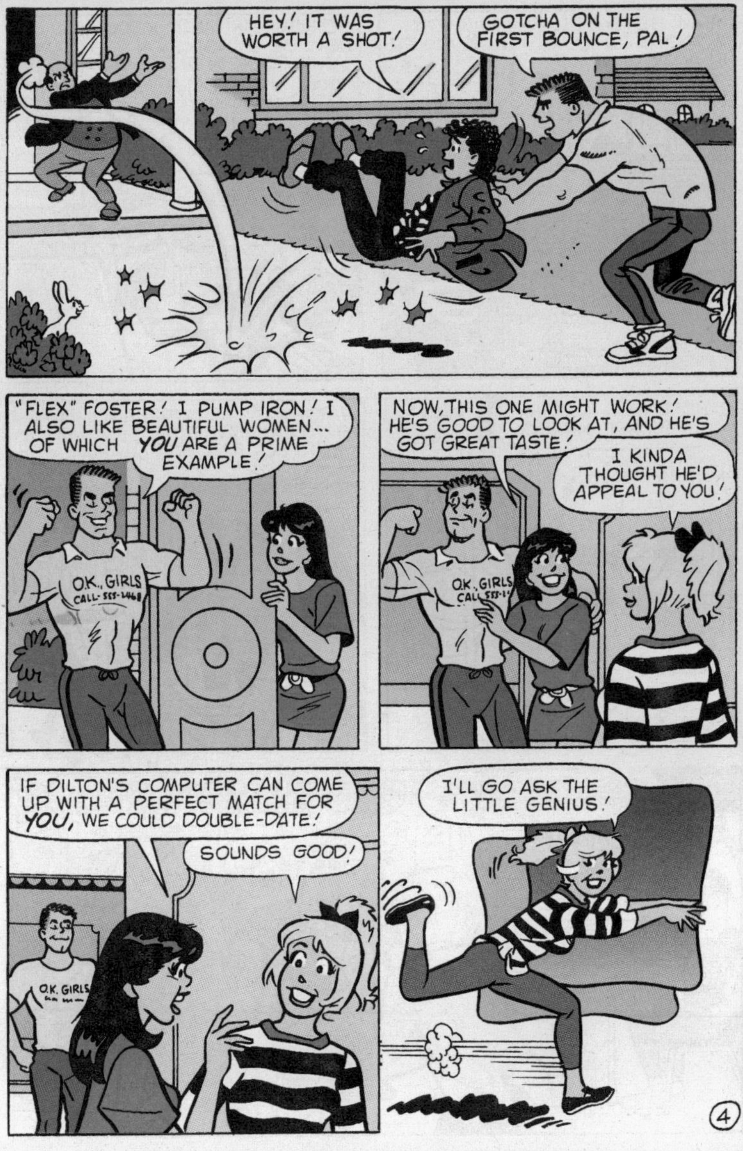
HEY! IT WAS WORTH A SHOT!
GOTCHA ON THE FIRST BOUNCE, PAL!
"FLEX" FOSTER! I PUMP IRON! I ALSO LIKE BEAUTIFUL WOMEN... OF WHICH YOU ARE A PRIME EXAMPLE!
O.K., GIRLS CALL-555-2468
NOW, THIS ONE MIGHT WORK! HE'S GOOD TO LOOK AT, AND HE'S GOT GREAT TASTE!
I KINDA THOUGHT HE'D APPEAL TO YOU!
IF DILTON'S COMPUTER CAN COME UP WITH A PERFECT MATCH FOR YOU, WE COULD DOUBLE-DATE!
SOUNDS GOOD!
O.K. GIRLS
I'LL GO ASK THE LITTLE GENIUS!
4

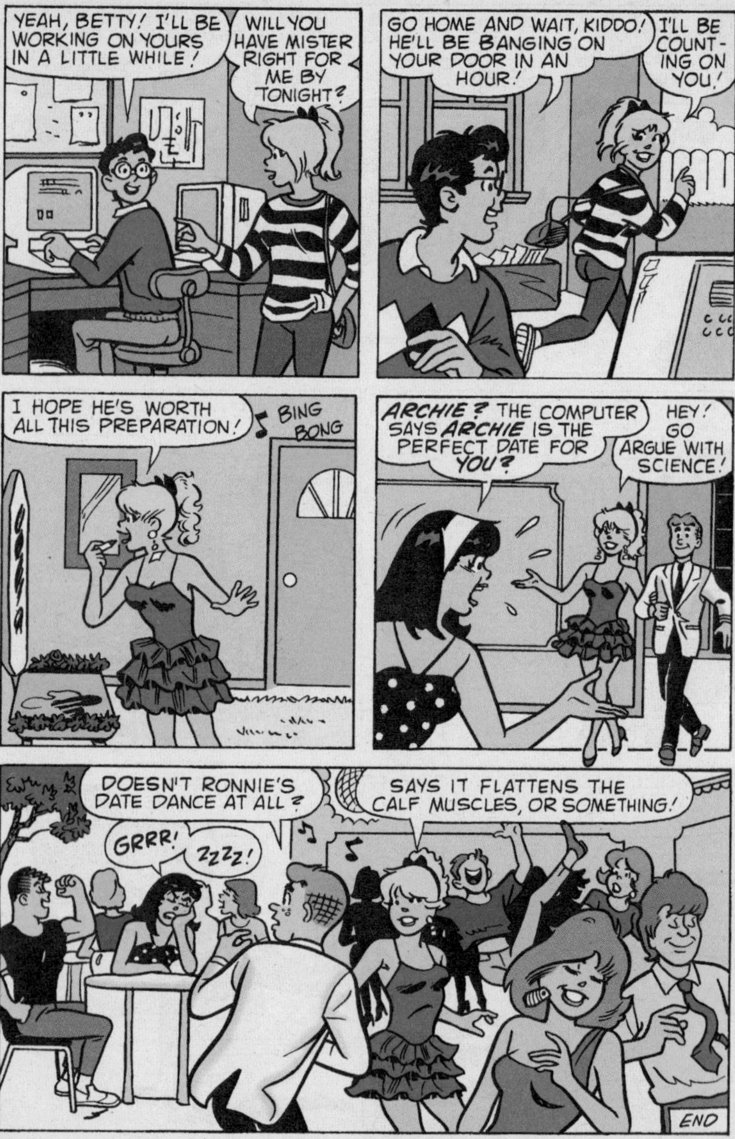
YEAH, BETTY! I'LL BE WORKING ON YOURS IN A LITTLE WHILE!
WILL YOU HAVE MISTER RIGHT FOR ME BY TONIGHT?
GO HOME AND WAIT, KIDDO! HE'LL BE BANGING ON YOUR DOOR IN AN HOUR!
I'LL BE COUNTING ON YOU!
I HOPE HE'S WORTH ALL THIS PREPARATION!
BING BONG
ARCHIE? THE COMPUTER SAYS ARCHIE IS THE PERFECT DATE FOR YOU?
HEY! GO ARGUE WITH SCIENCE!
DOESN'T RONNIE'S DATE DANCE AT ALL?
SAYS IT FLATTENS THE CALF MUSCLES, OR SOMETHING!
GRRR!
ZZZZ!
END

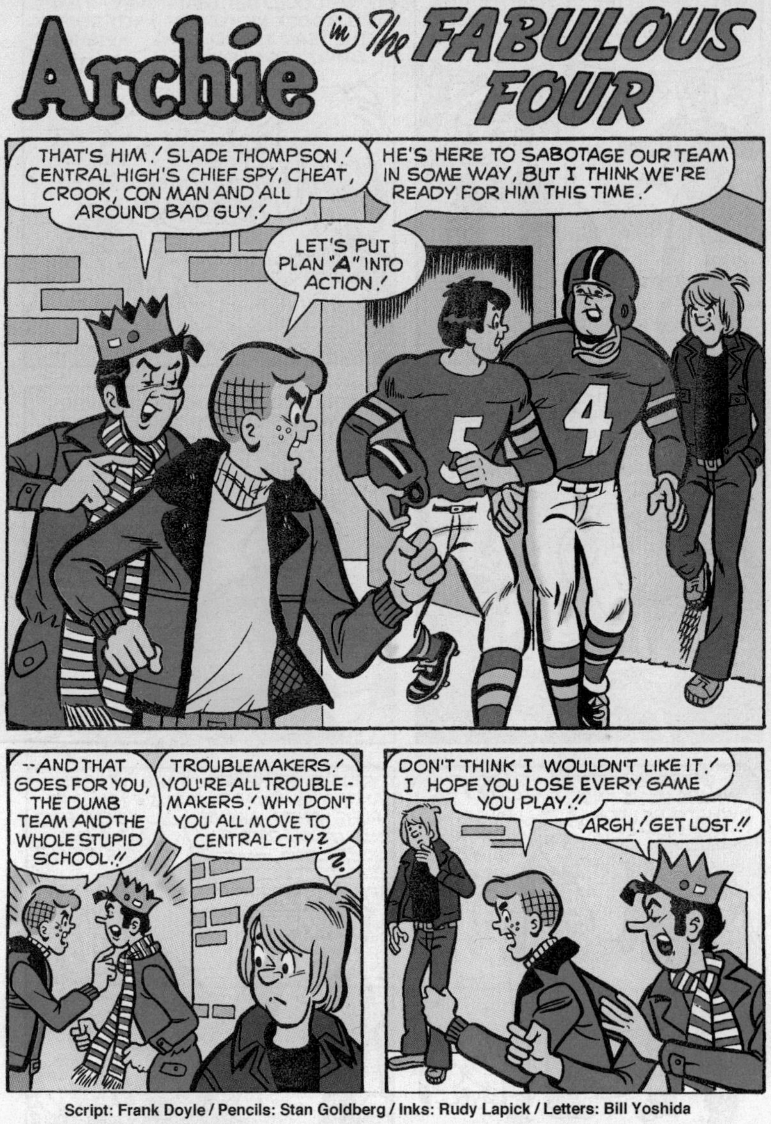
Archie in The FABULOUS FOUR
THAT'S HIM.! SLADE THOMPSON.! CENTRAL HIGH'S CHIEF SPY, CHEAT, CROOK, CON MAN AND ALL AROUND BAD GUY.!
HE'S HERE TO SABOTAGE OUR TEAM IN SOME WAY, BUT I THINK WE'RE READY FOR HIM THIS TIME.!
LET'S PUT PLAN "A" INTO ACTION.!
--AND THAT GOES FOR YOU, THE DUMB TEAM AND THE WHOLE STUPID SCHOOL.!!
TROUBLEMAKERS.! YOU'RE ALL TROUBLE-MAKERS.! WHY DON'T YOU ALL MOVE TO CENTRAL CITY?
DON'T THINK I WOULDN'T LIKE IT.! I HOPE YOU LOSE EVERY GAME YOU PLAY.!!
ARGH.! GET LOST.!!

Script: Frank Doyle / Pencils: Stan Goldberg / Inks: Rudy Lapick / Letters: Bill Yoshida

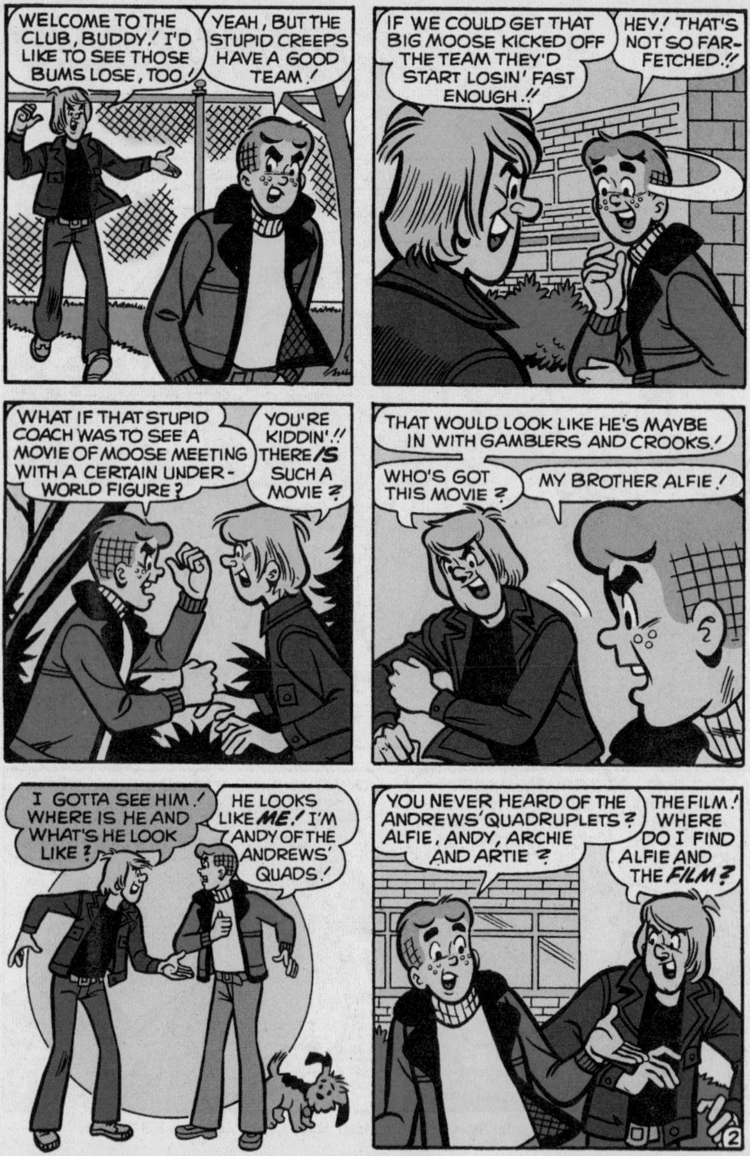
WELCOME TO THE CLUB, BUDDY! I'D LIKE TO SEE THOSE BUMS LOSE, TOO!
YEAH, BUT THE STUPID CREEPS HAVE A GOOD TEAM!
IF WE COULD GET THAT BIG MOOSE KICKED OFF THE TEAM THEY'D START LOSIN' FAST ENOUGH!!
HEY! THAT'S NOT SO FAR-FETCHED!!
WHAT IF THAT STUPID COACH WAS TO SEE A MOVIE OF MOOSE MEETING WITH A CERTAIN UNDER-WORLD FIGURE?
YOU'RE KIDDIN'!! THERE IS SUCH A MOVIE?
THAT WOULD LOOK LIKE HE'S MAYBE IN WITH GAMBLERS AND CROOKS!
WHO'S GOT THIS MOVIE?
MY BROTHER ALFIE!
I GOTTA SEE HIM! WHERE IS HE AND WHAT'S HE LOOK LIKE?
HE LOOKS LIKE ME! I'M ANDY OF THE ANDREWS' QUADS!
YOU NEVER HEARD OF THE ANDREWS' QUADRUPLETS? ALFIE, ANDY, ARCHIE AND ARTIE?
THE FILM! WHERE DO I FIND ALFIE AND THE FILM?
2

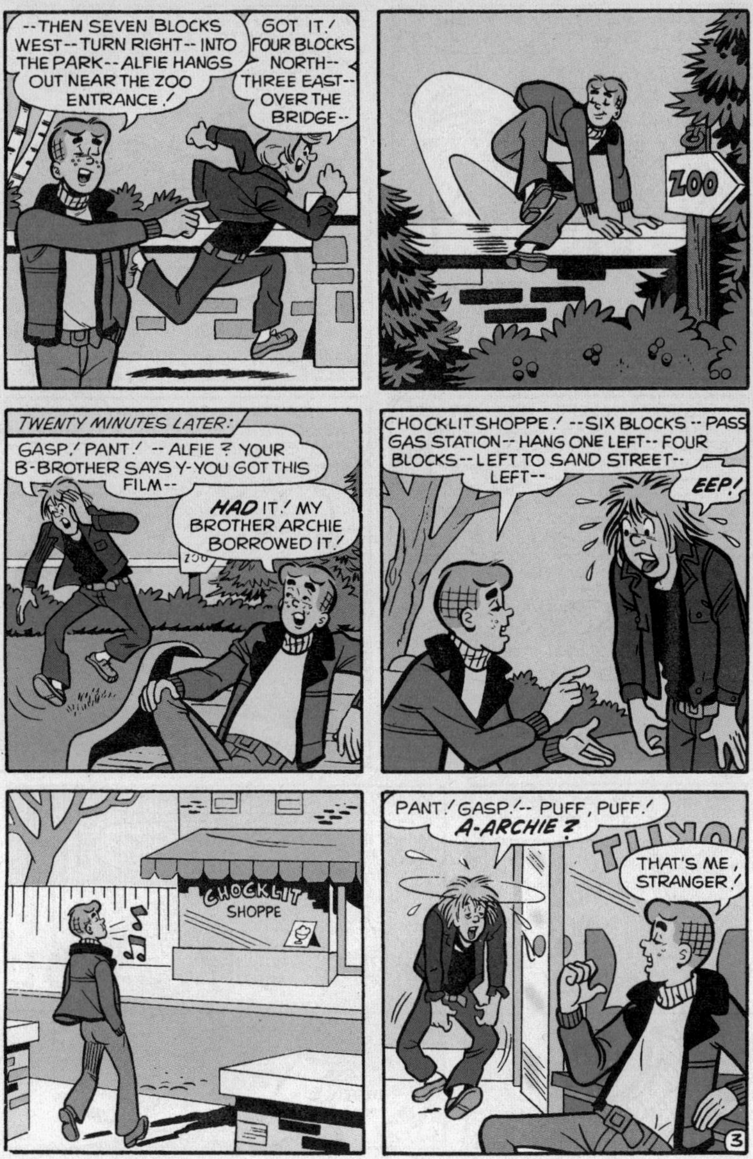
--THEN SEVEN BLOCKS WEST--TURN RIGHT--INTO THE PARK--ALFIE HANGS OUT NEAR THE ZOO ENTRANCE!
GOT IT! FOUR BLOCKS NORTH--THREE EAST--OVER THE BRIDGE--
ZOO
TWENTY MINUTES LATER:
GASP! PANT! --ALFIE? YOUR B-BROTHER SAYS Y-YOU GOT THIS FILM--
HAD IT! MY BROTHER ARCHIE BORROWED IT!
ZOO
CHOCKLIT SHOPPE! --SIX BLOCKS--PASS GAS STATION--HANG ONE LEFT--FOUR BLOCKS--LEFT TO SAND STREET--LEFT--
EEP!
CHOCKLIT SHOPPE
PANT! GASP!--PUFF, PUFF! A-ARCHIE?
THAT'S ME, STRANGER!
3

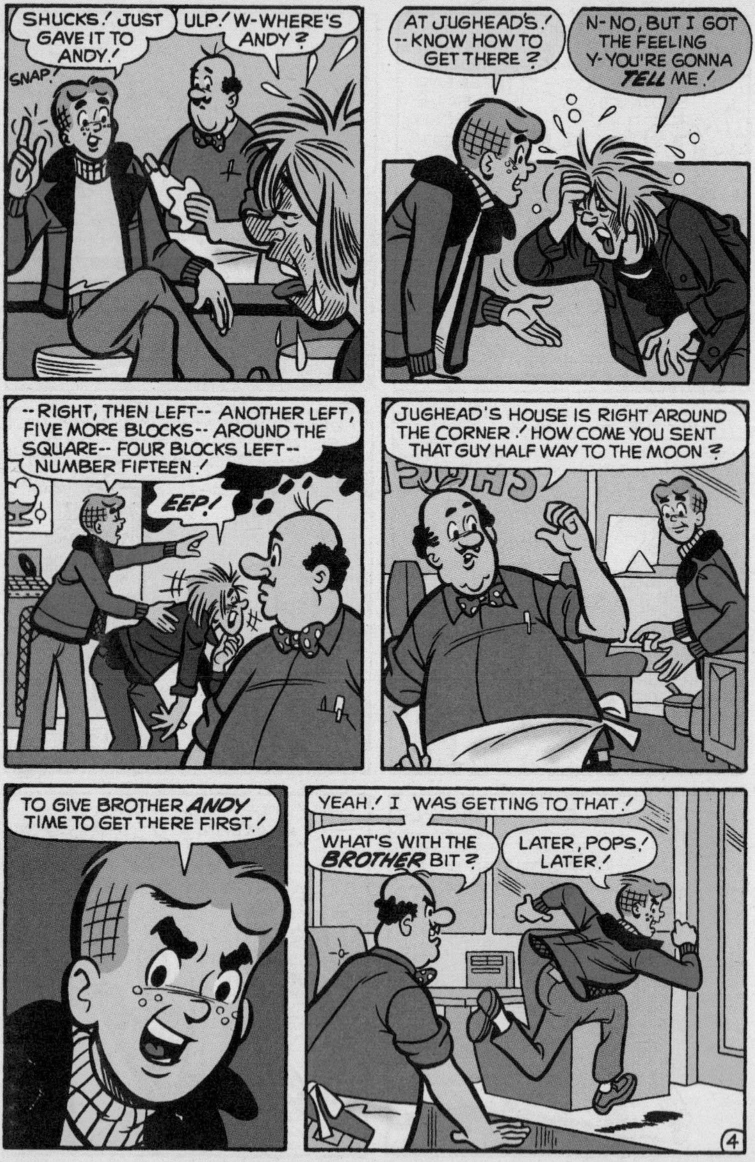
SHUCKS! JUST GAVE IT TO ANDY!
SNAP!
ULP! W-WHERE'S ANDY?
AT JUGHEAD'S! --KNOW HOW TO GET THERE?
N-NO, BUT I GOT THE FEELING Y-YOU'RE GONNA TELL ME!
--RIGHT, THEN LEFT-- ANOTHER LEFT, FIVE MORE BLOCKS-- AROUND THE SQUARE-- FOUR BLOCKS LEFT-- NUMBER FIFTEEN!
EEP!
JUGHEAD'S HOUSE IS RIGHT AROUND THE CORNER! HOW COME YOU SENT THAT GUY HALF WAY TO THE MOON?
TO GIVE BROTHER ANDY TIME TO GET THERE FIRST!
YEAH! I WAS GETTING TO THAT!
WHAT'S WITH THE BROTHER BIT?
LATER, POPS! LATER!
4

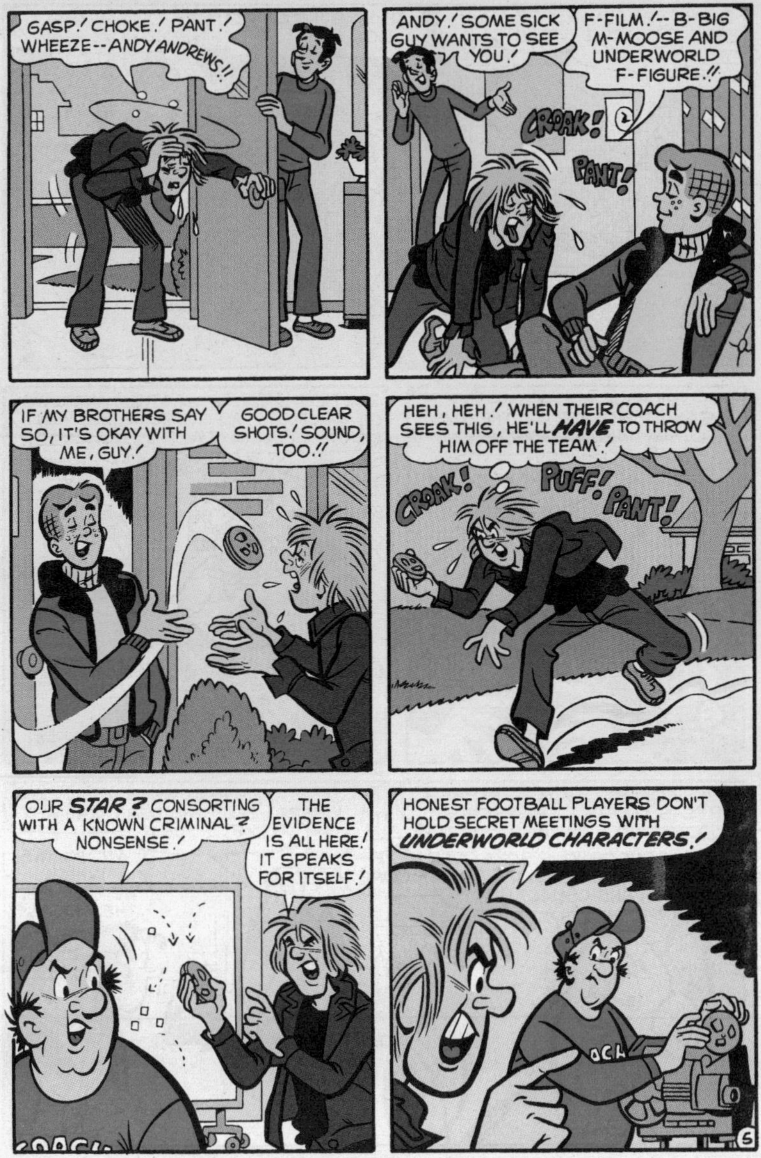
GASP.! CHOKE.! PANT.! WHEEZE--ANDY ANDREWS.!!
ANDY.! SOME SICK GUY WANTS TO SEE YOU.!
F-FILM.!--B-BIG M-MOOSE AND UNDERWORLD F-FIGURE.!!
CROAK!
PANT!
IF MY BROTHERS SAY SO, IT'S OKAY WITH ME, GUY.!
GOOD CLEAR SHOTS.! SOUND, TOO.!!
HEH, HEH.! WHEN THEIR COACH SEES THIS, HE'LL HAVE TO THROW HIM OFF THE TEAM.!
CROAK!
PUFF!
PANT!
OUR STAR? CONSORTING WITH A KNOWN CRIMINAL? NONSENSE.!
THE EVIDENCE IS ALL HERE! IT SPEAKS FOR ITSELF.!
HONEST FOOTBALL PLAYERS DON'T HOLD SECRET MEETINGS WITH UNDERWORLD CHARACTERS.!
5

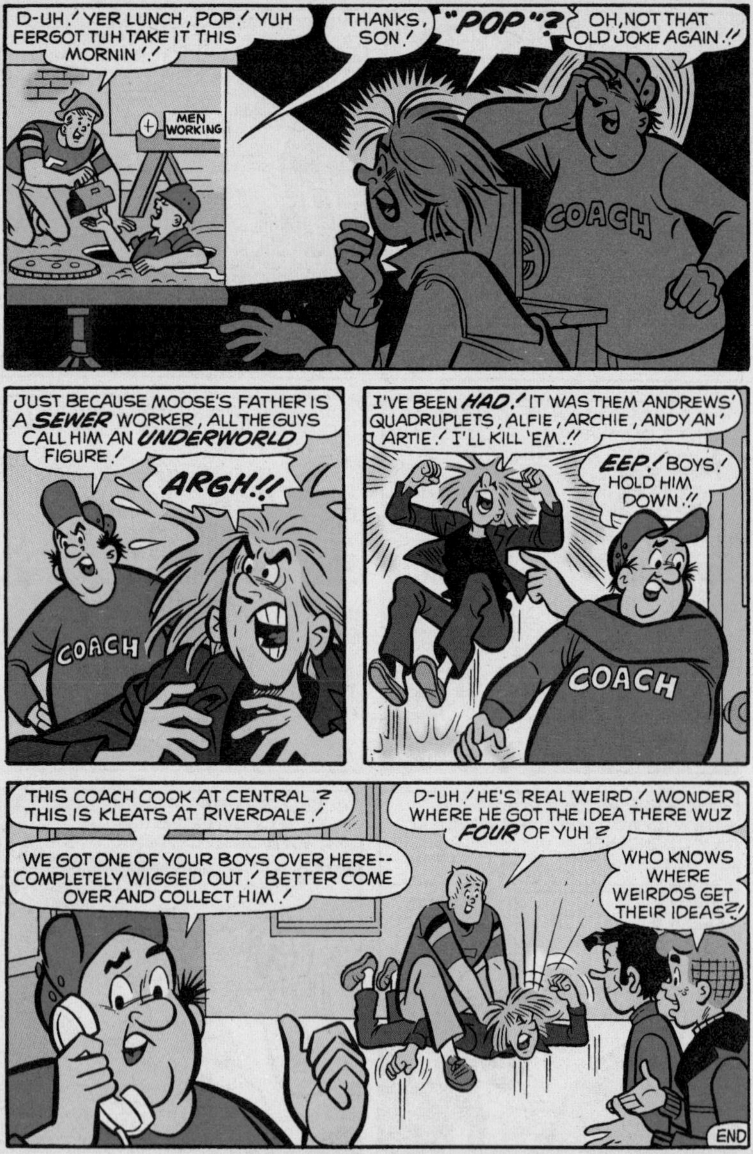
D-UH.! YER LUNCH, POP.! YUH FERGOT TUH TAKE IT THIS MORNIN'.!
MEN WORKING
THANKS, SON.!
"POP"?
OH, NOT THAT OLD JOKE AGAIN.!!
JUST BECAUSE MOOSE'S FATHER IS A SEWER WORKER, ALL THE GUYS CALL HIM AN UNDERWORLD FIGURE.!
ARGH!!!
COACH
I'VE BEEN HAD.! IT WAS THEM ANDREWS' QUADRUPLETS, ALFIE, ARCHIE, ANDY AN' ARTIE.! I'LL KILL 'EM.!!
EEP.! BOYS.! HOLD HIM DOWN.!!
COACH
THIS COACH COOK AT CENTRAL? THIS IS KLEATS AT RIVERDALE.!
WE GOT ONE OF YOUR BOYS OVER HERE-- COMPLETELY WIGGED OUT.! BETTER COME OVER AND COLLECT HIM.!
D-UH.! HE'S REAL WEIRD.! WONDER WHERE HE GOT THE IDEA THERE WUZ FOUR OF YUH?
WHO KNOWS WHERE WEIRDOS GET THEIR IDEAS?!
END

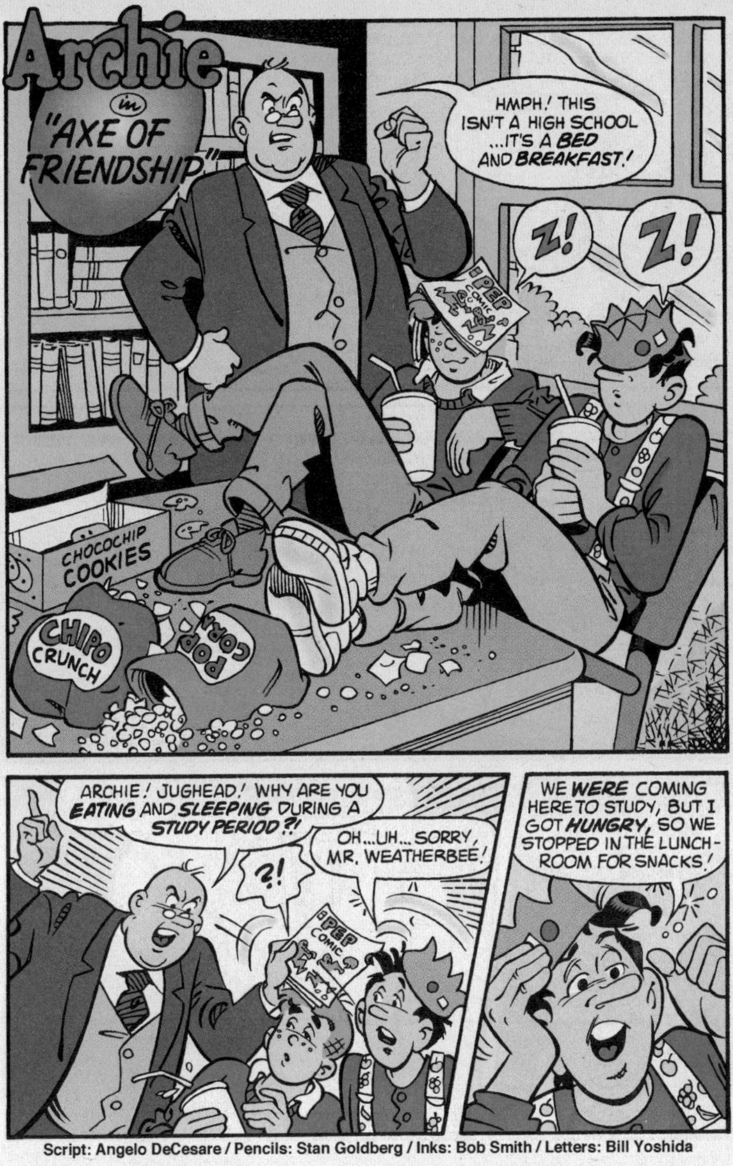
Archie
in
"AXE OF FRIENDSHIP"
HMPH! THIS ISN'T A HIGH SCHOOL ...IT'S A BED AND BREAKFAST!
Z!
Z!
PEP COMIC
CHOCOCHIP COOKIES
CHIPO CRUNCH
POP CORN
ARCHIE! JUGHEAD! WHY ARE YOU EATING AND SLEEPING DURING A STUDY PERIOD?!
?!
OH...UH... SORRY, MR. WEATHERBEE!
PEP COMIC
WE WERE COMING HERE TO STUDY, BUT I GOT HUNGRY, SO WE STOPPED IN THE LUNCH-ROOM FOR SNACKS!

Script: Angelo DeCesare / Pencils: Stan Goldberg / Inks: Bob Smith / Letters: Bill Yoshida

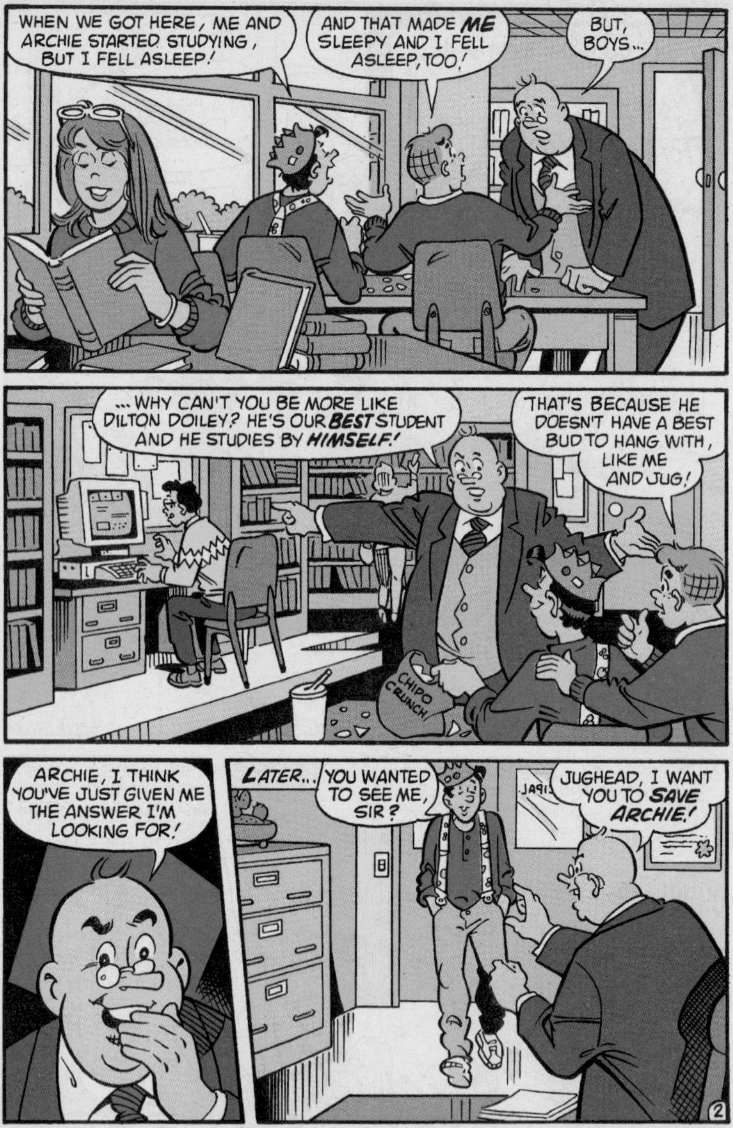
WHEN WE GOT HERE, ME AND ARCHIE STARTED STUDYING, BUT I FELL ASLEEP!
AND THAT MADE ME SLEEPY AND I FELL ASLEEP, TOO!
BUT, BOYS...
...WHY CAN'T YOU BE MORE LIKE DILTON DOILEY? HE'S OUR BEST STUDENT AND HE STUDIES BY HIMSELF!
THAT'S BECAUSE HE DOESN'T HAVE A BEST BUD TO HANG WITH, LIKE ME AND JUG!
CHIPO CRUNCH
ARCHIE, I THINK YOU'VE JUST GIVEN ME THE ANSWER I'M LOOKING FOR!
LATER...
YOU WANTED TO SEE ME, SIR?
JUGHEAD, I WANT YOU TO SAVE ARCHIE!
2

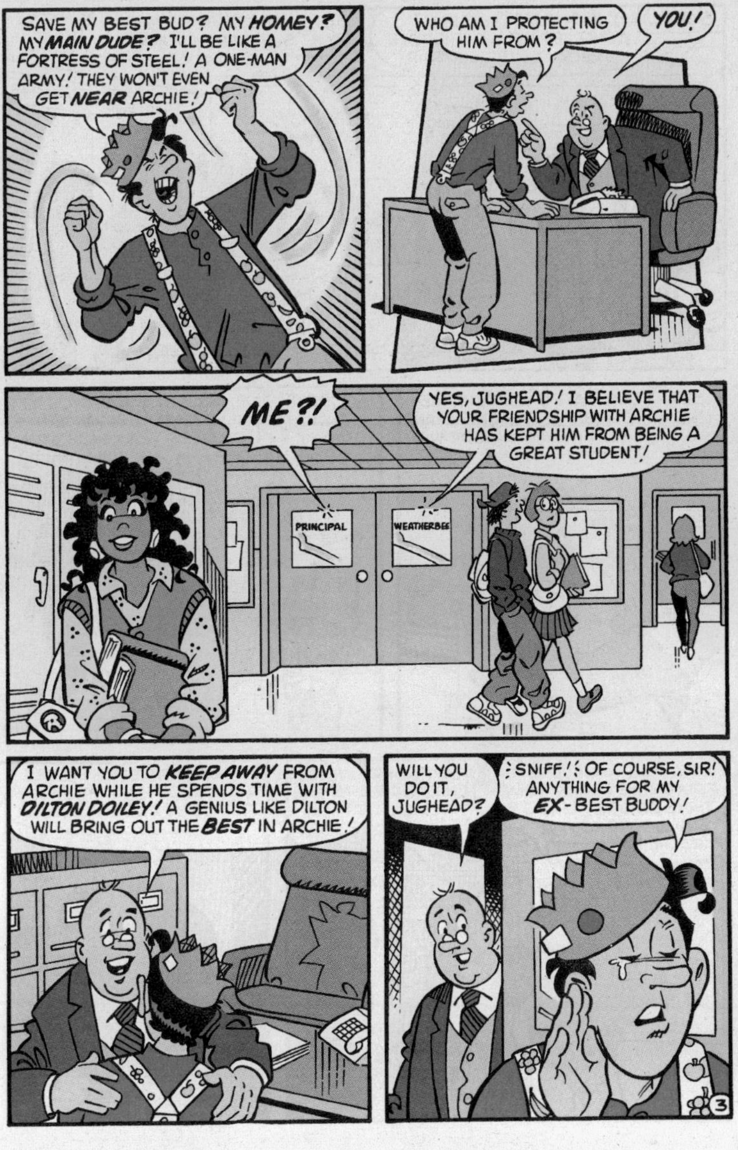
SAVE MY BEST BUD? MY HOMEY? MY MAIN DUDE? I'LL BE LIKE A FORTRESS OF STEEL! A ONE-MAN ARMY! THEY WON'T EVEN GET NEAR ARCHIE!
WHO AM I PROTECTING HIM FROM?
YOU!
ME?!
YES, JUGHEAD! I BELIEVE THAT YOUR FRIENDSHIP WITH ARCHIE HAS KEPT HIM FROM BEING A GREAT STUDENT!
PRINCIPAL
WEATHERBEE
I WANT YOU TO KEEP AWAY FROM ARCHIE WHILE HE SPENDS TIME WITH DILTON DOILEY! A GENIUS LIKE DILTON WILL BRING OUT THE BEST IN ARCHIE!
WILL YOU DO IT, JUGHEAD?
SNIFF! OF COURSE, SIR! ANYTHING FOR MY EX-BEST BUDDY!
3

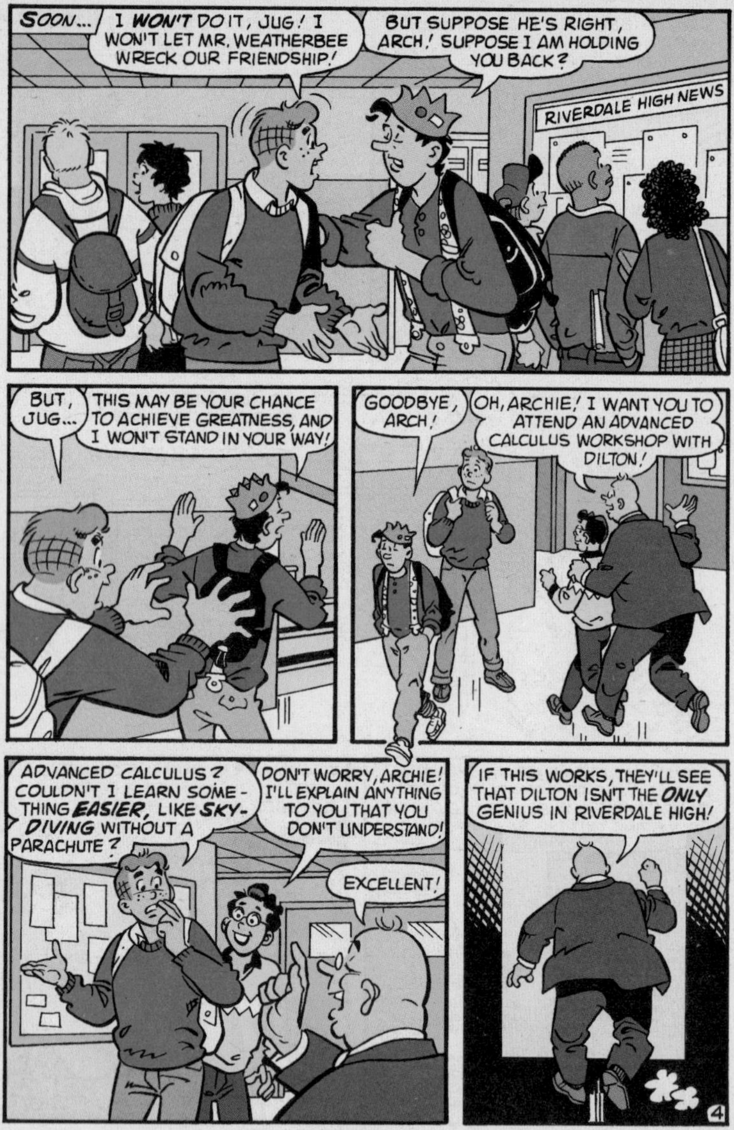
SOON...
I WON'T DO IT, JUG! I WON'T LET MR. WEATHERBEE WRECK OUR FRIENDSHIP!
BUT SUPPOSE HE'S RIGHT, ARCH! SUPPOSE I AM HOLDING YOU BACK?
RIVERDALE HIGH NEWS
BUT, JUG...
THIS MAY BE YOUR CHANCE TO ACHIEVE GREATNESS, AND I WON'T STAND IN YOUR WAY!
GOODBYE, ARCH!
OH, ARCHIE! I WANT YOU TO ATTEND AN ADVANCED CALCULUS WORKSHOP WITH DILTON!
ADVANCED CALCULUS? COULDN'T I LEARN SOME-THING EASIER, LIKE SKY-DIVING WITHOUT A PARACHUTE?
DON'T WORRY, ARCHIE! I'LL EXPLAIN ANYTHING TO YOU THAT YOU DON'T UNDERSTAND!
EXCELLENT!
IF THIS WORKS, THEY'LL SEE THAT DILTON ISN'T THE ONLY GENIUS IN RIVERDALE HIGH!
4

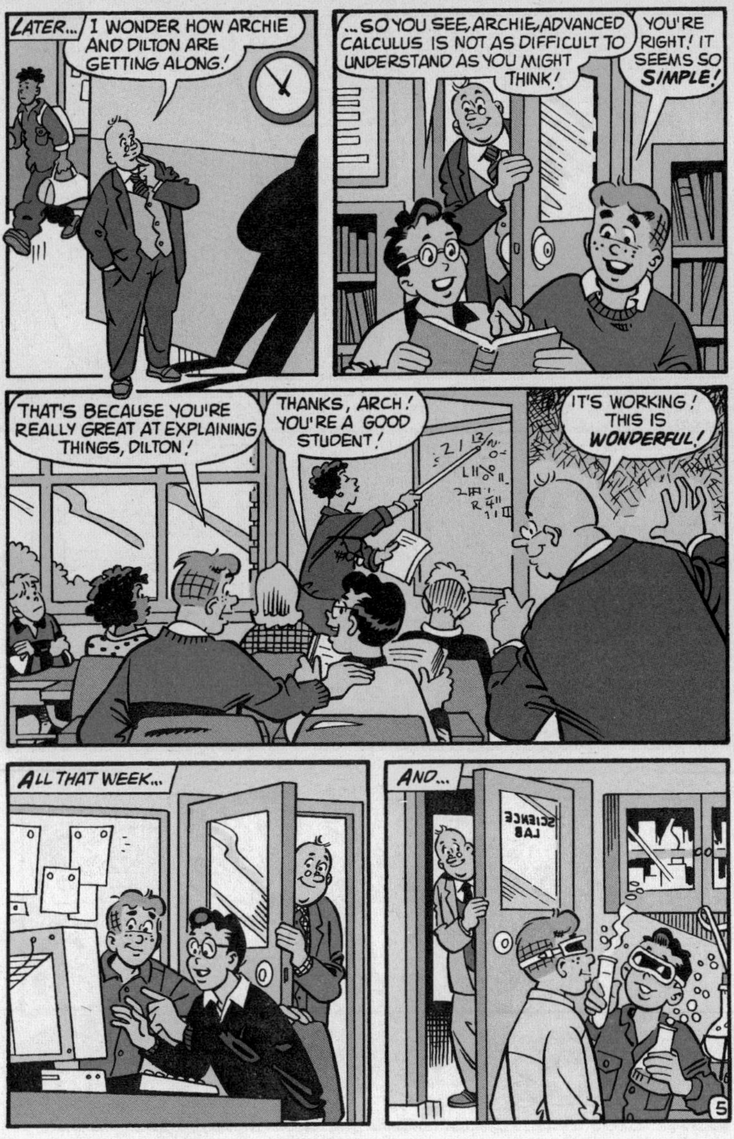
LATER...
I WONDER HOW ARCHIE AND DILTON ARE GETTING ALONG!
...SO YOU SEE, ARCHIE, ADVANCED CALCULUS IS NOT AS DIFFICULT TO UNDERSTAND AS YOU MIGHT THINK!
YOU'RE RIGHT! IT SEEMS SO SIMPLE!
THAT'S BECAUSE YOU'RE REALLY GREAT AT EXPLAINING THINGS, DILTON!
THANKS, ARCH! YOU'RE A GOOD STUDENT!
IT'S WORKING! THIS IS WONDERFUL!
ALL THAT WEEK...
AND...
SCIENCE LAB
5

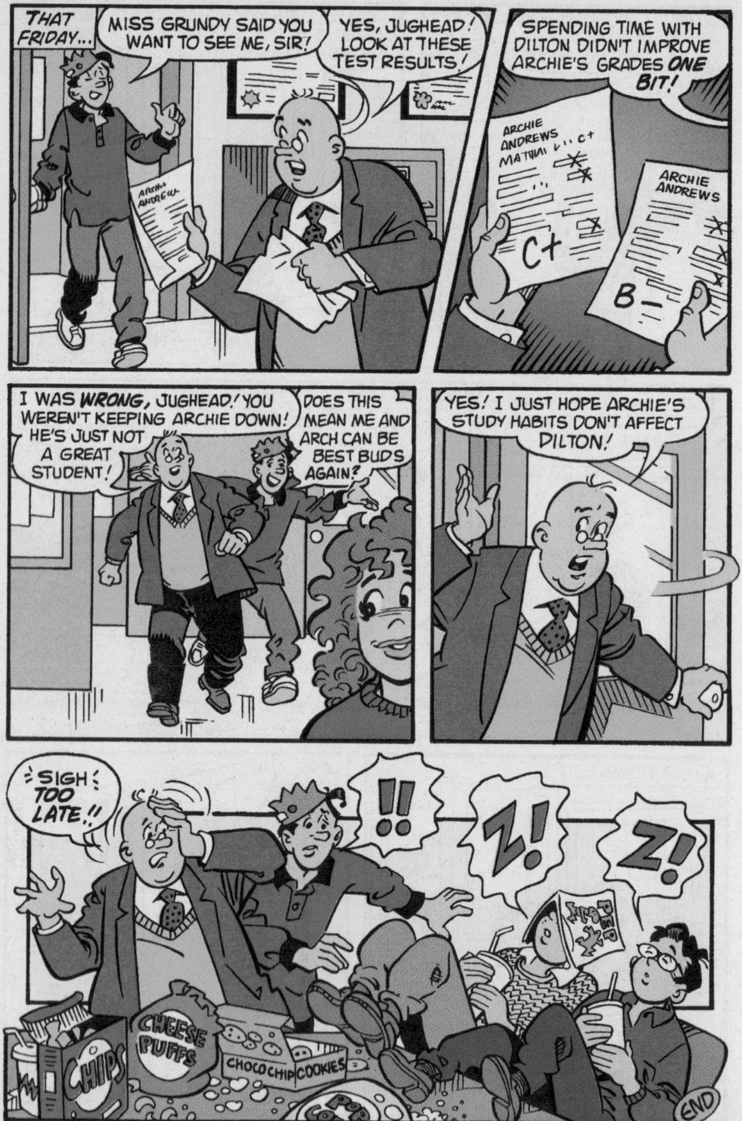
THAT FRIDAY...
MISS GRUNDY SAID YOU WANT TO SEE ME, SIR!
YES, JUGHEAD! LOOK AT THESE TEST RESULTS!
SPENDING TIME WITH DILTON DIDN'T IMPROVE ARCHIE'S GRADES ONE BIT!
ARCHIE ANDREWS
C+
ARCHIE ANDREWS
B–
I WAS WRONG, JUGHEAD! YOU WEREN'T KEEPING ARCHIE DOWN! HE'S JUST NOT A GREAT STUDENT!
DOES THIS MEAN ME AND ARCH CAN BE BEST BUDS AGAIN?
YES! I JUST HOPE ARCHIE'S STUDY HABITS DON'T AFFECT DILTON!
SIGH TOO LATE!!
!!
Z!
Z!
CHIPS
CHEESE PUFFS
CHOCO CHIP COOKIES
END

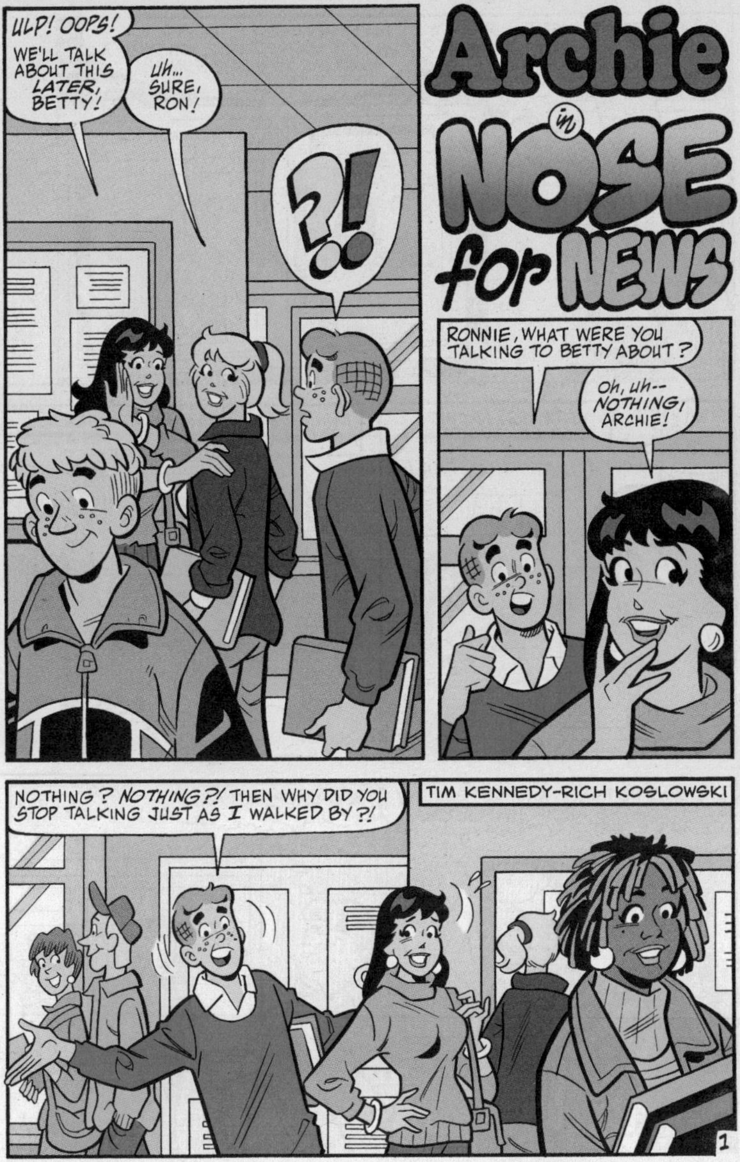
ULP! OOPS!
WE'LL TALK ABOUT THIS LATER, BETTY!
uh... SURE, RON!
?!
Archie in NOSE for NEWS
RONNIE, WHAT WERE YOU TALKING TO BETTY ABOUT?
Oh, uh-- NOTHING, ARCHIE!
NOTHING? NOTHING?! THEN WHY DID YOU STOP TALKING JUST AS I WALKED BY?!
TIM KENNEDY-RICH KOSLOWSKI
1

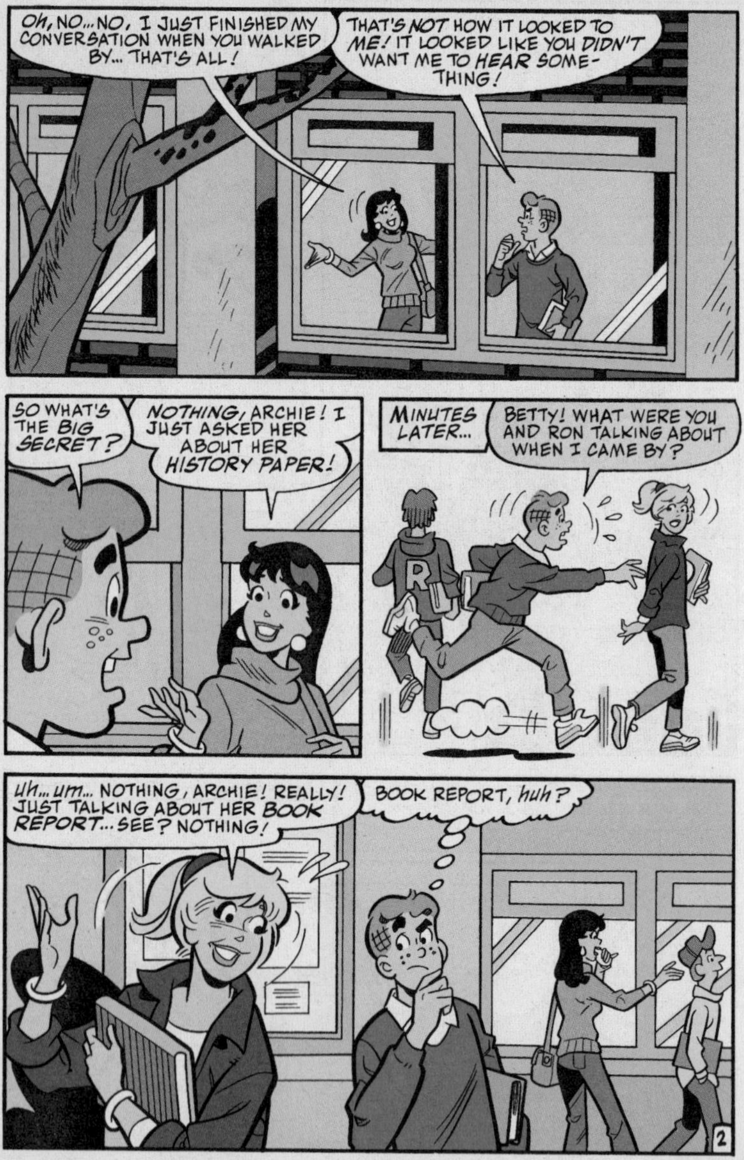

OH, NO... NO, I JUST FINISHED MY CONVERSATION WHEN YOU WALKED BY... THAT'S ALL!
THAT'S NOT HOW IT LOOKED TO ME! IT LOOKED LIKE YOU DIDN'T WANT ME TO HEAR SOMETHING!
SO WHAT'S THE BIG SECRET?
NOTHING, ARCHIE! I JUST ASKED HER ABOUT HER HISTORY PAPER!
MINUTES LATER...
BETTY! WHAT WERE YOU AND RON TALKING ABOUT WHEN I CAME BY?
UH... UM... NOTHING, ARCHIE! REALLY! JUST TALKING ABOUT HER BOOK REPORT... SEE? NOTHING!
BOOK REPORT, HUH?
2

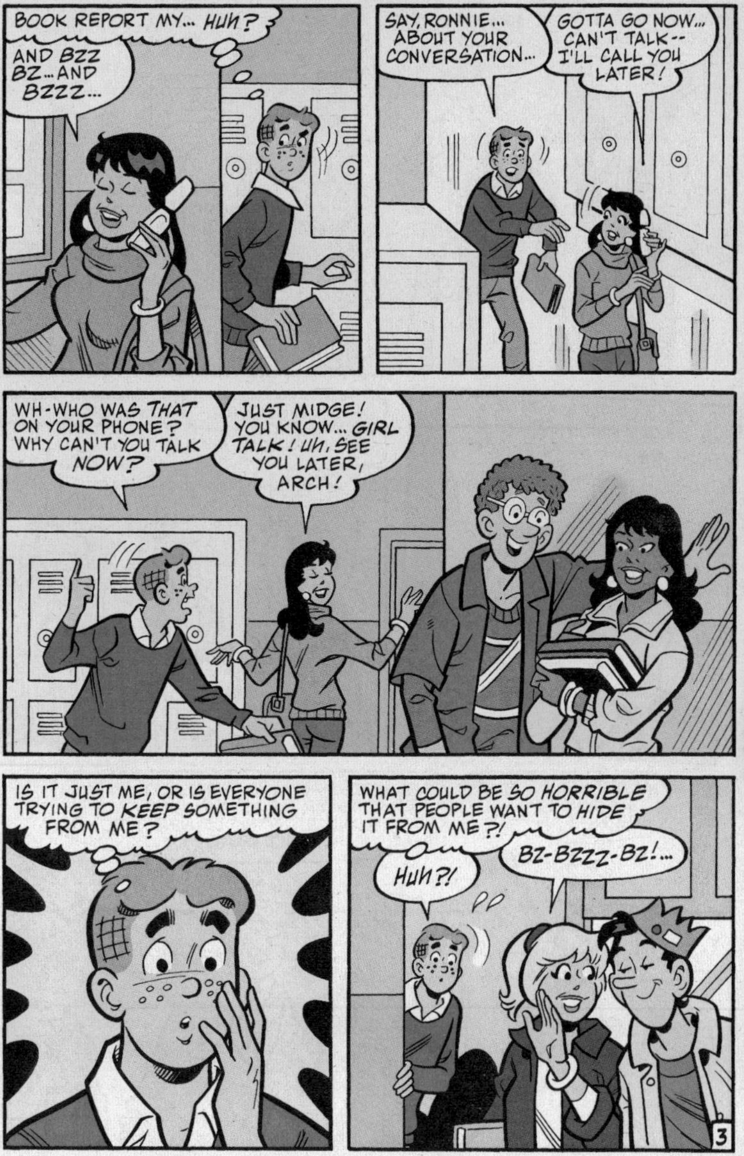
BOOK REPORT MY... HUH?
AND BZZ BZ... AND BZZZ...
SAY, RONNIE... ABOUT YOUR CONVERSATION...
GOTTA GO NOW... CAN'T TALK-- I'LL CALL YOU LATER!
WH-WHO WAS THAT ON YOUR PHONE? WHY CAN'T YOU TALK NOW?
JUST MIDGE! YOU KNOW... GIRL TALK! UH, SEE YOU LATER, ARCH!
IS IT JUST ME, OR IS EVERYONE TRYING TO KEEP SOMETHING FROM ME?
WHAT COULD BE SO HORRIBLE THAT PEOPLE WANT TO HIDE IT FROM ME?!
HUH?!
BZ-BZZZ-BZ!...
3

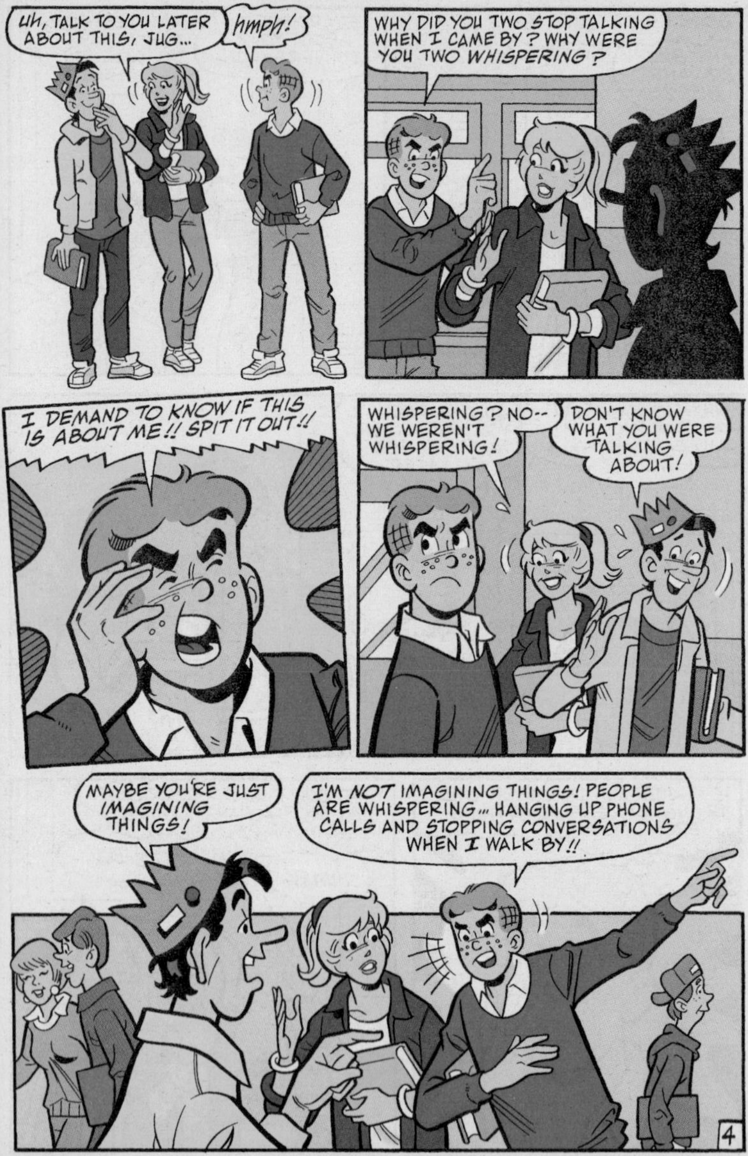

uh, TALK TO YOU LATER ABOUT THIS, JUG...
hmph!
WHY DID YOU TWO STOP TALKING WHEN I CAME BY? WHY WERE YOU TWO WHISPERING?
I DEMAND TO KNOW IF THIS IS ABOUT ME!! SPIT IT OUT!!
WHISPERING? NO-- WE WEREN'T WHISPERING!
DON'T KNOW WHAT YOU WERE TALKING ABOUT!
MAYBE YOU'RE JUST IMAGINING THINGS!
I'M NOT IMAGINING THINGS! PEOPLE ARE WHISPERING... HANGING UP PHONE CALLS AND STOPPING CONVERSATIONS WHEN I WALK BY!!
4

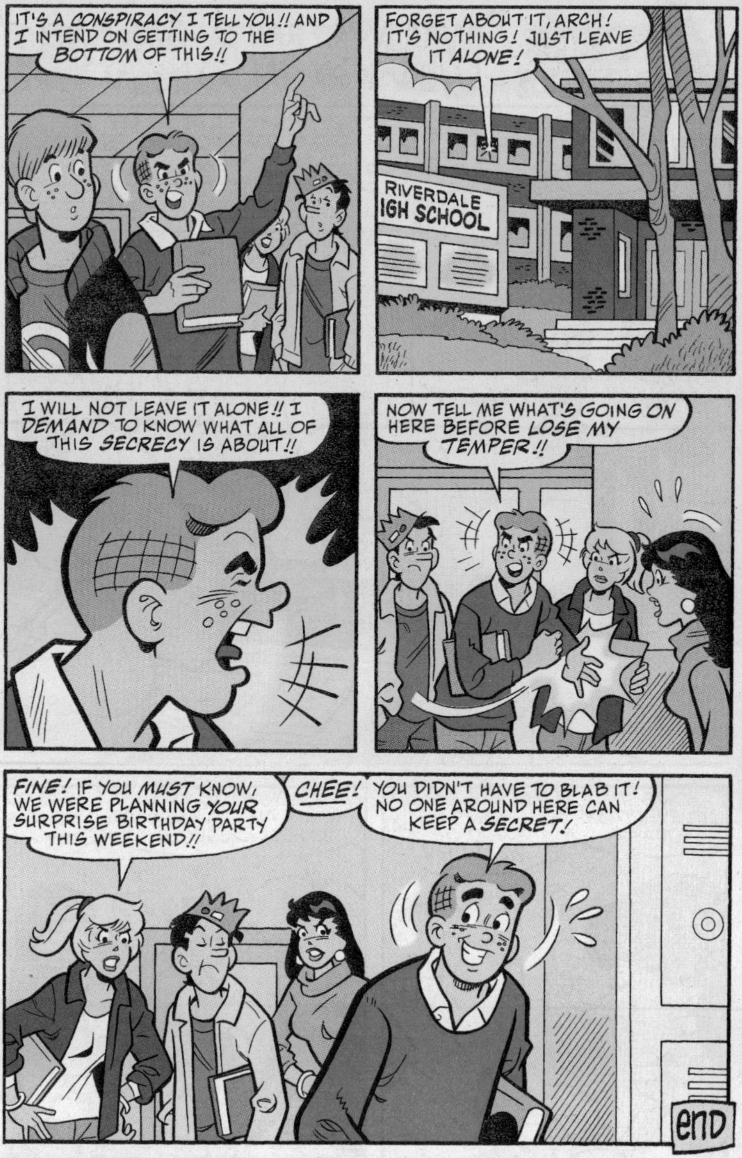

IT'S A CONSPIRACY I TELL YOU!! AND I INTEND ON GETTING TO THE BOTTOM OF THIS!!
FORGET ABOUT IT, ARCH! IT'S NOTHING! JUST LEAVE IT ALONE!
RIVERDALE
IGH SCHOOL
I WILL NOT LEAVE IT ALONE!! I DEMAND TO KNOW WHAT ALL OF THIS SECRECY IS ABOUT!!
NOW TELL ME WHAT'S GOING ON HERE BEFORE LOSE MY TEMPER!!
FINE! IF YOU MUST KNOW, WE WERE PLANNING YOUR SURPRISE BIRTHDAY PARTY THIS WEEKEND!!
CHEE!
YOU DIDN'T HAVE TO BLAB IT! NO ONE AROUND HERE CAN KEEP A SECRET!
END

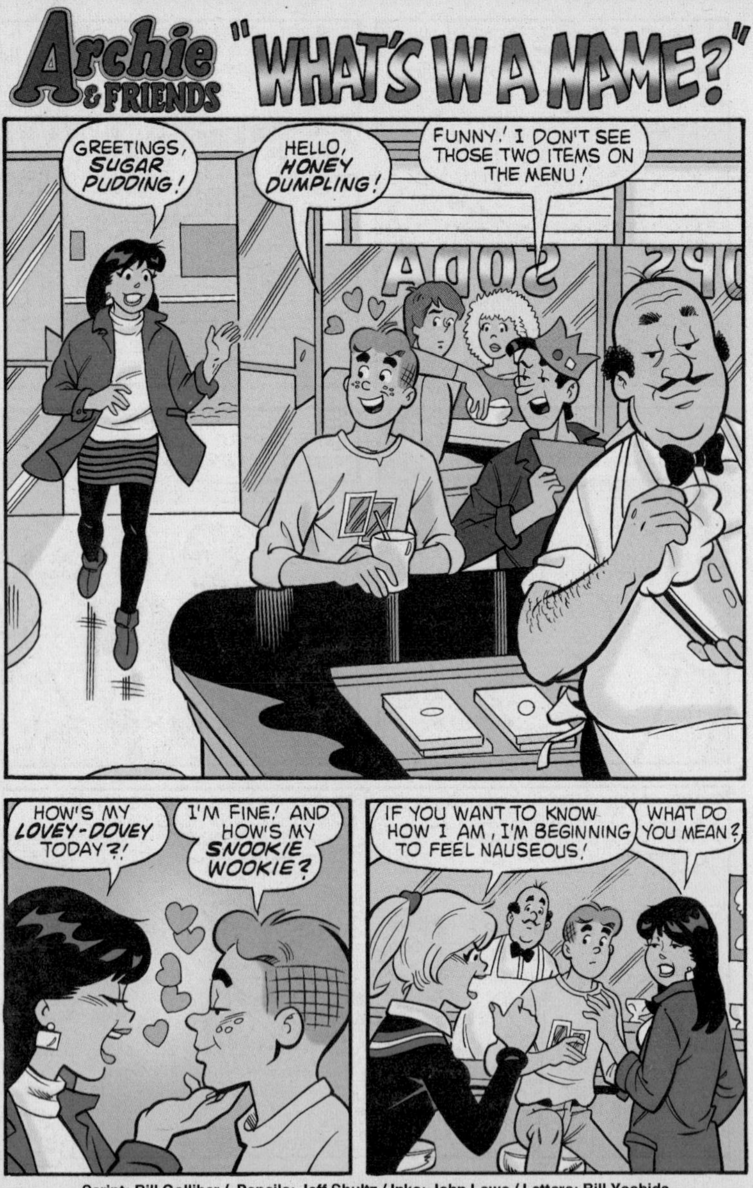
Archie & FRIENDS
"WHAT'S IN A NAME?"
GREETINGS, SUGAR PUDDING!
HELLO, HONEY DUMPLING!
FUNNY! I DON'T SEE THOSE TWO ITEMS ON THE MENU!
SODA
HOW'S MY LOVEY-DOVEY TODAY?!
I'M FINE! AND HOW'S MY SNOOKIE WOOKIE?
IF YOU WANT TO KNOW HOW I AM, I'M BEGINNING TO FEEL NAUSEOUS!
WHAT DO YOU MEAN?

Script: Bill Golliher / Pencils: Jeff Shultz / Inks: John Lowe / Letters: Bill Yoshida

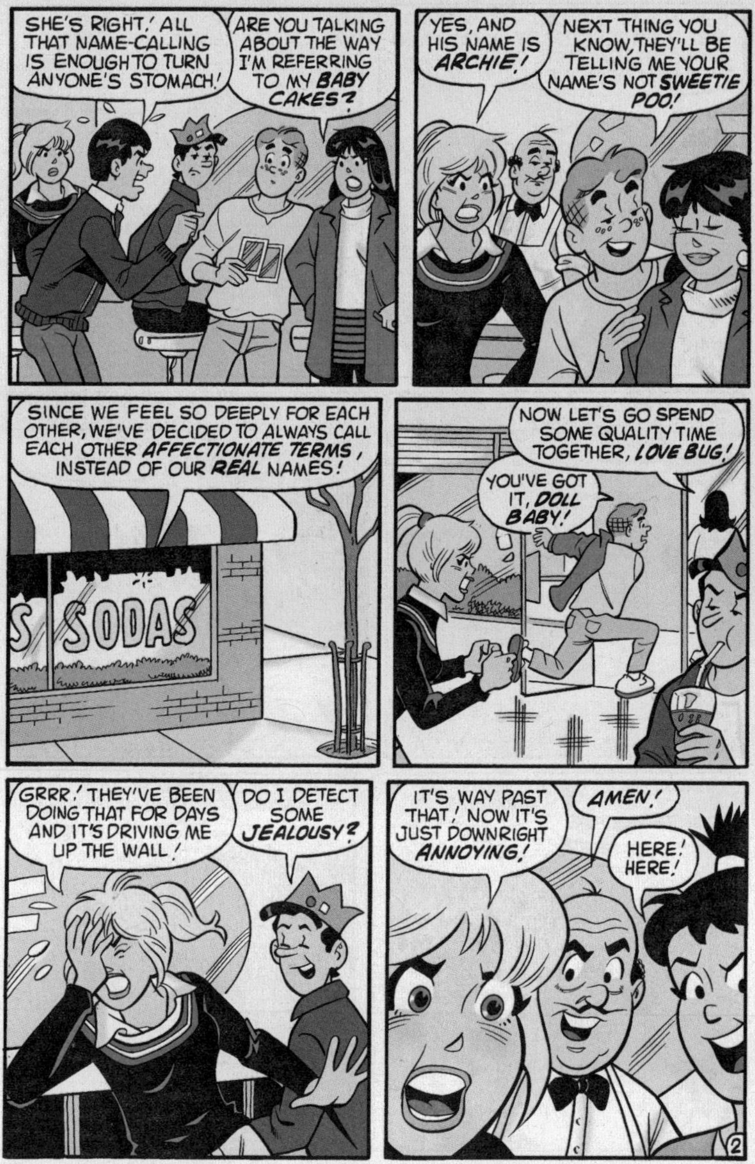
SHE'S RIGHT! ALL THAT NAME-CALLING IS ENOUGH TO TURN ANYONE'S STOMACH!
ARE YOU TALKING ABOUT THE WAY I'M REFERRING TO MY BABY CAKES?
YES, AND HIS NAME IS ARCHIE!
NEXT THING YOU KNOW, THEY'LL BE TELLING ME YOUR NAME'S NOT SWEETIE POO!
SINCE WE FEEL SO DEEPLY FOR EACH OTHER, WE'VE DECIDED TO ALWAYS CALL EACH OTHER AFFECTIONATE TERMS, INSTEAD OF OUR REAL NAMES!
SODAS
NOW LET'S GO SPEND SOME QUALITY TIME TOGETHER, LOVE BUG!
YOU'VE GOT IT, DOLL BABY!
GRRR! THEY'VE BEEN DOING THAT FOR DAYS AND IT'S DRIVING ME UP THE WALL!
DO I DETECT SOME JEALOUSY?
IT'S WAY PAST THAT! NOW IT'S JUST DOWNRIGHT ANNOYING!
AMEN!
HERE! HERE!
2

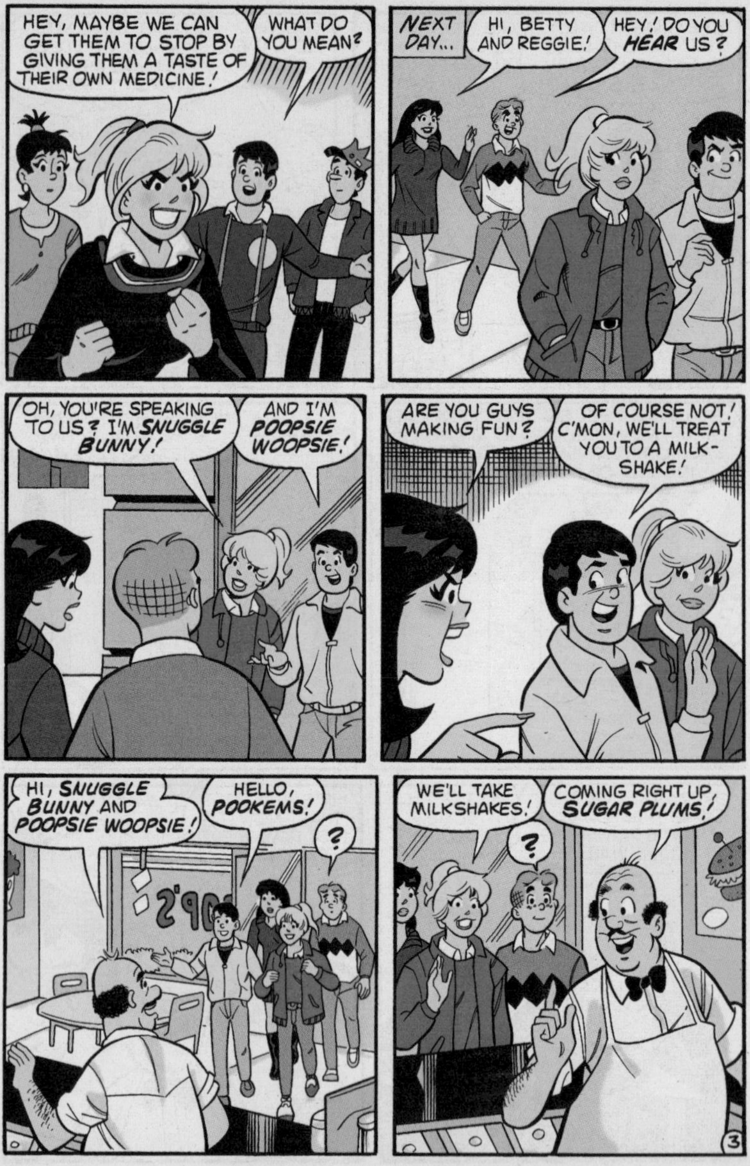
HEY, MAYBE WE CAN GET THEM TO STOP BY GIVING THEM A TASTE OF THEIR OWN MEDICINE!
WHAT DO YOU MEAN?
NEXT DAY...
HI, BETTY AND REGGIE!
HEY! DO YOU HEAR US?
OH, YOU'RE SPEAKING TO US? I'M SNUGGLE BUNNY!
AND I'M POOPSIE WOOPSIE!
ARE YOU GUYS MAKING FUN?
OF COURSE NOT! C'MON, WE'LL TREAT YOU TO A MILK-SHAKE!
HI, SNUGGLE BUNNY AND POOPSIE WOOPSIE!
HELLO, POOKEMS!
?
POP'S
WE'LL TAKE MILKSHAKES!
?
COMING RIGHT UP, SUGAR PLUMS!
3

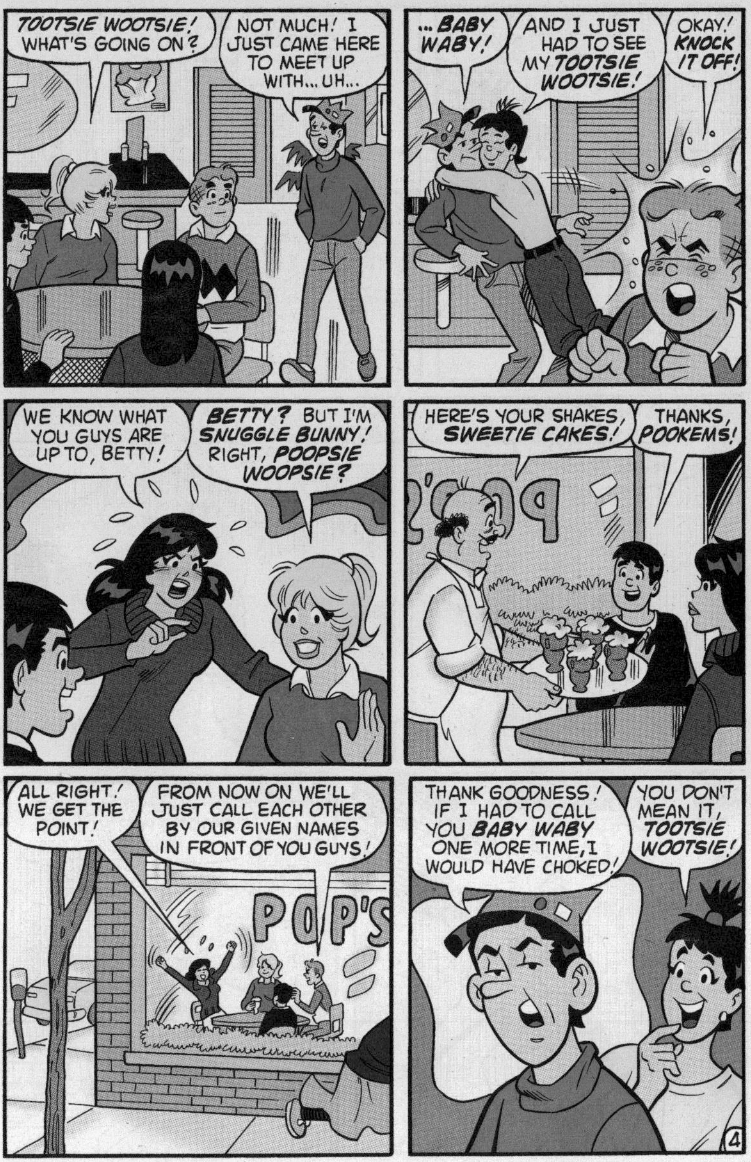

TOOTSIE WOOTSIE! WHAT'S GOING ON?
NOT MUCH! I JUST CAME HERE TO MEET UP WITH... UH...
...BABY WABY!
AND I JUST HAD TO SEE MY TOOTSIE WOOTSIE!
OKAY! KNOCK IT OFF!
WE KNOW WHAT YOU GUYS ARE UP TO, BETTY!
BETTY? BUT I'M SNUGGLE BUNNY! RIGHT, POOPSIE WOOPSIE?
HERE'S YOUR SHAKES, SWEETIE CAKES!
THANKS, POOKEMS!
POP'S
ALL RIGHT! WE GET THE POINT!
FROM NOW ON WE'LL JUST CALL EACH OTHER BY OUR GIVEN NAMES IN FRONT OF YOU GUYS!
POP'S
THANK GOODNESS! IF I HAD TO CALL YOU BABY WABY ONE MORE TIME, I WOULD HAVE CHOKED!
YOU DON'T MEAN IT, TOOTSIE WOOTSIE!
4

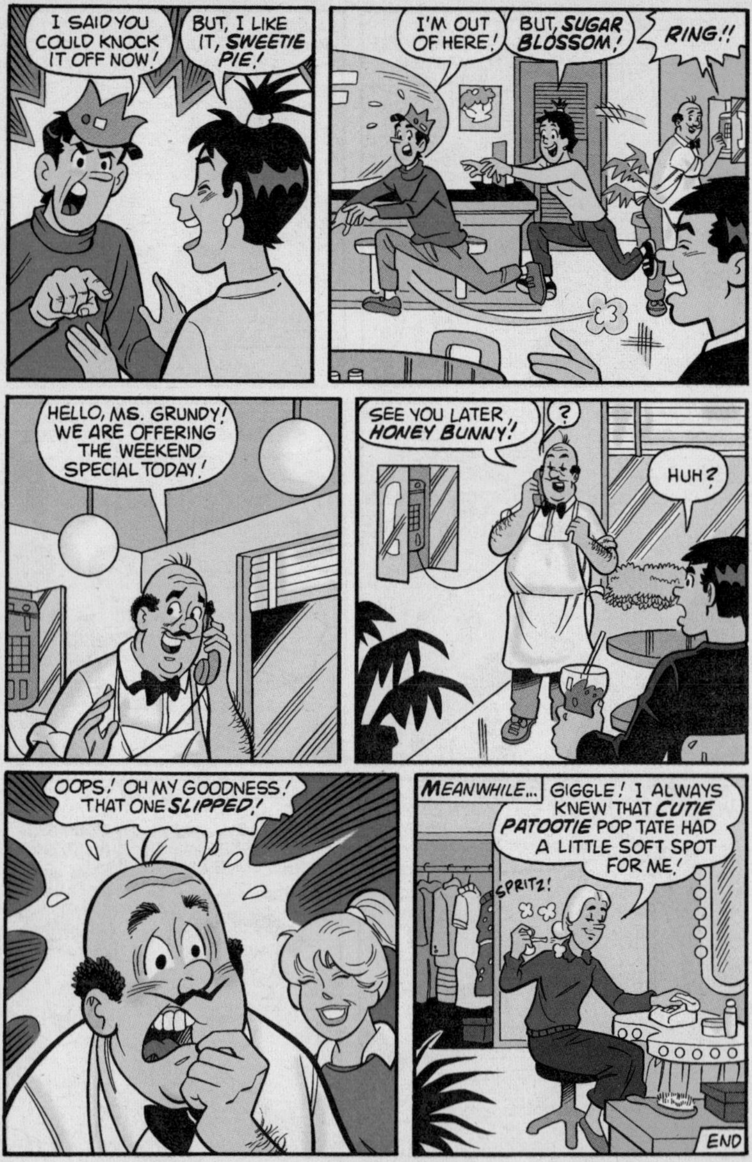
I SAID YOU COULD KNOCK IT OFF NOW!
BUT, I LIKE IT, SWEETIE PIE!
I'M OUT OF HERE!
BUT, SUGAR BLOSSOM!
RING!!
HELLO, MS. GRUNDY! WE ARE OFFERING THE WEEKEND SPECIAL TODAY!
SEE YOU LATER, HONEY BUNNY!
?
HUH?
OOPS! OH MY GOODNESS! THAT ONE SLIPPED!
MEANWHILE...
GIGGLE! I ALWAYS KNEW THAT CUTIE PATOOTIE POP TATE HAD A LITTLE SOFT SPOT FOR ME!
SPRITZ!
END

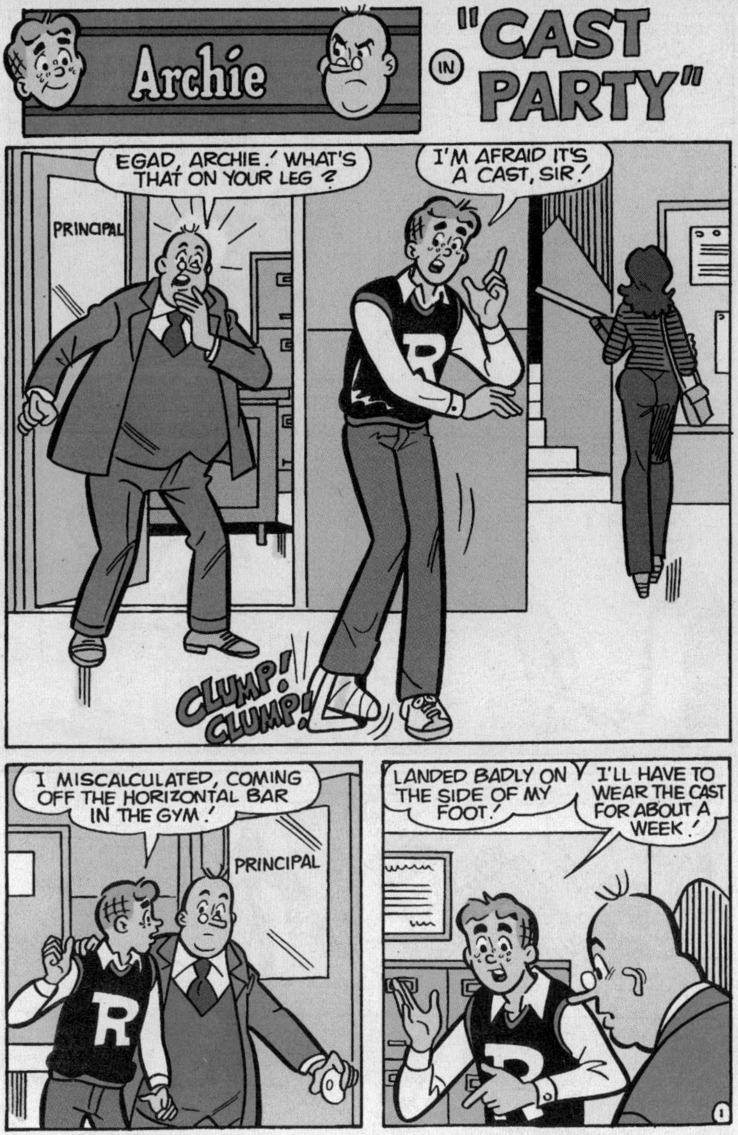
Archie
IN
"CAST PARTY"
EGAD, ARCHIE! WHAT'S THAT ON YOUR LEG ?
I'M AFRAID IT'S A CAST, SIR!
PRINCIPAL
CLUMP! CLUMP!
I MISCALCULATED, COMING OFF THE HORIZONTAL BAR IN THE GYM!
PRINCIPAL
LANDED BADLY ON THE SIDE OF MY FOOT!
I'LL HAVE TO WEAR THE CAST FOR ABOUT A WEEK!
1

Script: George Gladir / Pencils: Stan Goldberg / Inks: Rudy Lapick / Letters: Bill Yoshida

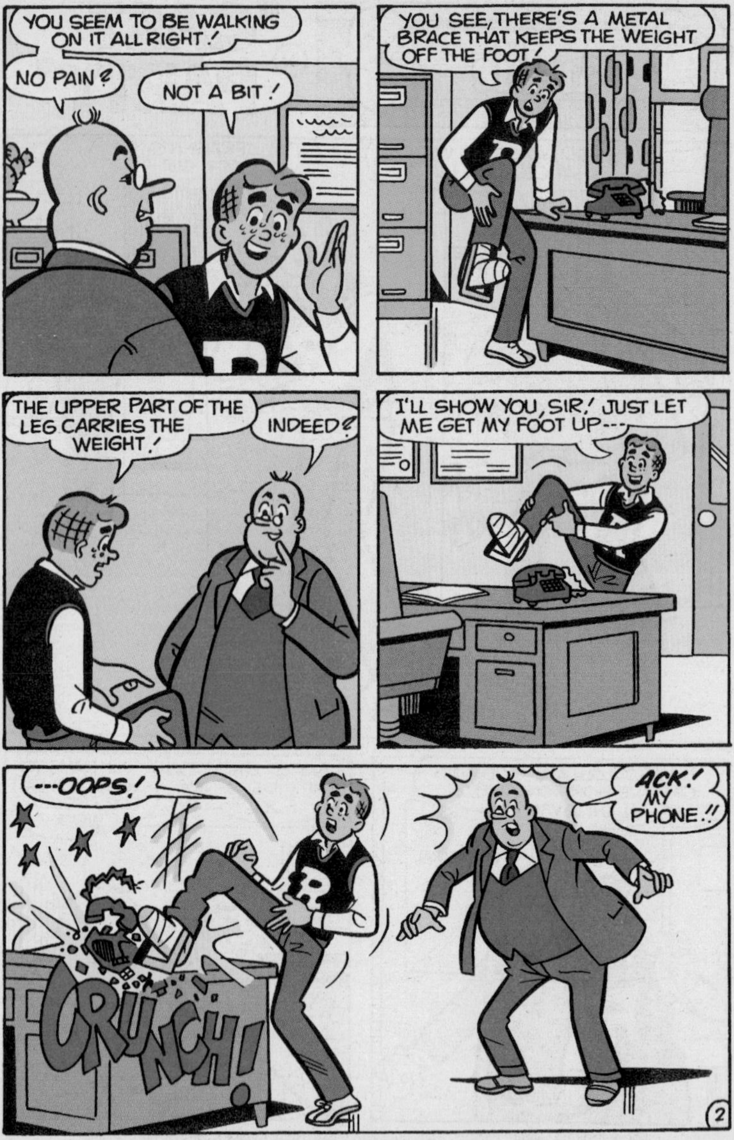
YOU SEEM TO BE WALKING ON IT ALL RIGHT!
NO PAIN?
NOT A BIT!
YOU SEE, THERE'S A METAL BRACE THAT KEEPS THE WEIGHT OFF THE FOOT!
THE UPPER PART OF THE LEG CARRIES THE WEIGHT!
INDEED?
I'LL SHOW YOU, SIR! JUST LET ME GET MY FOOT UP---
---OOPS!
ACK! MY PHONE!!
CRUNCH!
2

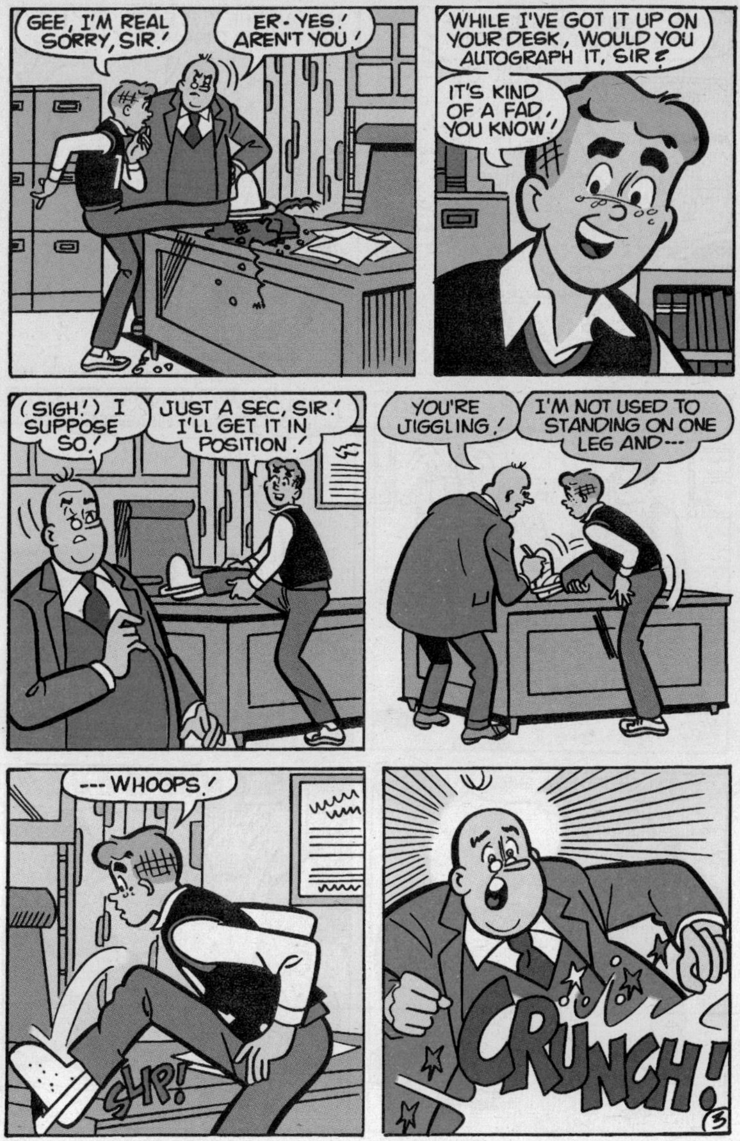
GEE, I'M REAL SORRY, SIR!
ER-YES! AREN'T YOU!
WHILE I'VE GOT IT UP ON YOUR DESK, WOULD YOU AUTOGRAPH IT, SIR?
IT'S KIND OF A FAD, YOU KNOW!
(SIGH!) I SUPPOSE SO!
JUST A SEC, SIR! I'LL GET IT IN POSITION!
YOU'RE JIGGLING!
I'M NOT USED TO STANDING ON ONE LEG AND---
---WHOOPS!
SLIP!
CRUNCH!
3

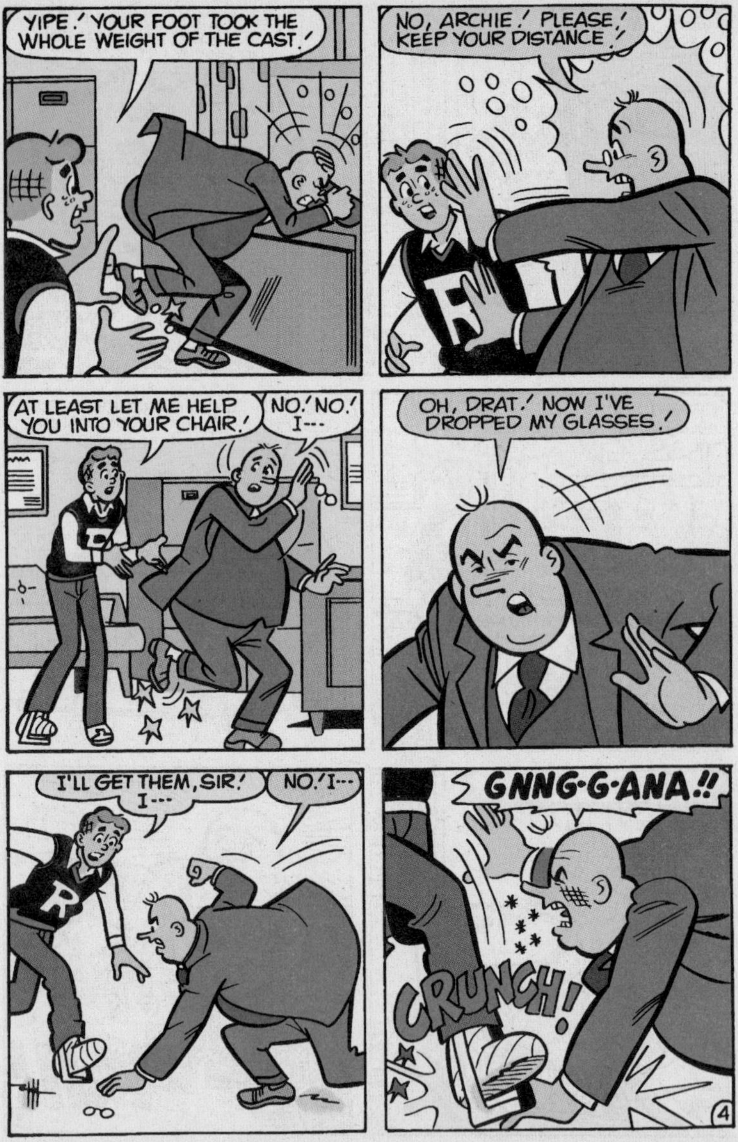
YIPE! YOUR FOOT TOOK THE WHOLE WEIGHT OF THE CAST!
NO, ARCHIE! PLEASE! KEEP YOUR DISTANCE!
AT LEAST LET ME HELP YOU INTO YOUR CHAIR!
NO! NO! I---
OH, DRAT! NOW I'VE DROPPED MY GLASSES!
I'LL GET THEM, SIR! I---
NO! I---
GNNG-G-ANA!!
CRUNCH!
4

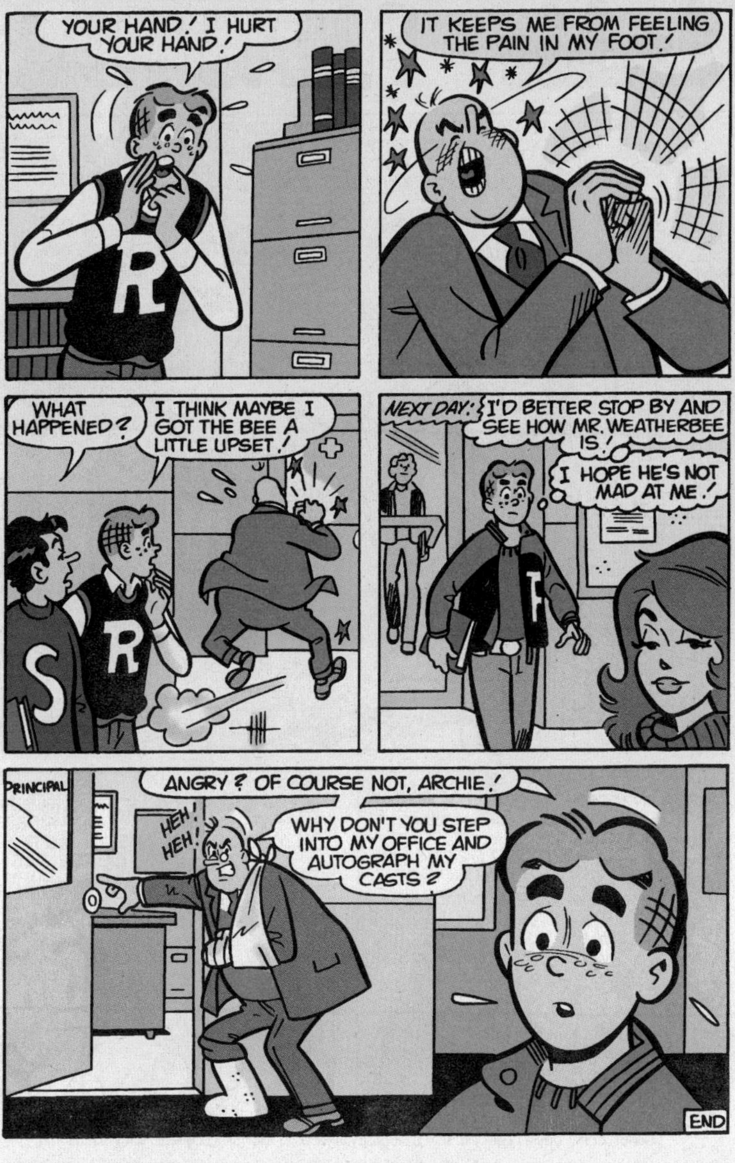

YOUR HAND! I HURT YOUR HAND!
IT KEEPS ME FROM FEELING THE PAIN IN MY FOOT!
WHAT HAPPENED?
I THINK MAYBE I GOT THE BEE A LITTLE UPSET!
NEXT DAY:
I'D BETTER STOP BY AND SEE HOW MR. WEATHERBEE IS!
I HOPE HE'S NOT MAD AT ME!
PRINCIPAL
ANGRY? OF COURSE NOT, ARCHIE!
HEH! HEH!
WHY DON'T YOU STEP INTO MY OFFICE AND AUTOGRAPH MY CASTS?
END

Archie in PRIME TIME

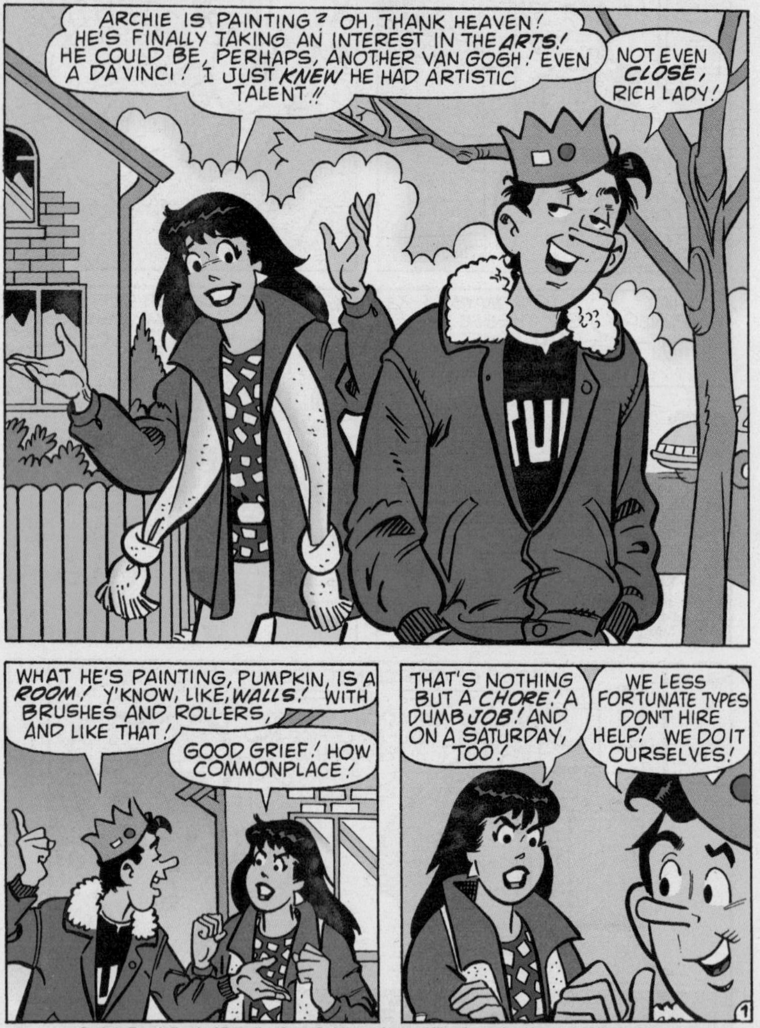
ARCHIE IS PAINTING? OH, THANK HEAVEN! HE'S FINALLY TAKING AN INTEREST IN THE ARTS! HE COULD BE, PERHAPS, ANOTHER VAN GOGH! EVEN A DA VINCI! I JUST KNEW HE HAD ARTISTIC TALENT!!
NOT EVEN CLOSE, RICH LADY!
WHAT HE'S PAINTING, PUMPKIN, IS A ROOM! Y'KNOW, LIKE, WALLS! WITH BRUSHES AND ROLLERS, AND LIKE THAT!
GOOD GRIEF! HOW COMMONPLACE!
THAT'S NOTHING BUT A CHORE! A DUMB JOB! AND ON A SATURDAY, TOO!
WE LESS FORTUNATE TYPES DON'T HIRE HELP! WE DO IT OURSELVES!
1

Script: Frank Doyle / Pencils: Stan Goldberg / Inks: Mike Esposito / Letters: Bill Yoshida

HEY, YOU TWO! WANT TO HAVE SOME GREAT FUN? COME ON IN AND HELP ME PAINT MY LIVING ROOM!

DIDN'T TOM SAWYER TRY THIS PLOY TO GET THE FENCE PAINTED?

HEY! DON'T KNOCK IT! I'VE GOT A NEAT IDEA!

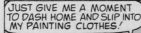

JUST GIVE ME A MOMENT TO DASH HOME AND SLIP INTO MY PAINTING CLOTHES!

YOU'RE TRYIN' TO CON US, RIGHT, PAL?

PERISH THE THOUGHT OL' BUDDY! PAINTING IS FUN!

OKAY! I'M READY IF YOU ARE!

IS THIS A PAINTING SESSION OR A FASHION SHOW?

JUST BECAUSE YOU'RE DOING MENIAL LABOR, IT DOESN'T MEAN YOU HAVE TO LOOK LIKE A SLOB!

2

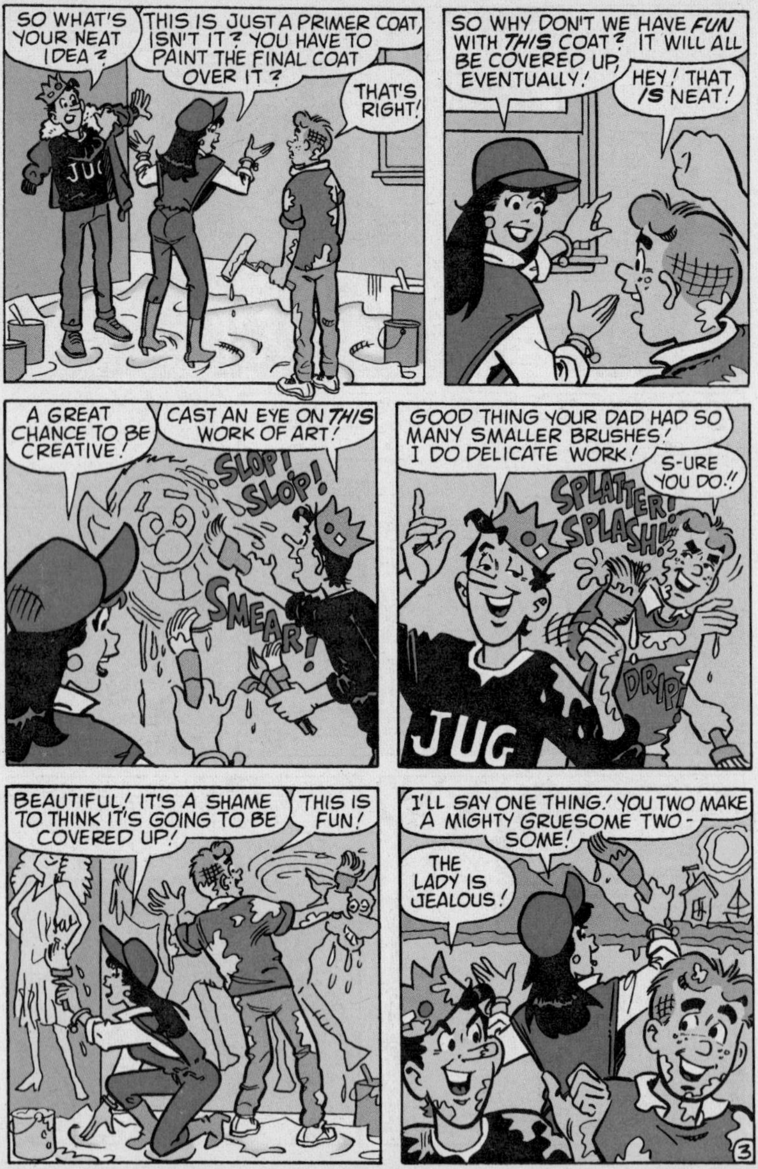
SO WHAT'S YOUR NEAT IDEA?
THIS IS JUST A PRIMER COAT, ISN'T IT? YOU HAVE TO PAINT THE FINAL COAT OVER IT?
THAT'S RIGHT!
JUG
SO WHY DON'T WE HAVE FUN WITH THIS COAT? IT WILL ALL BE COVERED UP, EVENTUALLY!
HEY! THAT IS NEAT!
A GREAT CHANCE TO BE CREATIVE!
CAST AN EYE ON THIS WORK OF ART!
SLOP! SLOP!
SMEAR!
GOOD THING YOUR DAD HAD SO MANY SMALLER BRUSHES! I DO DELICATE WORK!
S-URE YOU DO!!
SPLATTER! SPLASH!
JUG
DRIP!
BEAUTIFUL! IT'S A SHAME TO THINK IT'S GOING TO BE COVERED UP!
THIS IS FUN!
I'LL SAY ONE THING! YOU TWO MAKE A MIGHTY GRUESOME TWO-SOME!
THE LADY IS JEALOUS!
3

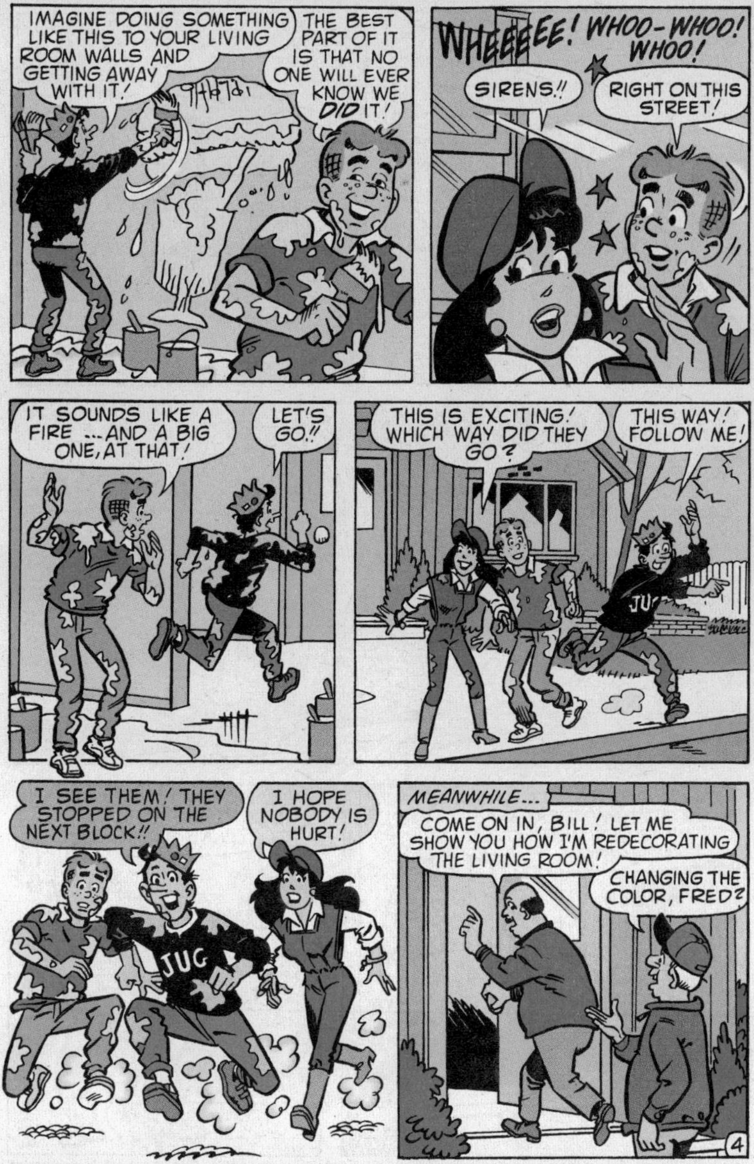
IMAGINE DOING SOMETHING LIKE THIS TO YOUR LIVING ROOM WALLS AND GETTING AWAY WITH IT!
THE BEST PART OF IT IS THAT NO ONE WILL EVER KNOW WE DID IT!
WHEEEEEE! WHOO-WHOO! WHOO!
SIRENS!!
RIGHT ON THIS STREET!
IT SOUNDS LIKE A FIRE ...AND A BIG ONE, AT THAT!
LET'S GO!!
THIS IS EXCITING! WHICH WAY DID THEY GO?
THIS WAY! FOLLOW ME!
JUG
I SEE THEM! THEY STOPPED ON THE NEXT BLOCK!!
I HOPE NOBODY IS HURT!
JUG
MEANWHILE...
COME ON IN, BILL! LET ME SHOW YOU HOW I'M REDECORATING THE LIVING ROOM!
CHANGING THE COLOR, FRED?
4

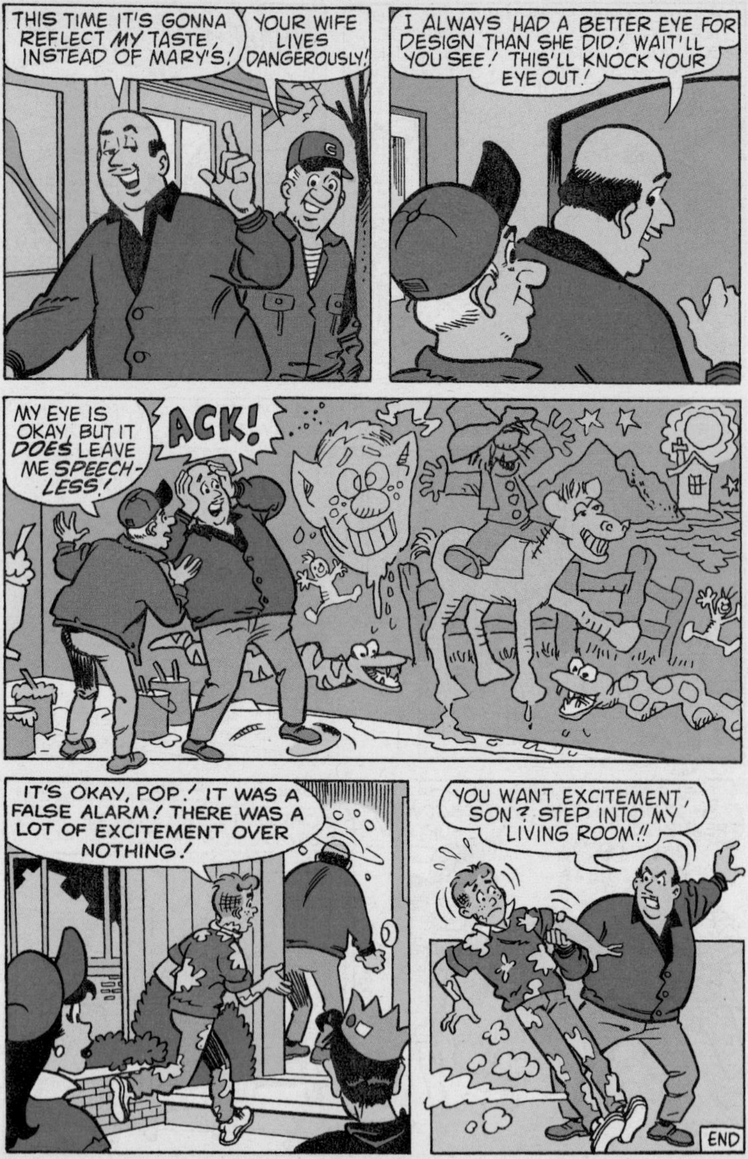
THIS TIME IT'S GONNA REFLECT MY TASTE, INSTEAD OF MARY'S!
YOUR WIFE LIVES DANGEROUSLY!
I ALWAYS HAD A BETTER EYE FOR DESIGN THAN SHE DID! WAIT'LL YOU SEE! THIS'LL KNOCK YOUR EYE OUT!
MY EYE IS OKAY, BUT IT DOES LEAVE ME SPEECH-LESS!
ACK!
IT'S OKAY, POP! IT WAS A FALSE ALARM! THERE WAS A LOT OF EXCITEMENT OVER NOTHING!
YOU WANT EXCITEMENT, SON? STEP INTO MY LIVING ROOM!!
END

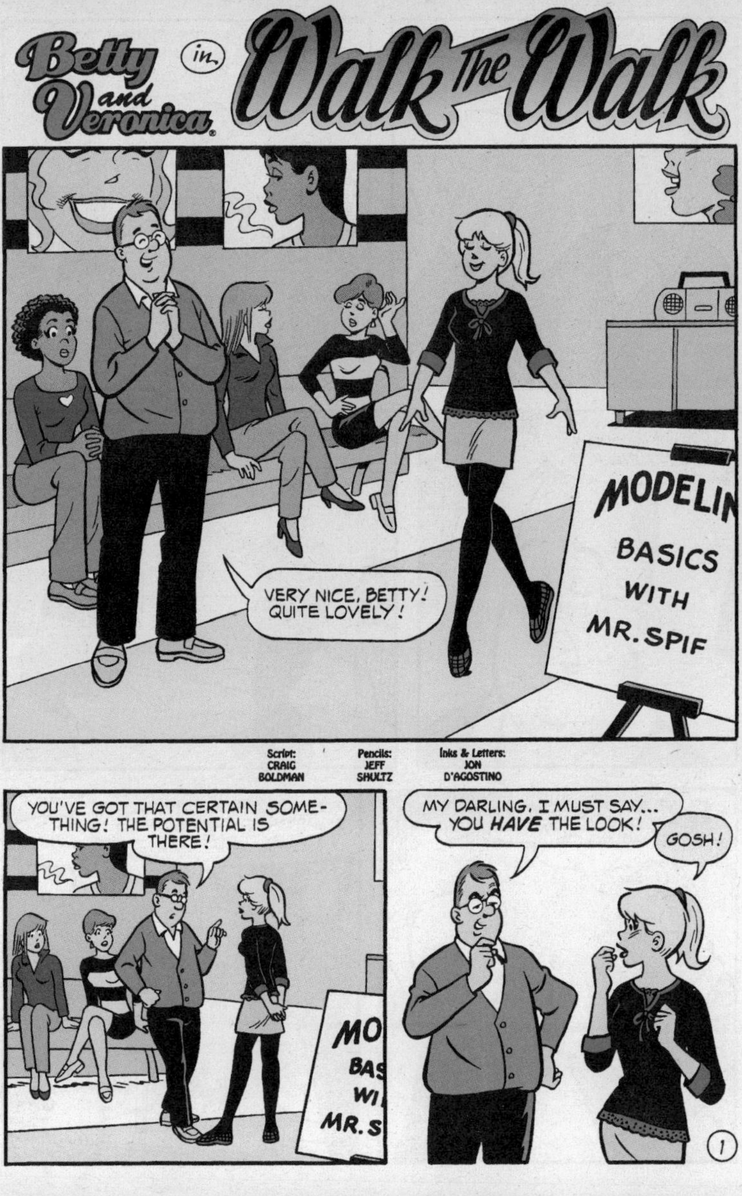

Betty and Veronica in Walk The Walk
MODELIN
BASICS
WITH
MR. SPIF
VERY NICE, BETTY! QUITE LOVELY!
Script: CRAIG BOLDMAN
Pencils: JEFF SHULTZ
Inks & Letters: JON D'AGOSTINO
YOU'VE GOT THAT CERTAIN SOME-THING! THE POTENTIAL IS THERE!
MO
BAS
WI
MR. S
MY DARLING, I MUST SAY... YOU *HAVE* THE LOOK!
GOSH!

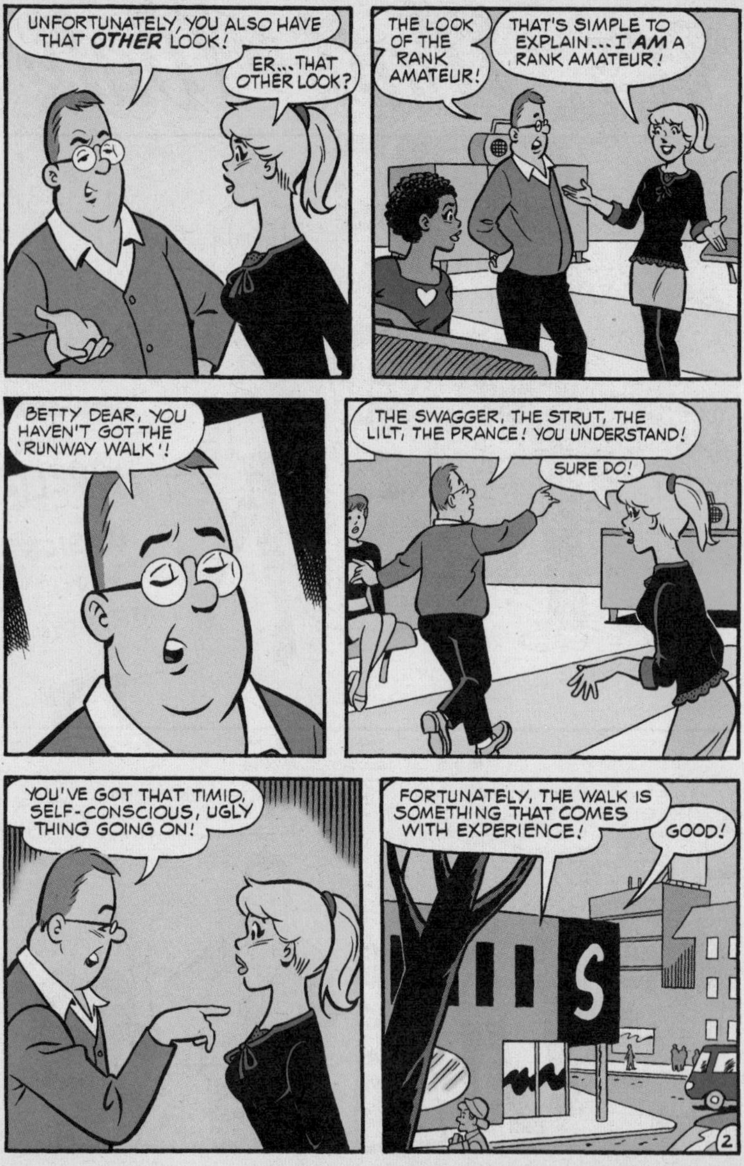

UNFORTUNATELY, YOU ALSO HAVE THAT OTHER LOOK!
ER...THAT OTHER LOOK?
THE LOOK OF THE RANK AMATEUR!
THAT'S SIMPLE TO EXPLAIN... I AM A RANK AMATEUR!
BETTY DEAR, YOU HAVEN'T GOT THE 'RUNWAY WALK'!
THE SWAGGER, THE STRUT, THE LILT, THE PRANCE! YOU UNDERSTAND!
SURE DO!
YOU'VE GOT THAT TIMID, SELF-CONSCIOUS, UGLY THING GOING ON!
FORTUNATELY, THE WALK IS SOMETHING THAT COMES WITH EXPERIENCE!
GOOD!
S
2

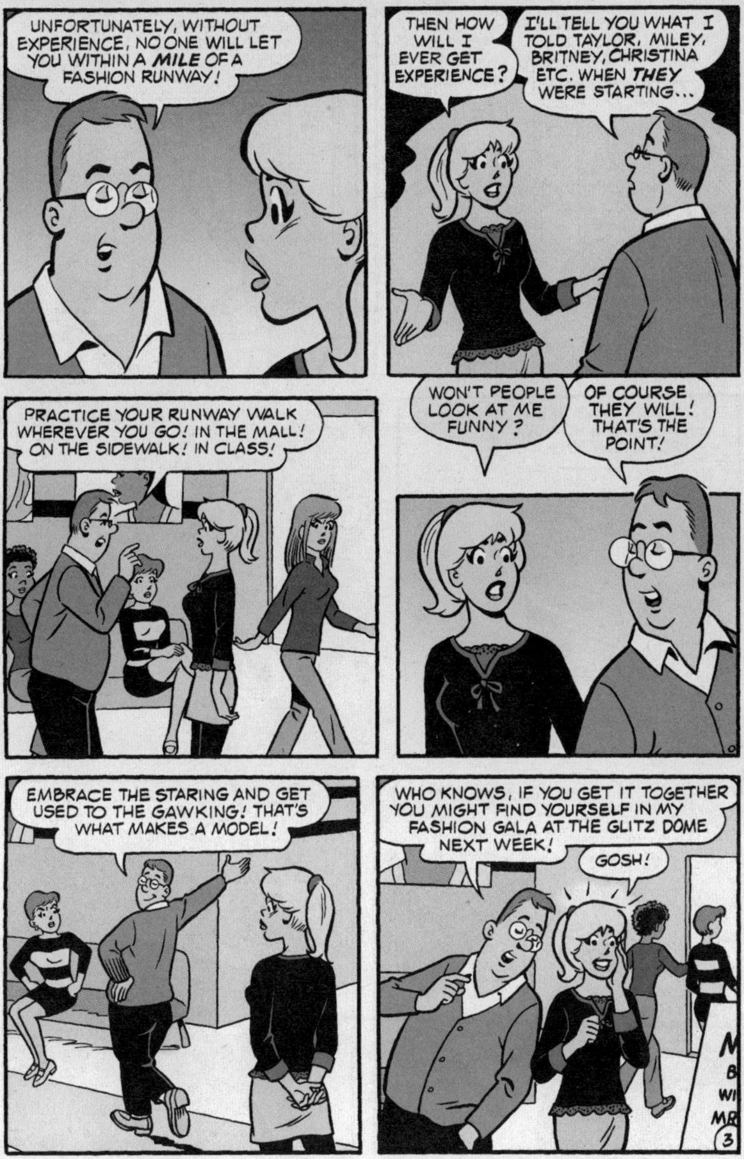

UNFORTUNATELY, WITHOUT EXPERIENCE, NO ONE WILL LET YOU WITHIN A **MILE** OF A FASHION RUNWAY!
THEN HOW WILL I EVER GET EXPERIENCE?
I'LL TELL YOU WHAT I TOLD TAYLOR, MILEY, BRITNEY, CHRISTINA ETC. WHEN **THEY** WERE STARTING...
PRACTICE YOUR RUNWAY WALK WHEREVER YOU GO! IN THE MALL! ON THE SIDEWALK! IN CLASS!
WON'T PEOPLE LOOK AT ME FUNNY?
OF COURSE THEY WILL! THAT'S THE POINT!
EMBRACE THE STARING AND GET USED TO THE GAWKING! THAT'S WHAT MAKES A MODEL!
WHO KNOWS, IF YOU GET IT TOGETHER YOU MIGHT FIND YOURSELF IN MY FASHION GALA AT THE GLITZ DOME NEXT WEEK!
GOSH!

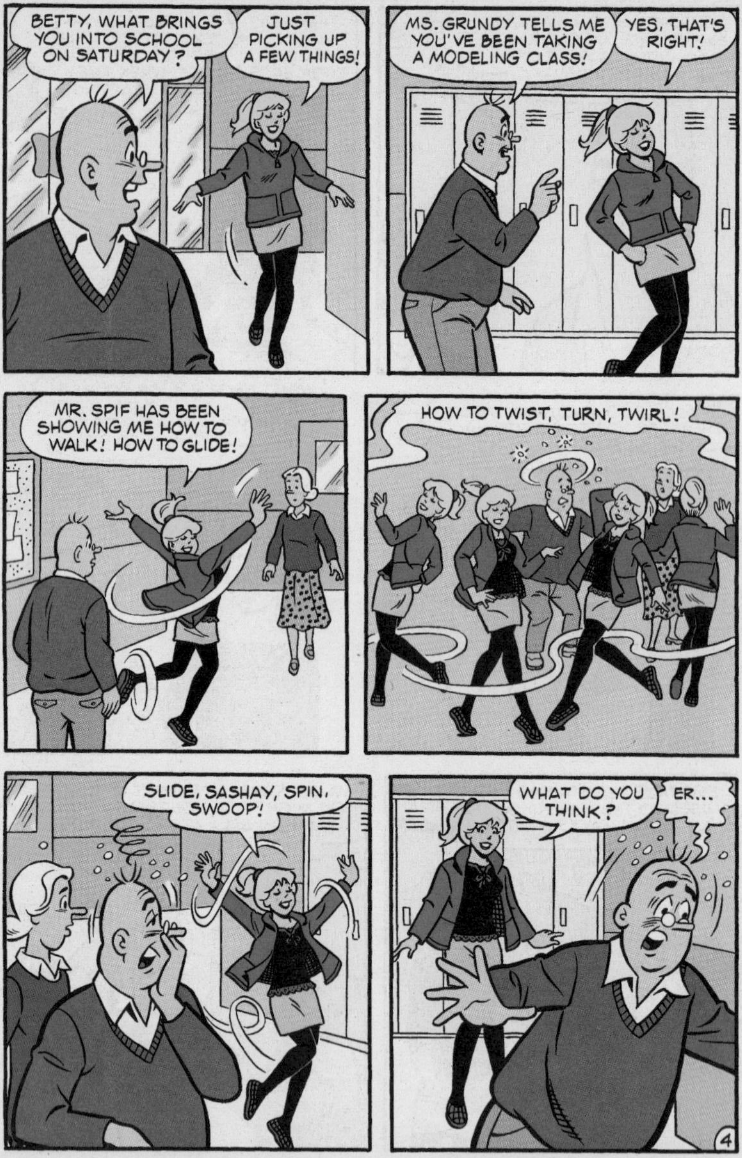
BETTY, WHAT BRINGS YOU INTO SCHOOL ON SATURDAY?
JUST PICKING UP A FEW THINGS!
MS. GRUNDY TELLS ME YOU'VE BEEN TAKING A MODELING CLASS!
YES, THAT'S RIGHT!
MR. SPIF HAS BEEN SHOWING ME HOW TO WALK! HOW TO GLIDE!
HOW TO TWIST, TURN, TWIRL!
SLIDE, SASHAY, SPIN, SWOOP!
WHAT DO YOU THINK?
ER...
4

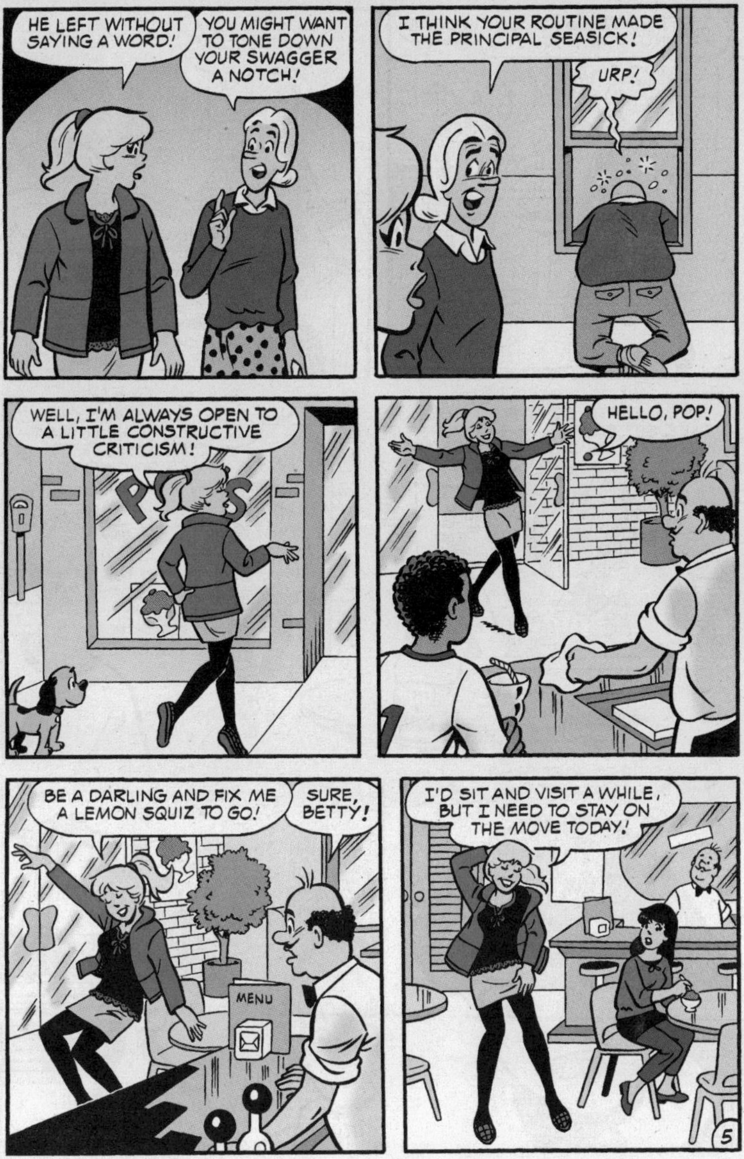
HE LEFT WITHOUT SAYING A WORD!
YOU MIGHT WANT TO TONE DOWN YOUR SWAGGER A NOTCH!
I THINK YOUR ROUTINE MADE THE PRINCIPAL SEASICK!
URP!
WELL, I'M ALWAYS OPEN TO A LITTLE CONSTRUCTIVE CRITICISM!
HELLO, POP!
BE A DARLING AND FIX ME A LEMON SQUIZ TO GO!
SURE, BETTY!
MENU
I'D SIT AND VISIT A WHILE, BUT I NEED TO STAY ON THE MOVE TODAY!
5

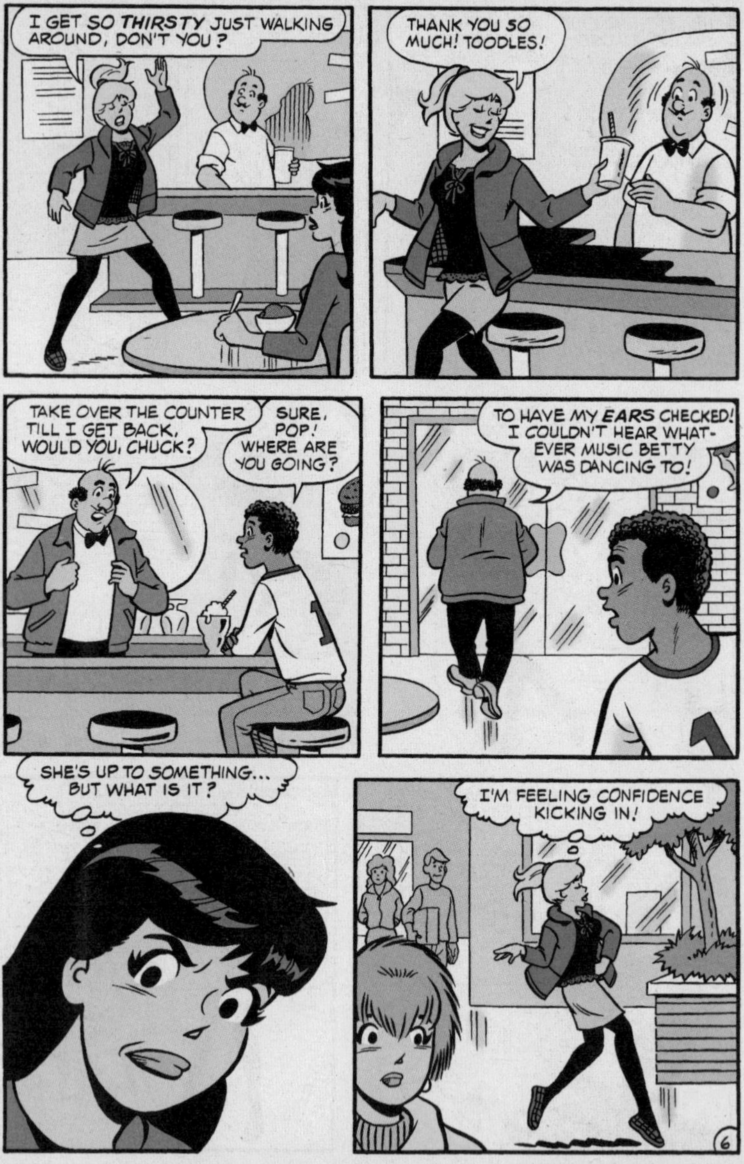
I GET SO THIRSTY JUST WALKING AROUND, DON'T YOU?
THANK YOU SO MUCH! TOODLES!
TAKE OVER THE COUNTER TILL I GET BACK, WOULD YOU, CHUCK?
SURE, POP! WHERE ARE YOU GOING?
TO HAVE MY EARS CHECKED! I COULDN'T HEAR WHATEVER MUSIC BETTY WAS DANCING TO!
SHE'S UP TO SOMETHING... BUT WHAT IS IT?
I'M FEELING CONFIDENCE KICKING IN!
6

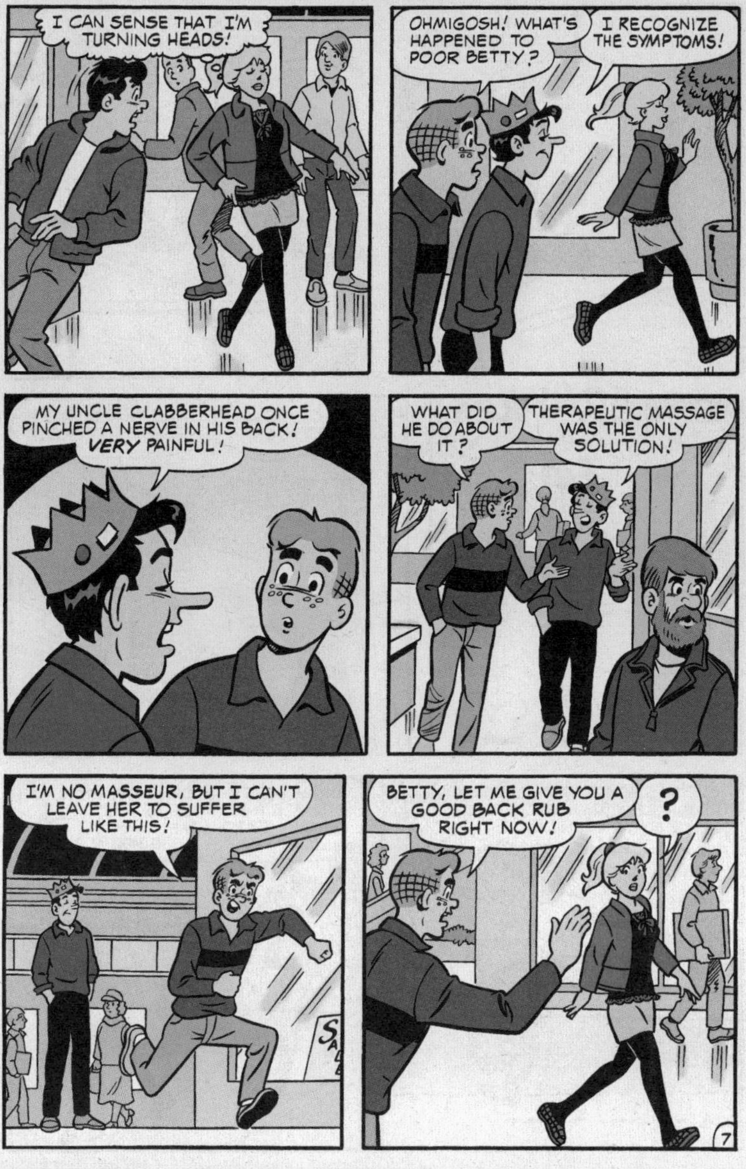
I CAN SENSE THAT I'M TURNING HEADS!
OHMIGOSH! WHAT'S HAPPENED TO POOR BETTY?
I RECOGNIZE THE SYMPTOMS!
MY UNCLE CLABBERHEAD ONCE PINCHED A NERVE IN HIS BACK! VERY PAINFUL!
WHAT DID HE DO ABOUT IT?
THERAPEUTIC MASSAGE WAS THE ONLY SOLUTION!
I'M NO MASSEUR, BUT I CAN'T LEAVE HER TO SUFFER LIKE THIS!
BETTY, LET ME GIVE YOU A GOOD BACK RUB RIGHT NOW!
?
7

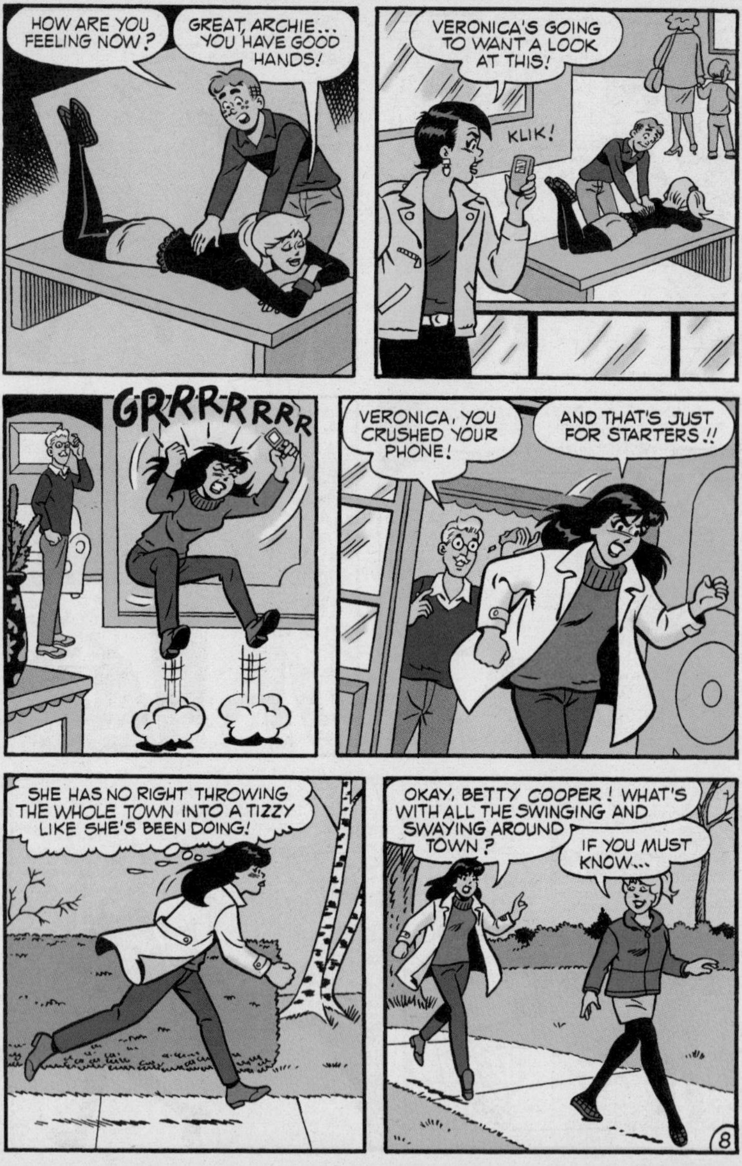
HOW ARE YOU FEELING NOW?
GREAT, ARCHIE... YOU HAVE GOOD HANDS!
VERONICA'S GOING TO WANT A LOOK AT THIS!
KLIK!
GRRRRRRRR
VERONICA, YOU CRUSHED YOUR PHONE!
AND THAT'S JUST FOR STARTERS!!
SHE HAS NO RIGHT THROWING THE WHOLE TOWN INTO A TIZZY LIKE SHE'S BEEN DOING!
OKAY, BETTY COOPER! WHAT'S WITH ALL THE SWINGING AND SWAYING AROUND TOWN?
IF YOU MUST KNOW...
8

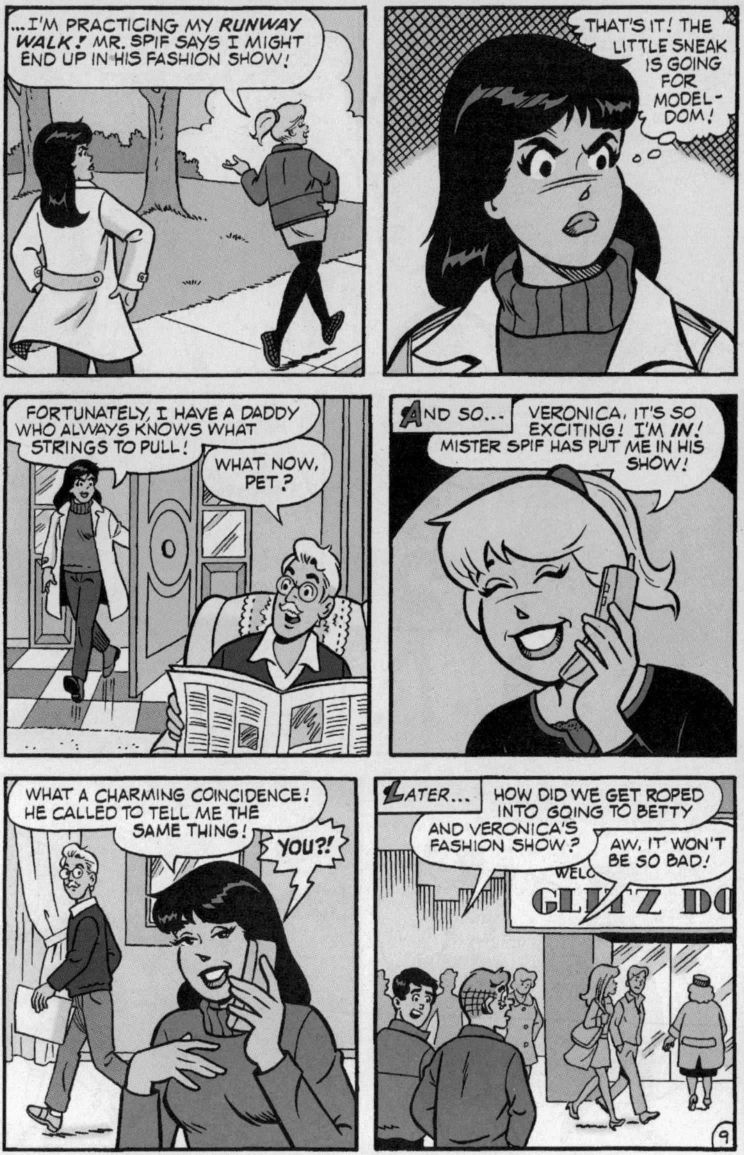
...I'M PRACTICING MY RUNWAY WALK! MR. SPIF SAYS I MIGHT END UP IN HIS FASHION SHOW!
THAT'S IT! THE LITTLE SNEAK IS GOING FOR MODEL-DOM!
FORTUNATELY, I HAVE A DADDY WHO ALWAYS KNOWS WHAT STRINGS TO PULL!
WHAT NOW, PET?
AND SO...
VERONICA, IT'S SO EXCITING! I'M IN! MISTER SPIF HAS PUT ME IN HIS SHOW!
WHAT A CHARMING COINCIDENCE! HE CALLED TO TELL ME THE SAME THING!
YOU?!
LATER...
HOW DID WE GET ROPED INTO GOING TO BETTY AND VERONICA'S FASHION SHOW?
AW, IT WON'T BE SO BAD!
WELC
GLITZ DO

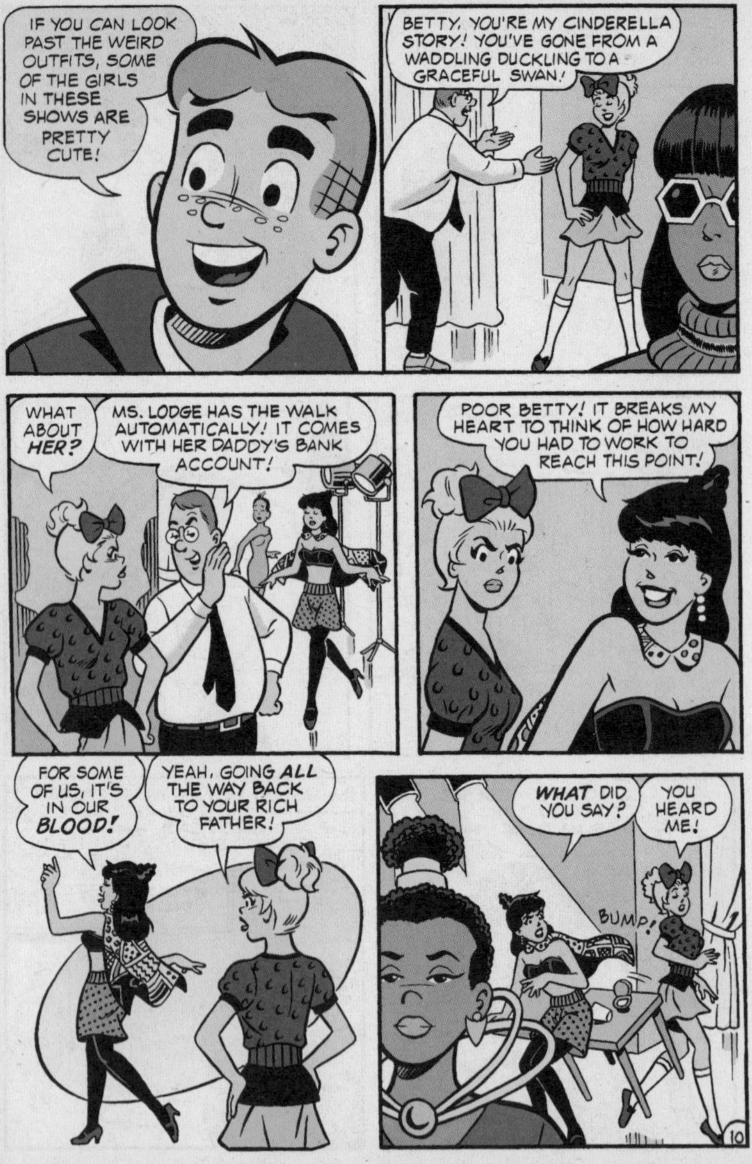
IF YOU CAN LOOK PAST THE WEIRD OUTFITS, SOME OF THE GIRLS IN THESE SHOWS ARE PRETTY CUTE!
BETTY, YOU'RE MY CINDERELLA STORY! YOU'VE GONE FROM A WADDLING DUCKLING TO A GRACEFUL SWAN!
WHAT ABOUT HER?
MS. LODGE HAS THE WALK AUTOMATICALLY! IT COMES WITH HER DADDY'S BANK ACCOUNT!
POOR BETTY! IT BREAKS MY HEART TO THINK OF HOW HARD YOU HAD TO WORK TO REACH THIS POINT!
FOR SOME OF US, IT'S IN OUR BLOOD!
YEAH, GOING ALL THE WAY BACK TO YOUR RICH FATHER!
WHAT DID YOU SAY?
YOU HEARD ME!
BUMP!
10

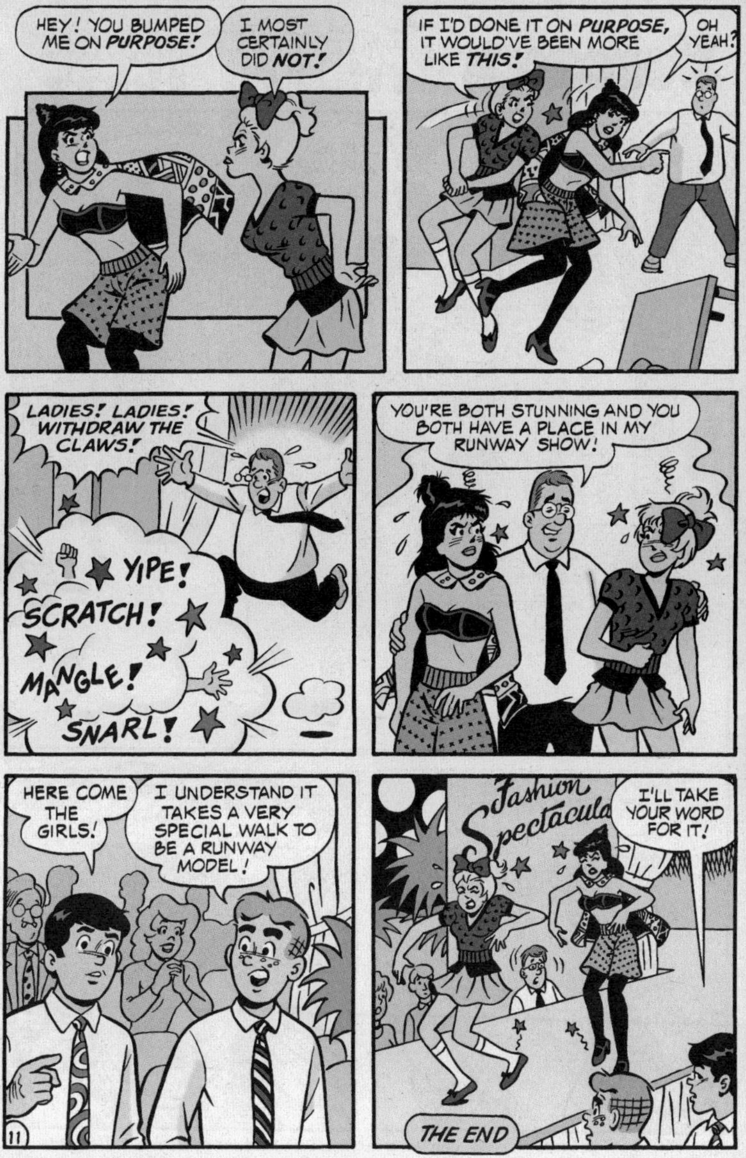
HEY! YOU BUMPED ME ON PURPOSE!
I MOST CERTAINLY DID NOT!
IF I'D DONE IT ON PURPOSE, IT WOULD'VE BEEN MORE LIKE THIS!
OH YEAH?
LADIES! LADIES! WITHDRAW THE CLAWS!
YIPE!
SCRATCH!
MANGLE!
SNARL!
YOU'RE BOTH STUNNING AND YOU BOTH HAVE A PLACE IN MY RUNWAY SHOW!
HERE COME THE GIRLS!
I UNDERSTAND IT TAKES A VERY SPECIAL WALK TO BE A RUNWAY MODEL!
Fashion Spectacula
I'LL TAKE YOUR WORD FOR IT!
THE END
11

Veronica in "PRESENT TENSE"

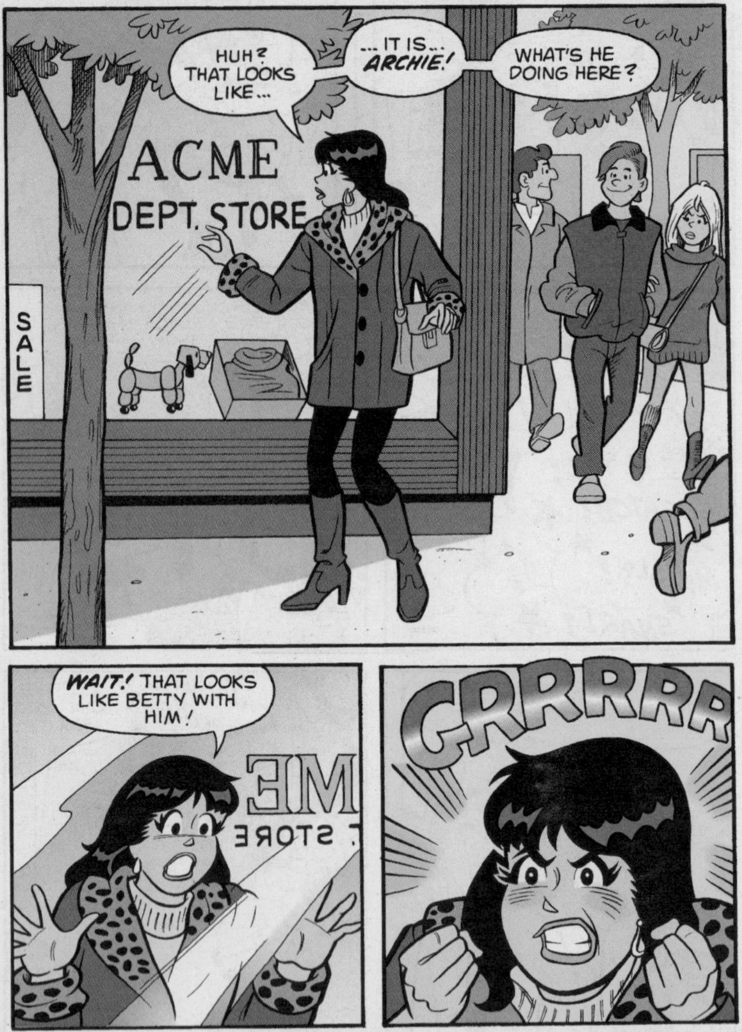
HUH? THAT LOOKS LIKE...
...IT IS... ARCHIE!
WHAT'S HE DOING HERE?
ACME
DEPT. STORE
SALE
WAIT! THAT LOOKS LIKE BETTY WITH HIM!
GRRRRR

Script: Joe Edwards / Pencils: Dan DeCarlo / Inks: Rich Koslowski / Letters: Bill Yoshida

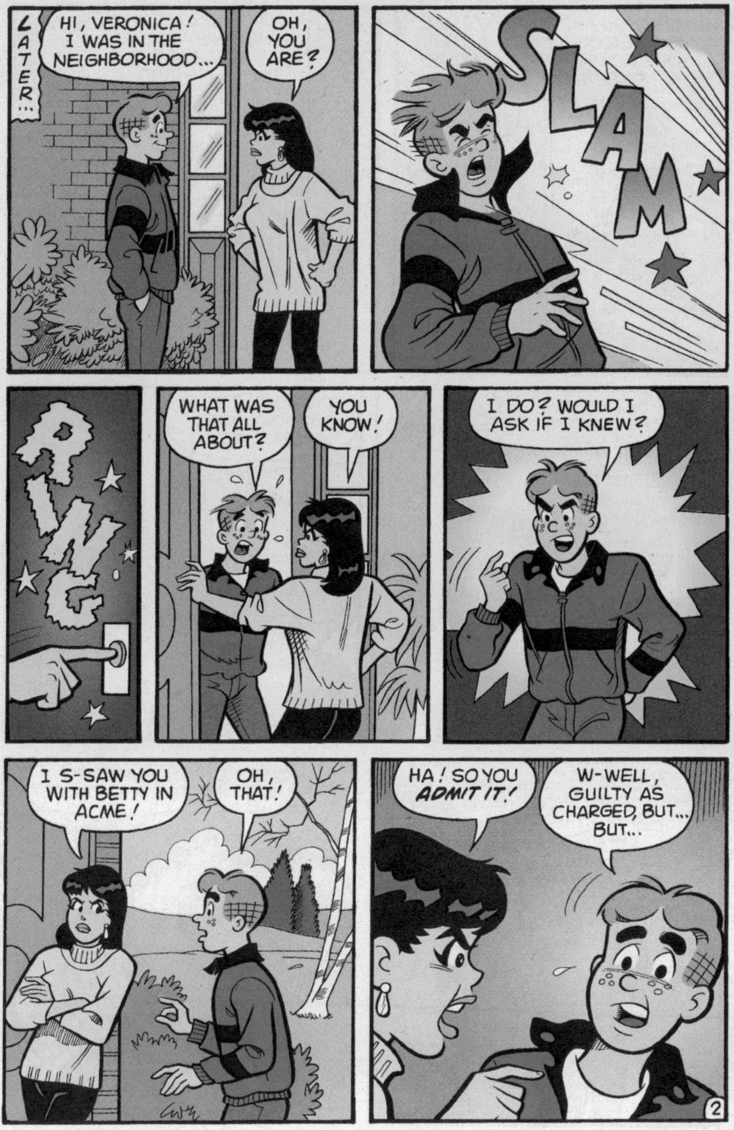
LATER...
HI, VERONICA! I WAS IN THE NEIGHBORHOOD...
OH, YOU ARE?
SLAM
RING
WHAT WAS THAT ALL ABOUT?
YOU KNOW!
I DO? WOULD I ASK IF I KNEW?
I S-SAW YOU WITH BETTY IN ACME!
OH, THAT!
HA! SO YOU ADMIT IT!
W-WELL, GUILTY AS CHARGED, BUT... BUT...
2

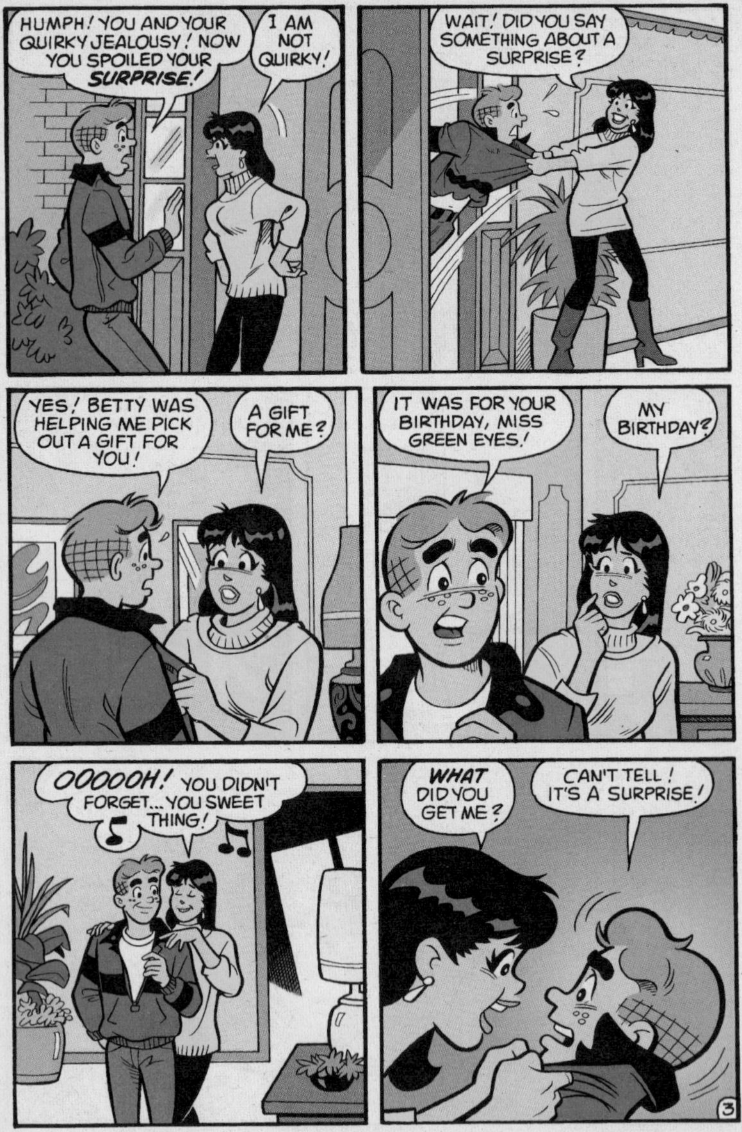
HUMPH! YOU AND YOUR QUIRKY JEALOUSY! NOW YOU SPOILED YOUR SURPRISE!
I AM NOT QUIRKY!
WAIT! DID YOU SAY SOMETHING ABOUT A SURPRISE?
YES! BETTY WAS HELPING ME PICK OUT A GIFT FOR YOU!
A GIFT FOR ME?
IT WAS FOR YOUR BIRTHDAY, MISS GREEN EYES!
MY BIRTHDAY?
OOOOOH! YOU DIDN'T FORGET... YOU SWEET THING!
WHAT DID YOU GET ME?
CAN'T TELL! IT'S A SURPRISE!
3

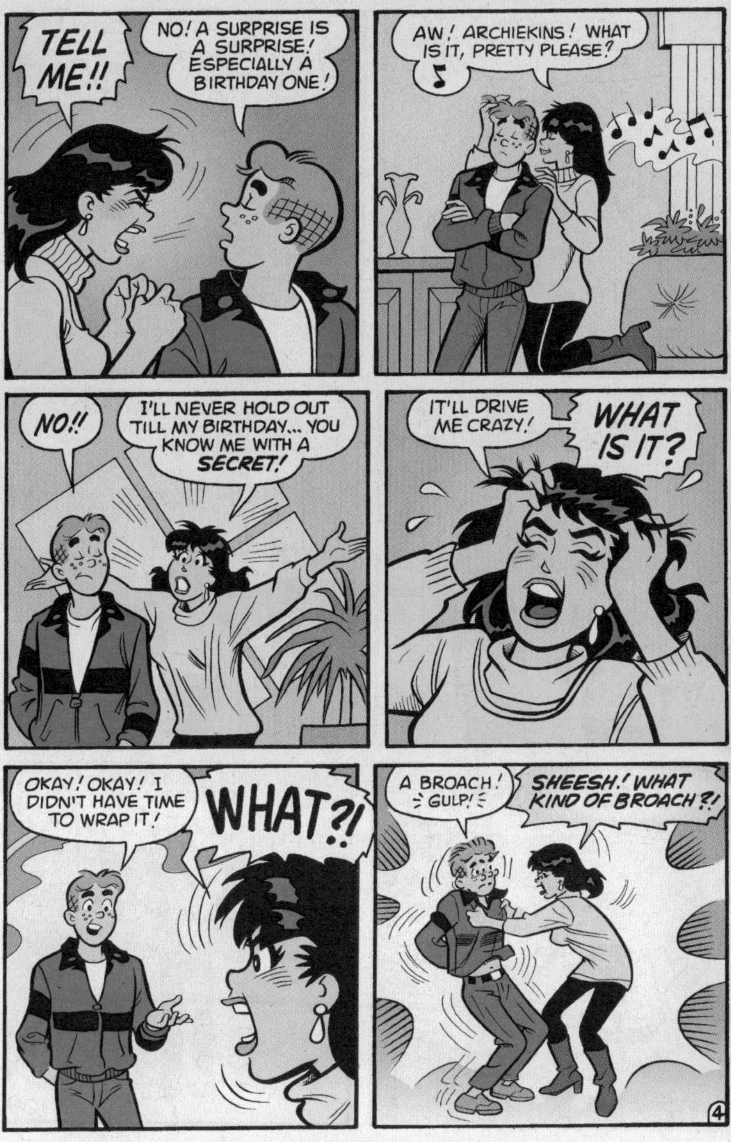
TELL ME!!
NO! A SURPRISE IS A SURPRISE! ESPECIALLY A BIRTHDAY ONE!
AW! ARCHIEKINS! WHAT IS IT, PRETTY PLEASE?
NO!!
I'LL NEVER HOLD OUT TILL MY BIRTHDAY... YOU KNOW ME WITH A SECRET!
IT'LL DRIVE ME CRAZY!
WHAT IS IT?
OKAY! OKAY! I DIDN'T HAVE TIME TO WRAP IT!
WHAT?!
A BROACH! GULP!
SHEESH! WHAT KIND OF BROACH?!
4

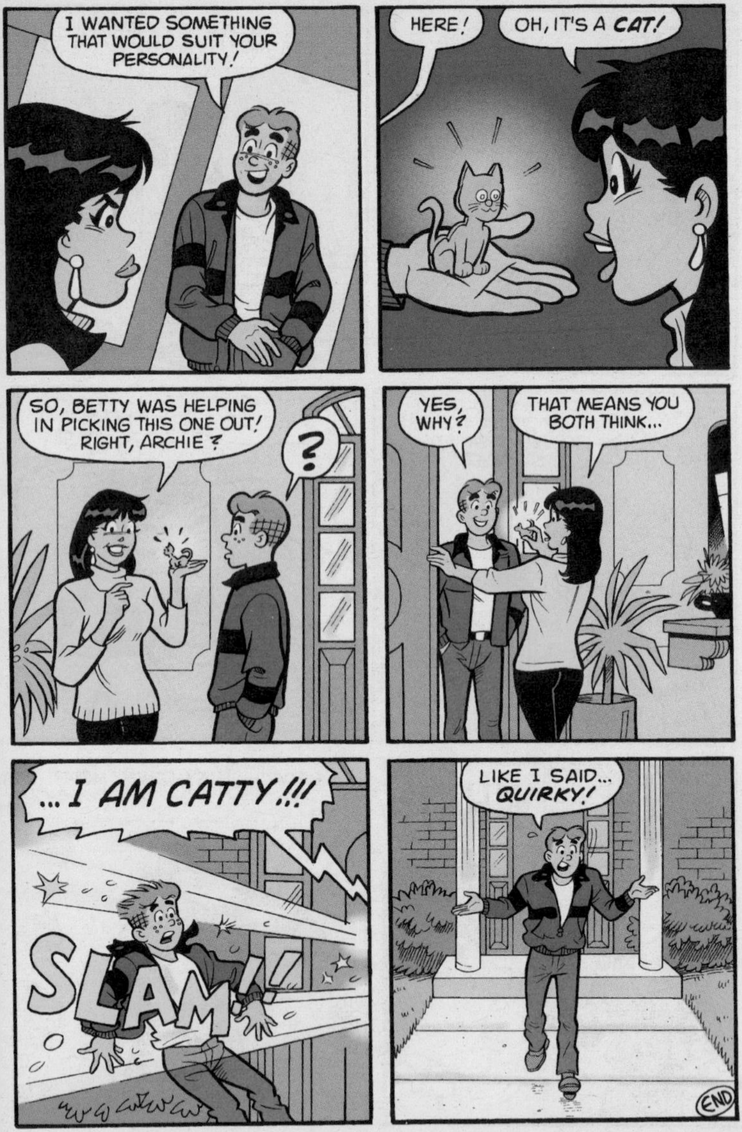
I WANTED SOMETHING THAT WOULD SUIT YOUR PERSONALITY!
HERE!
OH, IT'S A CAT!
SO, BETTY WAS HELPING IN PICKING THIS ONE OUT! RIGHT, ARCHIE?
?
YES, WHY?
THAT MEANS YOU BOTH THINK...
...I AM CATTY!!!
SLAM!!
LIKE I SAID... QUIRKY!
END

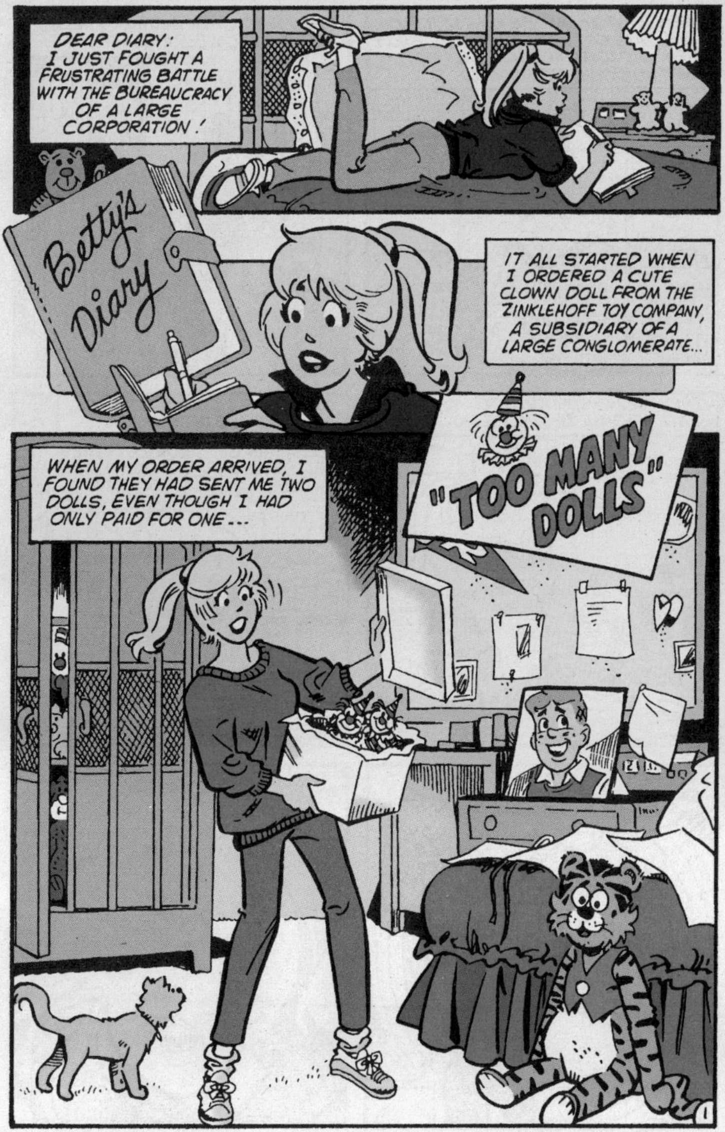
DEAR DIARY: I JUST FOUGHT A FRUSTRATING BATTLE WITH THE BUREAUCRACY OF A LARGE CORPORATION!
Betty's Diary
IT ALL STARTED WHEN I ORDERED A CUTE CLOWN DOLL FROM THE ZINKLEHOFF TOY COMPANY, A SUBSIDIARY OF A LARGE CONGLOMERATE...
"TOO MANY DOLLS"
WHEN MY ORDER ARRIVED, I FOUND THEY HAD SENT ME TWO DOLLS, EVEN THOUGH I HAD ONLY PAID FOR ONE...
1

Script: Hal Smith / Pencils: Stan Goldberg / Inks: Mike Esposito / Letters: Bill Yoshida

WELL, IT WOULDN'T BE HONEST TO TAKE ADVANTAGE OF THEIR ERROR, SO I WROTE THEM AND TOLD THEM THAT THEY SENT ME TWO DOLLS BY MISTAKE...

A FEW DAYS LATER ANOTHER PACKAGE ARRIVED FROM THE ZINKLEHOFF COMPANY...

THEY HAD MISUNDERSTOOD MY LETTER AND SENT ME TWO MORE DOLLS...

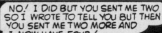

THIS TIME I DECIDED TO TRY CALLING THE COMPANY...

HELLO, THIS IS BETTY COOPER!

SORRY, THERE'S NO ONE HERE BY THAT NAME!

NO, NO, I'M BETTY COOPER! I ORDERED A CLOWN DOLL FROM YOU...

AND YOU HAVEN'T RECEIVED IT?

NO! I DID BUT YOU SENT ME TWO SO I WROTE TO TELL YOU BUT THEN YOU SENT ME TWO MORE AND I NOW HAVE FOUR!

I SEE...

2

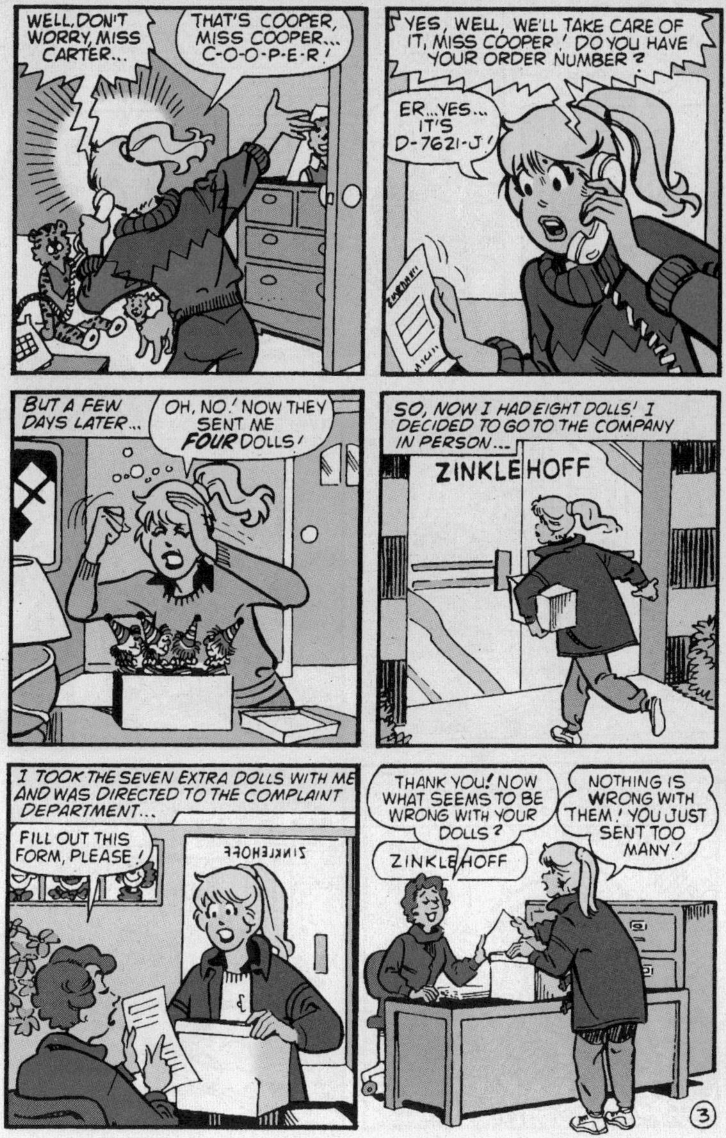
WELL, DON'T WORRY, MISS CARTER...
THAT'S COOPER, MISS COOPER... C-O-O-P-E-R!
YES, WELL, WE'LL TAKE CARE OF IT, MISS COOPER! DO YOU HAVE YOUR ORDER NUMBER?
ER...YES... IT'S D-7621-J!
BUT A FEW DAYS LATER...
OH, NO! NOW THEY SENT ME FOUR DOLLS!
SO, NOW I HAD EIGHT DOLLS! I DECIDED TO GO TO THE COMPANY IN PERSON...
ZINKLEHOFF
I TOOK THE SEVEN EXTRA DOLLS WITH ME AND WAS DIRECTED TO THE COMPLAINT DEPARTMENT...
FILL OUT THIS FORM, PLEASE!
ZINKLEHOFF
THANK YOU! NOW WHAT SEEMS TO BE WRONG WITH YOUR DOLLS?
ZINKLEHOFF
NOTHING IS WRONG WITH THEM! YOU JUST SENT TOO MANY!
3

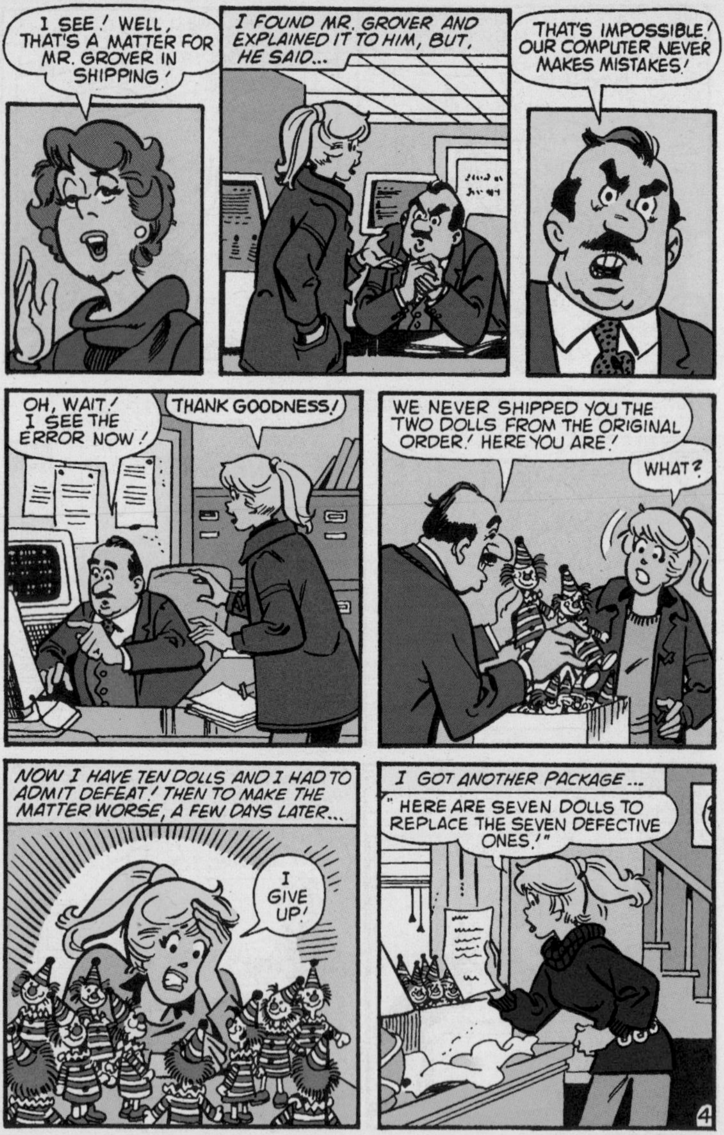
I SEE! WELL, THAT'S A MATTER FOR MR. GROVER IN SHIPPING!
I FOUND MR. GROVER AND EXPLAINED IT TO HIM, BUT, HE SAID...
THAT'S IMPOSSIBLE! OUR COMPUTER NEVER MAKES MISTAKES!
OH, WAIT! I SEE THE ERROR NOW!
THANK GOODNESS!
WE NEVER SHIPPED YOU THE TWO DOLLS FROM THE ORIGINAL ORDER! HERE YOU ARE!
WHAT?
NOW I HAVE TEN DOLLS AND I HAD TO ADMIT DEFEAT! THEN TO MAKE THE MATTER WORSE, A FEW DAYS LATER...
I GIVE UP!
I GOT ANOTHER PACKAGE...
" HERE ARE SEVEN DOLLS TO REPLACE THE SEVEN DEFECTIVE ONES!"
4

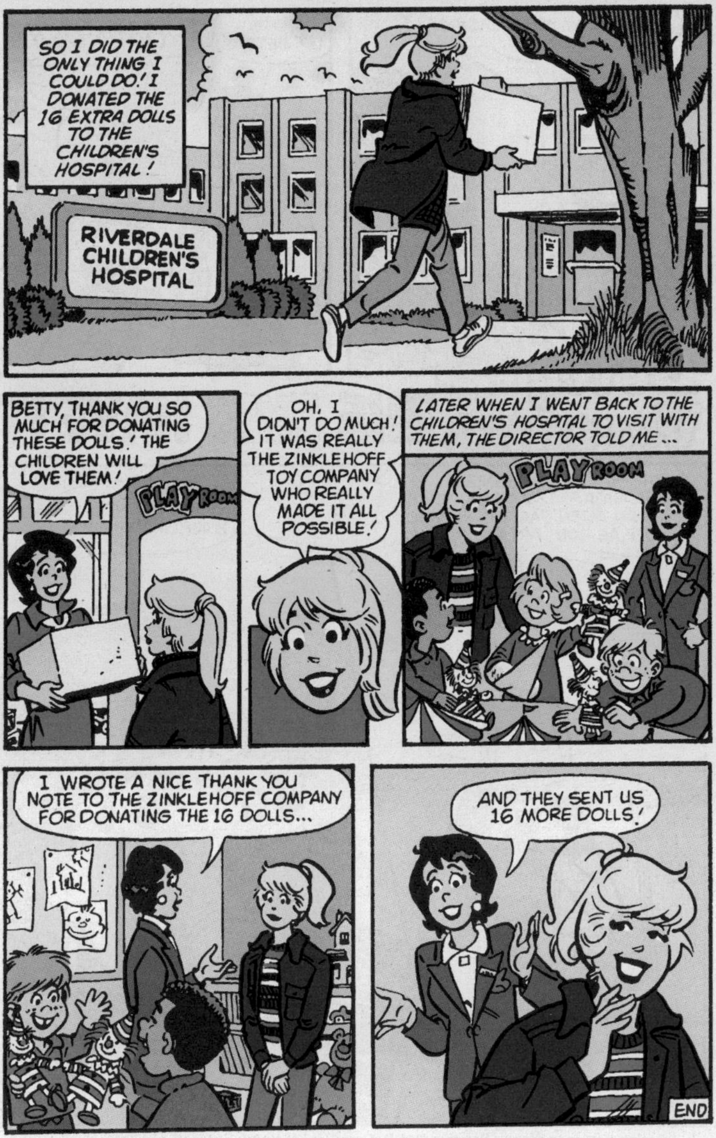
SO I DID THE ONLY THING I COULD DO! I DONATED THE 16 EXTRA DOLLS TO THE CHILDREN'S HOSPITAL!
RIVERDALE CHILDREN'S HOSPITAL
BETTY, THANK YOU SO MUCH FOR DONATING THESE DOLLS! THE CHILDREN WILL LOVE THEM!
PLAYROOM
OH, I DIDN'T DO MUCH! IT WAS REALLY THE ZINKLEHOFF TOY COMPANY WHO REALLY MADE IT ALL POSSIBLE!
LATER WHEN I WENT BACK TO THE CHILDREN'S HOSPITAL TO VISIT WITH THEM, THE DIRECTOR TOLD ME ...
PLAYROOM
I WROTE A NICE THANK YOU NOTE TO THE ZINKLEHOFF COMPANY FOR DONATING THE 16 DOLLS...
AND THEY SENT US 16 MORE DOLLS!
END

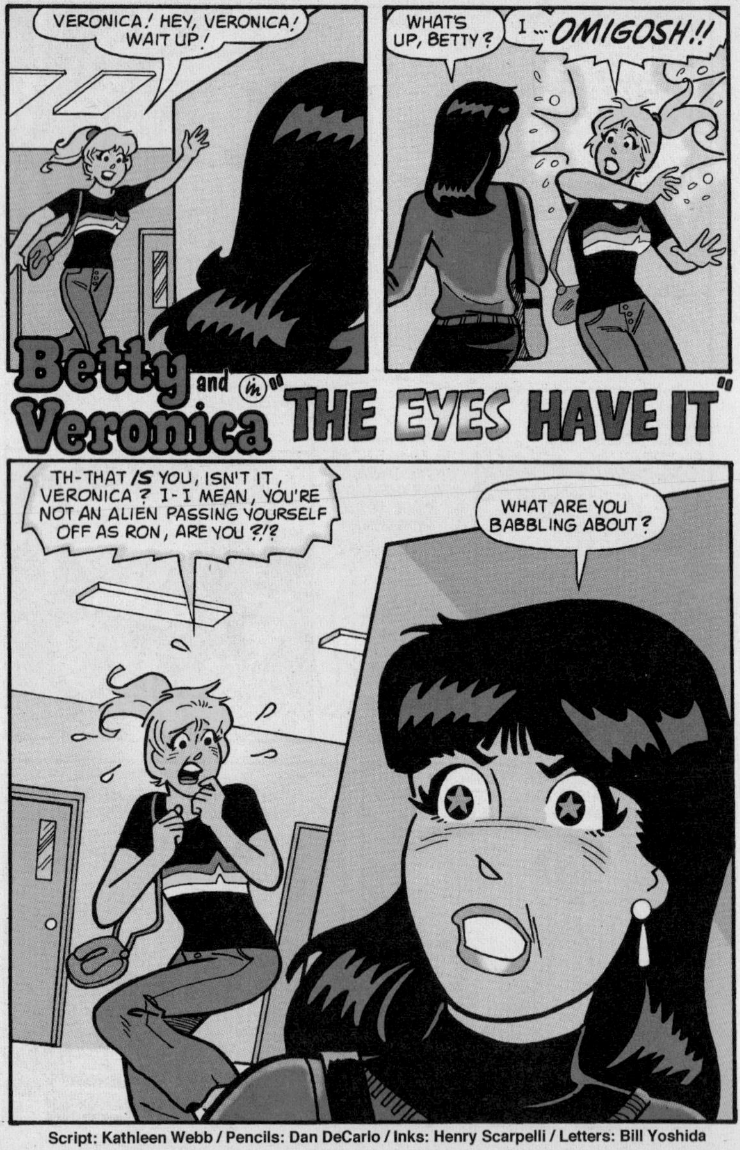
VERONICA! HEY, VERONICA! WAIT UP!
WHAT'S UP, BETTY?
I ... OMIGOSH!!
Betty and Veronica in "THE EYES HAVE IT"
TH-THAT IS YOU, ISN'T IT, VERONICA? I-I MEAN, YOU'RE NOT AN ALIEN PASSING YOURSELF OFF AS RON, ARE YOU?!?
WHAT ARE YOU BABBLING ABOUT?

Script: Kathleen Webb / Pencils: Dan DeCarlo / Inks: Henry Scarpelli / Letters: Bill Yoshida

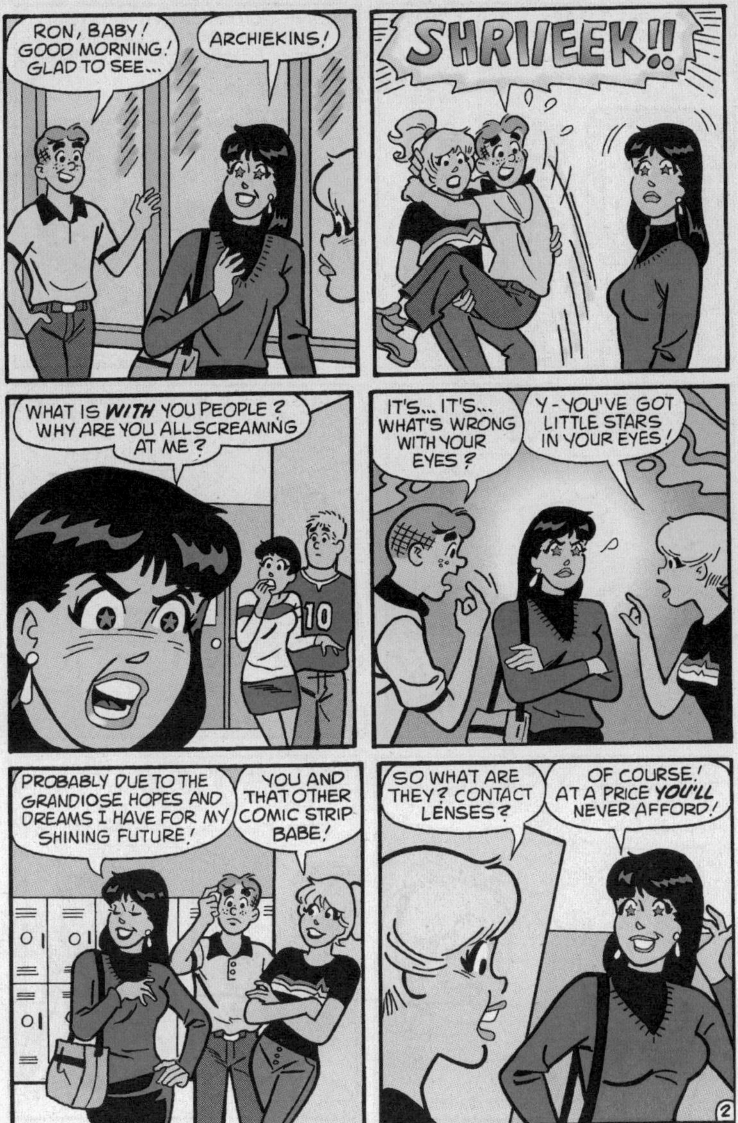
RON, BABY! GOOD MORNING! GLAD TO SEE...
ARCHIEKINS!
SHRIIEEK!!
WHAT IS WITH YOU PEOPLE? WHY ARE YOU ALL SCREAMING AT ME?
IT'S... IT'S... WHAT'S WRONG WITH YOUR EYES?
Y-YOU'VE GOT LITTLE STARS IN YOUR EYES!
PROBABLY DUE TO THE GRANDIOSE HOPES AND DREAMS I HAVE FOR MY SHINING FUTURE!
YOU AND THAT OTHER COMIC STRIP BABE!
SO WHAT ARE THEY? CONTACT LENSES?
OF COURSE! AT A PRICE YOU'LL NEVER AFFORD!
2

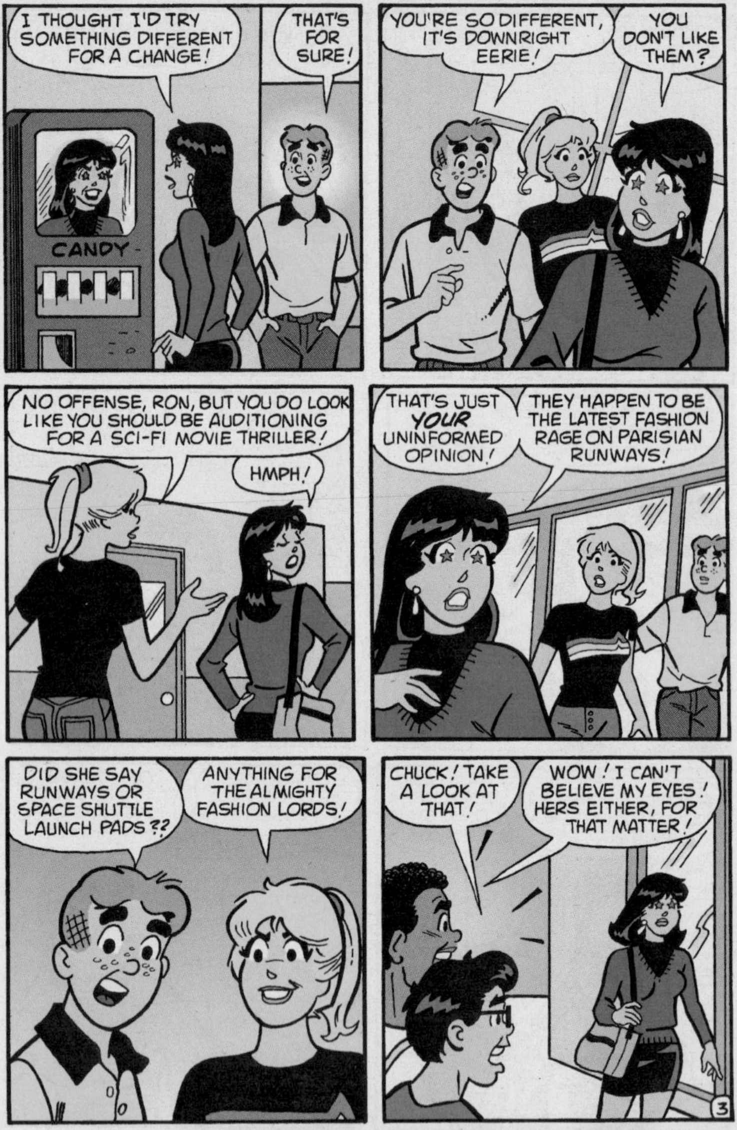
I THOUGHT I'D TRY SOMETHING DIFFERENT FOR A CHANGE!
THAT'S FOR SURE!
CANDY
YOU'RE SO DIFFERENT, IT'S DOWNRIGHT EERIE!
YOU DON'T LIKE THEM?
NO OFFENSE, RON, BUT YOU DO LOOK LIKE YOU SHOULD BE AUDITIONING FOR A SCI-FI MOVIE THRILLER!
HMPH!
THAT'S JUST YOUR UNINFORMED OPINION!
THEY HAPPEN TO BE THE LATEST FASHION RAGE ON PARISIAN RUNWAYS!
DID SHE SAY RUNWAYS OR SPACE SHUTTLE LAUNCH PADS??
ANYTHING FOR THE ALMIGHTY FASHION LORDS!
CHUCK! TAKE A LOOK AT THAT!
WOW! I CAN'T BELIEVE MY EYES! HERS EITHER, FOR THAT MATTER!
3

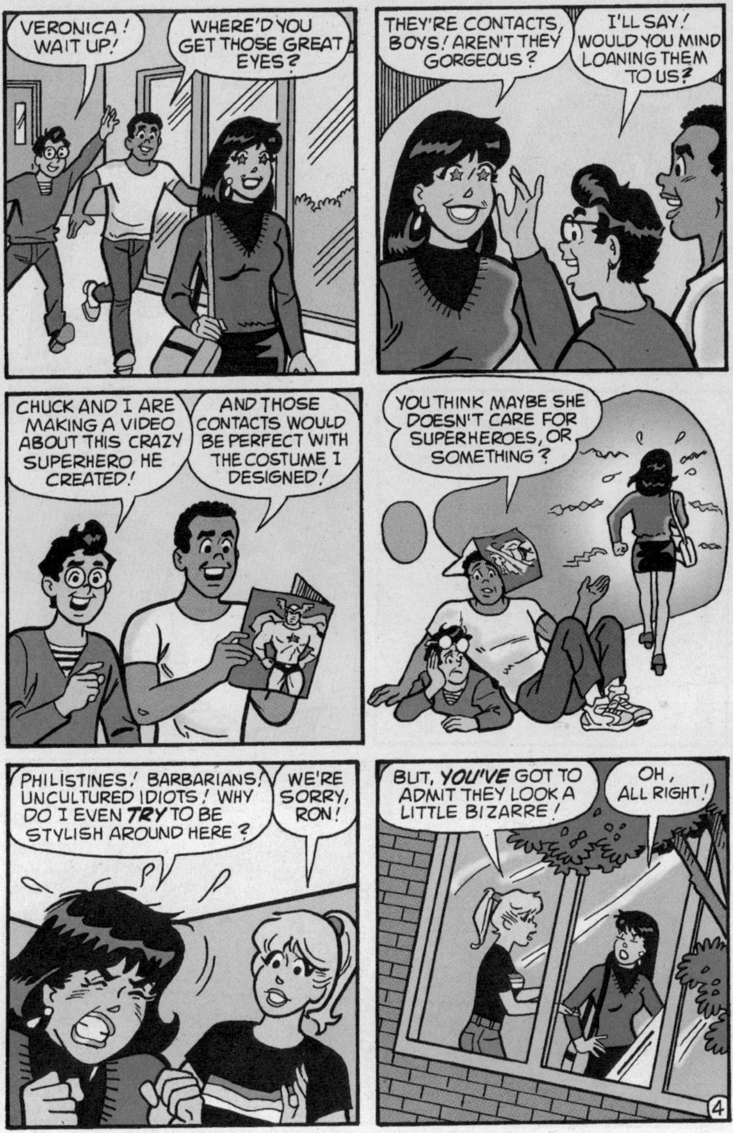

VERONICA! WAIT UP!
WHERE'D YOU GET THOSE GREAT EYES?
THEY'RE CONTACTS, BOYS! AREN'T THEY GORGEOUS?
I'LL SAY! WOULD YOU MIND LOANING THEM TO US?
CHUCK AND I ARE MAKING A VIDEO ABOUT THIS CRAZY SUPERHERO HE CREATED!
AND THOSE CONTACTS WOULD BE PERFECT WITH THE COSTUME I DESIGNED!
YOU THINK MAYBE SHE DOESN'T CARE FOR SUPERHEROES, OR SOMETHING?
PHILISTINES! BARBARIANS! UNCULTURED IDIOTS! WHY DO I EVEN TRY TO BE STYLISH AROUND HERE?
WE'RE SORRY, RON!
BUT, YOU'VE GOT TO ADMIT THEY LOOK A LITTLE BIZARRE!
OH, ALL RIGHT!
4

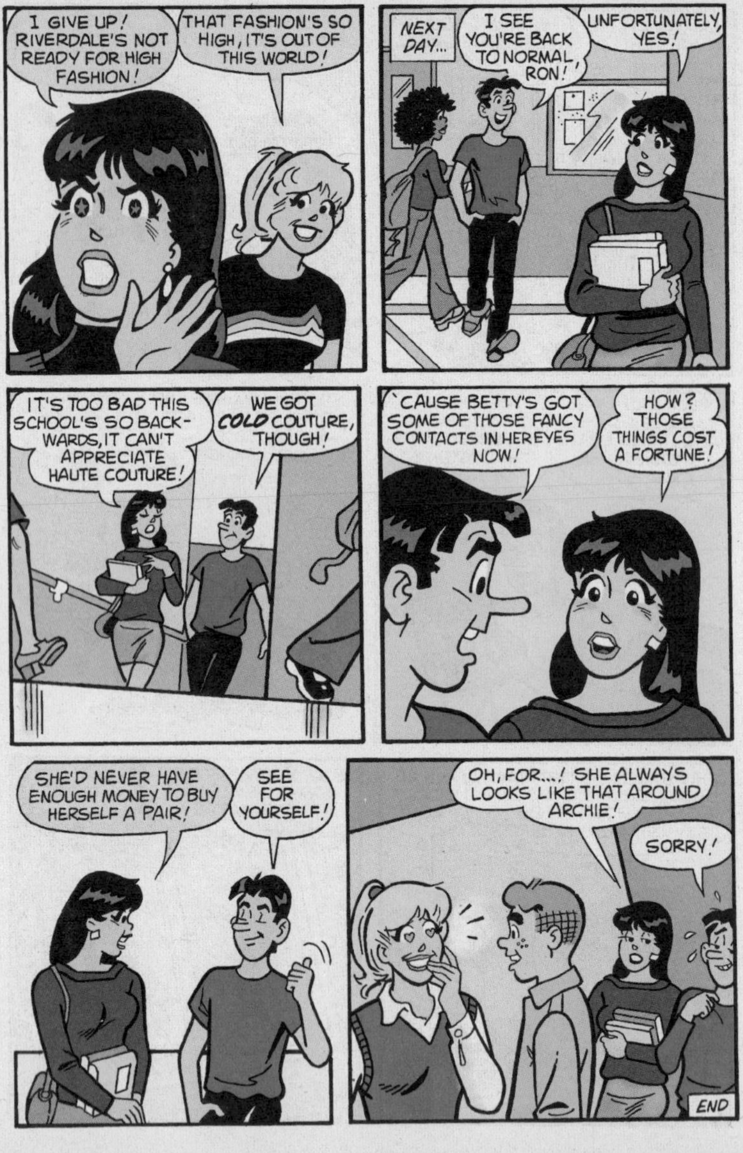
I GIVE UP! RIVERDALE'S NOT READY FOR HIGH FASHION!
THAT FASHION'S SO HIGH, IT'S OUT OF THIS WORLD!
NEXT DAY...
I SEE YOU'RE BACK TO NORMAL, RON!
UNFORTUNATELY, YES!
IT'S TOO BAD THIS SCHOOL'S SO BACK-WARDS, IT CAN'T APPRECIATE HAUTE COUTURE!
WE GOT COLD COUTURE, THOUGH!
`CAUSE BETTY'S GOT SOME OF THOSE FANCY CONTACTS IN HER EYES NOW!
HOW? THOSE THINGS COST A FORTUNE!
SHE'D NEVER HAVE ENOUGH MONEY TO BUY HERSELF A PAIR!
SEE FOR YOURSELF!
OH, FOR...! SHE ALWAYS LOOKS LIKE THAT AROUND ARCHIE!
SORRY!
END

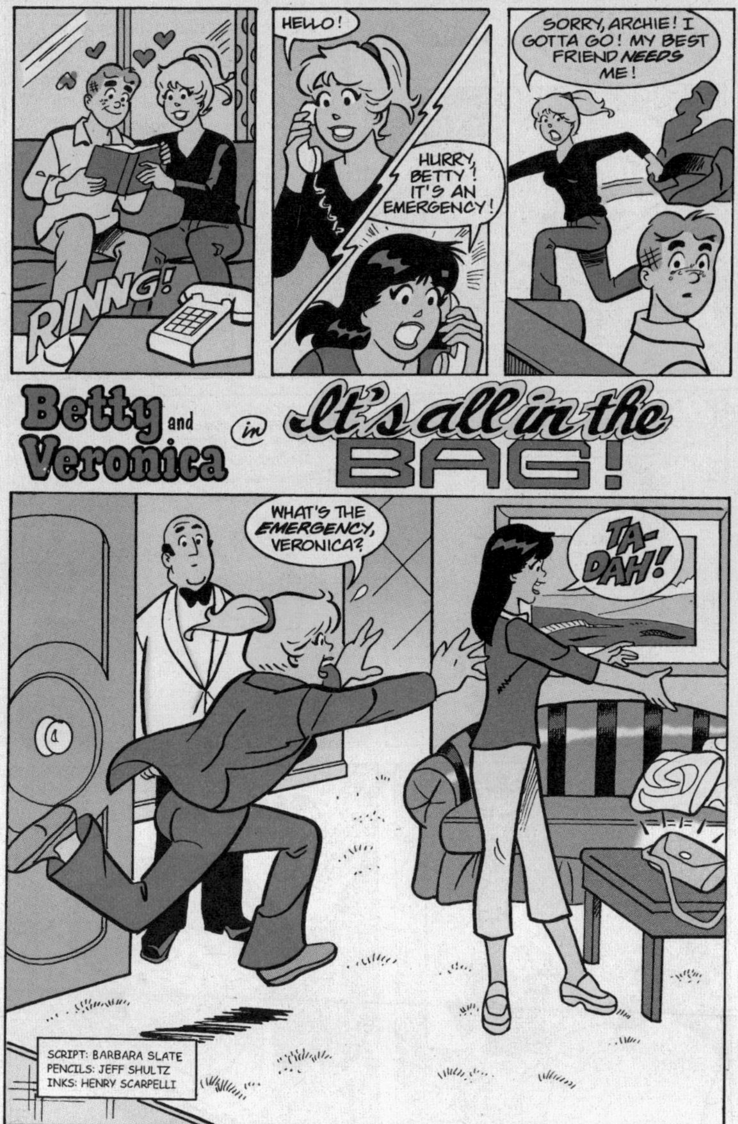
RINNG!
HELLO!
HURRY, BETTY! IT'S AN EMERGENCY!
SORRY, ARCHIE! I GOTTA GO! MY BEST FRIEND NEEDS ME!
Betty and Veronica in It's all in the BAG!
WHAT'S THE EMERGENCY, VERONICA?
TA-DAH!
SCRIPT: BARBARA SLATE
PENCILS: JEFF SHULTZ
INKS: HENRY SCARPELLI

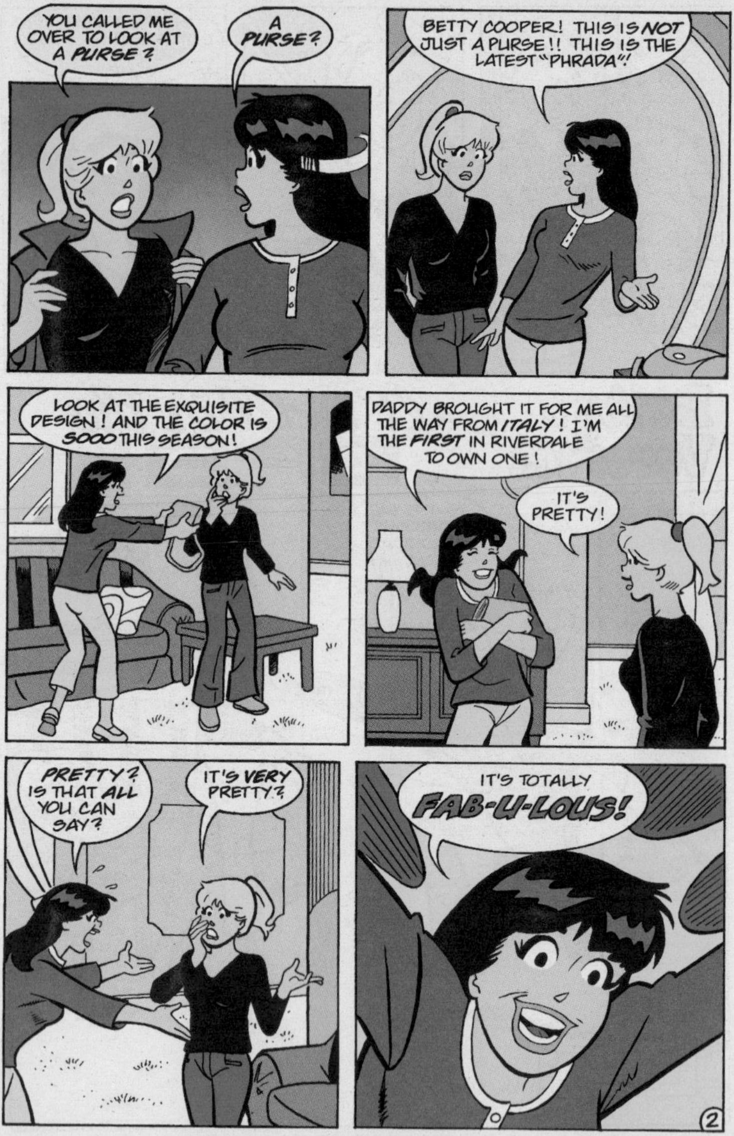

YOU CALLED ME OVER TO LOOK AT A PURSE?
A PURSE?
BETTY COOPER! THIS IS NOT JUST A PURSE!! THIS IS THE LATEST "PHRADA"!
LOOK AT THE EXQUISITE DESIGN! AND THE COLOR IS SOOO THIS SEASON!
DADDY BROUGHT IT FOR ME ALL THE WAY FROM ITALY! I'M THE FIRST IN RIVERDALE TO OWN ONE!
IT'S PRETTY!
PRETTY? IS THAT ALL YOU CAN SAY?
IT'S VERY PRETTY?
IT'S TOTALLY FAB-U-LOUS!
2

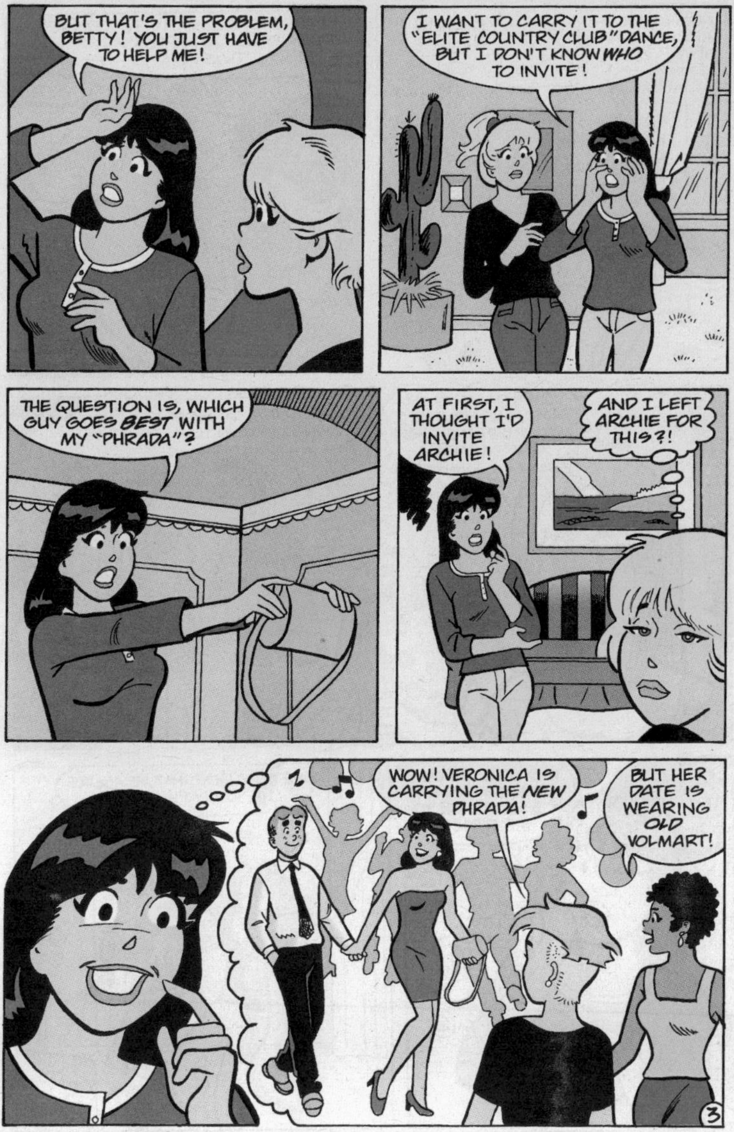
BUT THAT'S THE PROBLEM, BETTY! YOU JUST HAVE TO HELP ME!
I WANT TO CARRY IT TO THE "ELITE COUNTRY CLUB" DANCE, BUT I DON'T KNOW WHO TO INVITE!
THE QUESTION IS, WHICH GUY GOES BEST WITH MY "PHRADA"?
AT FIRST, I THOUGHT I'D INVITE ARCHIE!
AND I LEFT ARCHIE FOR THIS?!
WOW! VERONICA IS CARRYING THE NEW PHRADA!
BUT HER DATE IS WEARING OLD VOLMART!
3

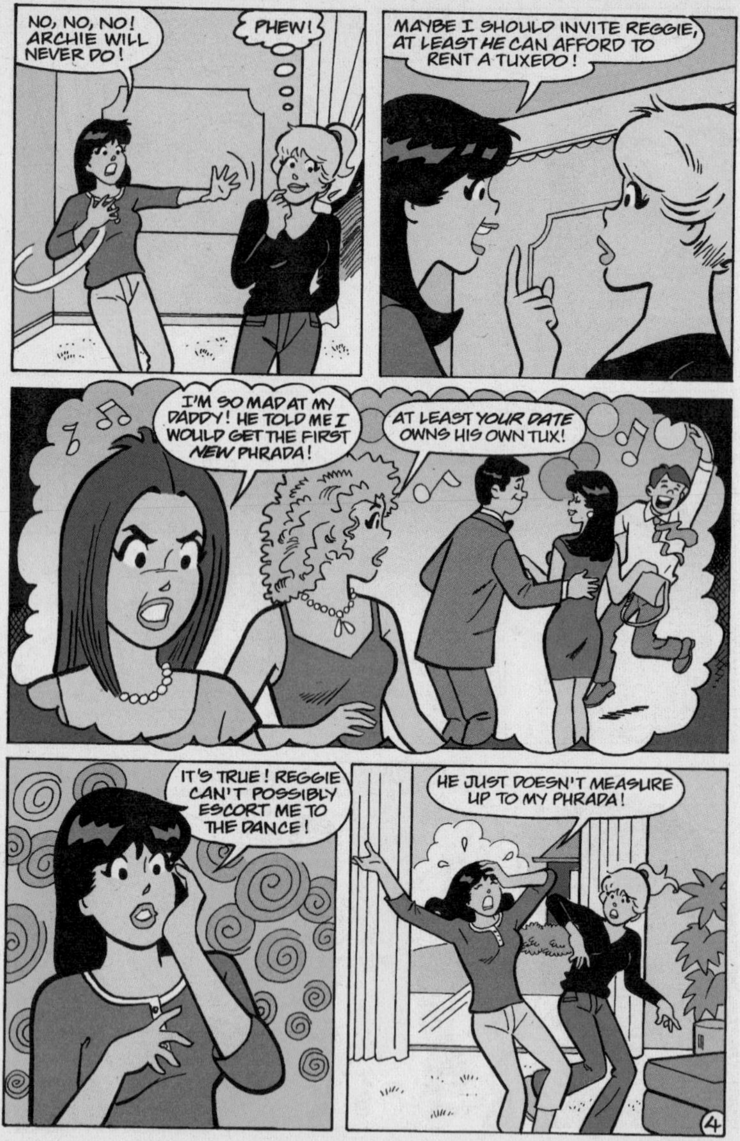
NO, NO, NO! ARCHIE WILL NEVER DO!
PHEW!
MAYBE I SHOULD INVITE REGGIE, AT LEAST HE CAN AFFORD TO RENT A TUXEDO!
I'M SO MAD AT MY DADDY! HE TOLD ME I WOULD GET THE FIRST NEW PHRADA!
AT LEAST YOUR DATE OWNS HIS OWN TUX!
IT'S TRUE! REGGIE CAN'T POSSIBLY ESCORT ME TO THE DANCE!
HE JUST DOESN'T MEASURE UP TO MY PHRADA!
4

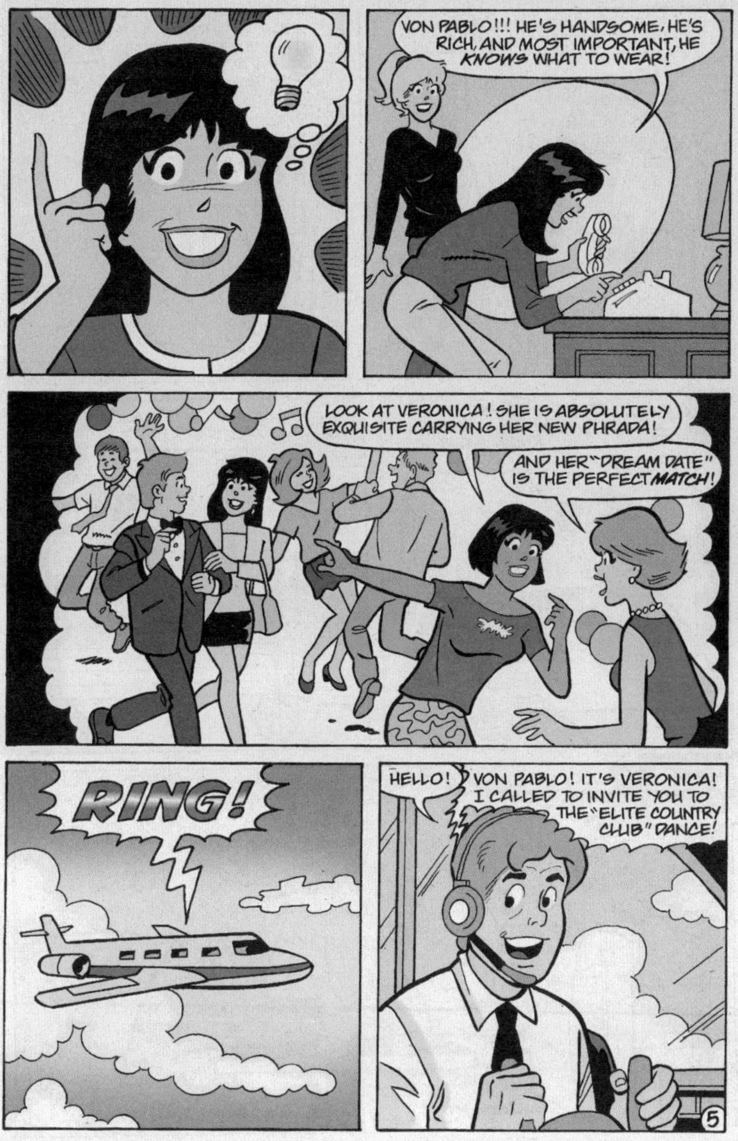
VON PABLO!!! HE'S HANDSOME, HE'S RICH, AND MOST IMPORTANT, HE KNOWS WHAT TO WEAR!
LOOK AT VERONICA! SHE IS ABSOLUTELY EXQUISITE CARRYING HER NEW PHRADA!
AND HER "DREAM DATE" IS THE PERFECT MATCH!
RING!
HELLO!
VON PABLO! IT'S VERONICA! I CALLED TO INVITE YOU TO THE "ELITE COUNTRY CLUB" DANCE!
5

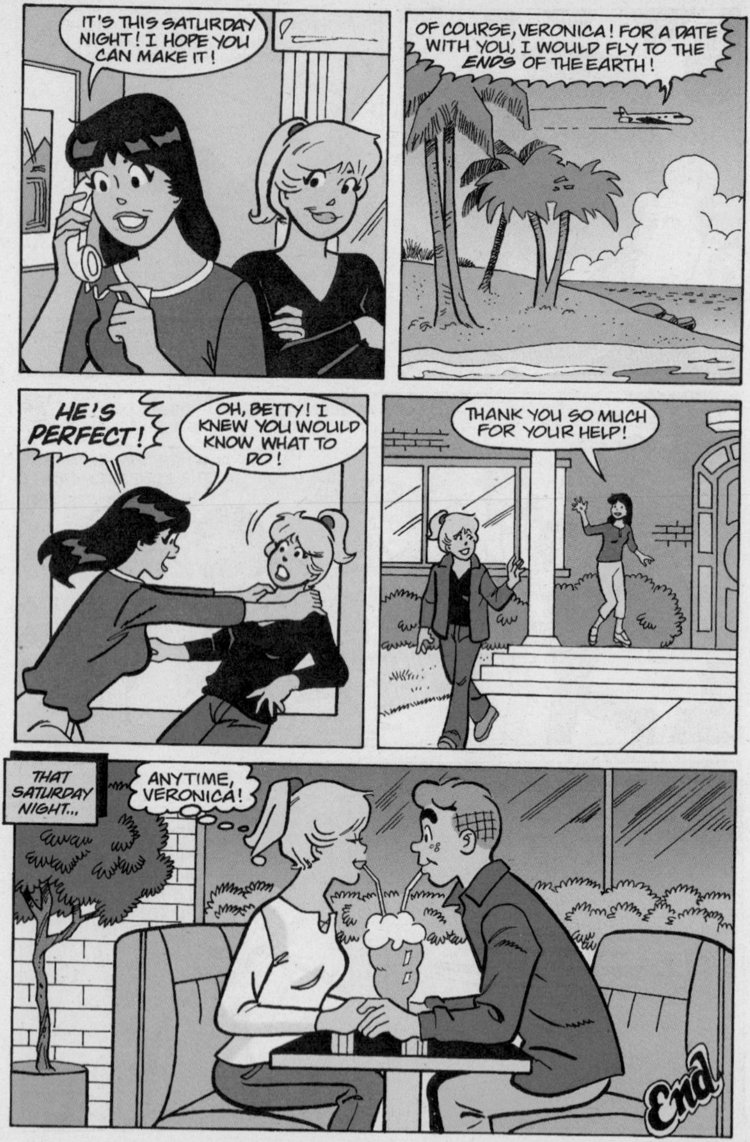
IT'S THIS SATURDAY NIGHT! I HOPE YOU CAN MAKE IT!
OF COURSE, VERONICA! FOR A DATE WITH YOU, I WOULD FLY TO THE ENDS OF THE EARTH!
HE'S PERFECT!
OH, BETTY! I KNEW YOU WOULD KNOW WHAT TO DO!
THANK YOU SO MUCH FOR YOUR HELP!
THAT SATURDAY NIGHT...
ANYTIME, VERONICA!
End

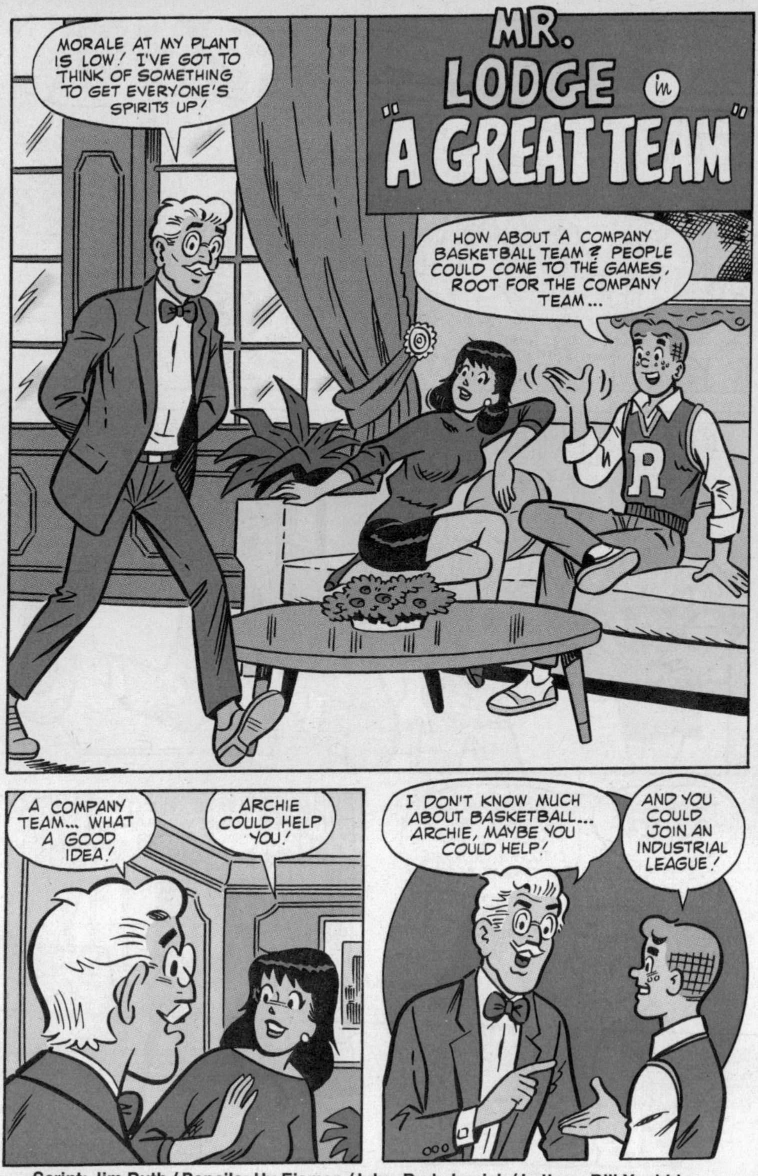
MR. LODGE in "A GREAT TEAM"
MORALE AT MY PLANT IS LOW! I'VE GOT TO THINK OF SOMETHING TO GET EVERYONE'S SPIRITS UP!
HOW ABOUT A COMPANY BASKETBALL TEAM? PEOPLE COULD COME TO THE GAMES, ROOT FOR THE COMPANY TEAM...
A COMPANY TEAM... WHAT A GOOD IDEA!
ARCHIE COULD HELP YOU!
I DON'T KNOW MUCH ABOUT BASKETBALL... ARCHIE, MAYBE YOU COULD HELP!
AND YOU COULD JOIN AN INDUSTRIAL LEAGUE!

Script: Jim Ruth / Pencils: Hy Eisman / Inks: Rudy Lapick / Letters: Bill Yoshida

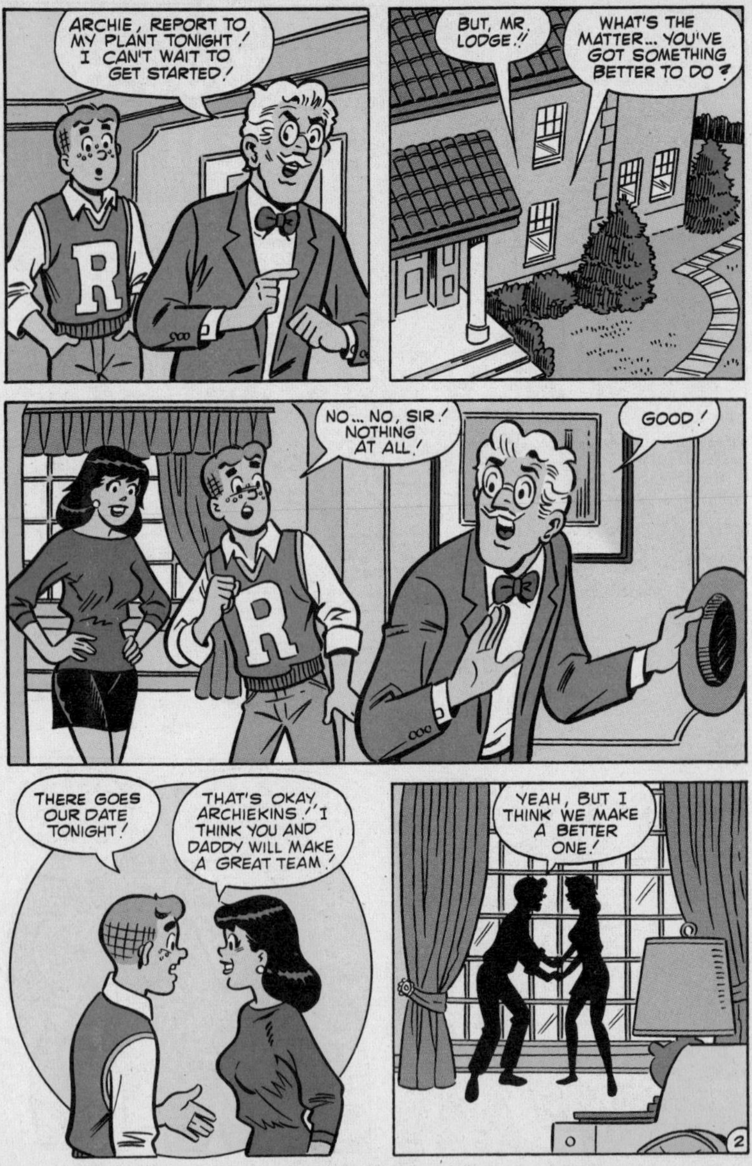
ARCHIE, REPORT TO MY PLANT TONIGHT! I CAN'T WAIT TO GET STARTED!
BUT, MR. LODGE!!
WHAT'S THE MATTER... YOU'VE GOT SOMETHING BETTER TO DO?
NO... NO, SIR! NOTHING AT ALL!
GOOD!
THERE GOES OUR DATE TONIGHT!
THAT'S OKAY, ARCHIEKINS! I THINK YOU AND DADDY WILL MAKE A GREAT TEAM!
YEAH, BUT I THINK WE MAKE A BETTER ONE!
2

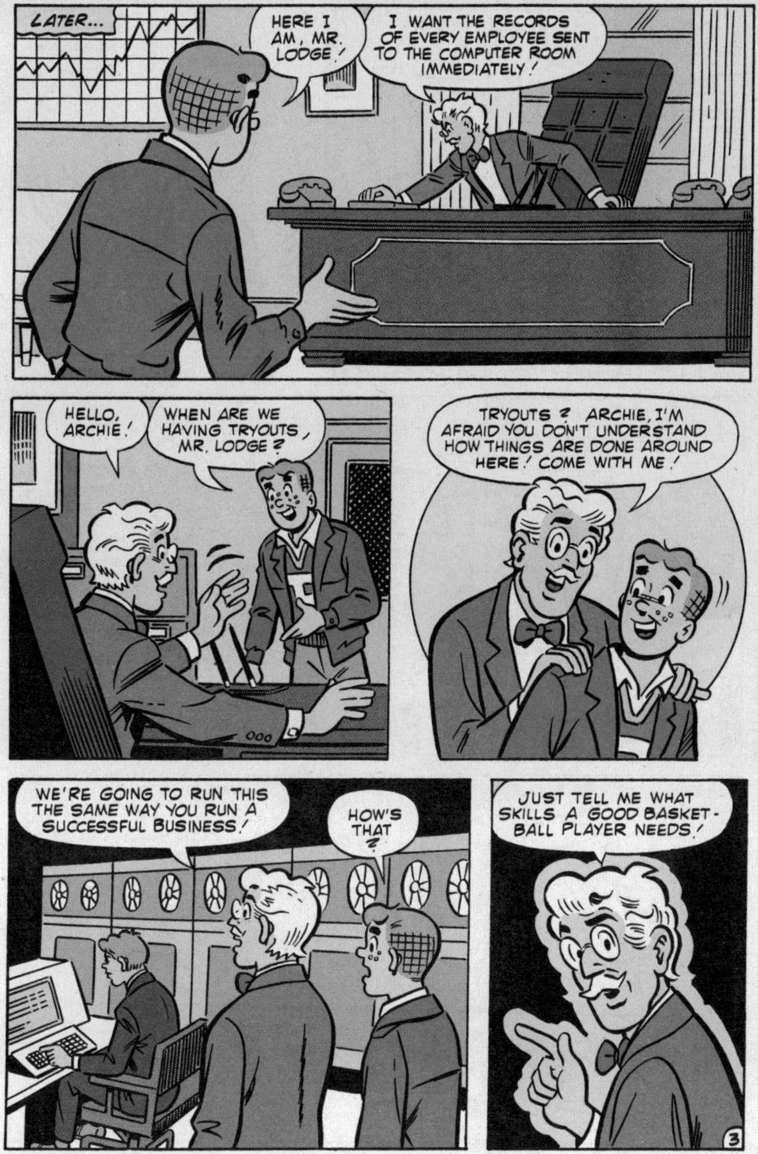
LATER...
HERE I AM, MR. LODGE!
I WANT THE RECORDS OF EVERY EMPLOYEE SENT TO THE COMPUTER ROOM IMMEDIATELY!
HELLO, ARCHIE!
WHEN ARE WE HAVING TRYOUTS, MR. LODGE?
TRYOUTS? ARCHIE, I'M AFRAID YOU DON'T UNDERSTAND HOW THINGS ARE DONE AROUND HERE! COME WITH ME!
WE'RE GOING TO RUN THIS THE SAME WAY YOU RUN A SUCCESSFUL BUSINESS!
HOW'S THAT?
JUST TELL ME WHAT SKILLS A GOOD BASKET-BALL PLAYER NEEDS!
3

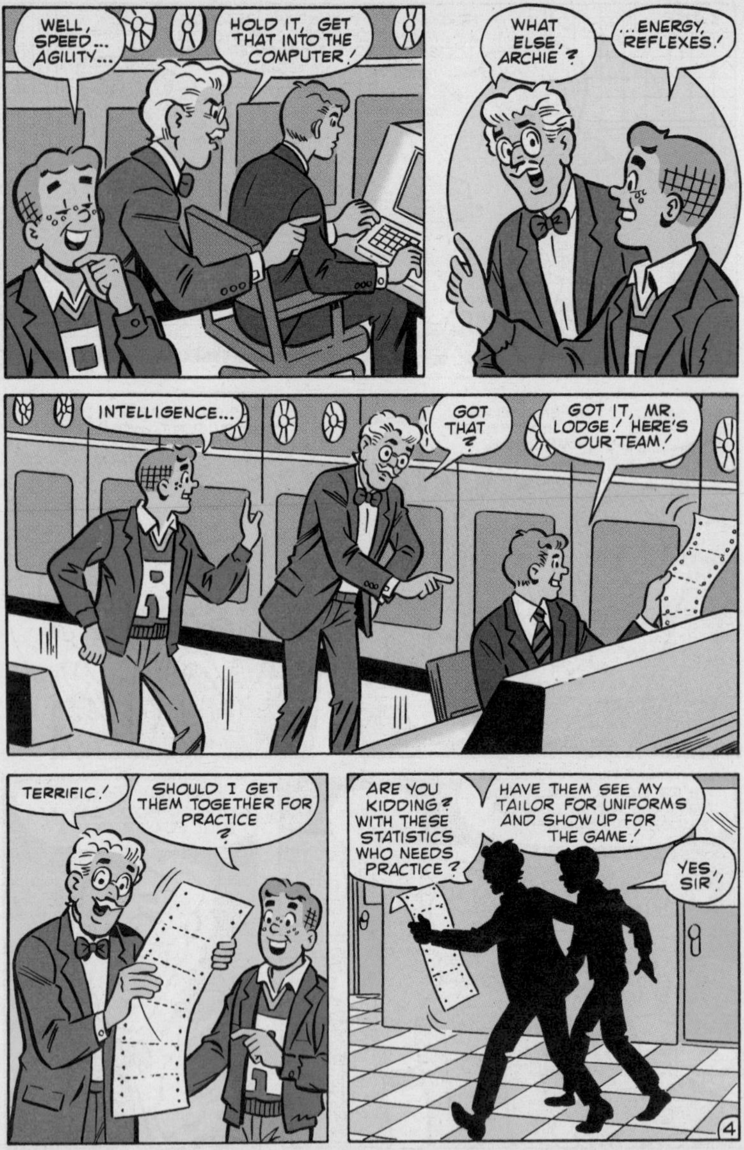
WELL, SPEED... AGILITY...
HOLD IT, GET THAT INTO THE COMPUTER!
WHAT ELSE, ARCHIE?
...ENERGY, REFLEXES!
INTELLIGENCE...
GOT THAT?
GOT IT, MR. LODGE! HERE'S OUR TEAM!
TERRIFIC!
SHOULD I GET THEM TOGETHER FOR PRACTICE?
ARE YOU KIDDING? WITH THESE STATISTICS WHO NEEDS PRACTICE?
HAVE THEM SEE MY TAILOR FOR UNIFORMS AND SHOW UP FOR THE GAME!
YES, SIR!
4

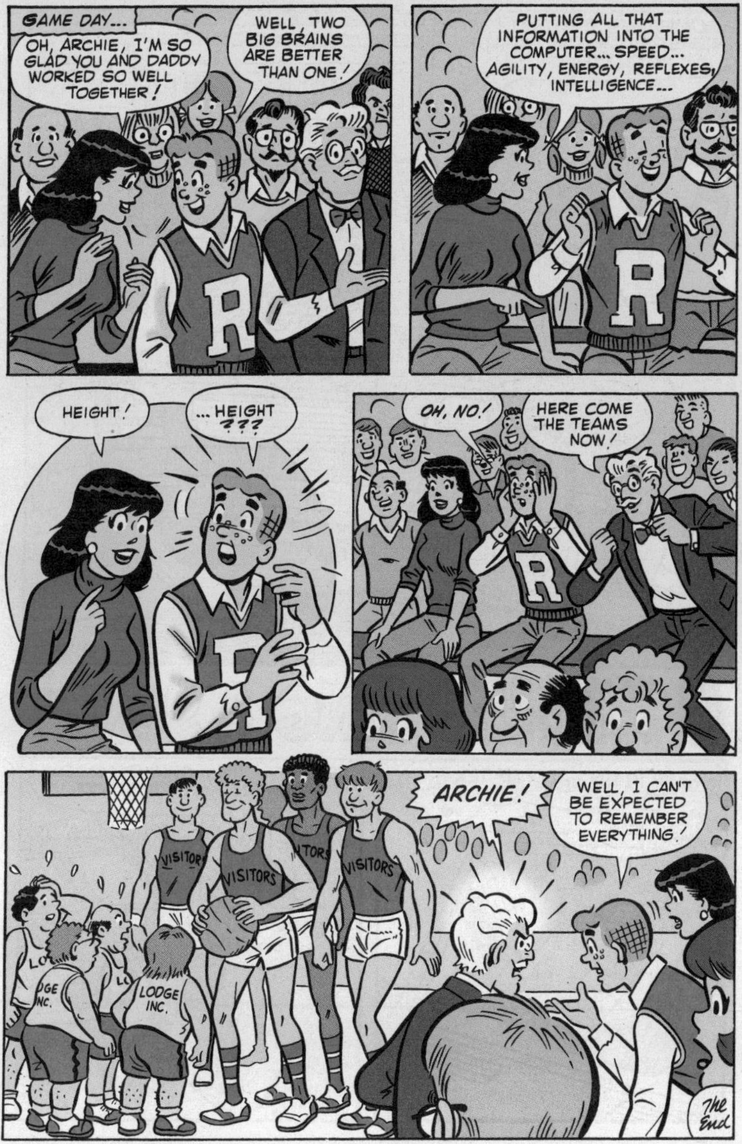
GAME DAY...
OH, ARCHIE, I'M SO GLAD YOU AND DADDY WORKED SO WELL TOGETHER!
WELL, TWO BIG BRAINS ARE BETTER THAN ONE!
PUTTING ALL THAT INFORMATION INTO THE COMPUTER... SPEED... AGILITY, ENERGY, REFLEXES, INTELLIGENCE...
HEIGHT!
... HEIGHT ???
OH, NO!
HERE COME THE TEAMS NOW!
VISITORS
VISITORS
VISITORS
LODGE INC.
ARCHIE!
WELL, I CAN'T BE EXPECTED TO REMEMBER EVERYTHING!
The End

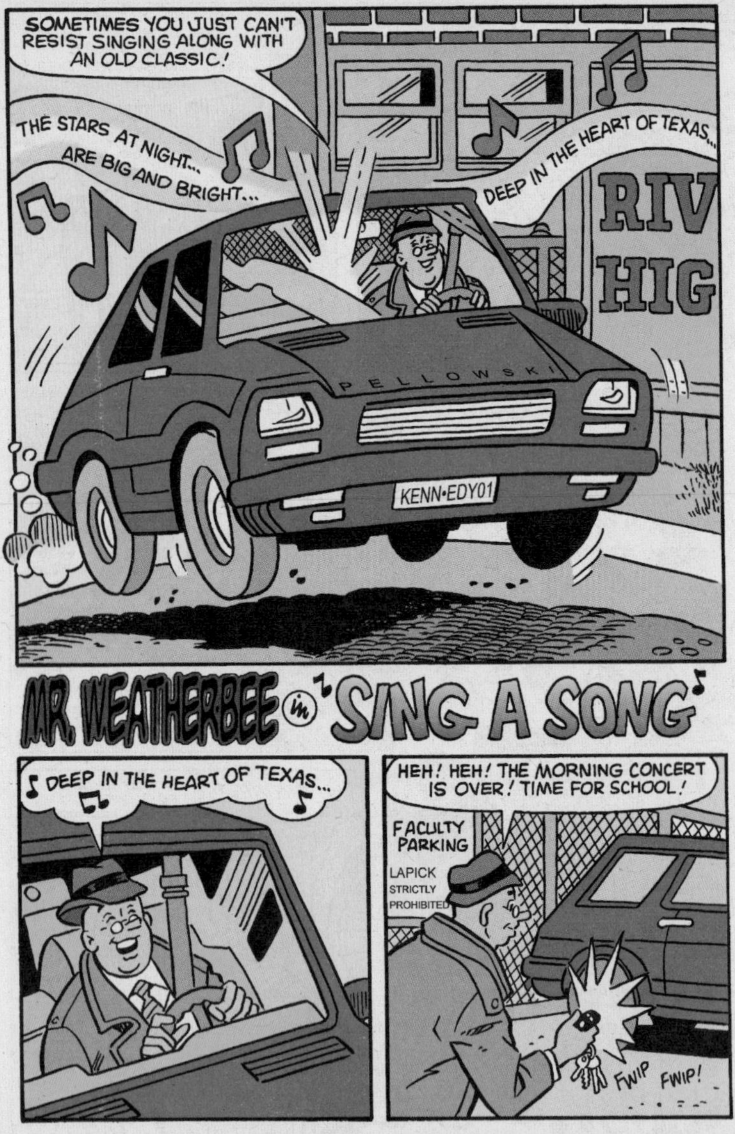
SOMETIMES YOU JUST CAN'T RESIST SINGING ALONG WITH AN OLD CLASSIC!
THE STARS AT NIGHT... ARE BIG AND BRIGHT...
DEEP IN THE HEART OF TEXAS...
RIV
HIG
PELLOWSKI
KENN•EDY01
MR. WEATHERBEE in "SING A SONG"
DEEP IN THE HEART OF TEXAS...
HEH! HEH! THE MORNING CONCERT IS OVER! TIME FOR SCHOOL!
FACULTY PARKING
LAPICK
STRICTLY
PROHIBITED
FWIP
FWIP!

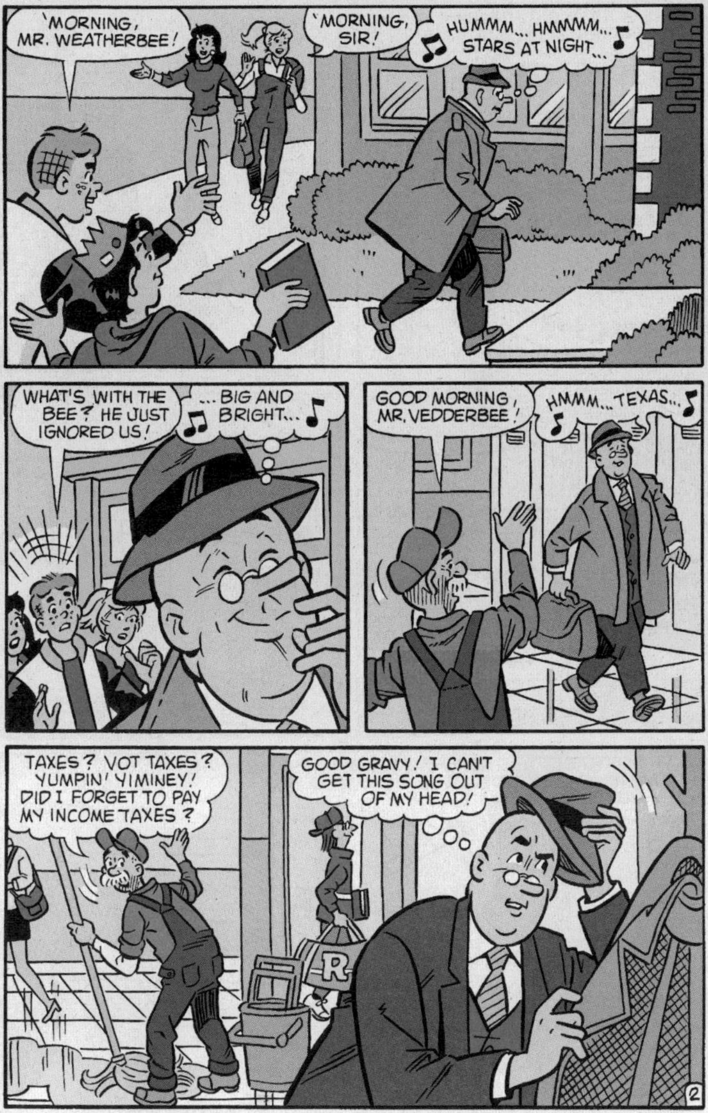
'MORNING, MR. WEATHERBEE!
'MORNING, SIR!
HUMMM... HMMMM... STARS AT NIGHT...
WHAT'S WITH THE BEE? HE JUST IGNORED US!
...BIG AND BRIGHT...
GOOD MORNING, MR. VEDDERBEE!
HMMM... TEXAS...
TAXES? VOT TAXES? YUMPIN' YIMINEY! DID I FORGET TO PAY MY INCOME TAXES?
GOOD GRAVY! I CAN'T GET THIS SONG OUT OF MY HEAD!
R
2

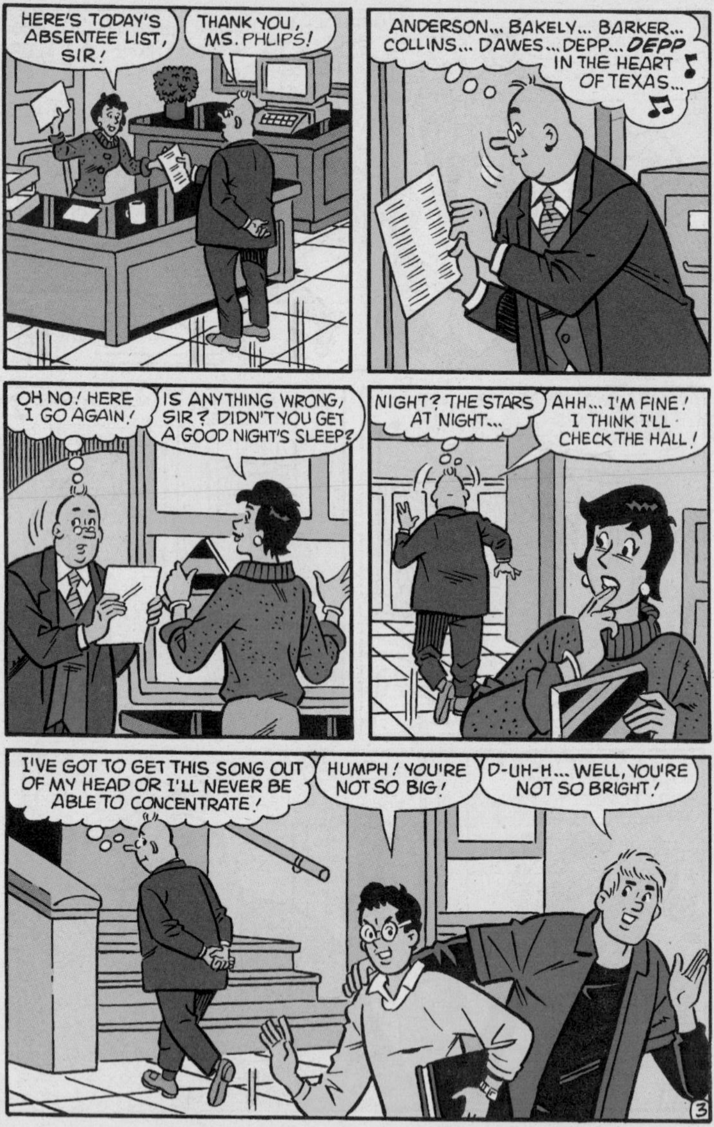
HERE'S TODAY'S ABSENTEE LIST, SIR!
THANK YOU, MS. PHLIPS!
ANDERSON... BAKELY... BARKER... COLLINS... DAWES... DEPP... DEPP IN THE HEART OF TEXAS...
OH NO! HERE I GO AGAIN!
IS ANYTHING WRONG, SIR? DIDN'T YOU GET A GOOD NIGHT'S SLEEP?
NIGHT? THE STARS AT NIGHT...
AHH... I'M FINE! I THINK I'LL CHECK THE HALL!
I'VE GOT TO GET THIS SONG OUT OF MY HEAD OR I'LL NEVER BE ABLE TO CONCENTRATE!
HUMPH! YOU'RE NOT SO BIG!
D-UH-H... WELL, YOU'RE NOT SO BRIGHT!
3

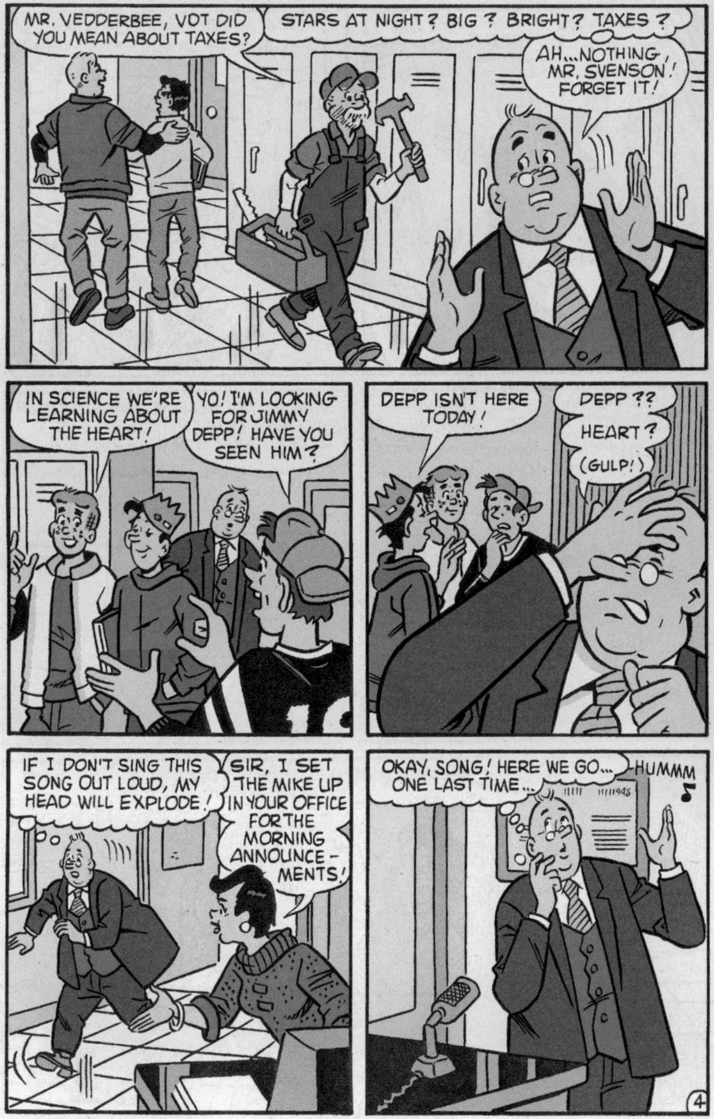
MR. VEDDERBEE, VOT DID YOU MEAN ABOUT TAXES?
STARS AT NIGHT? BIG? BRIGHT? TAXES?
AH...NOTHING, MR. SVENSON! FORGET IT!
IN SCIENCE WE'RE LEARNING ABOUT THE HEART!
YO! I'M LOOKING FOR JIMMY DEPP! HAVE YOU SEEN HIM?
DEPP ISN'T HERE TODAY!
DEPP??
HEART?
(GULP!)
IF I DON'T SING THIS SONG OUT LOUD, MY HEAD WILL EXPLODE!
SIR, I SET THE MIKE UP IN YOUR OFFICE FOR THE MORNING ANNOUNCE-MENTS!
OKAY, SONG! HERE WE GO... ONE LAST TIME...
HUMMM
4

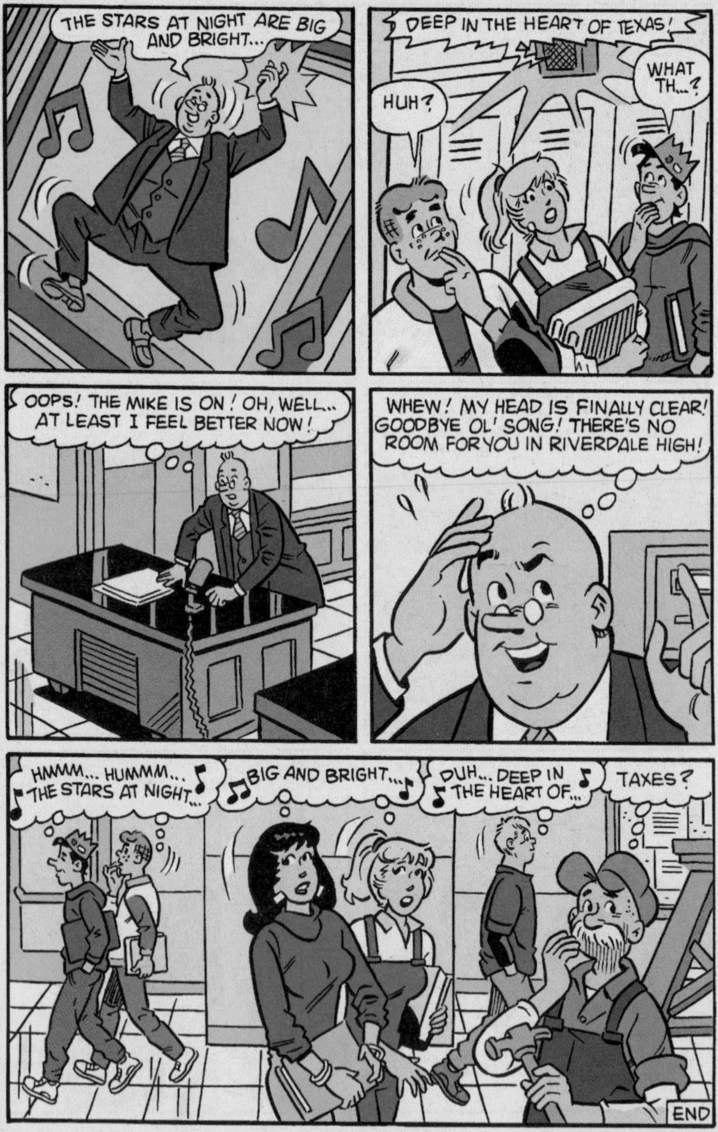
THE STARS AT NIGHT ARE BIG AND BRIGHT...
DEEP IN THE HEART OF TEXAS!
HUH?
WHAT TH...?
OOPS! THE MIKE IS ON! OH, WELL... AT LEAST I FEEL BETTER NOW!
WHEW! MY HEAD IS FINALLY CLEAR! GOODBYE OL' SONG! THERE'S NO ROOM FOR YOU IN RIVERDALE HIGH!
HMMM... HUMMM... THE STARS AT NIGHT...
BIG AND BRIGHT...
DUH... DEEP IN THE HEART OF...
TAXES?
END

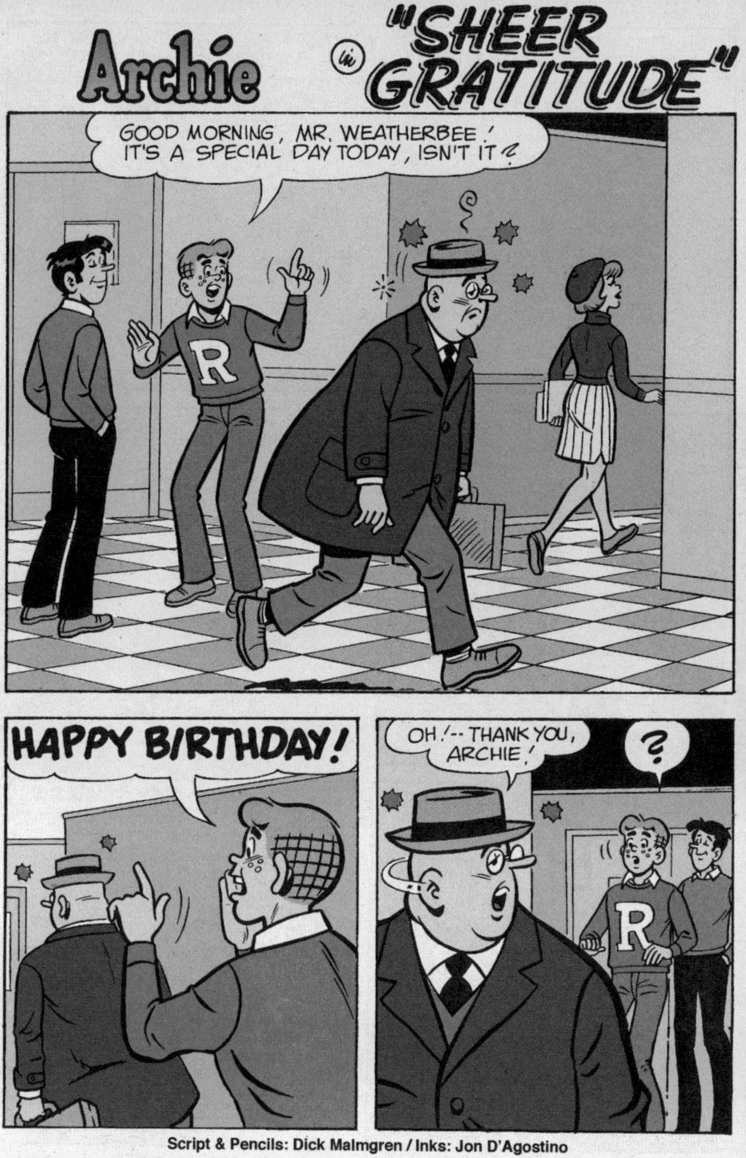
Archie in "SHEER GRATITUDE"
GOOD MORNING, MR. WEATHERBEE! IT'S A SPECIAL DAY TODAY, ISN'T IT?
HAPPY BIRTHDAY!
OH!-- THANK YOU, ARCHIE!
?

Script & Pencils: Dick Malmgren / Inks: Jon D'Agostino

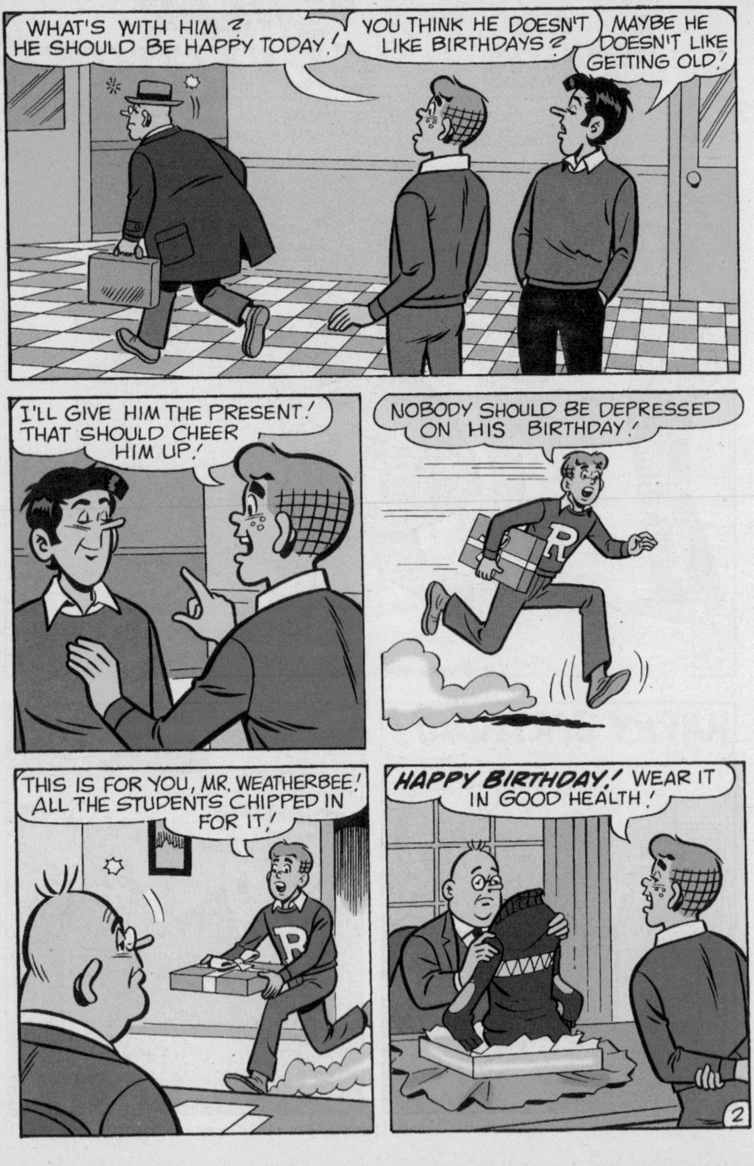
WHAT'S WITH HIM? HE SHOULD BE HAPPY TODAY!
YOU THINK HE DOESN'T LIKE BIRTHDAYS?
MAYBE HE DOESN'T LIKE GETTING OLD!
I'LL GIVE HIM THE PRESENT! THAT SHOULD CHEER HIM UP!
NOBODY SHOULD BE DEPRESSED ON HIS BIRTHDAY!
R
THIS IS FOR YOU, MR. WEATHERBEE! ALL THE STUDENTS CHIPPED IN FOR IT!
R
HAPPY BIRTHDAY! WEAR IT IN GOOD HEALTH!
2

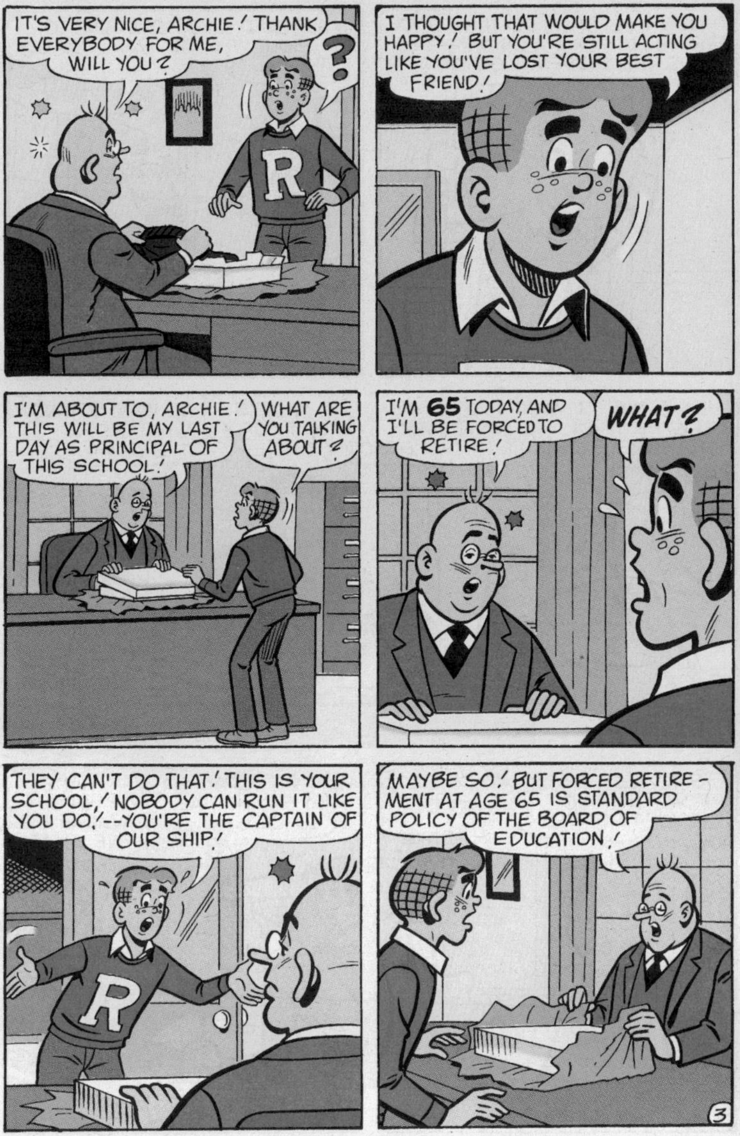
IT'S VERY NICE, ARCHIE! THANK EVERYBODY FOR ME, WILL YOU?
?
I THOUGHT THAT WOULD MAKE YOU HAPPY! BUT YOU'RE STILL ACTING LIKE YOU'VE LOST YOUR BEST FRIEND!
I'M ABOUT TO, ARCHIE! THIS WILL BE MY LAST DAY AS PRINCIPAL OF THIS SCHOOL!
WHAT ARE YOU TALKING ABOUT?
I'M 65 TODAY, AND I'LL BE FORCED TO RETIRE!
WHAT?
THEY CAN'T DO THAT! THIS IS YOUR SCHOOL! NOBODY CAN RUN IT LIKE YOU DO!--YOU'RE THE CAPTAIN OF OUR SHIP!
MAYBE SO! BUT FORCED RETIRE-MENT AT AGE 65 IS STANDARD POLICY OF THE BOARD OF EDUCATION!
3

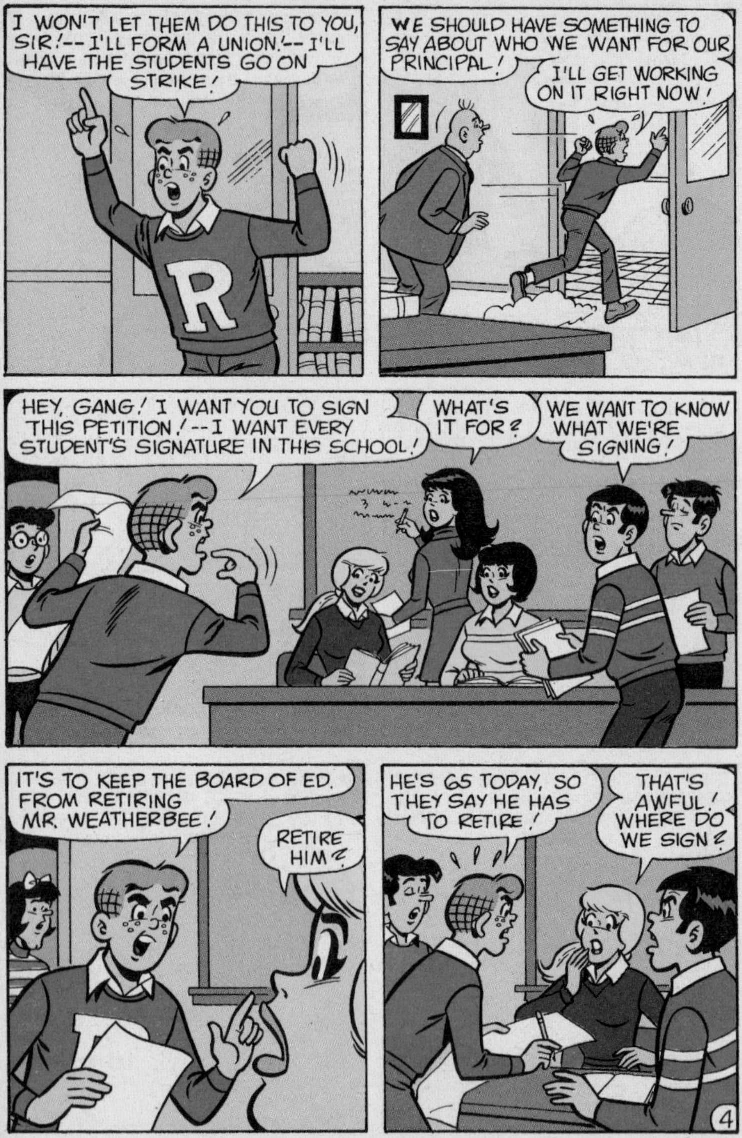
I WON'T LET THEM DO THIS TO YOU, SIR!--I'LL FORM A UNION!--I'LL HAVE THE STUDENTS GO ON STRIKE!
WE SHOULD HAVE SOMETHING TO SAY ABOUT WHO WE WANT FOR OUR PRINCIPAL!
I'LL GET WORKING ON IT RIGHT NOW!
HEY, GANG! I WANT YOU TO SIGN THIS PETITION!--I WANT EVERY STUDENT'S SIGNATURE IN THIS SCHOOL!
WHAT'S IT FOR?
WE WANT TO KNOW WHAT WE'RE SIGNING!
IT'S TO KEEP THE BOARD OF ED. FROM RETIRING MR. WEATHERBEE!
RETIRE HIM?
HE'S 65 TODAY, SO THEY SAY HE HAS TO RETIRE!
THAT'S AWFUL! WHERE DO WE SIGN?
4

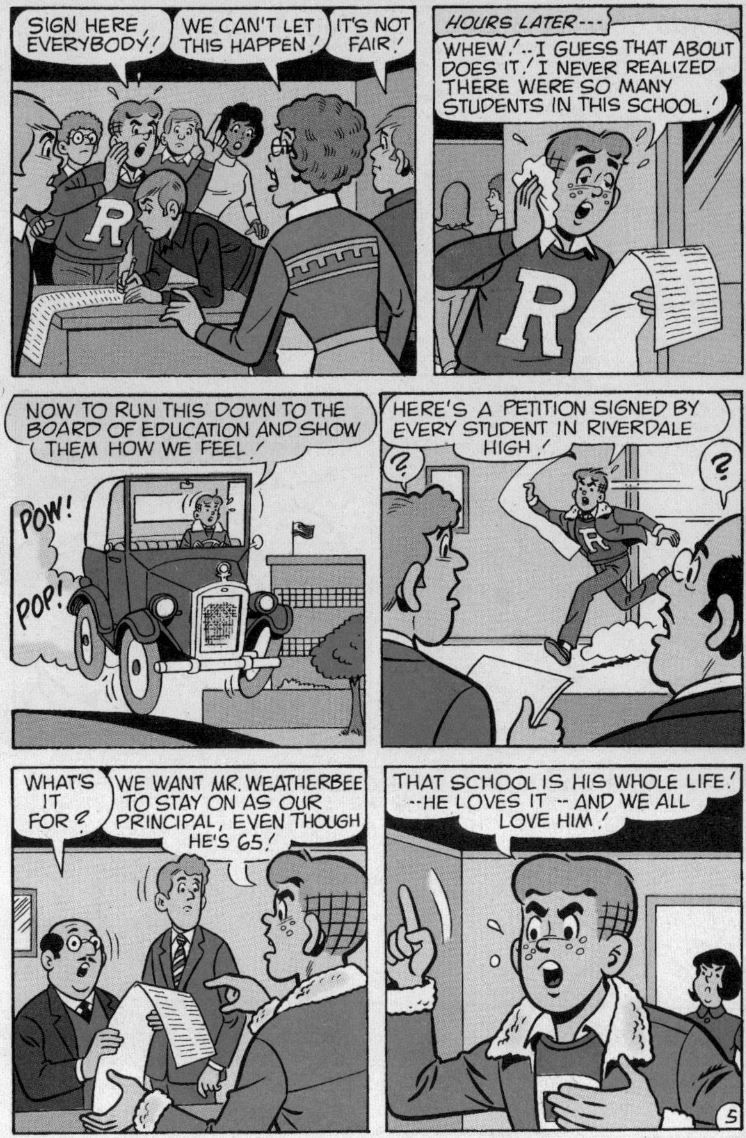
SIGN HERE, EVERYBODY!
WE CAN'T LET THIS HAPPEN!
IT'S NOT FAIR!
HOURS LATER---
WHEW! --I GUESS THAT ABOUT DOES IT! I NEVER REALIZED THERE WERE SO MANY STUDENTS IN THIS SCHOOL!
NOW TO RUN THIS DOWN TO THE BOARD OF EDUCATION AND SHOW THEM HOW WE FEEL!
POW!
POP!
HERE'S A PETITION SIGNED BY EVERY STUDENT IN RIVERDALE HIGH!
?
?
WHAT'S IT FOR?
WE WANT MR. WEATHERBEE TO STAY ON AS OUR PRINCIPAL, EVEN THOUGH HE'S 65!
THAT SCHOOL IS HIS WHOLE LIFE! --HE LOVES IT -- AND WE ALL LOVE HIM!
5

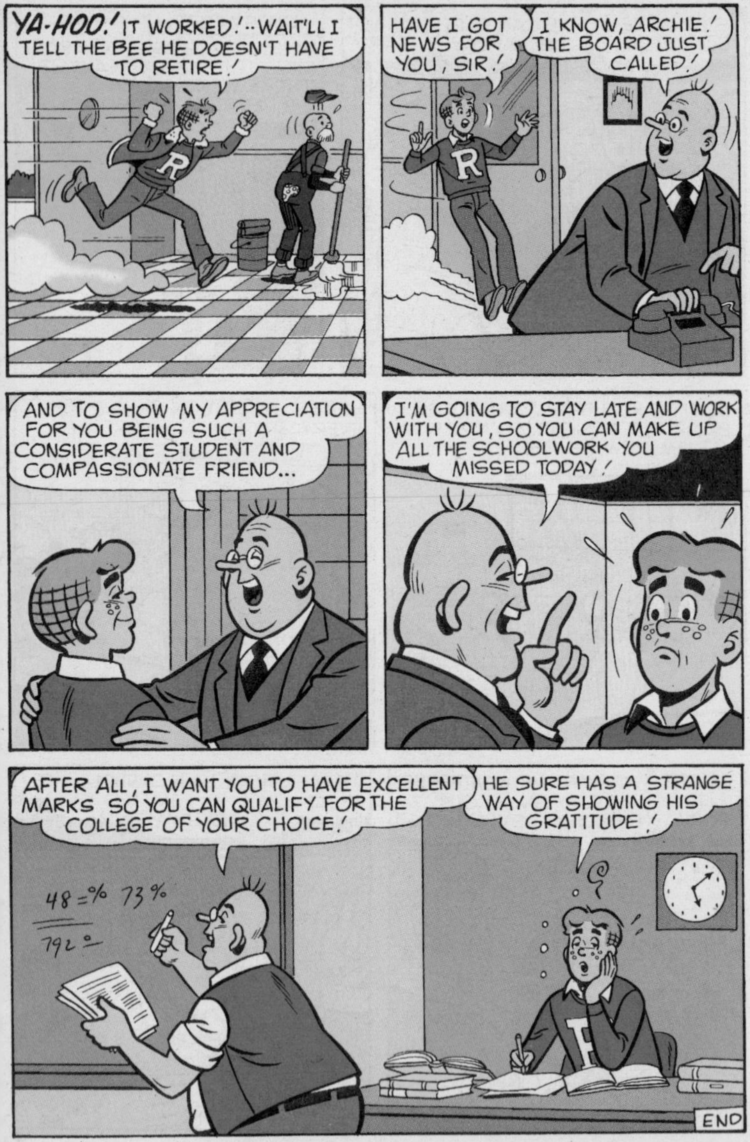
YA-HOO! IT WORKED! -- WAIT'LL I TELL THE BEE HE DOESN'T HAVE TO RETIRE!
HAVE I GOT NEWS FOR YOU, SIR!
I KNOW, ARCHIE! THE BOARD JUST CALLED!
AND TO SHOW MY APPRECIATION FOR YOU BEING SUCH A CONSIDERATE STUDENT AND COMPASSIONATE FRIEND...
I'M GOING TO STAY LATE AND WORK WITH YOU, SO YOU CAN MAKE UP ALL THE SCHOOLWORK YOU MISSED TODAY!
AFTER ALL, I WANT YOU TO HAVE EXCELLENT MARKS SO YOU CAN QUALIFY FOR THE COLLEGE OF YOUR CHOICE!
HE SURE HAS A STRANGE WAY OF SHOWING HIS GRATITUDE!
END

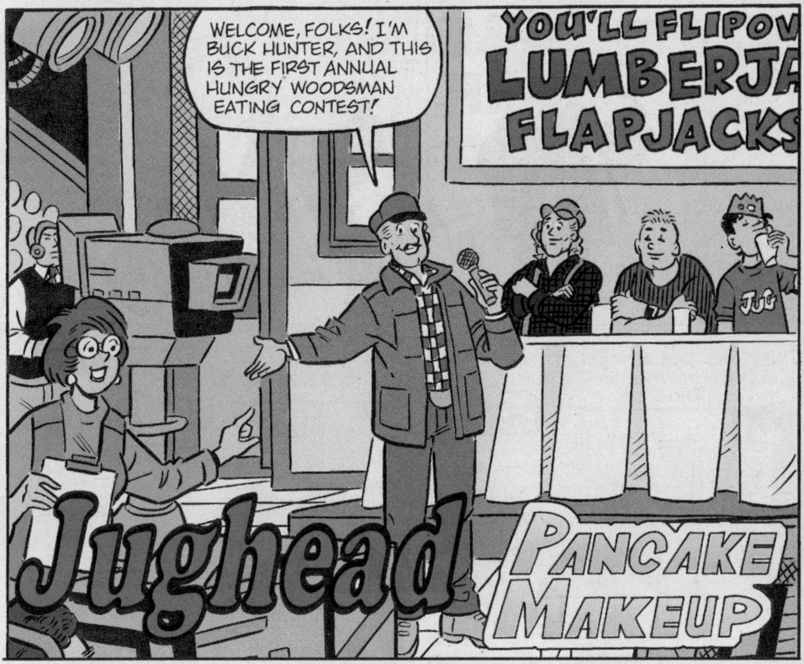
WELCOME, FOLKS! I'M BUCK HUNTER, AND THIS IS THE FIRST ANNUAL HUNGRY WOODSMAN EATING CONTEST!
YOU'LL FLIPOV
LUMBERJA
FLAPJACKS
Jughead
PANCAKE MAKEUP

SCRIPT: MIKE PELLOWSKI PENCILS: PAT KENNEDY INKS: RUDY LAPICK
LETTERS: DAN NAKROSIS

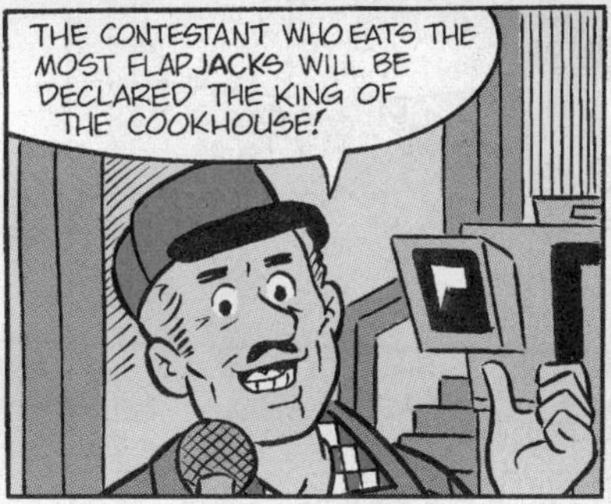
THE CONTESTANT WHO EATS THE MOST FLAPJACKS WILL BE DECLARED THE KING OF THE COOKHOUSE!

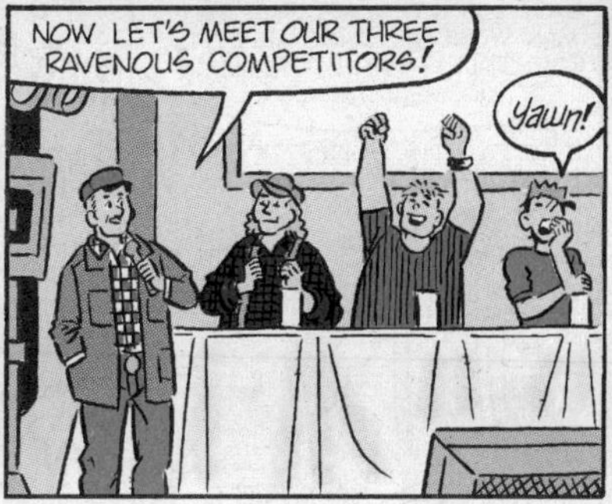
NOW LET'S MEET OUR THREE RAVENOUS COMPETITORS!
Yawn!

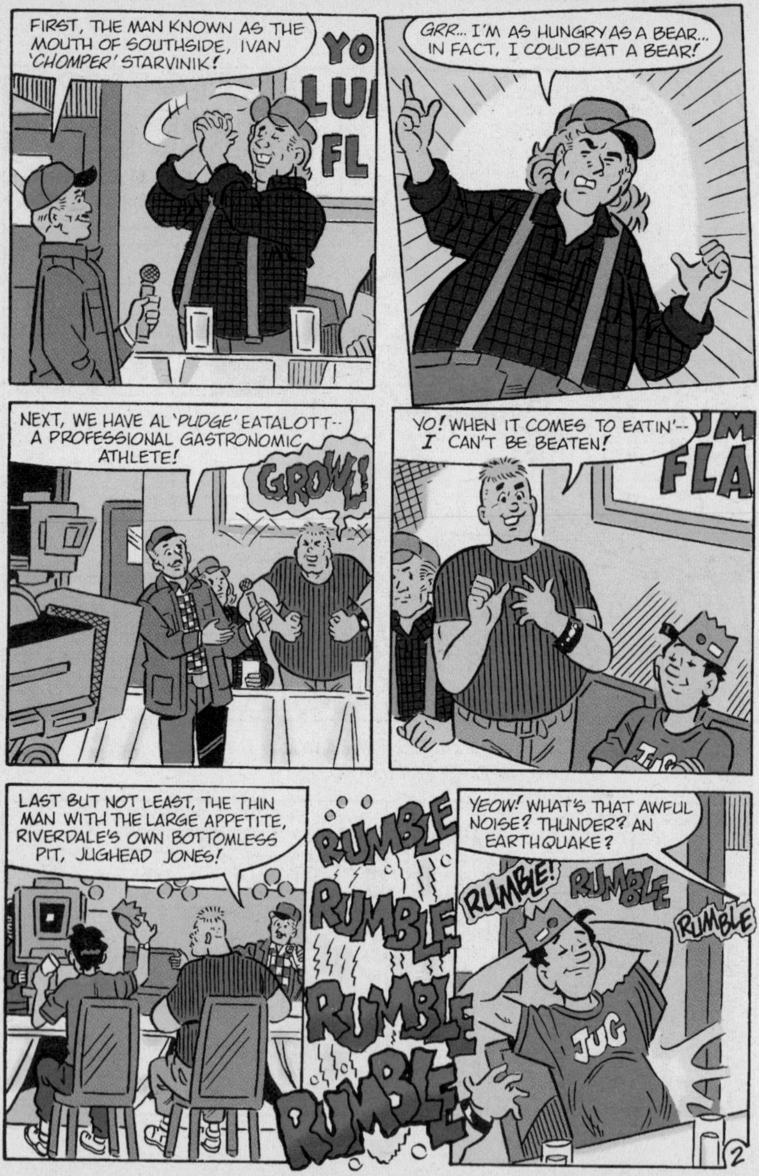
FIRST, THE MAN KNOWN AS THE MOUTH OF SOUTHSIDE, IVAN 'CHOMPER' STARVINIK!
GRR... I'M AS HUNGRY AS A BEAR... IN FACT, I COULD EAT A BEAR!
NEXT, WE HAVE AL 'PUDGE' EATALOTT-- A PROFESSIONAL GASTRONOMIC ATHLETE!
GROWL!
YO! WHEN IT COMES TO EATIN'-- I CAN'T BE BEATEN!
LAST BUT NOT LEAST, THE THIN MAN WITH THE LARGE APPETITE, RIVERDALE'S OWN BOTTOMLESS PIT, JUGHEAD JONES!
RUMBLE RUMBLE RUMBLE RUMBLE
YEOW! WHAT'S THAT AWFUL NOISE? THUNDER? AN EARTHQUAKE?
RUMBLE! RUMBLE RUMBLE
JUG
2

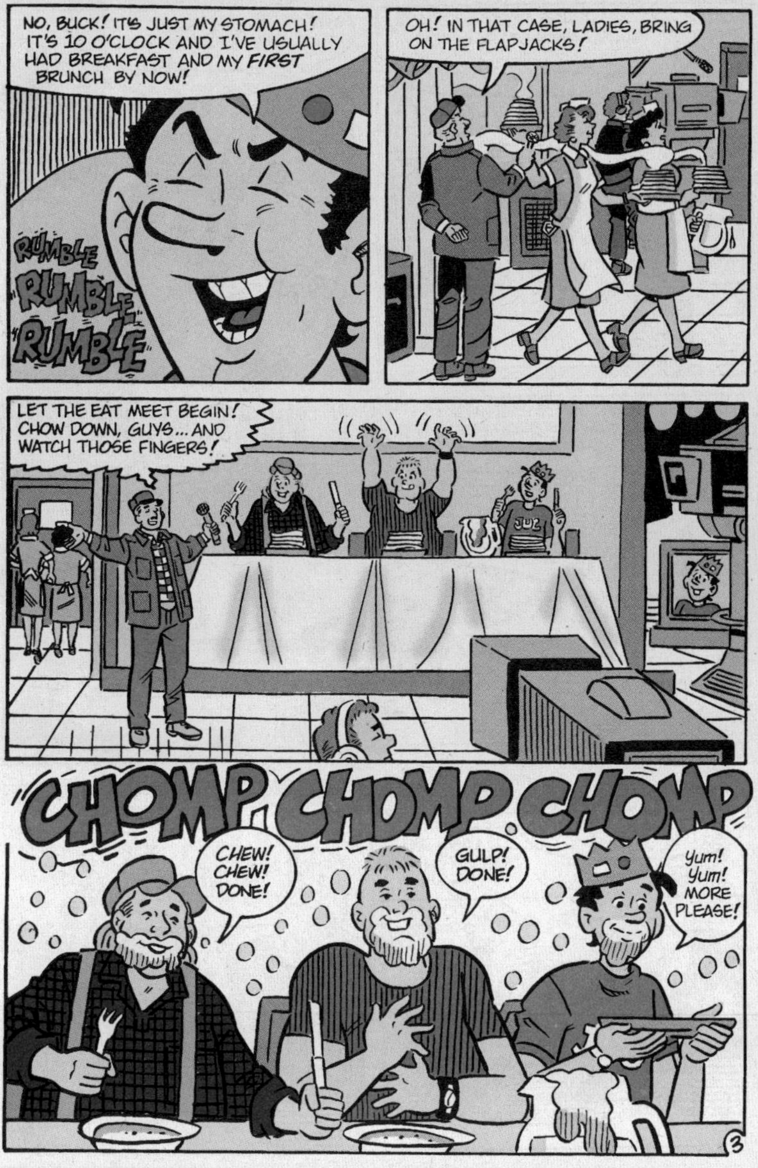
NO, BUCK! IT'S JUST MY STOMACH! IT'S 10 O'CLOCK AND I'VE USUALLY HAD BREAKFAST AND MY FIRST BRUNCH BY NOW!
RUMBLE
RUMBLE
RUMBLE
OH! IN THAT CASE, LADIES, BRING ON THE FLAPJACKS!
LET THE EAT MEET BEGIN! CHOW DOWN, GUYS... AND WATCH THOSE FINGERS!
CHOMP CHOMP CHOMP
CHEW! CHEW! DONE!
GULP! DONE!
Yum! Yum! MORE PLEASE!
3

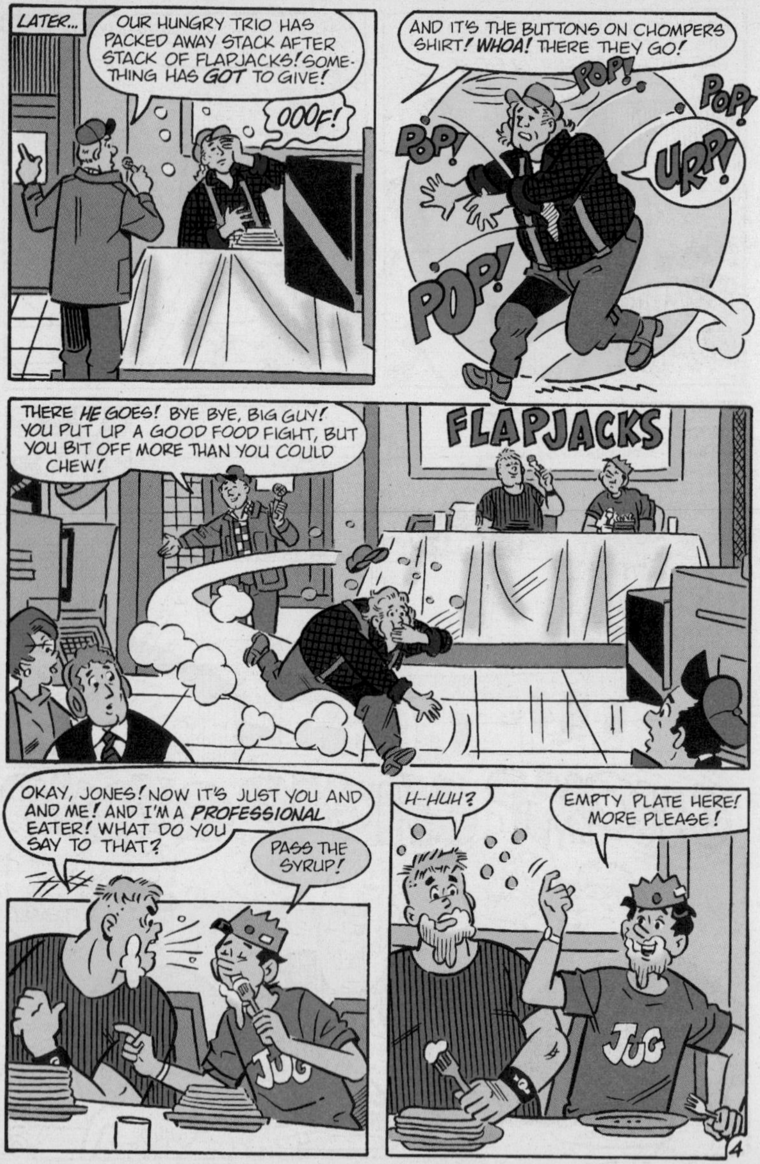
LATER...
OUR HUNGRY TRIO HAS PACKED AWAY STACK AFTER STACK OF FLAPJACKS! SOMETHING HAS GOT TO GIVE!
OOOF!
AND IT'S THE BUTTONS ON CHOMPERS SHIRT! WHOA! THERE THEY GO!
POP!
POP!
POP!
URP!
POP!
THERE HE GOES! BYE BYE, BIG GUY! YOU PUT UP A GOOD FOOD FIGHT, BUT YOU BIT OFF MORE THAN YOU COULD CHEW!
FLAPJACKS
OKAY, JONES! NOW IT'S JUST YOU AND AND ME! AND I'M A PROFESSIONAL EATER! WHAT DO YOU SAY TO THAT?
PASS THE SYRUP!
JUG
H--HUH?
EMPTY PLATE HERE! MORE PLEASE!
JUG

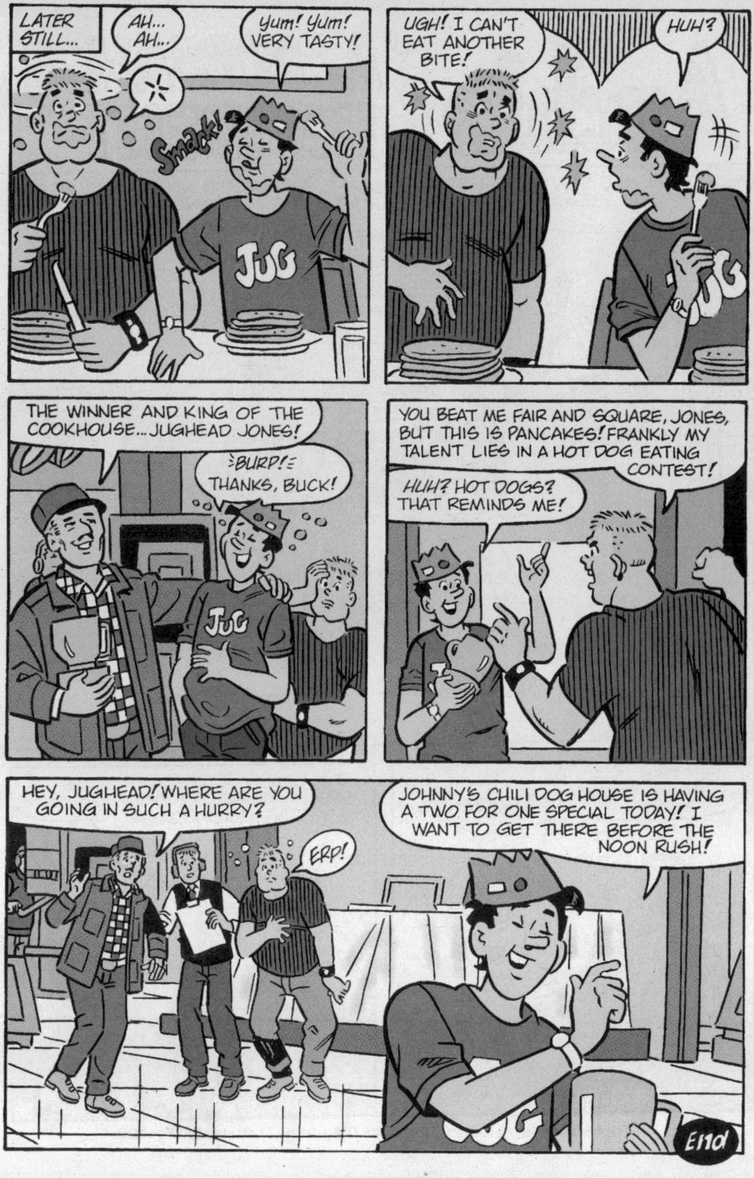
LATER STILL...
AH... AH...
Yum! Yum! VERY TASTY!
SMACK!
UGH! I CAN'T EAT ANOTHER BITE!
HUH?
THE WINNER AND KING OF THE COOKHOUSE...JUGHEAD JONES!
BURP! THANKS, BUCK!
YOU BEAT ME FAIR AND SQUARE, JONES, BUT THIS IS PANCAKES! FRANKLY MY TALENT LIES IN A HOT DOG EATING CONTEST!
HUH? HOT DOGS? THAT REMINDS ME!
HEY, JUGHEAD! WHERE ARE YOU GOING IN SUCH A HURRY?
ERP!
JOHNNY'S CHILI DOG HOUSE IS HAVING A TWO FOR ONE SPECIAL TODAY! I WANT TO GET THERE BEFORE THE NOON RUSH!
End

Archie in "A MYNAH INCIDENT"

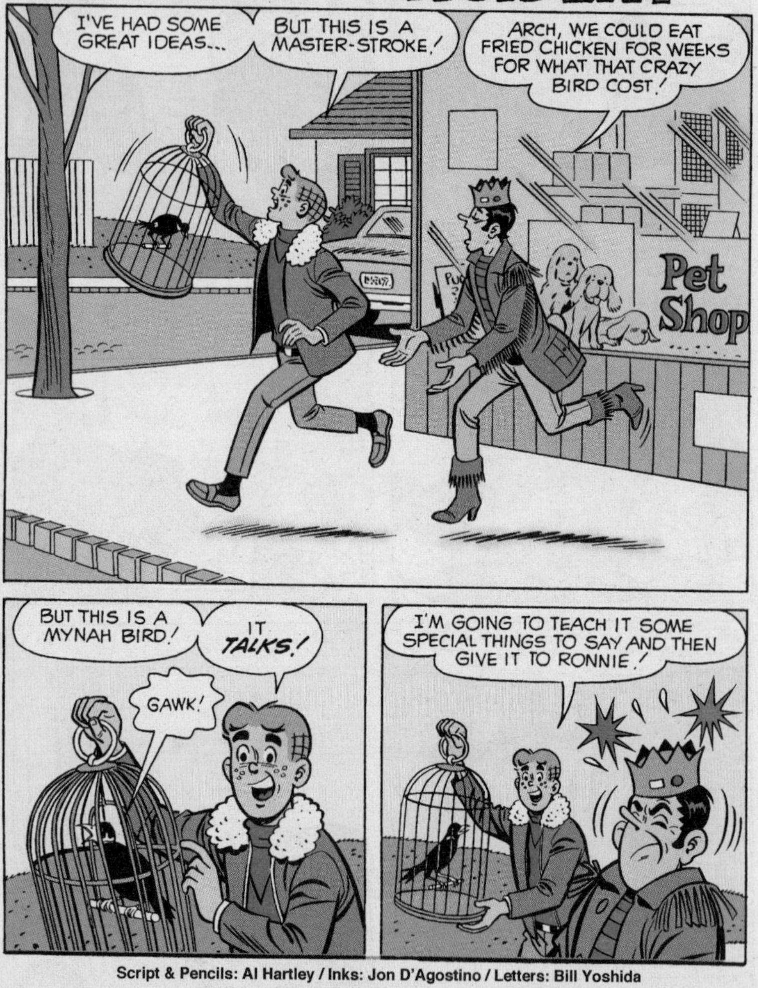
I'VE HAD SOME GREAT IDEAS...
BUT THIS IS A MASTER-STROKE!
ARCH, WE COULD EAT FRIED CHICKEN FOR WEEKS FOR WHAT THAT CRAZY BIRD COST!
Pet Shop
BUT THIS IS A MYNAH BIRD!
IT TALKS!
GAWK!
I'M GOING TO TEACH IT SOME SPECIAL THINGS TO SAY AND THEN GIVE IT TO RONNIE!

Script & Pencils: Al Hartley / Inks: Jon D'Agostino / Letters: Bill Yoshida

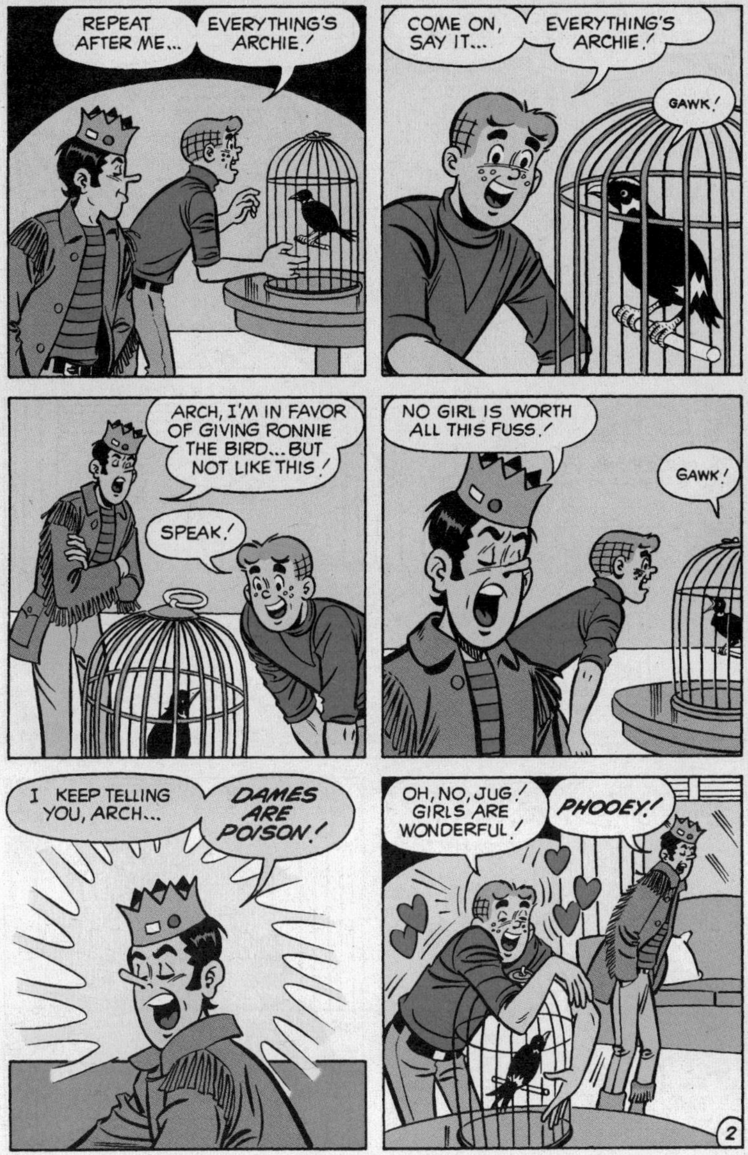
REPEAT AFTER ME...
EVERYTHING'S ARCHIE!
COME ON, SAY IT...
EVERYTHING'S ARCHIE!
GAWK!
ARCH, I'M IN FAVOR OF GIVING RONNIE THE BIRD... BUT NOT LIKE THIS!
SPEAK!
NO GIRL IS WORTH ALL THIS FUSS!
GAWK!
I KEEP TELLING YOU, ARCH...
DAMES ARE POISON!
OH, NO, JUG! GIRLS ARE WONDERFUL!
PHOOEY!
2

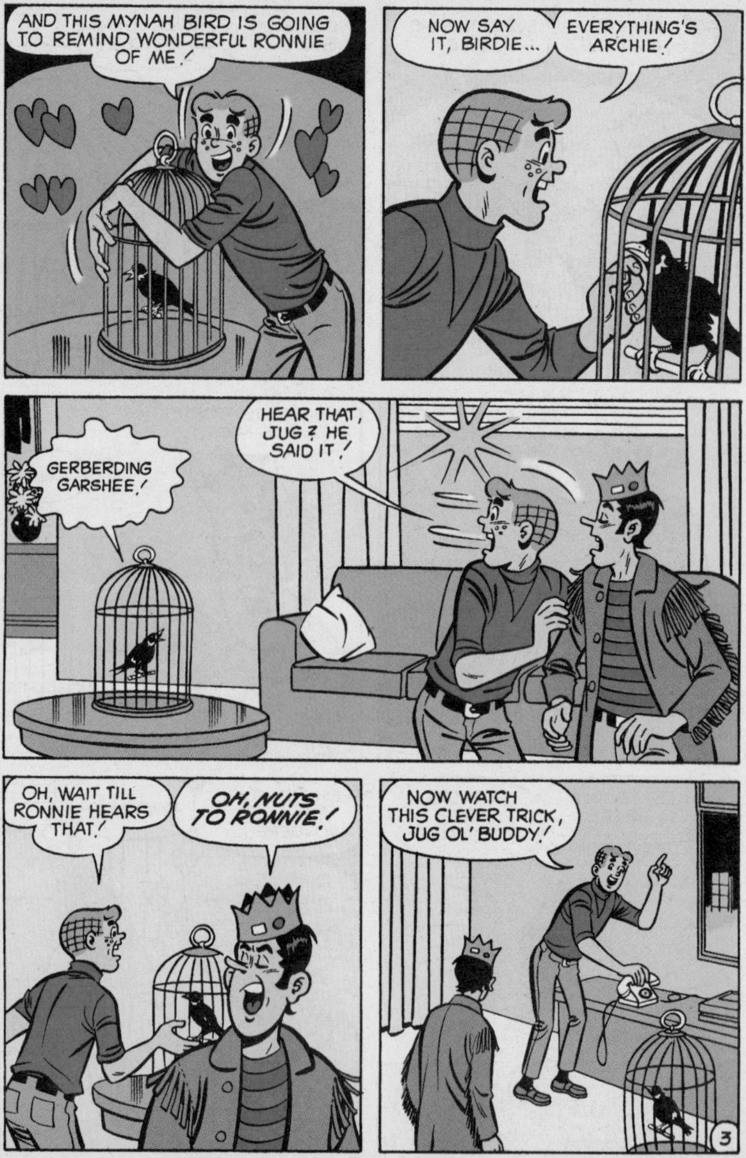
AND THIS MYNAH BIRD IS GOING TO REMIND WONDERFUL RONNIE OF ME!
NOW SAY IT, BIRDIE...
EVERYTHING'S ARCHIE!
GERBERDING GARSHEE!
HEAR THAT, JUG? HE SAID IT!
OH, WAIT TILL RONNIE HEARS THAT!
OH, NUTS TO RONNIE!
NOW WATCH THIS CLEVER TRICK, JUG OL' BUDDY!
3

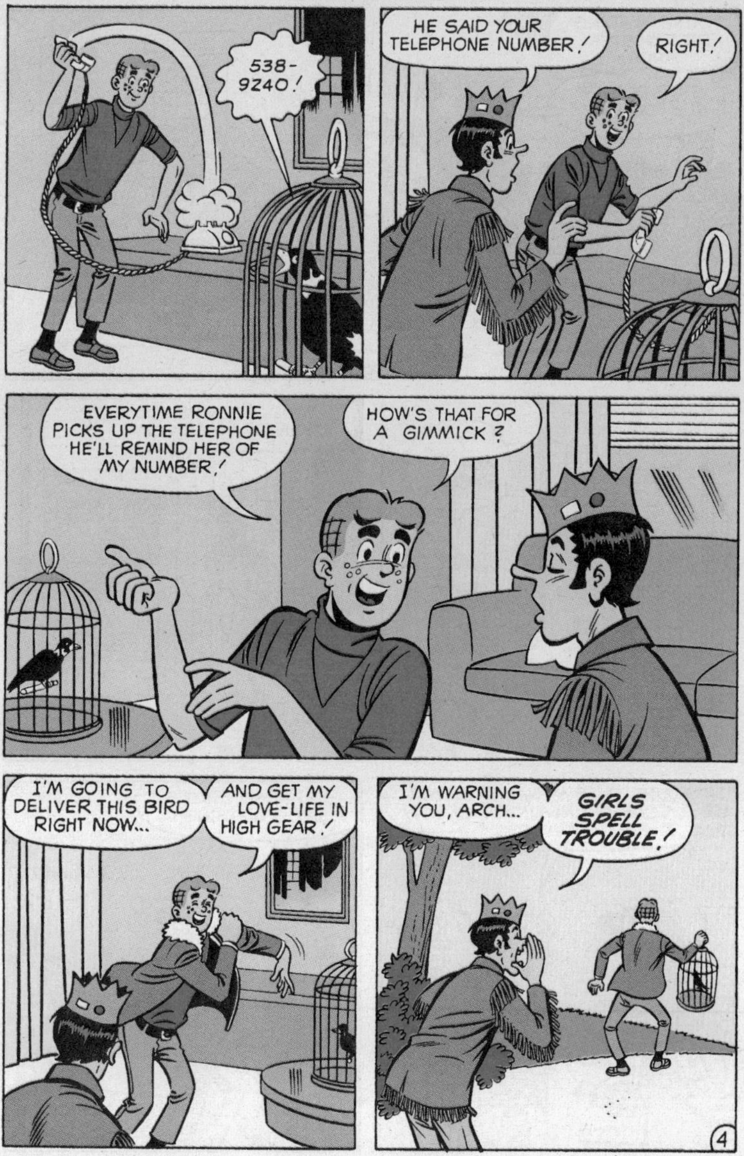

538-9240!
HE SAID YOUR TELEPHONE NUMBER!
RIGHT!
EVERYTIME RONNIE PICKS UP THE TELEPHONE HE'LL REMIND HER OF MY NUMBER!
HOW'S THAT FOR A GIMMICK?
I'M GOING TO DELIVER THIS BIRD RIGHT NOW...
AND GET MY LOVE-LIFE IN HIGH GEAR!
I'M WARNING YOU, ARCH...
GIRLS SPELL TROUBLE!
4

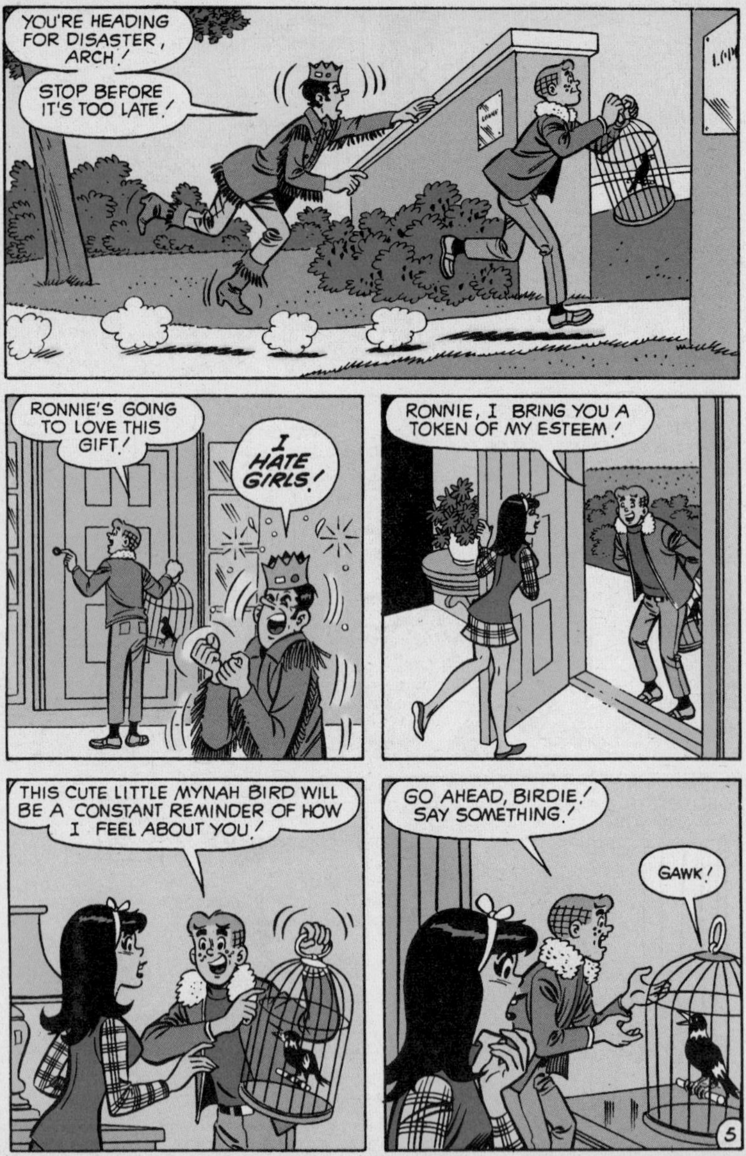

YOU'RE HEADING FOR DISASTER, ARCH!
STOP BEFORE IT'S TOO LATE!
RONNIE'S GOING TO LOVE THIS GIFT!
I HATE GIRLS!
RONNIE, I BRING YOU A TOKEN OF MY ESTEEM!
THIS CUTE LITTLE MYNAH BIRD WILL BE A CONSTANT REMINDER OF HOW I FEEL ABOUT YOU!
GO AHEAD, BIRDIE! SAY SOMETHING!
GAWK!
5

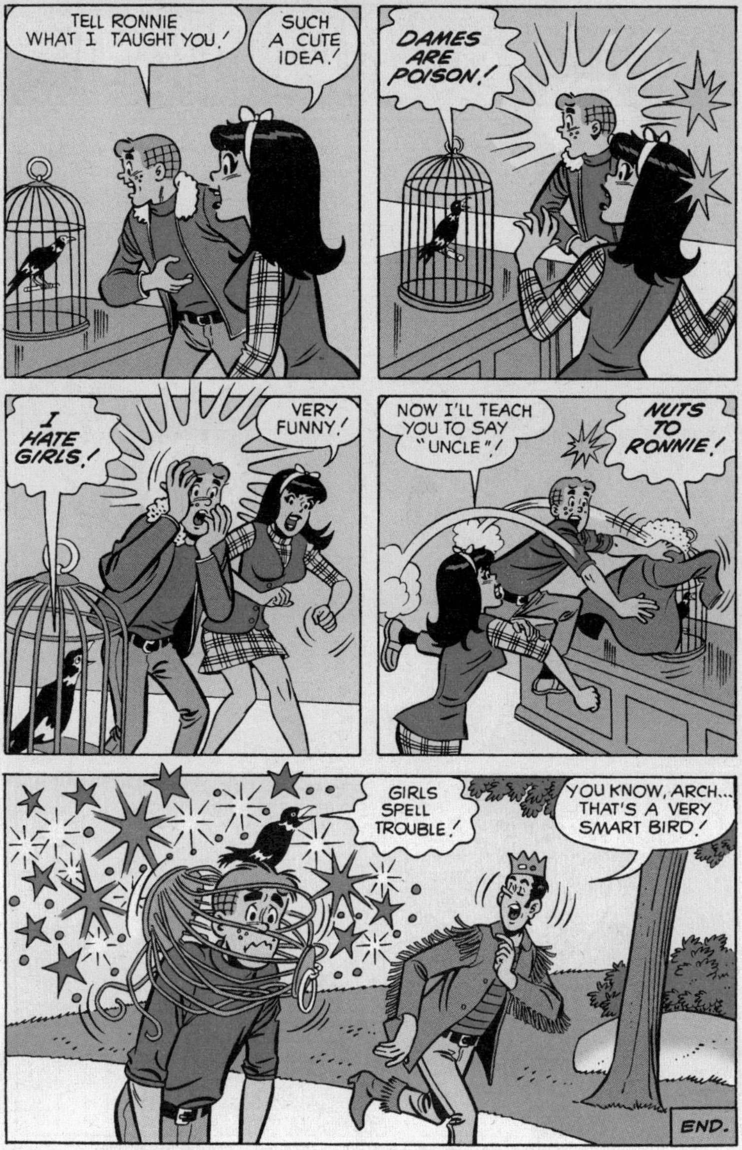
TELL RONNIE WHAT I TAUGHT YOU!
SUCH A CUTE IDEA!
DAMES ARE POISON!
I HATE GIRLS!
VERY FUNNY!
NOW I'LL TEACH YOU TO SAY "UNCLE"!
NUTS TO RONNIE!
GIRLS SPELL TROUBLE!
YOU KNOW, ARCH... THAT'S A VERY SMART BIRD!
END.

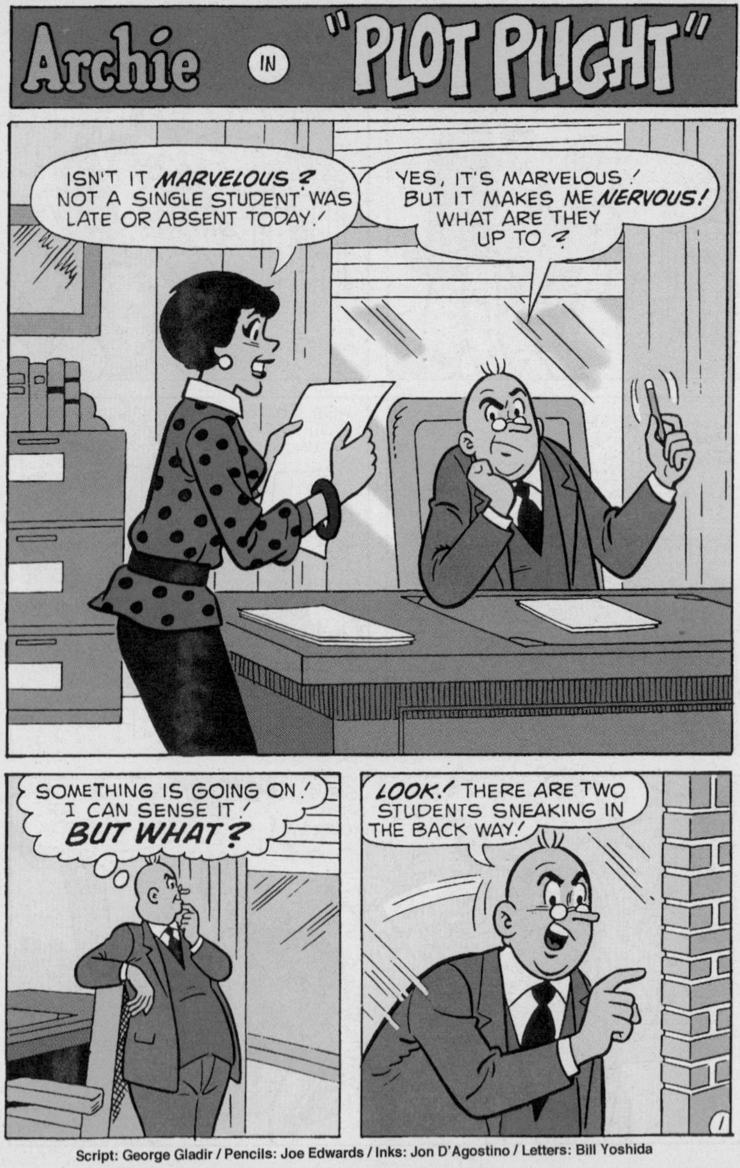
Archie IN "PLOT PLIGHT"
ISN'T IT MARVELOUS ? NOT A SINGLE STUDENT WAS LATE OR ABSENT TODAY!
YES, IT'S MARVELOUS! BUT IT MAKES ME NERVOUS! WHAT ARE THEY UP TO ?
SOMETHING IS GOING ON! I CAN SENSE IT! BUT WHAT?
LOOK! THERE ARE TWO STUDENTS SNEAKING IN THE BACK WAY!
1

Script: George Gladir / Pencils: Joe Edwards / Inks: Jon D'Agostino / Letters: Bill Yoshida

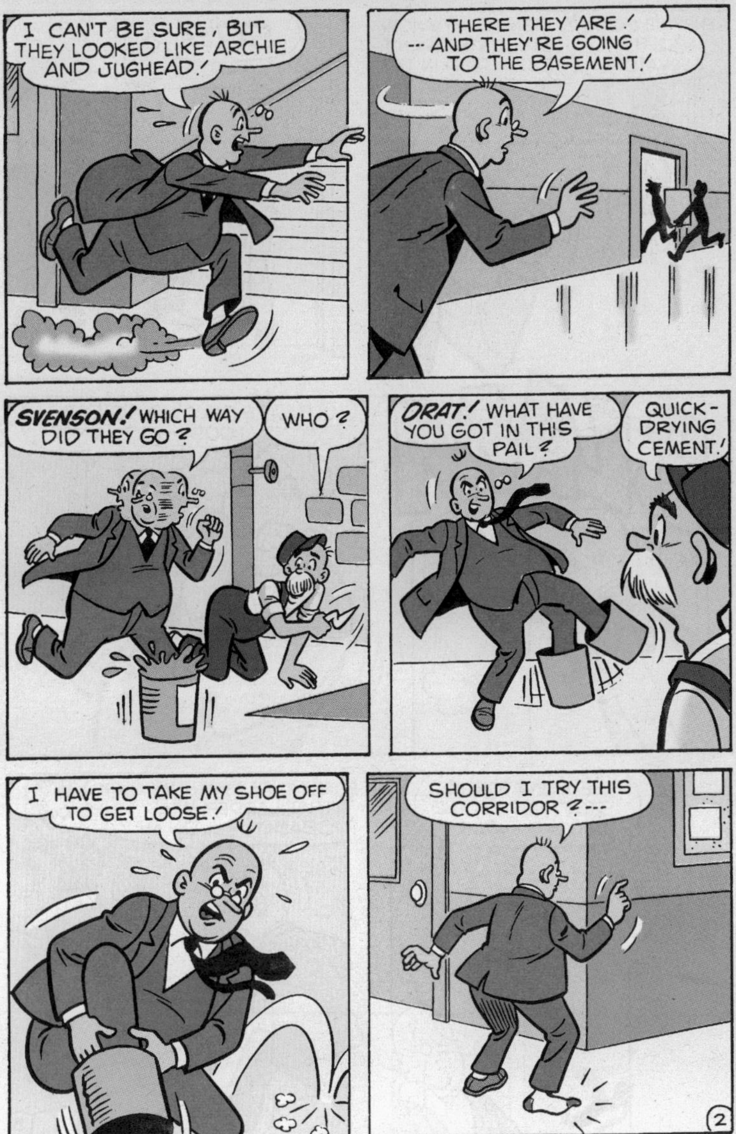

I CAN'T BE SURE, BUT THEY LOOKED LIKE ARCHIE AND JUGHEAD!
THERE THEY ARE! --- AND THEY'RE GOING TO THE BASEMENT!
SVENSON! WHICH WAY DID THEY GO?
WHO?
DRAT! WHAT HAVE YOU GOT IN THIS PAIL?
QUICK-DRYING CEMENT!
I HAVE TO TAKE MY SHOE OFF TO GET LOOSE!
SHOULD I TRY THIS CORRIDOR? ---
2

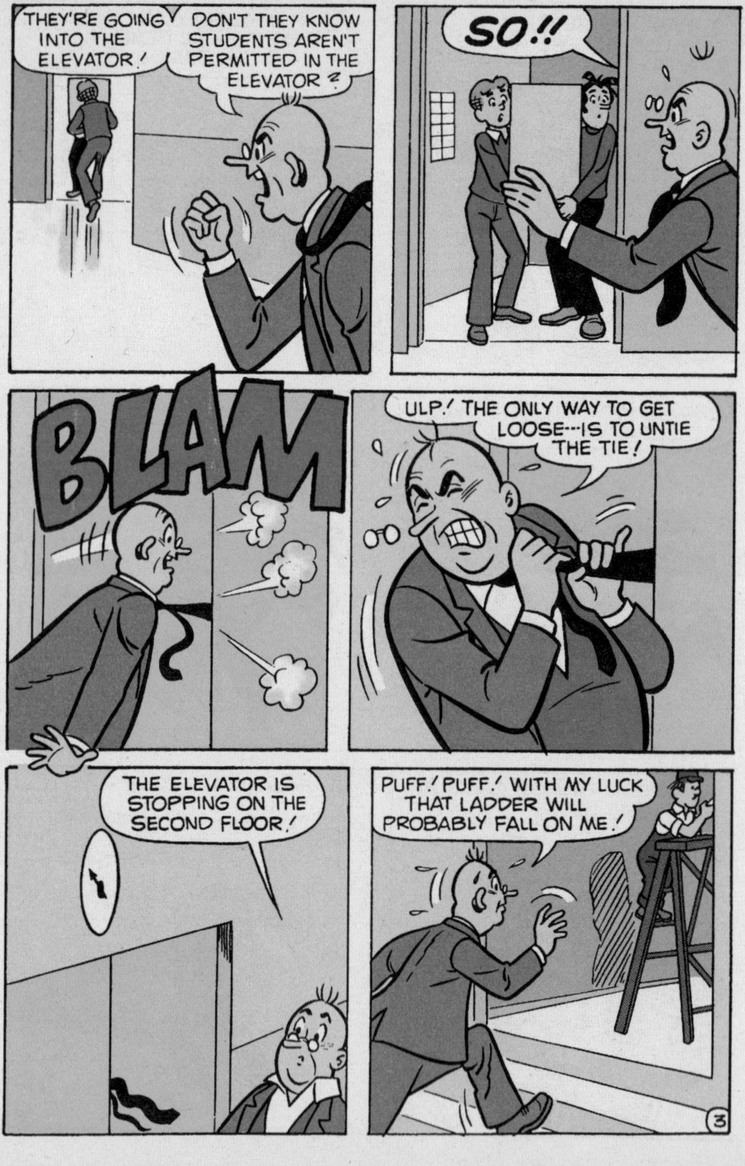
THEY'RE GOING INTO THE ELEVATOR!
DON'T THEY KNOW STUDENTS AREN'T PERMITTED IN THE ELEVATOR?
SO!!
BLAM
ULP! THE ONLY WAY TO GET LOOSE---IS TO UNTIE THE TIE!
THE ELEVATOR IS STOPPING ON THE SECOND FLOOR!
PUFF! PUFF! WITH MY LUCK THAT LADDER WILL PROBABLY FALL ON ME!
3

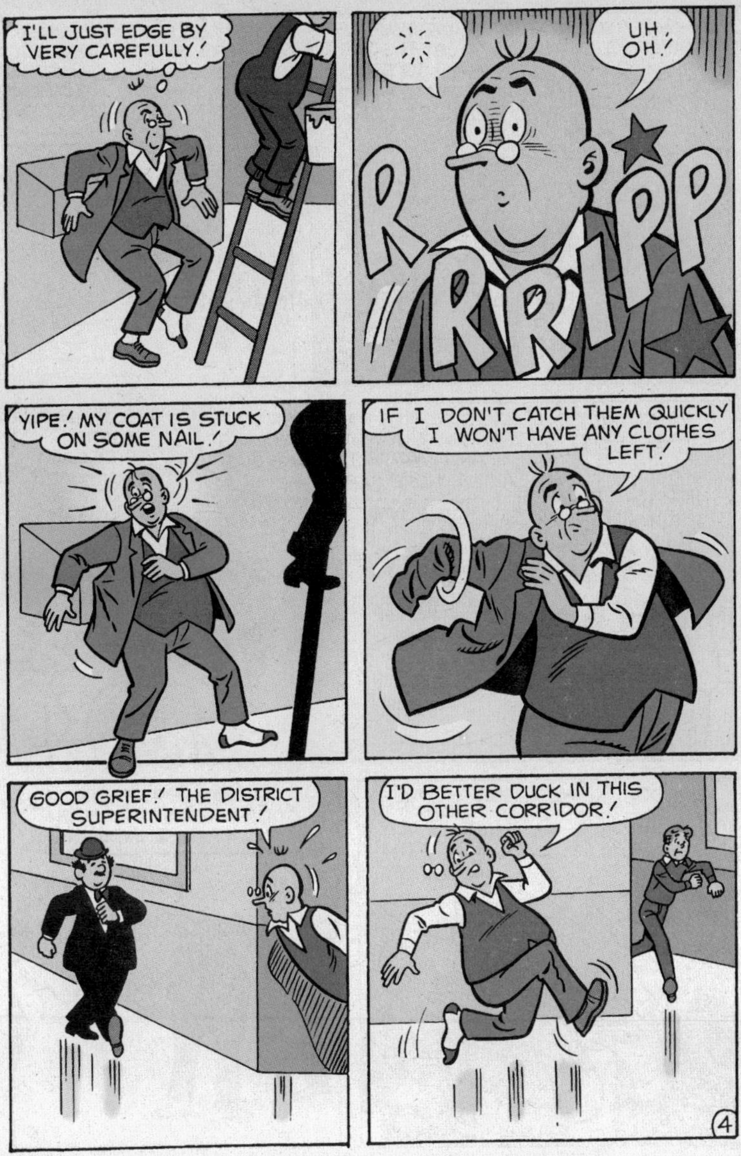
I'LL JUST EDGE BY VERY CAREFULLY!
UH, OH!
RRRIPP
YIPE! MY COAT IS STUCK ON SOME NAIL!
IF I DON'T CATCH THEM QUICKLY I WON'T HAVE ANY CLOTHES LEFT!
GOOD GRIEF! THE DISTRICT SUPERINTENDENT!
I'D BETTER DUCK IN THIS OTHER CORRIDOR!
4

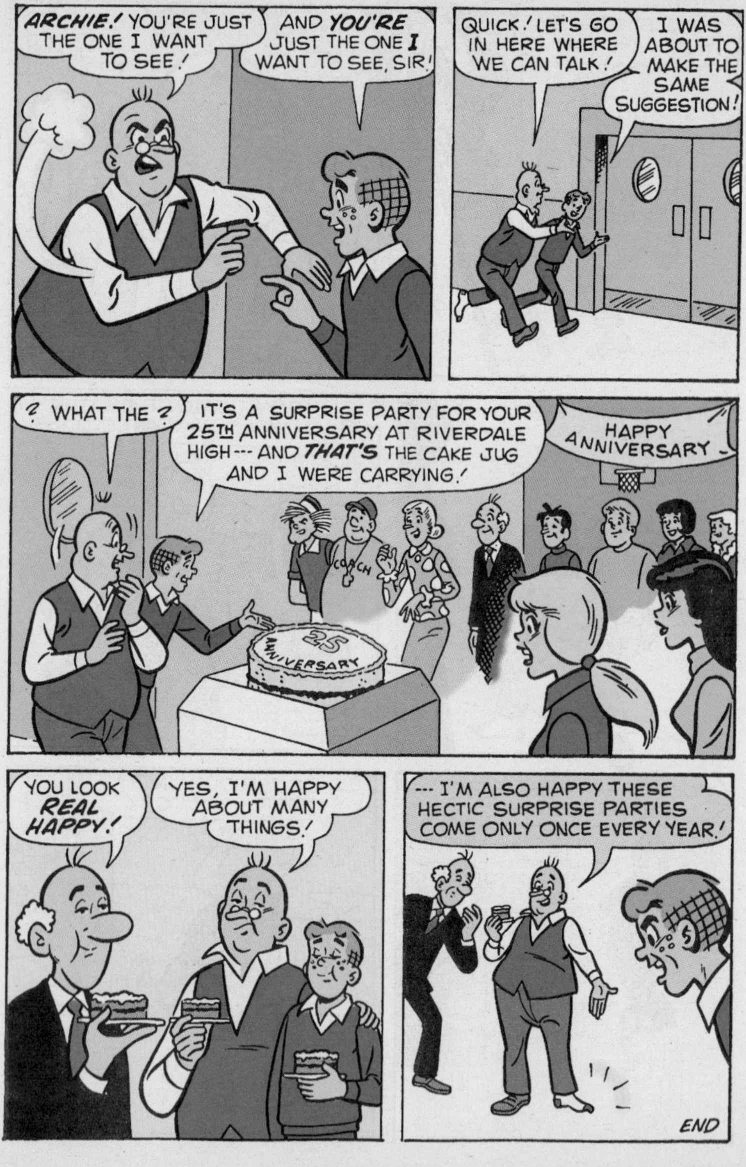

ARCHIE! YOU'RE JUST THE ONE I WANT TO SEE!
AND YOU'RE JUST THE ONE I WANT TO SEE, SIR!
QUICK! LET'S GO IN HERE WHERE WE CAN TALK!
I WAS ABOUT TO MAKE THE SAME SUGGESTION!
? WHAT THE ?
IT'S A SURPRISE PARTY FOR YOUR 25TH ANNIVERSARY AT RIVERDALE HIGH --- AND THAT'S THE CAKE JUG AND I WERE CARRYING!
HAPPY ANNIVERSARY
25 ANNIVERSARY
COACH
YOU LOOK REAL HAPPY!
YES, I'M HAPPY ABOUT MANY THINGS!
--- I'M ALSO HAPPY THESE HECTIC SURPRISE PARTIES COME ONLY ONCE EVERY YEAR!
END

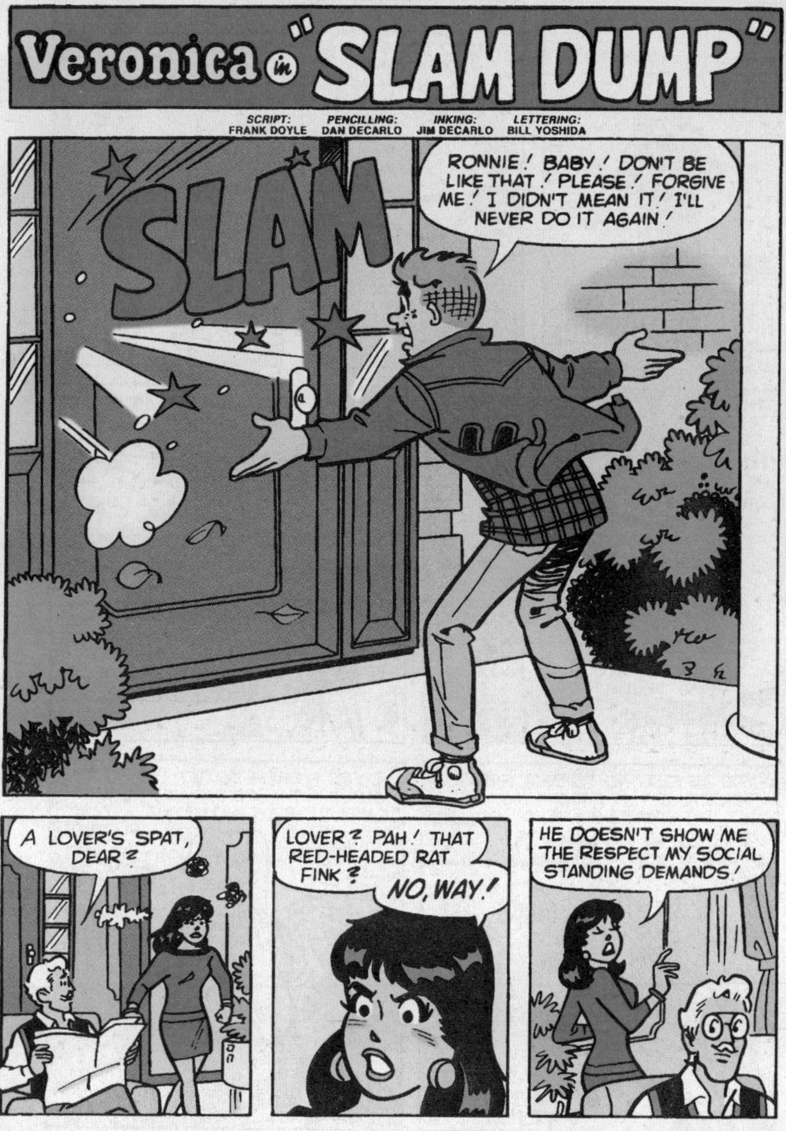

Veronica in "SLAM DUMP"
SCRIPT: FRANK DOYLE PENCILLING: DAN DECARLO INKING: JIM DECARLO LETTERING: BILL YOSHIDA
SLAM
RONNIE! BABY! DON'T BE LIKE THAT! PLEASE! FORGIVE ME! I DIDN'T MEAN IT! I'LL NEVER DO IT AGAIN!
A LOVER'S SPAT, DEAR?
LOVER? PAH! THAT RED-HEADED RAT FINK? NO, WAY!
HE DOESN'T SHOW ME THE RESPECT MY SOCIAL STANDING DEMANDS!

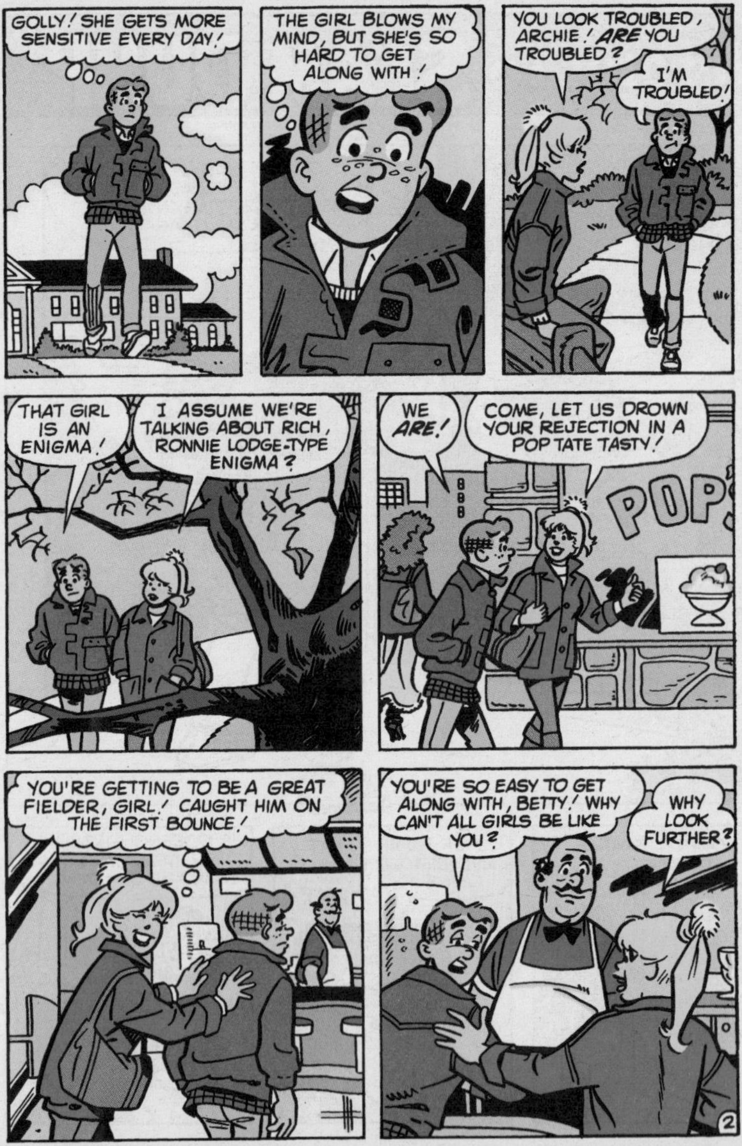
GOLLY! SHE GETS MORE SENSITIVE EVERY DAY!
THE GIRL BLOWS MY MIND, BUT SHE'S SO HARD TO GET ALONG WITH!
YOU LOOK TROUBLED, ARCHIE! ARE YOU TROUBLED?
I'M TROUBLED!
THAT GIRL IS AN ENIGMA!
I ASSUME WE'RE TALKING ABOUT RICH, RONNIE LODGE-TYPE ENIGMA?
WE ARE!
COME, LET US DROWN YOUR REJECTION IN A POP TATE TASTY!
POP'
YOU'RE GETTING TO BE A GREAT FIELDER, GIRL! CAUGHT HIM ON THE FIRST BOUNCE!
YOU'RE SO EASY TO GET ALONG WITH, BETTY! WHY CAN'T ALL GIRLS BE LIKE YOU?
WHY LOOK FURTHER?

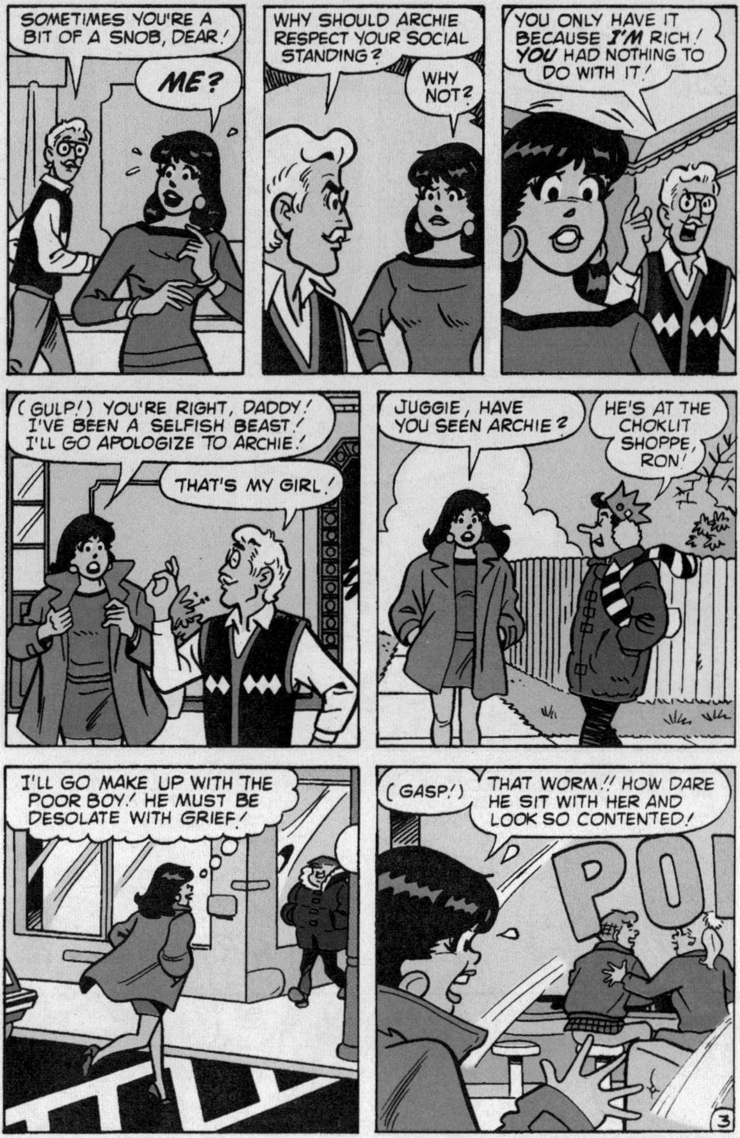
SOMETIMES YOU'RE A BIT OF A SNOB, DEAR!
ME?
WHY SHOULD ARCHIE RESPECT YOUR SOCIAL STANDING?
WHY NOT?
YOU ONLY HAVE IT BECAUSE I'M RICH! YOU HAD NOTHING TO DO WITH IT!
(GULP!) YOU'RE RIGHT, DADDY! I'VE BEEN A SELFISH BEAST! I'LL GO APOLOGIZE TO ARCHIE!
THAT'S MY GIRL!
JUGGIE, HAVE YOU SEEN ARCHIE?
HE'S AT THE CHOKLIT SHOPPE, RON!
I'LL GO MAKE UP WITH THE POOR BOY! HE MUST BE DESOLATE WITH GRIEF!
(GASP!)
THAT WORM!! HOW DARE HE SIT WITH HER AND LOOK SO CONTENTED!
PO
3

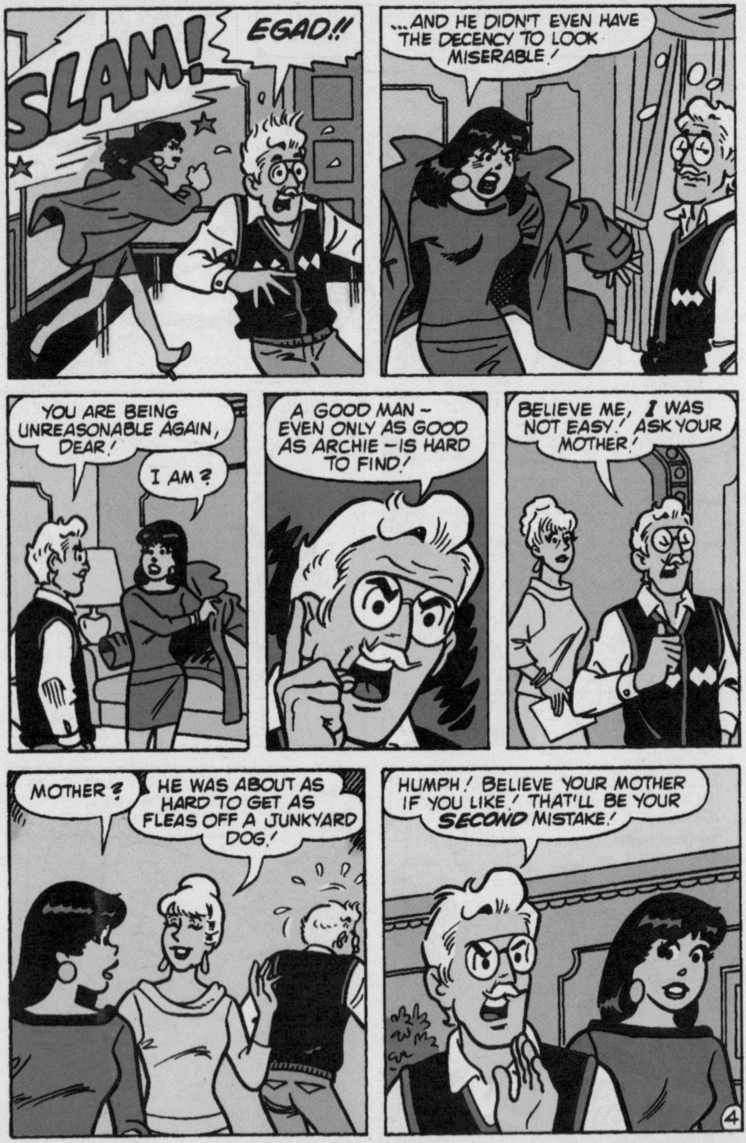
SLAM!
EGAD!!
...AND HE DIDN'T EVEN HAVE THE DECENCY TO LOOK MISERABLE!
YOU ARE BEING UNREASONABLE AGAIN, DEAR!
I AM?
A GOOD MAN – EVEN ONLY AS GOOD AS ARCHIE – IS HARD TO FIND!
BELIEVE ME, I WAS NOT EASY! ASK YOUR MOTHER!
MOTHER?
HE WAS ABOUT AS HARD TO GET AS FLEAS OFF A JUNKYARD DOG!
HUMPH! BELIEVE YOUR MOTHER IF YOU LIKE! THAT'LL BE YOUR SECOND MISTAKE!
4

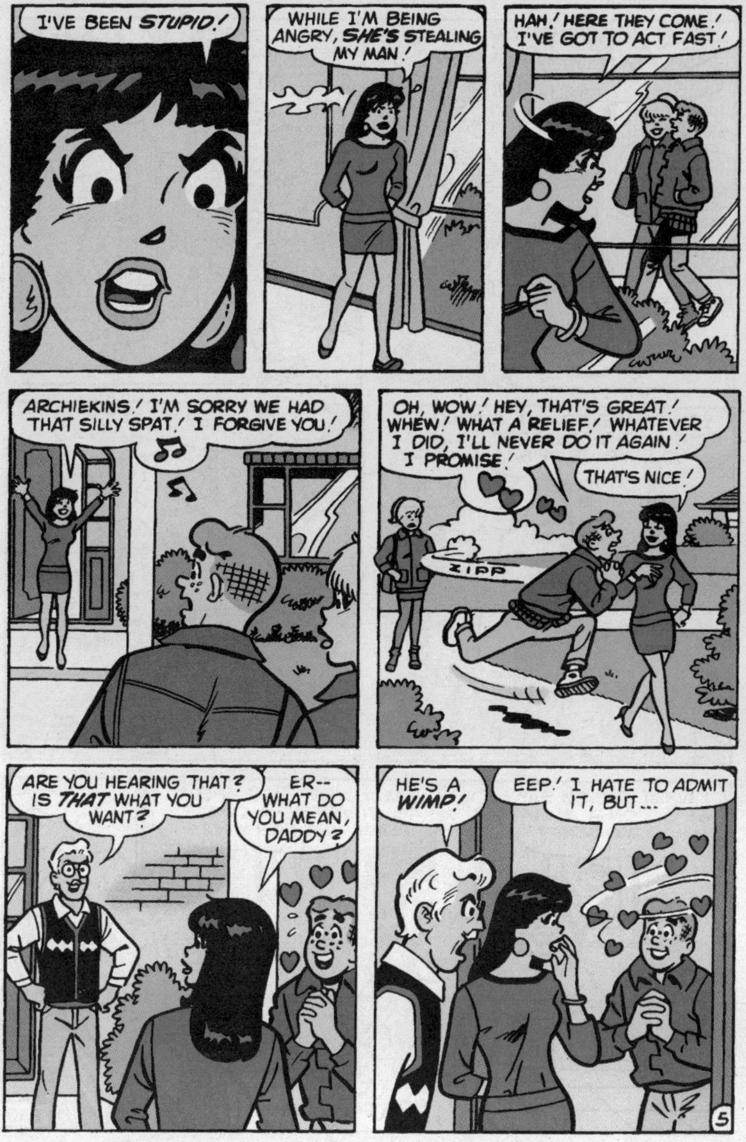
I'VE BEEN STUPID!
WHILE I'M BEING ANGRY, SHE'S STEALING MY MAN!
HAH! HERE THEY COME! I'VE GOT TO ACT FAST!
ARCHIEKINS! I'M SORRY WE HAD THAT SILLY SPAT! I FORGIVE YOU!
OH, WOW! HEY, THAT'S GREAT! WHEW! WHAT A RELIEF! WHATEVER I DID, I'LL NEVER DO IT AGAIN! I PROMISE!
THAT'S NICE!
ZIPP
ARE YOU HEARING THAT? IS THAT WHAT YOU WANT?
ER-- WHAT DO YOU MEAN, DADDY?
HE'S A WIMP!
EEP! I HATE TO ADMIT IT, BUT...
5

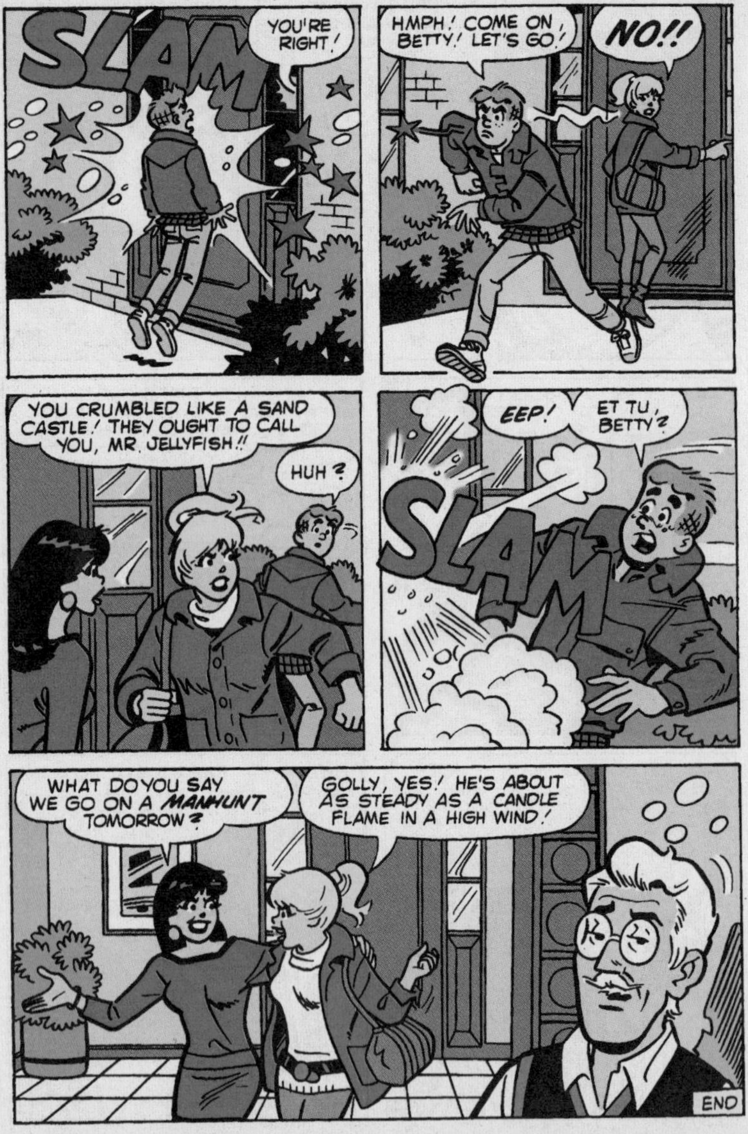
SLAM
YOU'RE RIGHT!
HMPH! COME ON, BETTY! LET'S GO!
NO!!
YOU CRUMBLED LIKE A SAND CASTLE! THEY OUGHT TO CALL YOU, MR. JELLYFISH!!
HUH?
EEP!
ET TU, BETTY?
SLAM
WHAT DO YOU SAY WE GO ON A MANHUNT TOMORROW?
GOLLY, YES! HE'S ABOUT AS STEADY AS A CANDLE FLAME IN A HIGH WIND!
END

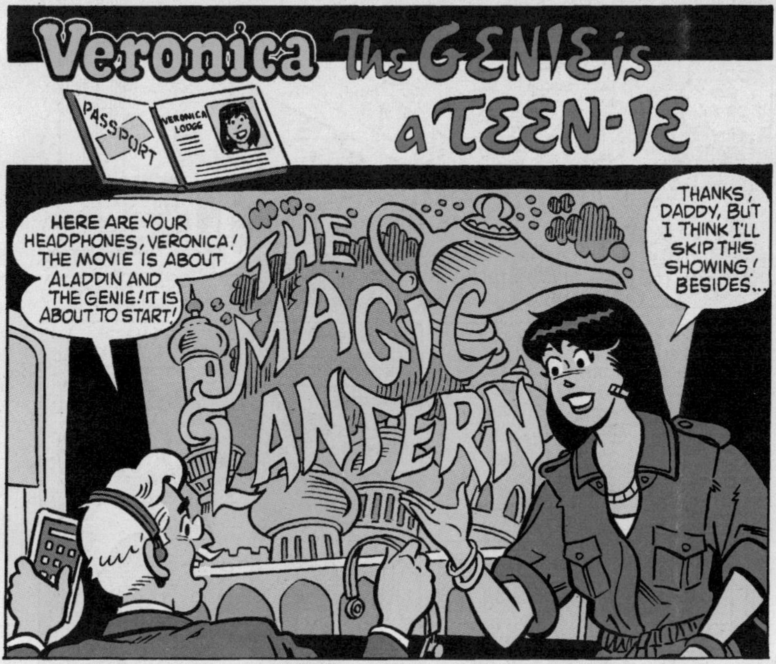
Veronica
The GENIE is a TEEN-IE
PASSPORT
VERONICA LODGE
THE MAGIC LANTERN
HERE ARE YOUR HEADPHONES, VERONICA! THE MOVIE IS ABOUT ALADDIN AND THE GENIE! IT IS ABOUT TO START!
THANKS, DADDY, BUT I THINK I'LL SKIP THIS SHOWING! BESIDES...

SCRIPT: ANGELO DECESARE PENCILLING: STAN GOLDBERG INKING: RUDY LAPICK LETTERING: BILL YOSHIDA COLORING: DAN PARENT

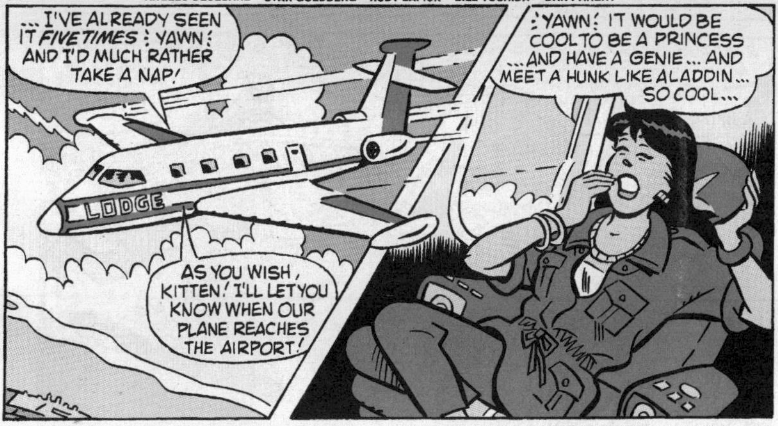
... I'VE ALREADY SEEN IT FIVE TIMES ⁝ YAWN ⁝ AND I'D MUCH RATHER TAKE A NAP!
⁝ YAWN ⁝ IT WOULD BE COOL TO BE A PRINCESS ... AND HAVE A GENIE ... AND MEET A HUNK LIKE ALADDIN... SO COOL...
LODGE
AS YOU WISH, KITTEN! I'LL LET YOU KNOW WHEN OUR PLANE REACHES THE AIRPORT!

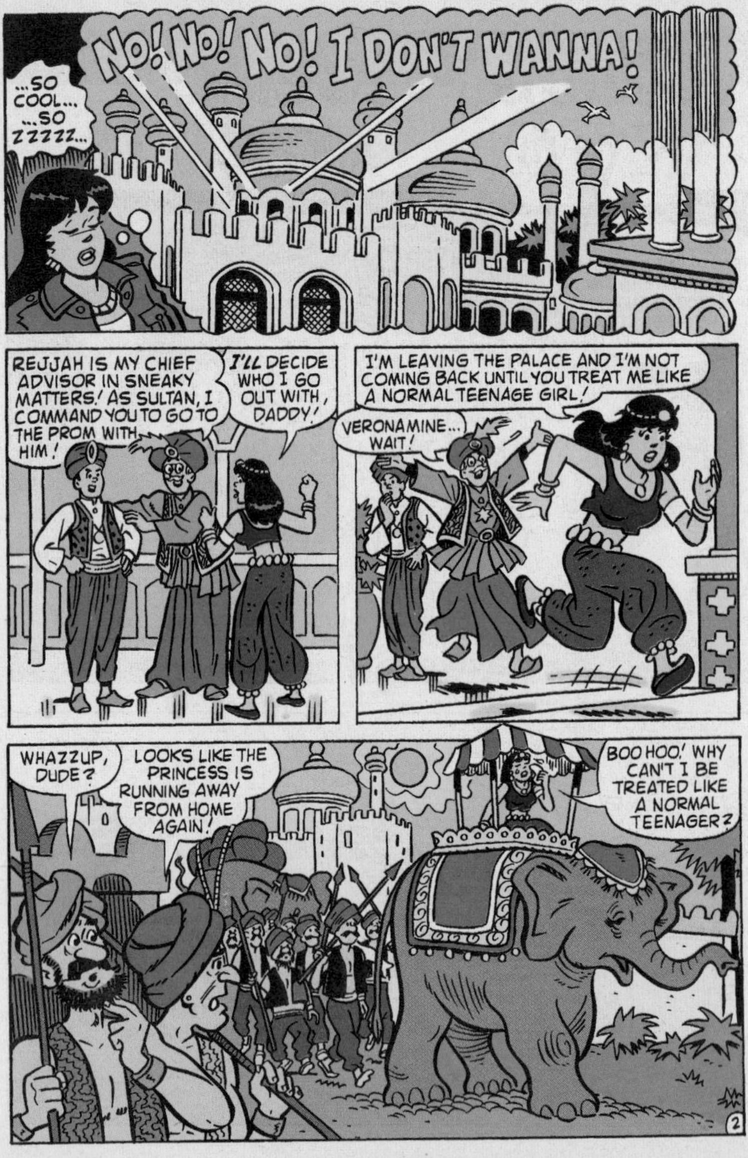
...SO COOL... ...SO ZZZZZ...
NO! NO! NO! I DON'T WANNA!
REJJAH IS MY CHIEF ADVISOR IN SNEAKY MATTERS! AS SULTAN, I COMMAND YOU TO GO TO THE PROM WITH HIM!
I'LL DECIDE WHO I GO OUT WITH, DADDY!
I'M LEAVING THE PALACE AND I'M NOT COMING BACK UNTIL YOU TREAT ME LIKE A NORMAL TEENAGE GIRL!
VERONAMINE... WAIT!
WHAZZUP, DUDE?
LOOKS LIKE THE PRINCESS IS RUNNING AWAY FROM HOME AGAIN!
BOO HOO! WHY CAN'T I BE TREATED LIKE A NORMAL TEENAGER?
2

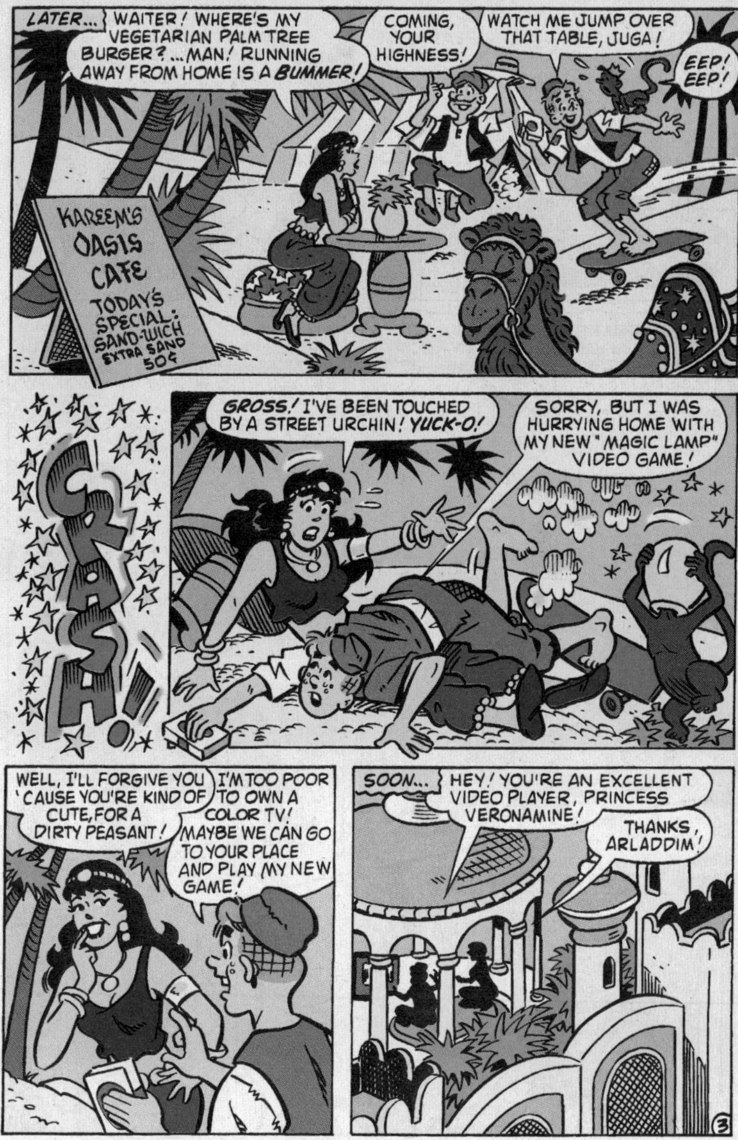

LATER...
WAITER! WHERE'S MY VEGETARIAN PALM TREE BURGER? ...MAN! RUNNING AWAY FROM HOME IS A BUMMER!
COMING, YOUR HIGHNESS!
WATCH ME JUMP OVER THAT TABLE, JUGA!
EEP! EEP!
KAREEM'S OASIS CAFE
TODAY'S SPECIAL: SAND-WICH
EXTRA SAND 50¢
CRASH!
GROSS! I'VE BEEN TOUCHED BY A STREET URCHIN! YUCK-O!
SORRY, BUT I WAS HURRYING HOME WITH MY NEW "MAGIC LAMP" VIDEO GAME!
WELL, I'LL FORGIVE YOU 'CAUSE YOU'RE KIND OF CUTE, FOR A DIRTY PEASANT!
I'M TOO POOR TO OWN A COLOR TV! MAYBE WE CAN GO TO YOUR PLACE AND PLAY MY NEW GAME!
SOON...
HEY! YOU'RE AN EXCELLENT VIDEO PLAYER, PRINCESS VERONAMINE!
THANKS, ARLADDIM!
3

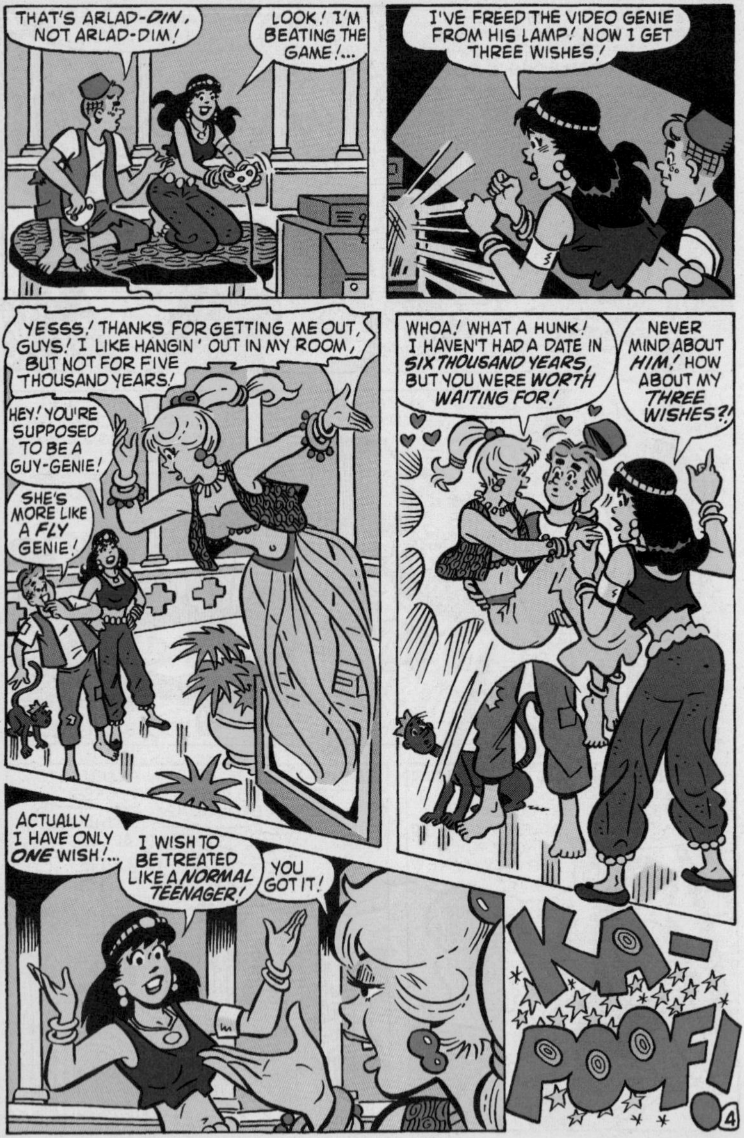

THAT'S ARLAD-DIN, NOT ARLAD-DIM!
LOOK! I'M BEATING THE GAME!...
I'VE FREED THE VIDEO GENIE FROM HIS LAMP! NOW I GET THREE WISHES!
YESSS! THANKS FOR GETTING ME OUT, GUYS! I LIKE HANGIN' OUT IN MY ROOM, BUT NOT FOR FIVE THOUSAND YEARS!
HEY! YOU'RE SUPPOSED TO BE A GUY-GENIE!
SHE'S MORE LIKE A FLY GENIE!
WHOA! WHAT A HUNK! I HAVEN'T HAD A DATE IN SIX THOUSAND YEARS, BUT YOU WERE WORTH WAITING FOR!
NEVER MIND ABOUT HIM! HOW ABOUT MY THREE WISHES?!
ACTUALLY I HAVE ONLY ONE WISH!...
I WISH TO BE TREATED LIKE A NORMAL TEENAGER!
YOU GOT IT!
KA-POOF!
4

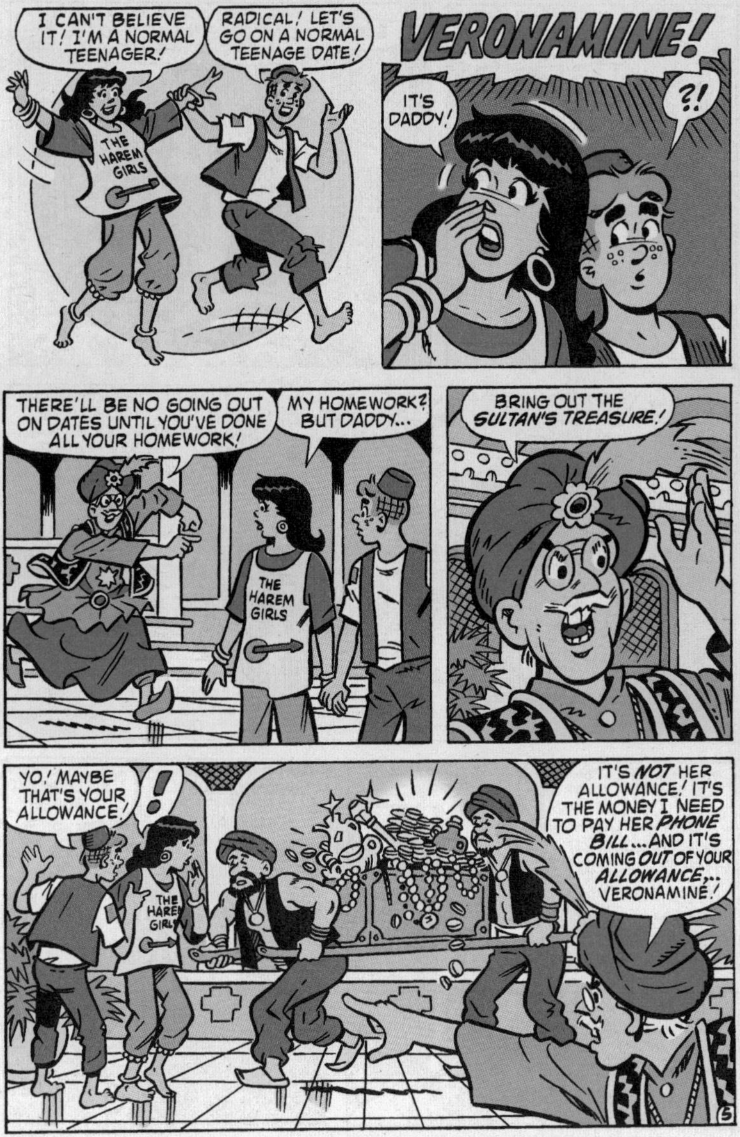
I CAN'T BELIEVE IT! I'M A NORMAL TEENAGER!
RADICAL! LET'S GO ON A NORMAL TEENAGE DATE!
THE HAREM GIRLS
VERONAMINE!
IT'S DADDY!
?!
THERE'LL BE NO GOING OUT ON DATES UNTIL YOU'VE DONE ALL YOUR HOMEWORK!
MY HOMEWORK? BUT DADDY...
THE HAREM GIRLS
BRING OUT THE SULTAN'S TREASURE!
YO! MAYBE THAT'S YOUR ALLOWANCE!
!
THE HAREM GIRLS
IT'S NOT HER ALLOWANCE! IT'S THE MONEY I NEED TO PAY HER PHONE BILL... AND IT'S COMING OUT OF YOUR ALLOWANCE,... VERONAMINE!
5

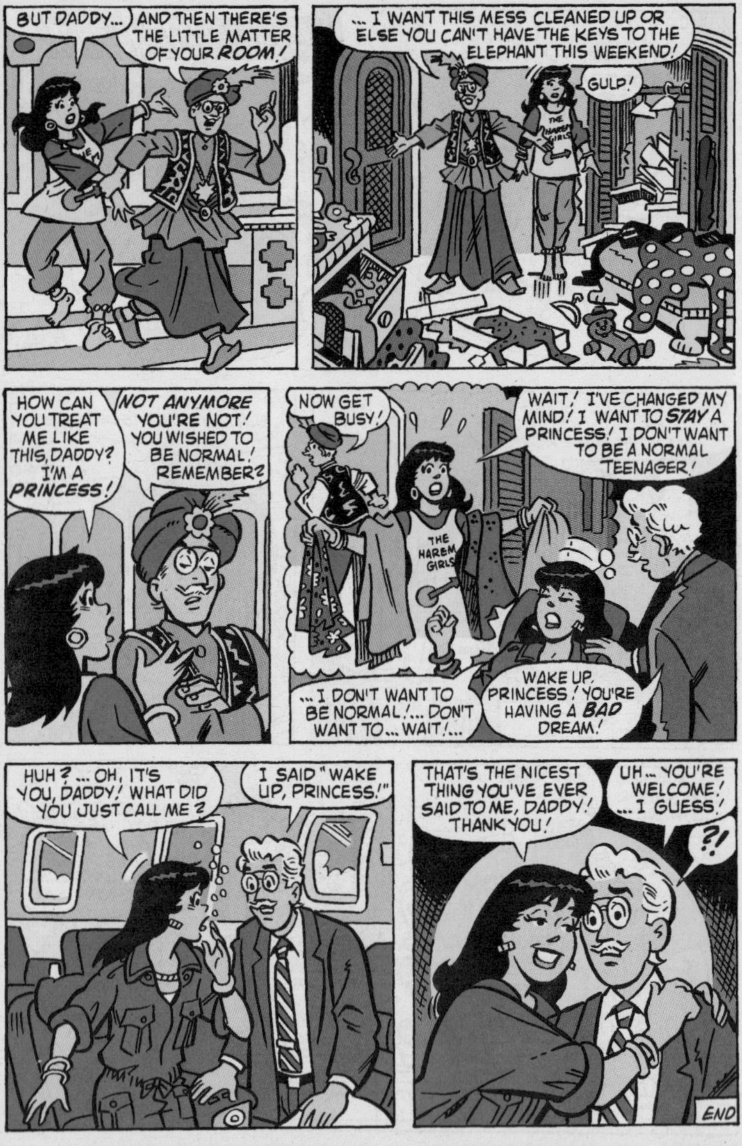
BUT DADDY...
AND THEN THERE'S THE LITTLE MATTER OF YOUR ROOM!
... I WANT THIS MESS CLEANED UP OR ELSE YOU CAN'T HAVE THE KEYS TO THE ELEPHANT THIS WEEKEND!
GULP!
THE HAREM GIRLS
HOW CAN YOU TREAT ME LIKE THIS, DADDY? I'M A PRINCESS!
NOT ANYMORE YOU'RE NOT! YOU WISHED TO BE NORMAL! REMEMBER?
NOW GET BUSY!
WAIT! I'VE CHANGED MY MIND! I WANT TO STAY A PRINCESS! I DON'T WANT TO BE A NORMAL TEENAGER!
THE HAREM GIRLS
... I DON'T WANT TO BE NORMAL!... DON'T WANT TO... WAIT!...
WAKE UP, PRINCESS! YOU'RE HAVING A BAD DREAM!
HUH? ... OH, IT'S YOU, DADDY! WHAT DID YOU JUST CALL ME?
I SAID "WAKE UP, PRINCESS!"
THAT'S THE NICEST THING YOU'VE EVER SAID TO ME, DADDY! THANK YOU!
UH... YOU'RE WELCOME! ... I GUESS!
?!
END

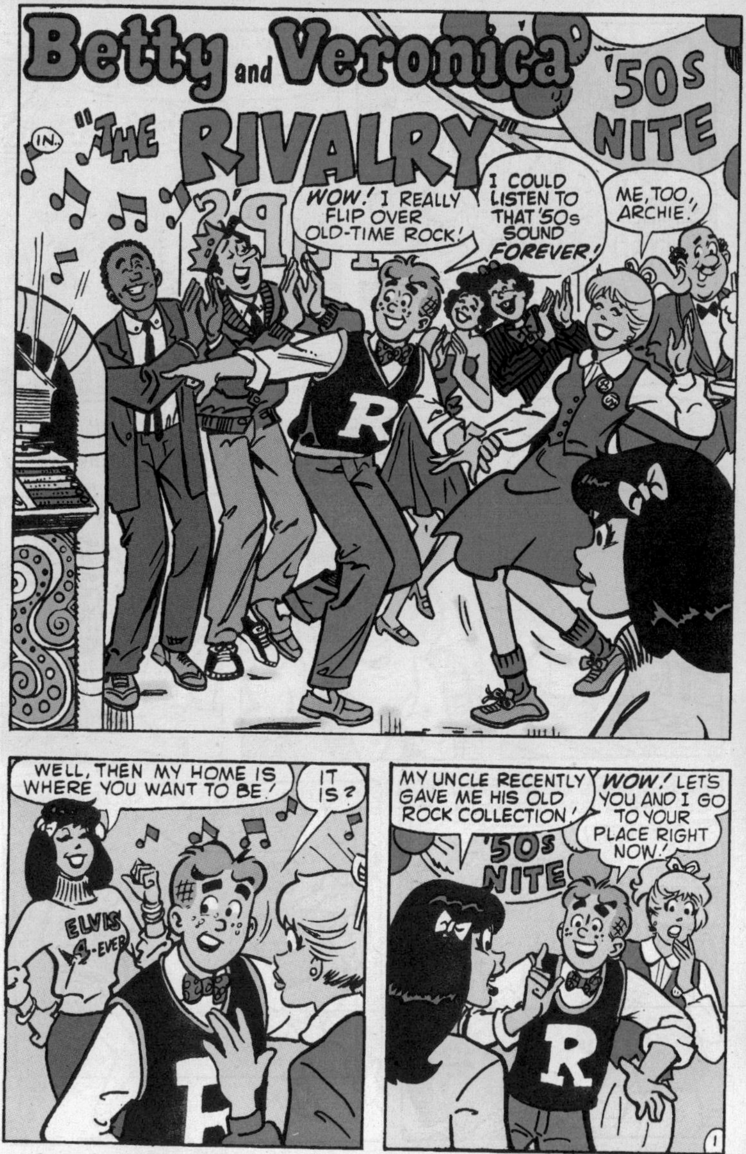
Betty and Veronica
in "THE RIVALRY"
'50s NITE
WOW! I REALLY FLIP OVER OLD-TIME ROCK!
I COULD LISTEN TO THAT '50s SOUND FOREVER!
ME, TOO, ARCHIE!
WELL, THEN MY HOME IS WHERE YOU WANT TO BE!
IT IS?
ELVIS 4-EVER
MY UNCLE RECENTLY GAVE ME HIS OLD ROCK COLLECTION!
WOW! LET'S YOU AND I GO TO YOUR PLACE RIGHT NOW!
'50s NITE
1

Script: George Gladir / Pencils: Stan Goldberg / Inks: Mike Esposito / Letters: Bill Yoshida

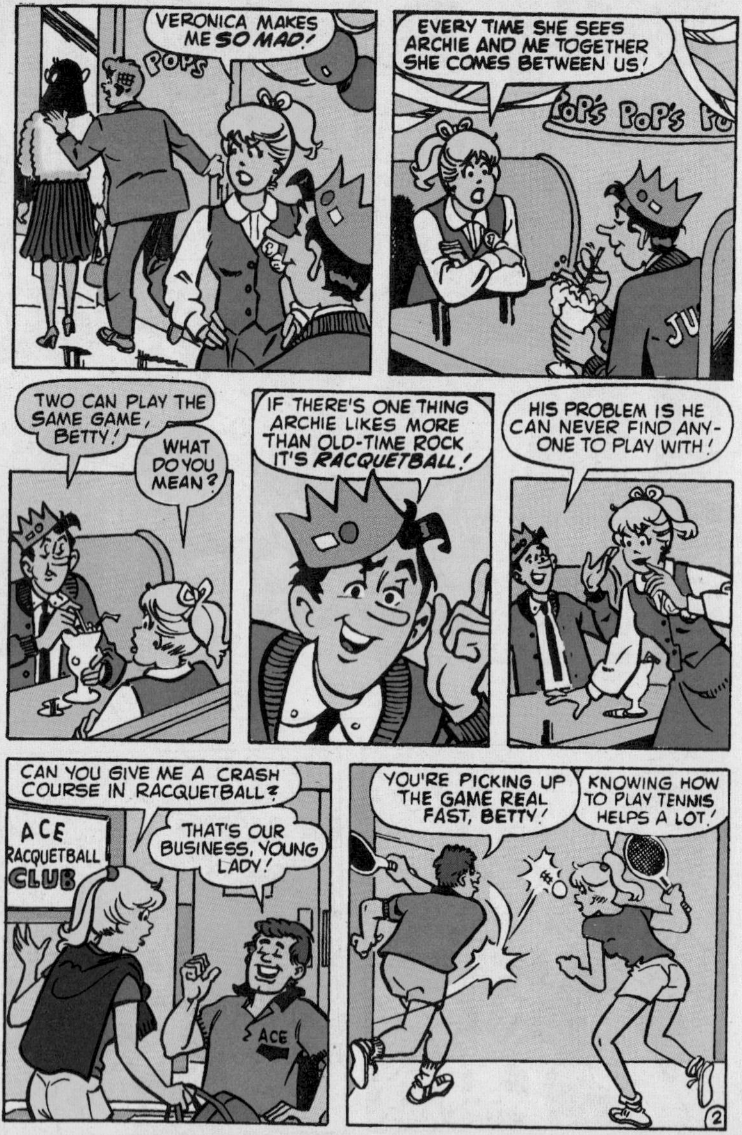
VERONICA MAKES ME SO MAD!
POP'S
EVERY TIME SHE SEES ARCHIE AND ME TOGETHER SHE COMES BETWEEN US!
POP'S POP'S
TWO CAN PLAY THE SAME GAME, BETTY!
WHAT DO YOU MEAN?
IF THERE'S ONE THING ARCHIE LIKES MORE THAN OLD-TIME ROCK IT'S RACQUETBALL!
HIS PROBLEM IS HE CAN NEVER FIND ANYONE TO PLAY WITH!
CAN YOU GIVE ME A CRASH COURSE IN RACQUETBALL?
ACE RACQUETBALL CLUB
THAT'S OUR BUSINESS, YOUNG LADY!
ACE
YOU'RE PICKING UP THE GAME REAL FAST, BETTY!
KNOWING HOW TO PLAY TENNIS HELPS A LOT!
2

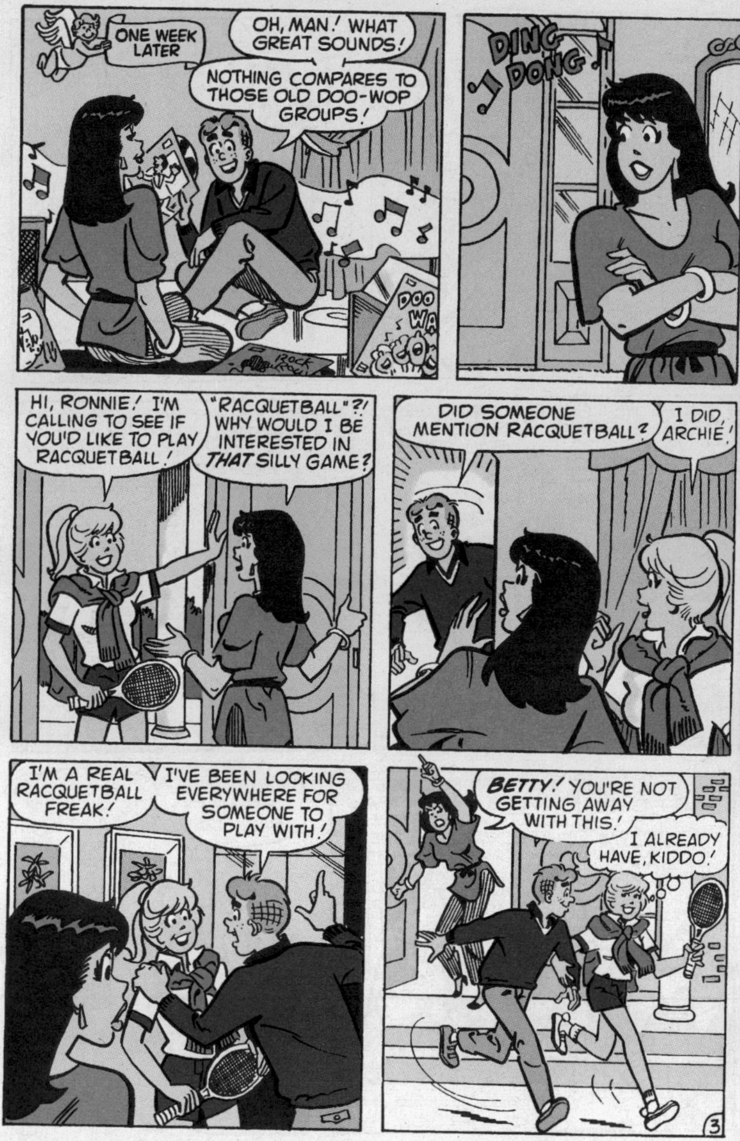
ONE WEEK LATER
OH, MAN! WHAT GREAT SOUNDS!
NOTHING COMPARES TO THOSE OLD DOO-WOP GROUPS!
DOO WA
ROCK ROLL
DING DONG
HI, RONNIE! I'M CALLING TO SEE IF YOU'D LIKE TO PLAY RACQUETBALL!
"RACQUETBALL"?! WHY WOULD I BE INTERESTED IN THAT SILLY GAME?
DID SOMEONE MENTION RACQUETBALL?
I DID, ARCHIE!
I'M A REAL RACQUETBALL FREAK!
I'VE BEEN LOOKING EVERYWHERE FOR SOMEONE TO PLAY WITH!
BETTY! YOU'RE NOT GETTING AWAY WITH THIS!
I ALREADY HAVE, KIDDO!
3

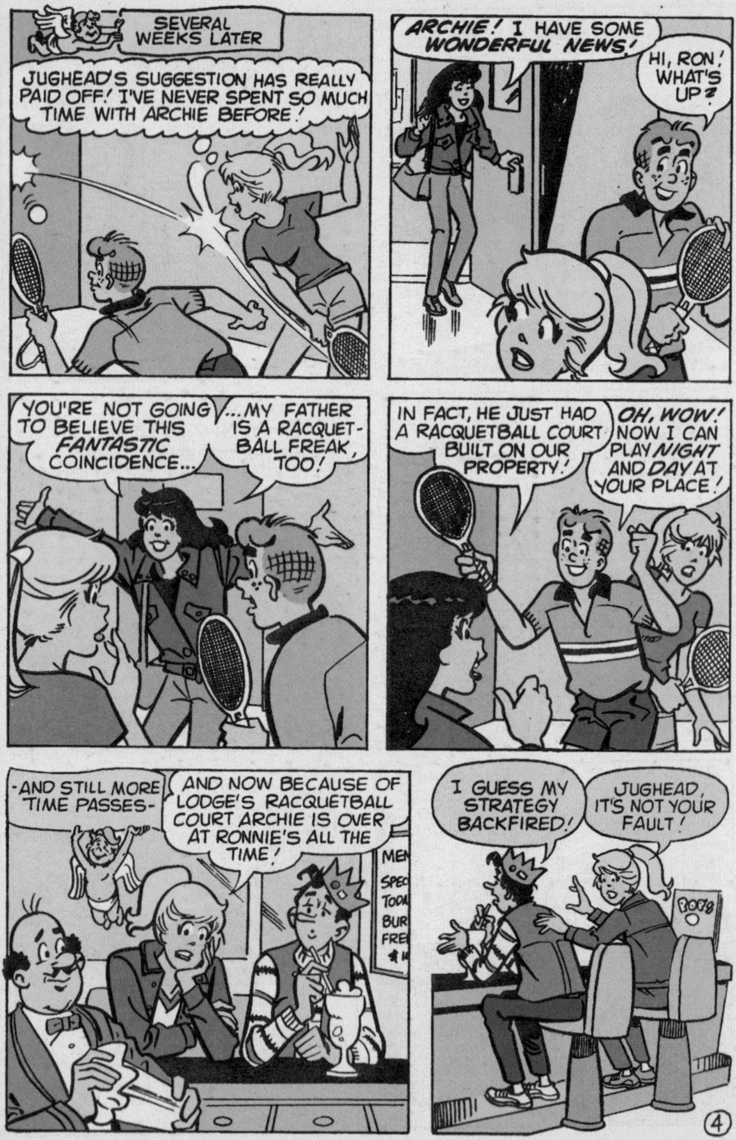

SEVERAL WEEKS LATER
JUGHEAD'S SUGGESTION HAS REALLY PAID OFF! I'VE NEVER SPENT SO MUCH TIME WITH ARCHIE BEFORE!
ARCHIE! I HAVE SOME WONDERFUL NEWS!
HI, RON! WHAT'S UP?
YOU'RE NOT GOING TO BELIEVE THIS FANTASTIC COINCIDENCE...
...MY FATHER IS A RACQUET-BALL FREAK, TOO!
IN FACT, HE JUST HAD A RACQUETBALL COURT BUILT ON OUR PROPERTY!
OH, WOW! NOW I CAN PLAY NIGHT AND DAY AT YOUR PLACE!
-AND STILL MORE TIME PASSES-
AND NOW BECAUSE OF LODGE'S RACQUETBALL COURT ARCHIE IS OVER AT RONNIE'S ALL THE TIME!
I GUESS MY STRATEGY BACKFIRED!
JUGHEAD, IT'S NOT YOUR FAULT!
POP'S

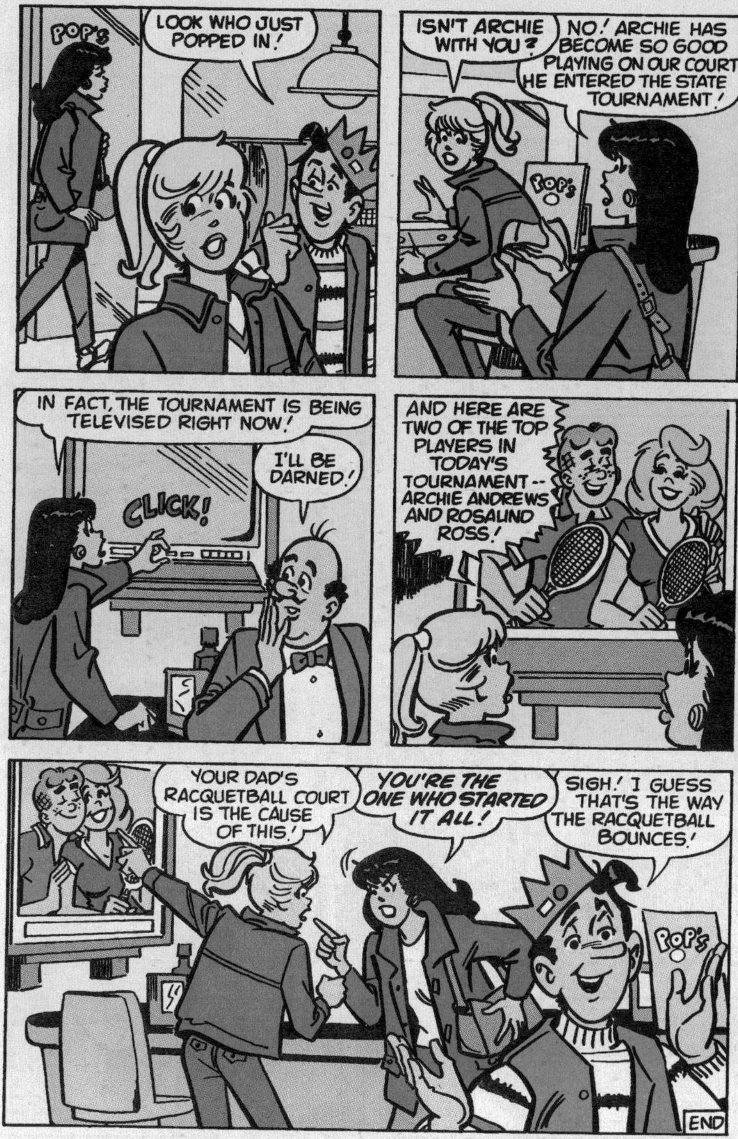
POP'S
LOOK WHO JUST POPPED IN!
ISN'T ARCHIE WITH YOU?
NO! ARCHIE HAS BECOME SO GOOD PLAYING ON OUR COURT HE ENTERED THE STATE TOURNAMENT!
POP'S
IN FACT, THE TOURNAMENT IS BEING TELEVISED RIGHT NOW!
CLICK!
I'LL BE DARNED!
AND HERE ARE TWO OF THE TOP PLAYERS IN TODAY'S TOURNAMENT -- ARCHIE ANDREWS AND ROSALIND ROSS!
YOUR DAD'S RACQUETBALL COURT IS THE CAUSE OF THIS!
YOU'RE THE ONE WHO STARTED IT ALL!
SIGH! I GUESS THAT'S THE WAY THE RACQUETBALL BOUNCES!
POP'S
END

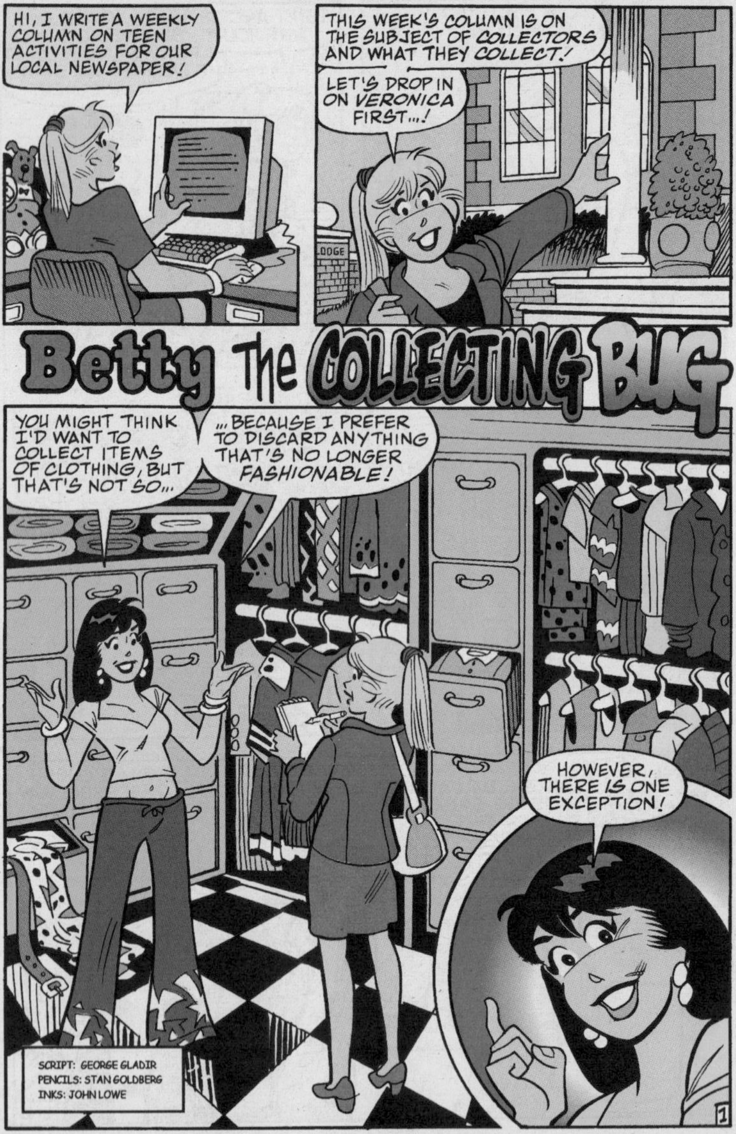
HI, I WRITE A WEEKLY COLUMN ON TEEN ACTIVITIES FOR OUR LOCAL NEWSPAPER!
THIS WEEK'S COLUMN IS ON THE SUBJECT OF COLLECTORS AND WHAT THEY COLLECT!
LET'S DROP IN ON VERONICA FIRST...!
LODGE
Betty The COLLECTING BUG
YOU MIGHT THINK I'D WANT TO COLLECT ITEMS OF CLOTHING, BUT THAT'S NOT SO...
...BECAUSE I PREFER TO DISCARD ANYTHING THAT'S NO LONGER FASHIONABLE!
HOWEVER, THERE IS ONE EXCEPTION!
SCRIPT: GEORGE GLADIR
PENCILS: STAN GOLDBERG
INKS: JOHN LOWE
1

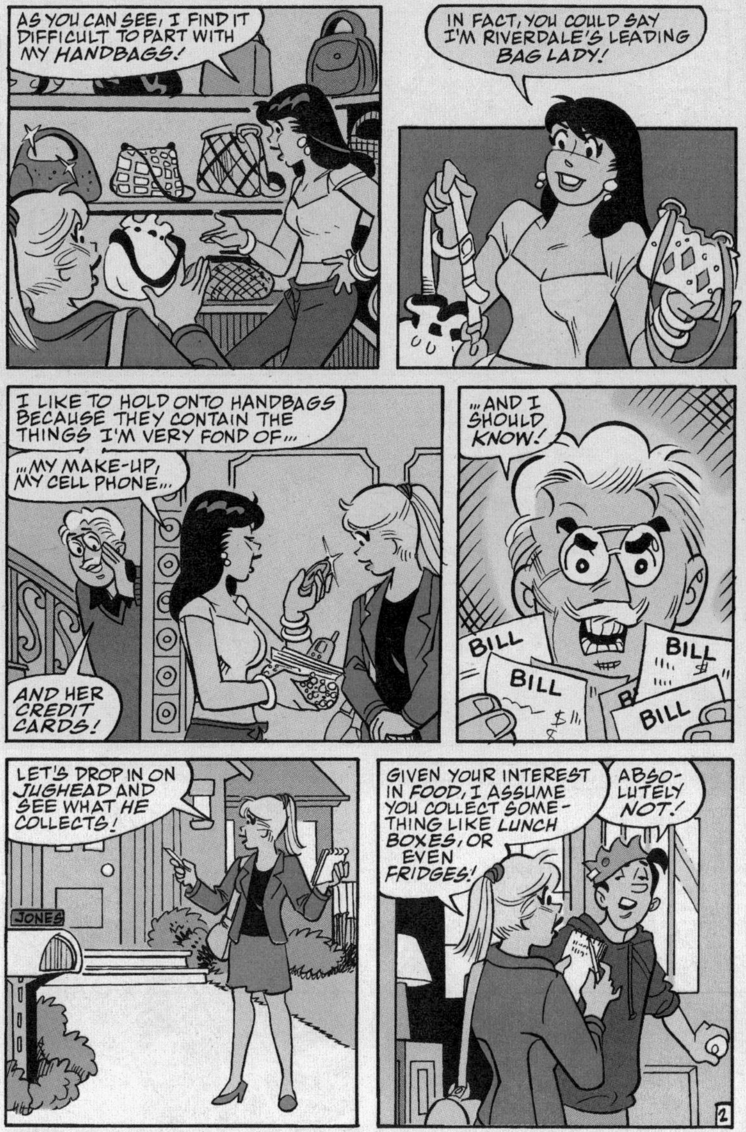

AS YOU CAN SEE, I FIND IT DIFFICULT TO PART WITH MY HANDBAGS!
IN FACT, YOU COULD SAY I'M RIVERDALE'S LEADING BAG LADY!
I LIKE TO HOLD ONTO HANDBAGS BECAUSE THEY CONTAIN THE THINGS I'M VERY FOND OF...
...MY MAKE-UP, MY CELL PHONE...
AND HER CREDIT CARDS!
...AND I SHOULD KNOW!
BILL
BILL
BILL
BILL
LET'S DROP IN ON JUGHEAD AND SEE WHAT HE COLLECTS!
JONES
GIVEN YOUR INTEREST IN FOOD, I ASSUME YOU COLLECT SOME-THING LIKE LUNCH BOXES, OR EVEN FRIDGES!
ABSO-LUTELY NOT!
2

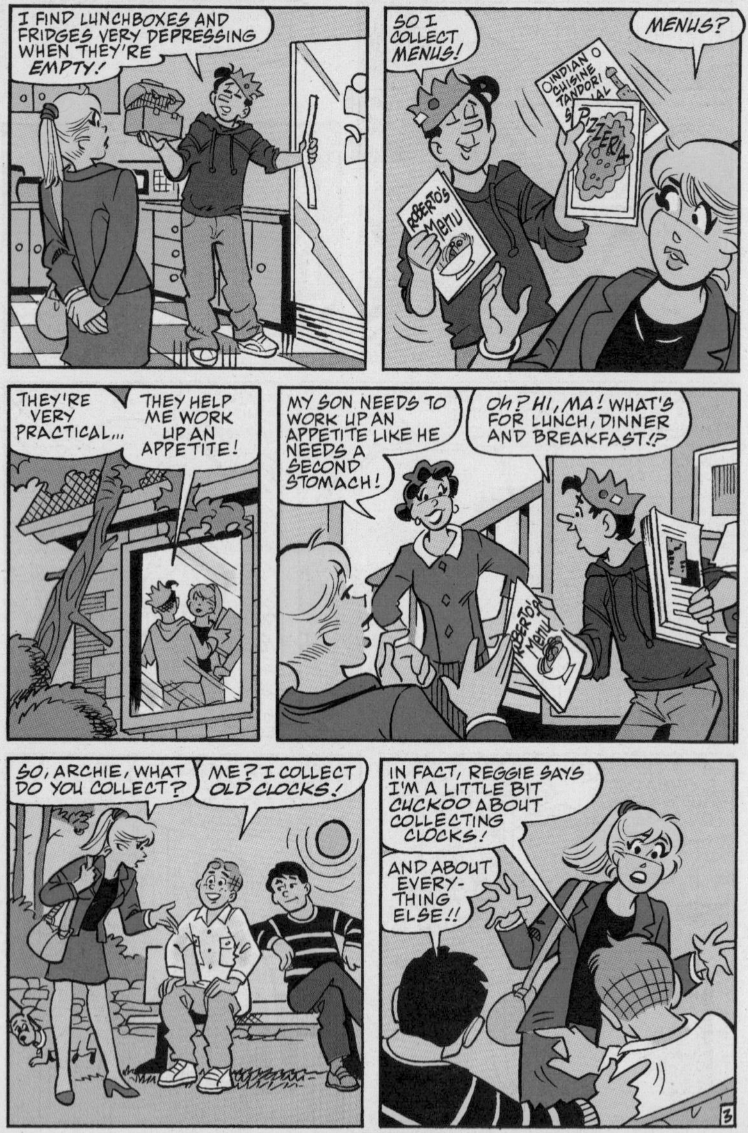

I FIND LUNCHBOXES AND FRIDGES VERY DEPRESSING WHEN THEY'RE EMPTY!
SO I COLLECT MENUS!
MENUS?
INDIAN CUISINE TANDORI
PIZZERIA
ROBERTO'S Menu
THEY'RE VERY PRACTICAL,...
THEY HELP ME WORK UP AN APPETITE!
MY SON NEEDS TO WORK UP AN APPETITE LIKE HE NEEDS A SECOND STOMACH!
Oh? HI, MA! WHAT'S FOR LUNCH, DINNER AND BREAKFAST!?
ROBERTO'S Menu
SO, ARCHIE, WHAT DO YOU COLLECT?
ME? I COLLECT OLD CLOCKS!
IN FACT, REGGIE SAYS I'M A LITTLE BIT CUCKOO ABOUT COLLECTING CLOCKS!
AND ABOUT EVERY-THING ELSE!!
3

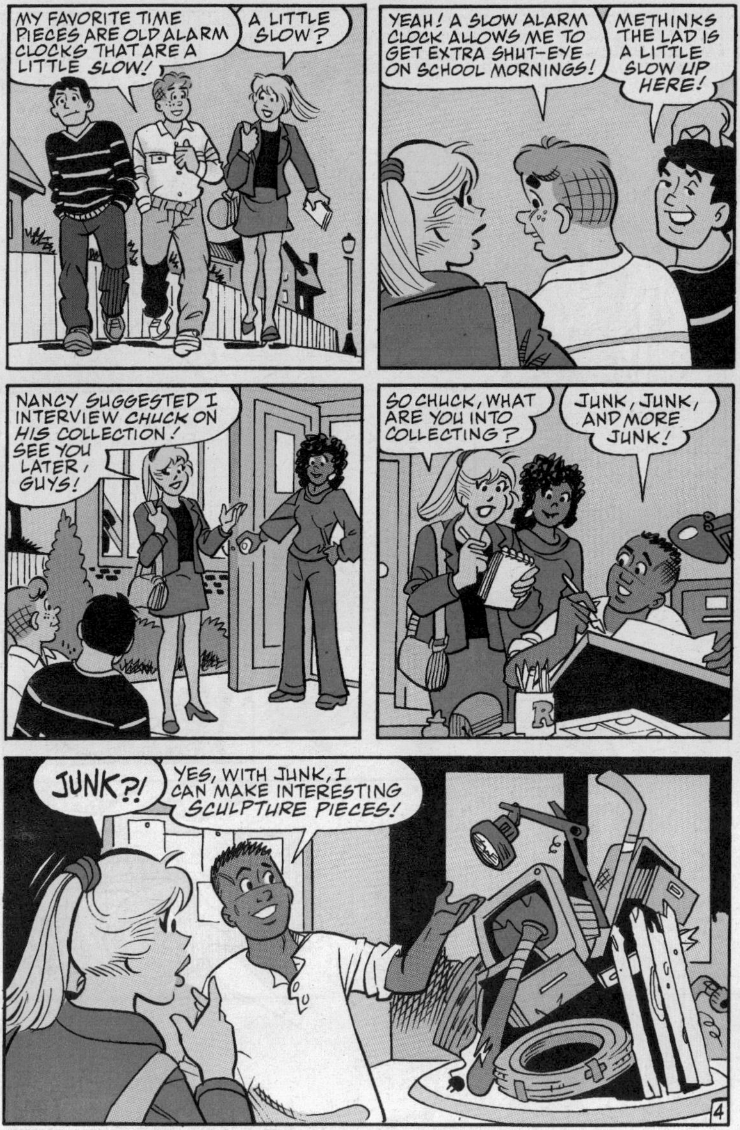
MY FAVORITE TIME PIECES ARE OLD ALARM CLOCKS THAT ARE A LITTLE SLOW!
A LITTLE SLOW?
YEAH! A SLOW ALARM CLOCK ALLOWS ME TO GET EXTRA SHUT-EYE ON SCHOOL MORNINGS!
METHINKS THE LAD IS A LITTLE SLOW UP HERE!
NANCY SUGGESTED I INTERVIEW CHUCK ON HIS COLLECTION! SEE YOU LATER, GUYS!
SO CHUCK, WHAT ARE YOU INTO COLLECTING?
JUNK, JUNK, AND MORE JUNK!
JUNK?!
YES, WITH JUNK, I CAN MAKE INTERESTING SCULPTURE PIECES!
4

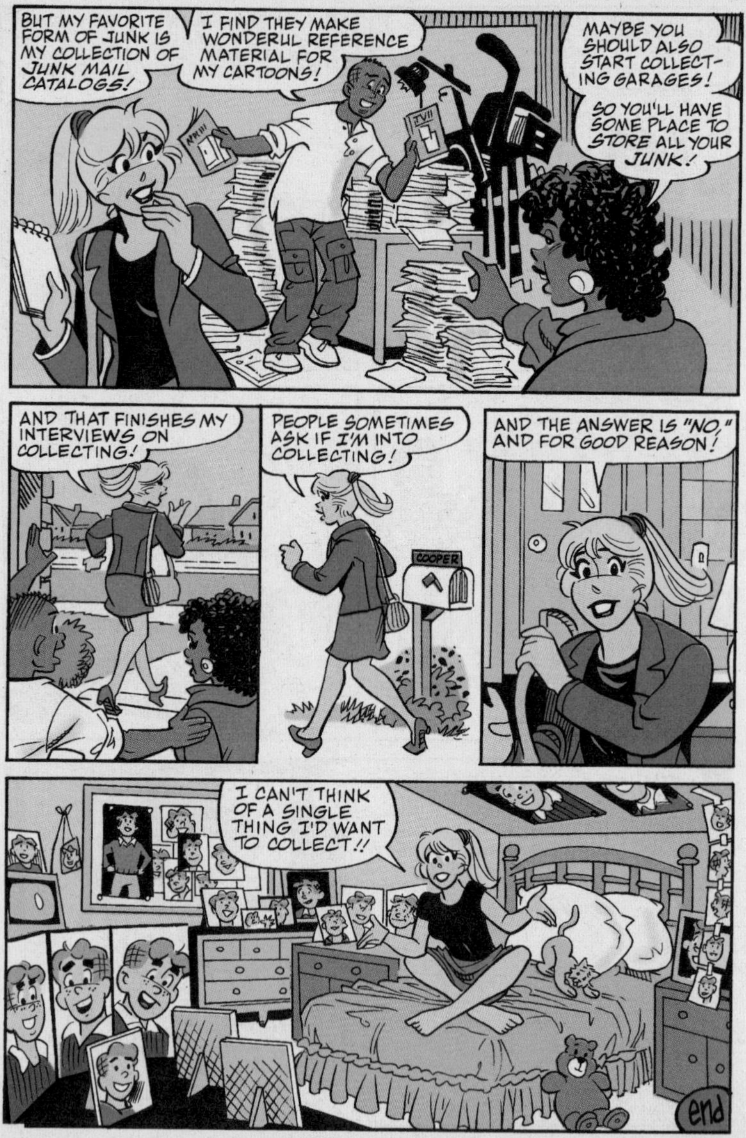
BUT MY FAVORITE FORM OF JUNK IS MY COLLECTION OF JUNK MAIL CATALOGS!
I FIND THEY MAKE WONDERUL REFERENCE MATERIAL FOR MY CARTOONS!
MAYBE YOU SHOULD ALSO START COLLECTING GARAGES!
SO YOU'LL HAVE SOME PLACE TO STORE ALL YOUR JUNK!
AND THAT FINISHES MY INTERVIEWS ON COLLECTING!
PEOPLE SOMETIMES ASK IF I'M INTO COLLECTING!
COOPER
AND THE ANSWER IS "NO," AND FOR GOOD REASON!
I CAN'T THINK OF A SINGLE THING I'D WANT TO COLLECT!!
end

Betty and Veronica in "STEADY NOW"

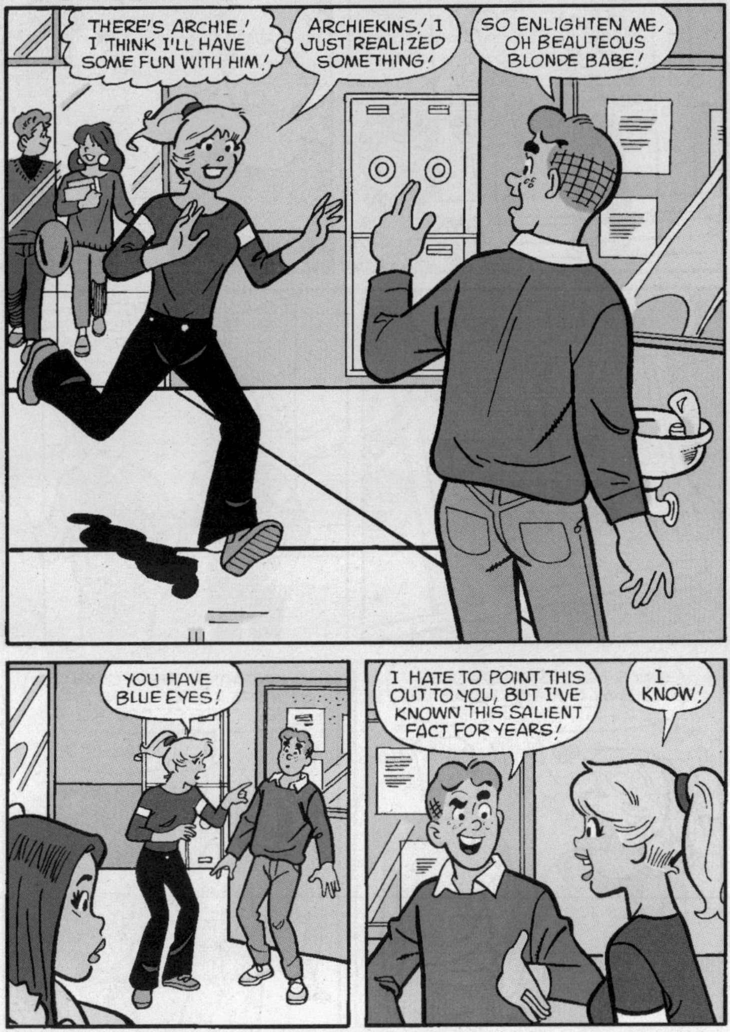
THERE'S ARCHIE! I THINK I'LL HAVE SOME FUN WITH HIM!
ARCHIEKINS! I JUST REALIZED SOMETHING!
SO ENLIGHTEN ME, OH BEAUTEOUS BLONDE BABE!
YOU HAVE BLUE EYES!
I HATE TO POINT THIS OUT TO YOU, BUT I'VE KNOWN THIS SALIENT FACT FOR YEARS!
I KNOW!

Script: Kathleen Webb / Pencils: Jeff Shultz / Inks: Henry Scarpelli / Letters: Bill Yoshida

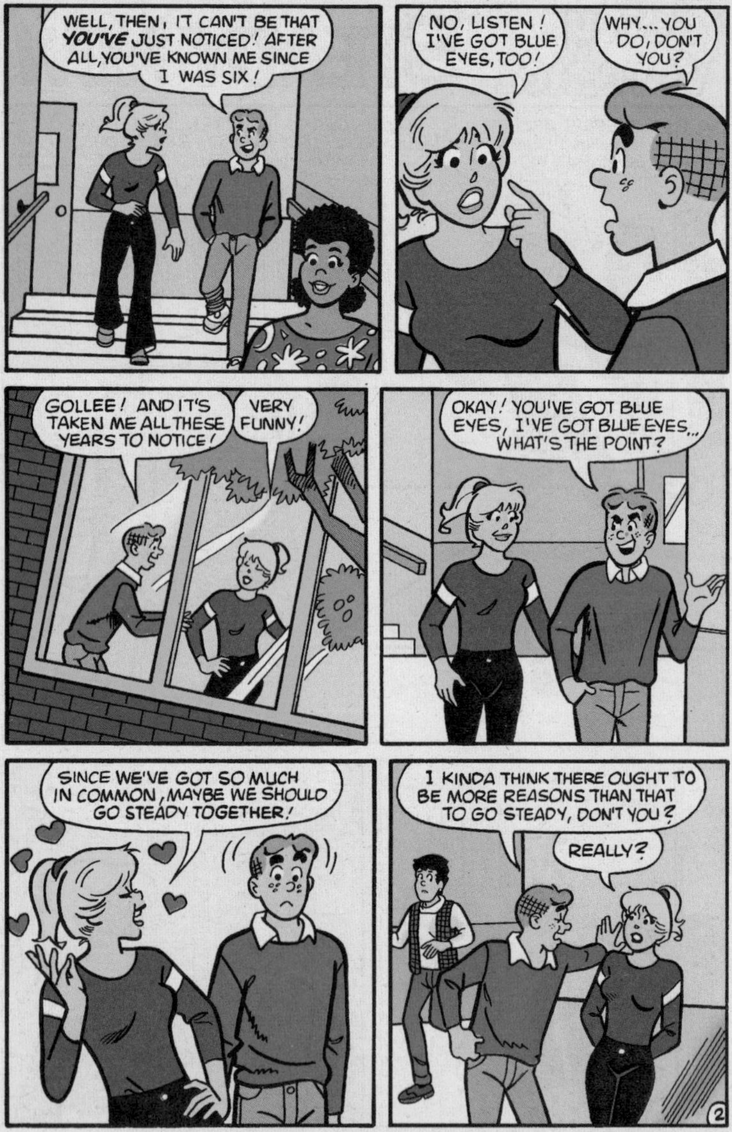

WELL, THEN, IT CAN'T BE THAT **YOU'VE** JUST NOTICED! AFTER ALL, YOU'VE KNOWN ME SINCE I WAS SIX!
NO, LISTEN! I'VE GOT BLUE EYES, TOO!
WHY... YOU DO, DON'T YOU?
GOLLEE! AND IT'S TAKEN ME ALL THESE YEARS TO NOTICE!
VERY FUNNY!
OKAY! YOU'VE GOT BLUE EYES, I'VE GOT BLUE EYES... WHAT'S THE POINT?
SINCE WE'VE GOT SO MUCH IN COMMON, MAYBE WE SHOULD GO STEADY TOGETHER!
I KINDA THINK THERE OUGHT TO BE MORE REASONS THAN THAT TO GO STEADY, DON'T YOU?
REALLY?
2

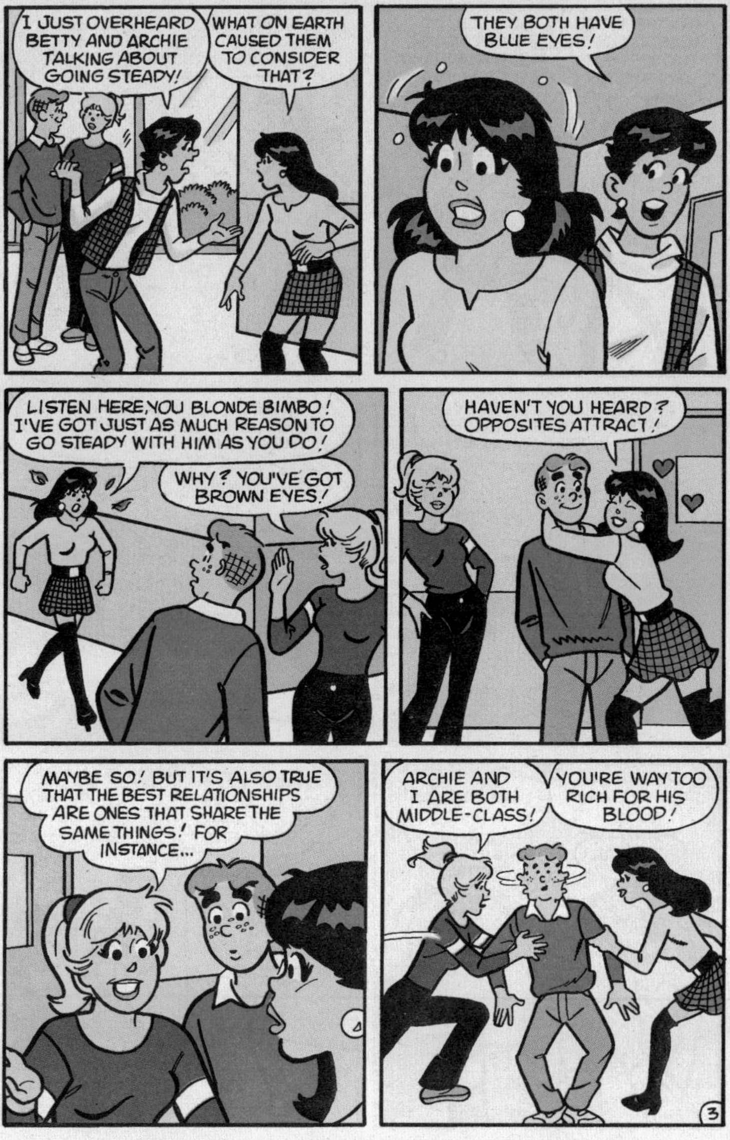
I JUST OVERHEARD BETTY AND ARCHIE TALKING ABOUT GOING STEADY!
WHAT ON EARTH CAUSED THEM TO CONSIDER THAT?
THEY BOTH HAVE BLUE EYES!
LISTEN HERE, YOU BLONDE BIMBO! I'VE GOT JUST AS MUCH REASON TO GO STEADY WITH HIM AS YOU DO!
WHY? YOU'VE GOT BROWN EYES!
HAVEN'T YOU HEARD? OPPOSITES ATTRACT!
MAYBE SO! BUT IT'S ALSO TRUE THAT THE BEST RELATIONSHIPS ARE ONES THAT SHARE THE SAME THINGS! FOR INSTANCE...
ARCHIE AND I ARE BOTH MIDDLE-CLASS!
YOU'RE WAY TOO RICH FOR HIS BLOOD!
3

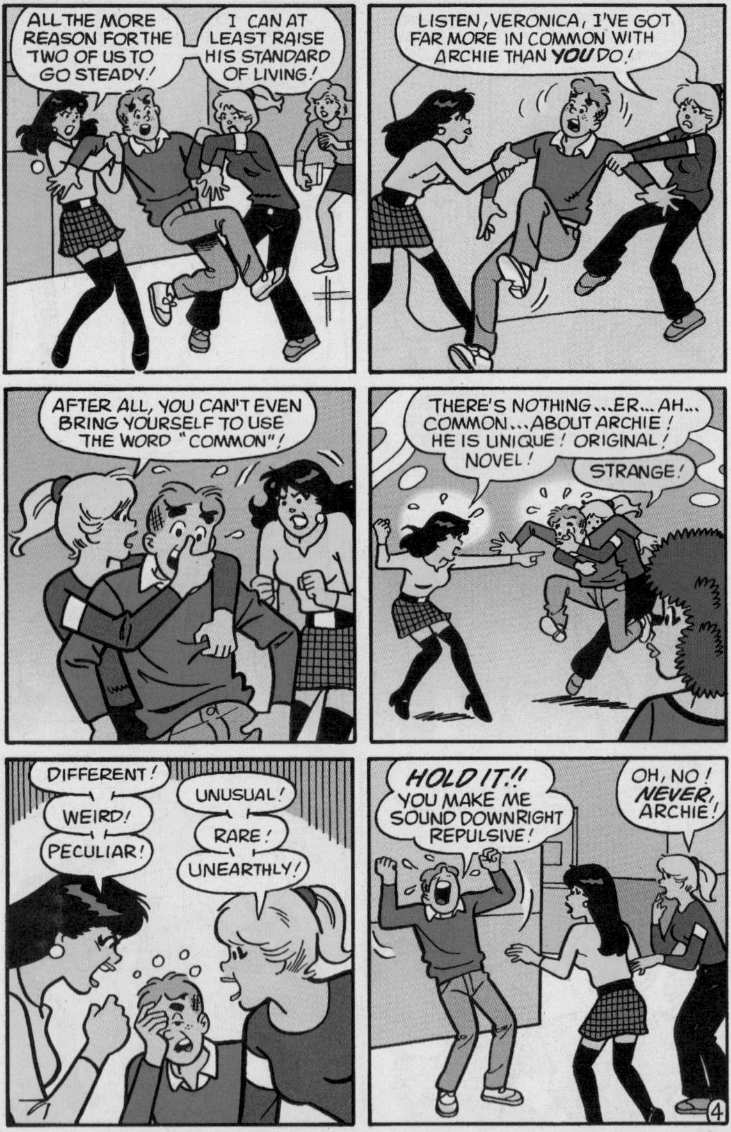

ALL THE MORE REASON FOR THE TWO OF US TO GO STEADY!
I CAN AT LEAST RAISE HIS STANDARD OF LIVING!
LISTEN, VERONICA, I'VE GOT FAR MORE IN COMMON WITH ARCHIE THAN YOU DO!
AFTER ALL, YOU CAN'T EVEN BRING YOURSELF TO USE THE WORD "COMMON"!
THERE'S NOTHING ...ER... AH... COMMON ... ABOUT ARCHIE! HE IS UNIQUE! ORIGINAL! NOVEL!
STRANGE!
DIFFERENT!
UNUSUAL!
WEIRD!
RARE!
PECULIAR!
UNEARTHLY!
HOLD IT!! YOU MAKE ME SOUND DOWNRIGHT REPULSIVE!
OH, NO! NEVER, ARCHIE!
4

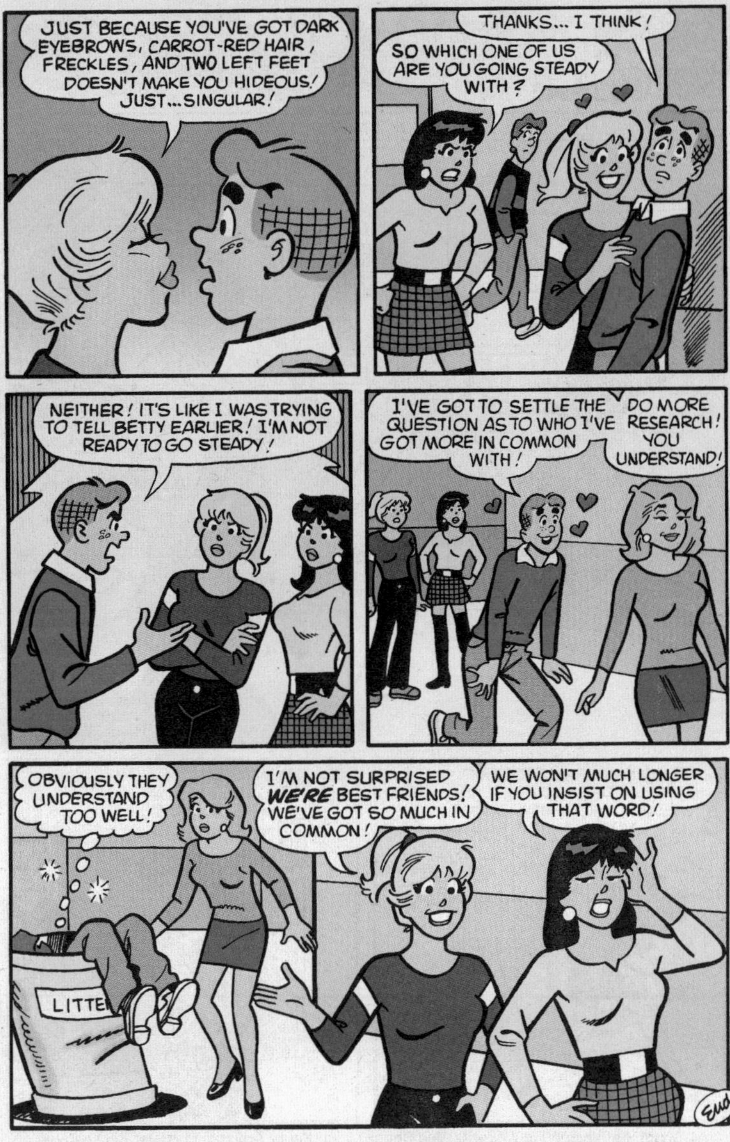
JUST BECAUSE YOU'VE GOT DARK EYEBROWS, CARROT-RED HAIR, FRECKLES, AND TWO LEFT FEET DOESN'T MAKE YOU HIDEOUS! JUST... SINGULAR!
THANKS... I THINK!
SO WHICH ONE OF US ARE YOU GOING STEADY WITH?
NEITHER! IT'S LIKE I WAS TRYING TO TELL BETTY EARLIER! I'M NOT READY TO GO STEADY!
I'VE GOT TO SETTLE THE QUESTION AS TO WHO I'VE GOT MORE IN COMMON WITH!
DO MORE RESEARCH! YOU UNDERSTAND!
OBVIOUSLY THEY UNDERSTAND TOO WELL!
I'M NOT SURPRISED WE'RE BEST FRIENDS! WE'VE GOT SO MUCH IN COMMON!
WE WON'T MUCH LONGER IF YOU INSIST ON USING THAT WORD!
LITTE
End

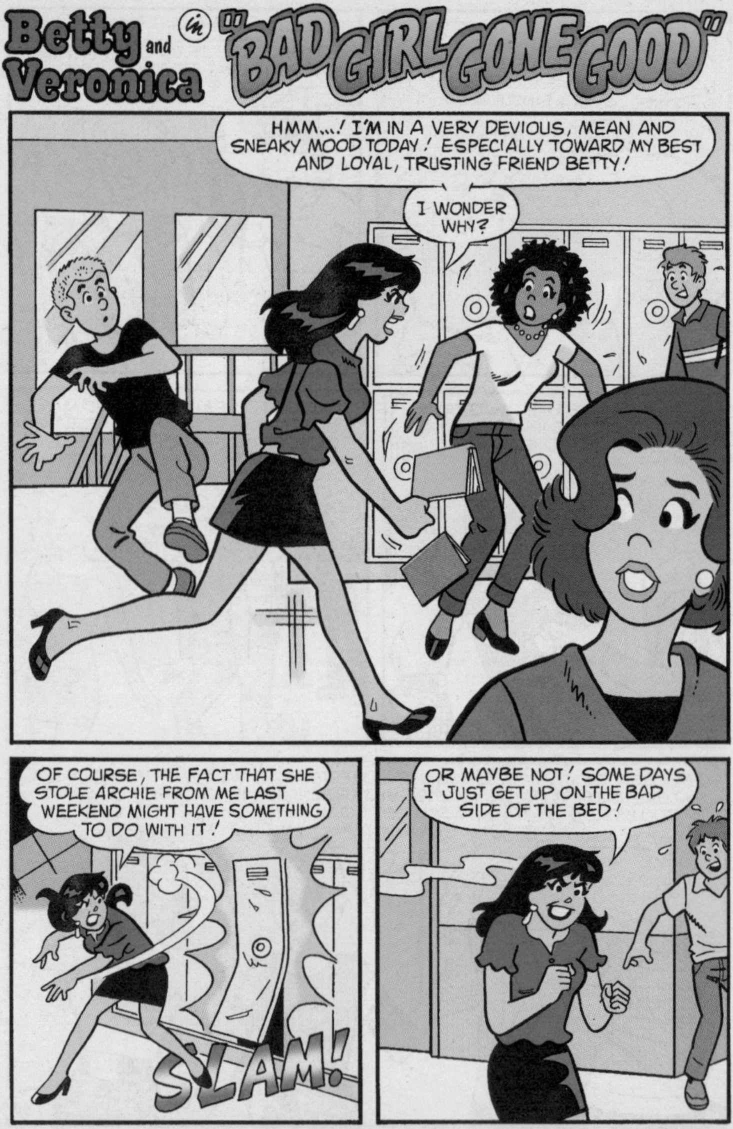
Betty and Veronica in
"BAD GIRL GONE GOOD"
HMM...! I'M IN A VERY DEVIOUS, MEAN AND SNEAKY MOOD TODAY! ESPECIALLY TOWARD MY BEST AND LOYAL, TRUSTING FRIEND BETTY!
I WONDER WHY?
OF COURSE, THE FACT THAT SHE STOLE ARCHIE FROM ME LAST WEEKEND MIGHT HAVE SOMETHING TO DO WITH IT!
SLAM!
OR MAYBE NOT! SOME DAYS I JUST GET UP ON THE BAD SIDE OF THE BED!

Script: Kathleen Webb / Pencils: Jeff Shultz / Inks: Henry Scarpelli / Letters: Bill Yoshida

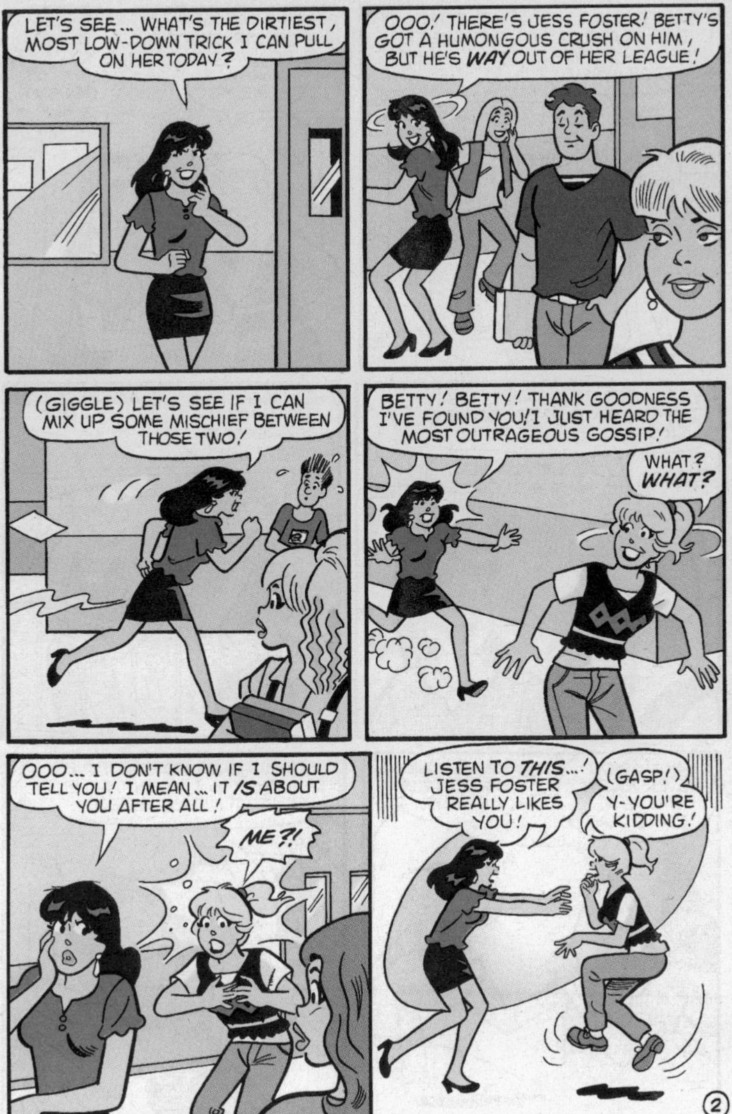

LET'S SEE... WHAT'S THE DIRTIEST, MOST LOW-DOWN TRICK I CAN PULL ON HER TODAY?
OOO! THERE'S JESS FOSTER! BETTY'S GOT A HUMONGOUS CRUSH ON HIM, BUT HE'S WAY OUT OF HER LEAGUE!
(GIGGLE) LET'S SEE IF I CAN MIX UP SOME MISCHIEF BETWEEN THOSE TWO!
BETTY! BETTY! THANK GOODNESS I'VE FOUND YOU! I JUST HEARD THE MOST OUTRAGEOUS GOSSIP!
WHAT? WHAT?
OOO... I DON'T KNOW IF I SHOULD TELL YOU! I MEAN... IT IS ABOUT YOU AFTER ALL!
ME?!
LISTEN TO THIS...! JESS FOSTER REALLY LIKES YOU!
(GASP!)
Y-YOU'RE KIDDING!
2

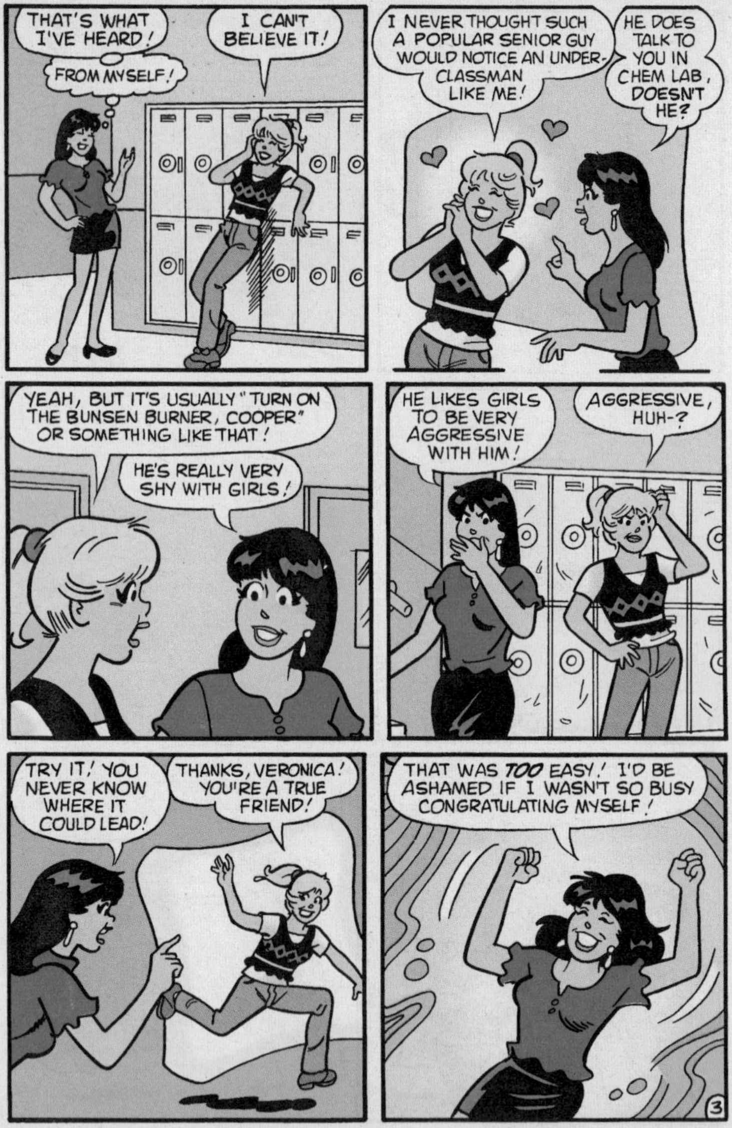
THAT'S WHAT I'VE HEARD!
FROM MYSELF!
I CAN'T BELIEVE IT!
I NEVER THOUGHT SUCH A POPULAR SENIOR GUY WOULD NOTICE AN UNDER-CLASSMAN LIKE ME!
HE DOES TALK TO YOU IN CHEM LAB, DOESN'T HE?
YEAH, BUT IT'S USUALLY "TURN ON THE BUNSEN BURNER, COOPER" OR SOMETHING LIKE THAT!
HE'S REALLY VERY SHY WITH GIRLS!
HE LIKES GIRLS TO BE VERY AGGRESSIVE WITH HIM!
AGGRESSIVE, HUH-?
TRY IT! YOU NEVER KNOW WHERE IT COULD LEAD!
THANKS, VERONICA! YOU'RE A TRUE FRIEND!
THAT WAS TOO EASY! I'D BE ASHAMED IF I WASN'T SO BUSY CONGRATULATING MYSELF!
3

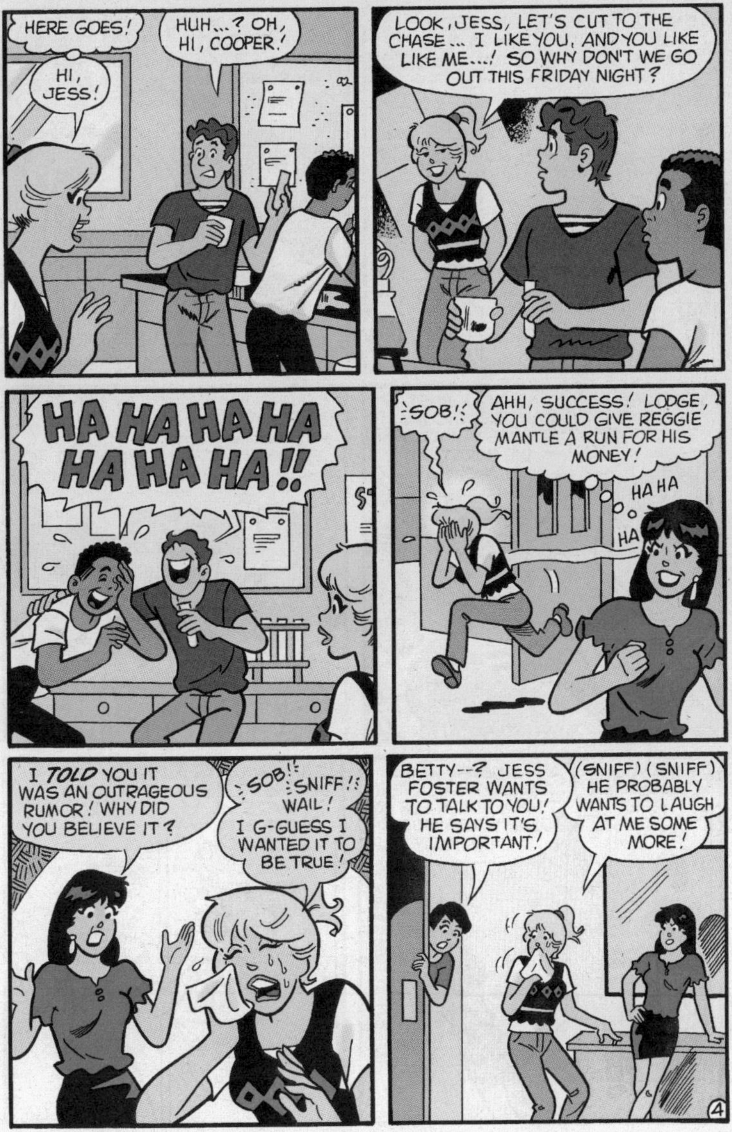
HERE GOES!
HI, JESS!
HUH...? OH, HI, COOPER!
LOOK, JESS, LET'S CUT TO THE CHASE... I LIKE YOU, AND YOU LIKE LIKE ME...! SO WHY DON'T WE GO OUT THIS FRIDAY NIGHT?
HA HA HA HA HA HA HA HA!!
SOB!
AHH, SUCCESS! LODGE, YOU COULD GIVE REGGIE MANTLE A RUN FOR HIS MONEY!
HA HA HA
I TOLD YOU IT WAS AN OUTRAGEOUS RUMOR! WHY DID YOU BELIEVE IT?
SOB! SNIFF! WAIL! I G-GUESS I WANTED IT TO BE TRUE!
BETTY--? JESS FOSTER WANTS TO TALK TO YOU! HE SAYS IT'S IMPORTANT!
(SNIFF) (SNIFF) HE PROBABLY WANTS TO LAUGH AT ME SOME MORE!
4

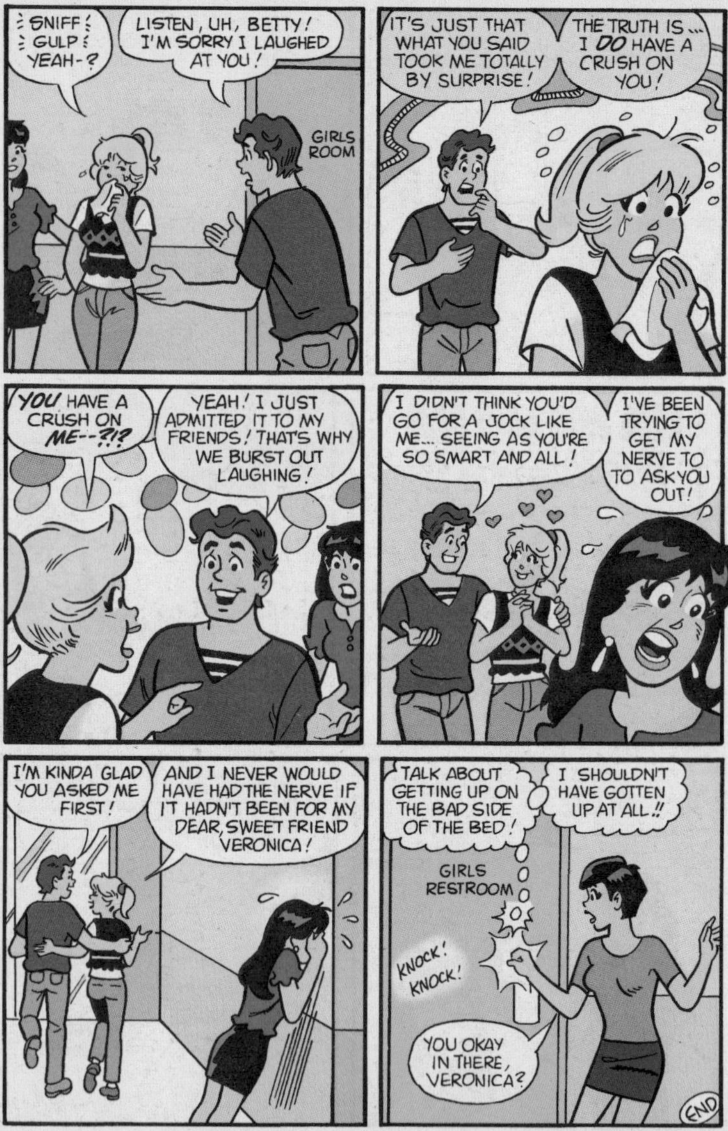
SNIFF! GULP! YEAH-?
LISTEN, UH, BETTY! I'M SORRY I LAUGHED AT YOU!
GIRLS ROOM
IT'S JUST THAT WHAT YOU SAID TOOK ME TOTALLY BY SURPRISE!
THE TRUTH IS... I DO HAVE A CRUSH ON YOU!
YOU HAVE A CRUSH ON ME--?!?
YEAH! I JUST ADMITTED IT TO MY FRIENDS! THAT'S WHY WE BURST OUT LAUGHING!
I DIDN'T THINK YOU'D GO FOR A JOCK LIKE ME... SEEING AS YOU'RE SO SMART AND ALL!
I'VE BEEN TRYING TO GET MY NERVE TO TO ASK YOU OUT!
I'M KINDA GLAD YOU ASKED ME FIRST!
AND I NEVER WOULD HAVE HAD THE NERVE IF IT HADN'T BEEN FOR MY DEAR, SWEET FRIEND VERONICA!
TALK ABOUT GETTING UP ON THE BAD SIDE OF THE BED!
I SHOULDN'T HAVE GOTTEN UP AT ALL!!
GIRLS RESTROOM
KNOCK! KNOCK!
YOU OKAY IN THERE, VERONICA?
END

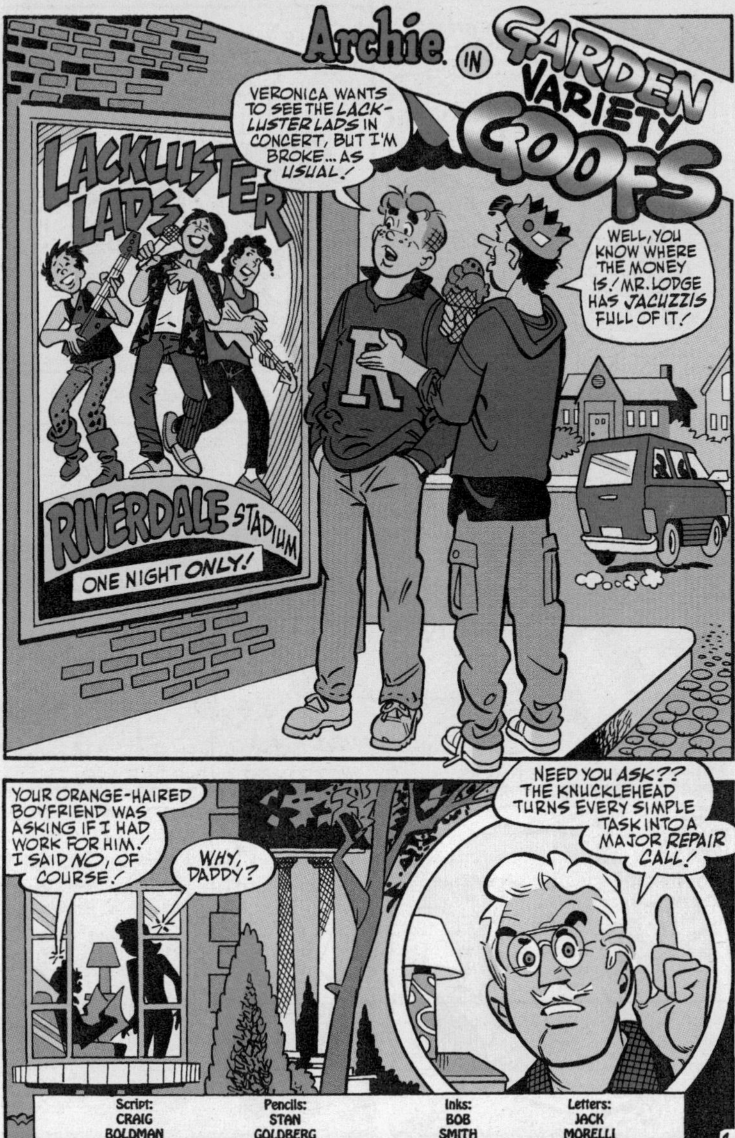
Archie IN GARDEN VARIETY GOOFS
VERONICA WANTS TO SEE THE LACK-LUSTER LADS IN CONCERT, BUT I'M BROKE... AS USUAL!
LACKLUSTER LADS
RIVERDALE STADIUM
ONE NIGHT ONLY!
WELL, YOU KNOW WHERE THE MONEY IS! MR. LODGE HAS JACUZZIS FULL OF IT!
YOUR ORANGE-HAIRED BOYFRIEND WAS ASKING IF I HAD WORK FOR HIM! I SAID NO, OF COURSE!
WHY, DADDY?
NEED YOU ASK?? THE KNUCKLEHEAD TURNS EVERY SIMPLE TASK INTO A MAJOR REPAIR CALL!
Script: CRAIG BOLDMAN
Pencils: STAN GOLDBERG
Inks: BOB SMITH
Letters: JACK MORELLI
1

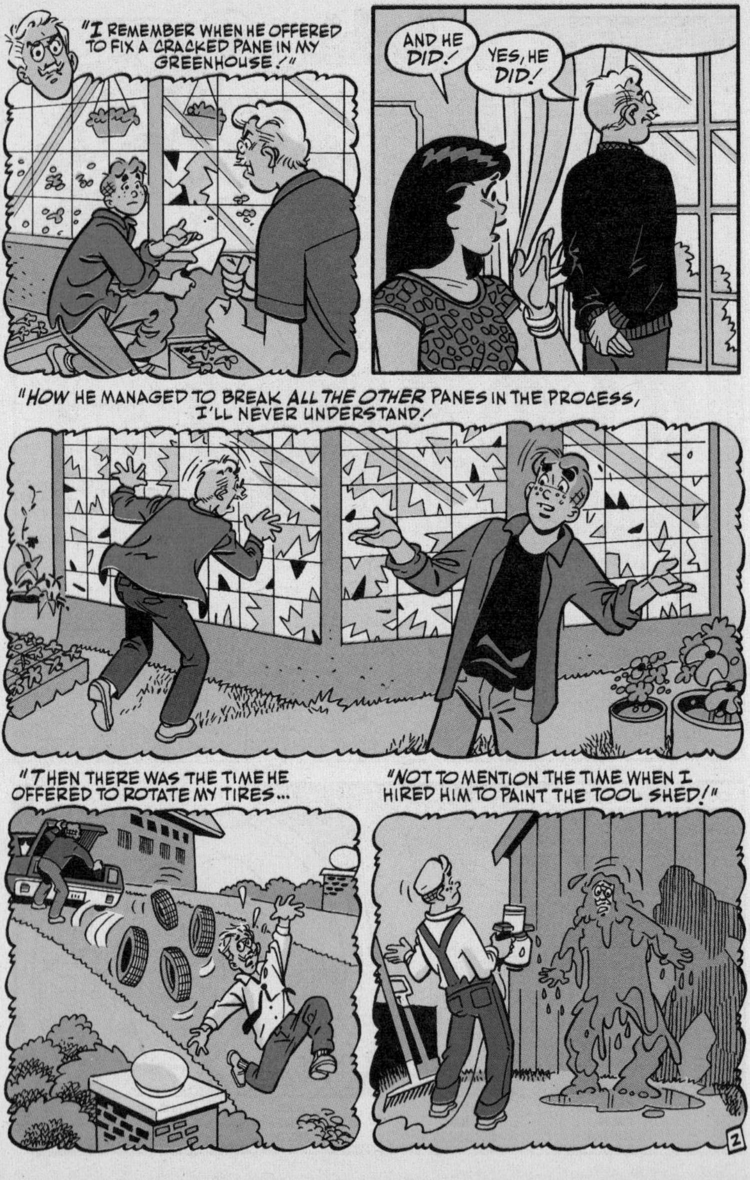
"I REMEMBER WHEN HE OFFERED TO FIX A CRACKED PANE IN MY GREENHOUSE!"
AND HE DID!
YES, HE DID!
"HOW HE MANAGED TO BREAK ALL THE OTHER PANES IN THE PROCESS, I'LL NEVER UNDERSTAND!
"THEN THERE WAS THE TIME HE OFFERED TO ROTATE MY TIRES...
"NOT TO MENTION THE TIME WHEN I HIRED HIM TO PAINT THE TOOL SHED!"

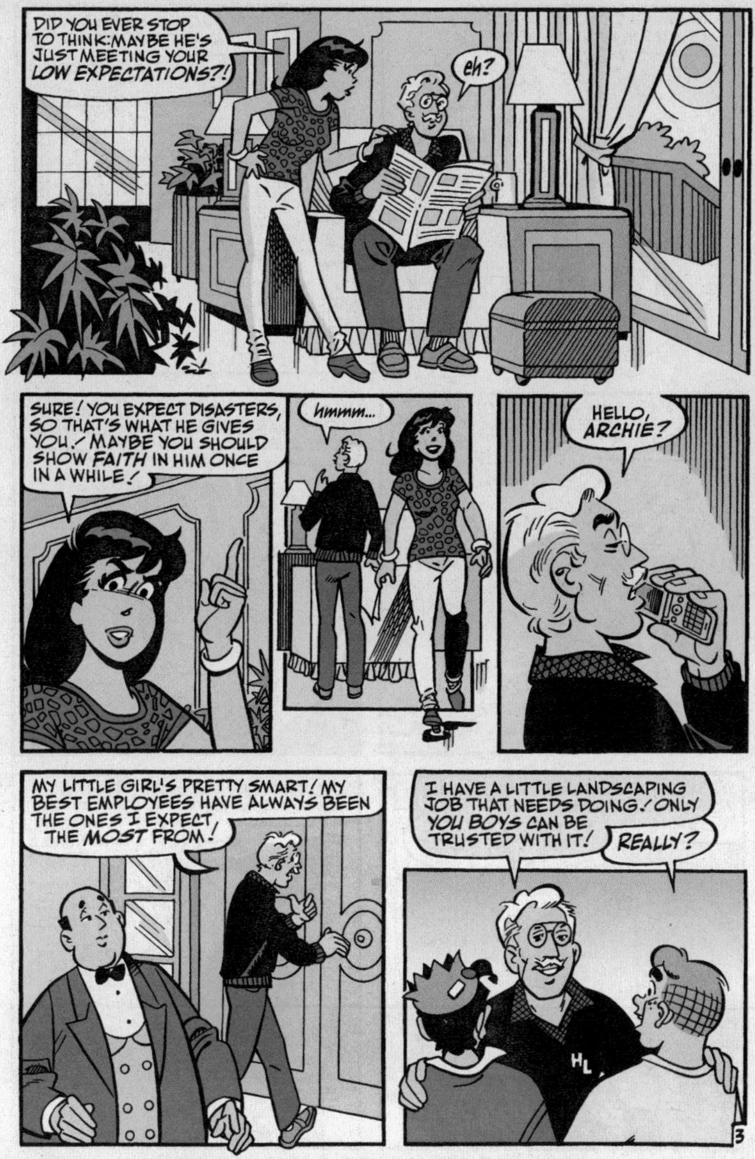
DID YOU EVER STOP TO THINK: MAYBE HE'S JUST MEETING YOUR LOW EXPECTATIONS?!
eh?
SURE! YOU EXPECT DISASTERS, SO THAT'S WHAT HE GIVES YOU! MAYBE YOU SHOULD SHOW FAITH IN HIM ONCE IN A WHILE!
hmmm...
HELLO, ARCHIE?
MY LITTLE GIRL'S PRETTY SMART! MY BEST EMPLOYEES HAVE ALWAYS BEEN THE ONES I EXPECT THE MOST FROM!
I HAVE A LITTLE LANDSCAPING JOB THAT NEEDS DOING! ONLY YOU BOYS CAN BE TRUSTED WITH IT!
REALLY?
HL

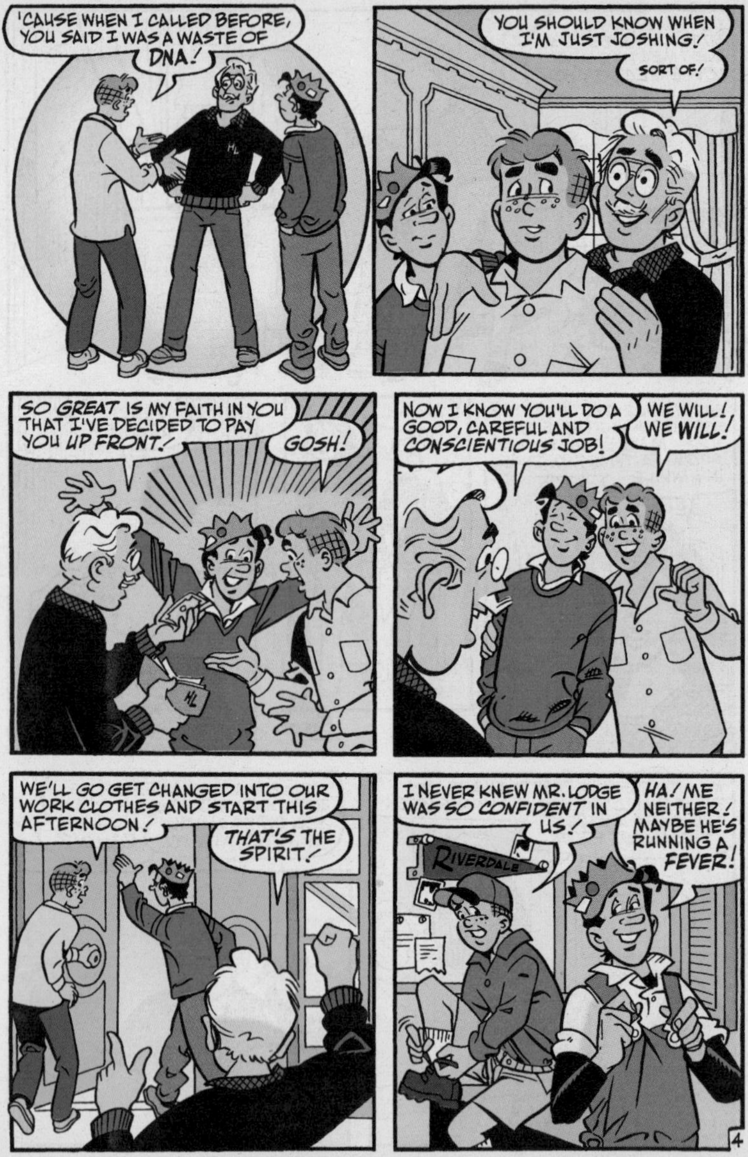
'CAUSE WHEN I CALLED BEFORE, YOU SAID I WAS A WASTE OF DNA!
YOU SHOULD KNOW WHEN I'M JUST JOSHING!
SORT OF!
SO GREAT IS MY FAITH IN YOU THAT I'VE DECIDED TO PAY YOU UP FRONT!
GOSH!
NOW I KNOW YOU'LL DO A GOOD, CAREFUL AND CONSCIENTIOUS JOB!
WE WILL! WE WILL!
WE'LL GO GET CHANGED INTO OUR WORK CLOTHES AND START THIS AFTERNOON!
THAT'S THE SPIRIT!
I NEVER KNEW MR. LODGE WAS SO CONFIDENT IN US!
HA! ME NEITHER! MAYBE HE'S RUNNING A FEVER!
RIVERDALE
4

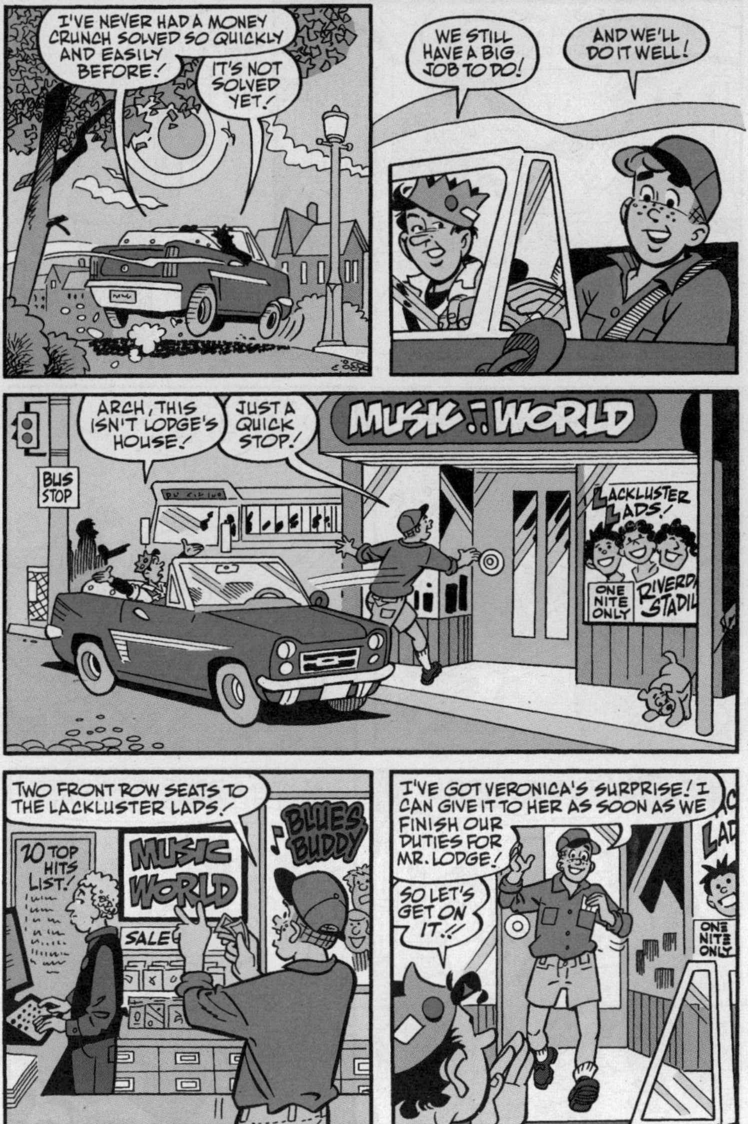
I'VE NEVER HAD A MONEY CRUNCH SOLVED SO QUICKLY AND EASILY BEFORE!
IT'S NOT SOLVED YET!
WE STILL HAVE A BIG JOB TO DO!
AND WE'LL DO IT WELL!
ARCH, THIS ISN'T LODGE'S HOUSE!
JUST A QUICK STOP!
MUSIC WORLD
BUS STOP
LACKLUSTER LADS!
ONE NITE ONLY
TWO FRONT ROW SEATS TO THE LACKLUSTER LADS!
20 TOP HITS LIST!
MUSIC WORLD
SALE
BLUES BUDDY
I'VE GOT VERONICA'S SURPRISE! I CAN GIVE IT TO HER AS SOON AS WE FINISH OUR DUTIES FOR MR. LODGE!
SO LET'S GET ON IT!!
ONE NITE ONLY

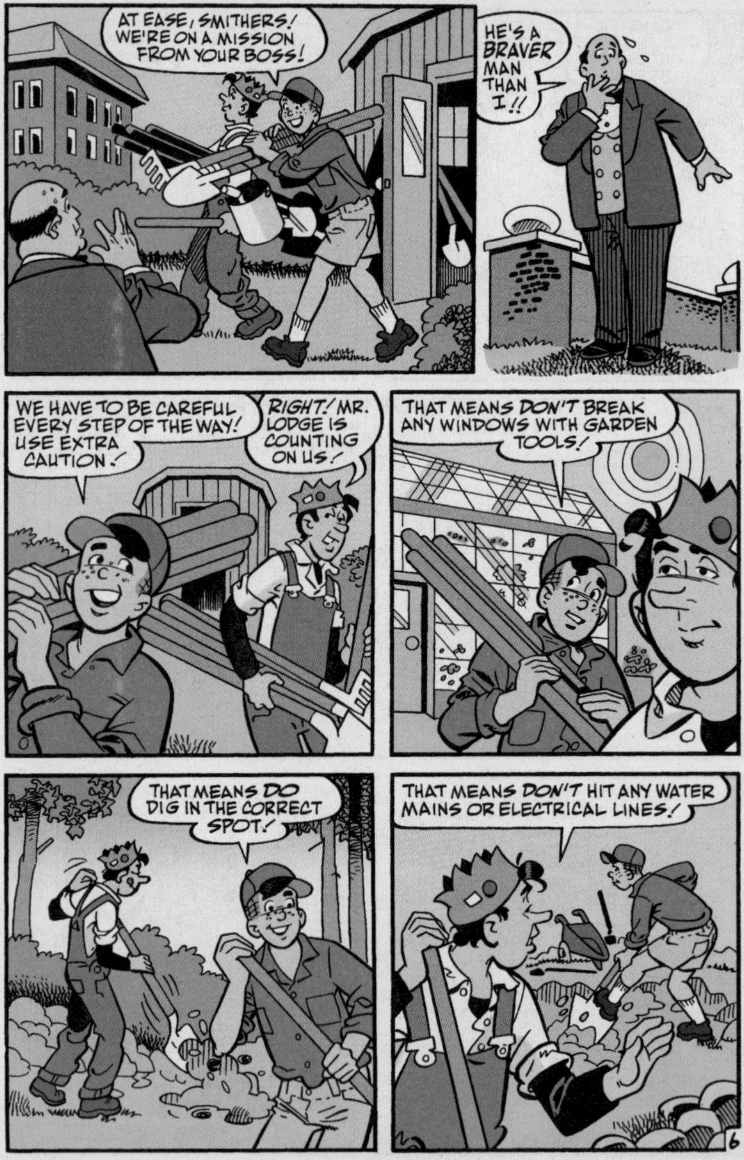
AT EASE, SMITHERS! WE'RE ON A MISSION FROM YOUR BOSS!
HE'S A BRAVER MAN THAN I!!
WE HAVE TO BE CAREFUL EVERY STEP OF THE WAY! USE EXTRA CAUTION!
RIGHT! MR. LODGE IS COUNTING ON US!
THAT MEANS DON'T BREAK ANY WINDOWS WITH GARDEN TOOLS!
THAT MEANS DO DIG IN THE CORRECT SPOT!
THAT MEANS DON'T HIT ANY WATER MAINS OR ELECTRICAL LINES!

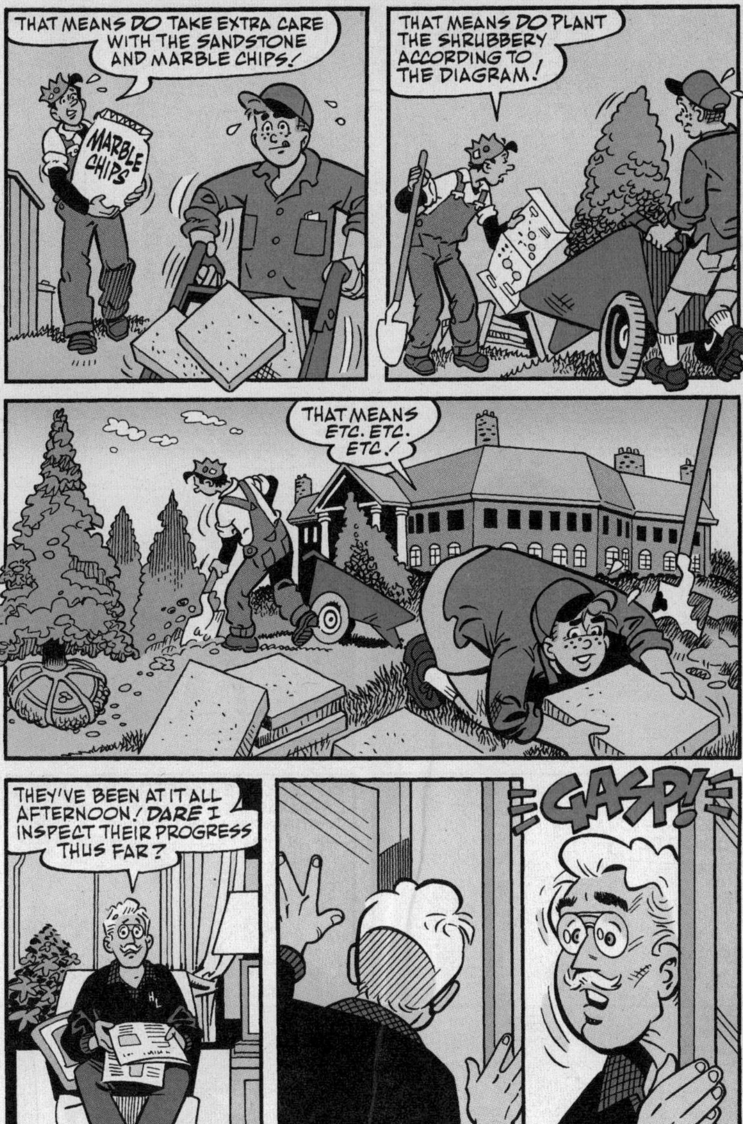
THAT MEANS DO TAKE EXTRA CARE WITH THE SANDSTONE AND MARBLE CHIPS!
MARBLE CHIPS
THAT MEANS DO PLANT THE SHRUBBERY ACCORDING TO THE DIAGRAM!
THAT MEANS ETC. ETC. ETC.!
THEY'VE BEEN AT IT ALL AFTERNOON! DARE I INSPECT THEIR PROGRESS THUS FAR?
GASP!

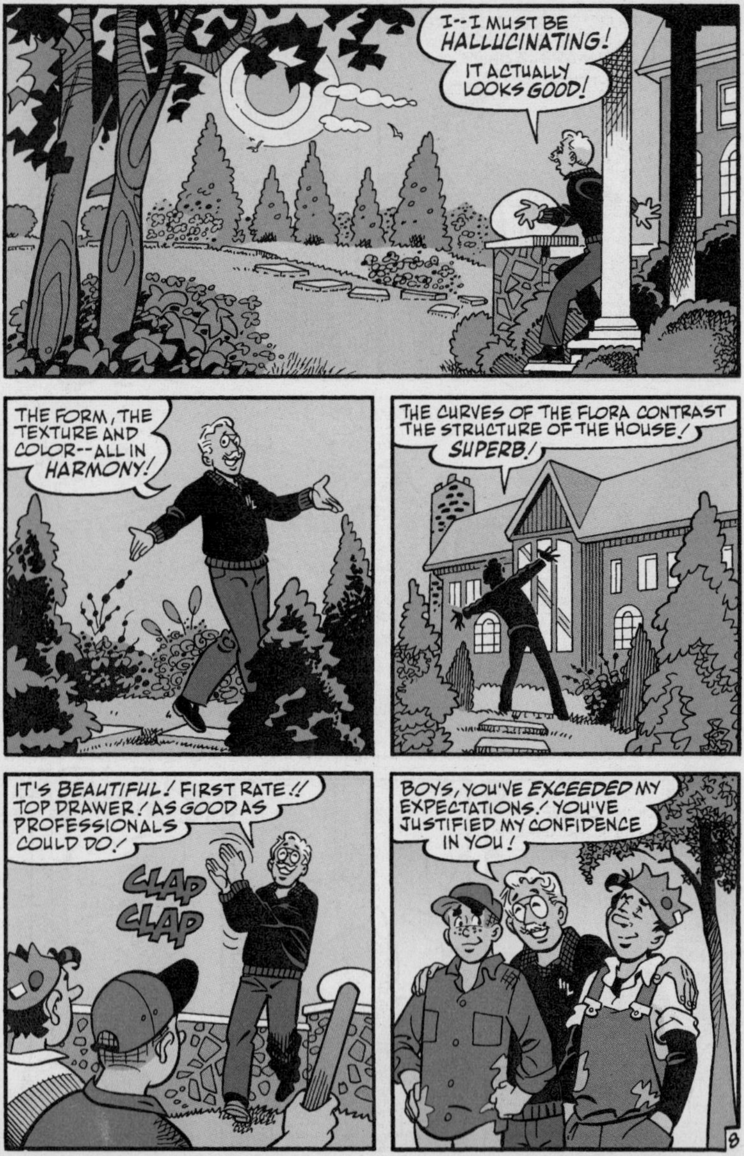
I--I MUST BE HALLUCINATING!
IT ACTUALLY LOOKS GOOD!
THE FORM, THE TEXTURE AND COLOR--ALL IN HARMONY!
THE CURVES OF THE FLORA CONTRAST THE STRUCTURE OF THE HOUSE!
SUPERB!
IT'S BEAUTIFUL! FIRST RATE!! TOP DRAWER! AS GOOD AS PROFESSIONALS COULD DO!
CLAP CLAP
BOYS, YOU'VE EXCEEDED MY EXPECTATIONS! YOU'VE JUSTIFIED MY CONFIDENCE IN YOU!
8

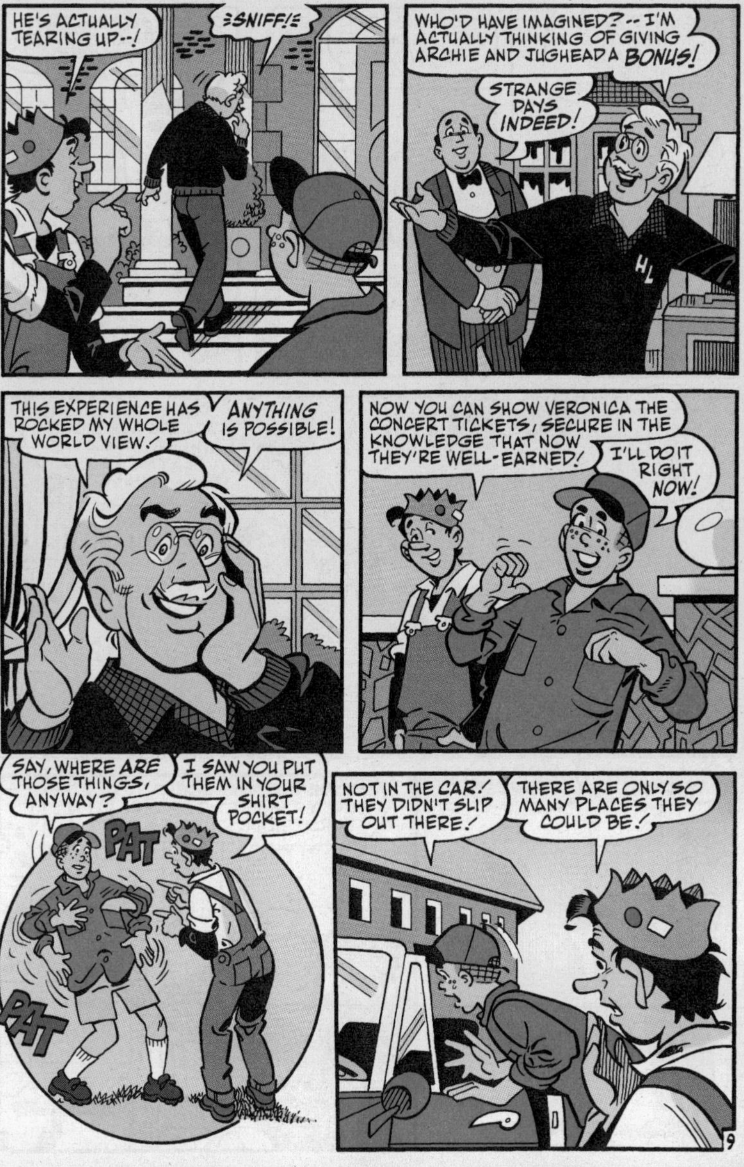

HE'S ACTUALLY TEARING UP--!
SNIFF!
WHO'D HAVE IMAGINED? -- I'M ACTUALLY THINKING OF GIVING ARCHIE AND JUGHEAD A BONUS!
STRANGE DAYS INDEED!
THIS EXPERIENCE HAS ROCKED MY WHOLE WORLD VIEW!
ANYTHING IS POSSIBLE!
NOW YOU CAN SHOW VERONICA THE CONCERT TICKETS, SECURE IN THE KNOWLEDGE THAT NOW THEY'RE WELL-EARNED!
I'LL DO IT RIGHT NOW!
SAY, WHERE ARE THOSE THINGS, ANYWAY?
I SAW YOU PUT THEM IN YOUR SHIRT POCKET!
PAT
PAT
NOT IN THE CAR! THEY DIDN'T SLIP OUT THERE!
THERE ARE ONLY SO MANY PLACES THEY COULD BE!

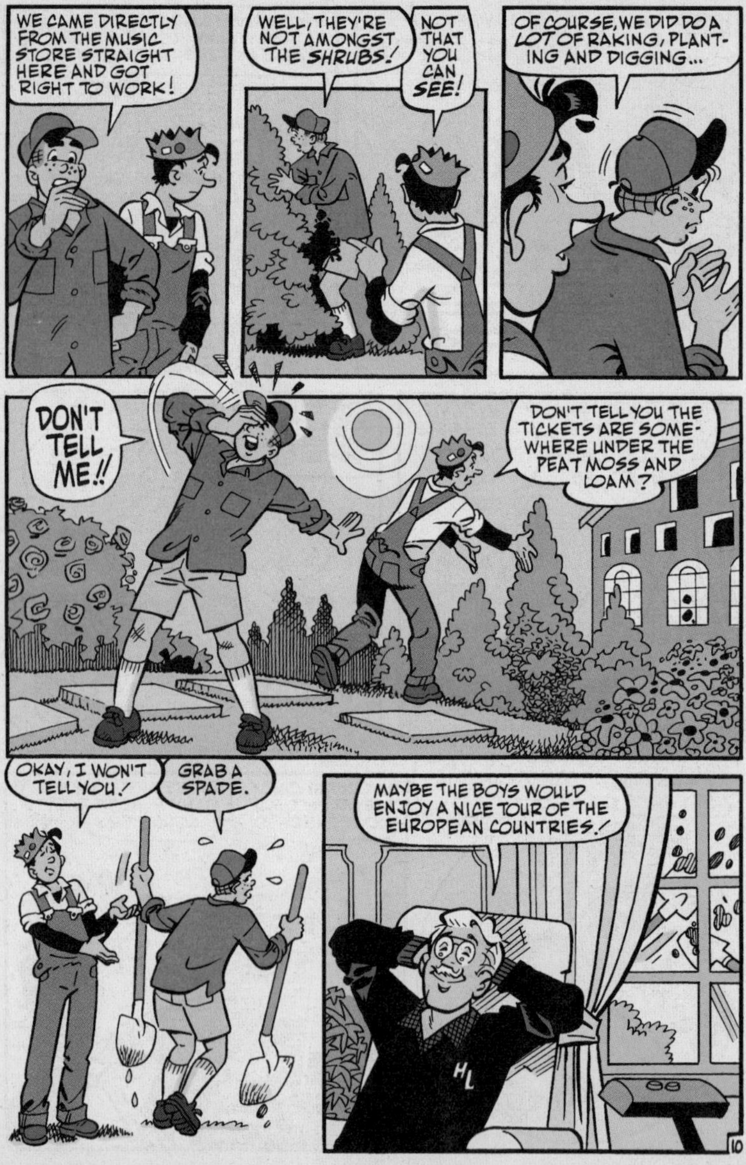
WE CAME DIRECTLY FROM THE MUSIC STORE STRAIGHT HERE AND GOT RIGHT TO WORK!
WELL, THEY'RE NOT AMONGST THE SHRUBS!
NOT THAT YOU CAN SEE!
OF COURSE, WE DID DO A LOT OF RAKING, PLANTING AND DIGGING...
DON'T TELL ME!!
DON'T TELL YOU THE TICKETS ARE SOMEWHERE UNDER THE PEAT MOSS AND LOAM?
OKAY, I WON'T TELL YOU!
GRAB A SPADE.
MAYBE THE BOYS WOULD ENJOY A NICE TOUR OF THE EUROPEAN COUNTRIES!
HL
10

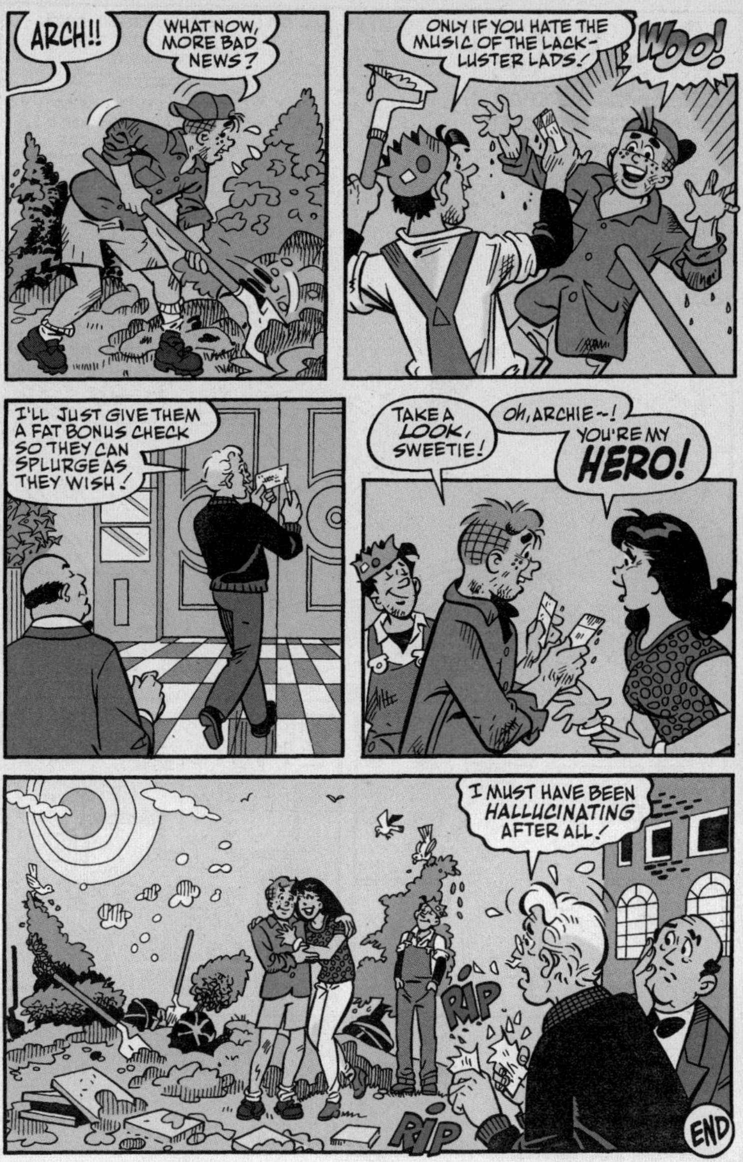
ARCH!!
WHAT NOW, MORE BAD NEWS?
ONLY IF YOU HATE THE MUSIC OF THE LACK-LUSTER LADS!
WOO!
I'LL JUST GIVE THEM A FAT BONUS CHECK SO THEY CAN SPLURGE AS THEY WISH!
TAKE A LOOK, SWEETIE!
Oh, ARCHIE--! YOU'RE MY HERO!
I MUST HAVE BEEN HALLUCINATING AFTER ALL!
RIP
RIP
END

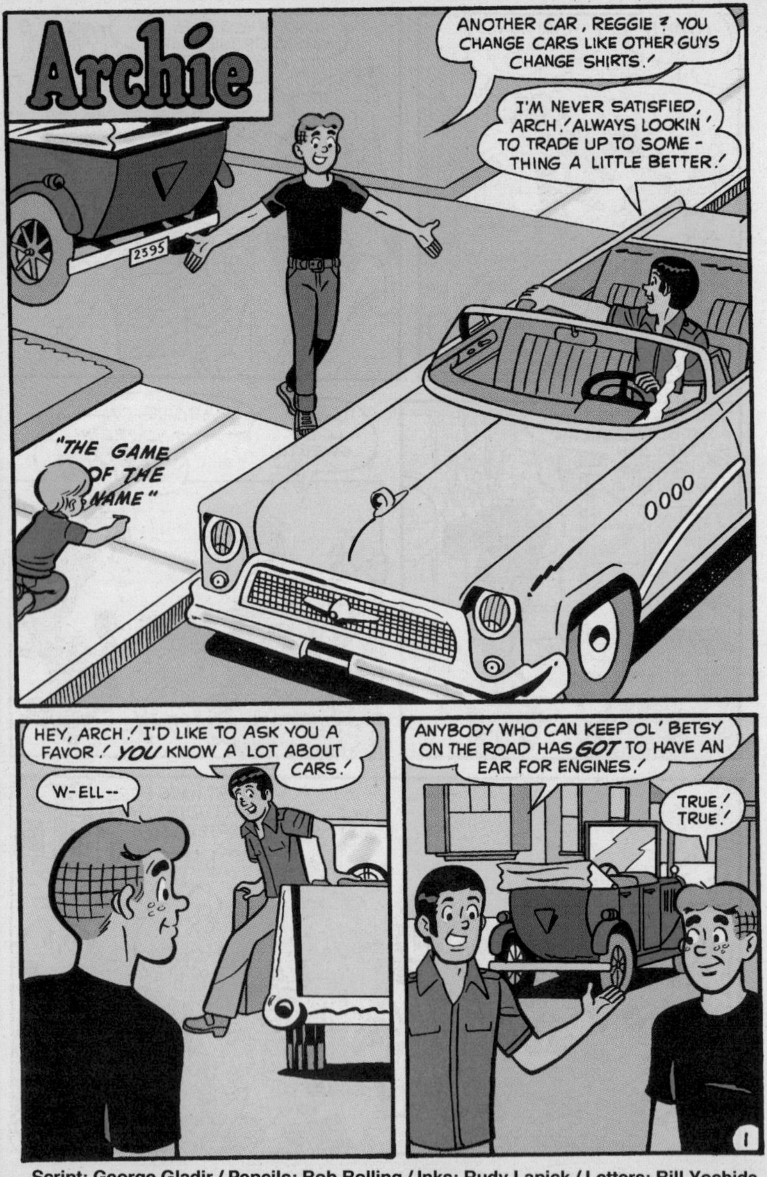
Archie
ANOTHER CAR, REGGIE ? YOU CHANGE CARS LIKE OTHER GUYS CHANGE SHIRTS!
I'M NEVER SATISFIED, ARCH! ALWAYS LOOKIN' TO TRADE UP TO SOME-THING A LITTLE BETTER!
"THE GAME OF THE NAME"
2395
0000
HEY, ARCH! I'D LIKE TO ASK YOU A FAVOR! YOU KNOW A LOT ABOUT CARS!
W-ELL--
ANYBODY WHO CAN KEEP OL' BETSY ON THE ROAD HAS GOT TO HAVE AN EAR FOR ENGINES!
TRUE! TRUE!
1

Script: George Gladir / Pencils: Bob Bolling / Inks: Rudy Lapick / Letters: Bill Yoshida

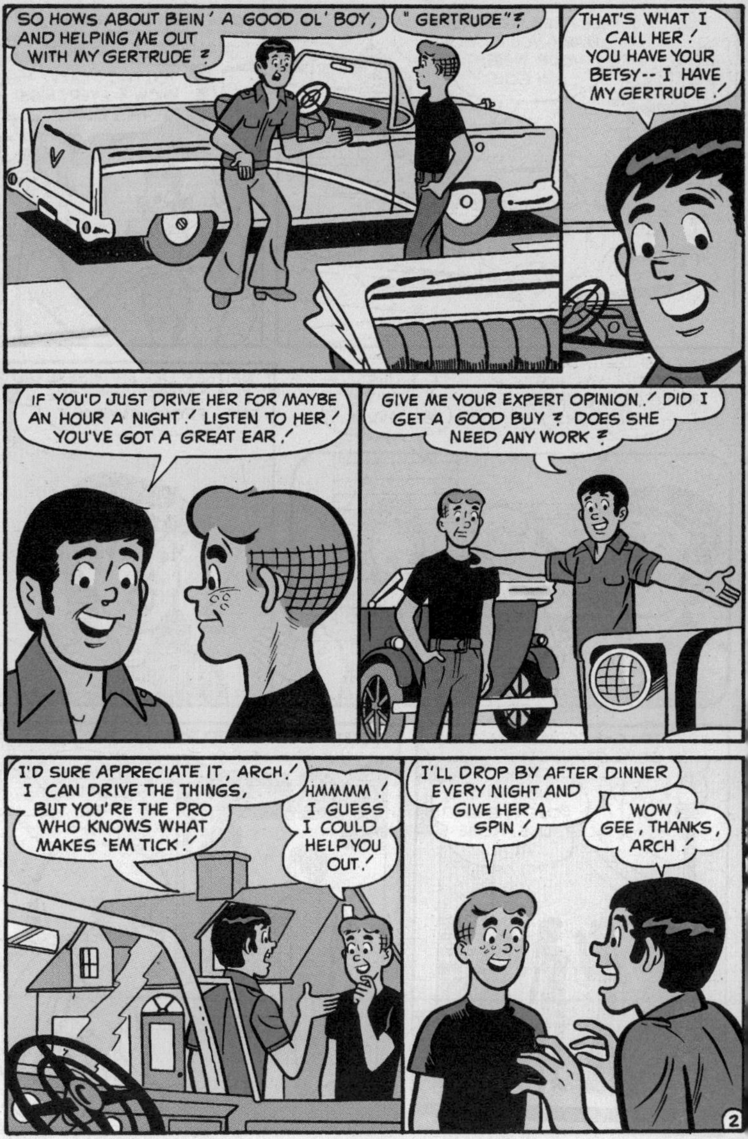

SO HOWS ABOUT BEIN' A GOOD OL' BOY, AND HELPING ME OUT WITH MY GERTRUDE ?
"GERTRUDE"?
THAT'S WHAT I CALL HER! YOU HAVE YOUR BETSY-- I HAVE MY GERTRUDE!
IF YOU'D JUST DRIVE HER FOR MAYBE AN HOUR A NIGHT! LISTEN TO HER! YOU'VE GOT A GREAT EAR!
GIVE ME YOUR EXPERT OPINION! DID I GET A GOOD BUY ? DOES SHE NEED ANY WORK ?
I'D SURE APPRECIATE IT, ARCH! I CAN DRIVE THE THINGS, BUT YOU'RE THE PRO WHO KNOWS WHAT MAKES 'EM TICK!
HMMMM! I GUESS I COULD HELP YOU OUT!
I'LL DROP BY AFTER DINNER EVERY NIGHT AND GIVE HER A SPIN!
WOW, GEE, THANKS, ARCH!
2

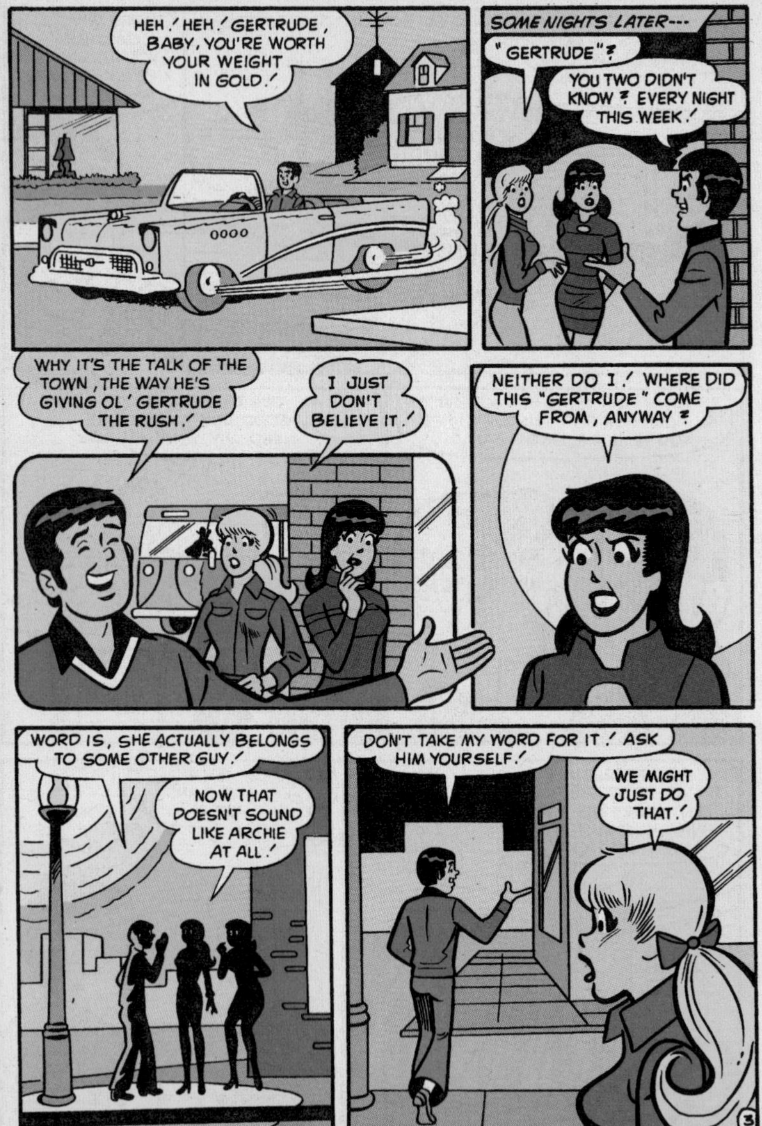

HEH.! HEH.! GERTRUDE, BABY, YOU'RE WORTH YOUR WEIGHT IN GOLD.!
0000
SOME NIGHTS LATER---
"GERTRUDE"?
YOU TWO DIDN'T KNOW? EVERY NIGHT THIS WEEK.!
WHY IT'S THE TALK OF THE TOWN, THE WAY HE'S GIVING OL' GERTRUDE THE RUSH.!
I JUST DON'T BELIEVE IT.!
NEITHER DO I.! WHERE DID THIS "GERTRUDE" COME FROM, ANYWAY?
WORD IS, SHE ACTUALLY BELONGS TO SOME OTHER GUY.!
NOW THAT DOESN'T SOUND LIKE ARCHIE AT ALL.!
DON'T TAKE MY WORD FOR IT.! ASK HIM YOURSELF.!
WE MIGHT JUST DO THAT.!
3

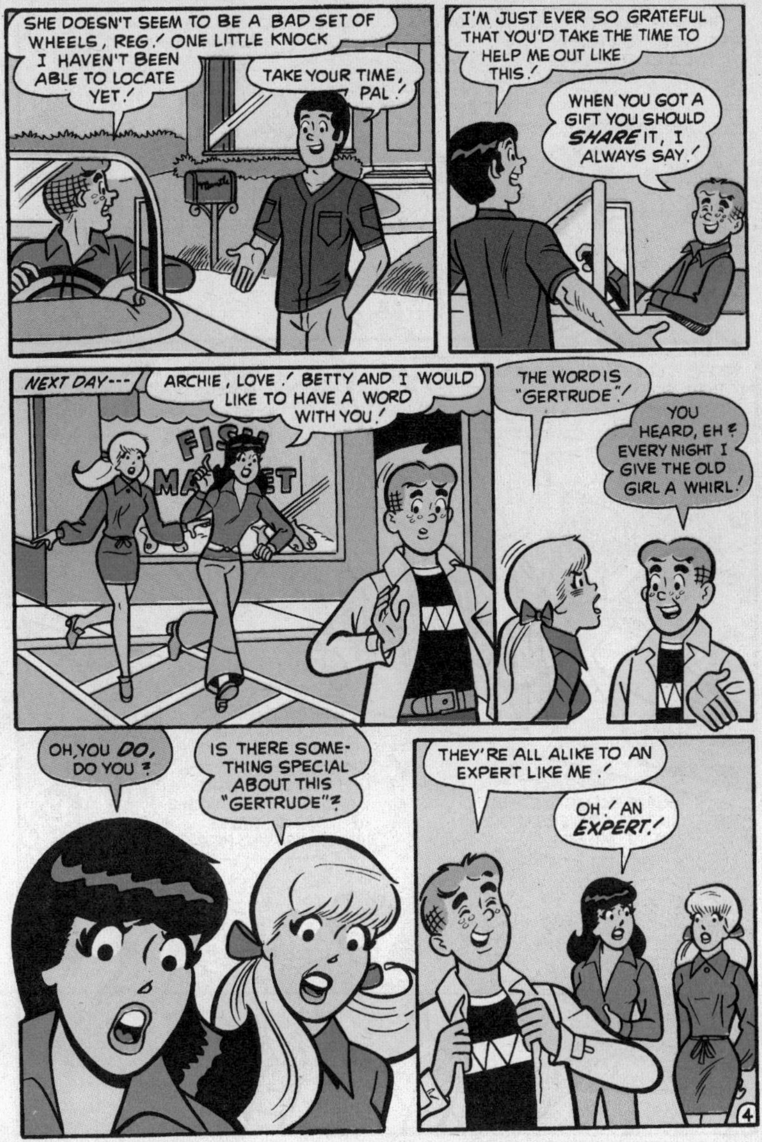

SHE DOESN'T SEEM TO BE A BAD SET OF WHEELS, REG.! ONE LITTLE KNOCK I HAVEN'T BEEN ABLE TO LOCATE YET.!
TAKE YOUR TIME, PAL!
I'M JUST EVER SO GRATEFUL THAT YOU'D TAKE THE TIME TO HELP ME OUT LIKE THIS.!
WHEN YOU GOT A GIFT YOU SHOULD SHARE IT, I ALWAYS SAY.!
NEXT DAY---
ARCHIE, LOVE.! BETTY AND I WOULD LIKE TO HAVE A WORD WITH YOU.!
FISH MARKET
THE WORD IS "GERTRUDE"!
YOU HEARD, EH? EVERY NIGHT I GIVE THE OLD GIRL A WHIRL!
OH, YOU DO, DO YOU?
IS THERE SOMETHING SPECIAL ABOUT THIS "GERTRUDE"?
THEY'RE ALL ALIKE TO AN EXPERT LIKE ME.!
OH.! AN EXPERT!
4

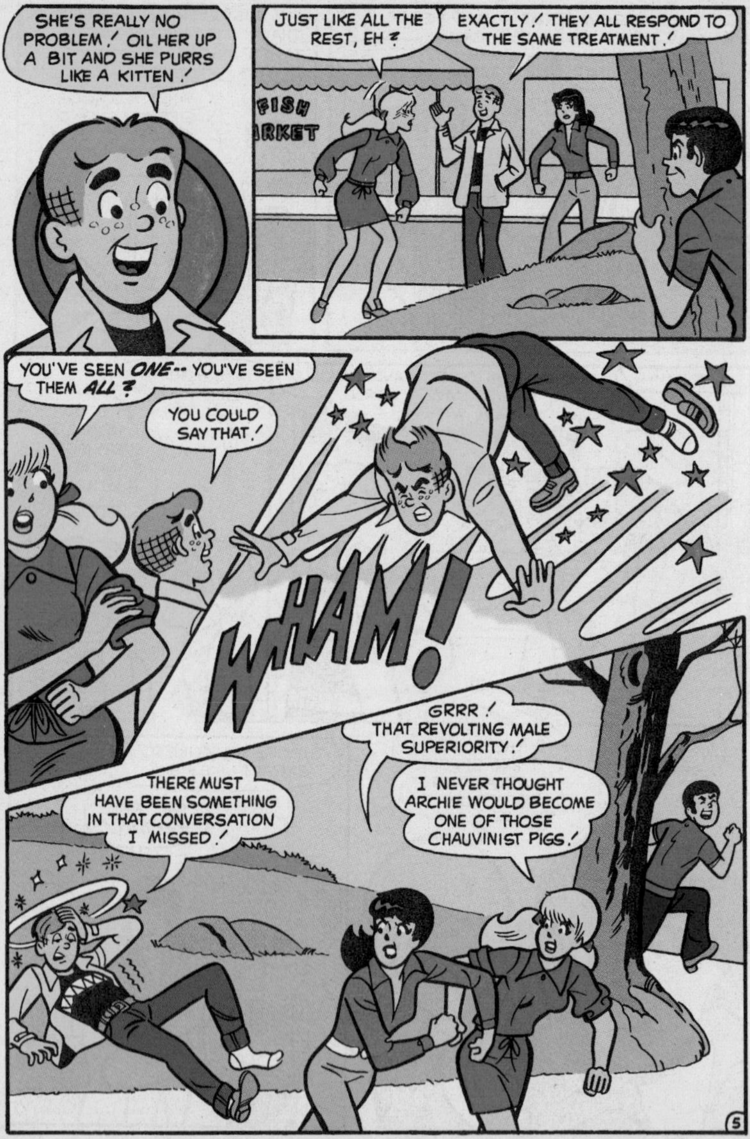
SHE'S REALLY NO PROBLEM! OIL HER UP A BIT AND SHE PURRS LIKE A KITTEN!
JUST LIKE ALL THE REST, EH?
EXACTLY! THEY ALL RESPOND TO THE SAME TREATMENT!
FISH
RKET
YOU'VE SEEN ONE-- YOU'VE SEEN THEM ALL?
YOU COULD SAY THAT!
WHAM!
GRRR! THAT REVOLTING MALE SUPERIORITY!
I NEVER THOUGHT ARCHIE WOULD BECOME ONE OF THOSE CHAUVINIST PIGS!
THERE MUST HAVE BEEN SOMETHING IN THAT CONVERSATION I MISSED!
5

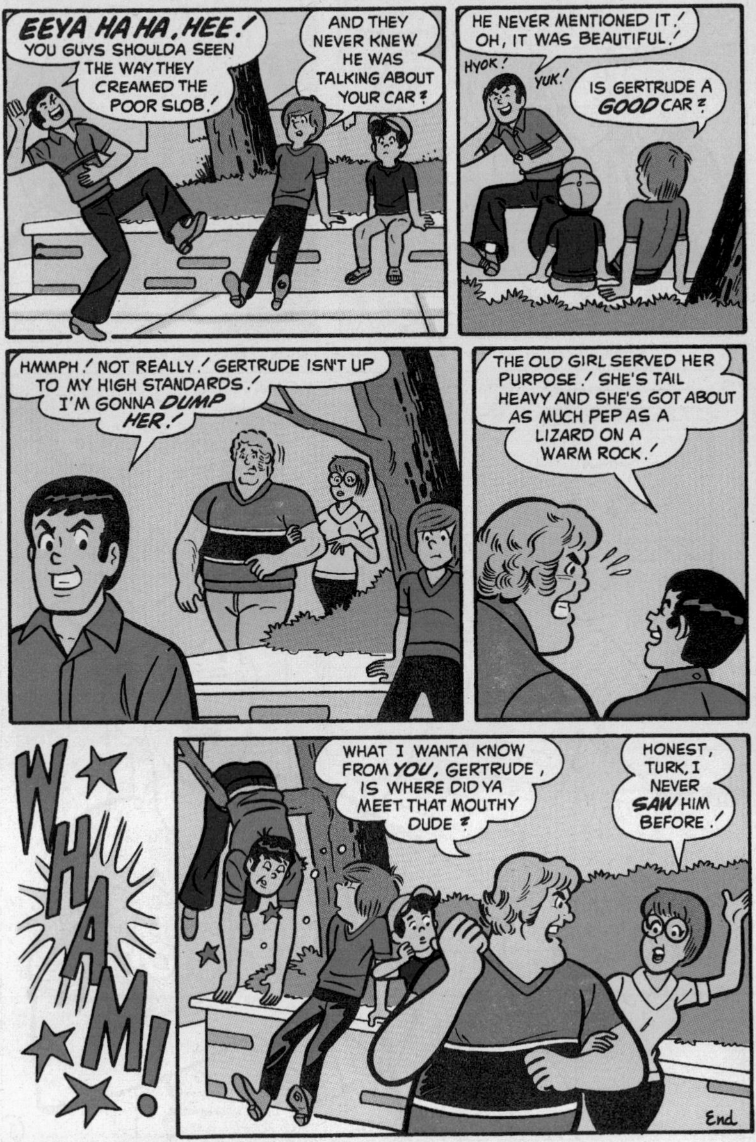
EEYA HA HA, HEE! YOU GUYS SHOULDA SEEN THE WAY THEY CREAMED THE POOR SLOB!
AND THEY NEVER KNEW HE WAS TALKING ABOUT YOUR CAR?
HE NEVER MENTIONED IT! OH, IT WAS BEAUTIFUL!
HYOK!
YUK!
IS GERTRUDE A GOOD CAR?
HMMPH! NOT REALLY! GERTRUDE ISN'T UP TO MY HIGH STANDARDS! I'M GONNA DUMP HER!
THE OLD GIRL SERVED HER PURPOSE! SHE'S TAIL HEAVY AND SHE'S GOT ABOUT AS MUCH PEP AS A LIZARD ON A WARM ROCK!
WHAM!
WHAT I WANTA KNOW FROM YOU, GERTRUDE, IS WHERE DID YA MEET THAT MOUTHY DUDE?
HONEST, TURK, I NEVER SAW HIM BEFORE!
End

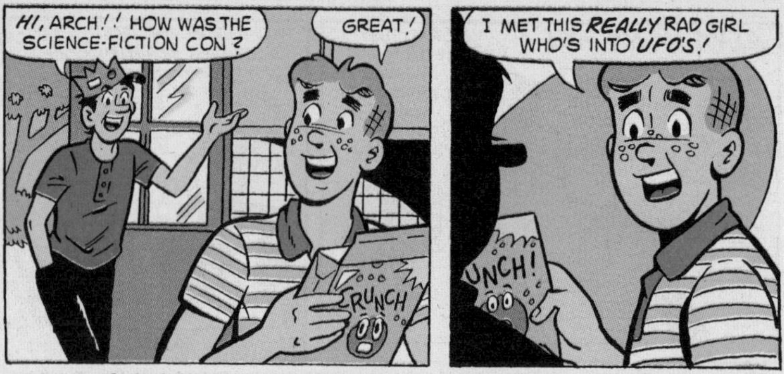
HI, ARCH!! HOW WAS THE SCIENCE-FICTION CON?
GREAT!
CRUNCH
I MET THIS REALLY RAD GIRL WHO'S INTO UFO'S!
UNCH!

Script & Pencils: Fernando Ruiz / Inks: Rudy Lapick / Letters: Bill Yoshida

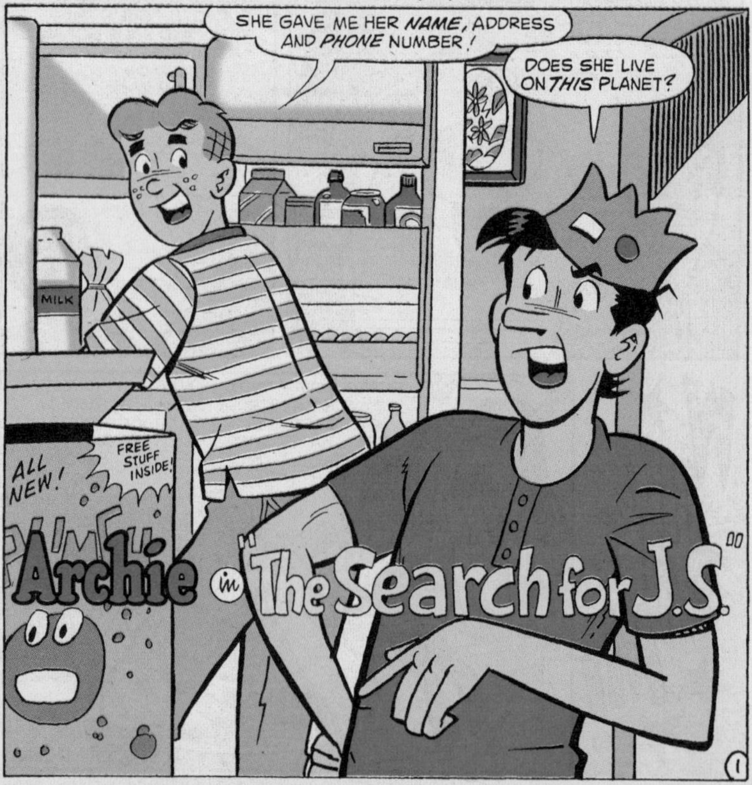
SHE GAVE ME HER NAME, ADDRESS AND PHONE NUMBER!
DOES SHE LIVE ON THIS PLANET?
MILK
ALL NEW!
FREE STUFF INSIDE!
Archie in "The Search for J.S."
1

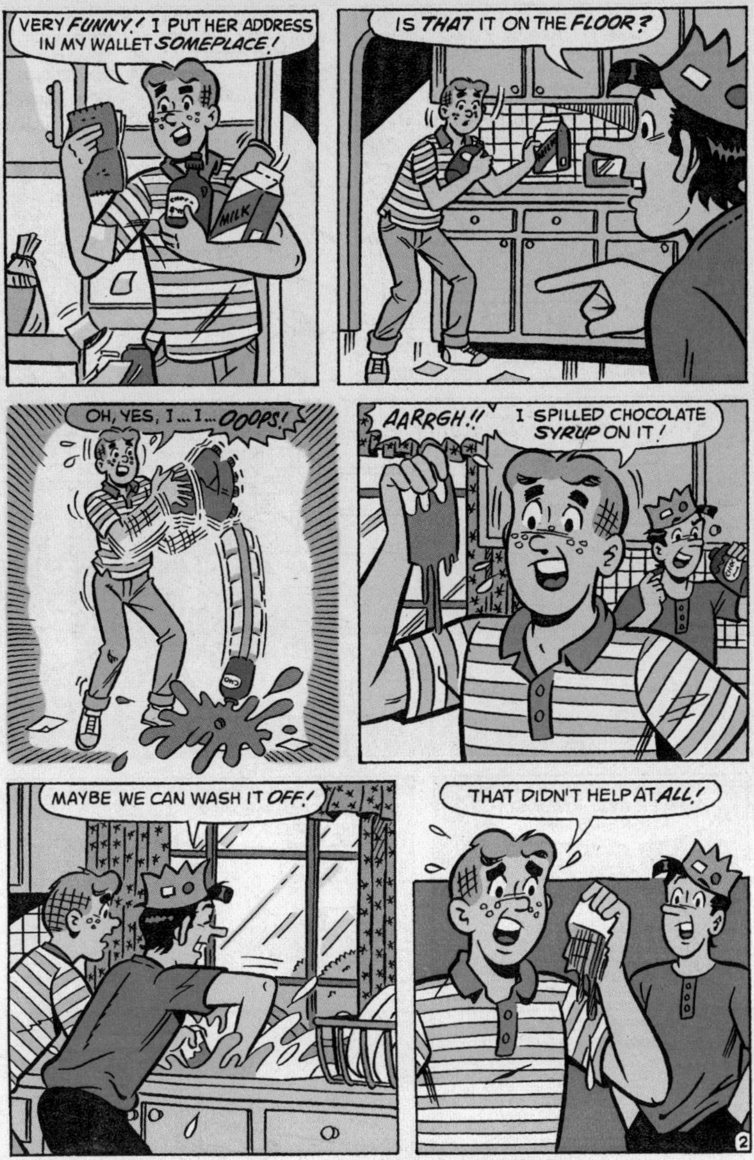
VERY FUNNY! I PUT HER ADDRESS IN MY WALLET SOMEPLACE!
MILK
IS THAT IT ON THE FLOOR?
OH, YES, I... I... OOOPS!
AARRGH!!
I SPILLED CHOCOLATE SYRUP ON IT!
MAYBE WE CAN WASH IT OFF!
THAT DIDN'T HELP AT ALL!
2

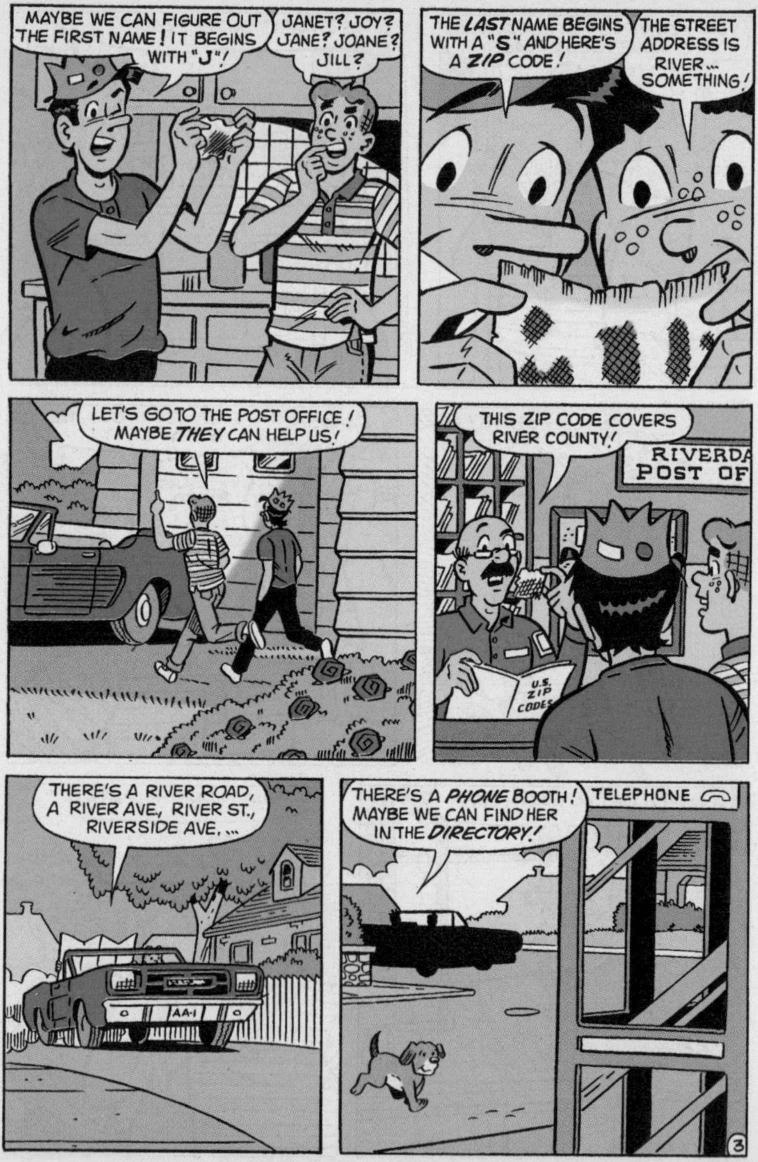

MAYBE WE CAN FIGURE OUT THE FIRST NAME! IT BEGINS WITH "J"!
JANET? JOY? JANE? JOANE? JILL?
THE LAST NAME BEGINS WITH A "S" AND HERE'S A ZIP CODE!
THE STREET ADDRESS IS RIVER... SOMETHING!
LET'S GO TO THE POST OFFICE! MAYBE THEY CAN HELP US!
THIS ZIP CODE COVERS RIVER COUNTY!
RIVERDA POST OF
U.S. ZIP CODES
THERE'S A RIVER ROAD, A RIVER AVE., RIVER ST., RIVERSIDE AVE. ...
AA-1
THERE'S A PHONE BOOTH! MAYBE WE CAN FIND HER IN THE DIRECTORY!
TELEPHONE
3

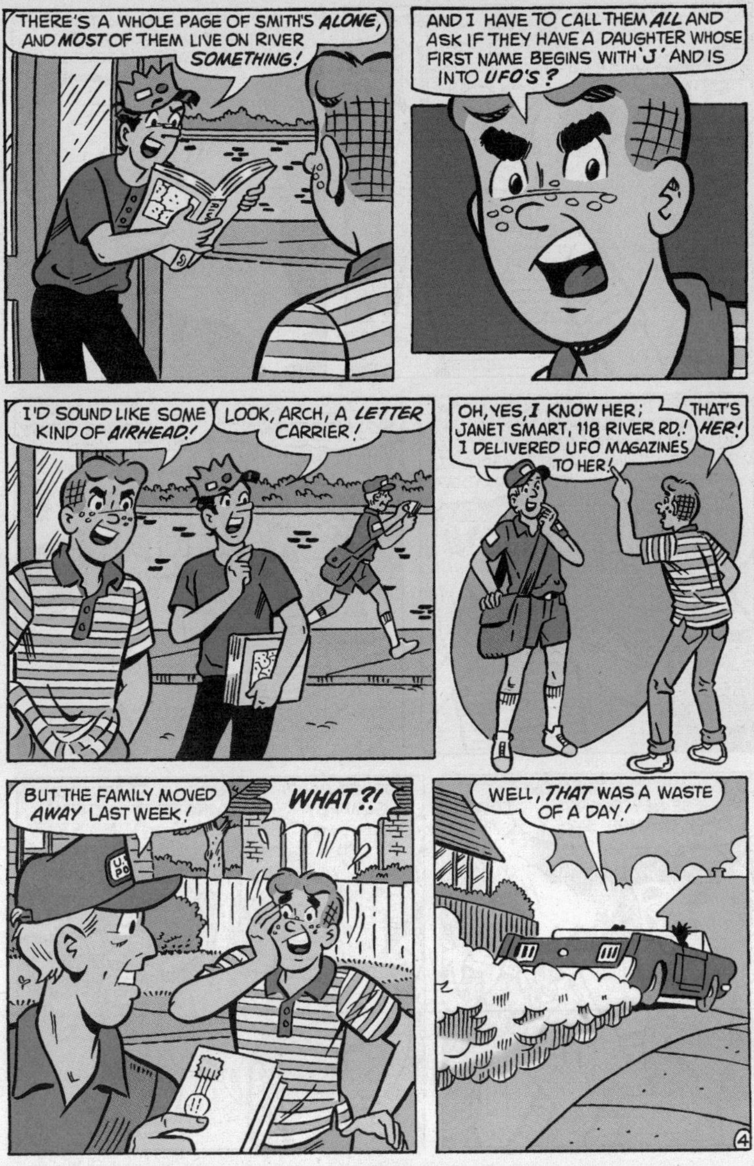
THERE'S A WHOLE PAGE OF SMITH'S ALONE, AND MOST OF THEM LIVE ON RIVER SOMETHING!
AND I HAVE TO CALL THEM ALL AND ASK IF THEY HAVE A DAUGHTER WHOSE FIRST NAME BEGINS WITH 'J' AND IS INTO UFO'S?
I'D SOUND LIKE SOME KIND OF AIRHEAD!
LOOK, ARCH, A LETTER CARRIER!
OH, YES, I KNOW HER; JANET SMART, 118 RIVER RD.! I DELIVERED UFO MAGAZINES TO HER!
THAT'S HER!
BUT THE FAMILY MOVED AWAY LAST WEEK!
WHAT?!
WELL, THAT WAS A WASTE OF A DAY!
4

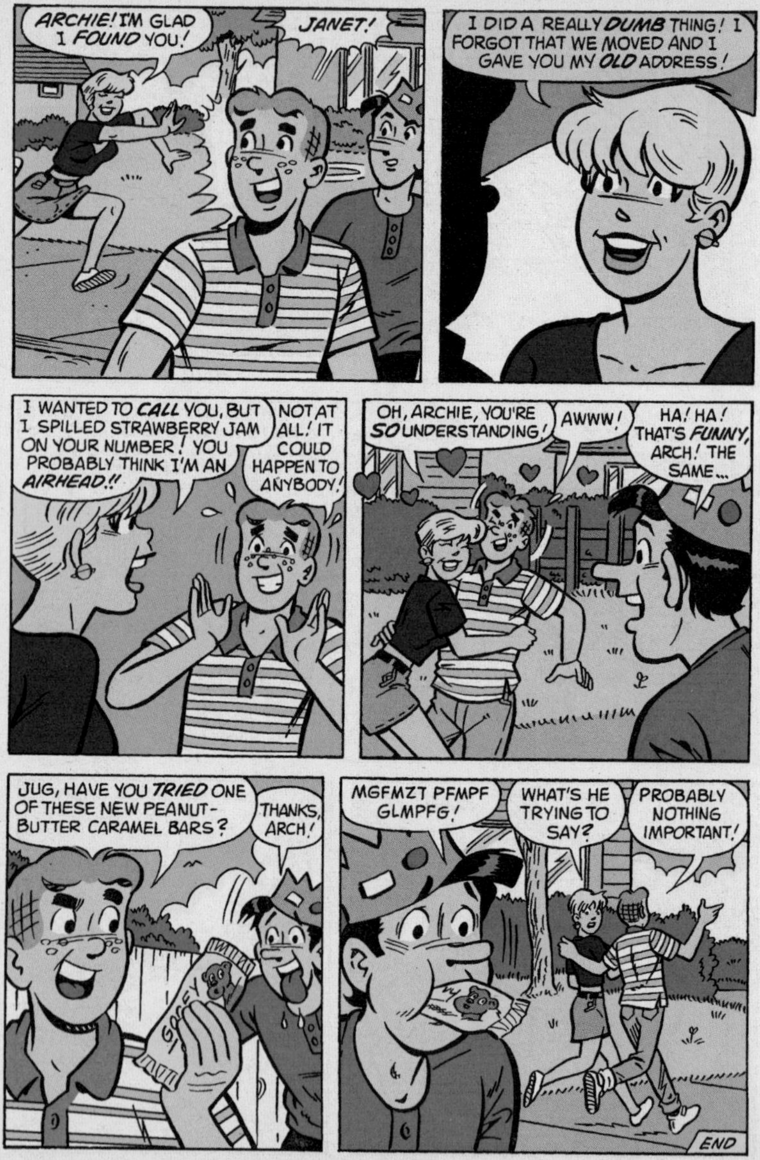
ARCHIE! I'M GLAD I FOUND YOU!
JANET!
I DID A REALLY DUMB THING! I FORGOT THAT WE MOVED AND I GAVE YOU MY OLD ADDRESS!
I WANTED TO CALL YOU, BUT I SPILLED STRAWBERRY JAM ON YOUR NUMBER! YOU PROBABLY THINK I'M AN AIRHEAD!!
NOT AT ALL! IT COULD HAPPEN TO ANYBODY!
OH, ARCHIE, YOU'RE SO UNDERSTANDING!
AWWW!
HA! HA! THAT'S FUNNY, ARCH! THE SAME...
JUG, HAVE YOU TRIED ONE OF THESE NEW PEANUT-BUTTER CARAMEL BARS?
THANKS, ARCH!
MGFMZT PFMPF GLMPFG!
WHAT'S HE TRYING TO SAY?
PROBABLY NOTHING IMPORTANT!
END

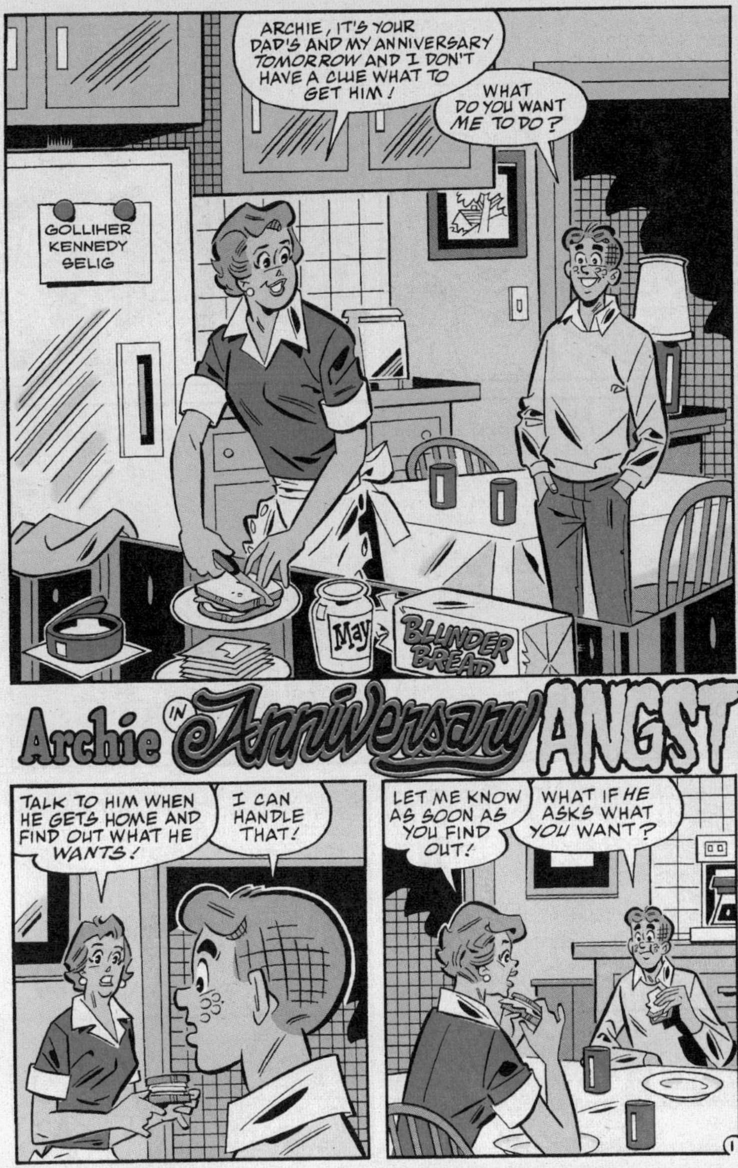

ARCHIE, IT'S YOUR DAD'S AND MY ANNIVERSARY TOMORROW AND I DON'T HAVE A CLUE WHAT TO GET HIM!
WHAT DO YOU WANT ME TO DO?
GOLLIHER KENNEDY SELIG
May
BLUNDER BREAD
Archie IN Anniversary ANGST
TALK TO HIM WHEN HE GETS HOME AND FIND OUT WHAT HE WANTS!
I CAN HANDLE THAT!
LET ME KNOW AS SOON AS YOU FIND OUT!
WHAT IF HE ASKS WHAT YOU WANT?
1

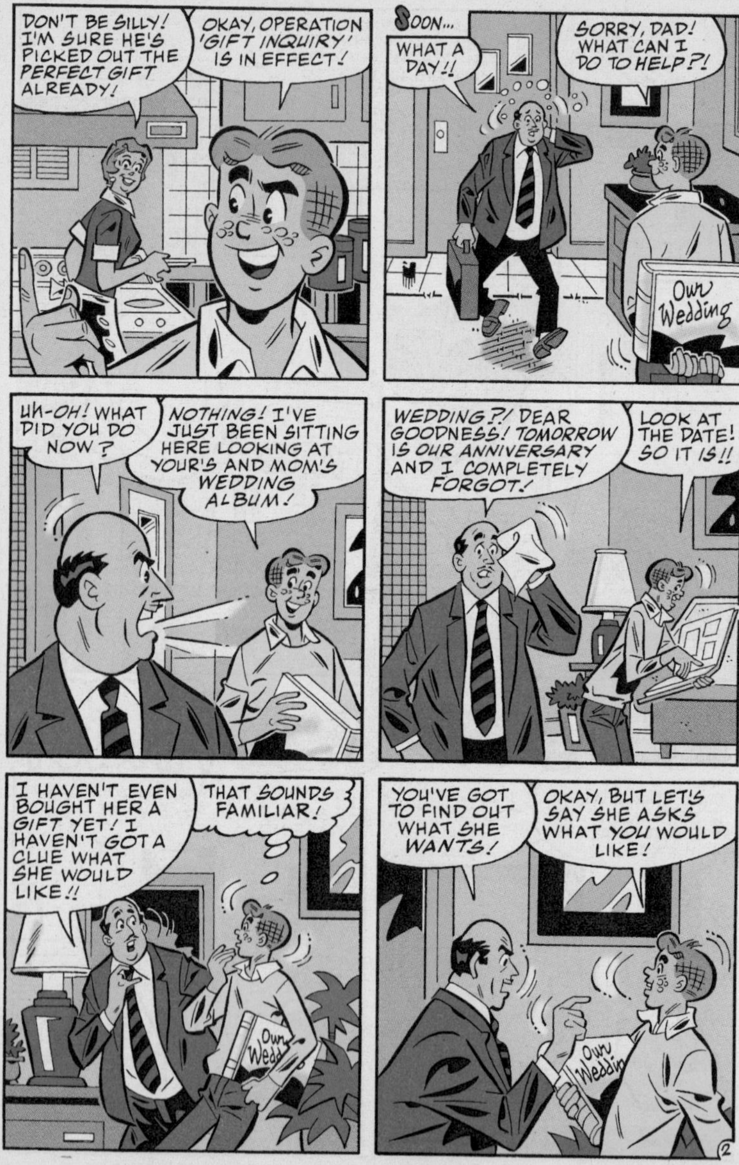
DON'T BE SILLY! I'M SURE HE'S PICKED OUT THE PERFECT GIFT ALREADY!
OKAY, OPERATION 'GIFT INQUIRY' IS IN EFFECT!
SOON...
WHAT A DAY!!
SORRY, DAD! WHAT CAN I DO TO HELP?!
Our Wedding
UH-OH! WHAT DID YOU DO NOW?
NOTHING! I'VE JUST BEEN SITTING HERE LOOKING AT YOUR'S AND MOM'S WEDDING ALBUM!
WEDDING?! DEAR GOODNESS! TOMORROW IS OUR ANNIVERSARY AND I COMPLETELY FORGOT!
LOOK AT THE DATE! SO IT IS!!
I HAVEN'T EVEN BOUGHT HER A GIFT YET! I HAVEN'T GOT A CLUE WHAT SHE WOULD LIKE!!
THAT SOUNDS FAMILIAR!
YOU'VE GOT TO FIND OUT WHAT SHE WANTS!
OKAY, BUT LET'S SAY SHE ASKS WHAT YOU WOULD LIKE!
2

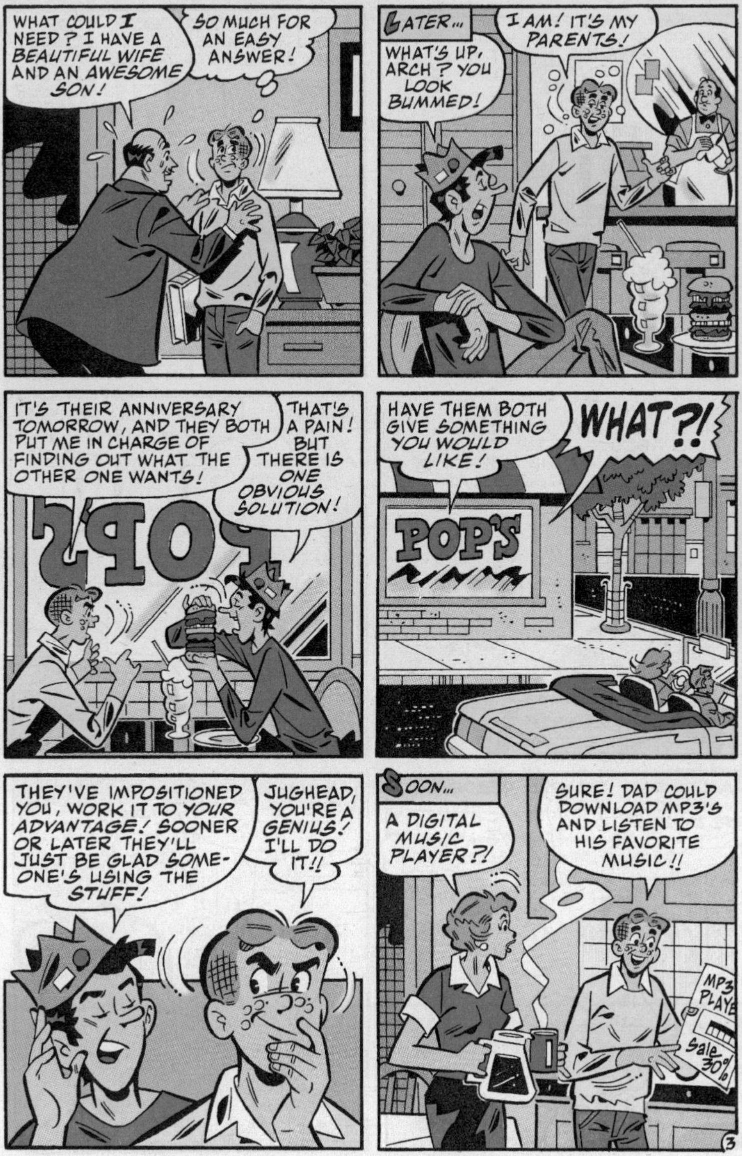
WHAT COULD I NEED? I HAVE A BEAUTIFUL WIFE AND AN AWESOME SON!
SO MUCH FOR AN EASY ANSWER!
LATER...
WHAT'S UP, ARCH? YOU LOOK BUMMED!
I AM! IT'S MY PARENTS!
IT'S THEIR ANNIVERSARY TOMORROW, AND THEY BOTH PUT ME IN CHARGE OF FINDING OUT WHAT THE OTHER ONE WANTS!
THAT'S A PAIN! BUT THERE IS ONE OBVIOUS SOLUTION!
POP'S
HAVE THEM BOTH GIVE SOMETHING YOU WOULD LIKE!
WHAT?!
POP'S
THEY'VE IMPOSITIONED YOU, WORK IT TO YOUR ADVANTAGE! SOONER OR LATER THEY'LL JUST BE GLAD SOME-ONE'S USING THE STUFF!
JUGHEAD, YOU'RE A GENIUS! I'LL DO IT!!
SOON...
A DIGITAL MUSIC PLAYER?!
SURE! DAD COULD DOWNLOAD MP3'S AND LISTEN TO HIS FAVORITE MUSIC!!
MP3 PLAYE
Sale 30%
3

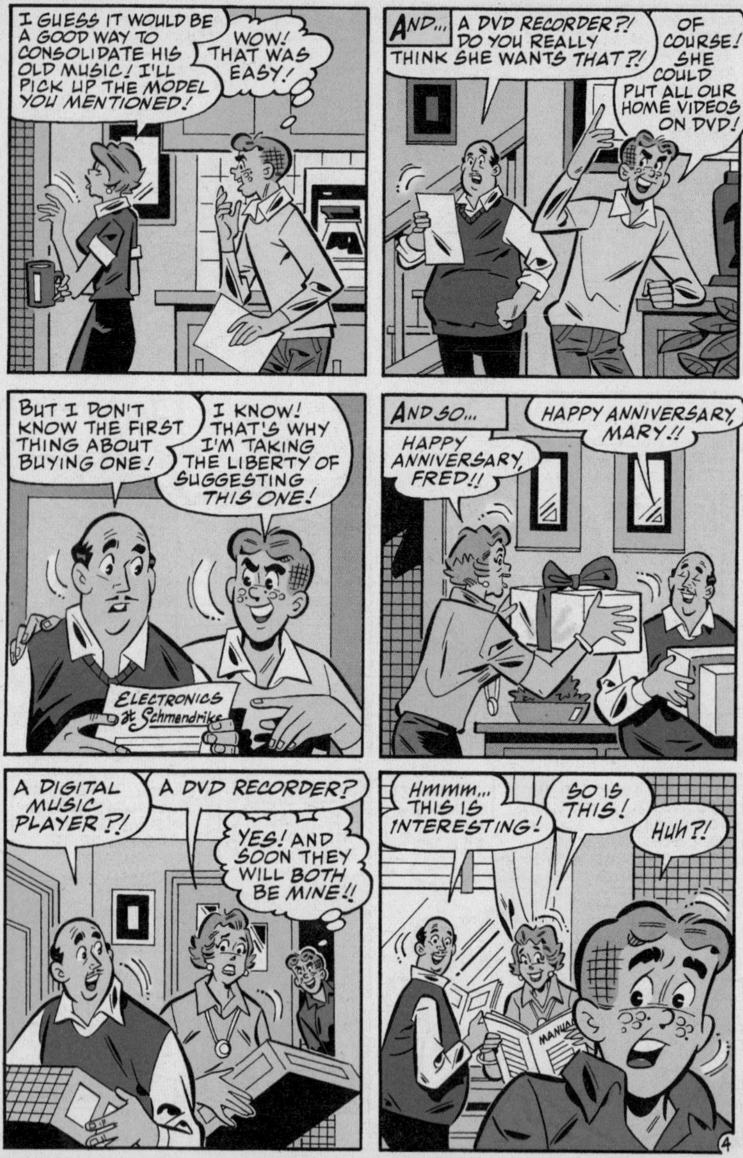
I GUESS IT WOULD BE A GOOD WAY TO CONSOLIDATE HIS OLD MUSIC! I'LL PICK UP THE MODEL YOU MENTIONED!
WOW! THAT WAS EASY!
AND...
A DVD RECORDER?! DO YOU REALLY THINK SHE WANTS THAT?!
OF COURSE! SHE COULD PUT ALL OUR HOME VIDEOS ON DVD!
BUT I DON'T KNOW THE FIRST THING ABOUT BUYING ONE!
I KNOW! THAT'S WHY I'M TAKING THE LIBERTY OF SUGGESTING THIS ONE!
ELECTRONICS at Schmendrike
AND SO...
HAPPY ANNIVERSARY, MARY!!
HAPPY ANNIVERSARY, FRED!!
A DIGITAL MUSIC PLAYER?!
A DVD RECORDER?
YES! AND SOON THEY WILL BOTH BE MINE!!
Hmmm... THIS IS INTERESTING!
SO IS THIS!
Huh?!
MANUAL
4

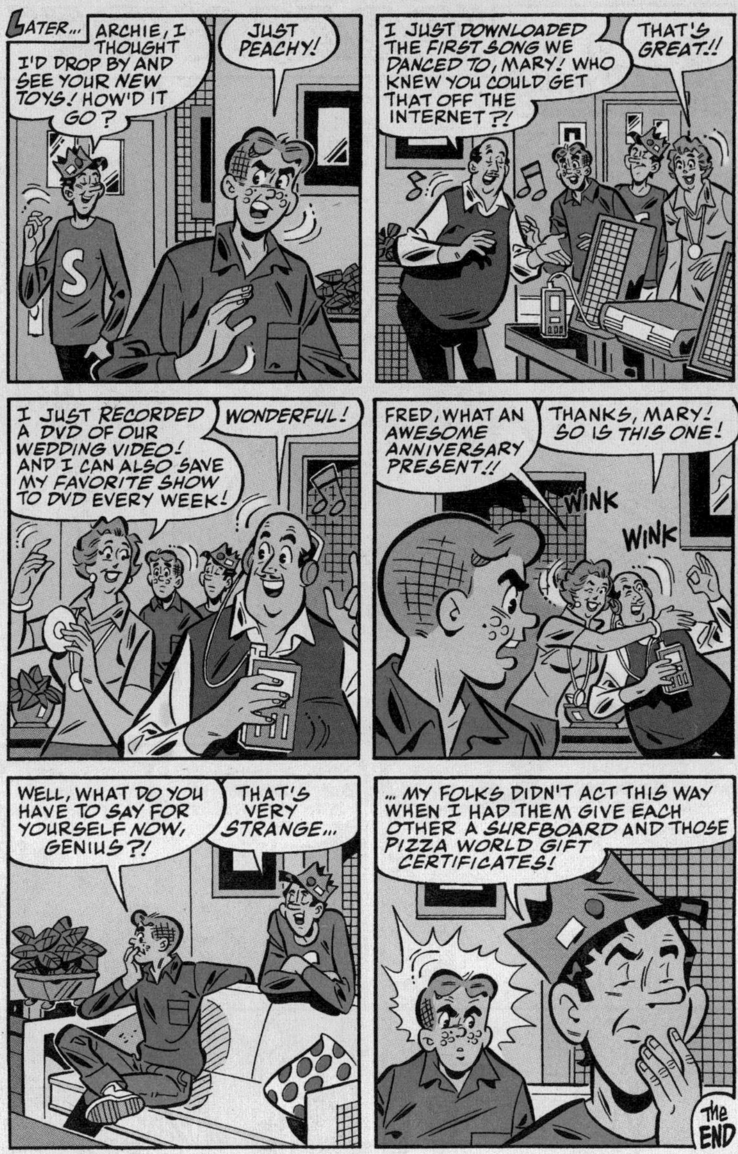

LATER...
ARCHIE, I THOUGHT I'D DROP BY AND SEE YOUR NEW TOYS! HOW'D IT GO?
JUST PEACHY!
I JUST DOWNLOADED THE FIRST SONG WE DANCED TO, MARY! WHO KNEW YOU COULD GET THAT OFF THE INTERNET?!
THAT'S GREAT!!
I JUST RECORDED A DVD OF OUR WEDDING VIDEO! AND I CAN ALSO SAVE MY FAVORITE SHOW TO DVD EVERY WEEK!
WONDERFUL!
FRED, WHAT AN AWESOME ANNIVERSARY PRESENT!!
THANKS, MARY! SO IS THIS ONE!
WINK
WINK
WELL, WHAT DO YOU HAVE TO SAY FOR YOURSELF NOW, GENIUS?!
THAT'S VERY STRANGE...
... MY FOLKS DIDN'T ACT THIS WAY WHEN I HAD THEM GIVE EACH OTHER A SURFBOARD AND THOSE PIZZA WORLD GIFT CERTIFICATES!
THE END

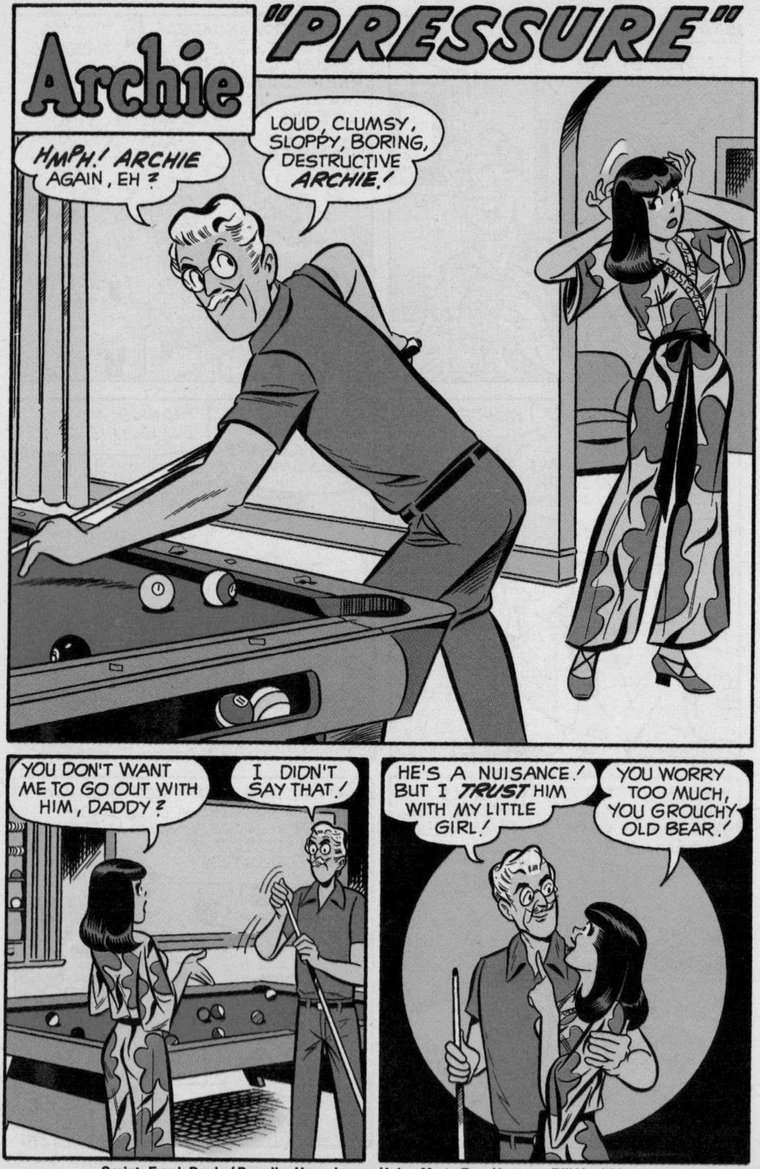

Archie
"PRESSURE"
HMPH! ARCHIE AGAIN, EH?
LOUD, CLUMSY, SLOPPY, BORING, DESTRUCTIVE ARCHIE!
YOU DON'T WANT ME TO GO OUT WITH HIM, DADDY?
I DIDN'T SAY THAT!
HE'S A NUISANCE! BUT I TRUST HIM WITH MY LITTLE GIRL!
YOU WORRY TOO MUCH, YOU GROUCHY OLD BEAR!

Script: Frank Doyle / Pencils: Harry Lucey / Inks: Marty Epp / Letters: Bill Yoshida

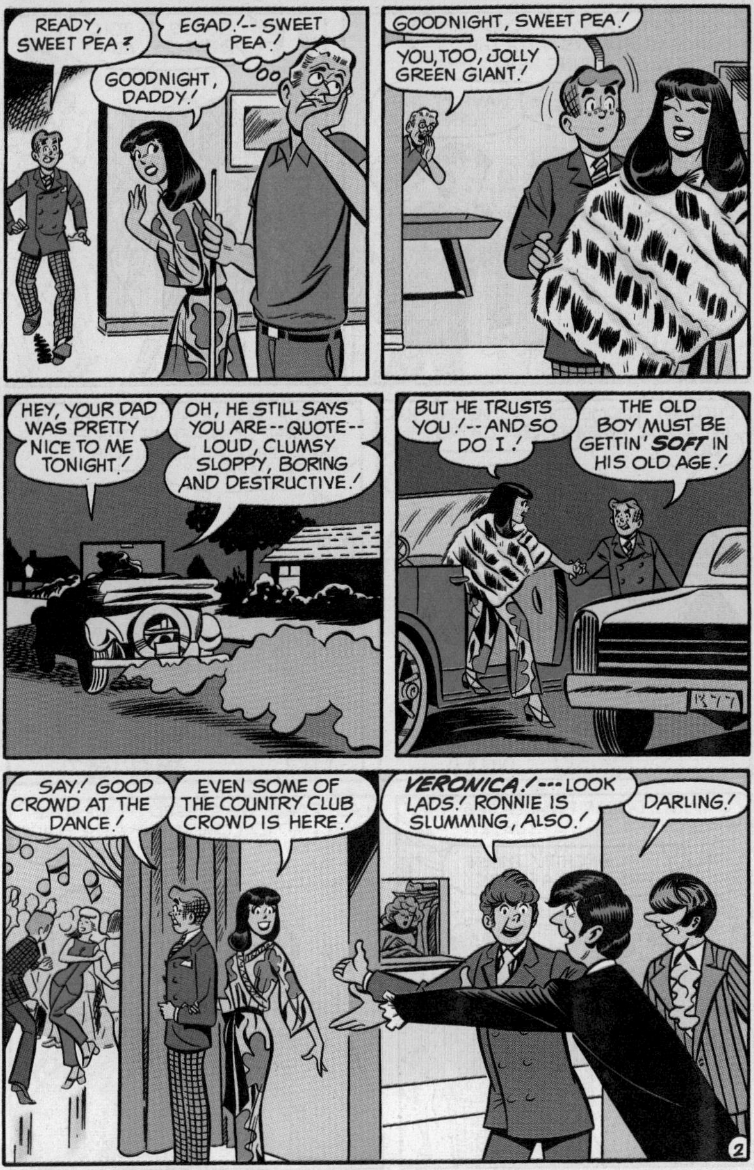

READY, SWEET PEA ?
EGAD!-- SWEET PEA!
GOODNIGHT, DADDY!
GOODNIGHT, SWEET PEA!
YOU,TOO, JOLLY GREEN GIANT!
HEY, YOUR DAD WAS PRETTY NICE TO ME TONIGHT!
OH, HE STILL SAYS YOU ARE--QUOTE-- LOUD, CLUMSY SLOPPY, BORING AND DESTRUCTIVE!
BUT HE TRUSTS YOU!--AND SO DO I!
THE OLD BOY MUST BE GETTIN' SOFT IN HIS OLD AGE!
SAY! GOOD CROWD AT THE DANCE!
EVEN SOME OF THE COUNTRY CLUB CROWD IS HERE!
VERONICA!--- LOOK LADS! RONNIE IS SLUMMING, ALSO!
DARLING!
2

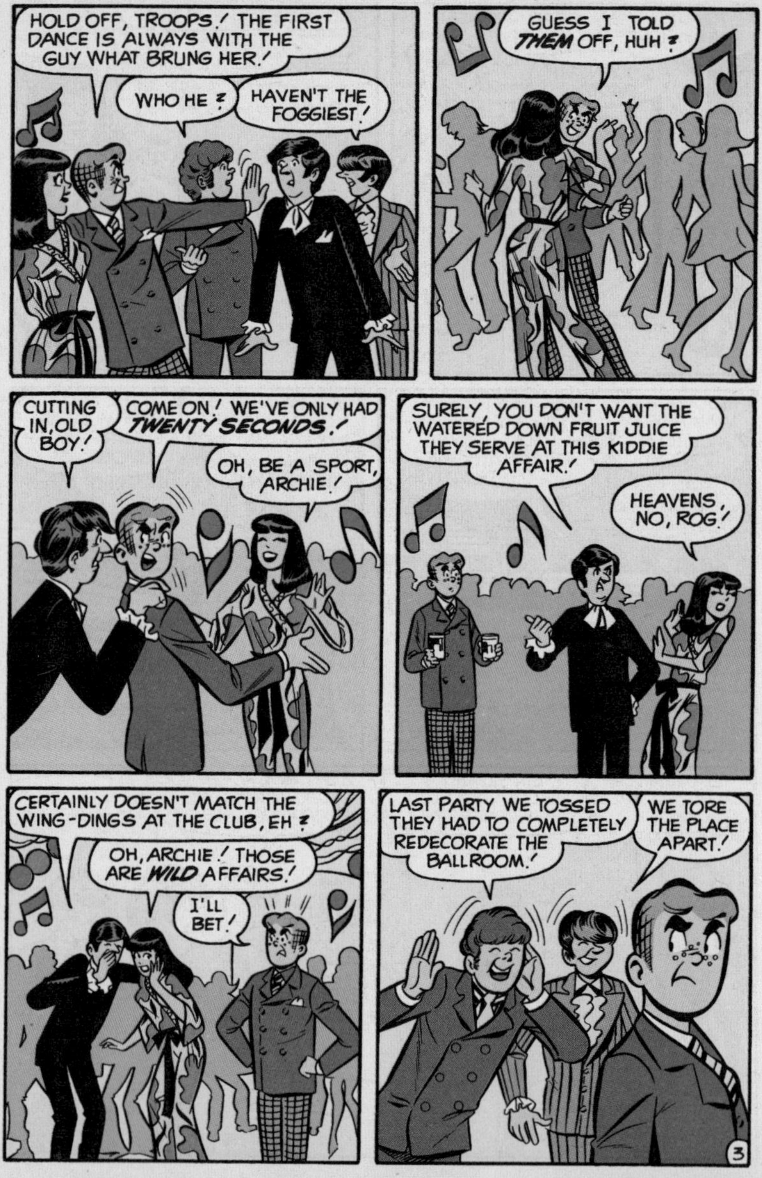

HOLD OFF, TROOPS! THE FIRST DANCE IS ALWAYS WITH THE GUY WHAT BRUNG HER!
WHO HE ?
HAVEN'T THE FOGGIEST!
GUESS I TOLD *THEM* OFF, HUH ?
CUTTING IN, OLD BOY!
COME ON! WE'VE ONLY HAD *TWENTY SECONDS*!
OH, BE A SPORT, ARCHIE!
SURELY, YOU DON'T WANT THE WATERED DOWN FRUIT JUICE THEY SERVE AT THIS KIDDIE AFFAIR!
HEAVENS, NO, ROG!
CERTAINLY DOESN'T MATCH THE WING-DINGS AT THE CLUB, EH ?
OH, ARCHIE! THOSE ARE *WILD* AFFAIRS!
I'LL BET!
LAST PARTY WE TOSSED THEY HAD TO COMPLETELY REDECORATE THE BALLROOM!
WE TORE THE PLACE APART!
3

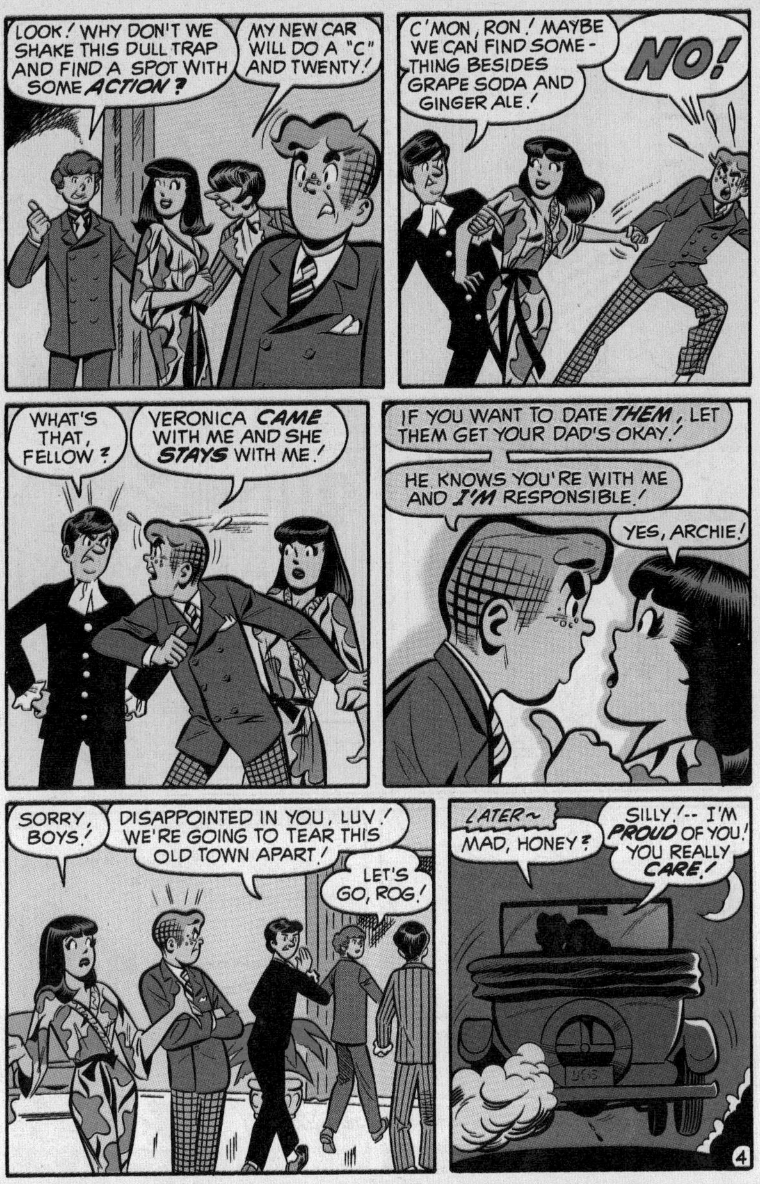
LOOK! WHY DON'T WE SHAKE THIS DULL TRAP AND FIND A SPOT WITH SOME ACTION?
MY NEW CAR WILL DO A "C" AND TWENTY!
C'MON, RON! MAYBE WE CAN FIND SOME-THING BESIDES GRAPE SODA AND GINGER ALE!
NO!
WHAT'S THAT, FELLOW?
VERONICA CAME WITH ME AND SHE STAYS WITH ME!
IF YOU WANT TO DATE THEM, LET THEM GET YOUR DAD'S OKAY!
HE KNOWS YOU'RE WITH ME AND I'M RESPONSIBLE!
YES, ARCHIE!
SORRY, BOYS!
DISAPPOINTED IN YOU, LUV! WE'RE GOING TO TEAR THIS OLD TOWN APART!
LET'S GO, ROG!
LATER~
MAD, HONEY?
SILLY!-- I'M PROUD OF YOU! YOU REALLY CARE!
4

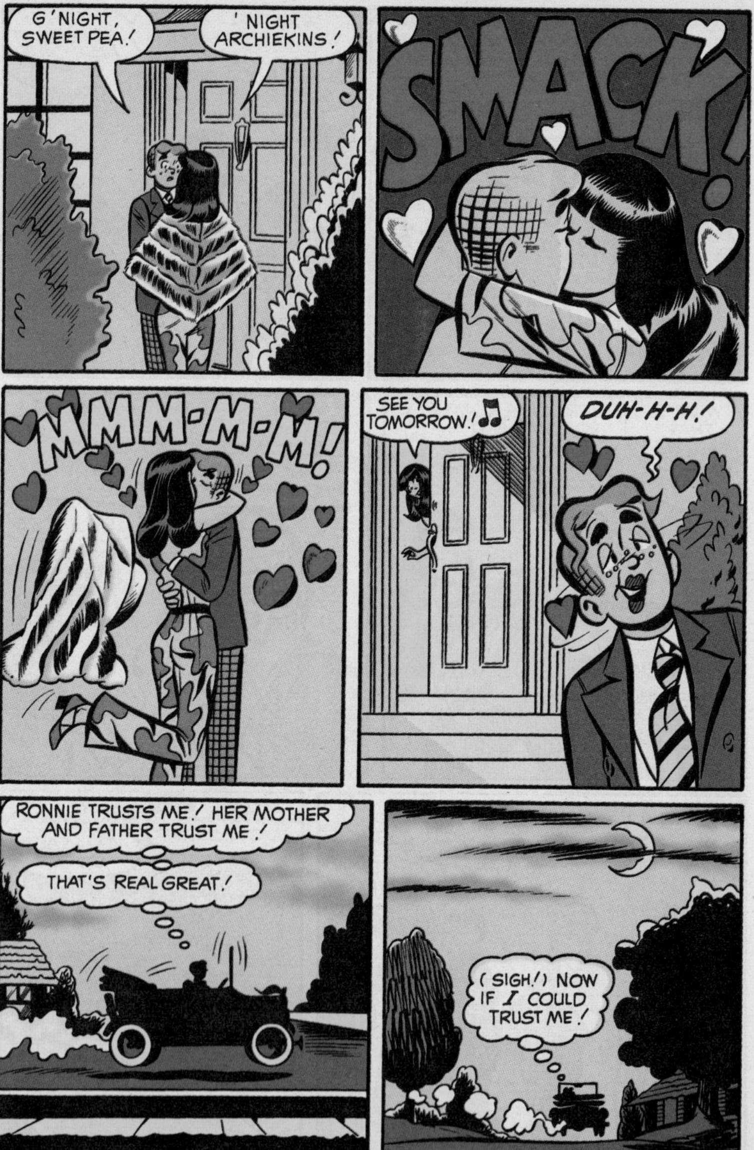
G'NIGHT, SWEET PEA!
'NIGHT ARCHIEKINS!
SMACK!
MMM-M-M!
SEE YOU TOMORROW!
DUH-H-H!
RONNIE TRUSTS ME! HER MOTHER AND FATHER TRUST ME!
THAT'S REAL GREAT!
(SIGH!) NOW IF I COULD TRUST ME!
THE END

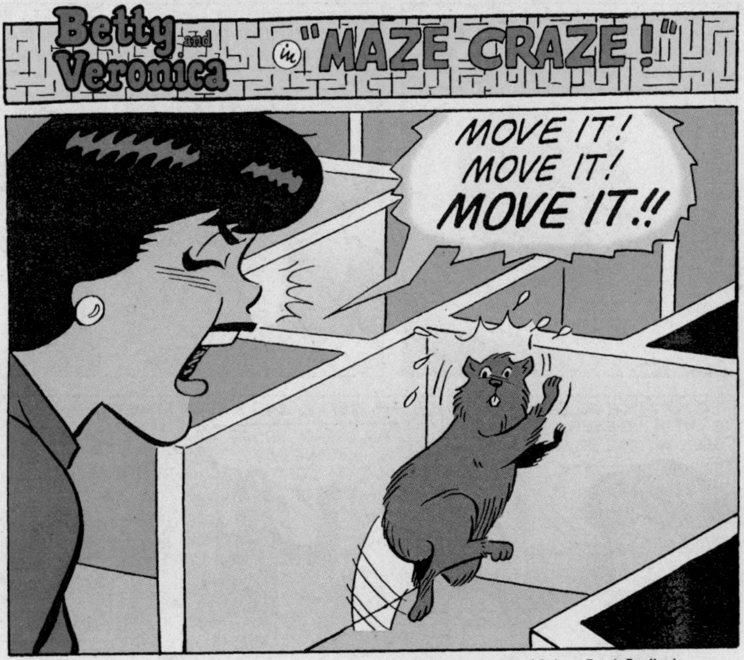
Betty and Veronica in "MAZE CRAZE!"
MOVE IT! MOVE IT! MOVE IT!!

Script & Pencils: Fernando Ruiz / Inks: Rudy Lapick / Letters: Bill Yoshida / Colors: Frank Gagliardo

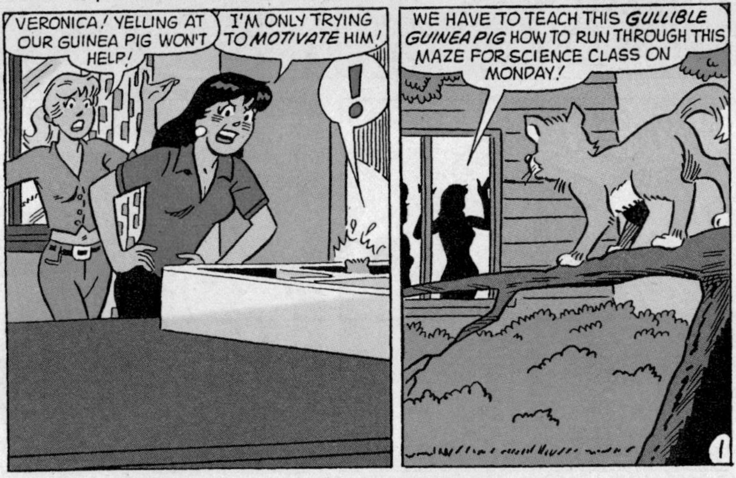
VERONICA! YELLING AT OUR GUINEA PIG WON'T HELP!
I'M ONLY TRYING TO MOTIVATE HIM!
!
WE HAVE TO TEACH THIS GULLIBLE GUINEA PIG HOW TO RUN THROUGH THIS MAZE FOR SCIENCE CLASS ON MONDAY!
1

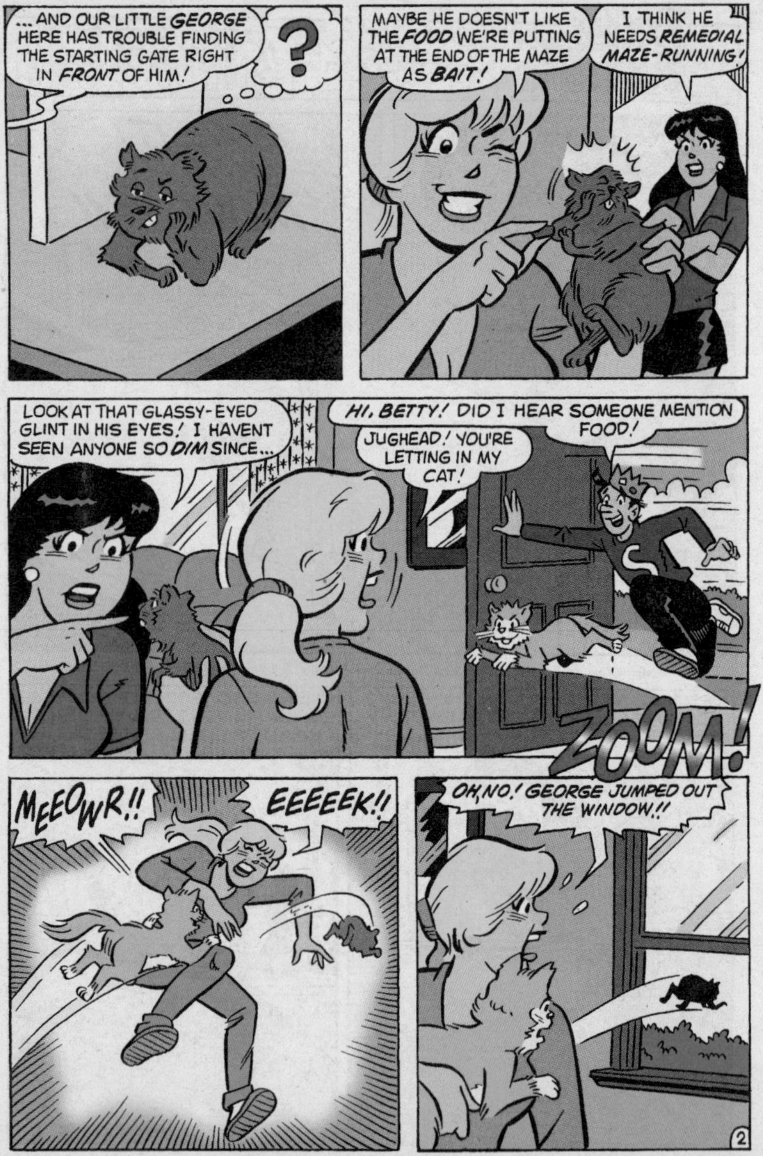
...AND OUR LITTLE GEORGE HERE HAS TROUBLE FINDING THE STARTING GATE RIGHT IN FRONT OF HIM!
?
MAYBE HE DOESN'T LIKE THE FOOD WE'RE PUTTING AT THE END OF THE MAZE AS BAIT!
I THINK HE NEEDS REMEDIAL MAZE-RUNNING!
LOOK AT THAT GLASSY-EYED GLINT IN HIS EYES! I HAVENT SEEN ANYONE SO DIM SINCE...
HI, BETTY! DID I HEAR SOMEONE MENTION FOOD!
JUGHEAD! YOU'RE LETTING IN MY CAT!
ZOOM!
MEEOWR!!
EEEEEK!!
OH, NO! GEORGE JUMPED OUT THE WINDOW!!
2

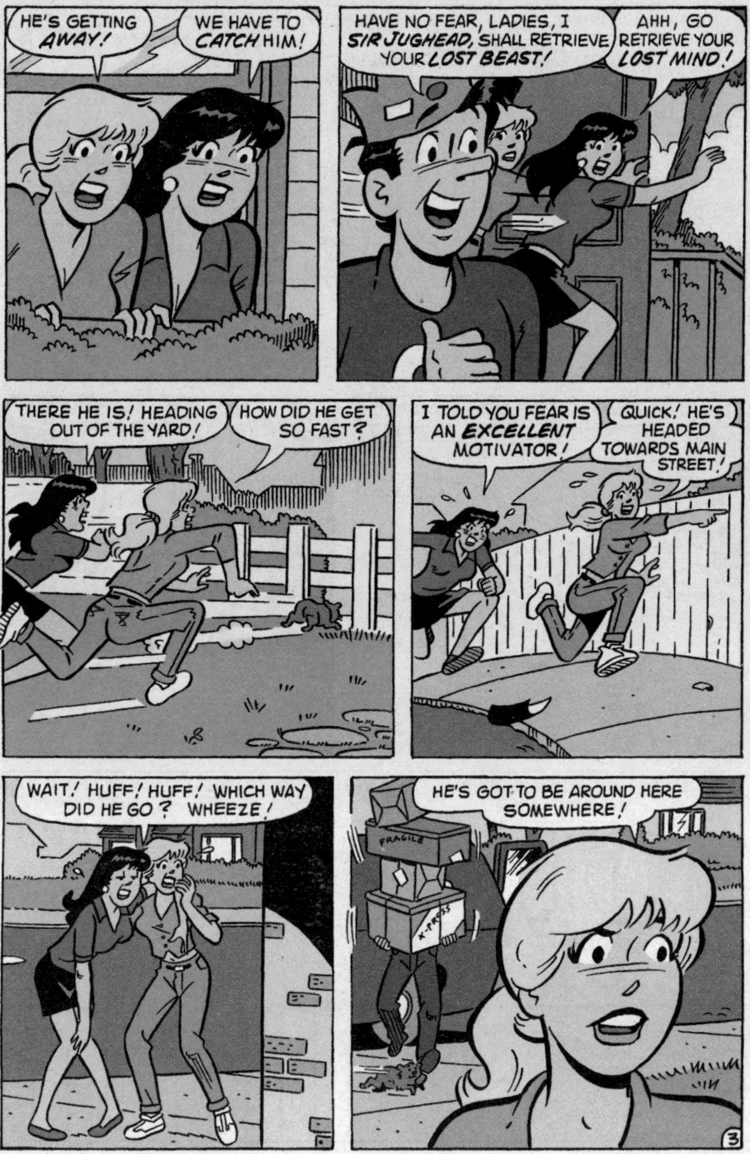
HE'S GETTING AWAY!
WE HAVE TO CATCH HIM!
HAVE NO FEAR, LADIES, I SIR JUGHEAD, SHALL RETRIEVE YOUR LOST BEAST!
AHH, GO RETRIEVE YOUR LOST MIND!
THERE HE IS! HEADING OUT OF THE YARD!
HOW DID HE GET SO FAST?
I TOLD YOU FEAR IS AN EXCELLENT MOTIVATOR!
QUICK! HE'S HEADED TOWARDS MAIN STREET!
WAIT! HUFF! HUFF! WHICH WAY DID HE GO? WHEEZE!
FRAGILE
X-PRESS
HE'S GOT TO BE AROUND HERE SOMEWHERE!
3

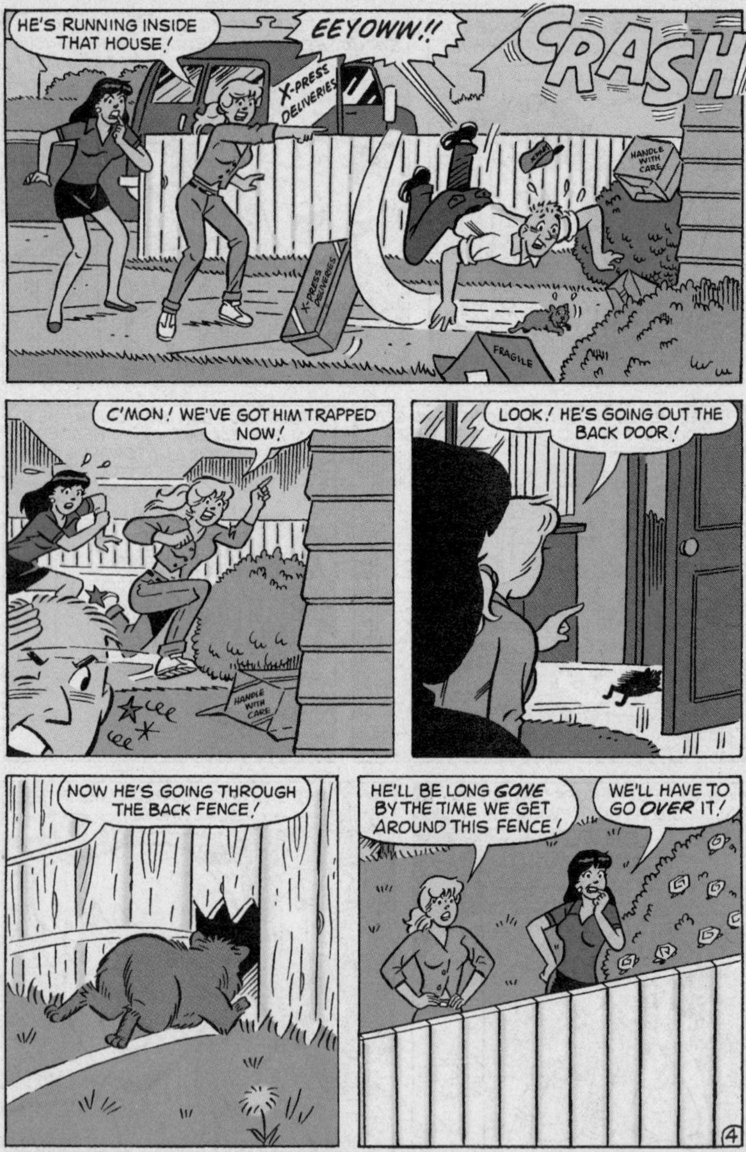
HE'S RUNNING INSIDE THAT HOUSE!
EEYOWW!!
CRASH
X-PRESS DELIVERIES
HANDLE WITH CARE
X-PRESS DELIVERIES
FRAGILE
C'MON! WE'VE GOT HIM TRAPPED NOW!
HANDLE WITH CARE
LOOK! HE'S GOING OUT THE BACK DOOR!
NOW HE'S GOING THROUGH THE BACK FENCE!
HE'LL BE LONG GONE BY THE TIME WE GET AROUND THIS FENCE!
WE'LL HAVE TO GO OVER IT!
4

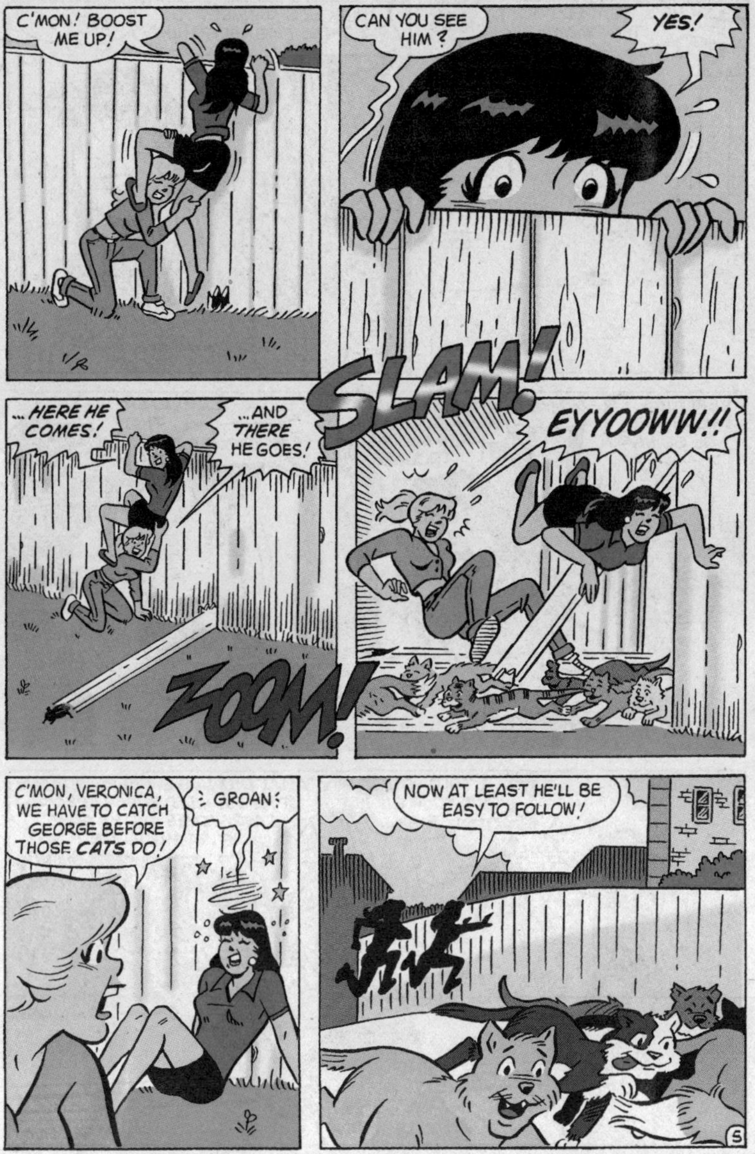
C'MON! BOOST ME UP!
CAN YOU SEE HIM?
YES!
SLAM!
...HERE HE COMES!
...AND THERE HE GOES!
ZOOM!
EYYOOWW!!
C'MON, VERONICA, WE HAVE TO CATCH GEORGE BEFORE THOSE CATS DO!
GROAN
NOW AT LEAST HE'LL BE EASY TO FOLLOW!
5

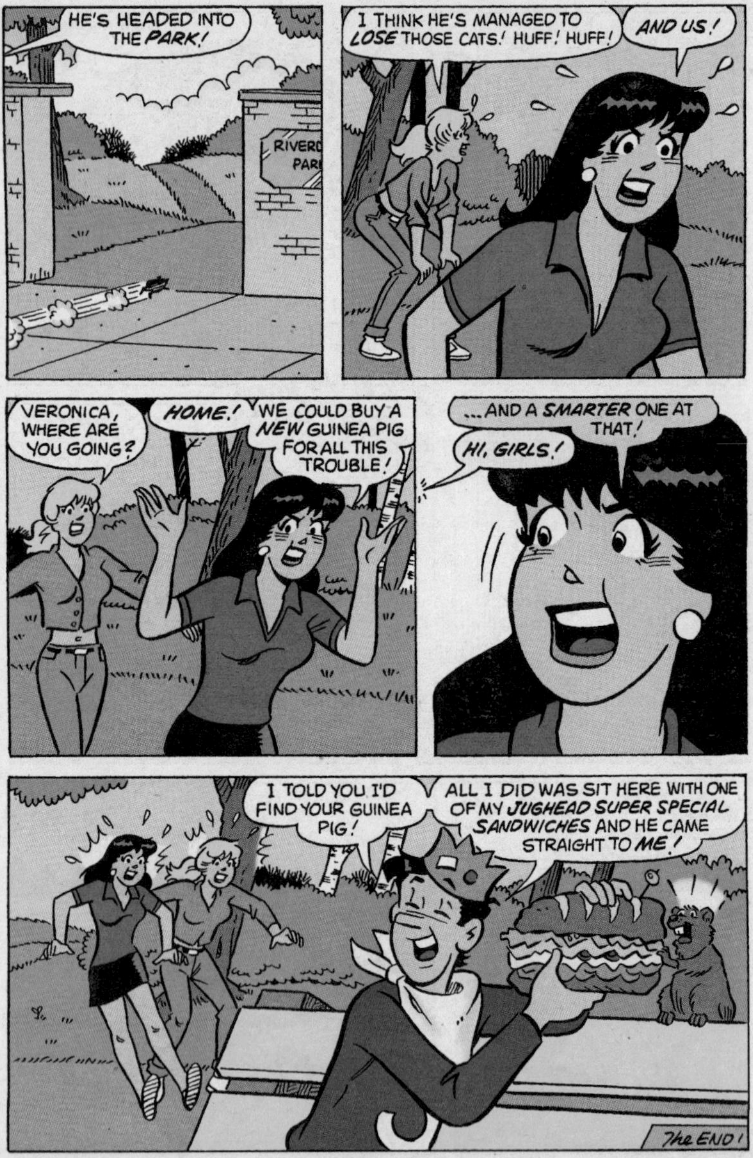

HE'S HEADED INTO THE PARK!
RIVERD
PAR
I THINK HE'S MANAGED TO LOSE THOSE CATS! HUFF! HUFF!
AND US!
VERONICA, WHERE ARE YOU GOING?
HOME!
WE COULD BUY A NEW GUINEA PIG FOR ALL THIS TROUBLE!
...AND A SMARTER ONE AT THAT!
HI, GIRLS!
I TOLD YOU I'D FIND YOUR GUINEA PIG!
ALL I DID WAS SIT HERE WITH ONE OF MY JUGHEAD SUPER SPECIAL SANDWICHES AND HE CAME STRAIGHT TO ME!
The END!

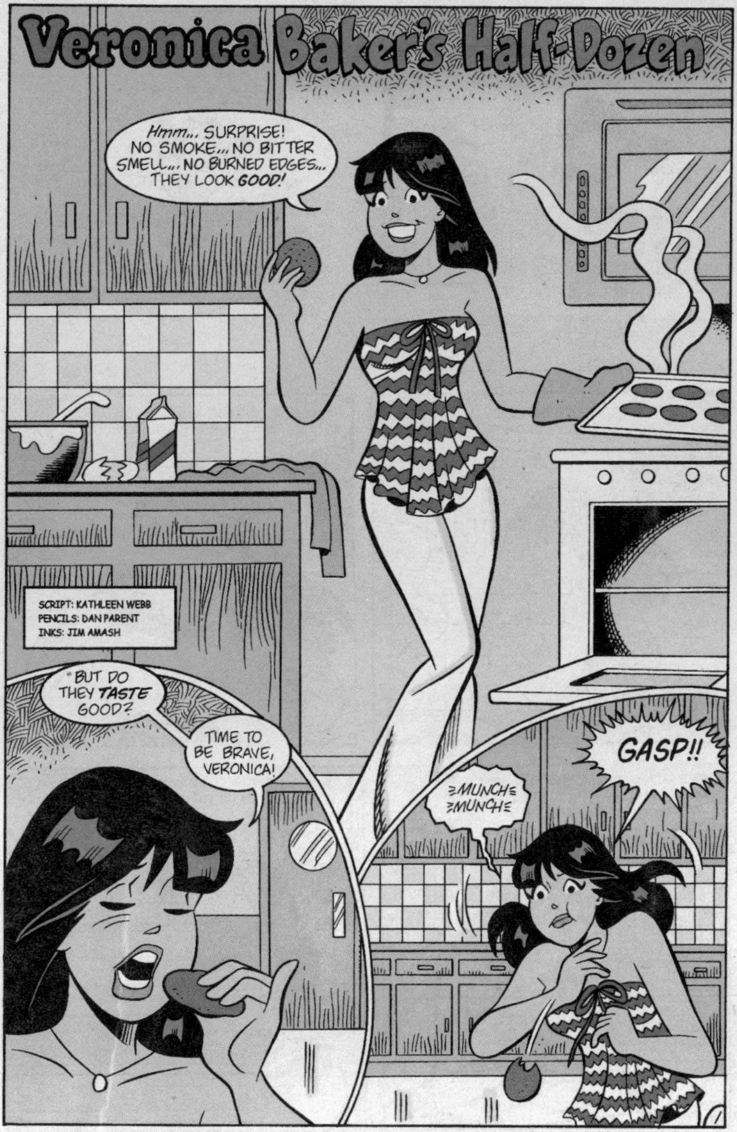

Veronica Baker's Half-Dozen
Hmm... SURPRISE! NO SMOKE... NO BITTER SMELL... NO BURNED EDGES... THEY LOOK GOOD!
SCRIPT: KATHLEEN WEBB
PENCILS: DAN PARENT
INKS: JIM AMASH
BUT DO THEY TASTE GOOD?
TIME TO BE BRAVE, VERONICA!
MUNCH MUNCH
GASP!!

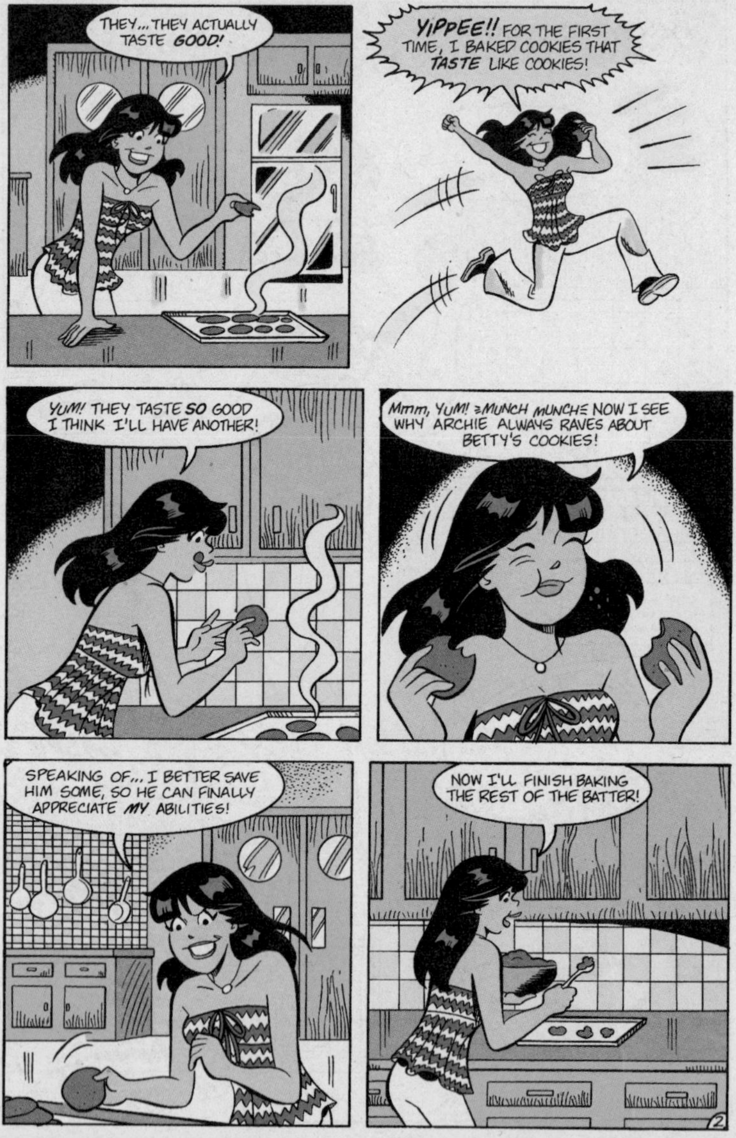

THEY... THEY ACTUALLY TASTE GOOD!
YIPPEE!! FOR THE FIRST TIME, I BAKED COOKIES THAT TASTE LIKE COOKIES!
YUM! THEY TASTE SO GOOD I THINK I'LL HAVE ANOTHER!
Mmm, YUM! ≋MUNCH MUNCH≋ NOW I SEE WHY ARCHIE ALWAYS RAVES ABOUT BETTY'S COOKIES!
SPEAKING OF... I BETTER SAVE HIM SOME, SO HE CAN FINALLY APPRECIATE MY ABILITIES!
NOW I'LL FINISH BAKING THE REST OF THE BATTER!
2

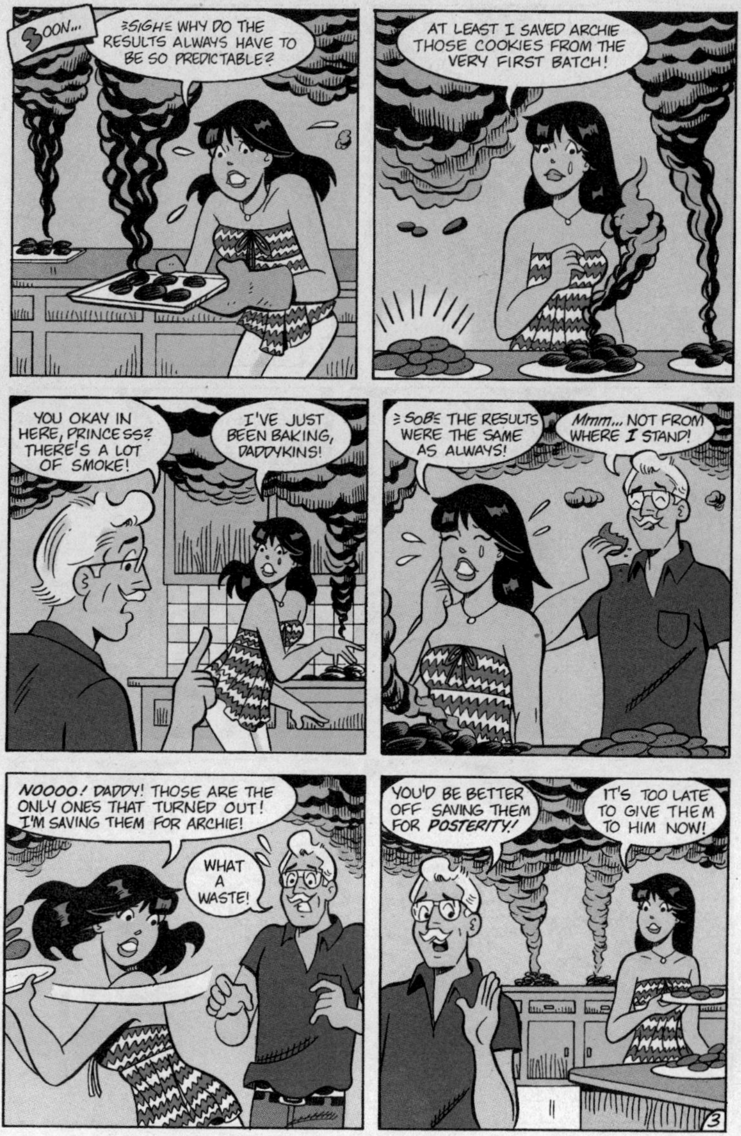
SOON...
≡SIGH≡ WHY DO THE RESULTS ALWAYS HAVE TO BE SO PREDICTABLE?
AT LEAST I SAVED ARCHIE THOSE COOKIES FROM THE VERY FIRST BATCH!
YOU OKAY IN HERE, PRINCESS? THERE'S A LOT OF SMOKE!
I'VE JUST BEEN BAKING, DADDYKINS!
≡SOB≡ THE RESULTS WERE THE SAME AS ALWAYS!
Mmm... NOT FROM WHERE I STAND!
NOOOO! DADDY! THOSE ARE THE ONLY ONES THAT TURNED OUT! I'M SAVING THEM FOR ARCHIE!
WHAT A WASTE!
YOU'D BE BETTER OFF SAVING THEM FOR POSTERITY!
IT'S TOO LATE TO GIVE THEM TO HIM NOW!
3

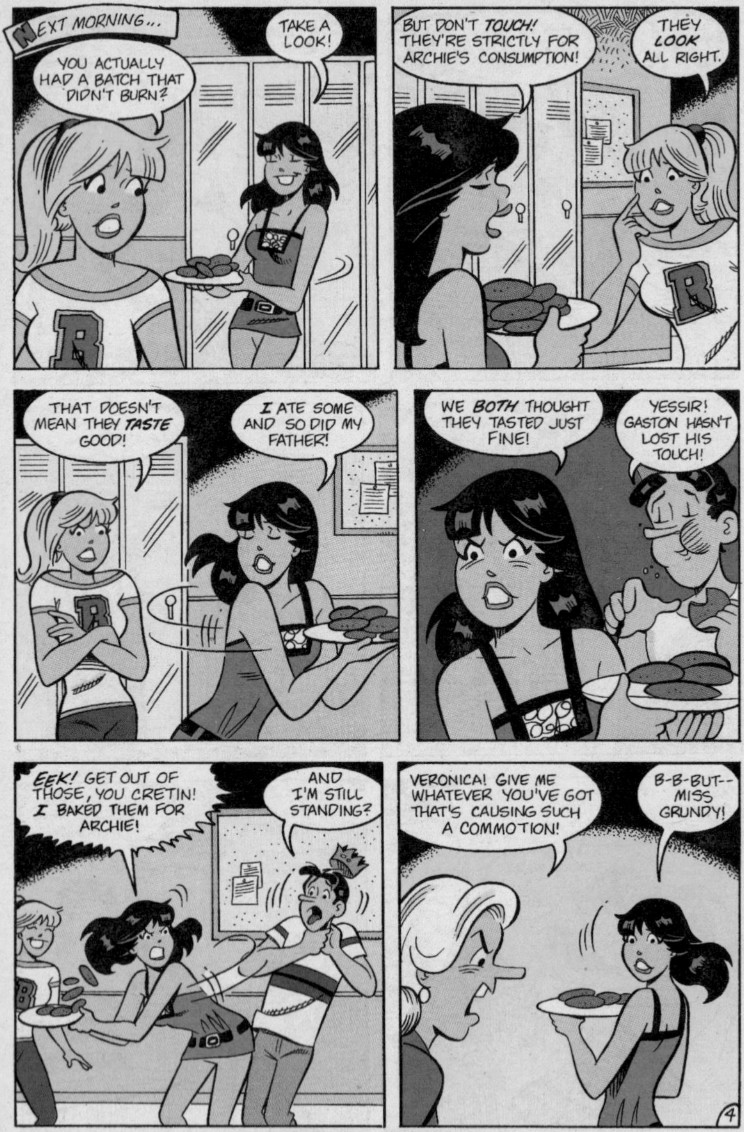
NEXT MORNING...
YOU ACTUALLY HAD A BATCH THAT DIDN'T BURN?
TAKE A LOOK!
BUT DON'T TOUCH! THEY'RE STRICTLY FOR ARCHIE'S CONSUMPTION!
THEY LOOK ALL RIGHT.
THAT DOESN'T MEAN THEY TASTE GOOD!
I ATE SOME AND SO DID MY FATHER!
WE BOTH THOUGHT THEY TASTED JUST FINE!
YESSIR! GASTON HASN'T LOST HIS TOUCH!
EEK! GET OUT OF THOSE, YOU CRETIN! I BAKED THEM FOR ARCHIE!
AND I'M STILL STANDING?
VERONICA! GIVE ME WHATEVER YOU'VE GOT THAT'S CAUSING SUCH A COMMOTION!
B-B-BUT-- MISS GRUNDY!
4

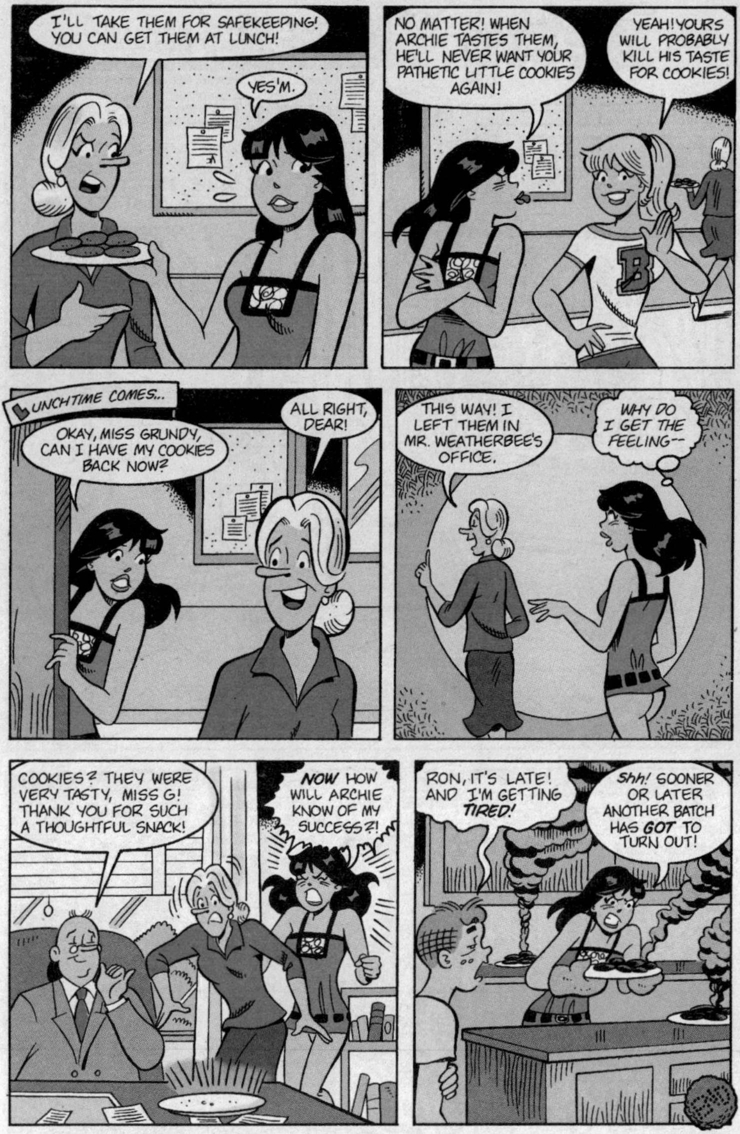
I'LL TAKE THEM FOR SAFEKEEPING! YOU CAN GET THEM AT LUNCH!
YES'M.
NO MATTER! WHEN ARCHIE TASTES THEM, HE'LL NEVER WANT YOUR PATHETIC LITTLE COOKIES AGAIN!
YEAH! YOURS WILL PROBABLY KILL HIS TASTE FOR COOKIES!
LUNCHTIME COMES...
OKAY, MISS GRUNDY, CAN I HAVE MY COOKIES BACK NOW?
ALL RIGHT, DEAR!
THIS WAY! I LEFT THEM IN MR. WEATHERBEE'S OFFICE.
WHY DO I GET THE FEELING--
COOKIES? THEY WERE VERY TASTY, MISS G! THANK YOU FOR SUCH A THOUGHTFUL SNACK!
NOW HOW WILL ARCHIE KNOW OF MY SUCCESS?!
RON, IT'S LATE! AND I'M GETTING TIRED!
Shh! SOONER OR LATER ANOTHER BATCH HAS GOT TO TURN OUT!

Betty in "MAKE BELIEVE"

Script: George Gladir / Pencils: Stan Goldberg
Inks: Rudy Lapick / Letters: Bill Yoshida

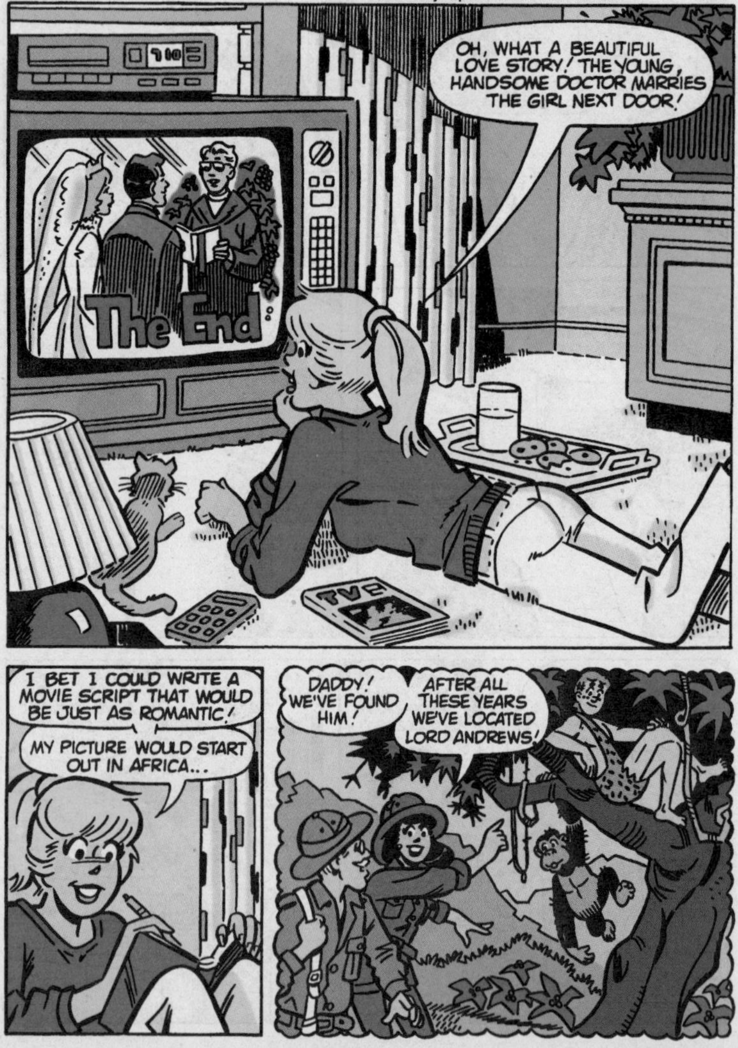
OH, WHAT A BEAUTIFUL LOVE STORY! THE YOUNG, HANDSOME DOCTOR MARRIES THE GIRL NEXT DOOR!
The End
TV
I BET I COULD WRITE A MOVIE SCRIPT THAT WOULD BE JUST AS ROMANTIC!
MY PICTURE WOULD START OUT IN AFRICA...
DADDY! WE'VE FOUND HIM!
AFTER ALL THESE YEARS WE'VE LOCATED LORD ANDREWS!

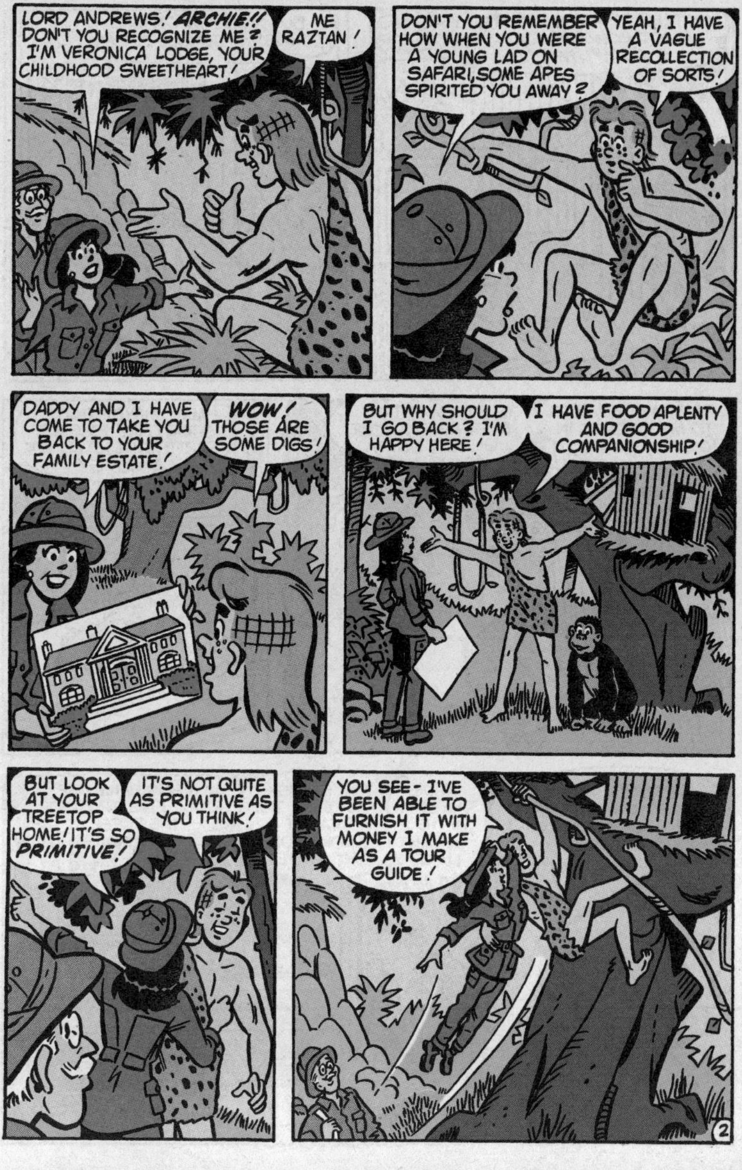

LORD ANDREWS! ARCHIE!! DON'T YOU RECOGNIZE ME? I'M VERONICA LODGE, YOUR CHILDHOOD SWEETHEART!
ME RAZTAN!
DON'T YOU REMEMBER HOW WHEN YOU WERE A YOUNG LAD ON SAFARI, SOME APES SPIRITED YOU AWAY?
YEAH, I HAVE A VAGUE RECOLLECTION OF SORTS!
DADDY AND I HAVE COME TO TAKE YOU BACK TO YOUR FAMILY ESTATE!
WOW! THOSE ARE SOME DIGS!
BUT WHY SHOULD I GO BACK? I'M HAPPY HERE!
I HAVE FOOD APLENTY AND GOOD COMPANIONSHIP!
BUT LOOK AT YOUR TREETOP HOME! IT'S SO PRIMITIVE!
IT'S NOT QUITE AS PRIMITIVE AS YOU THINK!
YOU SEE- I'VE BEEN ABLE TO FURNISH IT WITH MONEY I MAKE AS A TOUR GUIDE!
2

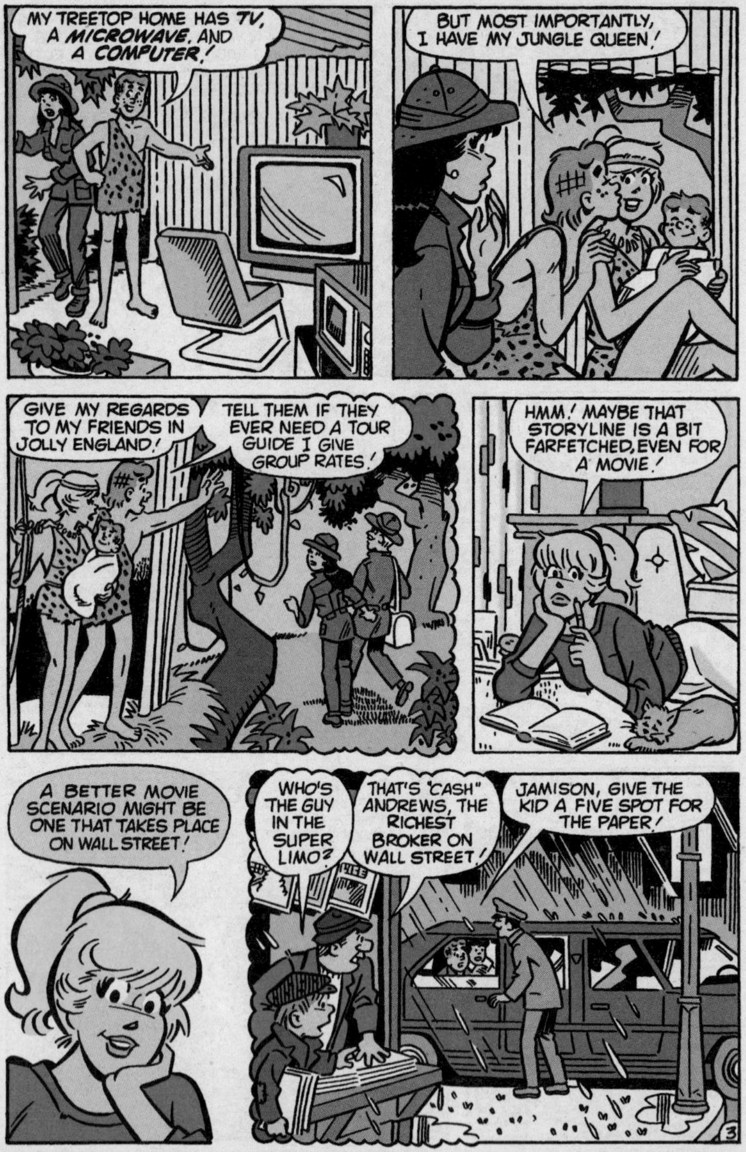
MY TREETOP HOME HAS TV, A MICROWAVE, AND A COMPUTER!
BUT MOST IMPORTANTLY, I HAVE MY JUNGLE QUEEN!
GIVE MY REGARDS TO MY FRIENDS IN JOLLY ENGLAND!
TELL THEM IF THEY EVER NEED A TOUR GUIDE I GIVE GROUP RATES!
HMM! MAYBE THAT STORYLINE IS A BIT FARFETCHED, EVEN FOR A MOVIE!
A BETTER MOVIE SCENARIO MIGHT BE ONE THAT TAKES PLACE ON WALL STREET!
WHO'S THE GUY IN THE SUPER LIMO?
THAT'S "CASH" ANDREWS, THE RICHEST BROKER ON WALL STREET!
JAMISON, GIVE THE KID A FIVE SPOT FOR THE PAPER!
3

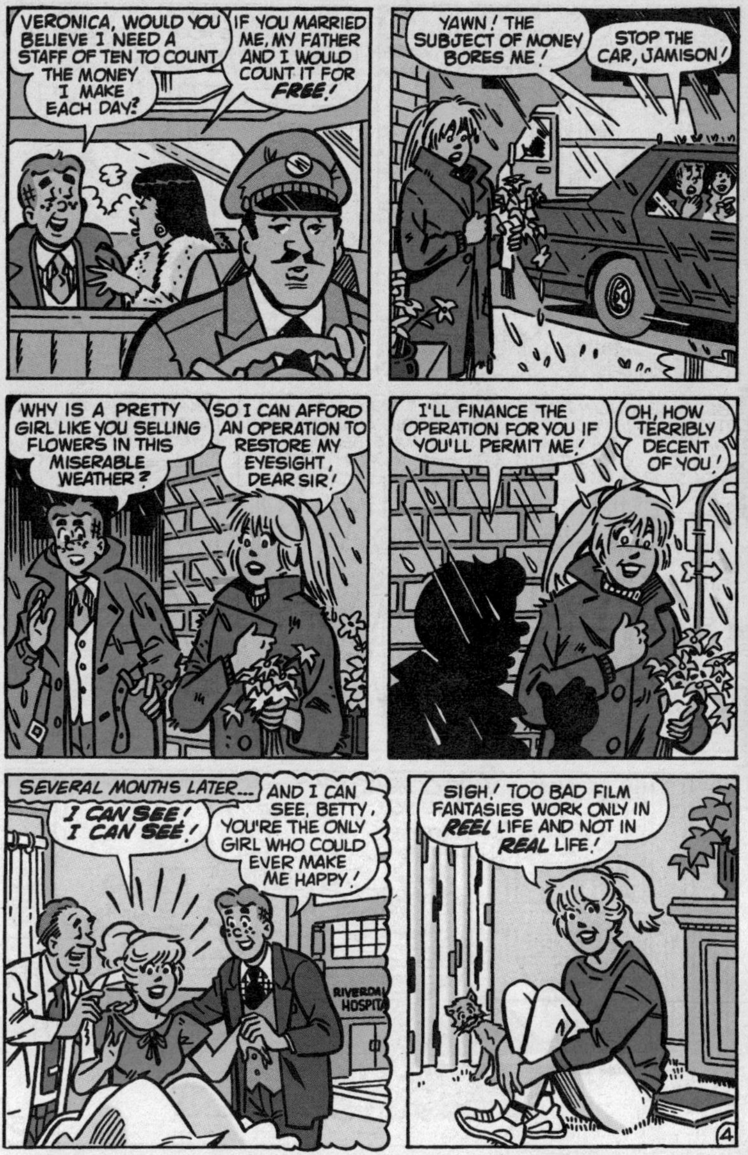

VERONICA, WOULD YOU BELIEVE I NEED A STAFF OF TEN TO COUNT THE MONEY I MAKE EACH DAY?
IF YOU MARRIED ME, MY FATHER AND I WOULD COUNT IT FOR FREE!
YAWN! THE SUBJECT OF MONEY BORES ME!
STOP THE CAR, JAMISON!
WHY IS A PRETTY GIRL LIKE YOU SELLING FLOWERS IN THIS MISERABLE WEATHER?
SO I CAN AFFORD AN OPERATION TO RESTORE MY EYESIGHT, DEAR SIR!
I'LL FINANCE THE OPERATION FOR YOU IF YOU'LL PERMIT ME!
OH, HOW TERRIBLY DECENT OF YOU!
SEVERAL MONTHS LATER...
I CAN SEE! I CAN SEE!
AND I CAN SEE, BETTY, YOU'RE THE ONLY GIRL WHO COULD EVER MAKE ME HAPPY!
SIGH! TOO BAD FILM FANTASIES WORK ONLY IN REEL LIFE AND NOT IN REAL LIFE!
4

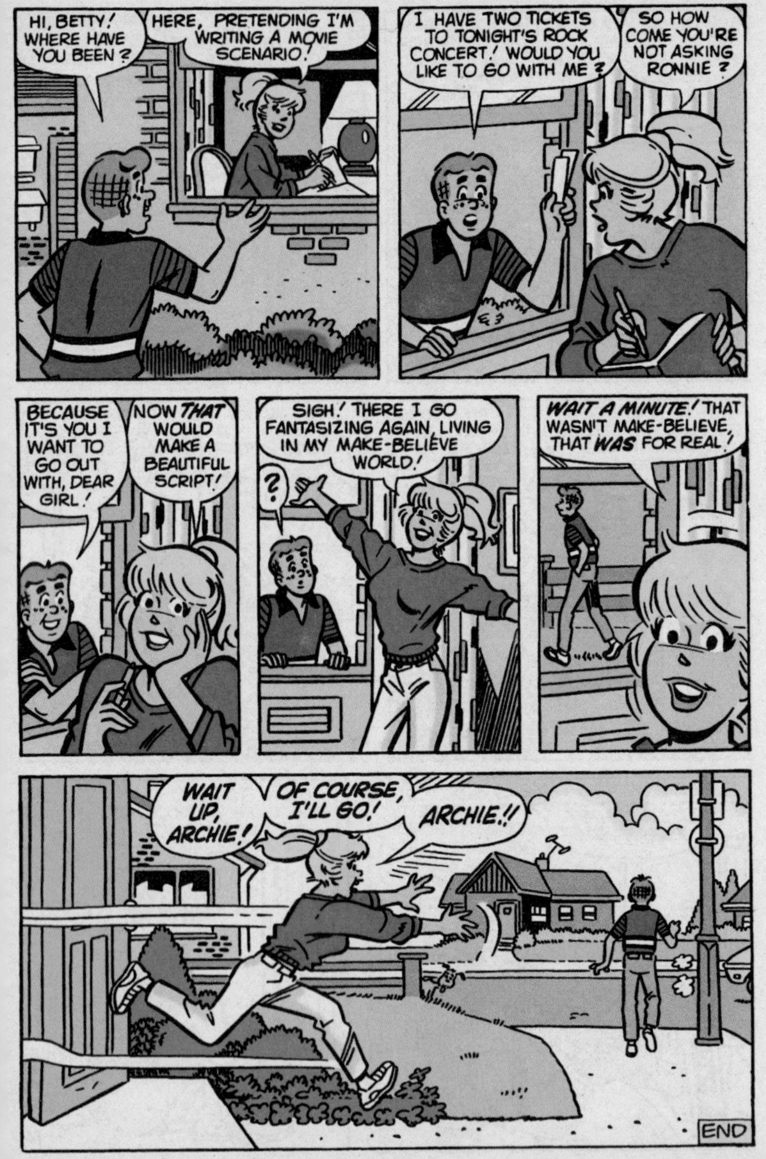
HI, BETTY! WHERE HAVE YOU BEEN?
HERE, PRETENDING I'M WRITING A MOVIE SCENARIO!
I HAVE TWO TICKETS TO TONIGHT'S ROCK CONCERT! WOULD YOU LIKE TO GO WITH ME?
SO HOW COME YOU'RE NOT ASKING RONNIE?
BECAUSE IT'S YOU I WANT TO GO OUT WITH, DEAR GIRL!
NOW THAT WOULD MAKE A BEAUTIFUL SCRIPT!
SIGH! THERE I GO FANTASIZING AGAIN, LIVING IN MY MAKE-BELIEVE WORLD!
?
WAIT A MINUTE! THAT WASN'T MAKE-BELIEVE, THAT WAS FOR REAL!
WAIT UP, ARCHIE!
OF COURSE, I'LL GO!
ARCHIE!!
END

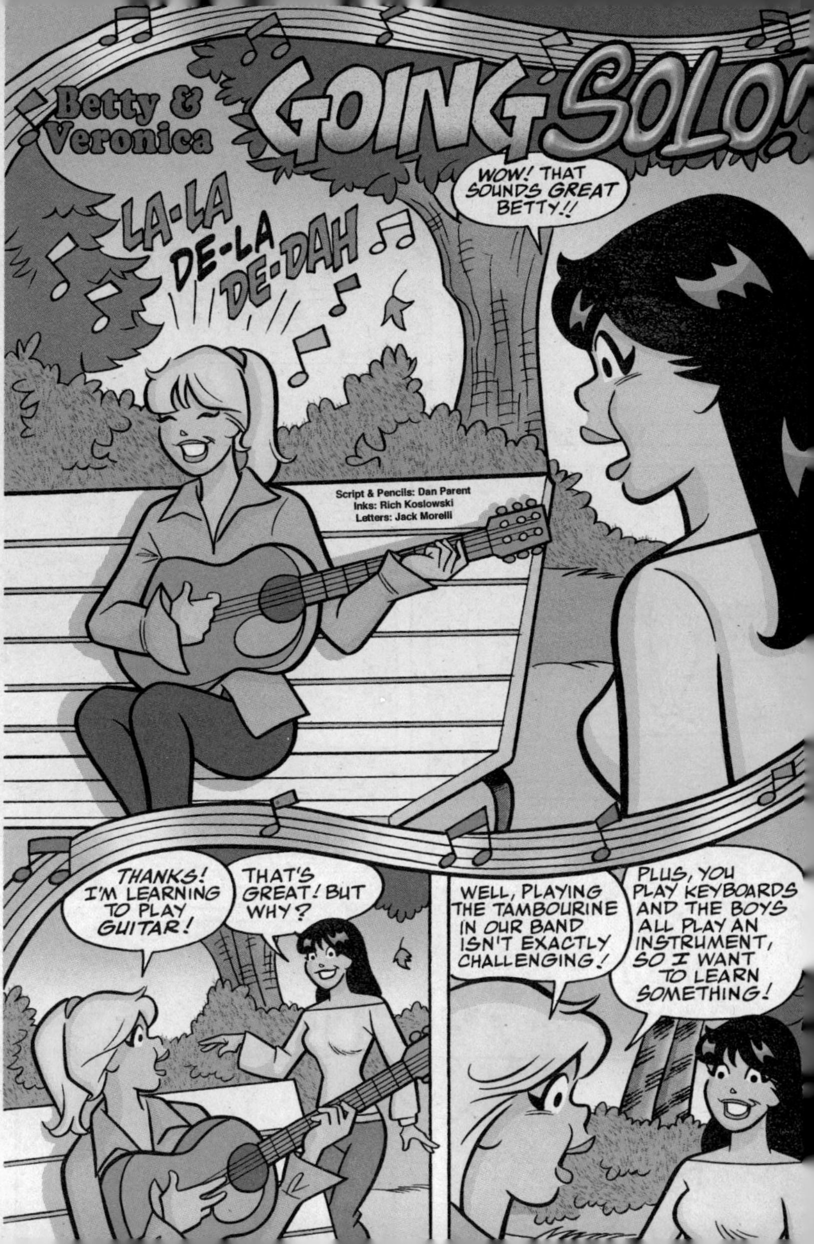
Betty & Veronica
GOING SOLO!
LA-LA DE-LA DE-DAH
WOW! THAT SOUNDS GREAT BETTY!!
Script & Pencils: Dan Parent
Inks: Rich Koslowski
Letters: Jack Morelli
THANKS! I'M LEARNING TO PLAY GUITAR!
THAT'S GREAT! BUT WHY?
WELL, PLAYING THE TAMBOURINE IN OUR BAND ISN'T EXACTLY CHALLENGING!
PLUS, YOU PLAY KEYBOARDS AND THE BOYS ALL PLAY AN INSTRUMENT, SO I WANT TO LEARN SOMETHING!

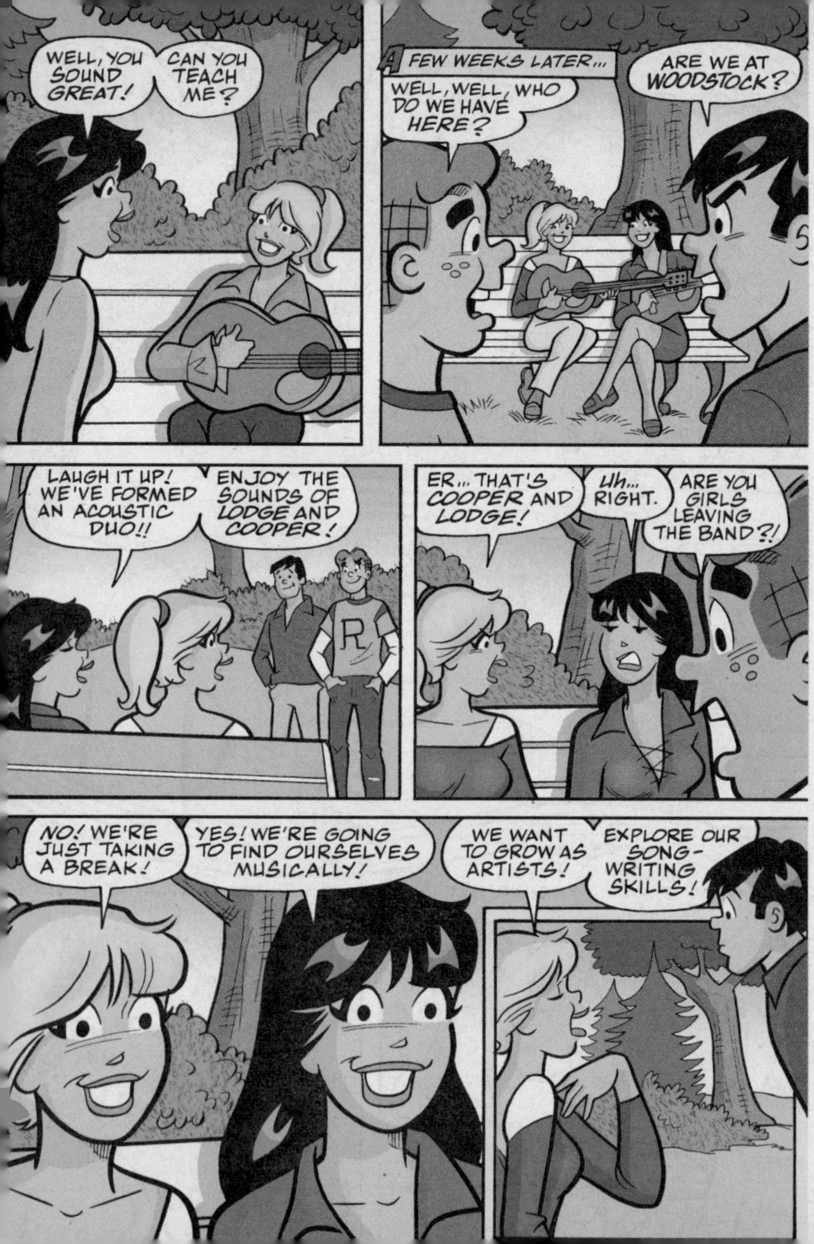
WELL, YOU SOUND GREAT!
CAN YOU TEACH ME?
A FEW WEEKS LATER...
WELL, WELL, WHO DO WE HAVE HERE?
ARE WE AT WOODSTOCK?
LAUGH IT UP! WE'VE FORMED AN ACOUSTIC DUO!!
ENJOY THE SOUNDS OF LODGE AND COOPER!
ER... THAT'S COOPER AND LODGE!
Uh... RIGHT.
ARE YOU GIRLS LEAVING THE BAND?!
NO! WE'RE JUST TAKING A BREAK!
YES! WE'RE GOING TO FIND OURSELVES MUSICALLY!
WE WANT TO GROW AS ARTISTS!
EXPLORE OUR SONG-WRITING SKILLS!

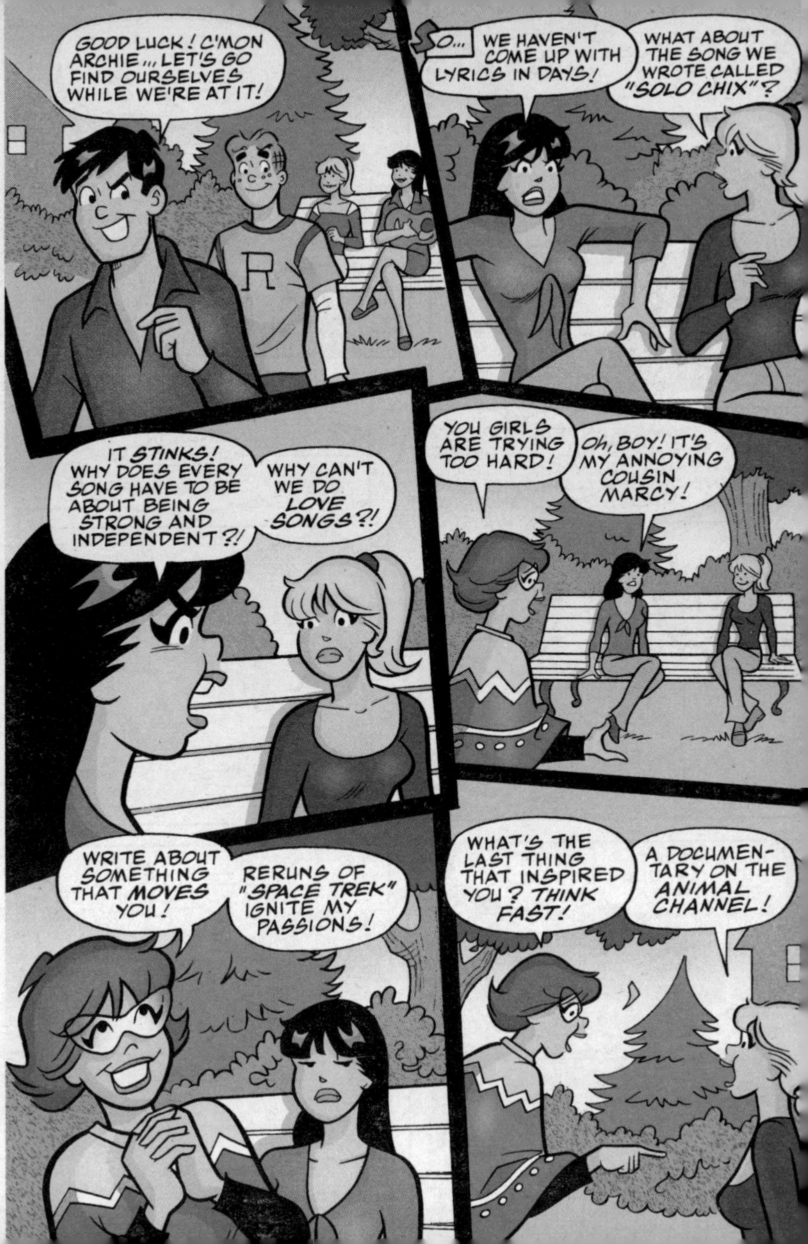
GOOD LUCK! C'MON ARCHIE... LET'S GO FIND OURSELVES WHILE WE'RE AT IT!
SO... WE HAVEN'T COME UP WITH LYRICS IN DAYS!
WHAT ABOUT THE SONG WE WROTE CALLED "SOLO CHIX"?
IT STINKS! WHY DOES EVERY SONG HAVE TO BE ABOUT BEING STRONG AND INDEPENDENT?!
WHY CAN'T WE DO LOVE SONGS?!
YOU GIRLS ARE TRYING TOO HARD!
Oh, BOY! IT'S MY ANNOYING COUSIN MARCY!
WRITE ABOUT SOMETHING THAT MOVES YOU!
RERUNS OF "SPACE TREK" IGNITE MY PASSIONS!
WHAT'S THE LAST THING THAT INSPIRED YOU? THINK FAST!
A DOCUMENTARY ON THE ANIMAL CHANNEL!

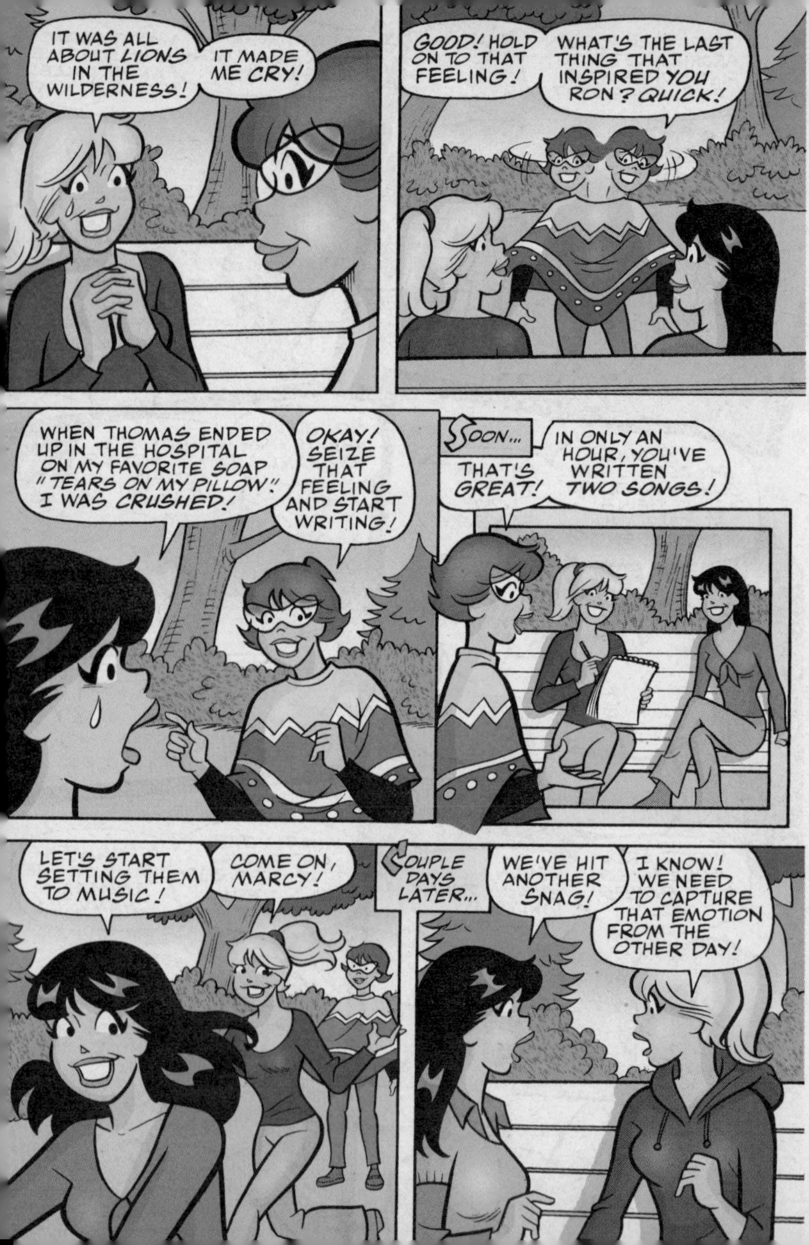
IT WAS ALL ABOUT LIONS IN THE WILDERNESS!
IT MADE ME CRY!
GOOD! HOLD ON TO THAT FEELING!
WHAT'S THE LAST THING THAT INSPIRED YOU RON? QUICK!
WHEN THOMAS ENDED UP IN THE HOSPITAL ON MY FAVORITE SOAP "TEARS ON MY PILLOW," I WAS CRUSHED!
OKAY! SEIZE THAT FEELING AND START WRITING!
SOON...
THAT'S GREAT!
IN ONLY AN HOUR, YOU'VE WRITTEN TWO SONGS!
LET'S START SETTING THEM TO MUSIC!
COME ON, MARCY!
COUPLE DAYS LATER...
WE'VE HIT ANOTHER SNAG!
I KNOW! WE NEED TO CAPTURE THAT EMOTION FROM THE OTHER DAY!

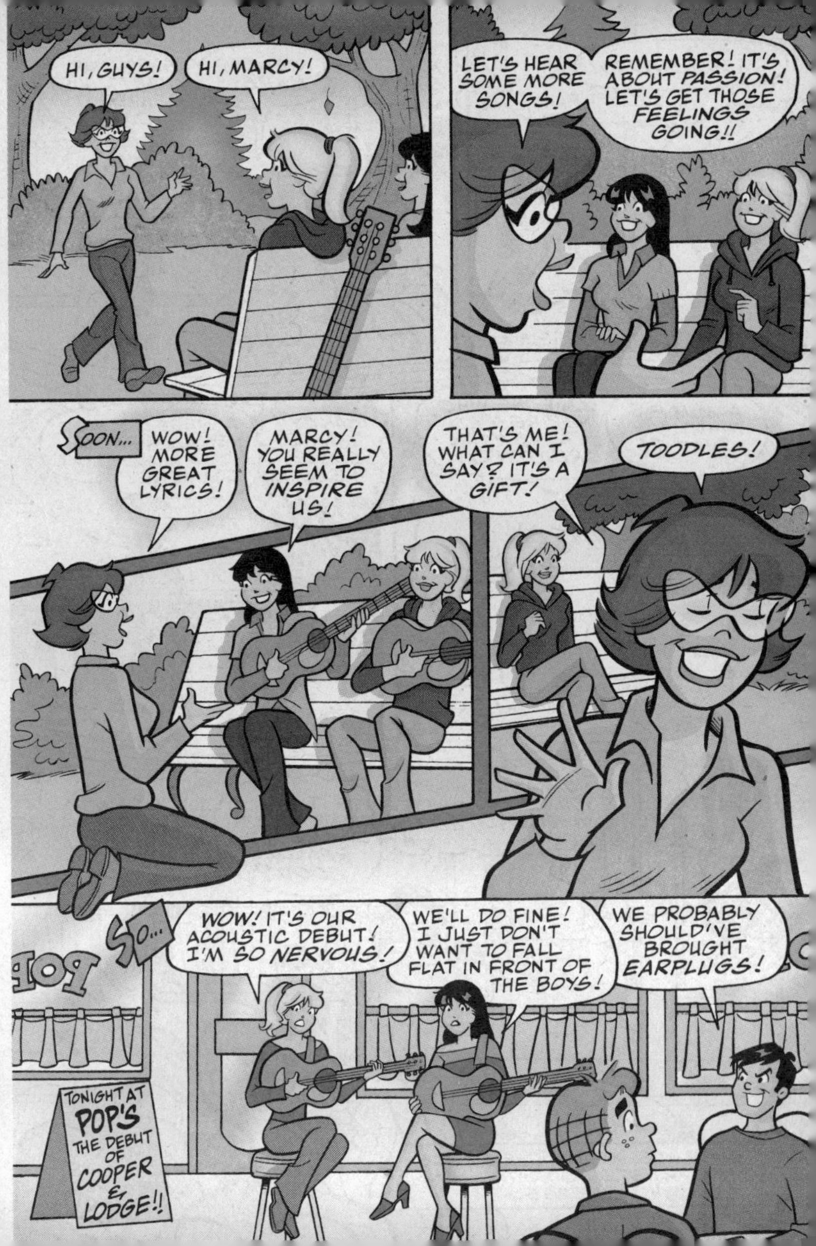
HI, GUYS!
HI, MARCY!
LET'S HEAR SOME MORE SONGS!
REMEMBER! IT'S ABOUT PASSION! LET'S GET THOSE FEELINGS GOING!!
SOON...
WOW! MORE GREAT LYRICS!
MARCY! YOU REALLY SEEM TO INSPIRE US!
THAT'S ME! WHAT CAN I SAY? IT'S A GIFT!
TOODLES!
SO...
WOW! IT'S OUR ACOUSTIC DEBUT! I'M SO NERVOUS!
WE'LL DO FINE! I JUST DON'T WANT TO FALL FLAT IN FRONT OF THE BOYS!
WE PROBABLY SHOULD'VE BROUGHT EARPLUGS!
TONIGHT AT POP'S THE DEBUT OF COOPER & LODGE!!

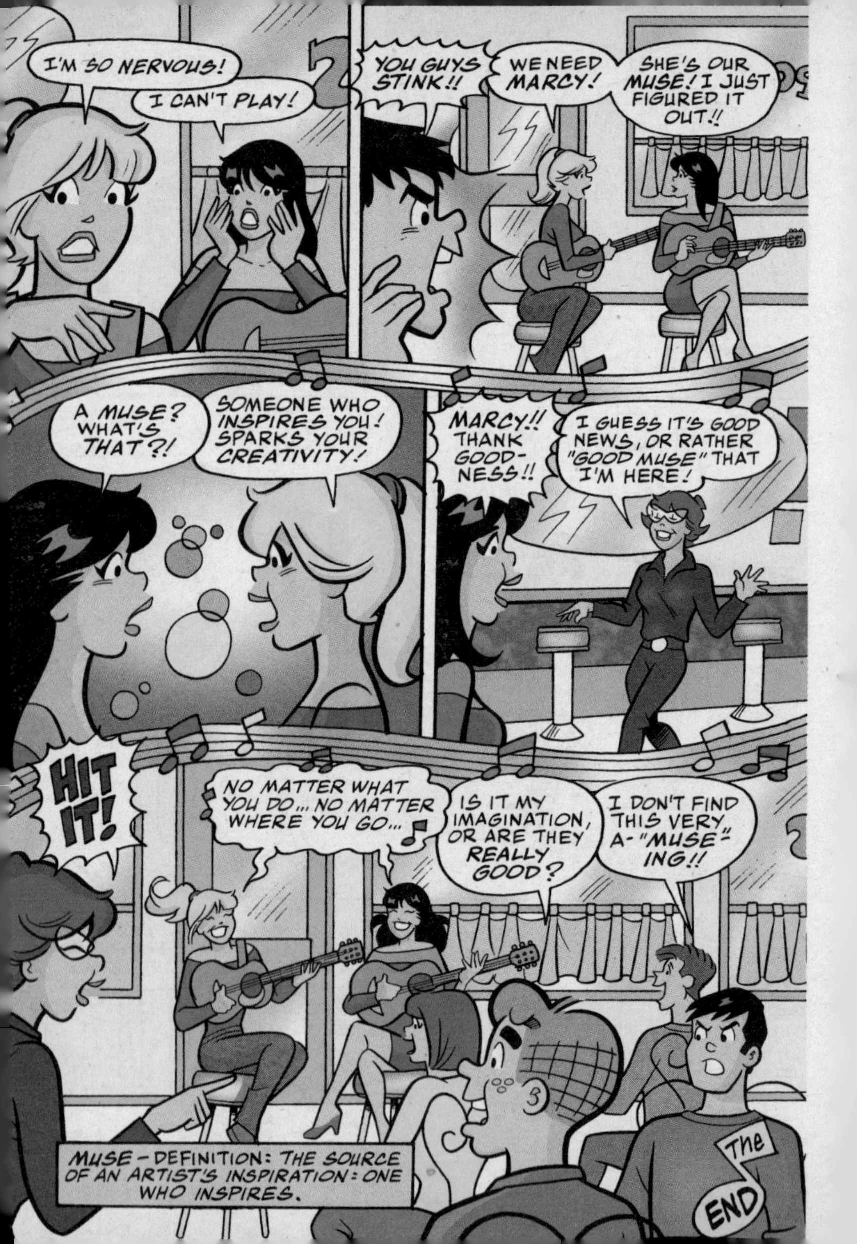
I'M SO NERVOUS!
I CAN'T PLAY!
YOU GUYS STINK!!
WE NEED MARCY!
SHE'S OUR MUSE! I JUST FIGURED IT OUT!!
A MUSE? WHAT'S THAT?!
SOMEONE WHO INSPIRES YOU! SPARKS YOUR CREATIVITY!
MARCY!! THANK GOODNESS!!
I GUESS IT'S GOOD NEWS, OR RATHER "GOOD MUSE" THAT I'M HERE!
HIT IT!
NO MATTER WHAT YOU DO... NO MATTER WHERE YOU GO...
IS IT MY IMAGINATION, OR ARE THEY REALLY GOOD?
I DON'T FIND THIS VERY A-"MUSE"-ING!!
MUSE – DEFINITION: THE SOURCE OF AN ARTIST'S INSPIRATION: ONE WHO INSPIRES.
The END

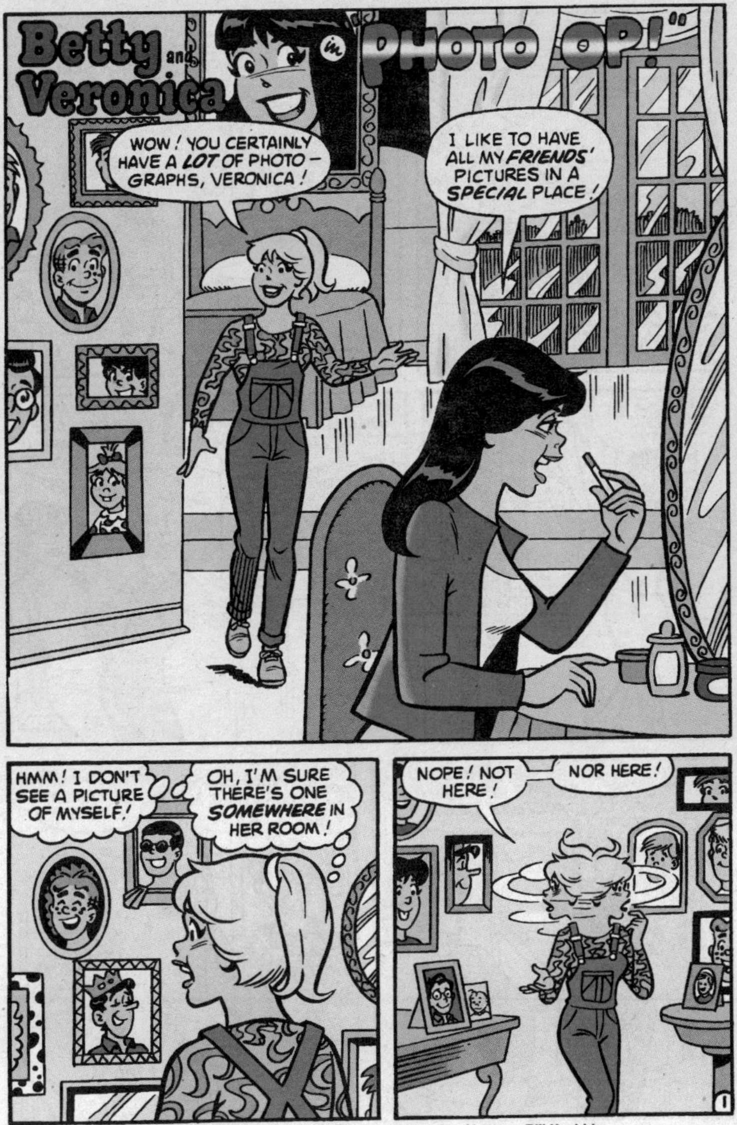
Betty and Veronica in "PHOTO OP!"
WOW! YOU CERTAINLY HAVE A LOT OF PHOTO-GRAPHS, VERONICA!
I LIKE TO HAVE ALL MY FRIENDS' PICTURES IN A SPECIAL PLACE!
HMM! I DON'T SEE A PICTURE OF MYSELF!
OH, I'M SURE THERE'S ONE SOMEWHERE IN HER ROOM!
NOPE! NOT HERE!
NOR HERE!
1

Script & Pencils: Dan Parent / Inks: Jon D'Agostino / Letters: Bill Yoshida

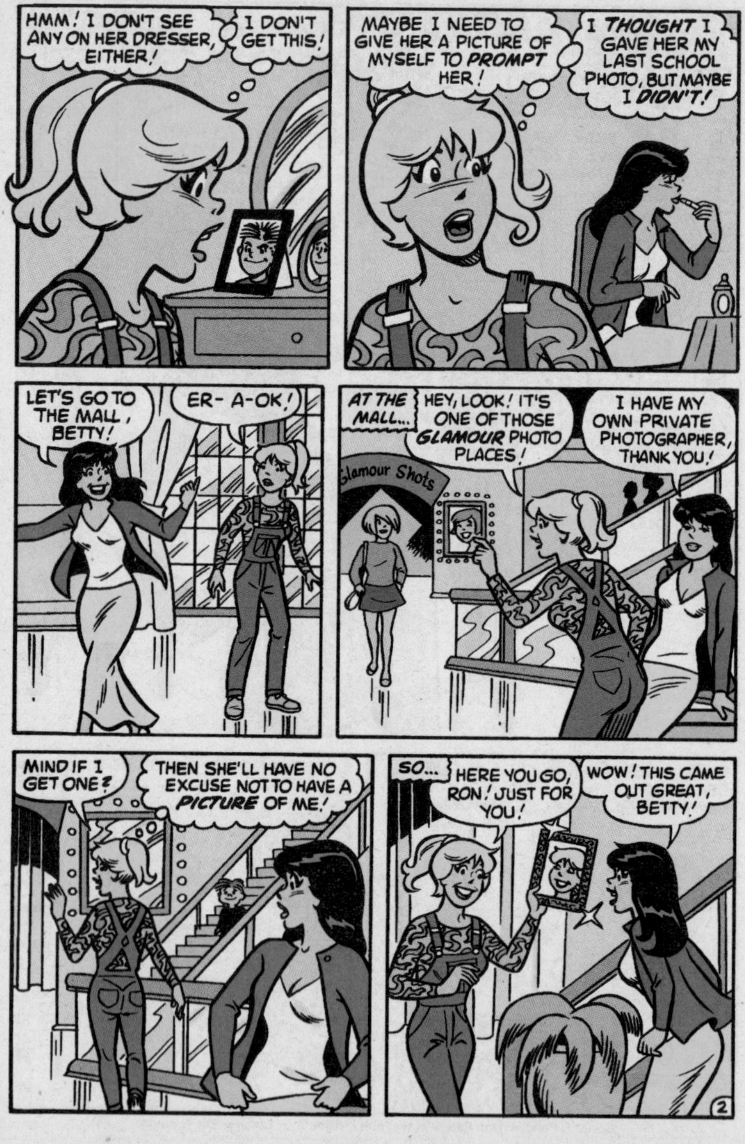

HMM! I DON'T SEE ANY ON HER DRESSER, EITHER!
I DON'T GET THIS!
MAYBE I NEED TO GIVE HER A PICTURE OF MYSELF TO *PROMPT* HER!
I *THOUGHT* I GAVE HER MY LAST SCHOOL PHOTO, BUT MAYBE I *DIDN'T*!
LET'S GO TO THE MALL, BETTY!
ER- A-OK!
AT THE MALL...
HEY, LOOK! IT'S ONE OF THOSE *GLAMOUR* PHOTO PLACES!
Glamour Shots
I HAVE MY OWN PRIVATE PHOTOGRAPHER, THANK YOU!
MIND IF I GET ONE?
THEN SHE'LL HAVE NO EXCUSE NOT TO HAVE A *PICTURE* OF ME!
SO...
HERE YOU GO, RON! JUST FOR YOU!
WOW! THIS CAME OUT GREAT, BETTY!
2

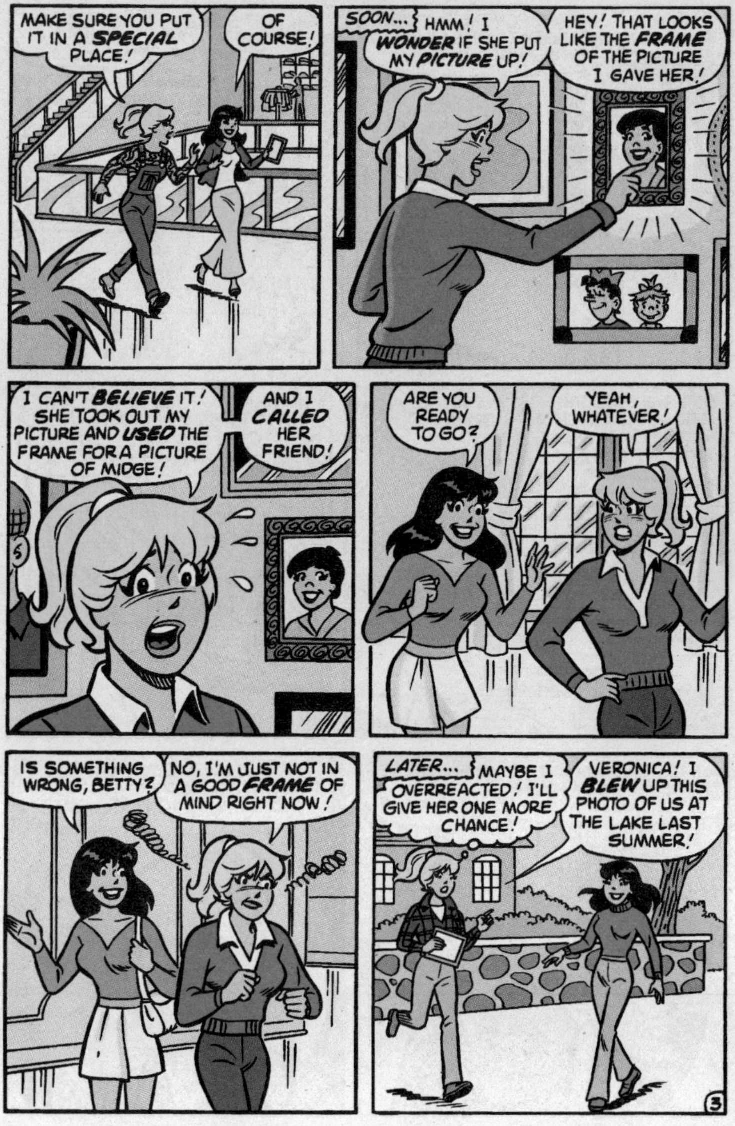
MAKE SURE YOU PUT IT IN A SPECIAL PLACE!
OF COURSE!
SOON...
HMM! I WONDER IF SHE PUT MY PICTURE UP!
HEY! THAT LOOKS LIKE THE FRAME OF THE PICTURE I GAVE HER!
I CAN'T BELIEVE IT! SHE TOOK OUT MY PICTURE AND USED THE FRAME FOR A PICTURE OF MIDGE!
AND I CALLED HER FRIEND!
ARE YOU READY TO GO?
YEAH, WHATEVER!
IS SOMETHING WRONG, BETTY?
NO, I'M JUST NOT IN A GOOD FRAME OF MIND RIGHT NOW!
LATER...
MAYBE I OVERREACTED! I'LL GIVE HER ONE MORE CHANCE!
VERONICA! I BLEW UP THIS PHOTO OF US AT THE LAKE LAST SUMMER!
3

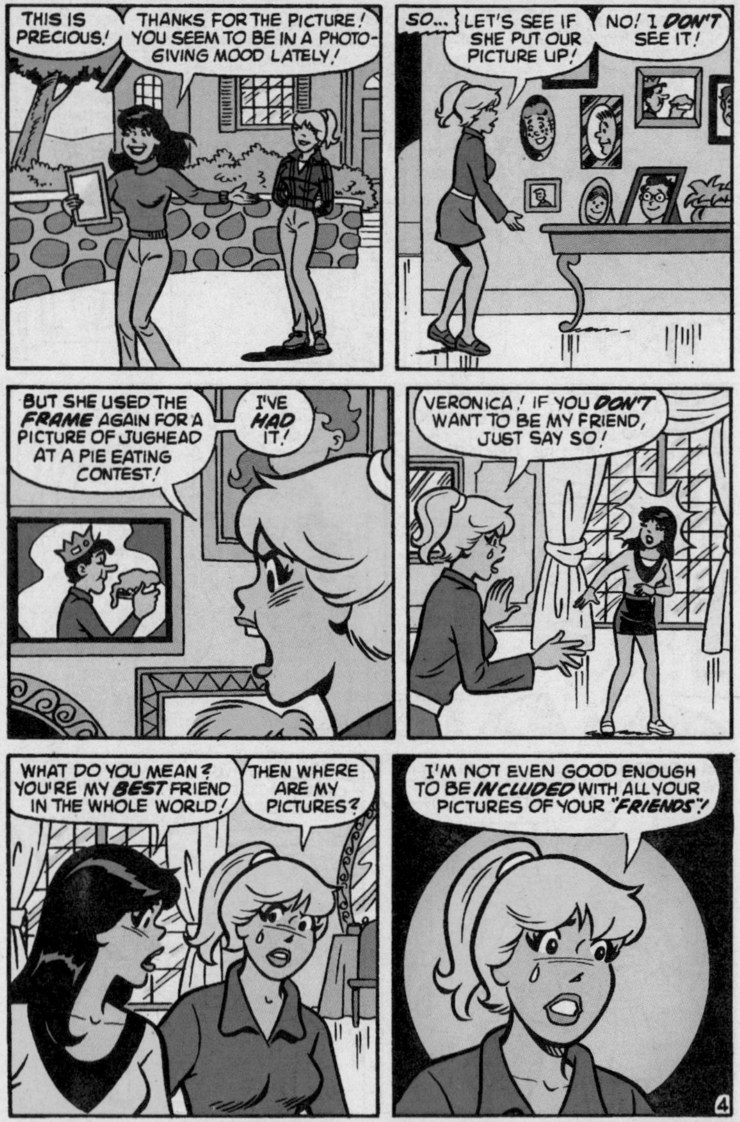
THIS IS PRECIOUS!
THANKS FOR THE PICTURE! YOU SEEM TO BE IN A PHOTO-GIVING MOOD LATELY!
SO...
LET'S SEE IF SHE PUT OUR PICTURE UP!
NO! I DON'T SEE IT!
BUT SHE USED THE FRAME AGAIN FOR A PICTURE OF JUGHEAD AT A PIE EATING CONTEST!
I'VE HAD IT!
VERONICA! IF YOU DON'T WANT TO BE MY FRIEND, JUST SAY SO!
WHAT DO YOU MEAN? YOU'RE MY BEST FRIEND IN THE WHOLE WORLD!
THEN WHERE ARE MY PICTURES?
I'M NOT EVEN GOOD ENOUGH TO BE INCLUDED WITH ALL YOUR PICTURES OF YOUR "FRIENDS"!
4

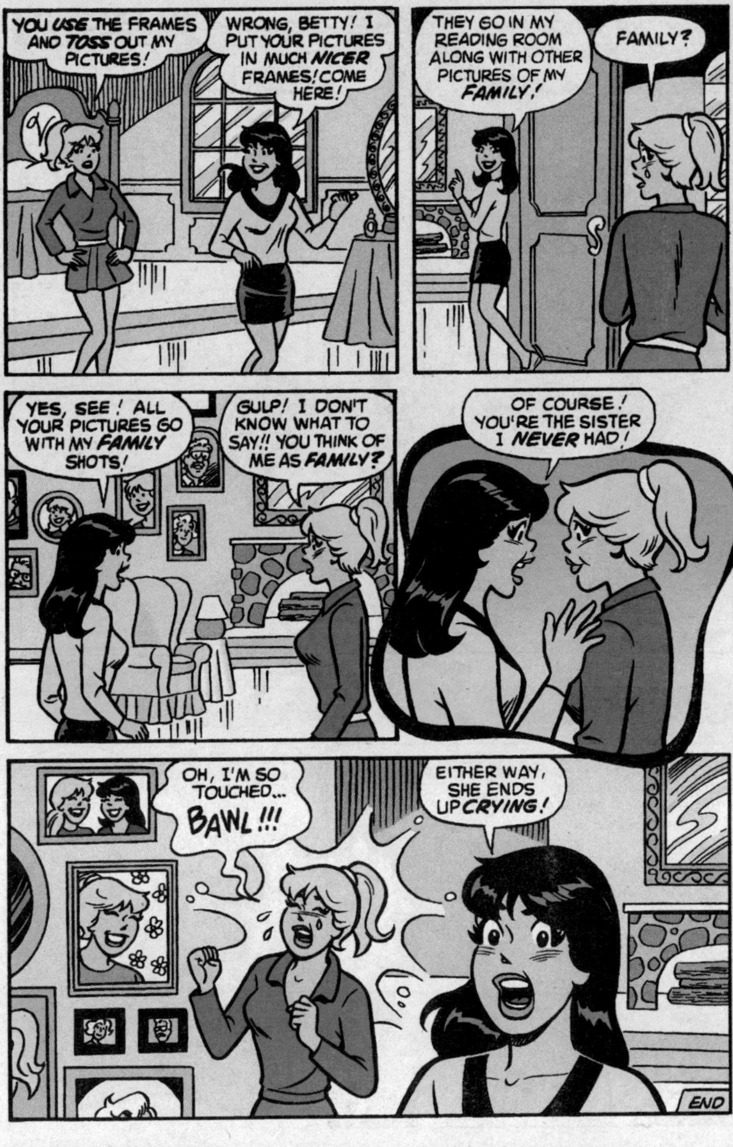
YOU USE THE FRAMES AND TOSS OUT MY PICTURES!
WRONG, BETTY! I PUT YOUR PICTURES IN MUCH NICER FRAMES! COME HERE!
THEY GO IN MY READING ROOM ALONG WITH OTHER PICTURES OF MY FAMILY!
FAMILY?
YES, SEE! ALL YOUR PICTURES GO WITH MY FAMILY SHOTS!
GULP! I DON'T KNOW WHAT TO SAY!! YOU THINK OF ME AS FAMILY?
OF COURSE! YOU'RE THE SISTER I NEVER HAD!
OH, I'M SO TOUCHED... BAWL!!!
EITHER WAY, SHE ENDS UP CRYING!
END

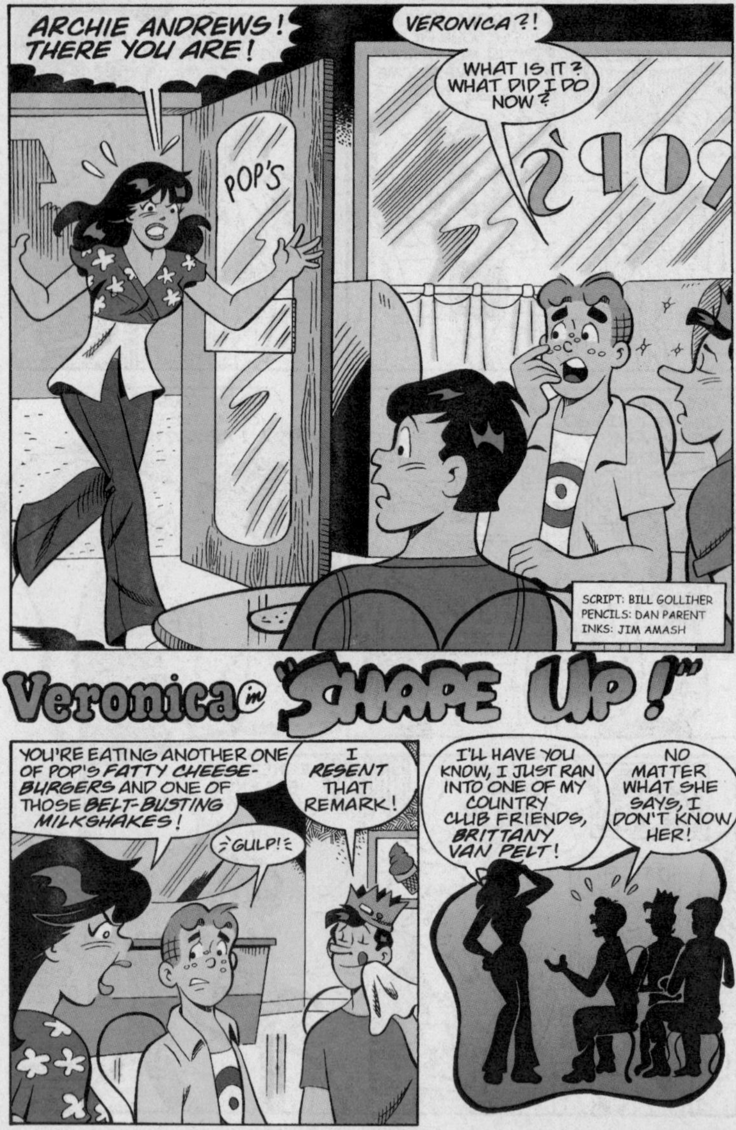
ARCHIE ANDREWS! THERE YOU ARE!
POP'S
VERONICA?!
WHAT IS IT? WHAT DID I DO NOW?
POP'S
SCRIPT: BILL GOLLIHER
PENCILS: DAN PARENT
INKS: JIM AMASH
Veronica in "SHAPE UP!"
YOU'RE EATING ANOTHER ONE OF POP'S FATTY CHEESE-BURGERS AND ONE OF THOSE BELT-BUSTING MILKSHAKES!
GULP!
I RESENT THAT REMARK!
I'LL HAVE YOU KNOW, I JUST RAN INTO ONE OF MY COUNTRY CLUB FRIENDS, BRITTANY VAN PELT!
NO MATTER WHAT SHE SAYS, I DON'T KNOW HER!

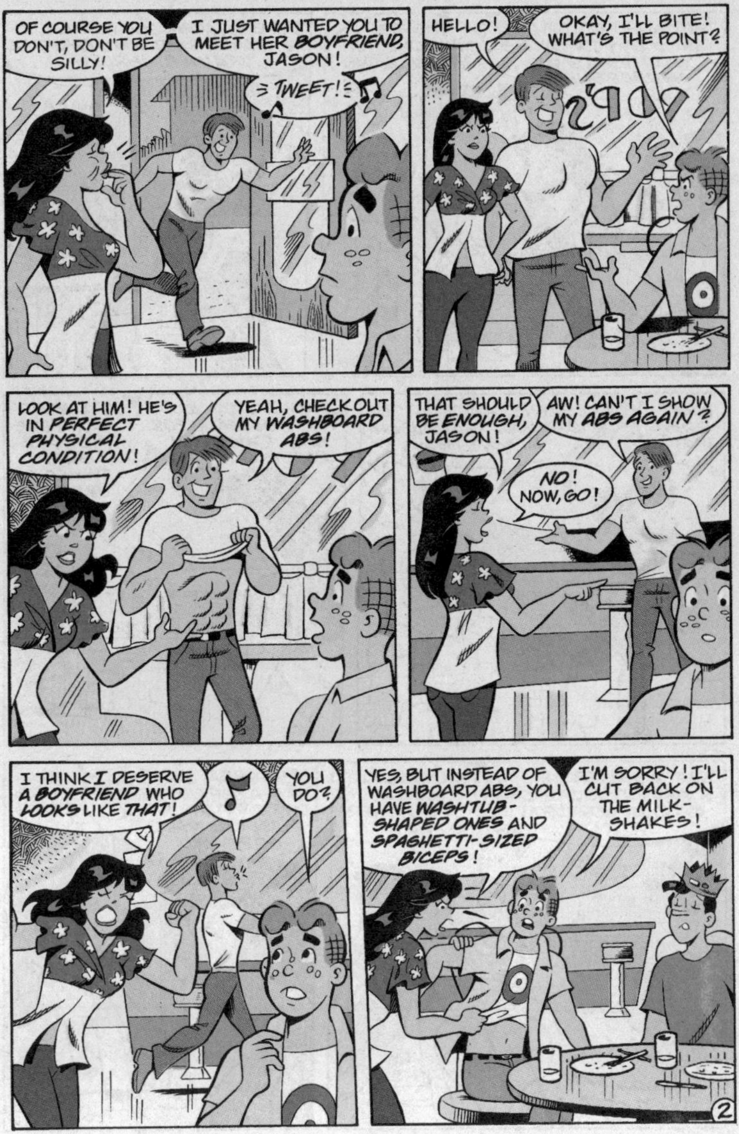

OF COURSE YOU DON'T, DON'T BE SILLY!
I JUST WANTED YOU TO MEET HER BOYFRIEND, JASON!
TWEET!
HELLO!
OKAY, I'LL BITE! WHAT'S THE POINT?
POP'S
LOOK AT HIM! HE'S IN PERFECT PHYSICAL CONDITION!
YEAH, CHECK OUT MY WASHBOARD ABS!
THAT SHOULD BE ENOUGH, JASON!
AW! CAN'T I SHOW MY ABS AGAIN?
NO! NOW, GO!
I THINK I DESERVE A BOYFRIEND WHO LOOKS LIKE THAT!
YOU DO?
YES, BUT INSTEAD OF WASHBOARD ABS, YOU HAVE WASHTUB-SHAPED ONES AND SPAGHETTI-SIZED BICEPS!
I'M SORRY! I'LL CUT BACK ON THE MILK-SHAKES!
2

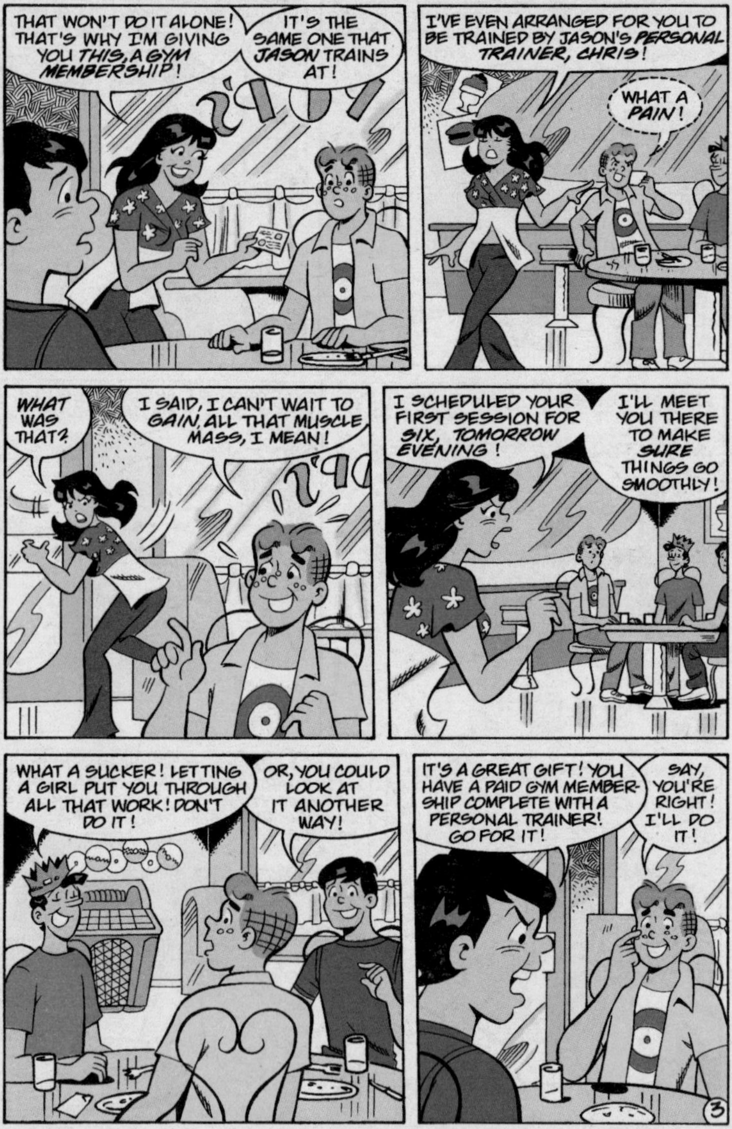
THAT WON'T DO IT ALONE! THAT'S WHY I'M GIVING YOU *THIS*, A GYM *MEMBERSHIP*!
IT'S THE SAME ONE THAT *JASON* TRAINS AT!
POP'S
I'VE EVEN ARRANGED FOR YOU TO BE TRAINED BY JASON'S *PERSONAL TRAINER, CHRIS*!
WHAT A *PAIN*!
WHAT WAS THAT?
I SAID, I CAN'T WAIT TO *GAIN*, ALL THAT MUSCLE MASS, I MEAN!
I SCHEDULED YOUR FIRST SESSION FOR *SIX, TOMORROW EVENING*!
I'LL MEET YOU THERE TO MAKE *SURE* THINGS GO SMOOTHLY!
WHAT A SUCKER! LETTING A GIRL PUT YOU THROUGH ALL THAT WORK! DON'T DO IT!
OR, YOU COULD LOOK AT IT ANOTHER WAY!
IT'S A GREAT GIFT! YOU HAVE A PAID GYM MEMBERSHIP COMPLETE WITH A PERSONAL TRAINER! GO FOR IT!
SAY, YOU'RE RIGHT! I'LL DO IT!
3

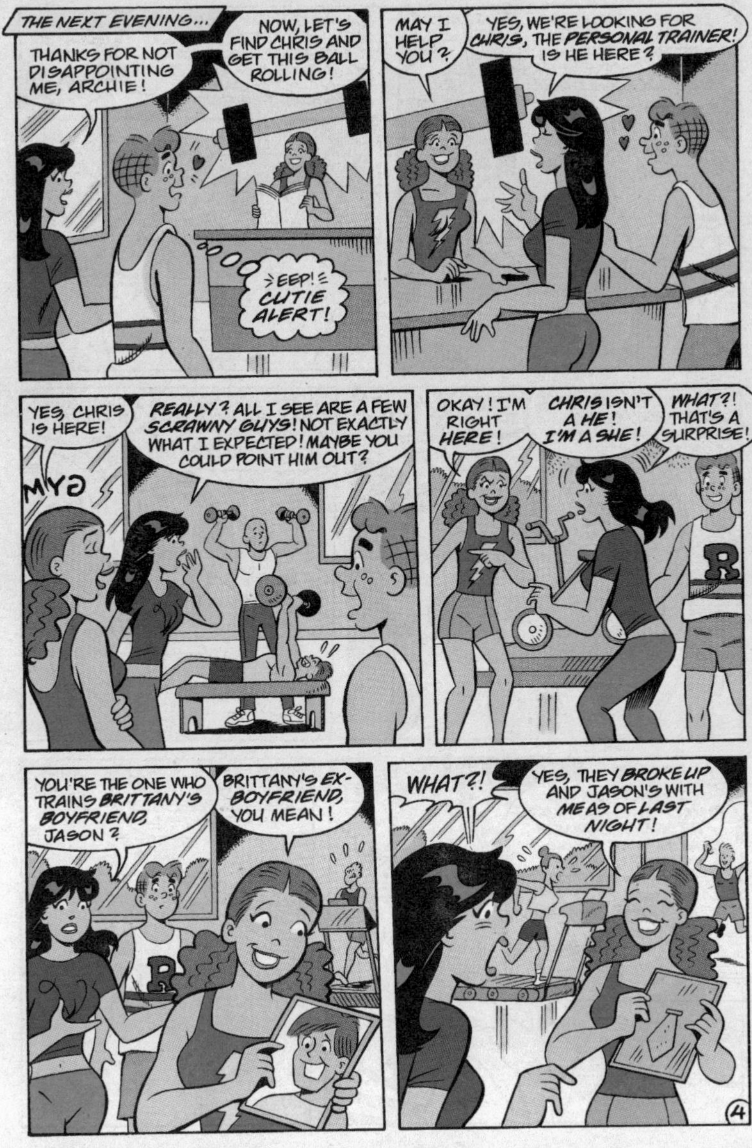
THE NEXT EVENING...
THANKS FOR NOT DISAPPOINTING ME, ARCHIE!
NOW, LET'S FIND CHRIS AND GET THIS BALL ROLLING!
EEP! CUTIE ALERT!
MAY I HELP YOU?
YES, WE'RE LOOKING FOR CHRIS, THE PERSONAL TRAINER! IS HE HERE?
YES, CHRIS IS HERE!
REALLY? ALL I SEE ARE A FEW SCRAWNY GUYS! NOT EXACTLY WHAT I EXPECTED! MAYBE YOU COULD POINT HIM OUT?
OKAY! I'M RIGHT HERE!
CHRIS ISN'T A HE! I'M A SHE!
WHAT?! THAT'S A SURPRISE!
YOU'RE THE ONE WHO TRAINS BRITTANY'S BOYFRIEND, JASON?
BRITTANY'S EX-BOYFRIEND, YOU MEAN!
WHAT?!
YES, THEY BROKE UP AND JASON'S WITH ME AS OF LAST NIGHT!
4

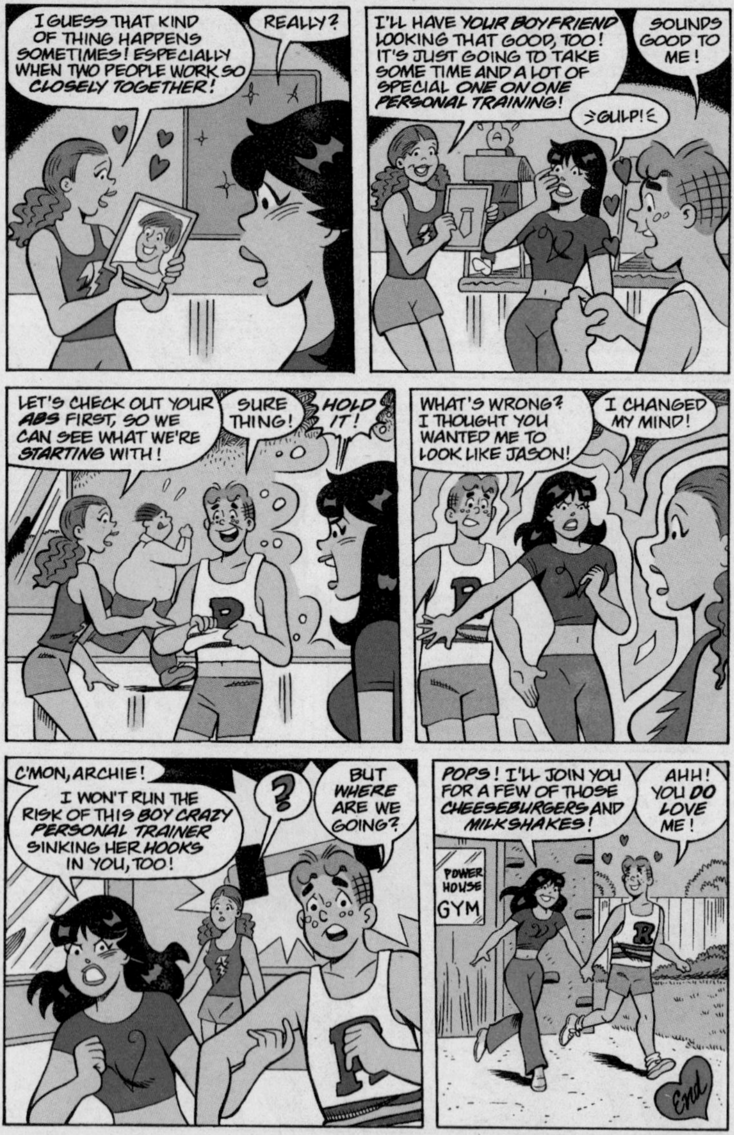
I GUESS THAT KIND OF THING HAPPENS SOMETIMES! ESPECIALLY WHEN TWO PEOPLE WORK SO CLOSELY TOGETHER!
REALLY?
I'LL HAVE YOUR BOYFRIEND LOOKING THAT GOOD, TOO! IT'S JUST GOING TO TAKE SOME TIME AND A LOT OF SPECIAL ONE ON ONE PERSONAL TRAINING!
SOUNDS GOOD TO ME!
GULP!
LET'S CHECK OUT YOUR ABS FIRST, SO WE CAN SEE WHAT WE'RE STARTING WITH!
SURE THING!
HOLD IT!
WHAT'S WRONG? I THOUGHT YOU WANTED ME TO LOOK LIKE JASON!
I CHANGED MY MIND!
C'MON, ARCHIE!
I WON'T RUN THE RISK OF THIS BOY CRAZY PERSONAL TRAINER SINKING HER HOOKS IN YOU, TOO!
?
BUT WHERE ARE WE GOING?
POPS! I'LL JOIN YOU FOR A FEW OF THOSE CHEESEBURGERS AND MILKSHAKES!
AHH! YOU DO LOVE ME!
POWER HOUSE GYM
End

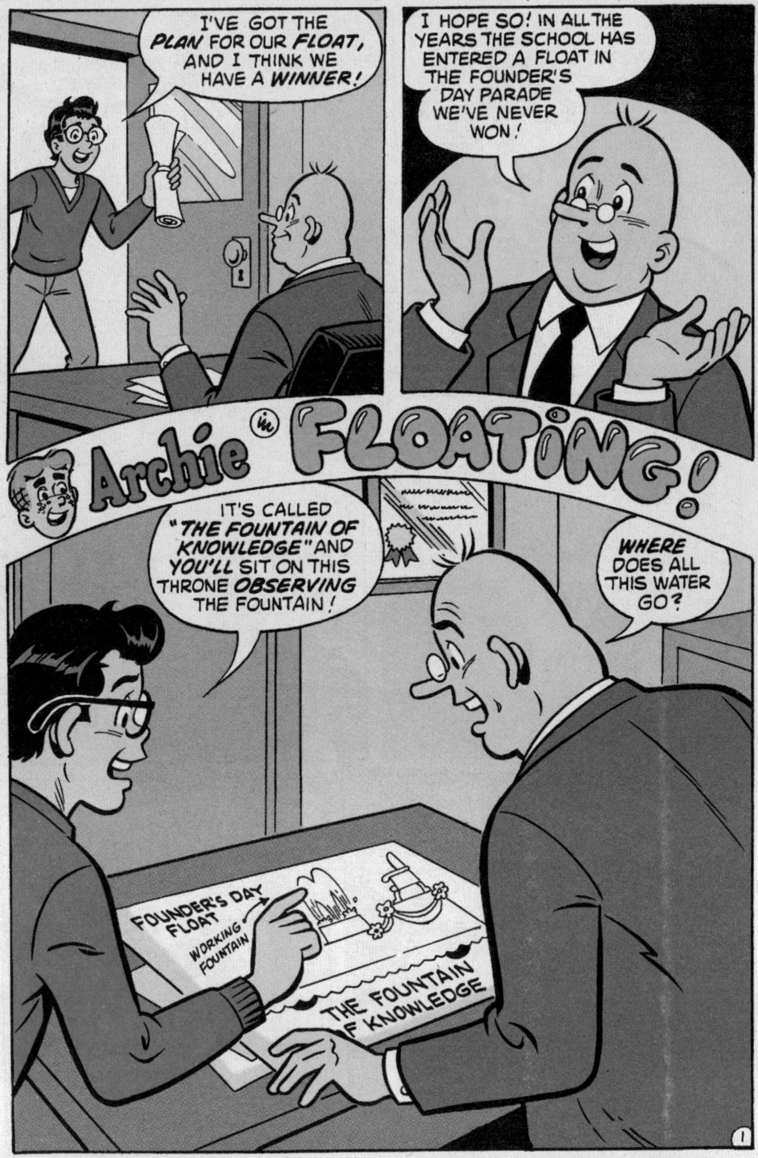
I'VE GOT THE PLAN FOR OUR FLOAT, AND I THINK WE HAVE A WINNER!
I HOPE SO! IN ALL THE YEARS THE SCHOOL HAS ENTERED A FLOAT IN THE FOUNDER'S DAY PARADE WE'VE NEVER WON!
Archie in FLOATING!
IT'S CALLED "THE FOUNTAIN OF KNOWLEDGE" AND YOU'LL SIT ON THIS THRONE OBSERVING THE FOUNTAIN!
WHERE DOES ALL THIS WATER GO?
FOUNDER'S DAY FLOAT
WORKING FOUNTAIN
THE FOUNTAIN OF KNOWLEDGE
1

Script & Pencils: Bill Golliher / Ink: Jon D'Agostino / Letters: Bill Yoshida

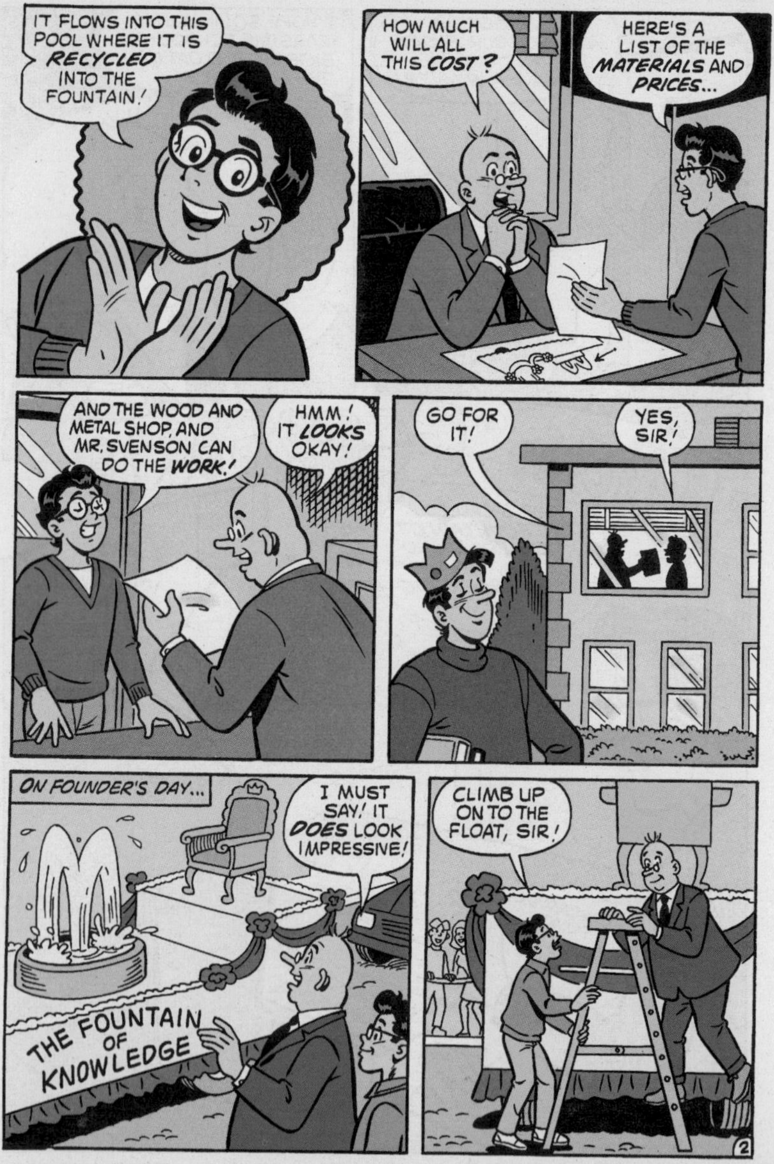
IT FLOWS INTO THIS POOL WHERE IT IS RECYCLED INTO THE FOUNTAIN!
HOW MUCH WILL ALL THIS COST?
HERE'S A LIST OF THE MATERIALS AND PRICES...
AND THE WOOD AND METAL SHOP, AND MR. SVENSON CAN DO THE WORK!
HMM! IT LOOKS OKAY!
GO FOR IT!
YES, SIR!
ON FOUNDER'S DAY...
I MUST SAY! IT DOES LOOK IMPRESSIVE!
THE FOUNTAIN OF KNOWLEDGE
CLIMB UP ON TO THE FLOAT, SIR!
2

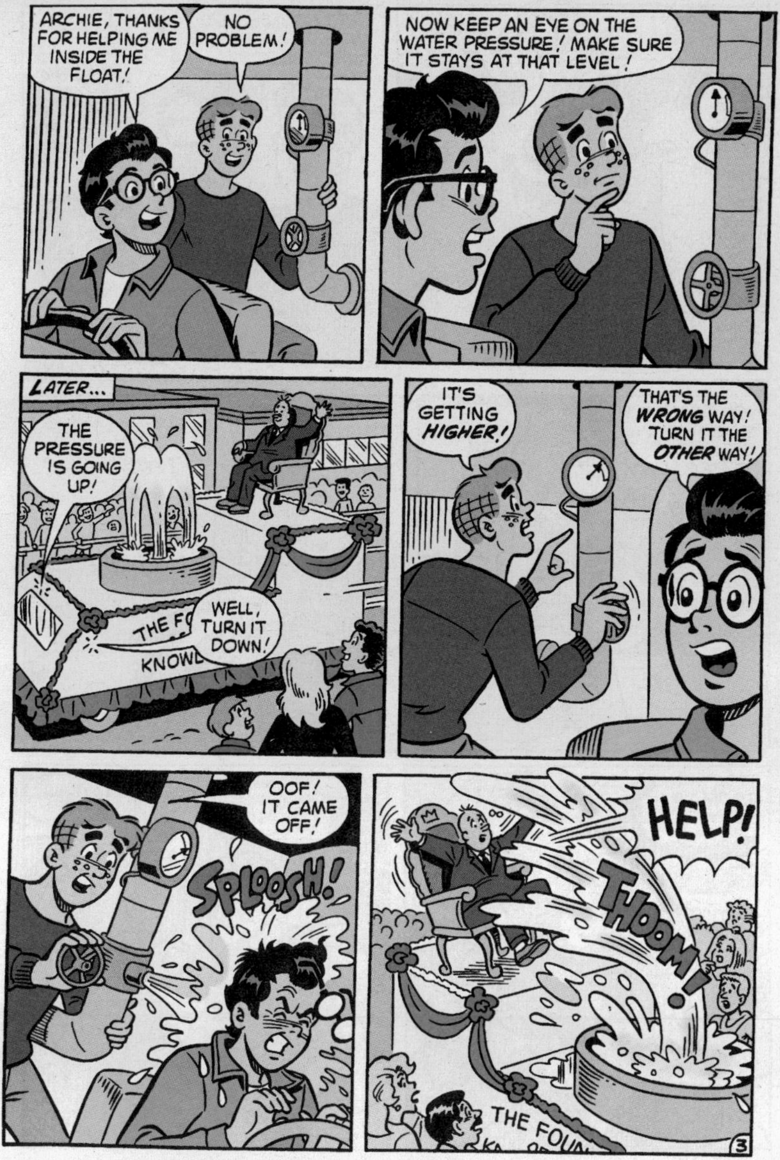

ARCHIE, THANKS FOR HELPING ME INSIDE THE FLOAT!
NO PROBLEM!
NOW KEEP AN EYE ON THE WATER PRESSURE! MAKE SURE IT STAYS AT THAT LEVEL!
LATER...
THE PRESSURE IS GOING UP!
THE FO
KNOWL
WELL, TURN IT DOWN!
IT'S GETTING HIGHER!
THAT'S THE WRONG WAY! TURN IT THE OTHER WAY!
OOF! IT CAME OFF!
SPLOOSH!
HELP!
THOOM!
THE FOUN
3

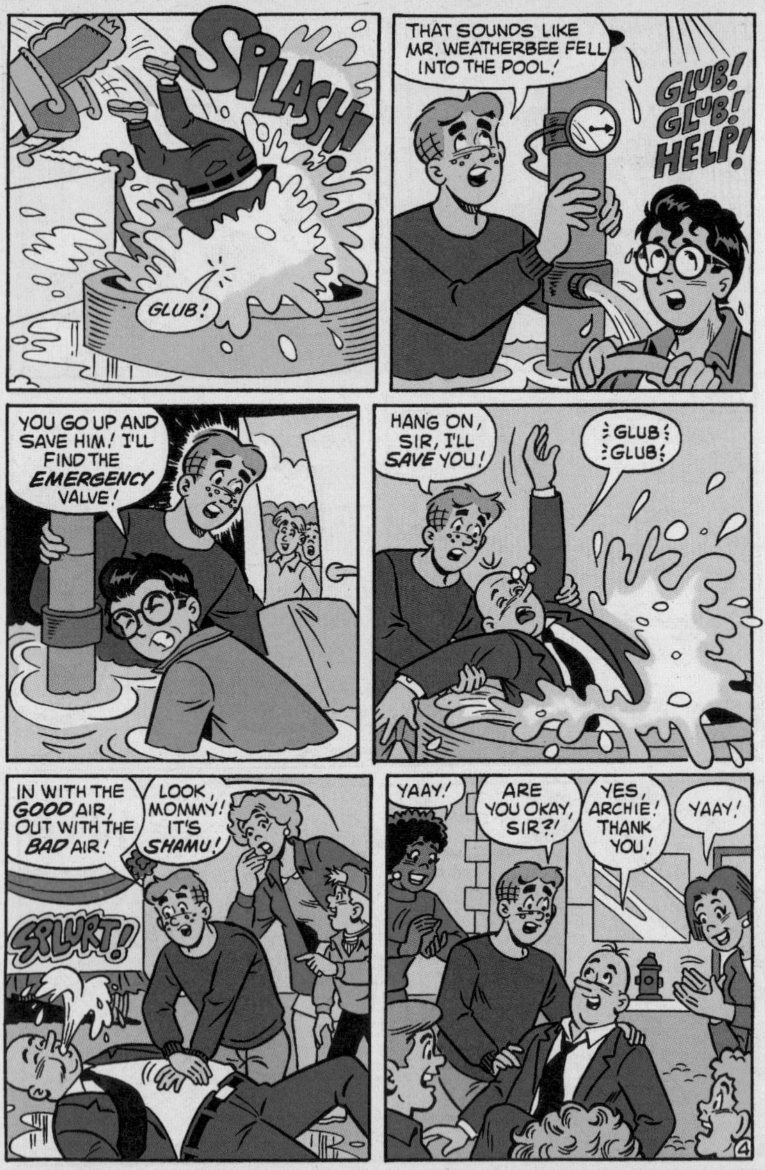
SPLASH!
GLUB!
THAT SOUNDS LIKE MR. WEATHERBEE FELL INTO THE POOL!
GLUB! GLUB! HELP!
YOU GO UP AND SAVE HIM! I'LL FIND THE EMERGENCY VALVE!
HANG ON, SIR, I'LL SAVE YOU!
GLUB GLUB!
IN WITH THE GOOD AIR, OUT WITH THE BAD AIR!
LOOK, MOMMY! IT'S SHAMU!
SPLURT!
YAAY!
ARE YOU OKAY, SIR?!
YES, ARCHIE! THANK YOU!
YAAY!
4

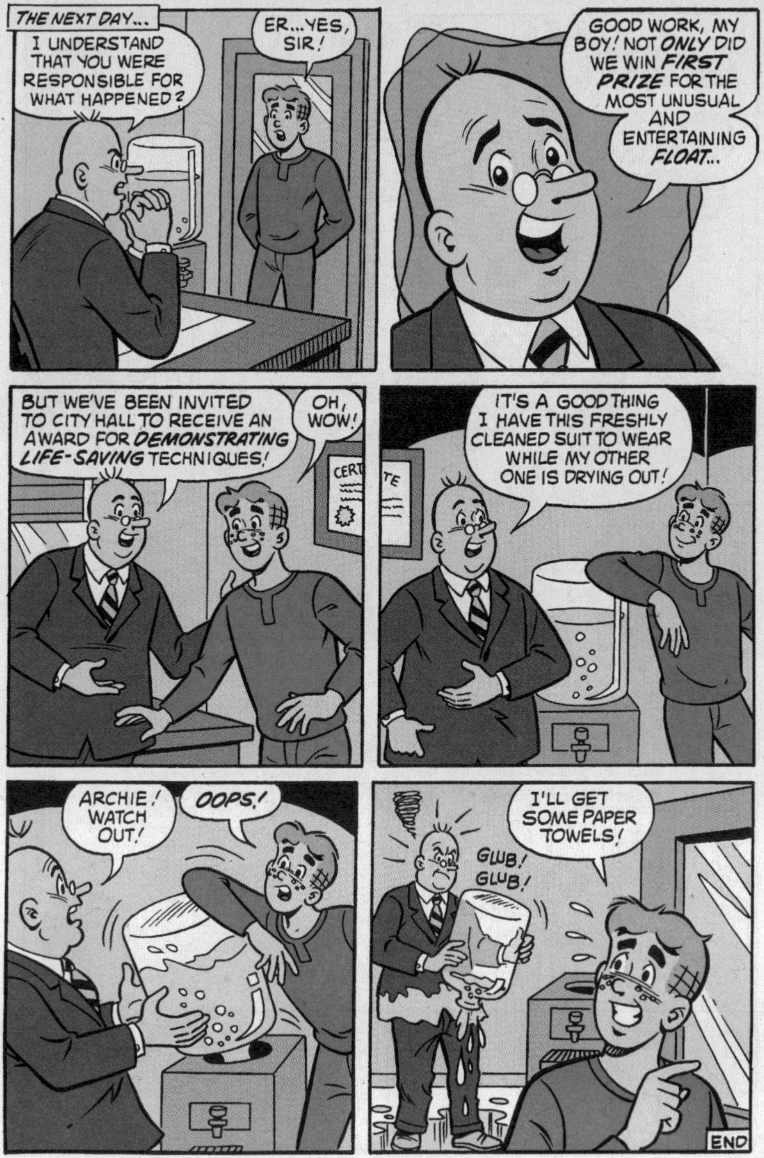
THE NEXT DAY...
I UNDERSTAND THAT YOU WERE RESPONSIBLE FOR WHAT HAPPENED?
ER...YES, SIR!
GOOD WORK, MY BOY! NOT ONLY DID WE WIN FIRST PRIZE FOR THE MOST UNUSUAL AND ENTERTAINING FLOAT...
BUT WE'VE BEEN INVITED TO CITY HALL TO RECEIVE AN AWARD FOR DEMONSTRATING LIFE-SAVING TECHNIQUES!
OH, WOW!
IT'S A GOOD THING I HAVE THIS FRESHLY CLEANED SUIT TO WEAR WHILE MY OTHER ONE IS DRYING OUT!
ARCHIE! WATCH OUT!
OOPS!
I'LL GET SOME PAPER TOWELS!
GLUB! GLUB!
END

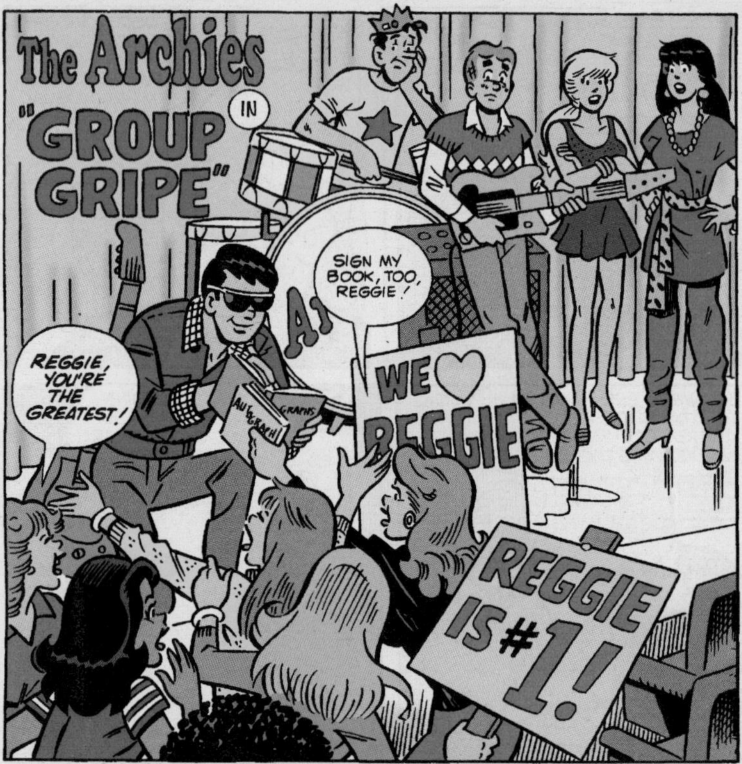
The Archies
IN
"GROUP GRIPE"
SIGN MY BOOK, TOO, REGGIE!
REGGIE, YOU'RE THE GREATEST!
AUTOGRAPHS
WE ♥ REGGIE
REGGIE IS #1!

Script: George Gladir / Pencils: Stan Goldberg / Inks: Rudy Lapick / Letters: Bill Yoshida

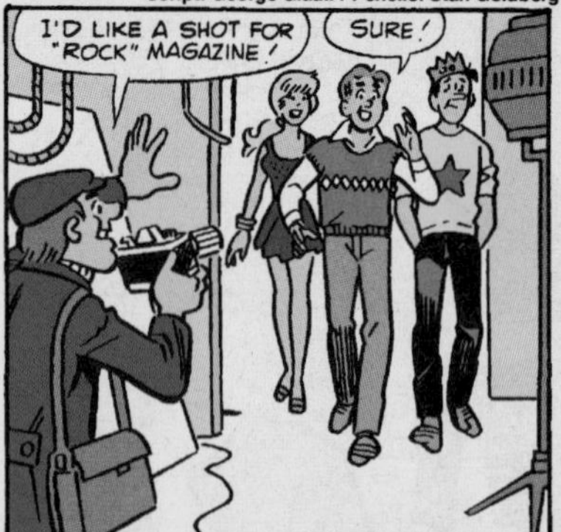
I'D LIKE A SHOT FOR "ROCK" MAGAZINE!
SURE!

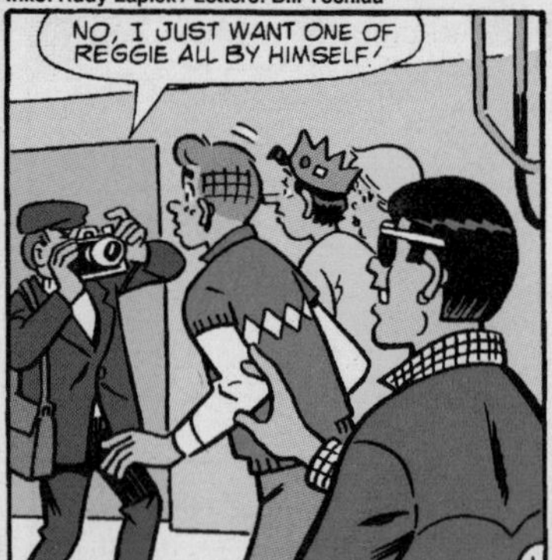
NO, I JUST WANT ONE OF REGGIE ALL BY HIMSELF!

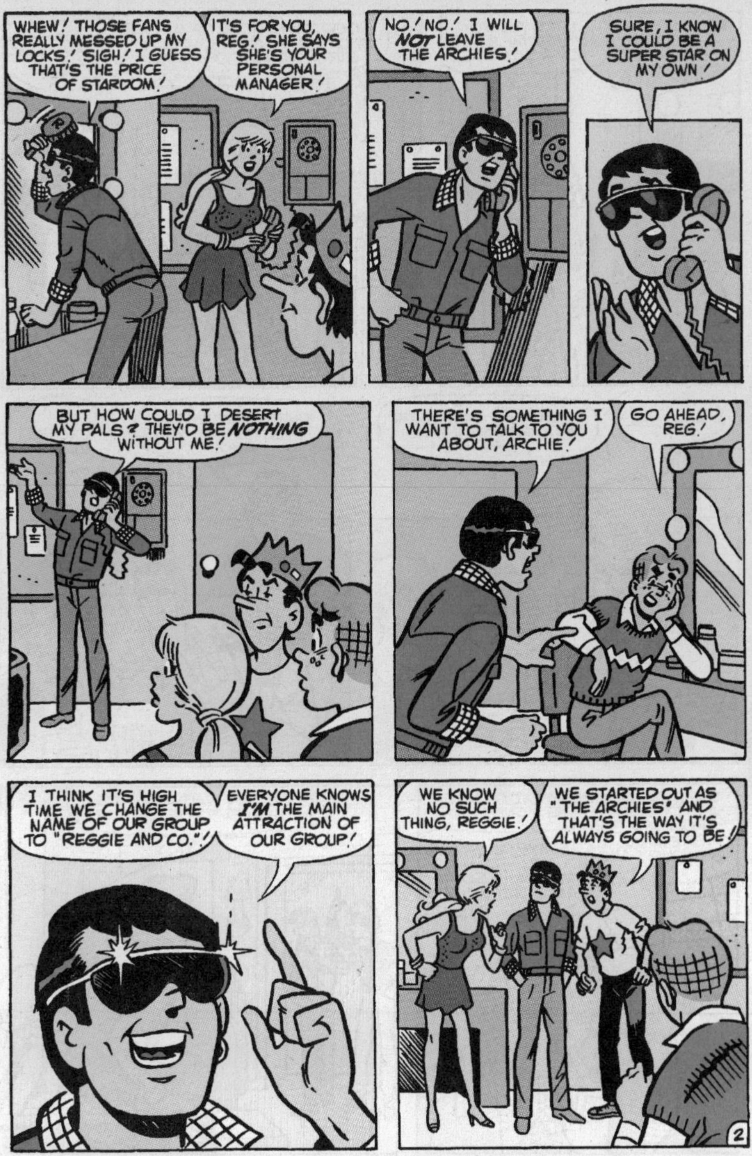
WHEW! THOSE FANS REALLY MESSED UP MY LOCKS! SIGH! I GUESS THAT'S THE PRICE OF STARDOM!
IT'S FOR YOU, REG! SHE SAYS SHE'S YOUR PERSONAL MANAGER!
NO! NO! I WILL NOT LEAVE THE ARCHIES!
SURE, I KNOW I COULD BE A SUPER STAR ON MY OWN!
BUT HOW COULD I DESERT MY PALS? THEY'D BE NOTHING WITHOUT ME!
THERE'S SOMETHING I WANT TO TALK TO YOU ABOUT, ARCHIE!
GO AHEAD, REG!
I THINK IT'S HIGH TIME WE CHANGE THE NAME OF OUR GROUP TO "REGGIE AND CO."!
EVERYONE KNOWS I'M THE MAIN ATTRACTION OF OUR GROUP!
WE KNOW NO SUCH THING, REGGIE!
WE STARTED OUT AS "THE ARCHIES" AND THAT'S THE WAY IT'S ALWAYS GOING TO BE!

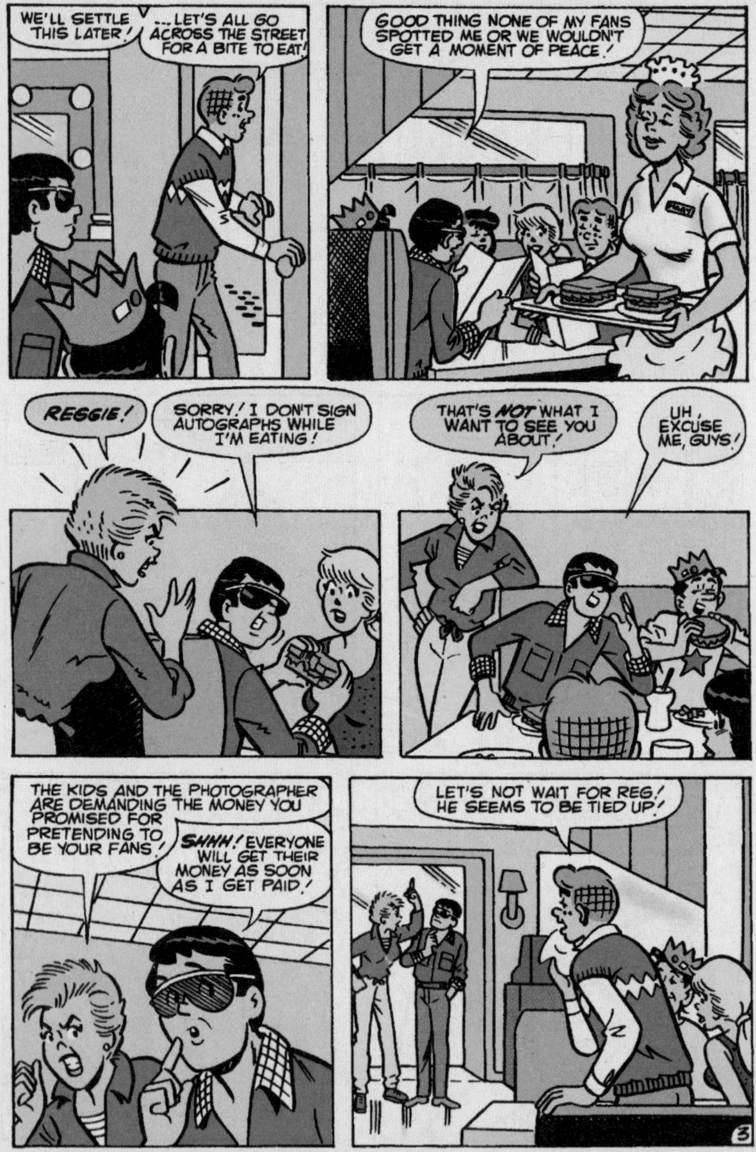
WE'LL SETTLE THIS LATER!
...LET'S ALL GO ACROSS THE STREET FOR A BITE TO EAT!
GOOD THING NONE OF MY FANS SPOTTED ME OR WE WOULDN'T GET A MOMENT OF PEACE!
REGGIE!
SORRY! I DON'T SIGN AUTOGRAPHS WHILE I'M EATING!
THAT'S NOT WHAT I WANT TO SEE YOU ABOUT!
UH, EXCUSE ME, GUYS!
THE KIDS AND THE PHOTOGRAPHER ARE DEMANDING THE MONEY YOU PROMISED FOR PRETENDING TO BE YOUR FANS!
SHHH! EVERYONE WILL GET THEIR MONEY AS SOON AS I GET PAID!
LET'S NOT WAIT FOR REG! HE SEEMS TO BE TIED UP!
3

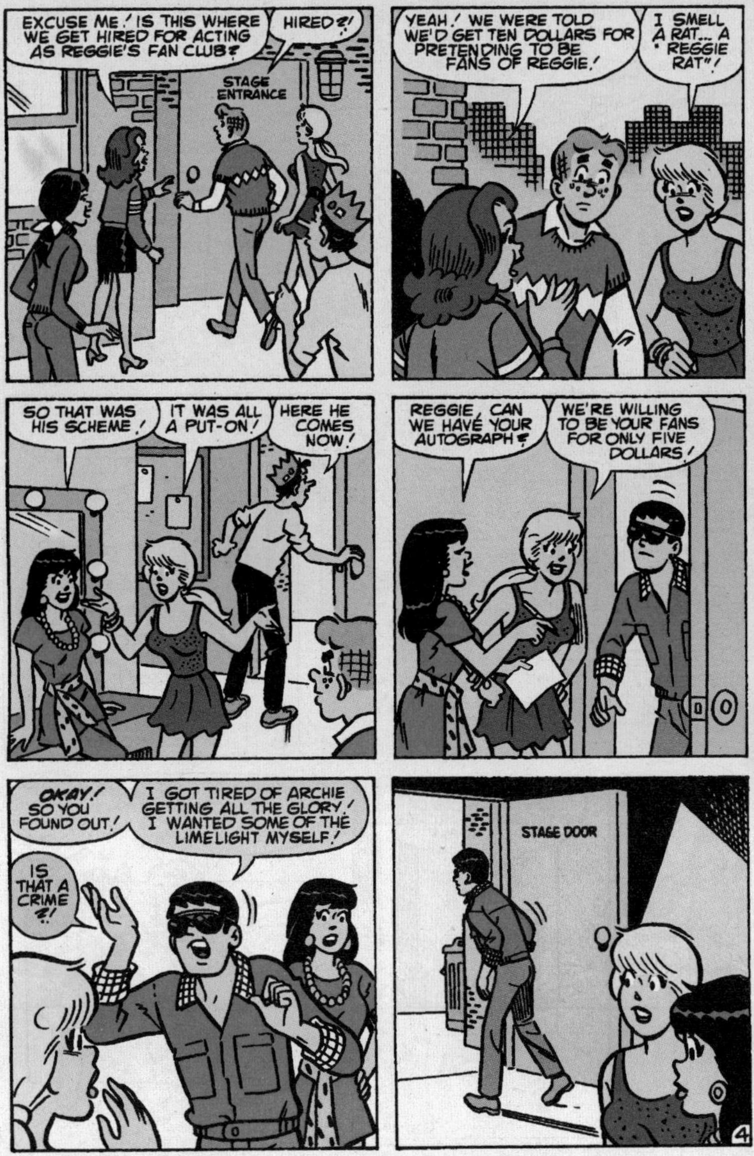

EXCUSE ME! IS THIS WHERE WE GET HIRED FOR ACTING AS REGGIE'S FAN CLUB?
HIRED?!
STAGE ENTRANCE
YEAH! WE WERE TOLD WE'D GET TEN DOLLARS FOR PRETENDING TO BE FANS OF REGGIE!
I SMELL A RAT... A "REGGIE RAT"!
SO THAT WAS HIS SCHEME!
IT WAS ALL A PUT-ON!
HERE HE COMES NOW!
REGGIE, CAN WE HAVE YOUR AUTOGRAPH?
WE'RE WILLING TO BE YOUR FANS FOR ONLY FIVE DOLLARS!
OKAY! SO YOU FOUND OUT!
I GOT TIRED OF ARCHIE GETTING ALL THE GLORY! I WANTED SOME OF THE LIMELIGHT MYSELF!
IS THAT A CRIME?!
STAGE DOOR
4

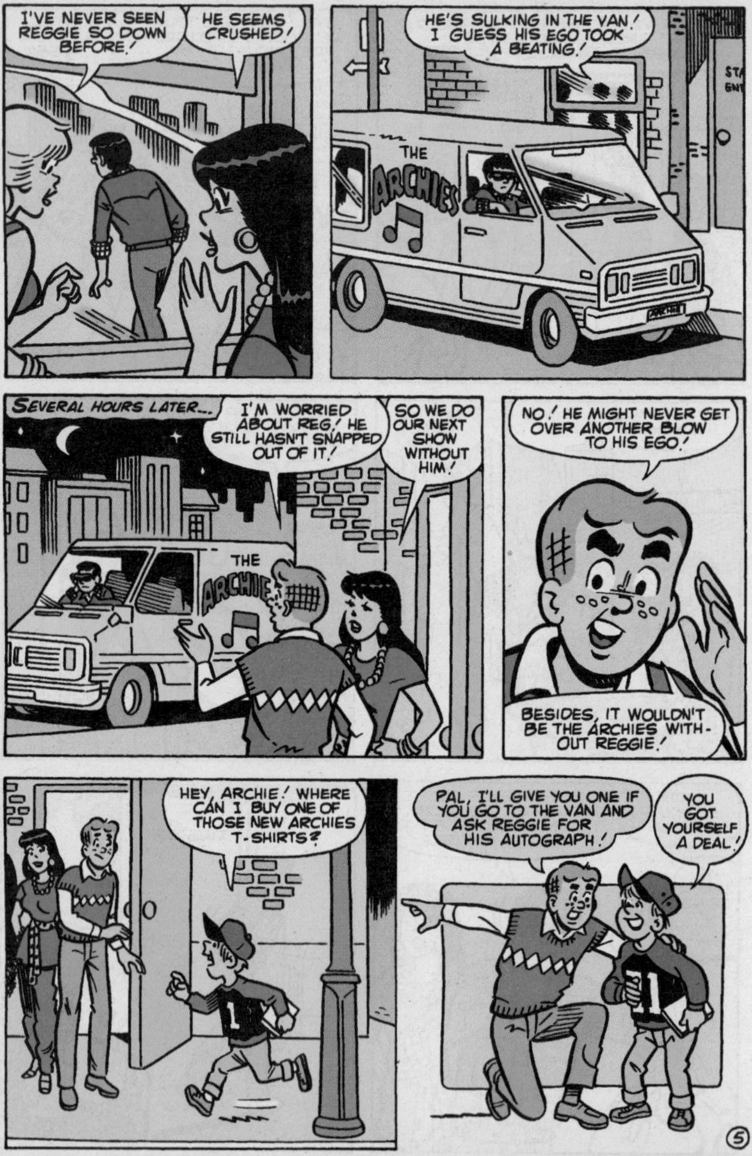
I'VE NEVER SEEN REGGIE SO DOWN BEFORE!
HE SEEMS CRUSHED!
HE'S SULKING IN THE VAN! I GUESS HIS EGO TOOK A BEATING!
THE ARCHIES
SEVERAL HOURS LATER...
I'M WORRIED ABOUT REG! HE STILL HASN'T SNAPPED OUT OF IT!
SO WE DO OUR NEXT SHOW WITHOUT HIM!
THE ARCHIE
NO! HE MIGHT NEVER GET OVER ANOTHER BLOW TO HIS EGO!
BESIDES, IT WOULDN'T BE THE ARCHIES WITH-OUT REGGIE!
HEY, ARCHIE! WHERE CAN I BUY ONE OF THOSE NEW ARCHIES T-SHIRTS?
PAL, I'LL GIVE YOU ONE IF YOU GO TO THE VAN AND ASK REGGIE FOR HIS AUTOGRAPH!
YOU GOT YOURSELF A DEAL!

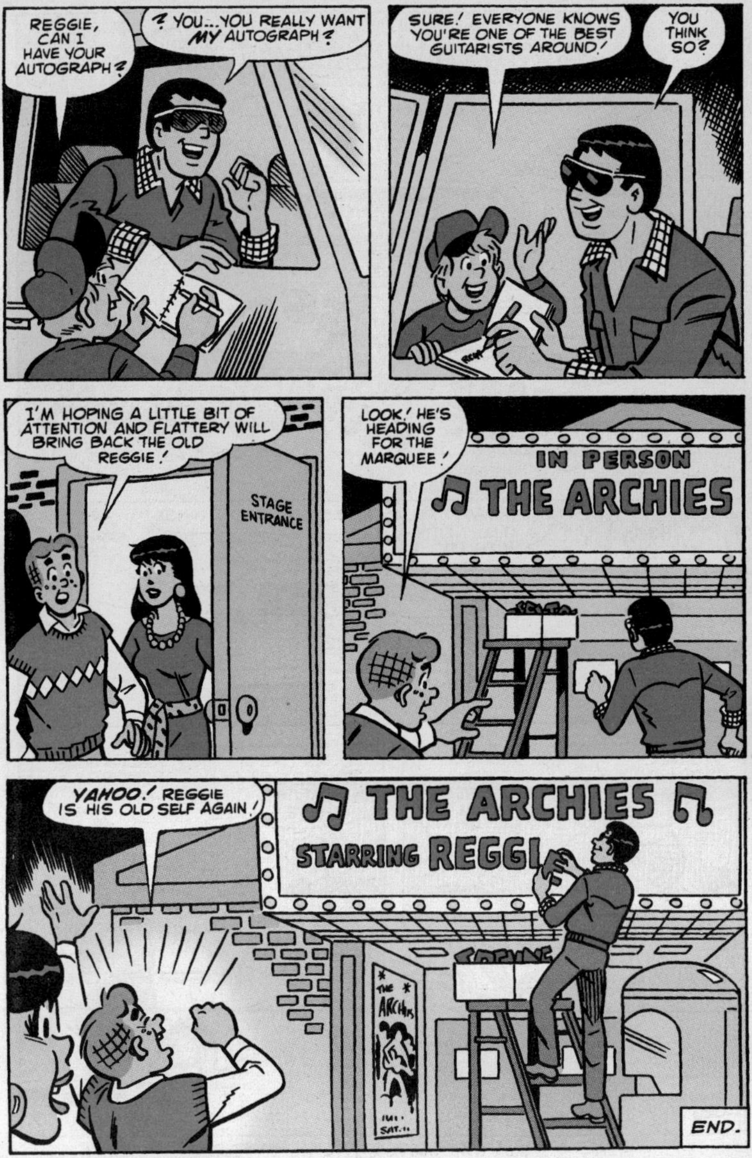

REGGIE, CAN I HAVE YOUR AUTOGRAPH?
? YOU...YOU REALLY WANT MY AUTOGRAPH?
SURE! EVERYONE KNOWS YOU'RE ONE OF THE BEST GUITARISTS AROUND!
YOU THINK SO?
I'M HOPING A LITTLE BIT OF ATTENTION AND FLATTERY WILL BRING BACK THE OLD REGGIE!
STAGE ENTRANCE
LOOK! HE'S HEADING FOR THE MARQUEE!
IN PERSON
THE ARCHIES
YAHOO! REGGIE IS HIS OLD SELF AGAIN!
THE ARCHIES
STARRING REGGI
THE ARCHIES
END.

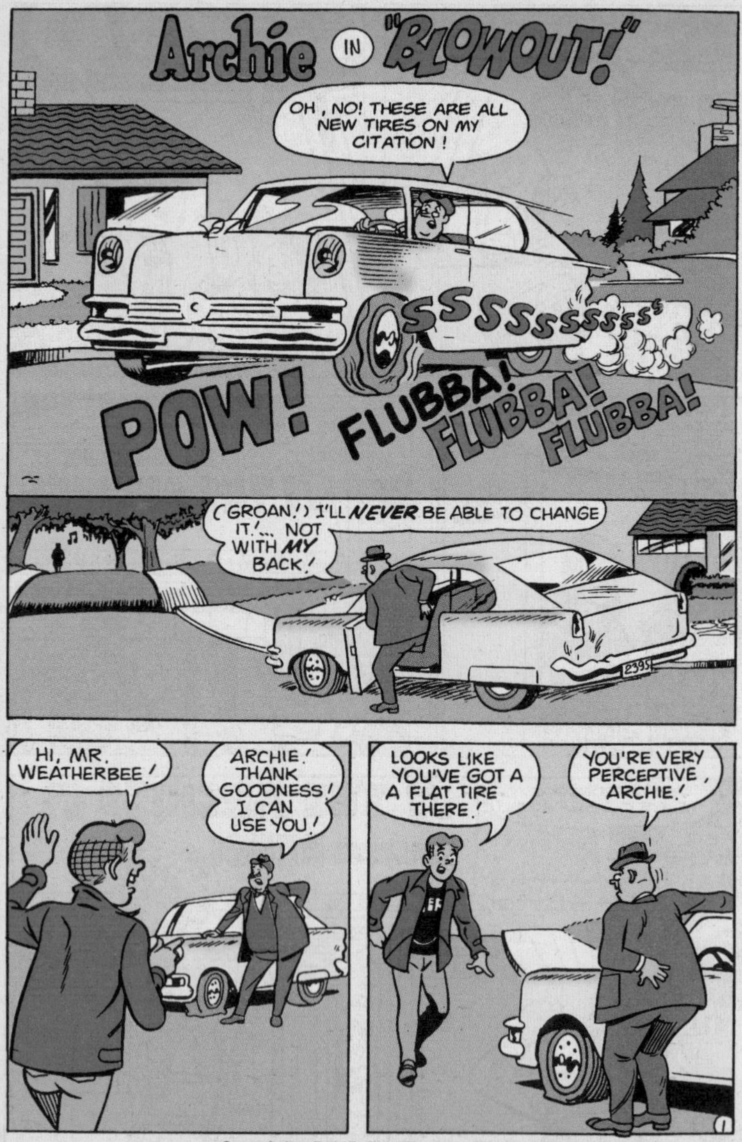
Archie IN "BLOWOUT!"
OH, NO! THESE ARE ALL NEW TIRES ON MY CITATION!
SSSSSSSSSS
POW!
FLUBBA! FLUBBA! FLUBBA!
(GROAN!) I'LL NEVER BE ABLE TO CHANGE IT!... NOT WITH MY BACK!
2395
HI, MR. WEATHERBEE!
ARCHIE! THANK GOODNESS! I CAN USE YOU!
LOOKS LIKE YOU'VE GOT A A FLAT TIRE THERE!
YOU'RE VERY PERCEPTIVE, ARCHIE!
1

Story & Art: Bob Bolling / Letters: Bill Yoshida

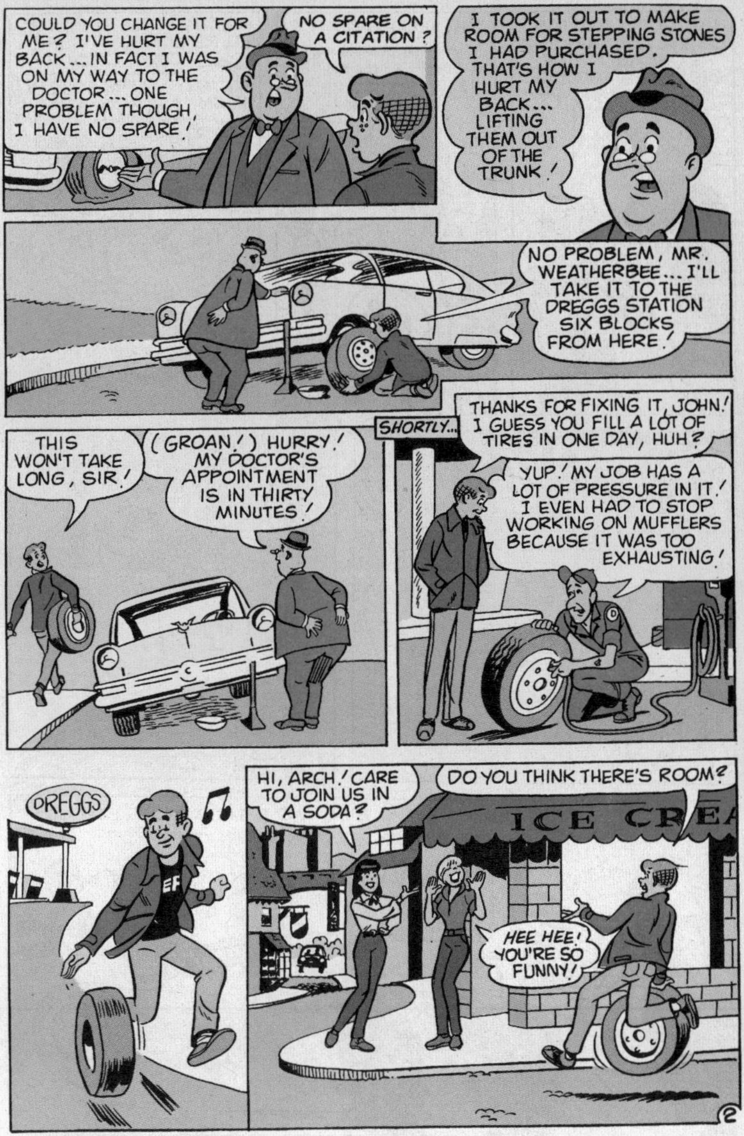
COULD YOU CHANGE IT FOR ME? I'VE HURT MY BACK... IN FACT I WAS ON MY WAY TO THE DOCTOR... ONE PROBLEM THOUGH, I HAVE NO SPARE!
NO SPARE ON A CITATION?
I TOOK IT OUT TO MAKE ROOM FOR STEPPING STONES I HAD PURCHASED. THAT'S HOW I HURT MY BACK... LIFTING THEM OUT OF THE TRUNK!
NO PROBLEM, MR. WEATHERBEE... I'LL TAKE IT TO THE DREGGS STATION SIX BLOCKS FROM HERE!
THIS WON'T TAKE LONG, SIR!
(GROAN!) HURRY! MY DOCTOR'S APPOINTMENT IS IN THIRTY MINUTES!
SHORTLY...
THANKS FOR FIXING IT, JOHN! I GUESS YOU FILL A LOT OF TIRES IN ONE DAY, HUH?
YUP! MY JOB HAS A LOT OF PRESSURE IN IT! I EVEN HAD TO STOP WORKING ON MUFFLERS BECAUSE IT WAS TOO EXHAUSTING!
DREGGS
HI, ARCH! CARE TO JOIN US IN A SODA?
DO YOU THINK THERE'S ROOM?
ICE CREA
HEE HEE! YOU'RE SO FUNNY!

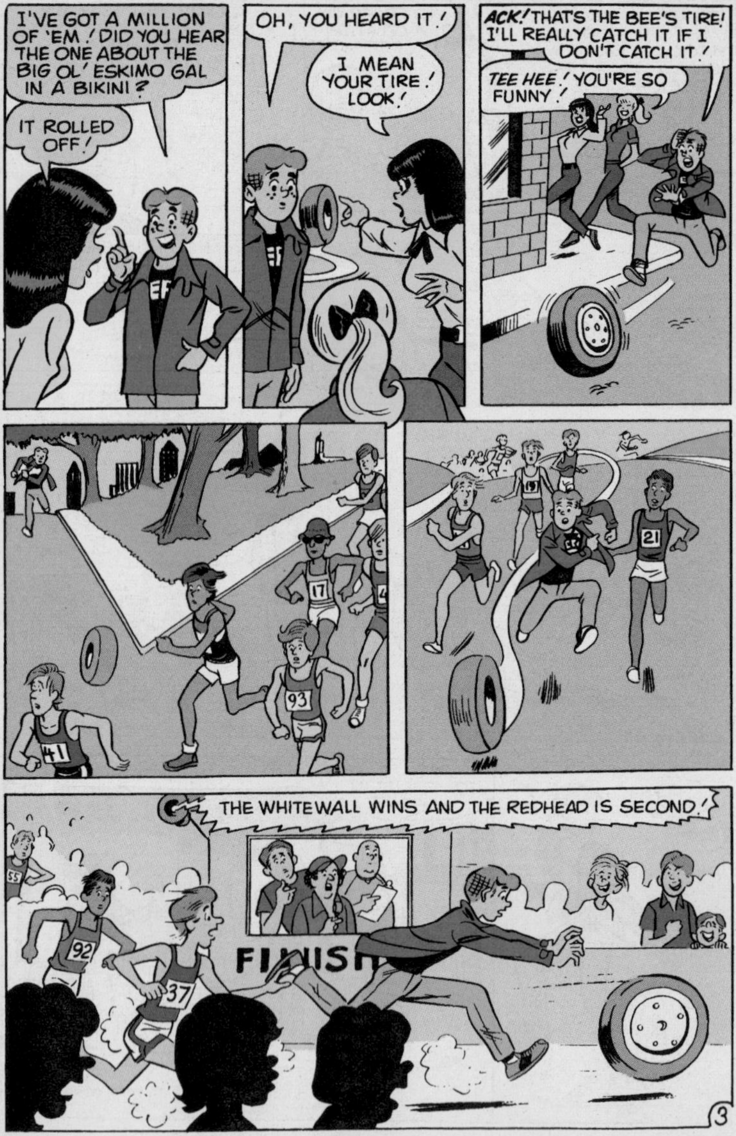
I'VE GOT A MILLION OF 'EM! DID YOU HEAR THE ONE ABOUT THE BIG OL' ESKIMO GAL IN A BIKINI?
IT ROLLED OFF!
OH, YOU HEARD IT!
I MEAN YOUR TIRE! LOOK!
ACK! THAT'S THE BEE'S TIRE! I'LL REALLY CATCH IT IF I DON'T CATCH IT!
TEE HEE! YOU'RE SO FUNNY!
THE WHITEWALL WINS AND THE REDHEAD IS SECOND!
FINISH

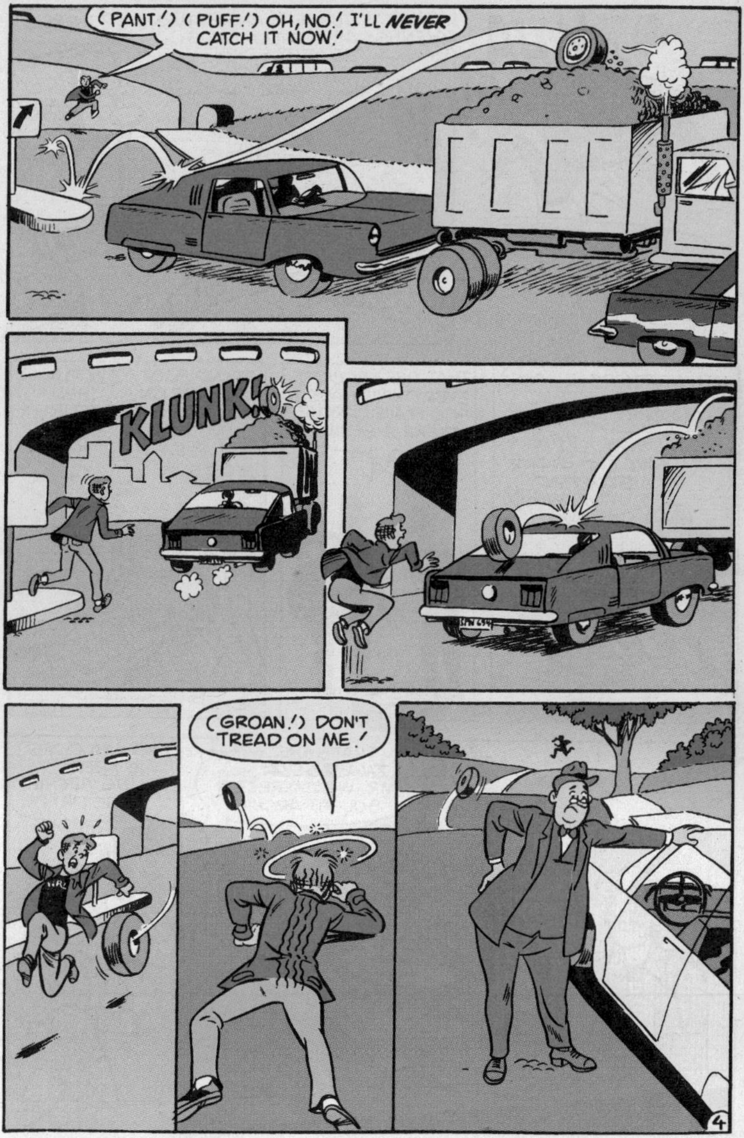

(PANT!) (PUFF!) OH, NO! I'LL NEVER CATCH IT NOW!
KLUNK!
(GROAN!) DON'T TREAD ON ME!
4

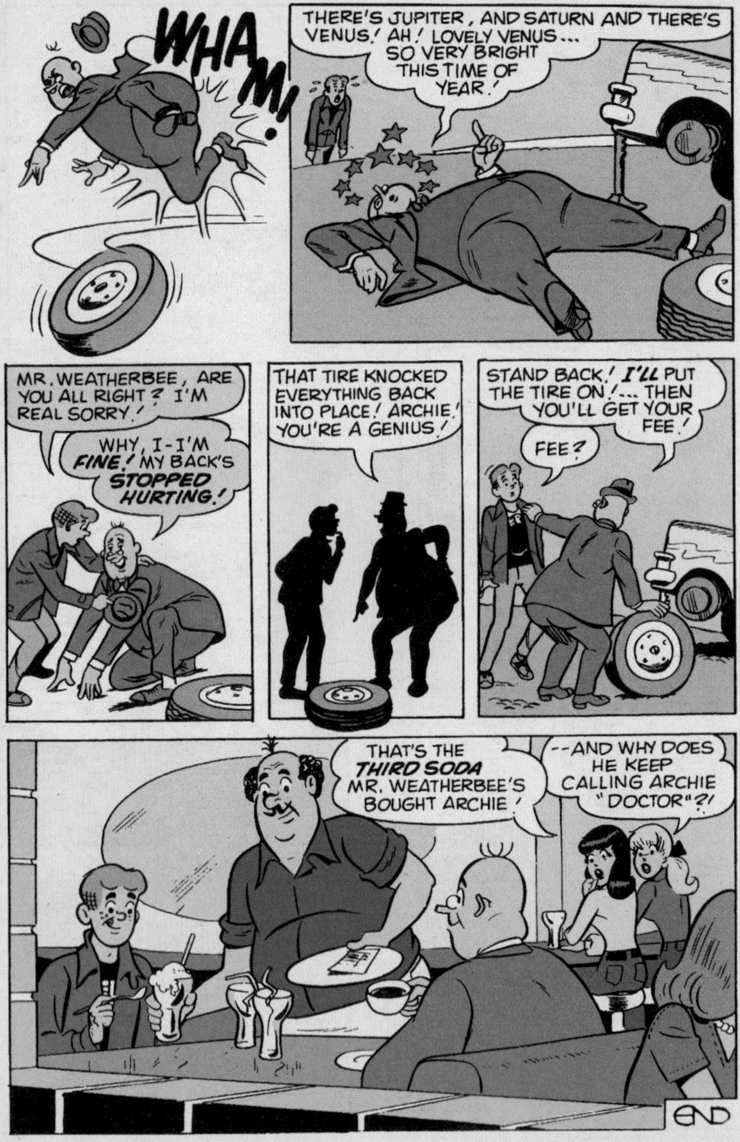
WHAM!
THERE'S JUPITER, AND SATURN AND THERE'S VENUS! AH! LOVELY VENUS... SO VERY BRIGHT THIS TIME OF YEAR!
MR. WEATHERBEE, ARE YOU ALL RIGHT? I'M REAL SORRY!
WHY, I-I'M FINE! MY BACK'S STOPPED HURTING!
THAT TIRE KNOCKED EVERYTHING BACK INTO PLACE! ARCHIE! YOU'RE A GENIUS!
STAND BACK! I'LL PUT THE TIRE ON!... THEN YOU'LL GET YOUR FEE!
FEE?
THAT'S THE THIRD SODA MR. WEATHERBEE'S BOUGHT ARCHIE!
--AND WHY DOES HE KEEP CALLING ARCHIE "DOCTOR"?!
END

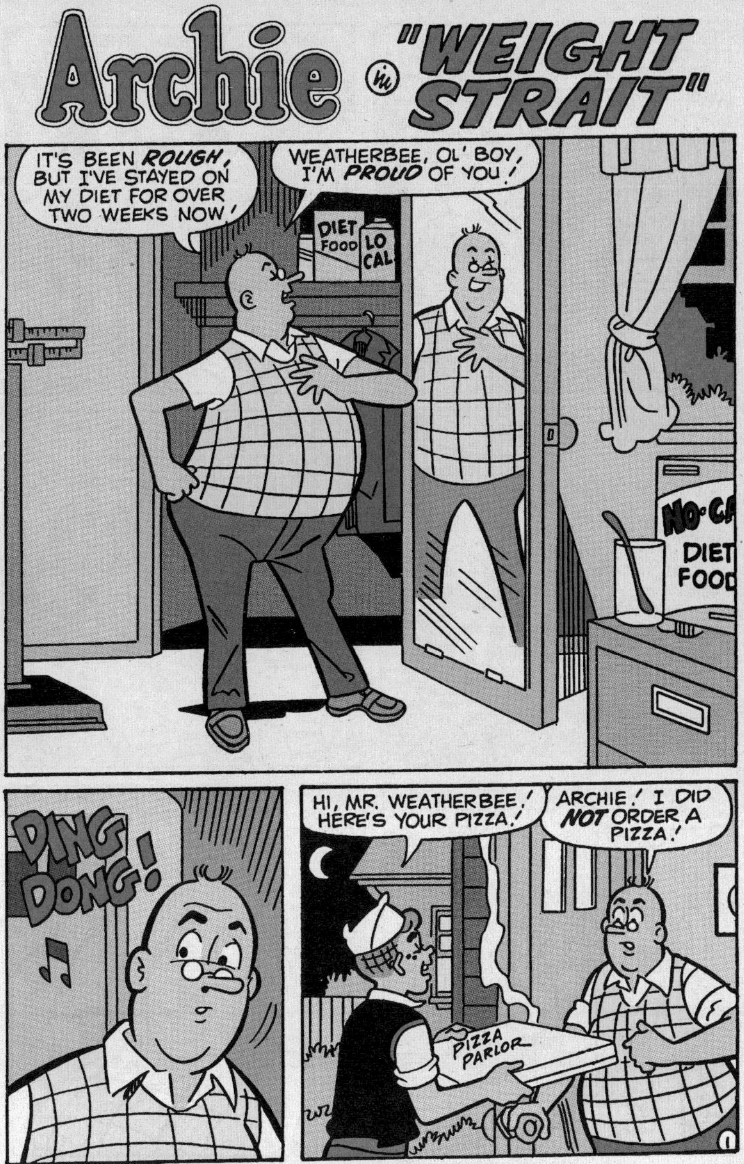
Archie in "WEIGHT STRAIT"
IT'S BEEN ROUGH, BUT I'VE STAYED ON MY DIET FOR OVER TWO WEEKS NOW!
WEATHERBEE, OL' BOY, I'M PROUD OF YOU!
DIET FOOD
LO CAL
NO-CA
DIET FOOD
DING DONG!
HI, MR. WEATHERBEE! HERE'S YOUR PIZZA!
ARCHIE! I DID NOT ORDER A PIZZA!
PIZZA PARLOR
1

Script: George Gladir / Art: Stan Goldberg / Letters: Bill Yoshida

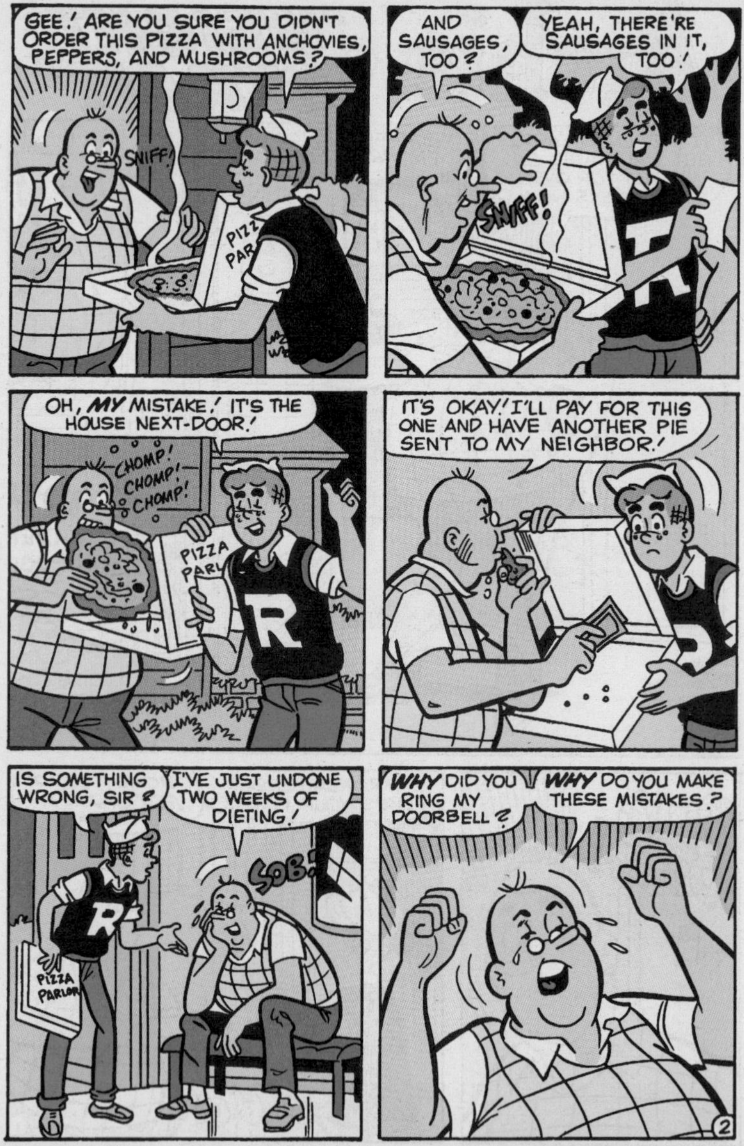
GEE! ARE YOU SURE YOU DIDN'T ORDER THIS PIZZA WITH ANCHOVIES, PEPPERS, AND MUSHROOMS?
SNIFF!
AND SAUSAGES, TOO?
YEAH, THERE'RE SAUSAGES IN IT, TOO!
SNIFF!
OH, *MY* MISTAKE! IT'S THE HOUSE NEXT-DOOR!
CHOMP! CHOMP! CHOMP!
PIZZA PARL
IT'S OKAY! I'LL PAY FOR THIS ONE AND HAVE ANOTHER PIE SENT TO MY NEIGHBOR!
IS SOMETHING WRONG, SIR?
I'VE JUST UNDONE TWO WEEKS OF DIETING!
SOB!
PIZZA PARLOR
WHY DID YOU RING MY DOORBELL?
WHY DO YOU MAKE THESE MISTAKES?
2

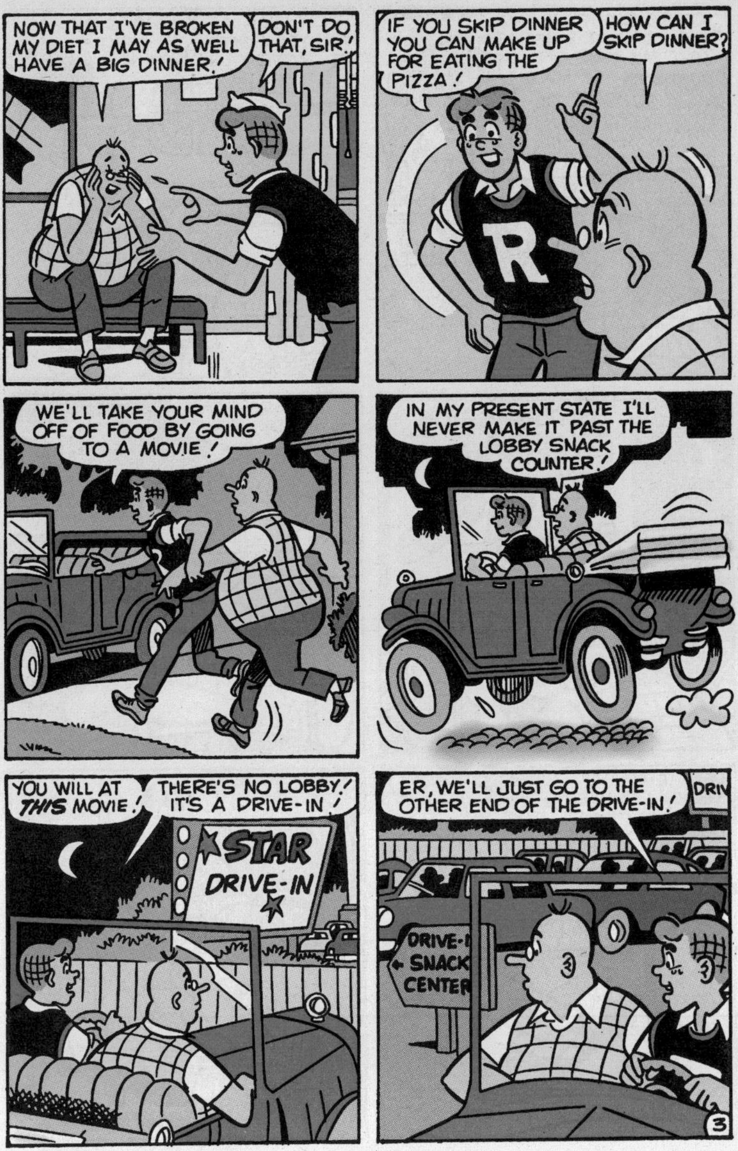
NOW THAT I'VE BROKEN MY DIET I MAY AS WELL HAVE A BIG DINNER!
DON'T DO THAT, SIR!
IF YOU SKIP DINNER YOU CAN MAKE UP FOR EATING THE PIZZA!
HOW CAN I SKIP DINNER?
WE'LL TAKE YOUR MIND OFF OF FOOD BY GOING TO A MOVIE!
IN MY PRESENT STATE I'LL NEVER MAKE IT PAST THE LOBBY SNACK COUNTER!
YOU WILL AT *THIS* MOVIE!
THERE'S NO LOBBY! IT'S A DRIVE-IN!
STAR DRIVE-IN
ER, WE'LL JUST GO TO THE OTHER END OF THE DRIVE-IN!
DRIV
DRIVE-I SNACK CENTER
3

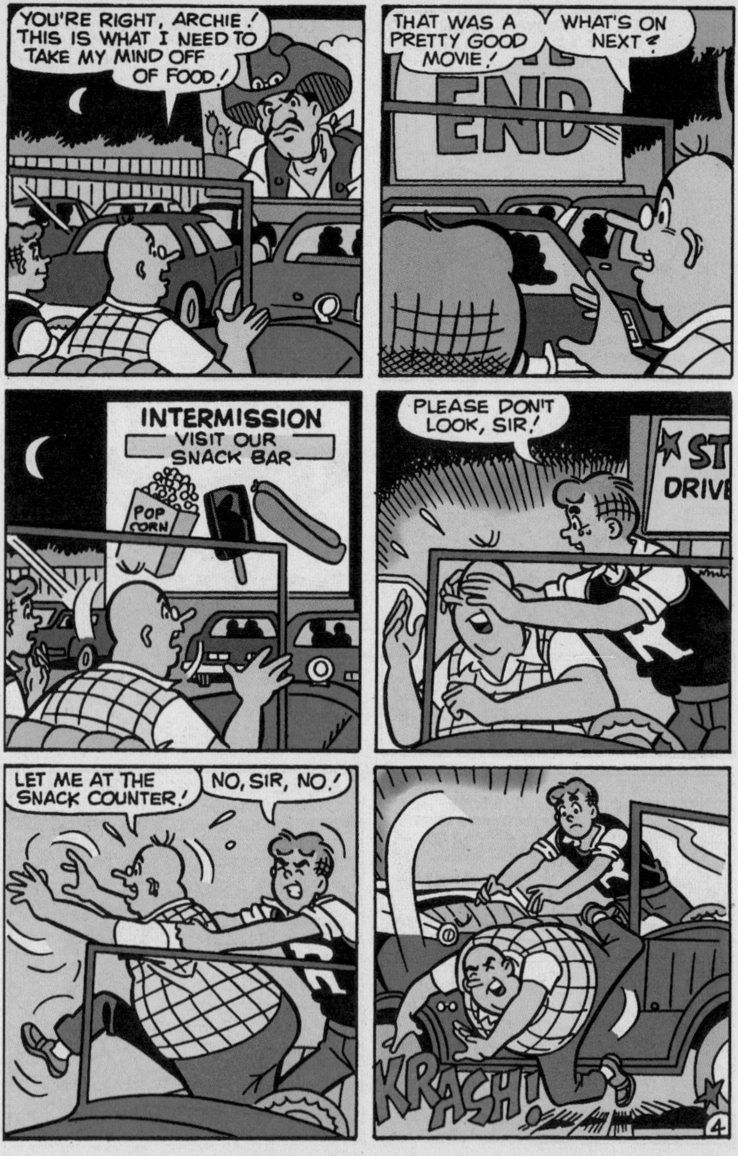
YOU'RE RIGHT, ARCHIE! THIS IS WHAT I NEED TO TAKE MY MIND OFF OF FOOD!
THAT WAS A PRETTY GOOD MOVIE!
WHAT'S ON NEXT?
END
INTERMISSION
VISIT OUR SNACK BAR
POP CORN
PLEASE DON'T LOOK, SIR!
DRIVE
LET ME AT THE SNACK COUNTER!
NO, SIR, NO!
KRASH!
4

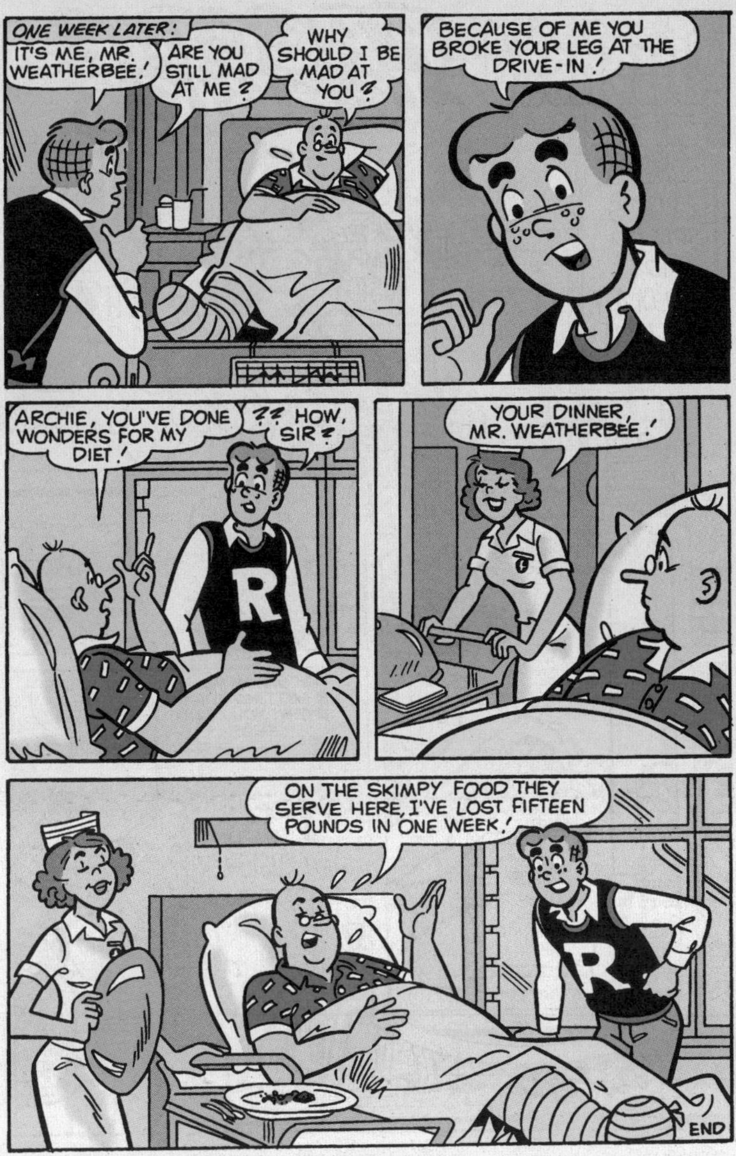

ONE WEEK LATER:
IT'S ME, MR. WEATHERBEE.!
ARE YOU STILL MAD AT ME?
WHY SHOULD I BE MAD AT YOU?
BECAUSE OF ME YOU BROKE YOUR LEG AT THE DRIVE-IN!
ARCHIE, YOU'VE DONE WONDERS FOR MY DIET!
?? HOW, SIR?
YOUR DINNER, MR. WEATHERBEE!
ON THE SKIMPY FOOD THEY SERVE HERE, I'VE LOST FIFTEEN POUNDS IN ONE WEEK!
END

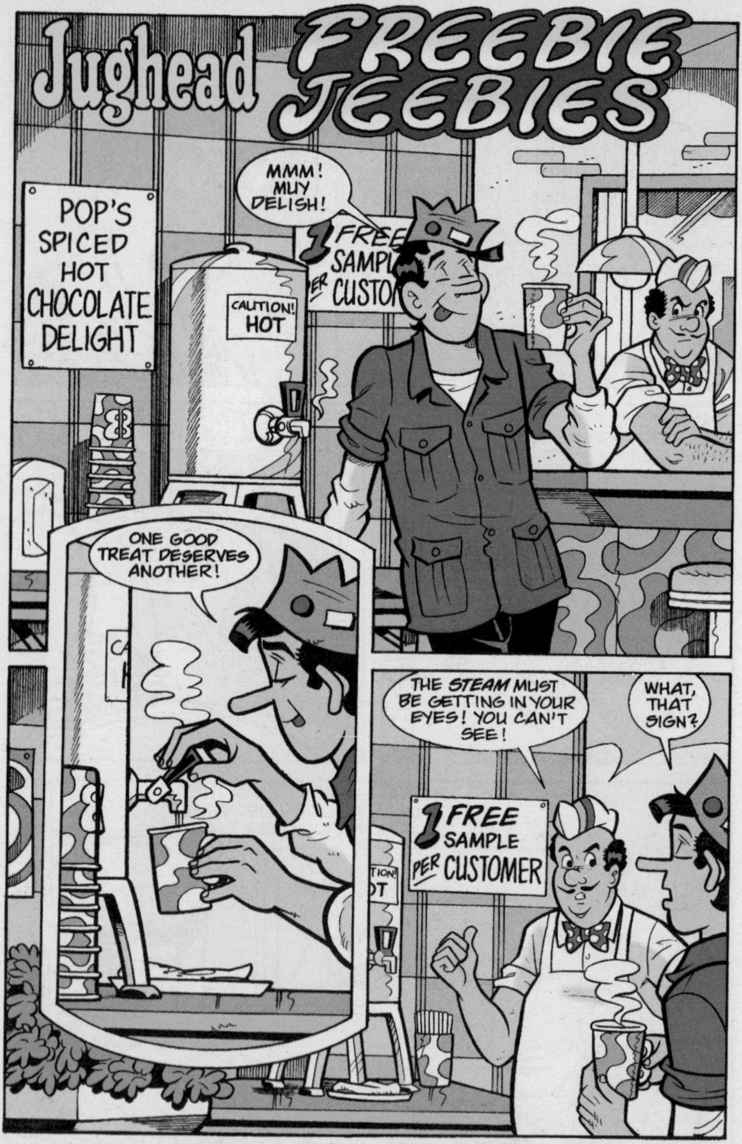

Jughead
FREEBIE JEEBIES
POP'S SPICED HOT CHOCOLATE DELIGHT
CAUTION! HOT
MMM! MUY DELISH!
1 FREE SAMPLE PER CUSTOMER
ONE GOOD TREAT DESERVES ANOTHER!
THE STEAM MUST BE GETTING IN YOUR EYES! YOU CAN'T SEE!
WHAT, THAT SIGN?
1 FREE SAMPLE PER CUSTOMER

SCRIPT: CRAIG BOLDMAN PENCILS: REX LINDSEY INKING: RICH KOSLOWSKI LETTERING: VICKIE WILLIAMS

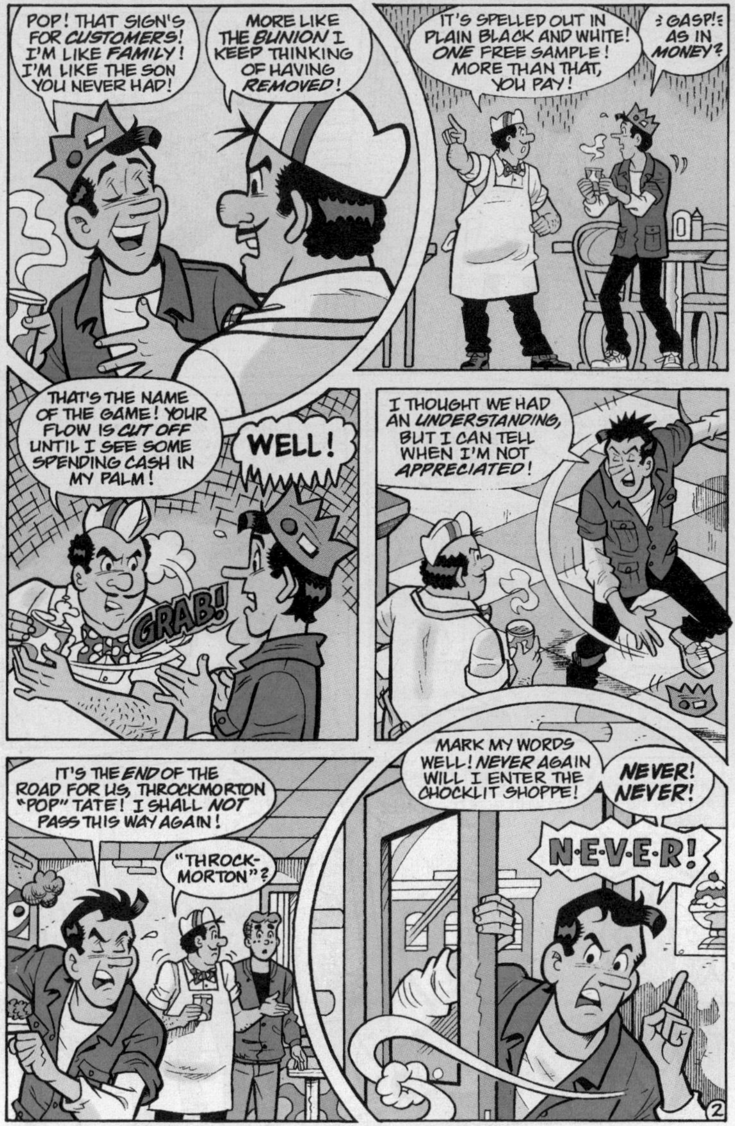
POP! THAT SIGN'S FOR CUSTOMERS! I'M LIKE FAMILY! I'M LIKE THE SON YOU NEVER HAD!
MORE LIKE THE BUNION I KEEP THINKING OF HAVING REMOVED!
IT'S SPELLED OUT IN PLAIN BLACK AND WHITE! ONE FREE SAMPLE! MORE THAN THAT, YOU PAY!
GASP! AS IN MONEY?
THAT'S THE NAME OF THE GAME! YOUR FLOW IS CUT OFF UNTIL I SEE SOME SPENDING CASH IN MY PALM!
WELL!
GRAB!
I THOUGHT WE HAD AN UNDERSTANDING, BUT I CAN TELL WHEN I'M NOT APPRECIATED!
IT'S THE END OF THE ROAD FOR US, THROCKMORTON "POP" TATE! I SHALL NOT PASS THIS WAY AGAIN!
"THROCK-MORTON"?
MARK MY WORDS WELL! NEVER AGAIN WILL I ENTER THE CHOCKLIT SHOPPE!
NEVER! NEVER!
N·E·V·E·R!
2

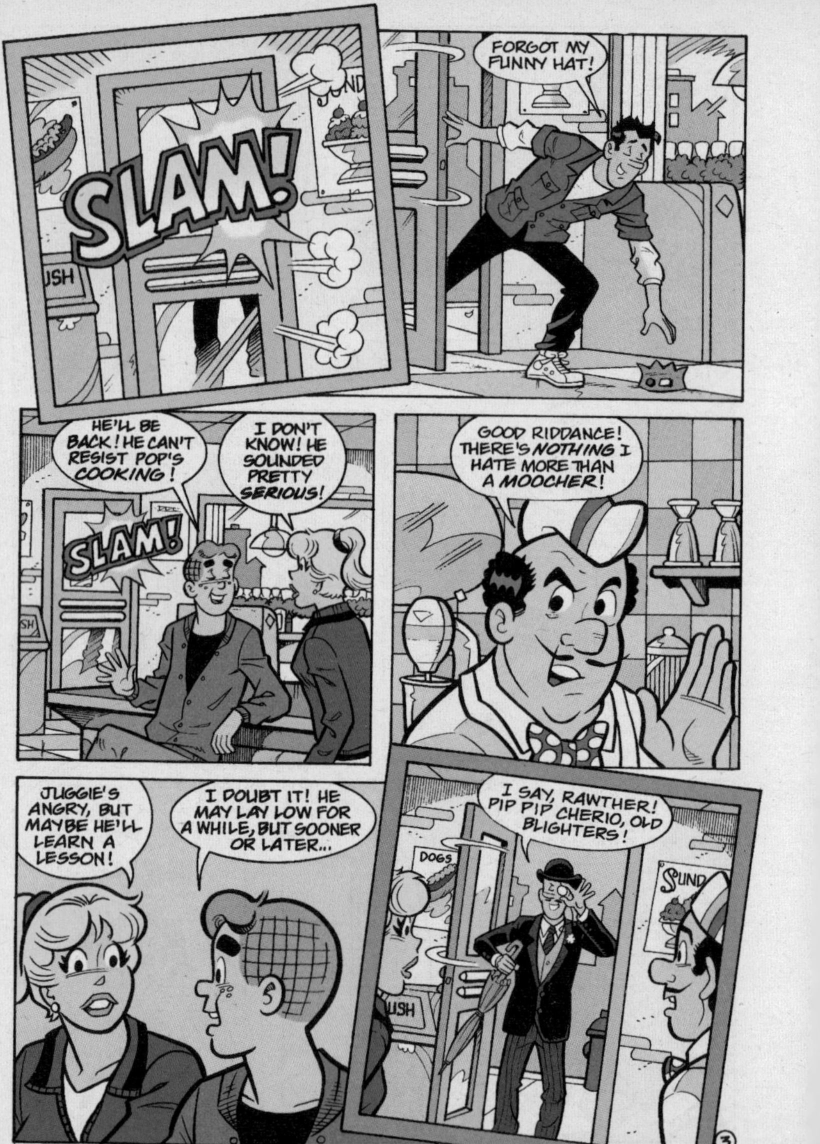
SLAM!
FORGOT MY FUNNY HAT!
HE'LL BE BACK! HE CAN'T RESIST POP'S COOKING!
I DON'T KNOW! HE SOUNDED PRETTY SERIOUS!
SLAM!
GOOD RIDDANCE! THERE'S NOTHING I HATE MORE THAN A MOOCHER!
JUGGIE'S ANGRY, BUT MAYBE HE'LL LEARN A LESSON!
I DOUBT IT! HE MAY LAY LOW FOR A WHILE, BUT SOONER OR LATER...
I SAY, RAWTHER! PIP PIP CHERIO, OLD BLIGHTERS!
DOGS
SUND

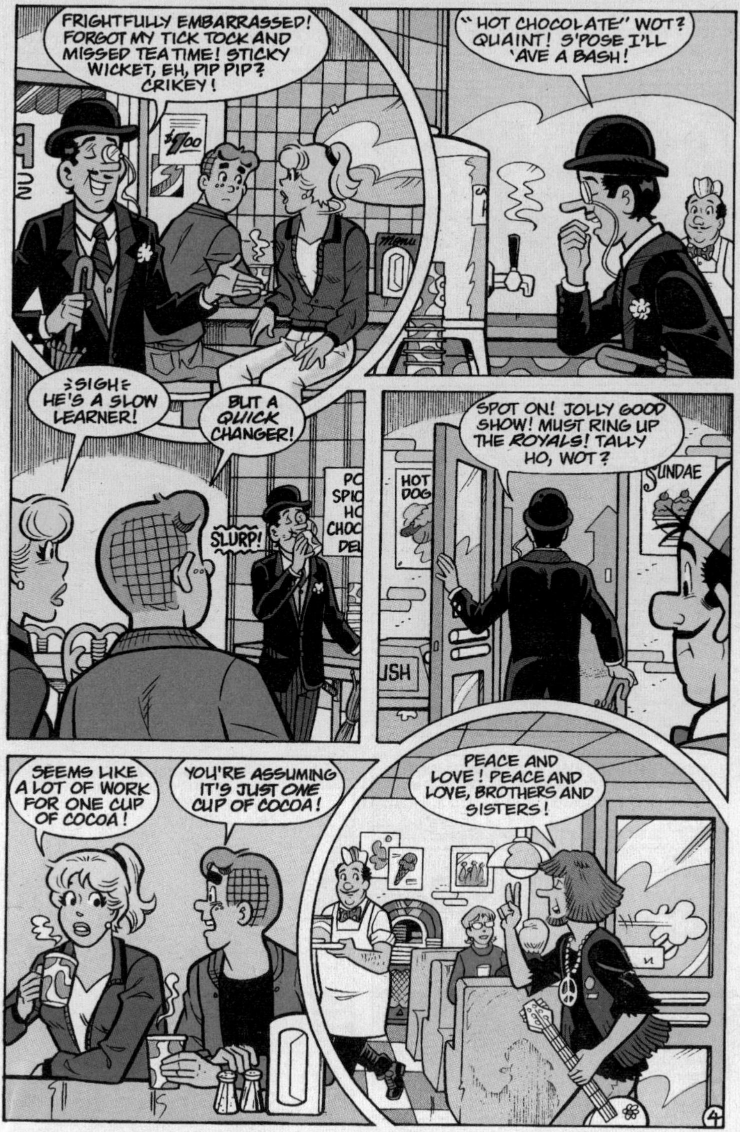
FRIGHTFULLY EMBARRASSED! FORGOT MY TICK TOCK AND MISSED TEA TIME! STICKY WICKET, EH, PIP PIP? CRIKEY!
"HOT CHOCOLATE" WOT? QUAINT! S'POSE I'LL 'AVE A BASH!
SIGH HE'S A SLOW LEARNER!
BUT A QUICK CHANGER!
SLURP!
SPOT ON! JOLLY GOOD SHOW! MUST RING UP THE ROYALS! TALLY HO, WOT?
SUNDAE
HOT DOG
PUSH
SEEMS LIKE A LOT OF WORK FOR ONE CUP OF COCOA!
YOU'RE ASSUMING IT'S JUST ONE CUP OF COCOA!
PEACE AND LOVE! PEACE AND LOVE, BROTHERS AND SISTERS!
4

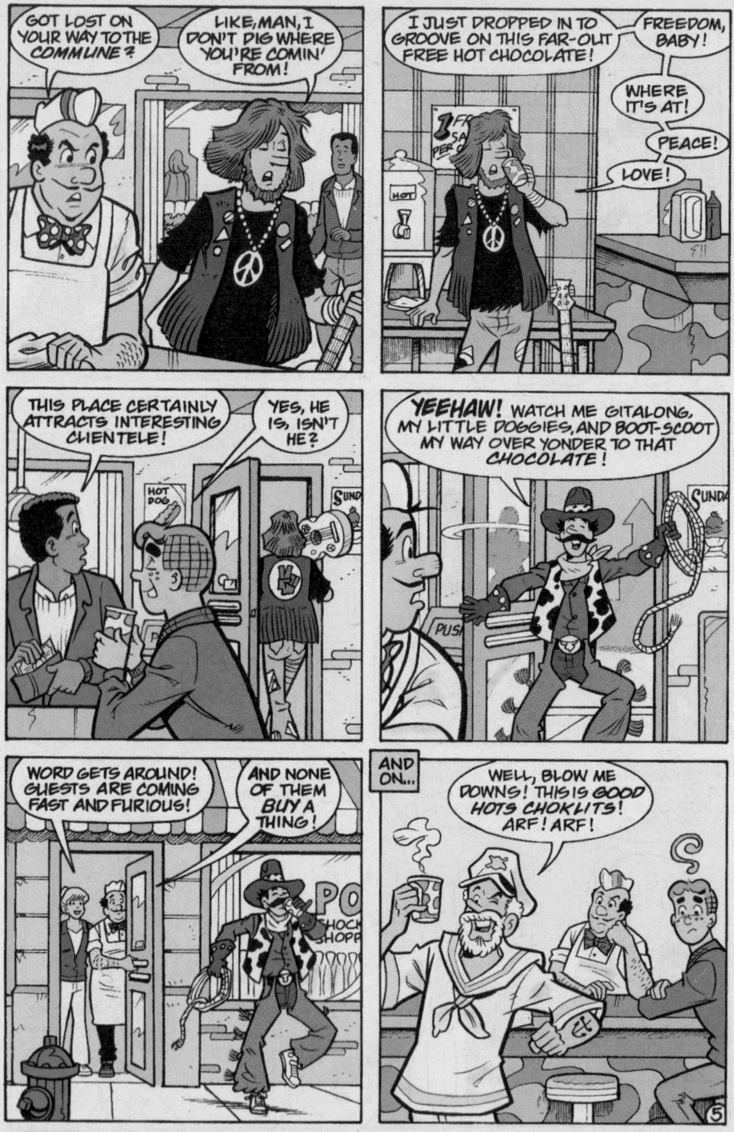
GOT LOST ON YOUR WAY TO THE COMMUNE?
LIKE, MAN, I DON'T DIG WHERE YOU'RE COMIN' FROM!
I JUST DROPPED IN TO GROOVE ON THIS FAR-OUT FREE HOT CHOCOLATE!
FREEDOM, BABY!
WHERE IT'S AT!
PEACE!
LOVE!
HOT
THIS PLACE CERTAINLY ATTRACTS INTERESTING CLIENTELE!
YES, HE IS, ISN'T HE?
HOT DOG
YEEHAW! WATCH ME GITALONG, MY LITTLE DOGGIES, AND BOOT-SCOOT MY WAY OVER YONDER TO THAT CHOCOLATE!
PUSH
WORD GETS AROUND! GUESTS ARE COMING FAST AND FURIOUS!
AND NONE OF THEM BUY A THING!
AND ON...
WELL, BLOW ME DOWNS! THIS IS GOOD HOTS CHOKLITS! ARF! ARF!
5

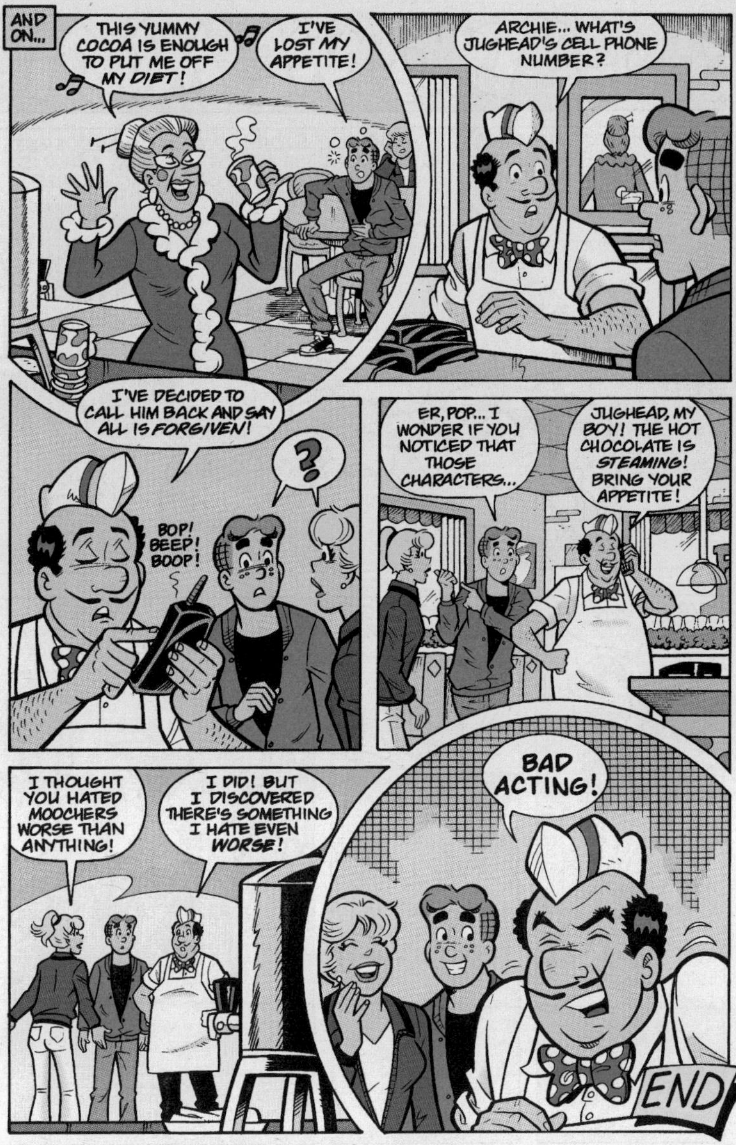
AND ON...
THIS YUMMY COCOA IS ENOUGH TO PUT ME OFF MY DIET!
I'VE LOST MY APPETITE!
ARCHIE... WHAT'S JUGHEAD'S CELL PHONE NUMBER?
I'VE DECIDED TO CALL HIM BACK AND SAY ALL IS FORGIVEN!
BOP! BEEP! BOOP!
?
ER, POP... I WONDER IF YOU NOTICED THAT THOSE CHARACTERS...
JUGHEAD, MY BOY! THE HOT CHOCOLATE IS STEAMING! BRING YOUR APPETITE!
I THOUGHT YOU HATED MOOCHERS WORSE THAN ANYTHING!
I DID! BUT I DISCOVERED THERE'S SOMETHING I HATE EVEN WORSE!
BAD ACTING!
END

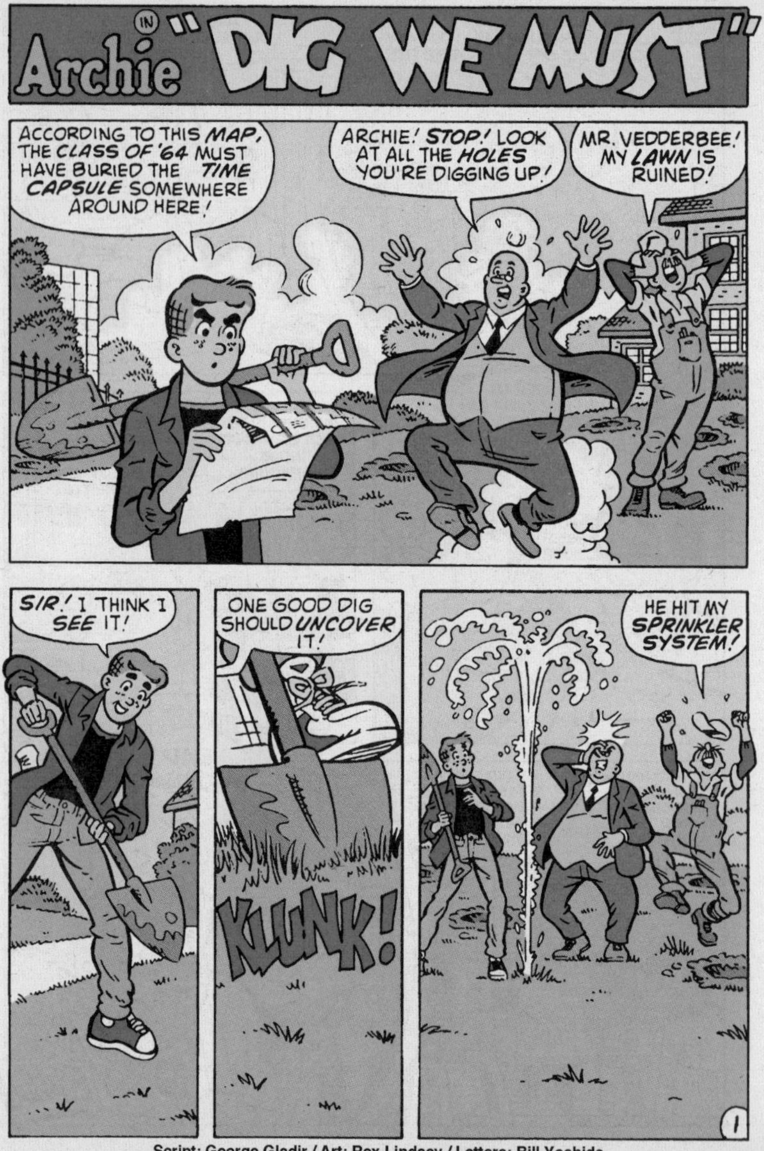
Archie in "DIG WE MUST"
ACCORDING TO THIS MAP, THE CLASS OF '64 MUST HAVE BURIED THE TIME CAPSULE SOMEWHERE AROUND HERE!
ARCHIE! STOP! LOOK AT ALL THE HOLES YOU'RE DIGGING UP!
MR. VEDDERBEE! MY LAWN IS RUINED!
SIR! I THINK I SEE IT!
ONE GOOD DIG SHOULD UNCOVER IT!
KLUNK!
HE HIT MY SPRINKLER SYSTEM!
1

Script: George Gladir / Art: Rex Lindsey / Letters: Bill Yoshida

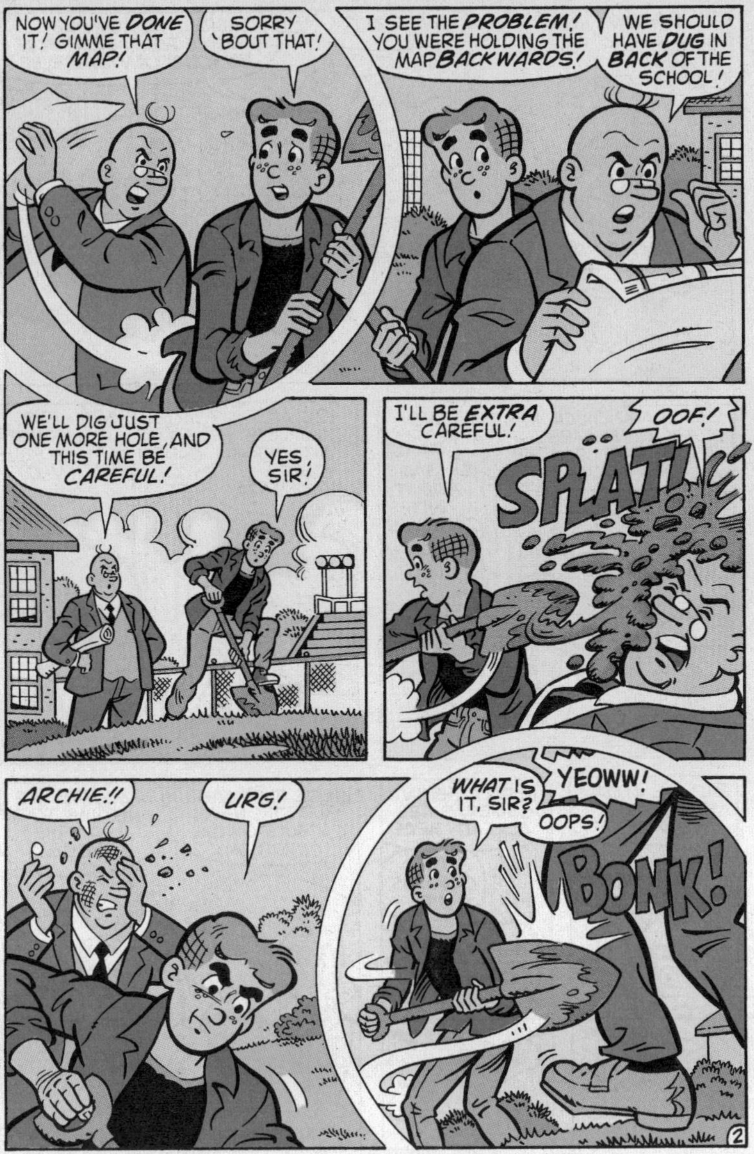
NOW YOU'VE DONE IT! GIMME THAT MAP!
SORRY 'BOUT THAT!
I SEE THE PROBLEM! YOU WERE HOLDING THE MAP BACKWARDS!
WE SHOULD HAVE DUG IN BACK OF THE SCHOOL!
WE'LL DIG JUST ONE MORE HOLE, AND THIS TIME BE CAREFUL!
YES, SIR!
I'LL BE EXTRA CAREFUL!
OOF!
SPLAT!
ARCHIE!!
URG!
WHAT IS IT, SIR?
YEOWW!
OOPS!
BONK!
2

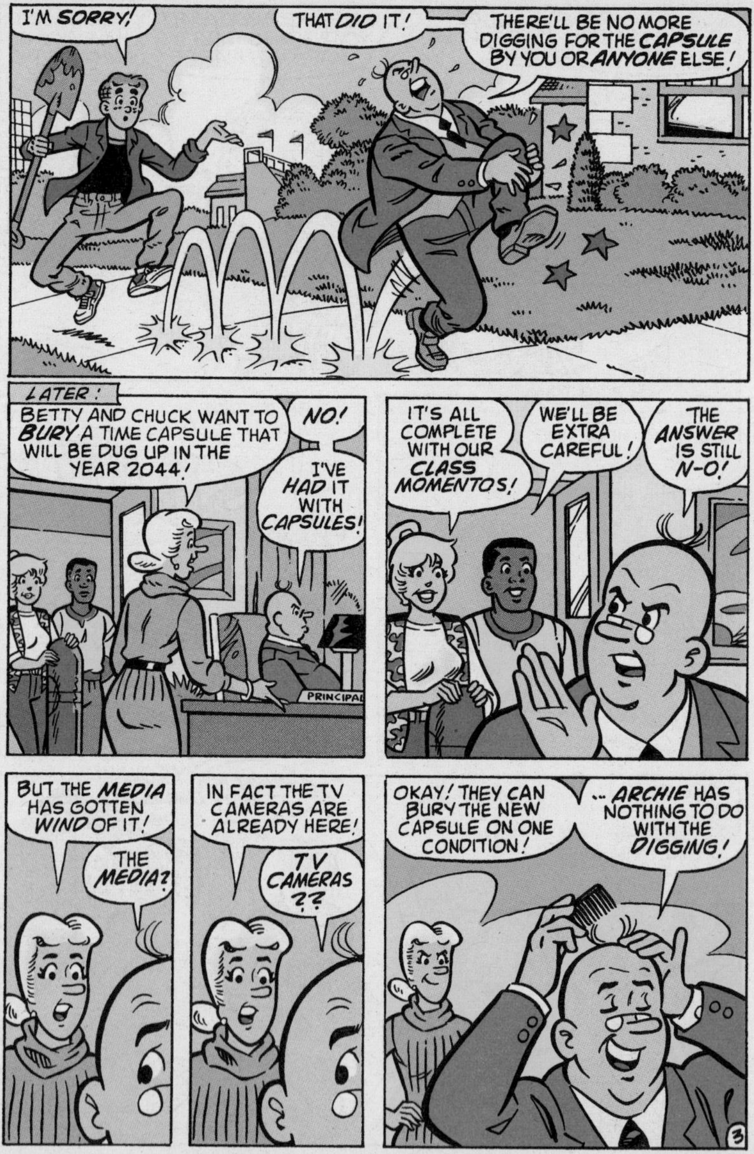

I'M SORRY!
THAT DID IT!
THERE'LL BE NO MORE DIGGING FOR THE CAPSULE BY YOU OR ANYONE ELSE!
LATER:
BETTY AND CHUCK WANT TO BURY A TIME CAPSULE THAT WILL BE DUG UP IN THE YEAR 2044!
NO!
I'VE HAD IT WITH CAPSULES!
PRINCIPAL
IT'S ALL COMPLETE WITH OUR CLASS MOMENTOS!
WE'LL BE EXTRA CAREFUL!
THE ANSWER IS STILL N-O!
BUT THE MEDIA HAS GOTTEN WIND OF IT!
THE MEDIA?
IN FACT THE TV CAMERAS ARE ALREADY HERE!
TV CAMERAS ??
OKAY! THEY CAN BURY THE NEW CAPSULE ON ONE CONDITION!
... ARCHIE HAS NOTHING TO DO WITH THE DIGGING!
3

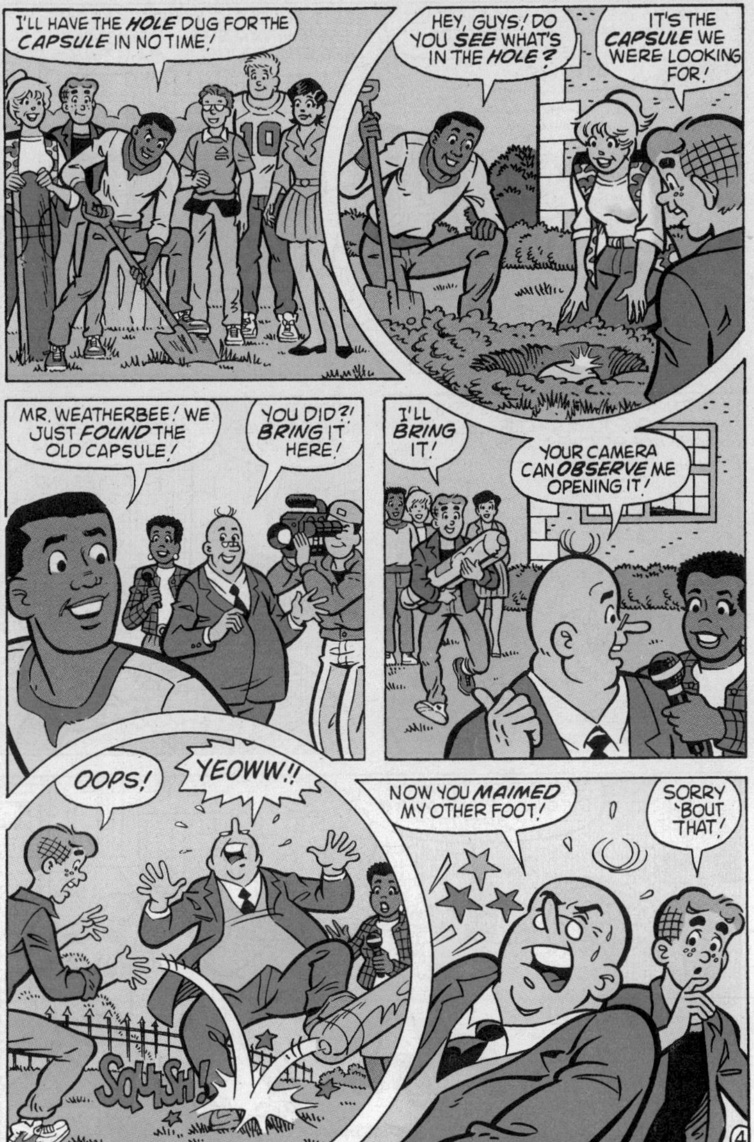
I'LL HAVE THE HOLE DUG FOR THE CAPSULE IN NO TIME!
HEY, GUYS! DO YOU SEE WHAT'S IN THE HOLE?
IT'S THE CAPSULE WE WERE LOOKING FOR!
MR. WEATHERBEE! WE JUST FOUND THE OLD CAPSULE!
YOU DID?! BRING IT HERE!
I'LL BRING IT!
YOUR CAMERA CAN OBSERVE ME OPENING IT!
OOPS!
YEOWW!!
SQUISH!
NOW YOU MAIMED MY OTHER FOOT!
SORRY 'BOUT THAT!
4

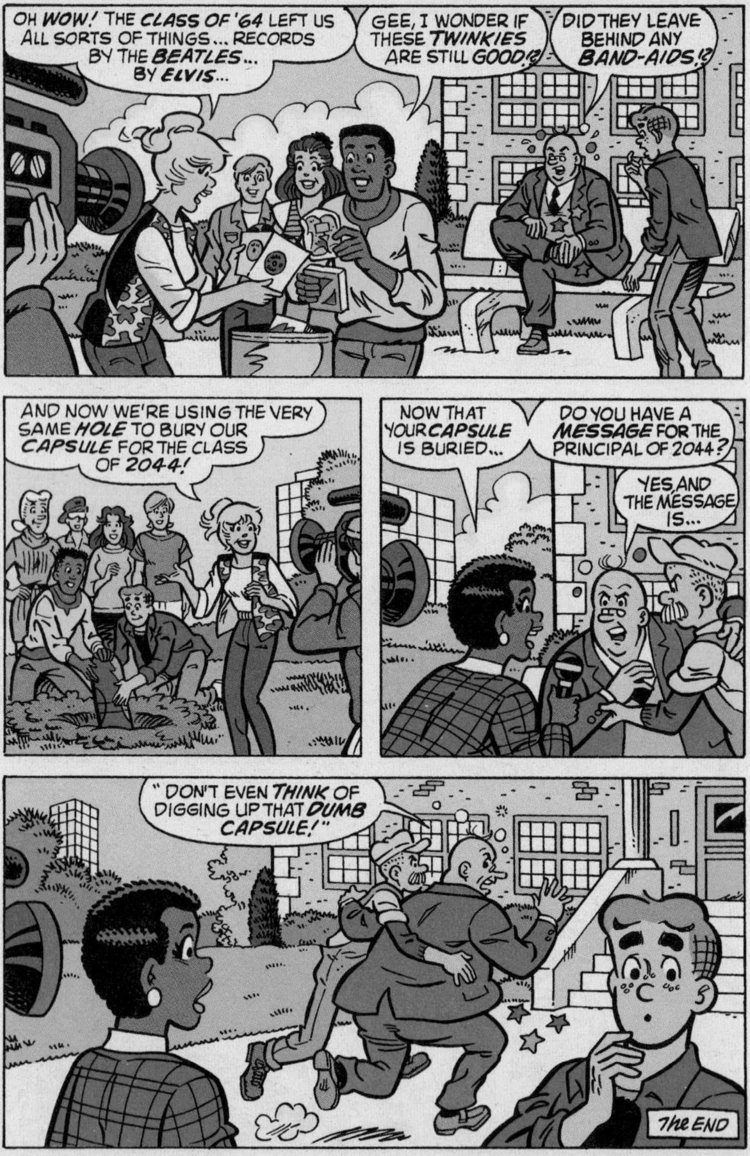
OH WOW! THE CLASS OF '64 LEFT US ALL SORTS OF THINGS... RECORDS BY THE BEATLES... BY ELVIS...
GEE, I WONDER IF THESE TWINKIES ARE STILL GOOD!?
DID THEY LEAVE BEHIND ANY BAND-AIDS!?
AND NOW WE'RE USING THE VERY SAME HOLE TO BURY OUR CAPSULE FOR THE CLASS OF 2044!
NOW THAT YOUR CAPSULE IS BURIED...
DO YOU HAVE A MESSAGE FOR THE PRINCIPAL OF 2044?
YES, AND THE MESSAGE IS...
"DON'T EVEN THINK OF DIGGING UP THAT DUMB CAPSULE!"
The END

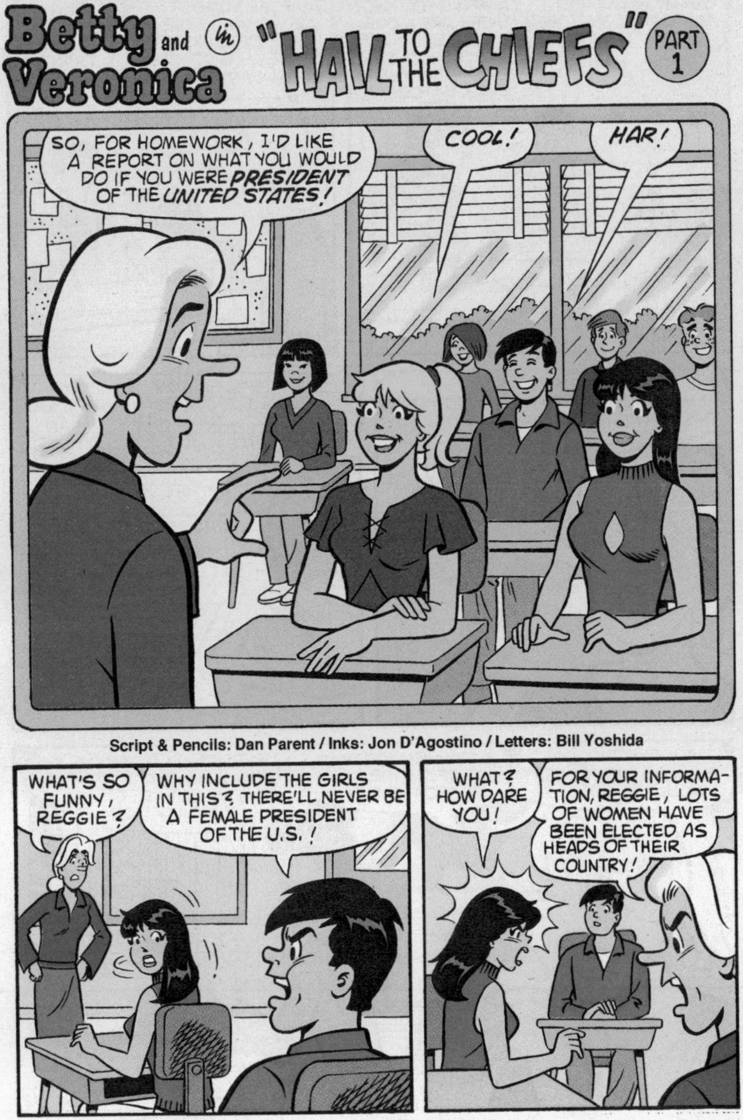
Betty and Veronica in "HAIL TO THE CHIEFS" PART 1
SO, FOR HOMEWORK, I'D LIKE A REPORT ON WHAT YOU WOULD DO IF YOU WERE PRESIDENT OF THE UNITED STATES!
COOL!
HAR!
Script & Pencils: Dan Parent / Inks: Jon D'Agostino / Letters: Bill Yoshida
WHAT'S SO FUNNY, REGGIE?
WHY INCLUDE THE GIRLS IN THIS? THERE'LL NEVER BE A FEMALE PRESIDENT OF THE U.S.!
WHAT? HOW DARE YOU!
FOR YOUR INFORMATION, REGGIE, LOTS OF WOMEN HAVE BEEN ELECTED AS HEADS OF THEIR COUNTRY!

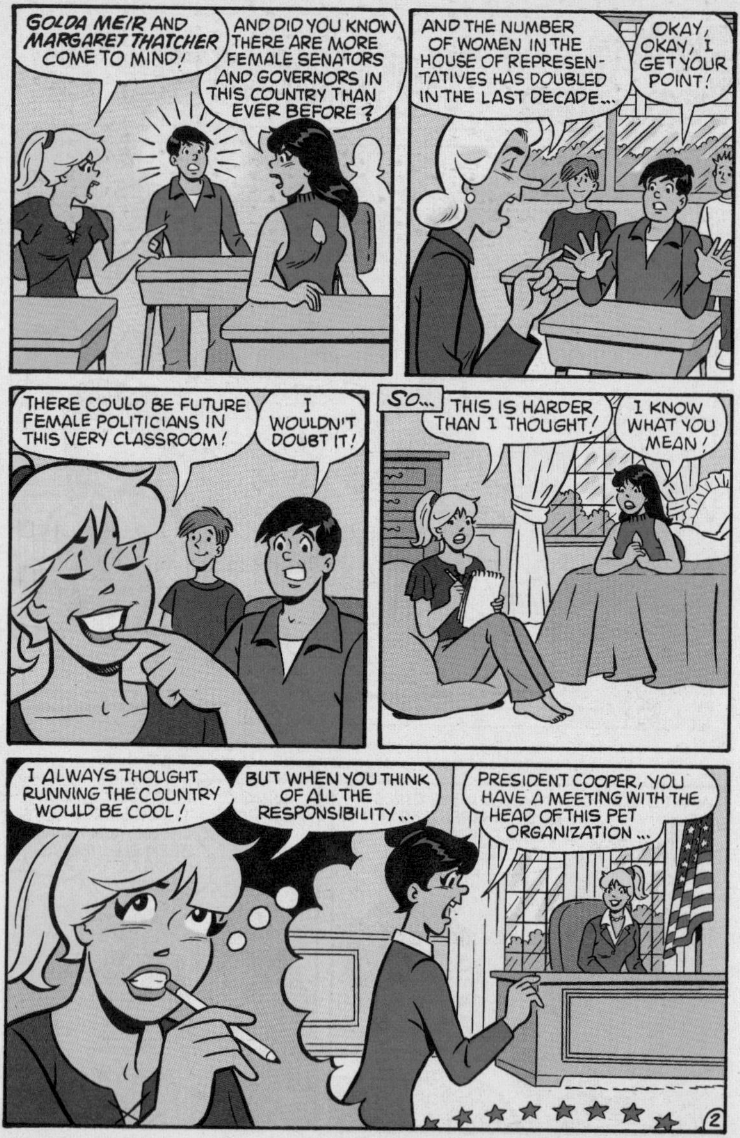

GOLDA MEIR AND MARGARET THATCHER COME TO MIND!
AND DID YOU KNOW THERE ARE MORE FEMALE SENATORS AND GOVERNORS IN THIS COUNTRY THAN EVER BEFORE?
AND THE NUMBER OF WOMEN IN THE HOUSE OF REPRESEN-TATIVES HAS DOUBLED IN THE LAST DECADE...
OKAY, OKAY, I GET YOUR POINT!
THERE COULD BE FUTURE FEMALE POLITICIANS IN THIS VERY CLASSROOM!
I WOULDN'T DOUBT IT!
SO...
THIS IS HARDER THAN I THOUGHT!
I KNOW WHAT YOU MEAN!
I ALWAYS THOUGHT RUNNING THE COUNTRY WOULD BE COOL!
BUT WHEN YOU THINK OF ALL THE RESPONSIBILITY...
PRESIDENT COOPER, YOU HAVE A MEETING WITH THE HEAD OF THIS PET ORGANIZATION...
2

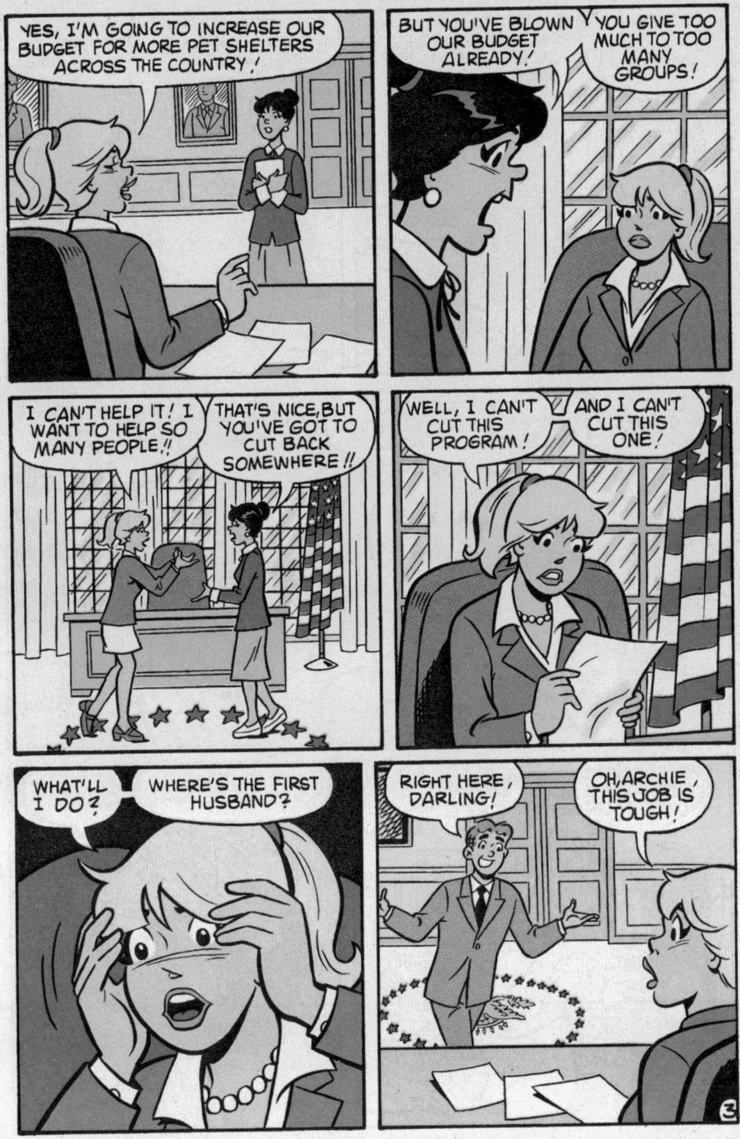
YES, I'M GOING TO INCREASE OUR BUDGET FOR MORE PET SHELTERS ACROSS THE COUNTRY!
BUT YOU'VE BLOWN OUR BUDGET ALREADY!
YOU GIVE TOO MUCH TO TOO MANY GROUPS!
I CAN'T HELP IT! I WANT TO HELP SO MANY PEOPLE!!
THAT'S NICE, BUT YOU'VE GOT TO CUT BACK SOMEWHERE!!
WELL, I CAN'T CUT THIS PROGRAM!
AND I CAN'T CUT THIS ONE!
WHAT'LL I DO?
WHERE'S THE FIRST HUSBAND?
RIGHT HERE, DARLING!
OH, ARCHIE, THIS JOB IS TOUGH!
3

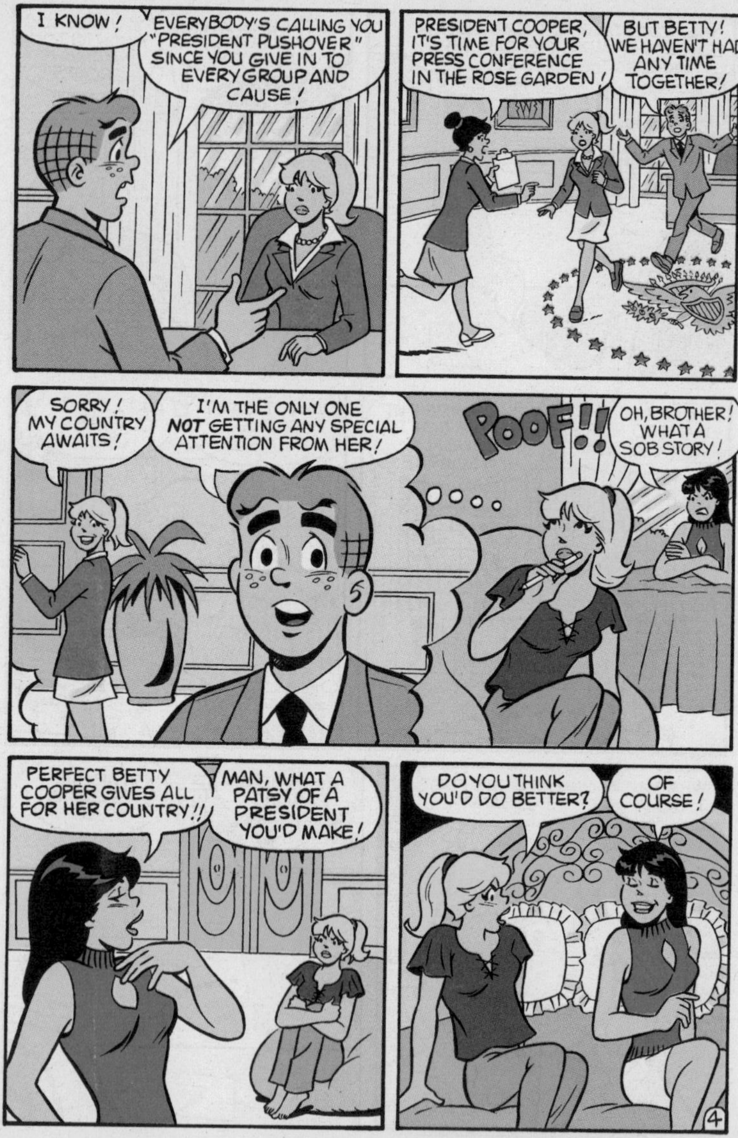
I KNOW!
EVERYBODY'S CALLING YOU "PRESIDENT PUSHOVER" SINCE YOU GIVE IN TO EVERY GROUP AND CAUSE!
PRESIDENT COOPER, IT'S TIME FOR YOUR PRESS CONFERENCE IN THE ROSE GARDEN!
BUT BETTY! WE HAVEN'T HAD ANY TIME TOGETHER!
SORRY! MY COUNTRY AWAITS!
I'M THE ONLY ONE NOT GETTING ANY SPECIAL ATTENTION FROM HER!
POOF!!
OH, BROTHER! WHAT A SOB STORY!
PERFECT BETTY COOPER GIVES ALL FOR HER COUNTRY!!
MAN, WHAT A PATSY OF A PRESIDENT YOU'D MAKE!
DO YOU THINK YOU'D DO BETTER?
OF COURSE!
4

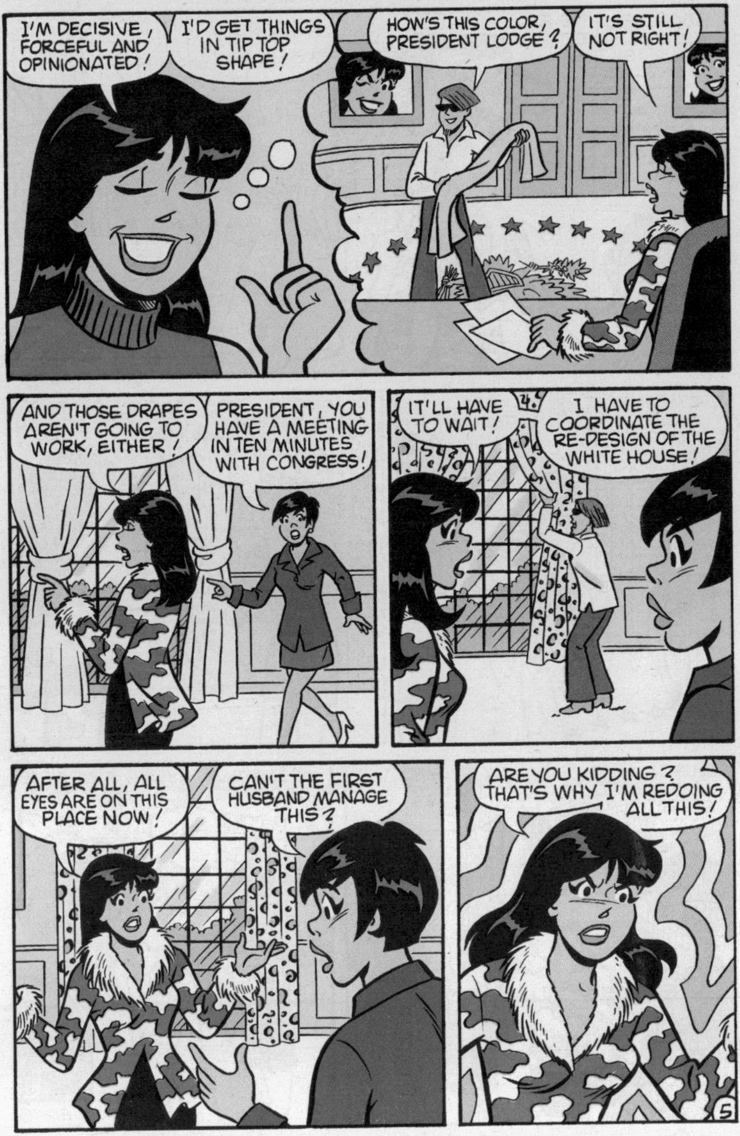
I'M DECISIVE, FORCEFUL AND OPINIONATED!
I'D GET THINGS IN TIP TOP SHAPE!
HOW'S THIS COLOR, PRESIDENT LODGE?
IT'S STILL NOT RIGHT!
AND THOSE DRAPES AREN'T GOING TO WORK, EITHER!
PRESIDENT, YOU HAVE A MEETING IN TEN MINUTES WITH CONGRESS!
IT'LL HAVE TO WAIT!
I HAVE TO COORDINATE THE RE-DESIGN OF THE WHITE HOUSE!
AFTER ALL, ALL EYES ARE ON THIS PLACE NOW!
CAN'T THE FIRST HUSBAND MANAGE THIS?
ARE YOU KIDDING? THAT'S WHY I'M REDOING ALL THIS!
5

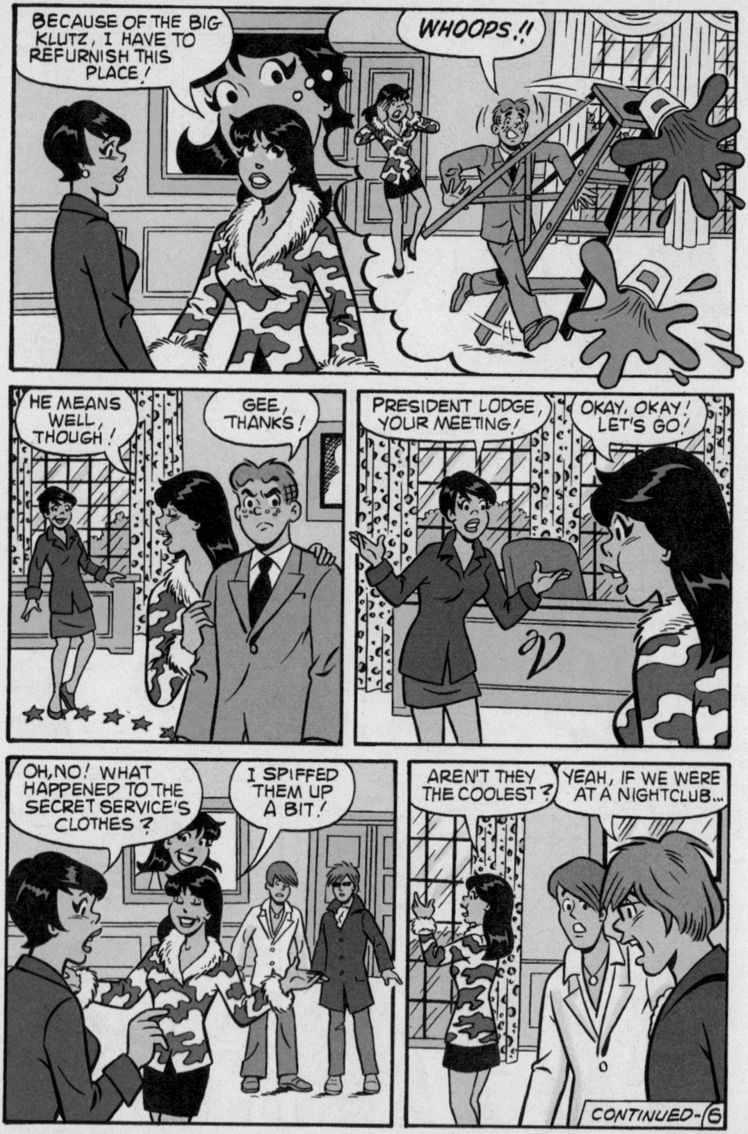
BECAUSE OF THE BIG KLUTZ, I HAVE TO REFURNISH THIS PLACE!
WHOOPS!!
HE MEANS WELL, THOUGH!
GEE, THANKS!
PRESIDENT LODGE, YOUR MEETING!
OKAY, OKAY! LET'S GO!
OH, NO! WHAT HAPPENED TO THE SECRET SERVICE'S CLOTHES?
I SPIFFED THEM UP A BIT!
AREN'T THEY THE COOLEST?
YEAH, IF WE WERE AT A NIGHTCLUB...
CONTINUED-6

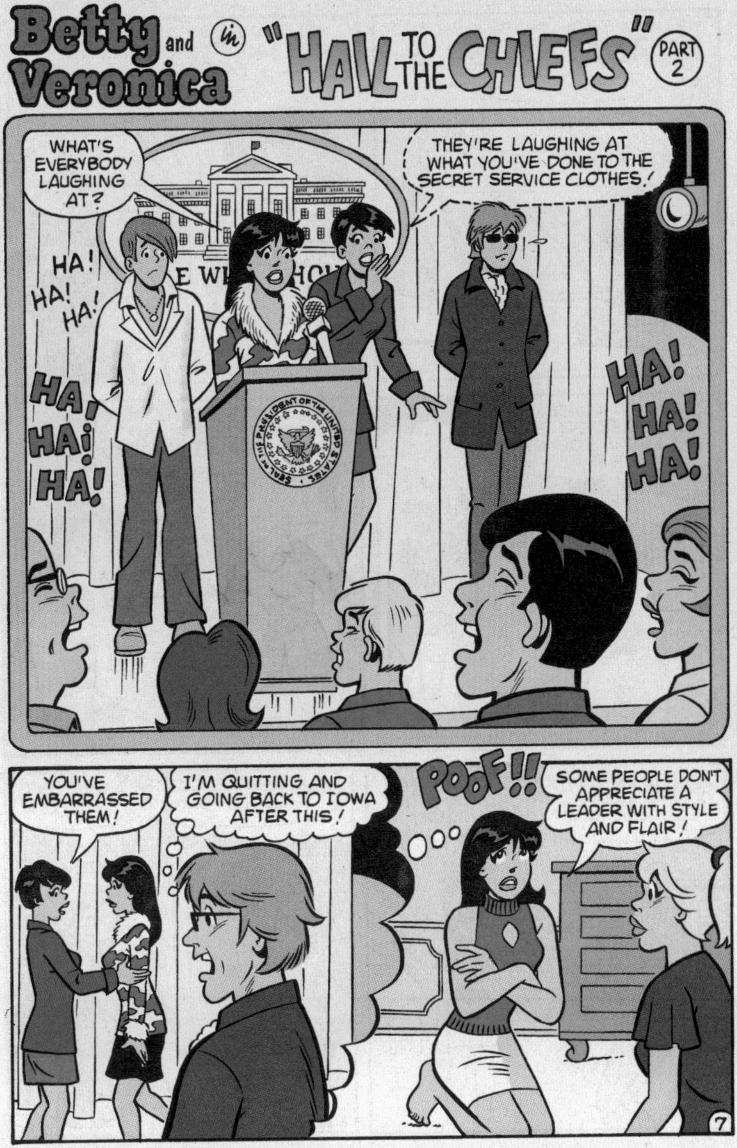

Betty and Veronica in "HAIL TO THE CHIEFS" PART 2
WHAT'S EVERYBODY LAUGHING AT?
THEY'RE LAUGHING AT WHAT YOU'VE DONE TO THE SECRET SERVICE CLOTHES!
HA! HA! HA!
HA! HA! HA!
HA! HA! HA!
YOU'VE EMBARRASSED THEM!
I'M QUITTING AND GOING BACK TO IOWA AFTER THIS!
POOF!!
SOME PEOPLE DON'T APPRECIATE A LEADER WITH STYLE AND FLAIR!

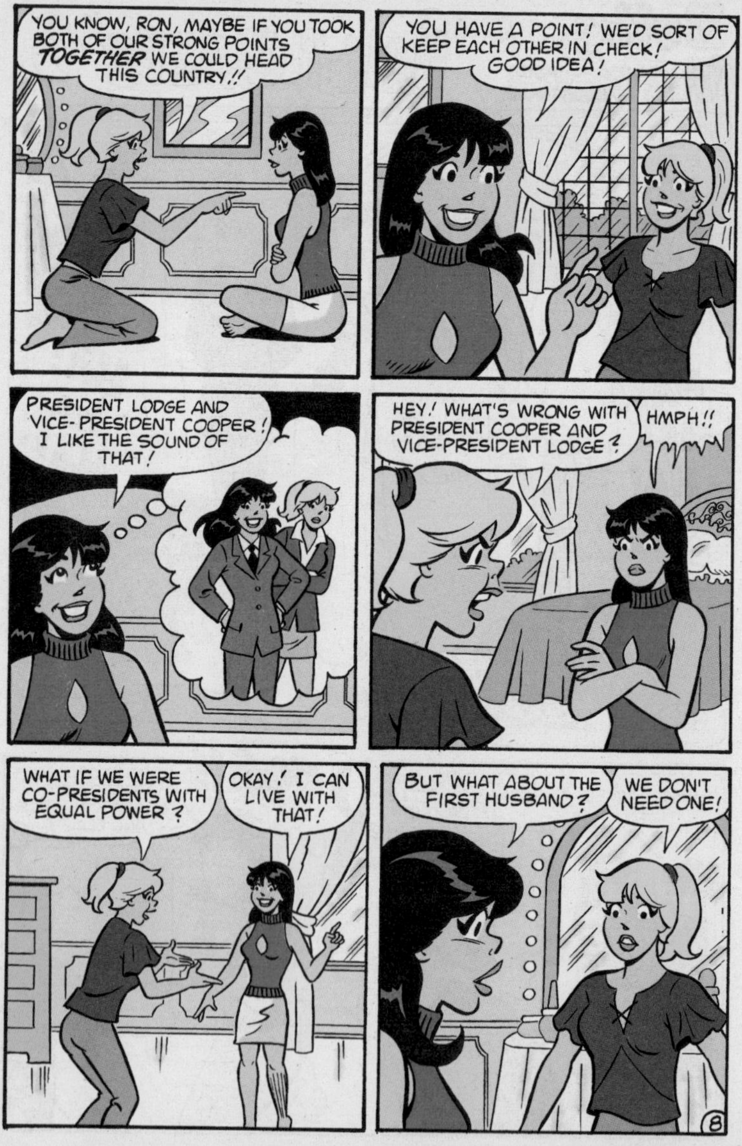
YOU KNOW, RON, MAYBE IF YOU TOOK BOTH OF OUR STRONG POINTS *TOGETHER* WE COULD HEAD THIS COUNTRY!!
YOU HAVE A POINT! WE'D SORT OF KEEP EACH OTHER IN CHECK! GOOD IDEA!
PRESIDENT LODGE AND VICE-PRESIDENT COOPER! I LIKE THE SOUND OF THAT!
HEY! WHAT'S WRONG WITH PRESIDENT COOPER AND VICE-PRESIDENT LODGE?
HMPH!!
WHAT IF WE WERE CO-PRESIDENTS WITH EQUAL POWER?
OKAY! I CAN LIVE WITH THAT!
BUT WHAT ABOUT THE FIRST HUSBAND?
WE DON'T NEED ONE!
8

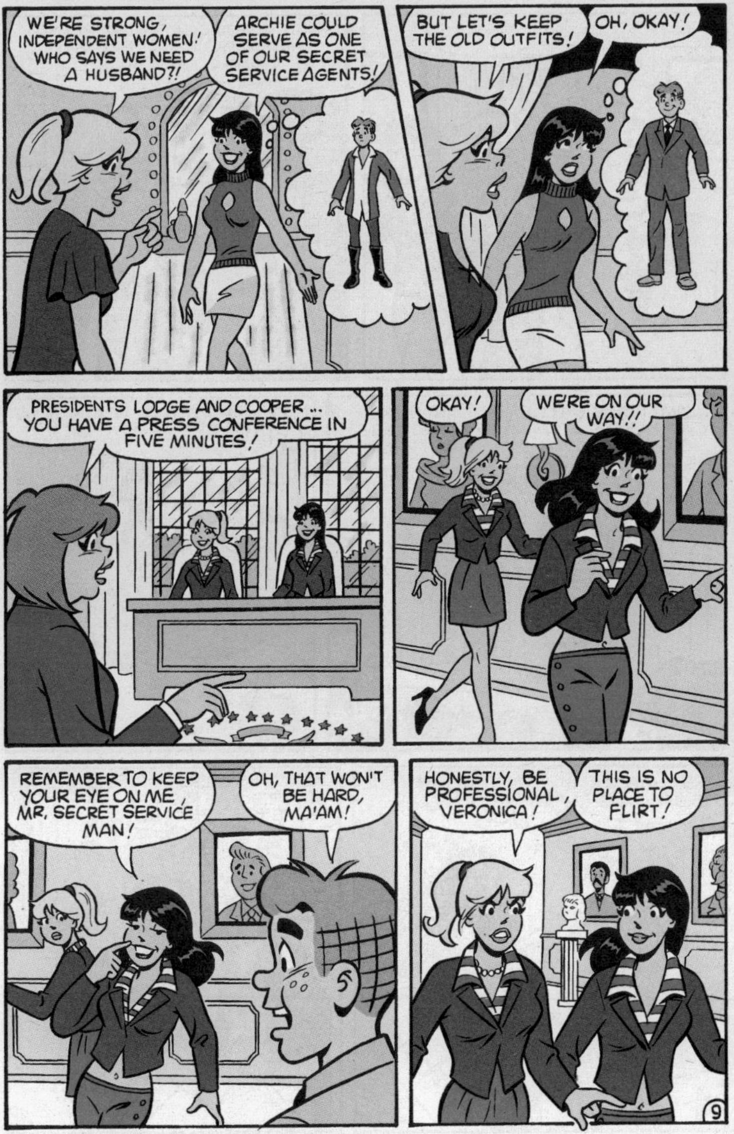
WE'RE STRONG, INDEPENDENT WOMEN! WHO SAYS WE NEED A HUSBAND?!
ARCHIE COULD SERVE AS ONE OF OUR SECRET SERVICE AGENTS!
BUT LET'S KEEP THE OLD OUTFITS!
OH, OKAY!
PRESIDENTS LODGE AND COOPER ... YOU HAVE A PRESS CONFERENCE IN FIVE MINUTES!
OKAY!
WE'RE ON OUR WAY!!
REMEMBER TO KEEP YOUR EYE ON ME, MR. SECRET SERVICE MAN!
OH, THAT WON'T BE HARD, MA'AM!
HONESTLY, BE PROFESSIONAL, VERONICA!
THIS IS NO PLACE TO FLIRT!
9

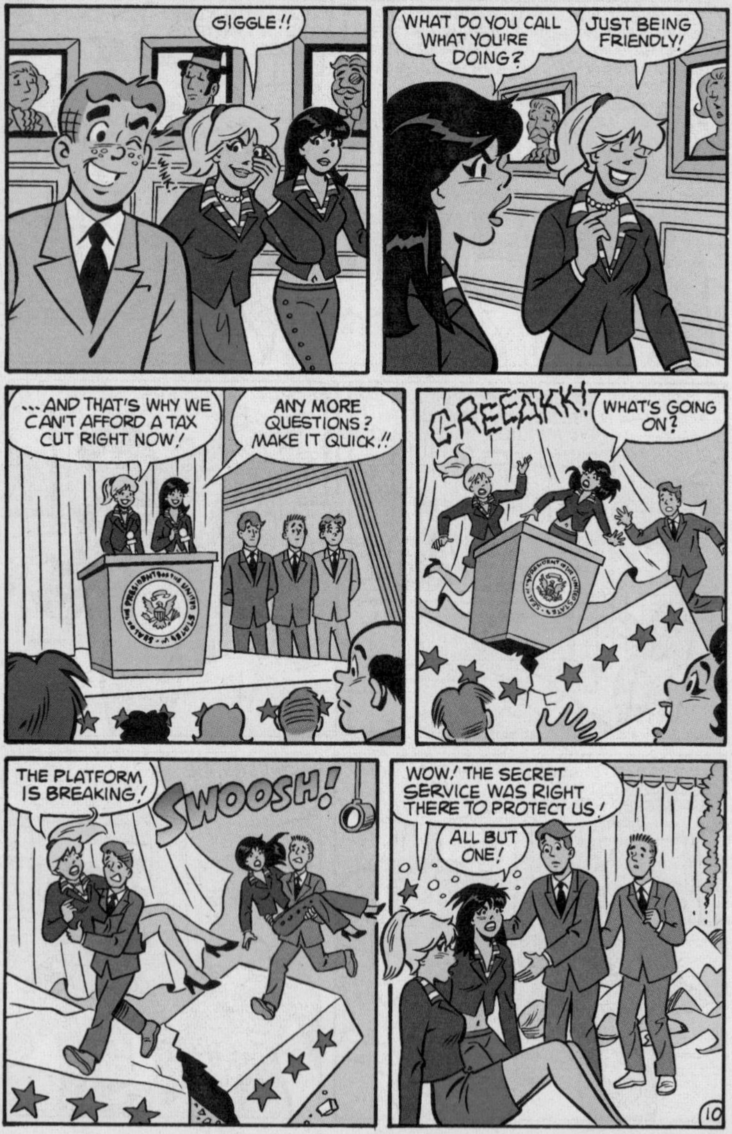
GIGGLE!!
WINK!
WHAT DO YOU CALL WHAT YOU'RE DOING?
JUST BEING FRIENDLY!
...AND THAT'S WHY WE CAN'T AFFORD A TAX CUT RIGHT NOW!
ANY MORE QUESTIONS? MAKE IT QUICK!!
CREEAKK!
WHAT'S GOING ON?
THE PLATFORM IS BREAKING!
SWOOSH!
WOW! THE SECRET SERVICE WAS RIGHT THERE TO PROTECT US!
ALL BUT ONE!
10

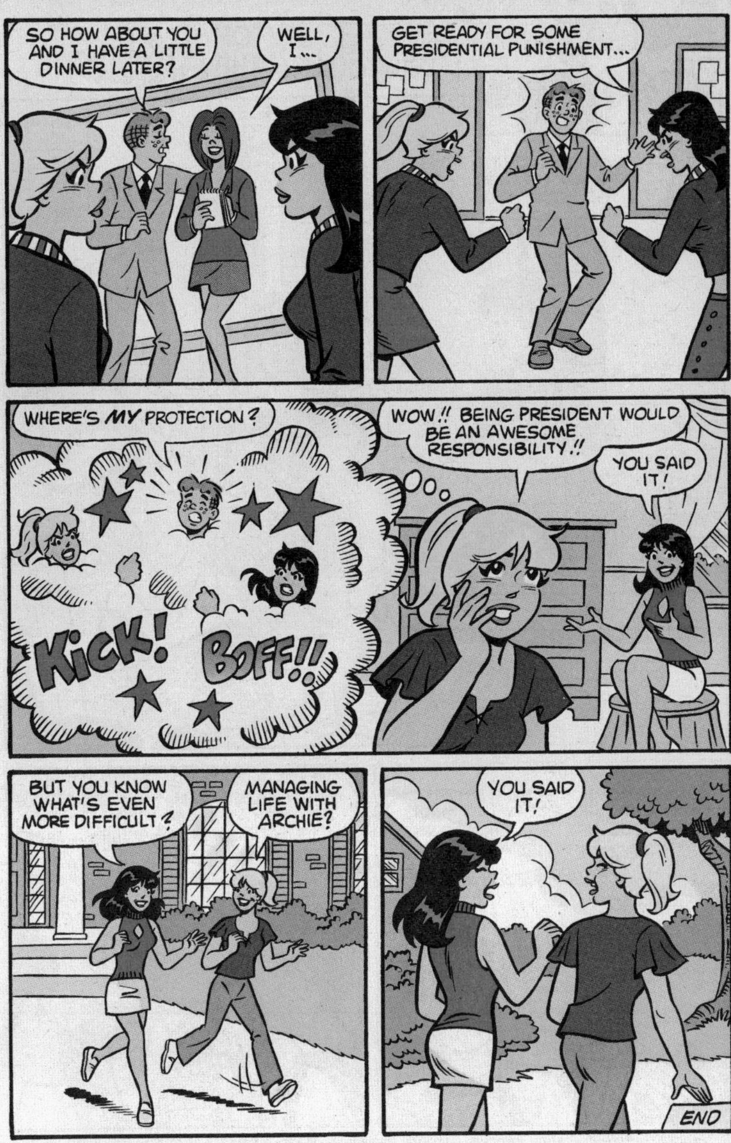
SO HOW ABOUT YOU AND I HAVE A LITTLE DINNER LATER?
WELL, I...
GET READY FOR SOME PRESIDENTIAL PUNISHMENT...
WHERE'S MY PROTECTION?
KICK!
BOFF!!
WOW!! BEING PRESIDENT WOULD BE AN AWESOME RESPONSIBILITY!!
YOU SAID IT!
BUT YOU KNOW WHAT'S EVEN MORE DIFFICULT?
MANAGING LIFE WITH ARCHIE?
YOU SAID IT!
END

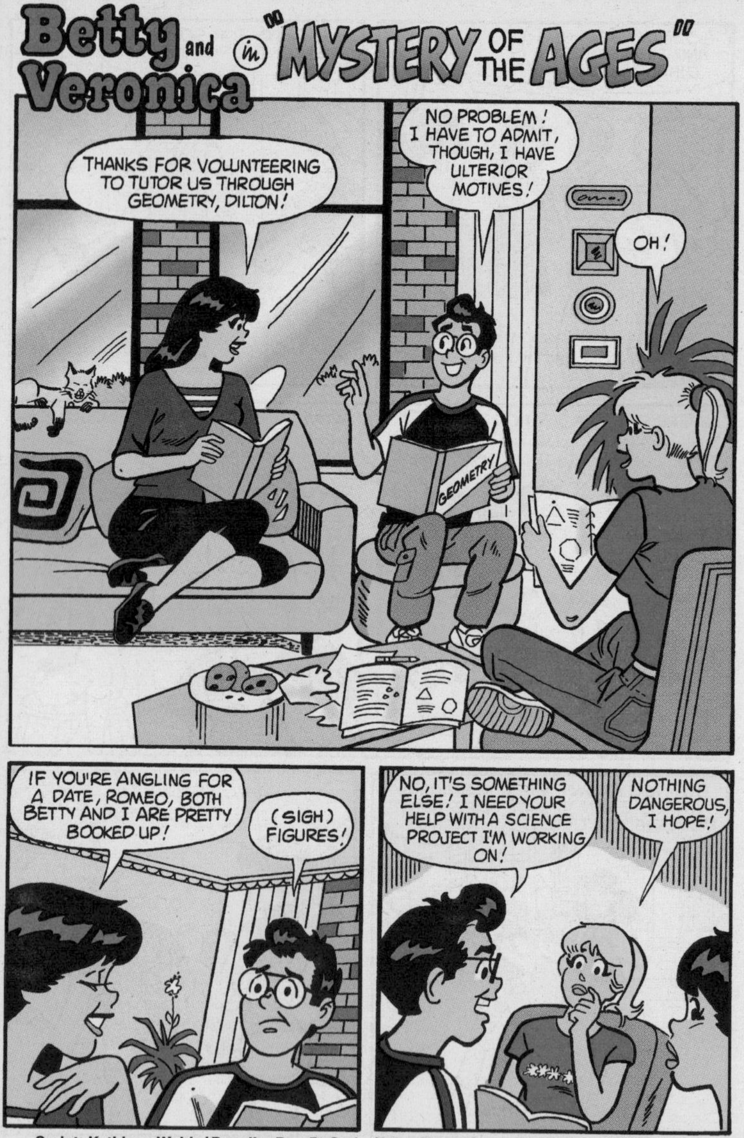
Betty and Veronica in "MYSTERY OF THE AGES"
THANKS FOR VOLUNTEERING TO TUTOR US THROUGH GEOMETRY, DILTON!
NO PROBLEM! I HAVE TO ADMIT, THOUGH, I HAVE ULTERIOR MOTIVES!
OH!
GEOMETRY
IF YOU'RE ANGLING FOR A DATE, ROMEO, BOTH BETTY AND I ARE PRETTY BOOKED UP!
(SIGH) FIGURES!
NO, IT'S SOMETHING ELSE! I NEED YOUR HELP WITH A SCIENCE PROJECT I'M WORKING ON!
NOTHING DANGEROUS, I HOPE!

Script: Kathleen Webb / Pencils: Dan DeCarlo / Inks: Henry Scarpelli / Letters: Bill Yoshida

Panel 1: ACTUALLY, IT FALLS UNDER THE BENIGN CATEGORY OF BEHAVIORAL SCIENCE!

WE DID OUR SCIENCE PROJECT ON THAT LAST YEAR!

Panel 2: YES... AND WE WON THE SCIENCE AWARD, TOO!

NO HARD FEELINGS, DILTON?

Panel 3: NONE TOWARDS YOU! IN FACT, SEEING YOUR SUCCESS, I CONSIDERED ASKING YOUR HELP WITH SOMETHING THAT'S BEEN INTRIGUING ME FOR SOME TIME!

Panel 4: I HAVE A LIST OF THINGS I'VE COMPILED THAT COME UNDER A VERY GENDER-SPECIFIC HEADING!

WHAT'S THAT?

Panel 5: "THINGS THAT ONLY THE FEMALE MIND COMPREHENDS"! I HOPE, PERHAPS, THAT YOU MIGHT BE ABLE TO ANSWER WHY!

WE'LL TRY!

Panel 6: FIRST, WHY DO GIRLS FEEL IT'S IMPORTANT TO HAVE SO MANY PAIRS OF SHOES?

OH, THAT'S AN EASY ONE!

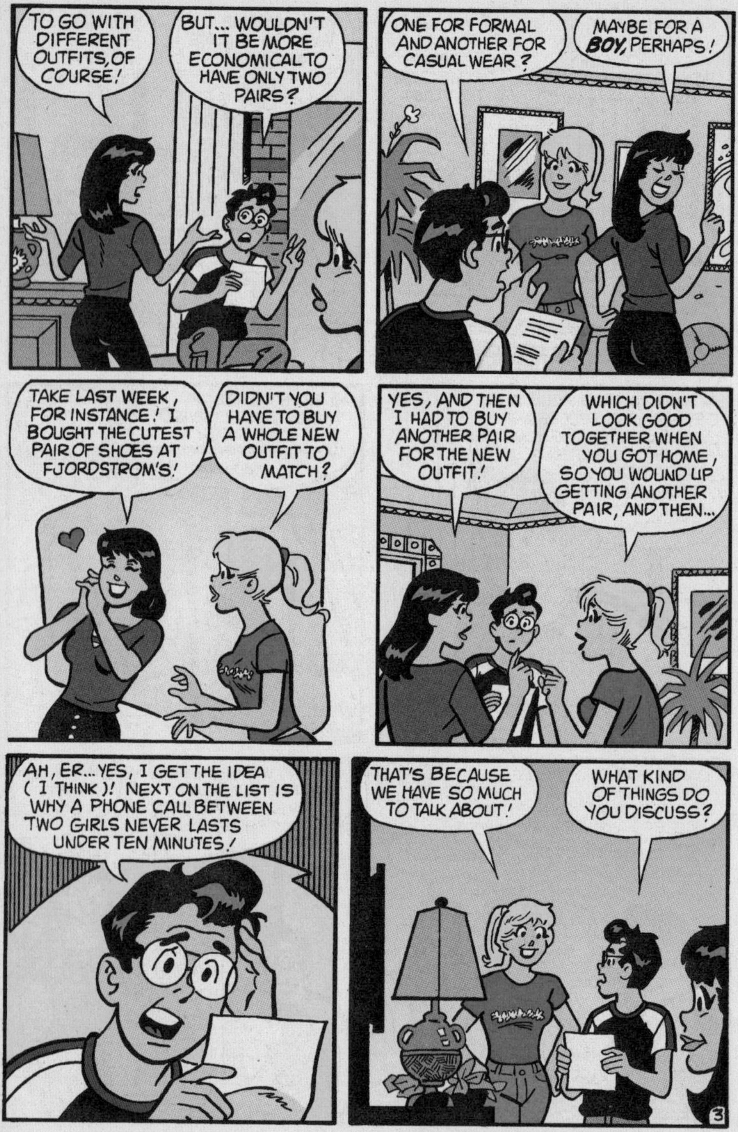
TO GO WITH DIFFERENT OUTFITS, OF COURSE!
BUT... WOULDN'T IT BE MORE ECONOMICAL TO HAVE ONLY TWO PAIRS?
ONE FOR FORMAL AND ANOTHER FOR CASUAL WEAR?
MAYBE FOR A BOY, PERHAPS!
TAKE LAST WEEK, FOR INSTANCE! I BOUGHT THE CUTEST PAIR OF SHOES AT FJORDSTROM'S!
DIDN'T YOU HAVE TO BUY A WHOLE NEW OUTFIT TO MATCH?
YES, AND THEN I HAD TO BUY ANOTHER PAIR FOR THE NEW OUTFIT!
WHICH DIDN'T LOOK GOOD TOGETHER WHEN YOU GOT HOME, SO YOU WOUND UP GETTING ANOTHER PAIR, AND THEN...
AH, ER... YES, I GET THE IDEA (I THINK)! NEXT ON THE LIST IS WHY A PHONE CALL BETWEEN TWO GIRLS NEVER LASTS UNDER TEN MINUTES!
THAT'S BECAUSE WE HAVE SO MUCH TO TALK ABOUT!
WHAT KIND OF THINGS DO YOU DISCUSS?
3

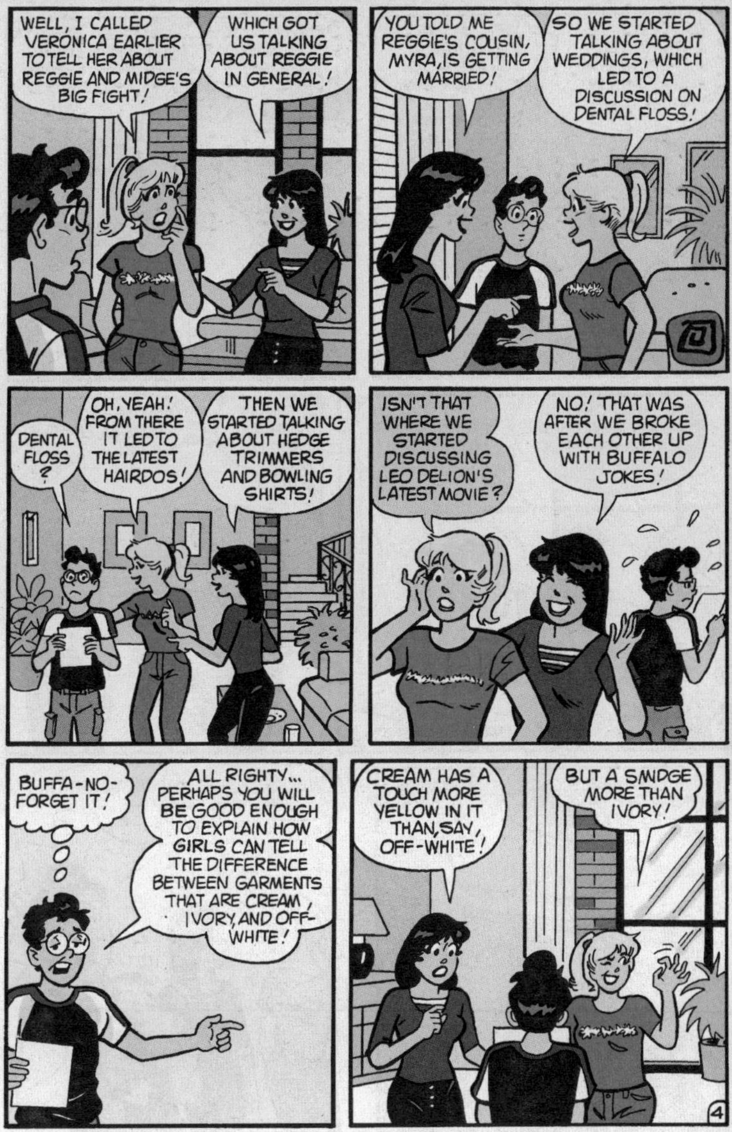
WELL, I CALLED VERONICA EARLIER TO TELL HER ABOUT REGGIE AND MIDGE'S BIG FIGHT!
WHICH GOT US TALKING ABOUT REGGIE IN GENERAL!
YOU TOLD ME REGGIE'S COUSIN, MYRA, IS GETTING MARRIED!
SO WE STARTED TALKING ABOUT WEDDINGS, WHICH LED TO A DISCUSSION ON DENTAL FLOSS!
DENTAL FLOSS?
OH, YEAH! FROM THERE IT LED TO THE LATEST HAIRDOS!
THEN WE STARTED TALKING ABOUT HEDGE TRIMMERS AND BOWLING SHIRTS!
ISN'T THAT WHERE WE STARTED DISCUSSING LEO DELION'S LATEST MOVIE?
NO! THAT WAS AFTER WE BROKE EACH OTHER UP WITH BUFFALO JOKES!
BUFFA-NO- FORGET IT!
ALL RIGHTY... PERHAPS YOU WILL BE GOOD ENOUGH TO EXPLAIN HOW GIRLS CAN TELL THE DIFFERENCE BETWEEN GARMENTS THAT ARE CREAM, IVORY, AND OFF-WHITE!
CREAM HAS A TOUCH MORE YELLOW IN IT THAN, SAY, OFF-WHITE!
BUT A SMIDGE MORE THAN IVORY!
4

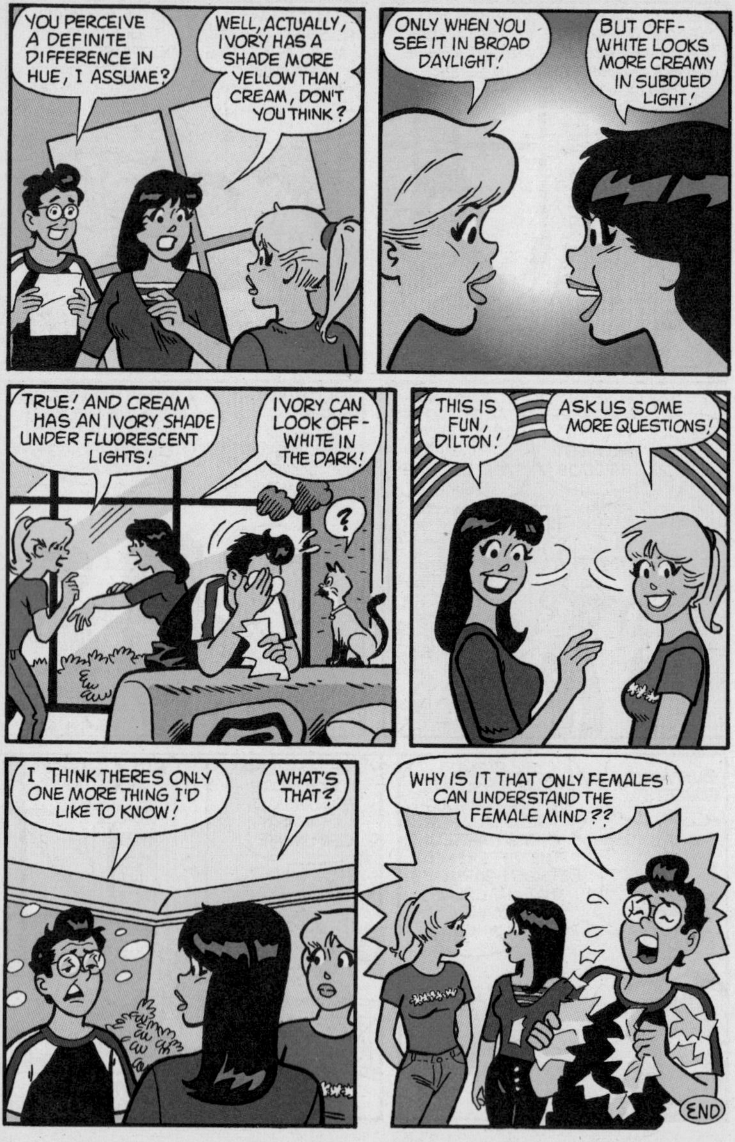
YOU PERCEIVE A DEFINITE DIFFERENCE IN HUE, I ASSUME?
WELL, ACTUALLY, IVORY HAS A SHADE MORE YELLOW THAN CREAM, DON'T YOU THINK?
ONLY WHEN YOU SEE IT IN BROAD DAYLIGHT!
BUT OFF-WHITE LOOKS MORE CREAMY IN SUBDUED LIGHT!
TRUE! AND CREAM HAS AN IVORY SHADE UNDER FLUORESCENT LIGHTS!
IVORY CAN LOOK OFF-WHITE IN THE DARK!
?
THIS IS FUN, DILTON!
ASK US SOME MORE QUESTIONS!
I THINK THERES ONLY ONE MORE THING I'D LIKE TO KNOW!
WHAT'S THAT?
WHY IS IT THAT ONLY FEMALES CAN UNDERSTAND THE FEMALE MIND??
END

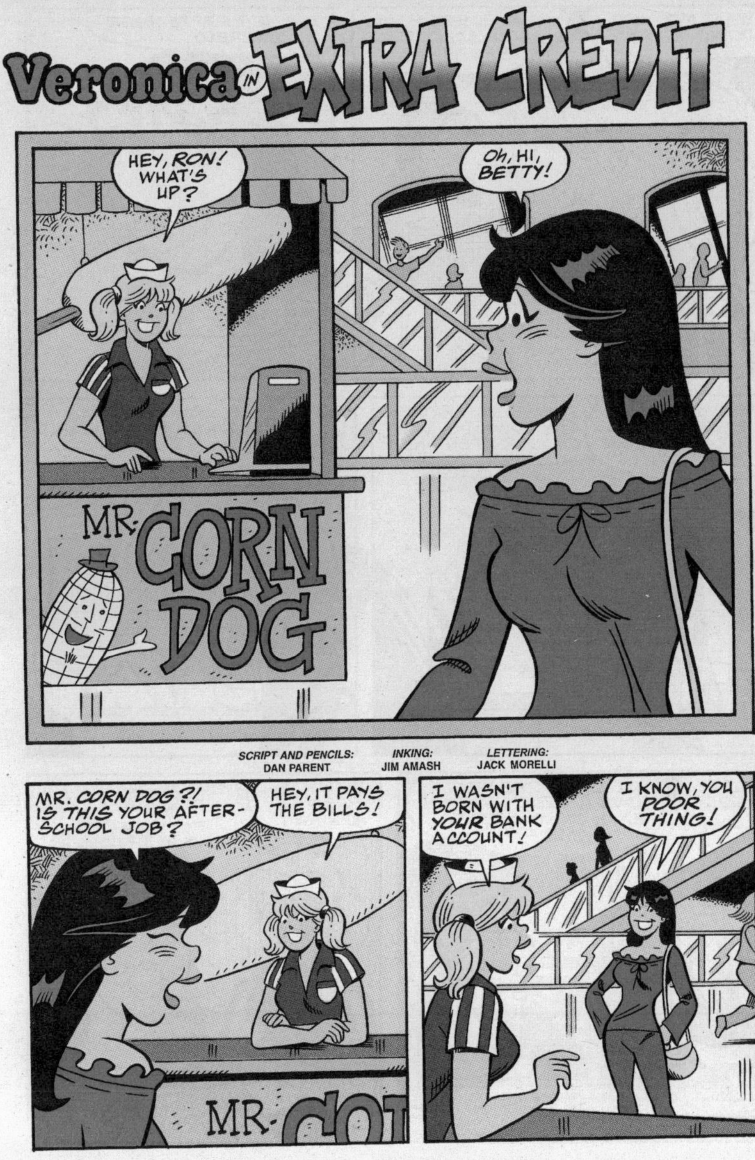
Veronica IN EXTRA CREDIT
HEY, RON! WHAT'S UP?
Oh, HI, BETTY!
MR. CORN DOG
SCRIPT AND PENCILS: DAN PARENT
INKING: JIM AMASH
LETTERING: JACK MORELLI
MR. CORN DOG?! IS THIS YOUR AFTER-SCHOOL JOB?
HEY, IT PAYS THE BILLS!
I WASN'T BORN WITH YOUR BANK ACCOUNT!
I KNOW, YOU POOR THING!

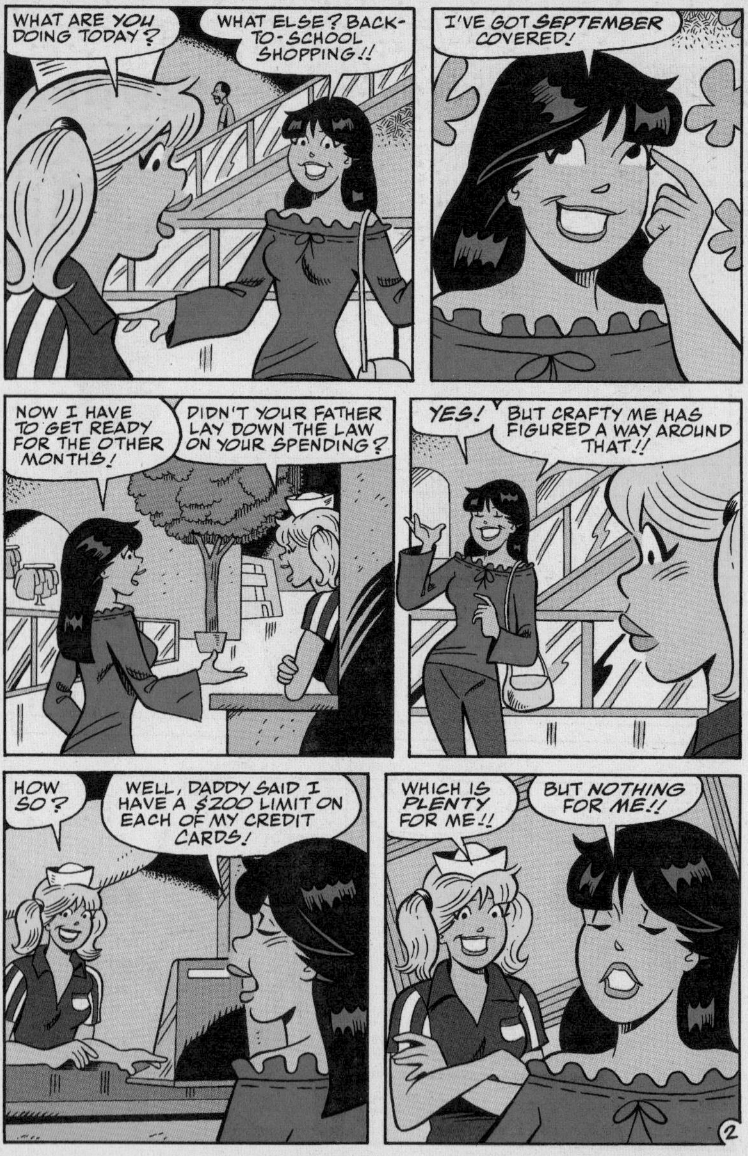
WHAT ARE YOU DOING TODAY?
WHAT ELSE? BACK-TO-SCHOOL SHOPPING!!
I'VE GOT SEPTEMBER COVERED!
NOW I HAVE TO GET READY FOR THE OTHER MONTHS!
DIDN'T YOUR FATHER LAY DOWN THE LAW ON YOUR SPENDING?
YES!
BUT CRAFTY ME HAS FIGURED A WAY AROUND THAT!!
HOW SO?
WELL, DADDY SAID I HAVE A $200 LIMIT ON EACH OF MY CREDIT CARDS!
WHICH IS PLENTY FOR ME!!
BUT NOTHING FOR ME!!
2

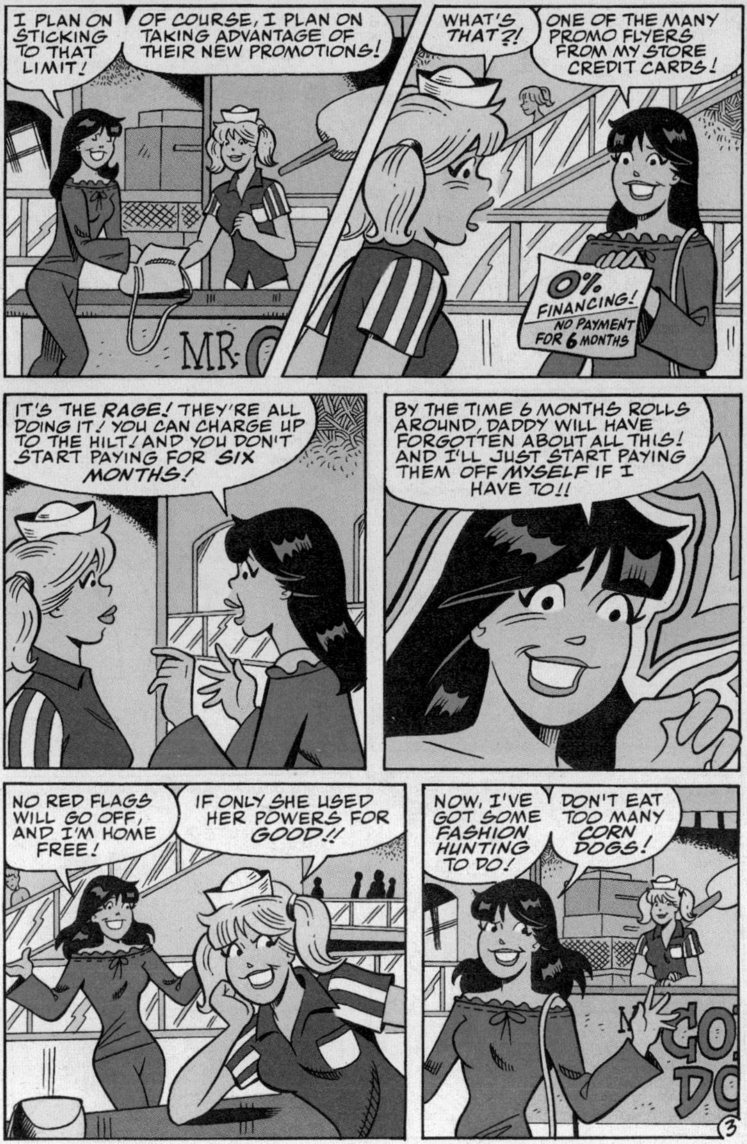

I PLAN ON STICKING TO THAT LIMIT!
OF COURSE, I PLAN ON TAKING ADVANTAGE OF THEIR NEW PROMOTIONS!
MR-
WHAT'S THAT?!
ONE OF THE MANY PROMO FLYERS FROM MY STORE CREDIT CARDS!
0% FINANCING! NO PAYMENT FOR 6 MONTHS
IT'S THE RAGE! THEY'RE ALL DOING IT! YOU CAN CHARGE UP TO THE HILT! AND YOU DON'T START PAYING FOR SIX MONTHS!
BY THE TIME 6 MONTHS ROLLS AROUND, DADDY WILL HAVE FORGOTTEN ABOUT ALL THIS! AND I'LL JUST START PAYING THEM OFF MYSELF IF I HAVE TO!!
NO RED FLAGS WILL GO OFF, AND I'M HOME FREE!
IF ONLY SHE USED HER POWERS FOR GOOD!!
NOW, I'VE GOT SOME FASHION HUNTING TO DO!
DON'T EAT TOO MANY CORN DOGS!

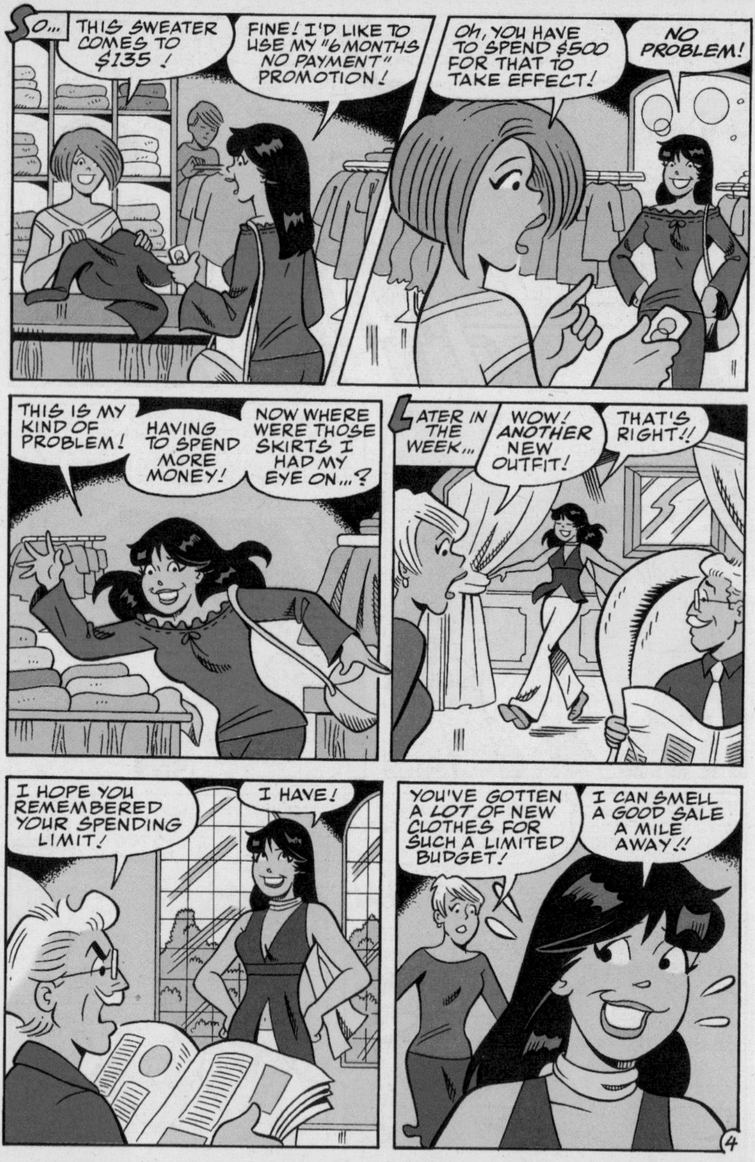
SO...
THIS SWEATER COMES TO $135 !
FINE! I'D LIKE TO USE MY "6 MONTHS NO PAYMENT" PROMOTION!
OH, YOU HAVE TO SPEND $500 FOR THAT TO TAKE EFFECT!
NO PROBLEM!
THIS IS MY KIND OF PROBLEM!
HAVING TO SPEND MORE MONEY!
NOW WHERE WERE THOSE SKIRTS I HAD MY EYE ON...?
LATER IN THE WEEK...
WOW! ANOTHER NEW OUTFIT!
THAT'S RIGHT!!
I HOPE YOU REMEMBERED YOUR SPENDING LIMIT!
I HAVE!
YOU'VE GOTTEN A LOT OF NEW CLOTHES FOR SUCH A LIMITED BUDGET!
I CAN SMELL A GOOD SALE A MILE AWAY!!
4

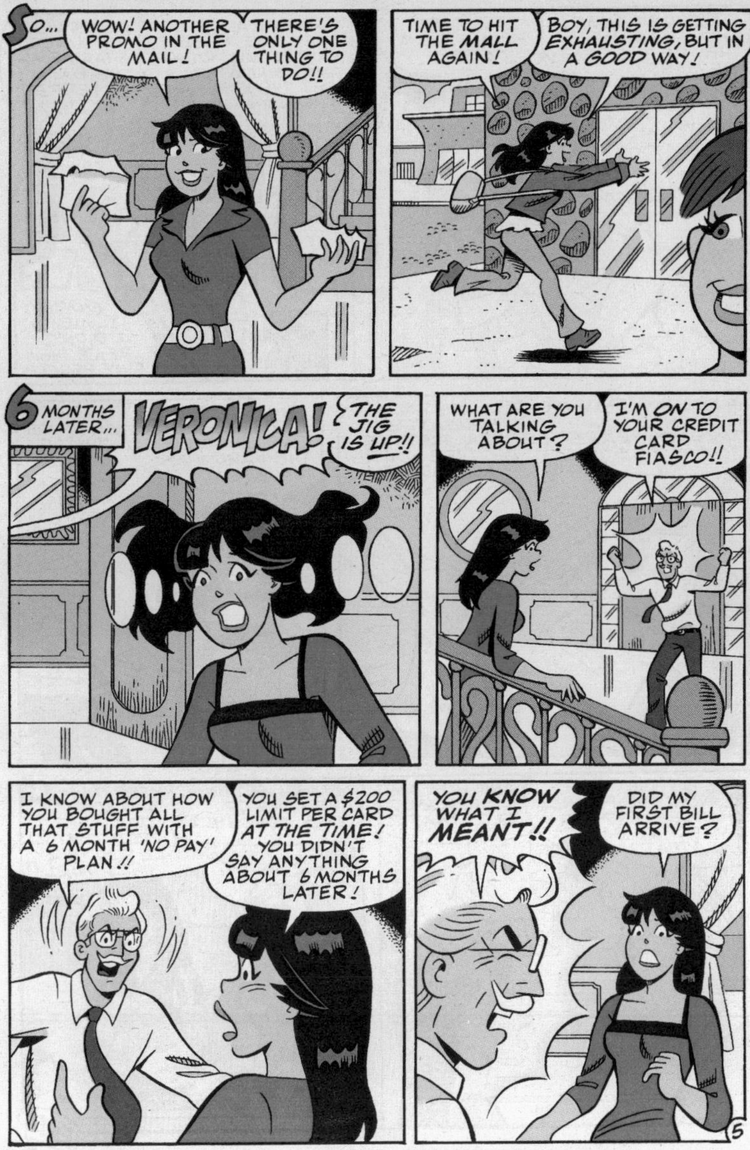
SO...
WOW! ANOTHER PROMO IN THE MAIL!
THERE'S ONLY ONE THING TO DO!!
TIME TO HIT THE MALL AGAIN!
BOY, THIS IS GETTING EXHAUSTING, BUT IN A GOOD WAY!
6 MONTHS LATER...
VERONICA!
THE JIG IS UP!!
WHAT ARE YOU TALKING ABOUT?
I'M ON TO YOUR CREDIT CARD FIASCO!!
I KNOW ABOUT HOW YOU BOUGHT ALL THAT STUFF WITH A 6 MONTH 'NO PAY' PLAN!!
YOU SET A $200 LIMIT PER CARD AT THE TIME! YOU DIDN'T SAY ANYTHING ABOUT 6 MONTHS LATER!
YOU KNOW WHAT I MEANT!!
DID MY FIRST BILL ARRIVE?
5

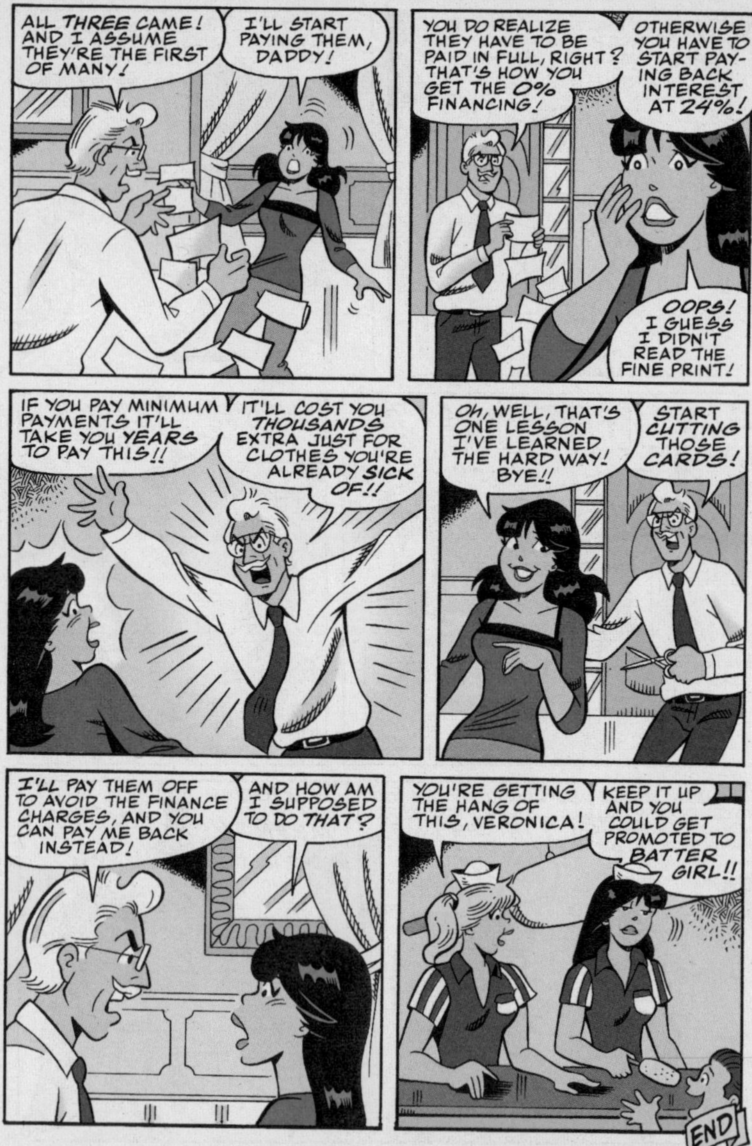
ALL THREE CAME! AND I ASSUME THEY'RE THE FIRST OF MANY!
I'LL START PAYING THEM, DADDY!
YOU DO REALIZE THEY HAVE TO BE PAID IN FULL, RIGHT? THAT'S HOW YOU GET THE 0% FINANCING!
OTHERWISE YOU HAVE TO START PAYING BACK INTEREST AT 24%!
OOPS! I GUESS I DIDN'T READ THE FINE PRINT!
IF YOU PAY MINIMUM PAYMENTS IT'LL TAKE YOU YEARS TO PAY THIS!!
IT'LL COST YOU THOUSANDS EXTRA JUST FOR CLOTHES YOU'RE ALREADY SICK OF!!
Oh, WELL, THAT'S ONE LESSON I'VE LEARNED THE HARD WAY! BYE!!
START CUTTING THOSE CARDS!
I'LL PAY THEM OFF TO AVOID THE FINANCE CHARGES, AND YOU CAN PAY ME BACK INSTEAD!
AND HOW AM I SUPPOSED TO DO THAT?
YOU'RE GETTING THE HANG OF THIS, VERONICA!
KEEP IT UP AND YOU COULD GET PROMOTED TO BATTER GIRL!!
END

Veronica FEAR FACTORS

WOW! LOOK WHO IS COMING TO TOWN FOR A BOOK SIGNING, RON!

Huh?

"CONQUER FEAR" by FAYE BATTLE
The #1 Best Seller!

Meet Faye Battle

AUTHOR OF "NO FEAR" & "CONQUER FEAR"

HERO
Conquer FEAR

PE
TH

SCRIPT: MIKE PELLOWSKI
PENCILS: DAN PARENT
INKS: JIM AMASH

SO? FAYE BATTLE IS COMING TO RIVERDALE! WHAT'S THE BIG DEAL, ETHEL?

FAYE BATTLE IS ONE OF THE WOMEN I MOST ADMIRE!

Meet Faye Battle

R OF NO FEAR & CONQUER FEAR

PETT THEF

I READ BOTH OF HER SELF-HELP BOOKS! SHE ISN'T AFRAID OF ANYTHING! HER LIFE IS AN AMAZING SUCCESS STORY!

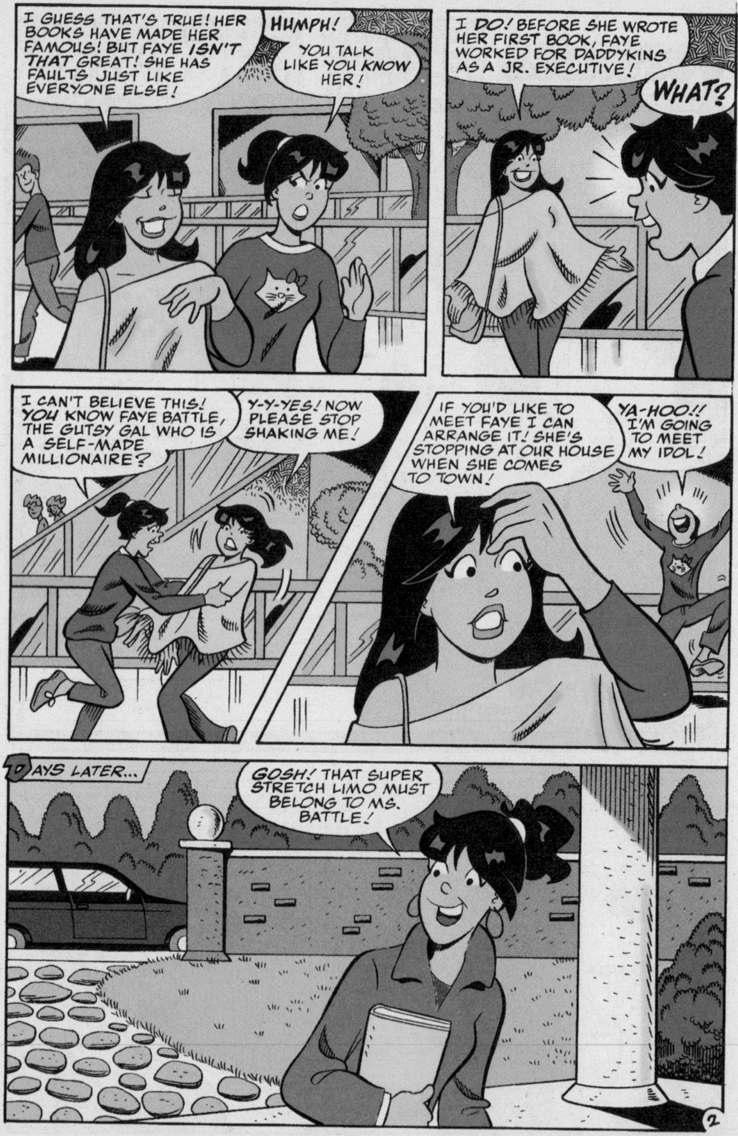
I GUESS THAT'S TRUE! HER BOOKS HAVE MADE HER FAMOUS! BUT FAYE ISN'T THAT GREAT! SHE HAS FAULTS JUST LIKE EVERYONE ELSE!
HUMPH!
YOU TALK LIKE YOU KNOW HER!
I DO! BEFORE SHE WROTE HER FIRST BOOK, FAYE WORKED FOR DADDYKINS AS A JR. EXECUTIVE!
WHAT?
I CAN'T BELIEVE THIS! YOU KNOW FAYE BATTLE, THE GUTSY GAL WHO IS A SELF-MADE MILLIONAIRE?
Y-Y-YES! NOW PLEASE STOP SHAKING ME!
IF YOU'D LIKE TO MEET FAYE I CAN ARRANGE IT! SHE'S STOPPING AT OUR HOUSE WHEN SHE COMES TO TOWN!
YA-HOO!! I'M GOING TO MEET MY IDOL!
DAYS LATER...
GOSH! THAT SUPER STRETCH LIMO MUST BELONG TO MS. BATTLE!
2

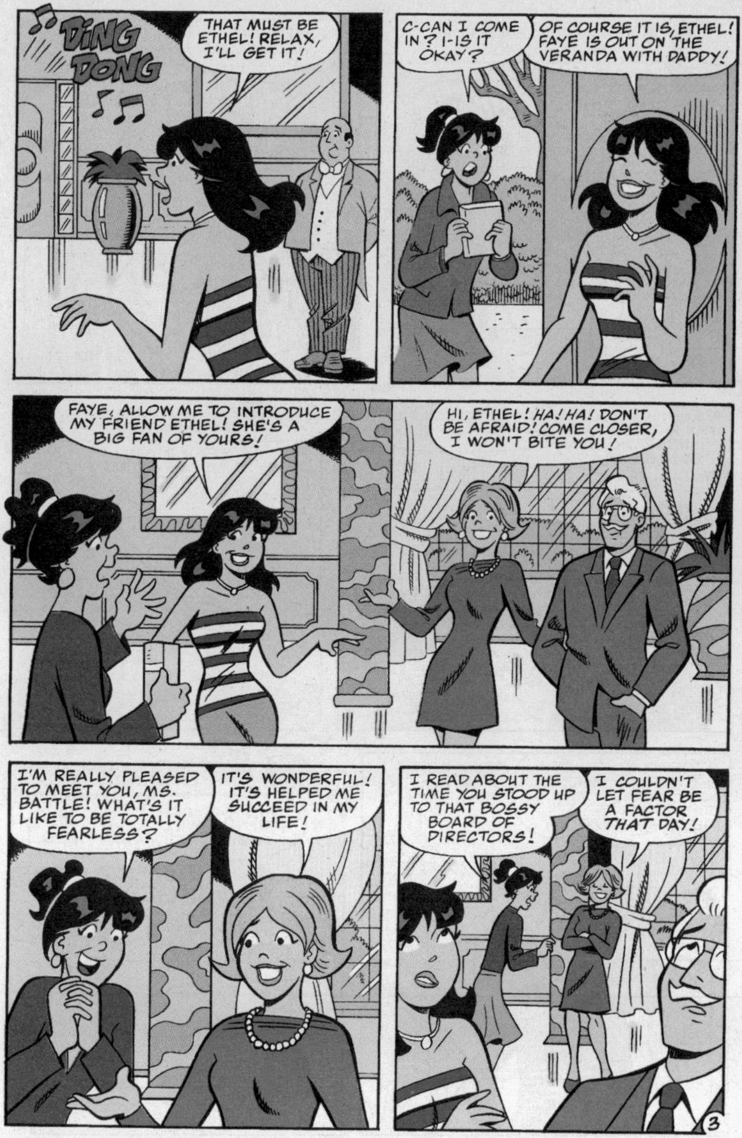
DING DONG
THAT MUST BE ETHEL! RELAX, I'LL GET IT!
C-CAN I COME IN? I-IS IT OKAY?
OF COURSE IT IS, ETHEL! FAYE IS OUT ON THE VERANDA WITH DADDY!
FAYE, ALLOW ME TO INTRODUCE MY FRIEND ETHEL! SHE'S A BIG FAN OF YOURS!
HI, ETHEL! HA! HA! DON'T BE AFRAID! COME CLOSER, I WON'T BITE YOU!
I'M REALLY PLEASED TO MEET YOU, MS. BATTLE! WHAT'S IT LIKE TO BE TOTALLY FEARLESS?
IT'S WONDERFUL! IT'S HELPED ME SUCCEED IN MY LIFE!
I READ ABOUT THE TIME YOU STOOD UP TO THAT BOSSY BOARD OF DIRECTORS!
I COULDN'T LET FEAR BE A FACTOR THAT DAY!
3

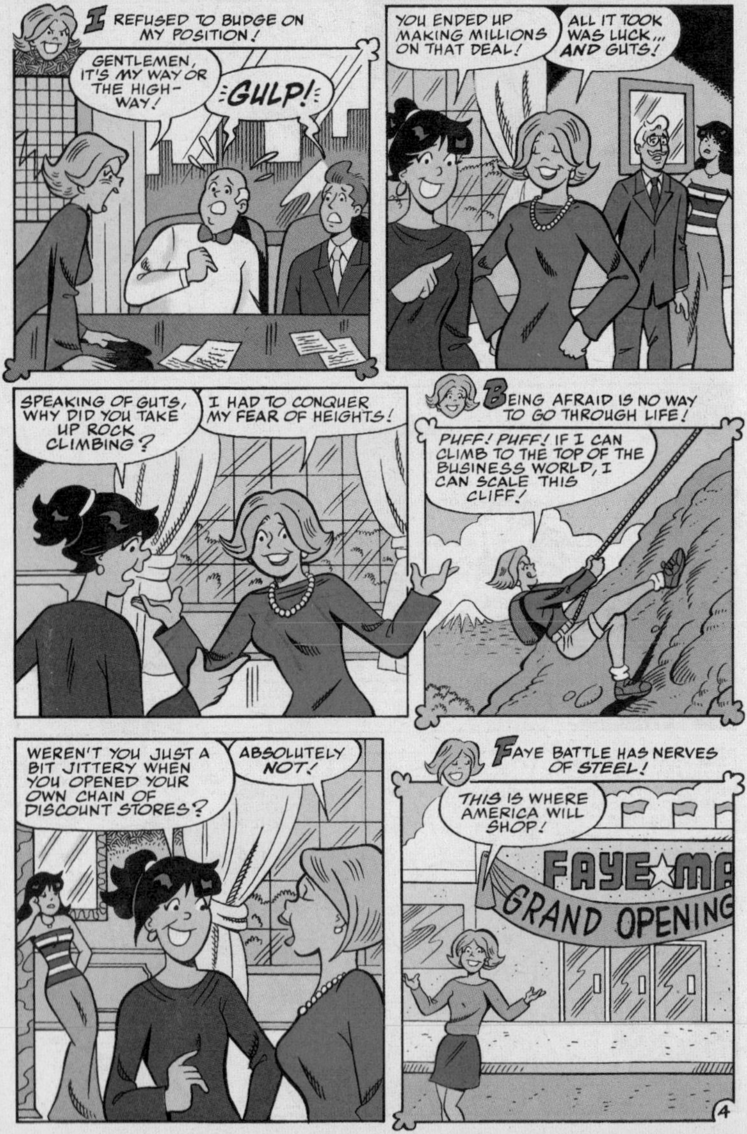
I REFUSED TO BUDGE ON MY POSITION!
GENTLEMEN, IT'S MY WAY OR THE HIGH-WAY!
GULP!
YOU ENDED UP MAKING MILLIONS ON THAT DEAL!
ALL IT TOOK WAS LUCK... AND GUTS!
SPEAKING OF GUTS, WHY DID YOU TAKE UP ROCK CLIMBING?
I HAD TO CONQUER MY FEAR OF HEIGHTS!
BEING AFRAID IS NO WAY TO GO THROUGH LIFE!
PUFF! PUFF! IF I CAN CLIMB TO THE TOP OF THE BUSINESS WORLD, I CAN SCALE THIS CLIFF!
WEREN'T YOU JUST A BIT JITTERY WHEN YOU OPENED YOUR OWN CHAIN OF DISCOUNT STORES?
ABSOLUTELY NOT!
FAYE BATTLE HAS NERVES OF STEEL!
THIS IS WHERE AMERICA WILL SHOP!
FAYE★MA
GRAND OPENING
4

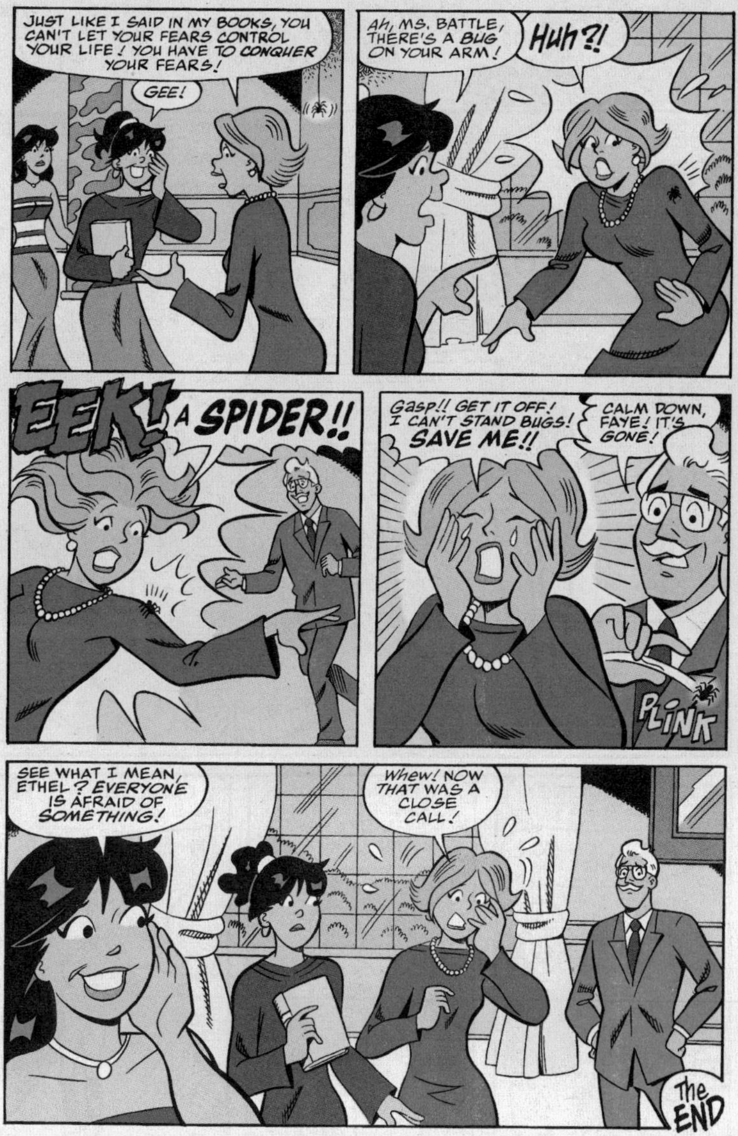

JUST LIKE I SAID IN MY BOOKS, YOU CAN'T LET YOUR FEARS CONTROL YOUR LIFE! YOU HAVE TO CONQUER YOUR FEARS!
GEE!
Ah, MS. BATTLE, THERE'S A BUG ON YOUR ARM!
Huh?!
EEK! A SPIDER!!
Gasp!! GET IT OFF! I CAN'T STAND BUGS! SAVE ME!!
CALM DOWN, FAYE! IT'S GONE!
PLINK
SEE WHAT I MEAN, ETHEL? EVERYONE IS AFRAID OF SOMETHING!
Whew! NOW THAT WAS A CLOSE CALL!
The END

Betty and Veronica in "Tongue Tied"

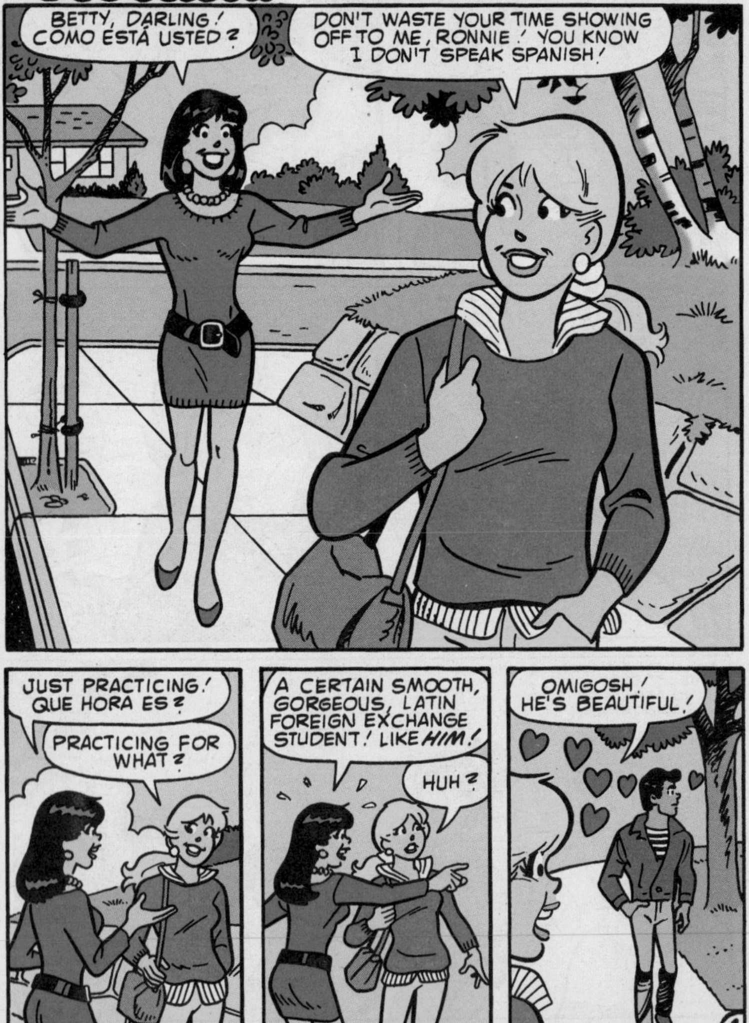
BETTY, DARLING! COMO ESTÁ USTED?
DON'T WASTE YOUR TIME SHOWING OFF TO ME, RONNIE! YOU KNOW I DON'T SPEAK SPANISH!
JUST PRACTICING! QUE HORA ES?
PRACTICING FOR WHAT?
A CERTAIN SMOOTH, GORGEOUS, LATIN FOREIGN EXCHANGE STUDENT! LIKE HIM!
HUH?
OMIGOSH! HE'S BEAUTIFUL!
1

Script: Frank Doyle / Pencils: Dan DeCarlo / Inks: Jimmy DeCarlo / Letters: Bill Yoshida

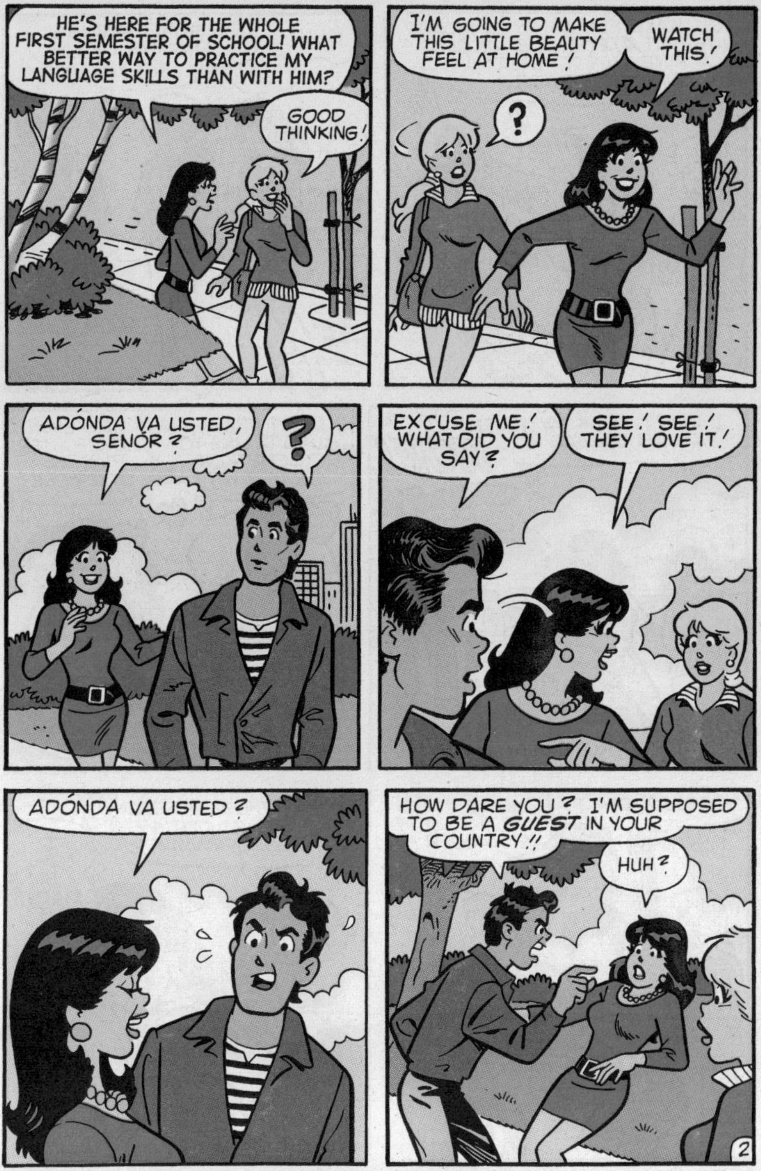

HE'S HERE FOR THE WHOLE FIRST SEMESTER OF SCHOOL! WHAT BETTER WAY TO PRACTICE MY LANGUAGE SKILLS THAN WITH HIM?
GOOD THINKING!
I'M GOING TO MAKE THIS LITTLE BEAUTY FEEL AT HOME!
WATCH THIS!
?
ADÓNDA VA USTED, SENÓR?
?
EXCUSE ME! WHAT DID YOU SAY?
SEE! SEE! THEY LOVE IT!
ADÓNDA VA USTED?
HOW DARE YOU? I'M SUPPOSED TO BE A *GUEST* IN YOUR COUNTRY!!
HUH?
2

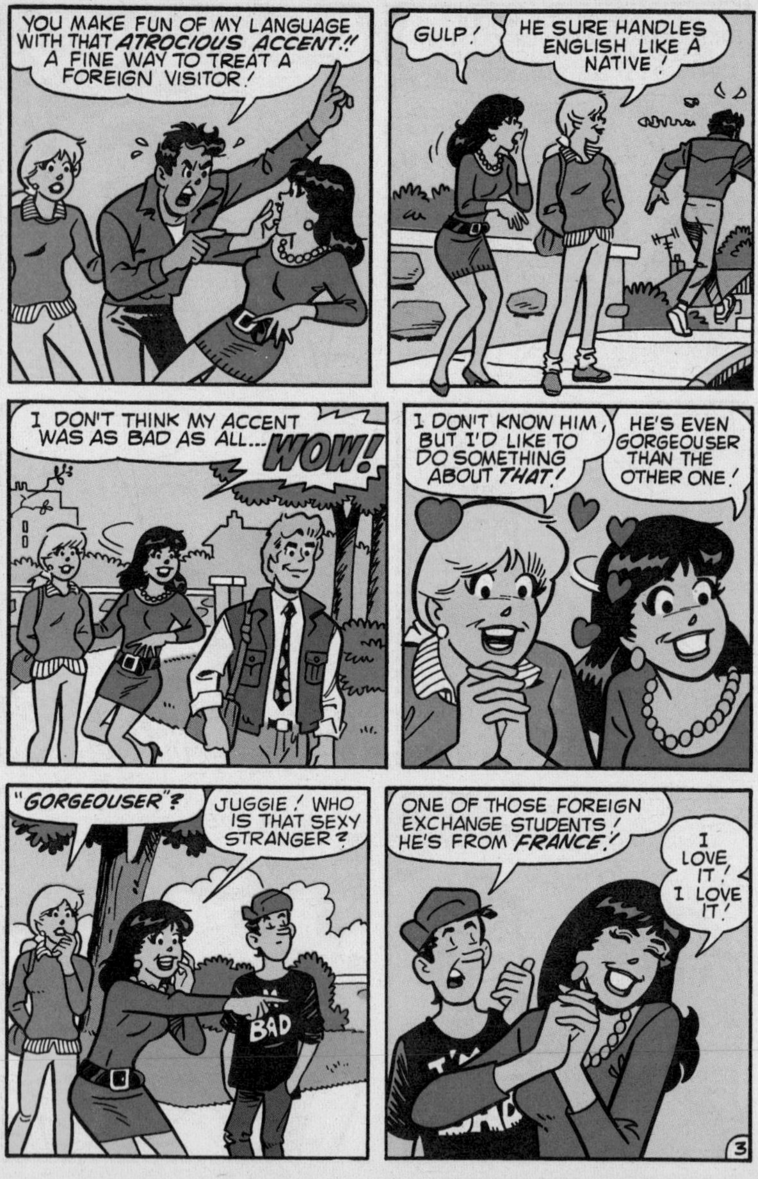

YOU MAKE FUN OF MY LANGUAGE WITH THAT ATROCIOUS ACCENT!! A FINE WAY TO TREAT A FOREIGN VISITOR!
GULP!
HE SURE HANDLES ENGLISH LIKE A NATIVE!
I DON'T THINK MY ACCENT WAS AS BAD AS ALL... WOW!
I DON'T KNOW HIM, BUT I'D LIKE TO DO SOMETHING ABOUT THAT!
HE'S EVEN GORGEOUSER THAN THE OTHER ONE!
"GORGEOUSER"?
JUGGIE! WHO IS THAT SEXY STRANGER?
BAD
ONE OF THOSE FOREIGN EXCHANGE STUDENTS! HE'S FROM FRANCE!
I LOVE IT! I LOVE IT!

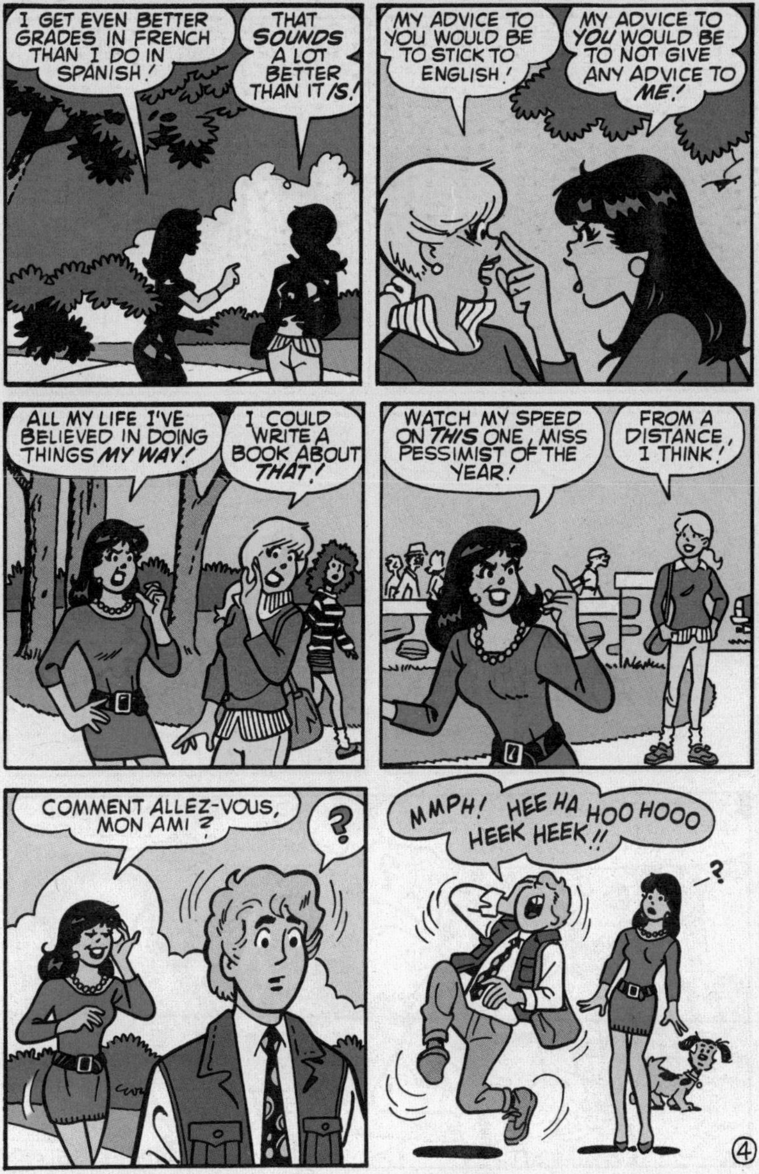
I GET EVEN BETTER GRADES IN FRENCH THAN I DO IN SPANISH!
THAT SOUNDS A LOT BETTER THAN IT IS!
MY ADVICE TO YOU WOULD BE TO STICK TO ENGLISH!
MY ADVICE TO YOU WOULD BE TO NOT GIVE ANY ADVICE TO ME!
ALL MY LIFE I'VE BELIEVED IN DOING THINGS MY WAY!
I COULD WRITE A BOOK ABOUT THAT!
WATCH MY SPEED ON THIS ONE, MISS PESSIMIST OF THE YEAR!
FROM A DISTANCE, I THINK!
COMMENT ALLEZ-VOUS, MON AMI?
?
MMPH! HEE HA HOO HOOO HEEK HEEK!!
?
4

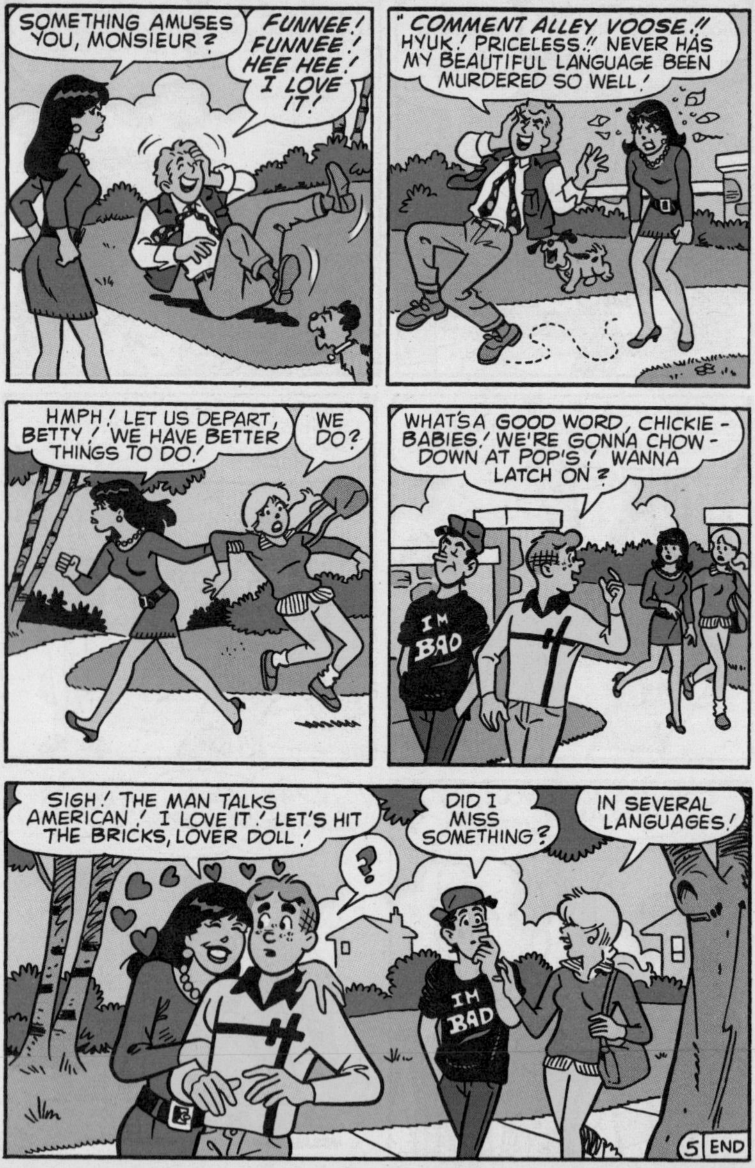
SOMETHING AMUSES YOU, MONSIEUR ?
FUNNEE! FUNNEE! HEE HEE! I LOVE IT!
" COMMENT ALLEY VOOSE !! HYUK! PRICELESS!! NEVER HAS MY BEAUTIFUL LANGUAGE BEEN MURDERED SO WELL!
HMPH! LET US DEPART, BETTY! WE HAVE BETTER THINGS TO DO!
WE DO?
WHAT'S A GOOD WORD, CHICKIE-BABIES! WE'RE GONNA CHOW-DOWN AT POP'S! WANNA LATCH ON ?
I'M BAD
SIGH! THE MAN TALKS AMERICAN! I LOVE IT! LET'S HIT THE BRICKS, LOVER DOLL!
?
DID I MISS SOMETHING?
IN SEVERAL LANGUAGES!
I'M BAD
5 END

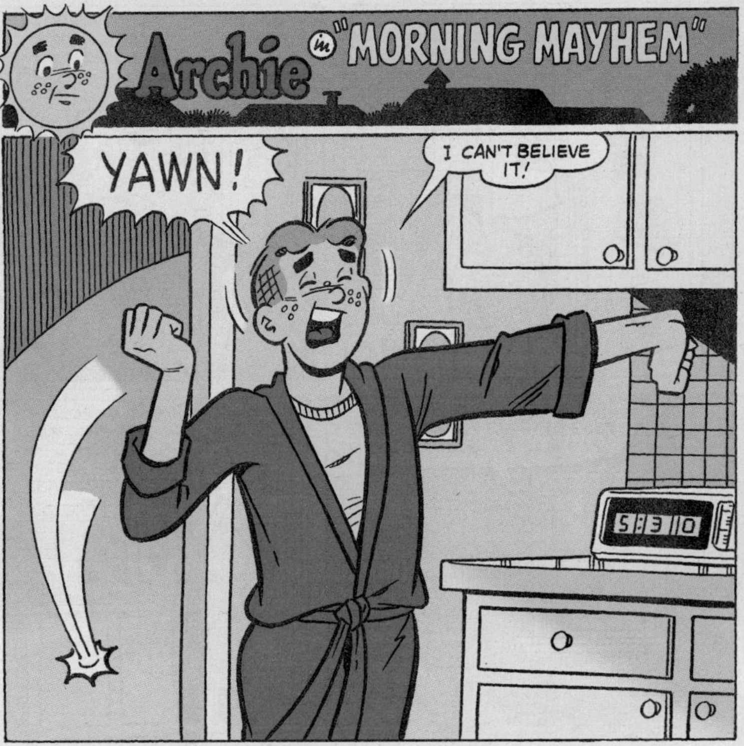
Archie in "MORNING MAYHEM"
YAWN!
I CAN'T BELIEVE IT!
5:30

Script & Pencils: Fernando Ruiz / Inks: Bob Smith / Letters: Bill Yoshida

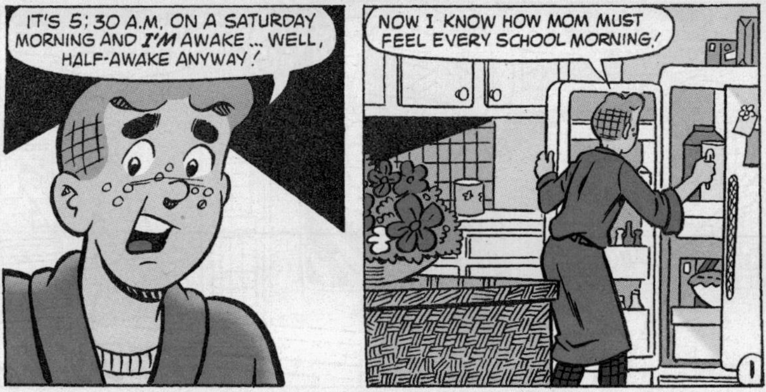
IT'S 5:30 A.M. ON A SATURDAY MORNING AND I'M AWAKE ... WELL, HALF-AWAKE ANYWAY!
NOW I KNOW HOW MOM MUST FEEL EVERY SCHOOL MORNING!
1

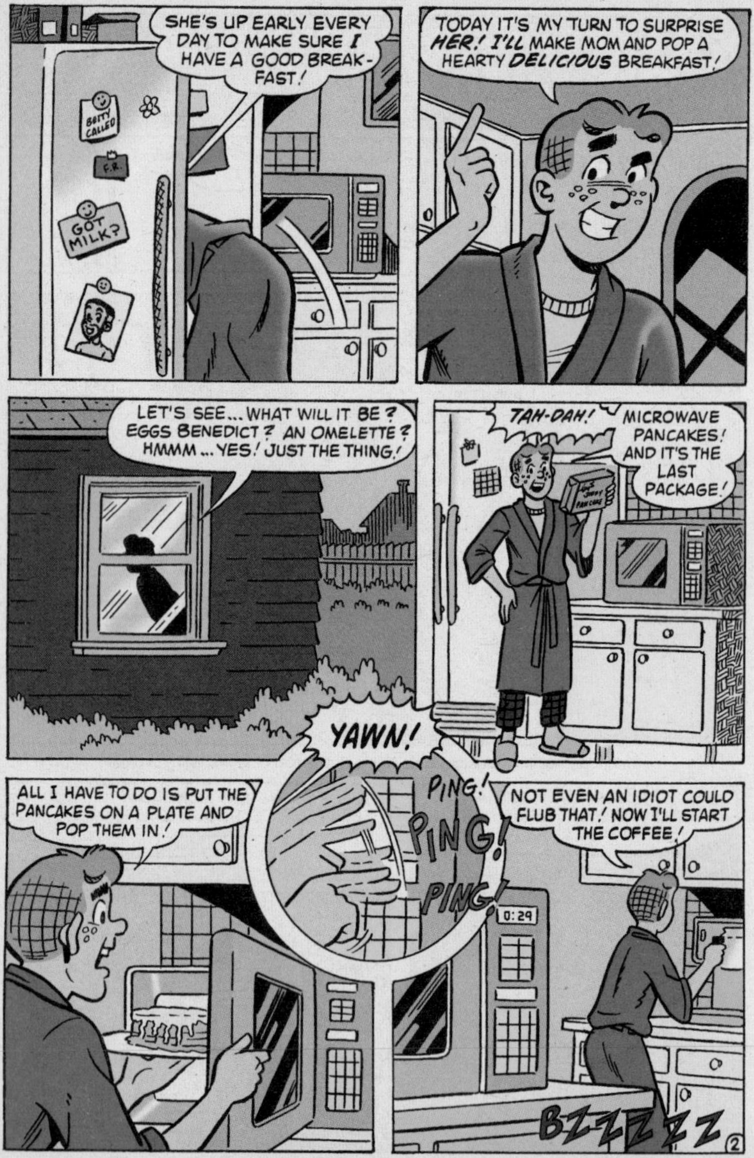
SHE'S UP EARLY EVERY DAY TO MAKE SURE *I* HAVE A GOOD BREAK-FAST!
BETTY CALLED
F.R.
GOT MILK?
TODAY IT'S MY TURN TO SURPRISE *HER!* *I'LL* MAKE MOM AND POP A HEARTY *DELICIOUS* BREAKFAST!
LET'S SEE... WHAT WILL IT BE? EGGS BENEDICT? AN OMELETTE? HMMM... YES! JUST THE THING!
TAH-DAH!
MICROWAVE PANCAKES! AND IT'S THE LAST PACKAGE!
YAWN!
ALL I HAVE TO DO IS PUT THE PANCAKES ON A PLATE AND POP THEM IN!
PING!
PING!
PING!
0:29
NOT EVEN AN IDIOT COULD FLUB THAT! NOW I'LL START THE COFFEE!
BZZZZZZ
2

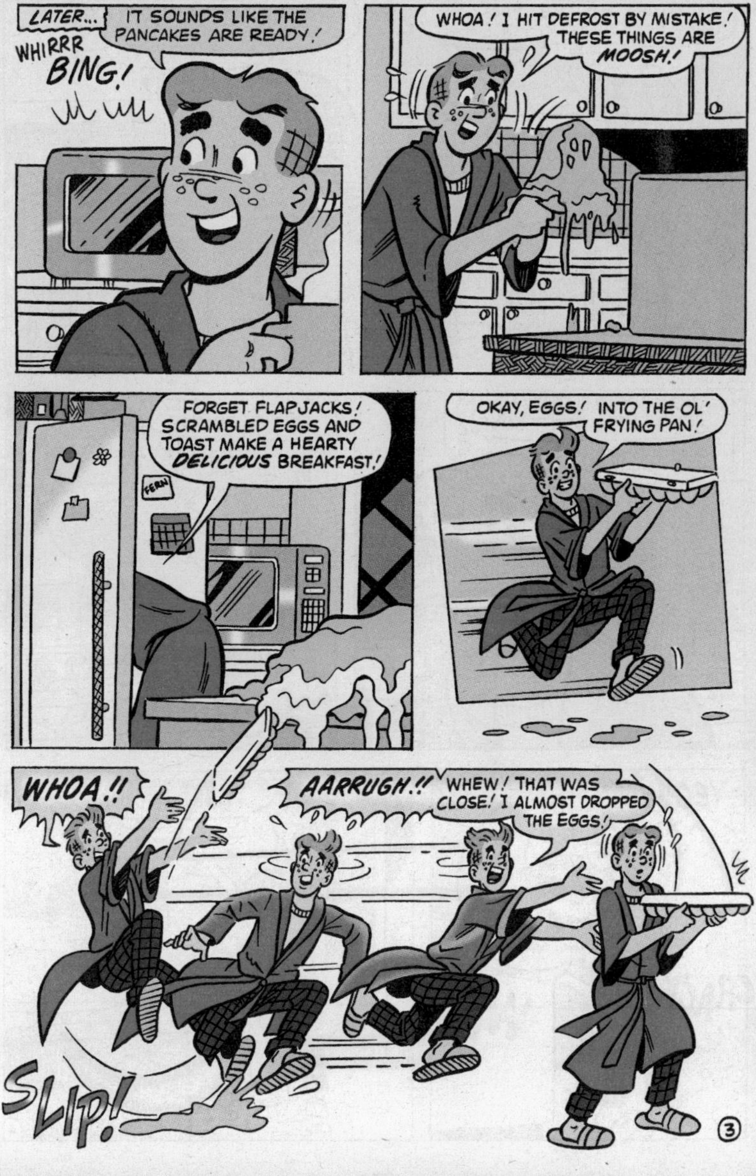
LATER...
IT SOUNDS LIKE THE PANCAKES ARE READY!
WHIRRR
BING!
WHOA! I HIT DEFROST BY MISTAKE! THESE THINGS ARE MOOSH!
FORGET FLAPJACKS! SCRAMBLED EGGS AND TOAST MAKE A HEARTY DELICIOUS BREAKFAST!
FERN
OKAY, EGGS! INTO THE OL' FRYING PAN!
WHOA.!!
AARRUGH.!!
WHEW! THAT WAS CLOSE! I ALMOST DROPPED THE EGGS!
SLIP!

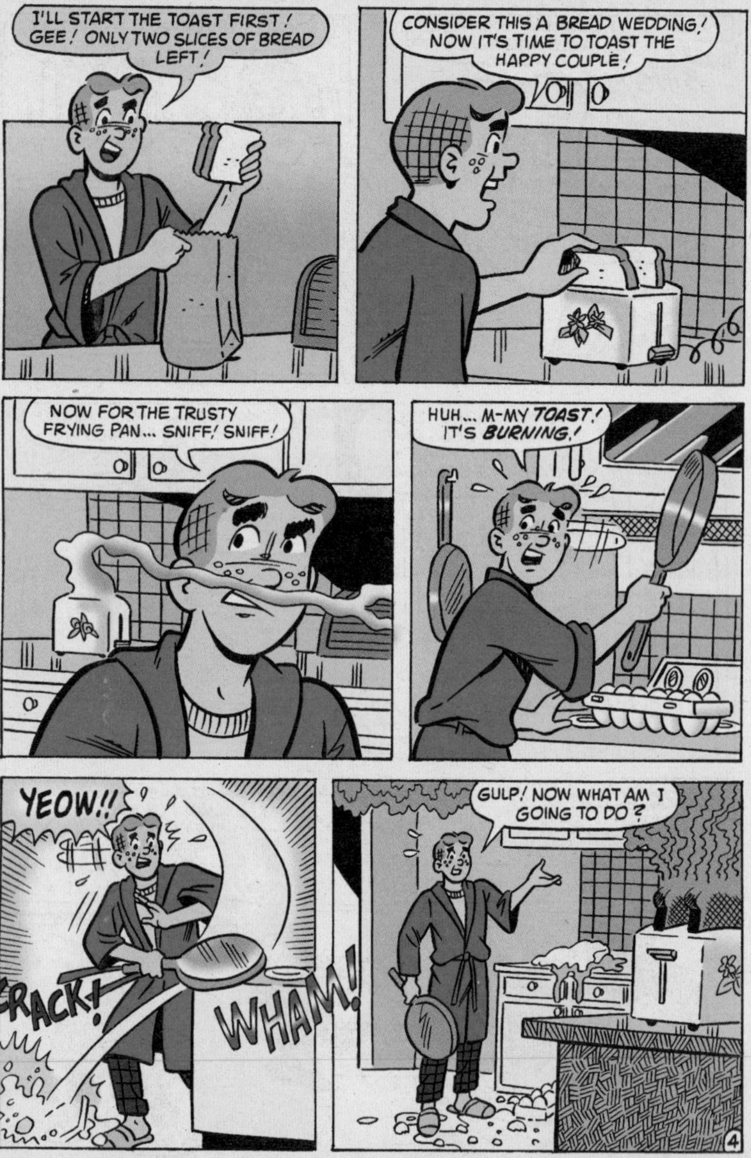
I'LL START THE TOAST FIRST! GEE! ONLY TWO SLICES OF BREAD LEFT!
CONSIDER THIS A BREAD WEDDING! NOW IT'S TIME TO TOAST THE HAPPY COUPLE!
NOW FOR THE TRUSTY FRYING PAN... SNIFF! SNIFF!
HUH... M-MY TOAST! IT'S BURNING!
YEOW!!
CRACK!
WHAM!
GULP! NOW WHAT AM I GOING TO DO?
4

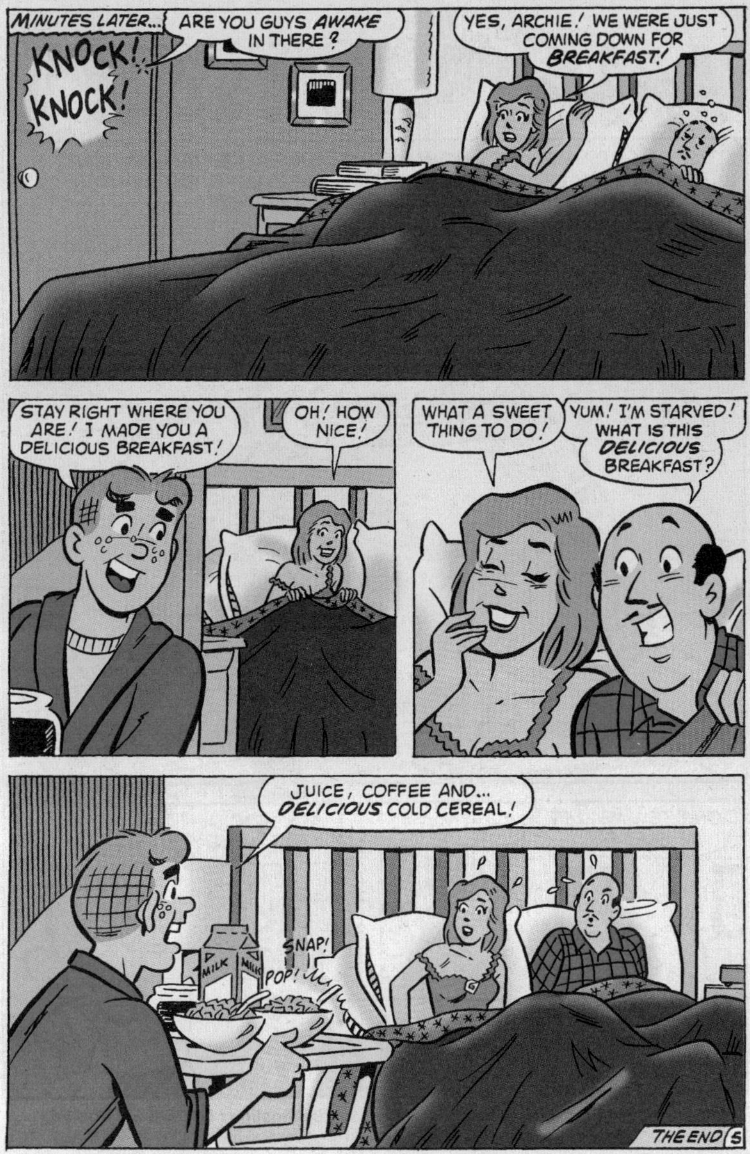

MINUTES LATER...
ARE YOU GUYS AWAKE IN THERE ?
KNOCK! KNOCK!
YES, ARCHIE! WE WERE JUST COMING DOWN FOR BREAKFAST!
STAY RIGHT WHERE YOU ARE! I MADE YOU A DELICIOUS BREAKFAST!
OH! HOW NICE!
WHAT A SWEET THING TO DO!
YUM! I'M STARVED! WHAT IS THIS DELICIOUS BREAKFAST?
JUICE, COFFEE AND... DELICIOUS COLD CEREAL!
SNAP!
POP!
MILK
THE END
5

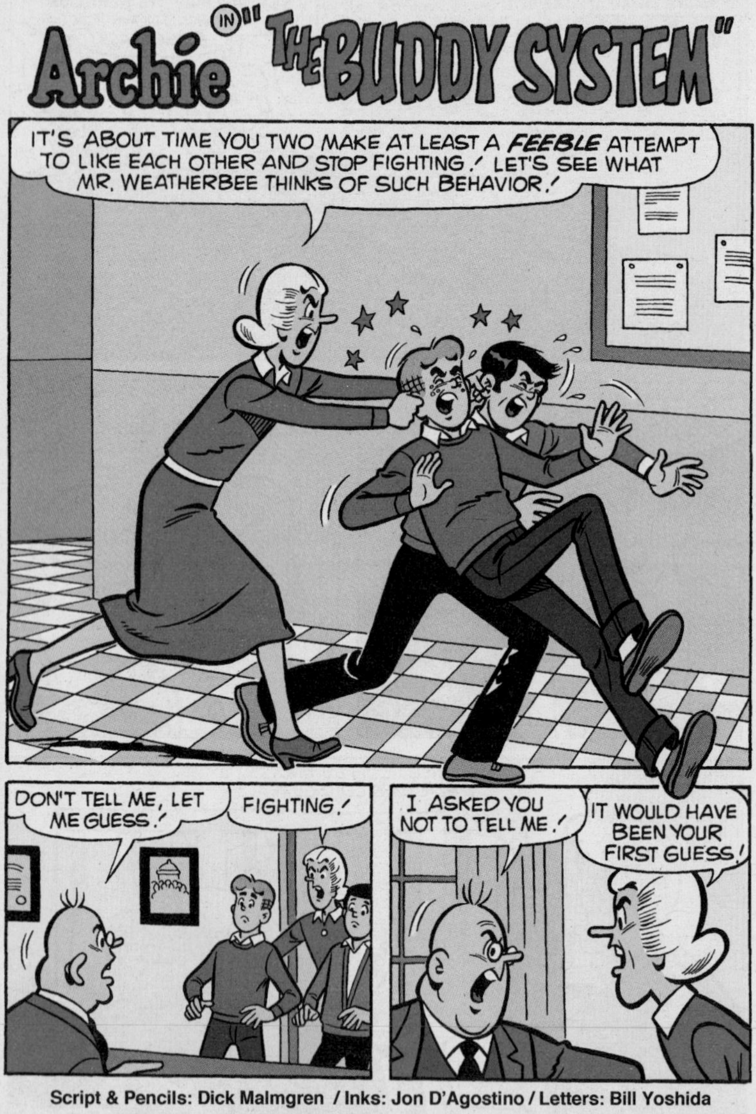
Archie in "THE BUDDY SYSTEM"
IT'S ABOUT TIME YOU TWO MAKE AT LEAST A FEEBLE ATTEMPT TO LIKE EACH OTHER AND STOP FIGHTING.! LET'S SEE WHAT MR. WEATHERBEE THINKS OF SUCH BEHAVIOR.!
DON'T TELL ME, LET ME GUESS.!
FIGHTING.!
I ASKED YOU NOT TO TELL ME.!
IT WOULD HAVE BEEN YOUR FIRST GUESS.!

Script & Pencils: Dick Malmgren / Inks: Jon D'Agostino / Letters: Bill Yoshida

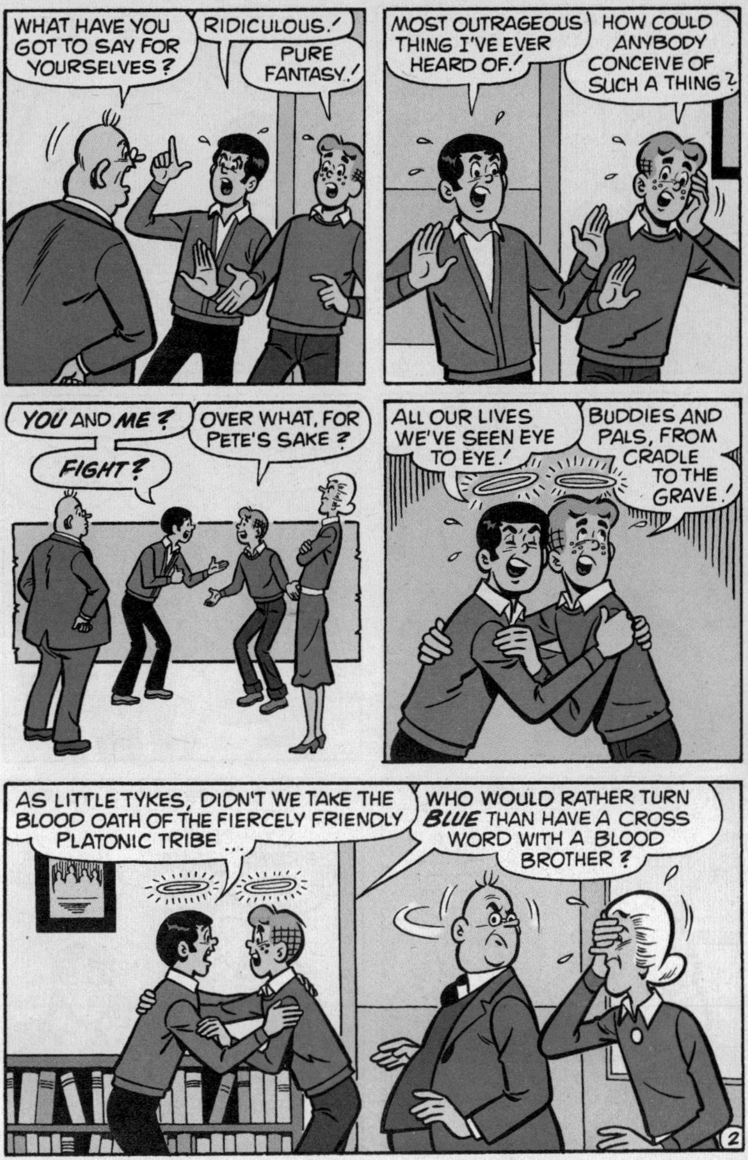

WHAT HAVE YOU GOT TO SAY FOR YOURSELVES ?
RIDICULOUS.!
PURE FANTASY.!
MOST OUTRAGEOUS THING I'VE EVER HEARD OF.!
HOW COULD ANYBODY CONCEIVE OF SUCH A THING ?
YOU AND ME ?
FIGHT ?
OVER WHAT, FOR PETE'S SAKE ?
ALL OUR LIVES WE'VE SEEN EYE TO EYE.!
BUDDIES AND PALS, FROM CRADLE TO THE GRAVE.!
AS LITTLE TYKES, DIDN'T WE TAKE THE BLOOD OATH OF THE FIERCELY FRIENDLY PLATONIC TRIBE ...
WHO WOULD RATHER TURN BLUE THAN HAVE A CROSS WORD WITH A BLOOD BROTHER ?

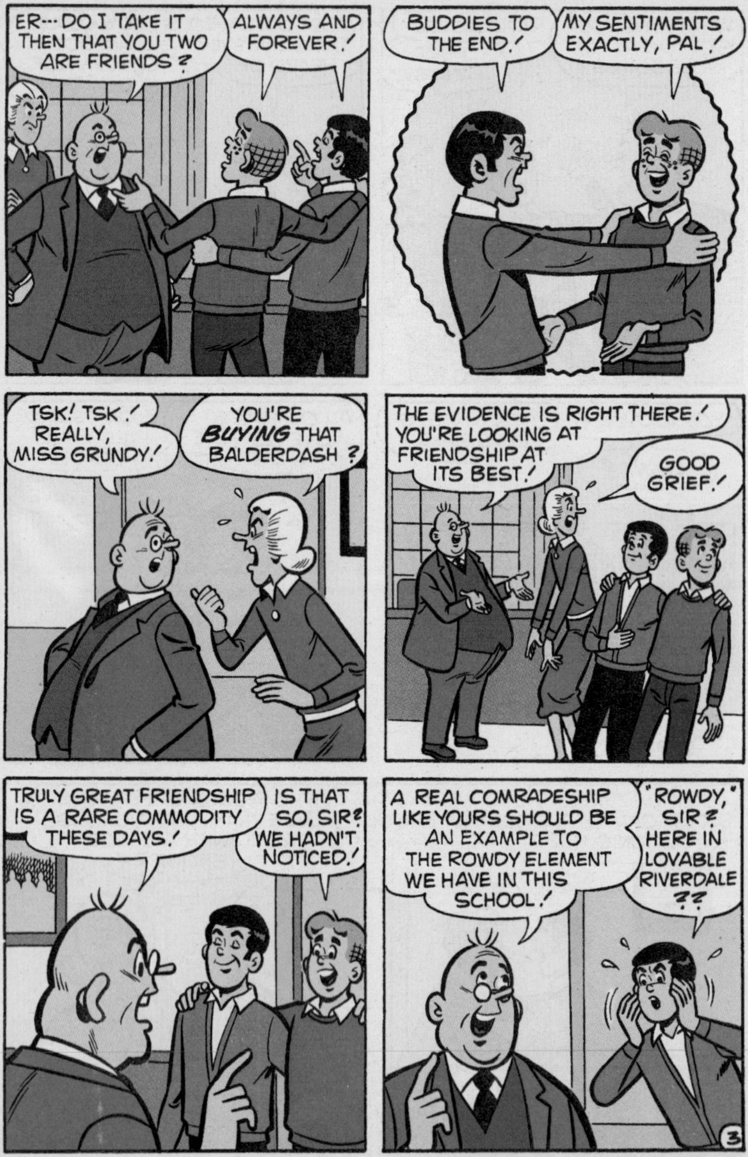
ER··· DO I TAKE IT THEN THAT YOU TWO ARE FRIENDS ?
ALWAYS AND FOREVER!
BUDDIES TO THE END!
MY SENTIMENTS EXACTLY, PAL!
TSK! TSK! REALLY, MISS GRUNDY!
YOU'RE BUYING THAT BALDERDASH ?
THE EVIDENCE IS RIGHT THERE! YOU'RE LOOKING AT FRIENDSHIP AT ITS BEST!
GOOD GRIEF!
TRULY GREAT FRIENDSHIP IS A RARE COMMODITY THESE DAYS!
IS THAT SO, SIR? WE HADN'T NOTICED!
A REAL COMRADESHIP LIKE YOURS SHOULD BE AN EXAMPLE TO THE ROWDY ELEMENT WE HAVE IN THIS SCHOOL!
"ROWDY," SIR? HERE IN LOVABLE RIVERDALE ??
3

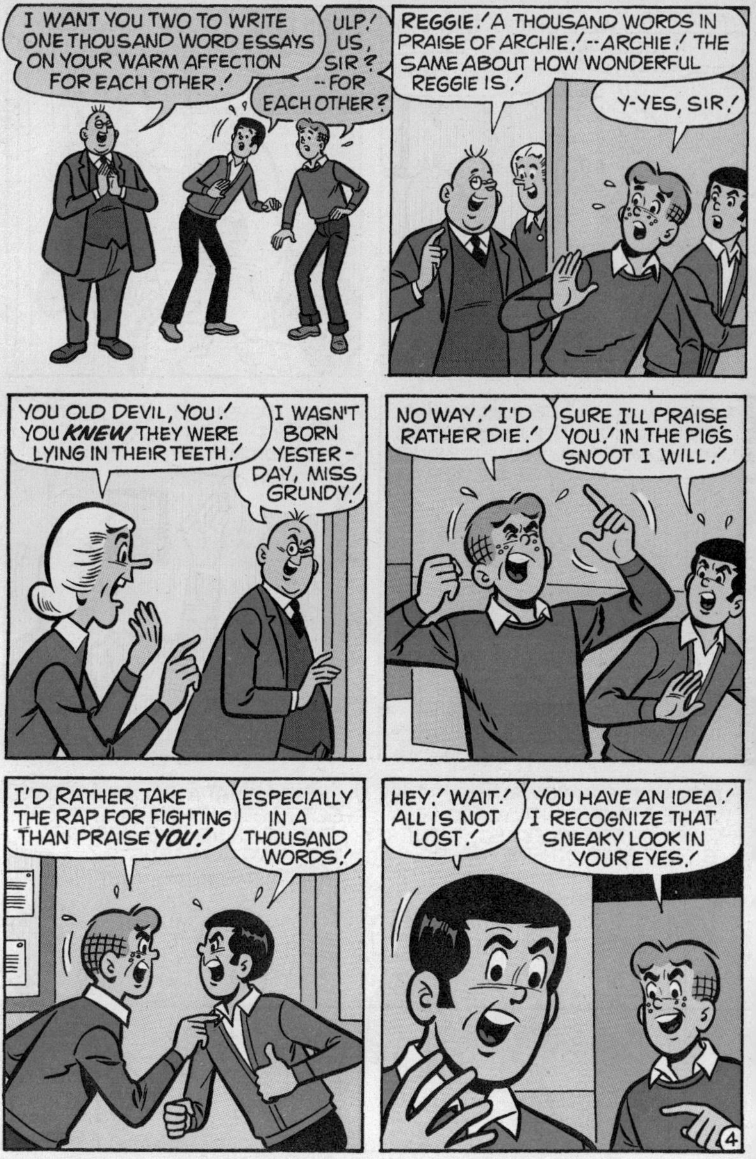
I WANT YOU TWO TO WRITE ONE THOUSAND WORD ESSAYS ON YOUR WARM AFFECTION FOR EACH OTHER!
ULP! US, SIR?
--FOR EACH OTHER?
REGGIE! A THOUSAND WORDS IN PRAISE OF ARCHIE! --ARCHIE! THE SAME ABOUT HOW WONDERFUL REGGIE IS!
Y-YES, SIR!
YOU OLD DEVIL, YOU! YOU KNEW THEY WERE LYING IN THEIR TEETH!
I WASN'T BORN YESTER-DAY, MISS GRUNDY!
NO WAY! I'D RATHER DIE!
SURE I'LL PRAISE YOU! IN THE PIG'S SNOOT I WILL!
I'D RATHER TAKE THE RAP FOR FIGHTING THAN PRAISE YOU!
ESPECIALLY IN A THOUSAND WORDS!
HEY! WAIT! ALL IS NOT LOST!
YOU HAVE AN IDEA! I RECOGNIZE THAT SNEAKY LOOK IN YOUR EYES!
4

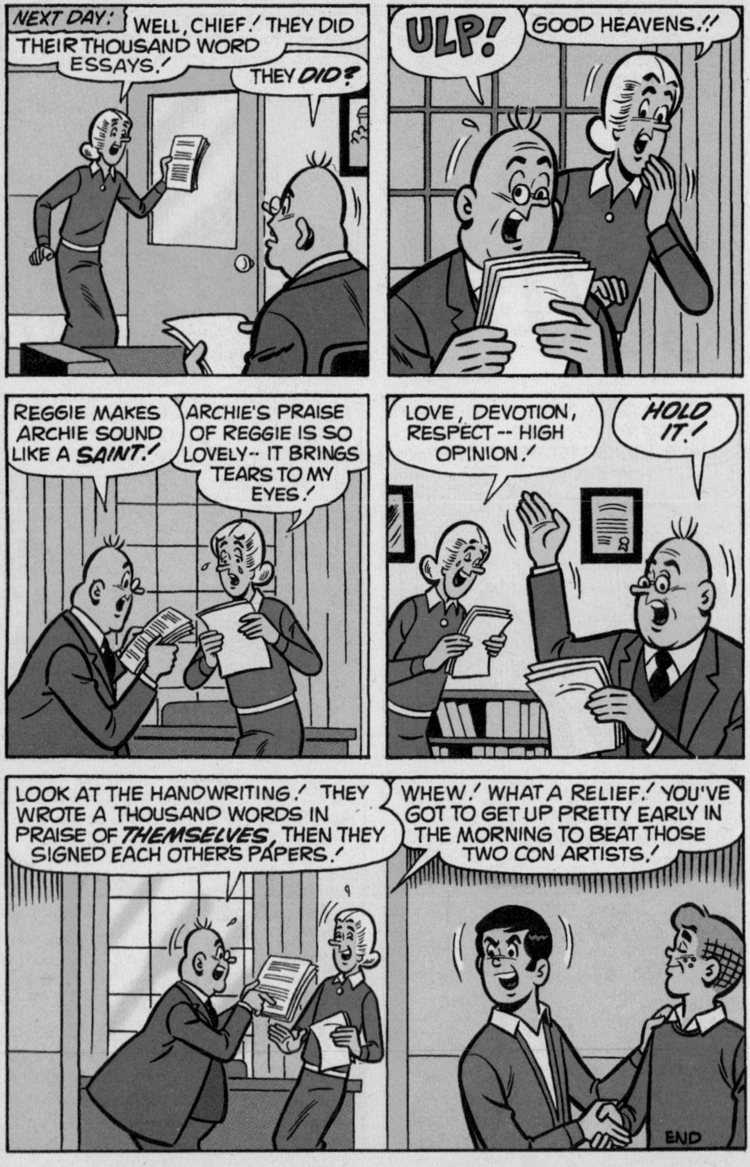
NEXT DAY:
WELL, CHIEF! THEY DID THEIR THOUSAND WORD ESSAYS!
THEY DID?
ULP!
GOOD HEAVENS!!
REGGIE MAKES ARCHIE SOUND LIKE A SAINT!
ARCHIE'S PRAISE OF REGGIE IS SO LOVELY-- IT BRINGS TEARS TO MY EYES!
LOVE, DEVOTION, RESPECT -- HIGH OPINION!
HOLD IT!
LOOK AT THE HANDWRITING! THEY WROTE A THOUSAND WORDS IN PRAISE OF THEMSELVES, THEN THEY SIGNED EACH OTHER'S PAPERS!
WHEW! WHAT A RELIEF! YOU'VE GOT TO GET UP PRETTY EARLY IN THE MORNING TO BEAT THOSE TWO CON ARTISTS!
END

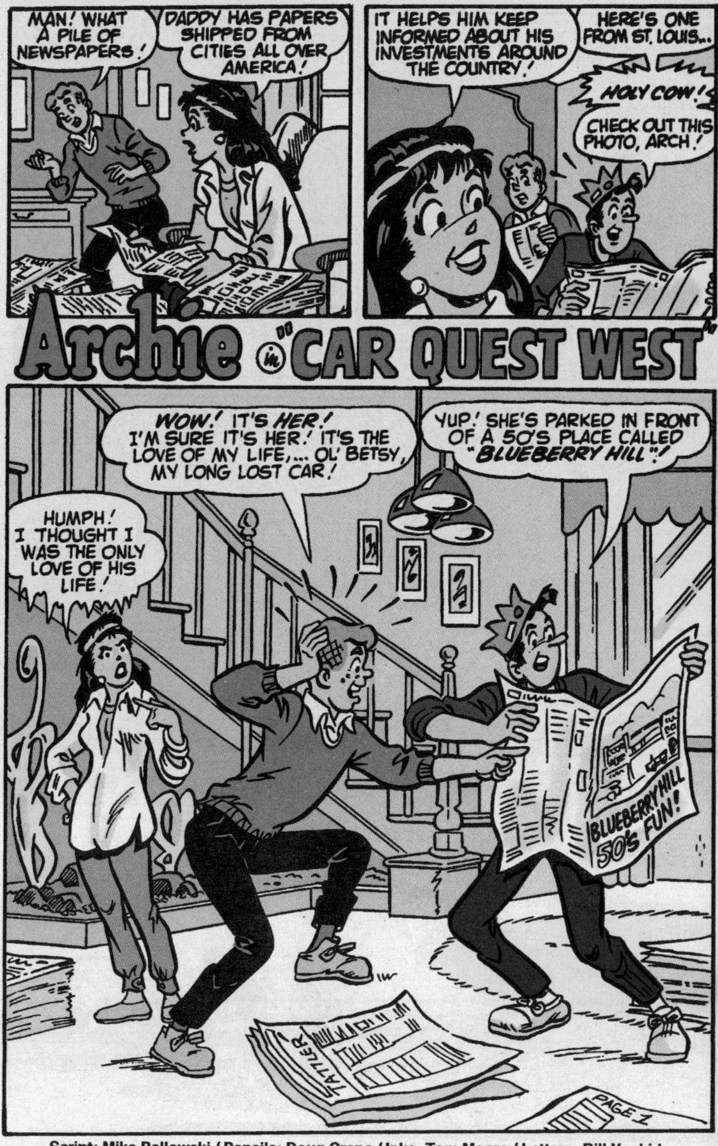
MAN! WHAT A PILE OF NEWSPAPERS!
DADDY HAS PAPERS SHIPPED FROM CITIES ALL OVER AMERICA!
IT HELPS HIM KEEP INFORMED ABOUT HIS INVESTMENTS AROUND THE COUNTRY!
HERE'S ONE FROM ST. LOUIS...
HOLY COW!
CHECK OUT THIS PHOTO, ARCH!
Archie in "CAR QUEST WEST"
WOW! IT'S HER! I'M SURE IT'S HER! IT'S THE LOVE OF MY LIFE,... OL' BETSY, MY LONG LOST CAR!
YUP! SHE'S PARKED IN FRONT OF A 50'S PLACE CALLED "BLUEBERRY HILL"!
HUMPH! I THOUGHT I WAS THE ONLY LOVE OF HIS LIFE!
BLUEBERRY HILL 50's FUN!
TATTLER
PAGE 1

Script: Mike Pellowski / Pencils: Doug Crane / Inks: Tom Moore / Letters: Bill Yoshida

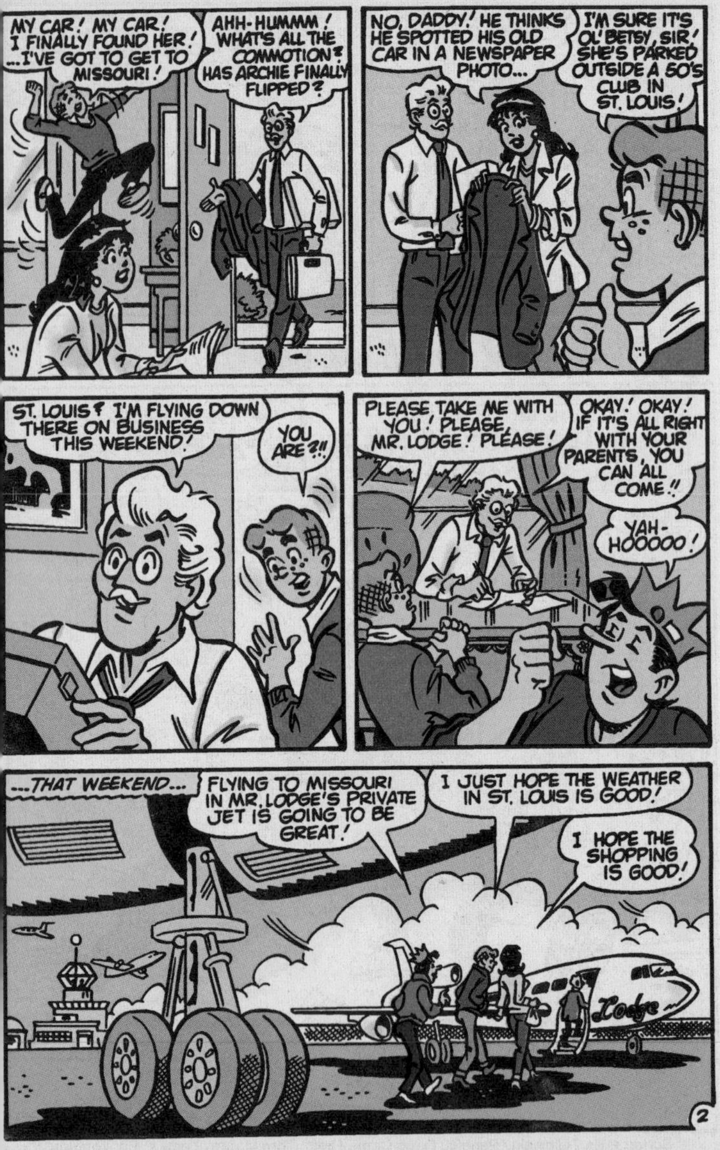
MY CAR! MY CAR! I FINALLY FOUND HER! ...I'VE GOT TO GET TO MISSOURI!
AHH-HUMMM! WHAT'S ALL THE COMMOTION? HAS ARCHIE FINALLY FLIPPED?
NO, DADDY! HE THINKS HE SPOTTED HIS OLD CAR IN A NEWSPAPER PHOTO...
I'M SURE IT'S OL' BETSY, SIR! SHE'S PARKED OUTSIDE A 50'S CLUB IN ST. LOUIS!
ST. LOUIS? I'M FLYING DOWN THERE ON BUSINESS THIS WEEKEND!
YOU ARE?!!
PLEASE TAKE ME WITH YOU! PLEASE, MR. LODGE! PLEASE!
OKAY! OKAY! IF IT'S ALL RIGHT WITH YOUR PARENTS, YOU CAN ALL COME!!
YAH-HOOOOO!
...THAT WEEKEND...
FLYING TO MISSOURI IN MR. LODGE'S PRIVATE JET IS GOING TO BE GREAT!
I JUST HOPE THE WEATHER IN ST. LOUIS IS GOOD!
I HOPE THE SHOPPING IS GOOD!
Lodge
2

WE'RE OFF! ST. LOUIS AND OL' BETSY... HERE I COME!"

LOOK OUT THERE, ARCHIE! IT'S "GATEWAY TO THE WEST," ARCH!

PLEASE FASTEN YOUR SEAT BELTS! WE'LL BE LANDING SHORTLY!

AT 630 FEET HIGH, IT'S THE LARGEST MONUMENT IN THE WORLD!

IF I FIND OL' BETSY, JUG, ...THE ARCH WILL BE MY *GATEWAY* TO HAPPINESS!

AFTER THE PLANE LANDS...

WE'LL SEE YOU TWO LATER! I HAVE BUSINESS TO TAKE CARE OF!

AND I HAVE SHOPPING TO DO! GOOD LUCK, ARCHIE!

AIRPORT SNACK

THANKS, RON! LET'S GO, JUG!

DO YOU KNOW A PLACE CALLED "BLUEBERRY HILL"?

SURE! EVERYONE IN ST. LOUIS DOES! HOP IN!

$2.00 per 1st
$1.00 Per Ext.

3

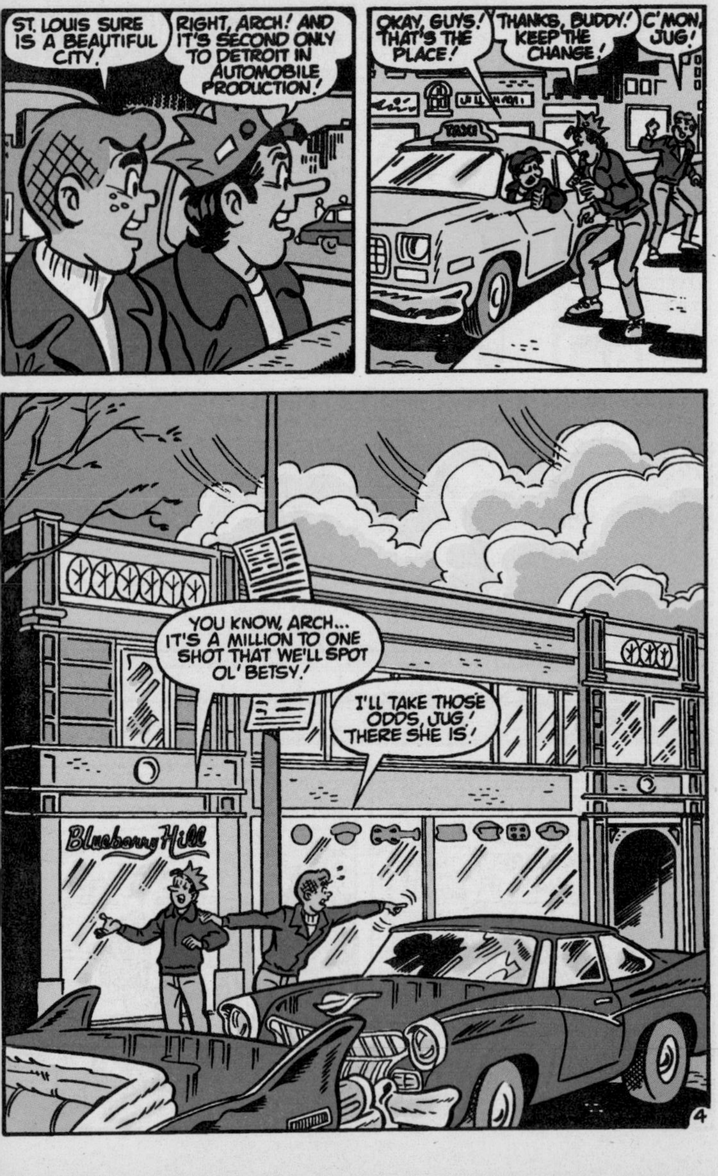
ST. LOUIS SURE IS A BEAUTIFUL CITY!
RIGHT, ARCH! AND IT'S SECOND ONLY TO DETROIT IN AUTOMOBILE PRODUCTION!
OKAY, GUYS! THAT'S THE PLACE!
THANKS, BUDDY! KEEP THE CHANGE!
C'MON, JUG!
YOU KNOW, ARCH... IT'S A MILLION TO ONE SHOT THAT WE'LL SPOT OL' BETSY!
I'LL TAKE THOSE ODDS, JUG! THERE SHE IS!
Blueberry Hill

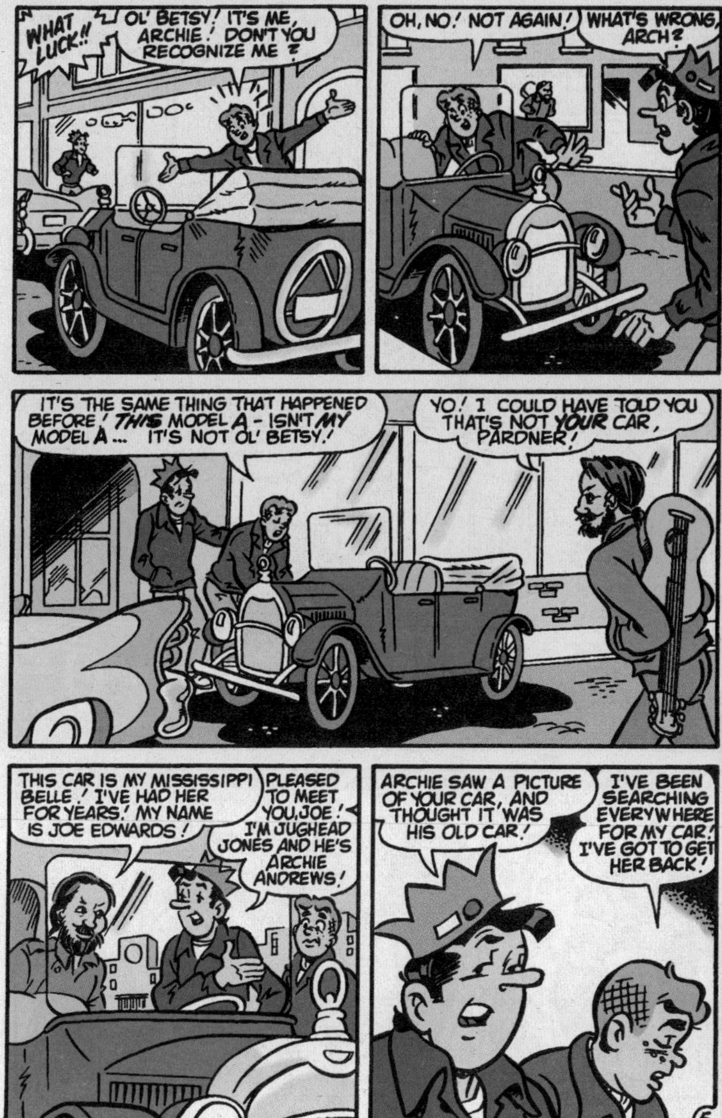
WHAT LUCK!!
OL' BETSY! IT'S ME, ARCHIE! DON'T YOU RECOGNIZE ME ?
OH, NO! NOT AGAIN!
WHAT'S WRONG, ARCH?
IT'S THE SAME THING THAT HAPPENED BEFORE! THIS MODEL A - ISN'T MY MODEL A... IT'S NOT OL' BETSY!
YO! I COULD HAVE TOLD YOU THAT'S NOT YOUR CAR, PARDNER!
THIS CAR IS MY MISSISSIPPI BELLE! I'VE HAD HER FOR YEARS! MY NAME IS JOE EDWARDS!
PLEASED TO MEET YOU, JOE! I'M JUGHEAD JONES AND HE'S ARCHIE ANDREWS!
ARCHIE SAW A PICTURE OF YOUR CAR, AND THOUGHT IT WAS HIS OLD CAR!
I'VE BEEN SEARCHING EVERYWHERE FOR MY CAR! I'VE GOT TO GET HER BACK!

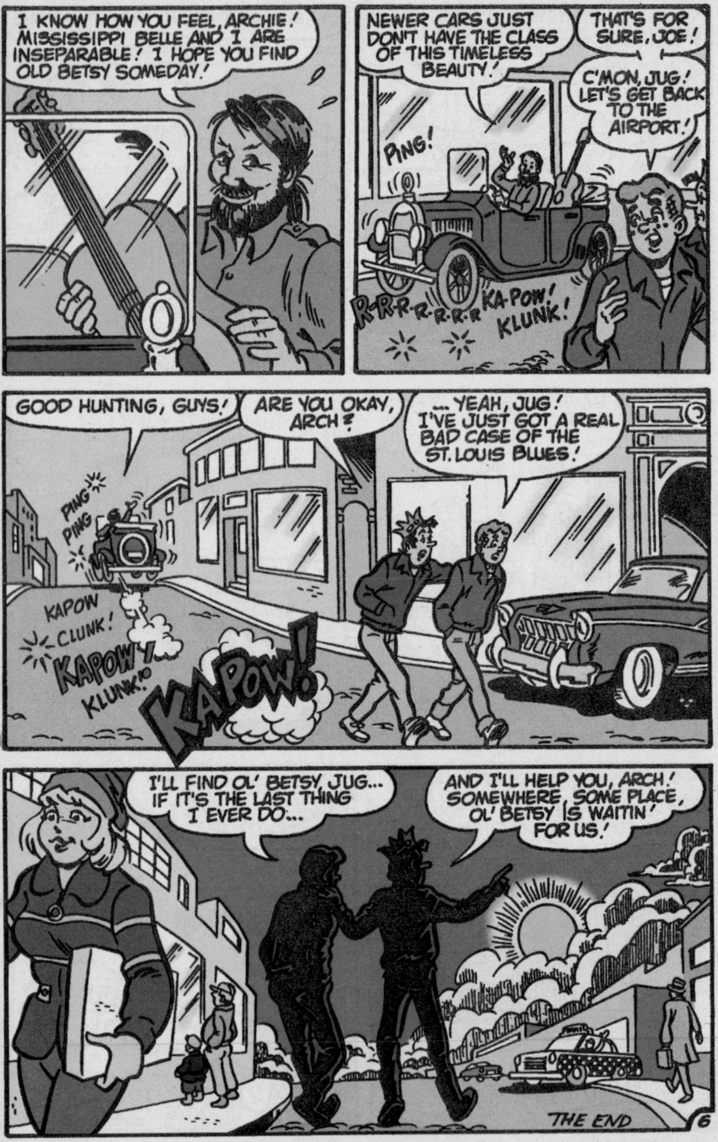

I KNOW HOW YOU FEEL, ARCHIE! MISSISSIPPI BELLE AND I ARE INSEPARABLE! I HOPE YOU FIND OLD BETSY SOMEDAY!
NEWER CARS JUST DON'T HAVE THE CLASS OF THIS TIMELESS BEAUTY!
THAT'S FOR SURE, JOE!
C'MON, JUG! LET'S GET BACK TO THE AIRPORT!
PING!
R-R-R-R-R-R-R-R
KA-POW! KLUNK!
GOOD HUNTING, GUYS!
ARE YOU OKAY, ARCH?
... YEAH, JUG! I'VE JUST GOT A REAL BAD CASE OF THE ST. LOUIS BLUES!
PING PING
KAPOW CLUNK!
KAPOW! KLUNK!
KAPOW!
I'LL FIND OL' BETSY, JUG... IF IT'S THE LAST THING I EVER DO...
AND I'LL HELP YOU, ARCH! SOMEWHERE, SOME PLACE, OL' BETSY IS WAITIN' FOR US!
THE END

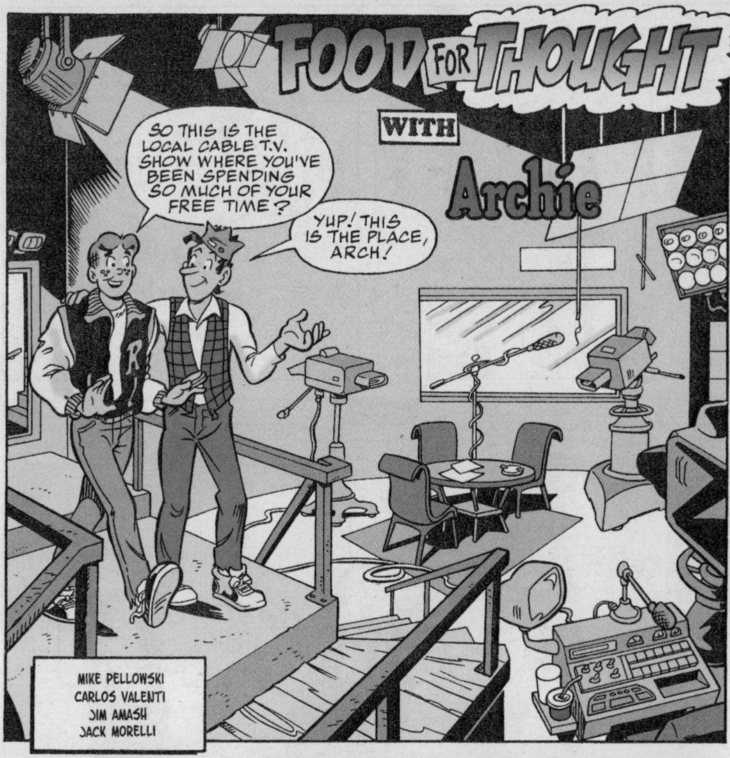
FOOD FOR THOUGHT
WITH
Archie
SO THIS IS THE LOCAL CABLE T.V. SHOW WHERE YOU'VE BEEN SPENDING SO MUCH OF YOUR FREE TIME?
YUP! THIS IS THE PLACE, ARCH!
MIKE PELLOWSKI
CARLOS VALENTI
JIM AMASH
JACK MORELLI

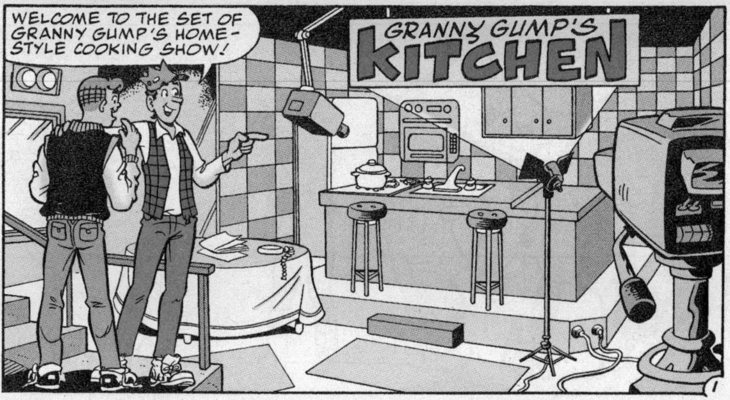
WELCOME TO THE SET OF GRANNY GUMP'S HOME-STYLE COOKING SHOW!
GRANNY GUMP'S KITCHEN

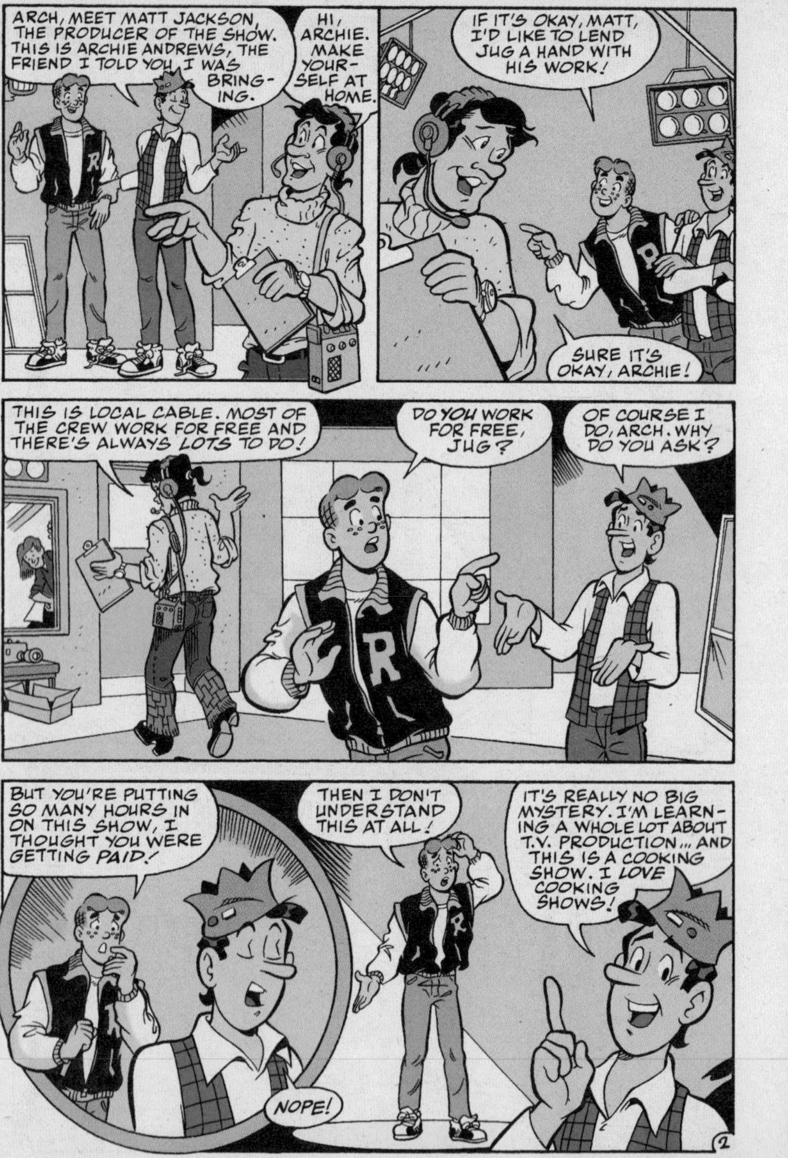
ARCH, MEET MATT JACKSON, THE PRODUCER OF THE SHOW. THIS IS ARCHIE ANDREWS, THE FRIEND I TOLD YOU I WAS BRING-ING.
HI, ARCHIE. MAKE YOUR-SELF AT HOME.
IF IT'S OKAY, MATT, I'D LIKE TO LEND JUG A HAND WITH HIS WORK!
SURE IT'S OKAY, ARCHIE!
THIS IS LOCAL CABLE. MOST OF THE CREW WORK FOR FREE AND THERE'S ALWAYS LOTS TO DO!
DO YOU WORK FOR FREE, JUG?
OF COURSE I DO, ARCH. WHY DO YOU ASK?
BUT YOU'RE PUTTING SO MANY HOURS IN ON THIS SHOW, I THOUGHT YOU WERE GETTING PAID!
NOPE!
THEN I DON'T UNDERSTAND THIS AT ALL!
IT'S REALLY NO BIG MYSTERY. I'M LEARN-ING A WHOLE LOT ABOUT T.V. PRODUCTION... AND THIS IS A COOKING SHOW. I LOVE COOKING SHOWS!
2

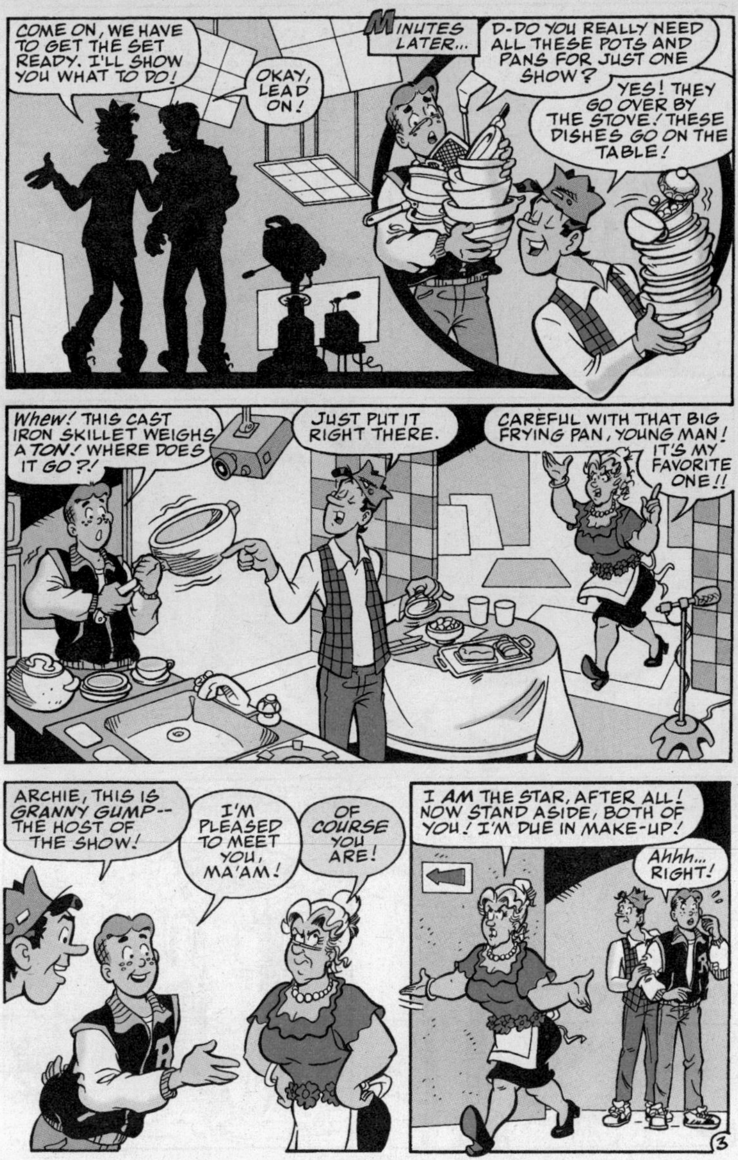
COME ON, WE HAVE TO GET THE SET READY. I'LL SHOW YOU WHAT TO DO!
OKAY, LEAD ON!
MINUTES LATER...
D-DO YOU REALLY NEED ALL THESE POTS AND PANS FOR JUST ONE SHOW?
YES! THEY GO OVER BY THE STOVE! THESE DISHES GO ON THE TABLE!
Whew! THIS CAST IRON SKILLET WEIGHS A TON! WHERE DOES IT GO?!
JUST PUT IT RIGHT THERE.
CAREFUL WITH THAT BIG FRYING PAN, YOUNG MAN! IT'S MY FAVORITE ONE!!
ARCHIE, THIS IS GRANNY GUMP--THE HOST OF THE SHOW!
I'M PLEASED TO MEET YOU, MA'AM!
OF COURSE YOU ARE!
I AM THE STAR, AFTER ALL! NOW STAND ASIDE, BOTH OF YOU! I'M DUE IN MAKE-UP!
Ahhh... RIGHT!
3

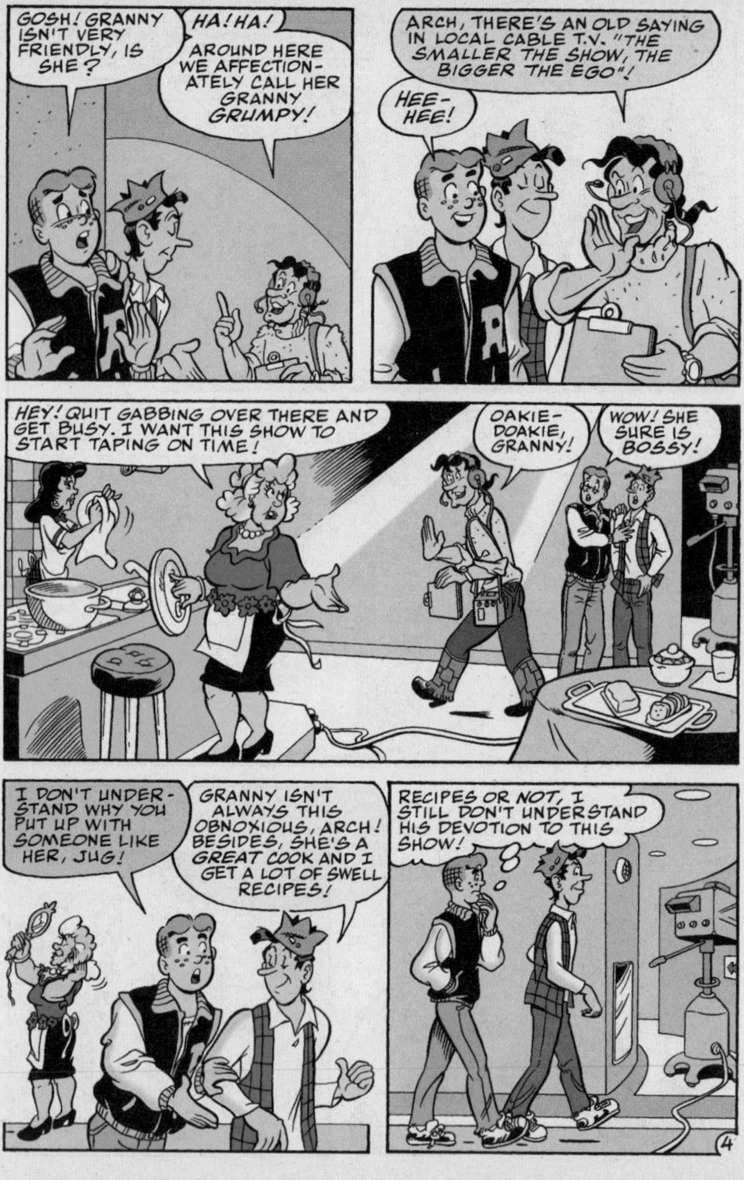
GOSH! GRANNY ISN'T VERY FRIENDLY, IS SHE?
HA! HA!
AROUND HERE WE AFFECTION-ATELY CALL HER GRANNY GRUMPY!
ARCH, THERE'S AN OLD SAYING IN LOCAL CABLE T.V. "THE SMALLER THE SHOW, THE BIGGER THE EGO"!
HEE-HEE!
HEY! QUIT GABBING OVER THERE AND GET BUSY. I WANT THIS SHOW TO START TAPING ON TIME!
OAKIE-DOAKIE, GRANNY!
WOW! SHE SURE IS BOSSY!
I DON'T UNDER-STAND WHY YOU PUT UP WITH SOMEONE LIKE HER, JUG!
GRANNY ISN'T ALWAYS THIS OBNOXIOUS, ARCH! BESIDES, SHE'S A GREAT COOK AND I GET A LOT OF SWELL RECIPES!
RECIPES OR NOT, I STILL DON'T UNDERSTAND HIS DEVOTION TO THIS SHOW!

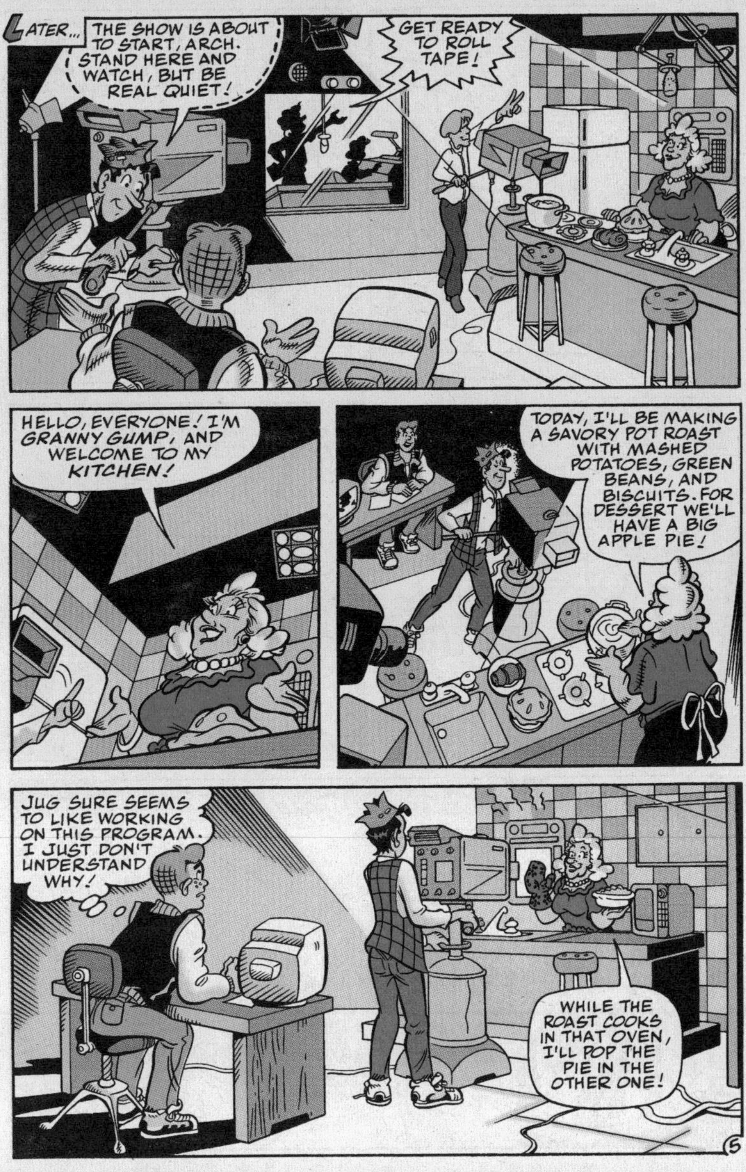
LATER...
THE SHOW IS ABOUT TO START, ARCH. STAND HERE AND WATCH, BUT BE REAL QUIET!
GET READY TO ROLL TAPE!
HELLO, EVERYONE! I'M GRANNY GUMP, AND WELCOME TO MY KITCHEN!
TODAY, I'LL BE MAKING A SAVORY POT ROAST WITH MASHED POTATOES, GREEN BEANS, AND BISCUITS. FOR DESSERT WE'LL HAVE A BIG APPLE PIE!
JUG SURE SEEMS TO LIKE WORKING ON THIS PROGRAM. I JUST DON'T UNDERSTAND WHY!
WHILE THE ROAST COOKS IN THAT OVEN, I'LL POP THE PIE IN THE OTHER ONE!

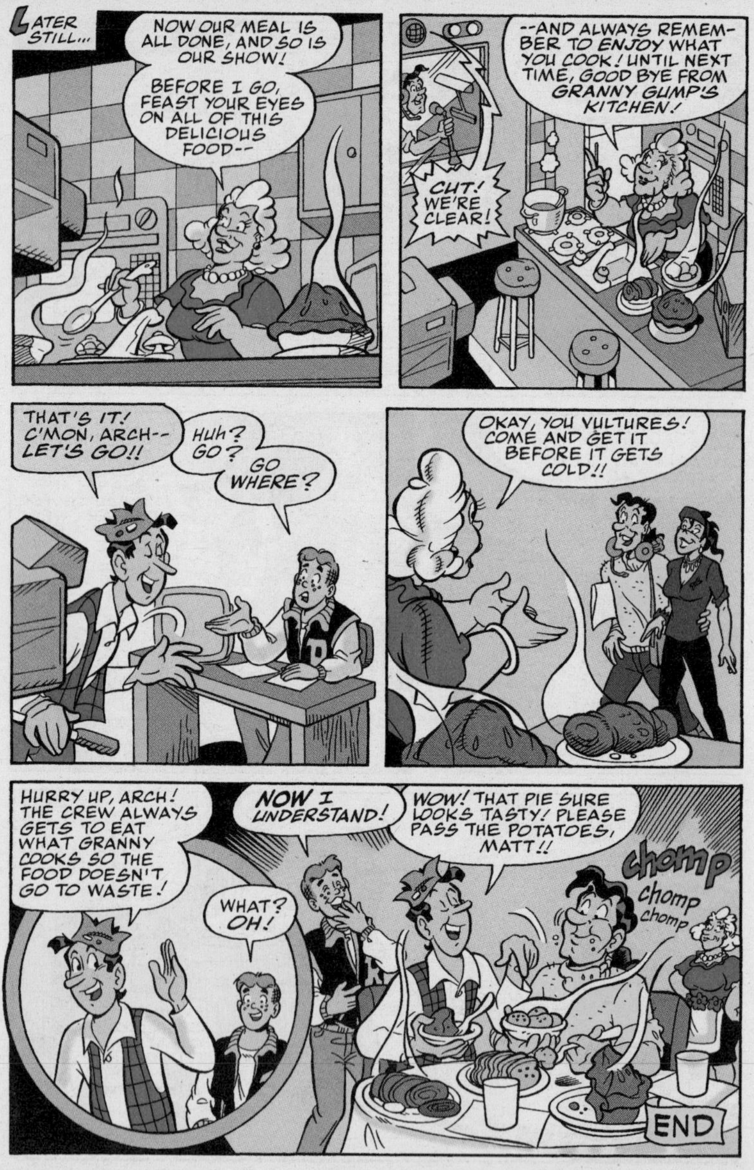
LATER STILL...
NOW OUR MEAL IS ALL DONE, AND SO IS OUR SHOW!
BEFORE I GO, FEAST YOUR EYES ON ALL OF THIS DELICIOUS FOOD--
--AND ALWAYS REMEMBER TO ENJOY WHAT YOU COOK! UNTIL NEXT TIME, GOOD BYE FROM GRANNY GUMP'S KITCHEN!
CUT! WE'RE CLEAR!
THAT'S IT! C'MON, ARCH-- LET'S GO!!
Huh? GO?
GO WHERE?
OKAY, YOU VULTURES! COME AND GET IT BEFORE IT GETS COLD!!
HURRY UP, ARCH! THE CREW ALWAYS GETS TO EAT WHAT GRANNY COOKS SO THE FOOD DOESN'T GO TO WASTE!
WHAT? OH!
NOW I UNDERSTAND!
WOW! THAT PIE SURE LOOKS TASTY! PLEASE PASS THE POTATOES, MATT!!
chomp
chomp
chomp
END

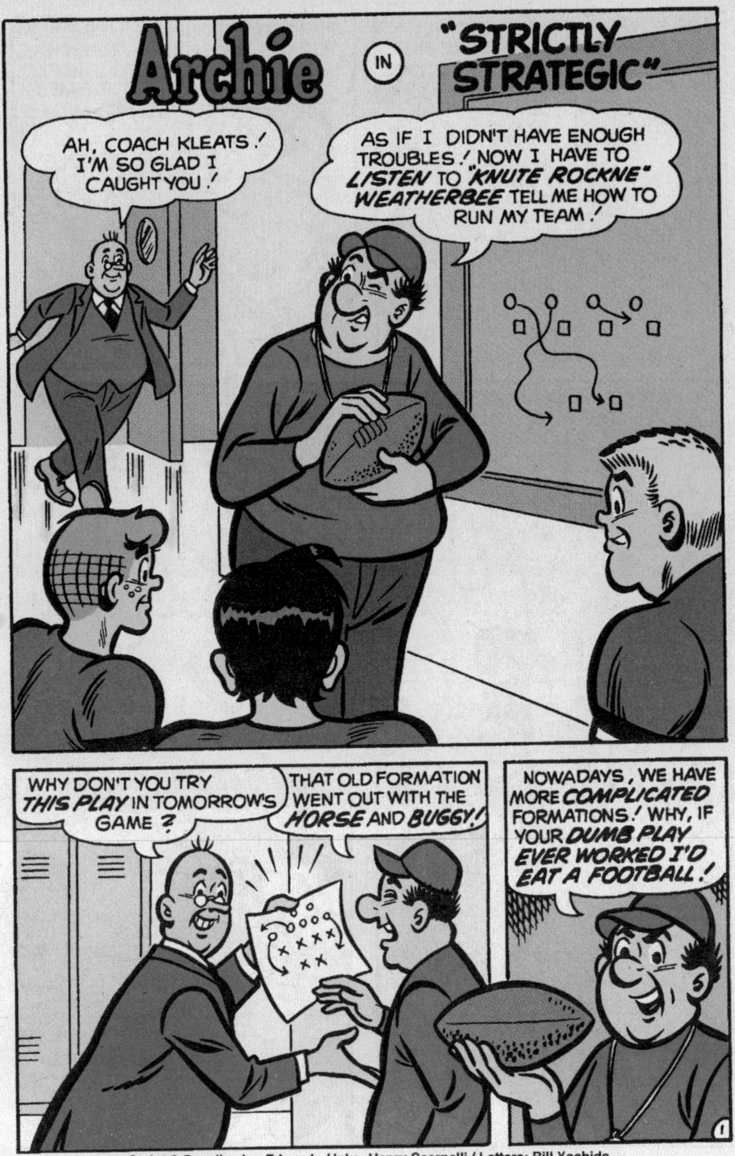
Archie IN "STRICTLY STRATEGIC"
AH, COACH KLEATS! I'M SO GLAD I CAUGHT YOU!
AS IF I DIDN'T HAVE ENOUGH TROUBLES! NOW I HAVE TO LISTEN TO "KNUTE ROCKNE" WEATHERBEE TELL ME HOW TO RUN MY TEAM!
WHY DON'T YOU TRY THIS PLAY IN TOMORROW'S GAME?
THAT OLD FORMATION WENT OUT WITH THE HORSE AND BUGGY!
NOWADAYS, WE HAVE MORE COMPLICATED FORMATIONS! WHY, IF YOUR DUMB PLAY EVER WORKED I'D EAT A FOOTBALL!
1

Script & Pencils: Joe Edwards / Inks: Henry Scarpelli / Letters: Bill Yoshida

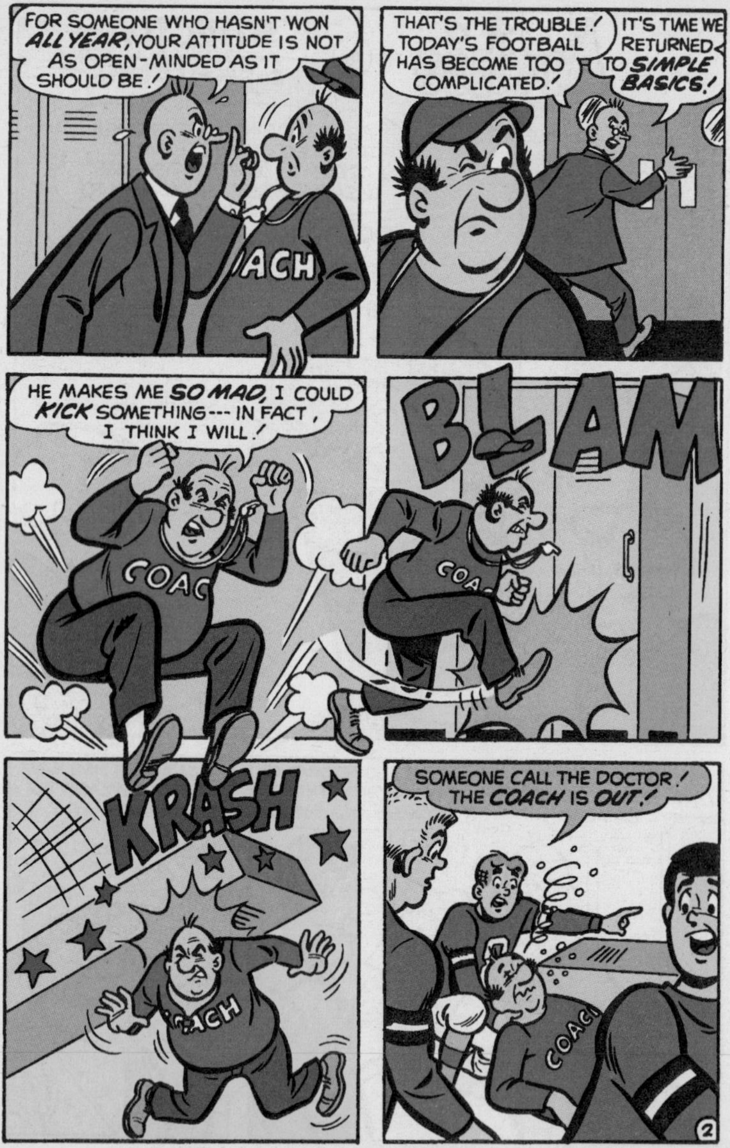

FOR SOMEONE WHO HASN'T WON ALL YEAR, YOUR ATTITUDE IS NOT AS OPEN-MINDED AS IT SHOULD BE!
ACH
THAT'S THE TROUBLE! TODAY'S FOOTBALL HAS BECOME TOO COMPLICATED!
IT'S TIME WE RETURNED TO SIMPLE BASICS!
HE MAKES ME SO MAD, I COULD KICK SOMETHING--- IN FACT, I THINK I WILL!
COAC
BLAM
COAC
KRASH
COACH
SOMEONE CALL THE DOCTOR! THE COACH IS OUT!
COAC
2

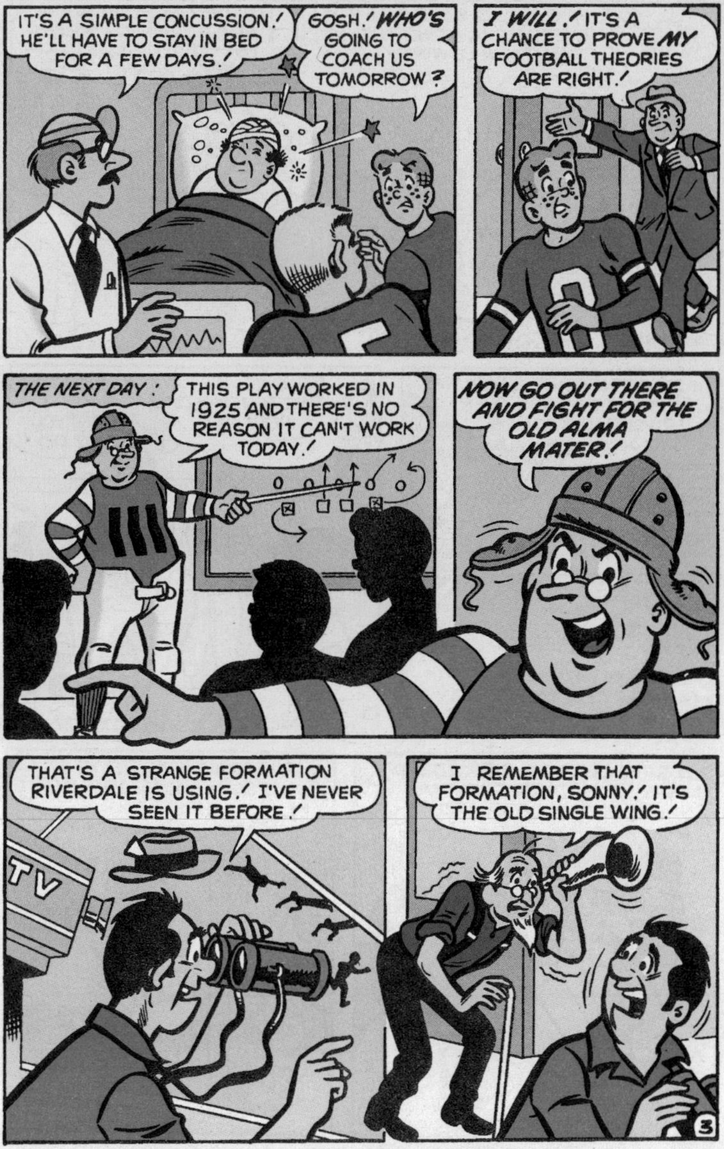
IT'S A SIMPLE CONCUSSION! HE'LL HAVE TO STAY IN BED FOR A FEW DAYS!
GOSH! WHO'S GOING TO COACH US TOMORROW?
I WILL! IT'S A CHANCE TO PROVE MY FOOTBALL THEORIES ARE RIGHT!
THE NEXT DAY:
THIS PLAY WORKED IN 1925 AND THERE'S NO REASON IT CAN'T WORK TODAY!
NOW GO OUT THERE AND FIGHT FOR THE OLD ALMA MATER!
THAT'S A STRANGE FORMATION RIVERDALE IS USING! I'VE NEVER SEEN IT BEFORE!
TV
I REMEMBER THAT FORMATION, SONNY! IT'S THE OLD SINGLE WING!
3

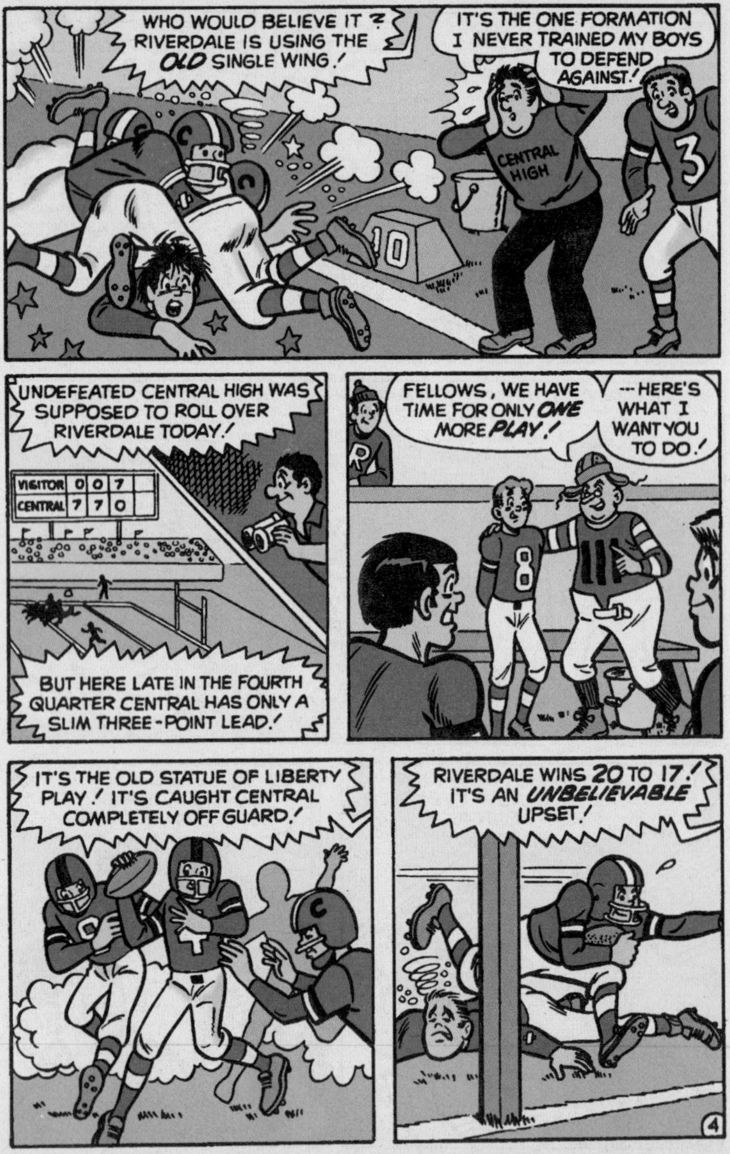

WHO WOULD BELIEVE IT ? RIVERDALE IS USING THE OLD SINGLE WING!
IT'S THE ONE FORMATION I NEVER TRAINED MY BOYS TO DEFEND AGAINST!
CENTRAL HIGH
10
3
UNDEFEATED CENTRAL HIGH WAS SUPPOSED TO ROLL OVER RIVERDALE TODAY!
VISITOR 0 0 7
CENTRAL 7 7 0
BUT HERE LATE IN THE FOURTH QUARTER CENTRAL HAS ONLY A SLIM THREE-POINT LEAD!
FELLOWS, WE HAVE TIME FOR ONLY ONE MORE PLAY!
--- HERE'S WHAT I WANT YOU TO DO!
IT'S THE OLD STATUE OF LIBERTY PLAY! IT'S CAUGHT CENTRAL COMPLETELY OFF GUARD!
RIVERDALE WINS 20 TO 17! IT'S AN UNBELIEVABLE UPSET!

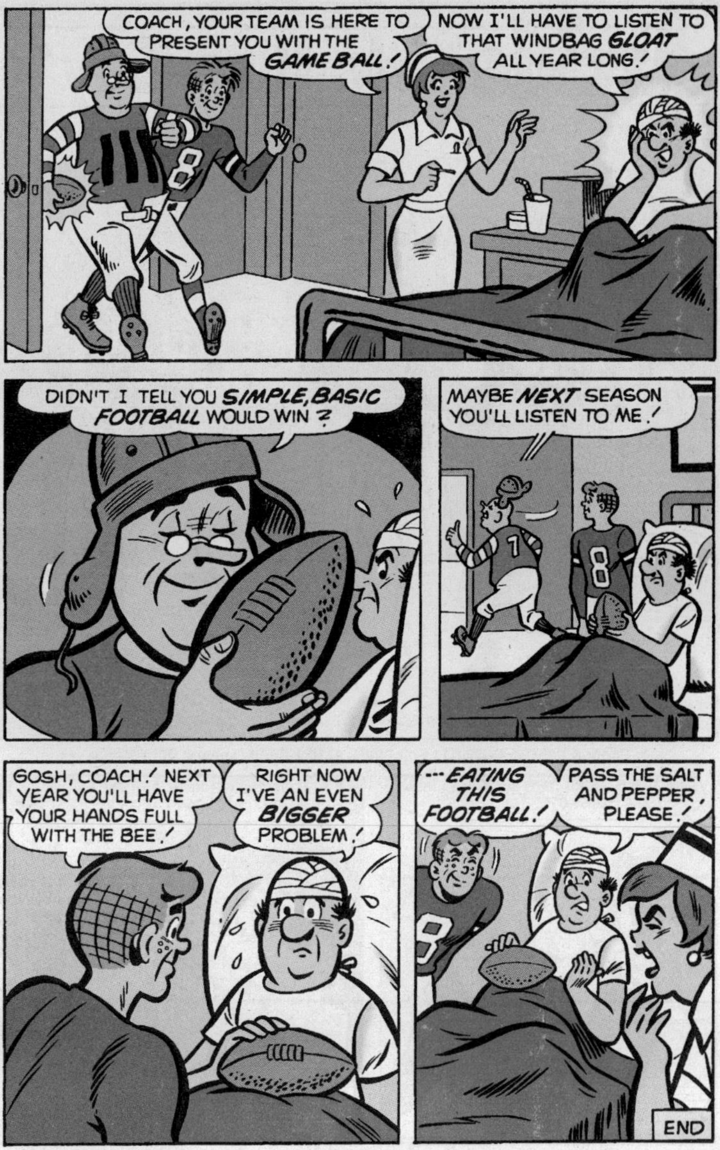
COACH, YOUR TEAM IS HERE TO PRESENT YOU WITH THE GAME BALL!
NOW I'LL HAVE TO LISTEN TO THAT WINDBAG GLOAT ALL YEAR LONG!
DIDN'T I TELL YOU SIMPLE, BASIC FOOTBALL WOULD WIN?
MAYBE NEXT SEASON YOU'LL LISTEN TO ME!
GOSH, COACH! NEXT YEAR YOU'LL HAVE YOUR HANDS FULL WITH THE BEE!
RIGHT NOW I'VE AN EVEN BIGGER PROBLEM!
---EATING THIS FOOTBALL!
PASS THE SALT AND PEPPER, PLEASE!
END

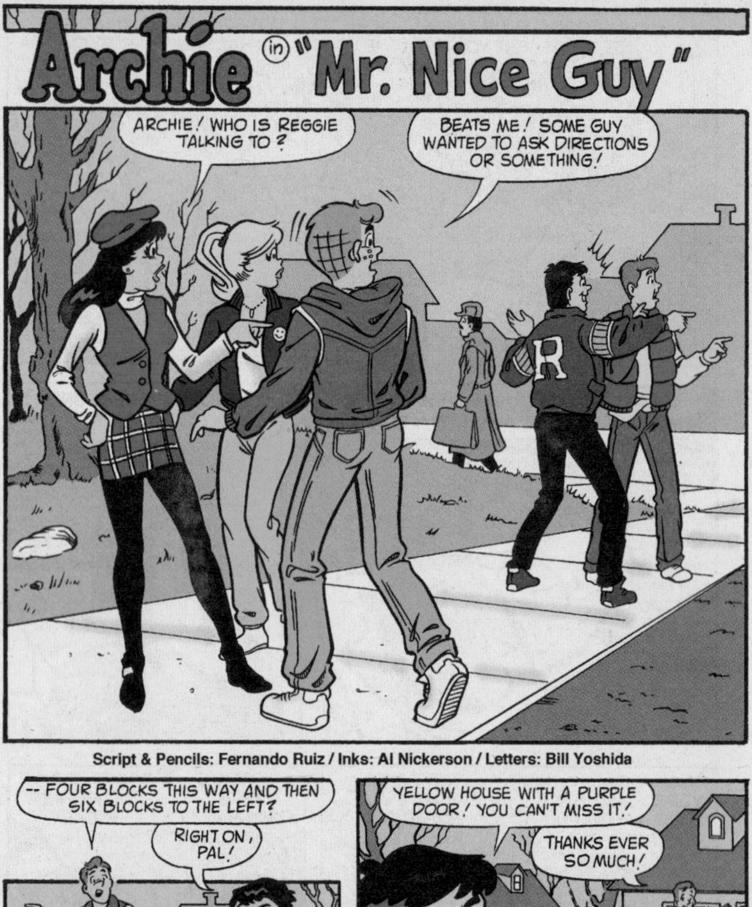
Archie in "Mr. Nice Guy"
ARCHIE! WHO IS REGGIE TALKING TO?
BEATS ME! SOME GUY WANTED TO ASK DIRECTIONS OR SOMETHING!

Script & Pencils: Fernando Ruiz / Inks: Al Nickerson / Letters: Bill Yoshida

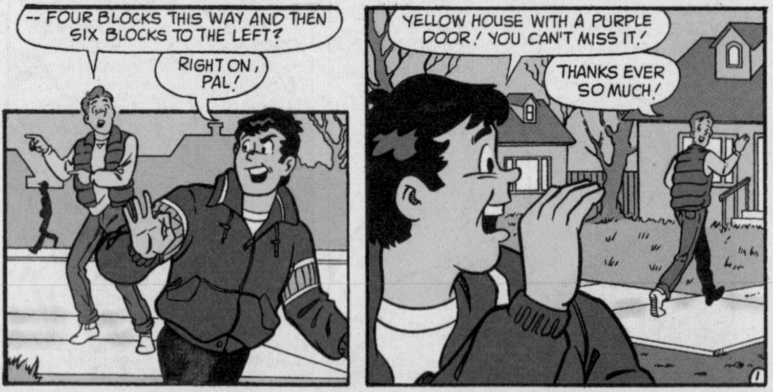
-- FOUR BLOCKS THIS WAY AND THEN SIX BLOCKS TO THE LEFT?
RIGHT ON, PAL!
YELLOW HOUSE WITH A PURPLE DOOR! YOU CAN'T MISS IT!
THANKS EVER SO MUCH!
1

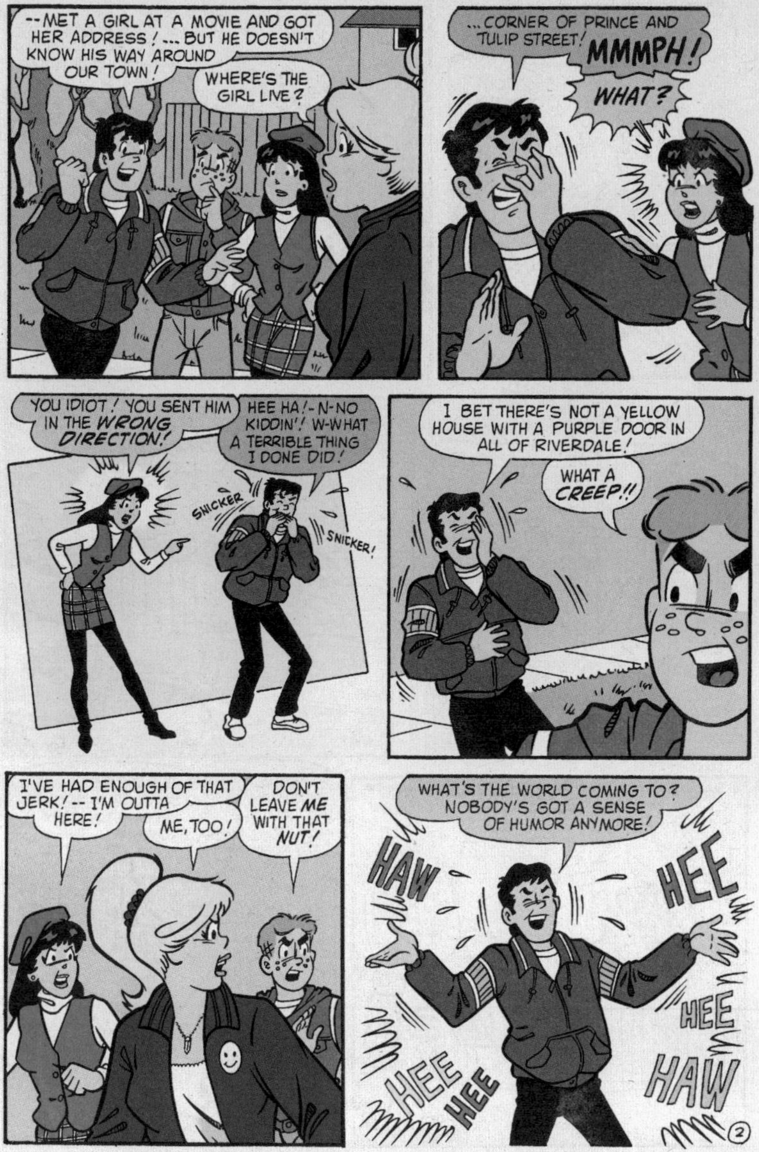

--MET A GIRL AT A MOVIE AND GOT HER ADDRESS! ... BUT HE DOESN'T KNOW HIS WAY AROUND OUR TOWN!
WHERE'S THE GIRL LIVE?
...CORNER OF PRINCE AND TULIP STREET!
MMMPH!
WHAT?
YOU IDIOT! YOU SENT HIM IN THE WRONG DIRECTION!
HEE HA!-N-NO KIDDIN'! W-WHAT A TERRIBLE THING I DONE DID!
SNICKER
SNICKER!
I BET THERE'S NOT A YELLOW HOUSE WITH A PURPLE DOOR IN ALL OF RIVERDALE!
WHAT A CREEP!!
I'VE HAD ENOUGH OF THAT JERK! -- I'M OUTTA HERE!
ME, TOO!
DON'T LEAVE ME WITH THAT NUT!
WHAT'S THE WORLD COMING TO? NOBODY'S GOT A SENSE OF HUMOR ANYMORE!
HAW
HEE
HEE
HEE
HEE
HAW
2

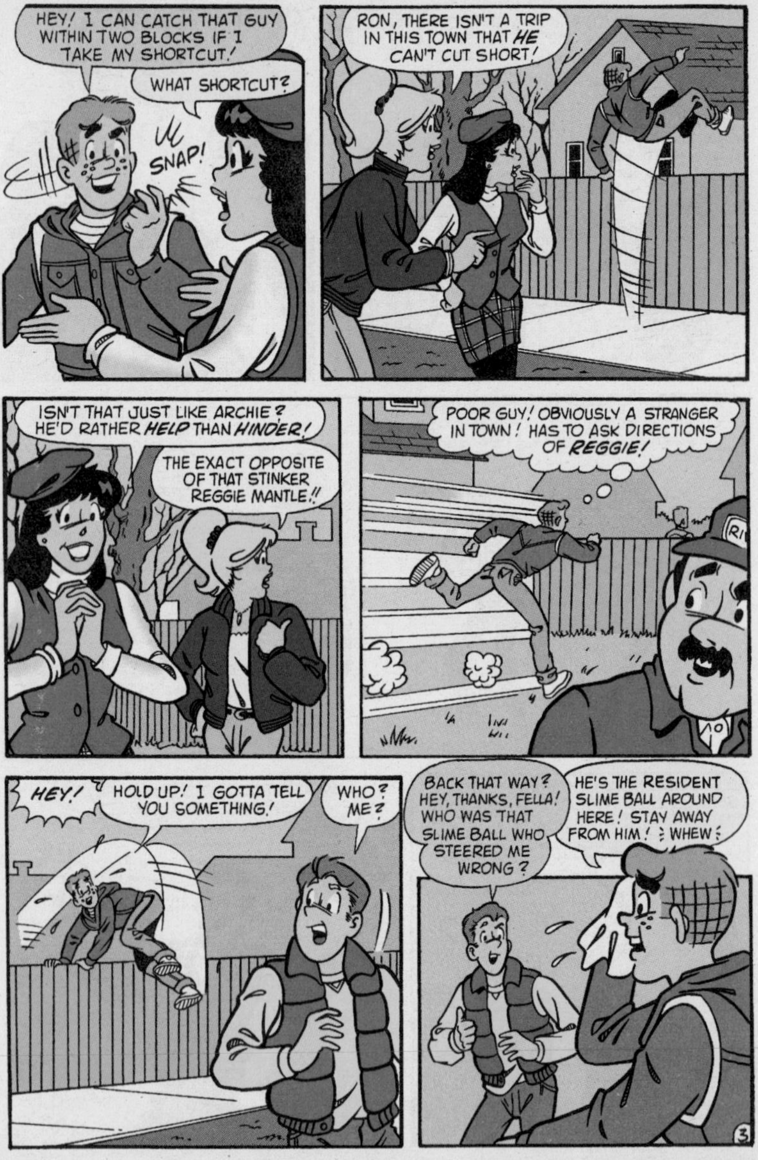
HEY! I CAN CATCH THAT GUY WITHIN TWO BLOCKS IF I TAKE MY SHORTCUT!
WHAT SHORTCUT?
SNAP!
RON, THERE ISN'T A TRIP IN THIS TOWN THAT HE CAN'T CUT SHORT!
ISN'T THAT JUST LIKE ARCHIE? HE'D RATHER HELP THAN HINDER!
THE EXACT OPPOSITE OF THAT STINKER REGGIE MANTLE!!
POOR GUY! OBVIOUSLY A STRANGER IN TOWN! HAS TO ASK DIRECTIONS OF REGGIE!
HEY!
HOLD UP! I GOTTA TELL YOU SOMETHING!
WHO? ME?
BACK THAT WAY? HEY, THANKS, FELLA! WHO WAS THAT SLIME BALL WHO STEERED ME WRONG?
HE'S THE RESIDENT SLIME BALL AROUND HERE! STAY AWAY FROM HIM! WHEW
3

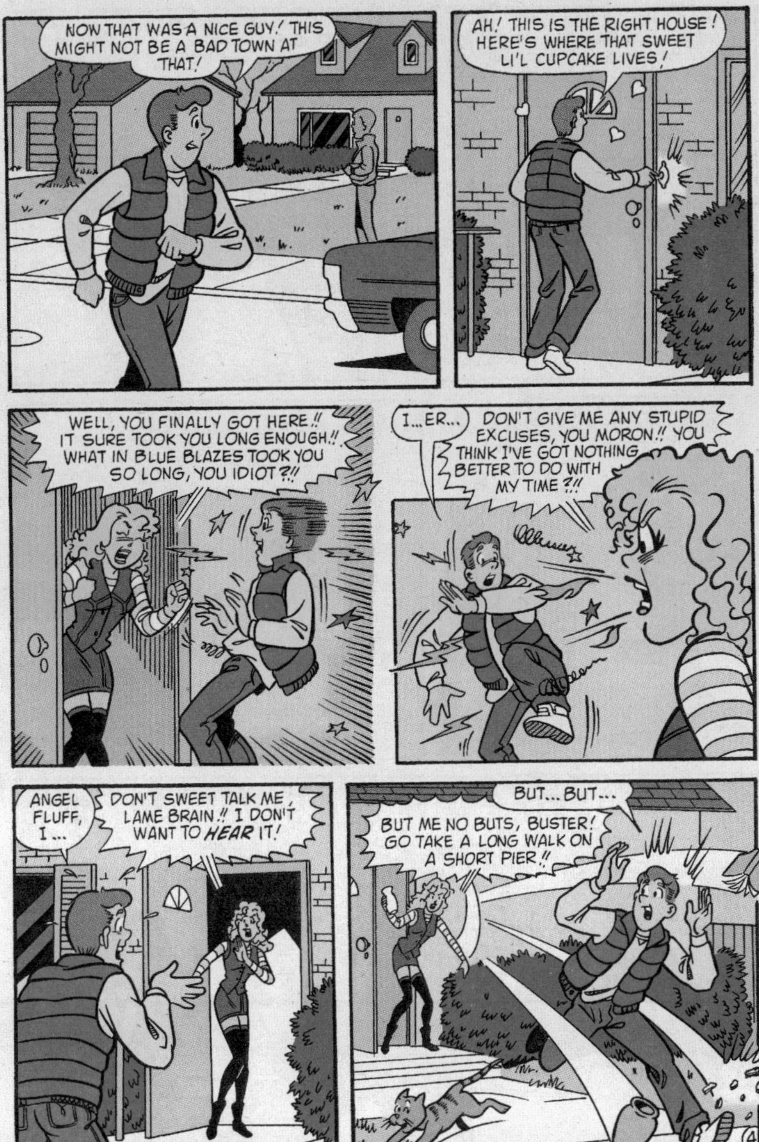
NOW THAT WAS A NICE GUY! THIS MIGHT NOT BE A BAD TOWN AT THAT!
AH! THIS IS THE RIGHT HOUSE! HERE'S WHERE THAT SWEET LI'L CUPCAKE LIVES!
WELL, YOU FINALLY GOT HERE!! IT SURE TOOK YOU LONG ENOUGH!! WHAT IN BLUE BLAZES TOOK YOU SO LONG, YOU IDIOT?!!
I...ER...
DON'T GIVE ME ANY STUPID EXCUSES, YOU MORON!! YOU THINK I'VE GOT NOTHING BETTER TO DO WITH MY TIME?!!
ANGEL FLUFF, I...
DON'T SWEET TALK ME, LAME BRAIN!! I DON'T WANT TO HEAR IT!
BUT... BUT...
BUT ME NO BUTS, BUSTER! GO TAKE A LONG WALK ON A SHORT PIER!!
4

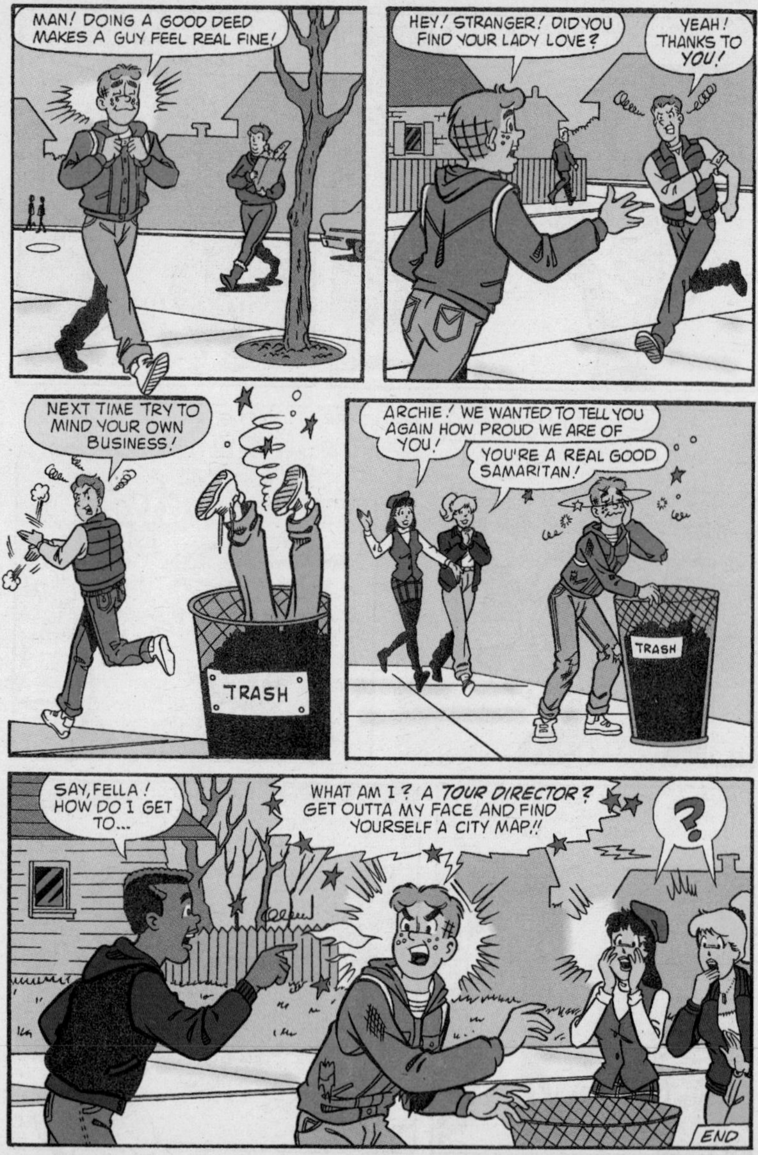
MAN! DOING A GOOD DEED MAKES A GUY FEEL REAL FINE!
HEY! STRANGER! DID YOU FIND YOUR LADY LOVE?
YEAH! THANKS TO YOU!
NEXT TIME TRY TO MIND YOUR OWN BUSINESS!
TRASH
ARCHIE! WE WANTED TO TELL YOU AGAIN HOW PROUD WE ARE OF YOU!
YOU'RE A REAL GOOD SAMARITAN!
TRASH
SAY, FELLA! HOW DO I GET TO...
WHAT AM I? A TOUR DIRECTOR? GET OUTTA MY FACE AND FIND YOURSELF A CITY MAP!!
?
END

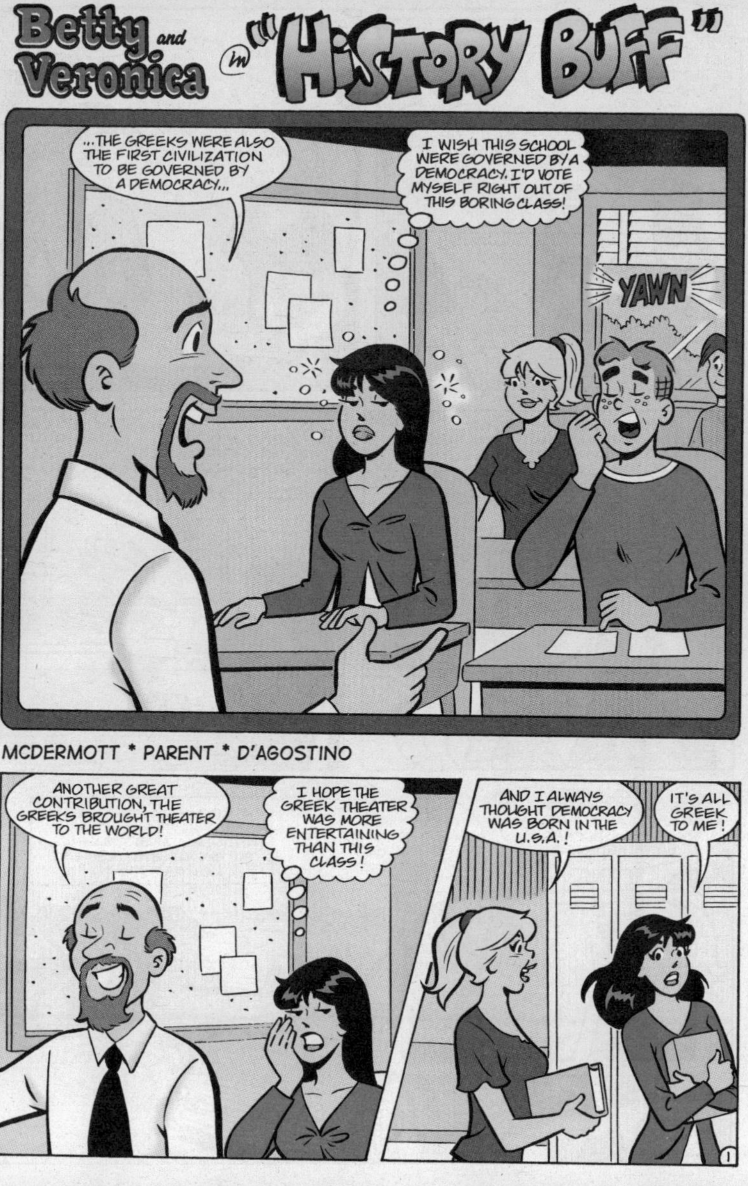
Betty and Veronica in "HISTORY BUFF"
...THE GREEKS WERE ALSO THE FIRST CIVILIZATION TO BE GOVERNED BY A DEMOCRACY...
I WISH THIS SCHOOL WERE GOVERNED BY A DEMOCRACY. I'D VOTE MYSELF RIGHT OUT OF THIS BORING CLASS!
YAWN
MCDERMOTT * PARENT * D'AGOSTINO
ANOTHER GREAT CONTRIBUTION, THE GREEKS BROUGHT THEATER TO THE WORLD!
I HOPE THE GREEK THEATER WAS MORE ENTERTAINING THAN THIS CLASS!
AND I ALWAYS THOUGHT DEMOCRACY WAS BORN IN THE U.S.A.!
IT'S ALL GREEK TO ME!
1

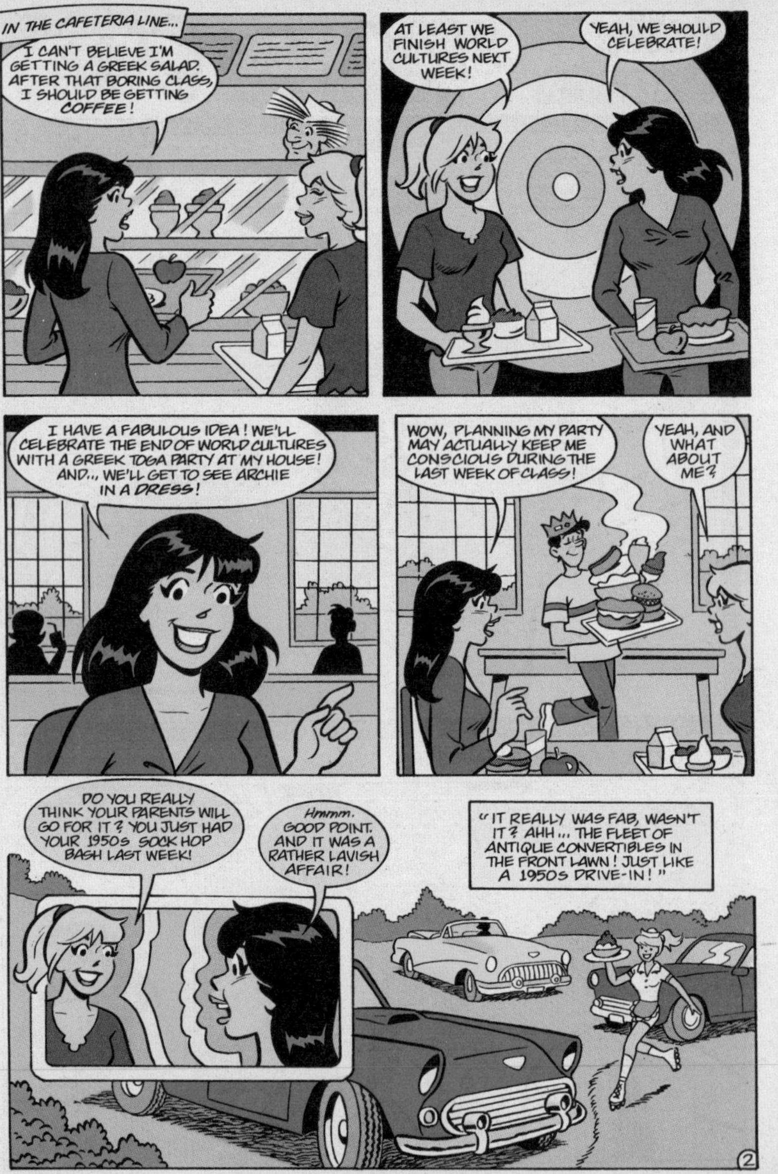
IN THE CAFETERIA LINE...
I CAN'T BELIEVE I'M GETTING A GREEK SALAD. AFTER THAT BORING CLASS, I SHOULD BE GETTING COFFEE!
AT LEAST WE FINISH WORLD CULTURES NEXT WEEK!
YEAH, WE SHOULD CELEBRATE!
I HAVE A FABULOUS IDEA! WE'LL CELEBRATE THE END OF WORLD CULTURES WITH A GREEK TOGA PARTY AT MY HOUSE! AND... WE'LL GET TO SEE ARCHIE IN A DRESS!
WOW, PLANNING MY PARTY MAY ACTUALLY KEEP ME CONSCIOUS DURING THE LAST WEEK OF CLASS!
YEAH, AND WHAT ABOUT ME?
DO YOU REALLY THINK YOUR PARENTS WILL GO FOR IT? YOU JUST HAD YOUR 1950s SOCK HOP BASH LAST WEEK!
Hmmm. GOOD POINT. AND IT WAS A RATHER LAVISH AFFAIR!
"IT REALLY WAS FAB, WASN'T IT? AHH... THE FLEET OF ANTIQUE CONVERTIBLES IN THE FRONT LAWN! JUST LIKE A 1950s DRIVE-IN!"
2

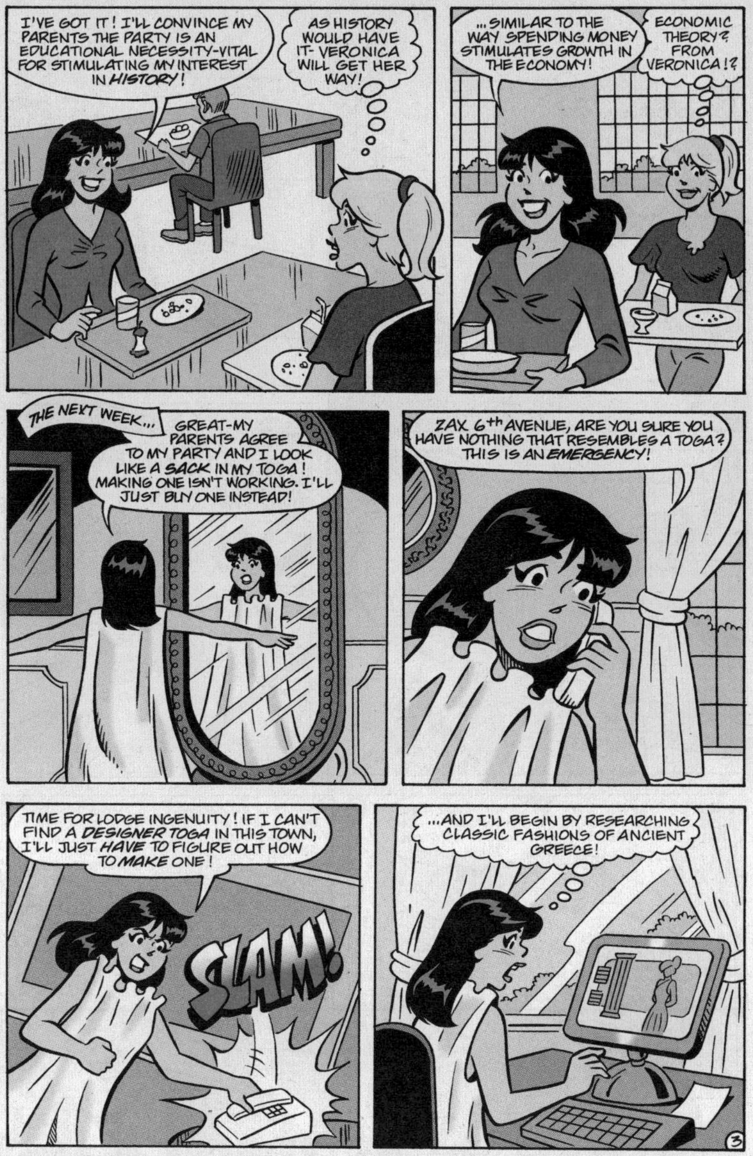
I'VE GOT IT! I'LL CONVINCE MY PARENTS THE PARTY IS AN EDUCATIONAL NECESSITY-VITAL FOR STIMULATING MY INTEREST IN HISTORY!
AS HISTORY WOULD HAVE IT- VERONICA WILL GET HER WAY!
...SIMILAR TO THE WAY SPENDING MONEY STIMULATES GROWTH IN THE ECONOMY!
ECONOMIC THEORY? FROM VERONICA!?
THE NEXT WEEK...
GREAT-MY PARENTS AGREE TO MY PARTY AND I LOOK LIKE A SACK IN MY TOGA! MAKING ONE ISN'T WORKING. I'LL JUST BUY ONE INSTEAD!
ZAX 6th AVENUE, ARE YOU SURE YOU HAVE NOTHING THAT RESEMBLES A TOGA? THIS IS AN EMERGENCY!
TIME FOR LODGE INGENUITY! IF I CAN'T FIND A DESIGNER TOGA IN THIS TOWN, I'LL JUST HAVE TO FIGURE OUT HOW TO MAKE ONE!
SLAM!
...AND I'LL BEGIN BY RESEARCHING CLASSIC FASHIONS OF ANCIENT GREECE!
3

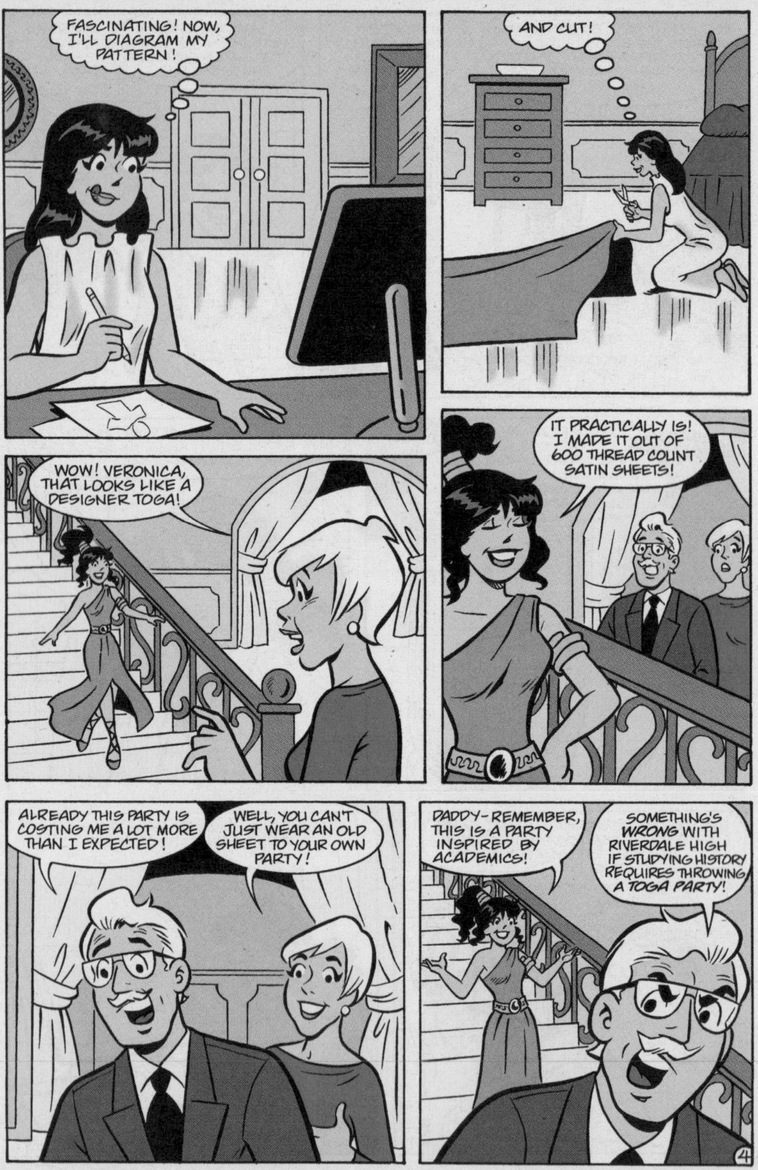
FASCINATING! NOW, I'LL DIAGRAM MY PATTERN!
AND CUT!
WOW! VERONICA, THAT LOOKS LIKE A DESIGNER TOGA!
IT PRACTICALLY IS! I MADE IT OUT OF 600 THREAD COUNT SATIN SHEETS!
ALREADY THIS PARTY IS COSTING ME A LOT MORE THAN I EXPECTED!
WELL, YOU CAN'T JUST WEAR AN OLD SHEET TO YOUR OWN PARTY!
DADDY- REMEMBER, THIS IS A PARTY INSPIRED BY ACADEMICS!
SOMETHING'S WRONG WITH RIVERDALE HIGH IF STUDYING HISTORY REQUIRES THROWING A TOGA PARTY!
4

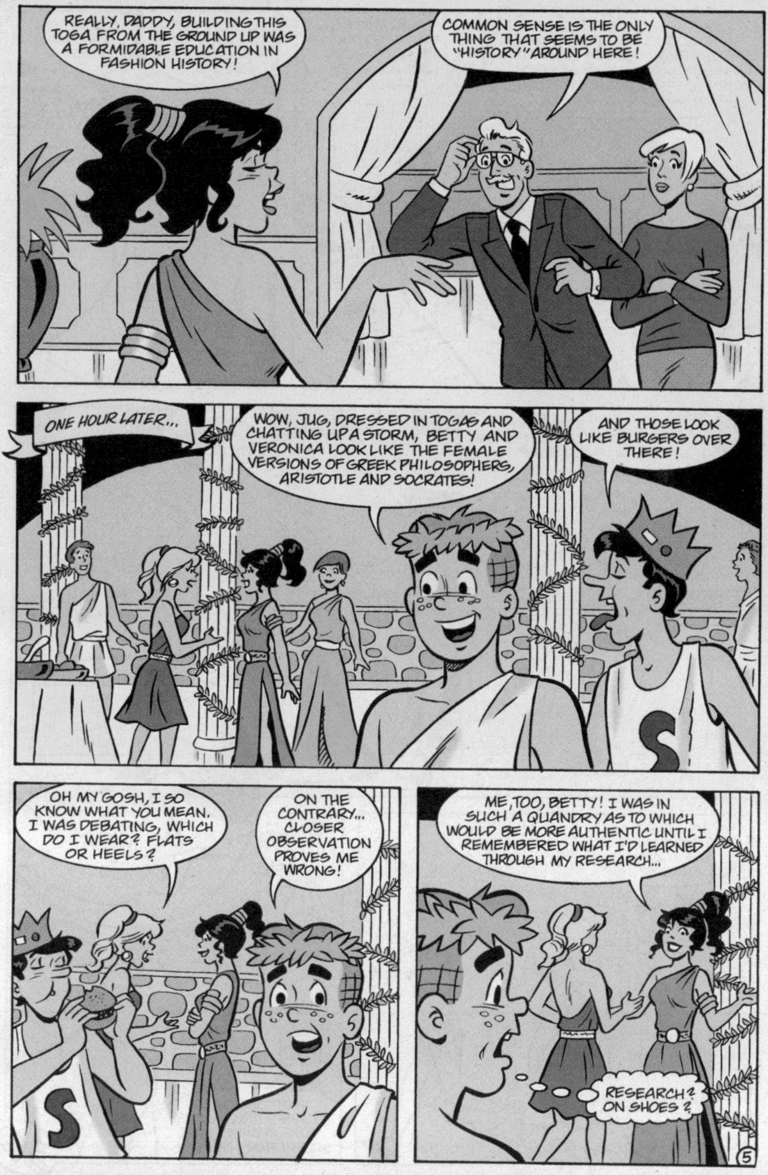
REALLY, DADDY, BUILDING THIS TOGA FROM THE GROUND UP WAS A FORMIDABLE EDUCATION IN FASHION HISTORY!
COMMON SENSE IS THE ONLY THING THAT SEEMS TO BE "HISTORY" AROUND HERE!
ONE HOUR LATER...
WOW, JUG, DRESSED IN TOGAS AND CHATTING UP A STORM, BETTY AND VERONICA LOOK LIKE THE FEMALE VERSIONS OF GREEK PHILOSOPHERS, ARISTOTLE AND SOCRATES!
AND THOSE LOOK LIKE BURGERS OVER THERE!
OH MY GOSH, I SO KNOW WHAT YOU MEAN. I WAS DEBATING, WHICH DO I WEAR? FLATS OR HEELS?
ON THE CONTRARY... CLOSER OBSERVATION PROVES ME WRONG!
ME, TOO, BETTY! I WAS IN SUCH A QUANDRY AS TO WHICH WOULD BE MORE AUTHENTIC UNTIL I REMEMBERED WHAT I'D LEARNED THROUGH MY RESEARCH...
RESEARCH? ON SHOES?
5

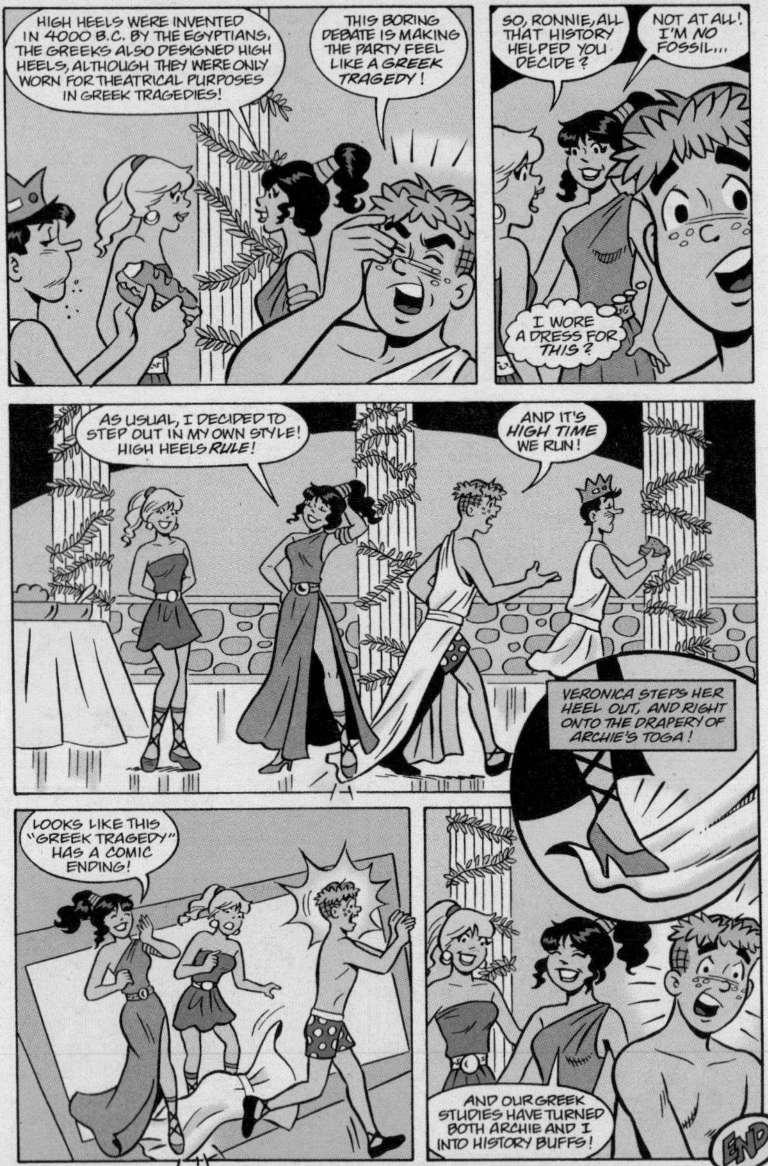
HIGH HEELS WERE INVENTED IN 4000 B.C. BY THE EGYPTIANS. THE GREEKS ALSO DESIGNED HIGH HEELS, ALTHOUGH THEY WERE ONLY WORN FOR THEATRICAL PURPOSES IN GREEK TRAGEDIES!
THIS BORING DEBATE IS MAKING THE PARTY FEEL LIKE A GREEK TRAGEDY!
SO, RONNIE, ALL THAT HISTORY HELPED YOU DECIDE?
NOT AT ALL! I'M NO FOSSIL...
I WORE A DRESS FOR THIS?
AS USUAL, I DECIDED TO STEP OUT IN MY OWN STYLE! HIGH HEELS RULE!
AND IT'S HIGH TIME WE RUN!
VERONICA STEPS HER HEEL OUT, AND RIGHT ONTO THE DRAPERY OF ARCHIE'S TOGA!
LOOKS LIKE THIS "GREEK TRAGEDY" HAS A COMIC ENDING!
AND OUR GREEK STUDIES HAVE TURNED BOTH ARCHIE AND I INTO HISTORY BUFFS!
END

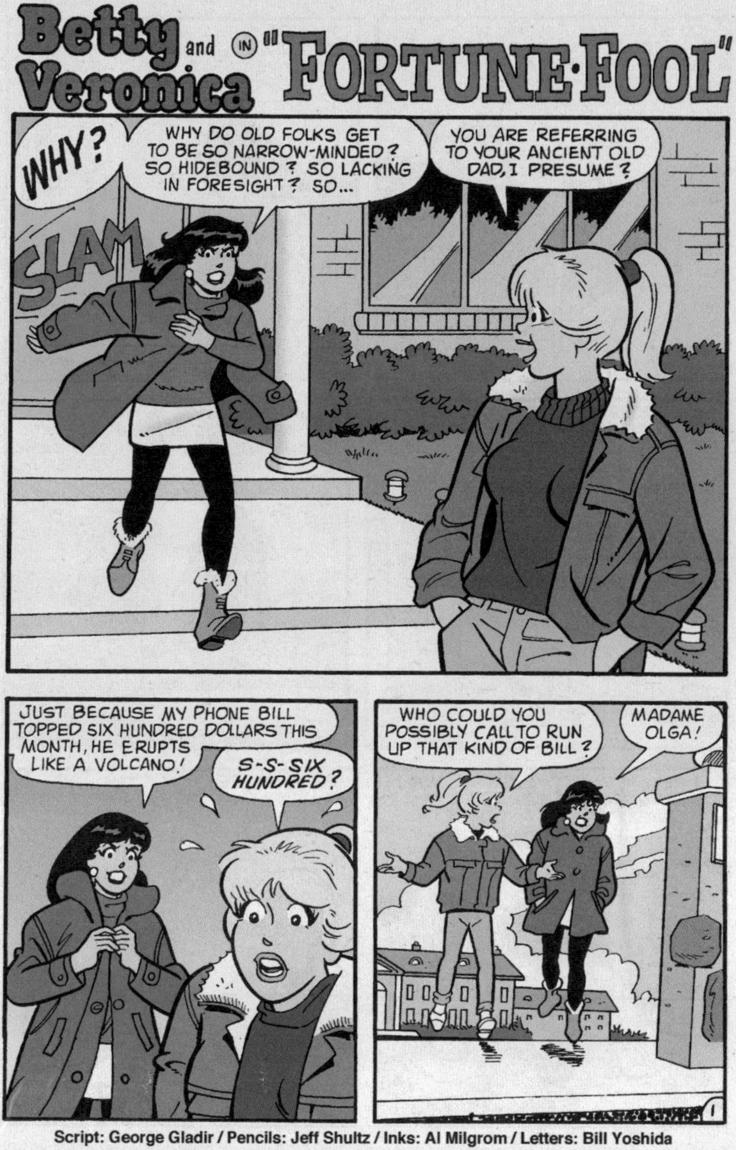
Betty and Veronica in "FORTUNE FOOL"
WHY?
WHY DO OLD FOLKS GET TO BE SO NARROW-MINDED? SO HIDEBOUND? SO LACKING IN FORESIGHT? SO...
SLAM
YOU ARE REFERRING TO YOUR ANCIENT OLD DAD, I PRESUME?
JUST BECAUSE MY PHONE BILL TOPPED SIX HUNDRED DOLLARS THIS MONTH, HE ERUPTS LIKE A VOLCANO!
S-S-SIX HUNDRED?
WHO COULD YOU POSSIBLY CALL TO RUN UP THAT KIND OF BILL?
MADAME OLGA!
1

Script: George Gladir / Pencils: Jeff Shultz / Inks: Al Milgrom / Letters: Bill Yoshida

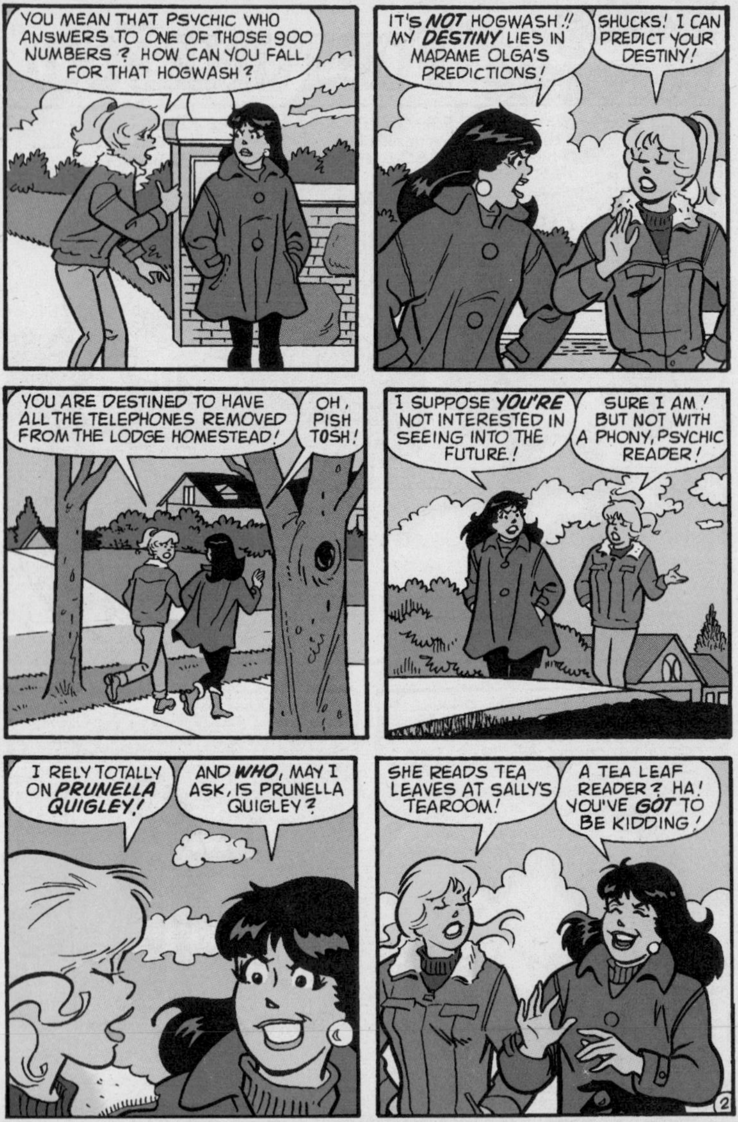
YOU MEAN THAT PSYCHIC WHO ANSWERS TO ONE OF THOSE 900 NUMBERS? HOW CAN YOU FALL FOR THAT HOGWASH?
IT'S NOT HOGWASH!! MY DESTINY LIES IN MADAME OLGA'S PREDICTIONS!
SHUCKS! I CAN PREDICT YOUR DESTINY!
YOU ARE DESTINED TO HAVE ALL THE TELEPHONES REMOVED FROM THE LODGE HOMESTEAD!
OH, PISH TOSH!
I SUPPOSE YOU'RE NOT INTERESTED IN SEEING INTO THE FUTURE!
SURE I AM! BUT NOT WITH A PHONY, PSYCHIC READER!
I RELY TOTALLY ON PRUNELLA QUIGLEY!
AND WHO, MAY I ASK, IS PRUNELLA QUIGLEY?
SHE READS TEA LEAVES AT SALLY'S TEAROOM!
A TEA LEAF READER? HA! YOU'VE GOT TO BE KIDDING!
2

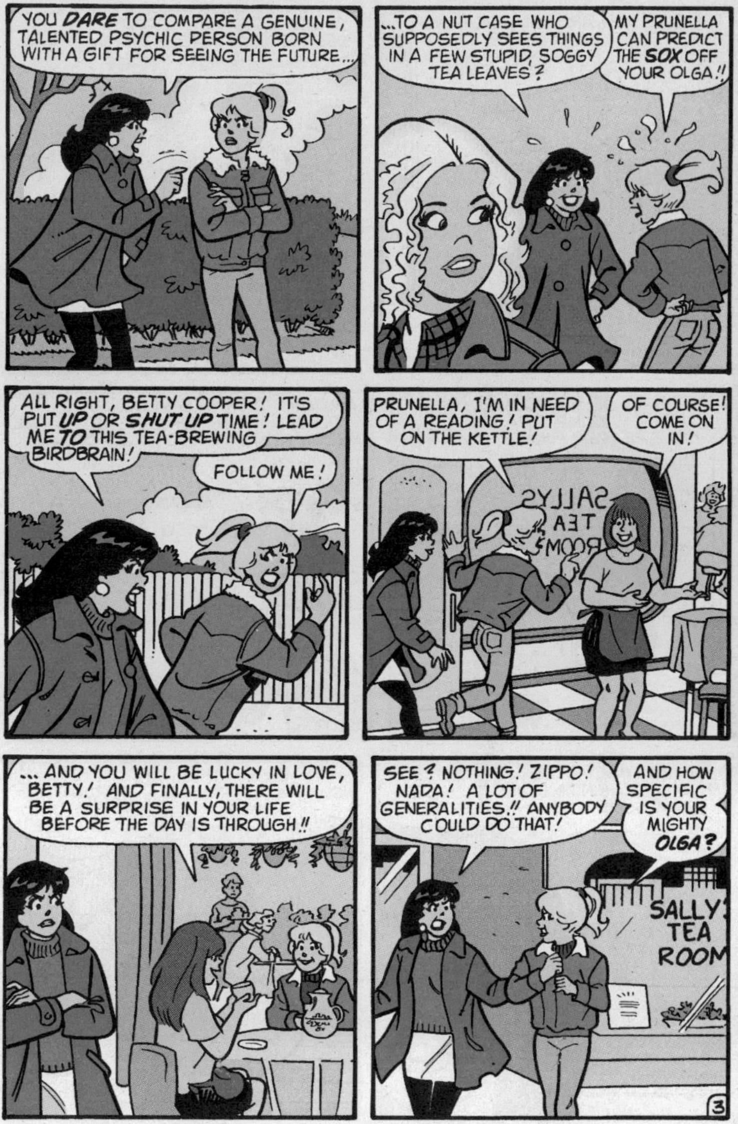
YOU DARE TO COMPARE A GENUINE, TALENTED PSYCHIC PERSON BORN WITH A GIFT FOR SEEING THE FUTURE...
...TO A NUT CASE WHO SUPPOSEDLY SEES THINGS IN A FEW STUPID, SOGGY TEA LEAVES?
MY PRUNELLA CAN PREDICT THE SOX OFF YOUR OLGA!!
ALL RIGHT, BETTY COOPER! IT'S PUT UP OR SHUT UP TIME! LEAD ME TO THIS TEA-BREWING BIRDBRAIN!
FOLLOW ME!
PRUNELLA, I'M IN NEED OF A READING! PUT ON THE KETTLE!
OF COURSE! COME ON IN!
SALLYS TEA ROOM
... AND YOU WILL BE LUCKY IN LOVE, BETTY! AND FINALLY, THERE WILL BE A SURPRISE IN YOUR LIFE BEFORE THE DAY IS THROUGH!!
SEE? NOTHING! ZIPPO! NADA! A LOT OF GENERALITIES!! ANYBODY COULD DO THAT!
AND HOW SPECIFIC IS YOUR MIGHTY OLGA?
SALLY'S TEA ROOM
3

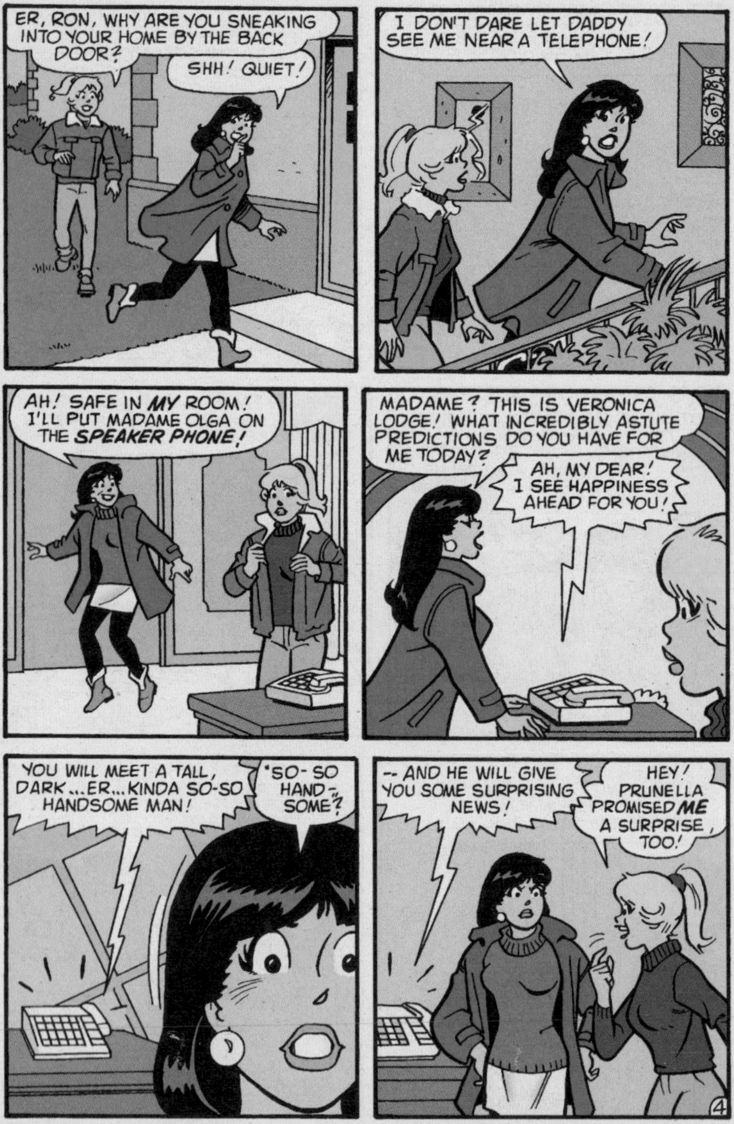
ER, RON, WHY ARE YOU SNEAKING INTO YOUR HOME BY THE BACK DOOR?
SHH! QUIET!
I DON'T DARE LET DADDY SEE ME NEAR A TELEPHONE!
AH! SAFE IN MY ROOM! I'LL PUT MADAME OLGA ON THE SPEAKER PHONE!
MADAME? THIS IS VERONICA LODGE! WHAT INCREDIBLY ASTUTE PREDICTIONS DO YOU HAVE FOR ME TODAY?
AH, MY DEAR! I SEE HAPPINESS AHEAD FOR YOU!
YOU WILL MEET A TALL, DARK...ER...KINDA SO-SO HANDSOME MAN!
"SO-SO HAND-SOME"?
-- AND HE WILL GIVE YOU SOME SURPRISING NEWS!
HEY! PRUNELLA PROMISED ME A SURPRISE, TOO!
4

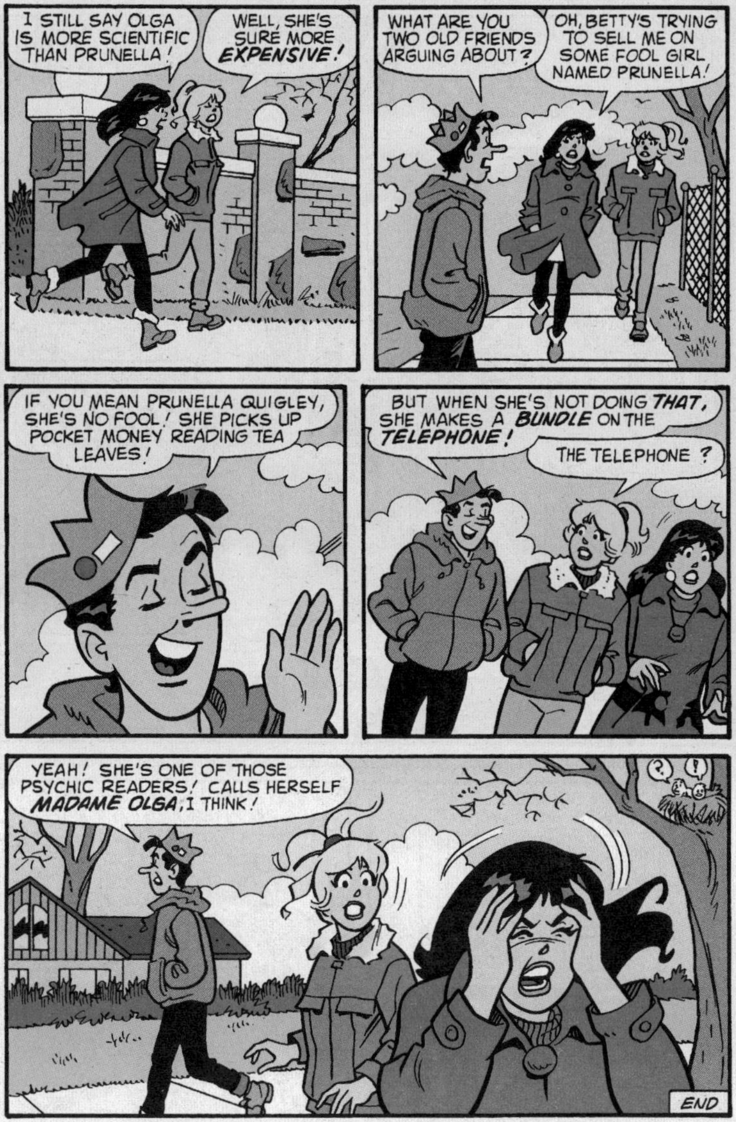
I STILL SAY OLGA IS MORE SCIENTIFIC THAN PRUNELLA!
WELL, SHE'S SURE MORE EXPENSIVE!
WHAT ARE YOU TWO OLD FRIENDS ARGUING ABOUT?
OH, BETTY'S TRYING TO SELL ME ON SOME FOOL GIRL NAMED PRUNELLA!
IF YOU MEAN PRUNELLA QUIGLEY, SHE'S NO FOOL! SHE PICKS UP POCKET MONEY READING TEA LEAVES!
BUT WHEN SHE'S NOT DOING THAT, SHE MAKES A BUNDLE ON THE TELEPHONE!
THE TELEPHONE?
YEAH! SHE'S ONE OF THOSE PSYCHIC READERS! CALLS HERSELF MADAME OLGA, I THINK!
?
!
END

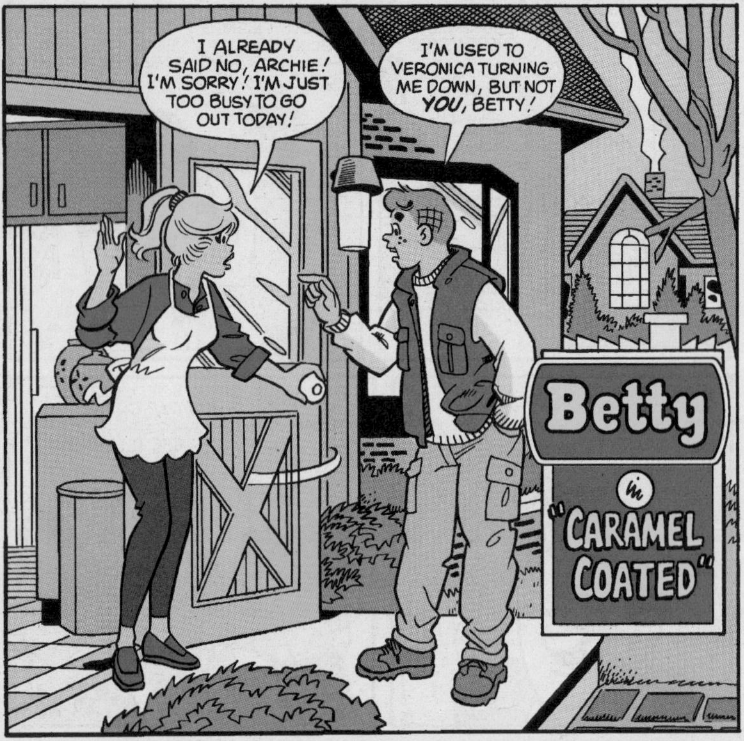
I ALREADY SAID NO, ARCHIE! I'M SORRY! I'M JUST TOO BUSY TO GO OUT TODAY!
I'M USED TO VERONICA TURNING ME DOWN, BUT NOT *YOU*, BETTY!
Betty
in
"CARAMEL COATED"

Script: Kathleen Webb / Pencils: Stan Goldberg / Inks: John Lowe / Letters: Bill Yoshida

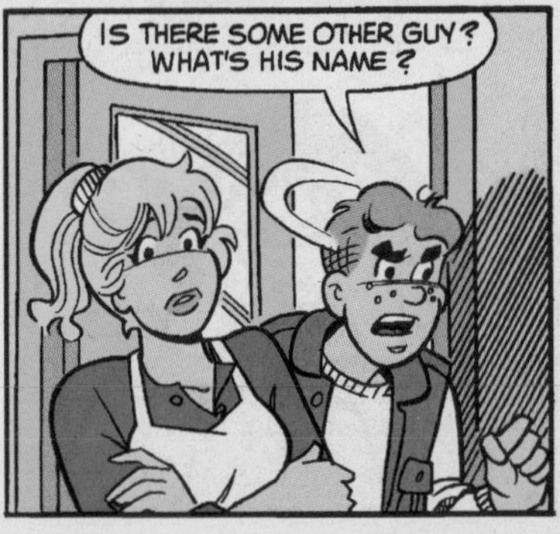
IS THERE SOME OTHER GUY? WHAT'S HIS NAME?

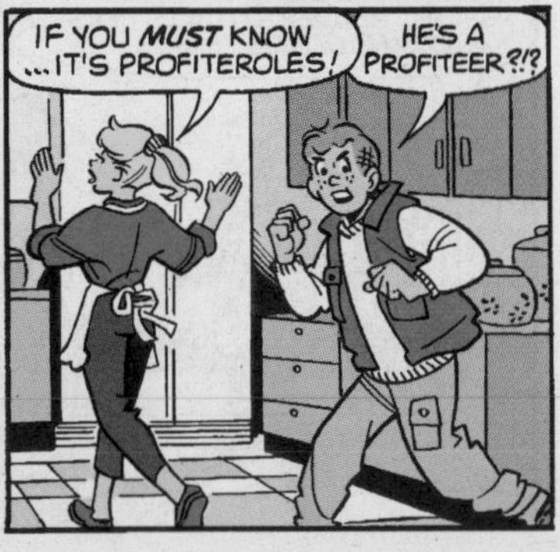
IF YOU *MUST* KNOW ...IT'S PROFITEROLES!
HE'S A PROFITEER?!?

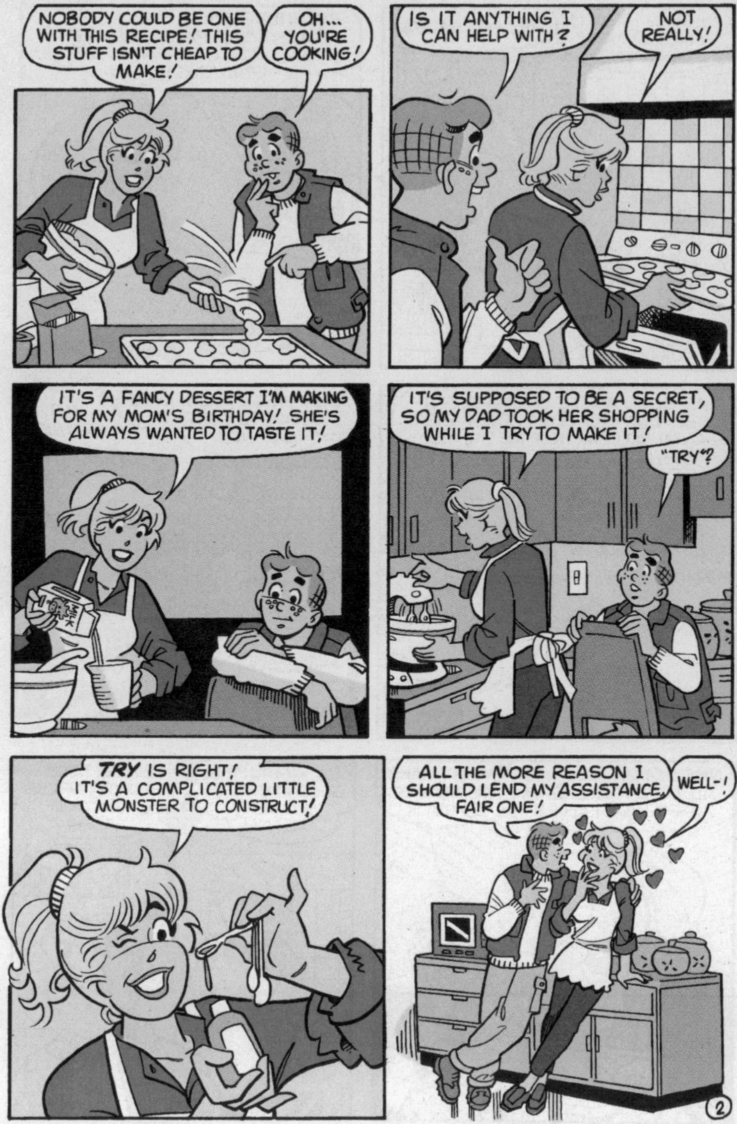
NOBODY COULD BE ONE WITH THIS RECIPE! THIS STUFF ISN'T CHEAP TO MAKE!
OH... YOU'RE COOKING!
IS IT ANYTHING I CAN HELP WITH?
NOT REALLY!
IT'S A FANCY DESSERT I'M MAKING FOR MY MOM'S BIRTHDAY! SHE'S ALWAYS WANTED TO TASTE IT!
MILK
IT'S SUPPOSED TO BE A SECRET, SO MY DAD TOOK HER SHOPPING WHILE I TRY TO MAKE IT!
"TRY"?
TRY IS RIGHT! IT'S A COMPLICATED LITTLE MONSTER TO CONSTRUCT!
ALL THE MORE REASON I SHOULD LEND MY ASSISTANCE, FAIR ONE!
WELL-!

WHAT IS "PROFIT FOR ROLAIDS," ANYWAY?

PROFITEROLES!

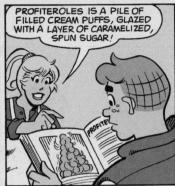

PROFITEROLES IS A PILE OF FILLED CREAM PUFFS, GLAZED WITH A LAYER OF CARAMELIZED, SPUN SUGAR!

PROFITE

AS SOON AS THE CREAM PUFFS ARE READY TO COME OUT OF THE OVEN, YOU CAN HELP ME FILL THEM!

THEY SMELL LIKE THEY'RE READY TO COME OUT NOW!

NO, ARCHIE!!

NICE GOING, ACE! NOW ALL MY LITTLE CREAM PUFFS HAVE FALLEN!

MIGHT MAKE THEM EASIER TO STACK!

ALL RIGHT...THE SECOND BATCH IS ALMOST READY!

LET *ME* TAKE THEM OUT OF THE OVEN, OKAY, ARCHIE?

YES'M!

3

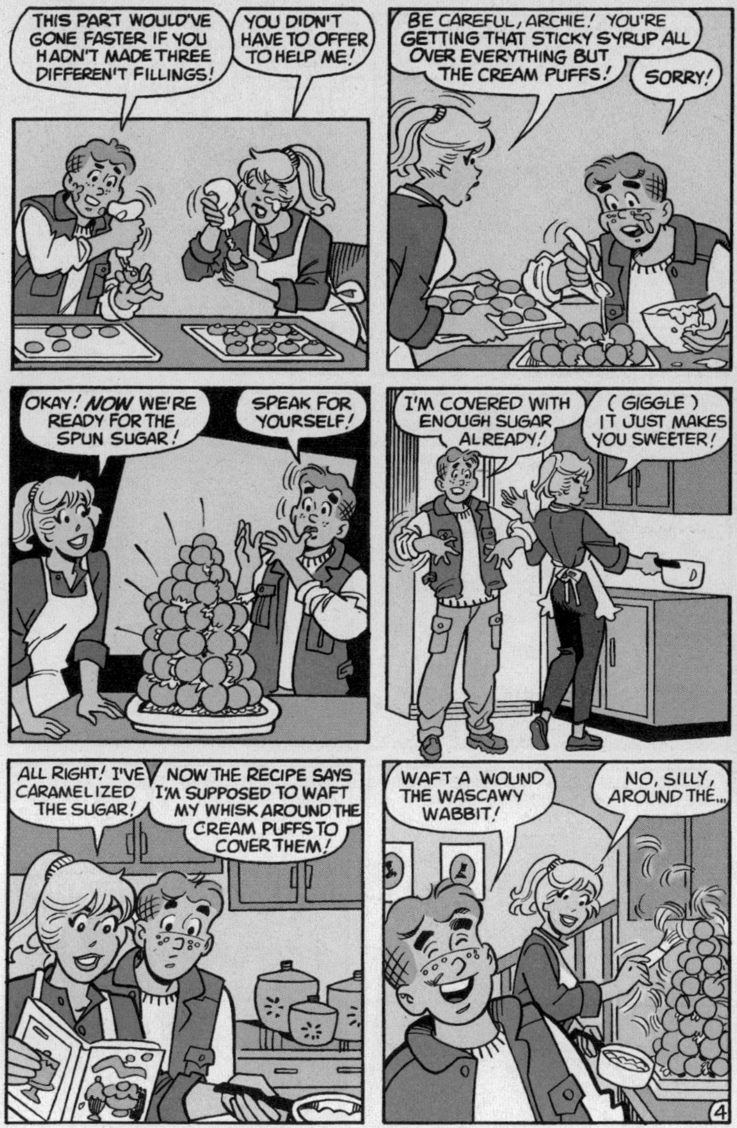

THIS PART WOULD'VE GONE FASTER IF YOU HADN'T MADE THREE DIFFERENT FILLINGS!
YOU DIDN'T HAVE TO OFFER TO HELP ME!
BE CAREFUL, ARCHIE! YOU'RE GETTING THAT STICKY SYRUP ALL OVER EVERYTHING BUT THE CREAM PUFFS!
SORRY!
OKAY! NOW WE'RE READY FOR THE SPUN SUGAR!
SPEAK FOR YOURSELF!
I'M COVERED WITH ENOUGH SUGAR ALREADY!
(GIGGLE) IT JUST MAKES YOU SWEETER!
ALL RIGHT! I'VE CARAMELIZED THE SUGAR!
NOW THE RECIPE SAYS I'M SUPPOSED TO WAFT MY WHISK AROUND THE CREAM PUFFS TO COVER THEM!
WAFT A WOUND THE WASCAWY WABBIT!
NO, SILLY, AROUND THE...
4

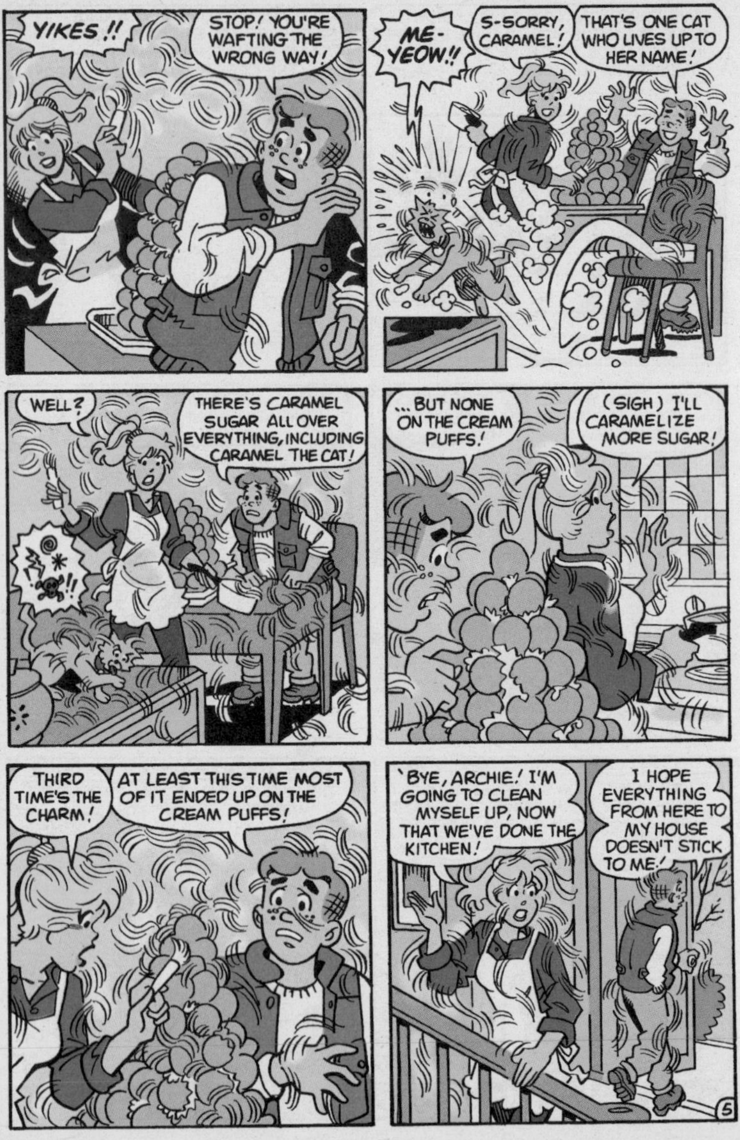
YIKES!!
STOP! YOU'RE WAFTING THE WRONG WAY!
ME-YEOW!!
S-SORRY, CARAMEL!
THAT'S ONE CAT WHO LIVES UP TO HER NAME!
WELL?
THERE'S CARAMEL SUGAR ALL OVER EVERYTHING, INCLUDING CARAMEL THE CAT!
...BUT NONE ON THE CREAM PUFFS!
(SIGH) I'LL CARAMELIZE MORE SUGAR!
THIRD TIME'S THE CHARM!
AT LEAST THIS TIME MOST OF IT ENDED UP ON THE CREAM PUFFS!
'BYE, ARCHIE! I'M GOING TO CLEAN MYSELF UP, NOW THAT WE'VE DONE THE KITCHEN!
I HOPE EVERYTHING FROM HERE TO MY HOUSE DOESN'T STICK TO ME!
5

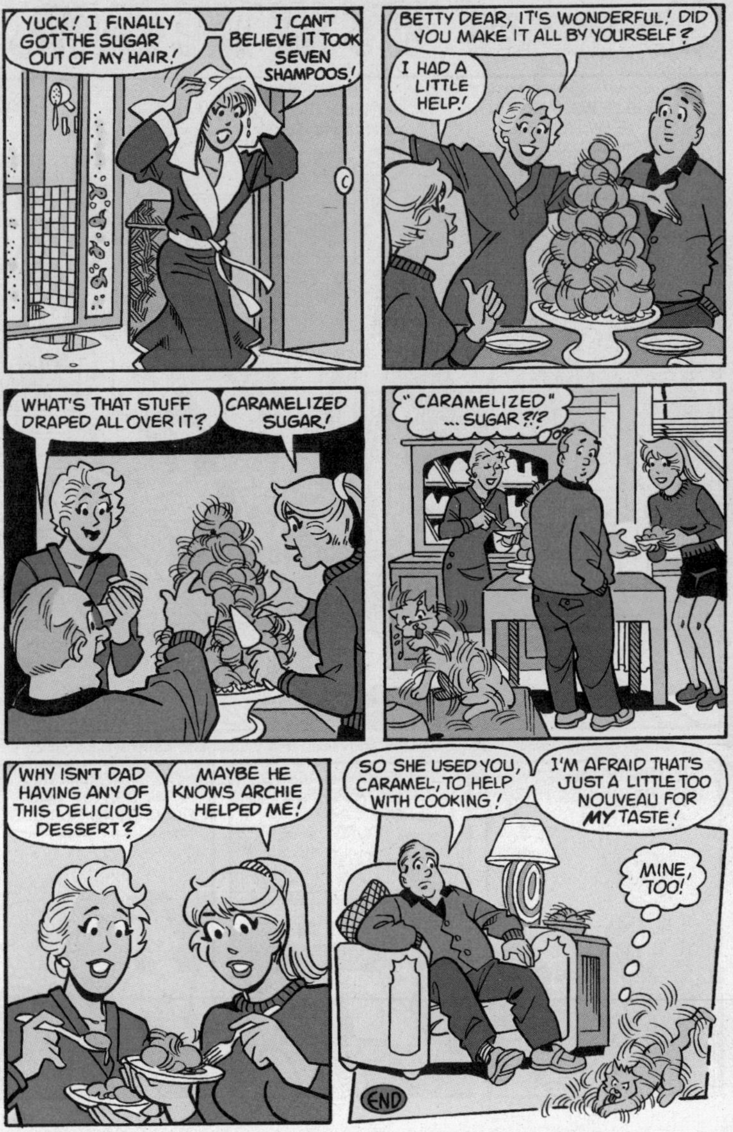

YUCK! I FINALLY GOT THE SUGAR OUT OF MY HAIR!
I CAN'T BELIEVE IT TOOK SEVEN SHAMPOOS!
BETTY DEAR, IT'S WONDERFUL! DID YOU MAKE IT ALL BY YOURSELF?
I HAD A LITTLE HELP!
WHAT'S THAT STUFF DRAPED ALL OVER IT?
CARAMELIZED SUGAR!
"CARAMELIZED" ... SUGAR?!?
WHY ISN'T DAD HAVING ANY OF THIS DELICIOUS DESSERT?
MAYBE HE KNOWS ARCHIE HELPED ME!
SO SHE USED YOU, CARAMEL, TO HELP WITH COOKING!
I'M AFRAID THAT'S JUST A LITTLE TOO NOUVEAU FOR MY TASTE!
MINE, TOO!
END

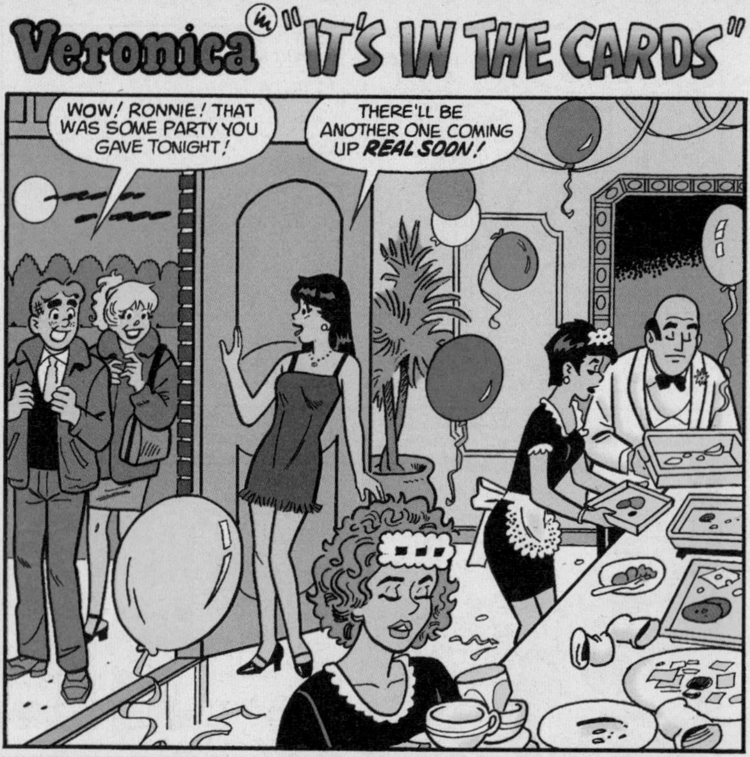
Veronica in "IT'S IN THE CARDS"
WOW! RONNIE! THAT WAS SOME PARTY YOU GAVE TONIGHT!
THERE'LL BE ANOTHER ONE COMING UP REAL SOON!

Script: George Gladir / Pencils: Dan DeCarlo / Inks: Henry Scarpelli / Letters: Bill Yoshida

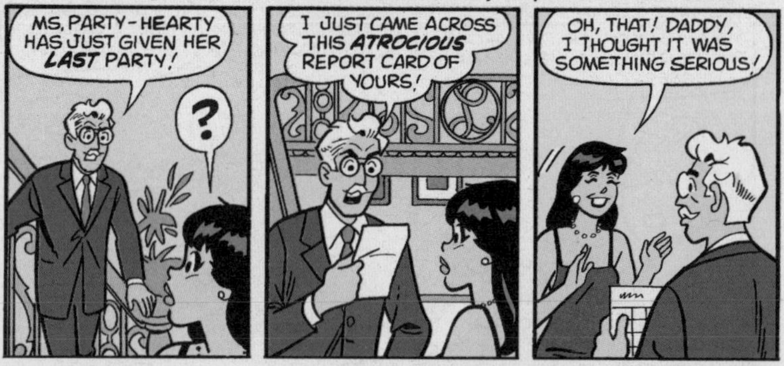
MS. PARTY-HEARTY HAS JUST GIVEN HER LAST PARTY!
?
I JUST CAME ACROSS THIS ATROCIOUS REPORT CARD OF YOURS!
OH, THAT! DADDY, I THOUGHT IT WAS SOMETHING SERIOUS!

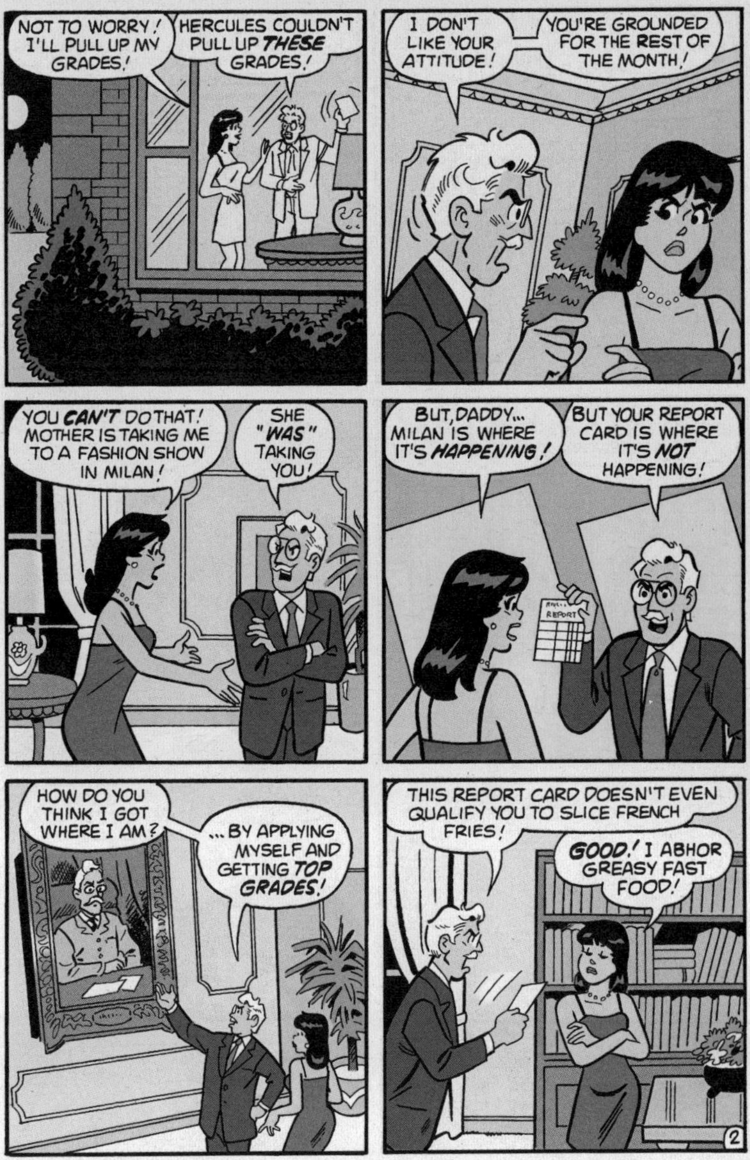
NOT TO WORRY! I'LL PULL UP MY GRADES!
HERCULES COULDN'T PULL UP THESE GRADES!
I DON'T LIKE YOUR ATTITUDE!
YOU'RE GROUNDED FOR THE REST OF THE MONTH!
YOU CAN'T DO THAT! MOTHER IS TAKING ME TO A FASHION SHOW IN MILAN!
SHE "WAS" TAKING YOU!
BUT, DADDY... MILAN IS WHERE IT'S HAPPENING!
BUT YOUR REPORT CARD IS WHERE IT'S NOT HAPPENING!
REPORT
HOW DO YOU THINK I GOT WHERE I AM?
...BY APPLYING MYSELF AND GETTING TOP GRADES!
THIS REPORT CARD DOESN'T EVEN QUALIFY YOU TO SLICE FRENCH FRIES!
GOOD! I ABHOR GREASY FAST FOOD!

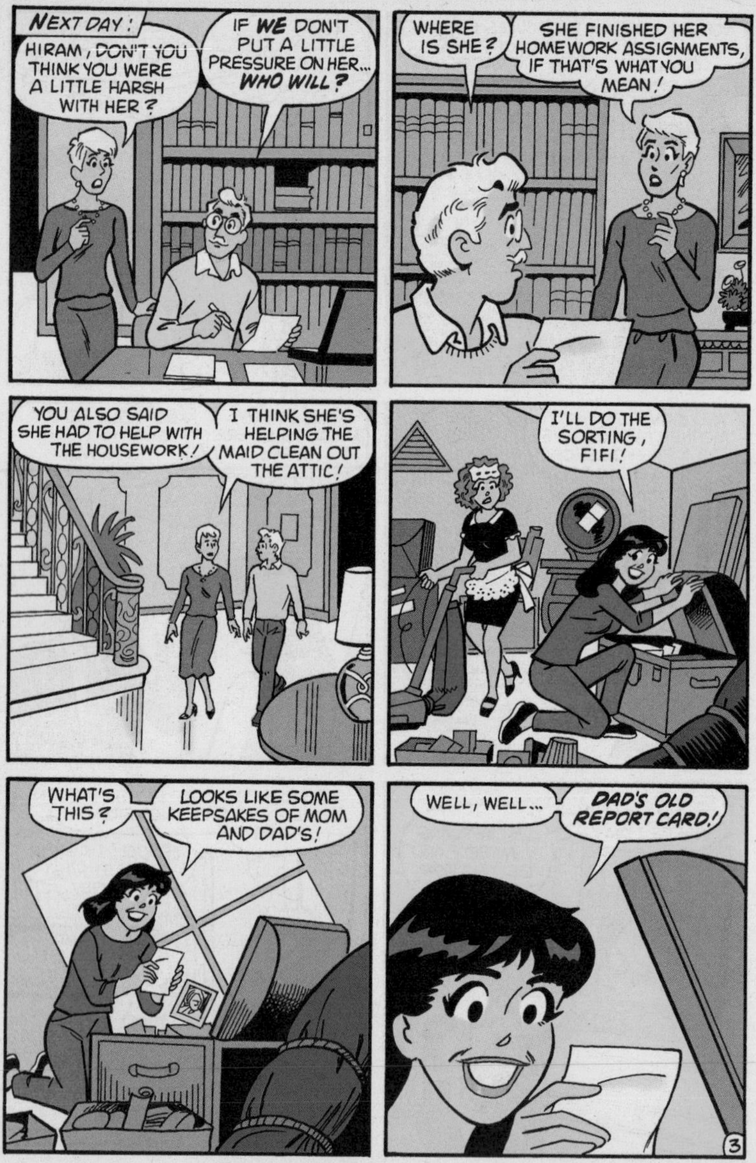

NEXT DAY:
HIRAM, DON'T YOU THINK YOU WERE A LITTLE HARSH WITH HER?
IF WE DON'T PUT A LITTLE PRESSURE ON HER... WHO WILL?
WHERE IS SHE?
SHE FINISHED HER HOMEWORK ASSIGNMENTS, IF THAT'S WHAT YOU MEAN!
YOU ALSO SAID SHE HAD TO HELP WITH THE HOUSEWORK!
I THINK SHE'S HELPING THE MAID CLEAN OUT THE ATTIC!
I'LL DO THE SORTING, FIFI!
WHAT'S THIS?
LOOKS LIKE SOME KEEPSAKES OF MOM AND DAD'S!
WELL, WELL...
DAD'S OLD REPORT CARD!
3

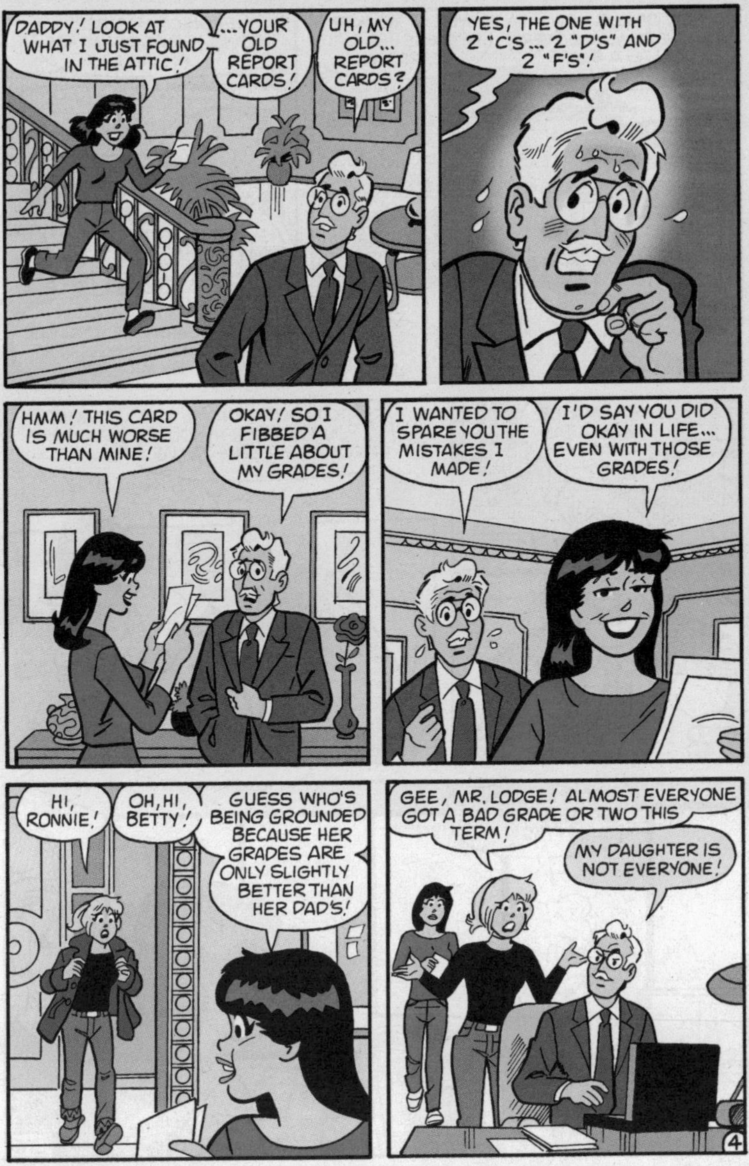

DADDY! LOOK AT WHAT I JUST FOUND IN THE ATTIC!
...YOUR OLD REPORT CARDS!
UH, MY OLD... REPORT CARDS?
YES, THE ONE WITH 2 "C'S... 2 "D'S" AND 2 "F'S"!
HMM! THIS CARD IS MUCH WORSE THAN MINE!
OKAY! SO I FIBBED A LITTLE ABOUT MY GRADES!
I WANTED TO SPARE YOU THE MISTAKES I MADE!
I'D SAY YOU DID OKAY IN LIFE... EVEN WITH THOSE GRADES!
HI, RONNIE!
OH, HI, BETTY!
GUESS WHO'S BEING GROUNDED BECAUSE HER GRADES ARE ONLY SLIGHTLY BETTER THAN HER DAD'S!
GEE, MR. LODGE! ALMOST EVERYONE GOT A BAD GRADE OR TWO THIS TERM!
MY DAUGHTER IS NOT EVERYONE!

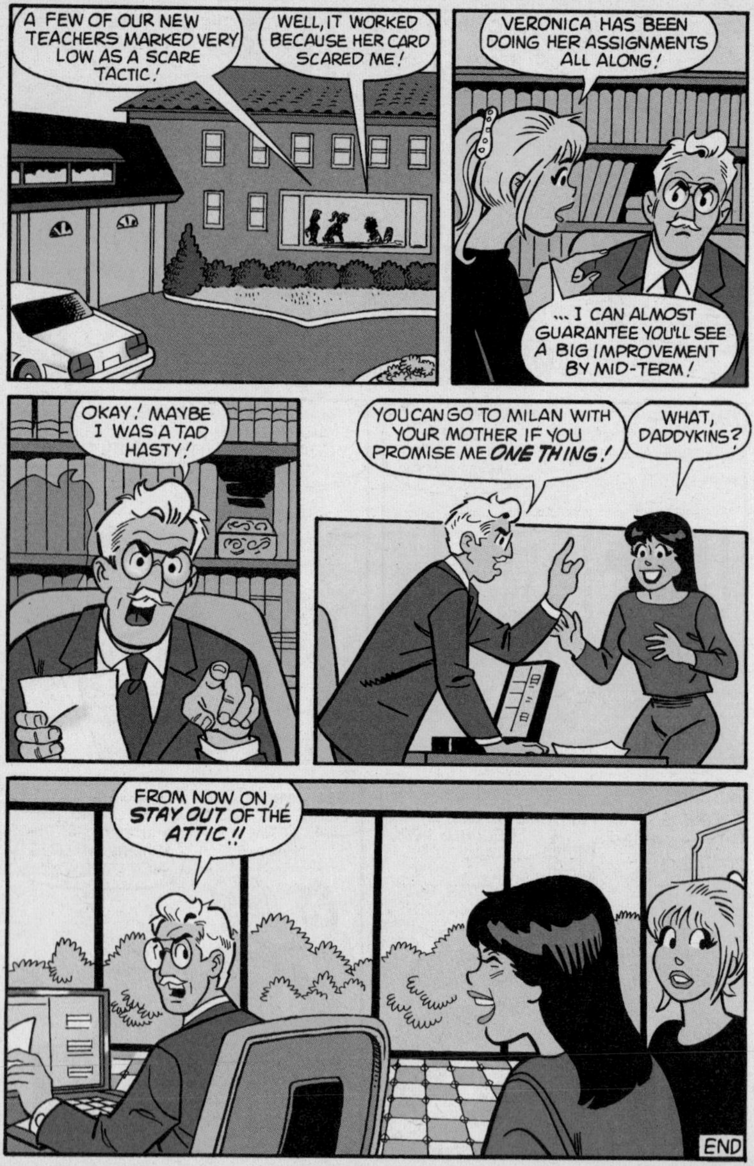
A FEW OF OUR NEW TEACHERS MARKED VERY LOW AS A SCARE TACTIC!
WELL, IT WORKED BECAUSE HER CARD SCARED ME!
VERONICA HAS BEEN DOING HER ASSIGNMENTS ALL ALONG!
... I CAN ALMOST GUARANTEE YOU'LL SEE A BIG IMPROVEMENT BY MID-TERM!
OKAY! MAYBE I WAS A TAD HASTY!
YOU CAN GO TO MILAN WITH YOUR MOTHER IF YOU PROMISE ME ONE THING!
WHAT, DADDYKINS?
FROM NOW ON, STAY OUT OF THE ATTIC!!
END

Betty in "GROWING PAINS"

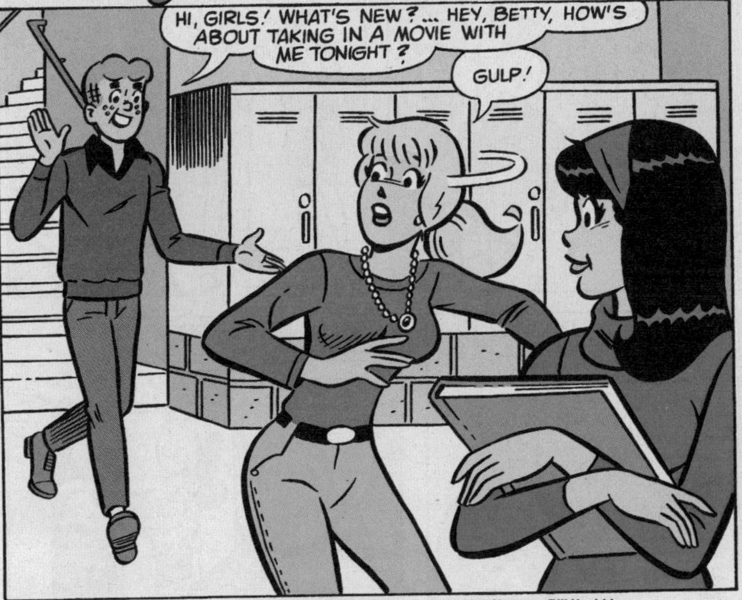
HI, GIRLS! WHAT'S NEW? ... HEY, BETTY, HOW'S ABOUT TAKING IN A MOVIE WITH ME TONIGHT?
GULP!

Script: Frank Doyle / Pencils: Bob Bolling / Inks: Rudy Lapick / Letters: Bill Yoshida

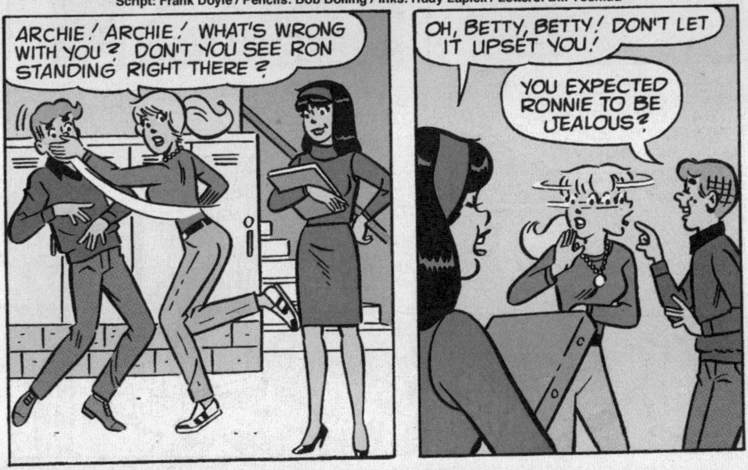
ARCHIE! ARCHIE! WHAT'S WRONG WITH YOU? DON'T YOU SEE RON STANDING RIGHT THERE?
OH, BETTY, BETTY! DON'T LET IT UPSET YOU!
YOU EXPECTED RONNIE TO BE JEALOUS?

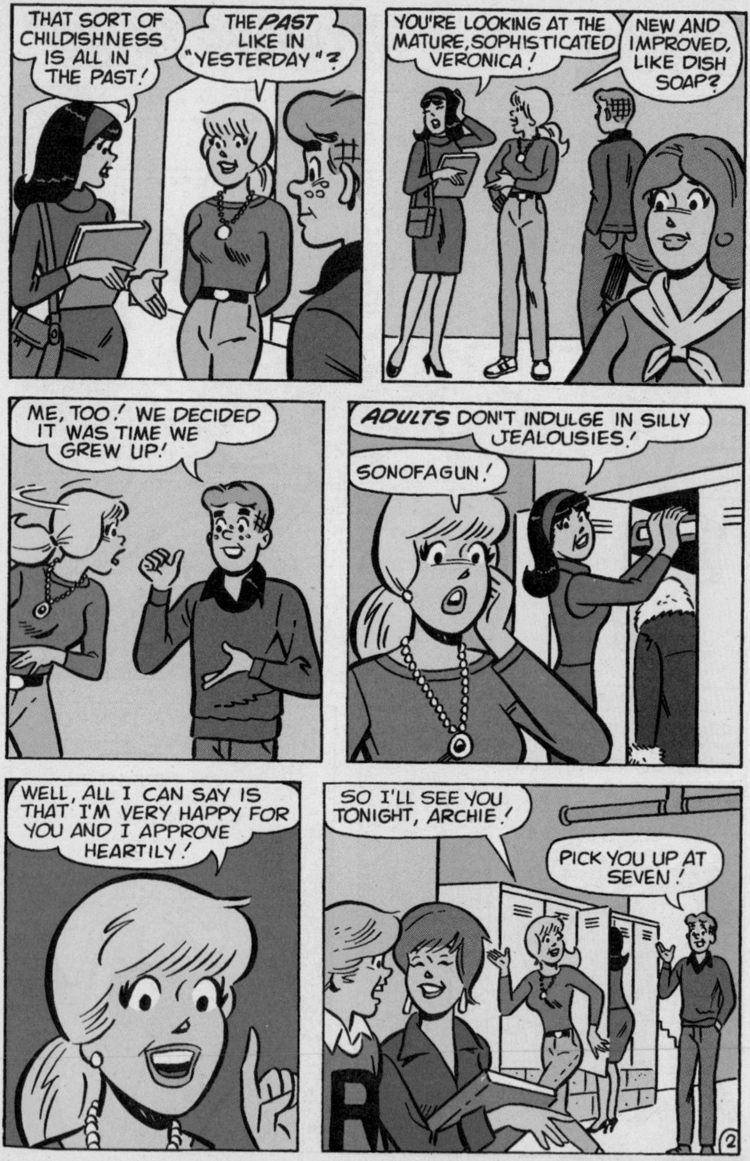
THAT SORT OF CHILDISHNESS IS ALL IN THE PAST!
THE *PAST* LIKE IN "YESTERDAY"?
YOU'RE LOOKING AT THE MATURE, SOPHISTICATED VERONICA!
NEW AND IMPROVED, LIKE DISH SOAP?
ME, TOO! WE DECIDED IT WAS TIME WE GREW UP!
ADULTS DON'T INDULGE IN SILLY JEALOUSIES!
SONOFAGUN!
WELL, ALL I CAN SAY IS THAT I'M VERY HAPPY FOR YOU AND I APPROVE HEARTILY!
SO I'LL SEE YOU TONIGHT, ARCHIE!
PICK YOU UP AT SEVEN!
R
2

AND SO... THEY SAY THIS IS A GOOD MOVIE!

I'VE BEEN LOOKING FORWARD TO SEEING IT!

NOW SHOWING
GLITZY BEACH

I STILL CAN'T GET OVER RONNIE'S NEW, ADULT ATTITUDE!

IT WAS ALL *HER* IDEA!

HERE ARE TWO SEATS, GORDON! LET'S SIT HERE!

HUH?

WELL HOW ABOUT THAT? TALK ABOUT YOUR COINCIDENCES!!

YEAH! LET'S *DO* THAT!

GOOD MOVIE! NICE RUNNING INTO YOU TWO!

NOW SHOWING
GLITZY BEACH

SMALL WORLD, ISN'T IT?

CHOCKLIT SHOPPE?

SOUNDS GOOD TO ME!

ANDREWS 9

3

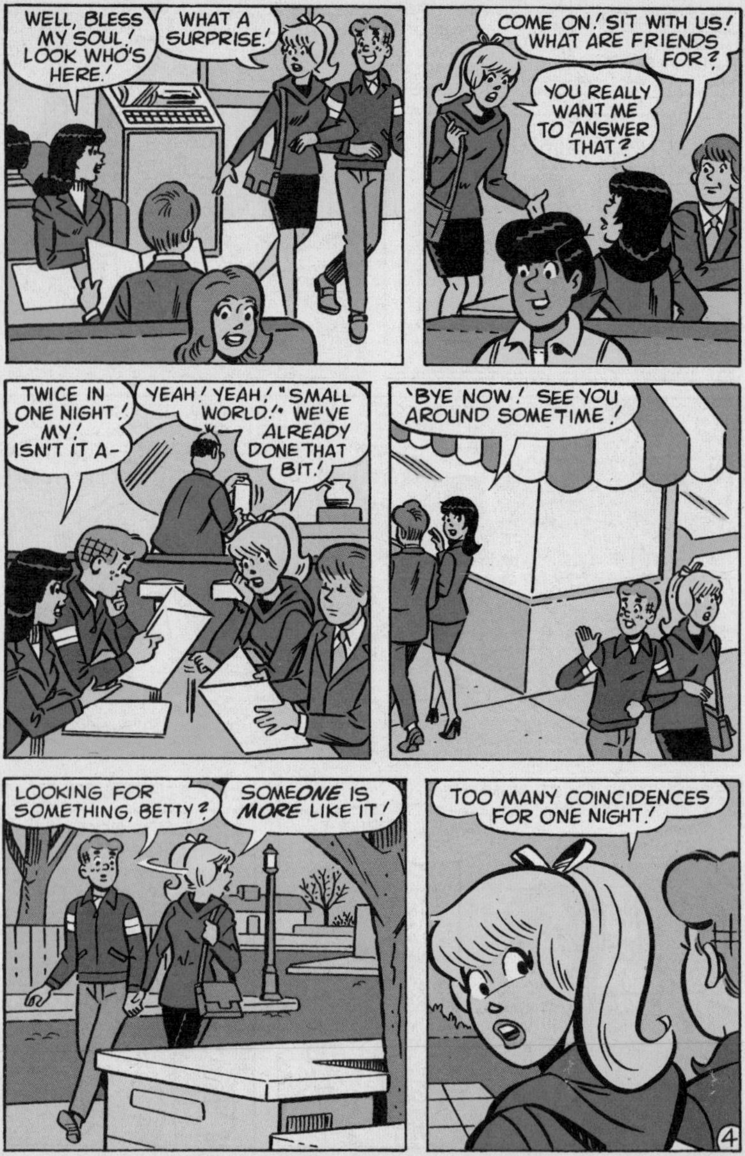
WELL, BLESS MY SOUL! LOOK WHO'S HERE!
WHAT A SURPRISE!
COME ON! SIT WITH US! WHAT ARE FRIENDS FOR?
YOU REALLY WANT ME TO ANSWER THAT?
TWICE IN ONE NIGHT! MY! ISN'T IT A-
YEAH! YEAH! "SMALL WORLD!" WE'VE ALREADY DONE THAT BIT!
'BYE NOW! SEE YOU AROUND SOMETIME!
LOOKING FOR SOMETHING, BETTY?
SOMEONE IS MORE LIKE IT!
TOO MANY COINCIDENCES FOR ONE NIGHT!
4

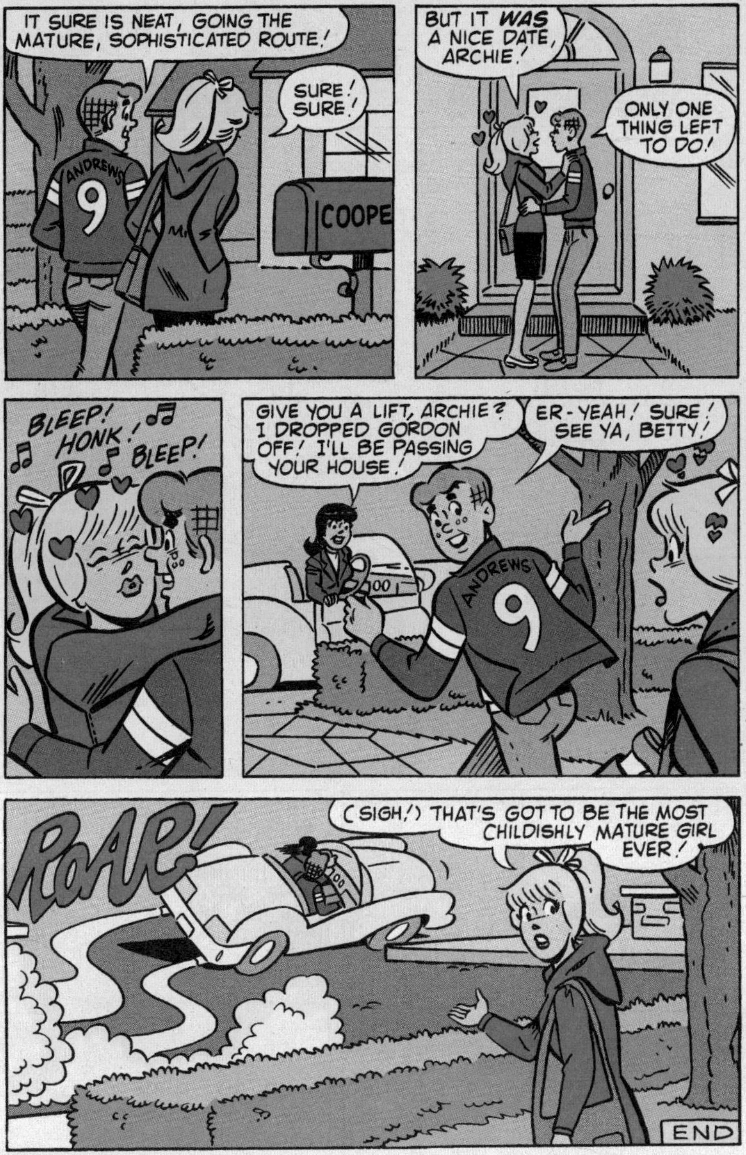
IT SURE IS NEAT, GOING THE MATURE, SOPHISTICATED ROUTE!
SURE! SURE!
ANDREWS
9
COOPE
BUT IT WAS A NICE DATE, ARCHIE!
ONLY ONE THING LEFT TO DO!
BLEEP! HONK! BLEEP!
GIVE YOU A LIFT, ARCHIE? I DROPPED GORDON OFF! I'LL BE PASSING YOUR HOUSE!
ER-YEAH! SURE! SEE YA, BETTY!
ANDREWS
9
ROAR!
(SIGH!) THAT'S GOT TO BE THE MOST CHILDISHLY MATURE GIRL EVER!
END

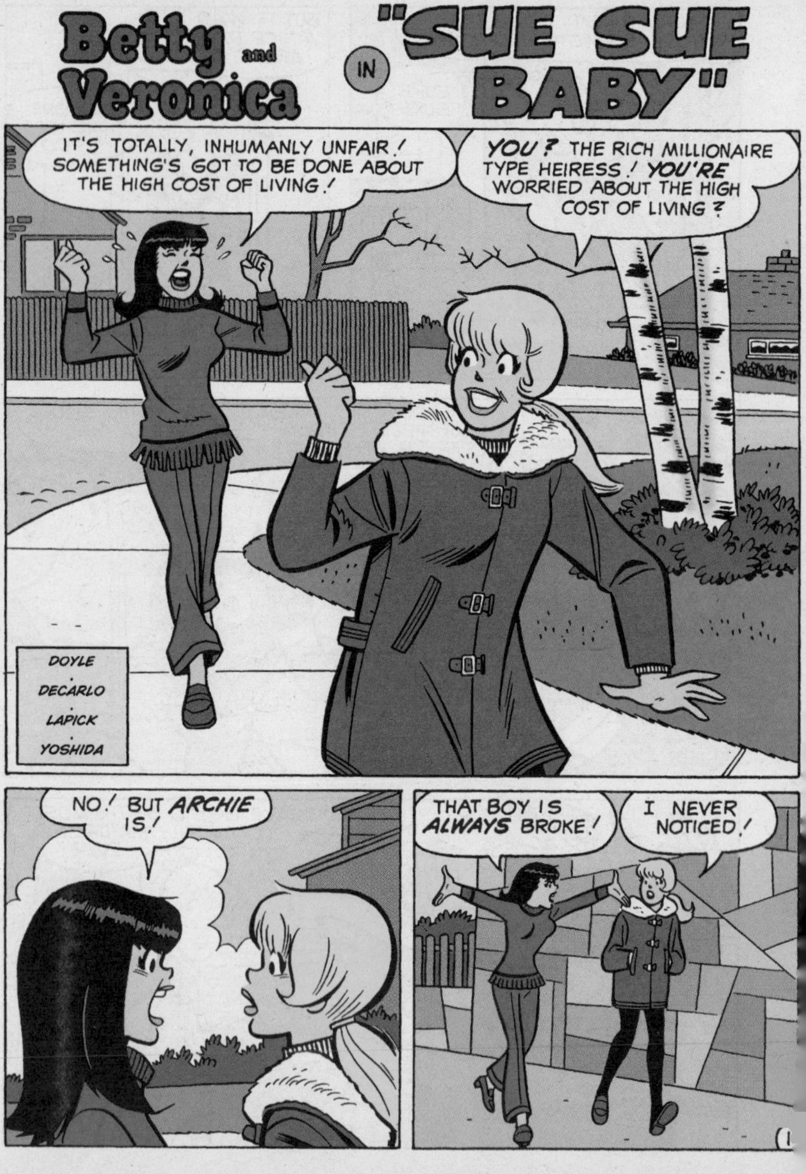
Betty and Veronica IN "SUE SUE BABY"
IT'S TOTALLY, INHUMANLY UNFAIR! SOMETHING'S GOT TO BE DONE ABOUT THE HIGH COST OF LIVING!
YOU? THE RICH MILLIONAIRE TYPE HEIRESS! YOU'RE WORRIED ABOUT THE HIGH COST OF LIVING?
DOYLE · DECARLO · LAPICK · YOSHIDA
NO! BUT ARCHIE IS!
THAT BOY IS ALWAYS BROKE!
I NEVER NOTICED!

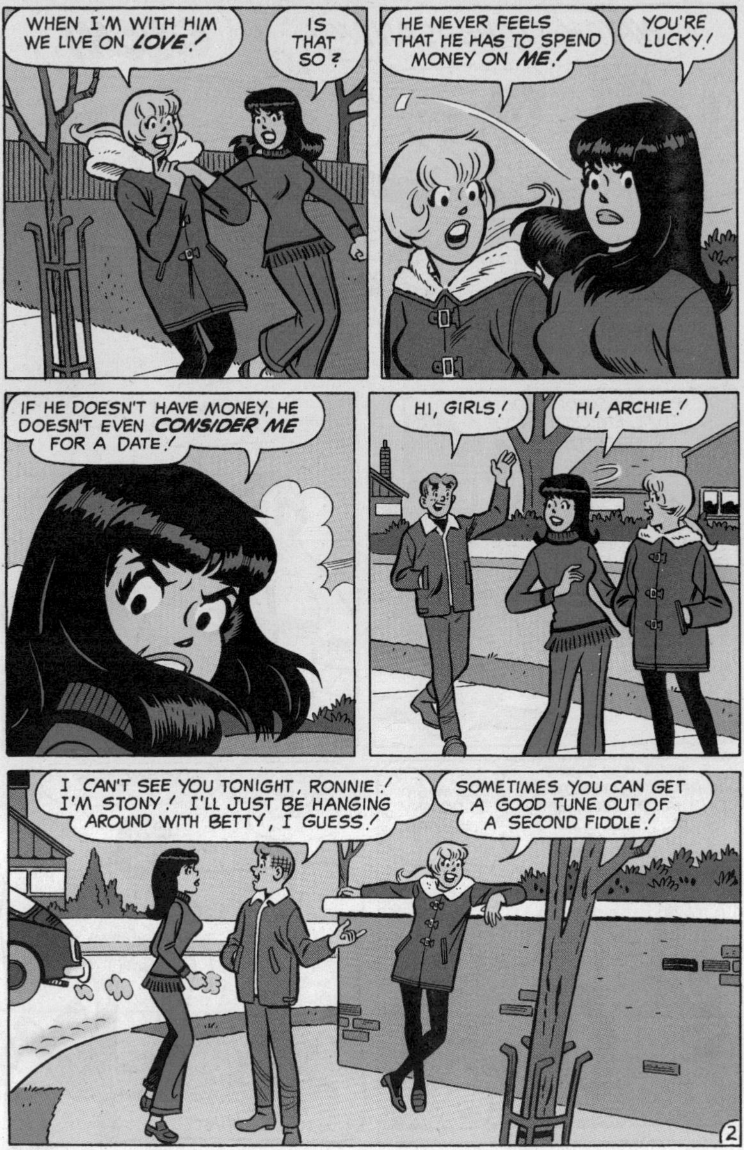
WHEN I'M WITH HIM WE LIVE ON LOVE!
IS THAT SO?
HE NEVER FEELS THAT HE HAS TO SPEND MONEY ON ME!
YOU'RE LUCKY!
IF HE DOESN'T HAVE MONEY, HE DOESN'T EVEN CONSIDER ME FOR A DATE!
HI, GIRLS!
HI, ARCHIE!
I CAN'T SEE YOU TONIGHT, RONNIE! I'M STONY! I'LL JUST BE HANGING AROUND WITH BETTY, I GUESS!
SOMETIMES YOU CAN GET A GOOD TUNE OUT OF A SECOND FIDDLE!
2

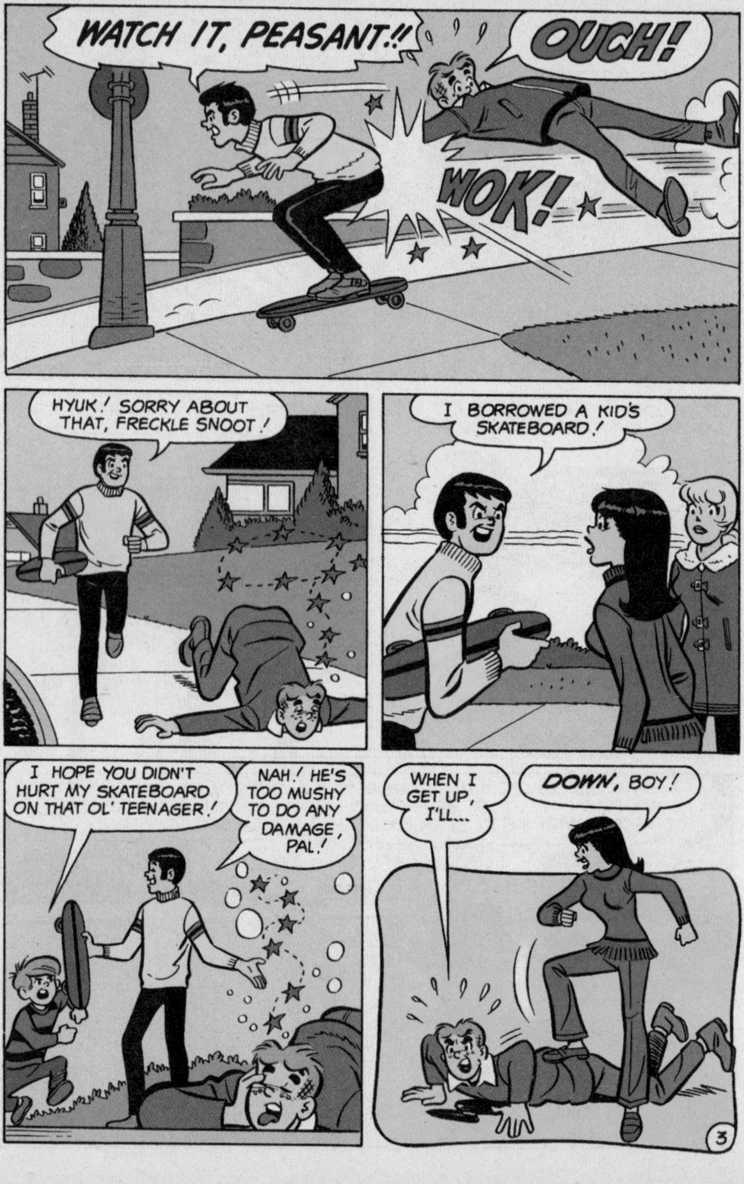

WATCH IT, PEASANT.!!
OUCH!
WOK!
HYUK! SORRY ABOUT THAT, FRECKLE SNOOT!
I BORROWED A KID'S SKATEBOARD!
I HOPE YOU DIDN'T HURT MY SKATEBOARD ON THAT OL' TEENAGER!
NAH! HE'S TOO MUSHY TO DO ANY DAMAGE, PAL!
WHEN I GET UP, I'LL...
DOWN, BOY!
3

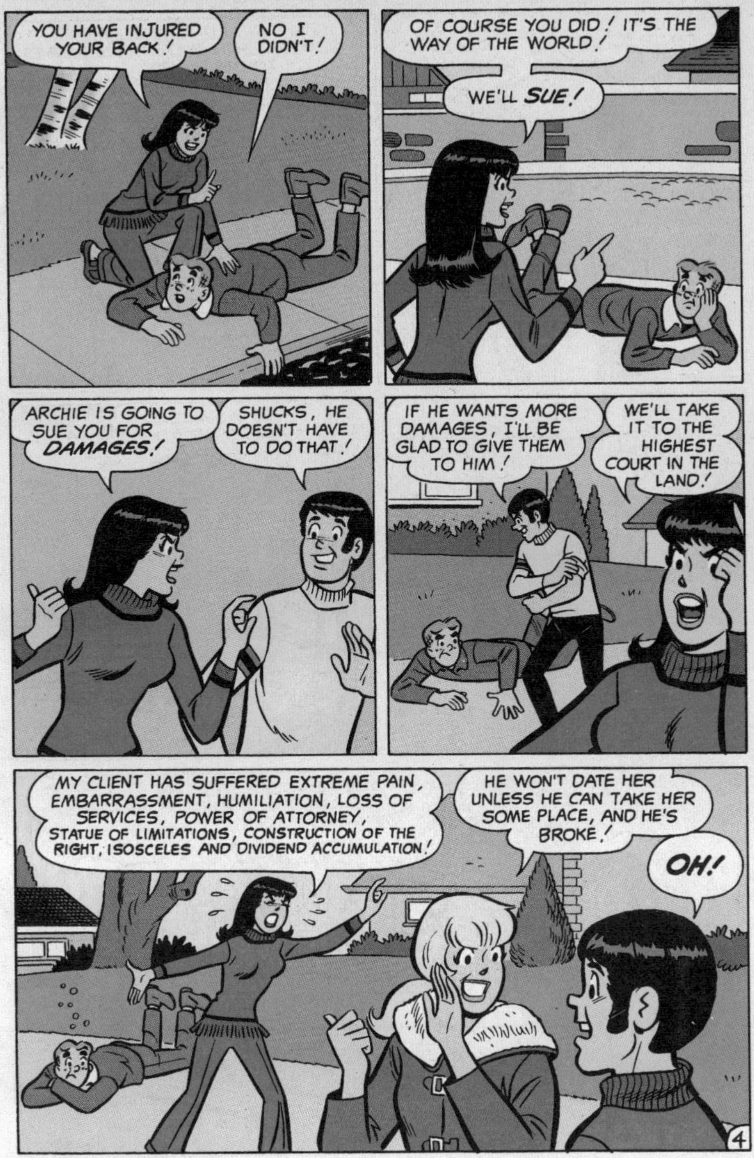
YOU HAVE INJURED YOUR BACK!
NO I DIDN'T!
OF COURSE YOU DID! IT'S THE WAY OF THE WORLD!
WE'LL SUE!
ARCHIE IS GOING TO SUE YOU FOR DAMAGES!
SHUCKS, HE DOESN'T HAVE TO DO THAT!
IF HE WANTS MORE DAMAGES, I'LL BE GLAD TO GIVE THEM TO HIM!
WE'LL TAKE IT TO THE HIGHEST COURT IN THE LAND!
MY CLIENT HAS SUFFERED EXTREME PAIN, EMBARRASSMENT, HUMILIATION, LOSS OF SERVICES, POWER OF ATTORNEY, STATUE OF LIMITATIONS, CONSTRUCTION OF THE RIGHT, ISOSCELES AND DIVIDEND ACCUMULATION!
HE WON'T DATE HER UNLESS HE CAN TAKE HER SOME PLACE, AND HE'S BROKE!
OH!
4

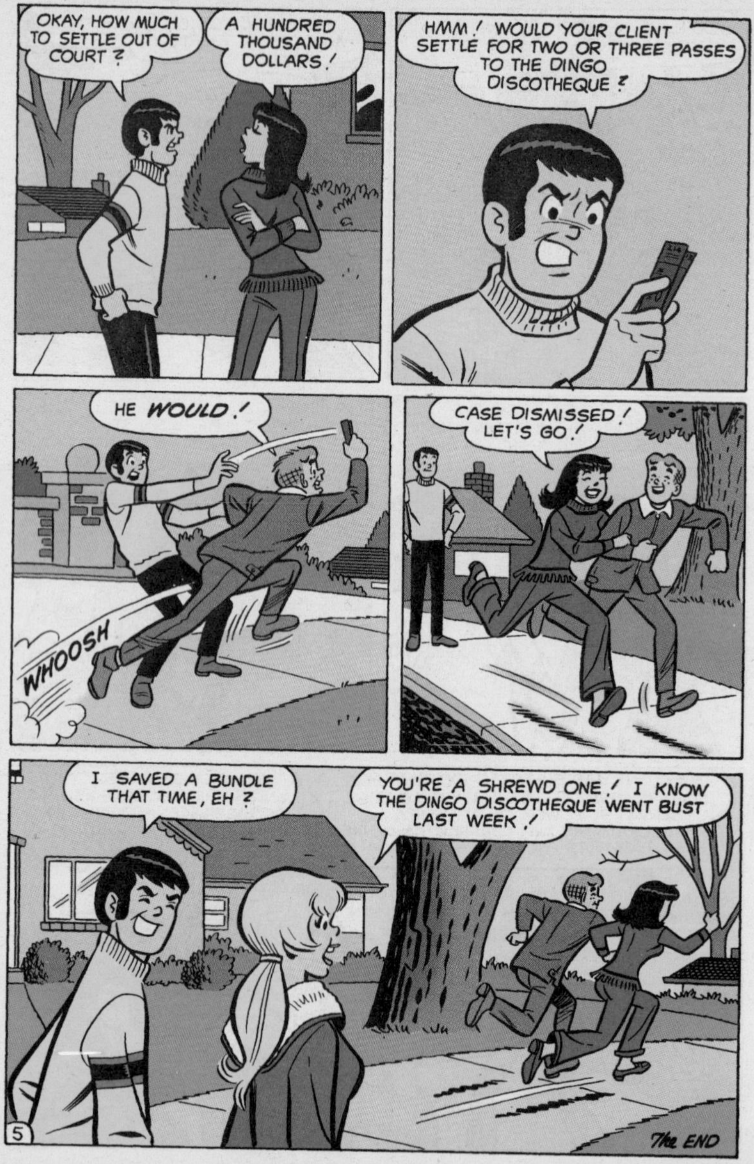
OKAY, HOW MUCH TO SETTLE OUT OF COURT ?
A HUNDRED THOUSAND DOLLARS !
HMM ! WOULD YOUR CLIENT SETTLE FOR TWO OR THREE PASSES TO THE DINGO DISCOTHEQUE ?
HE WOULD !
WHOOSH
CASE DISMISSED ! LET'S GO !
I SAVED A BUNDLE THAT TIME, EH ?
YOU'RE A SHREWD ONE ! I KNOW THE DINGO DISCOTHEQUE WENT BUST LAST WEEK !
5
The END

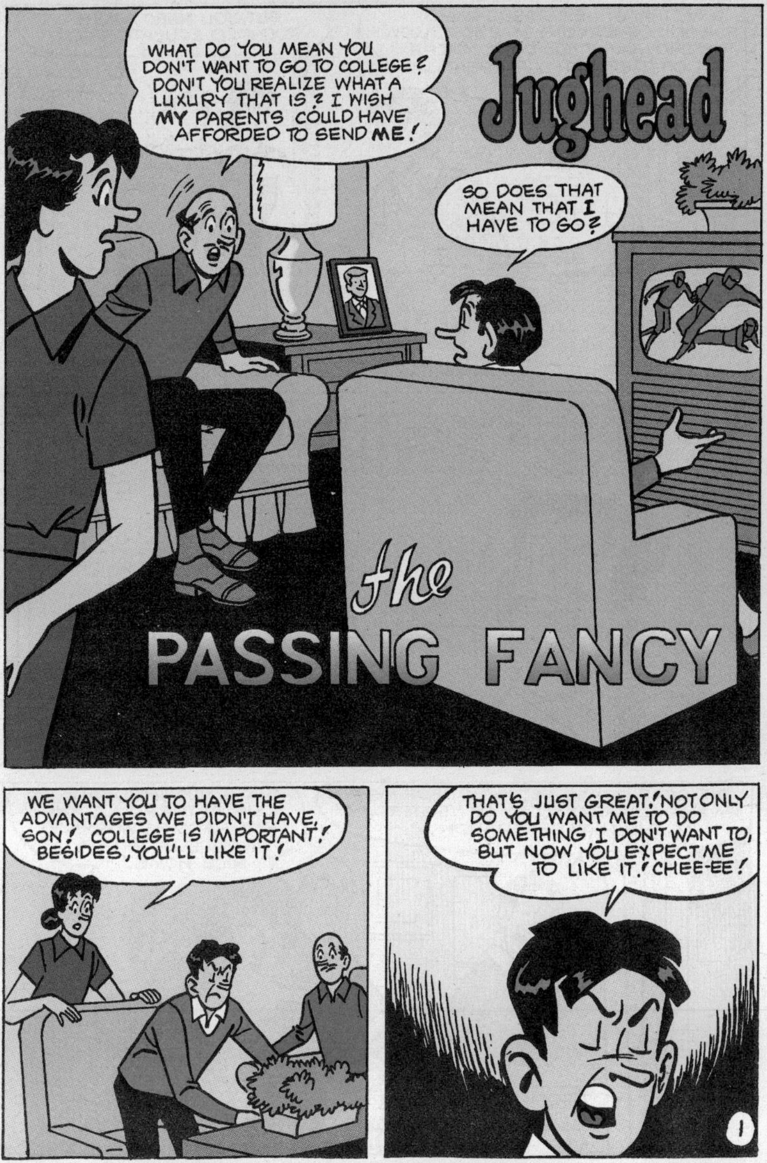
Jughead
WHAT DO YOU MEAN YOU DON'T WANT TO GO TO COLLEGE? DON'T YOU REALIZE WHAT A LUXURY THAT IS? I WISH MY PARENTS COULD HAVE AFFORDED TO SEND ME!
SO DOES THAT MEAN THAT I HAVE TO GO?
the PASSING FANCY
WE WANT YOU TO HAVE THE ADVANTAGES WE DIDN'T HAVE, SON! COLLEGE IS IMPORTANT! BESIDES, YOU'LL LIKE IT!
THAT'S JUST GREAT! NOT ONLY DO YOU WANT ME TO DO SOMETHING I DON'T WANT TO, BUT NOW YOU EXPECT ME TO LIKE IT! CHEE-EE!
1

Script: Dick Malmgren / Art & Letters: Samm Schwartz

BOY! THAT'S THE ESTABLISHMENT FOR YOU! EVERYONE HAS TO FOLLOW THE CROWD! IF YOU DON'T, YOU'RE OUT OF STEP WITH OUR GREAT SOCIETY!

BUT YOU NEED A WELL-ROUNDED EDUCATION, SON!

WHY? SO I CAN SOME DAY LIVE IN A MORTGAGED HOUSE AND RIDE AROUND IN A MORTGAGED CAR? NEGATIVE, POP!

THAT'S NOT MY BAG! I WANT MORE OUT OF LIFE THAN THAT!

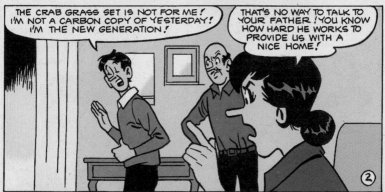

THE CRAB GRASS SET IS NOT FOR ME! I'M NOT A CARBON COPY OF YESTERDAY! I'M THE NEW GENERATION!

THAT'S NO WAY TO TALK TO YOUR FATHER! YOU KNOW HOW HARD HE WORKS TO PROVIDE US WITH A NICE HOME!

②

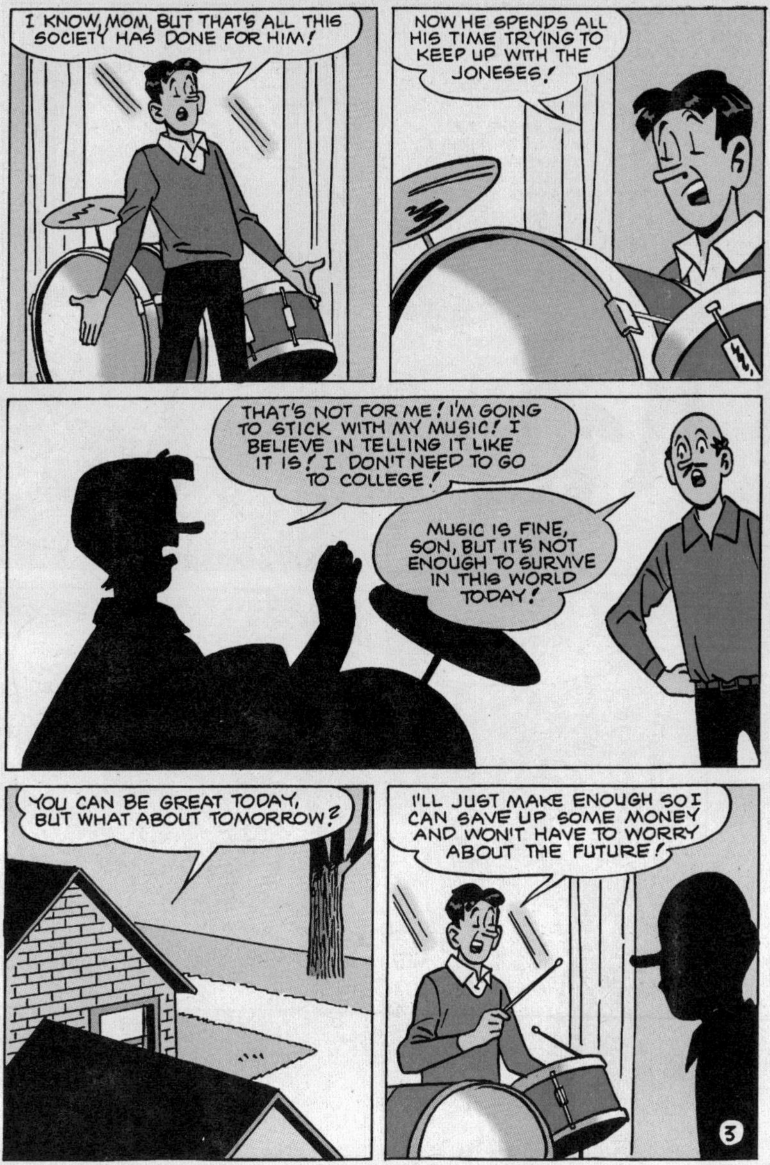
I KNOW, MOM, BUT THAT'S ALL THIS SOCIETY HAS DONE FOR HIM!
NOW HE SPENDS ALL HIS TIME TRYING TO KEEP UP WITH THE JONESES!
THAT'S NOT FOR ME! I'M GOING TO STICK WITH MY MUSIC! I BELIEVE IN TELLING IT LIKE IT IS! I DON'T NEED TO GO TO COLLEGE!
MUSIC IS FINE, SON, BUT IT'S NOT ENOUGH TO SURVIVE IN THIS WORLD TODAY!
YOU CAN BE GREAT TODAY, BUT WHAT ABOUT TOMORROW?
I'LL JUST MAKE ENOUGH SO I CAN SAVE UP SOME MONEY AND WON'T HAVE TO WORRY ABOUT THE FUTURE!
3

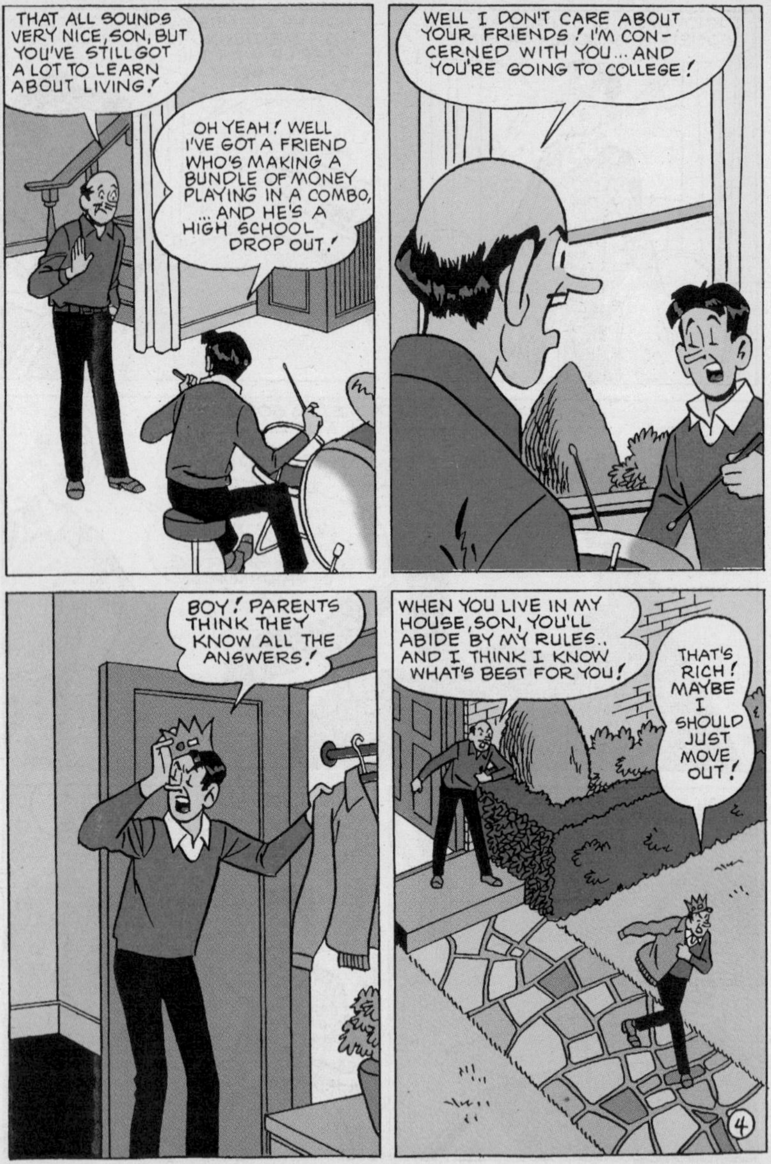
THAT ALL SOUNDS VERY NICE, SON, BUT YOU'VE STILL GOT A LOT TO LEARN ABOUT LIVING!
OH YEAH! WELL I'VE GOT A FRIEND WHO'S MAKING A BUNDLE OF MONEY PLAYING IN A COMBO, ... AND HE'S A HIGH SCHOOL DROP OUT!
WELL I DON'T CARE ABOUT YOUR FRIENDS! I'M CONCERNED WITH YOU... AND YOU'RE GOING TO COLLEGE!
BOY! PARENTS THINK THEY KNOW ALL THE ANSWERS!
WHEN YOU LIVE IN MY HOUSE, SON, YOU'LL ABIDE BY MY RULES.. AND I THINK I KNOW WHAT'S BEST FOR YOU!
THAT'S RICH! MAYBE I SHOULD JUST MOVE OUT!
4

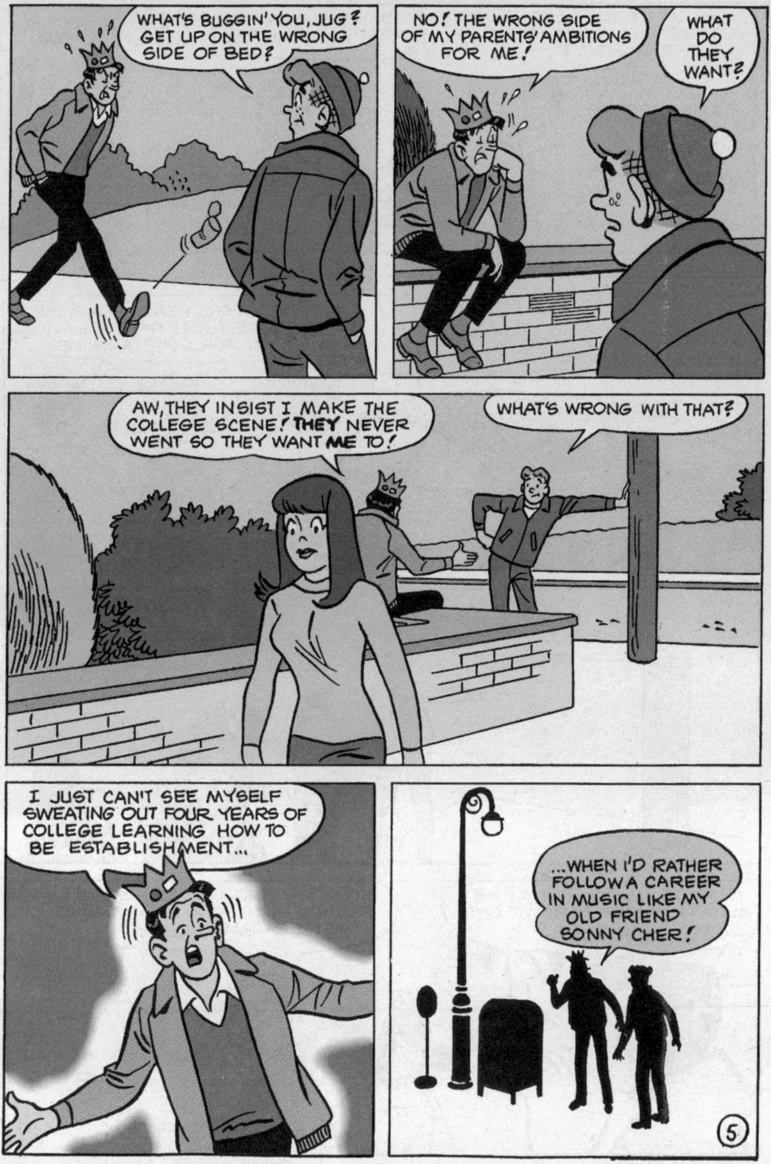
WHAT'S BUGGIN' YOU, JUG? GET UP ON THE WRONG SIDE OF BED?
NO! THE WRONG SIDE OF MY PARENTS' AMBITIONS FOR ME!
WHAT DO THEY WANT?
AW, THEY INSIST I MAKE THE COLLEGE SCENE! THEY NEVER WENT SO THEY WANT ME TO!
WHAT'S WRONG WITH THAT?
I JUST CAN'T SEE MYSELF SWEATING OUT FOUR YEARS OF COLLEGE LEARNING HOW TO BE ESTABLISHMENT...
...WHEN I'D RATHER FOLLOW A CAREER IN MUSIC LIKE MY OLD FRIEND SONNY CHER!
5

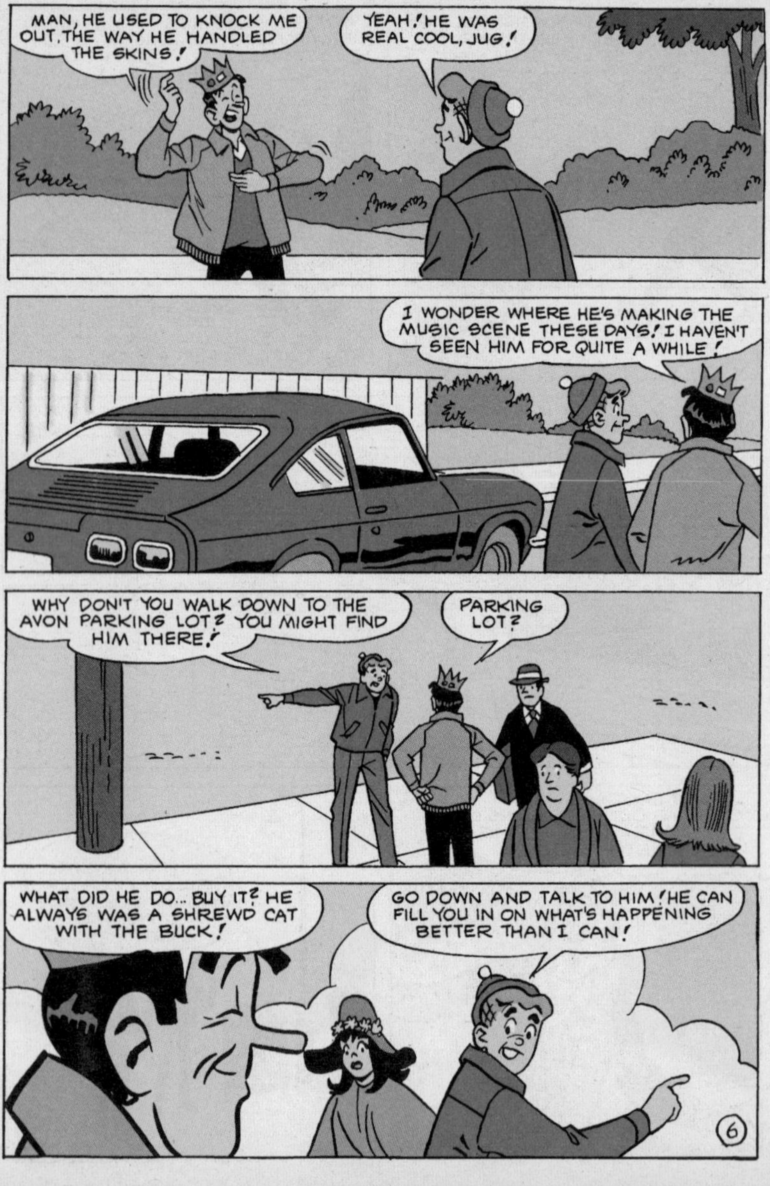

MAN, HE USED TO KNOCK ME OUT. THE WAY HE HANDLED THE SKINS!
YEAH! HE WAS REAL COOL, JUG!
I WONDER WHERE HE'S MAKING THE MUSIC SCENE THESE DAYS! I HAVEN'T SEEN HIM FOR QUITE A WHILE!
WHY DON'T YOU WALK DOWN TO THE AVON PARKING LOT? YOU MIGHT FIND HIM THERE!
PARKING LOT?
WHAT DID HE DO... BUY IT? HE ALWAYS WAS A SHREWD CAT WITH THE BUCK!
GO DOWN AND TALK TO HIM! HE CAN FILL YOU IN ON WHAT'S HAPPENING BETTER THAN I CAN!
6

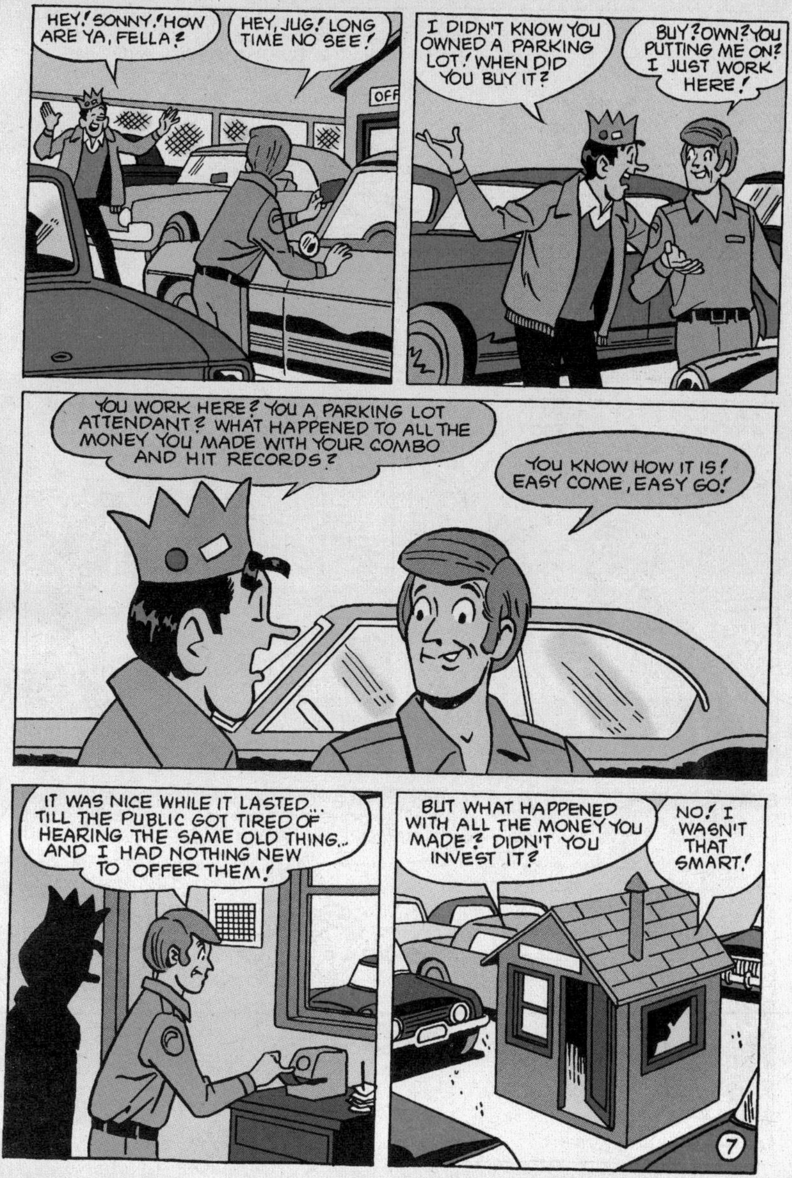
HEY! SONNY! HOW ARE YA, FELLA?
HEY, JUG! LONG TIME NO SEE!
I DIDN'T KNOW YOU OWNED A PARKING LOT! WHEN DID YOU BUY IT?
BUY? OWN? YOU PUTTING ME ON? I JUST WORK HERE!
YOU WORK HERE? YOU A PARKING LOT ATTENDANT? WHAT HAPPENED TO ALL THE MONEY YOU MADE WITH YOUR COMBO AND HIT RECORDS?
YOU KNOW HOW IT IS! EASY COME, EASY GO!
IT WAS NICE WHILE IT LASTED... TILL THE PUBLIC GOT TIRED OF HEARING THE SAME OLD THING... AND I HAD NOTHING NEW TO OFFER THEM!
BUT WHAT HAPPENED WITH ALL THE MONEY YOU MADE? DIDN'T YOU INVEST IT?
NO! I WASN'T THAT SMART!
7

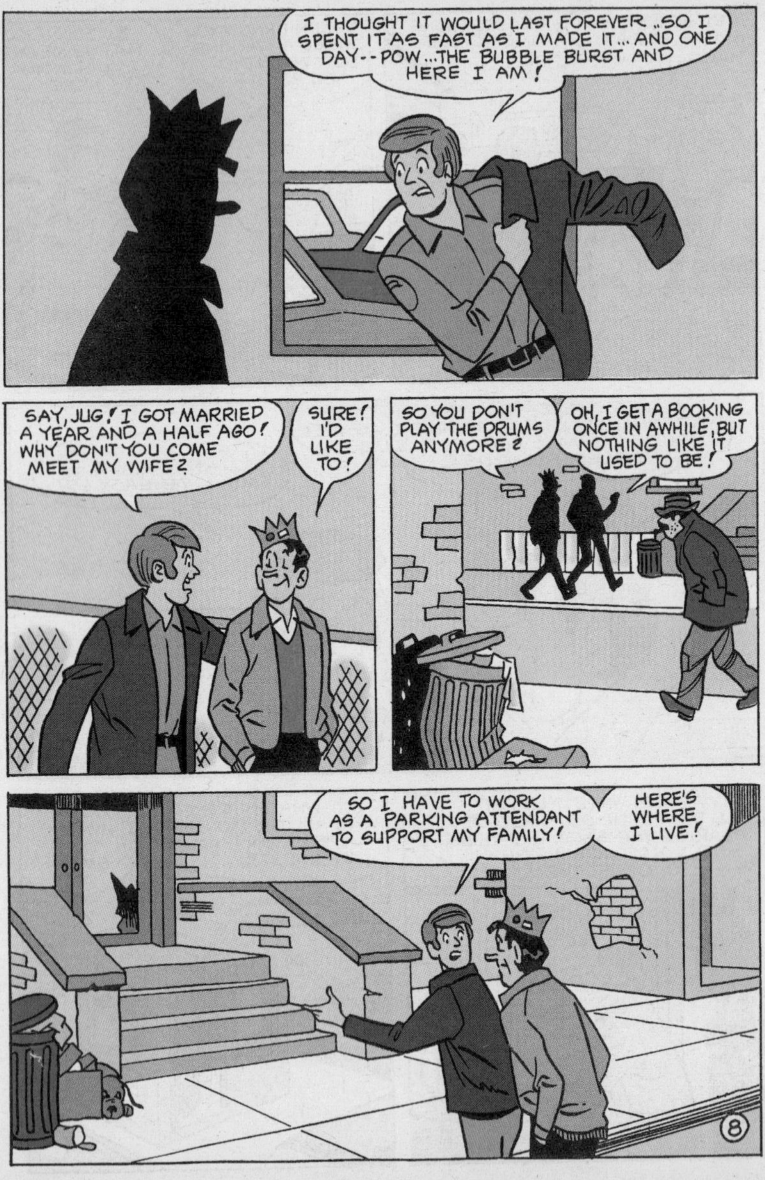
I THOUGHT IT WOULD LAST FOREVER ..SO I SPENT IT AS FAST AS I MADE IT... AND ONE DAY--POW...THE BUBBLE BURST AND HERE I AM!
SAY, JUG! I GOT MARRIED A YEAR AND A HALF AGO! WHY DON'T YOU COME MEET MY WIFE?
SURE! I'D LIKE TO!
SO YOU DON'T PLAY THE DRUMS ANYMORE?
OH, I GET A BOOKING ONCE IN AWHILE, BUT NOTHING LIKE IT USED TO BE!
SO I HAVE TO WORK AS A PARKING ATTENDANT TO SUPPORT MY FAMILY!
HERE'S WHERE I LIVE!
8

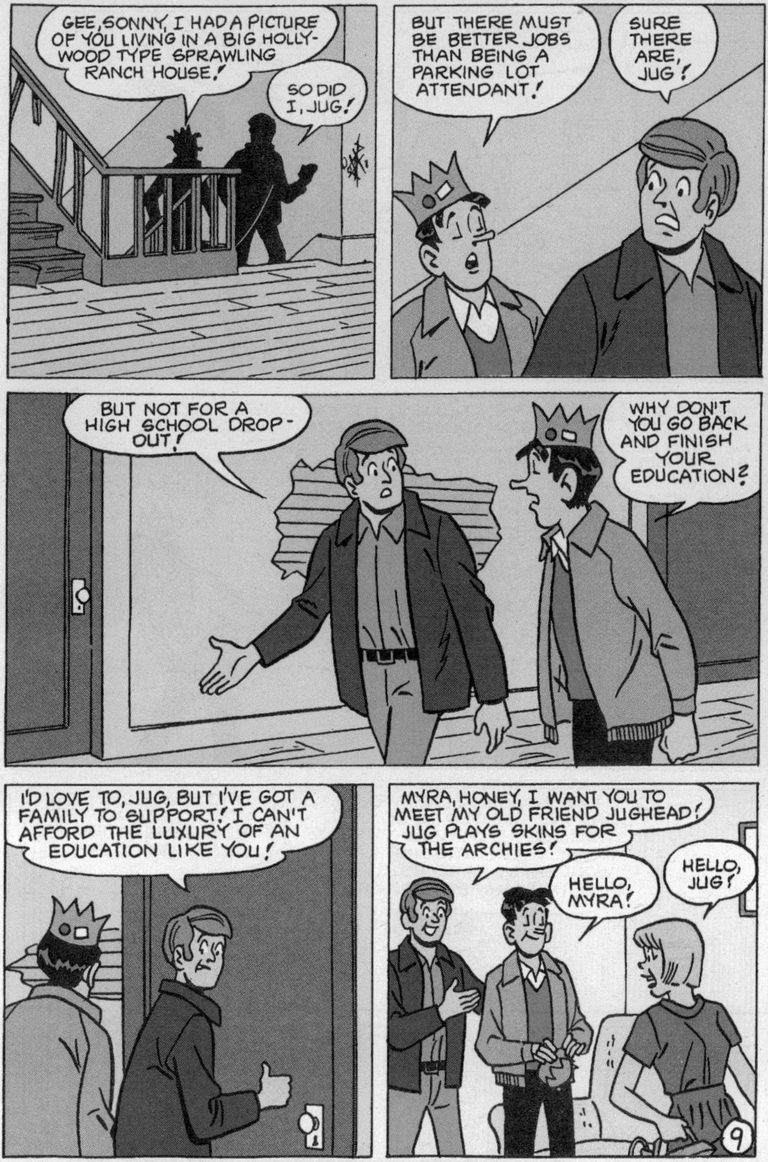
GEE, SONNY, I HAD A PICTURE OF YOU LIVING IN A BIG HOLLY-WOOD TYPE SPRAWLING RANCH HOUSE!
SO DID I, JUG!
BUT THERE MUST BE BETTER JOBS THAN BEING A PARKING LOT ATTENDANT!
SURE THERE ARE, JUG!
BUT NOT FOR A HIGH SCHOOL DROP-OUT!
WHY DON'T YOU GO BACK AND FINISH YOUR EDUCATION?
I'D LOVE TO, JUG, BUT I'VE GOT A FAMILY TO SUPPORT! I CAN'T AFFORD THE LUXURY OF AN EDUCATION LIKE YOU!
MYRA, HONEY, I WANT YOU TO MEET MY OLD FRIEND JUGHEAD! JUG PLAYS SKINS FOR THE ARCHIES!
HELLO, MYRA!
HELLO, JUG!
9

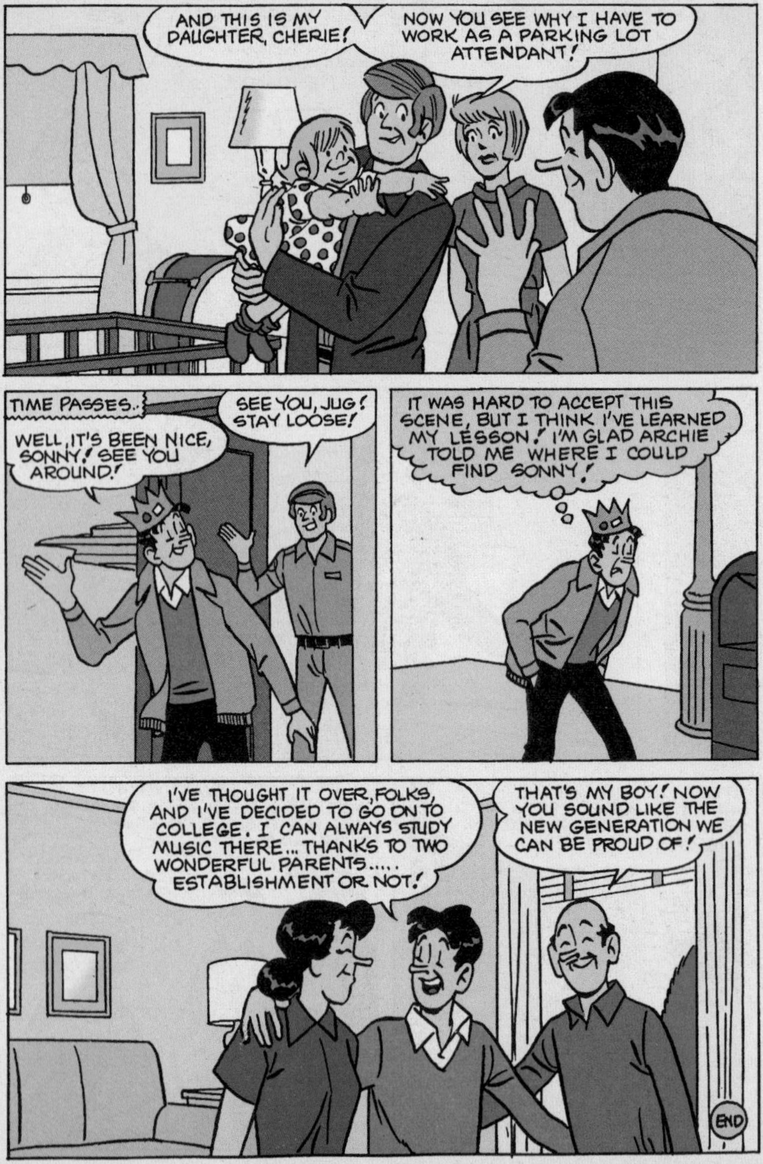
AND THIS IS MY DAUGHTER, CHERIE!
NOW YOU SEE WHY I HAVE TO WORK AS A PARKING LOT ATTENDANT!
TIME PASSES..
WELL, IT'S BEEN NICE, SONNY! SEE YOU AROUND!
SEE YOU, JUG! STAY LOOSE!
IT WAS HARD TO ACCEPT THIS SCENE, BUT I THINK I'VE LEARNED MY LESSON! I'M GLAD ARCHIE TOLD ME WHERE I COULD FIND SONNY!
I'VE THOUGHT IT OVER, FOLKS, AND I'VE DECIDED TO GO ON TO COLLEGE. I CAN ALWAYS STUDY MUSIC THERE... THANKS TO TWO WONDERFUL PARENTS..... ESTABLISHMENT OR NOT!
THAT'S MY BOY! NOW YOU SOUND LIKE THE NEW GENERATION WE CAN BE PROUD OF!
END

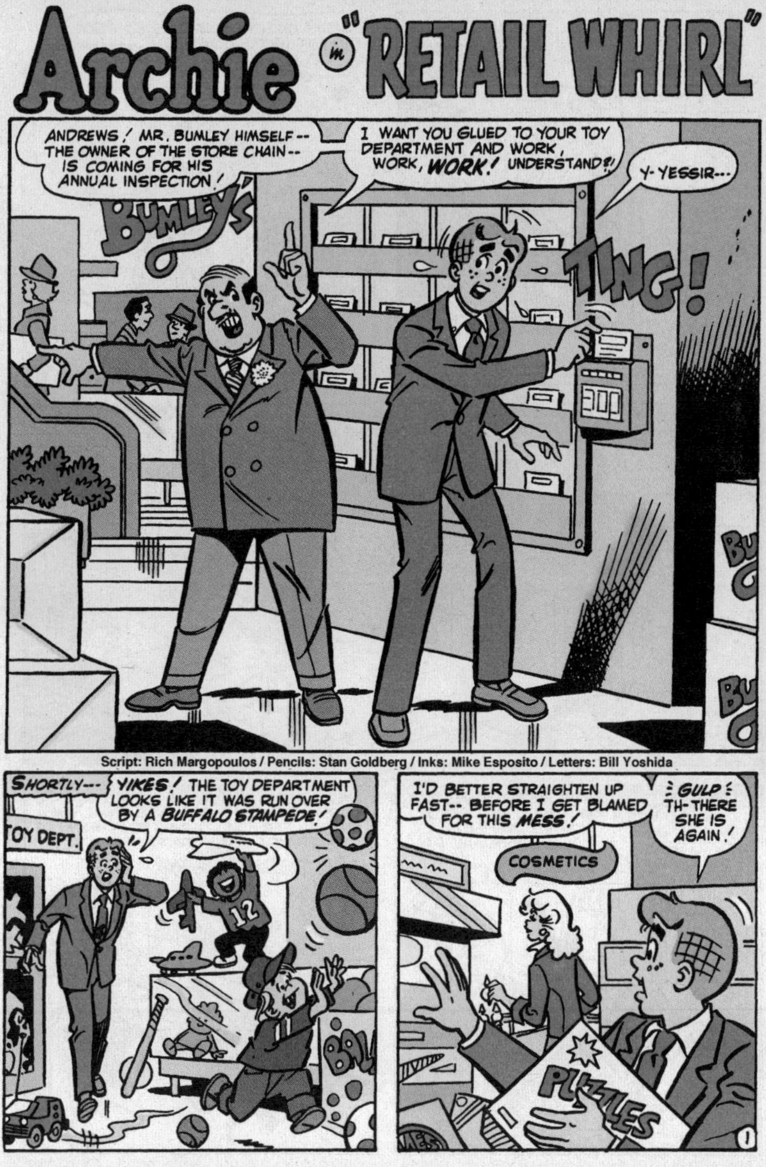

Archie in "RETAIL WHIRL"
ANDREWS! MR. BUMLEY HIMSELF -- THE OWNER OF THE STORE CHAIN -- IS COMING FOR HIS ANNUAL INSPECTION!
I WANT YOU GLUED TO YOUR TOY DEPARTMENT AND WORK, WORK, WORK! UNDERSTAND?!
Y-YESSIR---
BUMLEY'S
TING!
Script: Rich Margopoulos / Pencils: Stan Goldberg / Inks: Mike Esposito / Letters: Bill Yoshida
SHORTLY---
YIKES! THE TOY DEPARTMENT LOOKS LIKE IT WAS RUN OVER BY A BUFFALO STAMPEDE!
TOY DEPT.
I'D BETTER STRAIGHTEN UP FAST-- BEFORE I GET BLAMED FOR THIS MESS!
GULP TH-THERE SHE IS AGAIN!
COSMETICS
PUZZLES
1

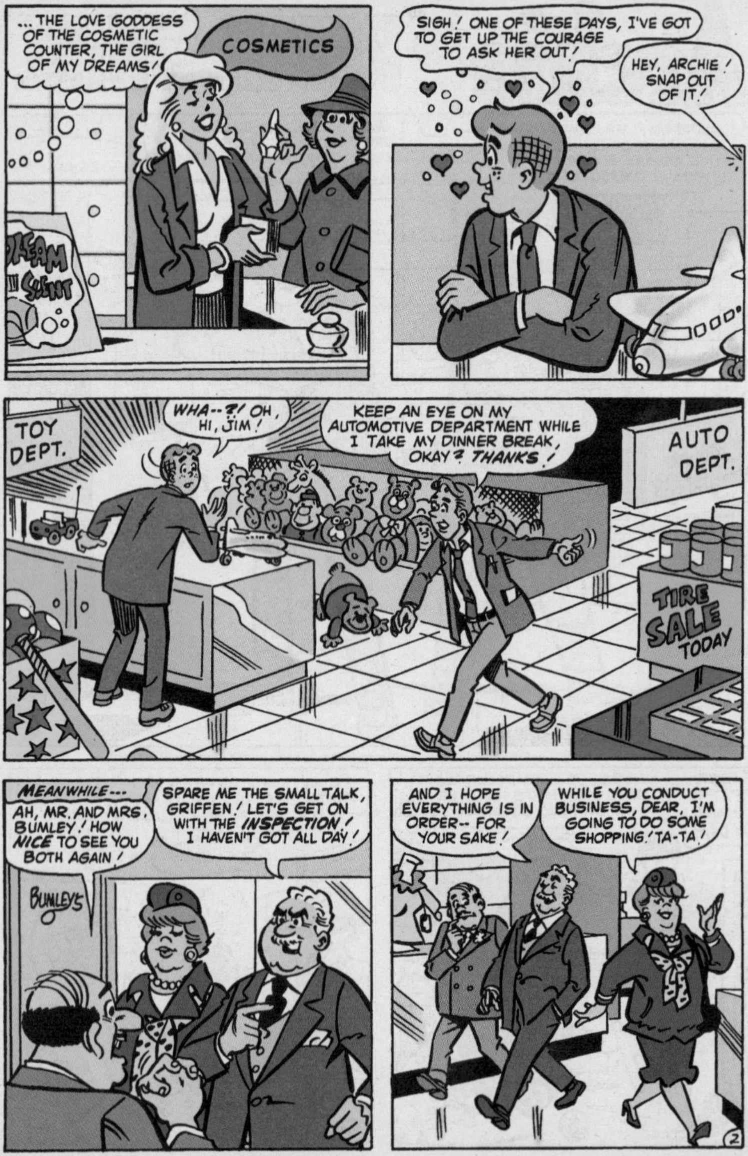
...THE LOVE GODDESS OF THE COSMETIC COUNTER, THE GIRL OF MY DREAMS!
COSMETICS
SIGH! ONE OF THESE DAYS, I'VE GOT TO GET UP THE COURAGE TO ASK HER OUT!
HEY, ARCHIE! SNAP OUT OF IT!
TOY DEPT.
WHA--?! OH, HI, JIM!
KEEP AN EYE ON MY AUTOMOTIVE DEPARTMENT WHILE I TAKE MY DINNER BREAK, OKAY? THANKS!
AUTO DEPT.
TIRE SALE TODAY
MEANWHILE---
AH, MR. AND MRS. BUMLEY! HOW NICE TO SEE YOU BOTH AGAIN!
SPARE ME THE SMALL TALK, GRIFFEN! LET'S GET ON WITH THE INSPECTION! I HAVEN'T GOT ALL DAY!
BUMLEY'S
AND I HOPE EVERYTHING IS IN ORDER-- FOR YOUR SAKE!
WHILE YOU CONDUCT BUSINESS, DEAR, I'M GOING TO DO SOME SHOPPING! TA-TA!
2

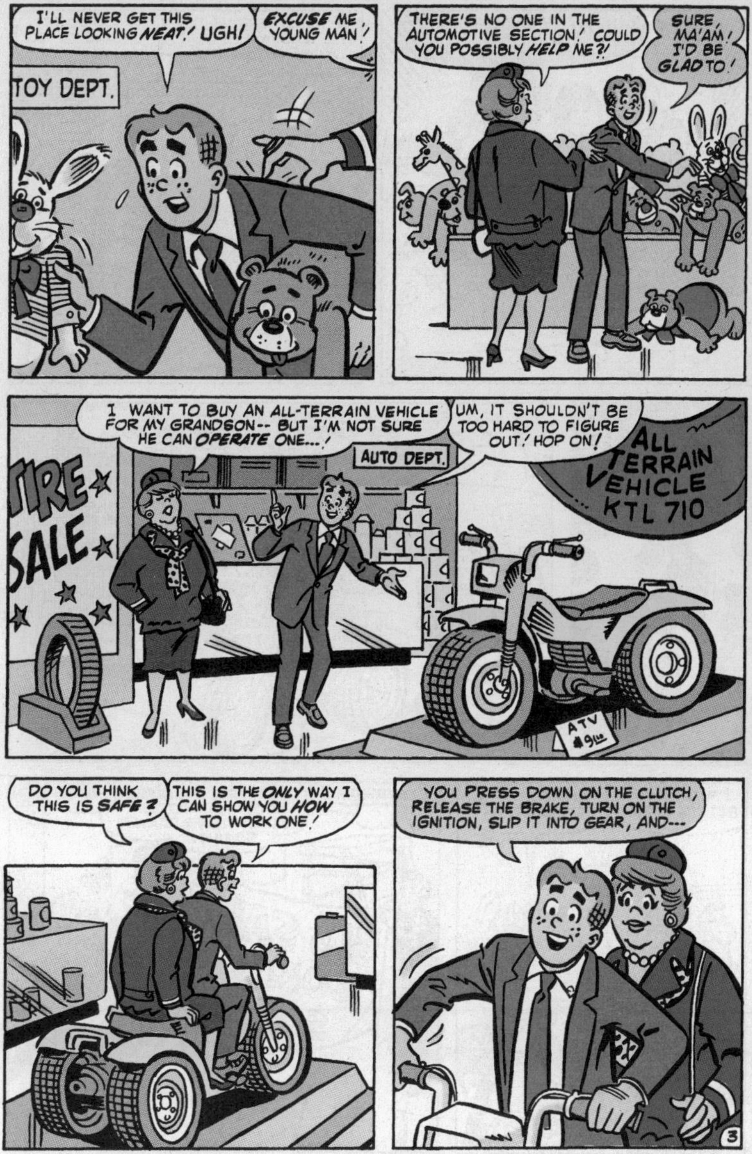

I'LL NEVER GET THIS PLACE LOOKING NEAT! UGH!
TOY DEPT.
EXCUSE ME, YOUNG MAN!
THERE'S NO ONE IN THE AUTOMOTIVE SECTION! COULD YOU POSSIBLY HELP ME?!
SURE, MA'AM! I'D BE GLAD TO!
I WANT TO BUY AN ALL-TERRAIN VEHICLE FOR MY GRANDSON-- BUT I'M NOT SURE HE CAN OPERATE ONE...!
UM, IT SHOULDN'T BE TOO HARD TO FIGURE OUT! HOP ON!
AUTO DEPT.
TIRE SALE
ALL TERRAIN VEHICLE KTL 710
ATV
DO YOU THINK THIS IS SAFE?
THIS IS THE ONLY WAY I CAN SHOW YOU HOW TO WORK ONE!
YOU PRESS DOWN ON THE CLUTCH, RELEASE THE BRAKE, TURN ON THE IGNITION, SLIP IT INTO GEAR, AND---

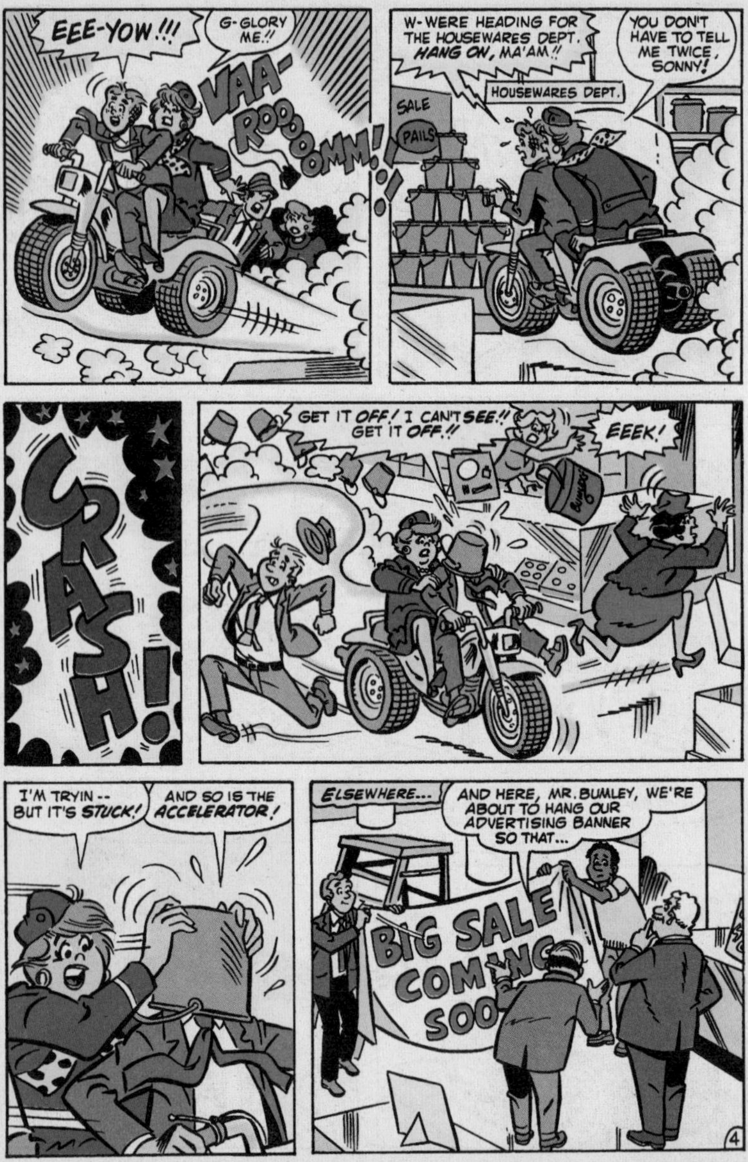
EEE-YOW!!!
G-GLORY ME.!!
VAA-ROOOOOMM!
W-WERE HEADING FOR THE HOUSEWARES DEPT. HANG ON, MA'AM!!
YOU DON'T HAVE TO TELL ME TWICE, SONNY!
HOUSEWARES DEPT.
SALE
PAILS
CRASH!
GET IT OFF! I CAN'T SEE!! GET IT OFF!!
EEEK!
I'M TRYIN -- BUT IT'S STUCK!
AND SO IS THE ACCELERATOR!
ELSEWHERE...
AND HERE, MR. BUMLEY, WE'RE ABOUT TO HANG OUR ADVERTISING BANNER SO THAT...
BIG SALE COMING SOO
4

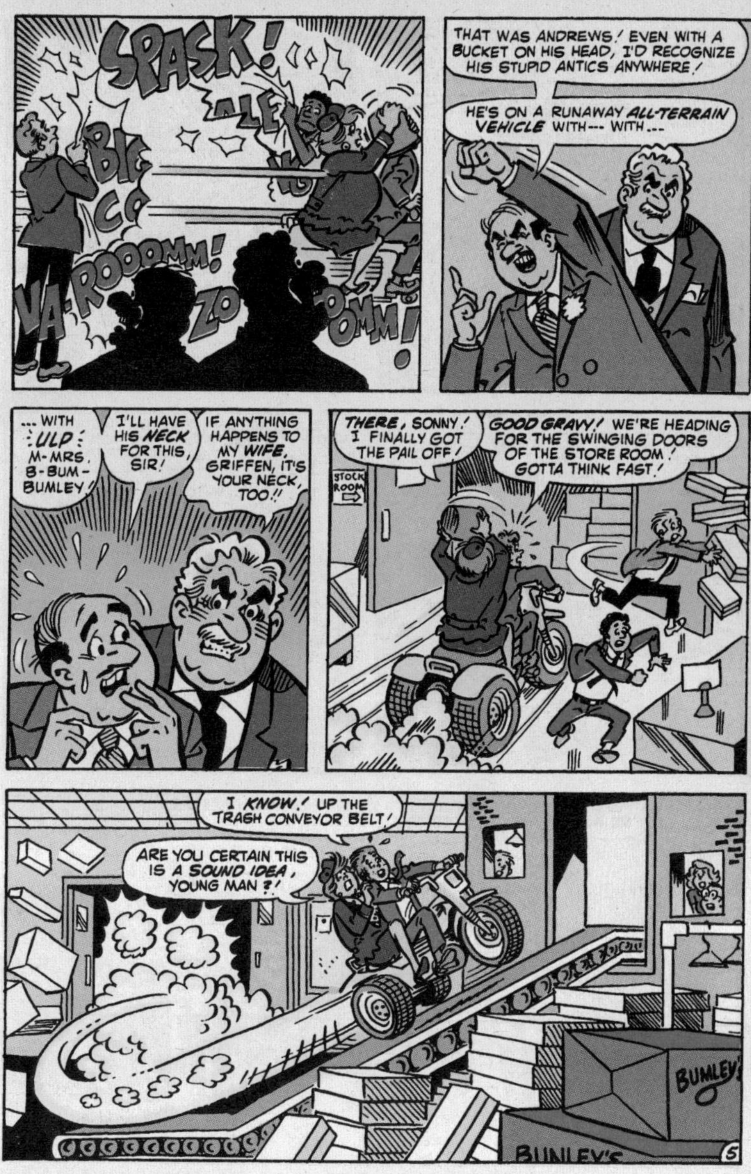
SPASK!
VA-ROOOMM!
THAT WAS ANDREWS! EVEN WITH A BUCKET ON HIS HEAD, I'D RECOGNIZE HIS STUPID ANTICS ANYWHERE!
HE'S ON A RUNAWAY ALL-TERRAIN VEHICLE WITH--- WITH---
--- WITH ULP M-MRS. B-BUM-BUMLEY!
I'LL HAVE HIS NECK FOR THIS, SIR!
IF ANYTHING HAPPENS TO MY WIFE, GRIFFEN, IT'S YOUR NECK, TOO!!
THERE, SONNY! I FINALLY GOT THE PAIL OFF!
GOOD GRAVY! WE'RE HEADING FOR THE SWINGING DOORS OF THE STORE ROOM! GOTTA THINK FAST!
STOCK ROOM
I KNOW! UP THE TRASH CONVEYOR BELT!
ARE YOU CERTAIN THIS IS A SOUND IDEA, YOUNG MAN ?!
BUMLEY'S

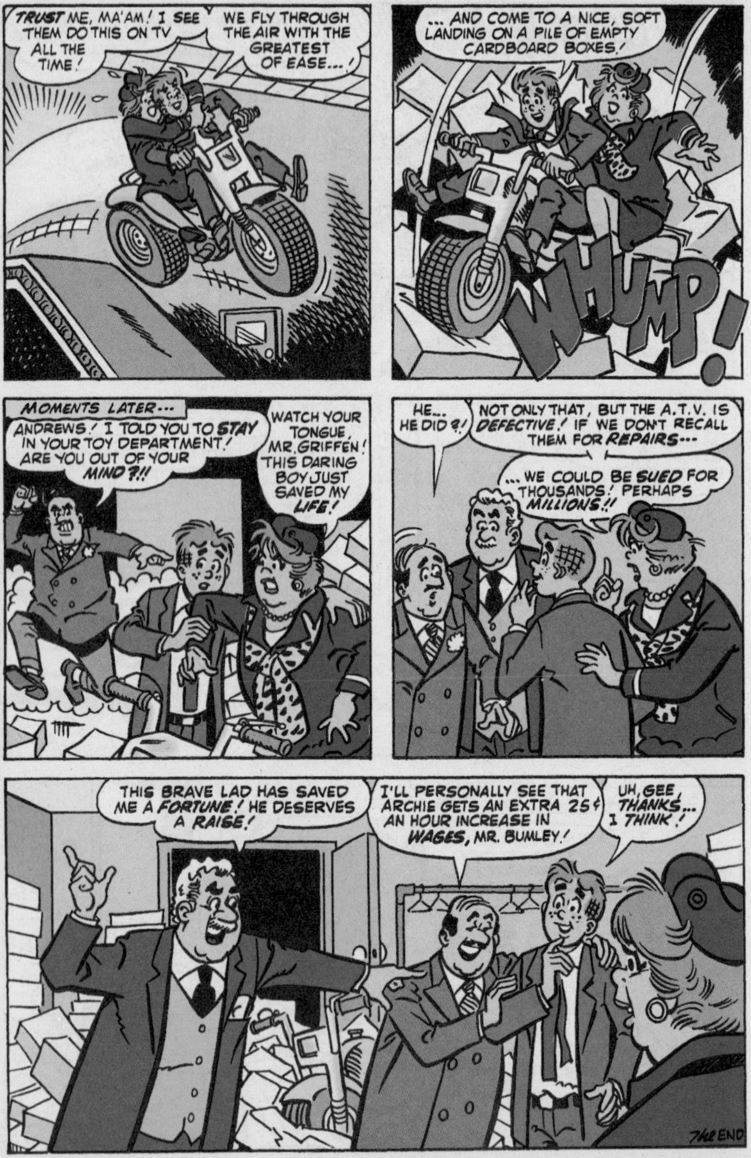

TRUST ME, MA'AM! I SEE THEM DO THIS ON TV ALL THE TIME!
WE FLY THROUGH THE AIR WITH THE GREATEST OF EASE...!
... AND COME TO A NICE, SOFT LANDING ON A PILE OF EMPTY CARDBOARD BOXES!
WHUMP!
MOMENTS LATER...
ANDREWS! I TOLD YOU TO STAY IN YOUR TOY DEPARTMENT! ARE YOU OUT OF YOUR MIND?!!
WATCH YOUR TONGUE, MR. GRIFFEN! THIS DARING BOY JUST SAVED MY LIFE!
HE... HE DID?!
NOT ONLY THAT, BUT THE A.T.V. IS DEFECTIVE! IF WE DON'T RECALL THEM FOR REPAIRS---
... WE COULD BE SUED FOR THOUSANDS! PERHAPS MILLIONS!!
THIS BRAVE LAD HAS SAVED ME A FORTUNE! HE DESERVES A RAISE!
I'LL PERSONALLY SEE THAT ARCHIE GETS AN EXTRA 25¢ AN HOUR INCREASE IN WAGES, MR. BUMLEY!
UH, GEE, THANKS... I THINK!
THE END

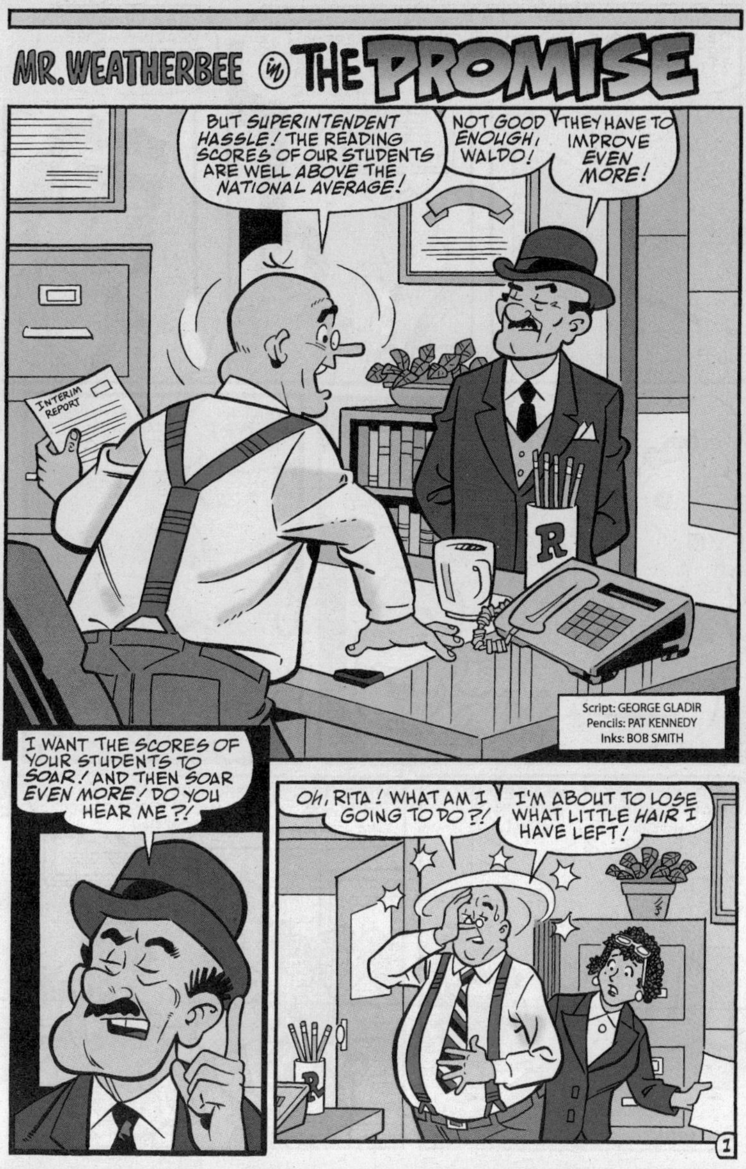
MR. WEATHERBEE in THE PROMISE
BUT SUPERINTENDENT HASSLE! THE READING SCORES OF OUR STUDENTS ARE WELL ABOVE THE NATIONAL AVERAGE!
NOT GOOD ENOUGH, WALDO!
THEY HAVE TO IMPROVE EVEN MORE!
INTERIM REPORT
R
Script: GEORGE GLADIR
Pencils: PAT KENNEDY
Inks: BOB SMITH
I WANT THE SCORES OF YOUR STUDENTS TO SOAR! AND THEN SOAR EVEN MORE! DO YOU HEAR ME?!
OH, RITA! WHAT AM I GOING TO DO?!
I'M ABOUT TO LOSE WHAT LITTLE HAIR I HAVE LEFT!
R
1

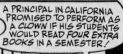 HERE'S A NEWS ITEM THAT MIGHT BE THE SOLUTION TO THE PROBLEM!

WHAT?

A PRINCIPAL IN CALIFORNIA PROMISED TO PERFORM AS A CLOWN IF HIS STUDENTS WOULD READ FOUR EXTRA BOOKS IN A SEMESTER!

 AS A RESULT, READING SCORES IMPROVED DRAMATICALLY!

 Hmmm... PERFORM AS A CLOWN!

 WHAT A SPLENDID IDEA!

I'VE ALWAYS HAD SHOWBIZ ASPIRATIONS!

 BUT WE CAN'T WAIT A WHOLE SCHOOL SEMESTER!

WE NEED ACTION NOW!

 WE'LL TELL ALL OUR STUDENTS I SHALL PERFORM AS A CLOWN IF THEY READ ONE EXTRA BOOK A MONTH!

2

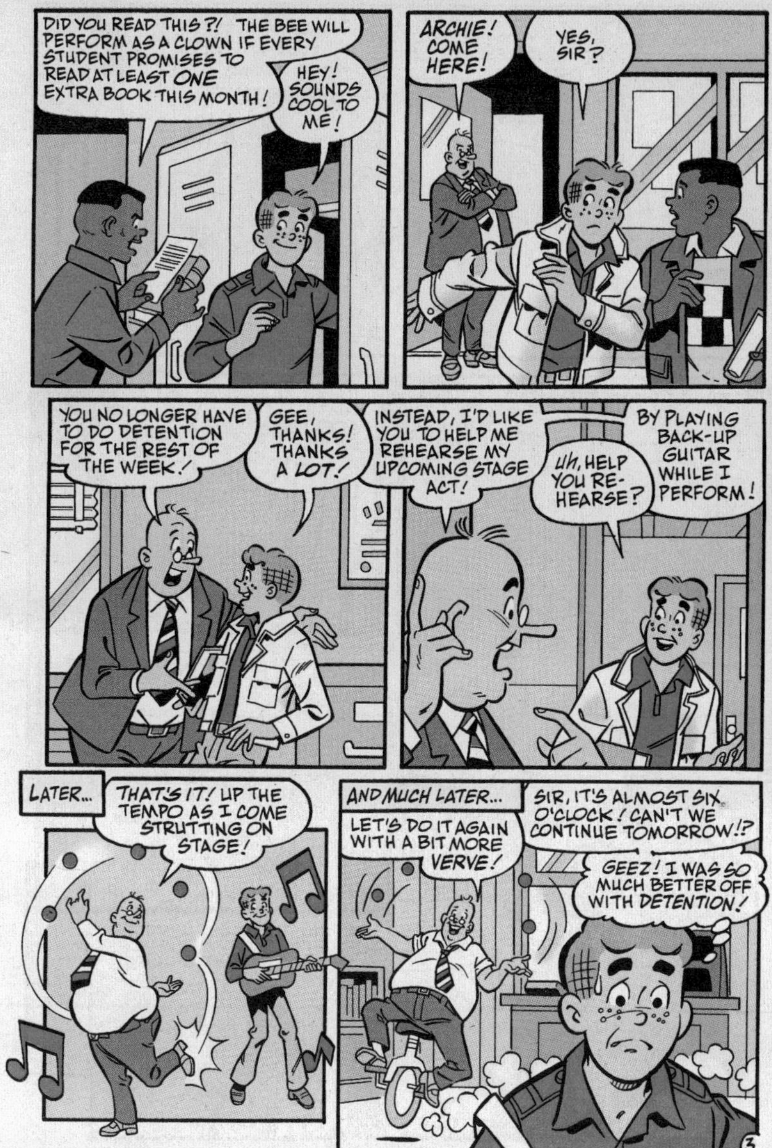
DID YOU READ THIS?! THE BEE WILL PERFORM AS A CLOWN IF EVERY STUDENT PROMISES TO READ AT LEAST ONE EXTRA BOOK THIS MONTH!
HEY! SOUNDS COOL TO ME!
ARCHIE! COME HERE!
YES, SIR?
YOU NO LONGER HAVE TO DO DETENTION FOR THE REST OF THE WEEK!
GEE, THANKS! THANKS A LOT!
INSTEAD, I'D LIKE YOU TO HELP ME REHEARSE MY UPCOMING STAGE ACT!
UH, HELP YOU RE-HEARSE?
BY PLAYING BACK-UP GUITAR WHILE I PERFORM!
LATER...
THAT'S IT! UP THE TEMPO AS I COME STRUTTING ON STAGE!
AND MUCH LATER...
LET'S DO IT AGAIN WITH A BIT MORE VERVE!
SIR, IT'S ALMOST SIX O'CLOCK! CAN'T WE CONTINUE TOMORROW!?
GEEZ! I WAS SO MUCH BETTER OFF WITH DETENTION!
3

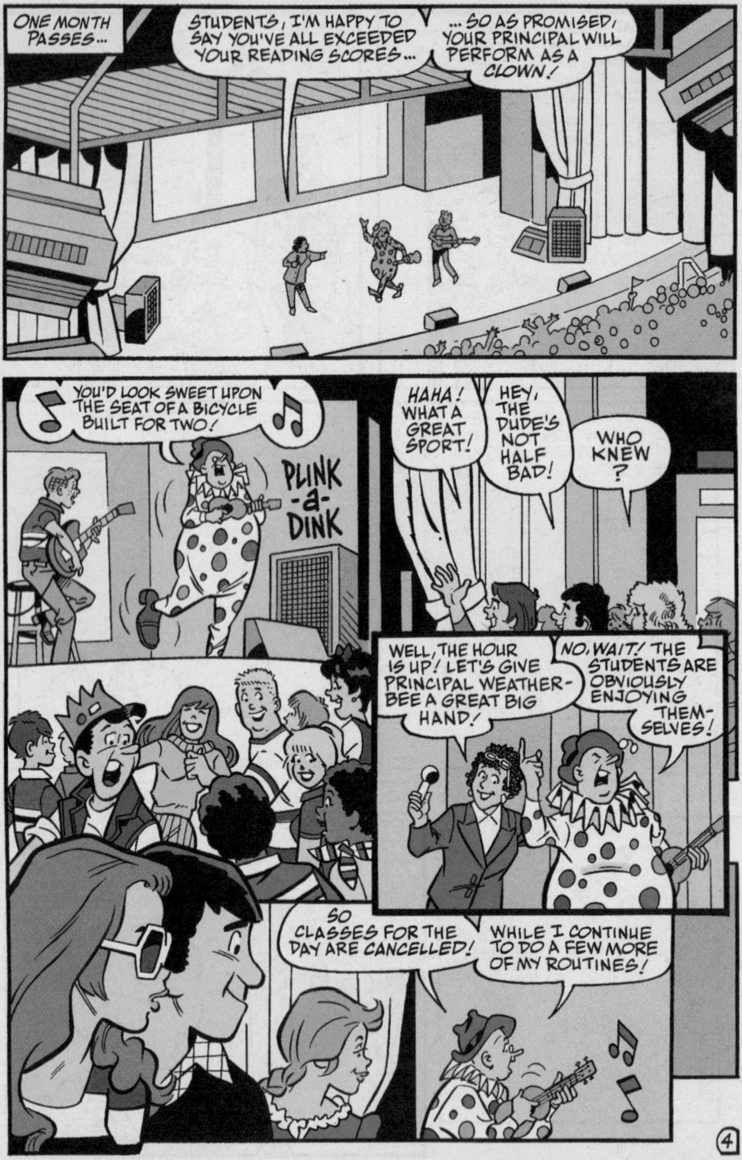
ONE MONTH PASSES...
STUDENTS, I'M HAPPY TO SAY YOU'VE ALL EXCEEDED YOUR READING SCORES...
...SO AS PROMISED, YOUR PRINCIPAL WILL PERFORM AS A CLOWN!
YOU'D LOOK SWEET UPON THE SEAT OF A BICYCLE BUILT FOR TWO!
PLINK -a- DINK
HAHA! WHAT A GREAT SPORT!
HEY, THE DUDE'S NOT HALF BAD!
WHO KNEW?
WELL, THE HOUR IS UP! LET'S GIVE PRINCIPAL WEATHERBEE A GREAT BIG HAND!
NO, WAIT! THE STUDENTS ARE OBVIOUSLY ENJOYING THEMSELVES!
SO CLASSES FOR THE DAY ARE CANCELLED!
WHILE I CONTINUE TO DO A FEW MORE OF MY ROUTINES!

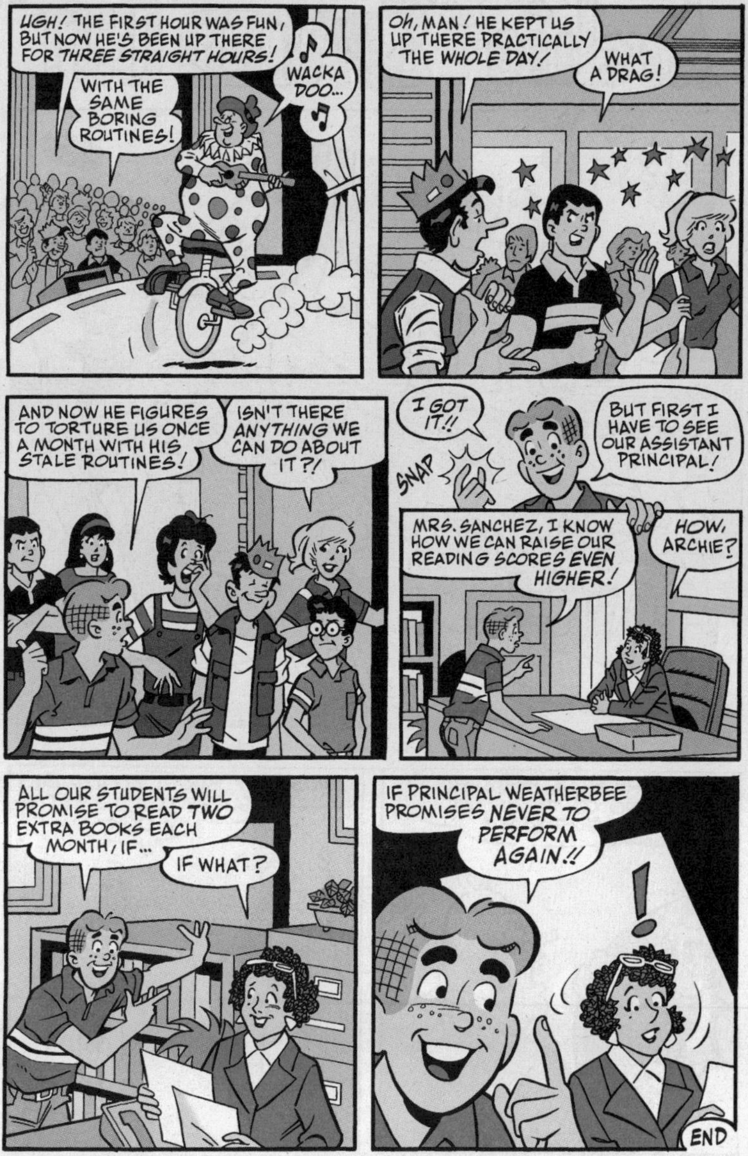
UGH! THE FIRST HOUR WAS FUN, BUT NOW HE'S BEEN UP THERE FOR THREE STRAIGHT HOURS!
WITH THE SAME BORING ROUTINES!
WACKA DOO...
Oh, MAN! HE KEPT US UP THERE PRACTICALLY THE WHOLE DAY!
WHAT A DRAG!
AND NOW HE FIGURES TO TORTURE US ONCE A MONTH WITH HIS STALE ROUTINES!
ISN'T THERE ANYTHING WE CAN DO ABOUT IT?!
I GOT IT!!
SNAP
BUT FIRST I HAVE TO SEE OUR ASSISTANT PRINCIPAL!
MRS. SANCHEZ, I KNOW HOW WE CAN RAISE OUR READING SCORES EVEN HIGHER!
HOW, ARCHIE?
ALL OUR STUDENTS WILL PROMISE TO READ TWO EXTRA BOOKS EACH MONTH, IF...
IF WHAT?
IF PRINCIPAL WEATHERBEE PROMISES NEVER TO PERFORM AGAIN!!
!
END

Archie in "SPACED OUT"

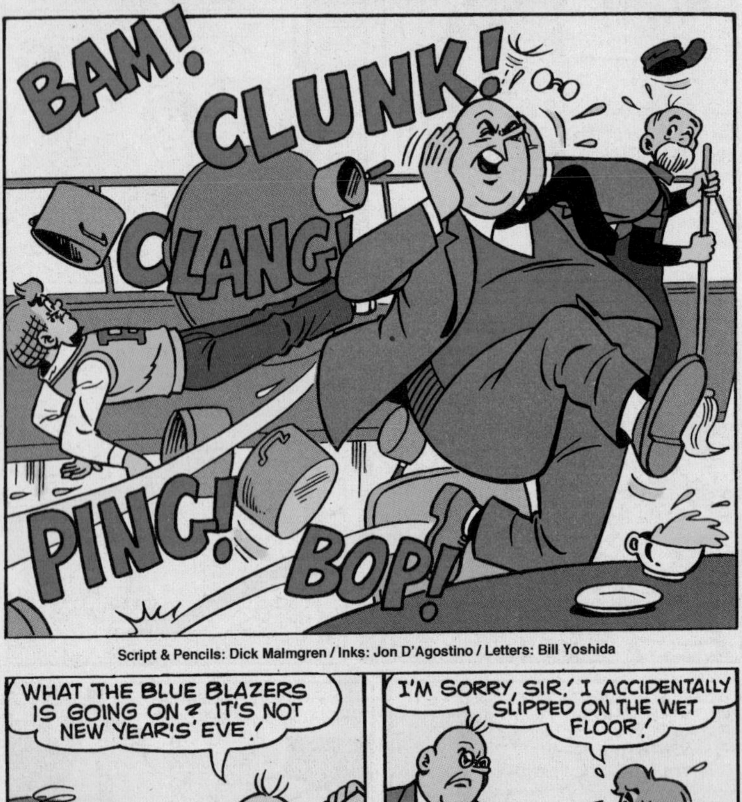
BAM!
CLUNK!
CLANG!
PING!
BOP!

Script & Pencils: Dick Malmgren / Inks: Jon D'Agostino / Letters: Bill Yoshida

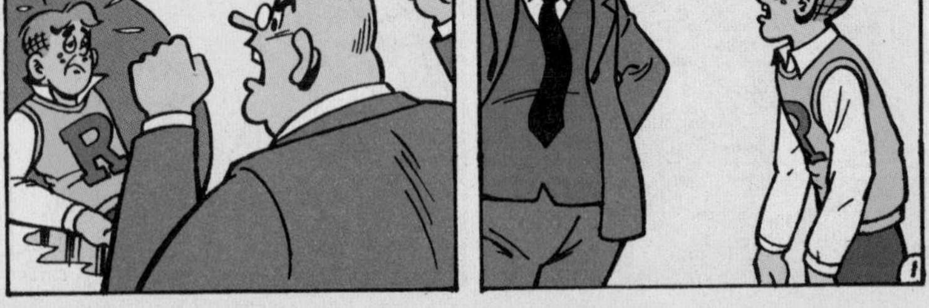
WHAT THE BLUE BLAZERS IS GOING ON? IT'S NOT NEW YEAR'S EVE!
I'M SORRY, SIR! I ACCIDENTALLY SLIPPED ON THE WET FLOOR!

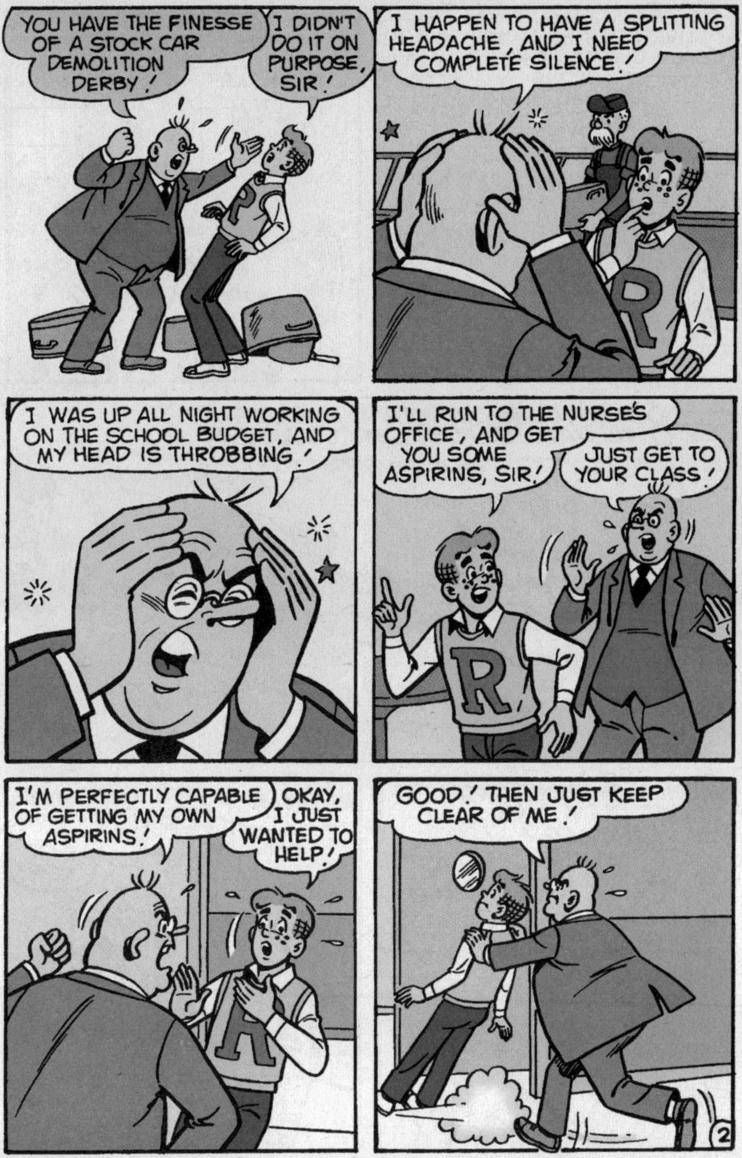

YOU HAVE THE FINESSE OF A STOCK CAR DEMOLITION DERBY!
I DIDN'T DO IT ON PURPOSE, SIR!
I HAPPEN TO HAVE A SPLITTING HEADACHE, AND I NEED COMPLETE SILENCE!
I WAS UP ALL NIGHT WORKING ON THE SCHOOL BUDGET, AND MY HEAD IS THROBBING!
I'LL RUN TO THE NURSE'S OFFICE, AND GET YOU SOME ASPIRINS, SIR!
JUST GET TO YOUR CLASS!
I'M PERFECTLY CAPABLE OF GETTING MY OWN ASPIRINS!
OKAY, I JUST WANTED TO HELP!
GOOD! THEN JUST KEEP CLEAR OF ME!
2

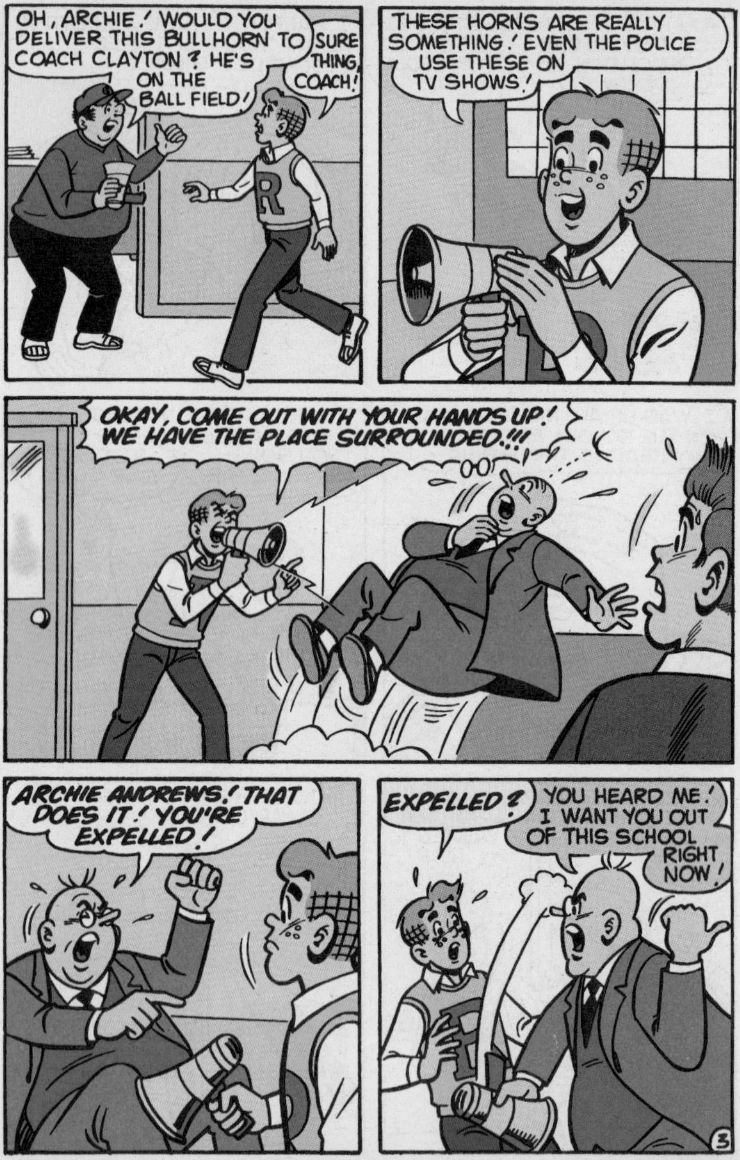

OH, ARCHIE! WOULD YOU DELIVER THIS BULLHORN TO COACH CLAYTON? HE'S ON THE BALL FIELD!
SURE THING, COACH!
THESE HORNS ARE REALLY SOMETHING! EVEN THE POLICE USE THESE ON TV SHOWS!
OKAY, COME OUT WITH YOUR HANDS UP! WE HAVE THE PLACE SURROUNDED!!!
ARCHIE ANDREWS! THAT DOES IT! YOU'RE EXPELLED!
EXPELLED?
YOU HEARD ME! I WANT YOU OUT OF THIS SCHOOL RIGHT NOW!
3

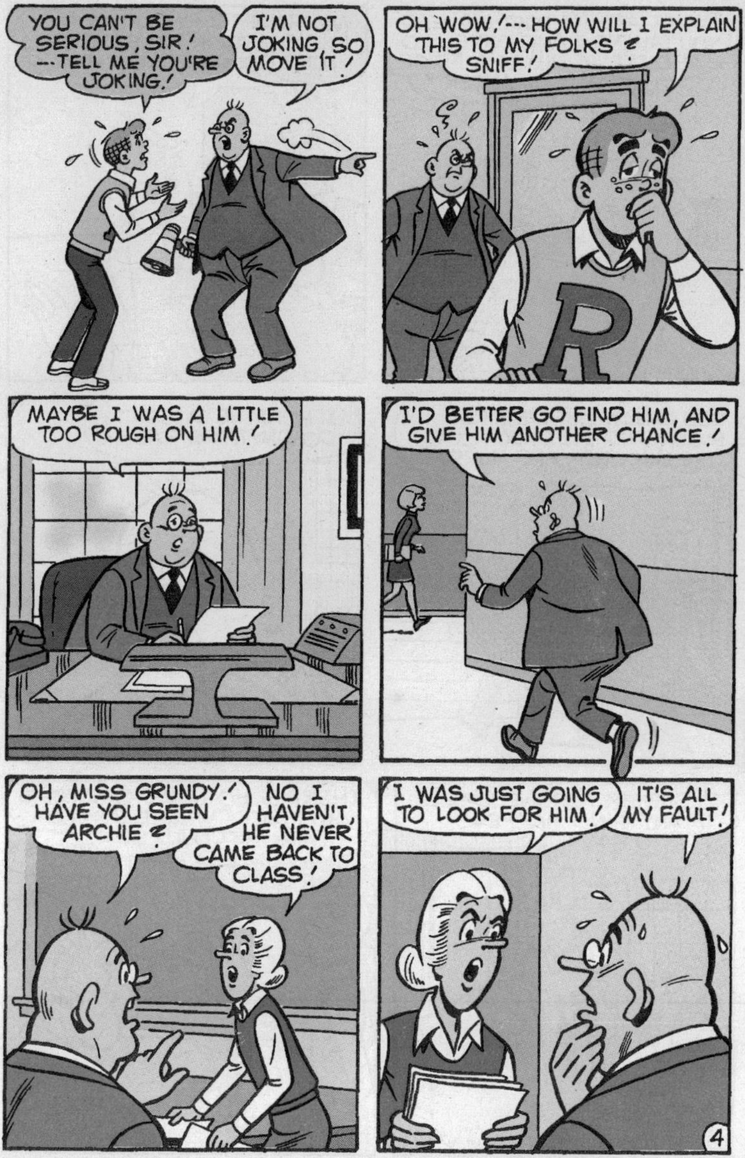

YOU CAN'T BE SERIOUS, SIR! --TELL ME YOU'RE JOKING!
I'M NOT JOKING, SO MOVE IT!
OH WOW!--- HOW WILL I EXPLAIN THIS TO MY FOLKS? SNIFF!
MAYBE I WAS A LITTLE TOO ROUGH ON HIM!
I'D BETTER GO FIND HIM, AND GIVE HIM ANOTHER CHANCE!
OH, MISS GRUNDY! HAVE YOU SEEN ARCHIE?
NO I HAVEN'T, HE NEVER CAME BACK TO CLASS!
I WAS JUST GOING TO LOOK FOR HIM!
IT'S ALL MY FAULT!
4

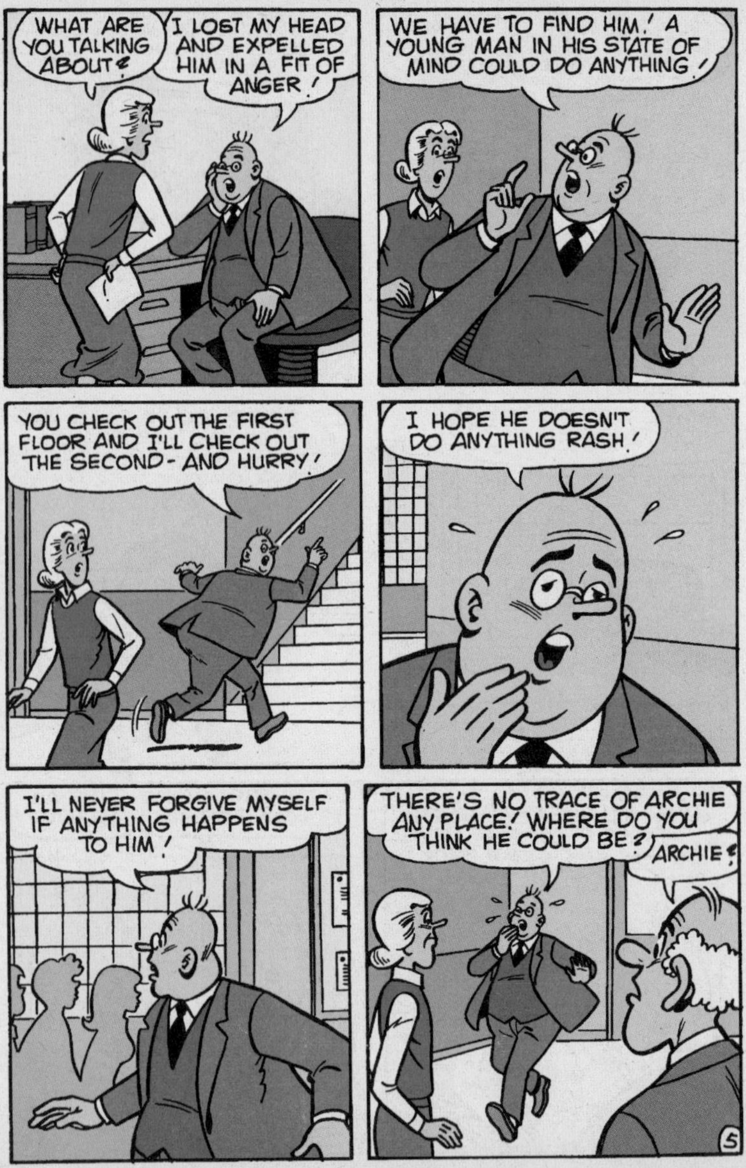

WHAT ARE YOU TALKING ABOUT?
I LOST MY HEAD AND EXPELLED HIM IN A FIT OF ANGER!
WE HAVE TO FIND HIM! A YOUNG MAN IN HIS STATE OF MIND COULD DO ANYTHING!
YOU CHECK OUT THE FIRST FLOOR AND I'LL CHECK OUT THE SECOND- AND HURRY!
I HOPE HE DOESN'T DO ANYTHING RASH!
I'LL NEVER FORGIVE MYSELF IF ANYTHING HAPPENS TO HIM!
THERE'S NO TRACE OF ARCHIE ANY PLACE! WHERE DO YOU THINK HE COULD BE?
ARCHIE?
5

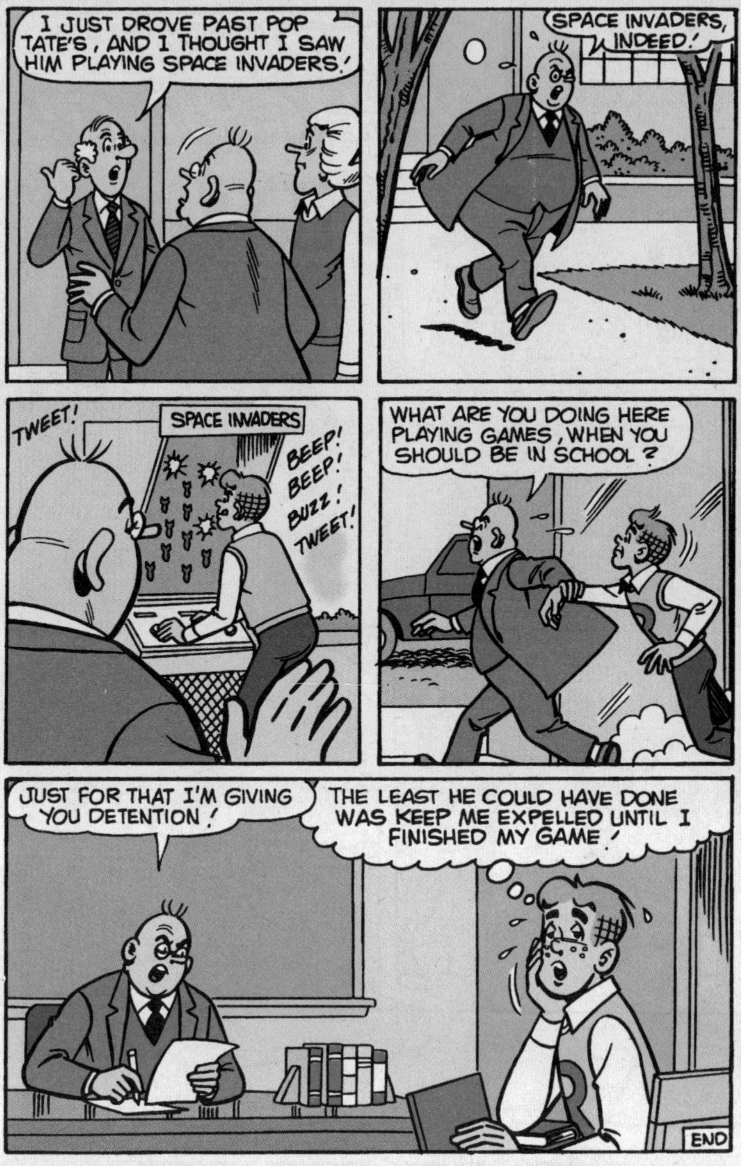
I JUST DROVE PAST POP TATE'S, AND I THOUGHT I SAW HIM PLAYING SPACE INVADERS!
SPACE INVADERS, INDEED!
TWEET!
SPACE INVADERS
BEEP! BEEP! BUZZ! TWEET!
WHAT ARE YOU DOING HERE PLAYING GAMES, WHEN YOU SHOULD BE IN SCHOOL?
JUST FOR THAT I'M GIVING YOU DETENTION!
THE LEAST HE COULD HAVE DONE WAS KEEP ME EXPELLED UNTIL I FINISHED MY GAME!
END

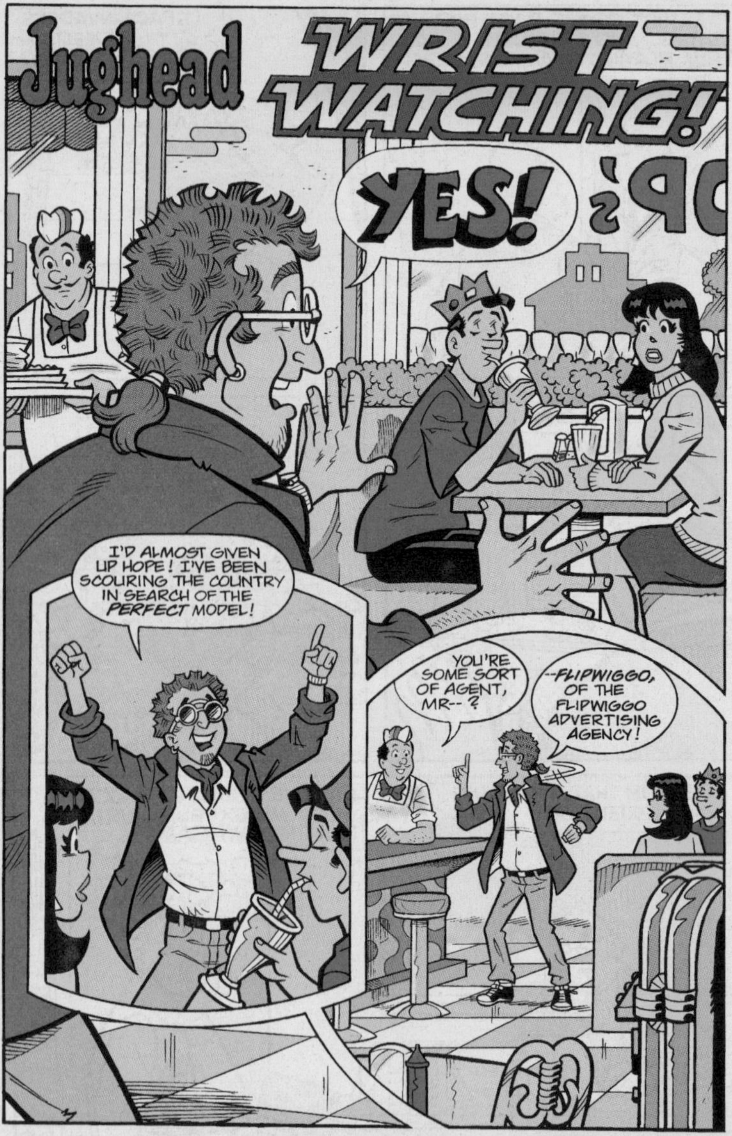
Jughead
WRIST WATCHING!
YES!
I'D ALMOST GIVEN UP HOPE! I'VE BEEN SCOURING THE COUNTRY IN SEARCH OF THE PERFECT MODEL!
YOU'RE SOME SORT OF AGENT, MR-- ?
--FLIPWIGGO, OF THE FLIPWIGGO ADVERTISING AGENCY!

SCRIPT: CRAIG BOLDMAN
PENCILS: REX LINDSEY
INKING: RICH KOSLOWSKI
LETTERING: VICKIE WILLIAMS

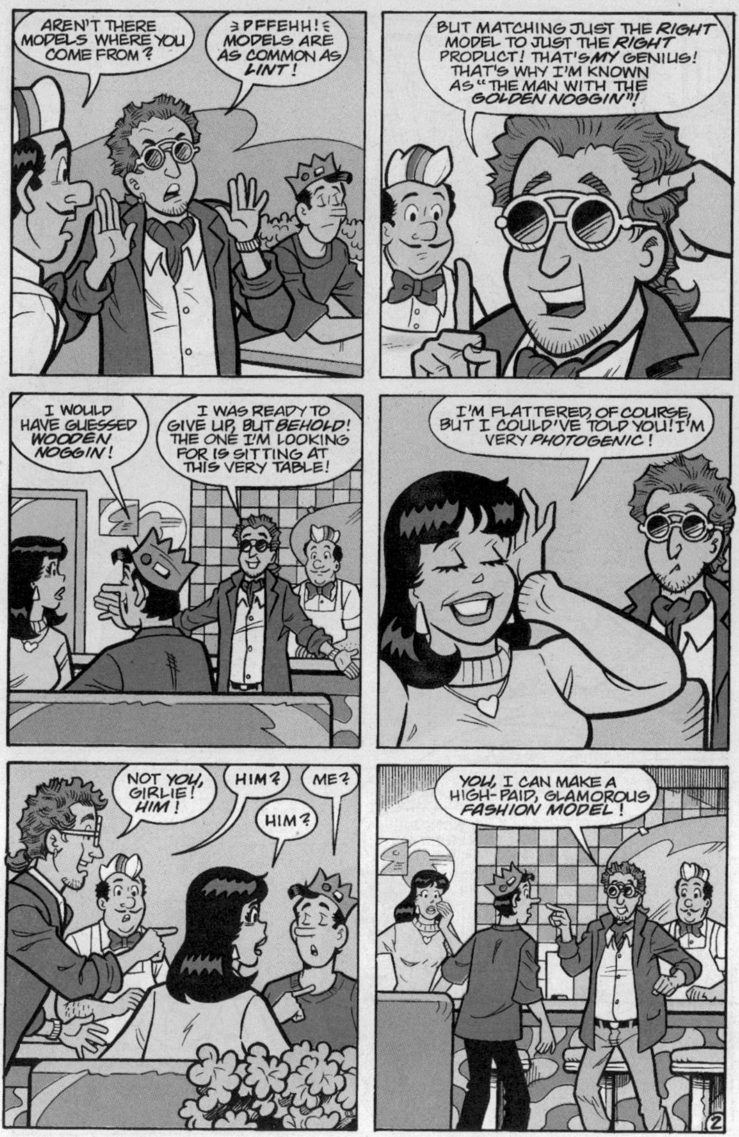
AREN'T THERE MODELS WHERE YOU COME FROM?
PFFEHH! MODELS ARE AS COMMON AS LINT!
BUT MATCHING JUST THE RIGHT MODEL TO JUST THE RIGHT PRODUCT! THAT'S MY GENIUS! THAT'S WHY I'M KNOWN AS "THE MAN WITH THE GOLDEN NOGGIN"!
I WOULD HAVE GUESSED WOODEN NOGGIN!
I WAS READY TO GIVE UP, BUT BEHOLD! THE ONE I'M LOOKING FOR IS SITTING AT THIS VERY TABLE!
I'M FLATTERED, OF COURSE, BUT I COULD'VE TOLD YOU! I'M VERY PHOTOGENIC!
NOT YOU, GIRLIE! HIM!
HIM?
ME?
HIM?
YOU, I CAN MAKE A HIGH-PAID, GLAMOROUS FASHION MODEL!
2

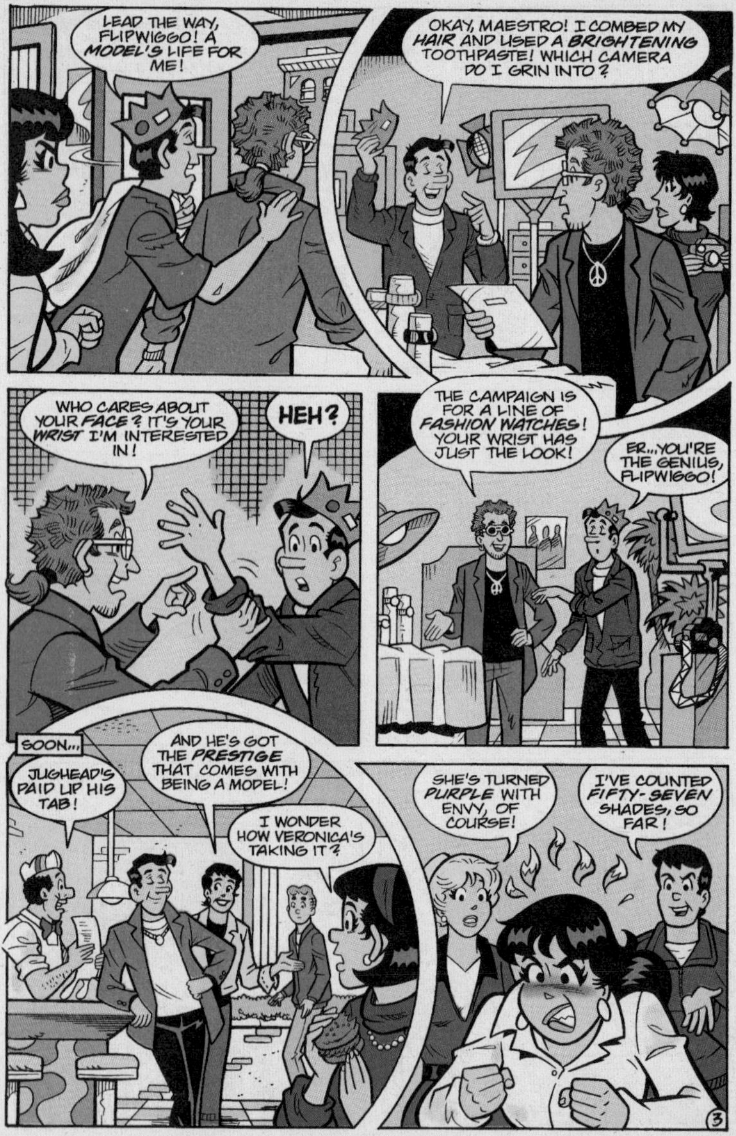
LEAD THE WAY, FLIPWIGGO! A MODEL'S LIFE FOR ME!
OKAY, MAESTRO! I COMBED MY HAIR AND USED A BRIGHTENING TOOTHPASTE! WHICH CAMERA DO I GRIN INTO?
WHO CARES ABOUT YOUR FACE? IT'S YOUR WRIST I'M INTERESTED IN!
HEH?
THE CAMPAIGN IS FOR A LINE OF FASHION WATCHES! YOUR WRIST HAS JUST THE LOOK!
ER...YOU'RE THE GENIUS, FLIPWIGGO!
SOON...
JUGHEAD'S PAID UP HIS TAB!
AND HE'S GOT THE PRESTIGE THAT COMES WITH BEING A MODEL!
I WONDER HOW VERONICA'S TAKING IT?
SHE'S TURNED PURPLE WITH ENVY, OF COURSE!
I'VE COUNTED FIFTY-SEVEN SHADES, SO FAR!
3

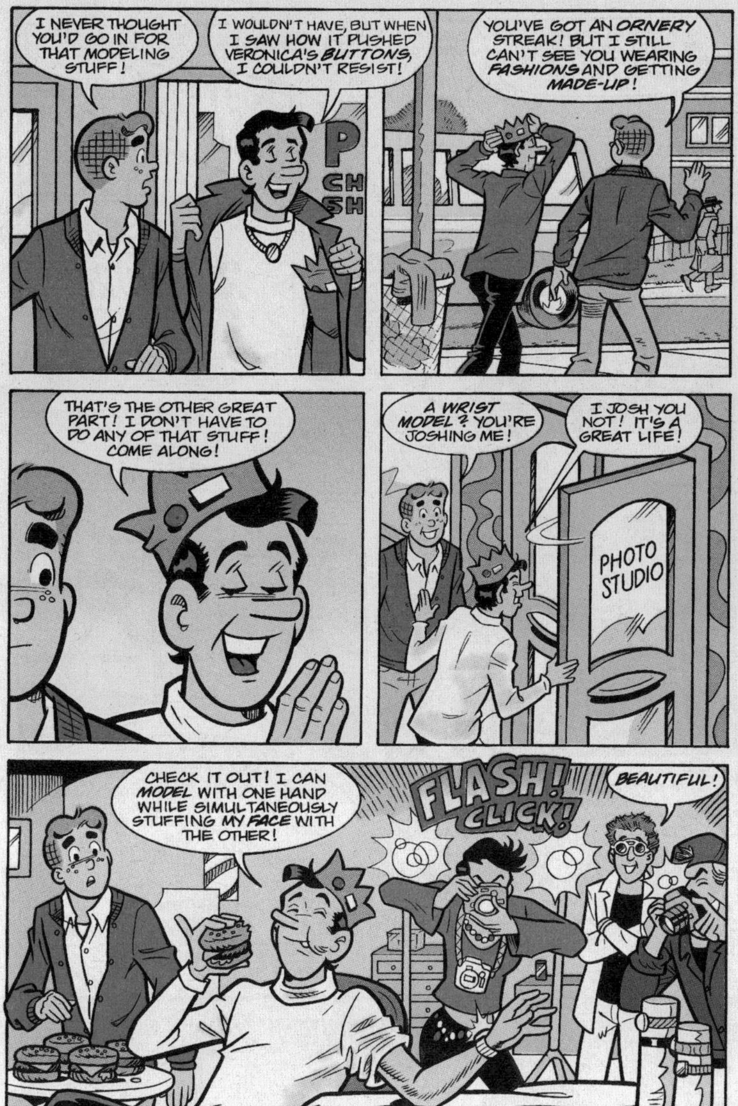
I NEVER THOUGHT YOU'D GO IN FOR THAT MODELING STUFF!
I WOULDN'T HAVE, BUT WHEN I SAW HOW IT PUSHED VERONICA'S BUTTONS, I COULDN'T RESIST!
YOU'VE GOT AN ORNERY STREAK! BUT I STILL CAN'T SEE YOU WEARING FASHIONS AND GETTING MADE-UP!
THAT'S THE OTHER GREAT PART! I DON'T HAVE TO DO ANY OF THAT STUFF! COME ALONG!
A WRIST MODEL? YOU'RE JOSHING ME!
I JOSH YOU NOT! IT'S A GREAT LIFE!
PHOTO STUDIO
CHECK IT OUT! I CAN MODEL WITH ONE HAND WHILE SIMULTANEOUSLY STUFFING MY FACE WITH THE OTHER!
FLASH! CLICK!
BEAUTIFUL!
4

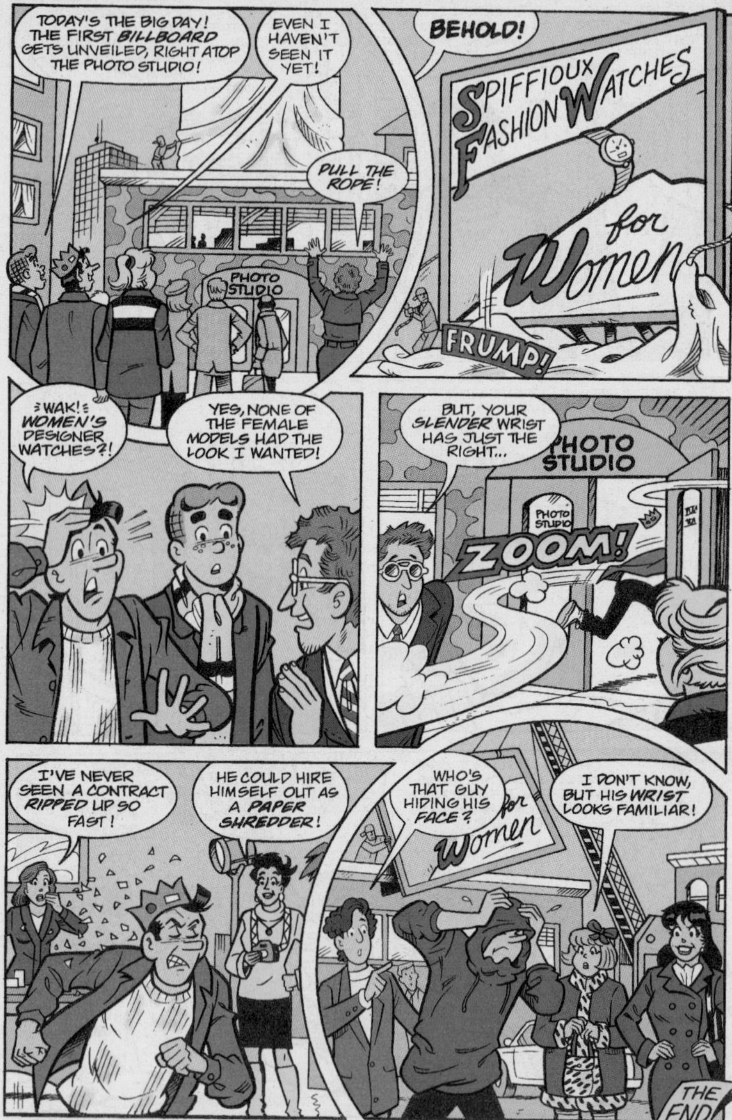
TODAY'S THE BIG DAY! THE FIRST BILLBOARD GETS UNVEILED, RIGHT ATOP THE PHOTO STUDIO!
EVEN I HAVEN'T SEEN IT YET!
PULL THE ROPE!
PHOTO STUDIO
BEHOLD!
SPIFFIOUX FASHION WATCHES for Women
FRUMP!
WAK! WOMEN'S DESIGNER WATCHES?!
YES, NONE OF THE FEMALE MODELS HAD THE LOOK I WANTED!
BUT, YOUR SLENDER WRIST HAS JUST THE RIGHT...
PHOTO STUDIO
PHOTO STUDIO
ZOOM!
I'VE NEVER SEEN A CONTRACT RIPPED UP SO FAST!
HE COULD HIRE HIMSELF OUT AS A PAPER SHREDDER!
WHO'S THAT GUY HIDING HIS FACE?
I DON'T KNOW, BUT HIS WRIST LOOKS FAMILIAR!
for Women
THE END

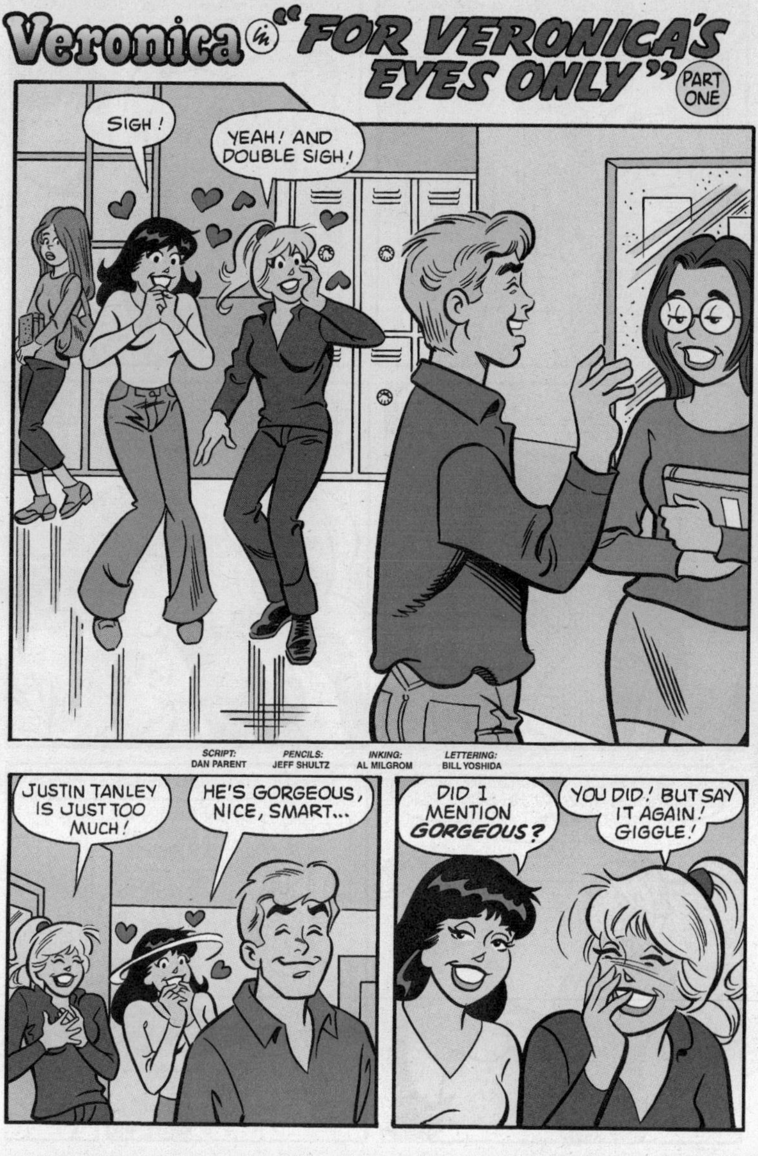
Veronica in "FOR VERONICA'S EYES ONLY" PART ONE
SIGH!
YEAH! AND DOUBLE SIGH!
SCRIPT: DAN PARENT PENCILS: JEFF SHULTZ INKING: AL MILGROM LETTERING: BILL YOSHIDA
JUSTIN TANLEY IS JUST TOO MUCH!
HE'S GORGEOUS, NICE, SMART...
DID I MENTION GORGEOUS?
YOU DID! BUT SAY IT AGAIN! GIGGLE!

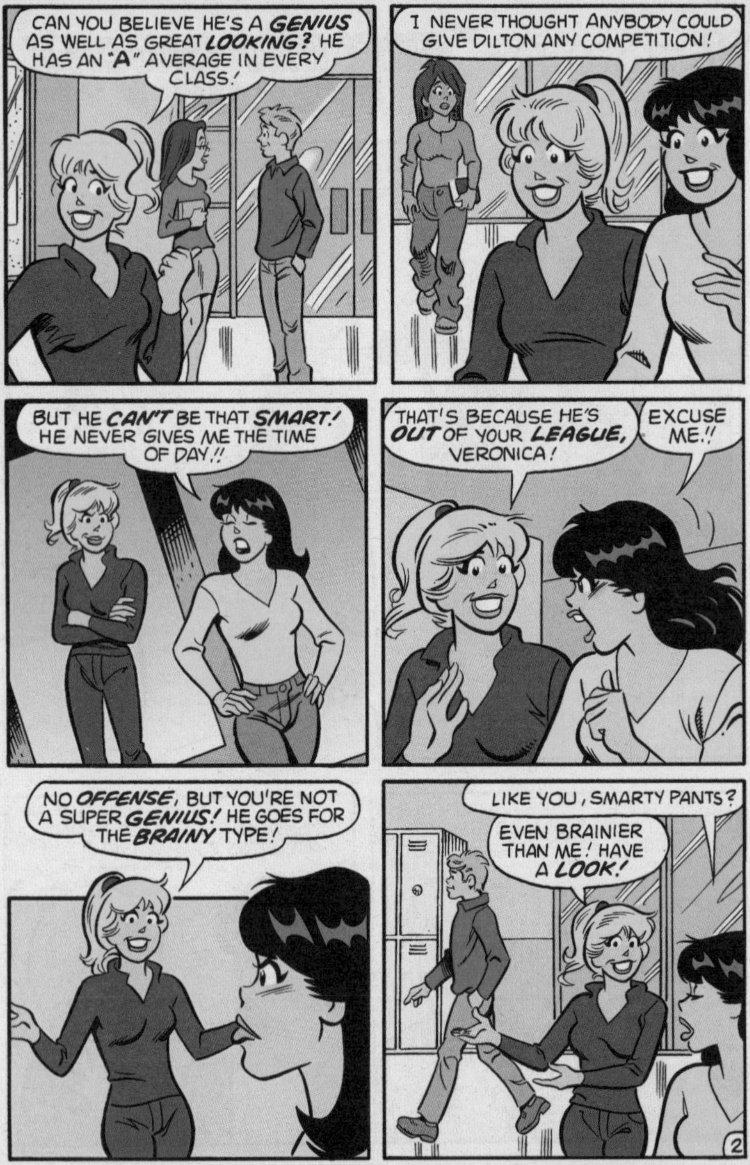

CAN YOU BELIEVE HE'S A GENIUS AS WELL AS GREAT LOOKING? HE HAS AN "A" AVERAGE IN EVERY CLASS!
I NEVER THOUGHT ANYBODY COULD GIVE DILTON ANY COMPETITION!
BUT HE CAN'T BE THAT SMART! HE NEVER GIVES ME THE TIME OF DAY!!
THAT'S BECAUSE HE'S OUT OF YOUR LEAGUE, VERONICA!
EXCUSE ME!!
NO OFFENSE, BUT YOU'RE NOT A SUPER GENIUS! HE GOES FOR THE BRAINY TYPE!
LIKE YOU, SMARTY PANTS?
EVEN BRAINIER THAN ME! HAVE A LOOK!
2

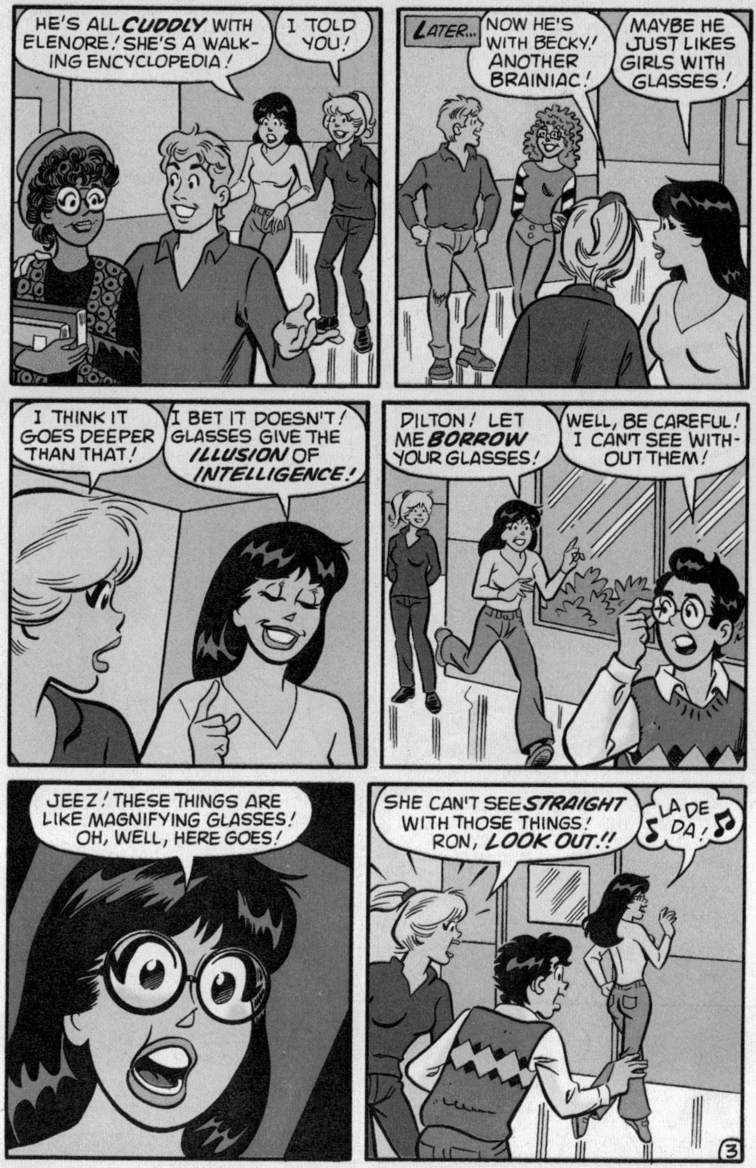
HE'S ALL CUDDLY WITH ELENORE! SHE'S A WALKING ENCYCLOPEDIA!
I TOLD YOU!
LATER...
NOW HE'S WITH BECKY! ANOTHER BRAINIAC!
MAYBE HE JUST LIKES GIRLS WITH GLASSES!
I THINK IT GOES DEEPER THAN THAT!
I BET IT DOESN'T! GLASSES GIVE THE ILLUSION OF INTELLIGENCE!
DILTON! LET ME BORROW YOUR GLASSES!
WELL, BE CAREFUL! I CAN'T SEE WITHOUT THEM!
JEEZ! THESE THINGS ARE LIKE MAGNIFYING GLASSES! OH, WELL, HERE GOES!
SHE CAN'T SEE STRAIGHT WITH THOSE THINGS! RON, LOOK OUT!!
LA DE DA!
3

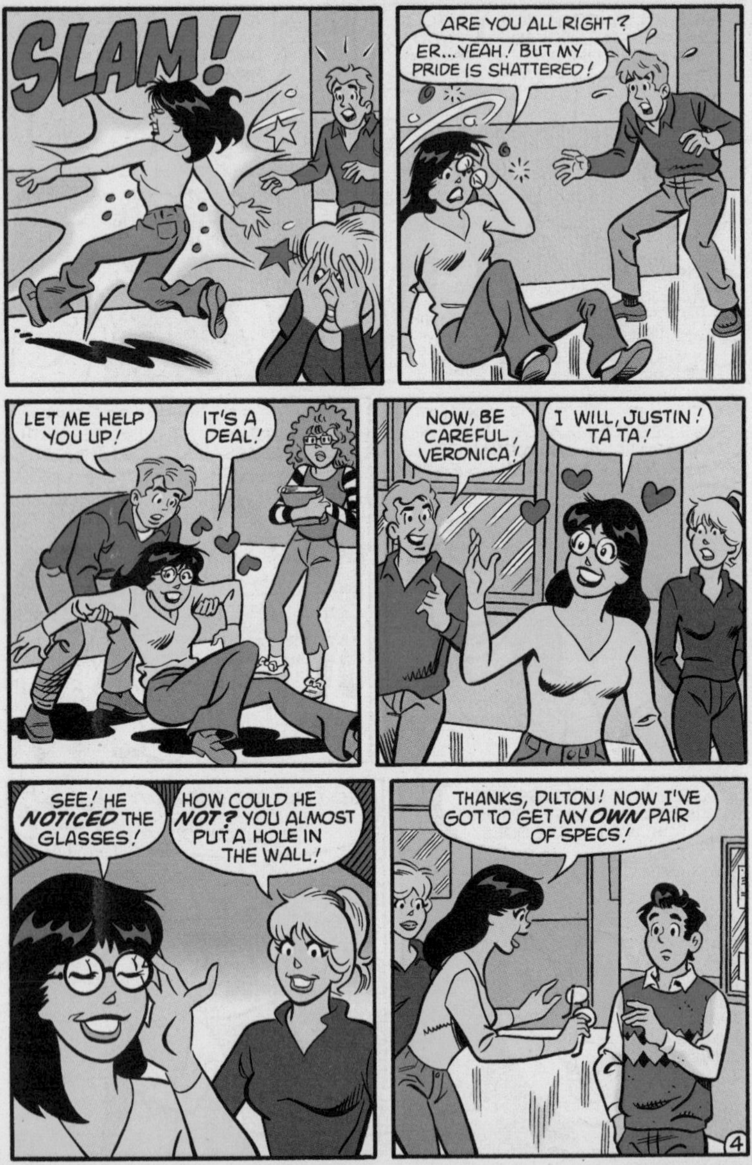
SLAM!
ARE YOU ALL RIGHT?
ER... YEAH! BUT MY PRIDE IS SHATTERED!
LET ME HELP YOU UP!
IT'S A DEAL!
NOW, BE CAREFUL, VERONICA!
I WILL, JUSTIN! TA TA!
SEE! HE NOTICED THE GLASSES!
HOW COULD HE NOT? YOU ALMOST PUT A HOLE IN THE WALL!
THANKS, DILTON! NOW I'VE GOT TO GET MY OWN PAIR OF SPECS!
4

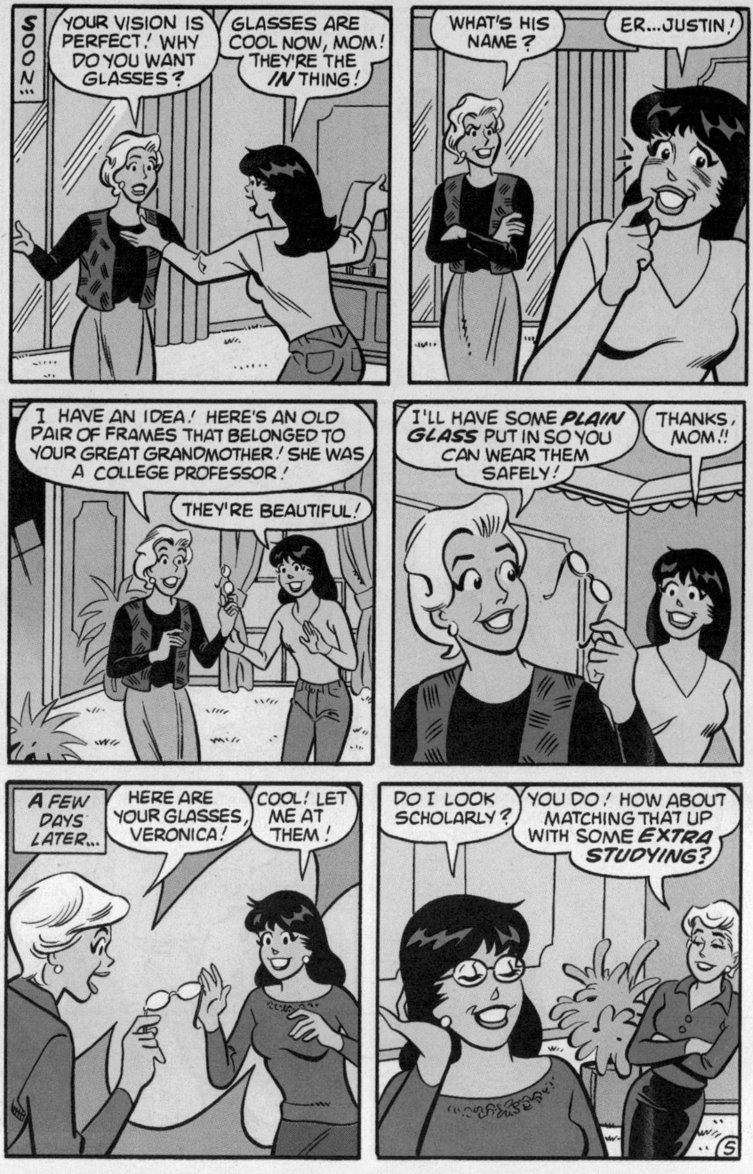
SOON...
YOUR VISION IS PERFECT! WHY DO YOU WANT GLASSES?
GLASSES ARE COOL NOW, MOM! THEY'RE THE IN THING!
WHAT'S HIS NAME?
ER...JUSTIN!
I HAVE AN IDEA! HERE'S AN OLD PAIR OF FRAMES THAT BELONGED TO YOUR GREAT GRANDMOTHER! SHE WAS A COLLEGE PROFESSOR!
THEY'RE BEAUTIFUL!
I'LL HAVE SOME PLAIN GLASS PUT IN SO YOU CAN WEAR THEM SAFELY!
THANKS, MOM!!
A FEW DAYS LATER...
HERE ARE YOUR GLASSES, VERONICA!
COOL! LET ME AT THEM!
DO I LOOK SCHOLARLY?
YOU DO! HOW ABOUT MATCHING THAT UP WITH SOME EXTRA STUDYING?
5

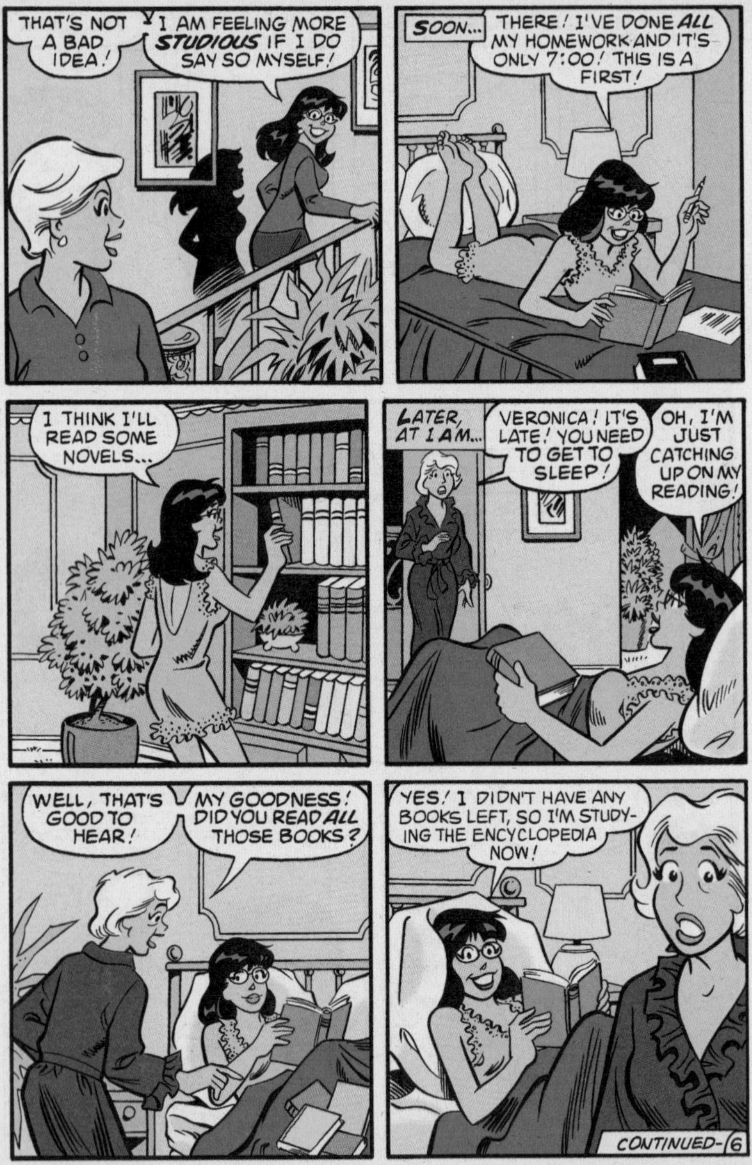
THAT'S NOT A BAD IDEA!
I AM FEELING MORE STUDIOUS IF I DO SAY SO MYSELF!
SOON...
THERE! I'VE DONE ALL MY HOMEWORK AND IT'S ONLY 7:00! THIS IS A FIRST!
I THINK I'LL READ SOME NOVELS...
LATER, AT 1 AM...
VERONICA! IT'S LATE! YOU NEED TO GET TO SLEEP!
OH, I'M JUST CATCHING UP ON MY READING!
WELL, THAT'S GOOD TO HEAR!
MY GOODNESS! DID YOU READ ALL THOSE BOOKS?
YES! I DIDN'T HAVE ANY BOOKS LEFT, SO I'M STUDYING THE ENCYCLOPEDIA NOW!
CONTINUED-6

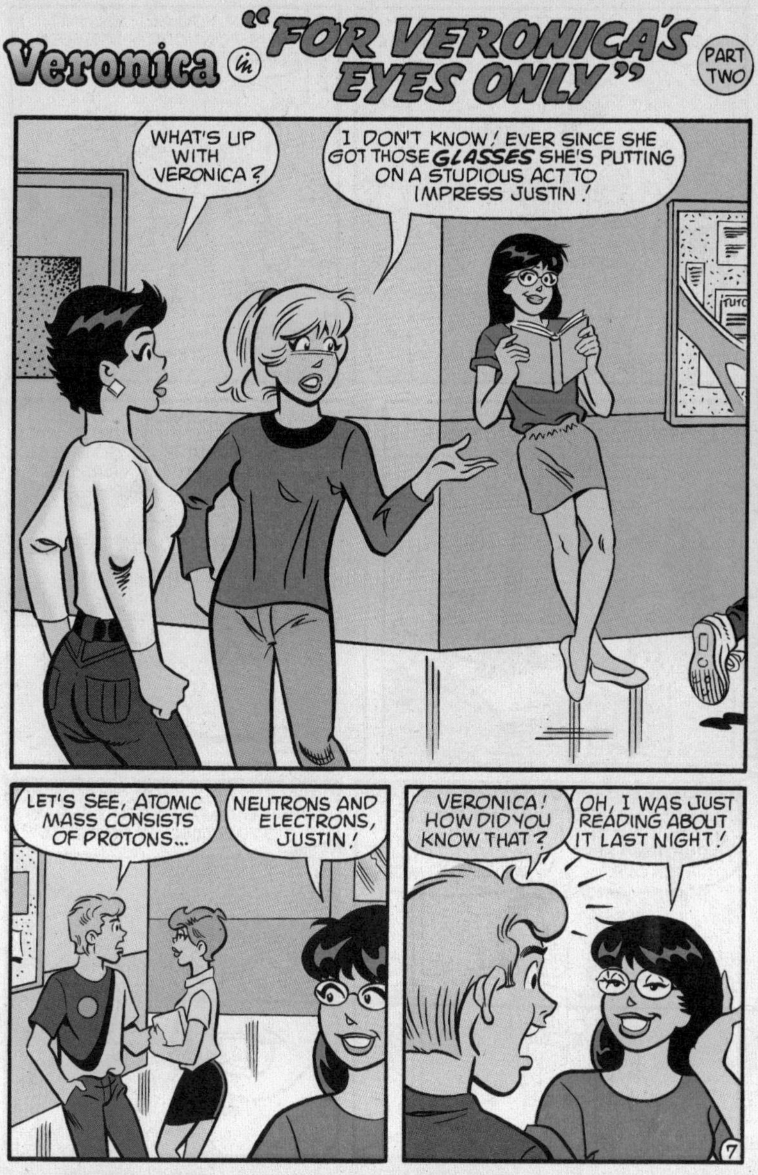

Veronica in
"FOR VERONICA'S EYES ONLY"
PART TWO
WHAT'S UP WITH VERONICA?
I DON'T KNOW! EVER SINCE SHE GOT THOSE GLASSES SHE'S PUTTING ON A STUDIOUS ACT TO IMPRESS JUSTIN!
LET'S SEE, ATOMIC MASS CONSISTS OF PROTONS...
NEUTRONS AND ELECTRONS, JUSTIN!
VERONICA! HOW DID YOU KNOW THAT?
OH, I WAS JUST READING ABOUT IT LAST NIGHT!

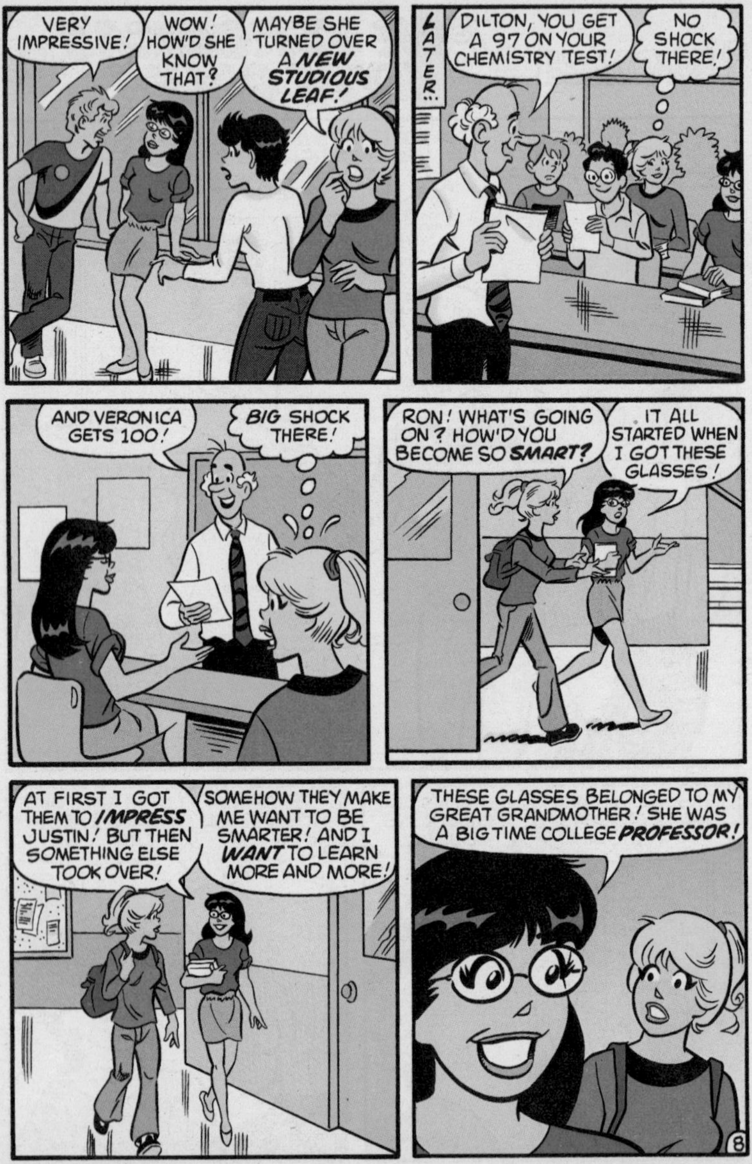
VERY IMPRESSIVE!
WOW! HOW'D SHE KNOW THAT?
MAYBE SHE TURNED OVER A NEW STUDIOUS LEAF!
LATER...
DILTON, YOU GET A 97 ON YOUR CHEMISTRY TEST!
NO SHOCK THERE!
AND VERONICA GETS 100!
BIG SHOCK THERE!
RON! WHAT'S GOING ON? HOW'D YOU BECOME SO SMART?
IT ALL STARTED WHEN I GOT THESE GLASSES!
AT FIRST I GOT THEM TO IMPRESS JUSTIN! BUT THEN SOMETHING ELSE TOOK OVER!
SOMEHOW THEY MAKE ME WANT TO BE SMARTER! AND I WANT TO LEARN MORE AND MORE!
THESE GLASSES BELONGED TO MY GREAT GRANDMOTHER! SHE WAS A BIG TIME COLLEGE PROFESSOR!
8

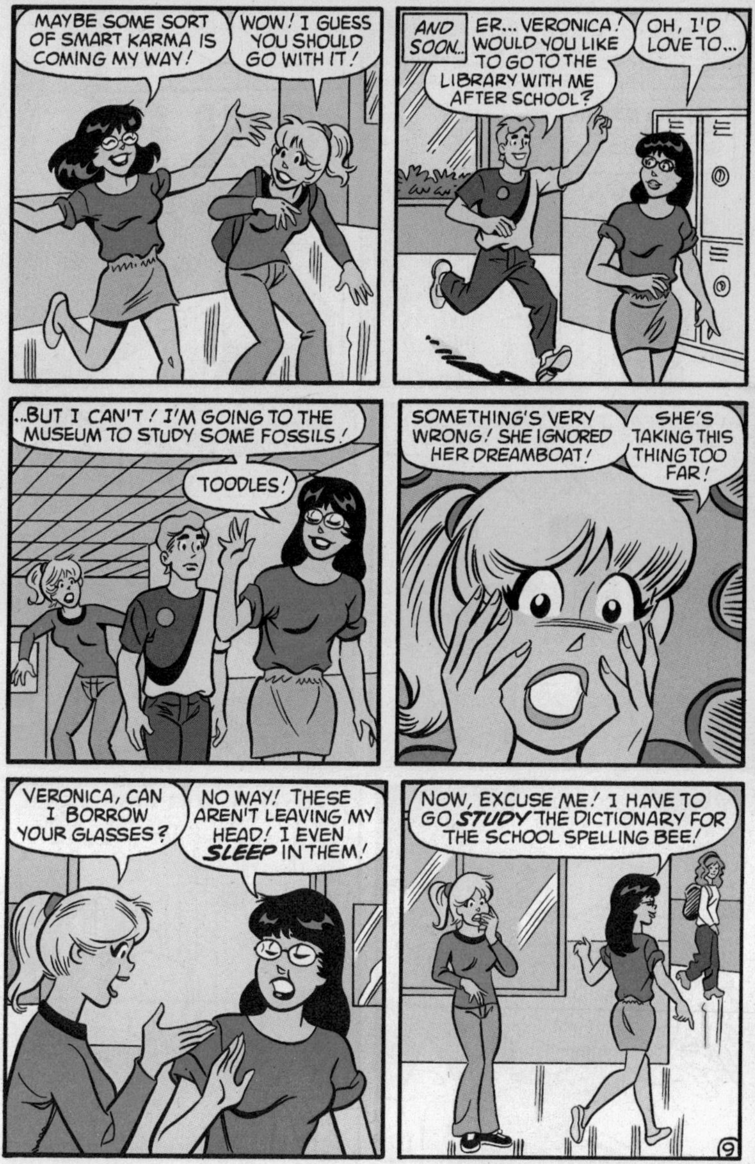

MAYBE SOME SORT OF SMART KARMA IS COMING MY WAY!
WOW! I GUESS YOU SHOULD GO WITH IT!
AND SOON...
ER... VERONICA! WOULD YOU LIKE TO GO TO THE LIBRARY WITH ME AFTER SCHOOL?
OH, I'D LOVE TO...
...BUT I CAN'T! I'M GOING TO THE MUSEUM TO STUDY SOME FOSSILS!
TOODLES!
SOMETHING'S VERY WRONG! SHE IGNORED HER DREAMBOAT!
SHE'S TAKING THIS THING TOO FAR!
VERONICA, CAN I BORROW YOUR GLASSES?
NO WAY! THESE AREN'T LEAVING MY HEAD! I EVEN SLEEP IN THEM!
NOW, EXCUSE ME! I HAVE TO GO STUDY THE DICTIONARY FOR THE SCHOOL SPELLING BEE!

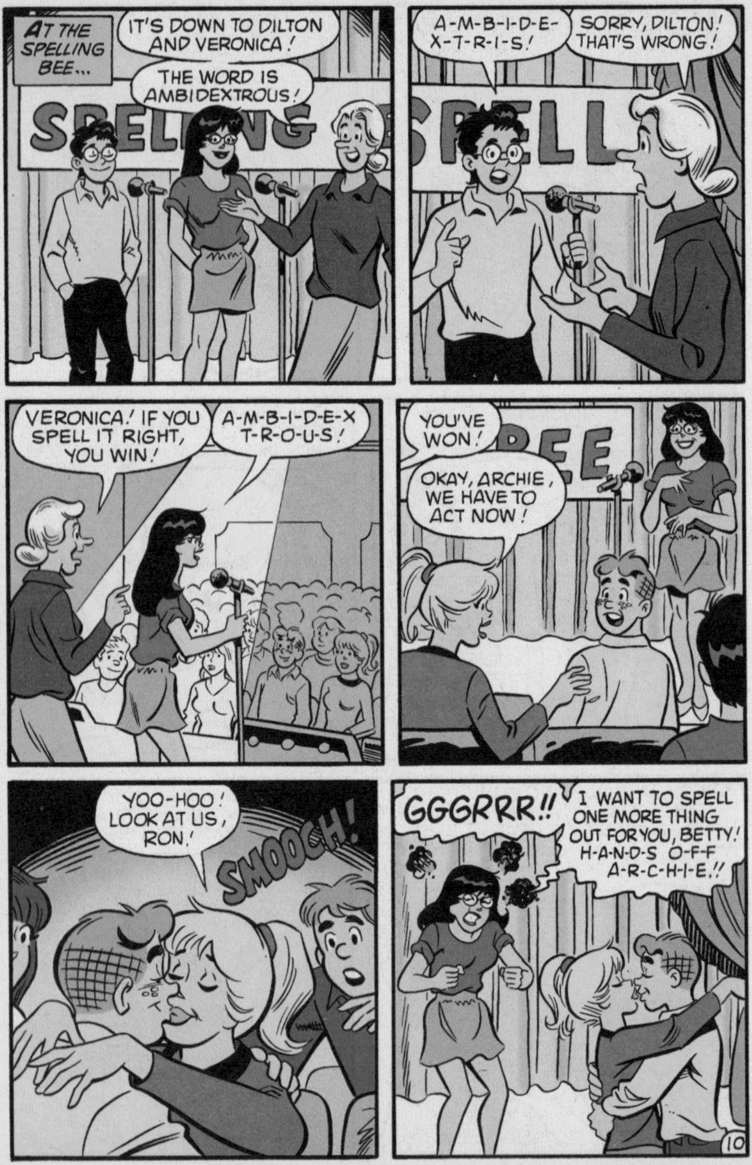
AT THE SPELLING BEE...
IT'S DOWN TO DILTON AND VERONICA!
THE WORD IS AMBIDEXTROUS!
SPELLING BEE
A-M-B-I-D-E-X-T-R-I-S!
SORRY, DILTON! THAT'S WRONG!
VERONICA! IF YOU SPELL IT RIGHT, YOU WIN!
A-M-B-I-D-E-X T-R-O-U-S!
YOU'VE WON!
OKAY, ARCHIE, WE HAVE TO ACT NOW!
YOO-HOO! LOOK AT US, RON!
SMOOCH!
GGGRRR!!
I WANT TO SPELL ONE MORE THING OUT FOR YOU, BETTY! H-A-N-D-S O-F-F A-R-C-H-I-E!!
10

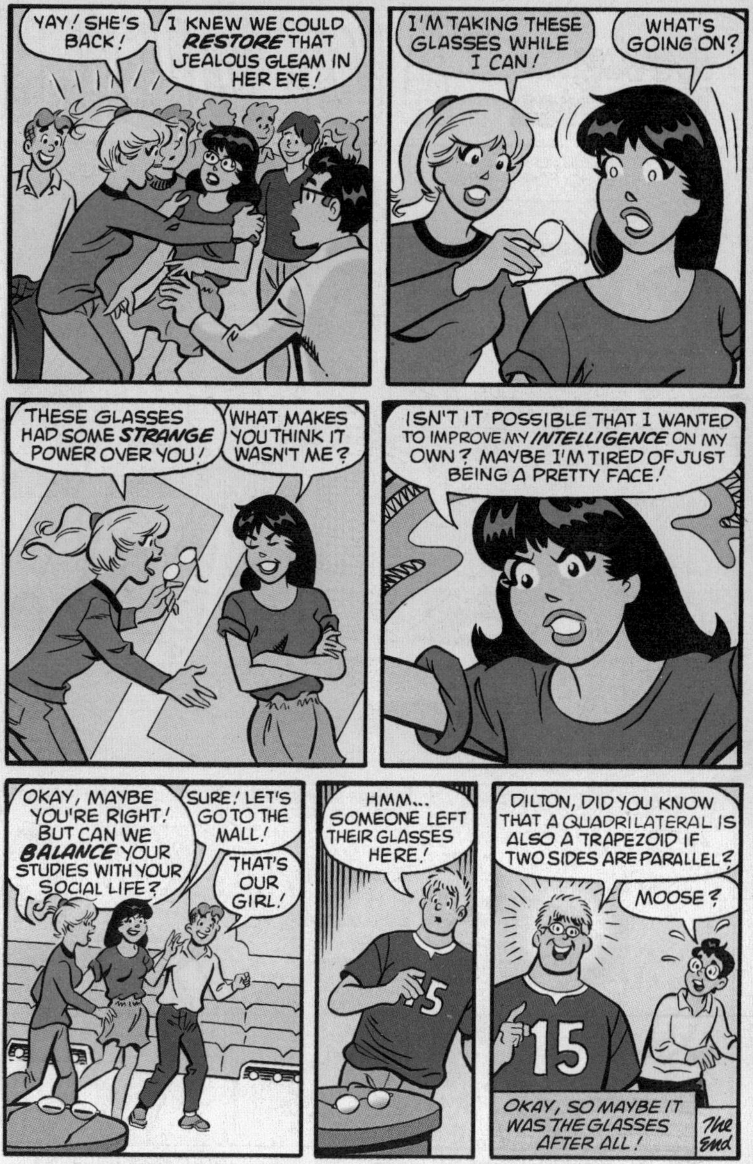
YAY! SHE'S BACK!
I KNEW WE COULD RESTORE THAT JEALOUS GLEAM IN HER EYE!
I'M TAKING THESE GLASSES WHILE I CAN!
WHAT'S GOING ON?
THESE GLASSES HAD SOME STRANGE POWER OVER YOU!
WHAT MAKES YOU THINK IT WASN'T ME?
ISN'T IT POSSIBLE THAT I WANTED TO IMPROVE MY INTELLIGENCE ON MY OWN? MAYBE I'M TIRED OF JUST BEING A PRETTY FACE!
OKAY, MAYBE YOU'RE RIGHT! BUT CAN WE BALANCE YOUR STUDIES WITH YOUR SOCIAL LIFE?
SURE! LET'S GO TO THE MALL!
THAT'S OUR GIRL!
HMM... SOMEONE LEFT THEIR GLASSES HERE!
15
DILTON, DID YOU KNOW THAT A QUADRILATERAL IS ALSO A TRAPEZOID IF TWO SIDES ARE PARALLEL?
MOOSE?
15
OKAY, SO MAYBE IT WAS THE GLASSES AFTER ALL!
The End

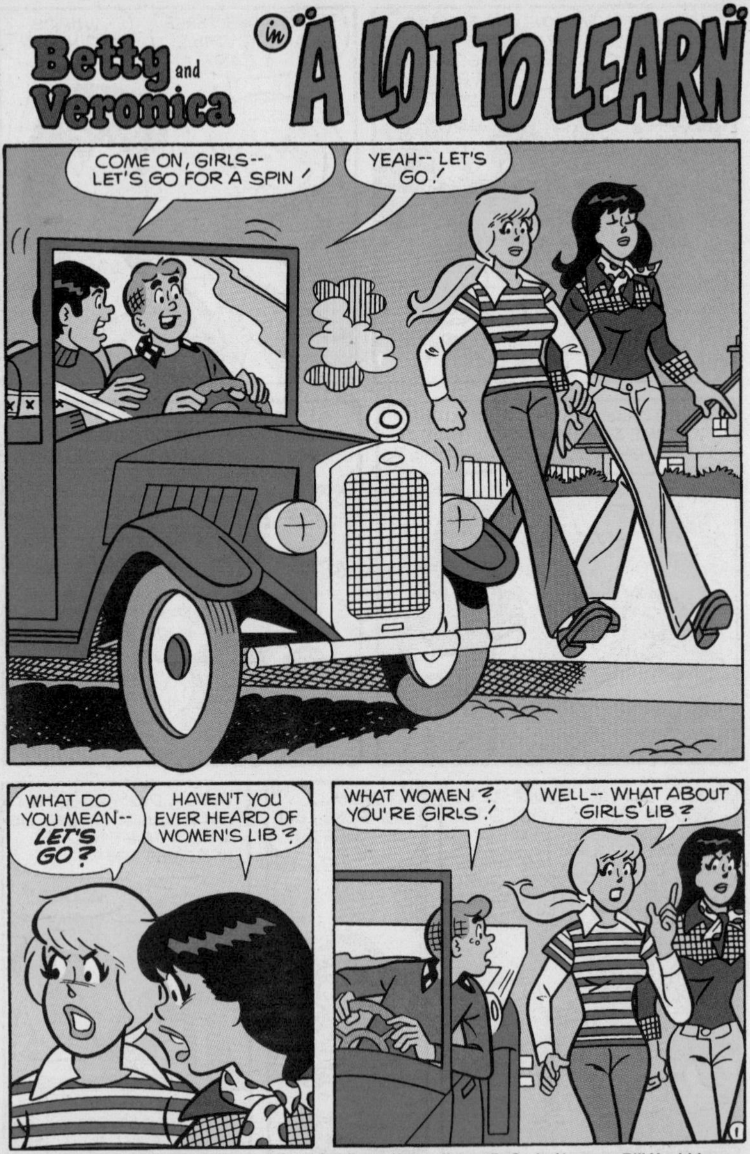
Betty and Veronica
in "A LOT TO LEARN"
COME ON, GIRLS-- LET'S GO FOR A SPIN!
YEAH-- LET'S GO.!
WHAT DO YOU MEAN-- LET'S GO?
HAVEN'T YOU EVER HEARD OF WOMEN'S LIB?
WHAT WOMEN? YOU'RE GIRLS!
WELL-- WHAT ABOUT GIRLS' LIB?
1

Script: Dick Malmgren / Pencils: Stan Goldberg / Inks: Jimmy DeCarlo / Letters: Bill Yoshida

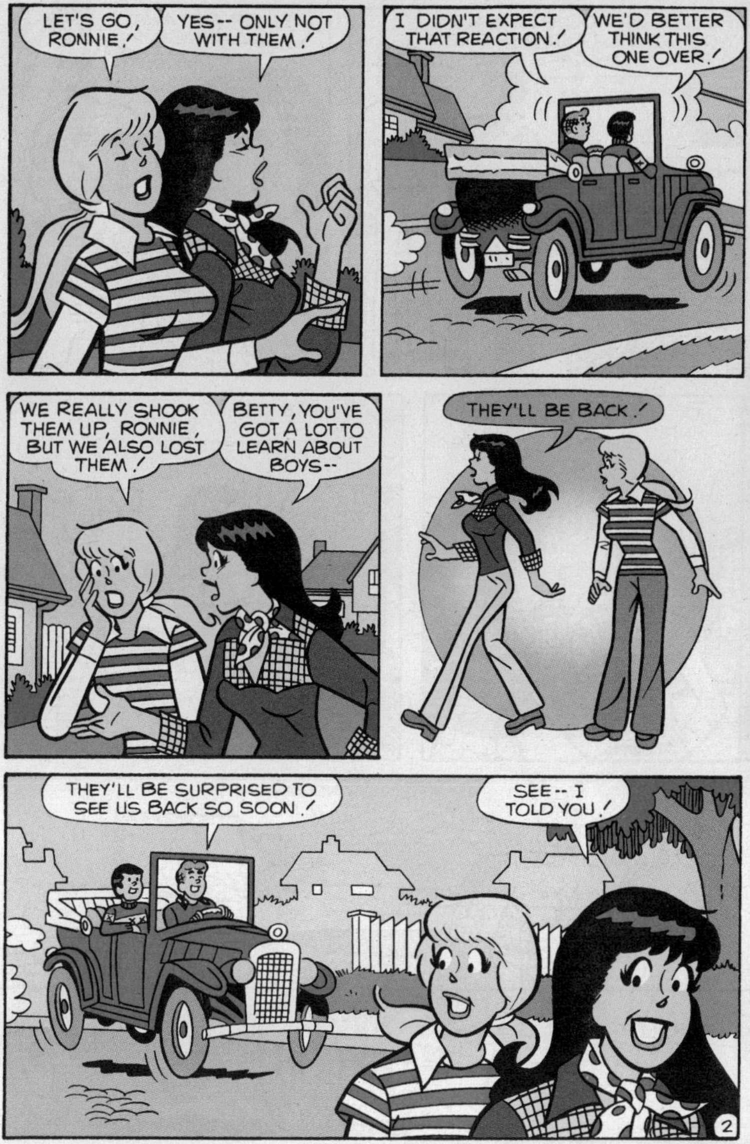
LET'S GO, RONNIE!
YES-- ONLY NOT WITH THEM!
I DIDN'T EXPECT THAT REACTION!
WE'D BETTER THINK THIS ONE OVER!
WE REALLY SHOOK THEM UP, RONNIE, BUT WE ALSO LOST THEM!
BETTY, YOU'VE GOT A LOT TO LEARN ABOUT BOYS--
THEY'LL BE BACK!
THEY'LL BE SURPRISED TO SEE US BACK SO SOON!
SEE-- I TOLD YOU!
2

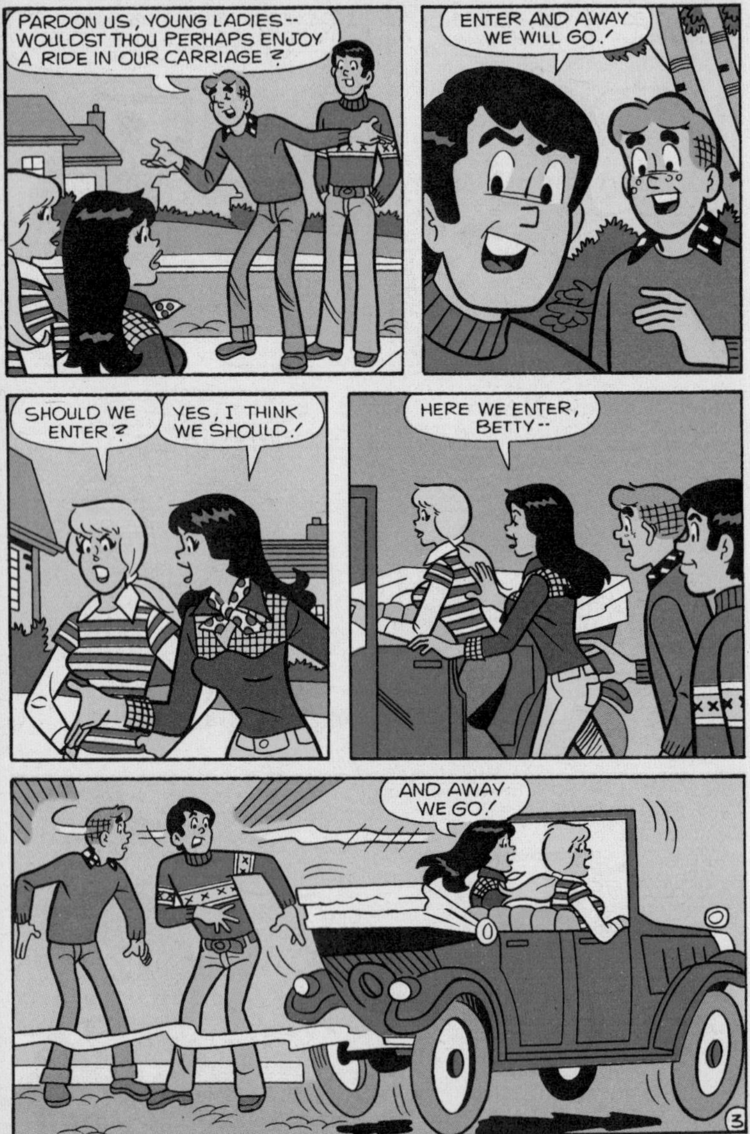
PARDON US, YOUNG LADIES-- WOULDST THOU PERHAPS ENJOY A RIDE IN OUR CARRIAGE?
ENTER AND AWAY WE WILL GO!
SHOULD WE ENTER?
YES, I THINK WE SHOULD!
HERE WE ENTER, BETTY--
AND AWAY WE GO!
3

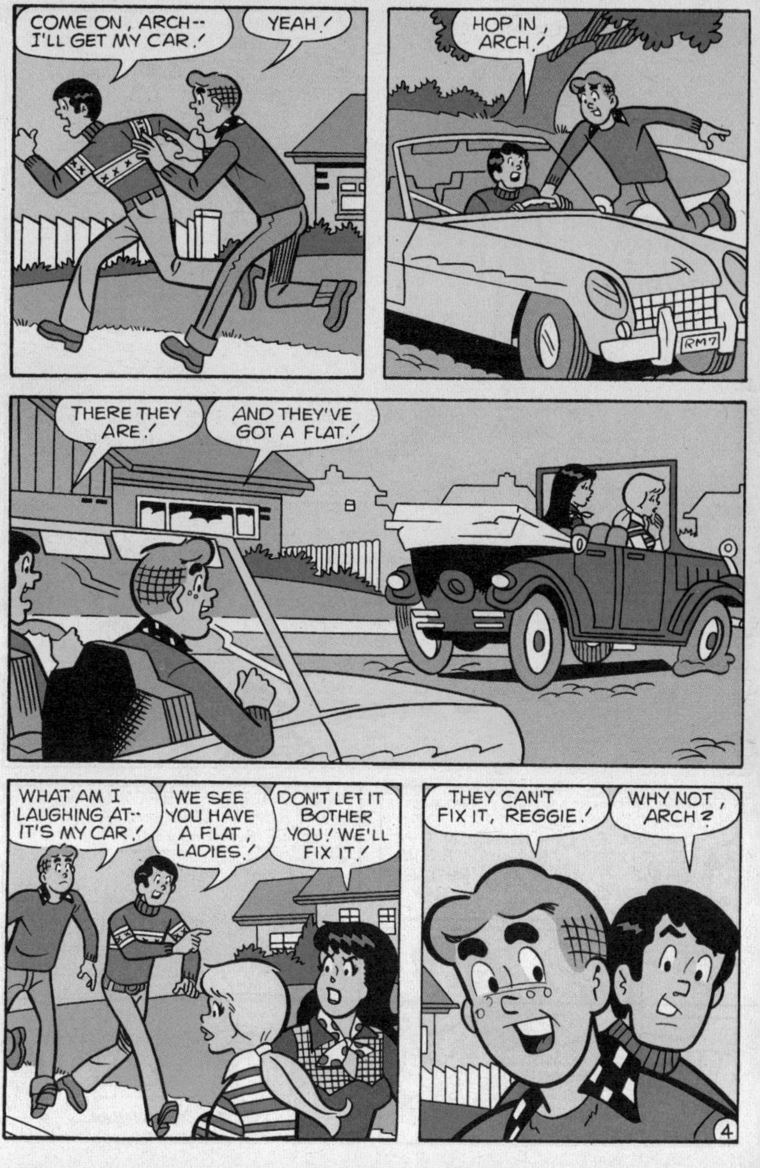
COME ON, ARCH-- I'LL GET MY CAR!
YEAH!
HOP IN, ARCH!
RM7
THERE THEY ARE!
AND THEY'VE GOT A FLAT!
WHAT AM I LAUGHING AT-- IT'S MY CAR!
WE SEE YOU HAVE A FLAT, LADIES!
DON'T LET IT BOTHER YOU! WE'LL FIX IT!
THEY CAN'T FIX IT, REGGIE!
WHY NOT, ARCH?
4

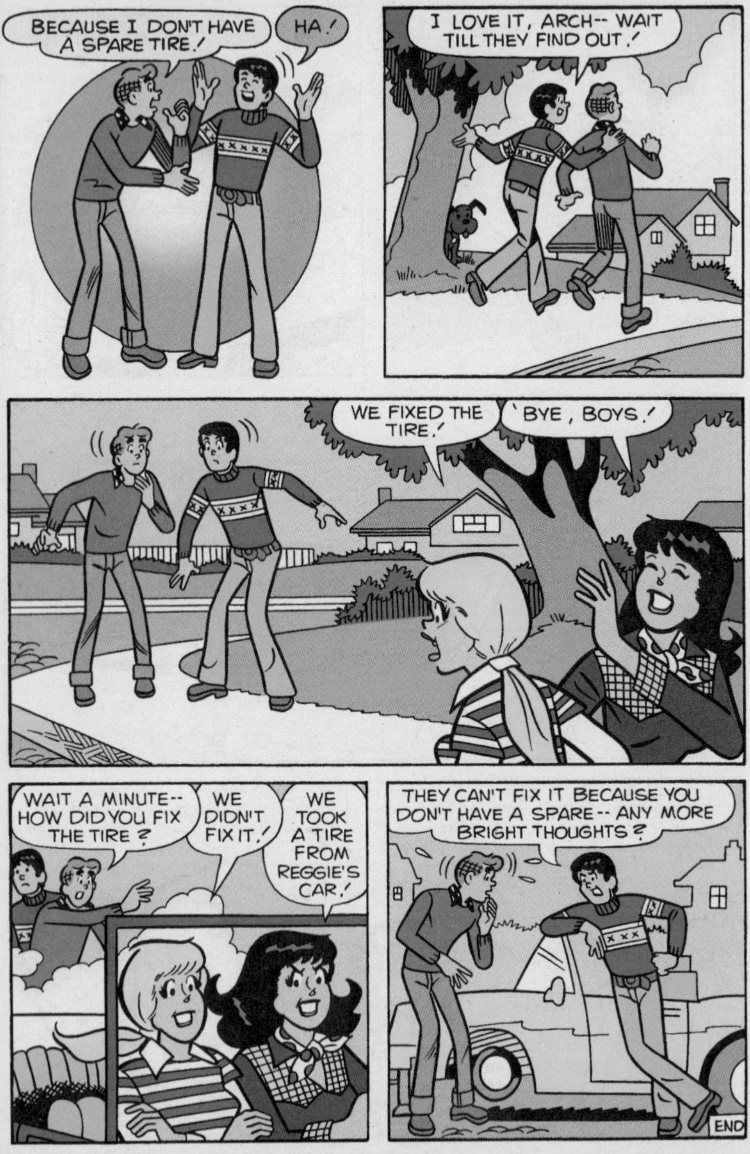
BECAUSE I DON'T HAVE A SPARE TIRE!
HA!
I LOVE IT, ARCH-- WAIT TILL THEY FIND OUT!
WE FIXED THE TIRE!
'BYE, BOYS!
WAIT A MINUTE-- HOW DID YOU FIX THE TIRE?
WE DIDN'T FIX IT!
WE TOOK A TIRE FROM REGGIE'S CAR!
THEY CAN'T FIX IT BECAUSE YOU DON'T HAVE A SPARE-- ANY MORE BRIGHT THOUGHTS?
END

Betty and Me in "PRACTICE SESSION"

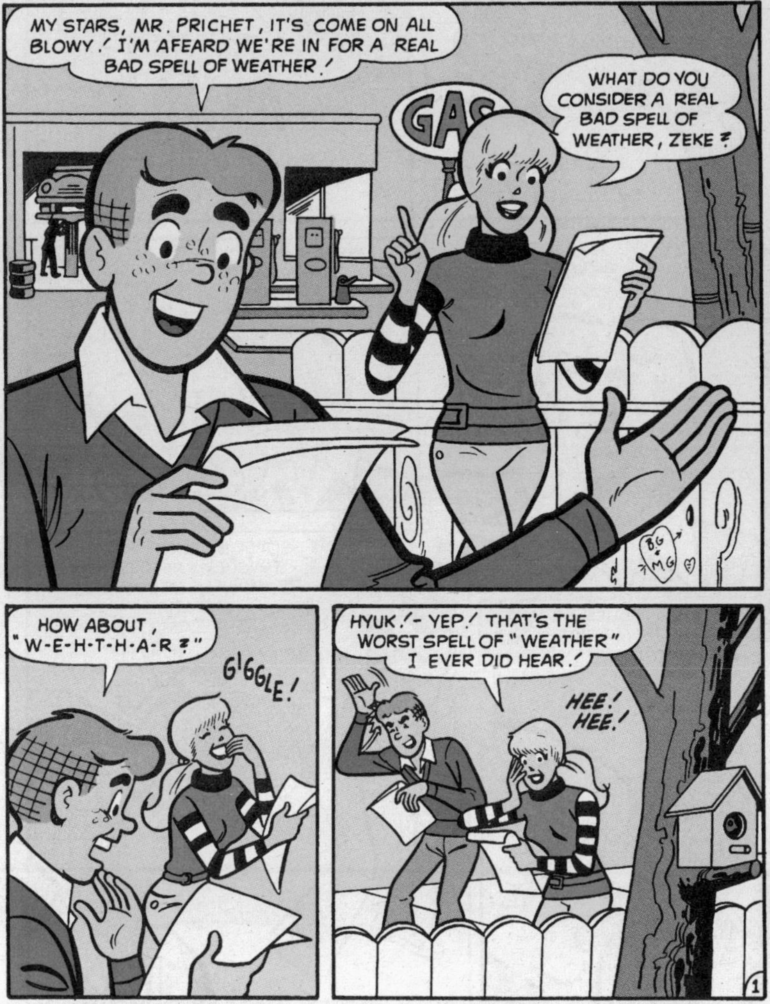

MY STARS, MR. PRICHET, IT'S COME ON ALL BLOWY! I'M AFEARD WE'RE IN FOR A REAL BAD SPELL OF WEATHER!
WHAT DO YOU CONSIDER A REAL BAD SPELL OF WEATHER, ZEKE?
GAS
B.G + M.G
HOW ABOUT, "W-E-H-T-H-A-R?"
GIGGLE!
HYUK!- YEP! THAT'S THE WORST SPELL OF "WEATHER" I EVER DID HEAR!
HEE! HEE!
1

Script: George Gladir / Pencils: Bob Bolling / Inks: Rudy Lapick / Letters: Bill Yoshida

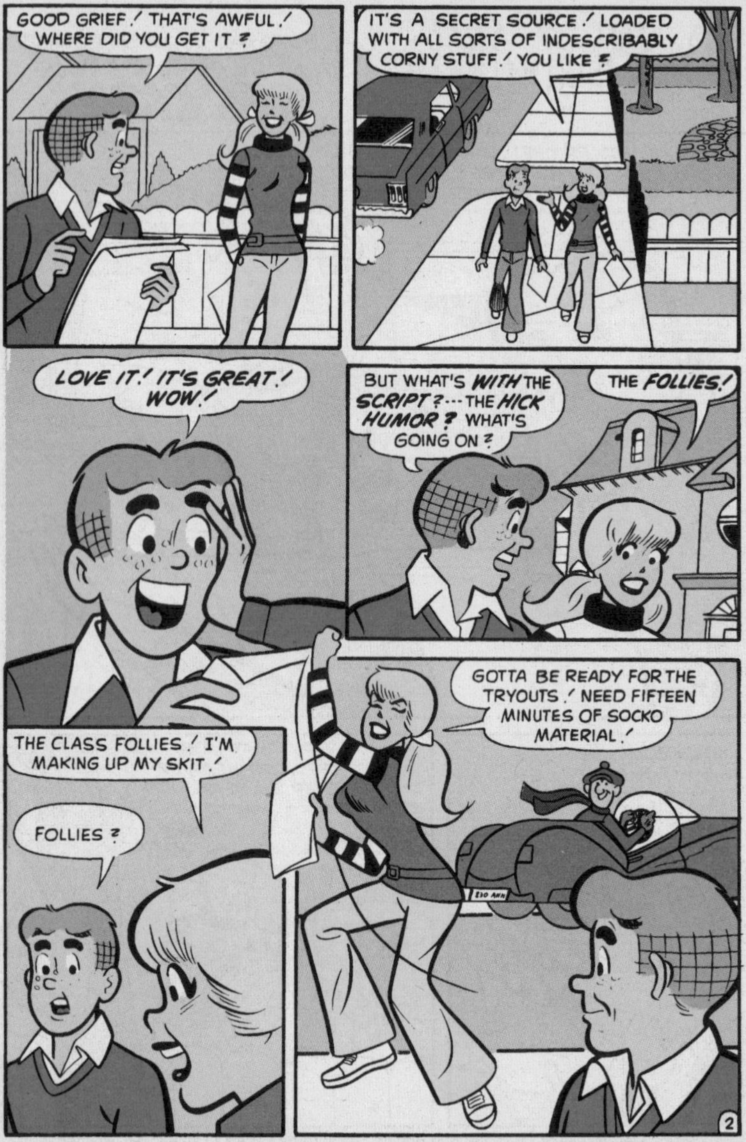
GOOD GRIEF! THAT'S AWFUL! WHERE DID YOU GET IT?
IT'S A SECRET SOURCE! LOADED WITH ALL SORTS OF INDESCRIBABLY CORNY STUFF! YOU LIKE?
LOVE IT! IT'S GREAT! WOW!
BUT WHAT'S WITH THE SCRIPT?--- THE HICK HUMOR? WHAT'S GOING ON?
THE FOLLIES!
THE CLASS FOLLIES! I'M MAKING UP MY SKIT!
FOLLIES?
GOTTA BE READY FOR THE TRYOUTS! NEED FIFTEEN MINUTES OF SOCKO MATERIAL!
2

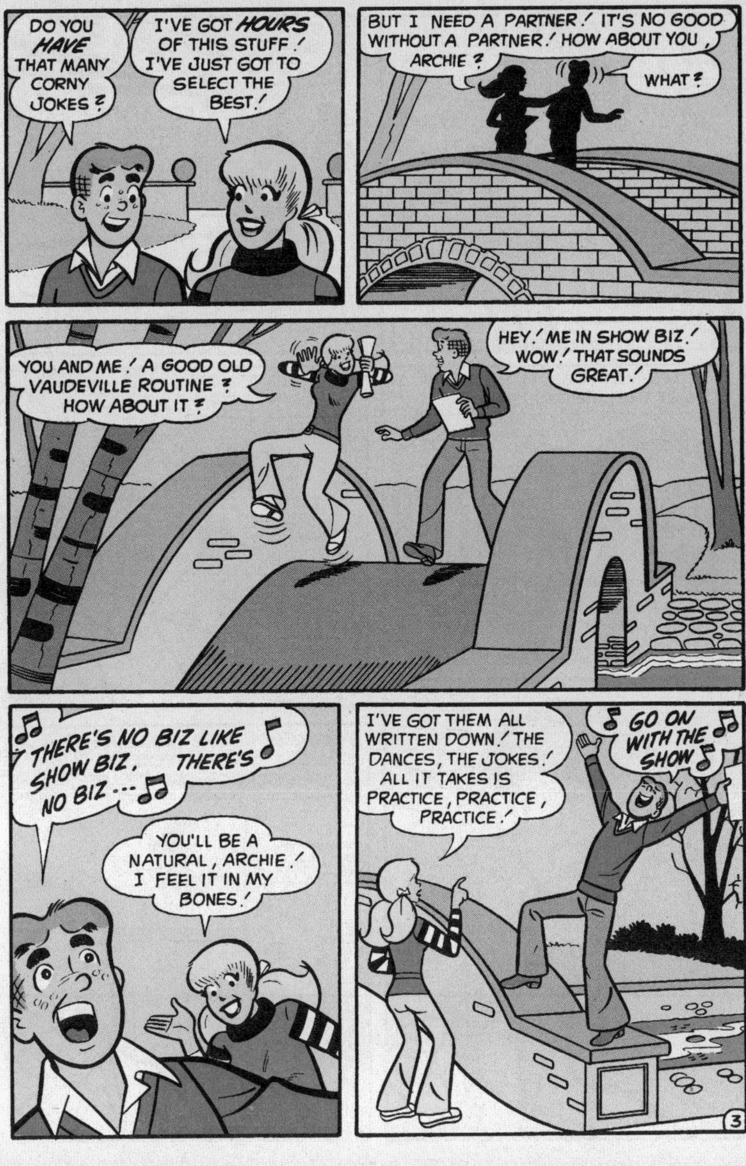
DO YOU HAVE THAT MANY CORNY JOKES?
I'VE GOT HOURS OF THIS STUFF! I'VE JUST GOT TO SELECT THE BEST!
BUT I NEED A PARTNER! IT'S NO GOOD WITHOUT A PARTNER! HOW ABOUT YOU, ARCHIE?
WHAT?
YOU AND ME! A GOOD OLD VAUDEVILLE ROUTINE? HOW ABOUT IT?
HEY! ME IN SHOW BIZ! WOW! THAT SOUNDS GREAT!
THERE'S NO BIZ LIKE SHOW BIZ, THERE'S NO BIZ...
YOU'LL BE A NATURAL, ARCHIE! I FEEL IT IN MY BONES!
I'VE GOT THEM ALL WRITTEN DOWN! THE DANCES, THE JOKES! ALL IT TAKES IS PRACTICE, PRACTICE, PRACTICE!
GO ON WITH THE SHOW

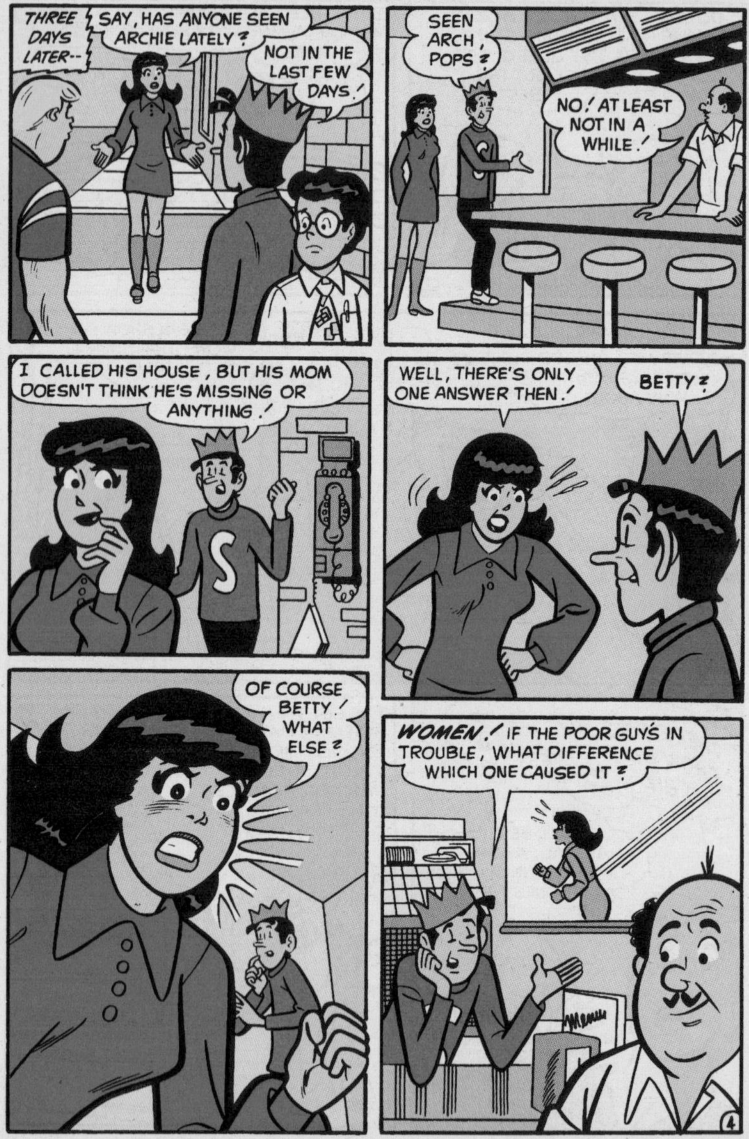
THREE DAYS LATER--
SAY, HAS ANYONE SEEN ARCHIE LATELY?
NOT IN THE LAST FEW DAYS!
SEEN ARCH, POPS?
NO! AT LEAST NOT IN A WHILE!
I CALLED HIS HOUSE, BUT HIS MOM DOESN'T THINK HE'S MISSING OR ANYTHING!
WELL, THERE'S ONLY ONE ANSWER THEN!
BETTY?
OF COURSE BETTY! WHAT ELSE?
WOMEN! IF THE POOR GUY'S IN TROUBLE, WHAT DIFFERENCE WHICH ONE CAUSED IT?
4

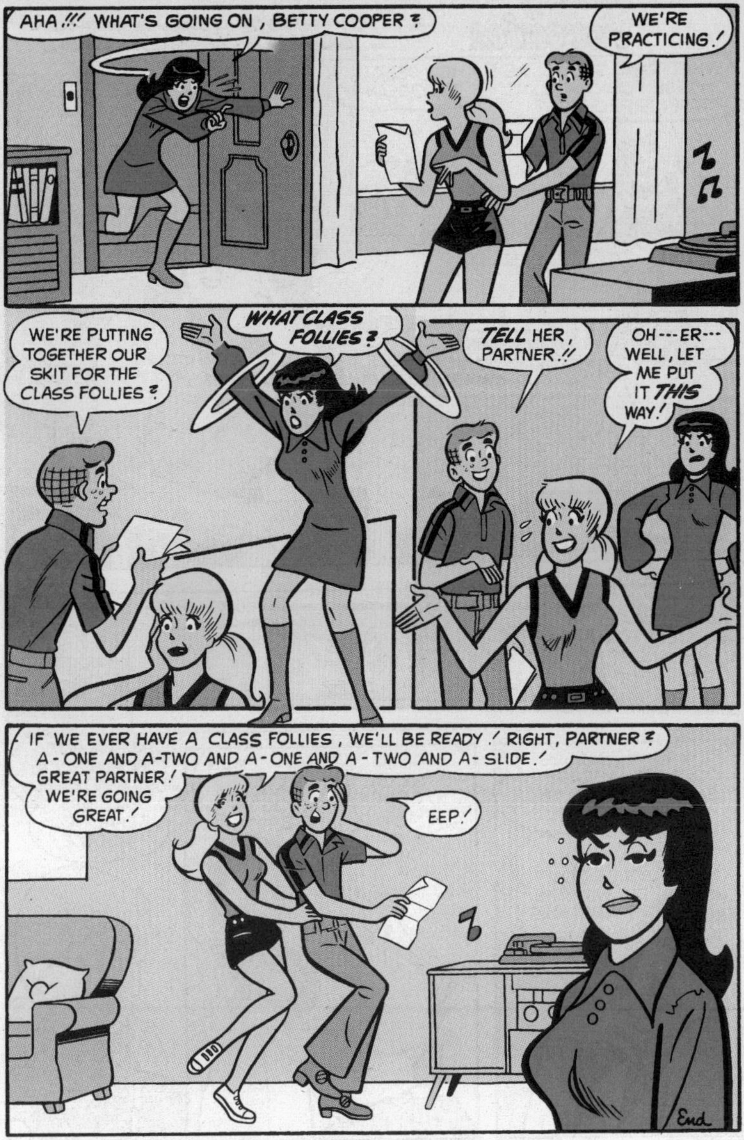
AHA !!! WHAT'S GOING ON , BETTY COOPER ?
WE'RE PRACTICING !
WE'RE PUTTING TOGETHER OUR SKIT FOR THE CLASS FOLLIES ?
WHAT CLASS FOLLIES ?
TELL HER, PARTNER !!
OH --- ER --- WELL, LET ME PUT IT THIS WAY !
IF WE EVER HAVE A CLASS FOLLIES , WE'LL BE READY ! RIGHT, PARTNER ? A - ONE AND A-TWO AND A - ONE AND A - TWO AND A- SLIDE ! GREAT PARTNER ! WE'RE GOING GREAT !
EEP !
End

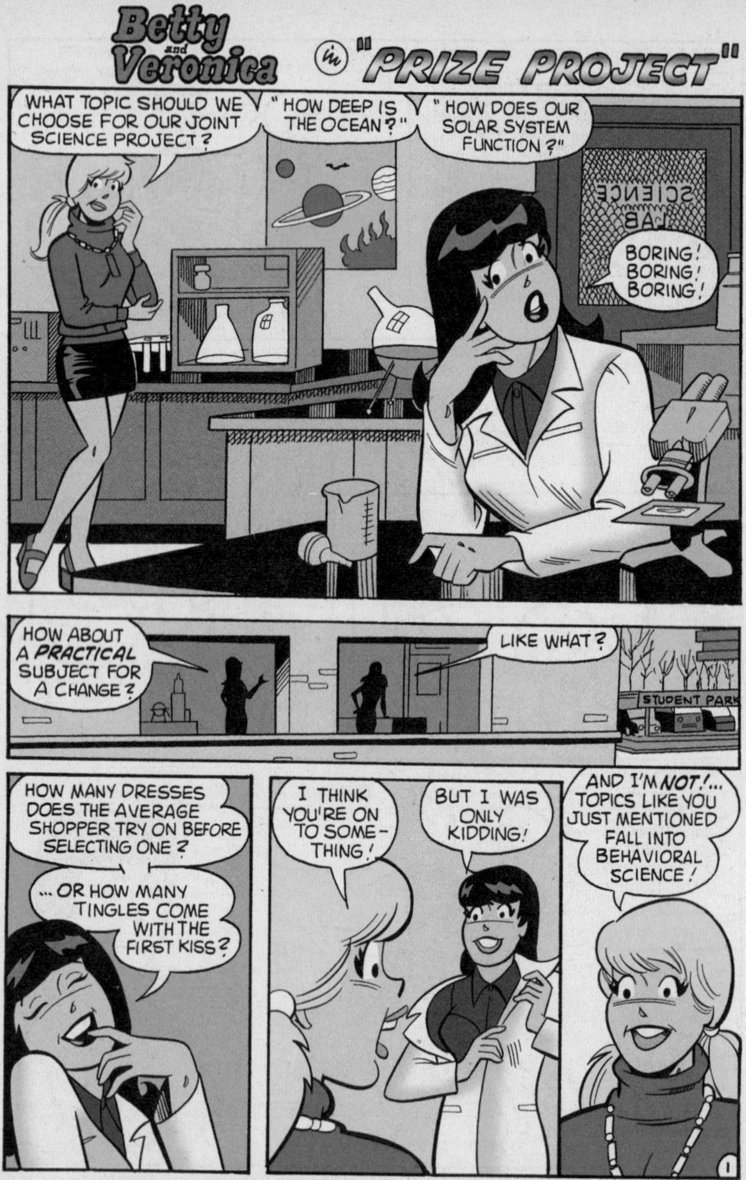
Betty and Veronica
in "PRIZE PROJECT"
WHAT TOPIC SHOULD WE CHOOSE FOR OUR JOINT SCIENCE PROJECT?
"HOW DEEP IS THE OCEAN?"
"HOW DOES OUR SOLAR SYSTEM FUNCTION?"
BORING! BORING! BORING!
HOW ABOUT A PRACTICAL SUBJECT FOR A CHANGE?
LIKE WHAT?
STUDENT PARK
HOW MANY DRESSES DOES THE AVERAGE SHOPPER TRY ON BEFORE SELECTING ONE?
... OR HOW MANY TINGLES COME WITH THE FIRST KISS?
I THINK YOU'RE ON TO SOME-THING!
BUT I WAS ONLY KIDDING!
AND I'M NOT!... TOPICS LIKE YOU JUST MENTIONED FALL INTO BEHAVIORAL SCIENCE!
1

Script: George Gladir / Pencils: Bob Bolling / Inks: Bob Smith / Letters: Bill Yoshida

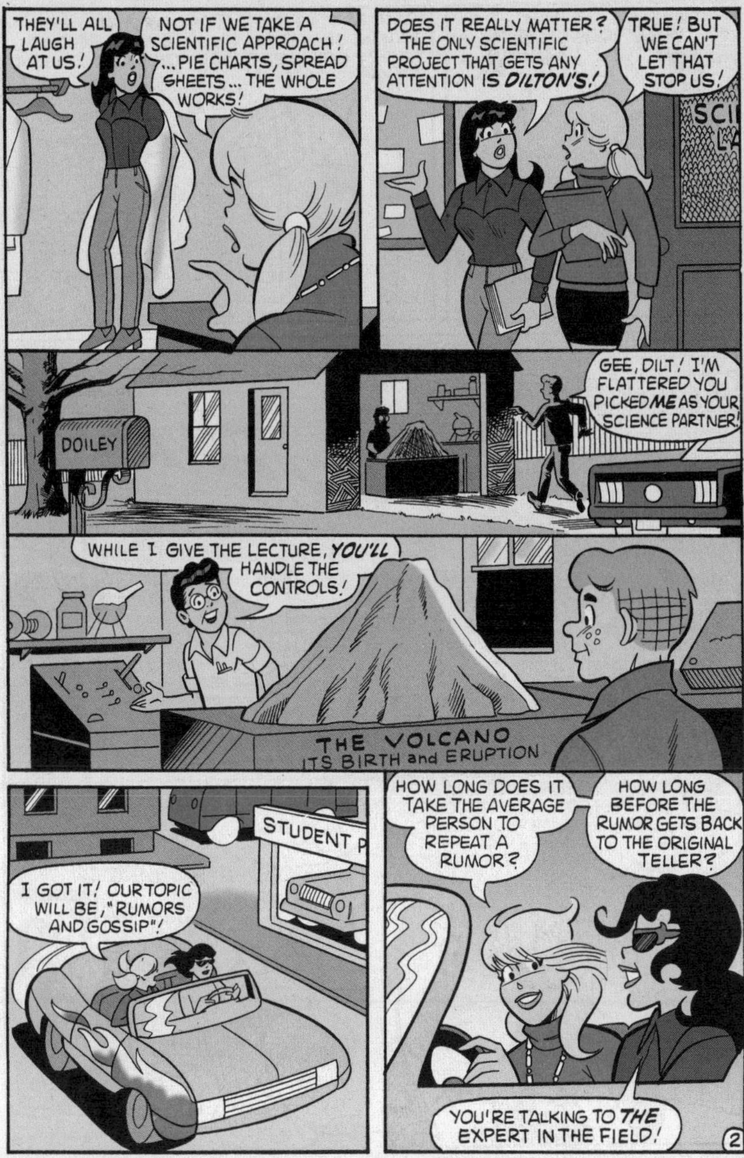
THEY'LL ALL LAUGH AT US!
NOT IF WE TAKE A SCIENTIFIC APPROACH! ...PIE CHARTS, SPREAD SHEETS ... THE WHOLE WORKS!
DOES IT REALLY MATTER? THE ONLY SCIENTIFIC PROJECT THAT GETS ANY ATTENTION IS DILTON'S!
TRUE! BUT WE CAN'T LET THAT STOP US!
DOILEY
GEE, DILT! I'M FLATTERED YOU PICKED ME AS YOUR SCIENCE PARTNER!
WHILE I GIVE THE LECTURE, YOU'LL HANDLE THE CONTROLS!
THE VOLCANO
ITS BIRTH and ERUPTION
STUDENT P
I GOT IT! OUR TOPIC WILL BE, "RUMORS AND GOSSIP"!
HOW LONG DOES IT TAKE THE AVERAGE PERSON TO REPEAT A RUMOR?
HOW LONG BEFORE THE RUMOR GETS BACK TO THE ORIGINAL TELLER?
YOU'RE TALKING TO THE EXPERT IN THE FIELD!
2

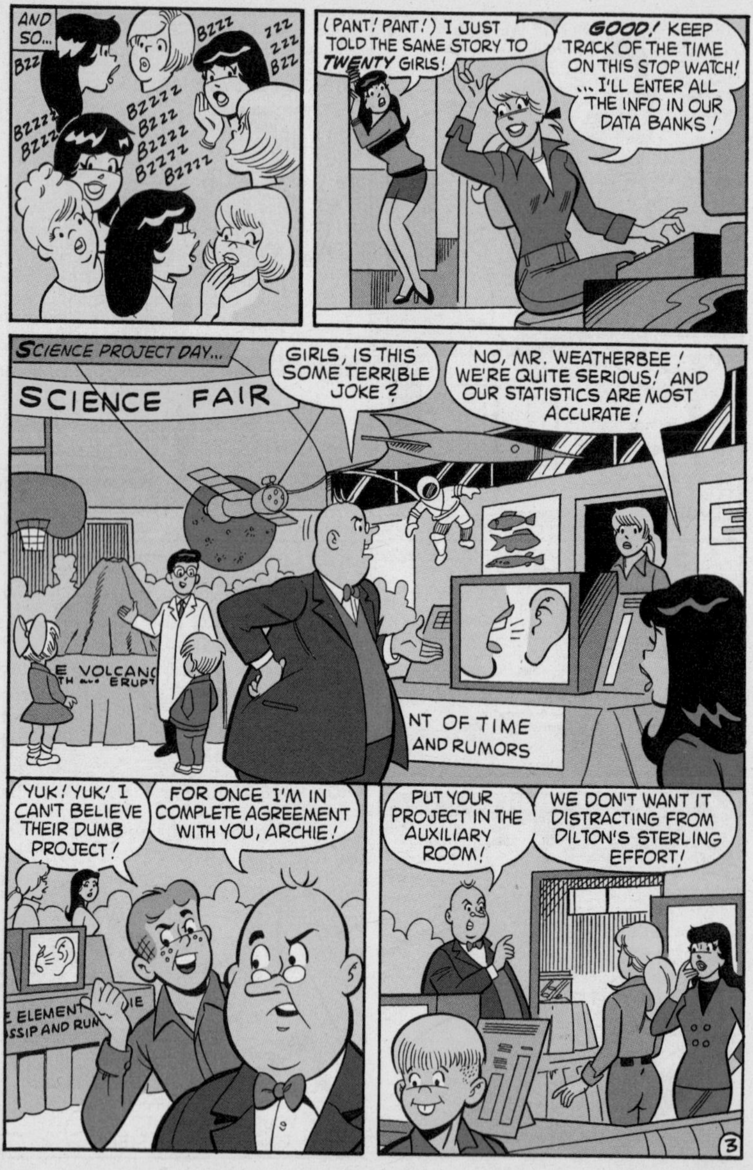

AND SO...
BZZ
BZZZ
ZZZ ZZZ BZZ
BZZZZ BZZZ
BZZZZ BZZZ BZZZZ BZZZZ BZZZZ
(PANT! PANT!) I JUST TOLD THE SAME STORY TO TWENTY GIRLS!
GOOD! KEEP TRACK OF THE TIME ON THIS STOP WATCH! ...I'LL ENTER ALL THE INFO IN OUR DATA BANKS!
SCIENCE PROJECT DAY...
SCIENCE FAIR
GIRLS, IS THIS SOME TERRIBLE JOKE?
NO, MR. WEATHERBEE! WE'RE QUITE SERIOUS! AND OUR STATISTICS ARE MOST ACCURATE!
E VOLCANO
NT OF TIME AND RUMORS
YUK! YUK! I CAN'T BELIEVE THEIR DUMB PROJECT!
FOR ONCE I'M IN COMPLETE AGREEMENT WITH YOU, ARCHIE!
E ELEMENT
SSIP AND RU
PUT YOUR PROJECT IN THE AUXILIARY ROOM!
WE DON'T WANT IT DISTRACTING FROM DILTON'S STERLING EFFORT!
3

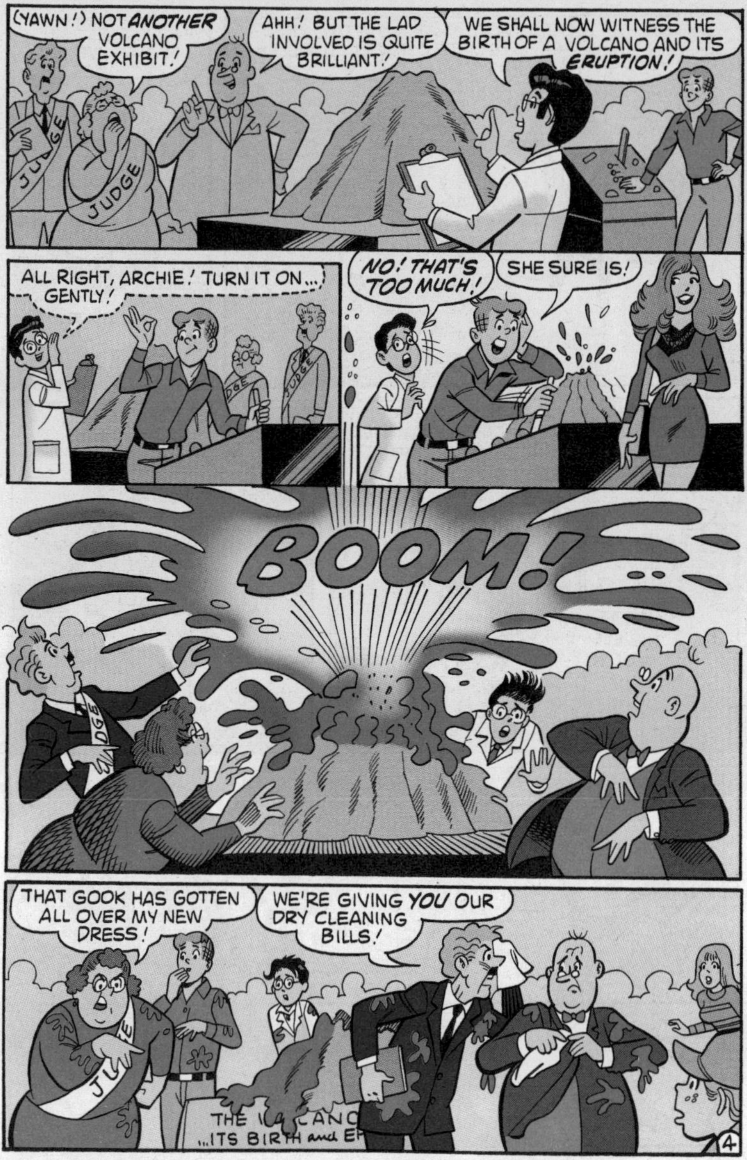
(YAWN!) NOT ANOTHER VOLCANO EXHIBIT!
AHH! BUT THE LAD INVOLVED IS QUITE BRILLIANT!
WE SHALL NOW WITNESS THE BIRTH OF A VOLCANO AND ITS ERUPTION!
JUDGE
JUDGE
ALL RIGHT, ARCHIE! TURN IT ON... GENTLY!
NO! THAT'S TOO MUCH!
SHE SURE IS!
BOOM!
THAT GOOK HAS GOTTEN ALL OVER MY NEW DRESS!
WE'RE GIVING YOU OUR DRY CLEANING BILLS!
THE VOLCANO
...ITS BIRTH and E

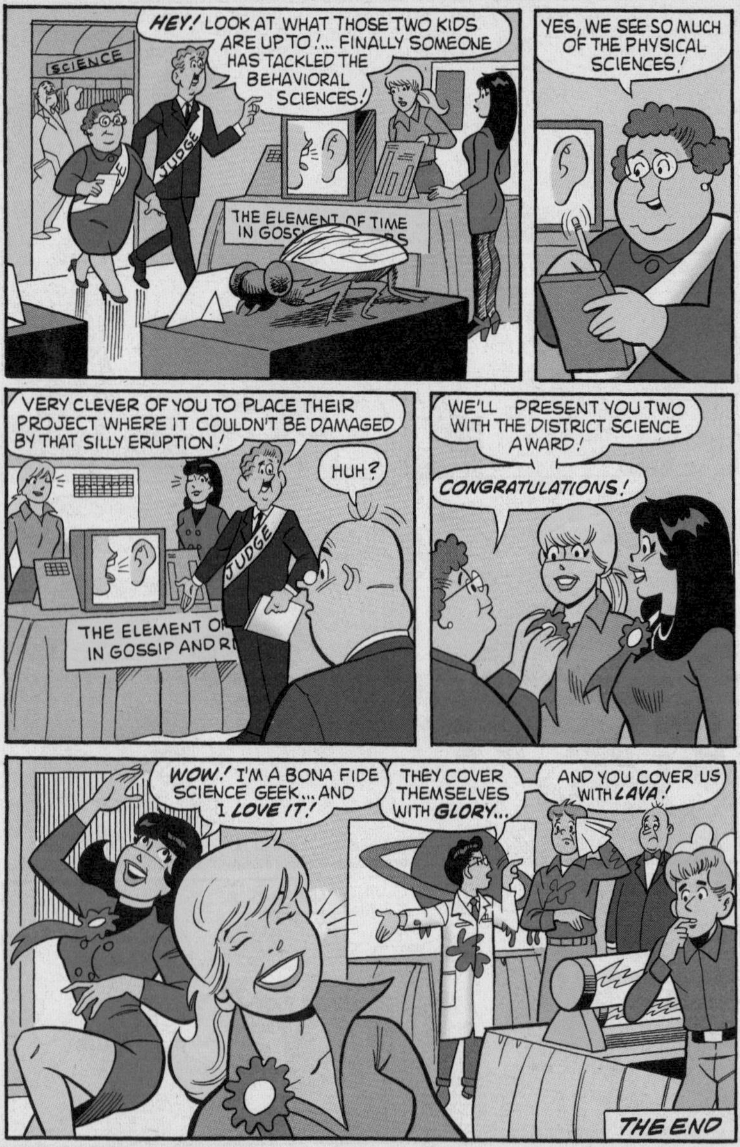

HEY! LOOK AT WHAT THOSE TWO KIDS ARE UP TO!... FINALLY SOMEONE HAS TACKLED THE BEHAVIORAL SCIENCES!
SCIENCE
JUDGE
THE ELEMENT OF TIME IN GOSS
YES, WE SEE SO MUCH OF THE PHYSICAL SCIENCES!
VERY CLEVER OF YOU TO PLACE THEIR PROJECT WHERE IT COULDN'T BE DAMAGED BY THAT SILLY ERUPTION!
HUH?
JUDGE
THE ELEMENT O
IN GOSSIP AND R
WE'LL PRESENT YOU TWO WITH THE DISTRICT SCIENCE AWARD!
CONGRATULATIONS!
WOW! I'M A BONA FIDE SCIENCE GEEK... AND I LOVE IT!
THEY COVER THEMSELVES WITH GLORY...
AND YOU COVER US WITH LAVA!
THE END

Betty and Veronica in THINKING POSITIVE!

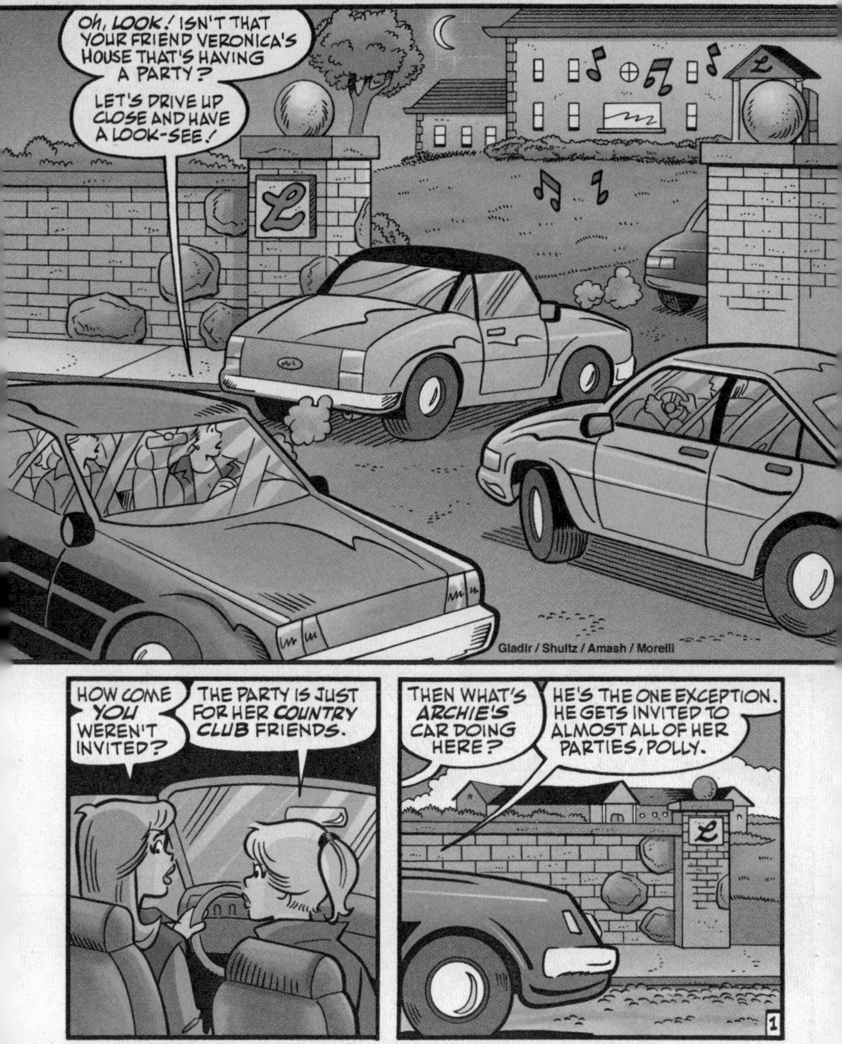

OH, LOOK! ISN'T THAT YOUR FRIEND VERONICA'S HOUSE THAT'S HAVING A PARTY?
LET'S DRIVE UP CLOSE AND HAVE A LOOK-SEE!
Gladir / Shultz / Amash / Morelli
HOW COME YOU WEREN'T INVITED?
THE PARTY IS JUST FOR HER COUNTRY CLUB FRIENDS.
THEN WHAT'S ARCHIE'S CAR DOING HERE?
HE'S THE ONE EXCEPTION. HE GETS INVITED TO ALMOST ALL OF HER PARTIES, POLLY.

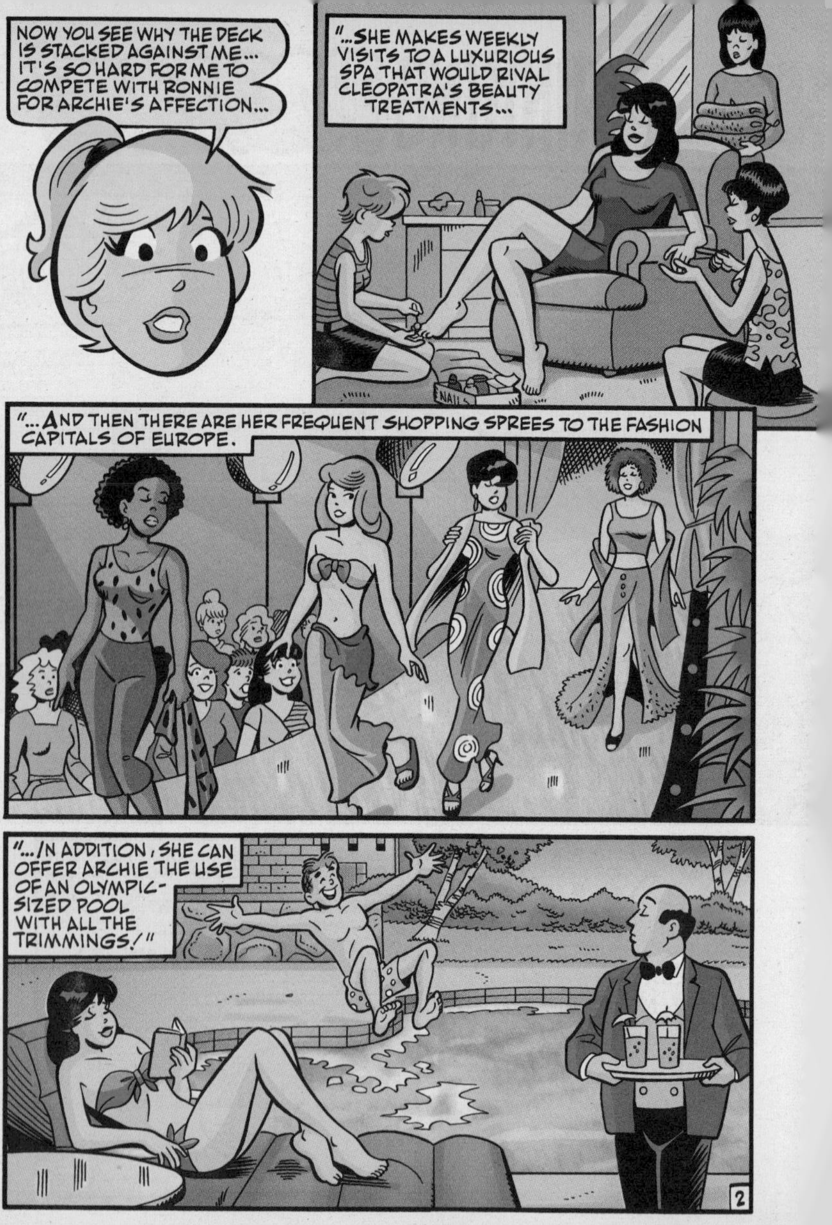
NOW YOU SEE WHY THE DECK IS STACKED AGAINST ME... IT'S SO HARD FOR ME TO COMPETE WITH RONNIE FOR ARCHIE'S AFFECTION...
"...SHE MAKES WEEKLY VISITS TO A LUXURIOUS SPA THAT WOULD RIVAL CLEOPATRA'S BEAUTY TREATMENTS...
NAILS
"...AND THEN THERE ARE HER FREQUENT SHOPPING SPREES TO THE FASHION CAPITALS OF EUROPE.
"...IN ADDITION, SHE CAN OFFER ARCHIE THE USE OF AN OLYMPIC-SIZED POOL WITH ALL THE TRIMMINGS!"
2

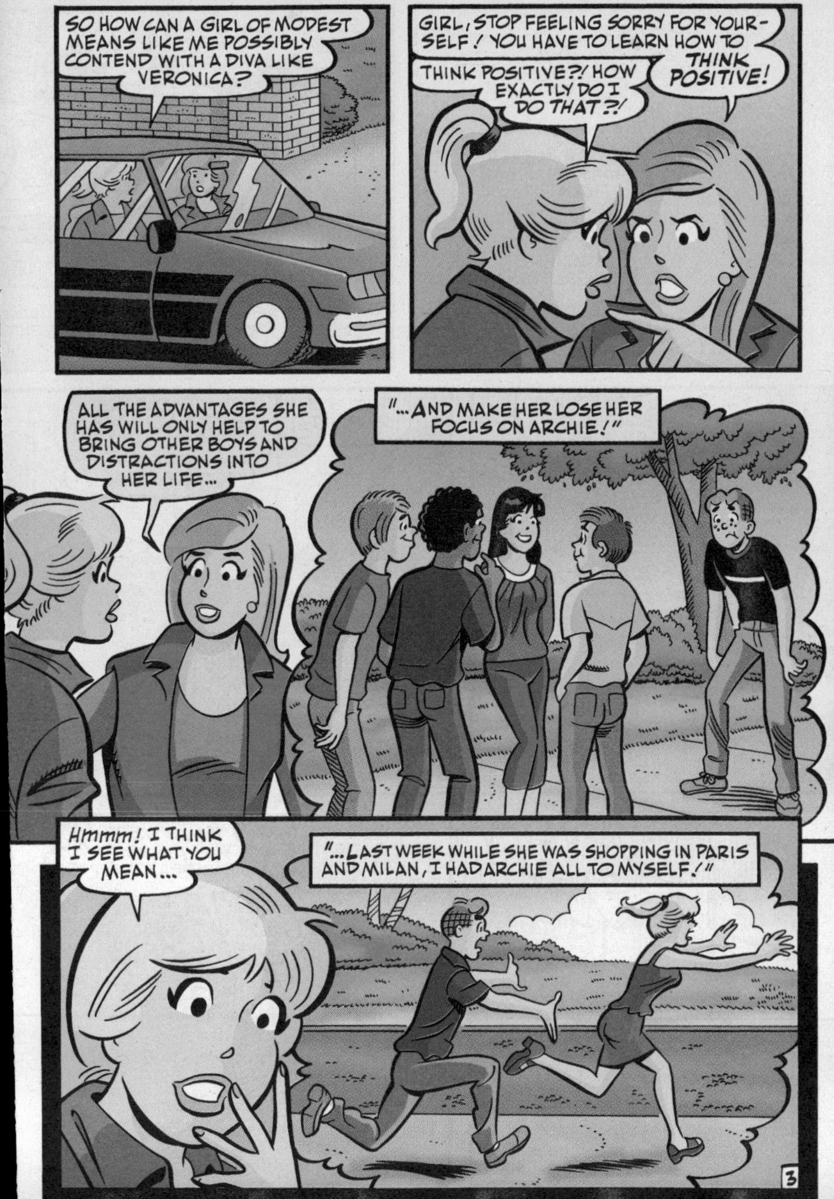
SO HOW CAN A GIRL OF MODEST MEANS LIKE ME POSSIBLY CONTEND WITH A DIVA LIKE VERONICA?
GIRL, STOP FEELING SORRY FOR YOUR-SELF! YOU HAVE TO LEARN HOW TO THINK POSITIVE!
THINK POSITIVE?! HOW EXACTLY DO I DO THAT?!
ALL THE ADVANTAGES SHE HAS WILL ONLY HELP TO BRING OTHER BOYS AND DISTRACTIONS INTO HER LIFE...
"...AND MAKE HER LOSE HER FOCUS ON ARCHIE!"
Hmmm! I THINK I SEE WHAT YOU MEAN...
"...LAST WEEK WHILE SHE WAS SHOPPING IN PARIS AND MILAN, I HAD ARCHIE ALL TO MYSELF!"

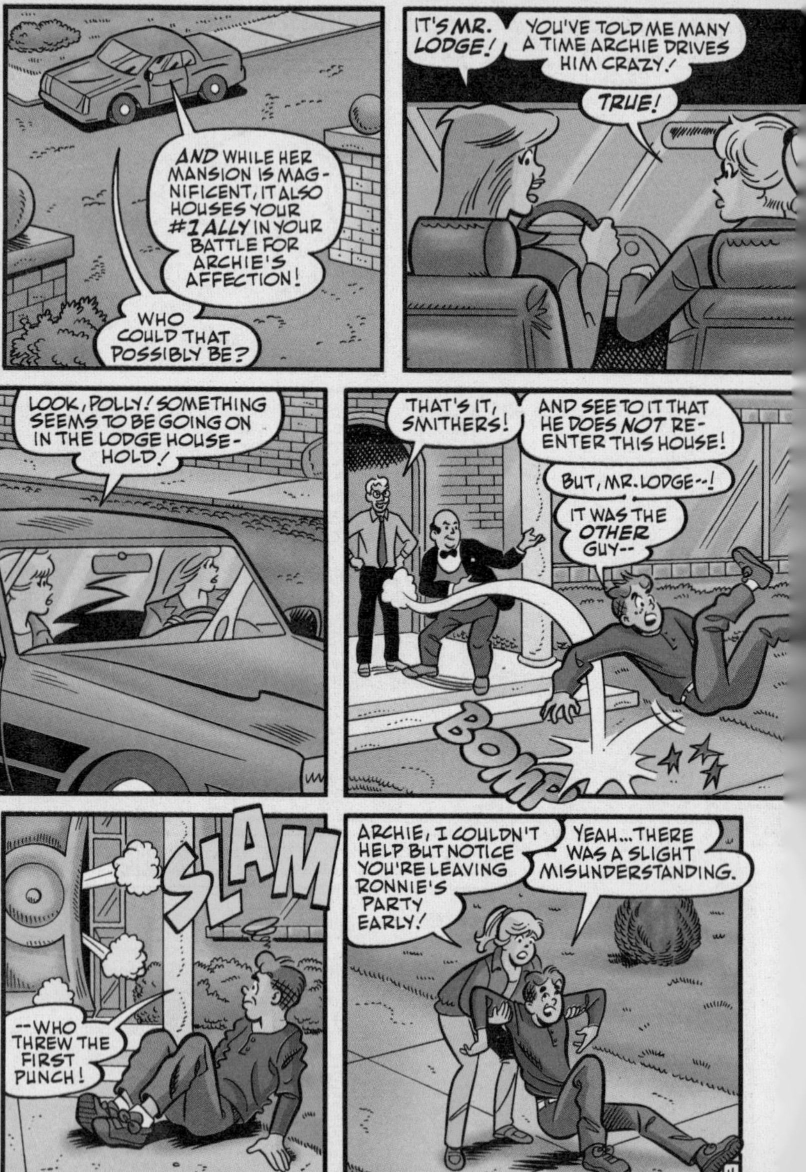
AND WHILE HER MANSION IS MAGNIFICENT, IT ALSO HOUSES YOUR #1 ALLY IN YOUR BATTLE FOR ARCHIE'S AFFECTION!
WHO COULD THAT POSSIBLY BE?
IT'S MR. LODGE!
YOU'VE TOLD ME MANY A TIME ARCHIE DRIVES HIM CRAZY!
TRUE!
LOOK, POLLY! SOMETHING SEEMS TO BE GOING ON IN THE LODGE HOUSEHOLD!
THAT'S IT, SMITHERS!
AND SEE TO IT THAT HE DOES NOT RE-ENTER THIS HOUSE!
BUT, MR. LODGE--!
IT WAS THE OTHER GUY--
BOMP
SLAM
--WHO THREW THE FIRST PUNCH!
ARCHIE, I COULDN'T HELP BUT NOTICE YOU'RE LEAVING RONNIE'S PARTY EARLY!
YEAH... THERE WAS A SLIGHT MISUNDERSTANDING.
4

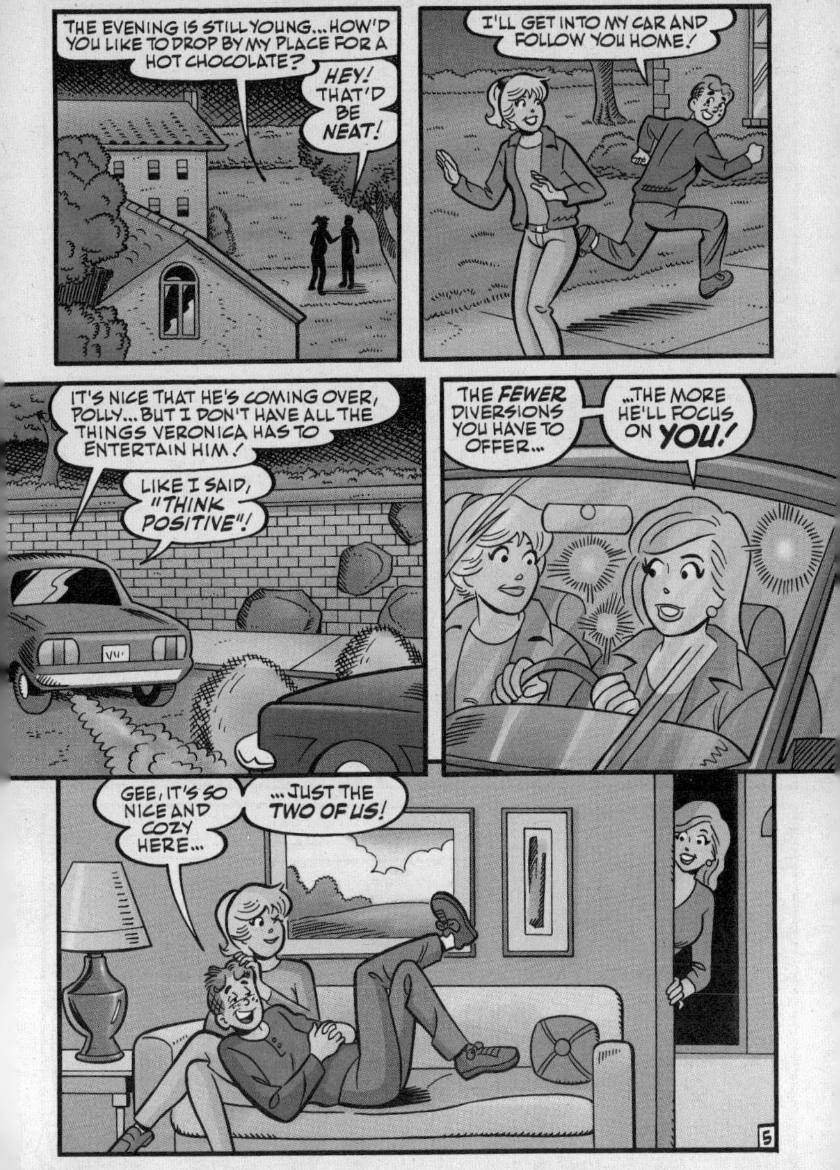
THE EVENING IS STILL YOUNG... HOW'D YOU LIKE TO DROP BY MY PLACE FOR A HOT CHOCOLATE?
HEY! THAT'D BE NEAT!
I'LL GET INTO MY CAR AND FOLLOW YOU HOME!
IT'S NICE THAT HE'S COMING OVER, POLLY... BUT I DON'T HAVE ALL THE THINGS VERONICA HAS TO ENTERTAIN HIM!
LIKE I SAID, "THINK POSITIVE"!
THE FEWER DIVERSIONS YOU HAVE TO OFFER...
...THE MORE HE'LL FOCUS ON YOU!
GEE, IT'S SO NICE AND COZY HERE...
...JUST THE TWO OF US!
5

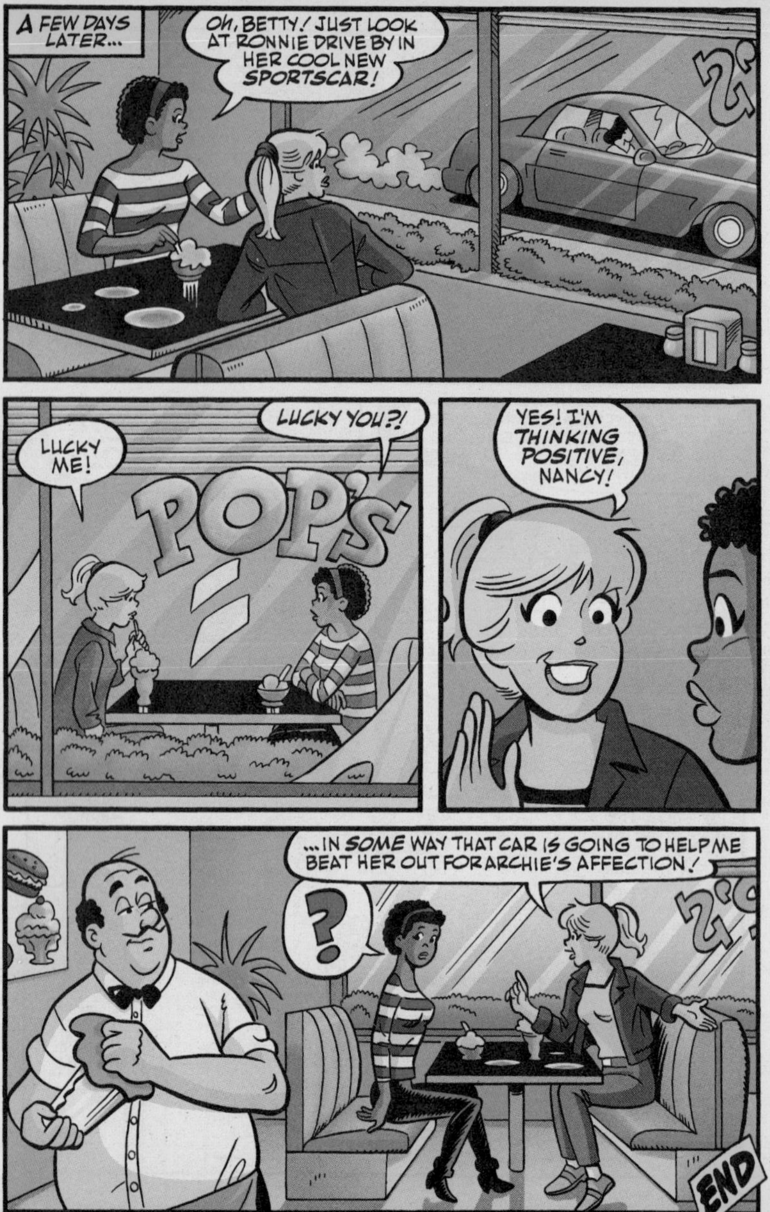
A FEW DAYS LATER...
OH, BETTY! JUST LOOK AT RONNIE DRIVE BY IN HER COOL NEW SPORTSCAR!
LUCKY ME!
LUCKY YOU?!
POP'S
YES! I'M THINKING POSITIVE, NANCY!
...IN SOME WAY THAT CAR IS GOING TO HELP ME BEAT HER OUT FOR ARCHIE'S AFFECTION!
?
END

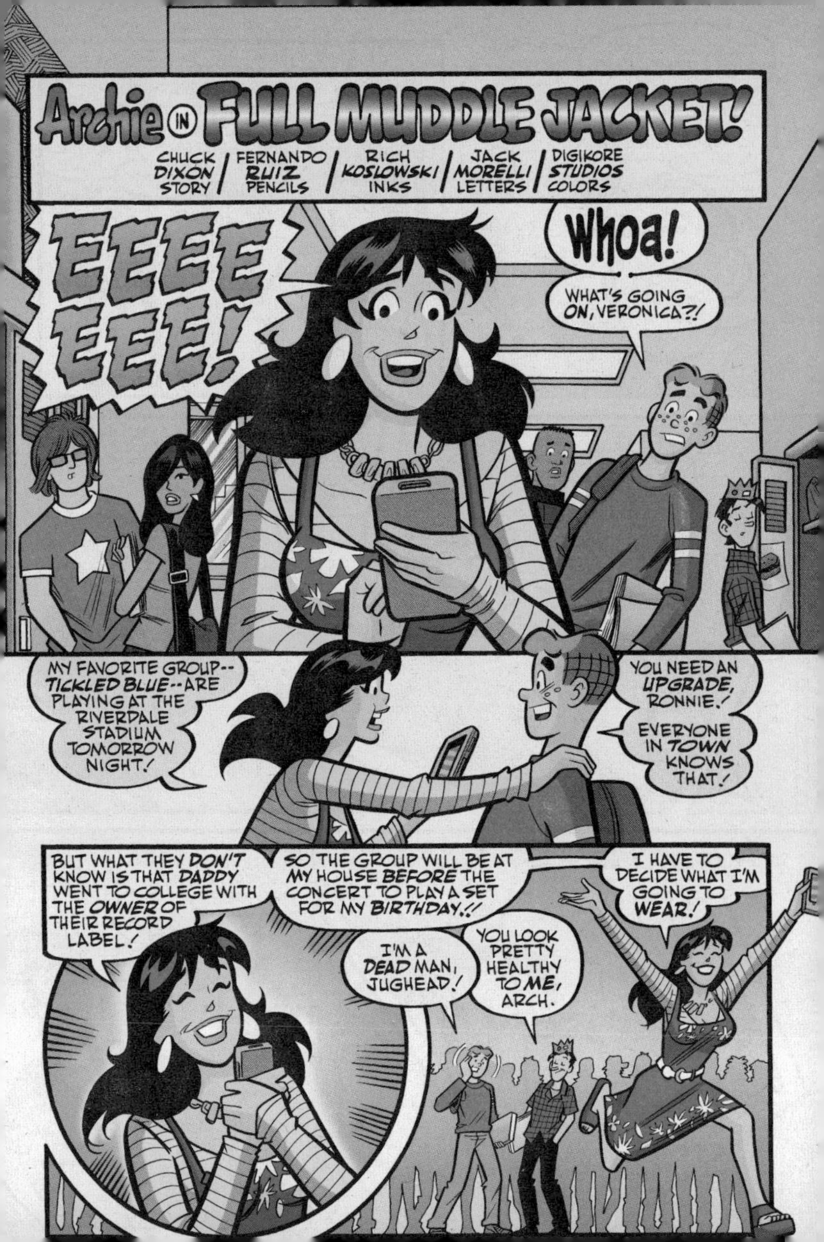
Archie in FULL MUDDLE JACKET!
CHUCK DIXON STORY / FERNANDO RUIZ PENCILS / RICH KOSLOWSKI INKS / JACK MORELLI LETTERS / DIGIKORE STUDIOS COLORS
EEEE EEE!
Whoa!
WHAT'S GOING ON, VERONICA?!
MY FAVORITE GROUP-- TICKLED BLUE--ARE PLAYING AT THE RIVERDALE STADIUM TOMORROW NIGHT!
YOU NEED AN UPGRADE, RONNIE!
EVERYONE IN TOWN KNOWS THAT!
BUT WHAT THEY DON'T KNOW IS THAT DADDY WENT TO COLLEGE WITH THE OWNER OF THEIR RECORD LABEL!
SO THE GROUP WILL BE AT MY HOUSE BEFORE THE CONCERT TO PLAY A SET FOR MY BIRTHDAY!!
I HAVE TO DECIDE WHAT I'M GOING TO WEAR!
I'M A DEAD MAN, JUGHEAD!
YOU LOOK PRETTY HEALTHY TO ME, ARCH.

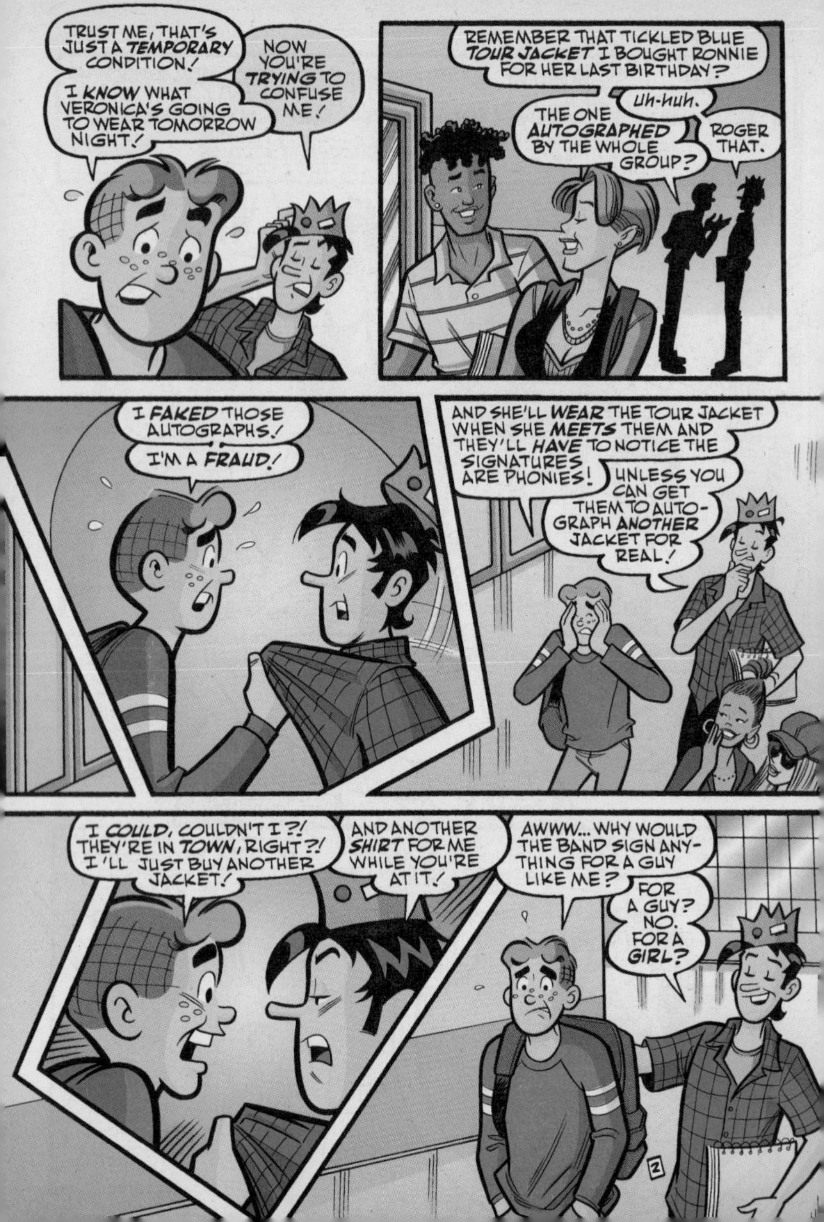

TRUST ME, THAT'S JUST A TEMPORARY CONDITION!
I KNOW WHAT VERONICA'S GOING TO WEAR TOMORROW NIGHT!
NOW YOU'RE TRYING TO CONFUSE ME!
REMEMBER THAT TICKLED BLUE TOUR JACKET I BOUGHT RONNIE FOR HER LAST BIRTHDAY?
UH-HUH.
THE ONE AUTOGRAPHED BY THE WHOLE GROUP?
ROGER THAT.
I FAKED THOSE AUTOGRAPHS!
I'M A FRAUD!
AND SHE'LL WEAR THE TOUR JACKET WHEN SHE MEETS THEM AND THEY'LL HAVE TO NOTICE THE SIGNATURES ARE PHONIES!
UNLESS YOU CAN GET THEM TO AUTO-GRAPH ANOTHER JACKET FOR REAL!
I COULD, COULDN'T I?! THEY'RE IN TOWN, RIGHT?! I'LL JUST BUY ANOTHER JACKET!
AND ANOTHER SHIRT FOR ME WHILE YOU'RE AT IT!
AWWW... WHY WOULD THE BAND SIGN ANY-THING FOR A GUY LIKE ME?
FOR A GUY? NO. FOR A GIRL?
2

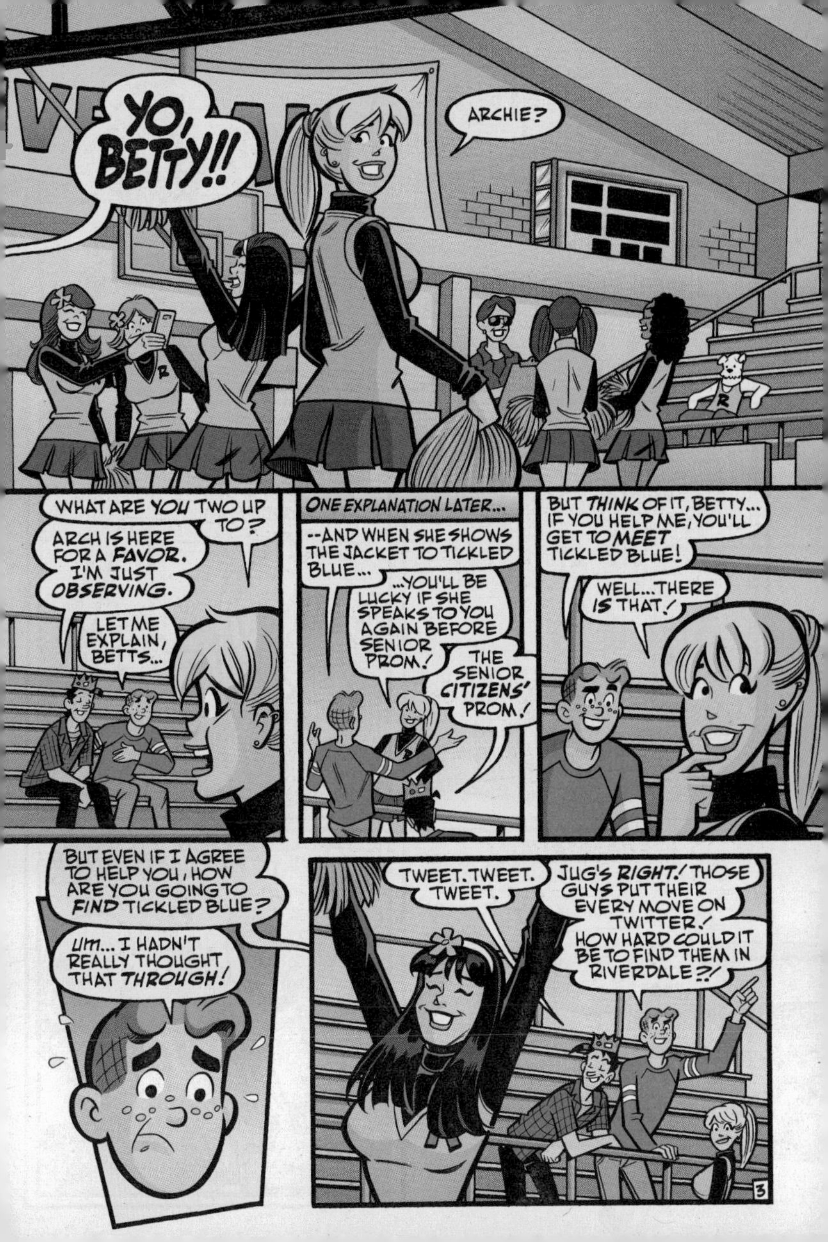
YO, BETTY!!
ARCHIE?
WHAT ARE YOU TWO UP TO?
ARCH IS HERE FOR A FAVOR. I'M JUST OBSERVING.
LET ME EXPLAIN, BETTS...
ONE EXPLANATION LATER...
--AND WHEN SHE SHOWS THE JACKET TO TICKLED BLUE...
...YOU'LL BE LUCKY IF SHE SPEAKS TO YOU AGAIN BEFORE SENIOR PROM!
THE SENIOR CITIZENS' PROM!
BUT THINK OF IT, BETTY... IF YOU HELP ME, YOU'LL GET TO MEET TICKLED BLUE!
WELL... THERE IS THAT!
BUT EVEN IF I AGREE TO HELP YOU, HOW ARE YOU GOING TO FIND TICKLED BLUE?
UM... I HADN'T REALLY THOUGHT THAT THROUGH!
TWEET. TWEET. TWEET.
JUG'S RIGHT! THOSE GUYS PUT THEIR EVERY MOVE ON TWITTER! HOW HARD COULD IT BE TO FIND THEM IN RIVERDALE?!
3

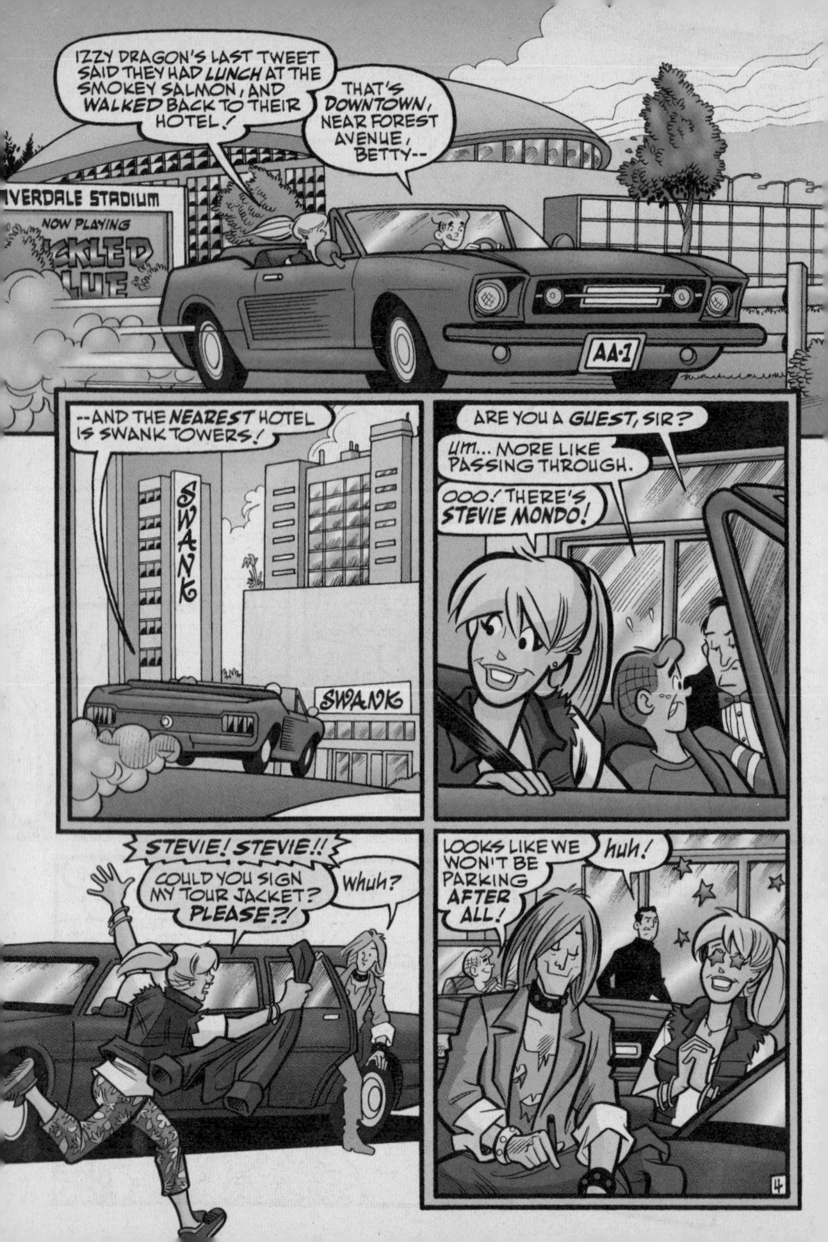
IZZY DRAGON'S LAST TWEET SAID THEY HAD LUNCH AT THE SMOKEY SALMON, AND WALKED BACK TO THEIR HOTEL!
THAT'S DOWNTOWN, NEAR FOREST AVENUE, BETTY--
RIVERDALE STADIUM
NOW PLAYING
AA-1
--AND THE NEAREST HOTEL IS SWANK TOWERS!
SWANK
SWANK
ARE YOU A GUEST, SIR?
UM... MORE LIKE PASSING THROUGH.
OOO! THERE'S STEVIE MONDO!
STEVIE! STEVIE!!
COULD YOU SIGN MY TOUR JACKET? PLEASE?!
Whuh?
LOOKS LIKE WE WON'T BE PARKING AFTER ALL!
huh!
4

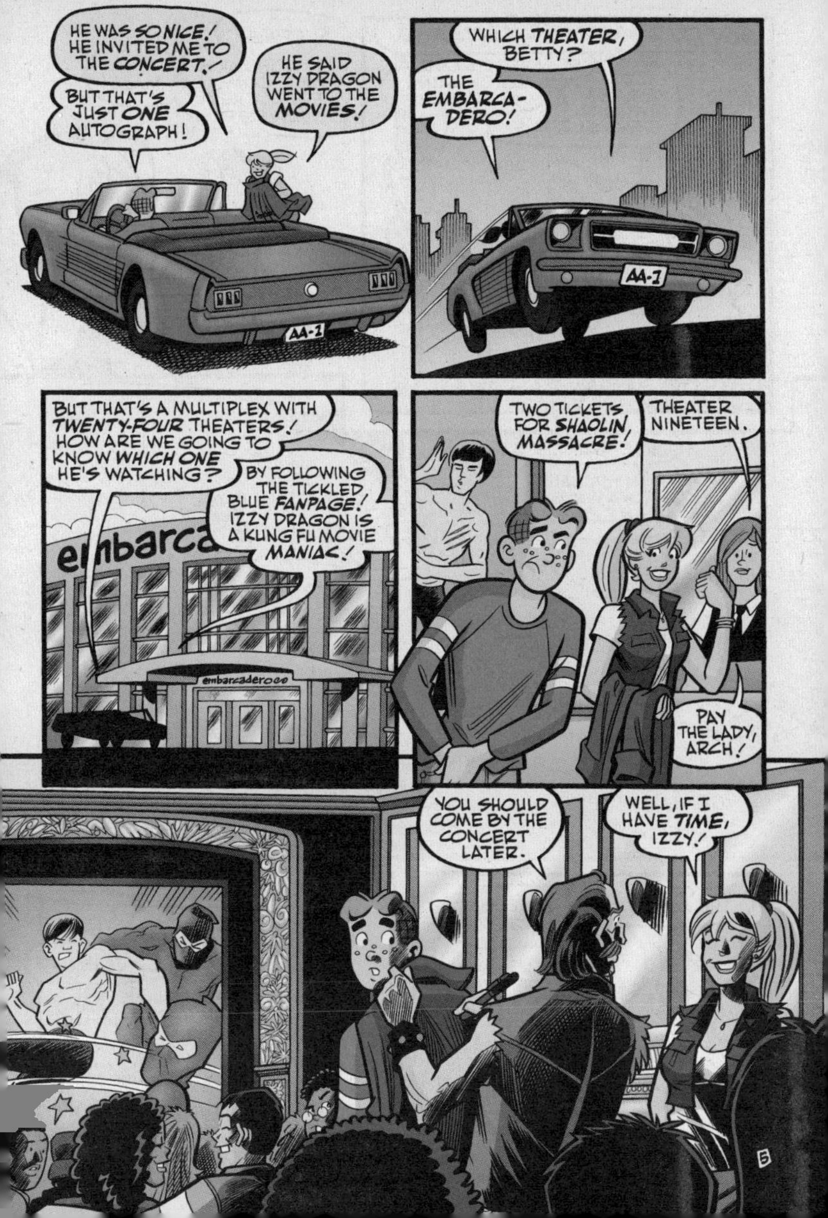
HE WAS SO NICE! HE INVITED ME TO THE CONCERT!
BUT THAT'S JUST ONE AUTOGRAPH!
HE SAID IZZY DRAGON WENT TO THE MOVIES!
AA-1
WHICH THEATER, BETTY?
THE EMBARCA-DERO!
AA-1
BUT THAT'S A MULTIPLEX WITH TWENTY-FOUR THEATERS! HOW ARE WE GOING TO KNOW WHICH ONE HE'S WATCHING?
BY FOLLOWING THE TICKLED BLUE FANPAGE! IZZY DRAGON IS A KUNG FU MOVIE MANIAC!
embarca
embarcadero
TWO TICKETS FOR SHAOLIN MASSACRE!
THEATER NINETEEN.
PAY THE LADY, ARCH!
YOU SHOULD COME BY THE CONCERT LATER.
WELL, IF I HAVE TIME, IZZY!
5

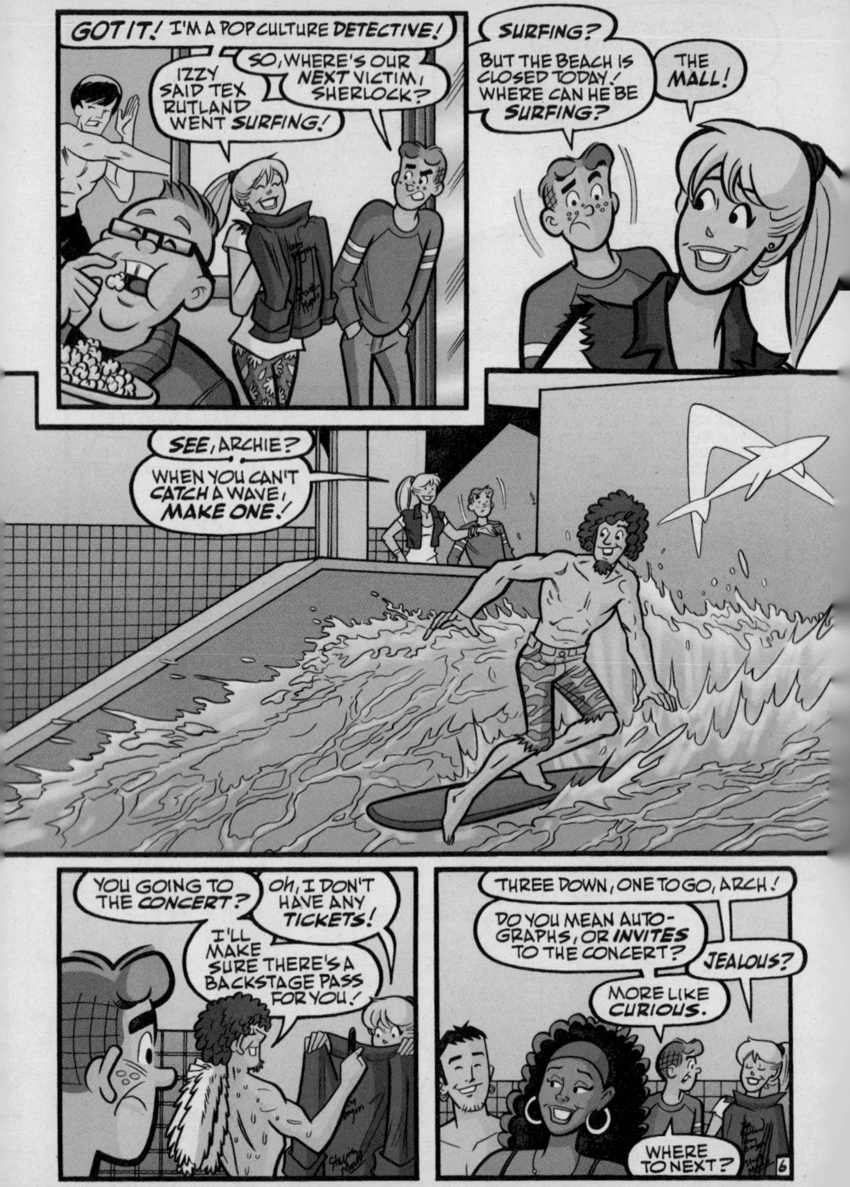
GOT IT! I'M A POP CULTURE DETECTIVE!
SO, WHERE'S OUR NEXT VICTIM, SHERLOCK?
IZZY SAID TEX RUTLAND WENT SURFING!
SURFING?
BUT THE BEACH IS CLOSED TODAY! WHERE CAN HE BE SURFING?
THE MALL!
SEE, ARCHIE?
WHEN YOU CAN'T CATCH A WAVE, MAKE ONE!
YOU GOING TO THE CONCERT?
OH, I DON'T HAVE ANY TICKETS!
I'LL MAKE SURE THERE'S A BACKSTAGE PASS FOR YOU!
THREE DOWN, ONE TO GO, ARCH!
DO YOU MEAN AUTO-GRAPHS, OR INVITES TO THE CONCERT?
JEALOUS?
MORE LIKE CURIOUS.
WHERE TO NEXT?
6

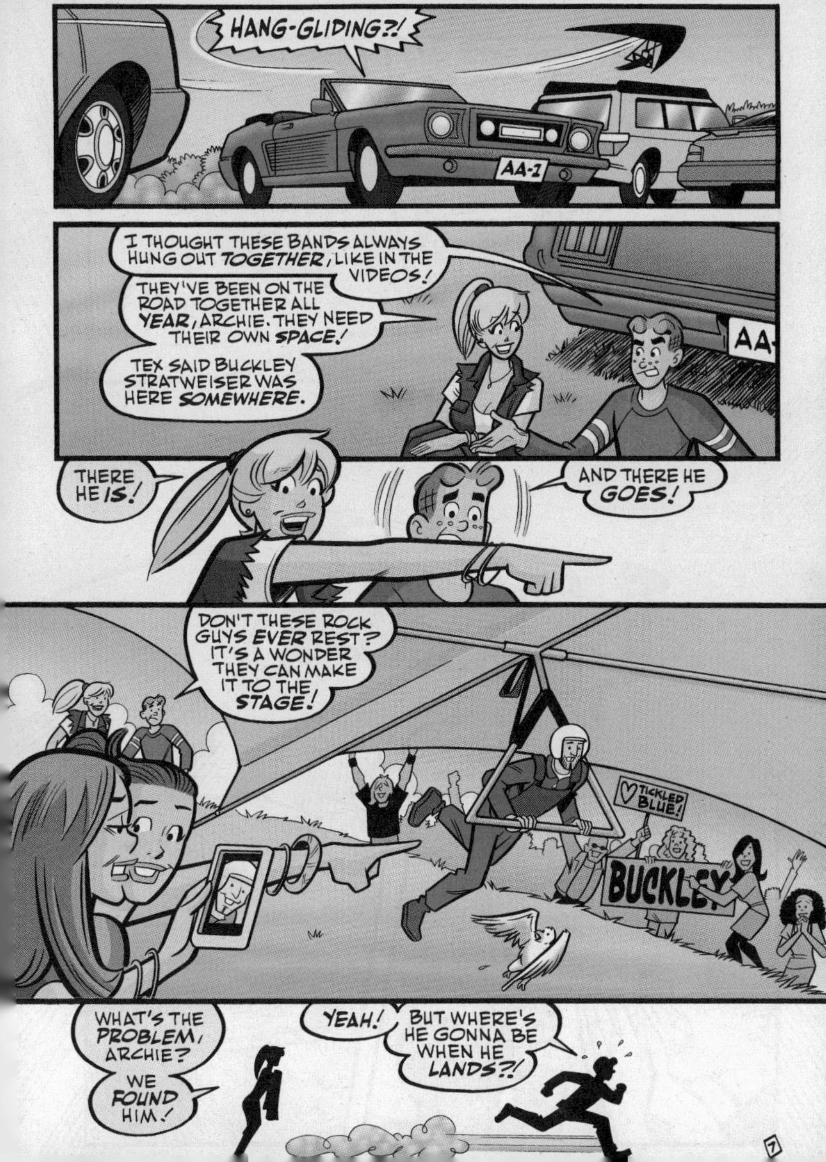
HANG-GLIDING?!
AA-1
I THOUGHT THESE BANDS ALWAYS HUNG OUT TOGETHER, LIKE IN THE VIDEOS!
THEY'VE BEEN ON THE ROAD TOGETHER ALL YEAR, ARCHIE. THEY NEED THEIR OWN SPACE!
TEX SAID BUCKLEY STRATWEISER WAS HERE SOMEWHERE.
THERE HE IS!
AND THERE HE GOES!
DON'T THESE ROCK GUYS EVER REST? IT'S A WONDER THEY CAN MAKE IT TO THE STAGE!
♡ TICKLED BLUE!
BUCKLEY
WHAT'S THE PROBLEM, ARCHIE?
WE FOUND HIM!
YEAH!
BUT WHERE'S HE GONNA BE WHEN HE LANDS?!

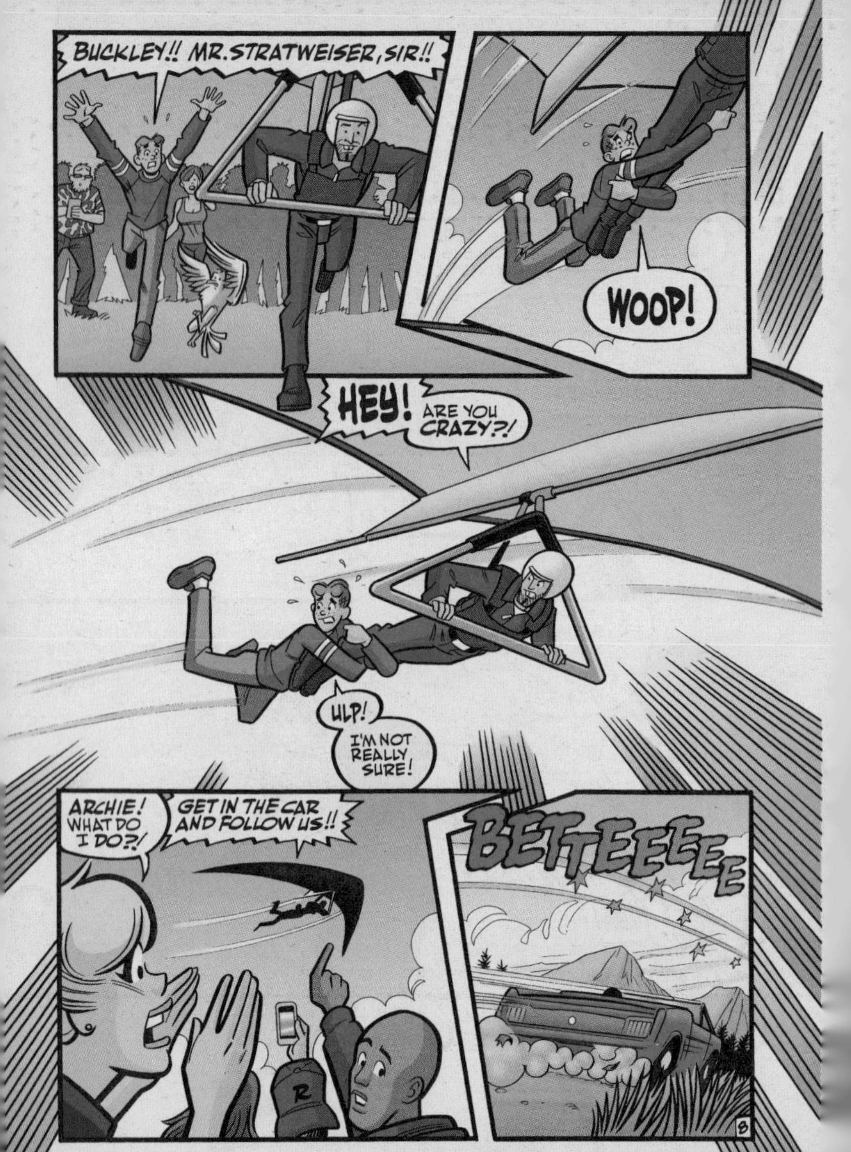
BUCKLEY!! MR.STRATWEISER, SIR!!
WOOP!
HEY! ARE YOU CRAZY?!
ULP!
I'M NOT REALLY SURE!
ARCHIE! WHAT DO I DO?!
GET IN THE CAR AND FOLLOW US!!
BETTEEEEEE
8

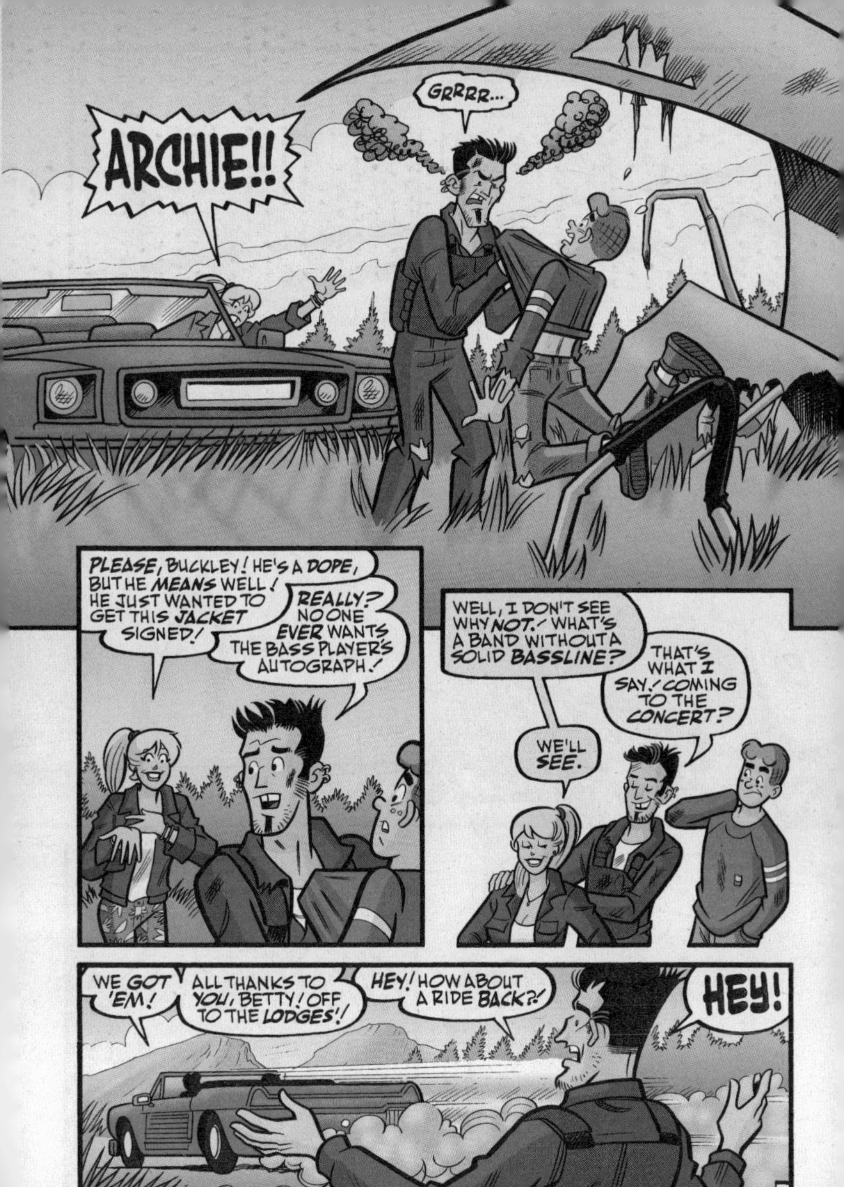
ARCHIE!!
GRRRR...
PLEASE, BUCKLEY! HE'S A DOPE, BUT HE MEANS WELL! HE JUST WANTED TO GET THIS JACKET SIGNED!
REALLY? NO ONE EVER WANTS THE BASS PLAYER'S AUTOGRAPH!
WELL, I DON'T SEE WHY NOT! WHAT'S A BAND WITHOUT A SOLID BASSLINE?
THAT'S WHAT I SAY! COMING TO THE CONCERT?
WE'LL SEE.
WE GOT 'EM!
ALL THANKS TO YOU, BETTY! OFF TO THE LODGES!
HEY! HOW ABOUT A RIDE BACK?!
HEY!
9

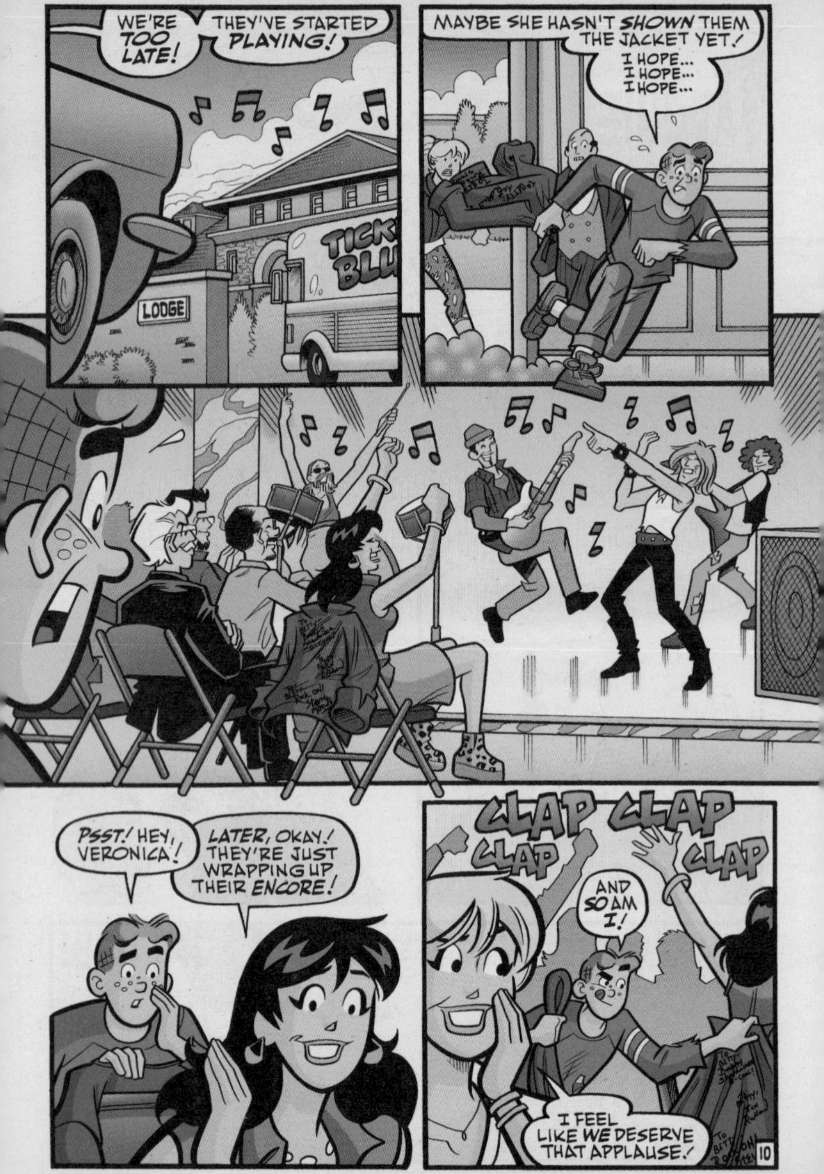

WE'RE TOO LATE!
THEY'VE STARTED PLAYING!
LODGE
MAYBE SHE HASN'T SHOWN THEM THE JACKET YET!
I HOPE... I HOPE... I HOPE...
PSST! HEY, VERONICA!
LATER, OKAY! THEY'RE JUST WRAPPING UP THEIR ENCORE!
CLAP CLAP CLAP CLAP
AND SO AM I!
I FEEL LIKE WE DESERVE THAT APPLAUSE!
10

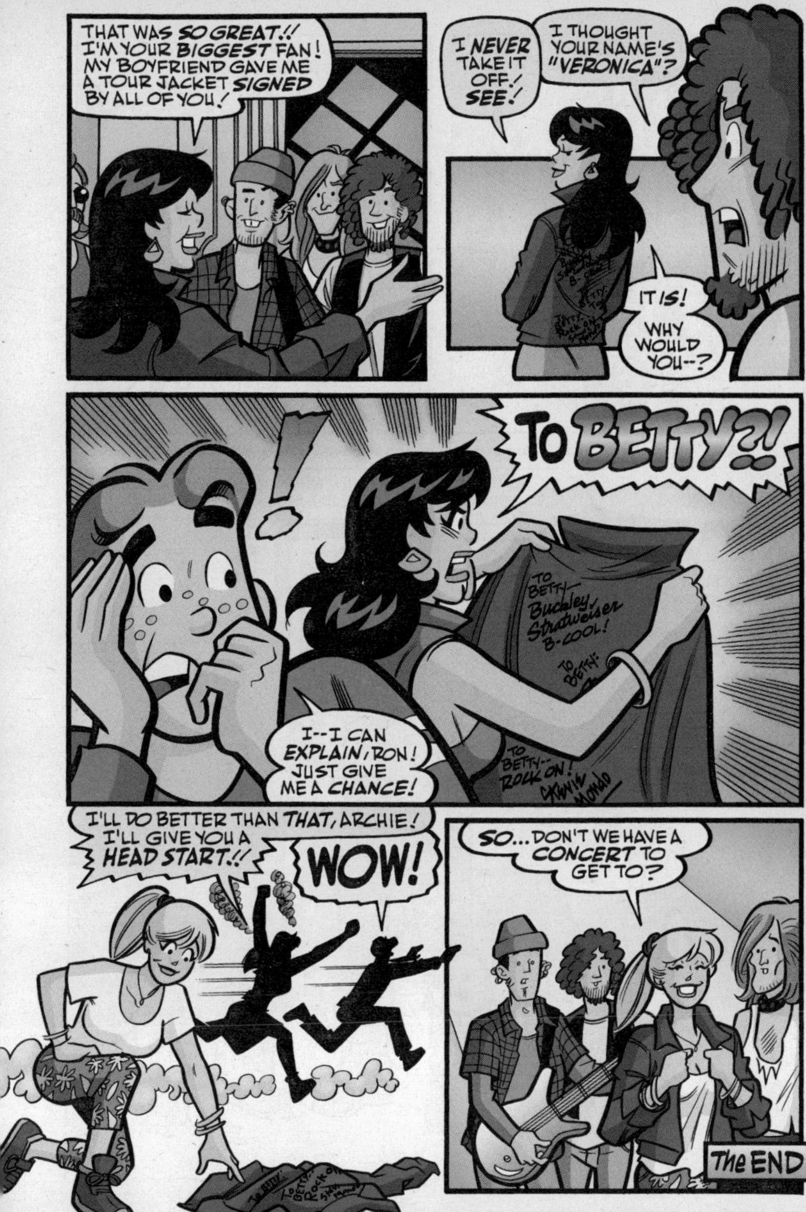
THAT WAS SO GREAT!! I'M YOUR BIGGEST FAN! MY BOYFRIEND GAVE ME A TOUR JACKET SIGNED BY ALL OF YOU!
I NEVER TAKE IT OFF! SEE!
I THOUGHT YOUR NAME'S "VERONICA"?
IT IS!
WHY WOULD YOU--?
TO BETTY?!
!
TO BETTY Buckley Stratweiser B-COOL!
I--I CAN EXPLAIN, RON! JUST GIVE ME A CHANCE!
TO BETTY-- ROCK ON!
I'LL DO BETTER THAN THAT, ARCHIE! I'LL GIVE YOU A HEAD START!!
WOW!
SO...DON'T WE HAVE A CONCERT TO GET TO?
The END

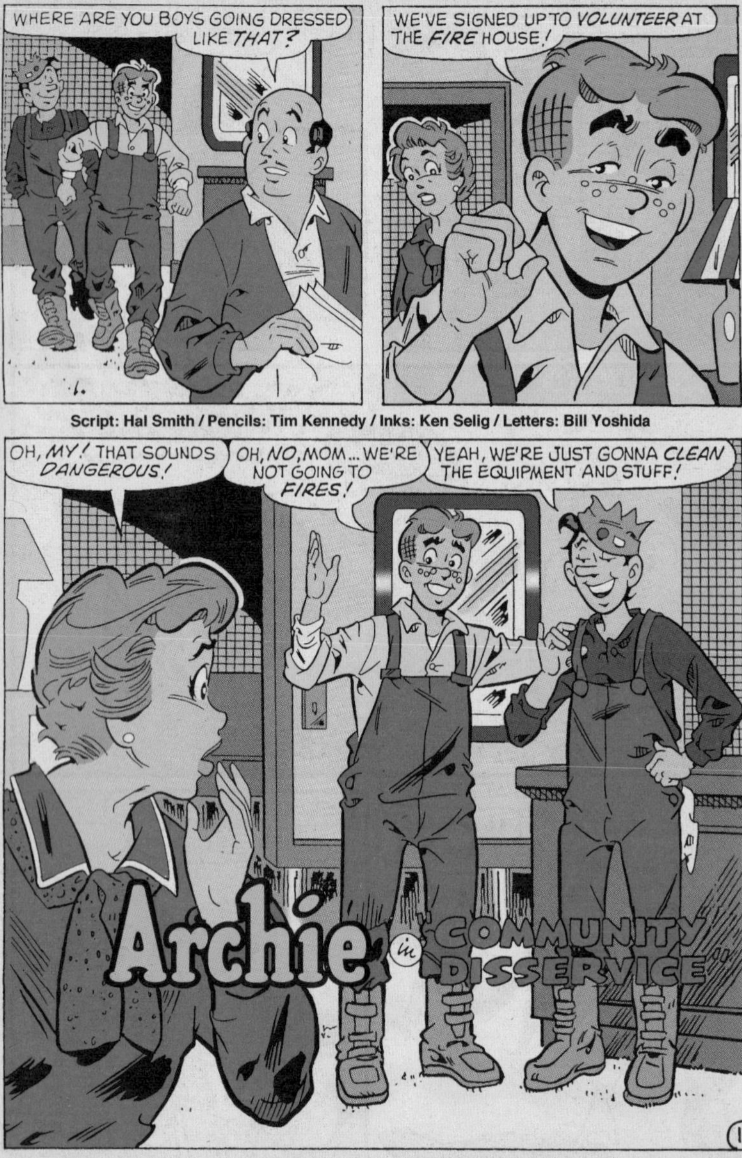
WHERE ARE YOU BOYS GOING DRESSED LIKE THAT?
WE'VE SIGNED UP TO VOLUNTEER AT THE FIRE HOUSE!
Script: Hal Smith / Pencils: Tim Kennedy / Inks: Ken Selig / Letters: Bill Yoshida
OH, MY! THAT SOUNDS DANGEROUS!
OH, NO, MOM... WE'RE NOT GOING TO FIRES!
YEAH, WE'RE JUST GONNA CLEAN THE EQUIPMENT AND STUFF!
Archie in "COMMUNITY DISSERVICE"
1

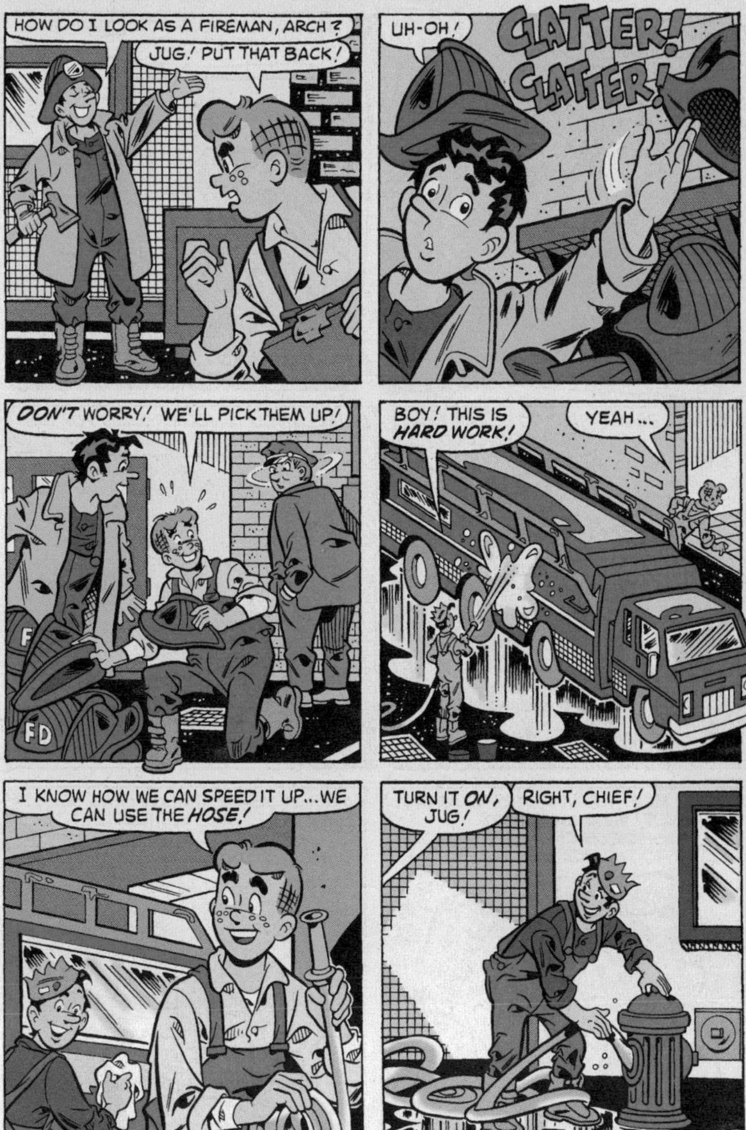
HOW DO I LOOK AS A FIREMAN, ARCH?
JUG! PUT THAT BACK!
UH-OH!
CLATTER! CLATTER!
DON'T WORRY! WE'LL PICK THEM UP!
F
FD
BOY! THIS IS HARD WORK!
YEAH...
I KNOW HOW WE CAN SPEED IT UP...WE CAN USE THE HOSE!
TURN IT ON, JUG!
RIGHT, CHIEF!
2

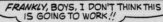

WOW! TOO MUCH PRESSURE!!

FRANKLY, BOYS, I DON'T THINK THIS IS GOING TO WORK!!

BUT WE REALLY WANT TO VOLUNTEER FOR *COMMUNITY SERVICE!!*

I HAVE AN IDEA...

LATER... YOU'VE VOLUNTEERED FOR THE COMMUNITY *WATCH* PATROL?

THAT SOUNDS *DANGEROUS!*

OH, NO, MOM... WE WON'T TRY TO ARREST CRIMINALS! WE JUST *REPORT* SUSPICIOUS CHARACTERS TO THE *POLICE!*

ARCH... *LOOK!*

YEAH! THAT GUY HAS BEEN STANDING IN THE ALLEY FOR A *LONG* TIME!

3

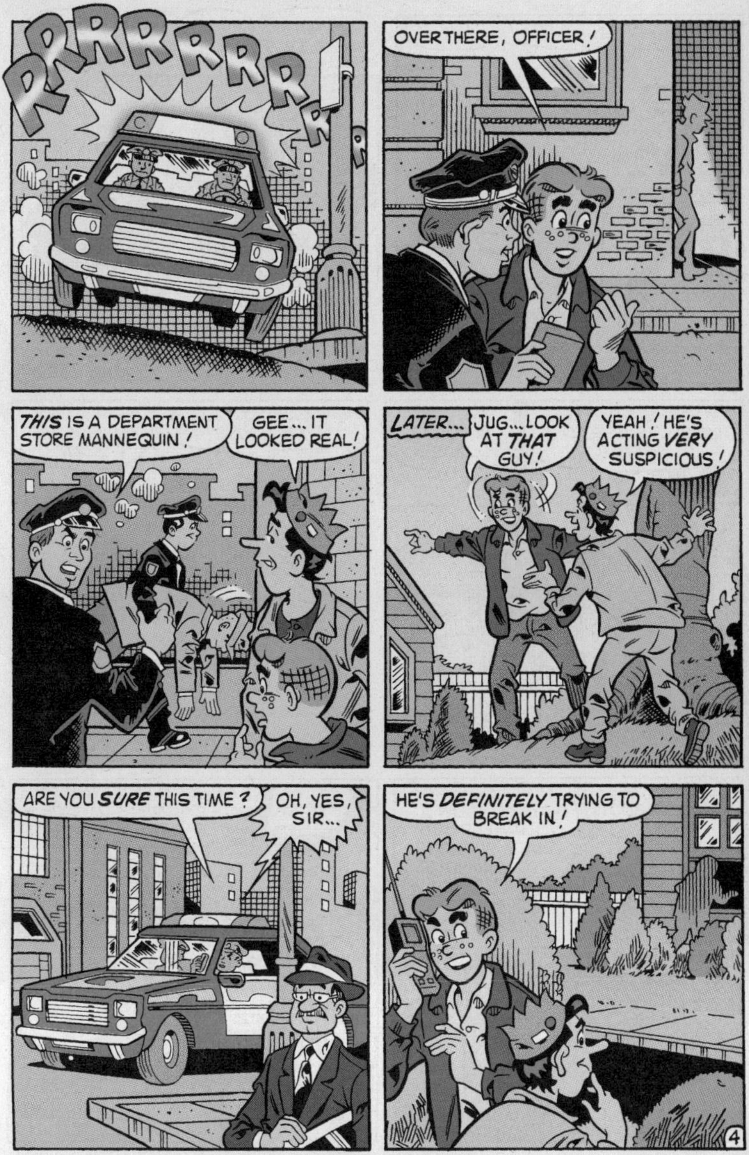
RRRRRRRRR
OVERTHERE, OFFICER!
THIS IS A DEPARTMENT STORE MANNEQUIN!
GEE... IT LOOKED REAL!
LATER...
JUG... LOOK AT THAT GUY!
YEAH! HE'S ACTING VERY SUSPICIOUS!
ARE YOU SURE THIS TIME?
OH, YES, SIR...
HE'S DEFINITELY TRYING TO BREAK IN!
4

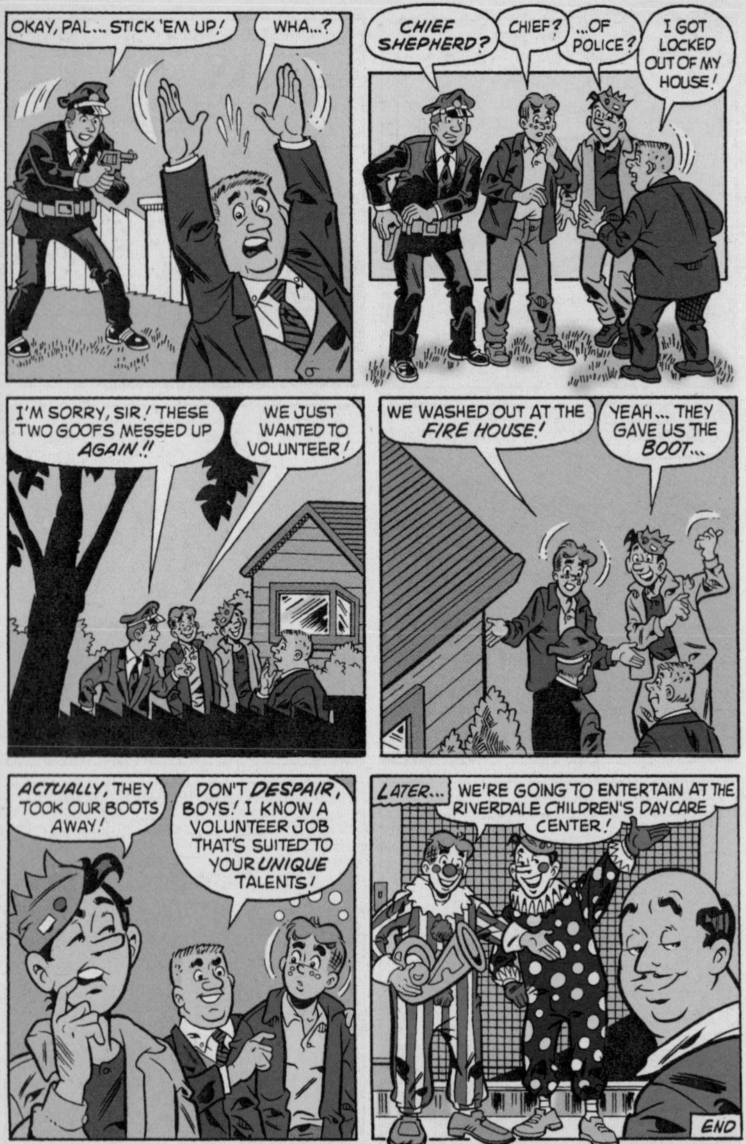
OKAY, PAL... STICK 'EM UP!
WHA...?
CHIEF SHEPHERD?
CHIEF?
...OF POLICE?
I GOT LOCKED OUT OF MY HOUSE!
I'M SORRY, SIR! THESE TWO GOOFS MESSED UP AGAIN!!
WE JUST WANTED TO VOLUNTEER!
WE WASHED OUT AT THE FIRE HOUSE!
YEAH... THEY GAVE US THE BOOT...
ACTUALLY, THEY TOOK OUR BOOTS AWAY!
DON'T DESPAIR, BOYS! I KNOW A VOLUNTEER JOB THAT'S SUITED TO YOUR UNIQUE TALENTS!
LATER...
WE'RE GOING TO ENTERTAIN AT THE RIVERDALE CHILDREN'S DAY CARE CENTER!
END

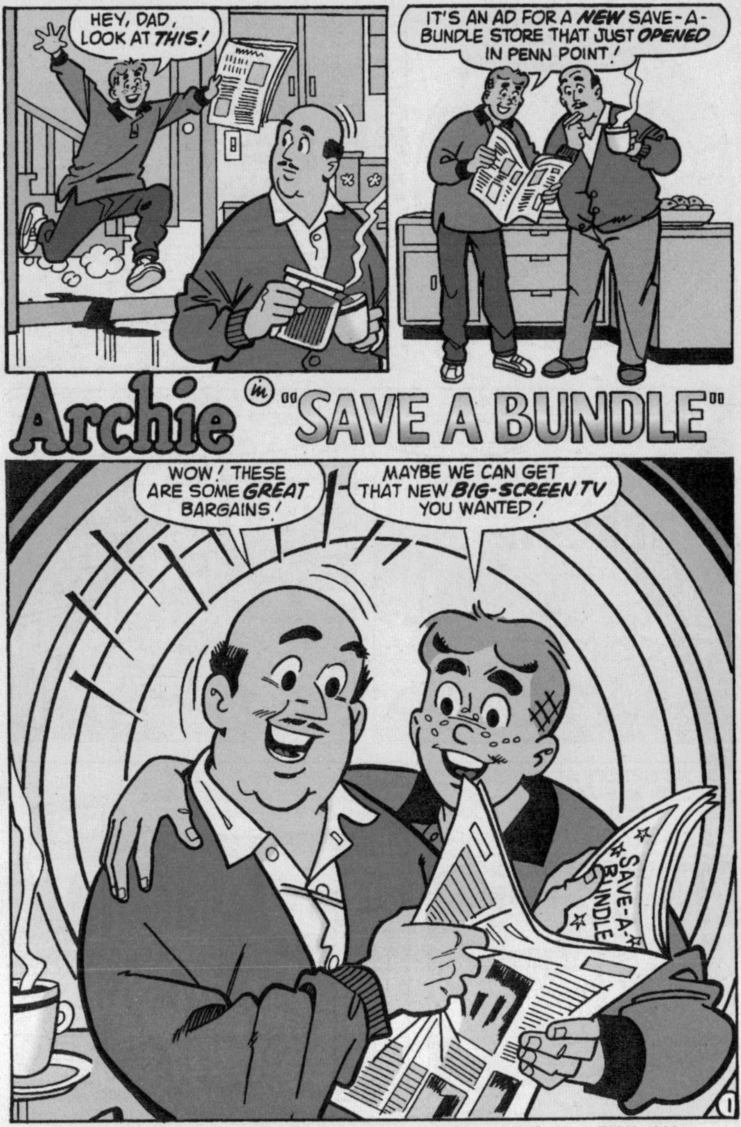

HEY, DAD, LOOK AT THIS!
IT'S AN AD FOR A NEW SAVE-A-BUNDLE STORE THAT JUST OPENED IN PENN POINT!
Archie in "SAVE A BUNDLE"
WOW! THESE ARE SOME GREAT BARGAINS!
MAYBE WE CAN GET THAT NEW BIG-SCREEN TV YOU WANTED!
SAVE-A-BUNDLE
1

Script: Hal Smith / Pencils: Stan Goldberg / Inks: Henry Scarpelli / Letters: Bill Yoshida

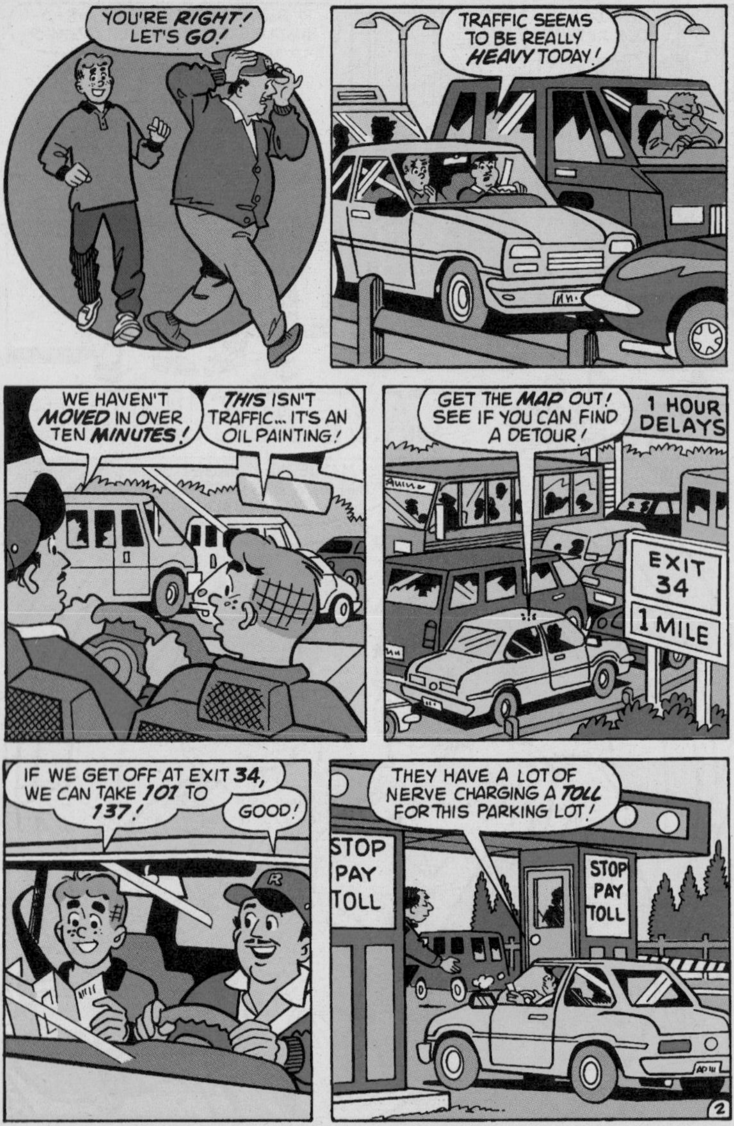
YOU'RE RIGHT! LET'S GO!
TRAFFIC SEEMS TO BE REALLY HEAVY TODAY!
WE HAVEN'T MOVED IN OVER TEN MINUTES!
THIS ISN'T TRAFFIC... IT'S AN OIL PAINTING!
GET THE MAP OUT! SEE IF YOU CAN FIND A DETOUR!
1 HOUR DELAYS
EXIT 34
1 MILE
IF WE GET OFF AT EXIT 34, WE CAN TAKE 101 TO 137!
GOOD!
THEY HAVE A LOT OF NERVE CHARGING A TOLL FOR THIS PARKING LOT!
STOP PAY TOLL
STOP PAY TOLL

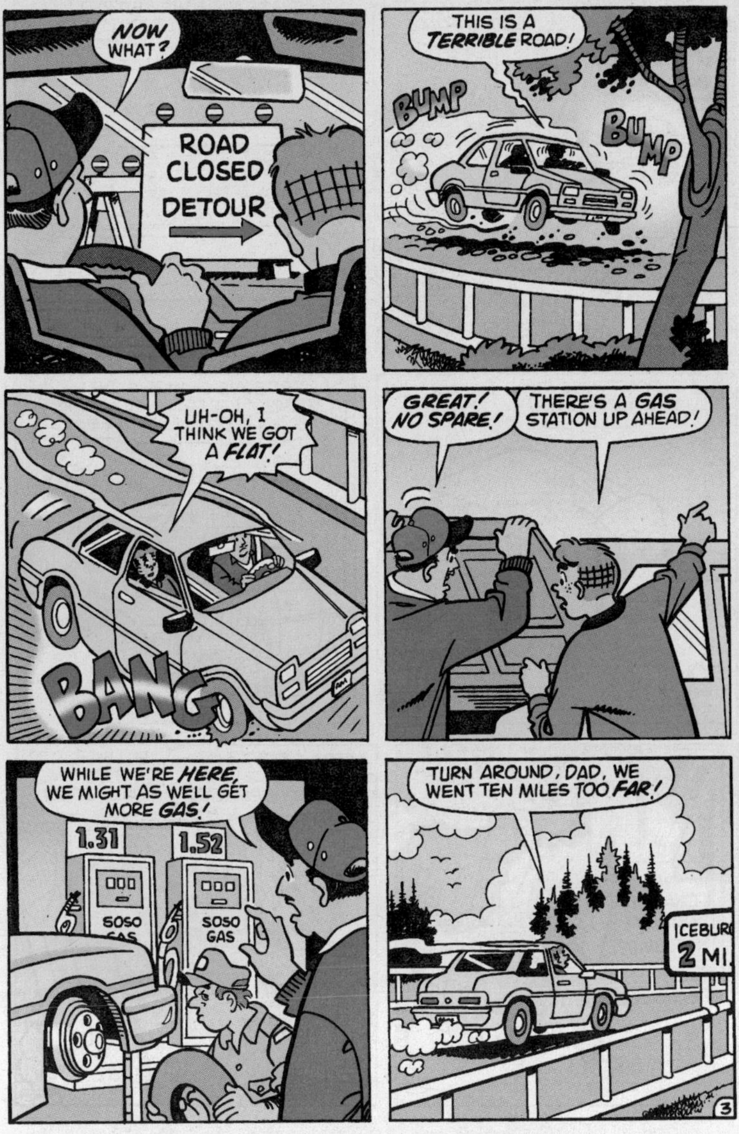
NOW WHAT?
ROAD CLOSED DETOUR
THIS IS A TERRIBLE ROAD!
BUMP
BUMP
UH-OH, I THINK WE GOT A FLAT!
BANG
GREAT! NO SPARE!
THERE'S A GAS STATION UP AHEAD!
WHILE WE'RE HERE, WE MIGHT AS WELL GET MORE GAS!
1.31
1.52
SOSO GAS
SOSO GAS
TURN AROUND, DAD, WE WENT TEN MILES TOO FAR!
2 MI.
3

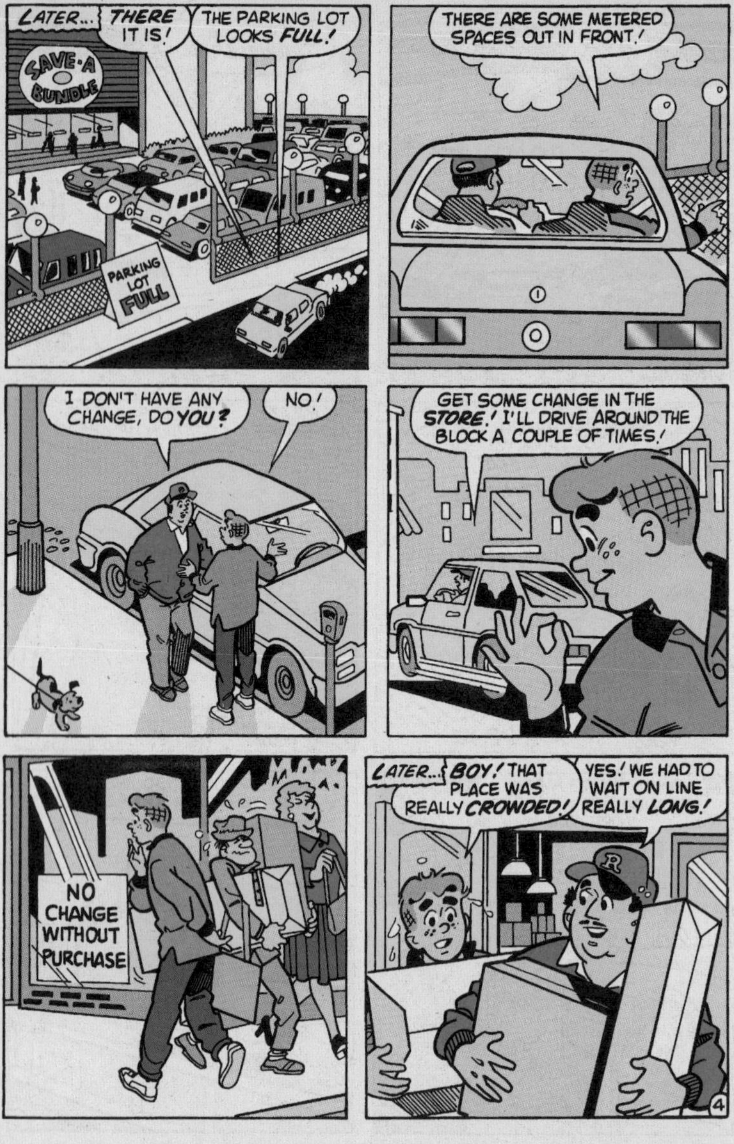
LATER...
THERE IT IS!
THE PARKING LOT LOOKS FULL!
SAVE-A BUNDLE
PARKING LOT FULL
THERE ARE SOME METERED SPACES OUT IN FRONT!
I DON'T HAVE ANY CHANGE, DO YOU?
NO!
GET SOME CHANGE IN THE STORE! I'LL DRIVE AROUND THE BLOCK A COUPLE OF TIMES!
NO CHANGE WITHOUT PURCHASE
LATER...
BOY! THAT PLACE WAS REALLY CROWDED!
YES! WE HAD TO WAIT ON LINE REALLY LONG!
4

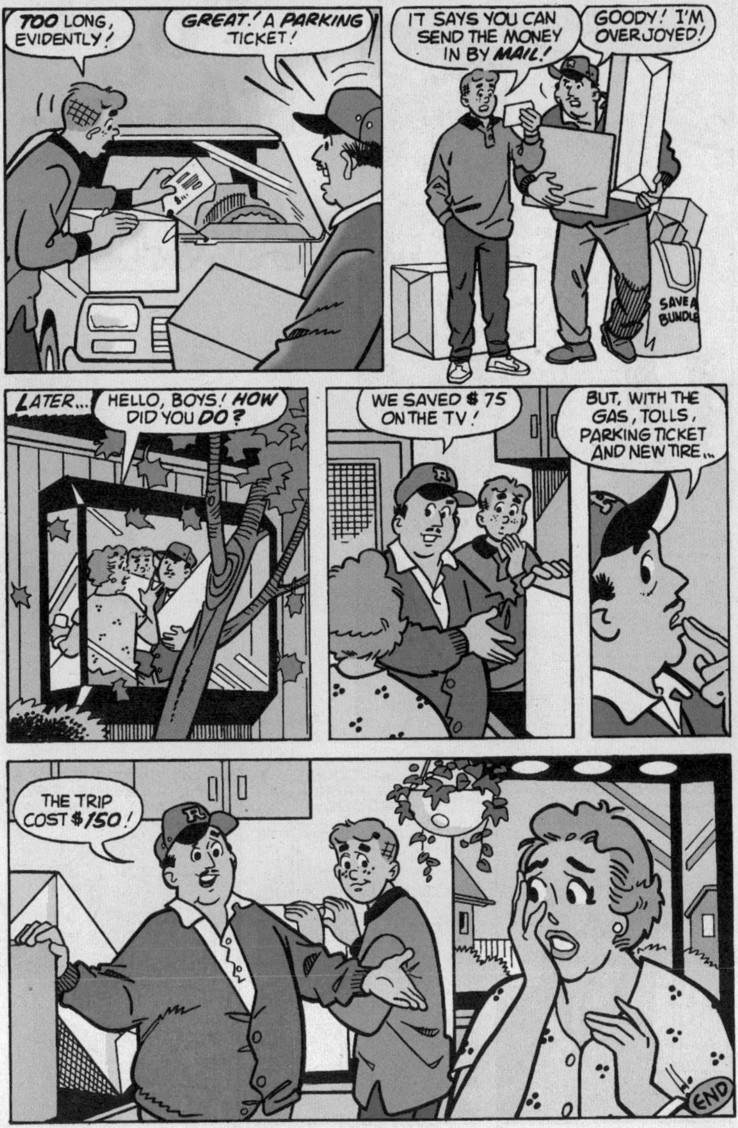
TOO LONG, EVIDENTLY!
GREAT! A PARKING TICKET!
IT SAYS YOU CAN SEND THE MONEY IN BY MAIL!
GOODY! I'M OVERJOYED!
SAVE A BUNDLE
LATER...
HELLO, BOYS! HOW DID YOU DO?
WE SAVED $ 75 ON THE TV!
BUT, WITH THE GAS, TOLLS, PARKING TICKET AND NEW TIRE...
THE TRIP COST $150!
END

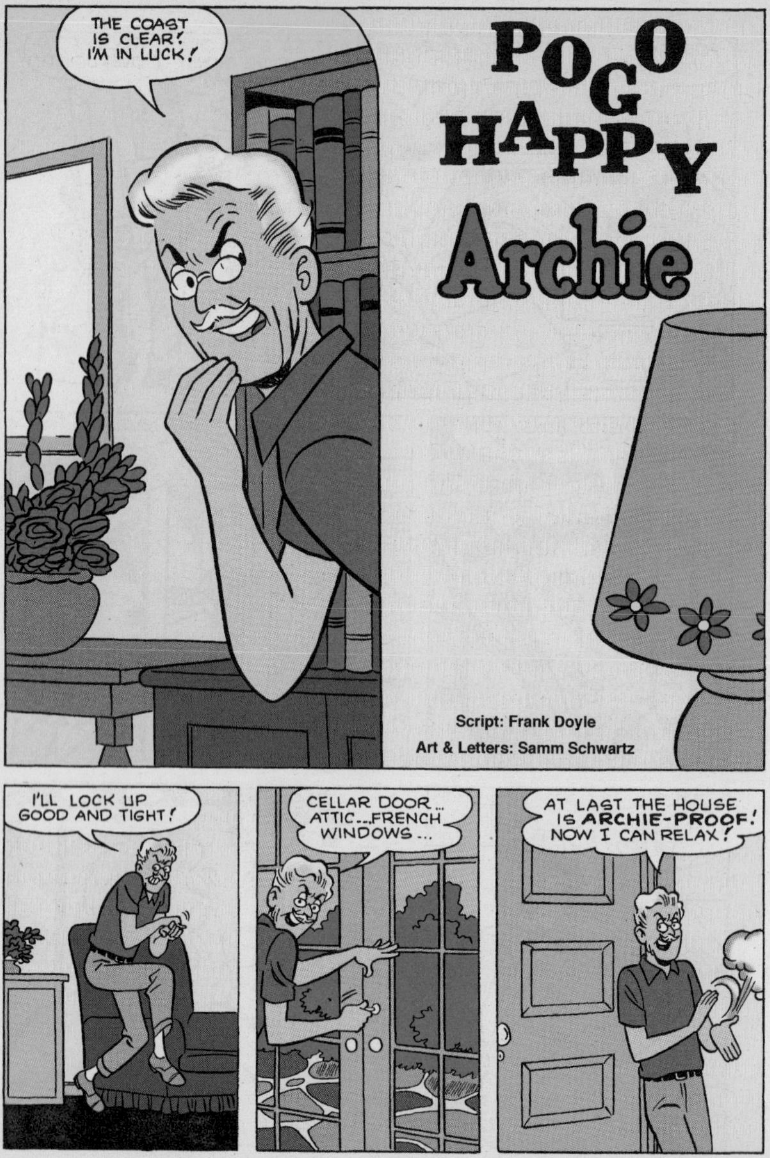
THE COAST IS CLEAR! I'M IN LUCK!
POGO HAPPY
Archie
Script: Frank Doyle
Art & Letters: Samm Schwartz
I'LL LOCK UP GOOD AND TIGHT!
CELLAR DOOR... ATTIC...FRENCH WINDOWS...
AT LAST THE HOUSE IS ARCHIE-PROOF! NOW I CAN RELAX!

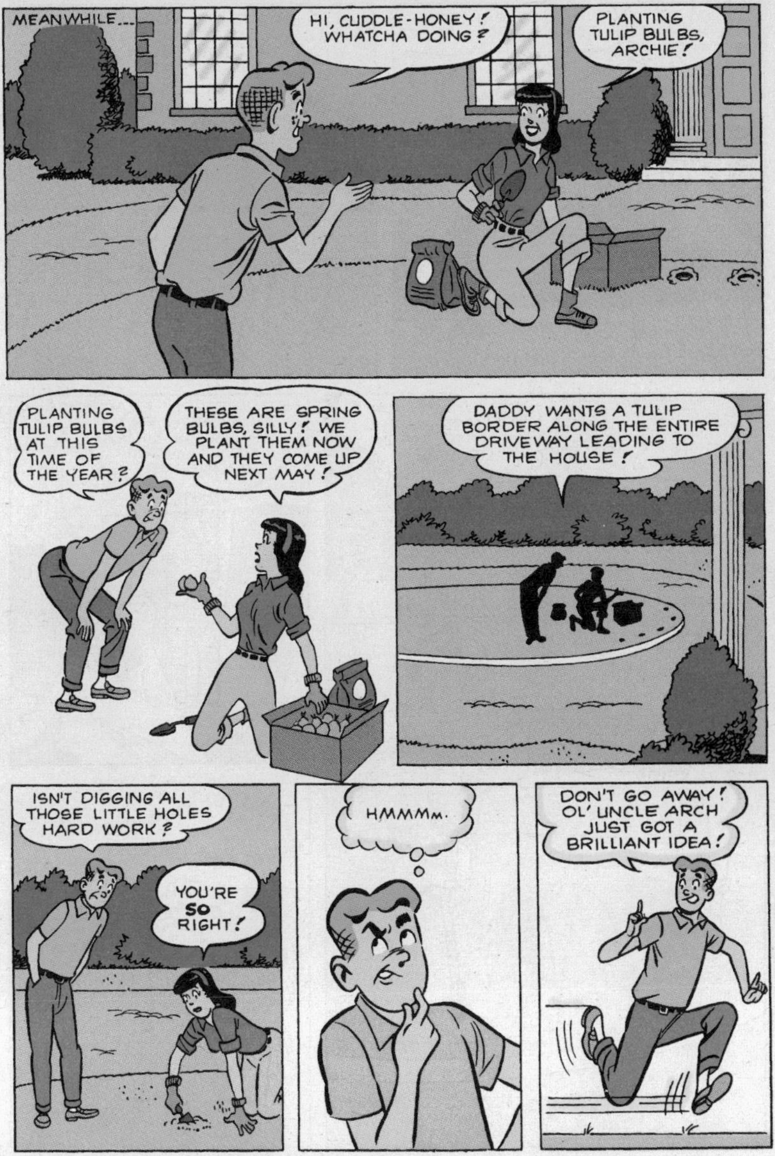
MEANWHILE...
HI, CUDDLE-HONEY! WHATCHA DOING?
PLANTING TULIP BULBS, ARCHIE!
PLANTING TULIP BULBS AT THIS TIME OF THE YEAR?
THESE ARE SPRING BULBS, SILLY! WE PLANT THEM NOW AND THEY COME UP NEXT MAY!
DADDY WANTS A TULIP BORDER ALONG THE ENTIRE DRIVEWAY LEADING TO THE HOUSE!
ISN'T DIGGING ALL THOSE LITTLE HOLES HARD WORK?
YOU'RE SO RIGHT!
HMMMM.
DON'T GO AWAY! OL' UNCLE ARCH JUST GOT A BRILLIANT IDEA!

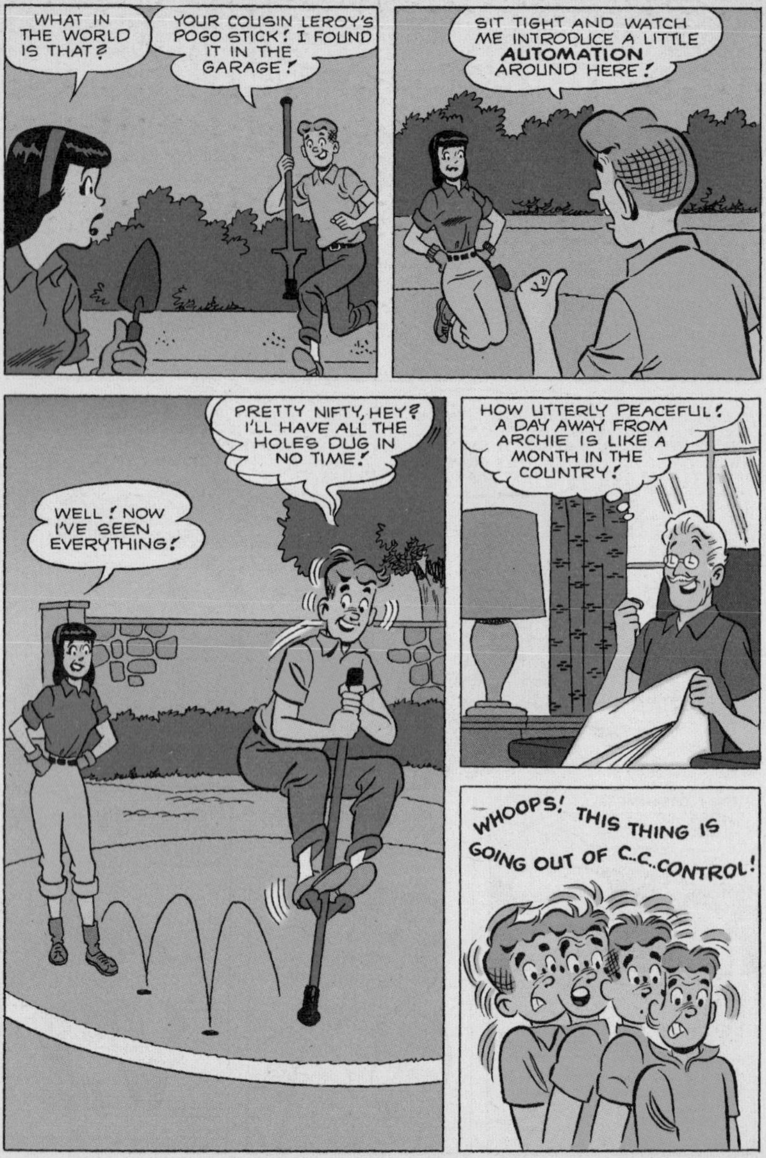
WHAT IN THE WORLD IS THAT?
YOUR COUSIN LEROY'S POGO STICK! I FOUND IT IN THE GARAGE!
SIT TIGHT AND WATCH ME INTRODUCE A LITTLE **AUTOMATION** AROUND HERE!
PRETTY NIFTY, HEY? I'LL HAVE ALL THE HOLES DUG IN NO TIME!
WELL! NOW I'VE SEEN EVERYTHING!
HOW UTTERLY PEACEFUL! A DAY AWAY FROM ARCHIE IS LIKE A MONTH IN THE COUNTRY!
WHOOPS! THIS THING IS GOING OUT OF C..C..CONTROL!

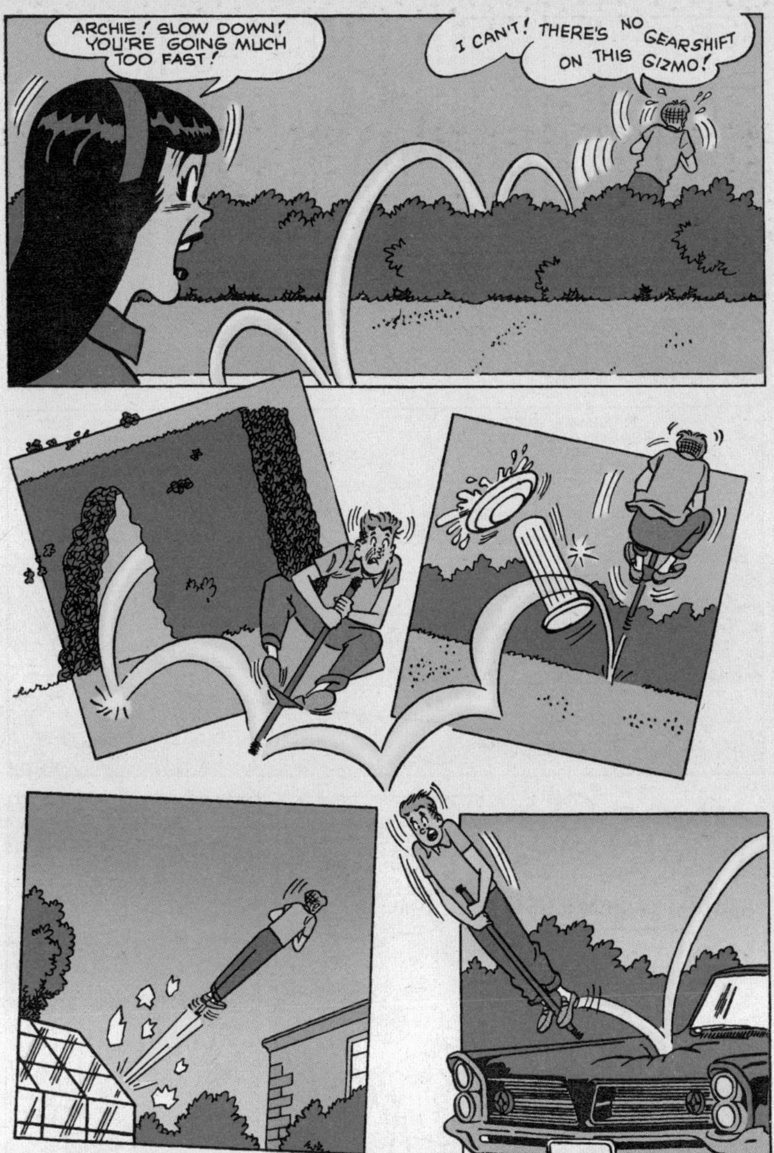
ARCHIE! SLOW DOWN! YOU'RE GOING MUCH TOO FAST!
I CAN'T! THERE'S NO GEARSHIFT ON THIS GIZMO!

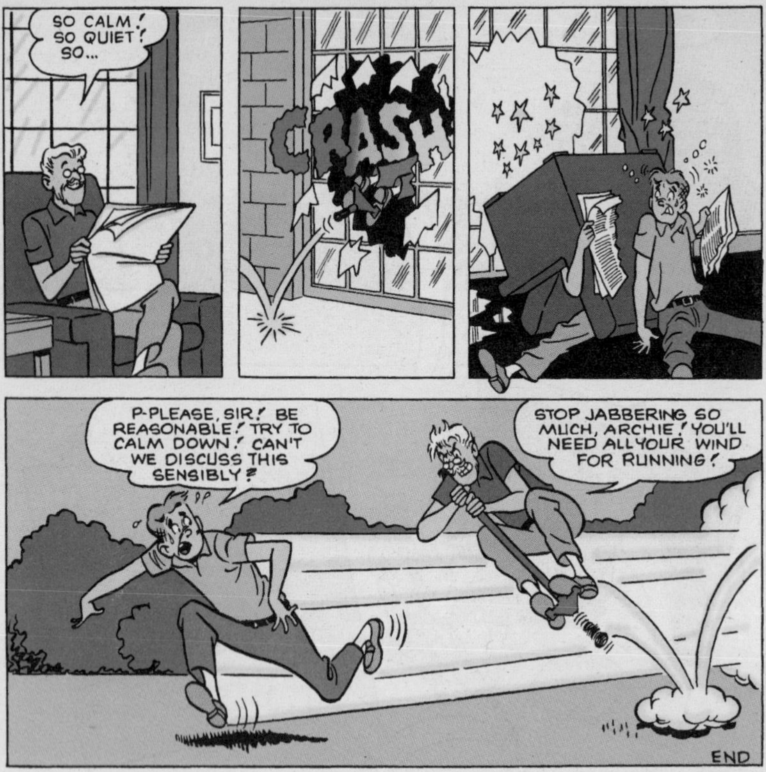
SO CALM! SO QUIET! SO...
CRASH
P-PLEASE, SIR! BE REASONABLE! TRY TO CALM DOWN! CAN'T WE DISCUSS THIS SENSIBLY?
STOP JABBERING SO MUCH, ARCHIE! YOU'LL NEED ALL YOUR WIND FOR RUNNING!
END

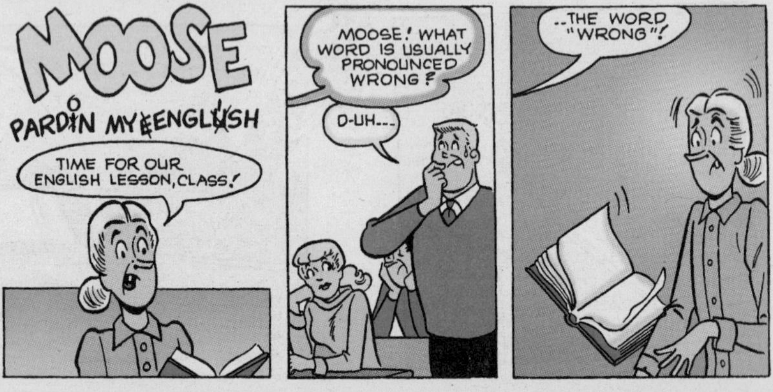
MOOSE
PARDON MY ENGLISH
TIME FOR OUR ENGLISH LESSON, CLASS!
MOOSE! WHAT WORD IS USUALLY PRONOUNCED WRONG?
D-UH...
..THE WORD "WRONG"!

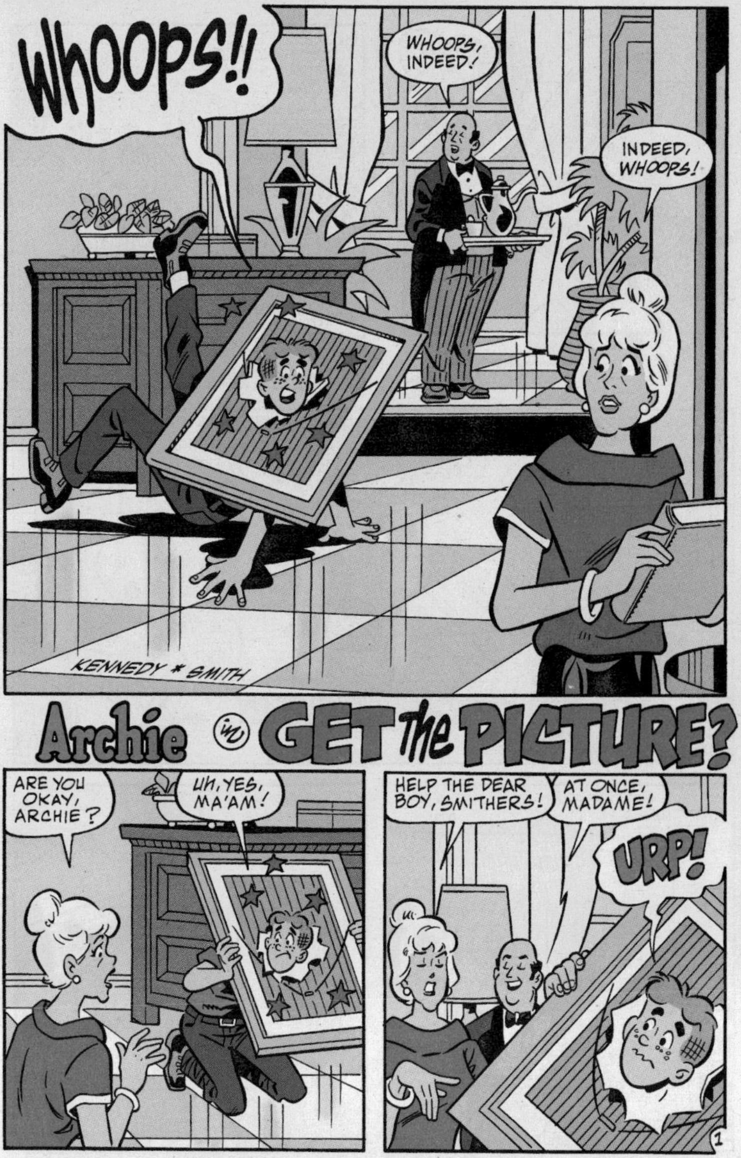
WHOOPS!!
WHOOPS, INDEED!
INDEED, WHOOPS!
KENNEDY * SMITH
Archie in GET the PICTURE?
ARE YOU OKAY, ARCHIE?
UH, YES, MA'AM!
HELP THE DEAR BOY, SMITHERS!
AT ONCE, MADAME!
URP!
1

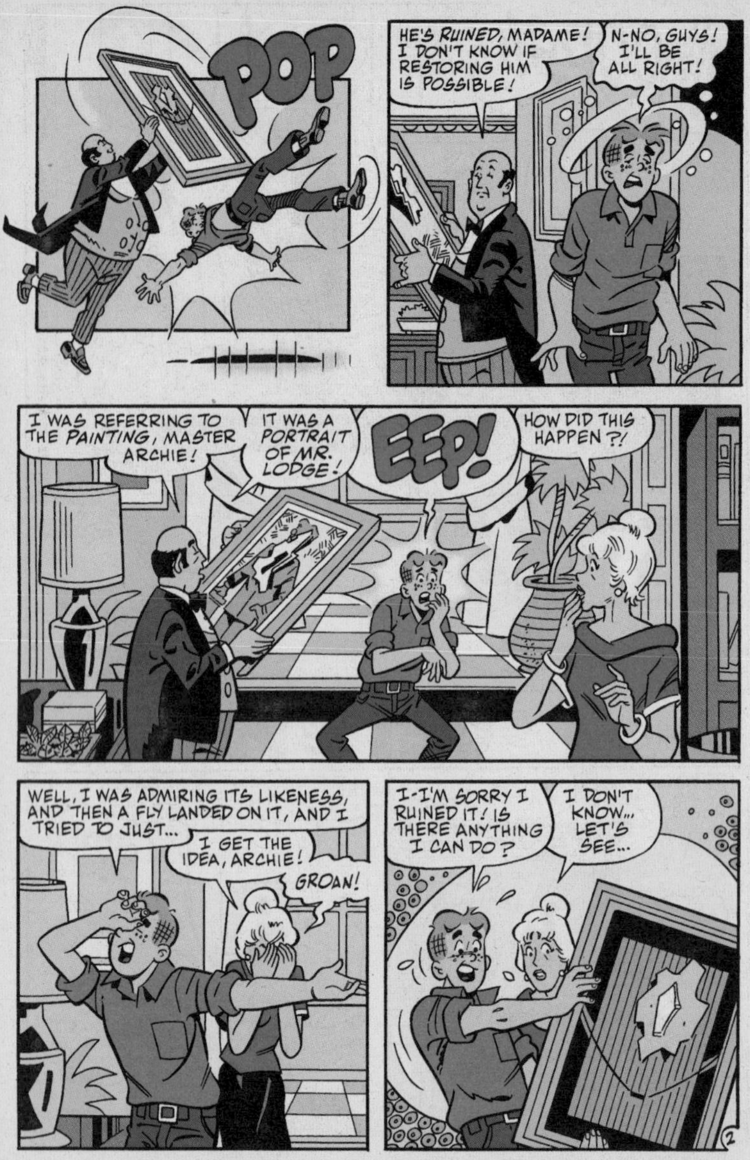
POP
HE'S RUINED, MADAME! I DON'T KNOW IF RESTORING HIM IS POSSIBLE!
N-NO, GUYS! I'LL BE ALL RIGHT!
I WAS REFERRING TO THE PAINTING, MASTER ARCHIE!
IT WAS A PORTRAIT OF MR. LODGE!
EEP!
HOW DID THIS HAPPEN?!
WELL, I WAS ADMIRING ITS LIKENESS, AND THEN A FLY LANDED ON IT, AND I TRIED TO JUST...
I GET THE IDEA, ARCHIE!
GROAN!
I-I'M SORRY I RUINED IT! IS THERE ANYTHING I CAN DO?
I DON'T KNOW... LET'S SEE...
2

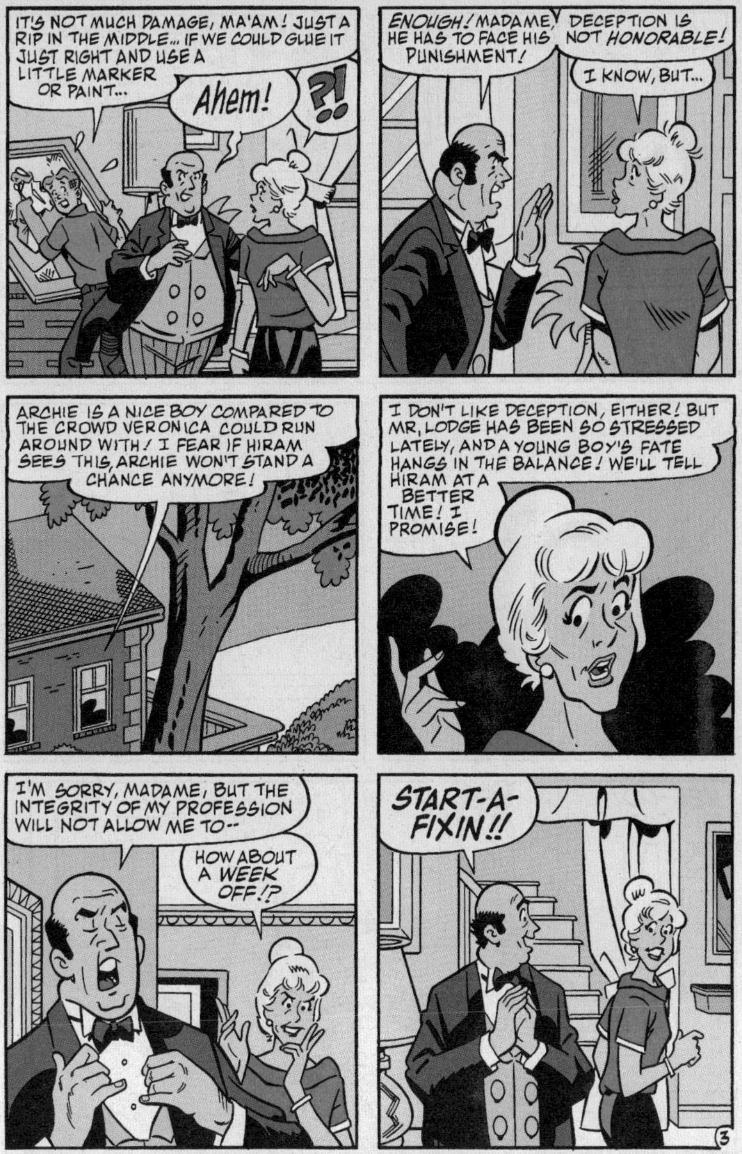

IT'S NOT MUCH DAMAGE, MA'AM! JUST A RIP IN THE MIDDLE... IF WE COULD GLUE IT JUST RIGHT AND USE A LITTLE MARKER OR PAINT...
Ahem!
?!
ENOUGH! MADAME, HE HAS TO FACE HIS PUNISHMENT!
DECEPTION IS NOT HONORABLE!
I KNOW, BUT...
ARCHIE IS A NICE BOY COMPARED TO THE CROWD VERONICA COULD RUN AROUND WITH! I FEAR IF HIRAM SEES THIS, ARCHIE WON'T STAND A CHANCE ANYMORE!
I DON'T LIKE DECEPTION, EITHER! BUT MR. LODGE HAS BEEN SO STRESSED LATELY, AND A YOUNG BOY'S FATE HANGS IN THE BALANCE! WE'LL TELL HIRAM AT A BETTER TIME! I PROMISE!
I'M SORRY, MADAME, BUT THE INTEGRITY OF MY PROFESSION WILL NOT ALLOW ME TO--
HOW ABOUT A WEEK OFF!?
START-A-FIXIN!!
3

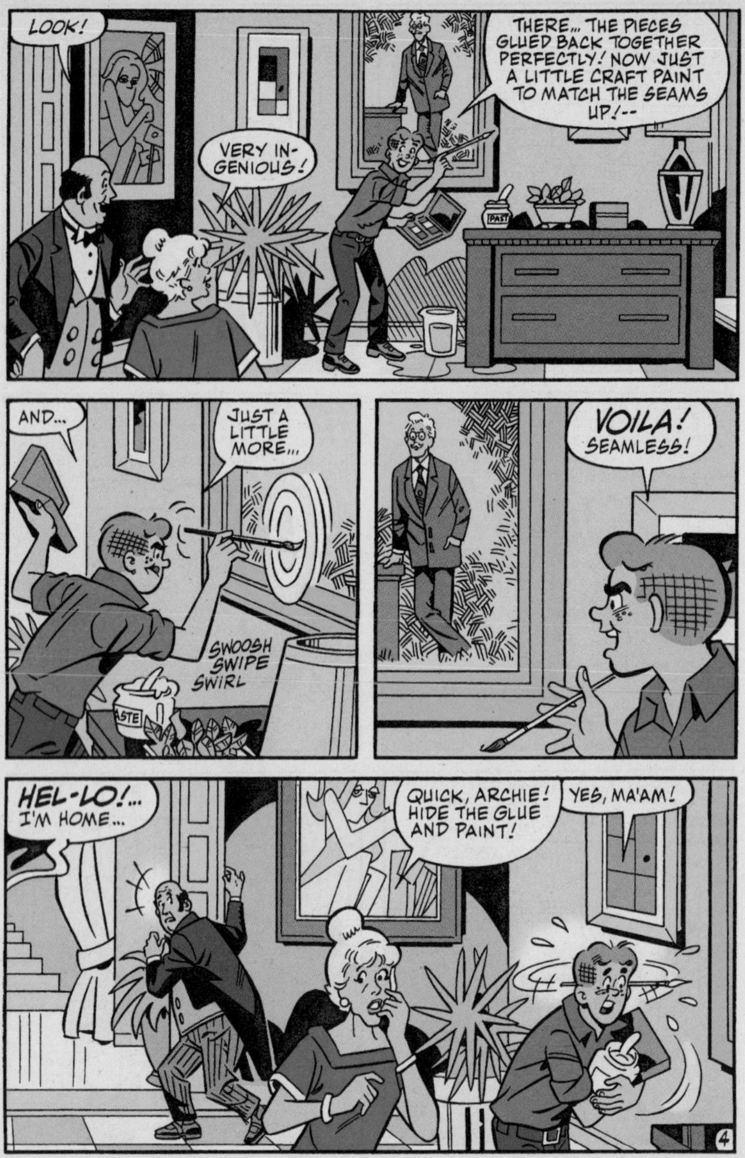
LOOK!
THERE... THE PIECES GLUED BACK TOGETHER PERFECTLY! NOW JUST A LITTLE CRAFT PAINT TO MATCH THE SEAMS UP!--
VERY IN-GENIOUS!
PASTE
AND...
JUST A LITTLE MORE...
SWOOSH SWIPE SWIRL
ASTE
VOILA! SEAMLESS!
HEL-LO!... I'M HOME...
QUICK, ARCHIE! HIDE THE GLUE AND PAINT!
YES, MA'AM!
4

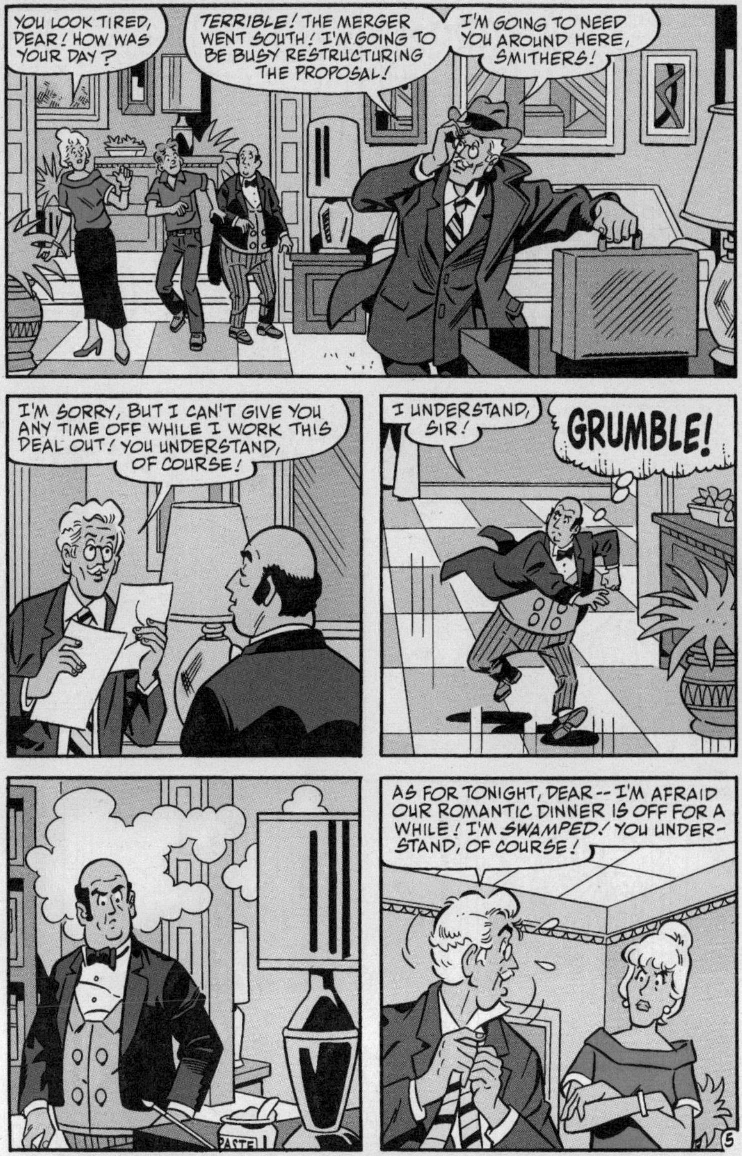
YOU LOOK TIRED, DEAR! HOW WAS YOUR DAY?
TERRIBLE! THE MERGER WENT SOUTH! I'M GOING TO BE BUSY RESTRUCTURING THE PROPOSAL!
I'M GOING TO NEED YOU AROUND HERE, SMITHERS!
I'M SORRY, BUT I CAN'T GIVE YOU ANY TIME OFF WHILE I WORK THIS DEAL OUT! YOU UNDERSTAND, OF COURSE!
I UNDERSTAND, SIR!
GRUMBLE!
AS FOR TONIGHT, DEAR -- I'M AFRAID OUR ROMANTIC DINNER IS OFF FOR A WHILE! I'M SWAMPED! YOU UNDERSTAND, OF COURSE!
PASTE
5

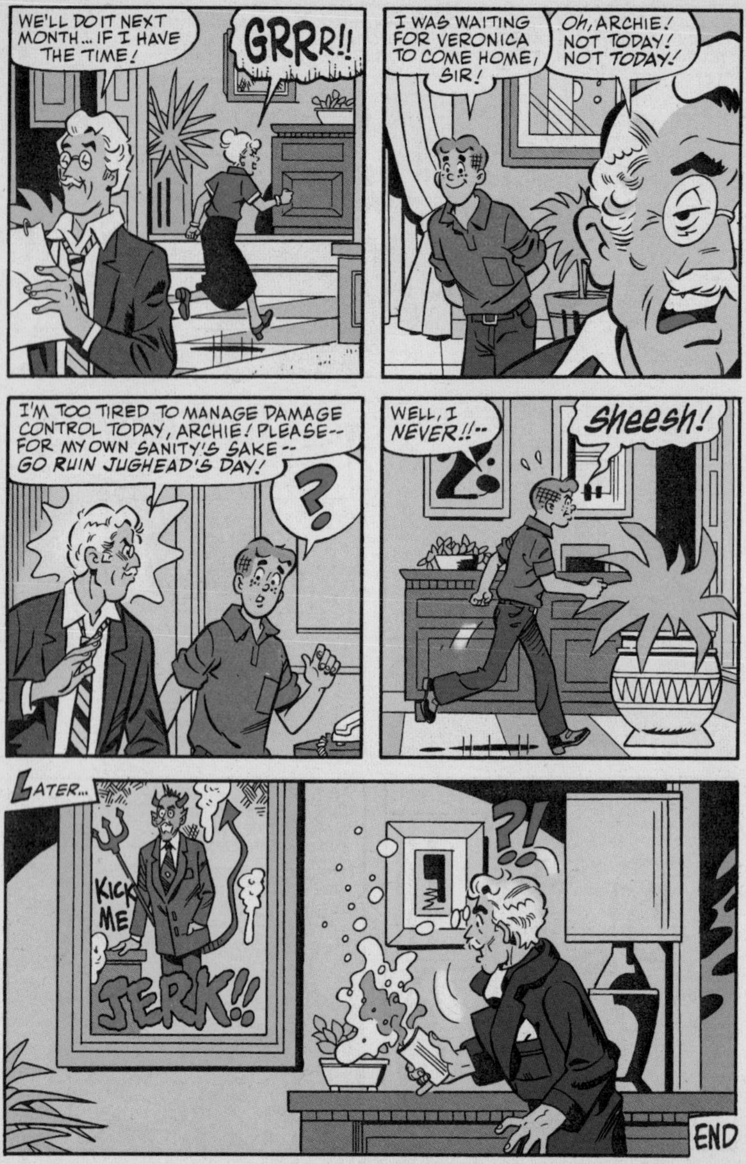
WE'LL DO IT NEXT MONTH... IF I HAVE THE TIME!
GRRR!!
I WAS WAITING FOR VERONICA TO COME HOME, SIR!
Oh, ARCHIE! NOT TODAY! NOT TODAY!
I'M TOO TIRED TO MANAGE DAMAGE CONTROL TODAY, ARCHIE! PLEASE-- FOR MY OWN SANITY'S SAKE -- GO RUIN JUGHEAD'S DAY!
?
WELL, I NEVER!!--
Sheesh!
LATER...
KICK ME
JERK!!
?!
END

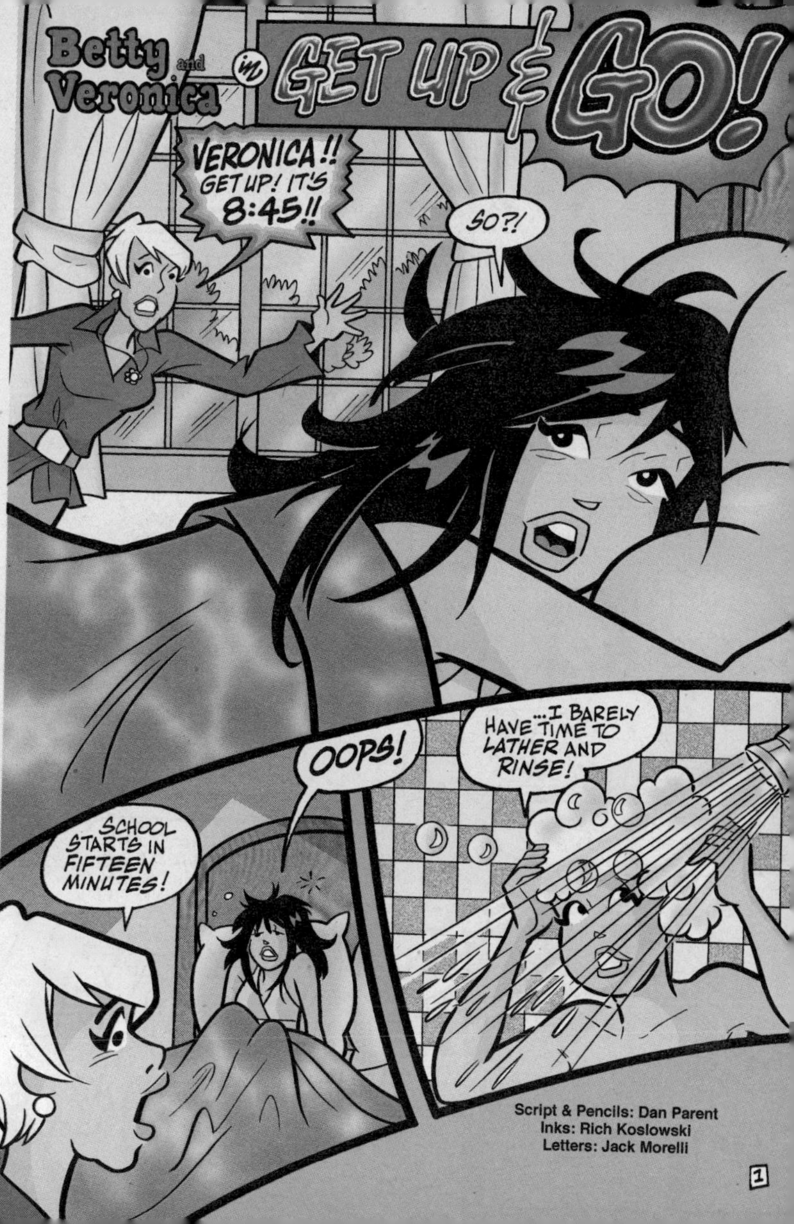
Betty and Veronica in GET UP & GO!
VERONICA!! GET UP! IT'S 8:45!!
SO?!
SCHOOL STARTS IN FIFTEEN MINUTES!
OOPS!
HAVE...I BARELY HAVE TIME TO LATHER AND RINSE!
Script & Pencils: Dan Parent
Inks: Rich Koslowski
Letters: Jack Morelli

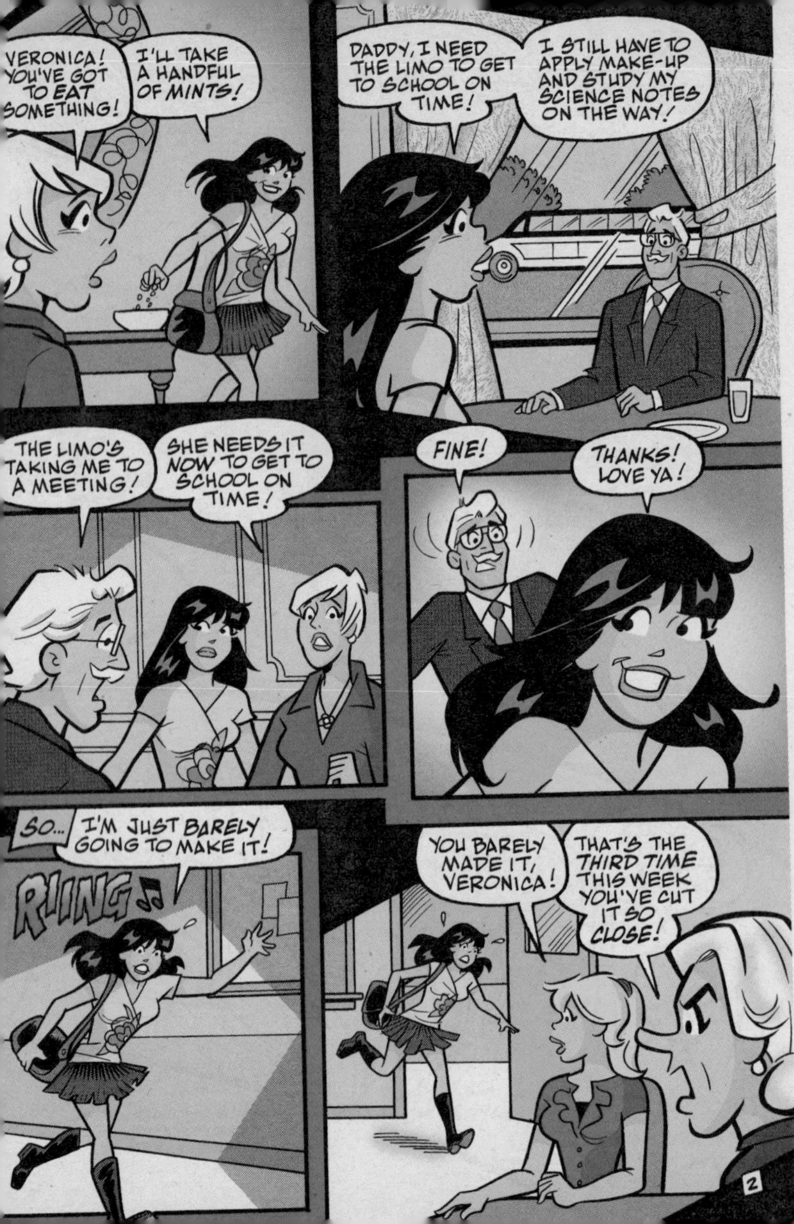
VERONICA! YOU'VE GOT TO EAT SOMETHING!
I'LL TAKE A HANDFUL OF MINTS!
DADDY, I NEED THE LIMO TO GET TO SCHOOL ON TIME!
I STILL HAVE TO APPLY MAKE-UP AND STUDY MY SCIENCE NOTES ON THE WAY!
THE LIMO'S TAKING ME TO A MEETING!
SHE NEEDS IT NOW TO GET TO SCHOOL ON TIME!
FINE!
THANKS! LOVE YA!
SO...
I'M JUST BARELY GOING TO MAKE IT!
RIING
YOU BARELY MADE IT, VERONICA!
THAT'S THE THIRD TIME THIS WEEK YOU'VE CUT IT SO CLOSE!
2

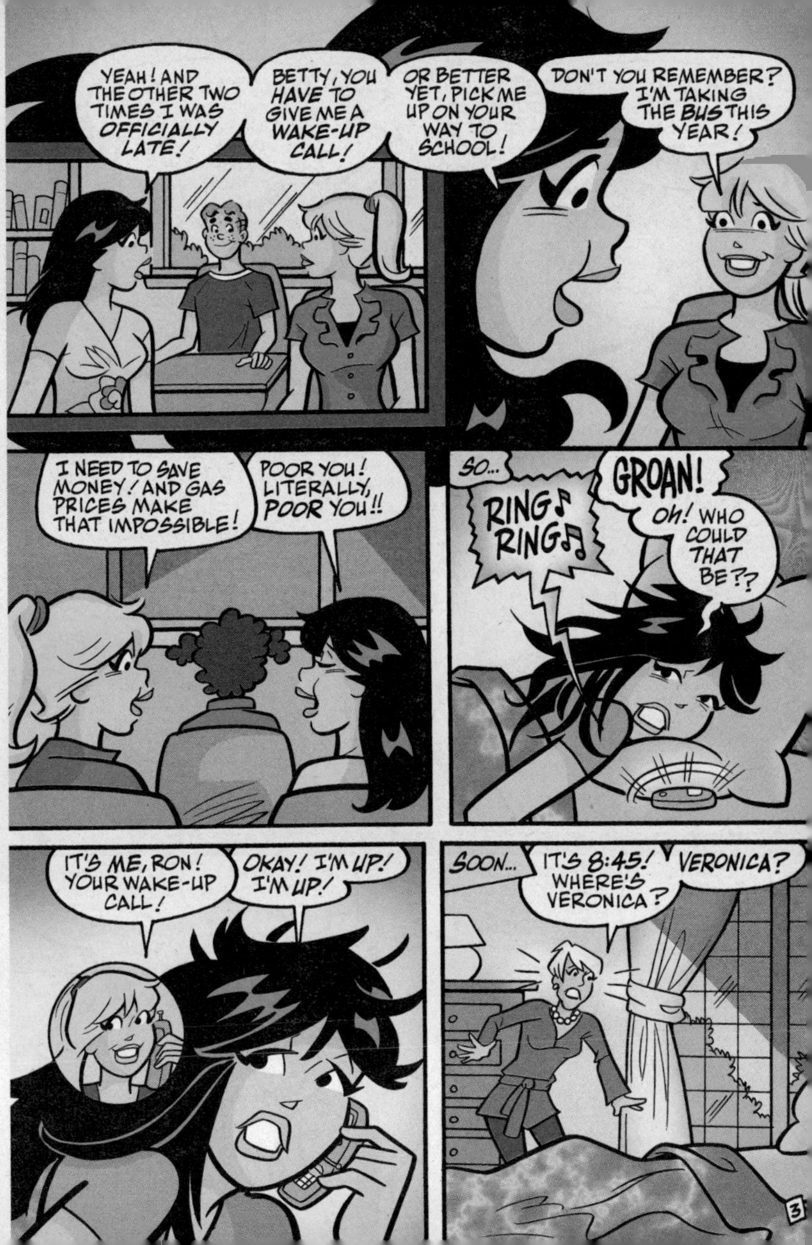
YEAH! AND THE OTHER TWO TIMES I WAS OFFICIALLY LATE!
BETTY, YOU HAVE TO GIVE ME A WAKE-UP CALL!
OR BETTER YET, PICK ME UP ON YOUR WAY TO SCHOOL!
DON'T YOU REMEMBER? I'M TAKING THE BUS THIS YEAR!
I NEED TO SAVE MONEY! AND GAS PRICES MAKE THAT IMPOSSIBLE!
POOR YOU! LITERALLY, POOR YOU!!
SO...
RING RING
GROAN!
Oh! WHO COULD THAT BE??
IT'S ME, RON! YOUR WAKE-UP CALL!
OKAY! I'M UP! I'M UP!
SOON...
IT'S 8:45! WHERE'S VERONICA?
VERONICA?
3

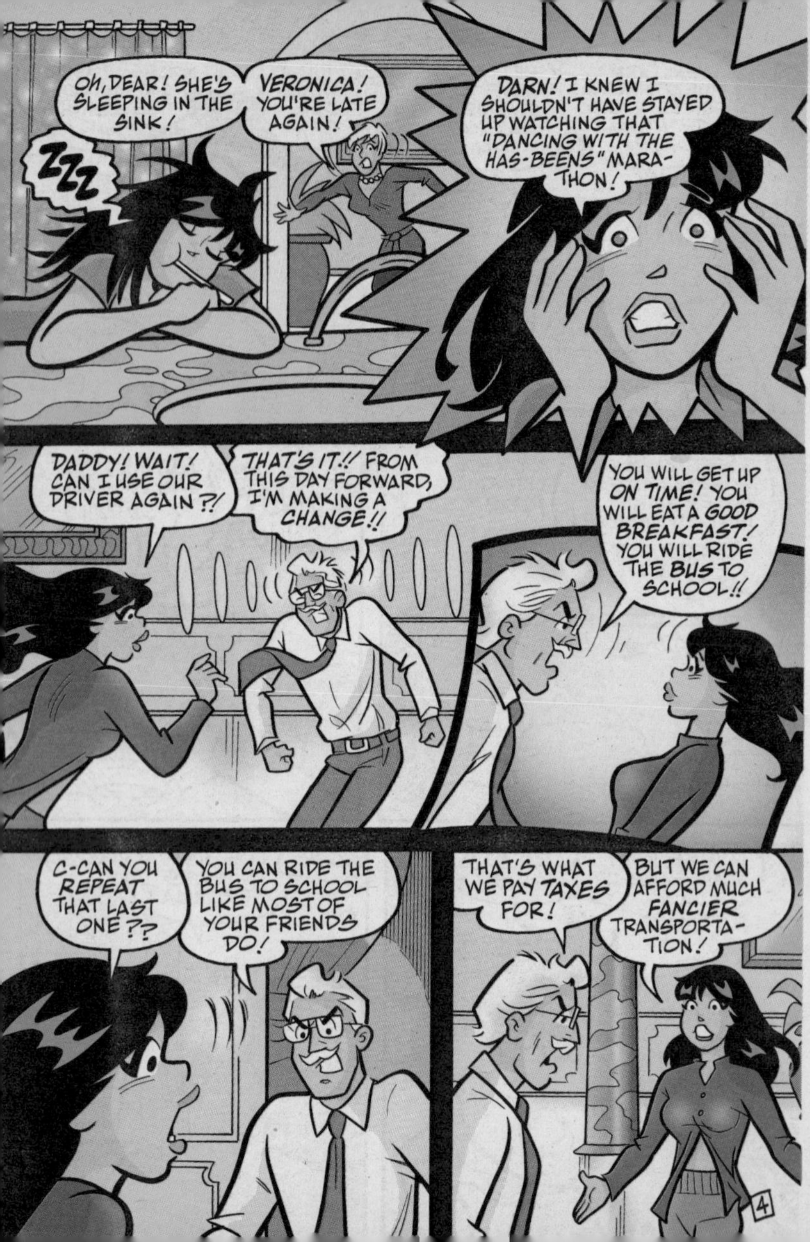

ZZZ
OH, DEAR! SHE'S SLEEPING IN THE SINK!
VERONICA! YOU'RE LATE AGAIN!
DARN! I KNEW I SHOULDN'T HAVE STAYED UP WATCHING THAT "DANCING WITH THE HAS-BEENS" MARATHON!
DADDY! WAIT! CAN I USE OUR DRIVER AGAIN?!
THAT'S IT!! FROM THIS DAY FORWARD, I'M MAKING A CHANGE!!
YOU WILL GET UP ON TIME! YOU WILL EAT A GOOD BREAKFAST! YOU WILL RIDE THE BUS TO SCHOOL!!
C-CAN YOU REPEAT THAT LAST ONE??
YOU CAN RIDE THE BUS TO SCHOOL LIKE MOST OF YOUR FRIENDS DO!
THAT'S WHAT WE PAY TAXES FOR!
BUT WE CAN AFFORD MUCH FANCIER TRANSPORTATION!
4

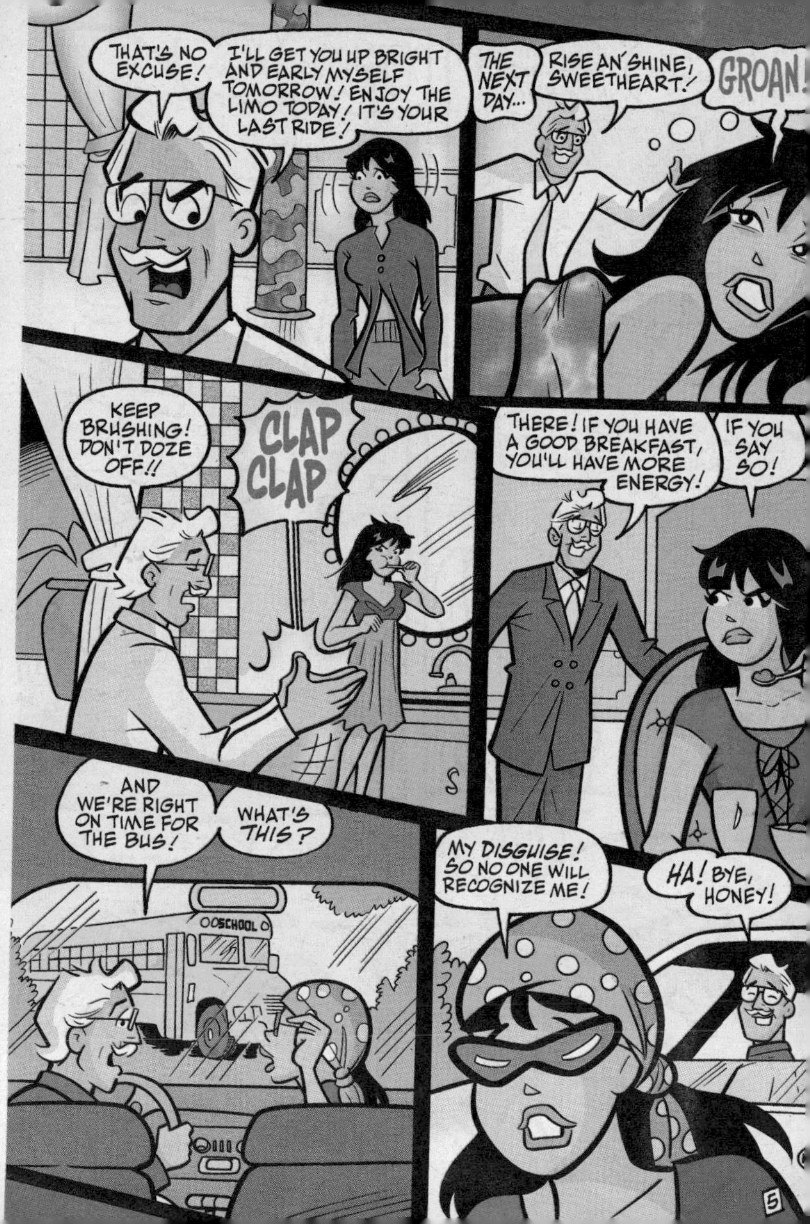
THAT'S NO EXCUSE!
I'LL GET YOU UP BRIGHT AND EARLY MYSELF TOMORROW! ENJOY THE LIMO TODAY! IT'S YOUR LAST RIDE!
THE NEXT DAY...
RISE AN' SHINE, SWEETHEART!
GROAN!
KEEP BRUSHING! DON'T DOZE OFF!!
CLAP CLAP
THERE! IF YOU HAVE A GOOD BREAKFAST, YOU'LL HAVE MORE ENERGY!
IF YOU SAY SO!
AND WE'RE RIGHT ON TIME FOR THE BUS!
WHAT'S THIS?
SCHOOL
MY DISGUISE! SO NO ONE WILL RECOGNIZE ME!
HA! BYE, HONEY!

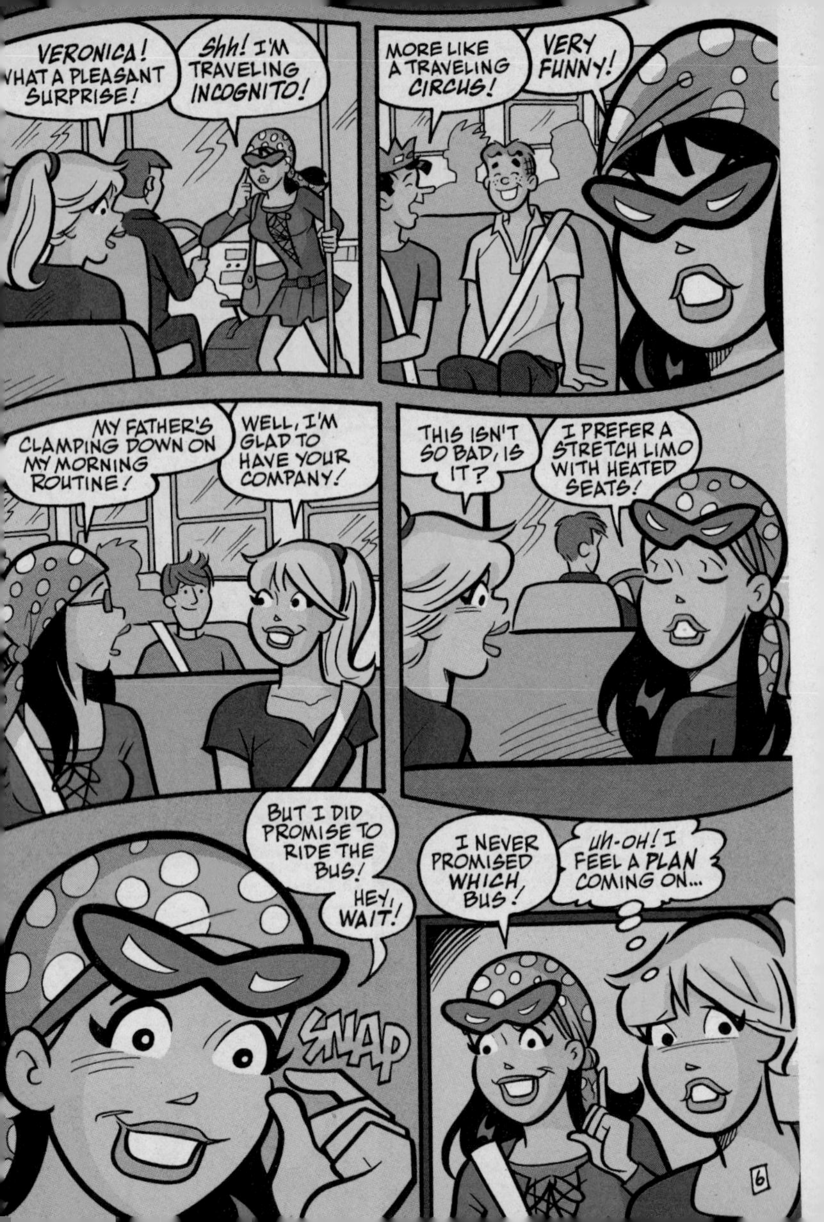
VERONICA! WHAT A PLEASANT SURPRISE!
Shh! I'M TRAVELING INCOGNITO!
MORE LIKE A TRAVELING CIRCUS!
VERY FUNNY!
MY FATHER'S CLAMPING DOWN ON MY MORNING ROUTINE!
WELL, I'M GLAD TO HAVE YOUR COMPANY!
THIS ISN'T SO BAD, IS IT?
I PREFER A STRETCH LIMO WITH HEATED SEATS!
BUT I DID PROMISE TO RIDE THE BUS!
HEY, WAIT!
SNAP
I NEVER PROMISED WHICH BUS!
UH-OH! I FEEL A PLAN COMING ON...
6

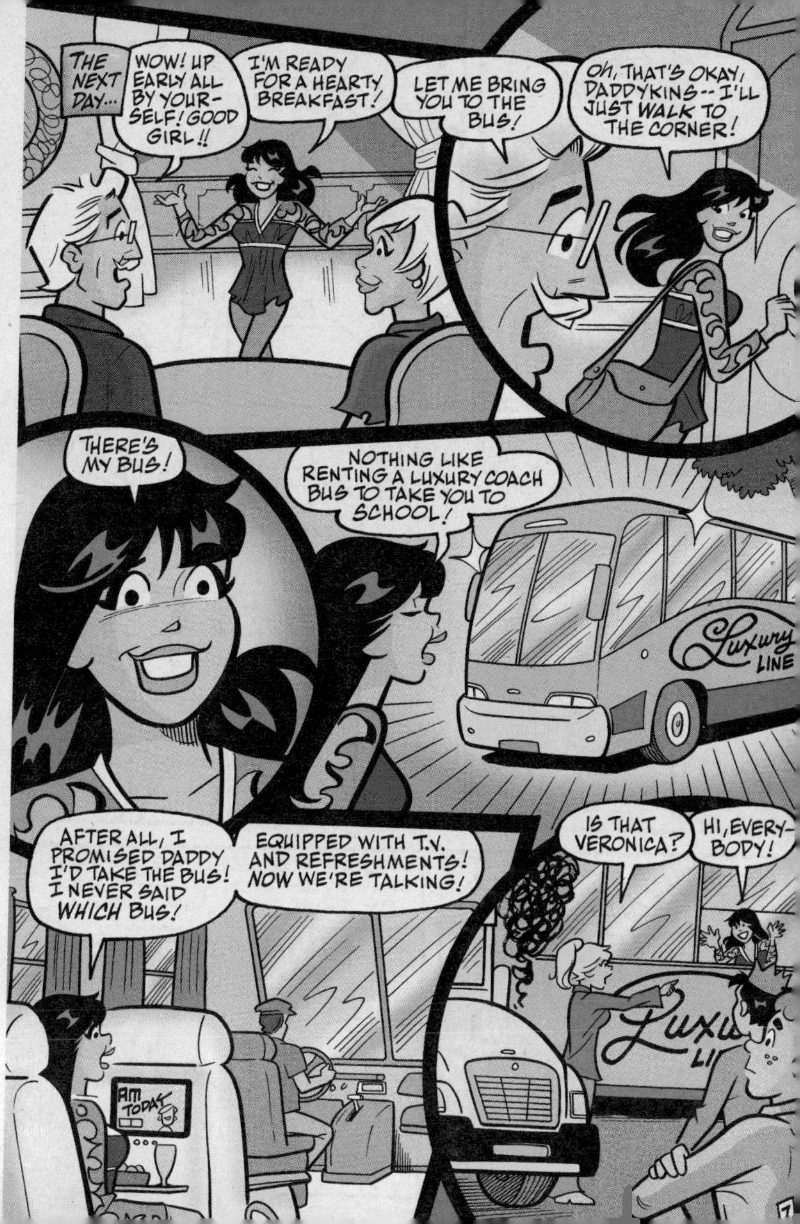

THE NEXT DAY...
WOW! UP EARLY ALL BY YOURSELF! GOOD GIRL!!
I'M READY FOR A HEARTY BREAKFAST!
LET ME BRING YOU TO THE BUS!
OH, THAT'S OKAY, DADDYKINS-- I'LL JUST WALK TO THE CORNER!
THERE'S MY BUS!
NOTHING LIKE RENTING A LUXURY COACH BUS TO TAKE YOU TO SCHOOL!
Luxury LINE
AFTER ALL, I PROMISED DADDY I'D TAKE THE BUS! I NEVER SAID WHICH BUS!
EQUIPPED WITH T.V. AND REFRESHMENTS! NOW WE'RE TALKING!
AM TODAY
IS THAT VERONICA?
HI, EVERYBODY!

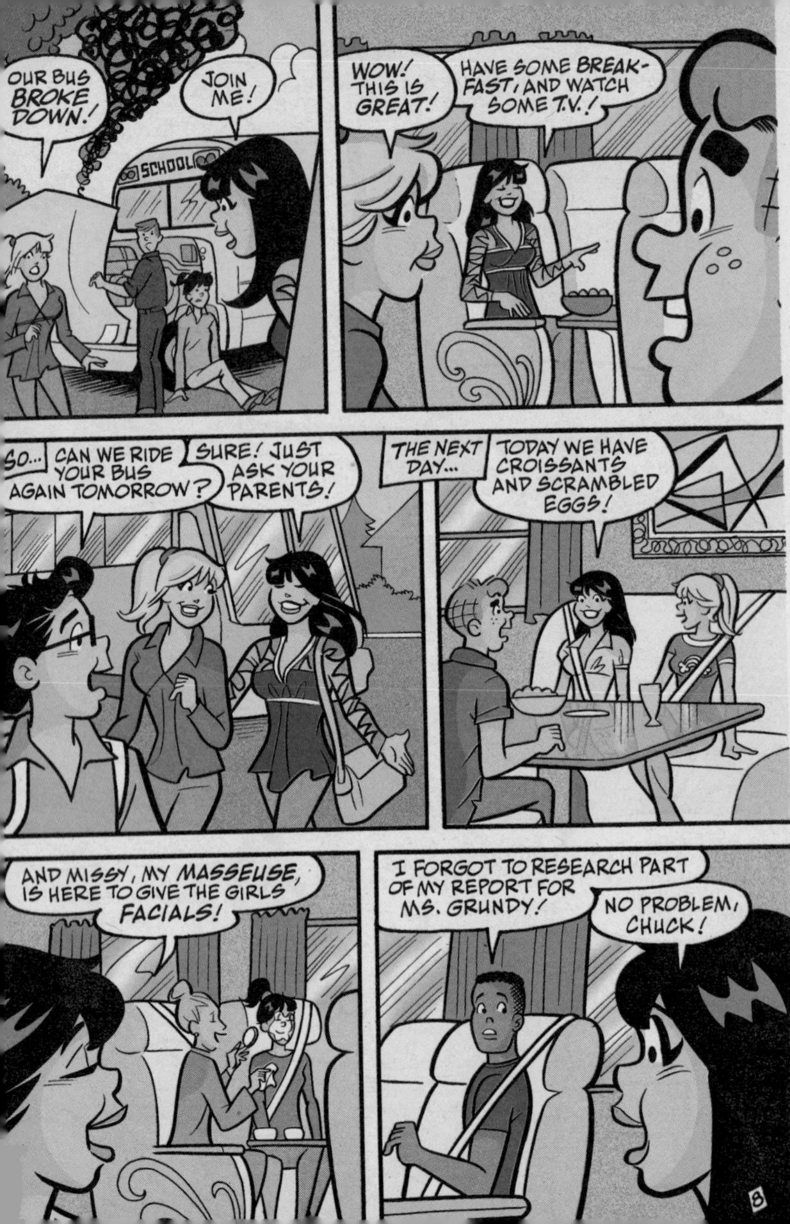
OUR BUS BROKE DOWN!
JOIN ME!
SCHOOL
WOW! THIS IS GREAT!
HAVE SOME BREAK-FAST, AND WATCH SOME T.V.!
SO... CAN WE RIDE YOUR BUS AGAIN TOMORROW?
SURE! JUST ASK YOUR PARENTS!
THE NEXT DAY...
TODAY WE HAVE CROISSANTS AND SCRAMBLED EGGS!
AND MISSY, MY MASSEUSE, IS HERE TO GIVE THE GIRLS FACIALS!
I FORGOT TO RESEARCH PART OF MY REPORT FOR MS. GRUNDY!
NO PROBLEM, CHUCK!
8

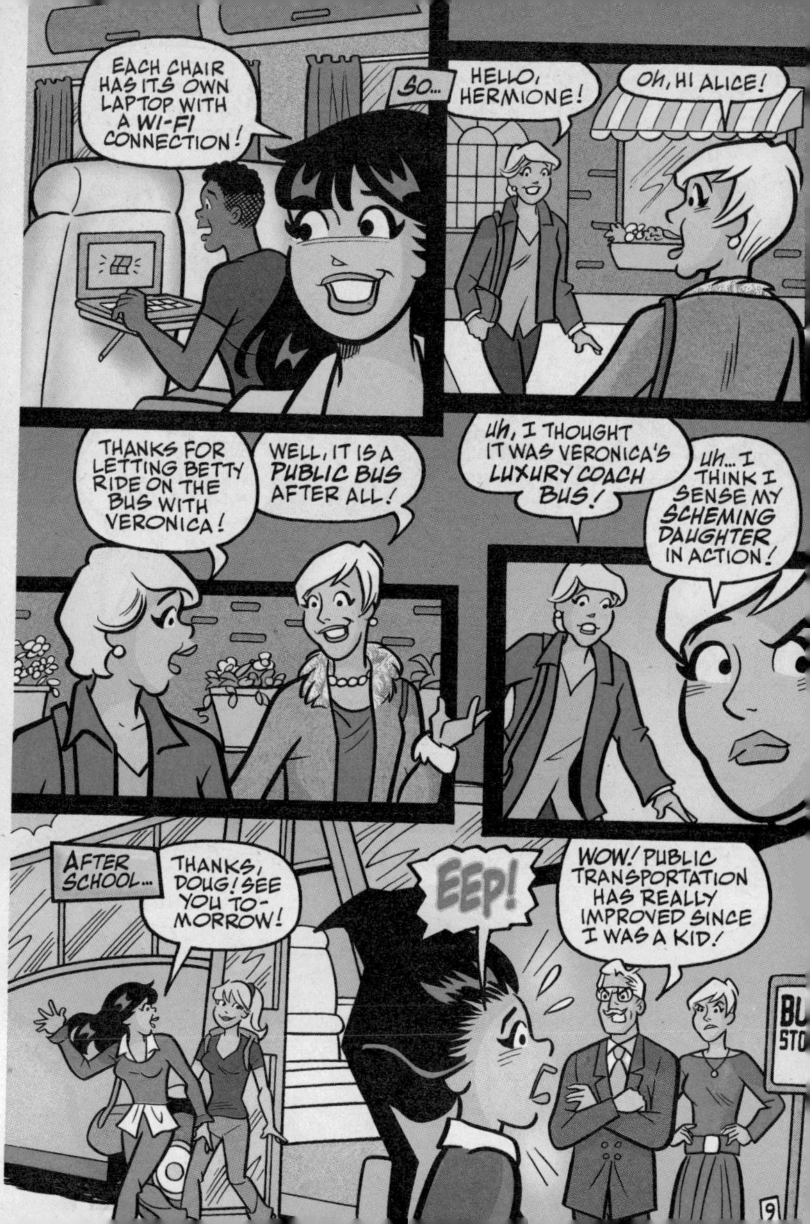
EACH CHAIR HAS ITS OWN LAPTOP WITH A WI-FI CONNECTION!
SO...
HELLO, HERMIONE!
OH, HI ALICE!
THANKS FOR LETTING BETTY RIDE ON THE BUS WITH VERONICA!
WELL, IT IS A PUBLIC BUS AFTER ALL!
UH, I THOUGHT IT WAS VERONICA'S LUXURY COACH BUS!
UH... I THINK I SENSE MY SCHEMING DAUGHTER IN ACTION!
AFTER SCHOOL...
THANKS, DOUG! SEE YOU TO-MORROW!
EEP!
WOW! PUBLIC TRANSPORTATION HAS REALLY IMPROVED SINCE I WAS A KID!
BU
STO

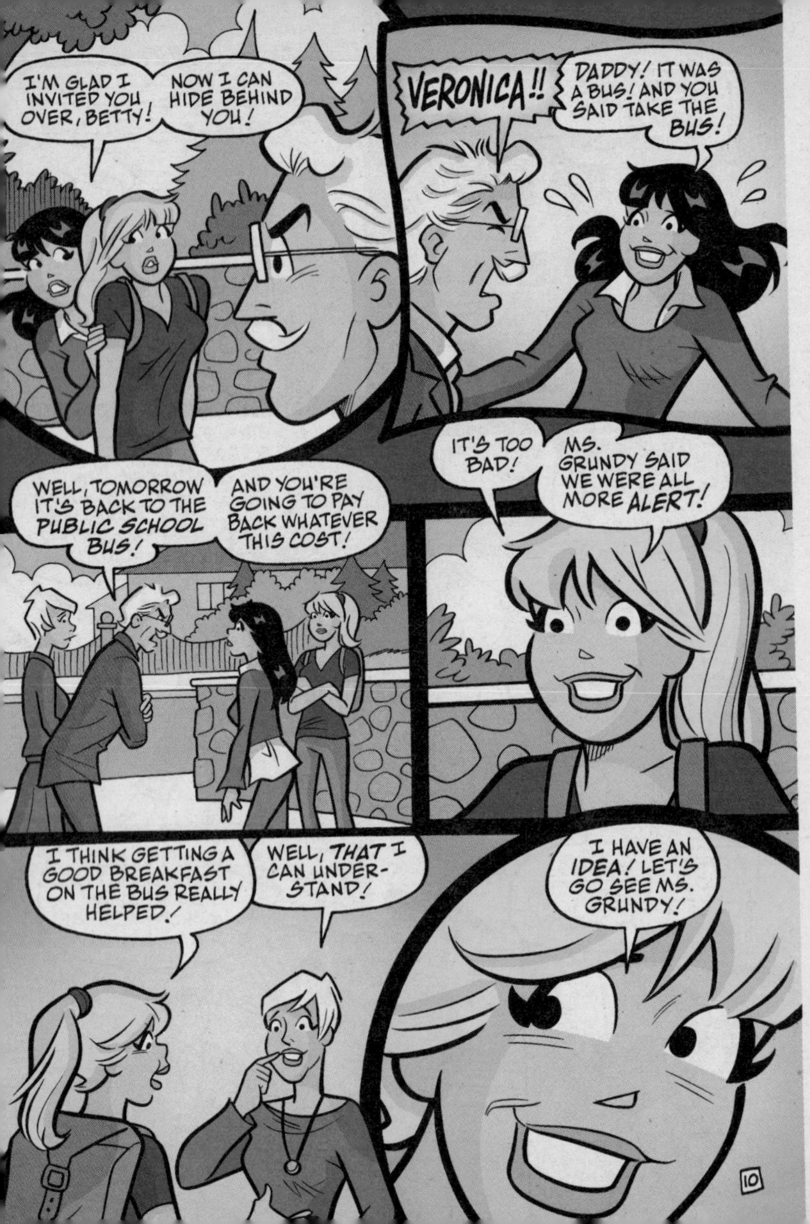
I'M GLAD I INVITED YOU OVER, BETTY!
NOW I CAN HIDE BEHIND YOU!
VERONICA!!
DADDY! IT WAS A BUS! AND YOU SAID TAKE THE BUS!
WELL, TOMORROW IT'S BACK TO THE PUBLIC SCHOOL BUS!
AND YOU'RE GOING TO PAY BACK WHATEVER THIS COST!
IT'S TOO BAD!
MS. GRUNDY SAID WE WERE ALL MORE ALERT!
I THINK GETTING A GOOD BREAKFAST ON THE BUS REALLY HELPED!
WELL, THAT I CAN UNDER-STAND!
I HAVE AN IDEA! LET'S GO SEE MS. GRUNDY!
10

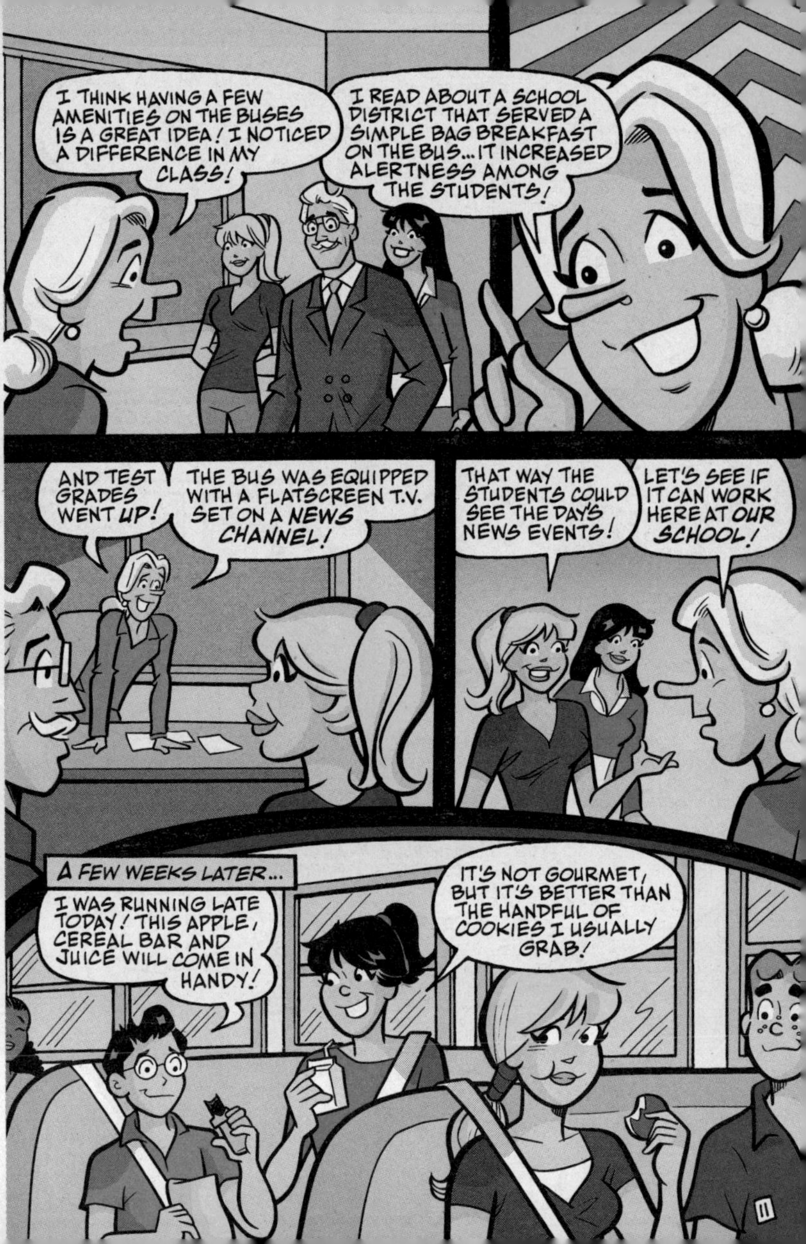
I THINK HAVING A FEW AMENITIES ON THE BUSES IS A GREAT IDEA! I NOTICED A DIFFERENCE IN MY CLASS!
I READ ABOUT A SCHOOL DISTRICT THAT SERVED A SIMPLE BAG BREAKFAST ON THE BUS... IT INCREASED ALERTNESS AMONG THE STUDENTS!
AND TEST GRADES WENT UP!
THE BUS WAS EQUIPPED WITH A FLATSCREEN T.V. SET ON A NEWS CHANNEL!
THAT WAY THE STUDENTS COULD SEE THE DAY'S NEWS EVENTS!
LET'S SEE IF IT CAN WORK HERE AT OUR SCHOOL!
A FEW WEEKS LATER...
I WAS RUNNING LATE TODAY! THIS APPLE, CEREAL BAR AND JUICE WILL COME IN HANDY!
IT'S NOT GOURMET, BUT IT'S BETTER THAN THE HANDFUL OF COOKIES I USUALLY GRAB!
11

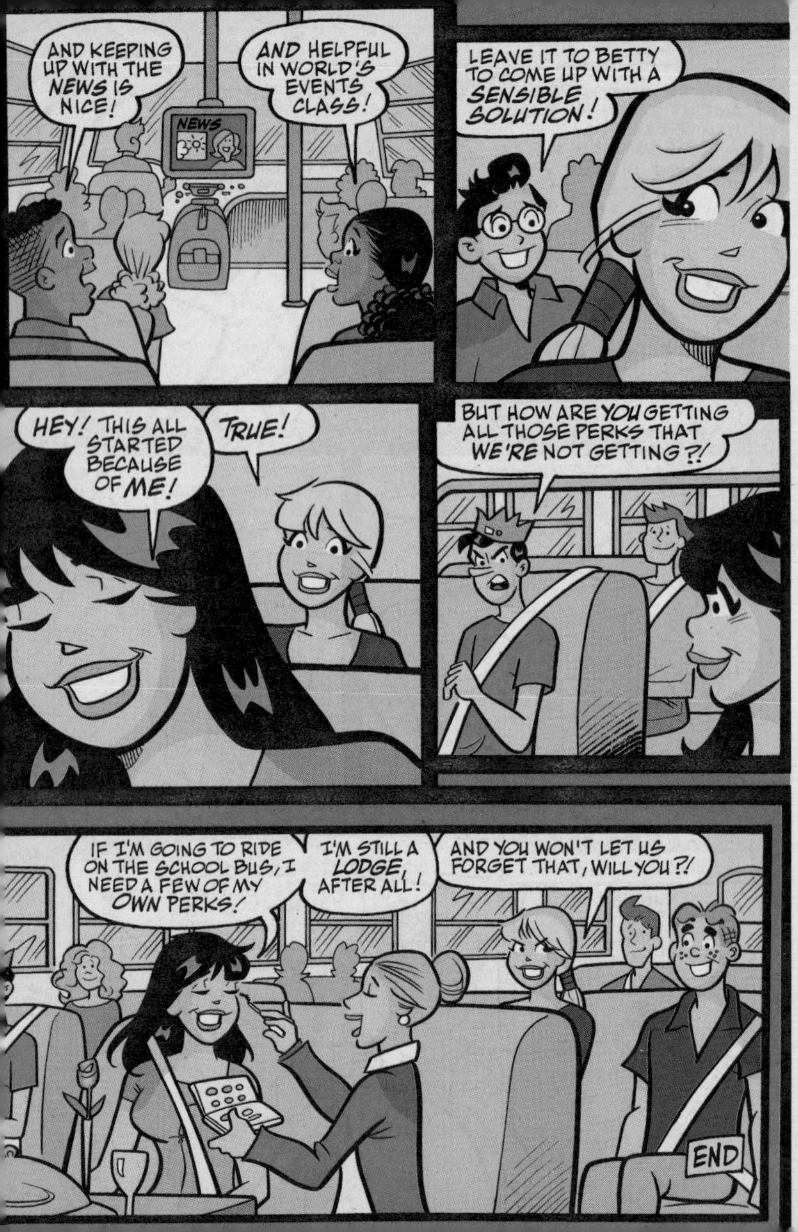

AND KEEPING UP WITH THE NEWS IS NICE!
AND HELPFUL IN WORLD'S EVENTS CLASS!
NEWS
LEAVE IT TO BETTY TO COME UP WITH A SENSIBLE SOLUTION!
HEY! THIS ALL STARTED BECAUSE OF ME!
TRUE!
BUT HOW ARE YOU GETTING ALL THOSE PERKS THAT WE'RE NOT GETTING?!
IF I'M GOING TO RIDE ON THE SCHOOL BUS, I NEED A FEW OF MY OWN PERKS!
I'M STILL A LODGE, AFTER ALL!
AND YOU WON'T LET US FORGET THAT, WILL YOU?!
END

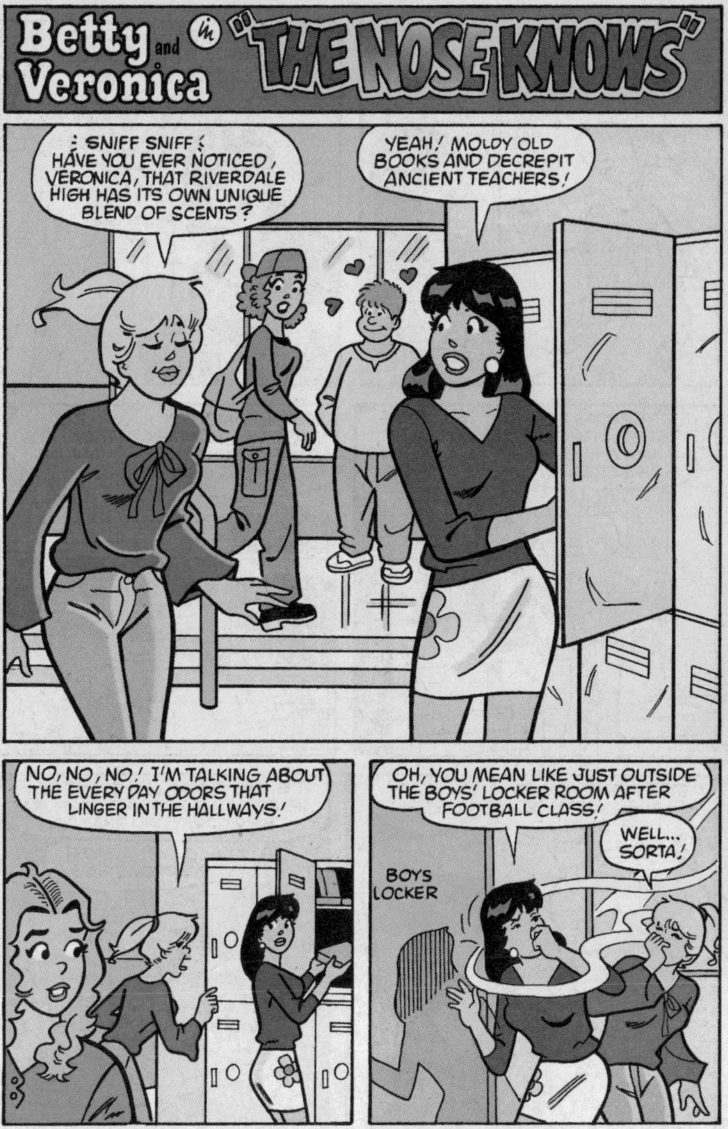
Betty and Veronica
in
"THE NOSE KNOWS"
: SNIFF SNIFF : HAVE YOU EVER NOTICED, VERONICA, THAT RIVERDALE HIGH HAS ITS OWN UNIQUE BLEND OF SCENTS?
YEAH! MOLDY OLD BOOKS AND DECREPIT ANCIENT TEACHERS!
NO, NO, NO! I'M TALKING ABOUT THE EVERY DAY ODORS THAT LINGER IN THE HALLWAYS!
OH, YOU MEAN LIKE JUST OUTSIDE THE BOYS' LOCKER ROOM AFTER FOOTBALL CLASS!
WELL... SORTA!
BOYS LOCKER

SCRIPT: KATHLEEN WEBB PENCILS: JEFF SHULTZ INKING: HENRY SCARPELLI LETTERING: BILL YOSHIDA

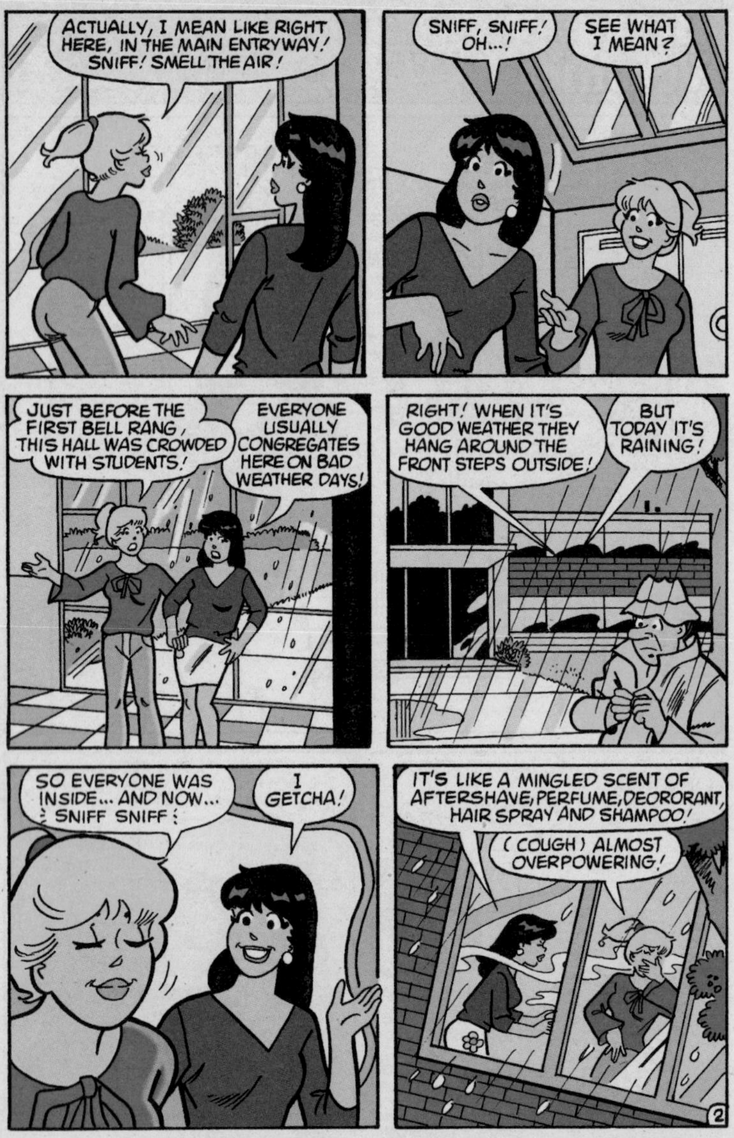
ACTUALLY, I MEAN LIKE RIGHT HERE, IN THE MAIN ENTRYWAY! SNIFF! SMELL THE AIR!
SNIFF, SNIFF! OH...!
SEE WHAT I MEAN?
JUST BEFORE THE FIRST BELL RANG, THIS HALL WAS CROWDED WITH STUDENTS!
EVERYONE USUALLY CONGREGATES HERE ON BAD WEATHER DAYS!
RIGHT! WHEN IT'S GOOD WEATHER THEY HANG AROUND THE FRONT STEPS OUTSIDE!
BUT TODAY IT'S RAINING!
SO EVERYONE WAS INSIDE... AND NOW... SNIFF SNIFF
I GETCHA!
IT'S LIKE A MINGLED SCENT OF AFTERSHAVE, PERFUME, DEORORANT, HAIR SPRAY AND SHAMPOO!
(COUGH) ALMOST OVERPOWERING!

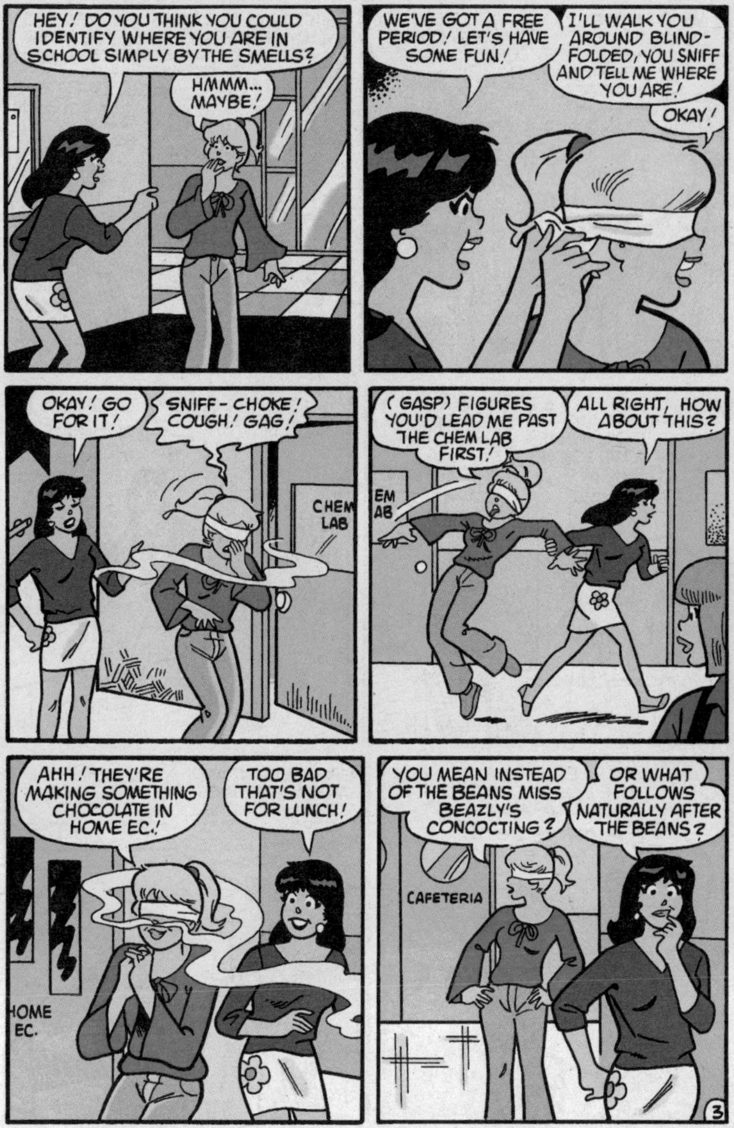
HEY! DO YOU THINK YOU COULD IDENTIFY WHERE YOU ARE IN SCHOOL SIMPLY BY THE SMELLS?
HMMM... MAYBE!
WE'VE GOT A FREE PERIOD! LET'S HAVE SOME FUN!
I'LL WALK YOU AROUND BLIND-FOLDED, YOU SNIFF AND TELL ME WHERE YOU ARE!
OKAY!
OKAY! GO FOR IT!
SNIFF - CHOKE! COUGH! GAG!
CHEM LAB
(GASP) FIGURES YOU'D LEAD ME PAST THE CHEM LAB FIRST!
ALL RIGHT, HOW ABOUT THIS?
EM AB
AHH! THEY'RE MAKING SOMETHING CHOCOLATE IN HOME EC.!
TOO BAD THAT'S NOT FOR LUNCH!
HOME EC.
YOU MEAN INSTEAD OF THE BEANS MISS BEAZLY'S CONCOCTING?
OR WHAT FOLLOWS NATURALLY AFTER THE BEANS?
CAFETERIA
3

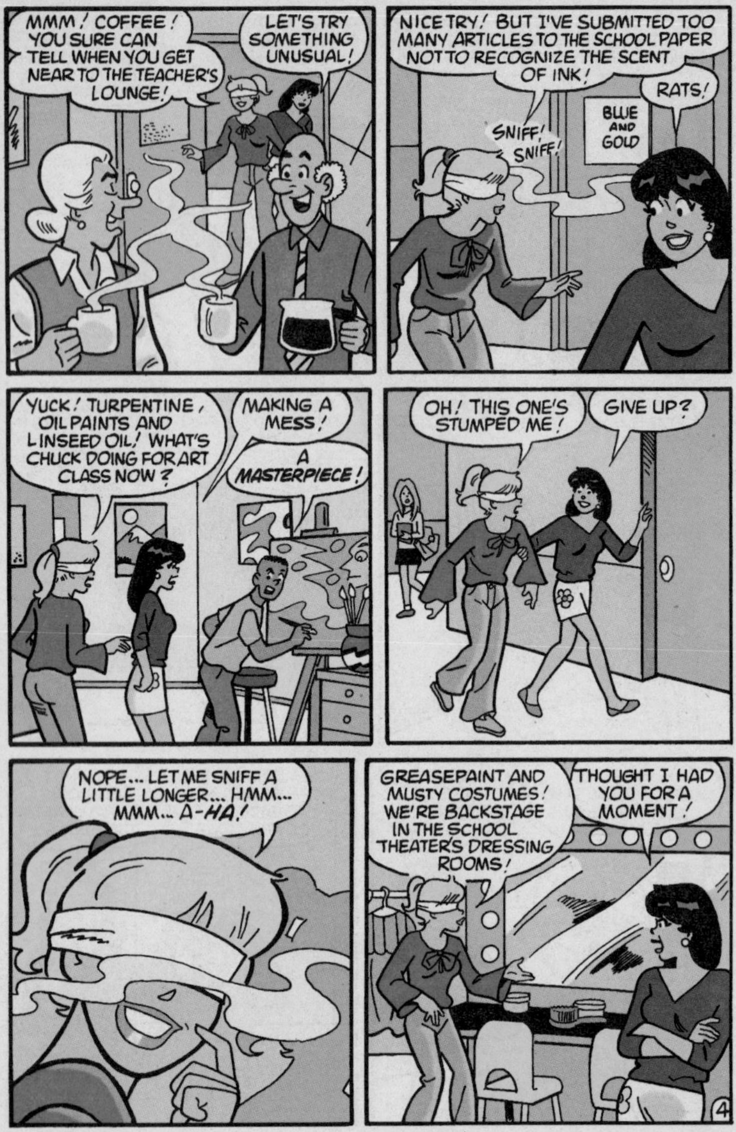
MMM! COFFEE! YOU SURE CAN TELL WHEN YOU GET NEAR TO THE TEACHER'S LOUNGE!
LET'S TRY SOMETHING UNUSUAL!
NICE TRY! BUT I'VE SUBMITTED TOO MANY ARTICLES TO THE SCHOOL PAPER NOT TO RECOGNIZE THE SCENT OF INK!
SNIFF! SNIFF!
BLUE AND GOLD
RATS!
YUCK! TURPENTINE, OIL PAINTS AND LINSEED OIL! WHAT'S CHUCK DOING FOR ART CLASS NOW?
MAKING A MESS!
A MASTERPIECE!
OH! THIS ONE'S STUMPED ME!
GIVE UP?
NOPE... LET ME SNIFF A LITTLE LONGER... HMM... MMM... A-HA!
GREASEPAINT AND MUSTY COSTUMES! WE'RE BACKSTAGE IN THE SCHOOL THEATER'S DRESSING ROOMS!
THOUGHT I HAD YOU FOR A MOMENT!
4

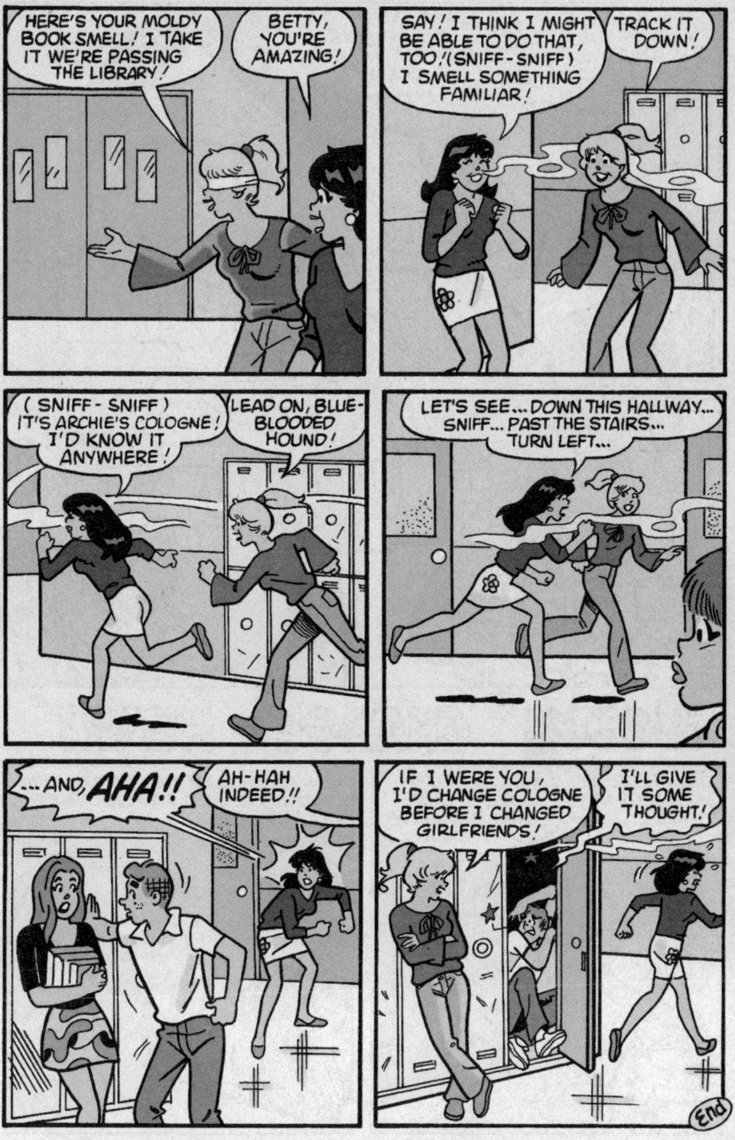
HERE'S YOUR MOLDY BOOK SMELL! I TAKE IT WE'RE PASSING THE LIBRARY!
BETTY, YOU'RE AMAZING!
SAY! I THINK I MIGHT BE ABLE TO DO THAT, TOO! (SNIFF-SNIFF) I SMELL SOMETHING FAMILIAR!
TRACK IT DOWN!
(SNIFF- SNIFF) IT'S ARCHIE'S COLOGNE! I'D KNOW IT ANYWHERE!
LEAD ON, BLUE-BLOODED HOUND!
LET'S SEE... DOWN THIS HALLWAY... SNIFF... PAST THE STAIRS... TURN LEFT...
... AND, AHA!!
AH-HAH INDEED!!
IF I WERE YOU, I'D CHANGE COLOGNE BEFORE I CHANGED GIRLFRIENDS!
I'LL GIVE IT SOME THOUGHT!
End

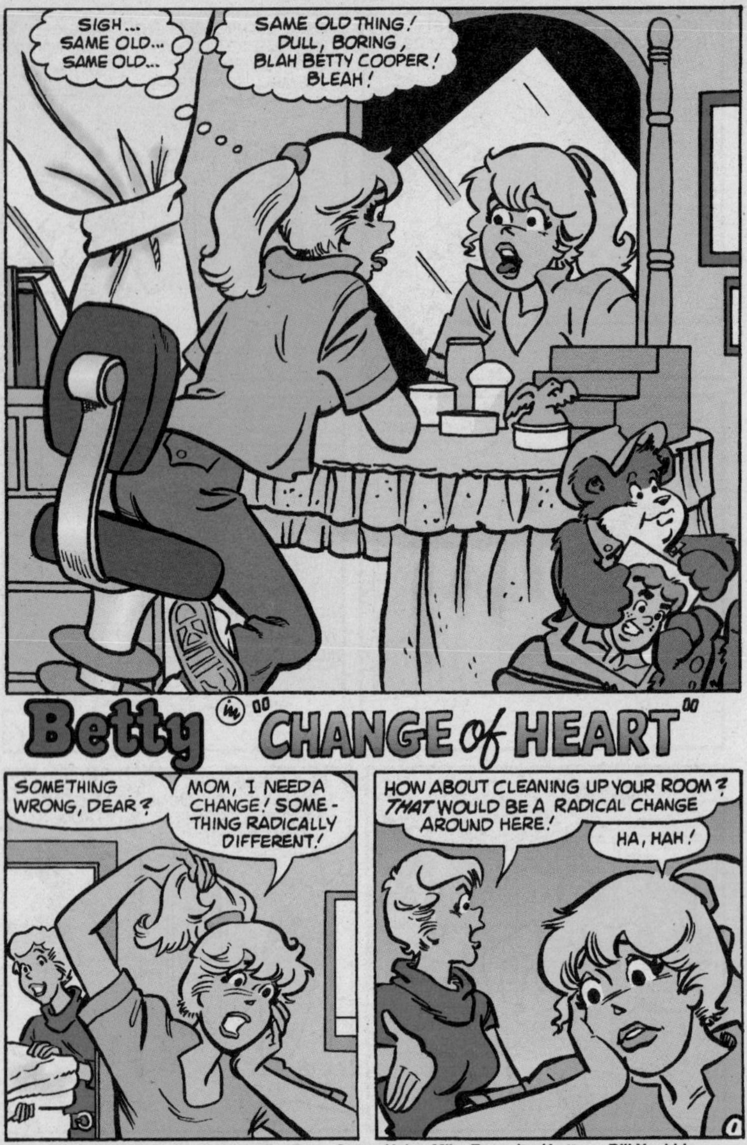
SIGH... SAME OLD... SAME OLD...
SAME OLD THING! DULL, BORING, BLAH BETTY COOPER! BLEAH!
Betty in "CHANGE of HEART"
SOMETHING WRONG, DEAR?
MOM, I NEED A CHANGE! SOME-THING RADICALLY DIFFERENT!
HOW ABOUT CLEANING UP YOUR ROOM? THAT WOULD BE A RADICAL CHANGE AROUND HERE!
HA, HAH!
1

Script: Kathleen Webb / Pencils: Doug Crane / Inks: Mike Esposito / Letters: Bill Yoshida

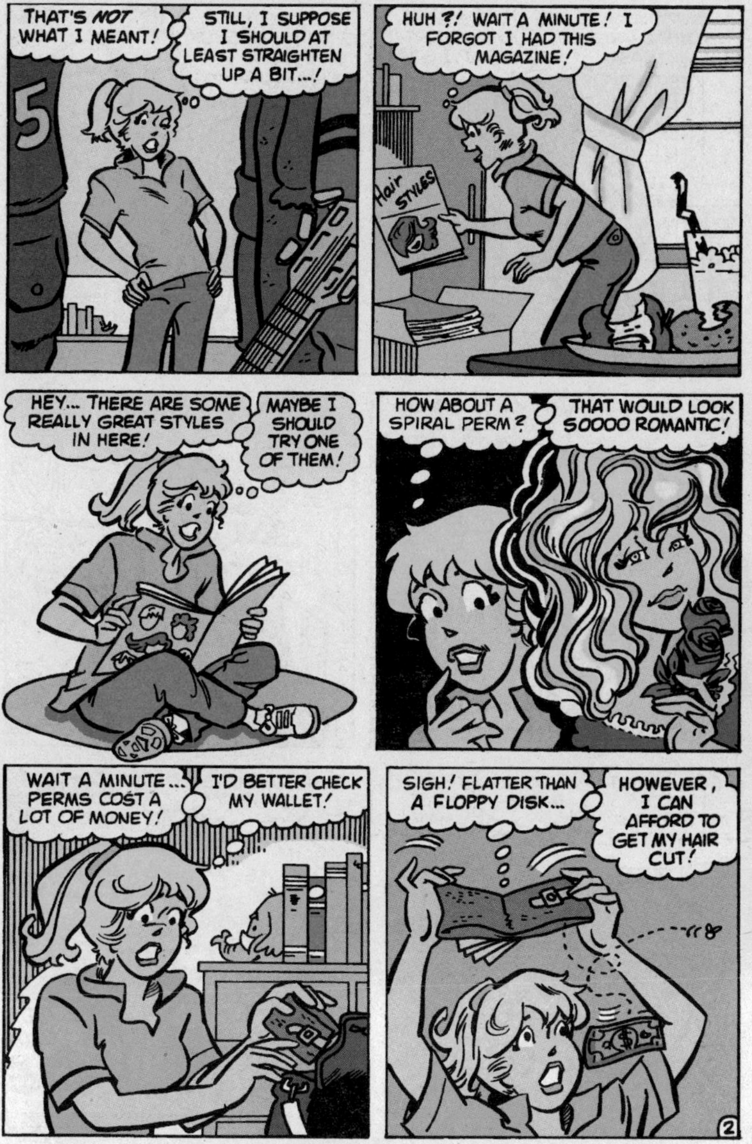
THAT'S NOT WHAT I MEANT!
STILL, I SUPPOSE I SHOULD AT LEAST STRAIGHTEN UP A BIT...!
HUH ?! WAIT A MINUTE! I FORGOT I HAD THIS MAGAZINE!
Hair STYLES
HEY... THERE ARE SOME REALLY GREAT STYLES IN HERE!
MAYBE I SHOULD TRY ONE OF THEM!
HOW ABOUT A SPIRAL PERM?
THAT WOULD LOOK SOOOO ROMANTIC!
WAIT A MINUTE... PERMS COST A LOT OF MONEY!
I'D BETTER CHECK MY WALLET!
SIGH! FLATTER THAN A FLOPPY DISK...
HOWEVER, I CAN AFFORD TO GET MY HAIR CUT!
2

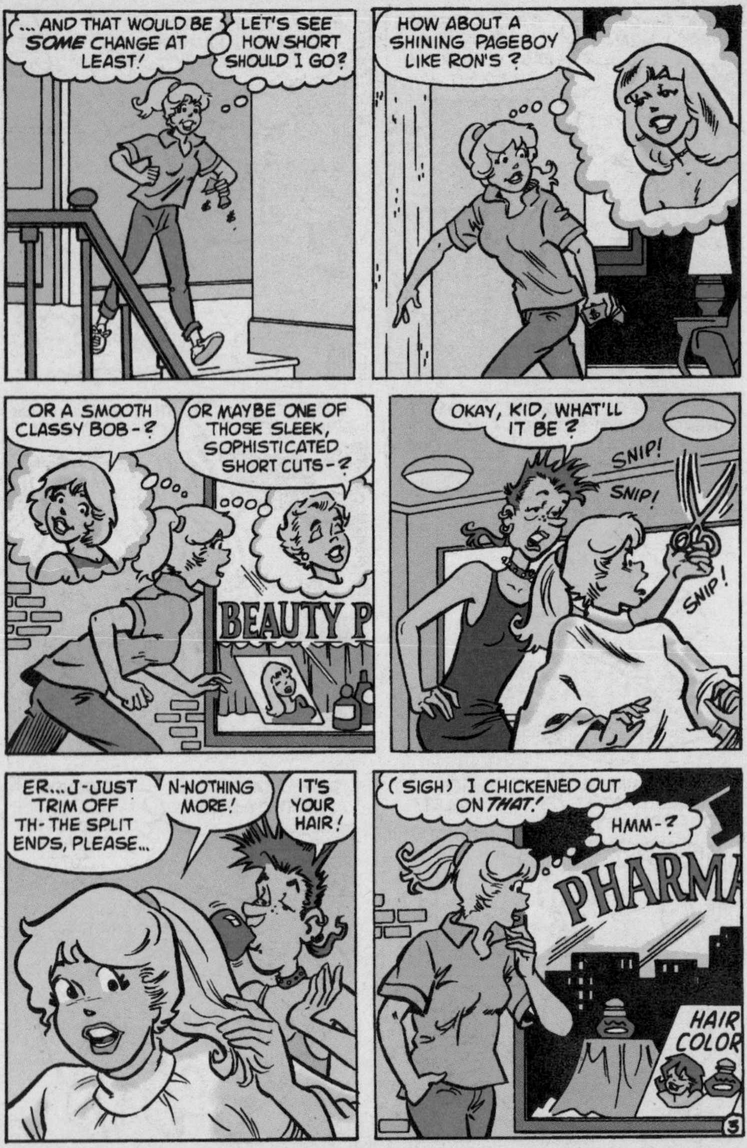

... AND THAT WOULD BE *SOME* CHANGE AT LEAST!
LET'S SEE HOW SHORT SHOULD I GO?
HOW ABOUT A SHINING PAGEBOY LIKE RON'S?
OR A SMOOTH CLASSY BOB-?
OR MAYBE ONE OF THOSE SLEEK, SOPHISTICATED SHORT CUTS-?
BEAUTY P
OKAY, KID, WHAT'LL IT BE?
SNIP!
SNIP!
SNIP!
ER... J-JUST TRIM OFF TH-THE SPLIT ENDS, PLEASE...
N-NOTHING MORE!
IT'S YOUR HAIR!
(SIGH) I CHICKENED OUT ON *THAT!*
HMM-?
PHARMA
HAIR COLOR
3

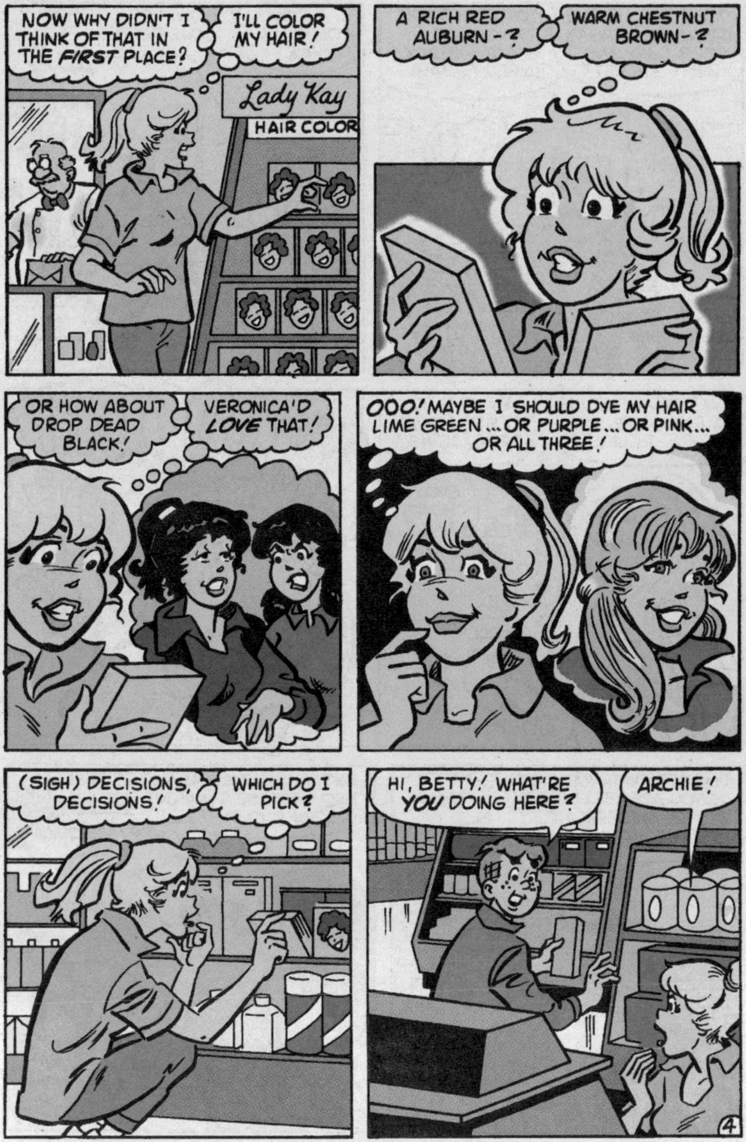
NOW WHY DIDN'T I THINK OF THAT IN THE FIRST PLACE?
I'LL COLOR MY HAIR!
Lady Kay
HAIR COLOR
A RICH RED AUBURN-?
WARM CHESTNUT BROWN-?
OR HOW ABOUT DROP DEAD BLACK!
VERONICA'D LOVE THAT!
OOO! MAYBE I SHOULD DYE MY HAIR LIME GREEN ... OR PURPLE ... OR PINK ... OR ALL THREE!
(SIGH) DECISIONS, DECISIONS!
WHICH DO I PICK?
HI, BETTY! WHAT'RE YOU DOING HERE?
ARCHIE!
4

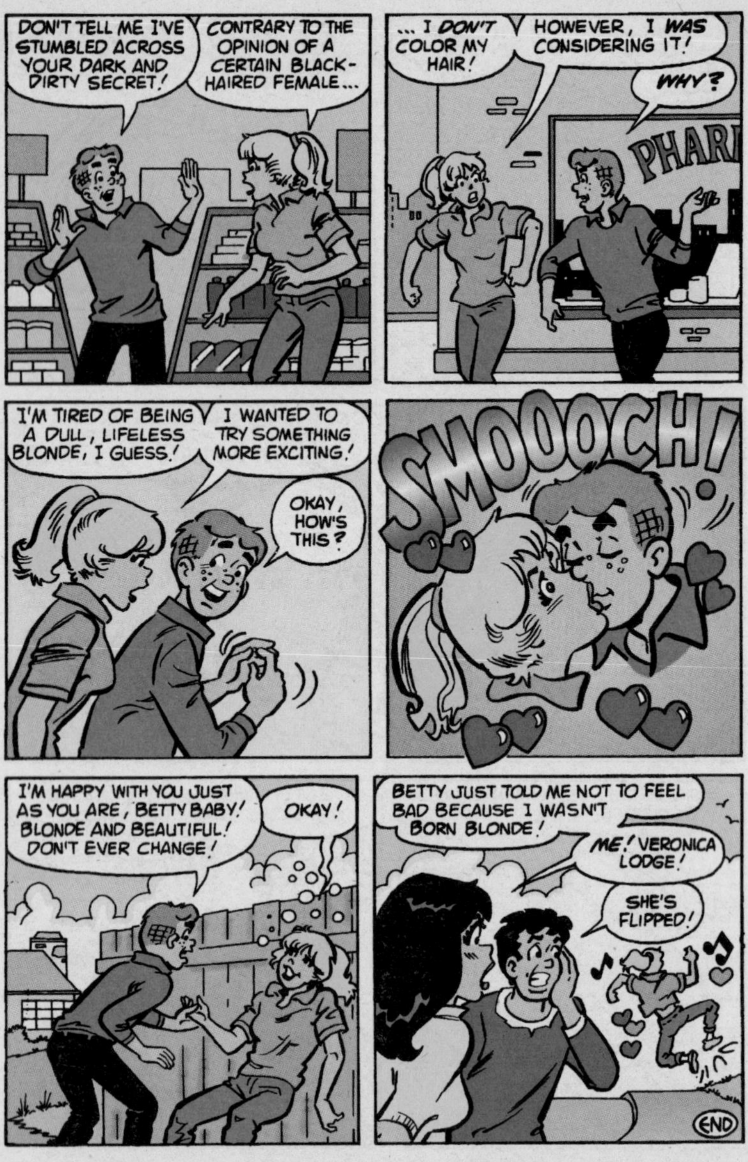
DON'T TELL ME I'VE STUMBLED ACROSS YOUR DARK AND DIRTY SECRET!
CONTRARY TO THE OPINION OF A CERTAIN BLACK-HAIRED FEMALE...
... I DON'T COLOR MY HAIR!
HOWEVER, I WAS CONSIDERING IT!
WHY?
PHAR
I'M TIRED OF BEING A DULL, LIFELESS BLONDE, I GUESS!
I WANTED TO TRY SOMETHING MORE EXCITING!
OKAY, HOW'S THIS?
SMOOOCH!
I'M HAPPY WITH YOU JUST AS YOU ARE, BETTY BABY! BLONDE AND BEAUTIFUL! DON'T EVER CHANGE!
OKAY!
BETTY JUST TOLD ME NOT TO FEEL BAD BECAUSE I WASN'T BORN BLONDE!
ME! VERONICA LODGE!
SHE'S FLIPPED!
END

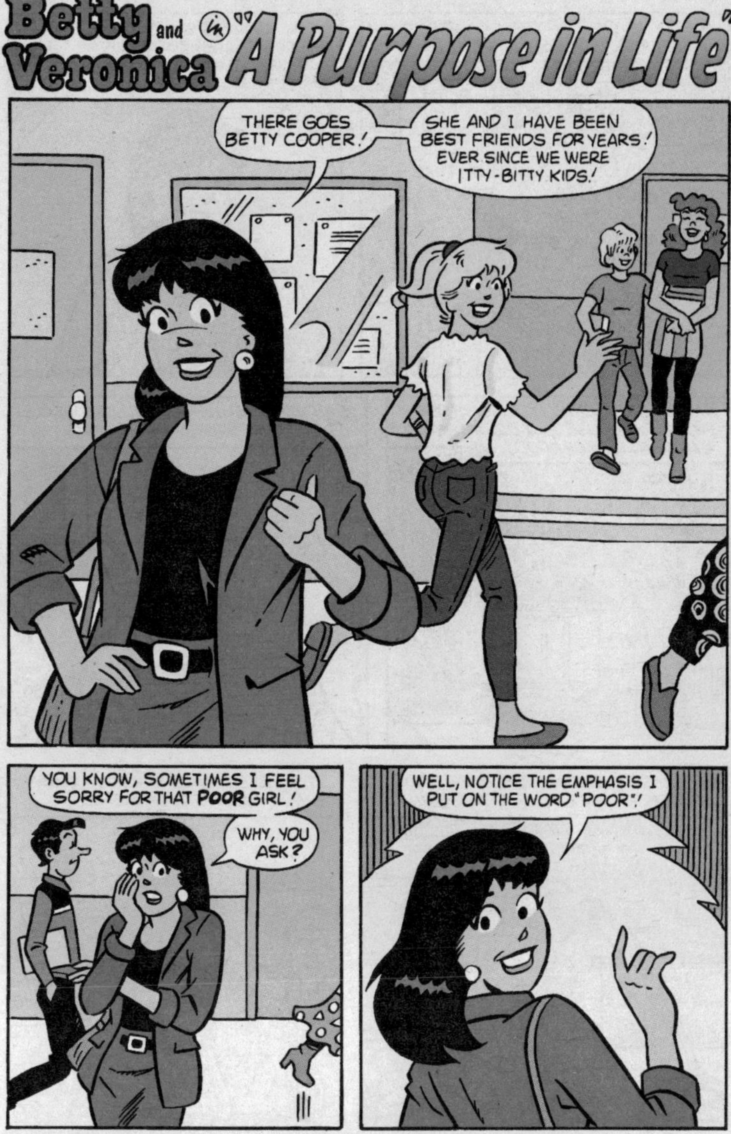
Betty and Veronica in "A Purpose in Life"
THERE GOES BETTY COOPER!
SHE AND I HAVE BEEN BEST FRIENDS FOR YEARS! EVER SINCE WE WERE ITTY-BITTY KIDS!
YOU KNOW, SOMETIMES I FEEL SORRY FOR THAT POOR GIRL!
WHY, YOU ASK?
WELL, NOTICE THE EMPHASIS I PUT ON THE WORD "POOR"!

Script: Kathleen Webb / Pencils: Jeff Shultz / Inks: Rudy Lapick / Letters: Bill Yoshida

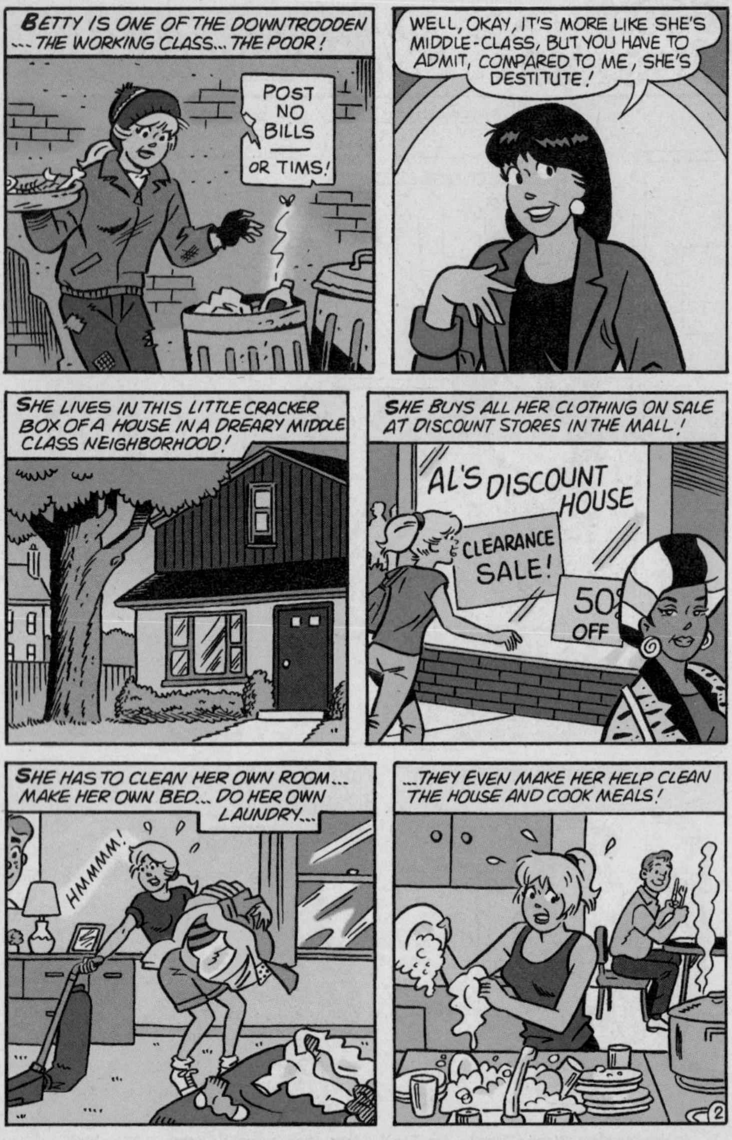
BETTY IS ONE OF THE DOWNTRODDEN ... THE WORKING CLASS... THE POOR!
POST NO BILLS
OR TIMS!
WELL, OKAY, IT'S MORE LIKE SHE'S MIDDLE-CLASS, BUT YOU HAVE TO ADMIT, COMPARED TO ME, SHE'S DESTITUTE!
SHE LIVES IN THIS LITTLE CRACKER BOX OF A HOUSE IN A DREARY MIDDLE CLASS NEIGHBORHOOD!
SHE BUYS ALL HER CLOTHING ON SALE AT DISCOUNT STORES IN THE MALL!
AL'S DISCOUNT HOUSE
CLEARANCE SALE!
50% OFF
SHE HAS TO CLEAN HER OWN ROOM... MAKE HER OWN BED... DO HER OWN LAUNDRY...
HMMMM!
...THEY EVEN MAKE HER HELP CLEAN THE HOUSE AND COOK MEALS!
2

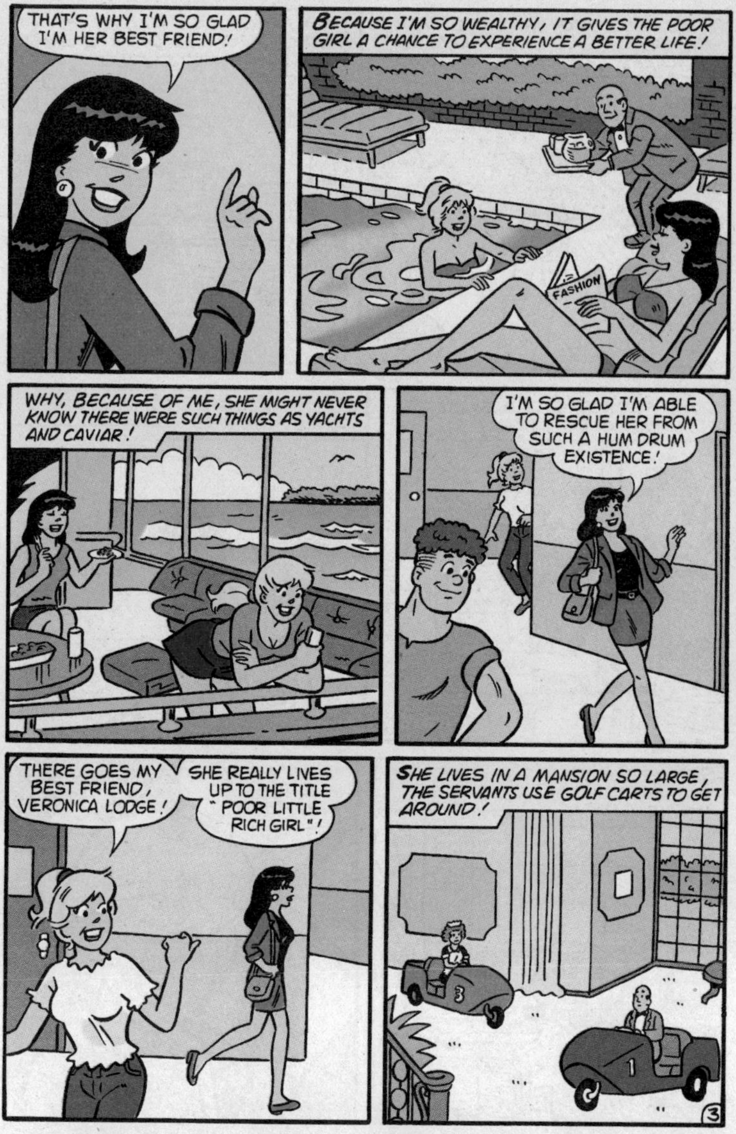
THAT'S WHY I'M SO GLAD I'M HER BEST FRIEND!
BECAUSE I'M SO WEALTHY, IT GIVES THE POOR GIRL A CHANCE TO EXPERIENCE A BETTER LIFE!
FASHION
WHY, BECAUSE OF ME, SHE MIGHT NEVER KNOW THERE WERE SUCH THINGS AS YACHTS AND CAVIAR!
I'M SO GLAD I'M ABLE TO RESCUE HER FROM SUCH A HUM DRUM EXISTENCE!
THERE GOES MY BEST FRIEND, VERONICA LODGE!
SHE REALLY LIVES UP TO THE TITLE "POOR LITTLE RICH GIRL"!
SHE LIVES IN A MANSION SO LARGE, THE SERVANTS USE GOLF CARTS TO GET AROUND!

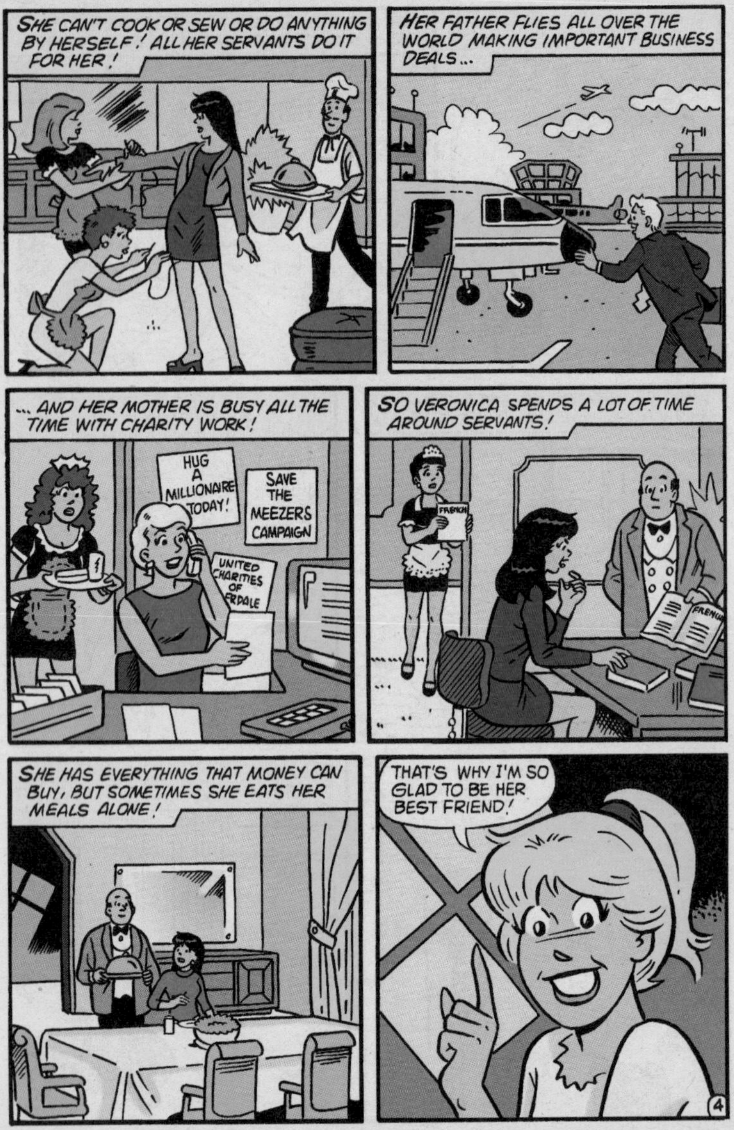
SHE CAN'T COOK OR SEW OR DO ANYTHING BY HERSELF! ALL HER SERVANTS DO IT FOR HER!
HER FATHER FLIES ALL OVER THE WORLD MAKING IMPORTANT BUSINESS DEALS...
... AND HER MOTHER IS BUSY ALL THE TIME WITH CHARITY WORK!
HUG A MILLIONAIRE TODAY!
SAVE THE MEEZERS CAMPAIGN
UNITED CHARITIES OF RIVERDALE
SO VERONICA SPENDS A LOT OF TIME AROUND SERVANTS!
FRENCH
SHE HAS EVERYTHING THAT MONEY CAN BUY, BUT SOMETIMES SHE EATS HER MEALS ALONE!
THAT'S WHY I'M SO GLAD TO BE HER BEST FRIEND!
4

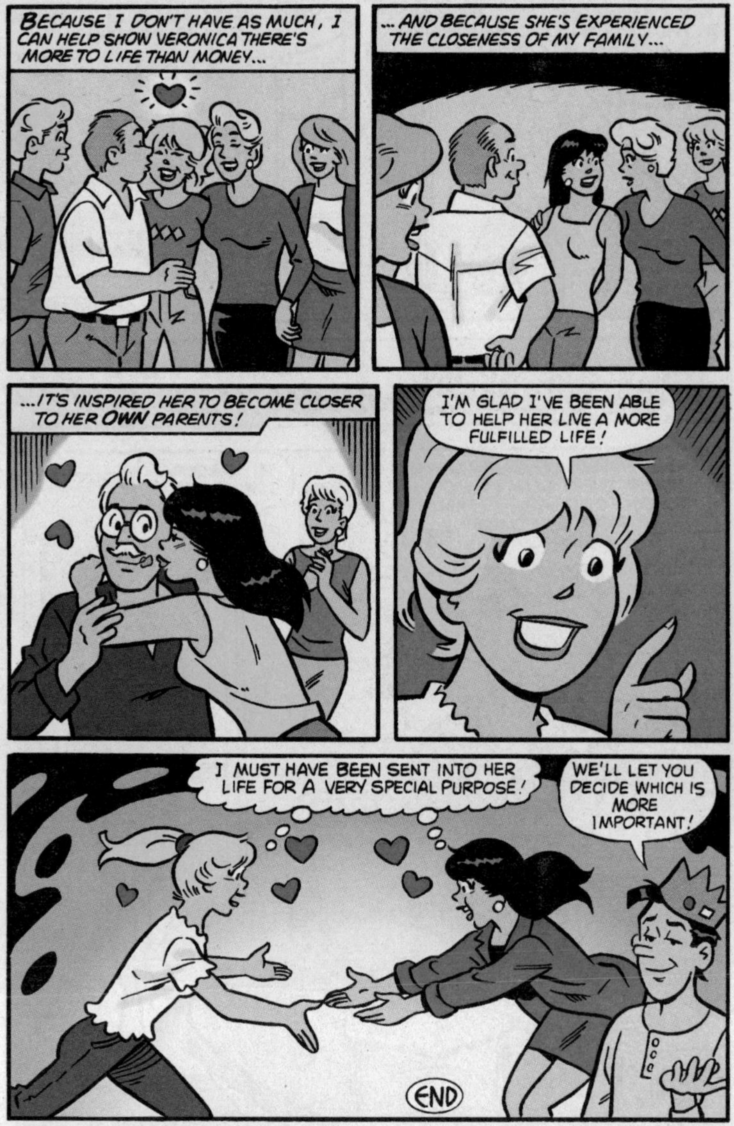
BECAUSE I DON'T HAVE AS MUCH, I CAN HELP SHOW VERONICA THERE'S MORE TO LIFE THAN MONEY...
... AND BECAUSE SHE'S EXPERIENCED THE CLOSENESS OF MY FAMILY...
...IT'S INSPIRED HER TO BECOME CLOSER TO HER OWN PARENTS!
I'M GLAD I'VE BEEN ABLE TO HELP HER LIVE A MORE FULFILLED LIFE!
I MUST HAVE BEEN SENT INTO HER LIFE FOR A VERY SPECIAL PURPOSE!
WE'LL LET YOU DECIDE WHICH IS MORE IMPORTANT!
END

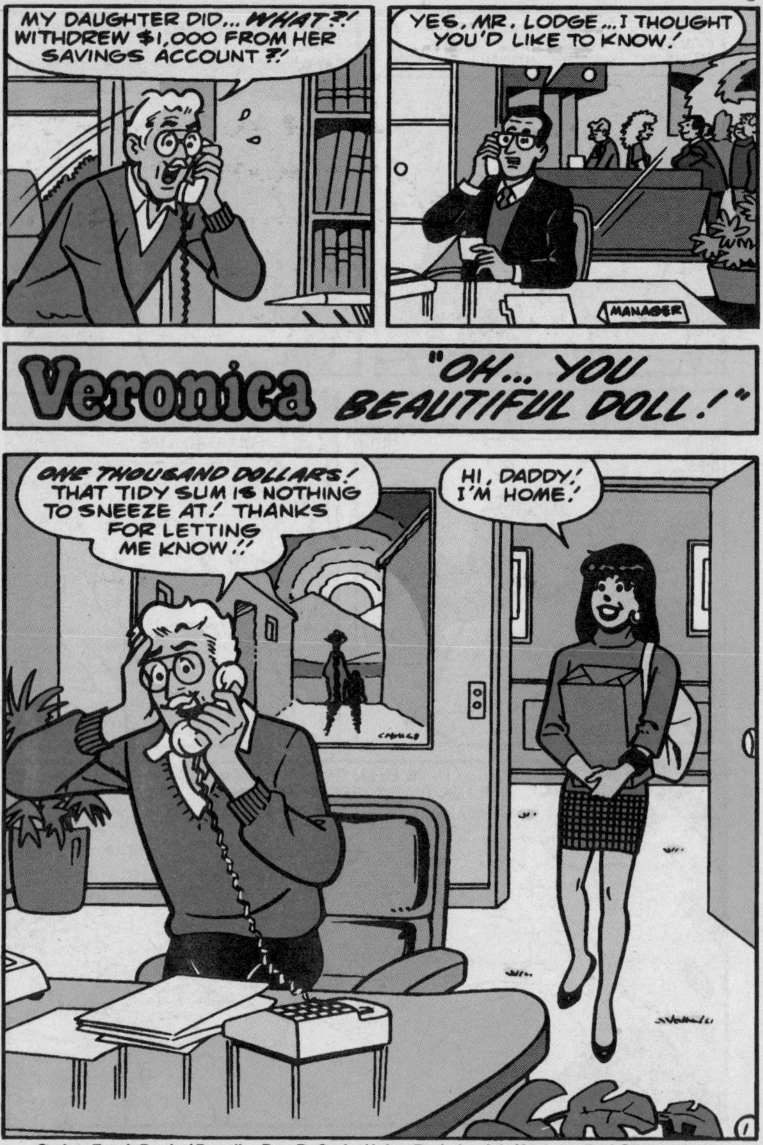

MY DAUGHTER DID... WHAT?! WITHDREW $1,000 FROM HER SAVINGS ACCOUNT?!
YES, MR. LODGE... I THOUGHT YOU'D LIKE TO KNOW!
MANAGER
Veronica
"OH... YOU BEAUTIFUL DOLL!"
ONE THOUSAND DOLLARS! THAT TIDY SUM IS NOTHING TO SNEEZE AT! THANKS FOR LETTING ME KNOW!!
HI, DADDY! I'M HOME!

Script: Frank Doyle / Pencils: Dan DeCarlo / Inks: Rudy Lapick / Letters: Rod Ollerenshaw

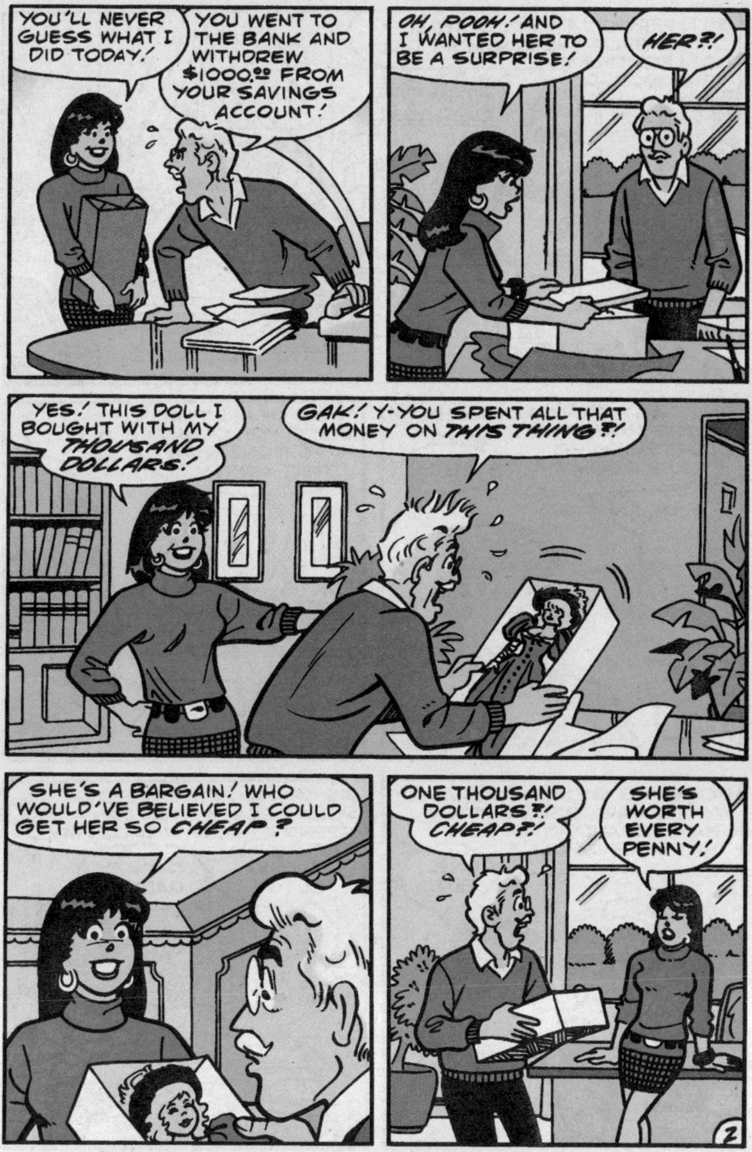

YOU'LL NEVER GUESS WHAT I DID TODAY!
YOU WENT TO THE BANK AND WITHDREW $1000.00 FROM YOUR SAVINGS ACCOUNT!
OH, POOH! AND I WANTED HER TO BE A SURPRISE!
HER?!
YES! THIS DOLL I BOUGHT WITH MY THOUSAND DOLLARS!
GAK! Y-YOU SPENT ALL THAT MONEY ON THIS THING?!
SHE'S A BARGAIN! WHO WOULD'VE BELIEVED I COULD GET HER SO CHEAP?
ONE THOUSAND DOLLARS?! CHEAP?!
SHE'S WORTH EVERY PENNY!
2

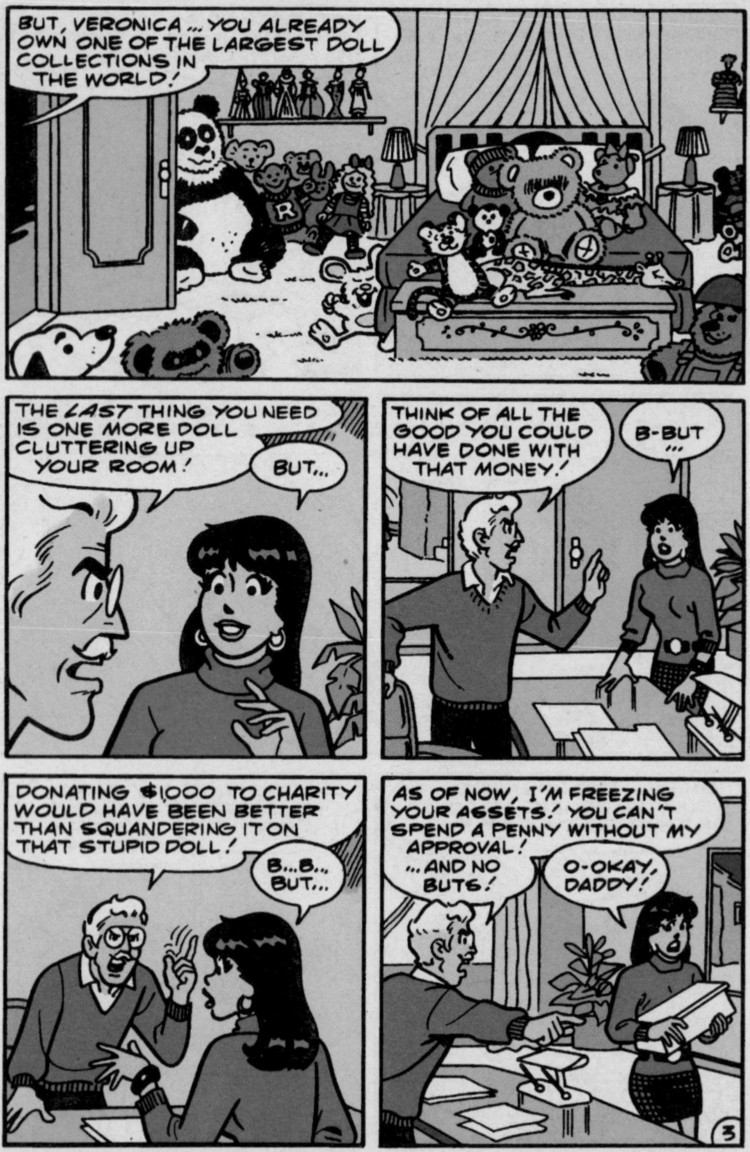
BUT, VERONICA ... YOU ALREADY OWN ONE OF THE LARGEST DOLL COLLECTIONS IN THE WORLD!
THE LAST THING YOU NEED IS ONE MORE DOLL CLUTTERING UP YOUR ROOM!
BUT...
THINK OF ALL THE GOOD YOU COULD HAVE DONE WITH THAT MONEY!
B-BUT ...
DONATING $1,000 TO CHARITY WOULD HAVE BEEN BETTER THAN SQUANDERING IT ON THAT STUPID DOLL!
B...B... BUT...
AS OF NOW, I'M FREEZING YOUR ASSETS! YOU CAN'T SPEND A PENNY WITHOUT MY APPROVAL!
...AND NO BUTS!
O-OKAY, DADDY!
3

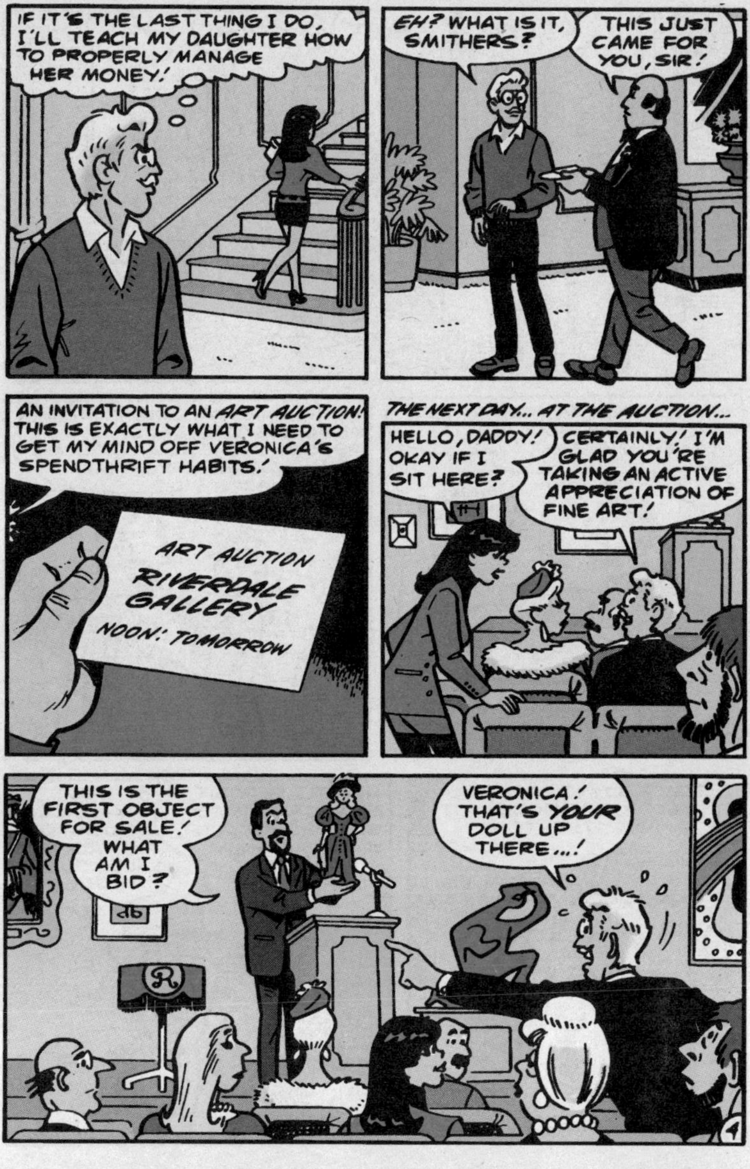

IF IT'S THE LAST THING I DO, I'LL TEACH MY DAUGHTER HOW TO PROPERLY MANAGE HER MONEY!
EH? WHAT IS IT, SMITHERS?
THIS JUST CAME FOR YOU, SIR!
AN INVITATION TO AN ART AUCTION! THIS IS EXACTLY WHAT I NEED TO GET MY MIND OFF VERONICA'S SPENDTHRIFT HABITS!
ART AUCTION
RIVERDALE GALLERY
NOON: TOMORROW
THE NEXT DAY... AT THE AUCTION...
HELLO, DADDY! OKAY IF I SIT HERE?
CERTAINLY! I'M GLAD YOU'RE TAKING AN ACTIVE APPRECIATION OF FINE ART!
THIS IS THE FIRST OBJECT FOR SALE! WHAT AM I BID?
VERONICA! THAT'S YOUR DOLL UP THERE...!
4

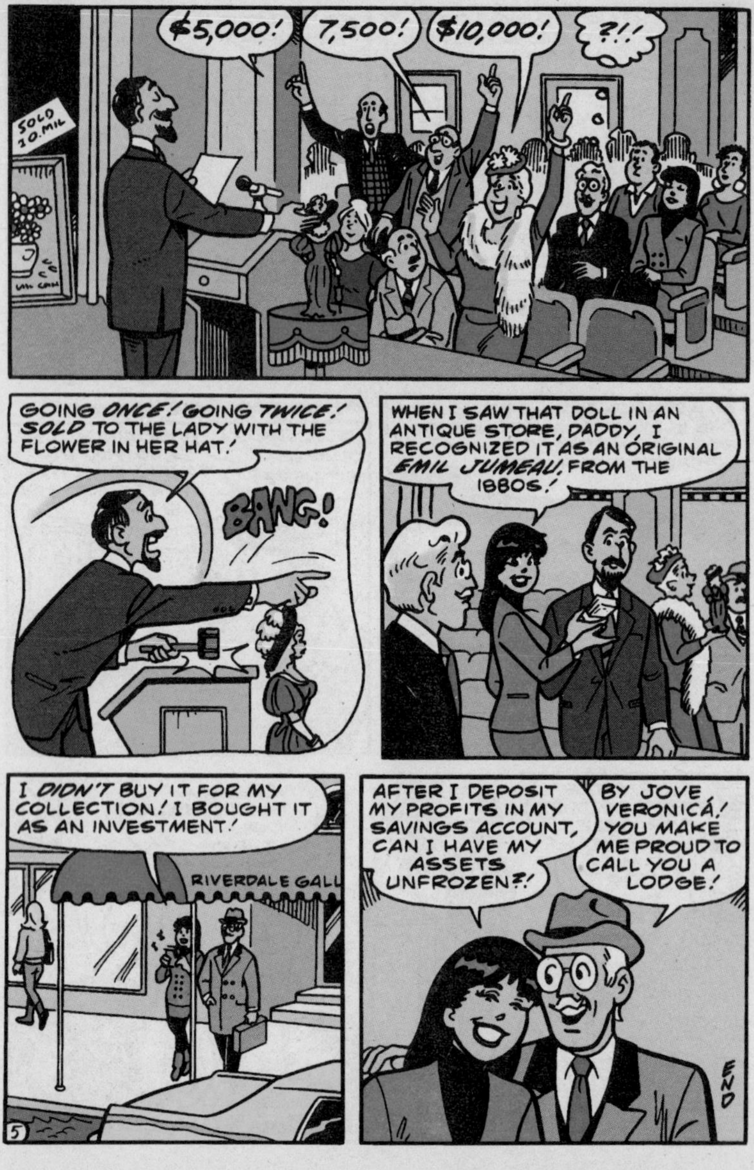
$5,000!
7,500!
$10,000!
?!!
SOLD 10. MIL
GOING ONCE! GOING TWICE! SOLD TO THE LADY WITH THE FLOWER IN HER HAT!
BANG!
WHEN I SAW THAT DOLL IN AN ANTIQUE STORE, DADDY, I RECOGNIZED IT AS AN ORIGINAL EMIL JUMEAU, FROM THE 1880S!
I DIDN'T BUY IT FOR MY COLLECTION! I BOUGHT IT AS AN INVESTMENT!
RIVERDALE GALL
5
AFTER I DEPOSIT MY PROFITS IN MY SAVINGS ACCOUNT, CAN I HAVE MY ASSETS UNFROZEN?!
BY JOVE VERONICA! YOU MAKE ME PROUD TO CALL YOU A LODGE!
END

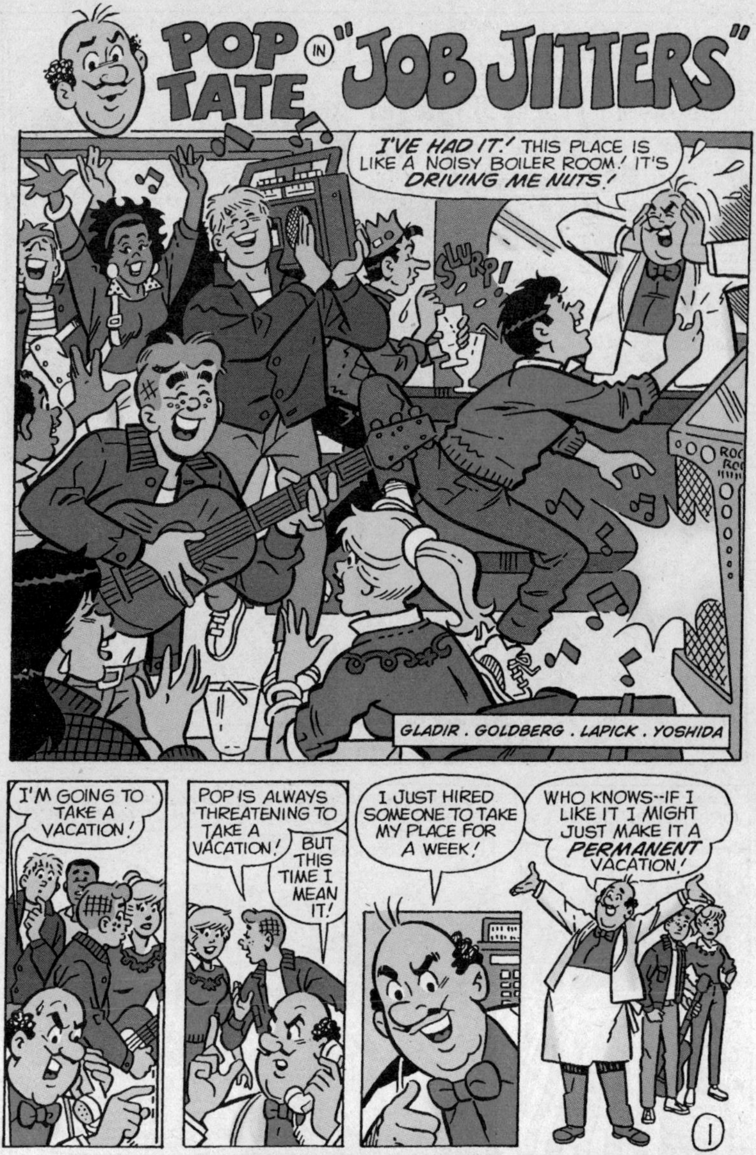

POP TATE IN "JOB JITTERS"
I'VE HAD IT! THIS PLACE IS LIKE A NOISY BOILER ROOM! IT'S DRIVING ME NUTS!
SLURP!
GLADIR . GOLDBERG . LAPICK . YOSHIDA
I'M GOING TO TAKE A VACATION!
POP IS ALWAYS THREATENING TO TAKE A VACATION!
BUT THIS TIME I MEAN IT!
I JUST HIRED SOMEONE TO TAKE MY PLACE FOR A WEEK!
WHO KNOWS--IF I LIKE IT I MIGHT JUST MAKE IT A PERMANENT VACATION!

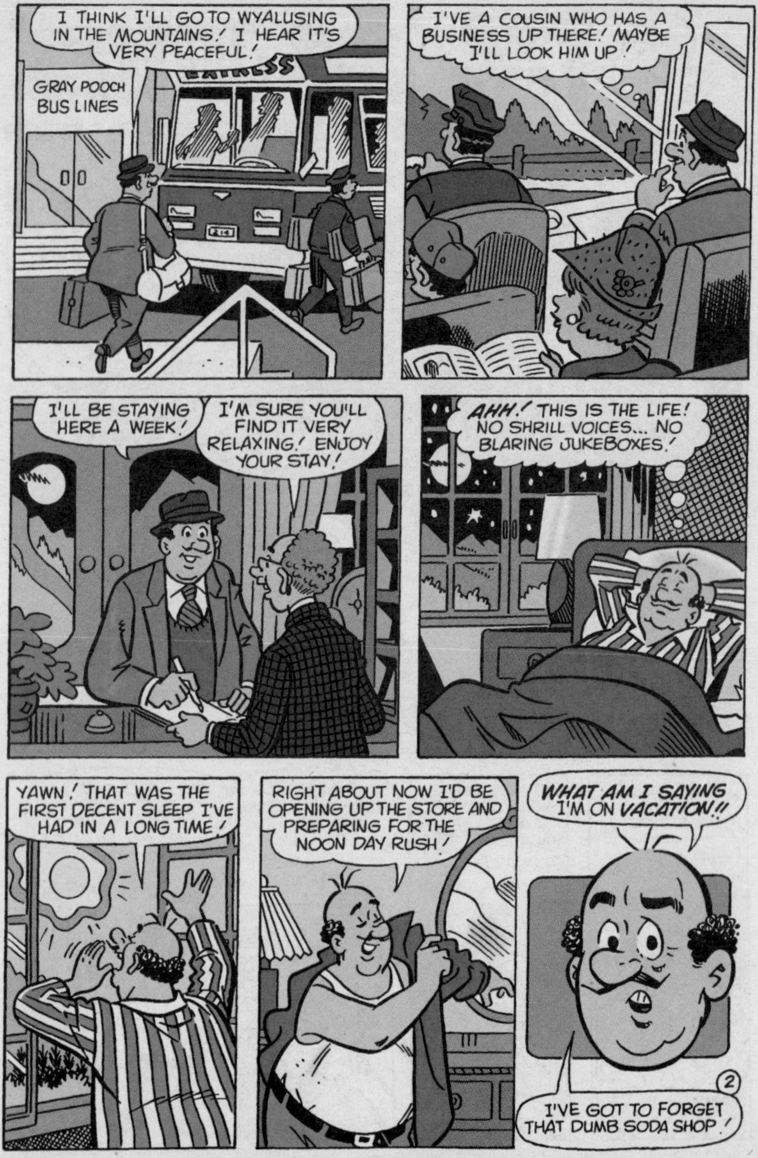
I THINK I'LL GO TO WYALUSING IN THE MOUNTAINS! I HEAR IT'S VERY PEACEFUL!
GRAY POOCH BUS LINES
I'VE A COUSIN WHO HAS A BUSINESS UP THERE! MAYBE I'LL LOOK HIM UP!
I'LL BE STAYING HERE A WEEK!
I'M SURE YOU'LL FIND IT VERY RELAXING! ENJOY YOUR STAY!
AHH! THIS IS THE LIFE! NO SHRILL VOICES... NO BLARING JUKEBOXES!
YAWN! THAT WAS THE FIRST DECENT SLEEP I'VE HAD IN A LONG TIME!
RIGHT ABOUT NOW I'D BE OPENING UP THE STORE AND PREPARING FOR THE NOON DAY RUSH!
WHAT AM I SAYING I'M ON VACATION!!
2
I'VE GOT TO FORGET THAT DUMB SODA SHOP!

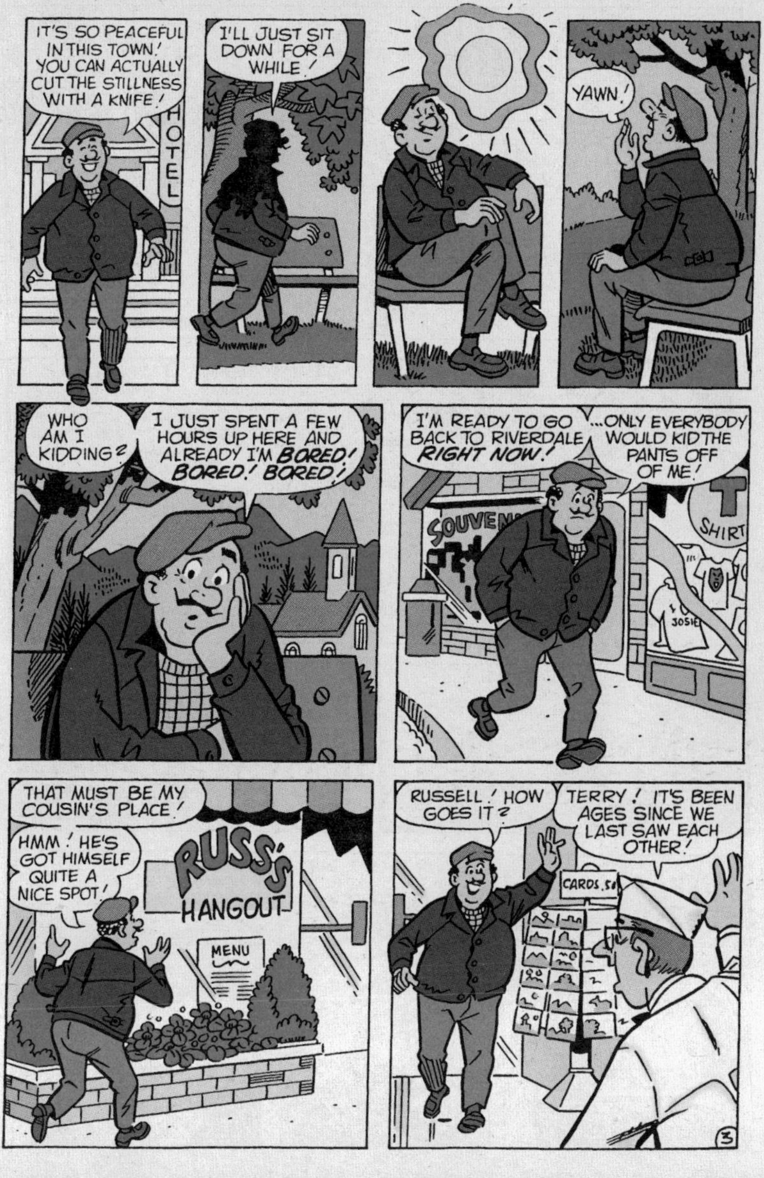
IT'S SO PEACEFUL IN THIS TOWN! YOU CAN ACTUALLY CUT THE STILLNESS WITH A KNIFE!
HOTEL
I'LL JUST SIT DOWN FOR A WHILE!
YAWN!
WHO AM I KIDDING?
I JUST SPENT A FEW HOURS UP HERE AND ALREADY I'M BORED! BORED! BORED!
I'M READY TO GO BACK TO RIVERDALE RIGHT NOW!
...ONLY EVERYBODY WOULD KID THE PANTS OFF OF ME!
T SHIRT
JOSIE
THAT MUST BE MY COUSIN'S PLACE!
HMM! HE'S GOT HIMSELF QUITE A NICE SPOT!
RUSS'S HANGOUT
MENU
RUSSELL! HOW GOES IT?
TERRY! IT'S BEEN AGES SINCE WE LAST SAW EACH OTHER!
CARDS

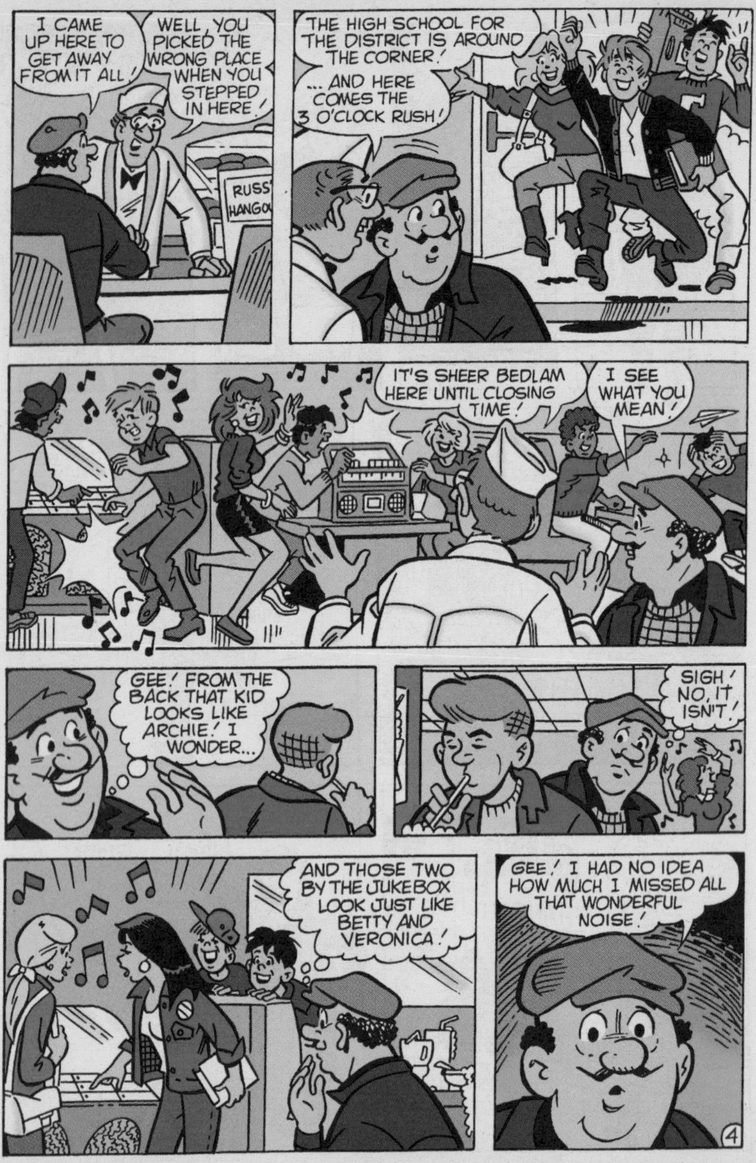
I CAME UP HERE TO GET AWAY FROM IT ALL!
WELL, YOU PICKED THE WRONG PLACE WHEN YOU STEPPED IN HERE!
RUSS' HANGOU
THE HIGH SCHOOL FOR THE DISTRICT IS AROUND THE CORNER!
... AND HERE COMES THE 3 O'CLOCK RUSH!
IT'S SHEER BEDLAM HERE UNTIL CLOSING TIME!
I SEE WHAT YOU MEAN!
GEE! FROM THE BACK THAT KID LOOKS LIKE ARCHIE! I WONDER...
SIGH! NO, IT ISN'T!
AND THOSE TWO BY THE JUKEBOX LOOK JUST LIKE BETTY AND VERONICA!
GEE! I HAD NO IDEA HOW MUCH I MISSED ALL THAT WONDERFUL NOISE!
4

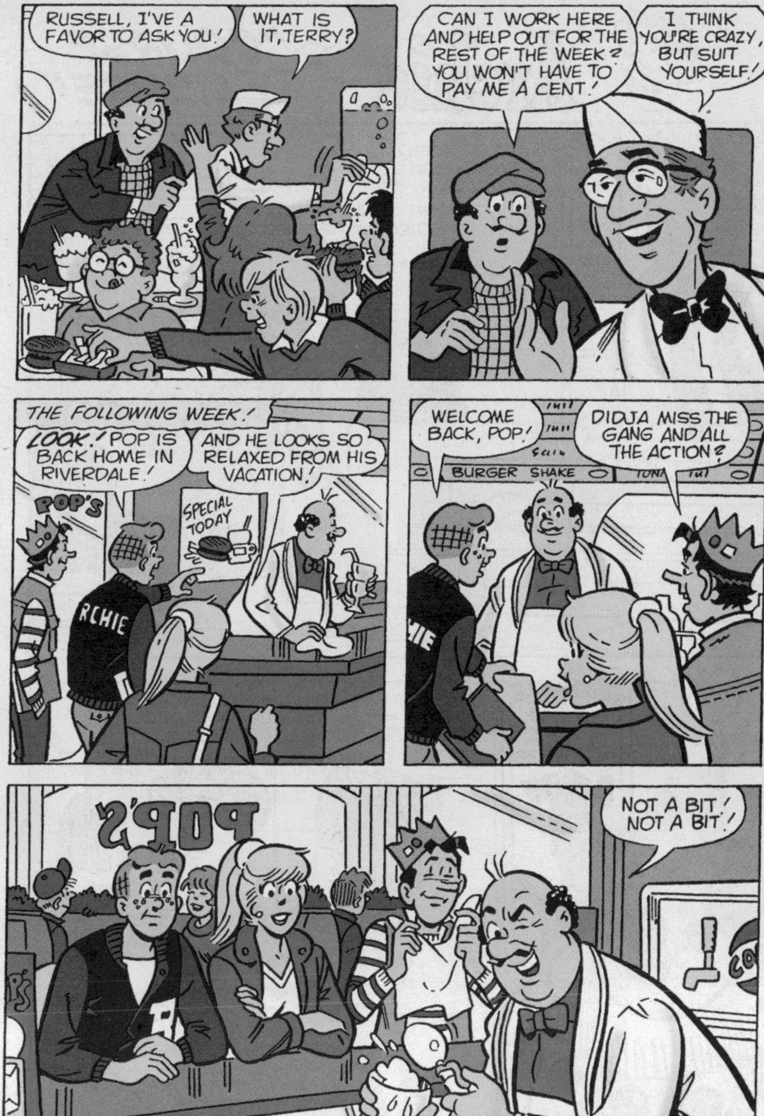
RUSSELL, I'VE A FAVOR TO ASK YOU!
WHAT IS IT, TERRY?
CAN I WORK HERE AND HELP OUT FOR THE REST OF THE WEEK? YOU WON'T HAVE TO PAY ME A CENT!
I THINK YOU'RE CRAZY, BUT SUIT YOURSELF!
THE FOLLOWING WEEK!
LOOK! POP IS BACK HOME IN RIVERDALE!
AND HE LOOKS SO RELAXED FROM HIS VACATION!
POP'S
SPECIAL TODAY
RCHIE
WELCOME BACK, POP!
DIDJA MISS THE GANG AND ALL THE ACTION?
BURGER SHAKE
POP'S
NOT A BIT! NOT A BIT!
END

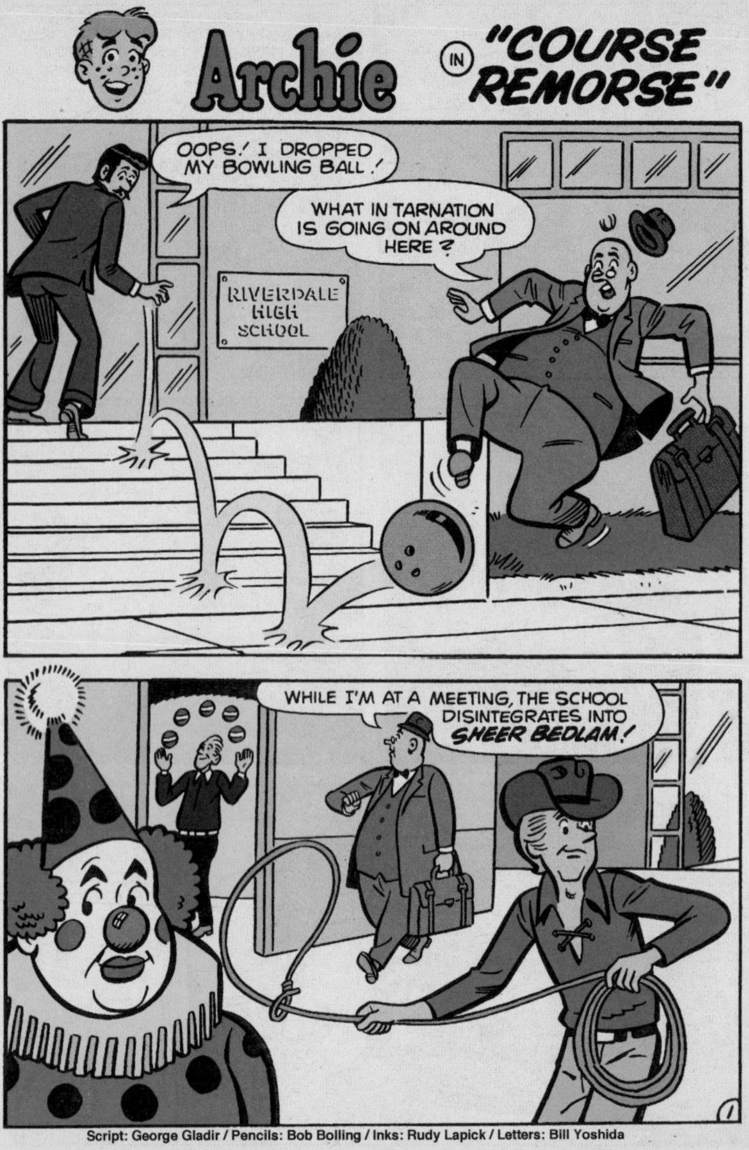
Archie
IN
"COURSE REMORSE"
OOPS! I DROPPED MY BOWLING BALL!
WHAT IN TARNATION IS GOING ON AROUND HERE?
RIVERDALE HIGH SCHOOL
WHILE I'M AT A MEETING, THE SCHOOL DISINTEGRATES INTO SHEER BEDLAM!
1

Script: George Gladir / Pencils: Bob Bolling / Inks: Rudy Lapick / Letters: Bill Yoshida

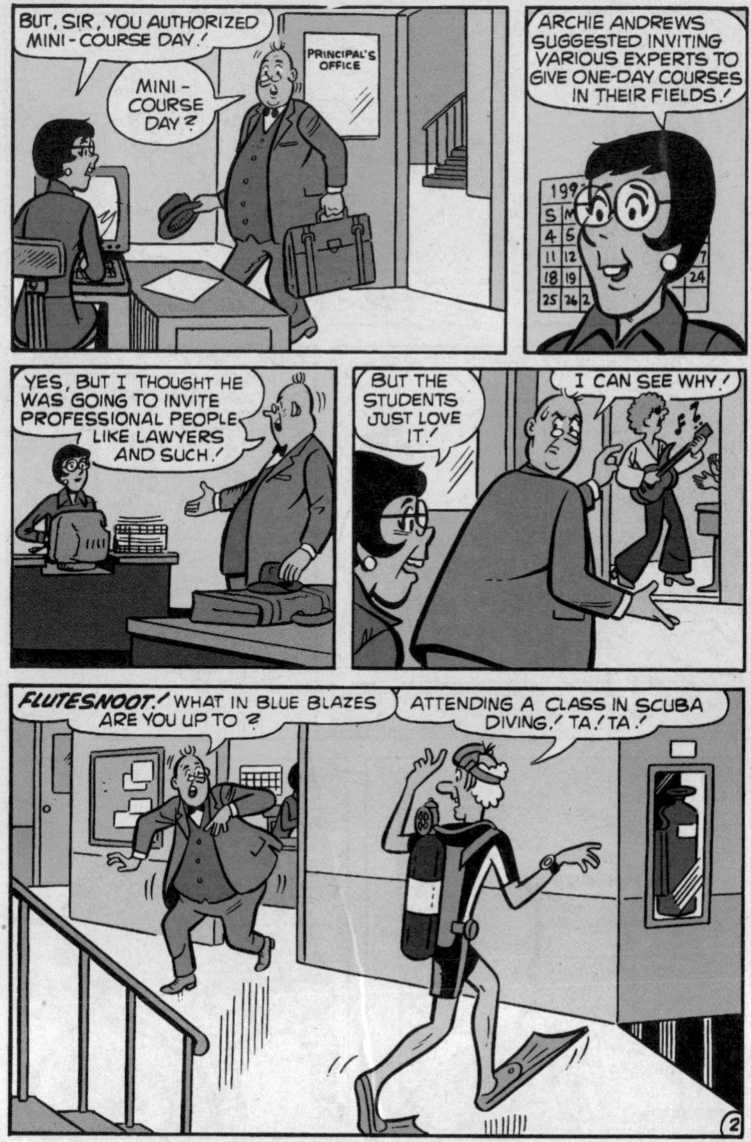
BUT, SIR, YOU AUTHORIZED MINI-COURSE DAY!
MINI-COURSE DAY?
PRINCIPAL'S OFFICE
ARCHIE ANDREWS SUGGESTED INVITING VARIOUS EXPERTS TO GIVE ONE-DAY COURSES IN THEIR FIELDS!
YES, BUT I THOUGHT HE WAS GOING TO INVITE PROFESSIONAL PEOPLE LIKE LAWYERS AND SUCH!
BUT THE STUDENTS JUST LOVE IT!
I CAN SEE WHY!
FLUTESNOOT! WHAT IN BLUE BLAZES ARE YOU UP TO?
ATTENDING A CLASS IN SCUBA DIVING! TA! TA!
2

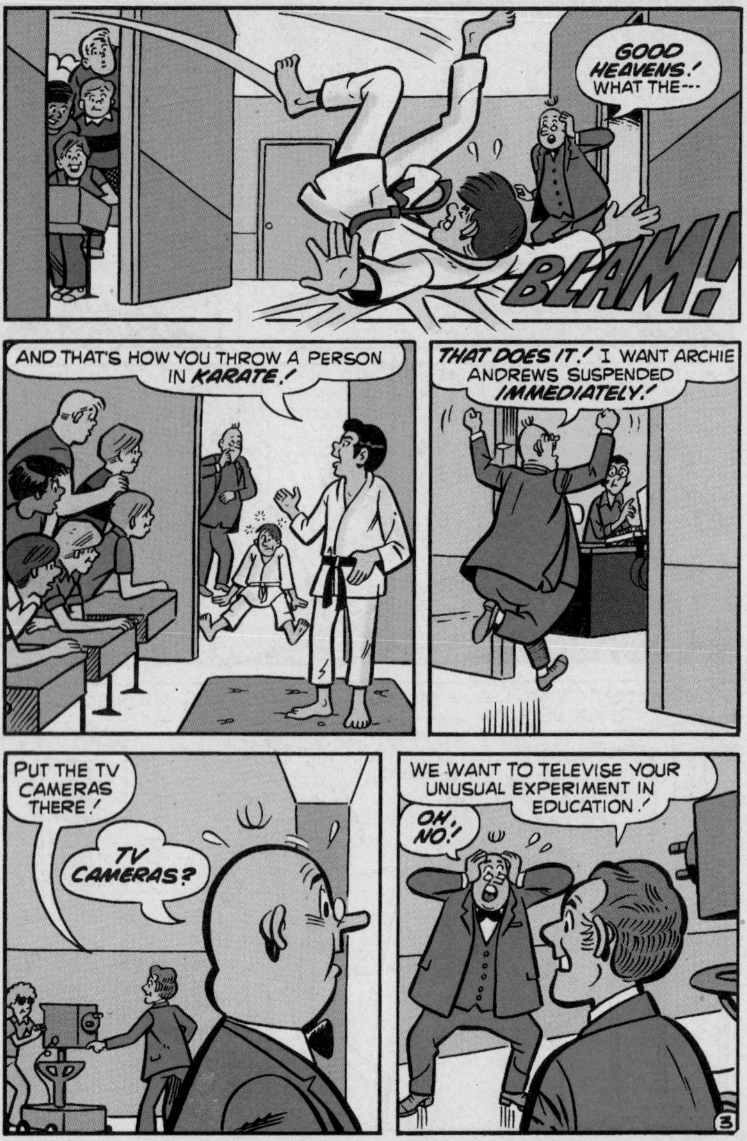
GOOD HEAVENS.! WHAT THE---
BLAM!
AND THAT'S HOW YOU THROW A PERSON IN KARATE.!
THAT DOES IT.! I WANT ARCHIE ANDREWS SUSPENDED IMMEDIATELY.!
PUT THE TV CAMERAS THERE.!
TV CAMERAS?
WE WANT TO TELEVISE YOUR UNUSUAL EXPERIMENT IN EDUCATION.!
OH, NO.!
3

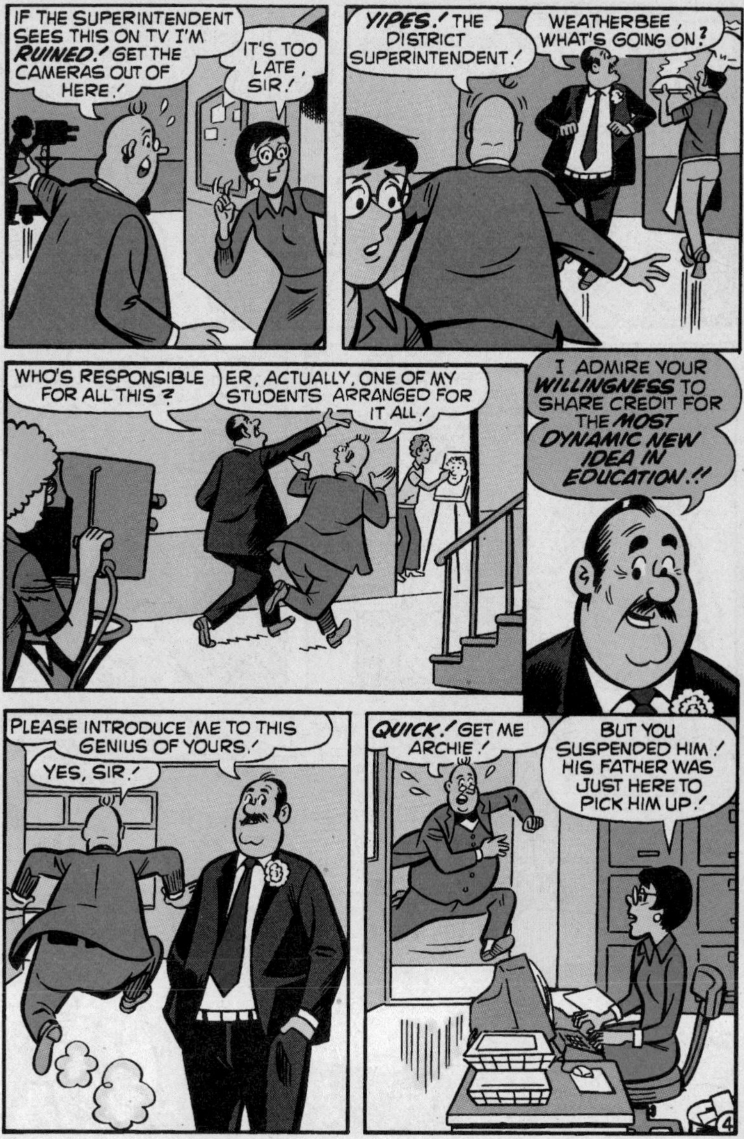
IF THE SUPERINTENDENT SEES THIS ON TV I'M RUINED! GET THE CAMERAS OUT OF HERE!
IT'S TOO LATE, SIR!
YIPES! THE DISTRICT SUPERINTENDENT!
WEATHERBEE, WHAT'S GOING ON?
WHO'S RESPONSIBLE FOR ALL THIS?
ER, ACTUALLY, ONE OF MY STUDENTS ARRANGED FOR IT ALL!
I ADMIRE YOUR WILLINGNESS TO SHARE CREDIT FOR THE MOST DYNAMIC NEW IDEA IN EDUCATION!!
PLEASE INTRODUCE ME TO THIS GENIUS OF YOURS!
YES, SIR!
QUICK! GET ME ARCHIE!
BUT YOU SUSPENDED HIM! HIS FATHER WAS JUST HERE TO PICK HIM UP!
4

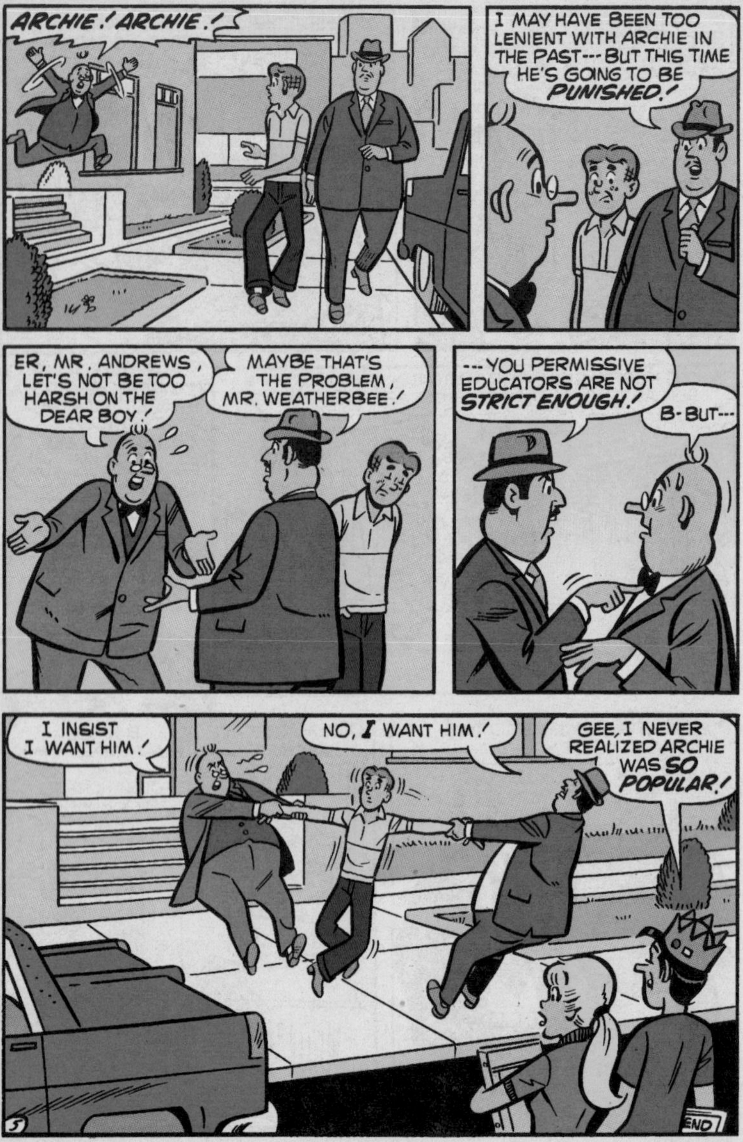
ARCHIE! ARCHIE!
I MAY HAVE BEEN TOO LENIENT WITH ARCHIE IN THE PAST--- BUT THIS TIME HE'S GOING TO BE PUNISHED!
ER, MR. ANDREWS, LET'S NOT BE TOO HARSH ON THE DEAR BOY!
MAYBE THAT'S THE PROBLEM, MR. WEATHERBEE!
---YOU PERMISSIVE EDUCATORS ARE NOT STRICT ENOUGH!
B-BUT---
I INSIST I WANT HIM!
NO, I WANT HIM!
GEE, I NEVER REALIZED ARCHIE WAS SO POPULAR!
5
END

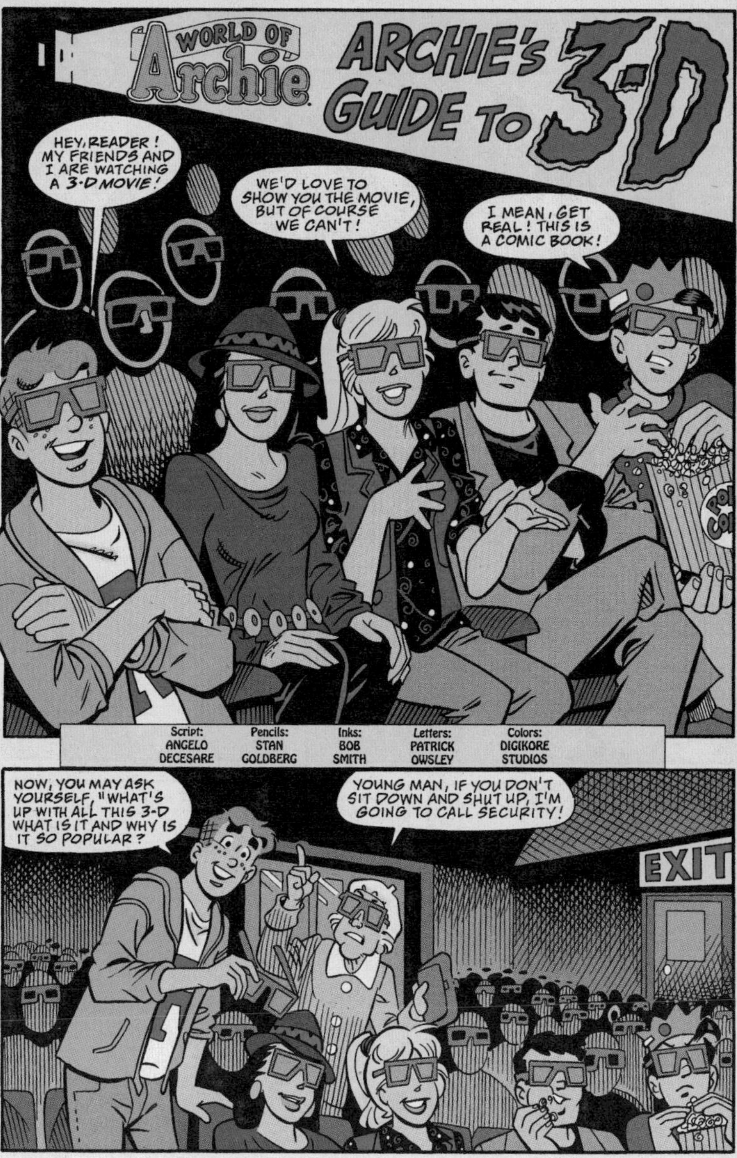
WORLD OF Archie
ARCHIE'S GUIDE TO 3-D
HEY, READER! MY FRIENDS AND I ARE WATCHING A 3-D MOVIE!
WE'D LOVE TO SHOW YOU THE MOVIE, BUT OF COURSE WE CAN'T!
I MEAN, GET REAL! THIS IS A COMIC BOOK!
Script: ANGELO DECESARE Pencils: STAN GOLDBERG Inks: BOB SMITH Letters: PATRICK OWSLEY Colors: DIGIKORE STUDIOS
NOW, YOU MAY ASK YOURSELF, "WHAT'S UP WITH ALL THIS 3-D WHAT IS IT AND WHY IS IT SO POPULAR?
YOUNG MAN, IF YOU DON'T SIT DOWN AND SHUT UP, I'M GOING TO CALL SECURITY!
EXIT

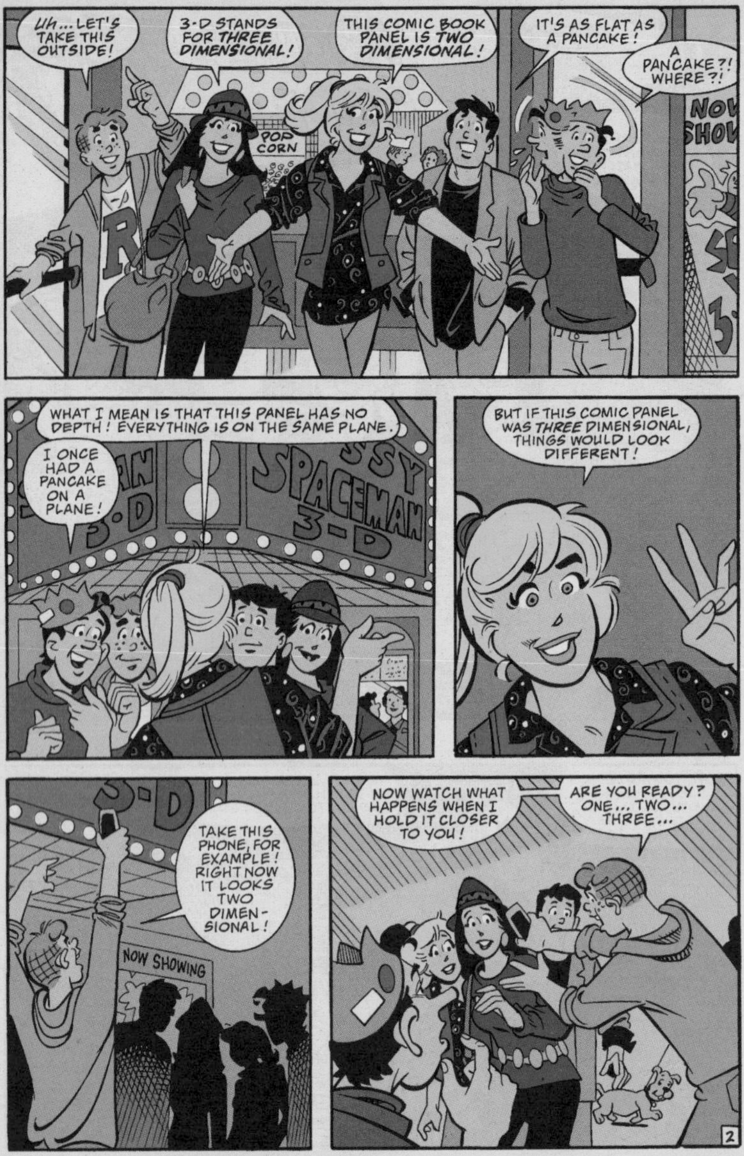
Uh... LET'S TAKE THIS OUTSIDE!
3-D STANDS FOR THREE DIMENSIONAL!
THIS COMIC BOOK PANEL IS TWO DIMENSIONAL!
IT'S AS FLAT AS A PANCAKE!
A PANCAKE?! WHERE?!
POP CORN
WHAT I MEAN IS THAT THIS PANEL HAS NO DEPTH! EVERYTHING IS ON THE SAME PLANE.
I ONCE HAD A PANCAKE ON A PLANE!
SPACEMAN 3-D
BUT IF THIS COMIC PANEL WAS THREE DIMENSIONAL, THINGS WOULD LOOK DIFFERENT!
TAKE THIS PHONE, FOR EXAMPLE! RIGHT NOW IT LOOKS TWO DIMEN-SIONAL!
NOW SHOWING
NOW WATCH WHAT HAPPENS WHEN I HOLD IT CLOSER TO YOU!
ARE YOU READY? ONE... TWO... THREE...
2

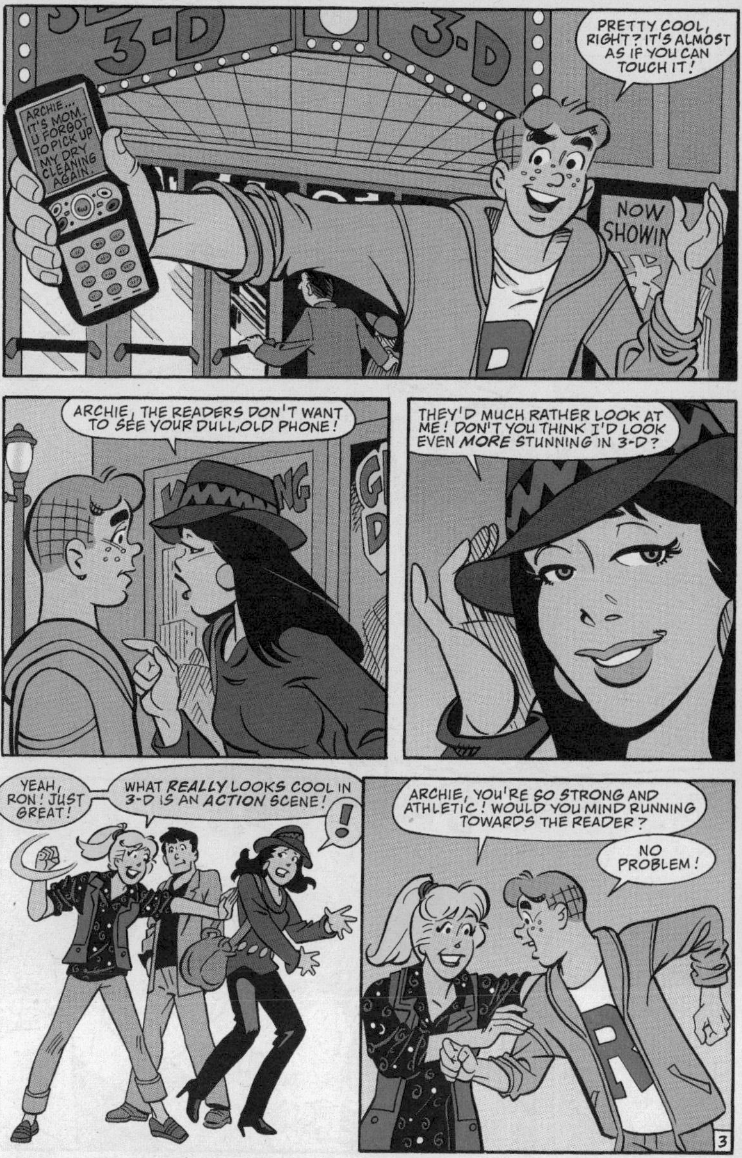
ARCHIE... IT'S MOM. U FORGOT TO PICK UP MY DRY CLEANING AGAIN.
3-D
3-D
PRETTY COOL, RIGHT? IT'S ALMOST AS IF YOU CAN TOUCH IT!
NOW SHOWIN
ARCHIE, THE READERS DON'T WANT TO SEE YOUR DULL, OLD PHONE!
THEY'D MUCH RATHER LOOK AT ME! DON'T YOU THINK I'D LOOK EVEN MORE STUNNING IN 3-D?
YEAH, RON! JUST GREAT!
WHAT REALLY LOOKS COOL IN 3-D IS AN ACTION SCENE!
!
ARCHIE, YOU'RE SO STRONG AND ATHLETIC! WOULD YOU MIND RUNNING TOWARDS THE READER?
NO PROBLEM!
3

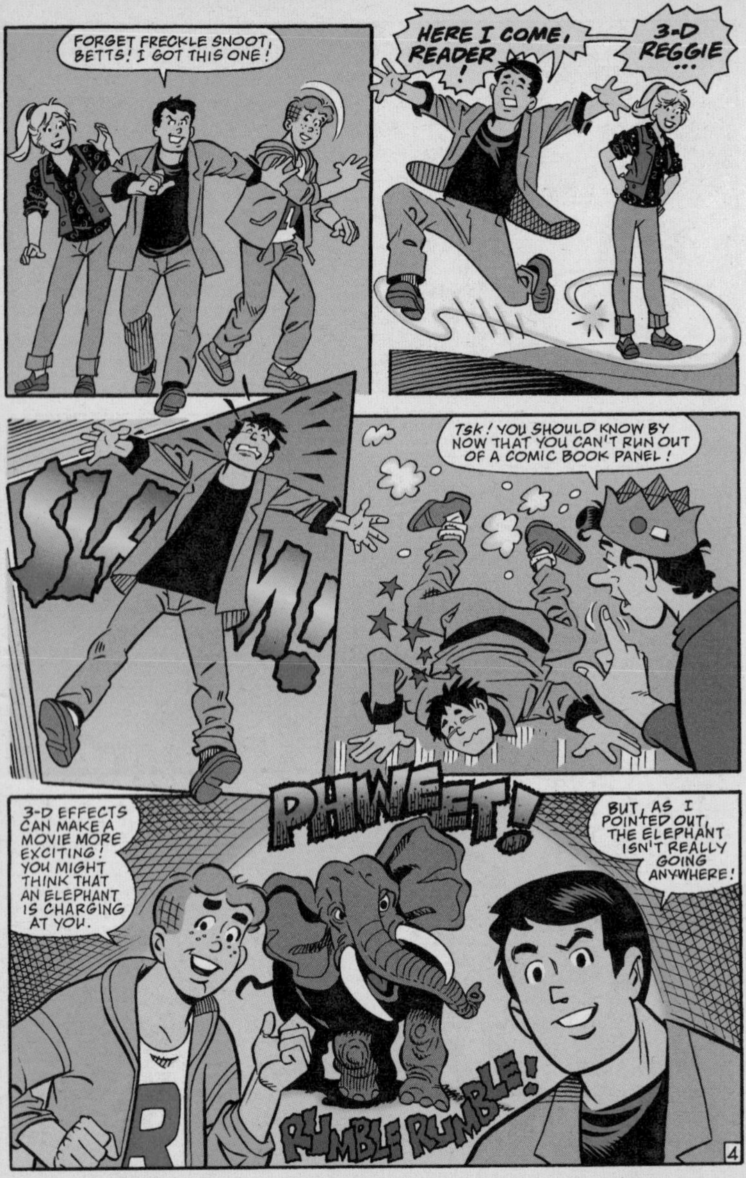
FORGET FRECKLE SNOOT, BETTS! I GOT THIS ONE!
HERE I COME, READER!
3-D REGGIE...
SLAM!
TSK! YOU SHOULD KNOW BY NOW THAT YOU CAN'T RUN OUT OF A COMIC BOOK PANEL!
PHWEET!
3-D EFFECTS CAN MAKE A MOVIE MORE EXCITING! YOU MIGHT THINK THAT AN ELEPHANT IS CHARGING AT YOU.
BUT, AS I POINTED OUT, THE ELEPHANT ISN'T REALLY GOING ANYWHERE!
RUMBLE RUMBLE!
4

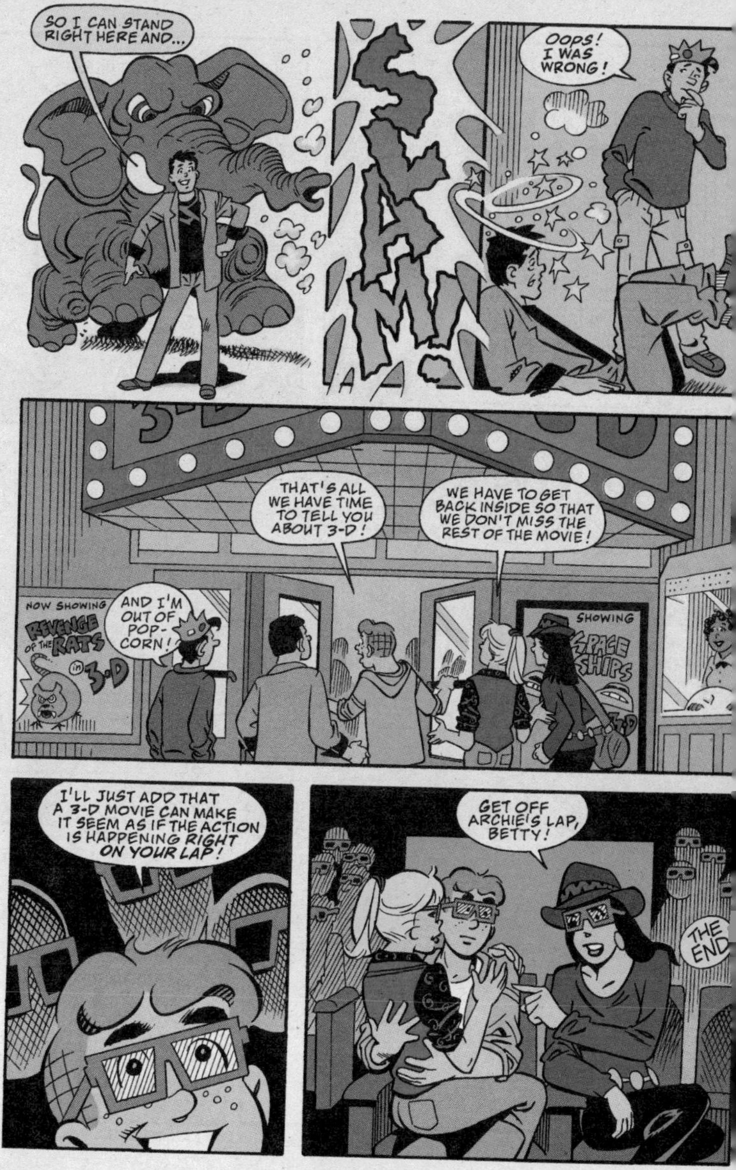
SO I CAN STAND RIGHT HERE AND...
SLAM
OOPS! I WAS WRONG!
THAT'S ALL WE HAVE TIME TO TELL YOU ABOUT 3-D!
WE HAVE TO GET BACK INSIDE SO THAT WE DON'T MISS THE REST OF THE MOVIE!
NOW SHOWING
REVENGE OF THE RATS in 3-D
AND I'M OUT OF POP-CORN!
SHOWING
SPACE SHIPS
I'LL JUST ADD THAT A 3-D MOVIE CAN MAKE IT SEEM AS IF THE ACTION IS HAPPENING RIGHT ON YOUR LAP!
GET OFF ARCHIE'S LAP, BETTY!
THE END

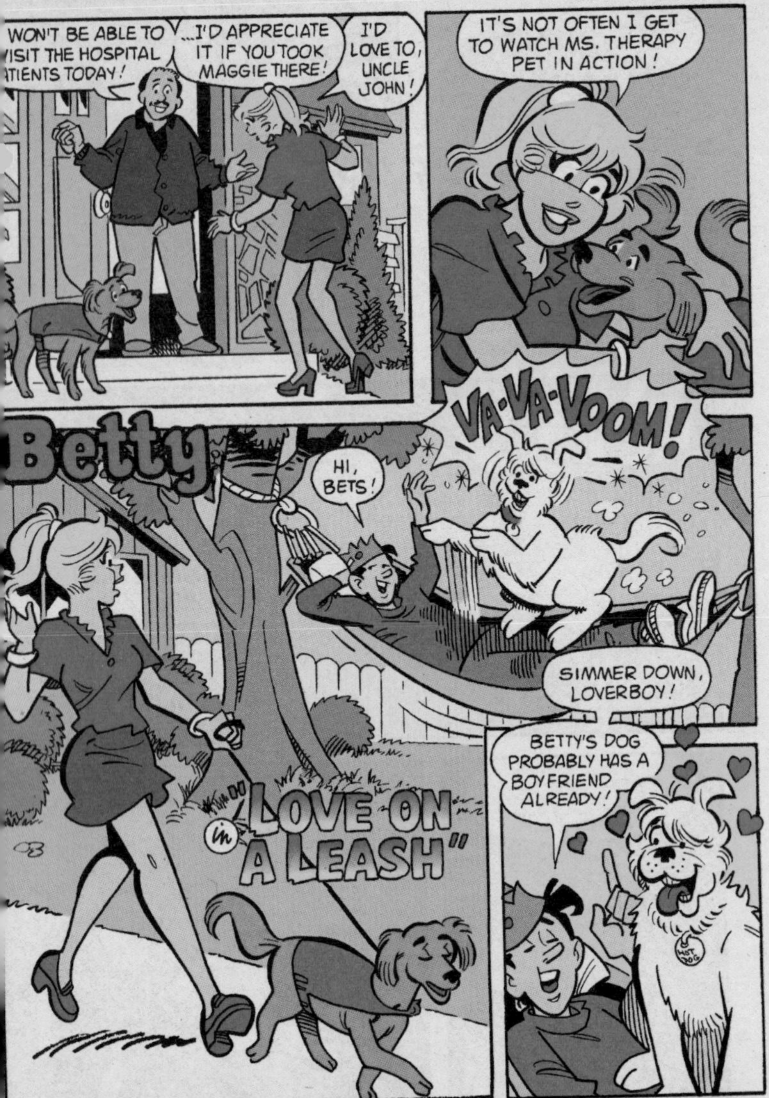
WON'T BE ABLE TO VISIT THE HOSPITAL PATIENTS TODAY!
...I'D APPRECIATE IT IF YOU TOOK MAGGIE THERE!
I'D LOVE TO, UNCLE JOHN!
IT'S NOT OFTEN I GET TO WATCH MS. THERAPY PET IN ACTION!
VA-VA-VOOM!
Betty
HI, BETS!
in "LOVE ON A LEASH"
SIMMER DOWN, LOVERBOY!
BETTY'S DOG PROBABLY HAS A BOYFRIEND ALREADY!

Script: George Gladir / Pencils: Stan Goldberg / Inks: John Lowe / Letters: Bill Yoshida

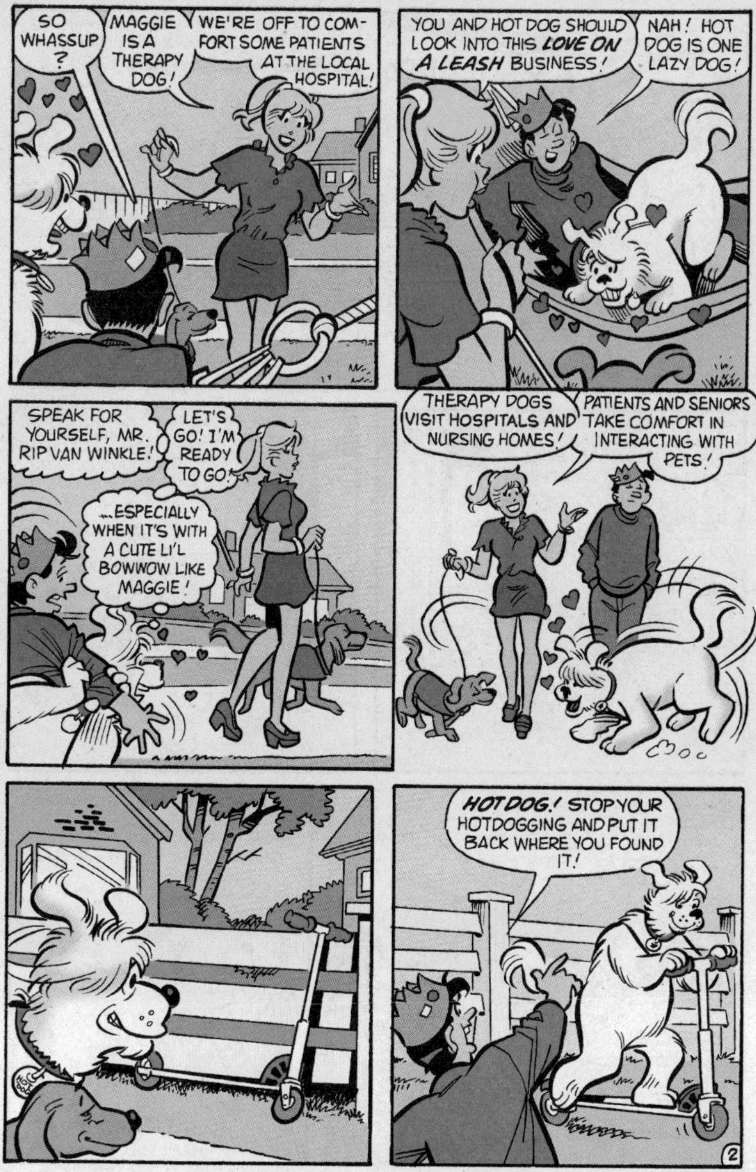
SO WHASSUP?
MAGGIE IS A THERAPY DOG!
WE'RE OFF TO COMFORT SOME PATIENTS AT THE LOCAL HOSPITAL!
YOU AND HOT DOG SHOULD LOOK INTO THIS LOVE ON A LEASH BUSINESS!
NAH! HOT DOG IS ONE LAZY DOG!
SPEAK FOR YOURSELF, MR. RIP VAN WINKLE!
LET'S GO! I'M READY TO GO!
...ESPECIALLY WHEN IT'S WITH A CUTE LI'L BOWWOW LIKE MAGGIE!
THERAPY DOGS VISIT HOSPITALS AND NURSING HOMES!
PATIENTS AND SENIORS TAKE COMFORT IN INTERACTING WITH PETS!
HOT DOG! STOP YOUR HOTDOGGING AND PUT IT BACK WHERE YOU FOUND IT!
2

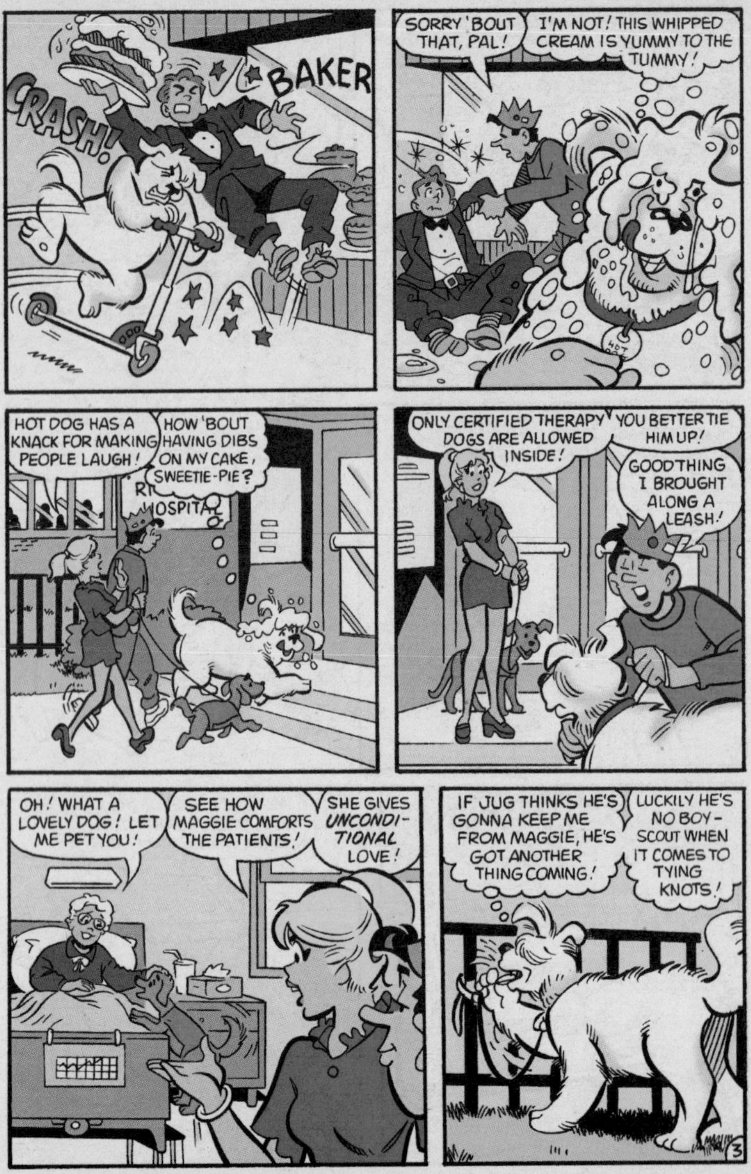
CRASH!
BAKER
SORRY 'BOUT THAT, PAL!
I'M NOT! THIS WHIPPED CREAM IS YUMMY TO THE TUMMY!
HOT DOG
HOT DOG HAS A KNACK FOR MAKING PEOPLE LAUGH!
HOW 'BOUT HAVING DIBS ON MY CAKE, SWEETIE-PIE?
HOSPITAL
ONLY CERTIFIED THERAPY DOGS ARE ALLOWED INSIDE!
YOU BETTER TIE HIM UP!
GOOD THING I BROUGHT ALONG A LEASH!
OH! WHAT A LOVELY DOG! LET ME PET YOU!
SEE HOW MAGGIE COMFORTS THE PATIENTS!
SHE GIVES UNCONDITIONAL LOVE!
IF JUG THINKS HE'S GONNA KEEP ME FROM MAGGIE, HE'S GOT ANOTHER THING COMING!
LUCKILY HE'S NO BOY-SCOUT WHEN IT COMES TO TYING KNOTS!
3

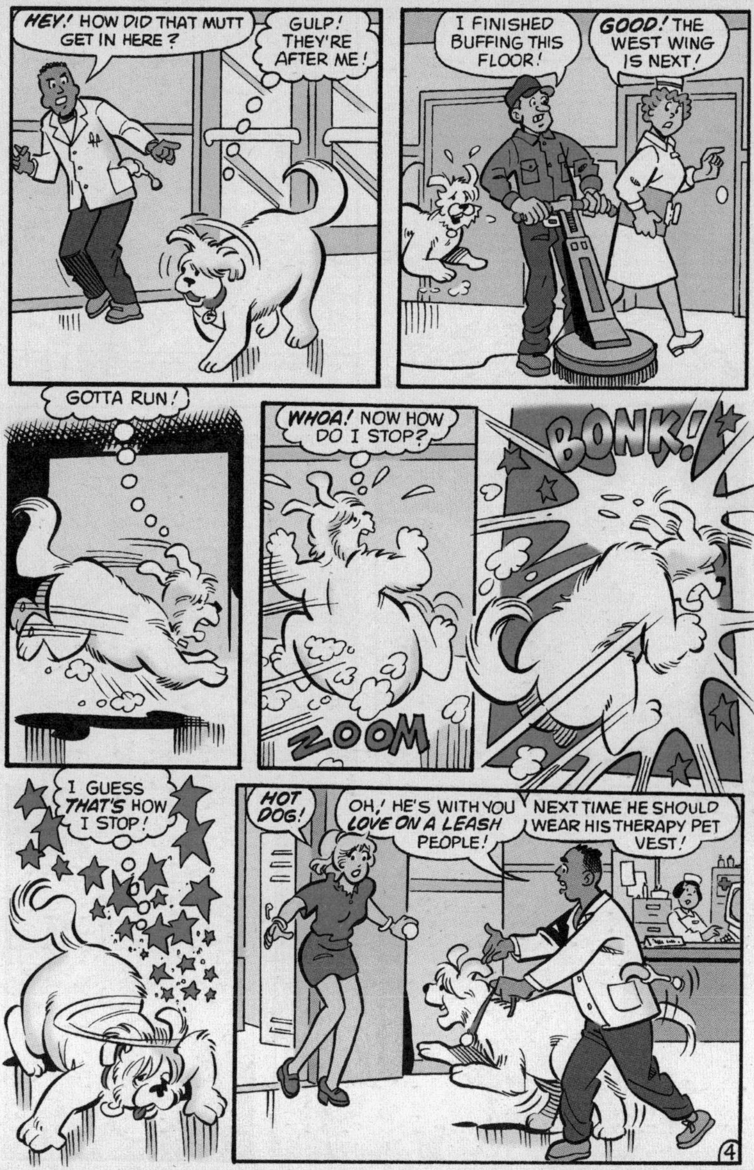
HEY! HOW DID THAT MUTT GET IN HERE?
GULP! THEY'RE AFTER ME!
I FINISHED BUFFING THIS FLOOR!
GOOD! THE WEST WING IS NEXT!
GOTTA RUN!
WHOA! NOW HOW DO I STOP?
ZOOM
BONK!
I GUESS THAT'S HOW I STOP!
HOT DOG!
OH,! HE'S WITH YOU LOVE ON A LEASH PEOPLE!
NEXT TIME HE SHOULD WEAR HIS THERAPY PET VEST!
4

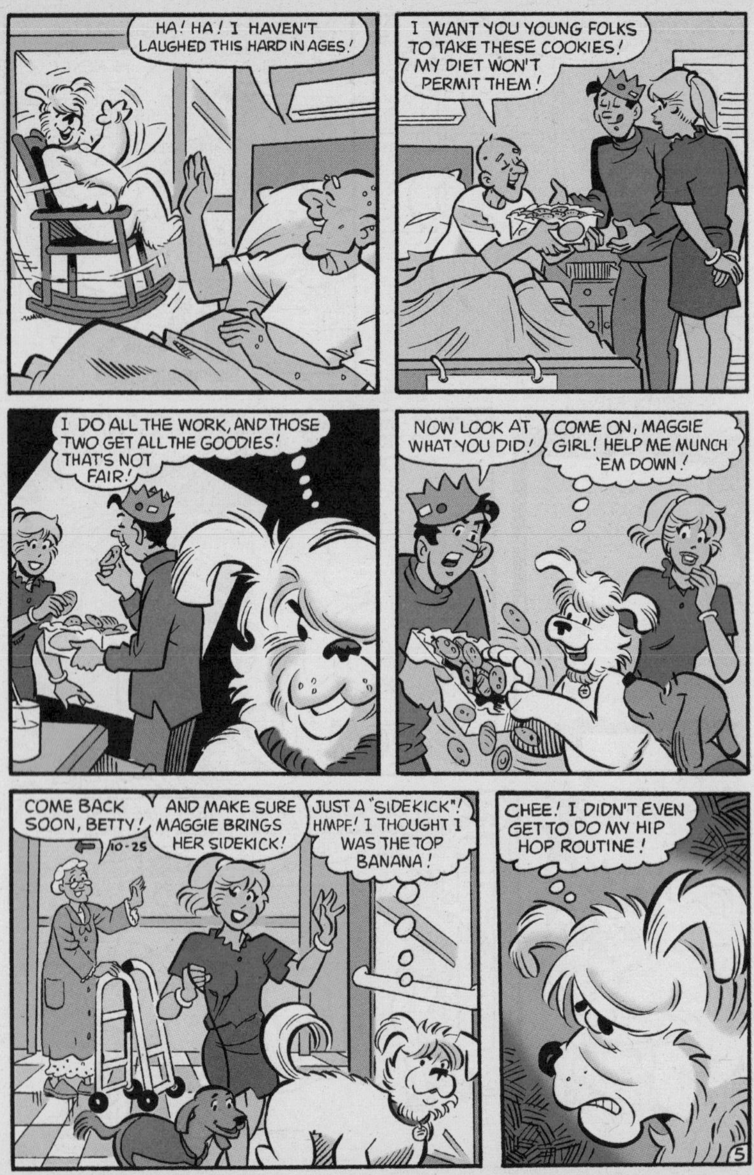
HA! HA! I HAVEN'T LAUGHED THIS HARD IN AGES!
I WANT YOU YOUNG FOLKS TO TAKE THESE COOKIES! MY DIET WON'T PERMIT THEM!
I DO ALL THE WORK, AND THOSE TWO GET ALL THE GOODIES! THAT'S NOT FAIR!
NOW LOOK AT WHAT YOU DID!
COME ON, MAGGIE GIRL! HELP ME MUNCH 'EM DOWN!
COME BACK SOON, BETTY!
AND MAKE SURE MAGGIE BRINGS HER SIDEKICK!
JUST A "SIDEKICK"! HMPF! I THOUGHT I WAS THE TOP BANANA!
10-25
CHEE! I DIDN'T EVEN GET TO DO MY HIP HOP ROUTINE!

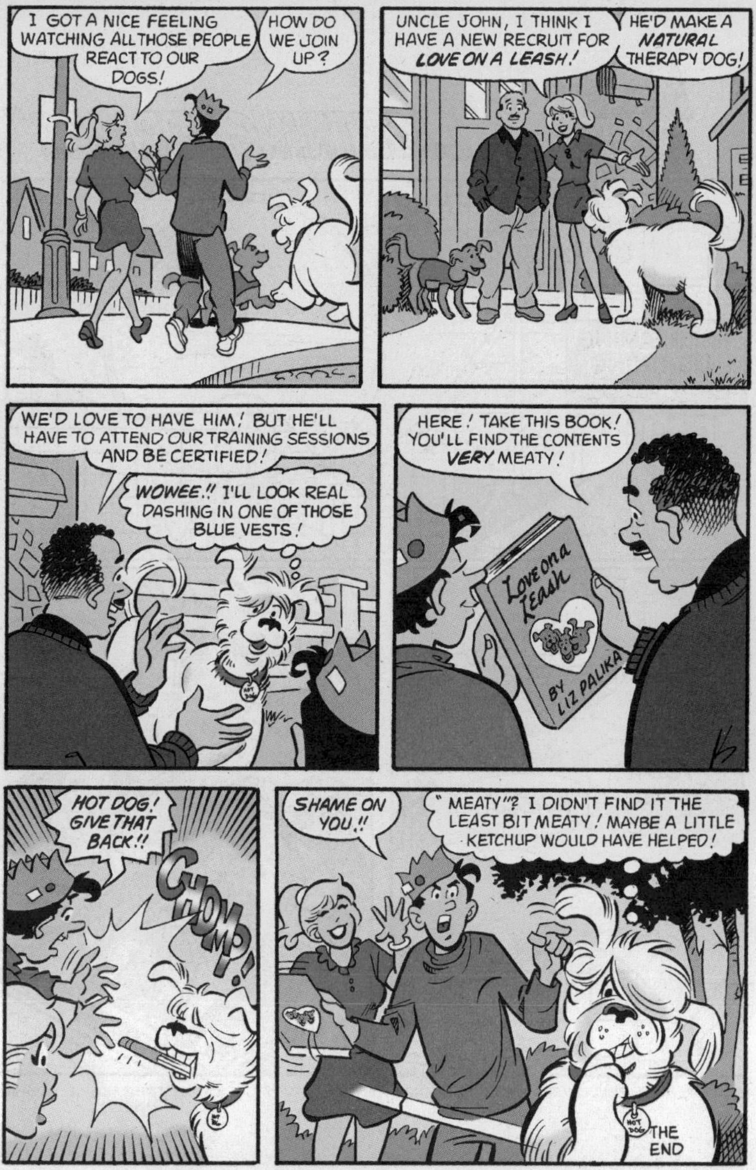
I GOT A NICE FEELING WATCHING ALL THOSE PEOPLE REACT TO OUR DOGS!
HOW DO WE JOIN UP?
UNCLE JOHN, I THINK I HAVE A NEW RECRUIT FOR LOVE ON A LEASH!
HE'D MAKE A NATURAL THERAPY DOG!
WE'D LOVE TO HAVE HIM! BUT HE'LL HAVE TO ATTEND OUR TRAINING SESSIONS AND BE CERTIFIED!
WOWEE!! I'LL LOOK REAL DASHING IN ONE OF THOSE BLUE VESTS!
HERE! TAKE THIS BOOK! YOU'LL FIND THE CONTENTS VERY MEATY!
Love on a Leash
BY LIZ PALIKA
HOT DOG! GIVE THAT BACK!!
CHOMP!
SHAME ON YOU!!
"MEATY"? I DIDN'T FIND IT THE LEAST BIT MEATY! MAYBE A LITTLE KETCHUP WOULD HAVE HELPED!
HOT DOG
THE END

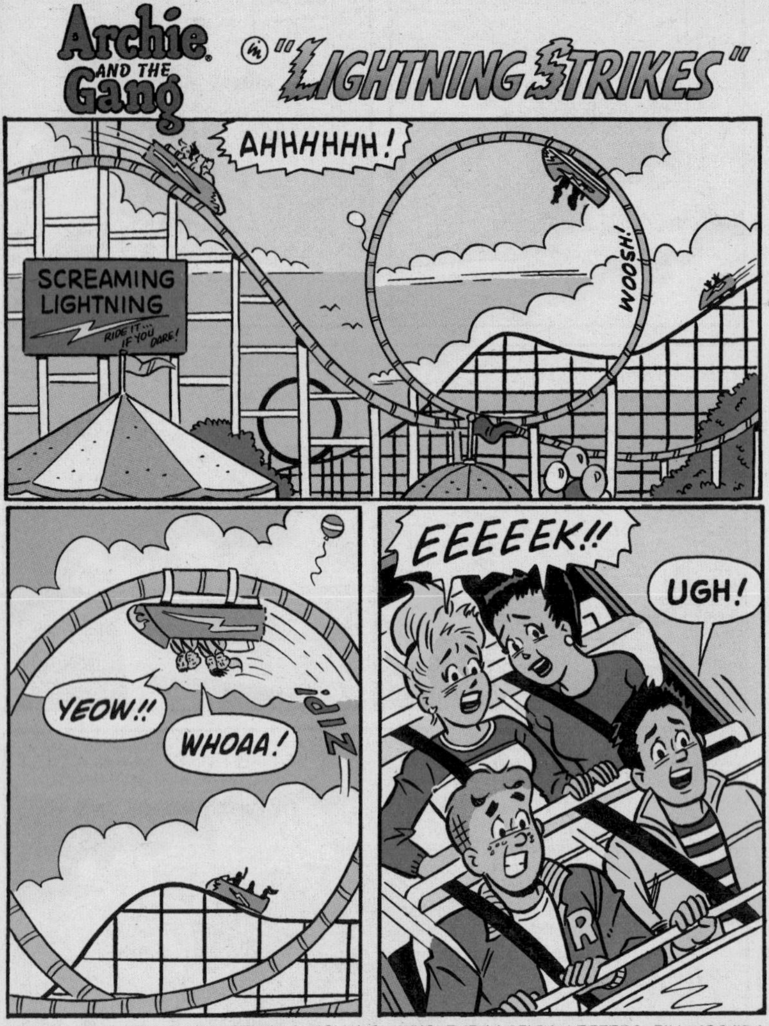
Archie AND THE Gang
in "LIGHTNING STRIKES"
AHHHHHH!
SCREAMING LIGHTNING
RIDE IT... IF YOU DARE!
WOOSH!
YEOW!!
WHOAA!
ZIP!
EEEEEK!!
UGH!

SCRIPT: MIKE PELLOWSKI PENCILS: HOLLY G. INKS: RUDY LAPICK LETTERS: BILL YOSHIDA

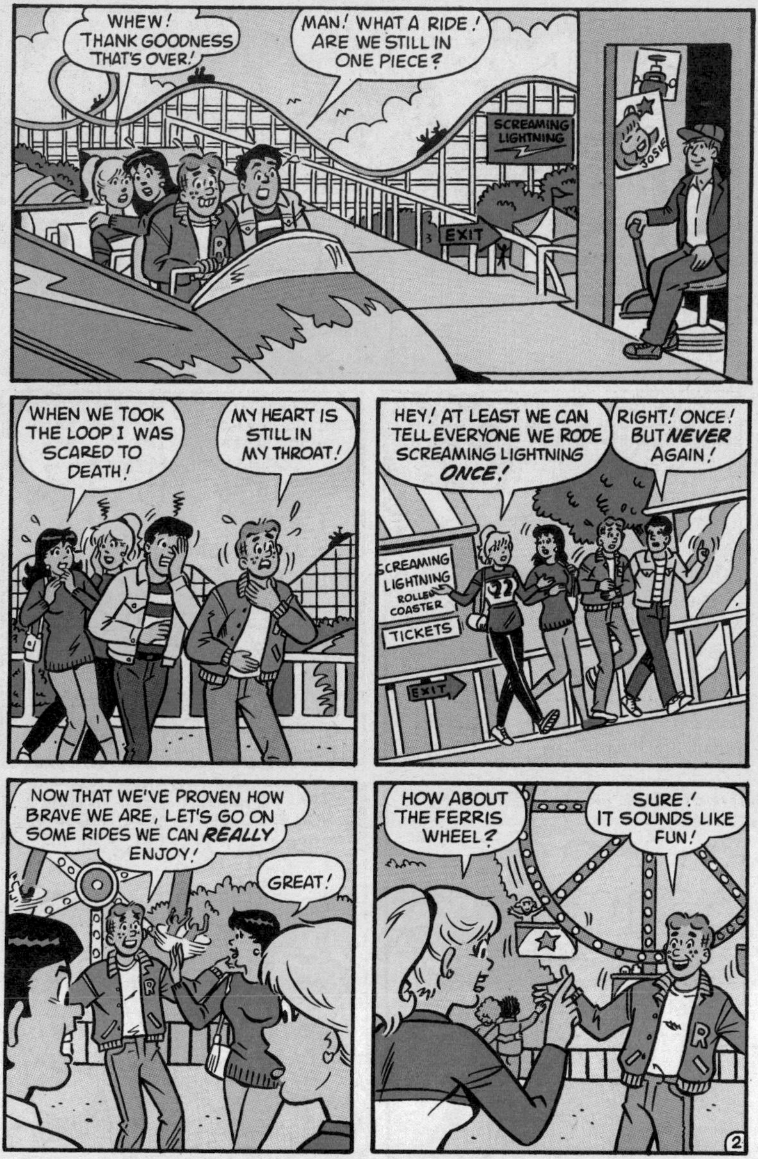
WHEW! THANK GOODNESS THAT'S OVER!
MAN! WHAT A RIDE! ARE WE STILL IN ONE PIECE?
SCREAMING LIGHTNING
EXIT
JOSIE
WHEN WE TOOK THE LOOP I WAS SCARED TO DEATH!
MY HEART IS STILL IN MY THROAT!
HEY! AT LEAST WE CAN TELL EVERYONE WE RODE SCREAMING LIGHTNING *ONCE!*
RIGHT! ONCE! BUT *NEVER* AGAIN!
SCREAMING LIGHTNING ROLLER COASTER
TICKETS
EXIT
NOW THAT WE'VE PROVEN HOW BRAVE WE ARE, LET'S GO ON SOME RIDES WE CAN *REALLY* ENJOY!
GREAT!
HOW ABOUT THE FERRIS WHEEL?
SURE! IT SOUNDS LIKE FUN!

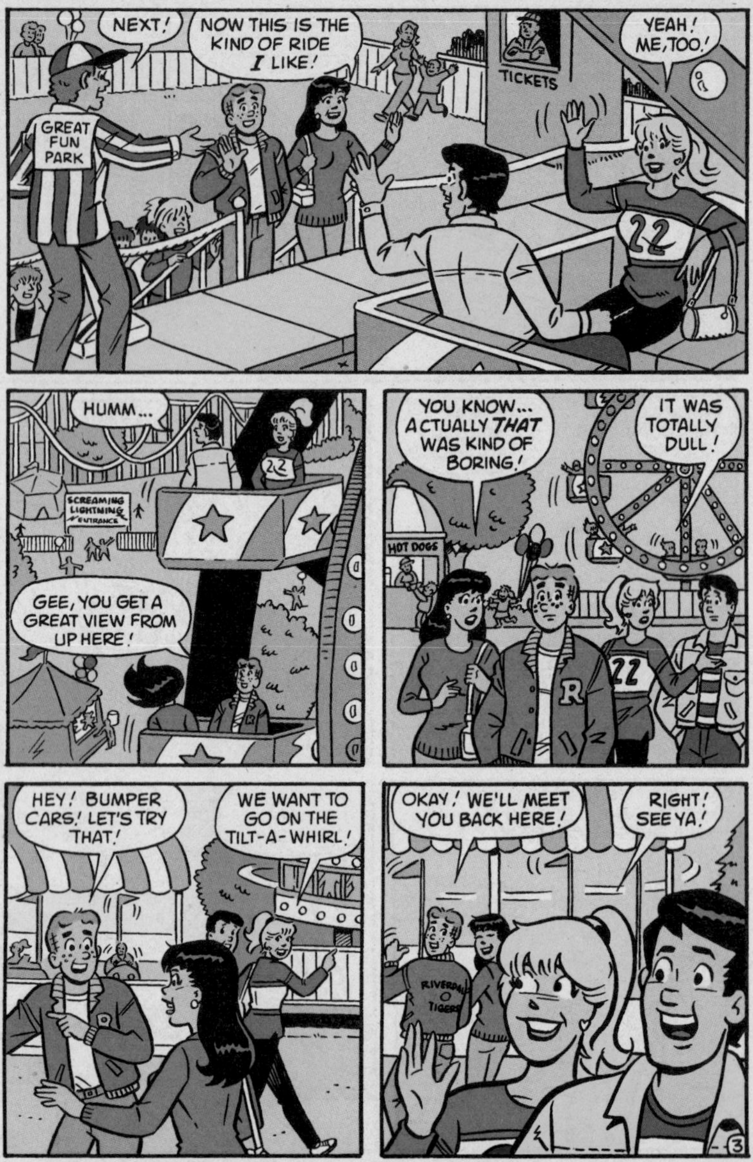
NEXT!
NOW THIS IS THE KIND OF RIDE I LIKE!
TICKETS
YEAH! ME, TOO!
GREAT FUN PARK
HUMM...
SCREAMING LIGHTNING ENTRANCE
GEE, YOU GET A GREAT VIEW FROM UP HERE!
YOU KNOW... ACTUALLY THAT WAS KIND OF BORING!
IT WAS TOTALLY DULL!
HOT DOGS
HEY! BUMPER CARS! LET'S TRY THAT!
WE WANT TO GO ON THE TILT-A-WHIRL!
OKAY! WE'LL MEET YOU BACK HERE!
RIGHT! SEE YA!
RIVERDALE TIGERS
3

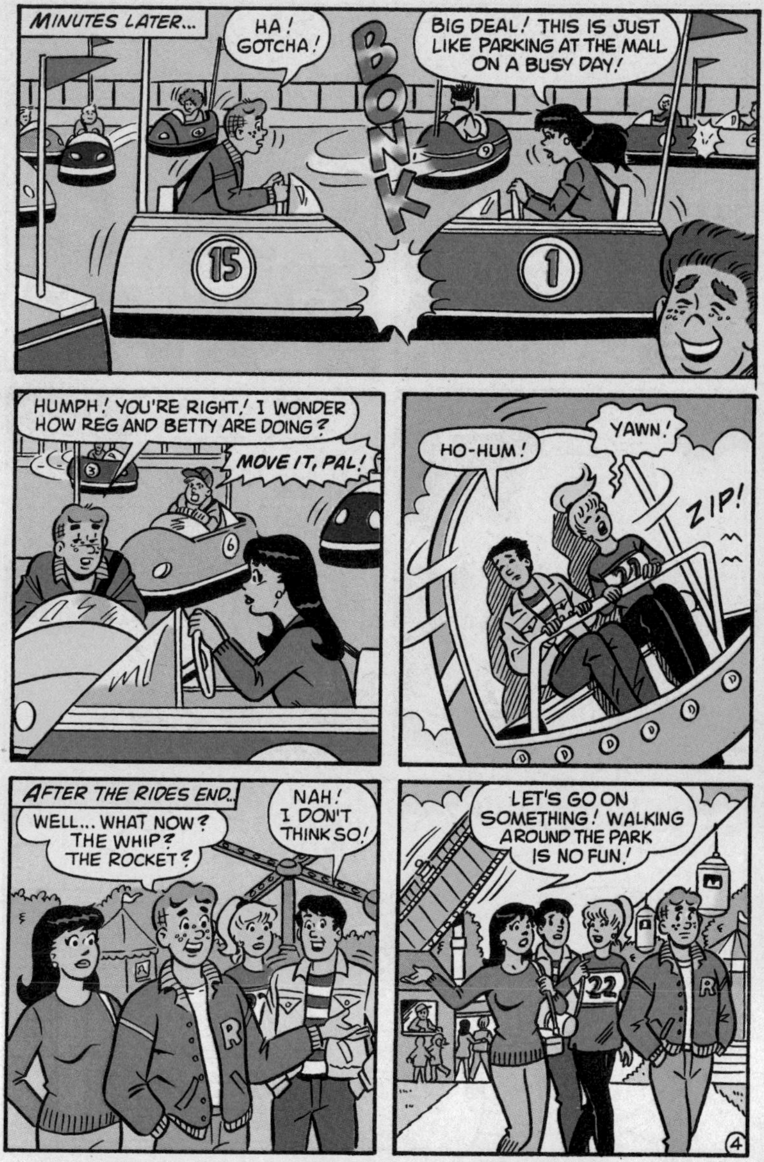
MINUTES LATER...
HA! GOTCHA!
BONK
BIG DEAL! THIS IS JUST LIKE PARKING AT THE MALL ON A BUSY DAY!
HUMPH! YOU'RE RIGHT! I WONDER HOW REG AND BETTY ARE DOING?
MOVE IT, PAL!
HO-HUM!
YAWN!
ZIP!
AFTER THE RIDES END...
WELL... WHAT NOW? THE WHIP? THE ROCKET?
NAH! I DON'T THINK SO!
LET'S GO ON SOMETHING! WALKING AROUND THE PARK IS NO FUN!
4

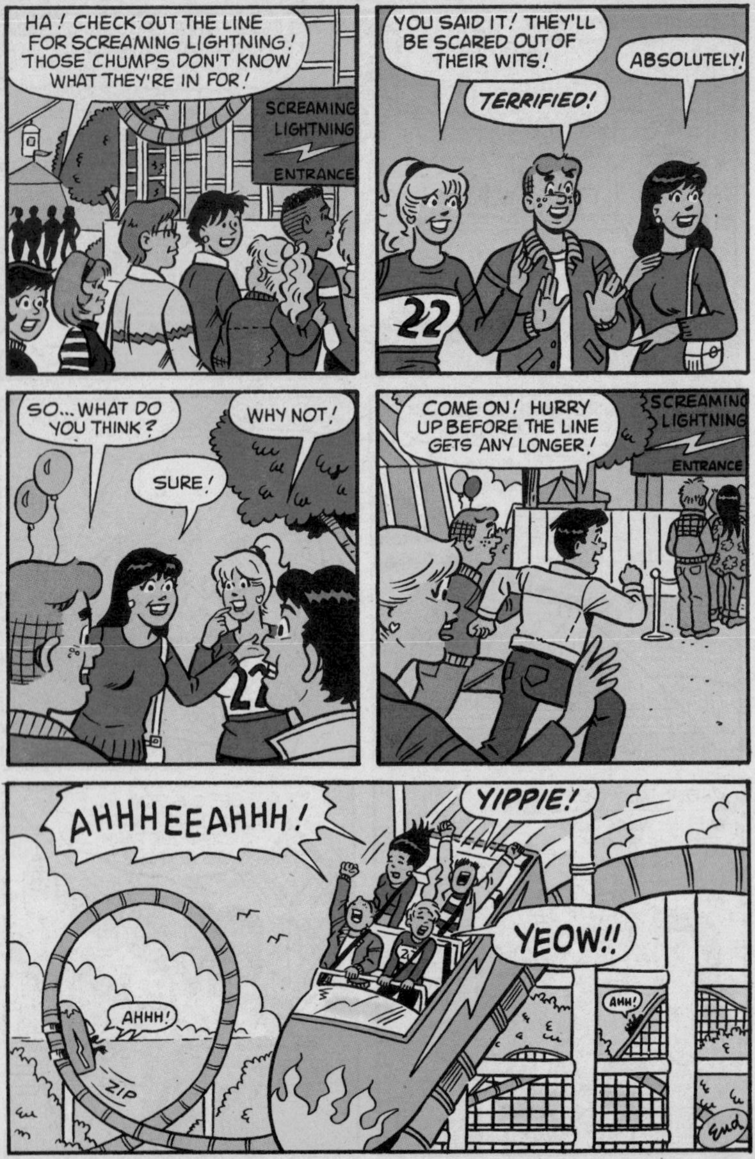
HA! CHECK OUT THE LINE FOR SCREAMING LIGHTNING! THOSE CHUMPS DON'T KNOW WHAT THEY'RE IN FOR!
SCREAMING LIGHTNING ENTRANCE
YOU SAID IT! THEY'LL BE SCARED OUT OF THEIR WITS!
TERRIFIED!
ABSOLUTELY!
22
SO... WHAT DO YOU THINK?
SURE!
WHY NOT!
COME ON! HURRY UP BEFORE THE LINE GETS ANY LONGER!
SCREAMING LIGHTNING ENTRANCE
AHHHEEAHHH!
YIPPIE!
YEOW!!
AHHH!
AHH!
ZIP
End

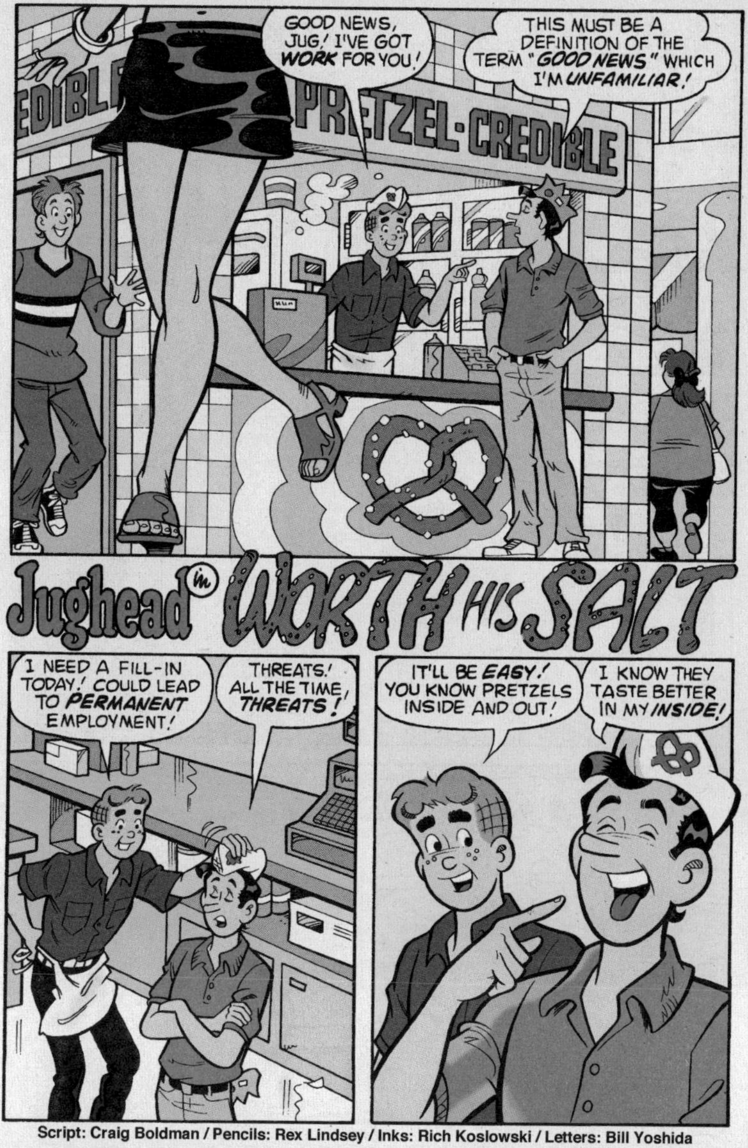

GOOD NEWS, JUG! I'VE GOT WORK FOR YOU!
THIS MUST BE A DEFINITION OF THE TERM "GOOD NEWS" WHICH I'M UNFAMILIAR!
PRETZEL-CREDIBLE
Jughead in WORTH HIS SALT
I NEED A FILL-IN TODAY! COULD LEAD TO PERMANENT EMPLOYMENT!
THREATS! ALL THE TIME, THREATS!
IT'LL BE EASY! YOU KNOW PRETZELS INSIDE AND OUT!
I KNOW THEY TASTE BETTER IN MY INSIDE!

Script: Craig Boldman / Pencils: Rex Lindsey / Inks: Rich Koslowski / Letters: Bill Yoshida

Panel 1:
YOU'LL WORK WITH *JAN* HERE!

WELL, YOU DON'T LOOK *TOO* MEAN!

Panel 2:
IT'S VERY SIMPLE! FIRST YOU KNEAD THE *DOUGH*...

YOU THINK I'D STAY HERE IF I DIDN'T NEED THE *DOUGH?*

Panel 3:
CUT OFF A STRIP, GIVE IT A *TWIST*, AND *VOILA!*

FLIP

TWIST

Panel 4:
THEN YOU PUT IT IN THE *OVEN*...

HOLD ON...

Panel 5:
I'M STILL WORKING ON *STEP 2!*

②

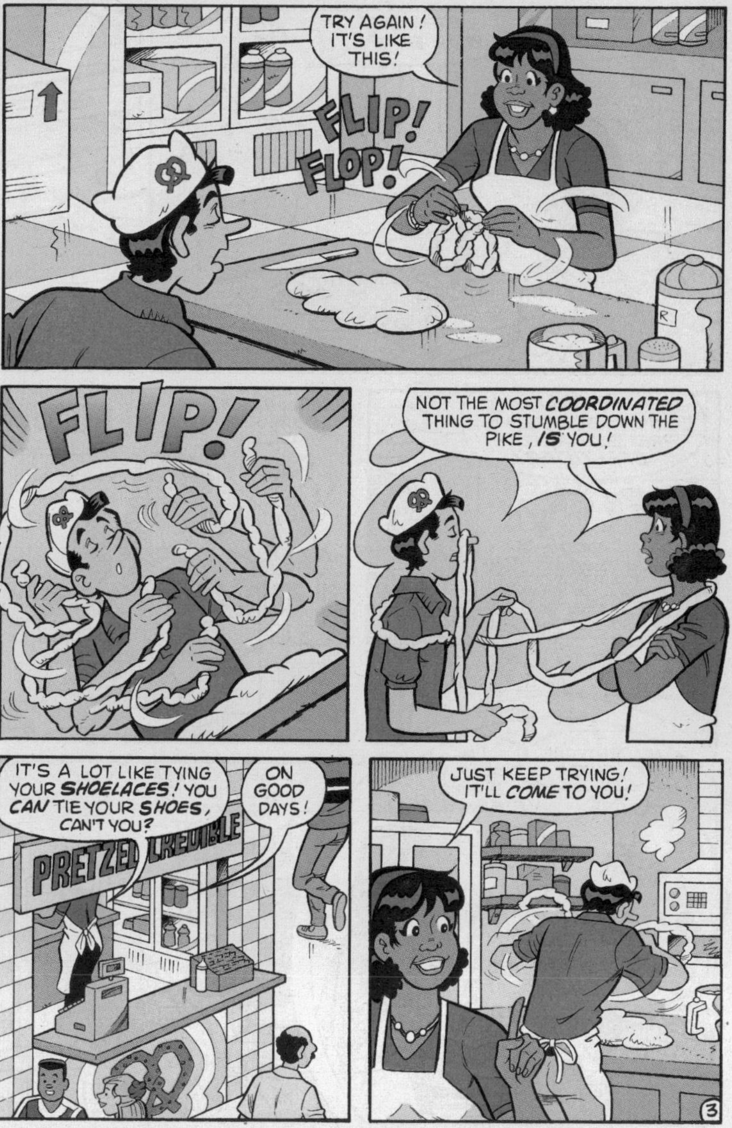
TRY AGAIN! IT'S LIKE THIS!
FLIP! FLOP!
FLIP!
NOT THE MOST COORDINATED THING TO STUMBLE DOWN THE PIKE, IS YOU!
IT'S A LOT LIKE TYING YOUR SHOELACES! YOU CAN TIE YOUR SHOES, CAN'T YOU?
ON GOOD DAYS!
JUST KEEP TRYING! IT'LL COME TO YOU!
3

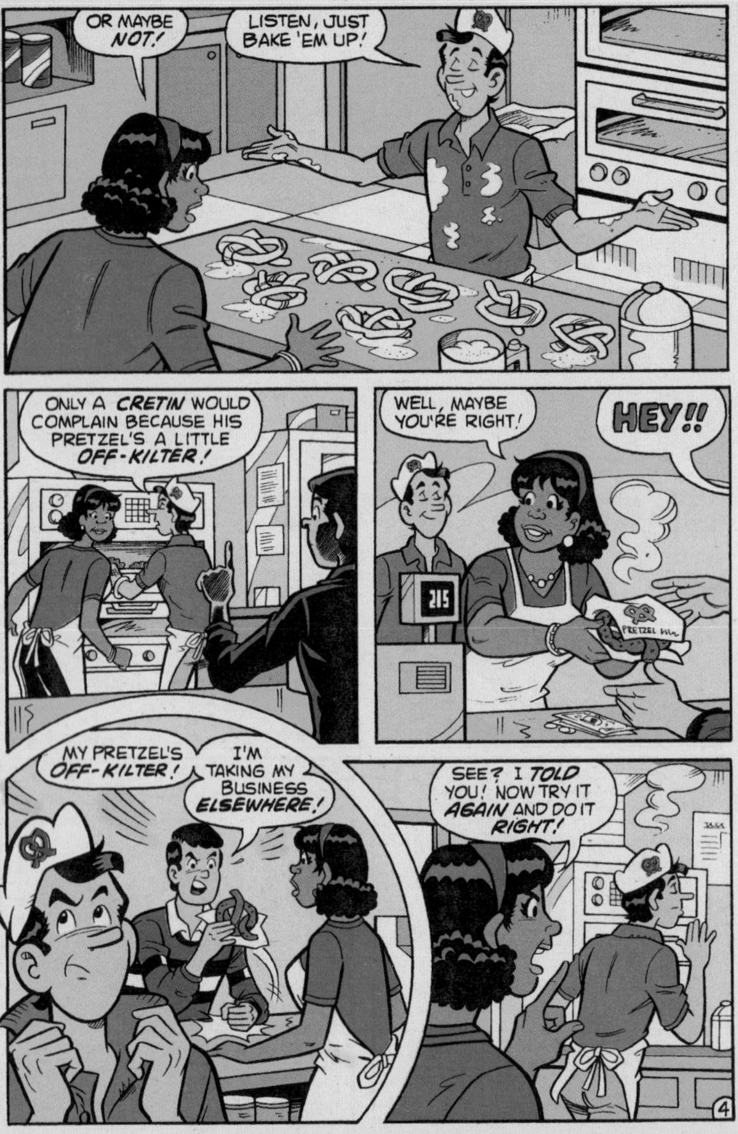
OR MAYBE NOT!
LISTEN, JUST BAKE 'EM UP!
ONLY A CRETIN WOULD COMPLAIN BECAUSE HIS PRETZEL'S A LITTLE OFF-KILTER!
WELL, MAYBE YOU'RE RIGHT!
HEY!!
215
PRETZEL
MY PRETZEL'S OFF-KILTER!
I'M TAKING MY BUSINESS ELSEWHERE!
SEE? I TOLD YOU! NOW TRY IT AGAIN AND DO IT RIGHT!
4

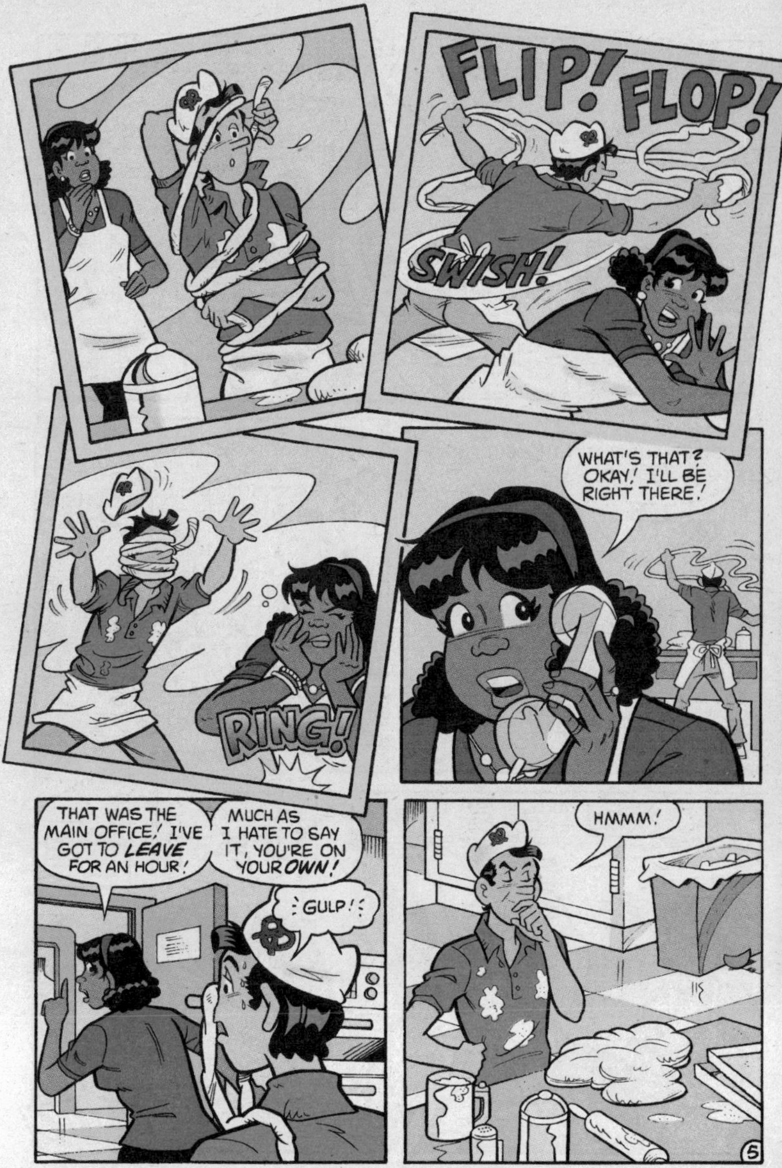
FLIP!
FLOP!
SWISH!
RING!
WHAT'S THAT? OKAY! I'LL BE RIGHT THERE!
THAT WAS THE MAIN OFFICE! I'VE GOT TO LEAVE FOR AN HOUR!
MUCH AS I HATE TO SAY IT, YOU'RE ON YOUR OWN!
GULP!
HMMM!

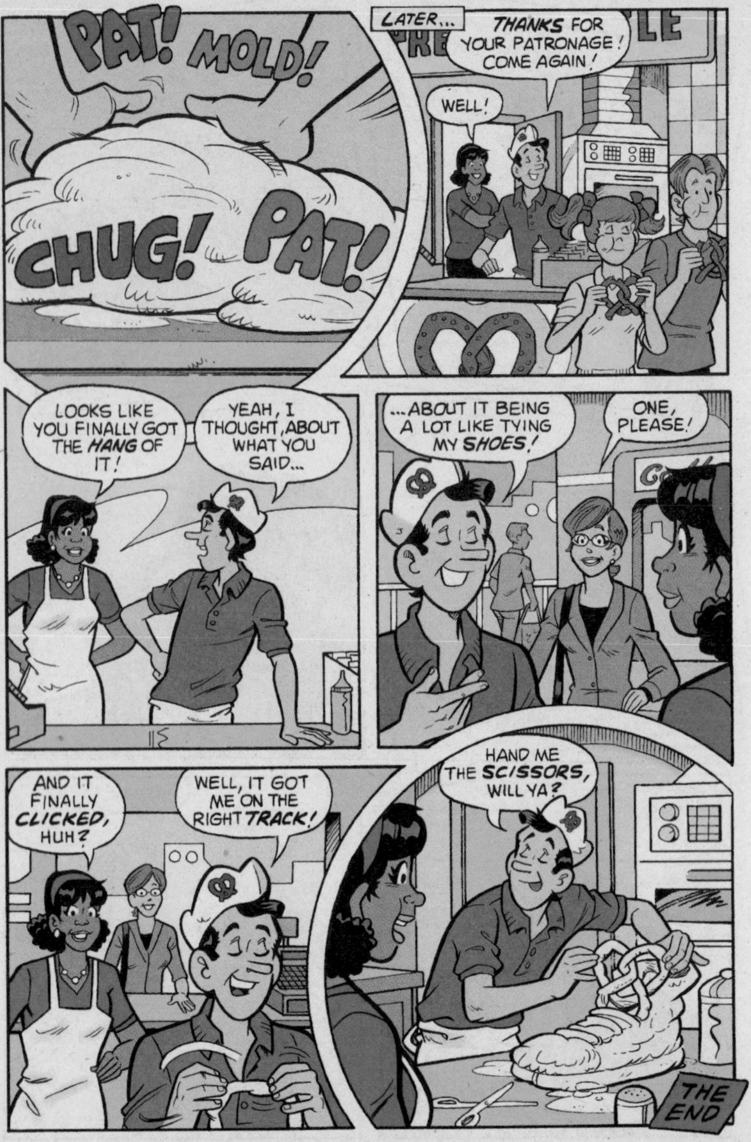
PAT! MOLD!
CHUG! PAT!
LATER...
THANKS FOR YOUR PATRONAGE! COME AGAIN!
WELL!
LOOKS LIKE YOU FINALLY GOT THE HANG OF IT!
YEAH, I THOUGHT, ABOUT WHAT YOU SAID...
...ABOUT IT BEING A LOT LIKE TYING MY SHOES!
ONE, PLEASE!
AND IT FINALLY CLICKED, HUH?
WELL, IT GOT ME ON THE RIGHT TRACK!
HAND ME THE SCISSORS, WILL YA?
THE END

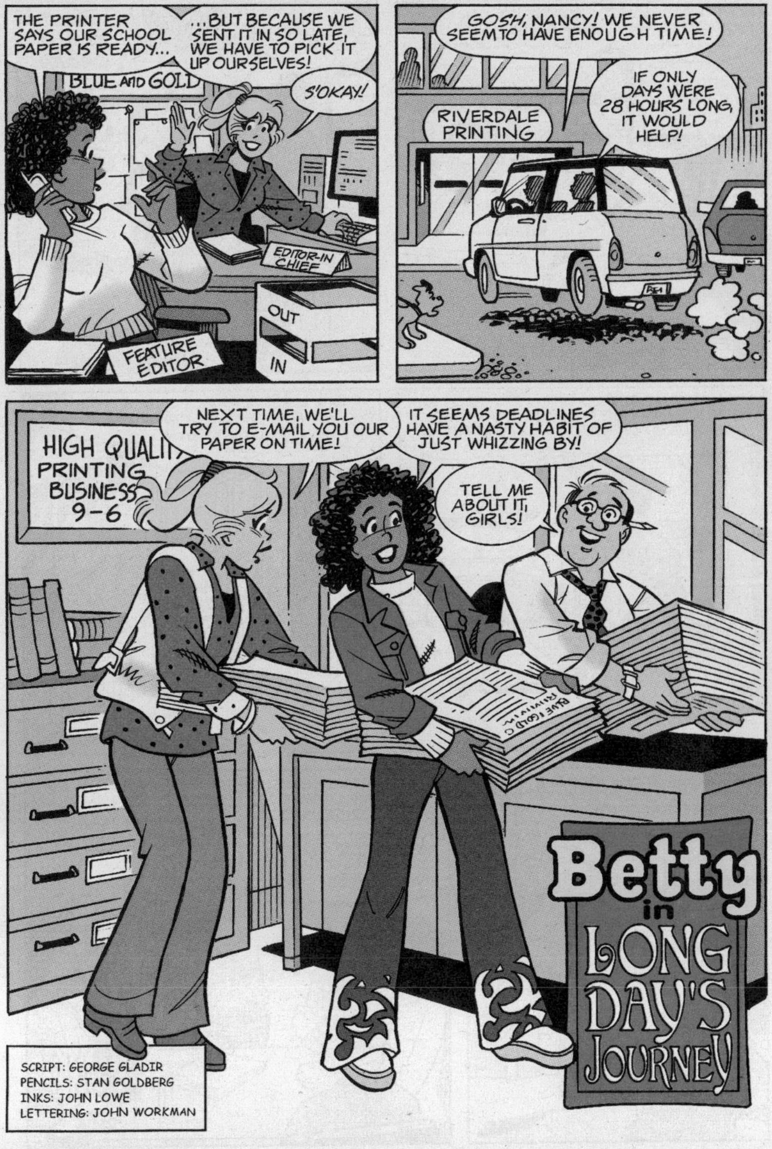
THE PRINTER SAYS OUR SCHOOL PAPER IS READY...
...BUT BECAUSE WE SENT IT IN SO LATE, WE HAVE TO PICK IT UP OURSELVES!
S'OKAY!
BLUE AND GOLD
EDITOR-IN CHIEF
FEATURE EDITOR
OUT
IN
GOSH, NANCY! WE NEVER SEEM TO HAVE ENOUGH TIME!
IF ONLY DAYS WERE 28 HOURS LONG, IT WOULD HELP!
RIVERDALE PRINTING
HIGH QUALITY PRINTING BUSINESS 9-6
NEXT TIME, WE'LL TRY TO E-MAIL YOU OUR PAPER ON TIME!
IT SEEMS DEADLINES HAVE A NASTY HABIT OF JUST WHIZZING BY!
TELL ME ABOUT IT, GIRLS!
Betty in LONG DAY'S JOURNEY
SCRIPT: GEORGE GLADIR
PENCILS: STAN GOLDBERG
INKS: JOHN LOWE
LETTERING: JOHN WORKMAN

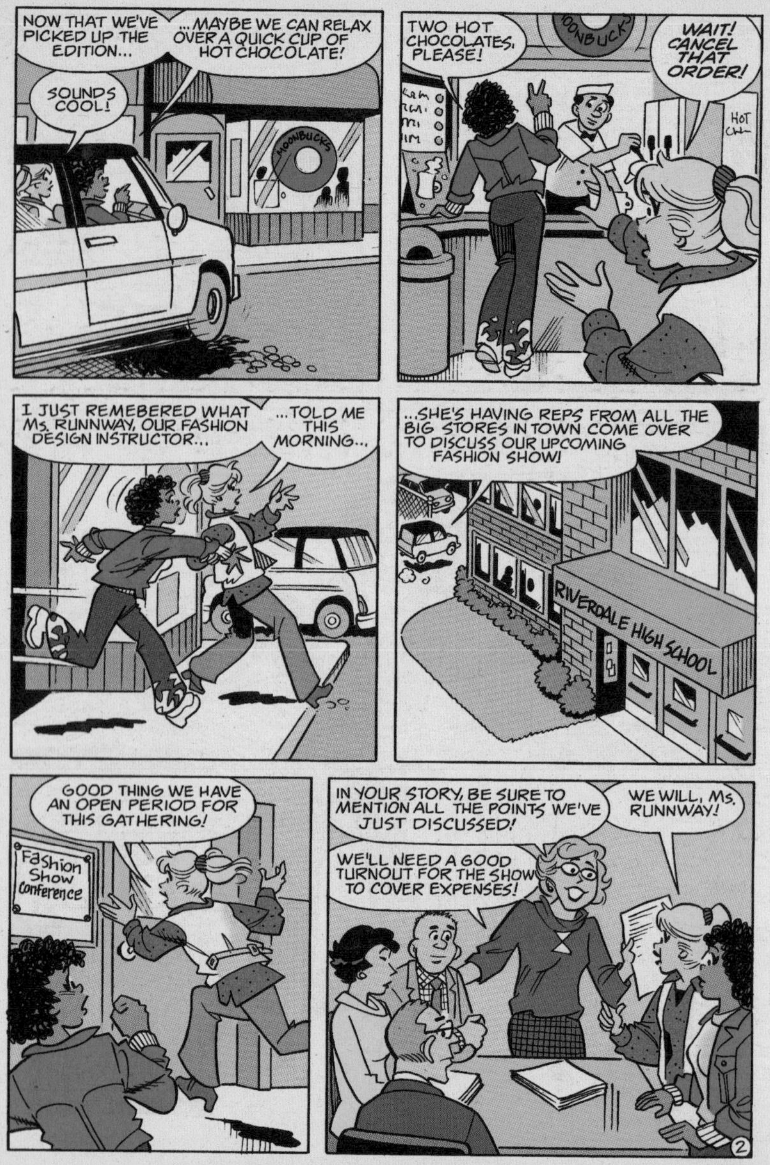
NOW THAT WE'VE PICKED UP THE EDITION...
...MAYBE WE CAN RELAX OVER A QUICK CUP OF HOT CHOCOLATE!
SOUNDS COOL!
MOONBUCKS
TWO HOT CHOCOLATES, PLEASE!
MOONBUCKS
WAIT! CANCEL THAT ORDER!
I JUST REMEBERED WHAT Ms. RUNNWAY, OUR FASHION DESIGN INSTRUCTOR...
...TOLD ME THIS MORNING...
...SHE'S HAVING REPS FROM ALL THE BIG STORES IN TOWN COME OVER TO DISCUSS OUR UPCOMING FASHION SHOW!
RIVERDALE HIGH SCHOOL
GOOD THING WE HAVE AN OPEN PERIOD FOR THIS GATHERING!
Fashion Show Conference
IN YOUR STORY, BE SURE TO MENTION ALL THE POINTS WE'VE JUST DISCUSSED!
WE WILL, Ms. RUNNWAY!
WE'LL NEED A GOOD TURNOUT FOR THE SHOW TO COVER EXPENSES!
2

CHUCK AND I KNEW YOU TWO WOULD BE BUSY... ...SO WE BROUGHT YOU YOUR LUNCHES!

YOU GUYS ARE LIFE-SAVERS!

BLUE AND GOLD

FEATURE EDITOR

MAYBE IF WE FOUND SOMEONE TO EAT OUR LUNCHES FOR US, WE'D *REALLY* SAVE TIME!

DO YOU THINK WE CAN GET JUGHEAD TO DO IT?

OUR FIRST AFTERNOON PERIOD IS COMING UP IN FIVE MINUTES!

WHAT?! WE HAVE FIVE MORE MINUTES TO GET THERE!

FEATURE EDITOR

WOW! THAT MEANS WE CAN WALK TO OUR CLASS AT A NICE LEISURELY PACE!

FOR A CHANGE!

BLUE AND GOLD

BETTY, I'D LIKE TO SEE YOU FOR A SECOND!

UH, YES, MR. WEATHERBEE!?!

MR. WEATHER PRINCIPAL

PARTS OF THIS EDITORIAL YOU WROTE IN OUR PAPER WERE QUITE CONTRO-VERSIAL!

I WAS MERELY TRYING TO COVER BOTH SIDES OF A THORNY ISSUE!

③

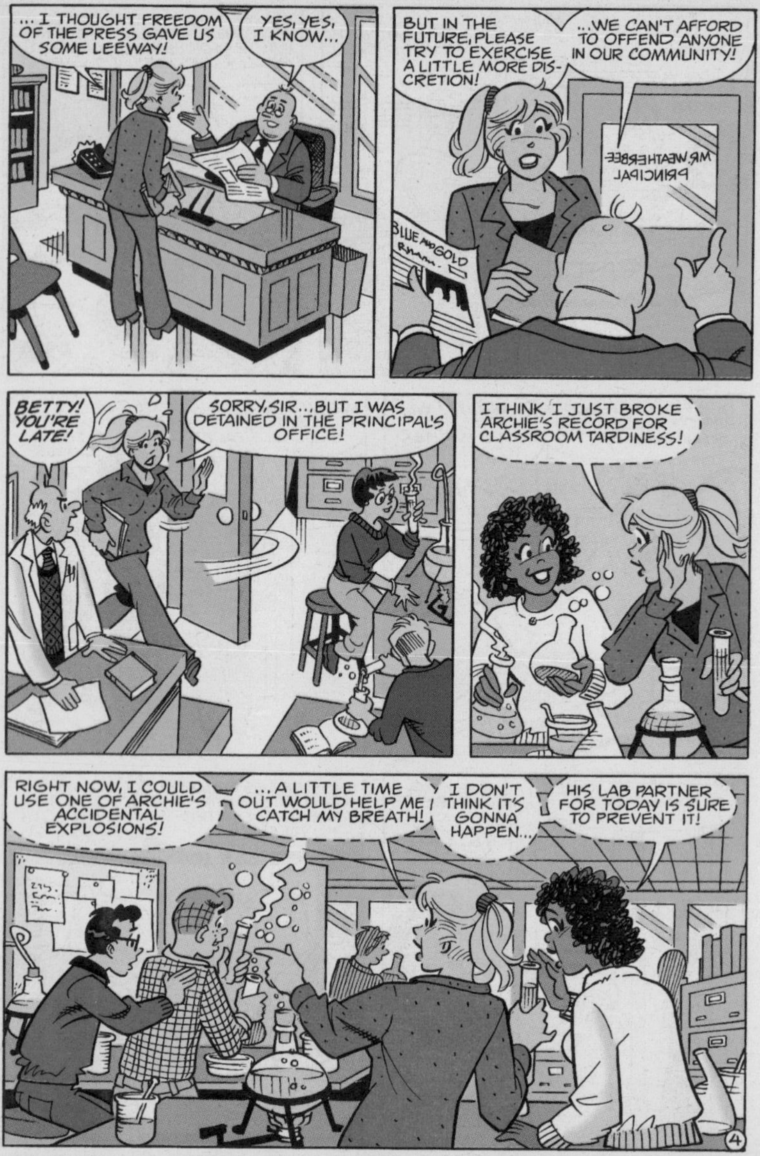
... I THOUGHT FREEDOM OF THE PRESS GAVE US SOME LEEWAY!
YES, YES, I KNOW...
BUT IN THE FUTURE, PLEASE TRY TO EXERCISE A LITTLE MORE DIS-CRETION!
...WE CAN'T AFFORD TO OFFEND ANYONE IN OUR COMMUNITY!
MR. WEATHERBEE PRINCIPAL
BLUE AND GOLD
BETTY! YOU'RE LATE!
SORRY, SIR... BUT I WAS DETAINED IN THE PRINCIPAL'S OFFICE!
I THINK I JUST BROKE ARCHIE'S RECORD FOR CLASSROOM TARDINESS!
RIGHT NOW, I COULD USE ONE OF ARCHIE'S ACCIDENTAL EXPLOSIONS!
...A LITTLE TIME OUT WOULD HELP ME CATCH MY BREATH!
I DON'T THINK IT'S GONNA HAPPEN...
HIS LAB PARTNER FOR TODAY IS SURE TO PREVENT IT!
4

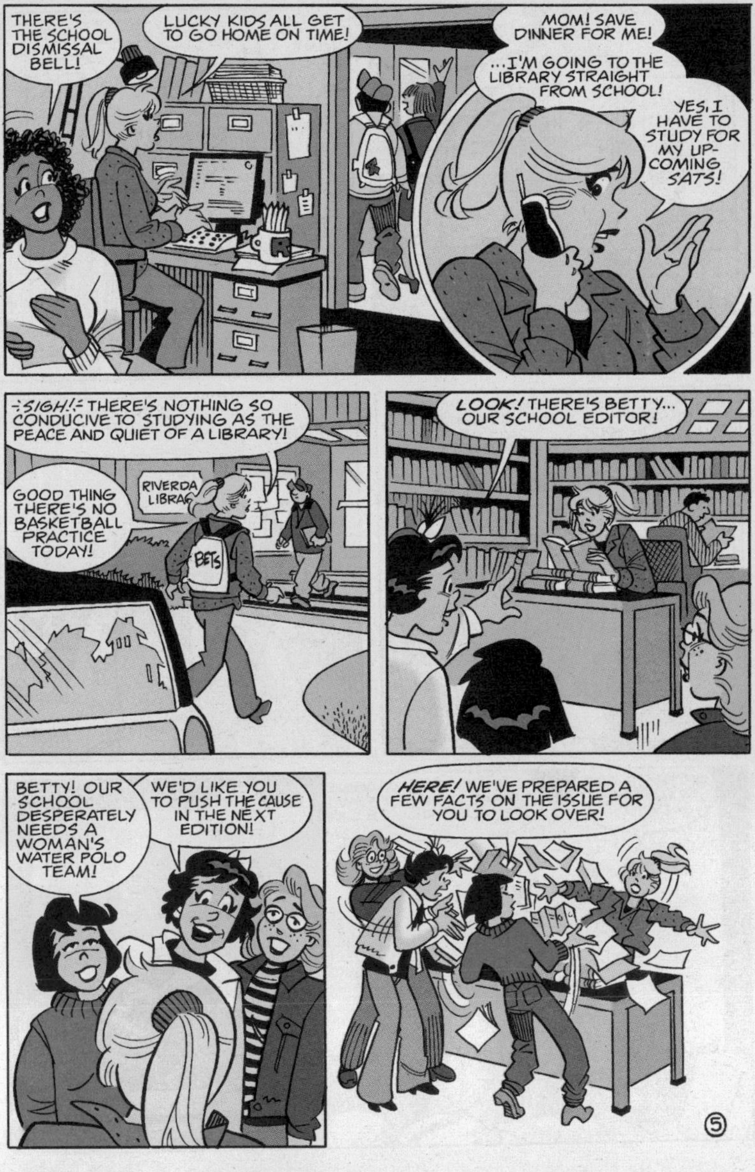

THERE'S THE SCHOOL DISMISSAL BELL!
LUCKY KIDS ALL GET TO GO HOME ON TIME!
MOM! SAVE DINNER FOR ME!
...I'M GOING TO THE LIBRARY STRAIGHT FROM SCHOOL!
YES, I HAVE TO STUDY FOR MY UP-COMING SATS!
-SIGH!- THERE'S NOTHING SO CONDUCIVE TO STUDYING AS THE PEACE AND QUIET OF A LIBRARY!
GOOD THING THERE'S NO BASKETBALL PRACTICE TODAY!
RIVERDA LIBRA
BETS
LOOK! THERE'S BETTY... OUR SCHOOL EDITOR!
BETTY! OUR SCHOOL DESPERATELY NEEDS A WOMAN'S WATER POLO TEAM!
WE'D LIKE YOU TO PUSH THE CAUSE IN THE NEXT EDITION!
HERE! WE'VE PREPARED A FEW FACTS ON THE ISSUE FOR YOU TO LOOK OVER!

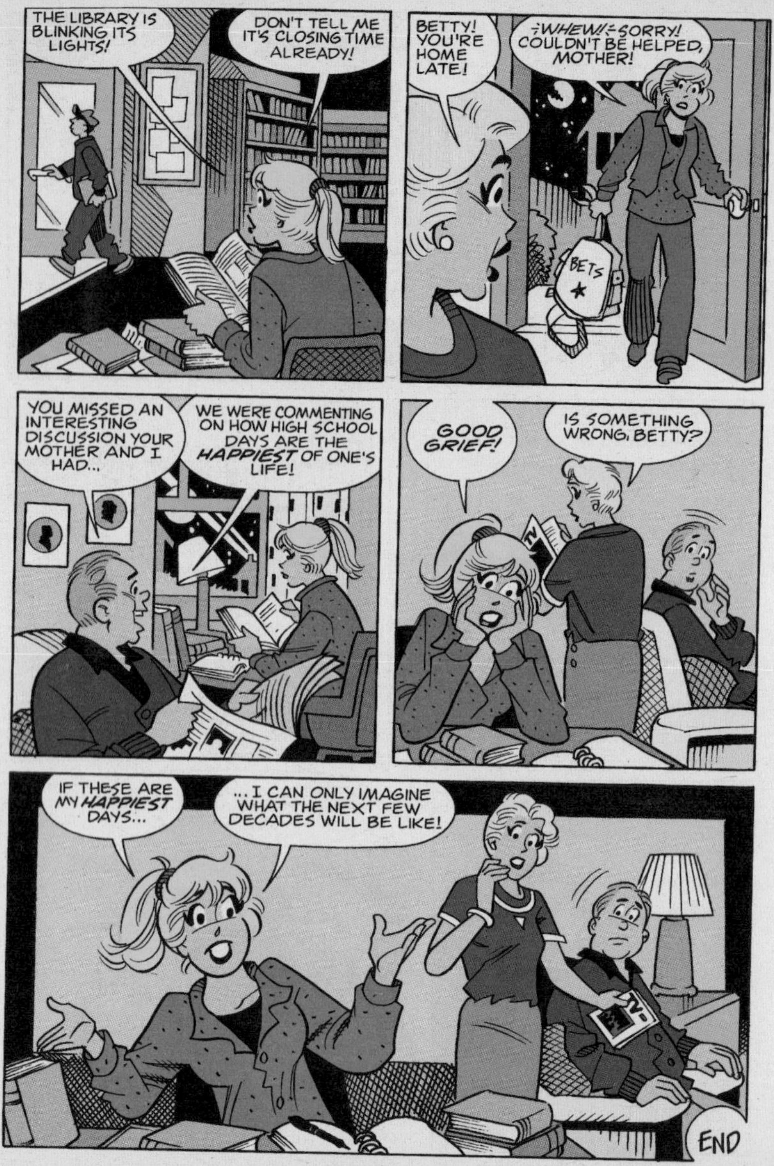
THE LIBRARY IS BLINKING ITS LIGHTS!
DON'T TELL ME IT'S CLOSING TIME ALREADY!
BETTY! YOU'RE HOME LATE!
WHEW! SORRY! COULDN'T BE HELPED, MOTHER!
BETS
YOU MISSED AN INTERESTING DISCUSSION YOUR MOTHER AND I HAD...
WE WERE COMMENTING ON HOW HIGH SCHOOL DAYS ARE THE HAPPIEST OF ONE'S LIFE!
GOOD GRIEF!
IS SOMETHING WRONG, BETTY?
IF THESE ARE MY HAPPIEST DAYS...
...I CAN ONLY IMAGINE WHAT THE NEXT FEW DECADES WILL BE LIKE!
END

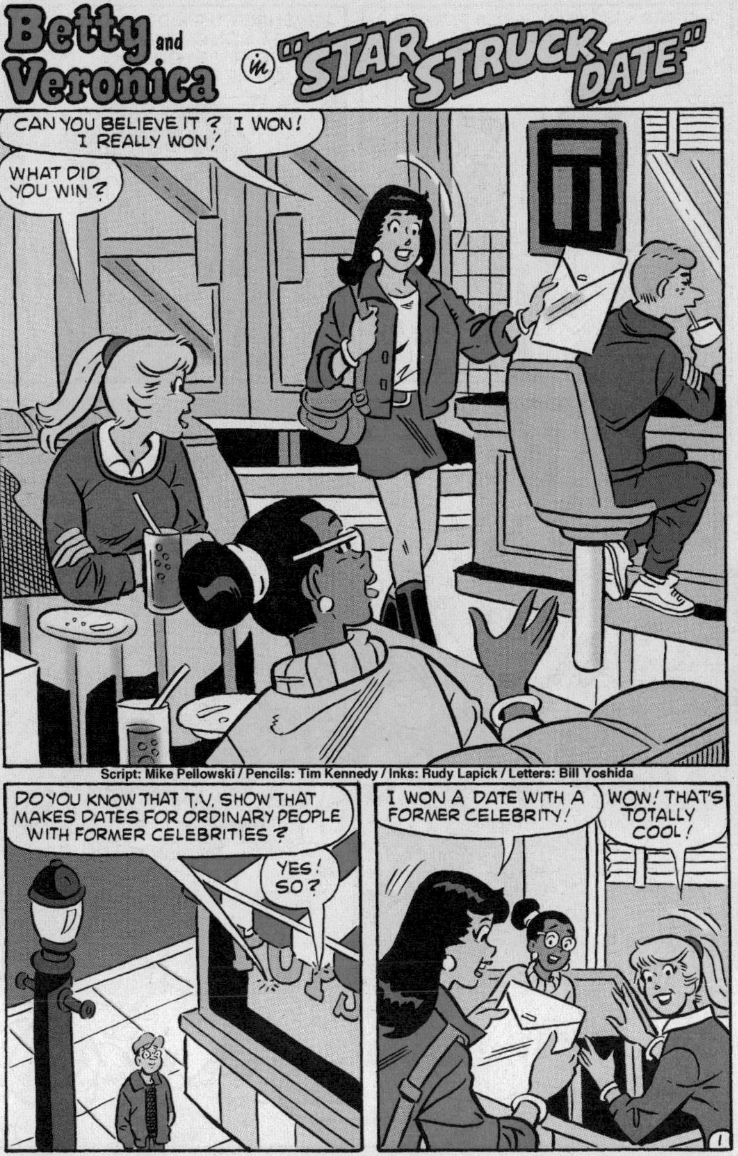
Betty and Veronica
in "STAR STRUCK DATE"
CAN YOU BELIEVE IT? I WON! I REALLY WON!
WHAT DID YOU WIN?
Script: Mike Pellowski / Pencils: Tim Kennedy / Inks: Rudy Lapick / Letters: Bill Yoshida
DO YOU KNOW THAT T.V. SHOW THAT MAKES DATES FOR ORDINARY PEOPLE WITH FORMER CELEBRITIES?
YES! SO?
I WON A DATE WITH A FORMER CELEBRITY!
WOW! THAT'S TOTALLY COOL!
1

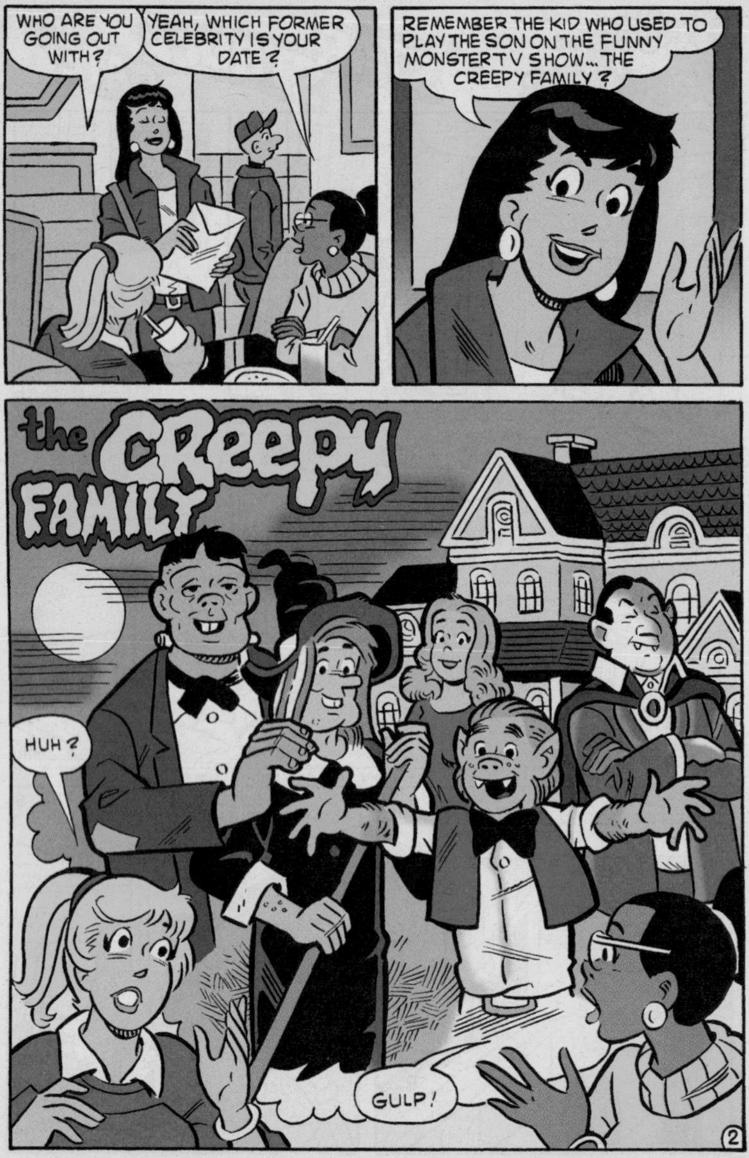
WHO ARE YOU GOING OUT WITH?
YEAH, WHICH FORMER CELEBRITY IS YOUR DATE?
REMEMBER THE KID WHO USED TO PLAY THE SON ON THE FUNNY MONSTER TV SHOW... THE CREEPY FAMILY?
the CREEPY FAMILY
HUH?
GULP!
2

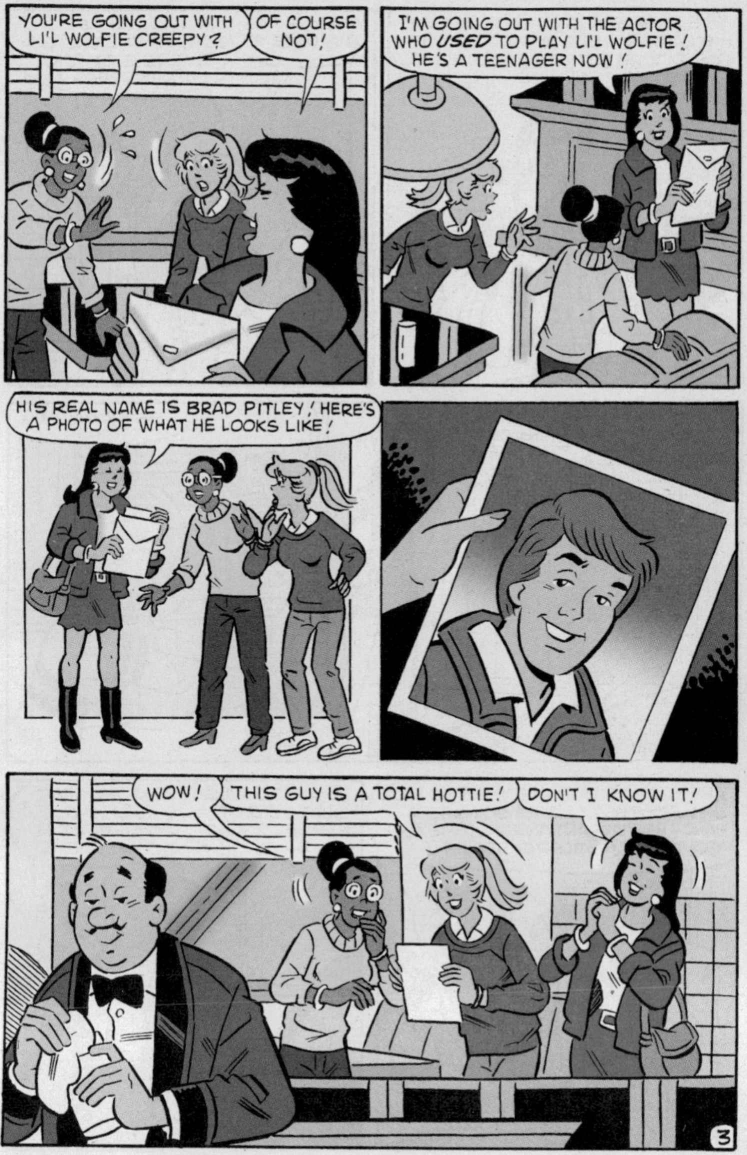
YOU'RE GOING OUT WITH LI'L WOLFIE CREEPY?
OF COURSE NOT!
I'M GOING OUT WITH THE ACTOR WHO USED TO PLAY LI'L WOLFIE! HE'S A TEENAGER NOW!
HIS REAL NAME IS BRAD PITLEY! HERE'S A PHOTO OF WHAT HE LOOKS LIKE!
WOW!
THIS GUY IS A TOTAL HOTTIE!
DON'T I KNOW IT!
3

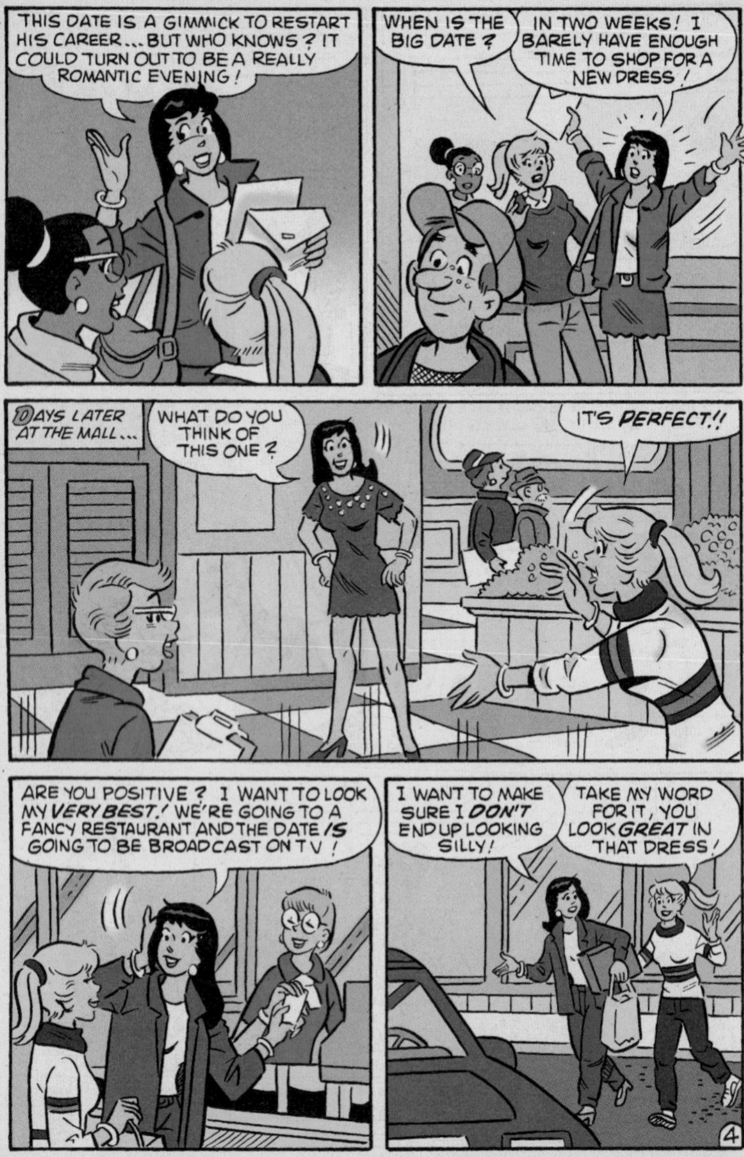

THIS DATE IS A GIMMICK TO RESTART HIS CAREER... BUT WHO KNOWS? IT COULD TURN OUT TO BE A REALLY ROMANTIC EVENING!
WHEN IS THE BIG DATE?
IN TWO WEEKS! I BARELY HAVE ENOUGH TIME TO SHOP FOR A NEW DRESS!
10 DAYS LATER AT THE MALL...
WHAT DO YOU THINK OF THIS ONE?
IT'S PERFECT!!
ARE YOU POSITIVE? I WANT TO LOOK MY VERY BEST! WE'RE GOING TO A FANCY RESTAURANT AND THE DATE IS GOING TO BE BROADCAST ON TV!
I WANT TO MAKE SURE I DON'T END UP LOOKING SILLY!
TAKE MY WORD FOR IT, YOU LOOK GREAT IN THAT DRESS!
4

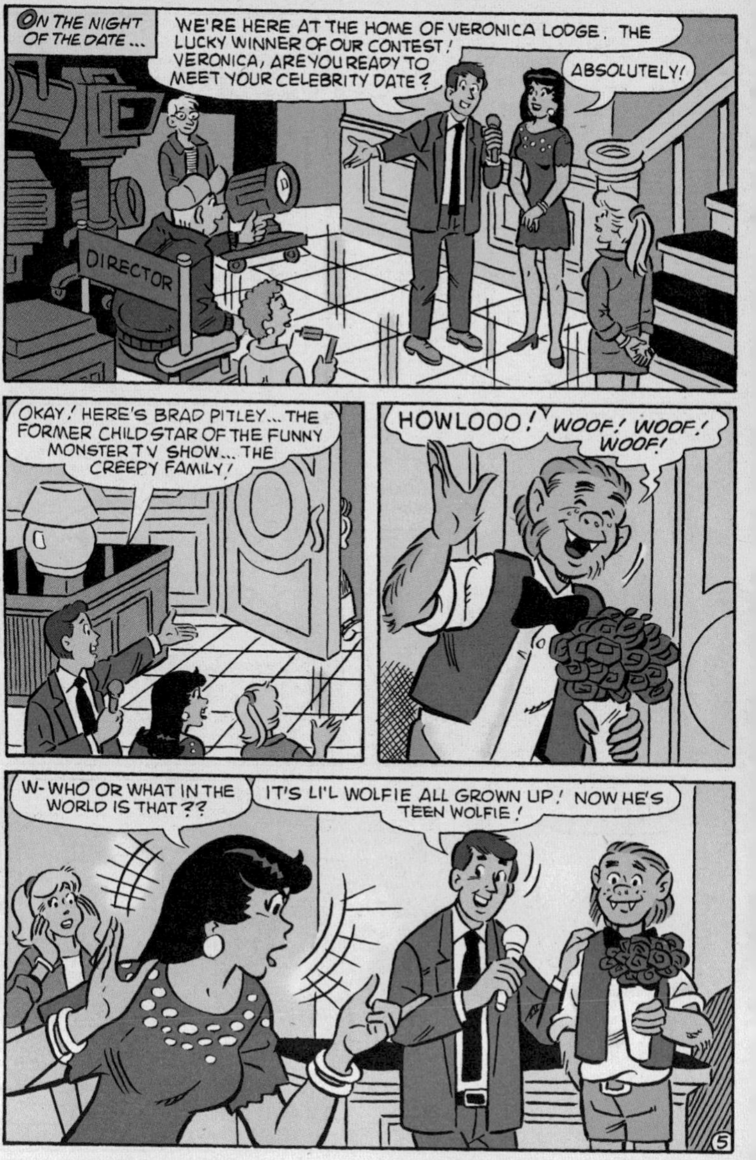
ON THE NIGHT OF THE DATE ...
WE'RE HERE AT THE HOME OF VERONICA LODGE, THE LUCKY WINNER OF OUR CONTEST! VERONICA, ARE YOU READY TO MEET YOUR CELEBRITY DATE?
ABSOLUTELY!
DIRECTOR
OKAY! HERE'S BRAD PITLEY... THE FORMER CHILD STAR OF THE FUNNY MONSTER TV SHOW... THE CREEPY FAMILY!
HOWLOOO!
WOOF! WOOF! WOOF!
W-WHO OR WHAT IN THE WORLD IS THAT??
IT'S LI'L WOLFIE ALL GROWN UP! NOW HE'S TEEN WOLFIE!
5

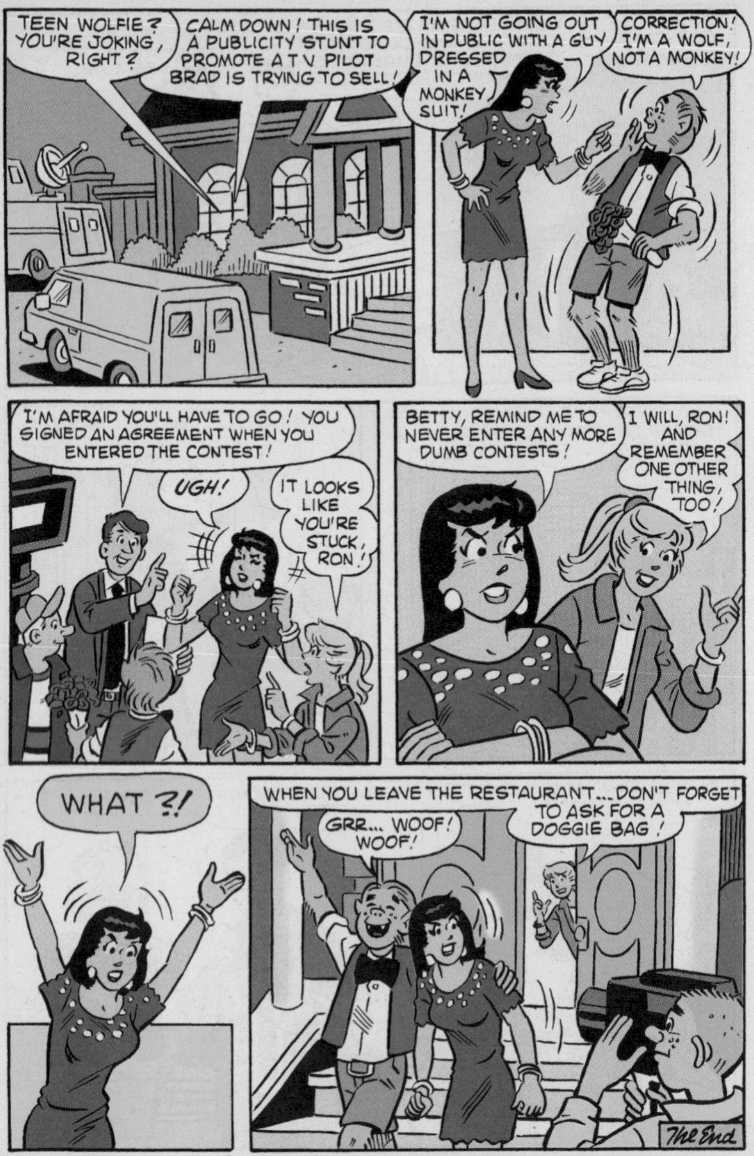
TEEN WOLFIE? YOU'RE JOKING, RIGHT?
CALM DOWN! THIS IS A PUBLICITY STUNT TO PROMOTE A T V PILOT BRAD IS TRYING TO SELL!
I'M NOT GOING OUT IN PUBLIC WITH A GUY DRESSED IN A MONKEY SUIT!
CORRECTION! I'M A WOLF, NOT A MONKEY!
I'M AFRAID YOU'LL HAVE TO GO! YOU SIGNED AN AGREEMENT WHEN YOU ENTERED THE CONTEST!
UGH!
IT LOOKS LIKE YOU'RE STUCK, RON!
BETTY, REMIND ME TO NEVER ENTER ANY MORE DUMB CONTESTS!
I WILL, RON! AND REMEMBER ONE OTHER THING, TOO!
WHAT ?!
WHEN YOU LEAVE THE RESTAURANT... DON'T FORGET TO ASK FOR A DOGGIE BAG!
GRR... WOOF! WOOF!
The End

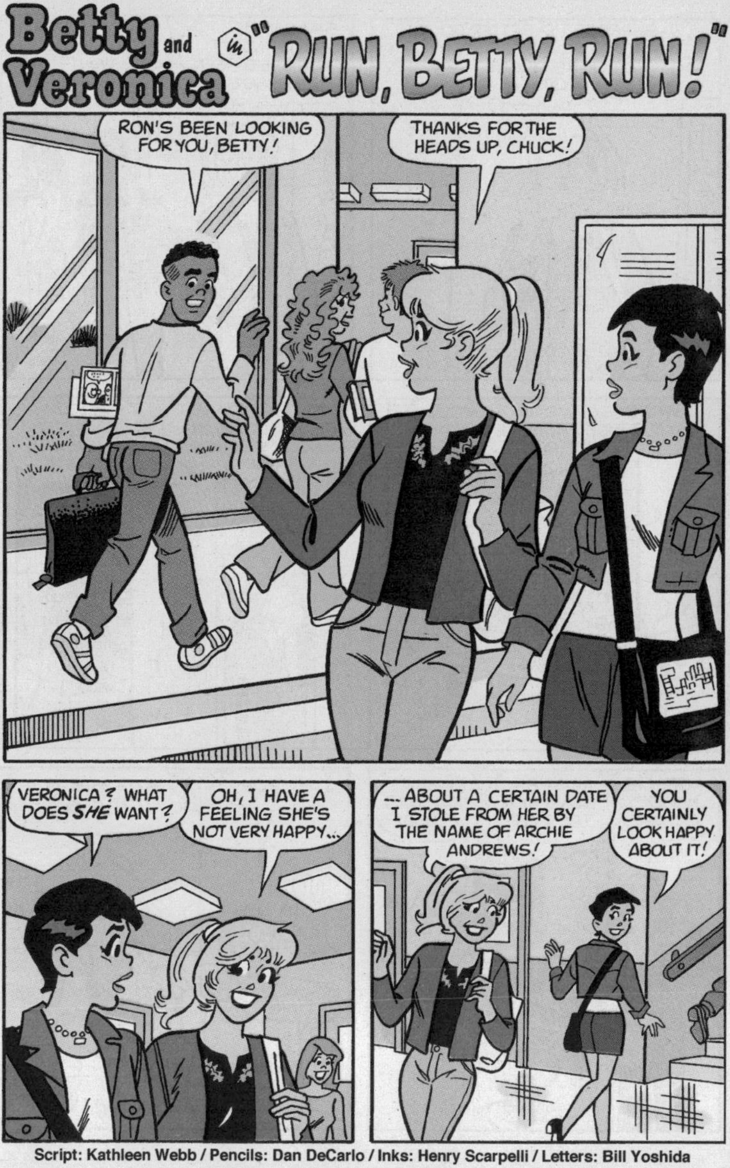
Betty and Veronica in "RUN, BETTY, RUN!"
RON'S BEEN LOOKING FOR YOU, BETTY!
THANKS FOR THE HEADS UP, CHUCK!
VERONICA? WHAT DOES SHE WANT?
OH, I HAVE A FEELING SHE'S NOT VERY HAPPY...
... ABOUT A CERTAIN DATE I STOLE FROM HER BY THE NAME OF ARCHIE ANDREWS!
YOU CERTAINLY LOOK HAPPY ABOUT IT!

Script: Kathleen Webb / Pencils: Dan DeCarlo / Inks: Henry Scarpelli / Letters: Bill Yoshida

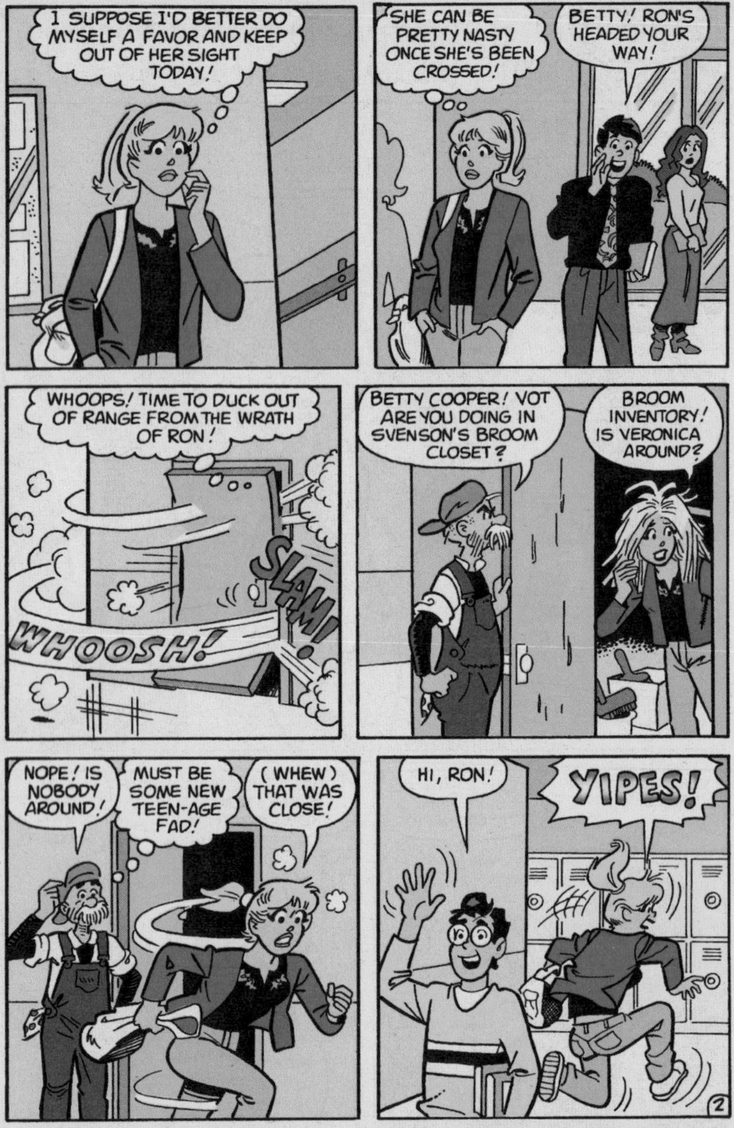
I SUPPOSE I'D BETTER DO MYSELF A FAVOR AND KEEP OUT OF HER SIGHT TODAY!
SHE CAN BE PRETTY NASTY ONCE SHE'S BEEN CROSSED!
BETTY! RON'S HEADED YOUR WAY!
WHOOPS! TIME TO DUCK OUT OF RANGE FROM THE WRATH OF RON!
SLAM!
WHOOSH!
BETTY COOPER! VOT ARE YOU DOING IN SVENSON'S BROOM CLOSET?
BROOM INVENTORY! IS VERONICA AROUND?
NOPE! IS NOBODY AROUND!
MUST BE SOME NEW TEEN-AGE FAD!
(WHEW) THAT WAS CLOSE!
HI, RON!
YIPES!
2

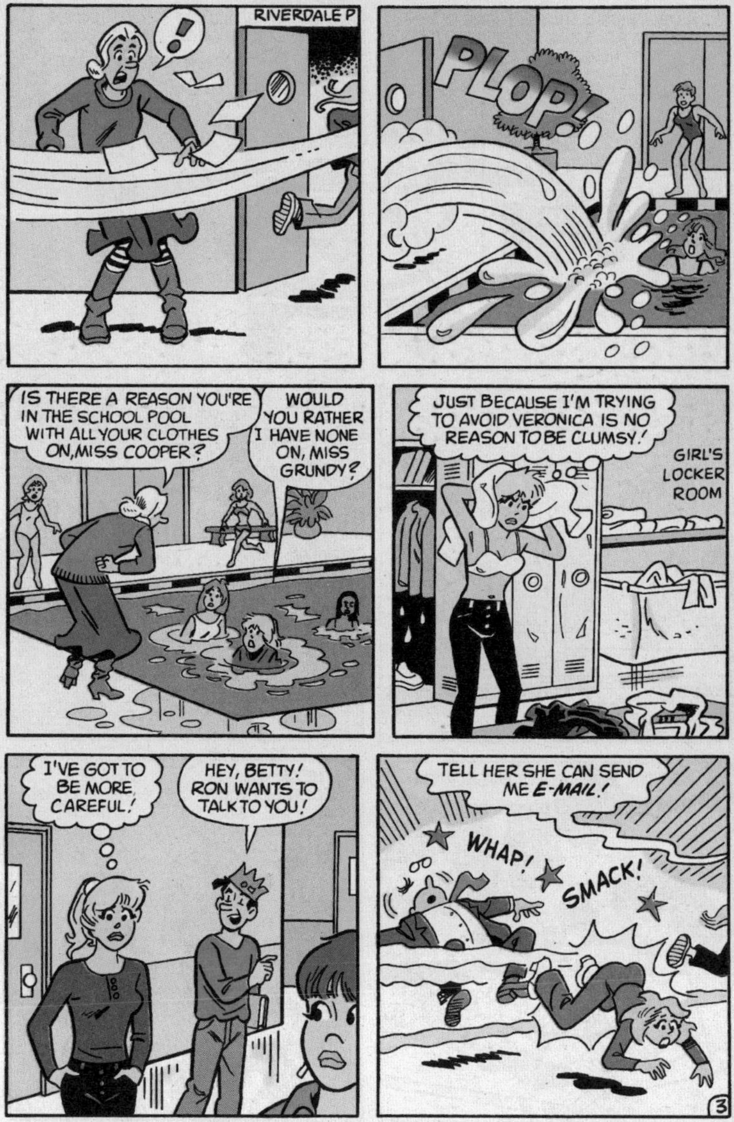
RIVERDALE P
PLOP!
IS THERE A REASON YOU'RE IN THE SCHOOL POOL WITH ALL YOUR CLOTHES ON, MISS COOPER?
WOULD YOU RATHER I HAVE NONE ON, MISS GRUNDY?
JUST BECAUSE I'M TRYING TO AVOID VERONICA IS NO REASON TO BE CLUMSY!
GIRL'S LOCKER ROOM
I'VE GOT TO BE MORE CAREFUL!
HEY, BETTY! RON WANTS TO TALK TO YOU!
TELL HER SHE CAN SEND ME E-MAIL!
WHAP!
SMACK!
3

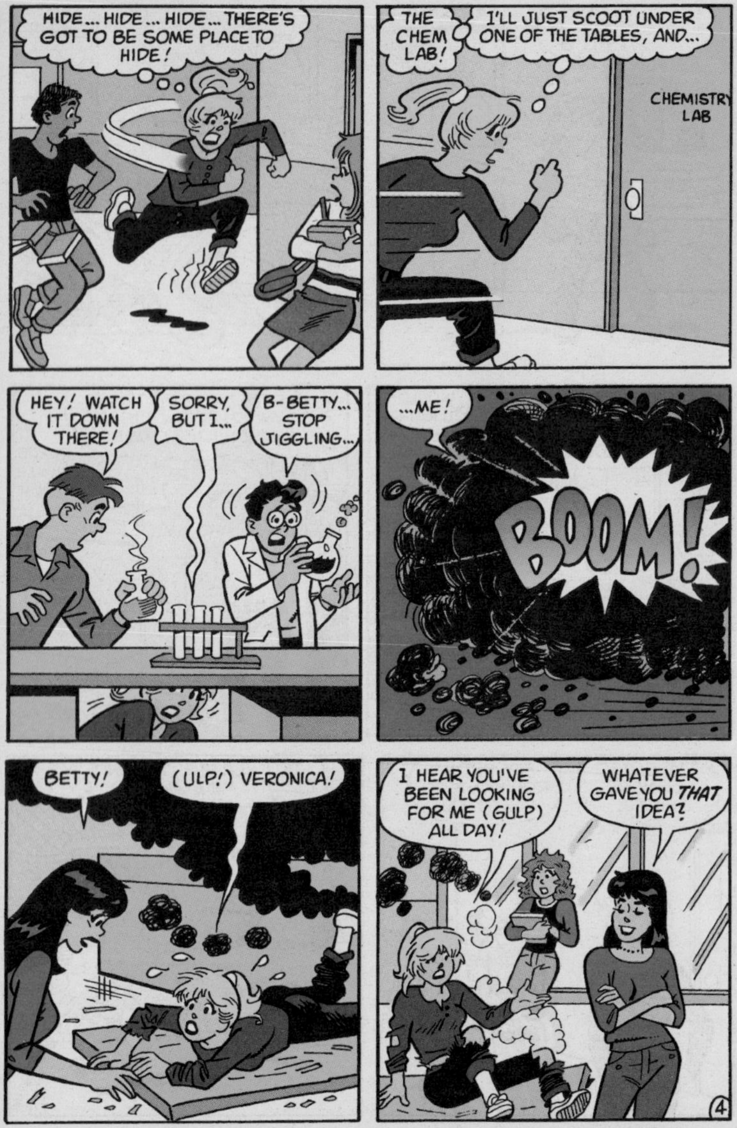
HIDE... HIDE... HIDE... THERE'S GOT TO BE SOME PLACE TO HIDE!
THE CHEM LAB!
I'LL JUST SCOOT UNDER ONE OF THE TABLES, AND...
CHEMISTRY LAB
HEY! WATCH IT DOWN THERE!
SORRY, BUT I...
B-BETTY... STOP JIGGLING...
...ME!
BOOM!
BETTY!
(ULP!) VERONICA!
I HEAR YOU'VE BEEN LOOKING FOR ME (GULP) ALL DAY!
WHATEVER GAVE YOU THAT IDEA?
4

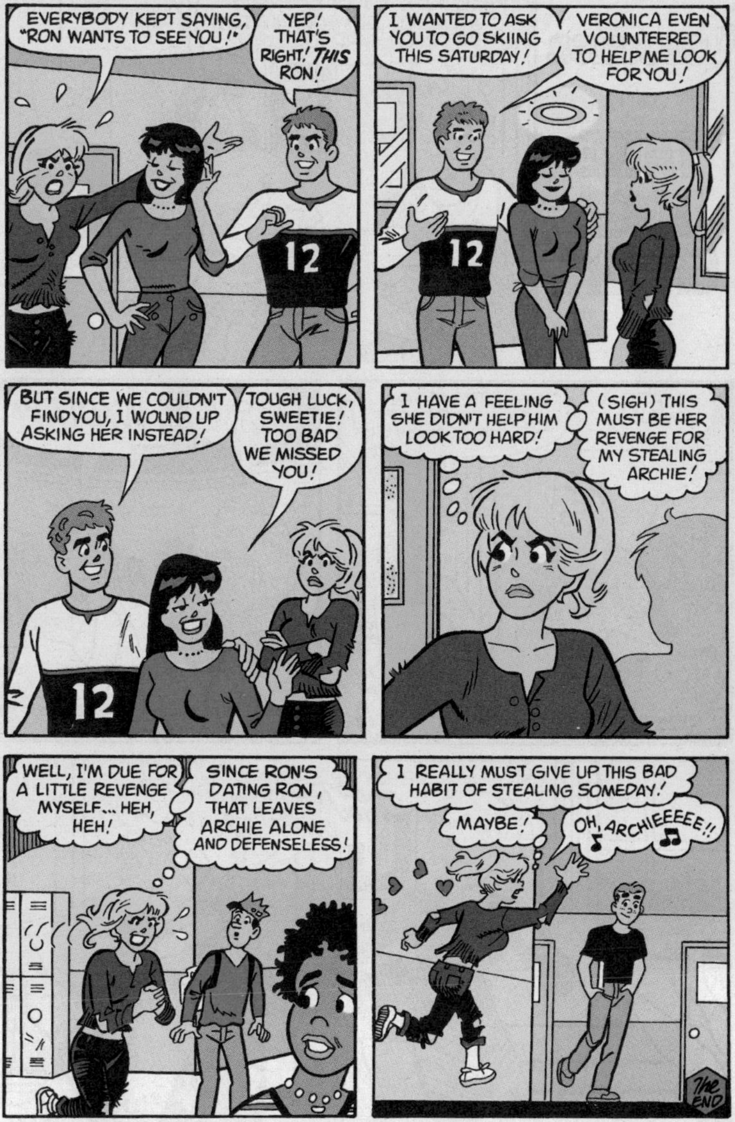
EVERYBODY KEPT SAYING, "RON WANTS TO SEE YOU!"
YEP! THAT'S RIGHT! THIS RON!
I WANTED TO ASK YOU TO GO SKIING THIS SATURDAY!
VERONICA EVEN VOLUNTEERED TO HELP ME LOOK FOR YOU!
BUT SINCE WE COULDN'T FIND YOU, I WOUND UP ASKING HER INSTEAD!
TOUGH LUCK, SWEETIE! TOO BAD WE MISSED YOU!
I HAVE A FEELING SHE DIDN'T HELP HIM LOOK TOO HARD!
(SIGH) THIS MUST BE HER REVENGE FOR MY STEALING ARCHIE!
WELL, I'M DUE FOR A LITTLE REVENGE MYSELF... HEH, HEH!
SINCE RON'S DATING RON, THAT LEAVES ARCHIE ALONE AND DEFENSELESS!
I REALLY MUST GIVE UP THIS BAD HABIT OF STEALING SOMEDAY!
MAYBE!
OH, ARCHIEEEEE!!
The END

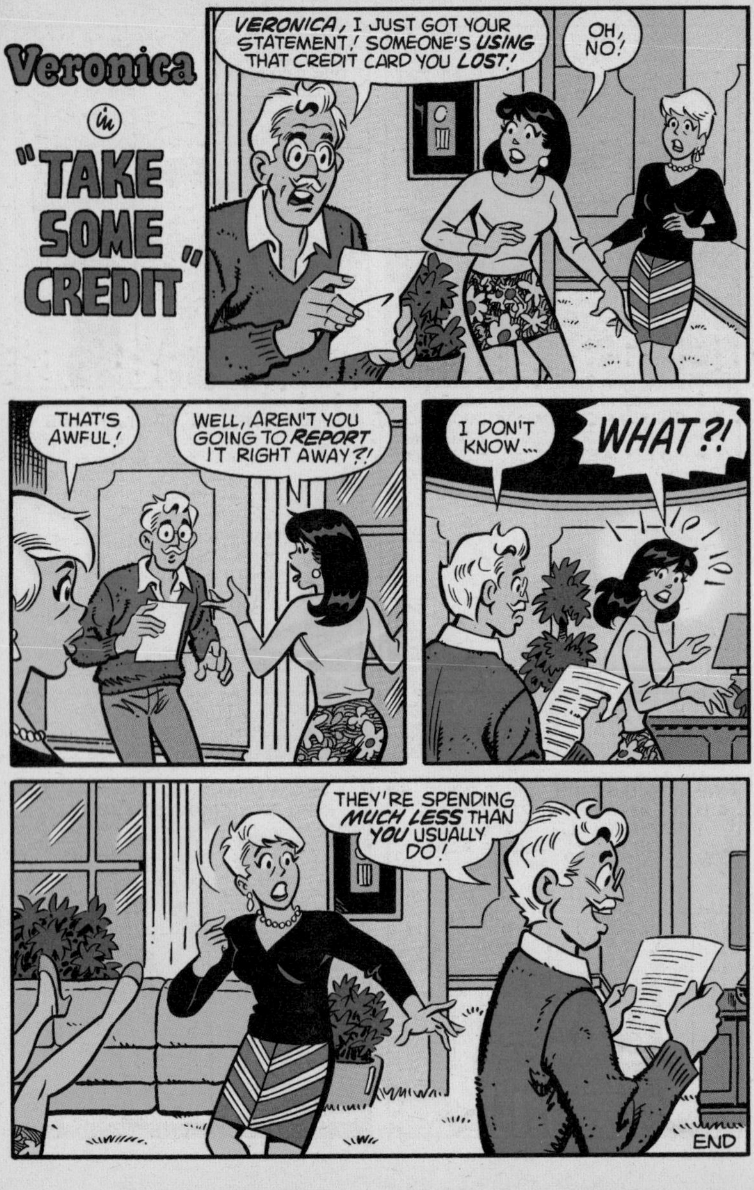
Veronica
in
"TAKE SOME CREDIT"
VERONICA, I JUST GOT YOUR STATEMENT! SOMEONE'S USING THAT CREDIT CARD YOU LOST!
OH, NO!
THAT'S AWFUL!
WELL, AREN'T YOU GOING TO REPORT IT RIGHT AWAY?!
I DON'T KNOW...
WHAT?!
THEY'RE SPENDING MUCH LESS THAN YOU USUALLY DO!
END

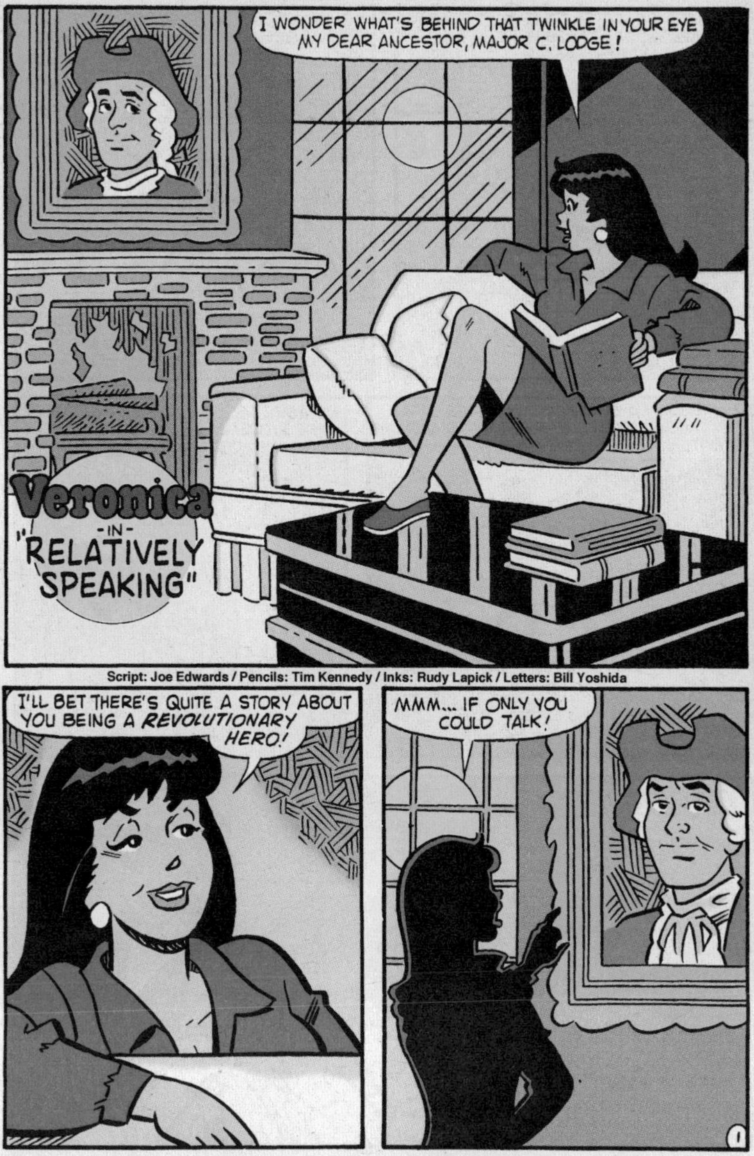

I WONDER WHAT'S BEHIND THAT TWINKLE IN YOUR EYE MY DEAR ANCESTOR, MAJOR C. LODGE!
Veronica
-IN-
"RELATIVELY SPEAKING"
Script: Joe Edwards / Pencils: Tim Kennedy / Inks: Rudy Lapick / Letters: Bill Yoshida
I'LL BET THERE'S QUITE A STORY ABOUT YOU BEING A *REVOLUTIONARY* HERO!
MMM... IF ONLY YOU COULD TALK!
1

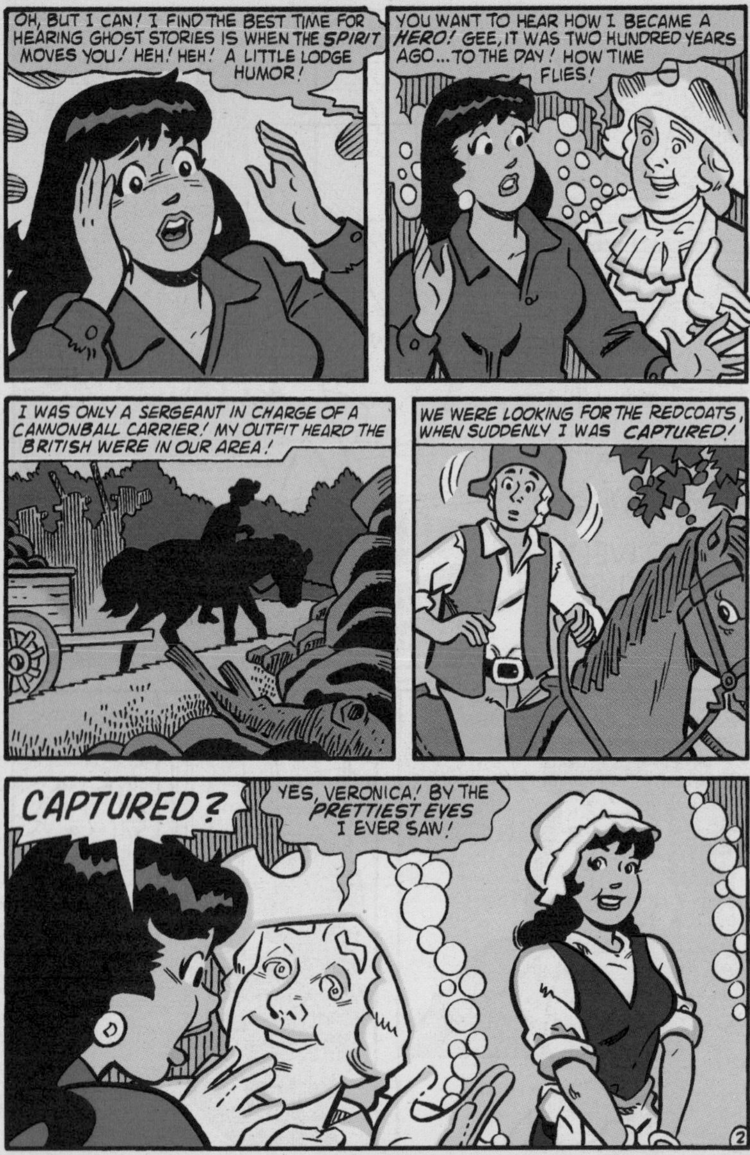
OH, BUT I CAN! I FIND THE BEST TIME FOR HEARING GHOST STORIES IS WHEN THE SPIRIT MOVES YOU! HEH! HEH! A LITTLE LODGE HUMOR!
YOU WANT TO HEAR HOW I BECAME A HERO! GEE, IT WAS TWO HUNDRED YEARS AGO... TO THE DAY! HOW TIME FLIES!
I WAS ONLY A SERGEANT IN CHARGE OF A CANNONBALL CARRIER! MY OUTFIT HEARD THE BRITISH WERE IN OUR AREA!
WE WERE LOOKING FOR THE REDCOATS, WHEN SUDDENLY I WAS CAPTURED!
CAPTURED?
YES, VERONICA! BY THE PRETTIEST EYES I EVER SAW!
2

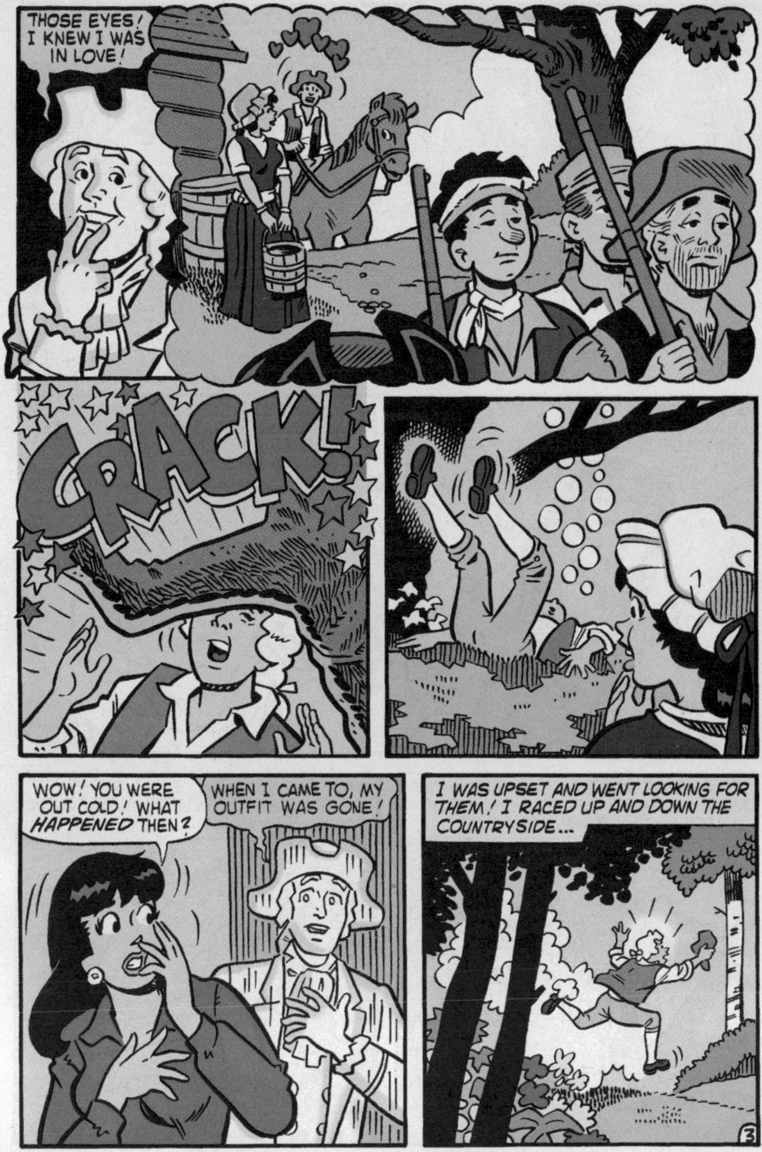
THOSE EYES! I KNEW I WAS IN LOVE!
CRACK!
WOW! YOU WERE OUT COLD! WHAT HAPPENED THEN?
WHEN I CAME TO, MY OUTFIT WAS GONE!
I WAS UPSET AND WENT LOOKING FOR THEM! I RACED UP AND DOWN THE COUNTRYSIDE...
3

IT WAS NO USE! I WAS ABSOLUTELY EXHAUSTED... AND RETURNED TO WHERE I LEFT THE CANNONBALL WAGON!

MY FEET WERE KILLING ME! YOU SEE, ARCHES FOR SHOES WEREN'T INVENTED UNTIL AFTER THE CIVIL WAR! HEARD THAT ON 'JEOPARDY'!

STOP WITH THE TRIVIA! I STILL DIDN'T HEAR HOW YOU BECAME A REVOLUTIONARY WAR HERO!

OKAY! BOY! YOU LODGES ARE IMPATIENT! I WAS COMING TO THE HERO PART! IT'S MY RIGHT AS A HERO TO DRAG IT OUT A BIT! AHEM! AS I WAS SAYING...

DOLLY! THAT WAS THE GORGEOUS GIRL'S NAME! I ASKED HER FOR A BUCKET OF WATER FOR MY BURNING FEET!

WHILE SHE WAS GONE, I THOUGHT IT WAS A GOOD IDEA TO ELEVATE MY FEET ON THE CANNONBALL WAGON...

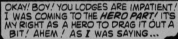

CREAK!

4

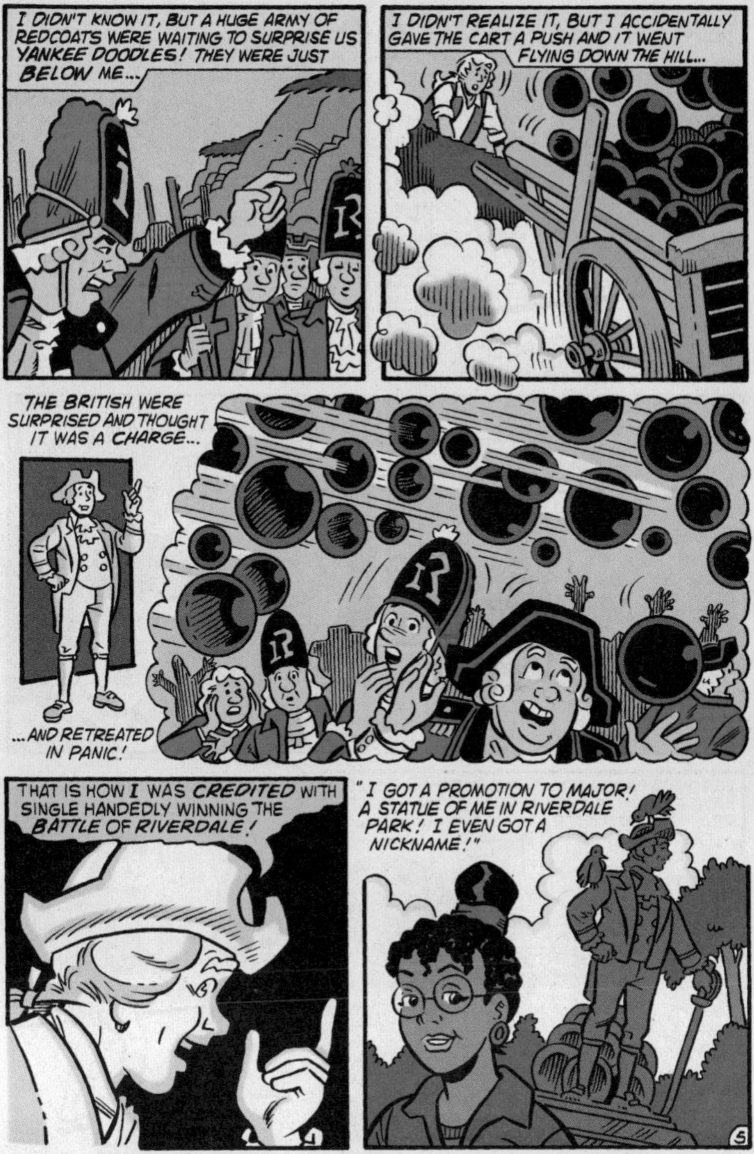
I DIDN'T KNOW IT, BUT A HUGE ARMY OF REDCOATS WERE WAITING TO SURPRISE US YANKEE DOODLES! THEY WERE JUST BELOW ME...
I DIDN'T REALIZE IT, BUT I ACCIDENTALLY GAVE THE CART A PUSH AND IT WENT FLYING DOWN THE HILL...
THE BRITISH WERE SURPRISED AND THOUGHT IT WAS A CHARGE...
...AND RETREATED IN PANIC!
THAT IS HOW I WAS CREDITED WITH SINGLE HANDEDLY WINNING THE BATTLE OF RIVERDALE!
"I GOT A PROMOTION TO MAJOR! A STATUE OF ME IN RIVERDALE PARK! I EVEN GOT A NICKNAME!"
5

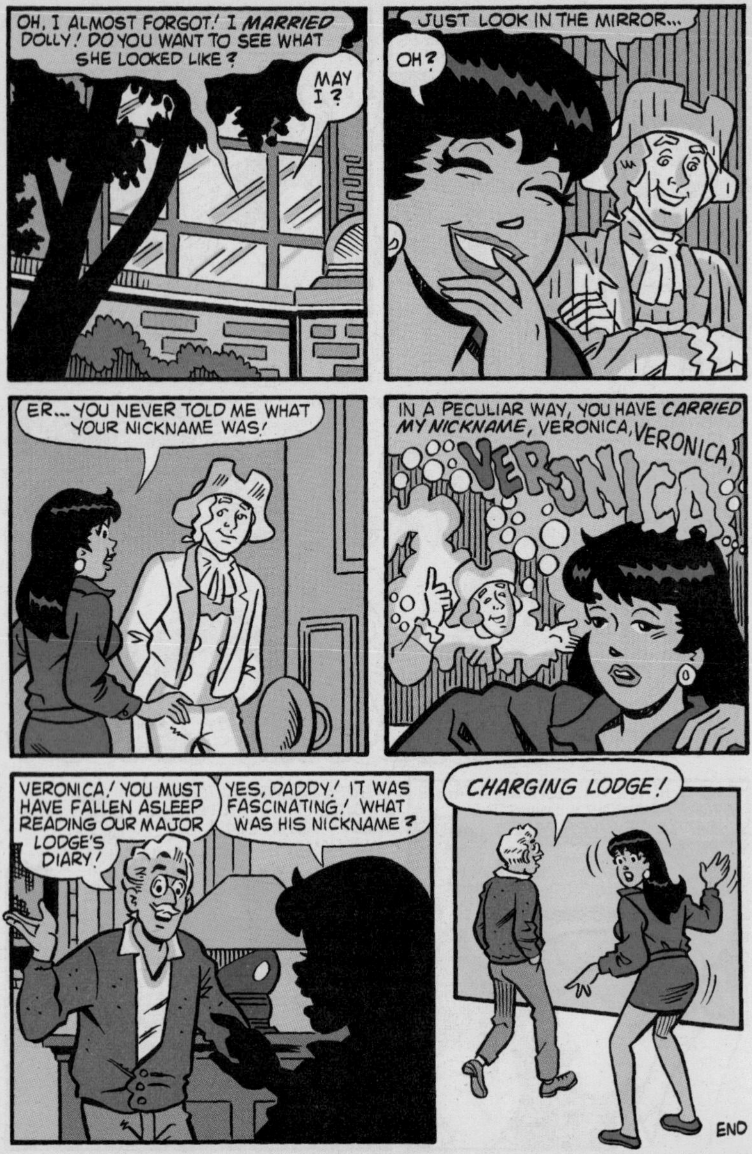
OH, I ALMOST FORGOT! I MARRIED DOLLY! DO YOU WANT TO SEE WHAT SHE LOOKED LIKE?
MAY I?
JUST LOOK IN THE MIRROR...
OH?
ER... YOU NEVER TOLD ME WHAT YOUR NICKNAME WAS!
IN A PECULIAR WAY, YOU HAVE CARRIED MY NICKNAME, VERONICA, VERONICA,
VERONICA
VERONICA! YOU MUST HAVE FALLEN ASLEEP READING OUR MAJOR LODGE'S DIARY!
YES, DADDY! IT WAS FASCINATING! WHAT WAS HIS NICKNAME?
CHARGING LODGE!
END

Betty in "CAMERA CLOSE-UP"

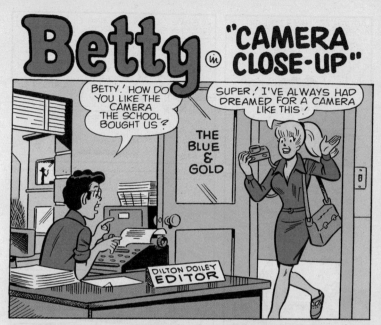

BETTY! HOW DO YOU LIKE THE CAMERA THE SCHOOL BOUGHT US?

SUPER! I'VE ALWAYS HAD DREAMED FOR A CAMERA LIKE THIS!

THE BLUE & GOLD

DILTON DOILEY EDITOR

LOOK! MY FIRST PHOTO--- TAKEN RIGHT HERE IN SCHOOL!

THAT'S A NICE SHOT OF THE FEEBLY TWINS EATING A GIANT MEATBALL SANDWICH!

NOT REALLY--- IT'S A DOUBLE EXPOSURE OF SAMMY SINGLETON PLAYING HIS STRING BASS!

THAT'S RATHER NEAT! HMMM!--- MAYBE YOU'D DO BETTER SHOOTING SOME ACTION!

Script & Pencils: Bob Bolling / Inks: Rudy Lapick / Letters: Bill Yoshida

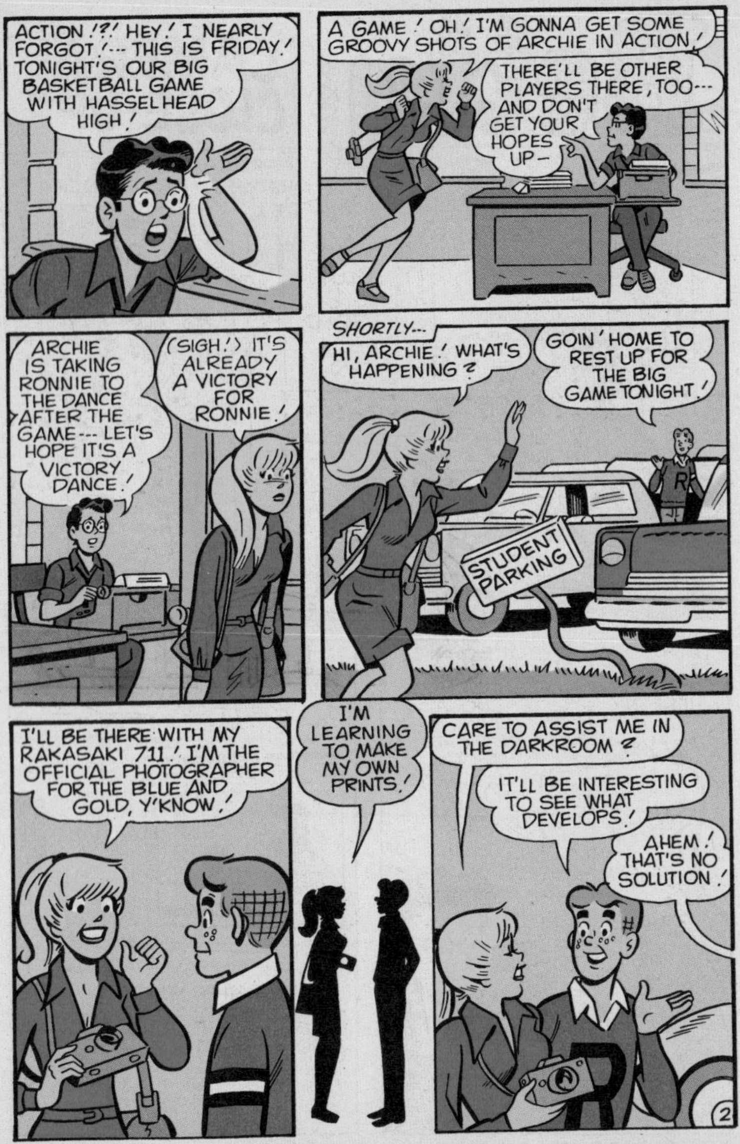

ACTION !?! HEY! I NEARLY FORGOT!--- THIS IS FRIDAY! TONIGHT'S OUR BIG BASKETBALL GAME WITH HASSELHEAD HIGH!
A GAME! OH! I'M GONNA GET SOME GROOVY SHOTS OF ARCHIE IN ACTION!
THERE'LL BE OTHER PLAYERS THERE, TOO--- AND DON'T GET YOUR HOPES UP–
ARCHIE IS TAKING RONNIE TO THE DANCE AFTER THE GAME--- LET'S HOPE IT'S A VICTORY DANCE!
(SIGH!) IT'S ALREADY A VICTORY FOR RONNIE!
SHORTLY...
HI, ARCHIE! WHAT'S HAPPENING?
GOIN' HOME TO REST UP FOR THE BIG GAME TONIGHT!
STUDENT PARKING
I'LL BE THERE WITH MY RAKASAKI 711! I'M THE OFFICIAL PHOTOGRAPHER FOR THE BLUE AND GOLD, Y'KNOW!
I'M LEARNING TO MAKE MY OWN PRINTS!
CARE TO ASSIST ME IN THE DARKROOM?
IT'LL BE INTERESTING TO SEE WHAT DEVELOPS!
AHEM! THAT'S NO SOLUTION!
2

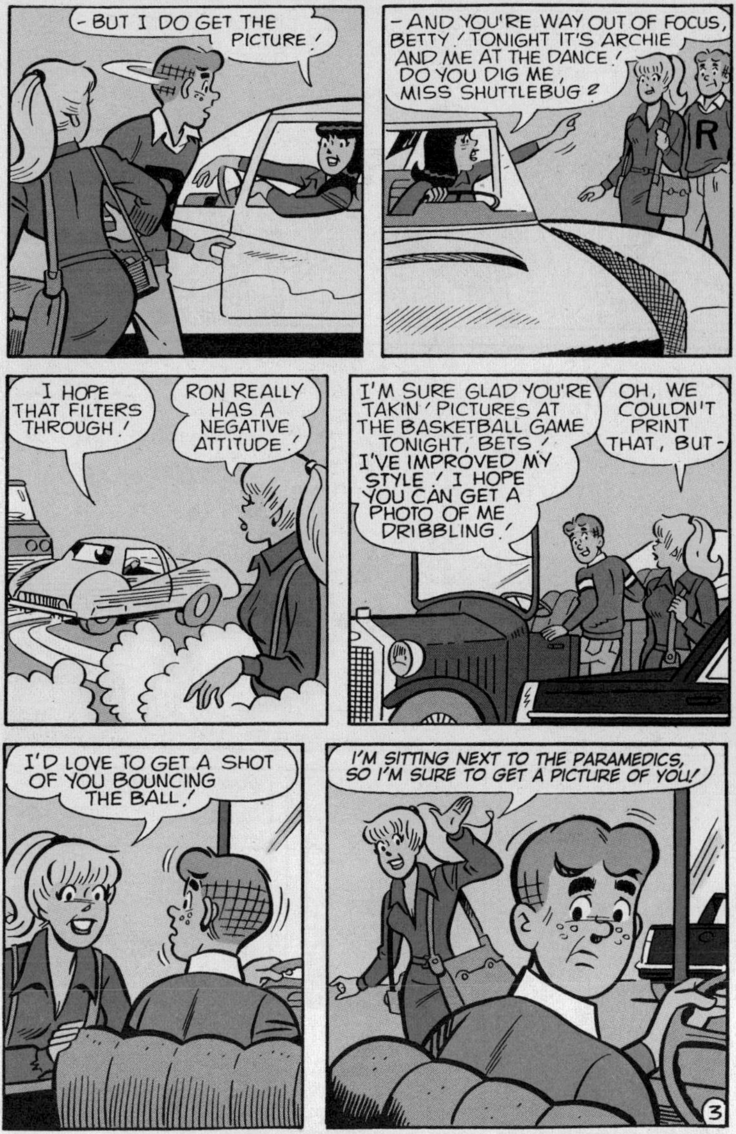
- BUT I DO GET THE PICTURE!
- AND YOU'RE WAY OUT OF FOCUS, BETTY! TONIGHT IT'S ARCHIE AND ME AT THE DANCE! DO YOU DIG ME, MISS SHUTTLEBUG?
R
I HOPE THAT FILTERS THROUGH!
RON REALLY HAS A NEGATIVE ATTITUDE!
I'M SURE GLAD YOU'RE TAKIN' PICTURES AT THE BASKETBALL GAME TONIGHT, BETS! I'VE IMPROVED MY STYLE! I HOPE YOU CAN GET A PHOTO OF ME DRIBBLING!
OH, WE COULDN'T PRINT THAT, BUT-
I'D LOVE TO GET A SHOT OF YOU BOUNCING THE BALL!
I'M SITTING NEXT TO THE PARAMEDICS, SO I'M SURE TO GET A PICTURE OF YOU!
3

THAT NIGHT...

HASSELHEAD 3i RIVERDALE 27

WOW! THE PLACE IS PACKED! OOOO! THERE'S ARCHIE WITH THE BALL!

FORGET ARCHIE, BETTY, AND GET BUSY WITH THE CAMERA--- TRY FOR SOME CROWD SHOTS!

PEANUTS 50¢

EX

HASSELHEAD, HASSELHEAD, HASSELHEAD HIGH!

YOU CAN WIN IT-

IF YOU TRY!

HASSELHEAD, HASSELHEAD, HASSELHEAD TEAM -

YOU'LL NEVER WIN IT -

YOU'VE RUN OUT OF STEAM!

I'D BETTER GET BACK DOWN ON THE FLOOR FOR SOME SHOTS OF THE PLAYERS!

3

HMMM --- HAVEN'T USED THIS ATTACHMENT YET---

NOW THE GAME IS IN ITS FINAL SECONDS--- HASSELHEAD LEADING BY A POINT, 73-72 THEN--

REGGIE STEALS THE BALL-

4

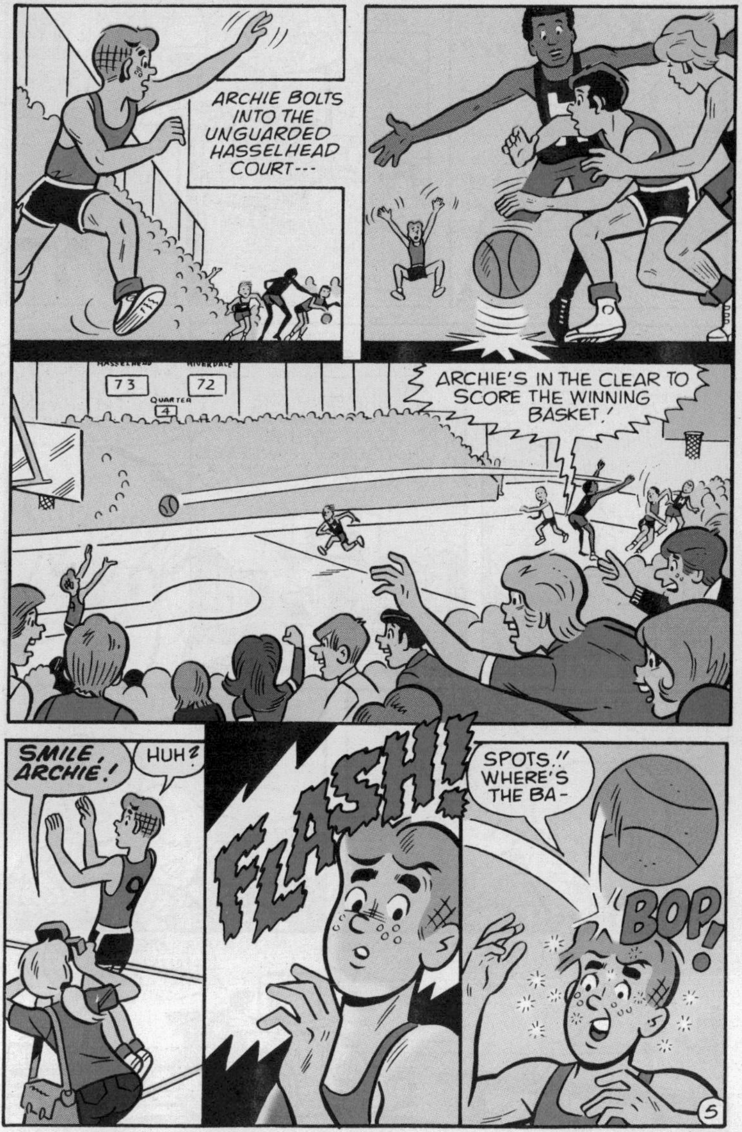
ARCHIE BOLTS INTO THE UNGUARDED HASSELHEAD COURT---
73
72
4
ARCHIE'S IN THE CLEAR TO SCORE THE WINNING BASKET!
SMILE, ARCHIE!
HUH?
FLASH!
SPOTS!! WHERE'S THE BA-
BOP!
5

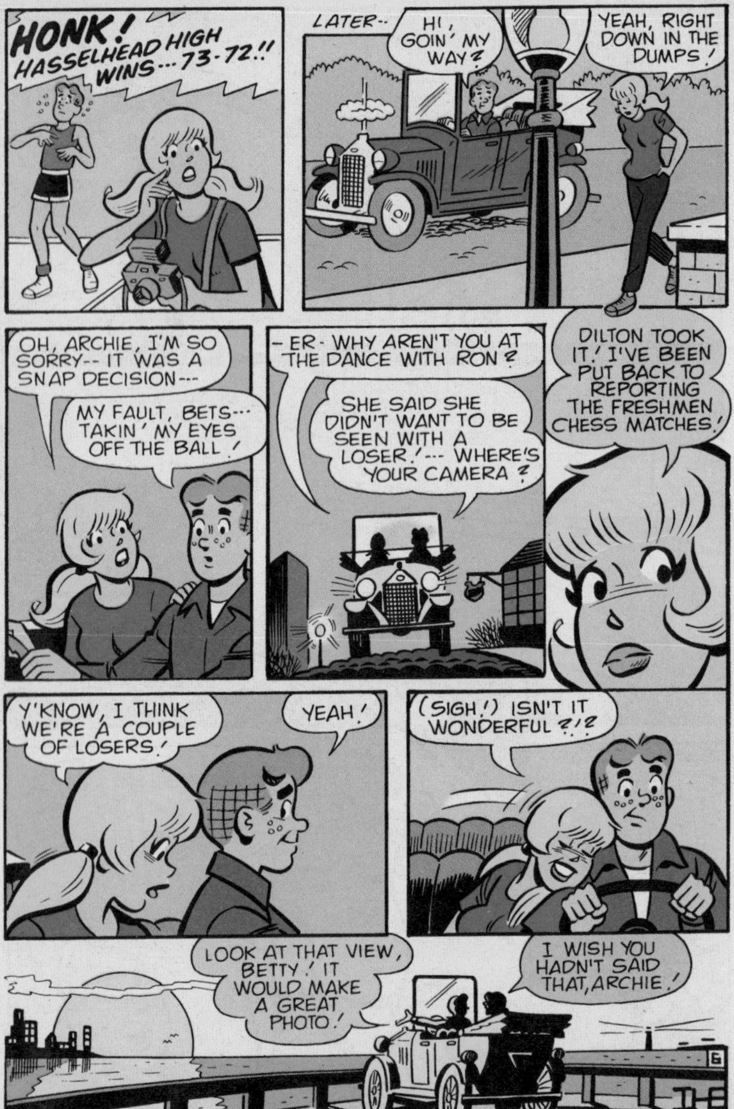
HONK!
HASSELHEAD HIGH WINS--- 73-72.!!
LATER--
HI, GOIN' MY WAY?
YEAH, RIGHT DOWN IN THE DUMPS!
OH, ARCHIE, I'M SO SORRY-- IT WAS A SNAP DECISION---
MY FAULT, BETS--- TAKIN' MY EYES OFF THE BALL!
-ER- WHY AREN'T YOU AT THE DANCE WITH RON?
SHE SAID SHE DIDN'T WANT TO BE SEEN WITH A LOSER!--- WHERE'S YOUR CAMERA?
DILTON TOOK IT! I'VE BEEN PUT BACK TO REPORTING THE FRESHMEN CHESS MATCHES!
Y'KNOW, I THINK WE'RE A COUPLE OF LOSERS!
YEAH!
(SIGH!) ISN'T IT WONDERFUL?!?
LOOK AT THAT VIEW, BETTY! IT WOULD MAKE A GREAT PHOTO!
I WISH YOU HADN'T SAID THAT, ARCHIE!
THE END
6

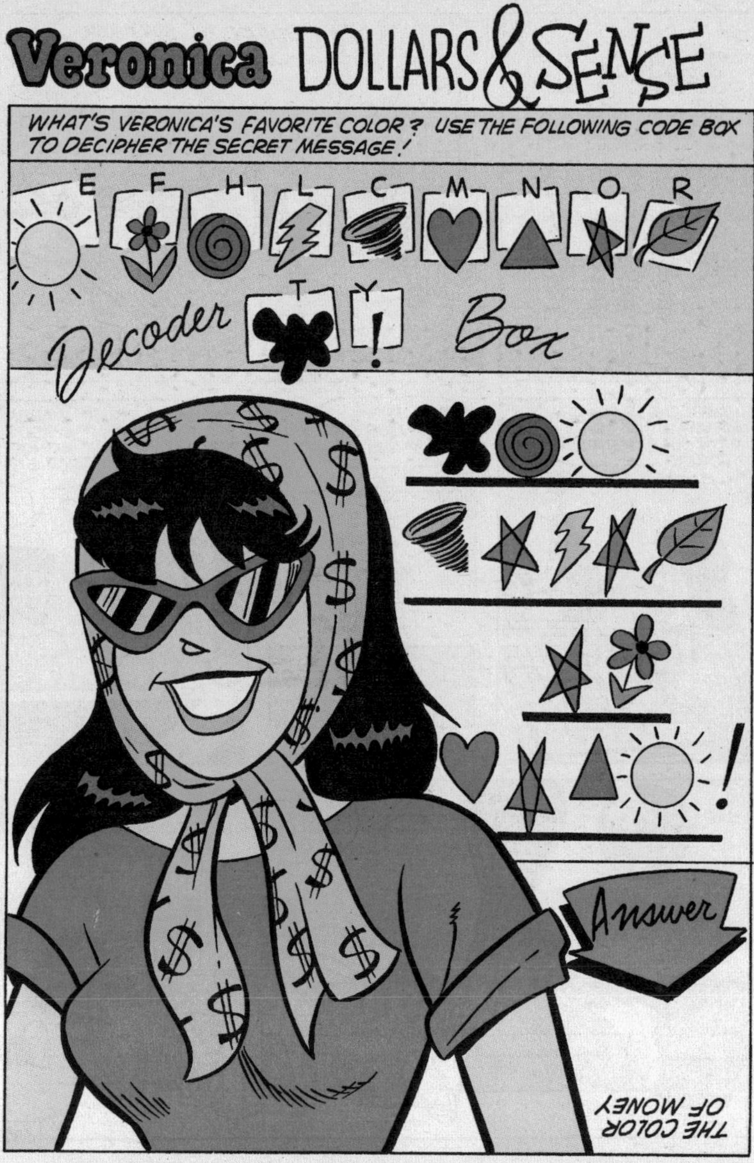
Veronica DOLLARS & SENSE
WHAT'S VERONICA'S FAVORITE COLOR? USE THE FOLLOWING CODE BOX TO DECIPHER THE SECRET MESSAGE!
E F H L C M N O R
T Y
Decoder Box
!
Answer
THE COLOR OF MONEY

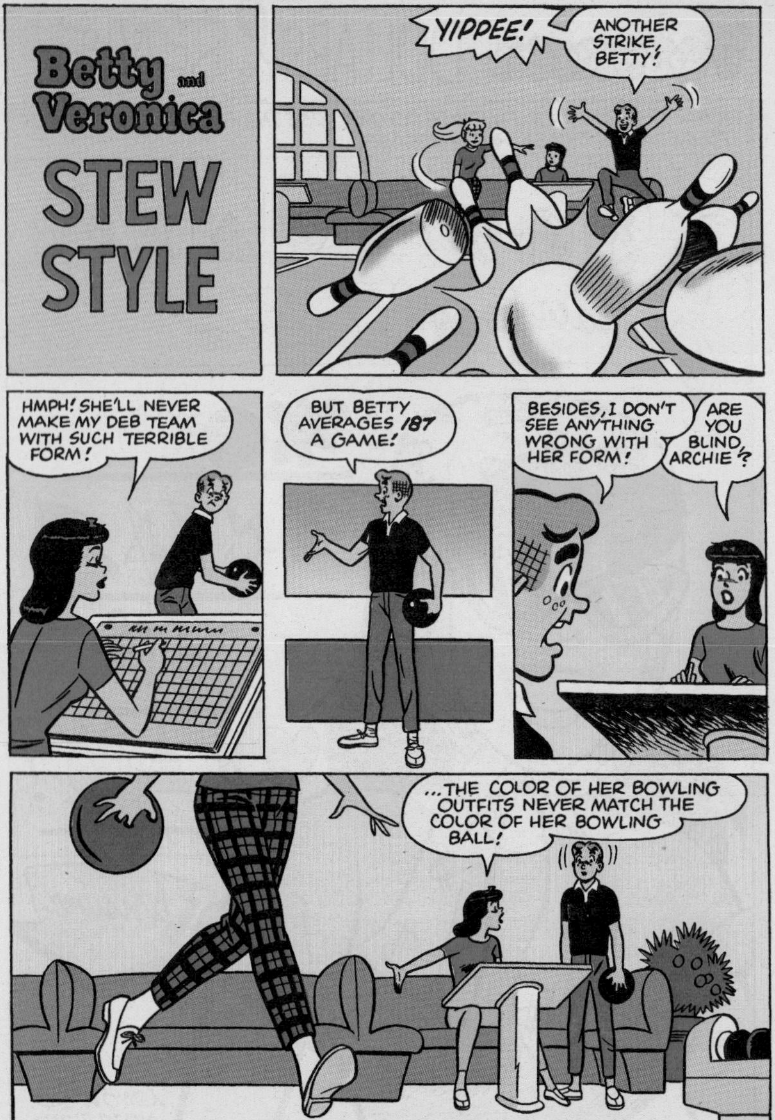
Betty and Veronica
STEW STYLE
YIPPEE!
ANOTHER STRIKE, BETTY!
HMPH! SHE'LL NEVER MAKE MY DEB TEAM WITH SUCH TERRIBLE FORM!
BUT BETTY AVERAGES 187 A GAME!
BESIDES, I DON'T SEE ANYTHING WRONG WITH HER FORM!
ARE YOU BLIND, ARCHIE?
...THE COLOR OF HER BOWLING OUTFITS NEVER MATCH THE COLOR OF HER BOWLING BALL!
END.

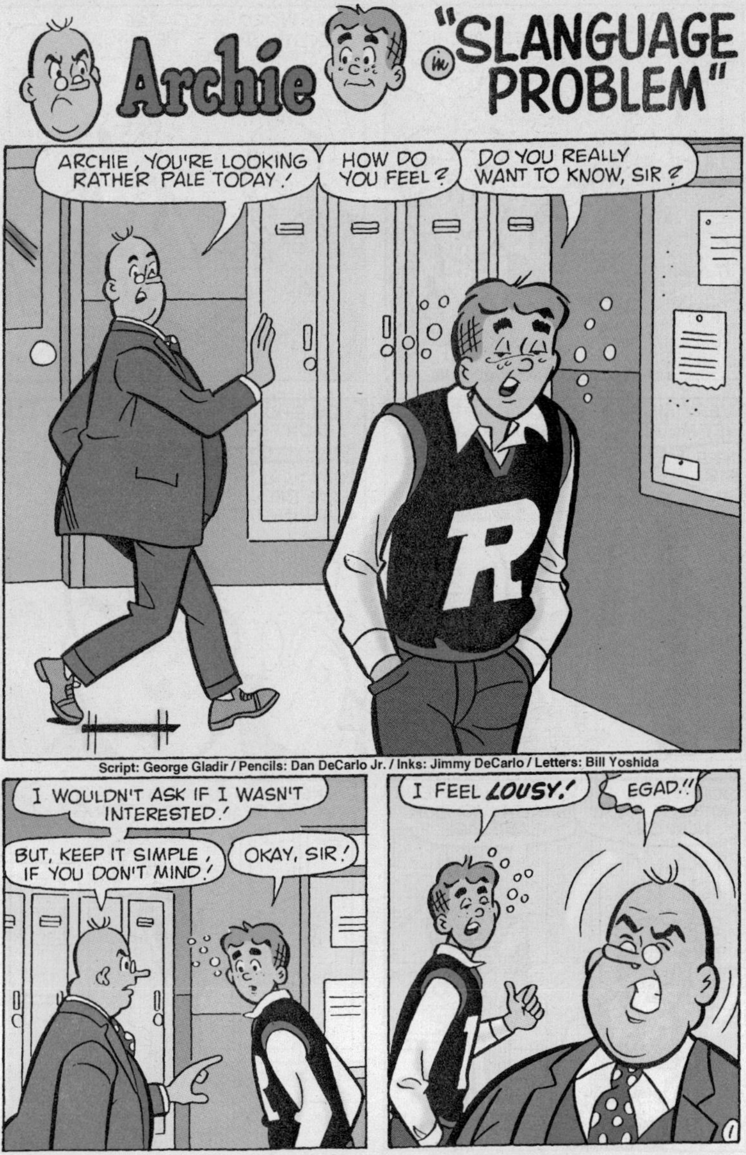
Archie in "SLANGUAGE PROBLEM"
ARCHIE, YOU'RE LOOKING RATHER PALE TODAY!
HOW DO YOU FEEL?
DO YOU REALLY WANT TO KNOW, SIR?
Script: George Gladir / Pencils: Dan DeCarlo Jr. / Inks: Jimmy DeCarlo / Letters: Bill Yoshida
I WOULDN'T ASK IF I WASN'T INTERESTED!
BUT, KEEP IT SIMPLE, IF YOU DON'T MIND!
OKAY, SIR!
I FEEL LOUSY!
EGAD!!
1

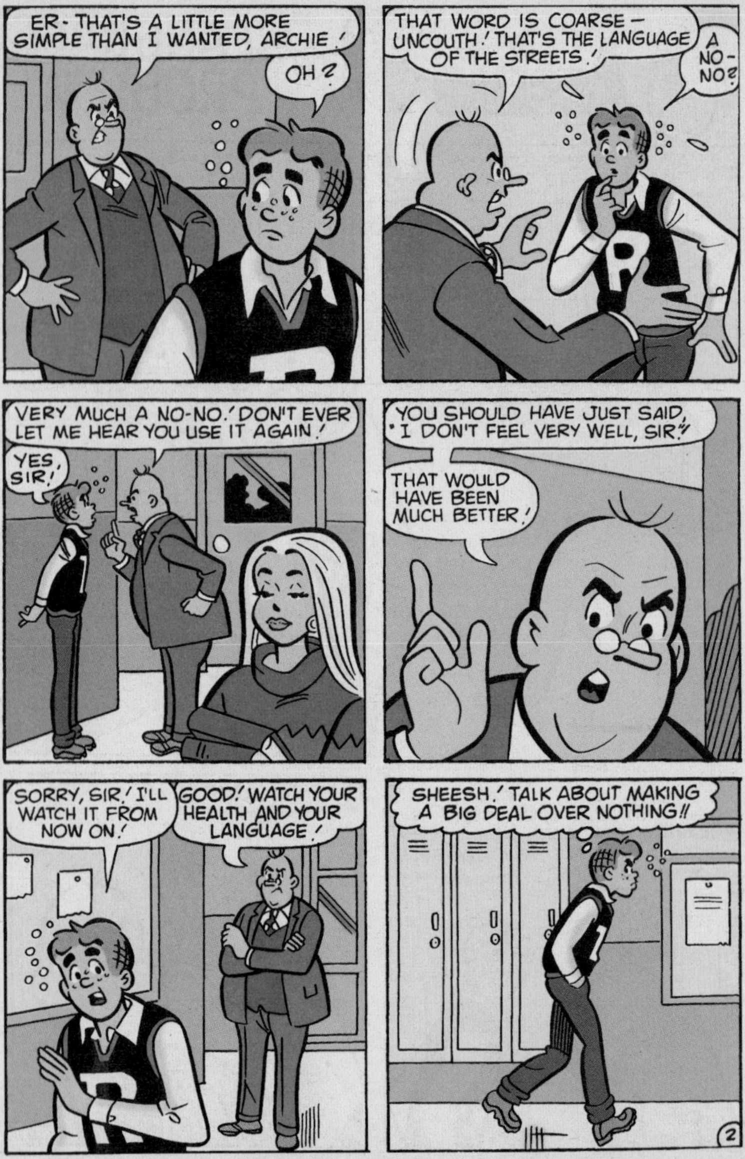
ER- THAT'S A LITTLE MORE SIMPLE THAN I WANTED, ARCHIE!
OH?
THAT WORD IS COARSE— UNCOUTH! THAT'S THE LANGUAGE OF THE STREETS!
A NO-NO?
VERY MUCH A NO-NO! DON'T EVER LET ME HEAR YOU USE IT AGAIN!
YES, SIR!
YOU SHOULD HAVE JUST SAID, "I DON'T FEEL VERY WELL, SIR"!
THAT WOULD HAVE BEEN MUCH BETTER!
SORRY, SIR! I'LL WATCH IT FROM NOW ON!
GOOD! WATCH YOUR HEALTH AND YOUR LANGUAGE!
SHEESH! TALK ABOUT MAKING A BIG DEAL OVER NOTHING!!
2

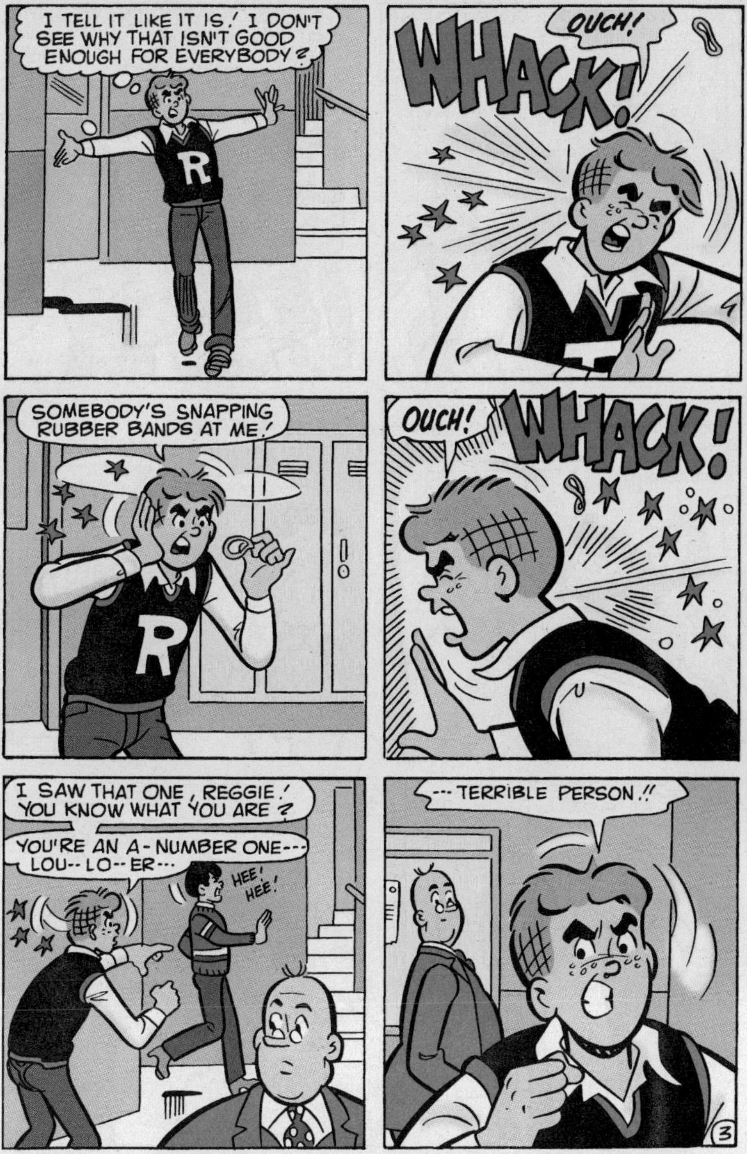
I TELL IT LIKE IT IS.! I DON'T SEE WHY THAT ISN'T GOOD ENOUGH FOR EVERYBODY?
WHACK!
OUCH!
SOMEBODY'S SNAPPING RUBBER BANDS AT ME!
OUCH!
WHACK!
I SAW THAT ONE, REGGIE! YOU KNOW WHAT YOU ARE?
YOU'RE AN A-NUMBER ONE--- LOU-- LO-- ER---
HEE! HEE!
--- TERRIBLE PERSON.!!
3

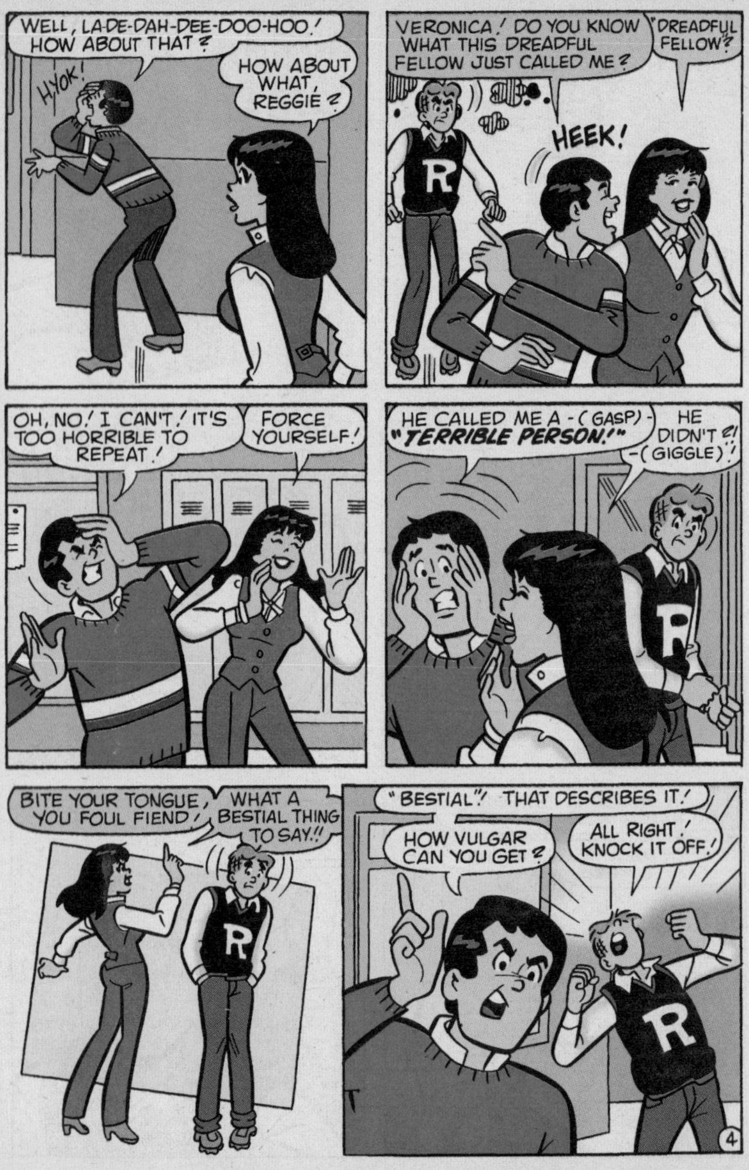
WELL, LA-DE-DAH-DEE-DOO-HOO! HOW ABOUT THAT?
H'YOK!
HOW ABOUT WHAT, REGGIE?
VERONICA! DO YOU KNOW WHAT THIS DREADFUL FELLOW JUST CALLED ME?
"DREADFUL FELLOW"?
HEEK!
OH, NO! I CAN'T! IT'S TOO HORRIBLE TO REPEAT!
FORCE YOURSELF!
HE CALLED ME A -(GASP)- "TERRIBLE PERSON!"
HE DIDN'T?! -(GIGGLE)-!
BITE YOUR TONGUE, YOU FOUL FIEND!
WHAT A BESTIAL THING TO SAY!!
"BESTIAL"! THAT DESCRIBES IT!
HOW VULGAR CAN YOU GET?
ALL RIGHT! KNOCK IT OFF!
4

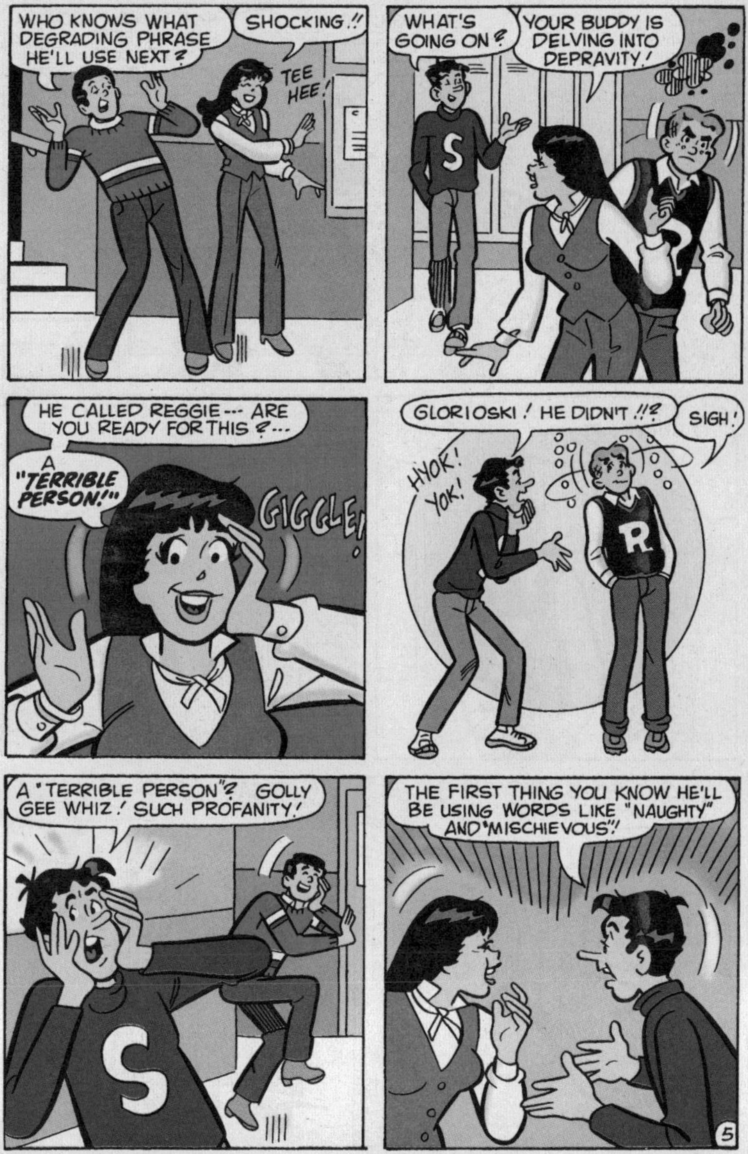
WHO KNOWS WHAT DEGRADING PHRASE HE'LL USE NEXT?
SHOCKING.!!
TEE HEE!
WHAT'S GOING ON?
YOUR BUDDY IS DELVING INTO DEPRAVITY!
HE CALLED REGGIE--- ARE YOU READY FOR THIS?...
A "TERRIBLE PERSON!"
GIGGLE!
GLORIOSKI! HE DIDN'T!!?
SIGH!
HYOK! YOK!
A "TERRIBLE PERSON"? GOLLY GEE WHIZ! SUCH PROFANITY!
THE FIRST THING YOU KNOW HE'LL BE USING WORDS LIKE "NAUGHTY" AND "MISCHIEVOUS"!
5

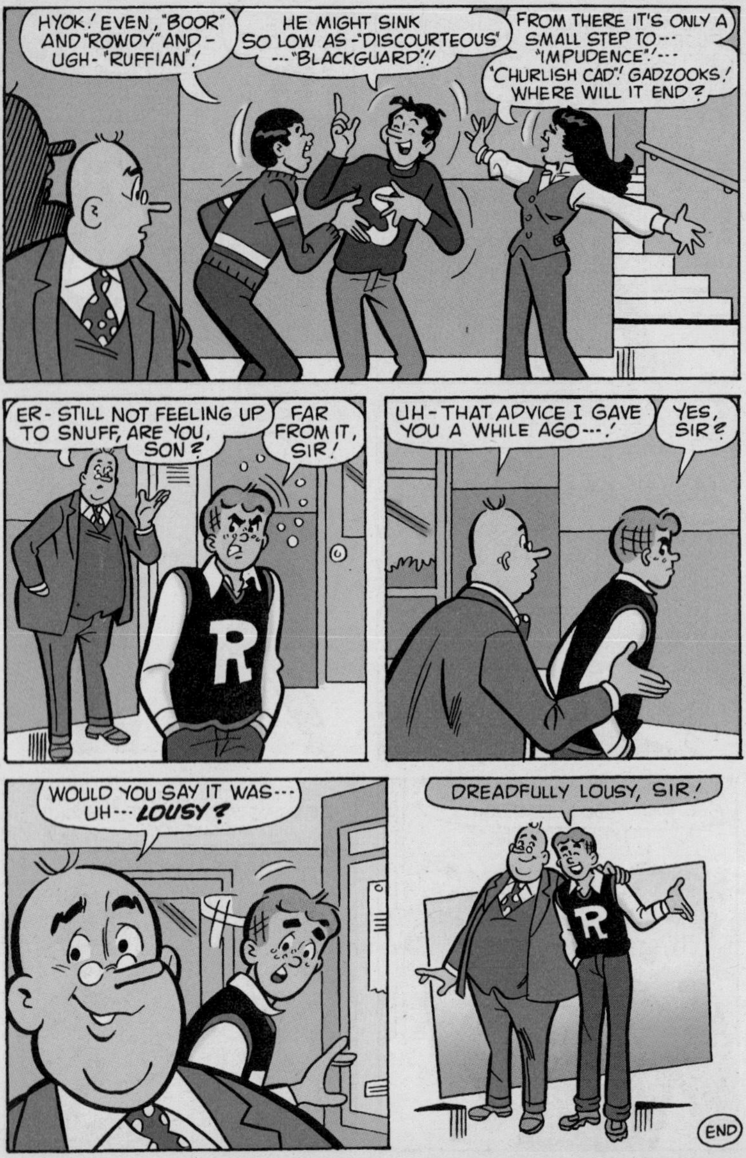
HYOK! EVEN, "BOOR" AND "ROWDY" AND - UGH - "RUFFIAN"!
HE MIGHT SINK SO LOW AS - "DISCOURTEOUS" --- "BLACKGUARD"!!
FROM THERE IT'S ONLY A SMALL STEP TO --- "IMPUDENCE"! --- "CHURLISH CAD"! GADZOOKS! WHERE WILL IT END?
ER - STILL NOT FEELING UP TO SNUFF, ARE YOU, SON?
FAR FROM IT, SIR!
UH - THAT ADVICE I GAVE YOU A WHILE AGO ---!
YES, SIR?
WOULD YOU SAY IT WAS --- UH --- LOUSY?
DREADFULLY LOUSY, SIR!
END

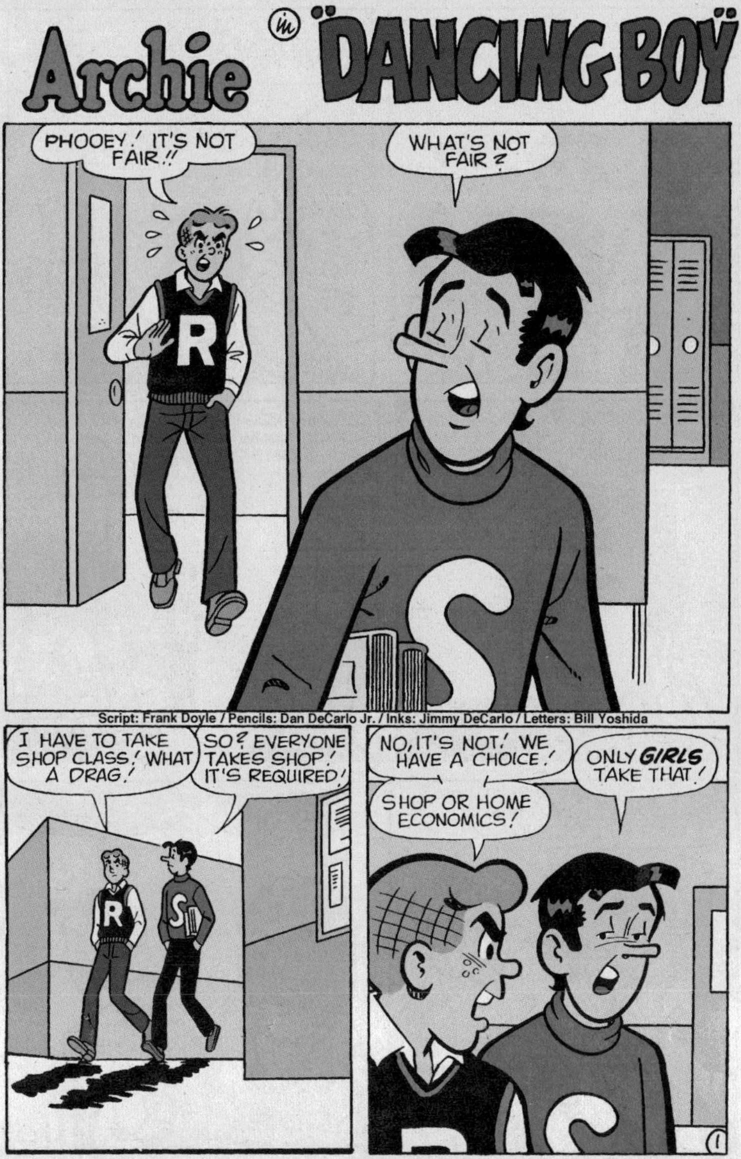Archie in "DANCING BOY"
PHOOEY! IT'S NOT FAIR!!
WHAT'S NOT FAIR?
Script: Frank Doyle / Pencils: Dan DeCarlo Jr. / Inks: Jimmy DeCarlo / Letters: Bill Yoshida
I HAVE TO TAKE SHOP CLASS! WHAT A DRAG!
SO? EVERYONE TAKES SHOP! IT'S REQUIRED!
NO, IT'S NOT! WE HAVE A CHOICE!
SHOP OR HOME ECONOMICS!
ONLY GIRLS TAKE THAT!
1

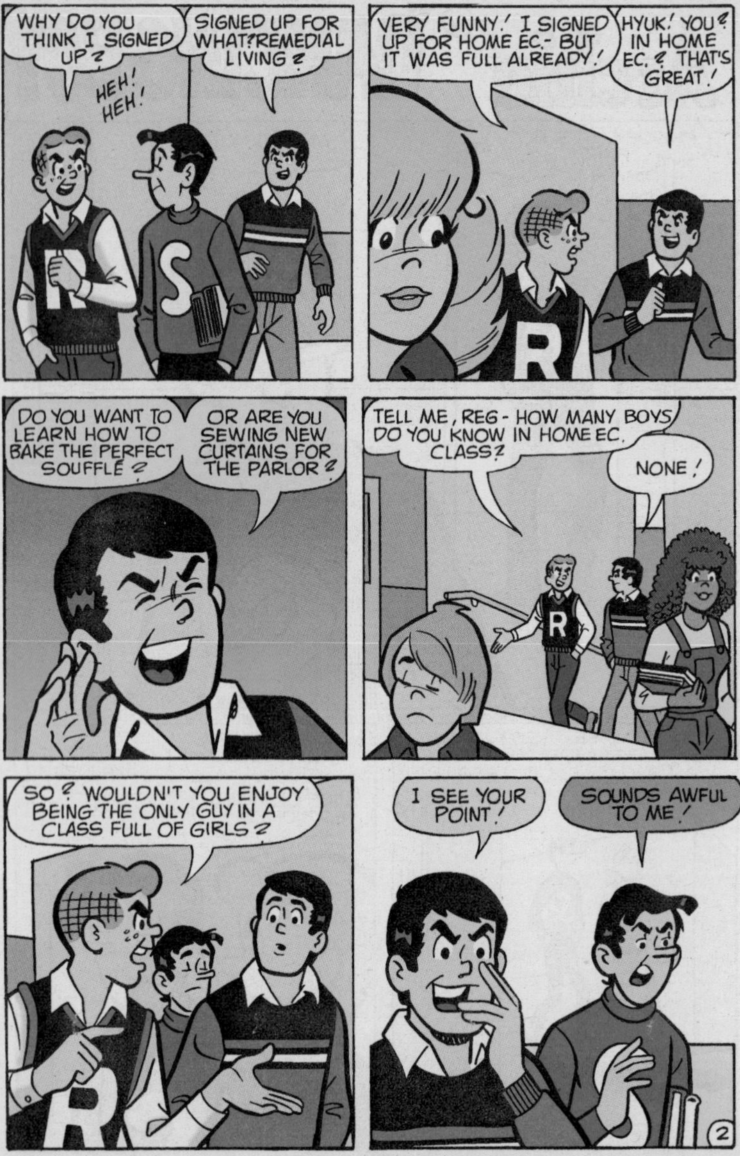
WHY DO YOU THINK I SIGNED UP?
HEH! HEH!
SIGNED UP FOR WHAT? REMEDIAL LIVING?
VERY FUNNY! I SIGNED UP FOR HOME EC.- BUT IT WAS FULL ALREADY!
HYUK! YOU? IN HOME EC.? THAT'S GREAT!
DO YOU WANT TO LEARN HOW TO BAKE THE PERFECT SOUFFLÉ?
OR ARE YOU SEWING NEW CURTAINS FOR THE PARLOR?
TELL ME, REG - HOW MANY BOYS DO YOU KNOW IN HOME EC. CLASS?
NONE!
SO? WOULDN'T YOU ENJOY BEING THE ONLY GUY IN A CLASS FULL OF GIRLS?
I SEE YOUR POINT!
SOUNDS AWFUL TO ME!
2

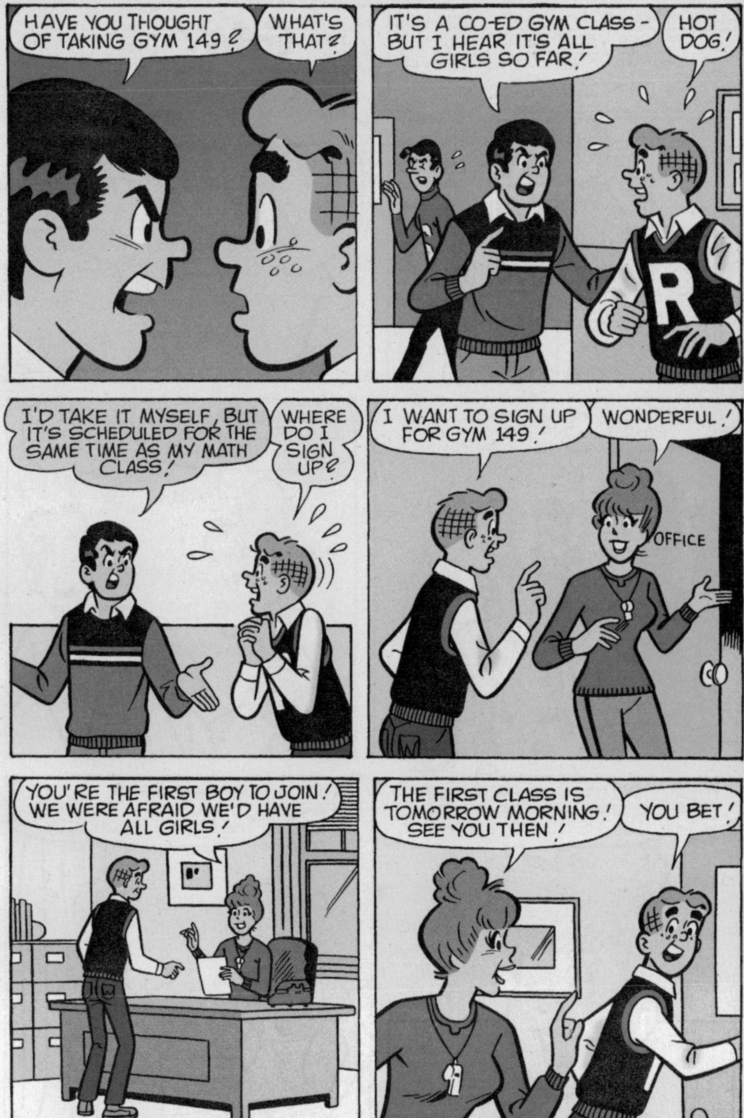
HAVE YOU THOUGHT OF TAKING GYM 149?
WHAT'S THAT?
IT'S A CO-ED GYM CLASS - BUT I HEAR IT'S ALL GIRLS SO FAR!
HOT DOG!
I'D TAKE IT MYSELF, BUT IT'S SCHEDULED FOR THE SAME TIME AS MY MATH CLASS!
WHERE DO I SIGN UP?
I WANT TO SIGN UP FOR GYM 149!
WONDERFUL!
OFFICE
YOU'RE THE FIRST BOY TO JOIN! WE WERE AFRAID WE'D HAVE ALL GIRLS!
THE FIRST CLASS IS TOMORROW MORNING! SEE YOU THEN!
YOU BET!
3

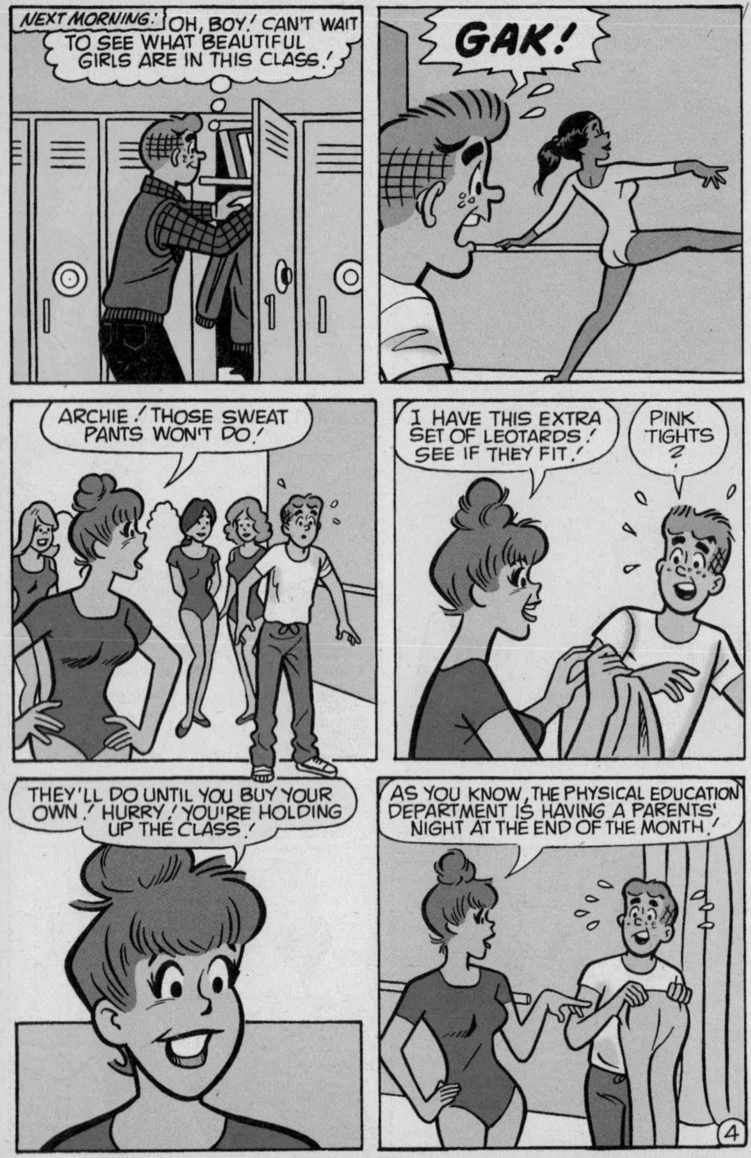

NEXT MORNING:
OH, BOY! CAN'T WAIT TO SEE WHAT BEAUTIFUL GIRLS ARE IN THIS CLASS!
GAK!
ARCHIE! THOSE SWEAT PANTS WON'T DO!
I HAVE THIS EXTRA SET OF LEOTARDS! SEE IF THEY FIT!
PINK TIGHTS?
THEY'LL DO UNTIL YOU BUY YOUR OWN! HURRY! YOU'RE HOLDING UP THE CLASS!
AS YOU KNOW, THE PHYSICAL EDUCATION DEPARTMENT IS HAVING A PARENTS' NIGHT AT THE END OF THE MONTH!
4

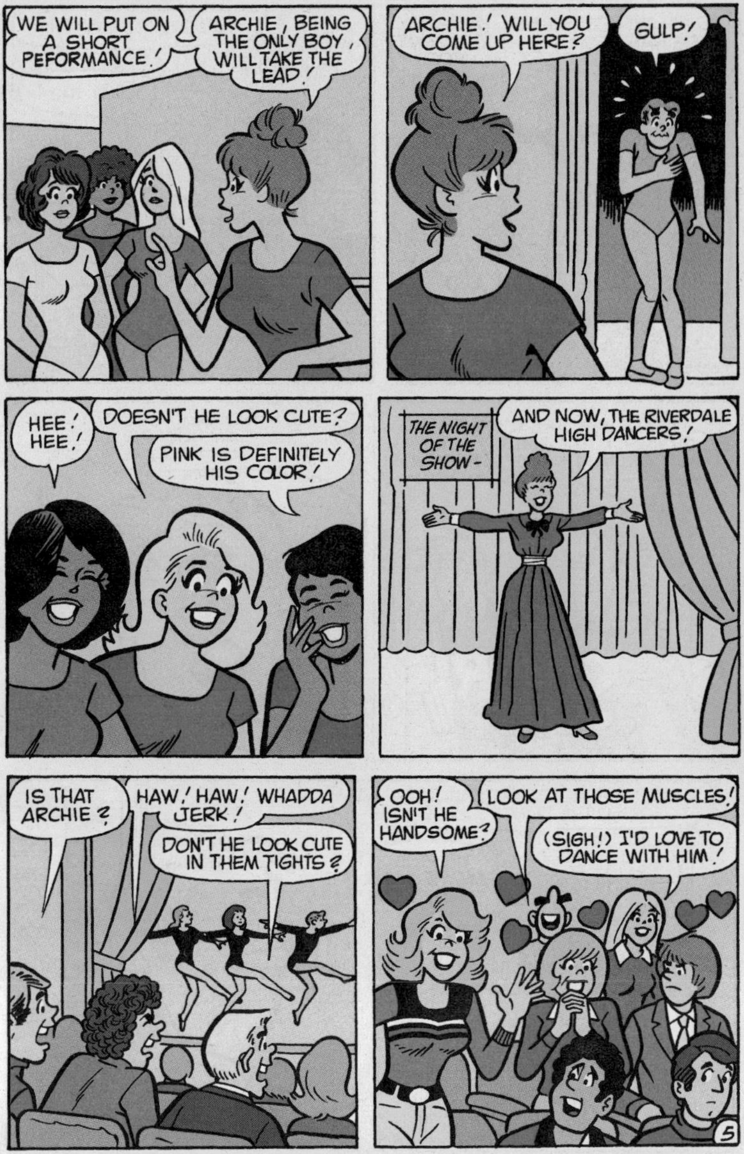
WE WILL PUT ON A SHORT PEFORMANCE!
ARCHIE, BEING THE ONLY BOY, WILL TAKE THE LEAD!
ARCHIE! WILL YOU COME UP HERE?
GULP!
HEE! HEE!
DOESN'T HE LOOK CUTE?
PINK IS DEFINITELY HIS COLOR!
THE NIGHT OF THE SHOW-
AND NOW, THE RIVERDALE HIGH DANCERS!
IS THAT ARCHIE?
HAW! HAW! WHADDA JERK!
DON'T HE LOOK CUTE IN THEM TIGHTS?
OOH! ISN'T HE HANDSOME?
LOOK AT THOSE MUSCLES!
(SIGH!) I'D LOVE TO DANCE WITH HIM!
5

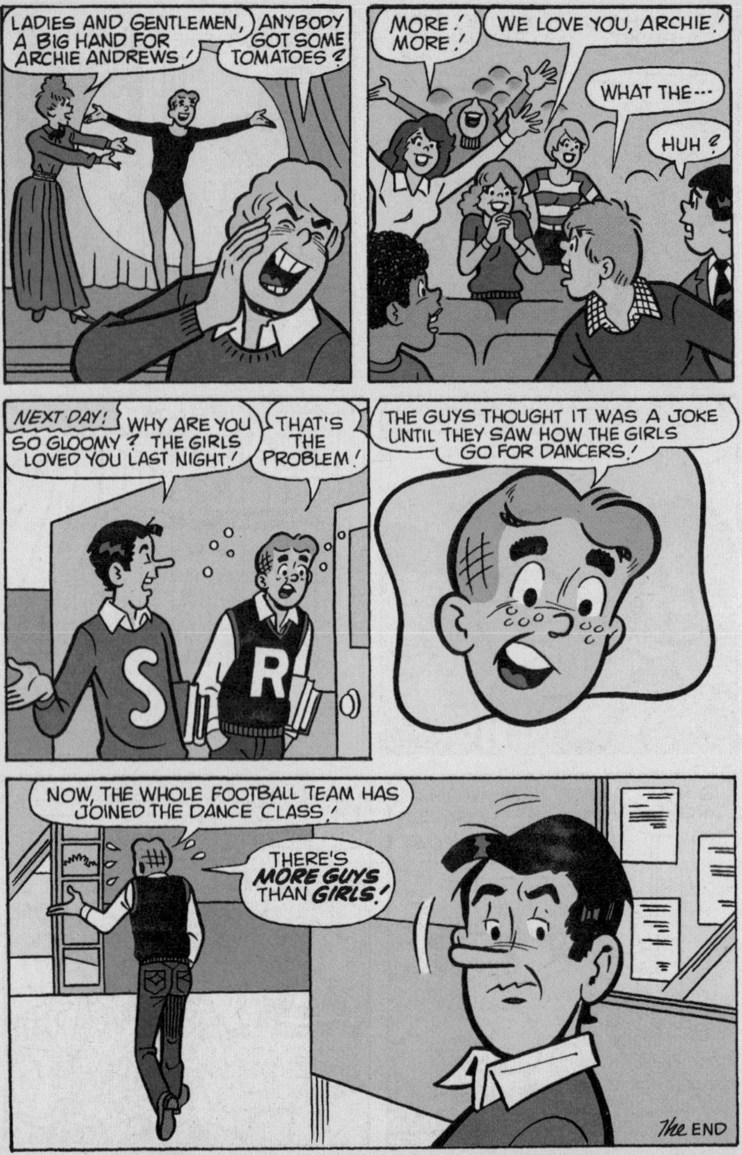
LADIES AND GENTLEMEN, A BIG HAND FOR ARCHIE ANDREWS!
ANYBODY GOT SOME TOMATOES?
MORE! MORE!
WE LOVE YOU, ARCHIE!
WHAT THE---
HUH?
NEXT DAY!
WHY ARE YOU SO GLOOMY? THE GIRLS LOVED YOU LAST NIGHT!
THAT'S THE PROBLEM!
THE GUYS THOUGHT IT WAS A JOKE UNTIL THEY SAW HOW THE GIRLS GO FOR DANCERS!
NOW, THE WHOLE FOOTBALL TEAM HAS JOINED THE DANCE CLASS!
THERE'S MORE GUYS THAN GIRLS!
The END

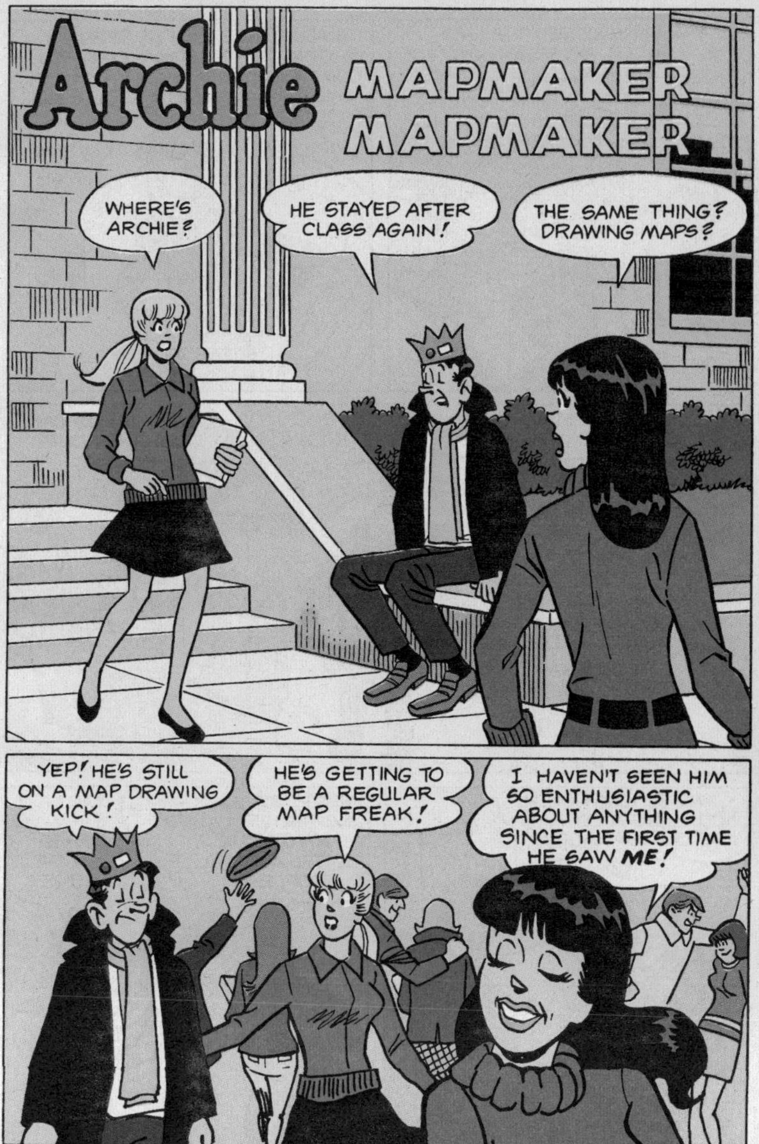
Archie
MAPMAKER MAPMAKER
WHERE'S ARCHIE?
HE STAYED AFTER CLASS AGAIN!
THE SAME THING? DRAWING MAPS?
YEP! HE'S STILL ON A MAP DRAWING KICK!
HE'S GETTING TO BE A REGULAR MAP FREAK!
I HAVEN'T SEEN HIM SO ENTHUSIASTIC ABOUT ANYTHING SINCE THE FIRST TIME HE SAW **ME**!

Script: Frank Doyle / Art & Letters: Samm Schwartz / Colors: Carlos Antunes

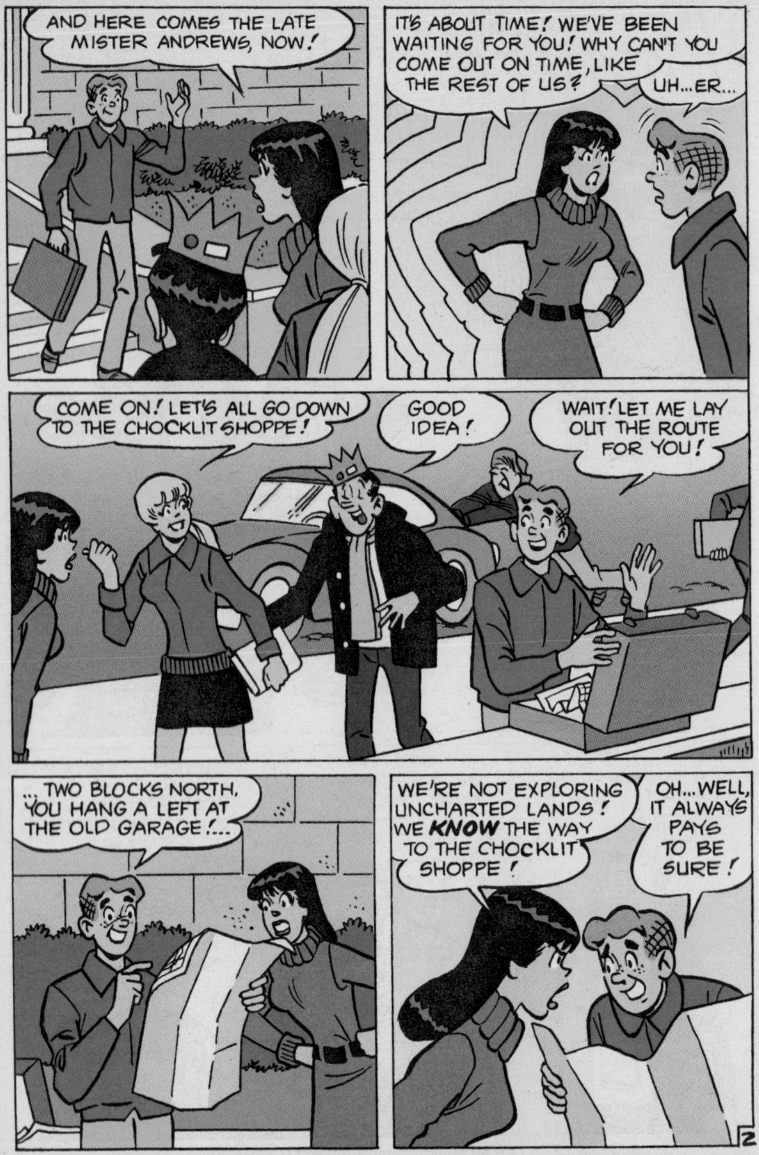
AND HERE COMES THE LATE MISTER ANDREWS, NOW!
IT'S ABOUT TIME! WE'VE BEEN WAITING FOR YOU! WHY CAN'T YOU COME OUT ON TIME, LIKE THE REST OF US?
UH...ER...
COME ON! LET'S ALL GO DOWN TO THE CHOCKLIT SHOPPE!
GOOD IDEA!
WAIT! LET ME LAY OUT THE ROUTE FOR YOU!
...TWO BLOCKS NORTH, YOU HANG A LEFT AT THE OLD GARAGE!...
WE'RE NOT EXPLORING UNCHARTED LANDS! WE KNOW THE WAY TO THE CHOCKLIT SHOPPE!
OH...WELL, IT ALWAYS PAYS TO BE SURE!
2

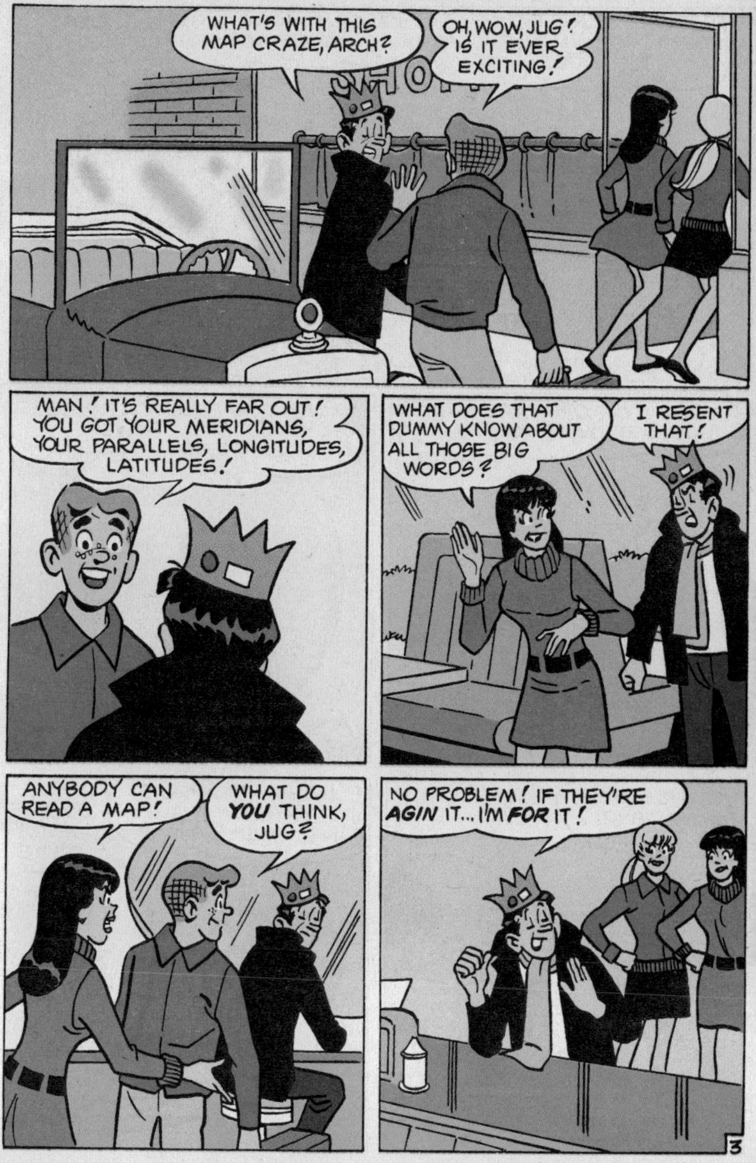
WHAT'S WITH THIS MAP CRAZE, ARCH?
OH, WOW, JUG! IS IT EVER EXCITING!
MAN! IT'S REALLY FAR OUT! YOU GOT YOUR MERIDIANS, YOUR PARALLELS, LONGITUDES, LATITUDES!
WHAT DOES THAT DUMMY KNOW ABOUT ALL THOSE BIG WORDS?
I RESENT THAT!
ANYBODY CAN READ A MAP!
WHAT DO **YOU** THINK, JUG?
NO PROBLEM! IF THEY'RE **AGIN** IT... I'M **FOR** IT!

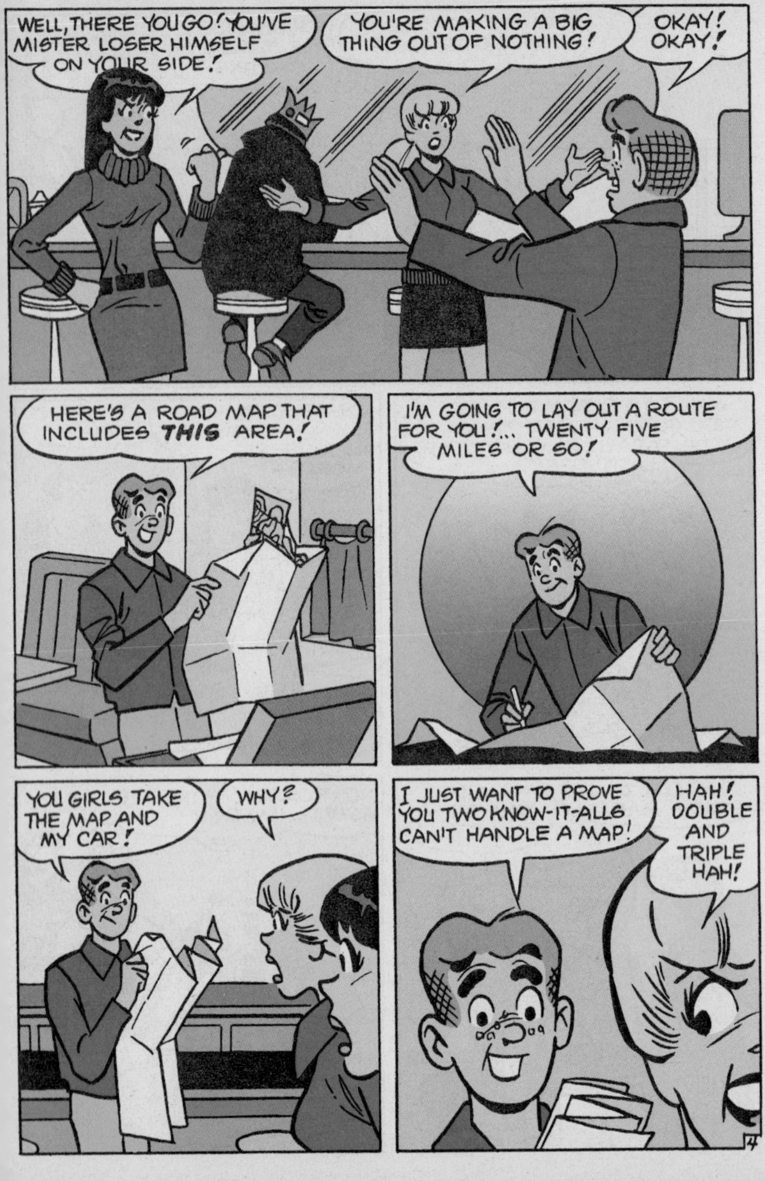
WELL, THERE YOU GO! YOU'VE MISTER LOSER HIMSELF ON YOUR SIDE!
YOU'RE MAKING A BIG THING OUT OF NOTHING!
OKAY! OKAY!
HERE'S A ROAD MAP THAT INCLUDES THIS AREA!
I'M GOING TO LAY OUT A ROUTE FOR YOU!... TWENTY FIVE MILES OR SO!
YOU GIRLS TAKE THE MAP AND MY CAR!
WHY?
I JUST WANT TO PROVE YOU TWO KNOW-IT-ALLS CAN'T HANDLE A MAP!
HAH! DOUBLE AND TRIPLE HAH!
4

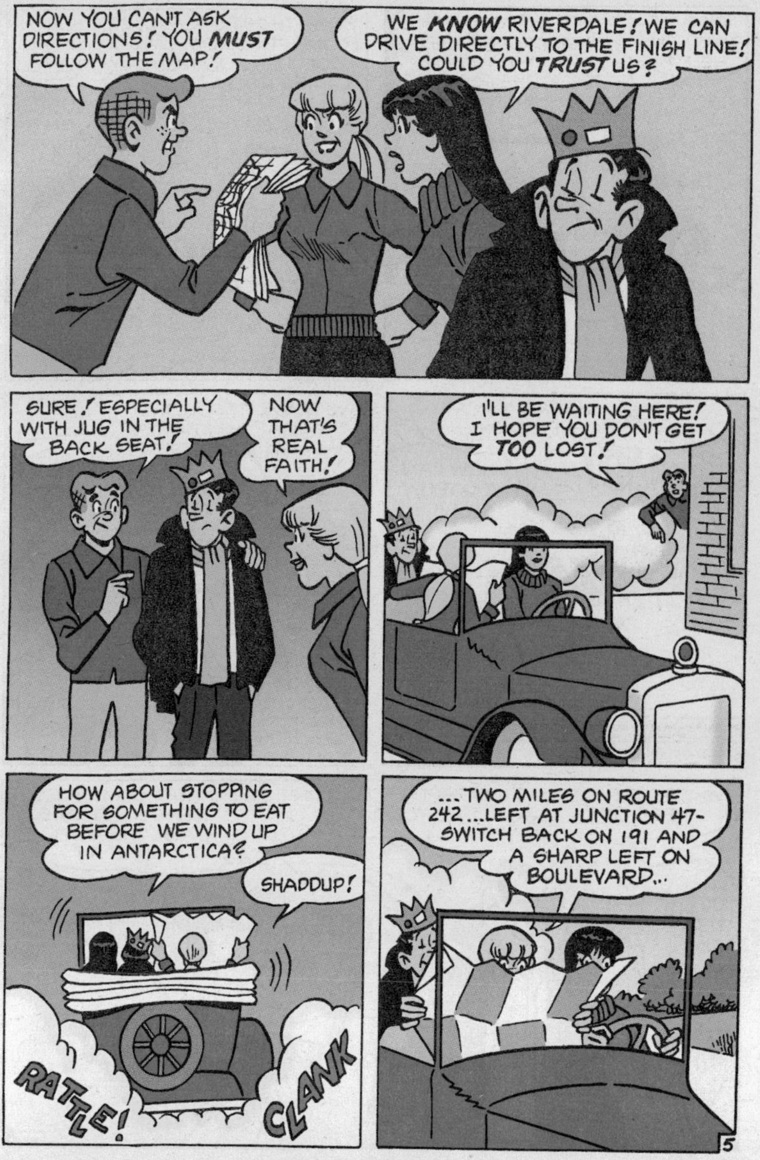
NOW YOU CAN'T ASK DIRECTIONS! YOU MUST FOLLOW THE MAP!
WE KNOW RIVERDALE! WE CAN DRIVE DIRECTLY TO THE FINISH LINE! COULD YOU TRUST US?
SURE! ESPECIALLY WITH JUG IN THE BACK SEAT!
NOW THAT'S REAL FAITH!
I'LL BE WAITING HERE! I HOPE YOU DON'T GET TOO LOST!
HOW ABOUT STOPPING FOR SOMETHING TO EAT BEFORE WE WIND UP IN ANTARCTICA?
SHADDUP!
RATTLE!
CLANK
...TWO MILES ON ROUTE 242...LEFT AT JUNCTION 47- SWITCH BACK ON 191 AND A SHARP LEFT ON BOULEVARD...

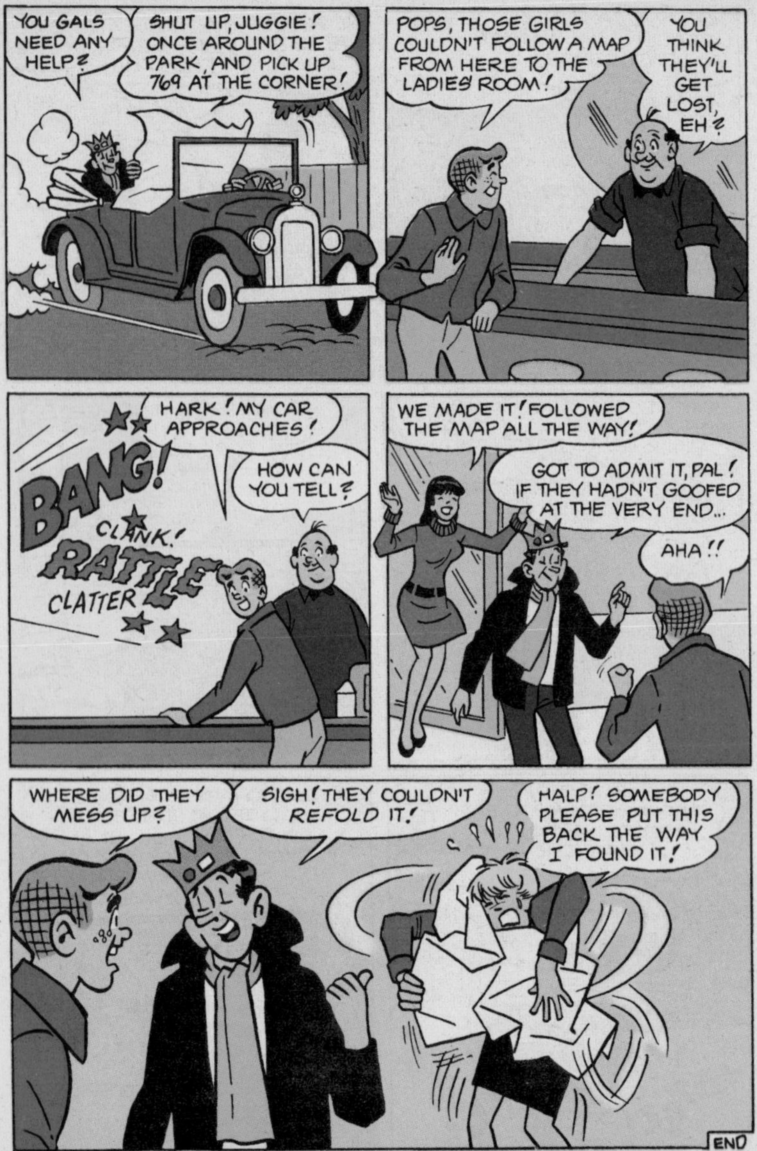

YOU GALS NEED ANY HELP?
SHUT UP, JUGGIE! ONCE AROUND THE PARK, AND PICK UP 769 AT THE CORNER!
POPS, THOSE GIRLS COULDN'T FOLLOW A MAP FROM HERE TO THE LADIES' ROOM!
YOU THINK THEY'LL GET LOST, EH?
HARK! MY CAR APPROACHES!
HOW CAN YOU TELL?
BANG!
CLANK!
RATTLE
CLATTER
WE MADE IT! FOLLOWED THE MAP ALL THE WAY!
GOT TO ADMIT IT, PAL! IF THEY HADN'T GOOFED AT THE VERY END...
AHA!!
WHERE DID THEY MESS UP?
SIGH! THEY COULDN'T REFOLD IT!
HALP! SOMEBODY PLEASE PUT THIS BACK THE WAY I FOUND IT!
END

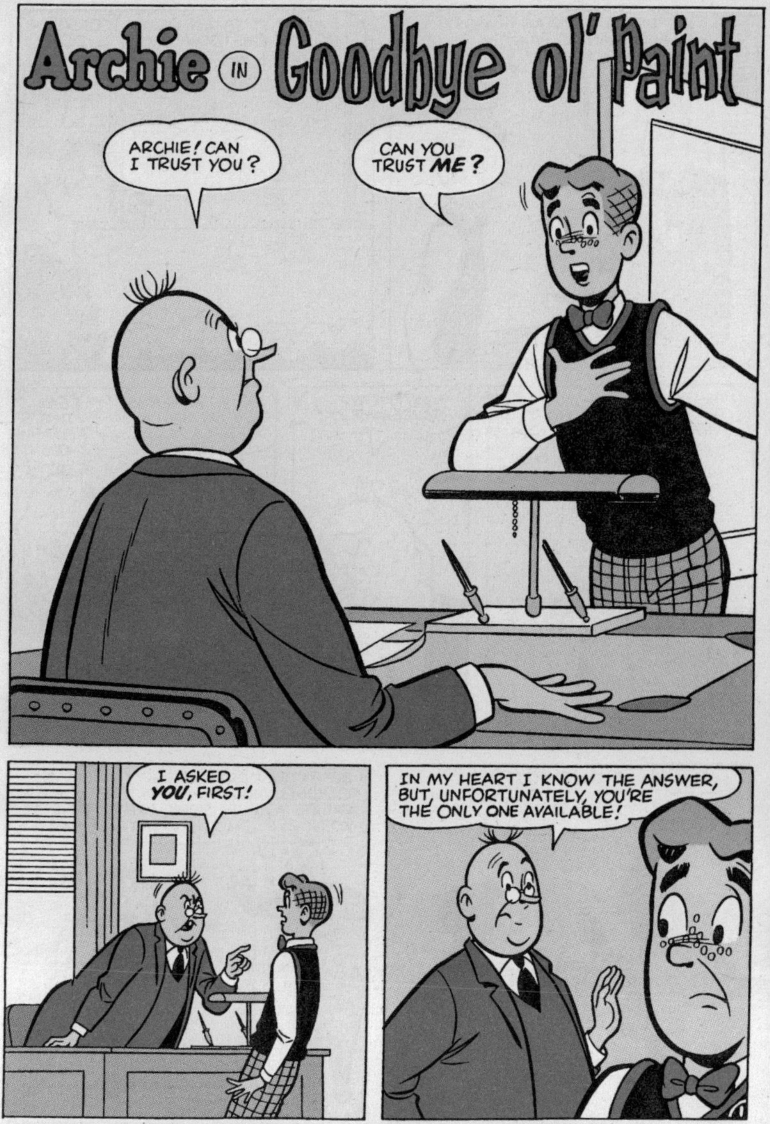
Archie IN Goodbye ol' Paint
ARCHIE! CAN I TRUST YOU?
CAN YOU TRUST ME?
I ASKED YOU, FIRST!
IN MY HEART I KNOW THE ANSWER, BUT, UNFORTUNATELY, YOU'RE THE ONLY ONE AVAILABLE!

Script: Frank Doyle / Pencils: Samm Schwartz / Inks: Marty Epp

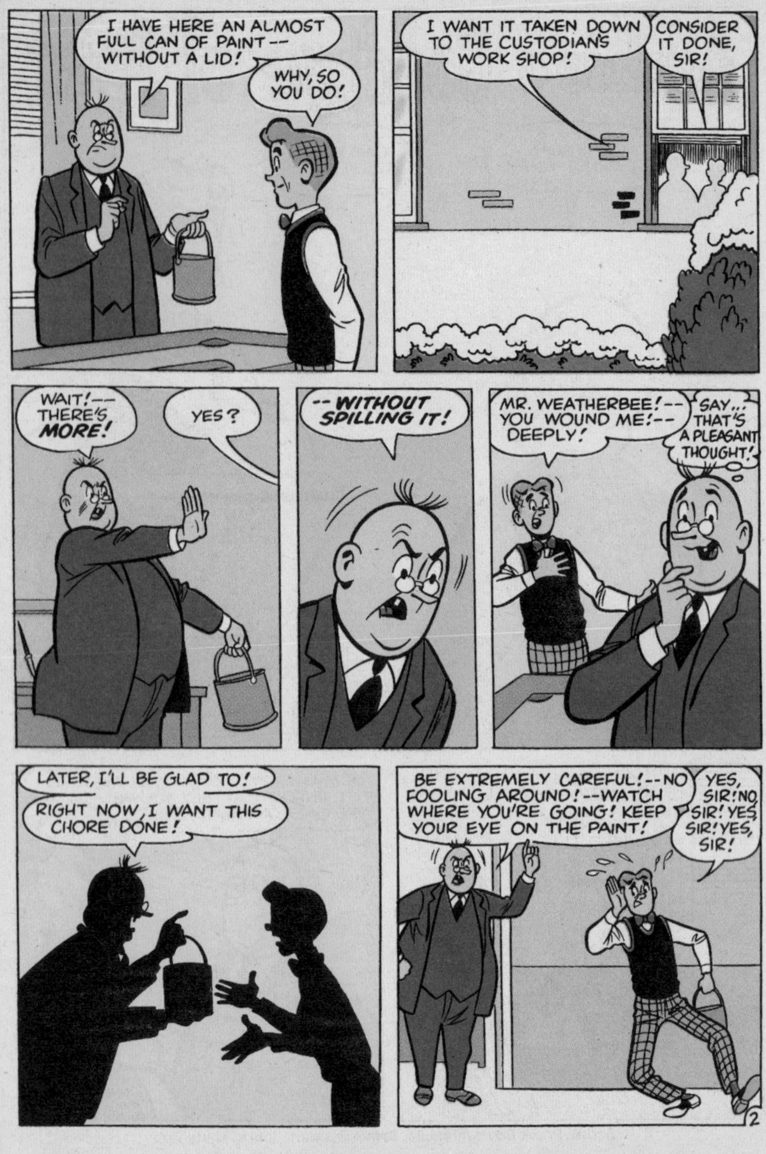
I HAVE HERE AN ALMOST FULL CAN OF PAINT -- WITHOUT A LID!
WHY, SO YOU DO!
I WANT IT TAKEN DOWN TO THE CUSTODIAN'S WORK SHOP!
CONSIDER IT DONE, SIR!
WAIT!-- THERE'S **MORE!**
YES?
-- **WITHOUT SPILLING IT!**
MR. WEATHERBEE!-- YOU WOUND ME!-- DEEPLY!
SAY... THAT'S A PLEASANT THOUGHT!
LATER, I'LL BE GLAD TO!
RIGHT NOW, I WANT THIS CHORE DONE!
BE EXTREMELY CAREFUL!--NO FOOLING AROUND!--WATCH WHERE YOU'RE GOING! KEEP YOUR EYE ON THE PAINT!
YES, SIR! NO, SIR! YES, SIR! YES, SIR!

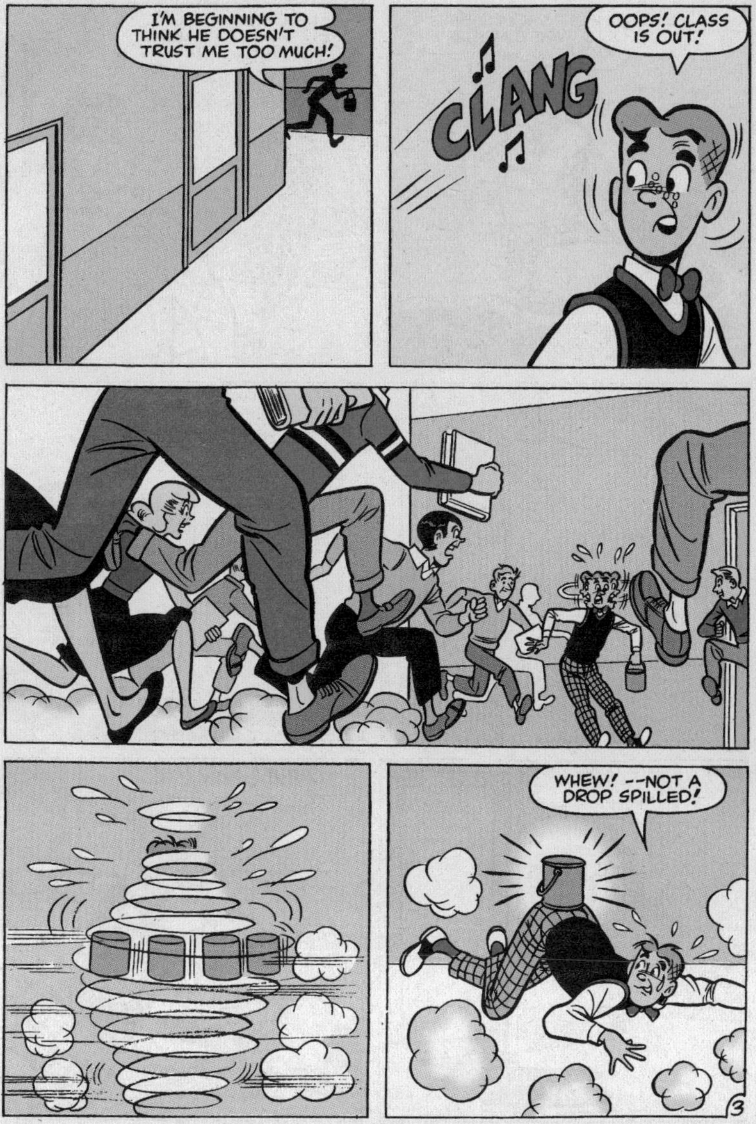

I'M BEGINNING TO THINK HE DOESN'T TRUST ME TOO MUCH!
OOPS! CLASS IS OUT!
CLANG
WHEW! --NOT A DROP SPILLED!
3

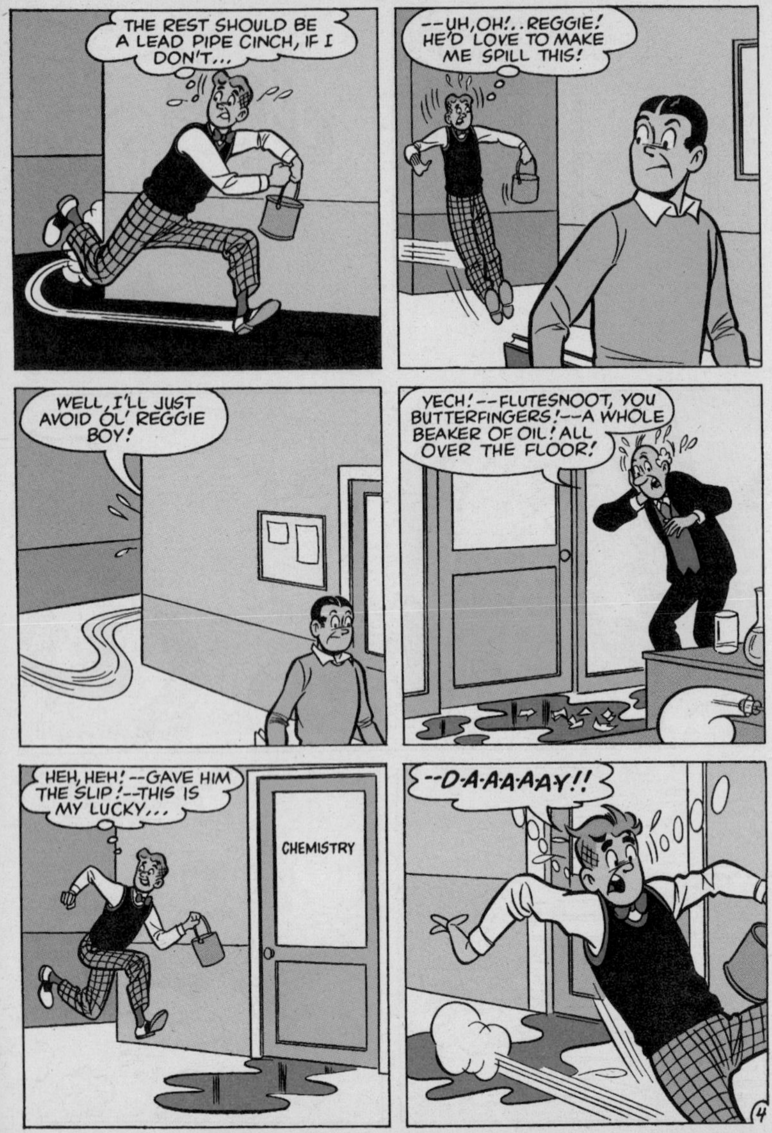
THE REST SHOULD BE A LEAD PIPE CINCH, IF I DON'T...
--UH,OH!..REGGIE! HE'D LOVE TO MAKE ME SPILL THIS!
WELL, I'LL JUST AVOID OL' REGGIE BOY!
YECH!--FLUTESNOOT, YOU BUTTERFINGERS!--A WHOLE BEAKER OF OIL! ALL OVER THE FLOOR!
HEH, HEH! --GAVE HIM THE SLIP!--THIS IS MY LUCKY...
CHEMISTRY
--D-A-A-A-A-A-Y!!
4

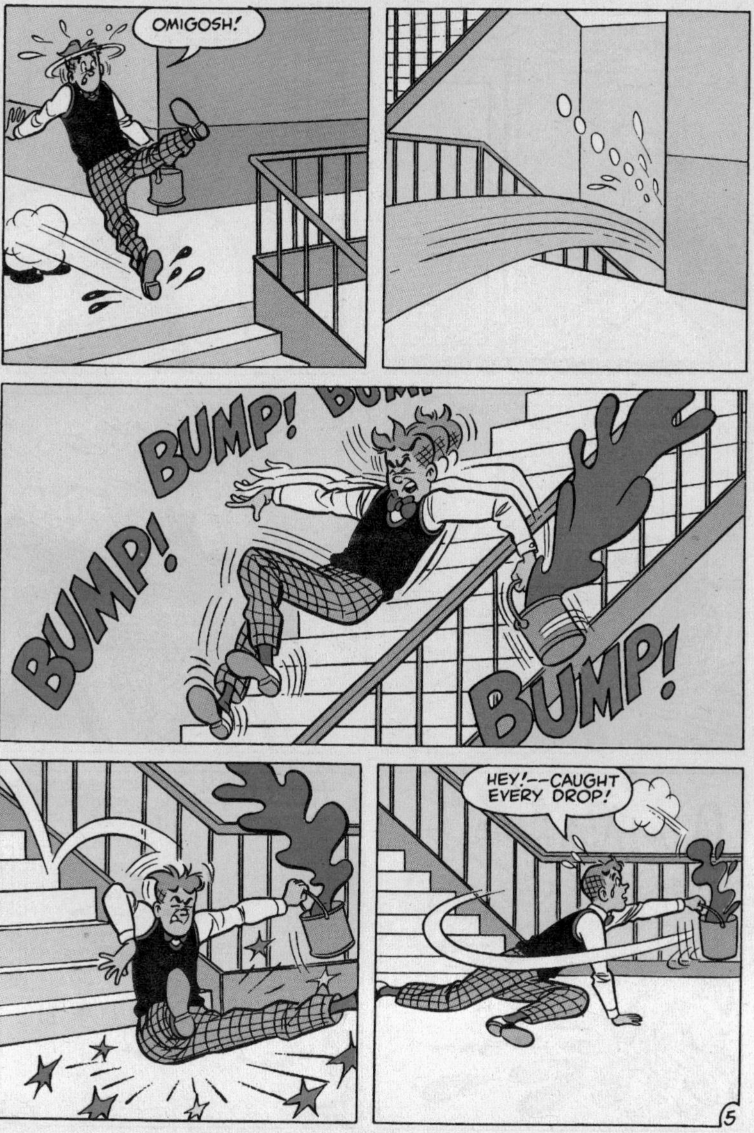
OMIGOSH!
BUMP!
BUMP!
BUMP!
HEY!--CAUGHT EVERY DROP!

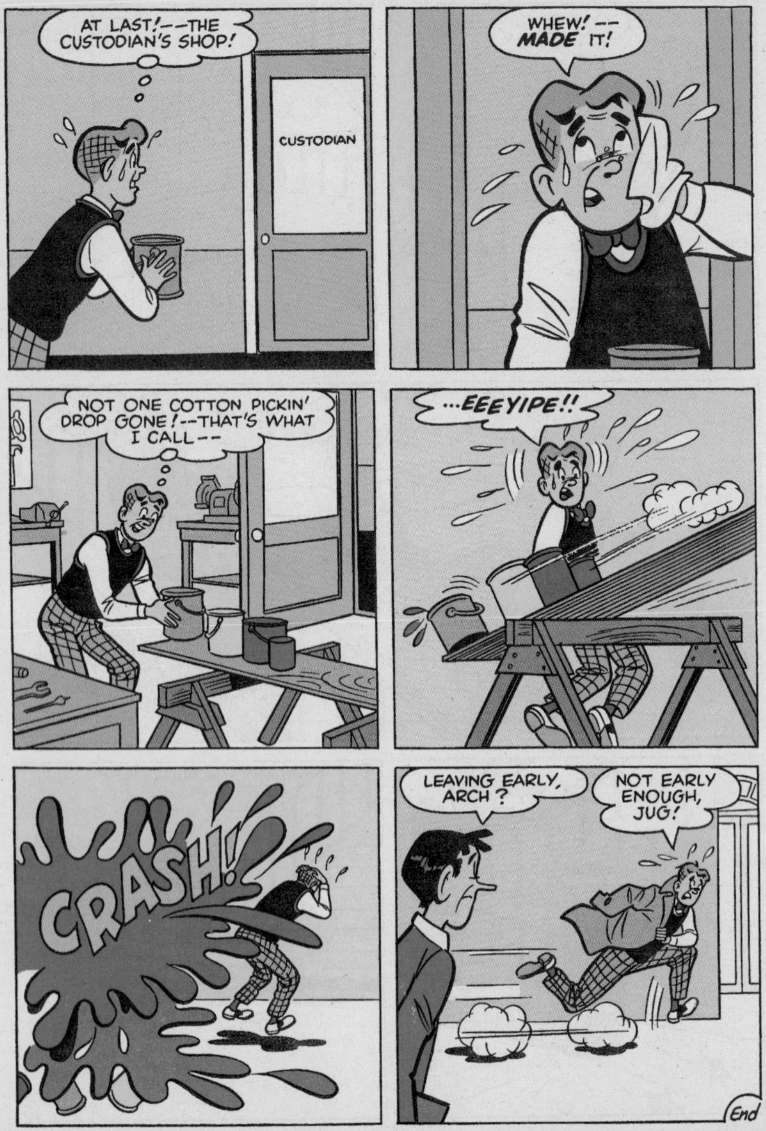
AT LAST!--THE CUSTODIAN'S SHOP!
CUSTODIAN
WHEW! -- MADE IT!
NOT ONE COTTON PICKIN' DROP GONE!--THAT'S WHAT I CALL--
...EEEYIPE!!
CRASH!
LEAVING EARLY, ARCH?
NOT EARLY ENOUGH, JUG!
End

ARCHIE·CHRISTMAS MAZE

ARCHIE WANTS TO WISH ALL HIS READERS A *"MERRY CHRISTMAS."* TRACE A PATH *THROUGH* THIS *WREATH MAZE* TO ARCHIE.

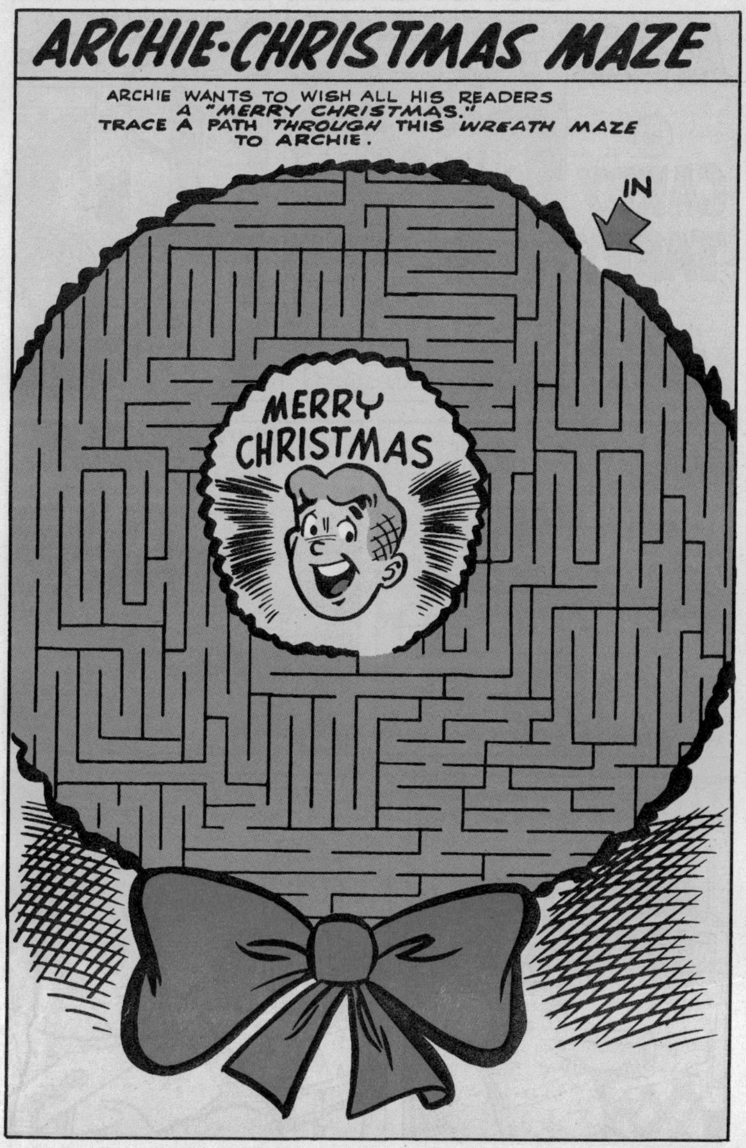
IN
MERRY CHRISTMAS

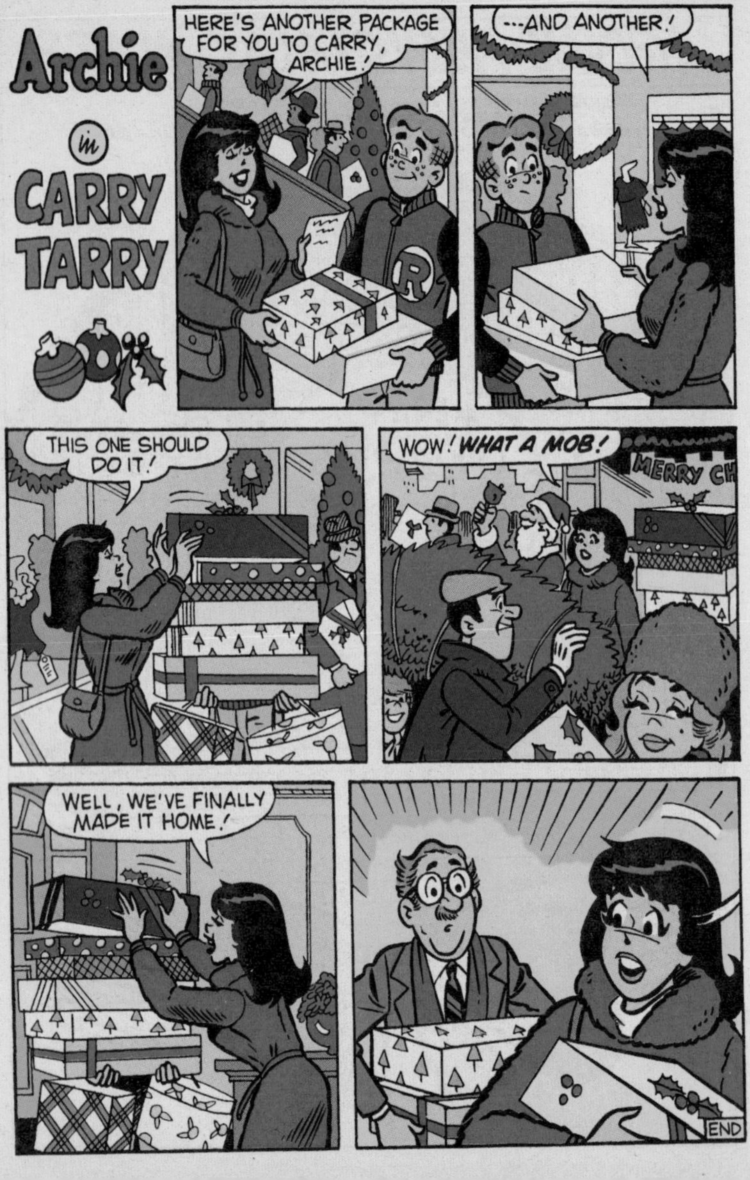
Archie
in
CARRY TARRY
HERE'S ANOTHER PACKAGE FOR YOU TO CARRY, ARCHIE!
---AND ANOTHER!
THIS ONE SHOULD DO IT!
WOW! WHAT A MOB!
MERRY CH
WELL, WE'VE FINALLY MADE IT HOME!
END

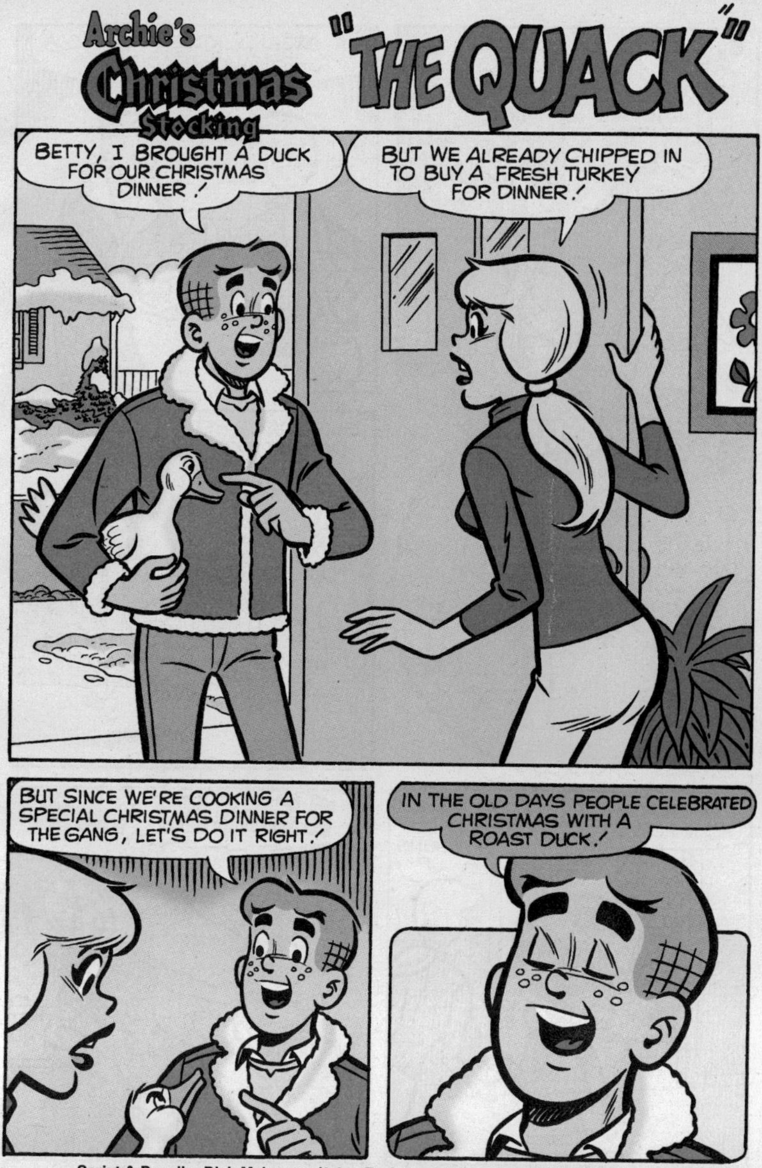
Archie's Christmas Stocking
"THE QUACK"
BETTY, I BROUGHT A DUCK FOR OUR CHRISTMAS DINNER!
BUT WE ALREADY CHIPPED IN TO BUY A FRESH TURKEY FOR DINNER!
BUT SINCE WE'RE COOKING A SPECIAL CHRISTMAS DINNER FOR THE GANG, LET'S DO IT RIGHT!
IN THE OLD DAYS PEOPLE CELEBRATED CHRISTMAS WITH A ROAST DUCK!

Script & Pencils: Dick Malmgren / Inks: Rudy Lapick / Letters: Bill Yoshida

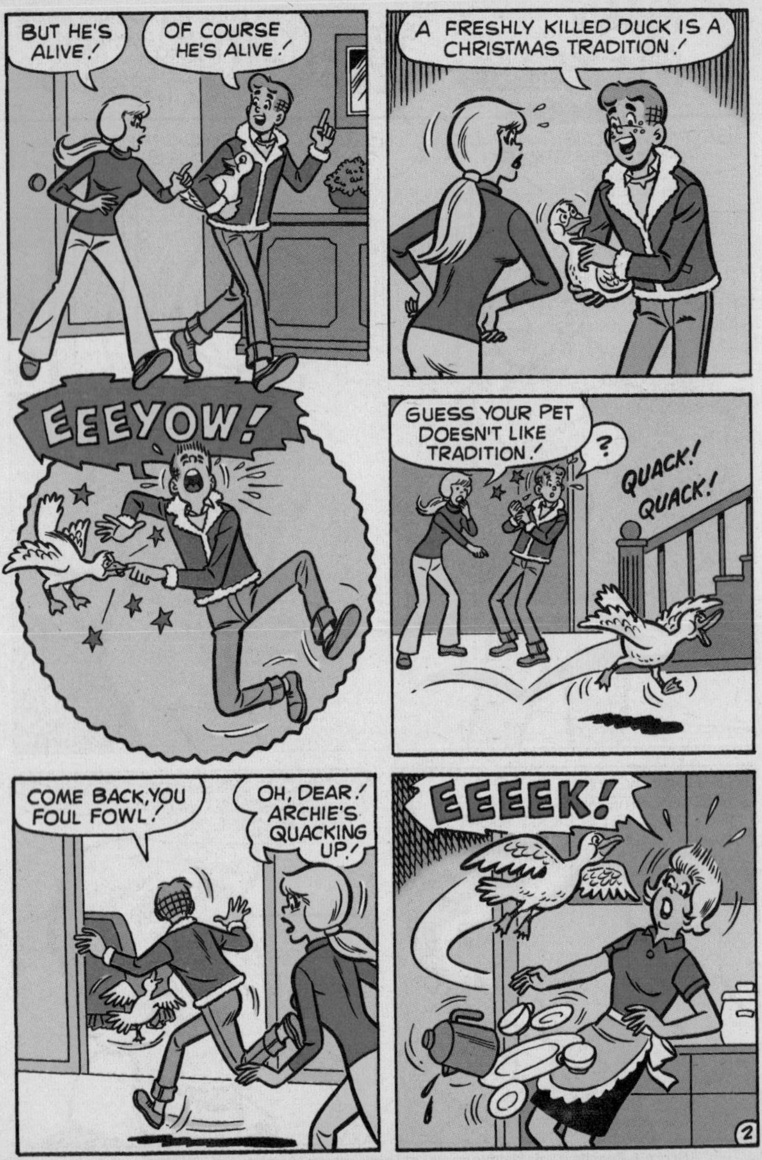
BUT HE'S ALIVE!
OF COURSE HE'S ALIVE!
A FRESHLY KILLED DUCK IS A CHRISTMAS TRADITION!
EEEYOW!
GUESS YOUR PET DOESN'T LIKE TRADITION!
?
QUACK! QUACK!
COME BACK, YOU FOUL FOWL!
OH, DEAR! ARCHIE'S QUACKING UP!
EEEEK!
2

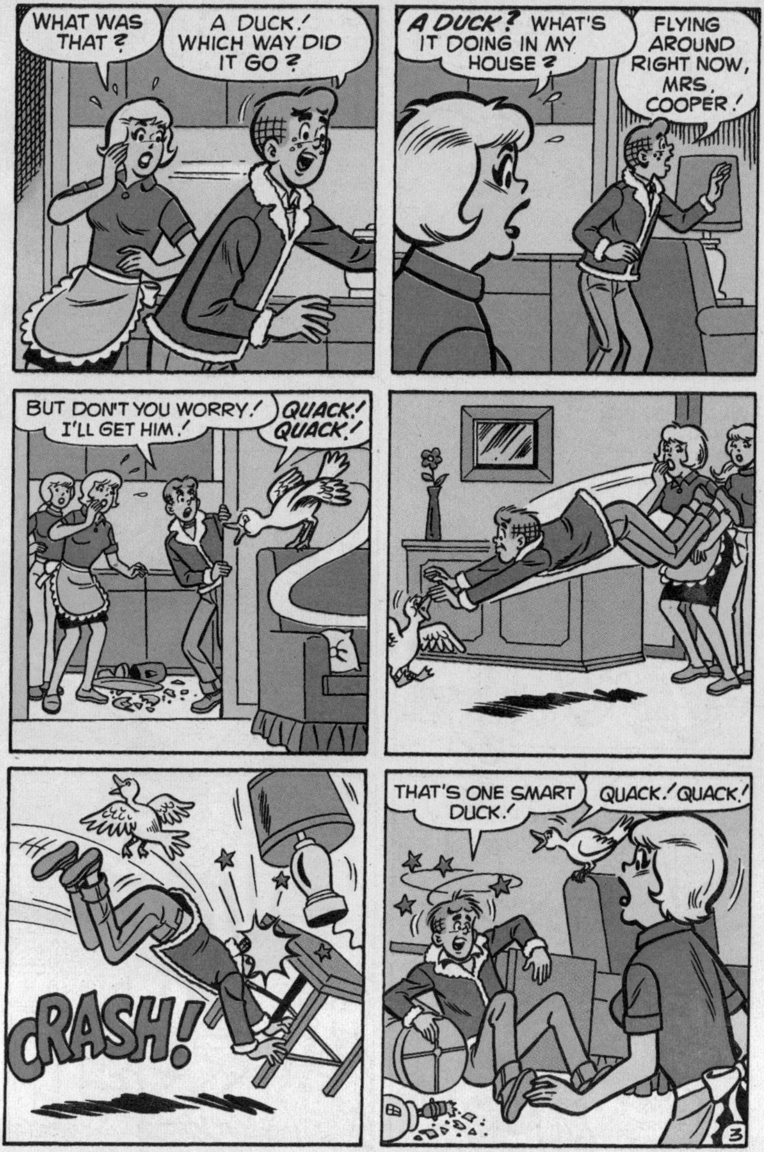
WHAT WAS THAT?
A DUCK! WHICH WAY DID IT GO?
A DUCK? WHAT'S IT DOING IN MY HOUSE?
FLYING AROUND RIGHT NOW, MRS. COOPER!
BUT DON'T YOU WORRY! I'LL GET HIM!
QUACK! QUACK!
CRASH!
THAT'S ONE SMART DUCK!
QUACK! QUACK!
3

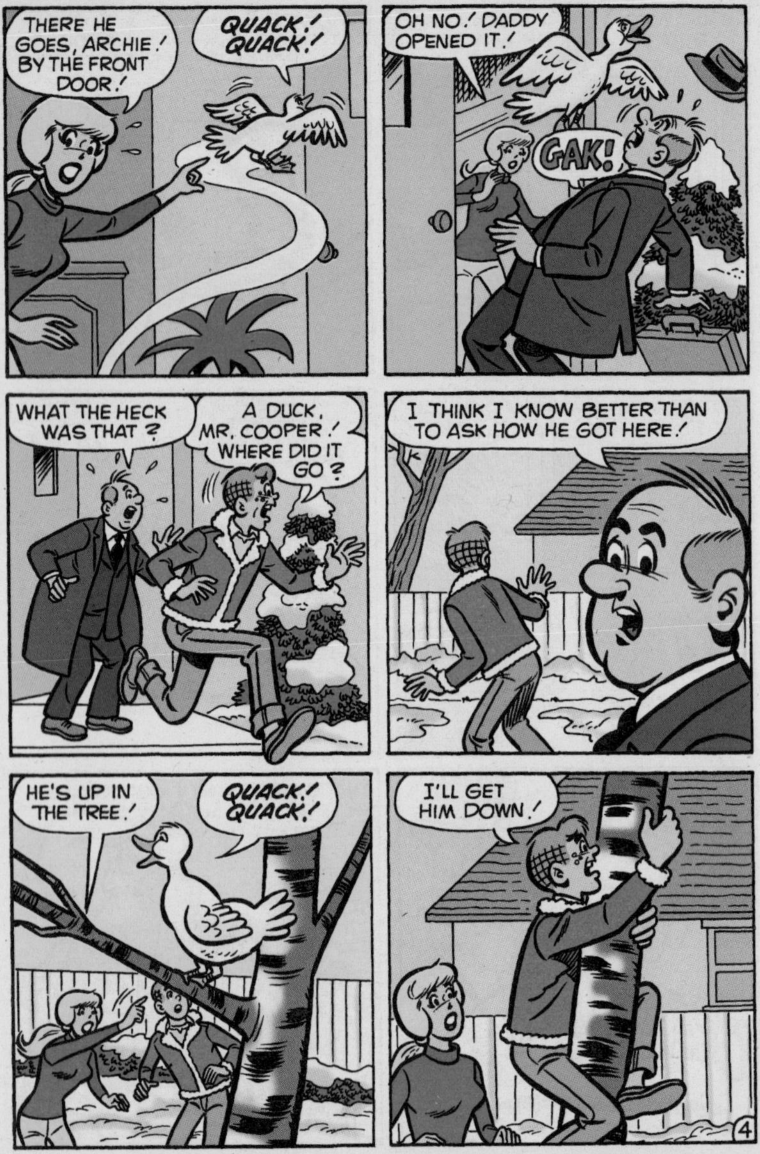
THERE HE GOES, ARCHIE! BY THE FRONT DOOR!
QUACK! QUACK!
OH NO! DADDY OPENED IT!
GAK!
WHAT THE HECK WAS THAT?
A DUCK, MR. COOPER! WHERE DID IT GO?
I THINK I KNOW BETTER THAN TO ASK HOW HE GOT HERE!
HE'S UP IN THE TREE!
QUACK! QUACK!
I'LL GET HIM DOWN!
4

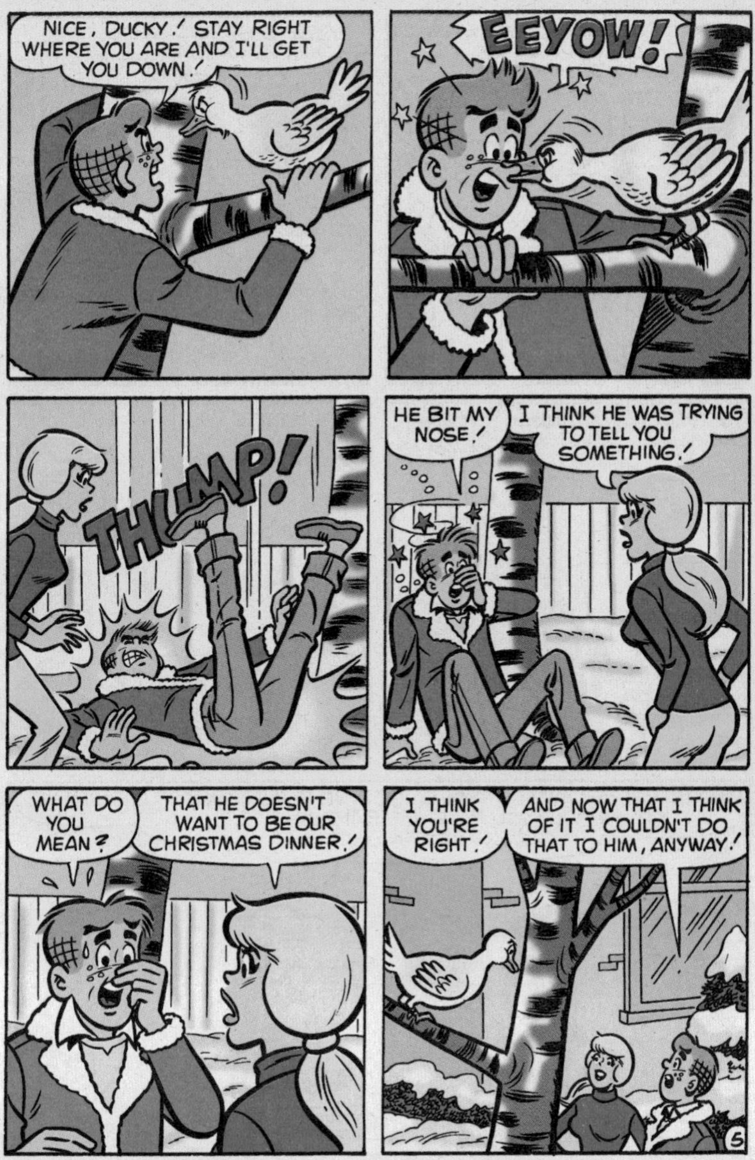
NICE, DUCKY! STAY RIGHT WHERE YOU ARE AND I'LL GET YOU DOWN!
EEYOW!
THUMP!
HE BIT MY NOSE!
I THINK HE WAS TRYING TO TELL YOU SOMETHING!
WHAT DO YOU MEAN?
THAT HE DOESN'T WANT TO BE OUR CHRISTMAS DINNER!
I THINK YOU'RE RIGHT!
AND NOW THAT I THINK OF IT I COULDN'T DO THAT TO HIM, ANYWAY!
5

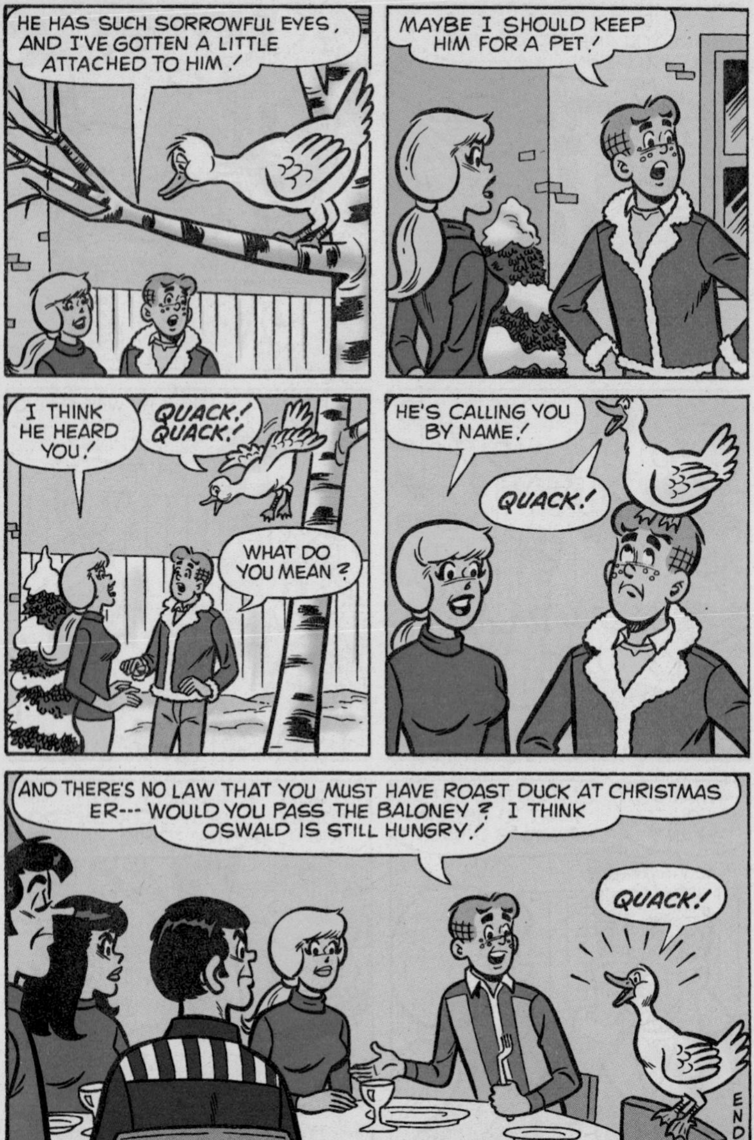
HE HAS SUCH SORROWFUL EYES, AND I'VE GOTTEN A LITTLE ATTACHED TO HIM!
MAYBE I SHOULD KEEP HIM FOR A PET!
I THINK HE HEARD YOU!
QUACK! QUACK!
WHAT DO YOU MEAN?
HE'S CALLING YOU BY NAME!
QUACK!
AND THERE'S NO LAW THAT YOU MUST HAVE ROAST DUCK AT CHRISTMAS ER--- WOULD YOU PASS THE BALONEY? I THINK OSWALD IS STILL HUNGRY!
QUACK!
END

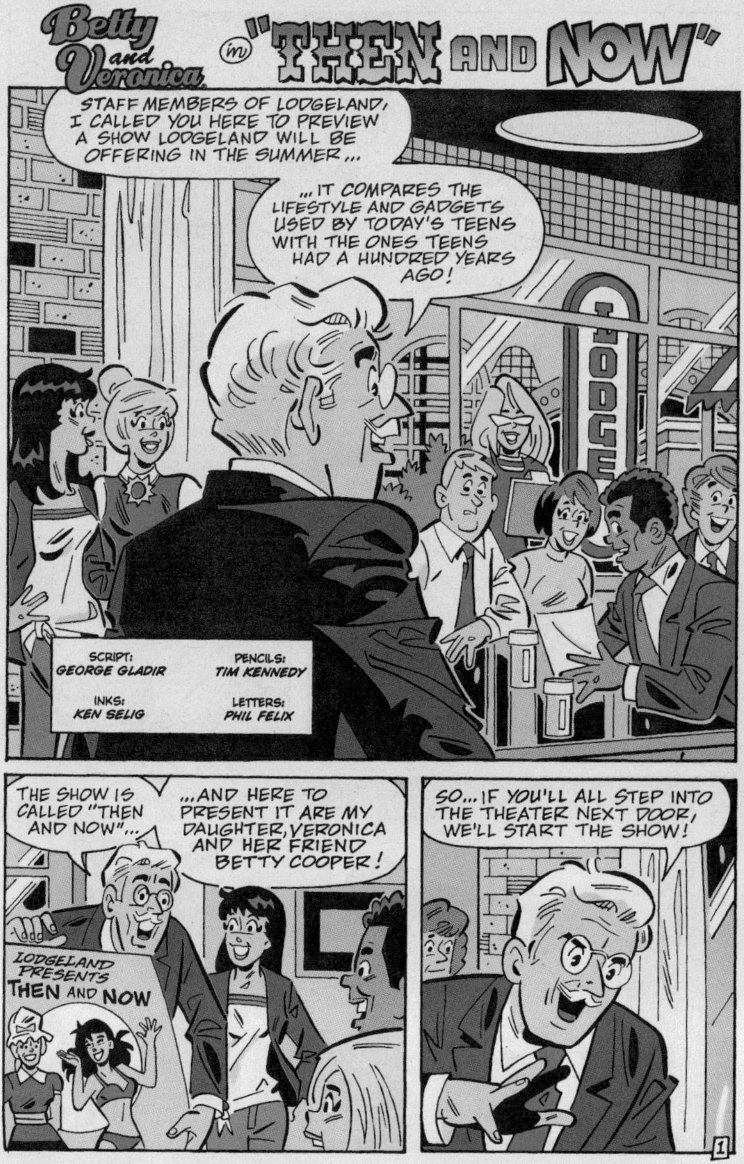
Betty and Veronica
in "THEN AND NOW"
STAFF MEMBERS OF LODGELAND, I CALLED YOU HERE TO PREVIEW A SHOW LODGELAND WILL BE OFFERING IN THE SUMMER...
...IT COMPARES THE LIFESTYLE AND GADGETS USED BY TODAY'S TEENS WITH THE ONES TEENS HAD A HUNDRED YEARS AGO!
LODGE
SCRIPT: GEORGE GLADIR
PENCILS: TIM KENNEDY
INKS: KEN SELIG
LETTERS: PHIL FELIX
THE SHOW IS CALLED "THEN AND NOW"...
...AND HERE TO PRESENT IT ARE MY DAUGHTER, VERONICA AND HER FRIEND BETTY COOPER!
LODGELAND PRESENTS THEN AND NOW
SO... IF YOU'LL ALL STEP INTO THE THEATER NEXT DOOR, WE'LL START THE SHOW!
1

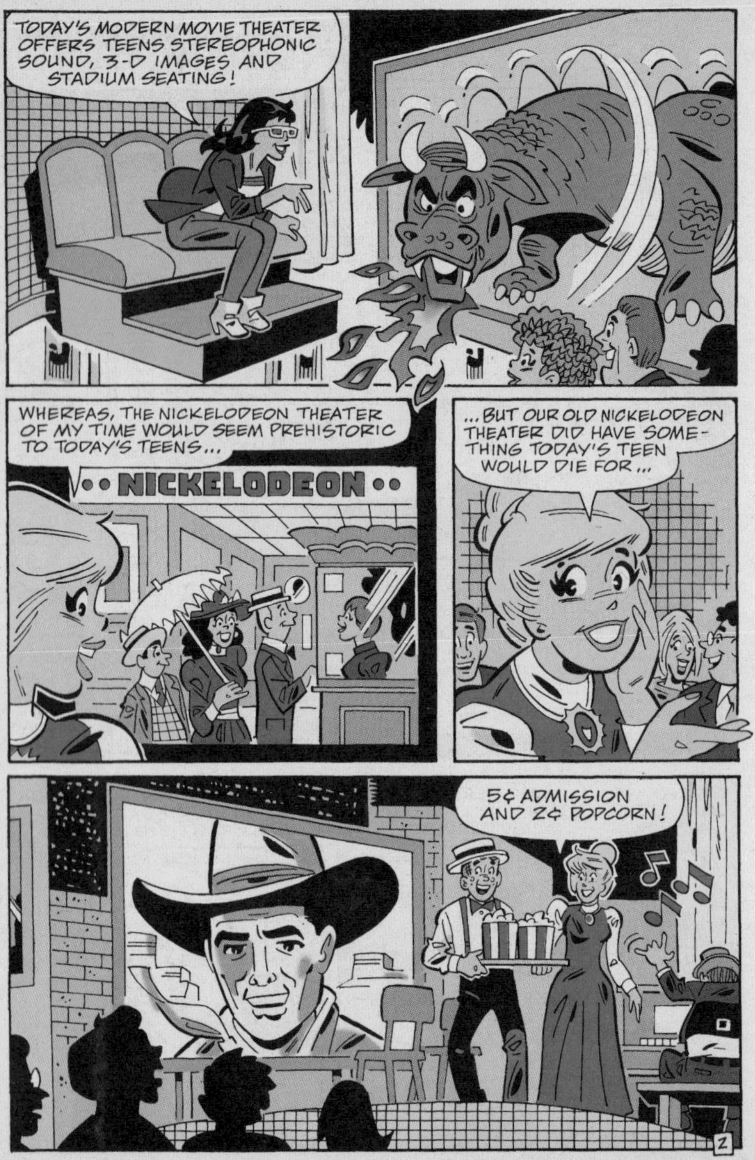
TODAY'S MODERN MOVIE THEATER OFFERS TEENS STEREOPHONIC SOUND, 3-D IMAGES AND STADIUM SEATING!
WHEREAS, THE NICKELODEON THEATER OF MY TIME WOULD SEEM PREHISTORIC TO TODAY'S TEENS...
NICKELODEON
...BUT OUR OLD NICKELODEON THEATER DID HAVE SOMETHING TODAY'S TEEN WOULD DIE FOR...
5¢ ADMISSION AND 2¢ POPCORN!
2

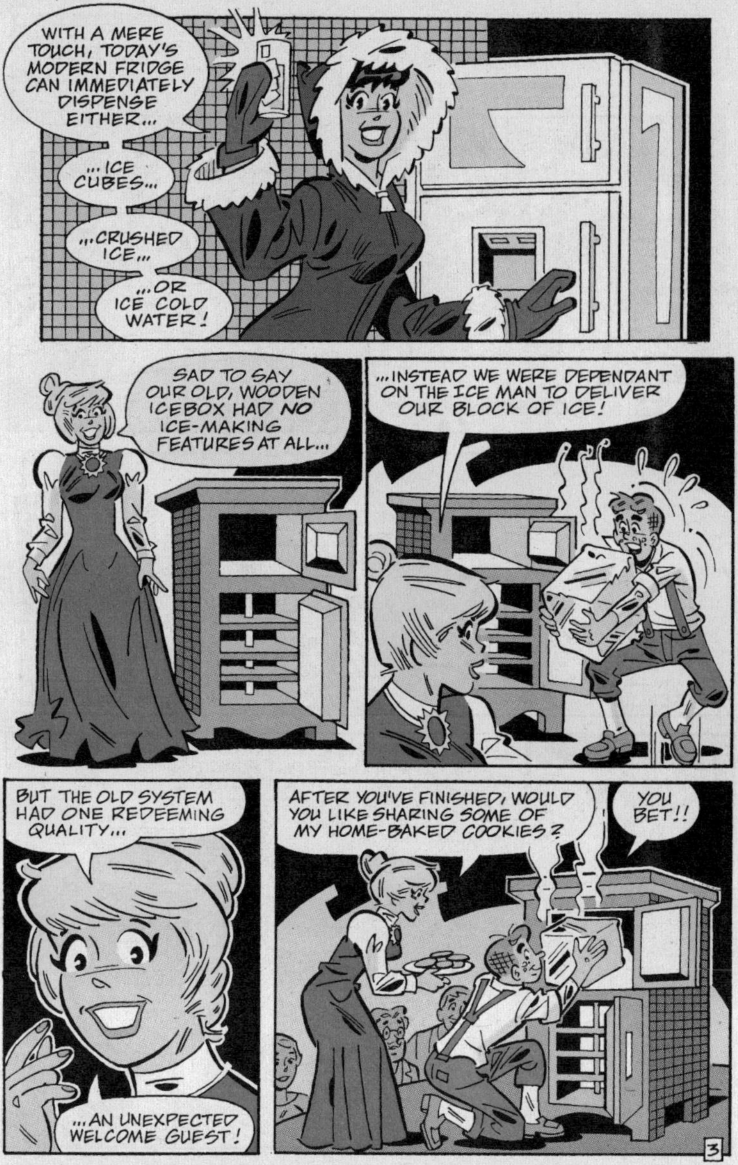
WITH A MERE TOUCH, TODAY'S MODERN FRIDGE CAN IMMEDIATELY DISPENSE EITHER...
...ICE CUBES...
...CRUSHED ICE...
...OR ICE COLD WATER!
SAD TO SAY OUR OLD, WOODEN ICEBOX HAD NO ICE-MAKING FEATURES AT ALL...
...INSTEAD WE WERE DEPENDANT ON THE ICE MAN TO DELIVER OUR BLOCK OF ICE!
BUT THE OLD SYSTEM HAD ONE REDEEMING QUALITY...
...AN UNEXPECTED WELCOME GUEST!
AFTER YOU'VE FINISHED, WOULD YOU LIKE SHARING SOME OF MY HOME-BAKED COOKIES?
YOU BET!!

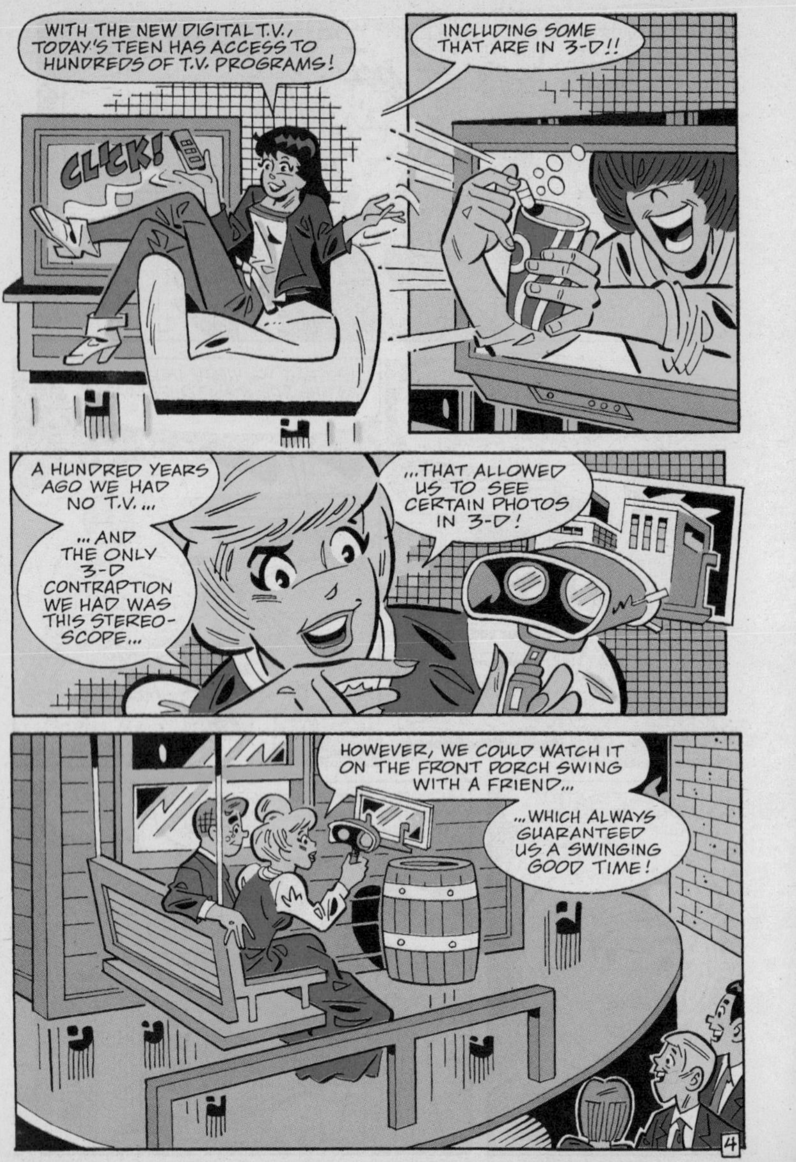
WITH THE NEW DIGITAL T.V., TODAY'S TEEN HAS ACCESS TO HUNDREDS OF T.V. PROGRAMS!
CLICK!
INCLUDING SOME THAT ARE IN 3-D!!
A HUNDRED YEARS AGO WE HAD NO T.V. ...
... AND THE ONLY 3-D CONTRAPTION WE HAD WAS THIS STEREO-SCOPE...
...THAT ALLOWED US TO SEE CERTAIN PHOTOS IN 3-D!
HOWEVER, WE COULD WATCH IT ON THE FRONT PORCH SWING WITH A FRIEND...
...WHICH ALWAYS GUARANTEED US A SWINGING GOOD TIME!
4

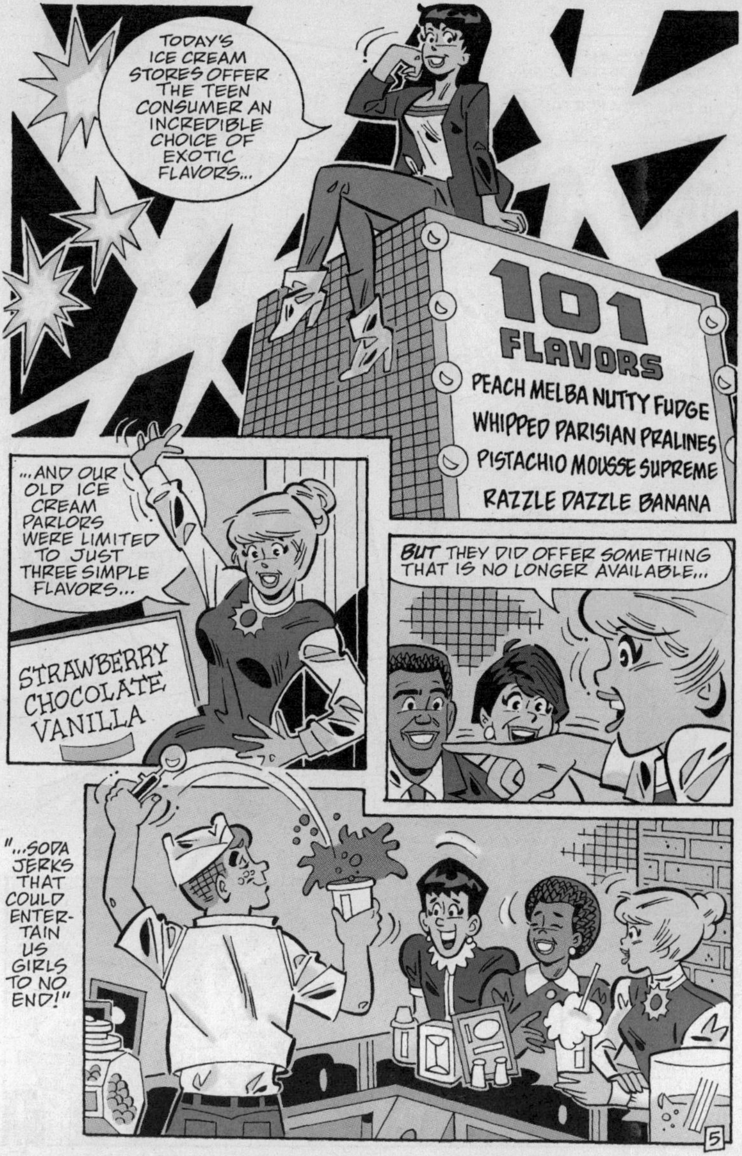
TODAY'S ICE CREAM STORES OFFER THE TEEN CONSUMER AN INCREDIBLE CHOICE OF EXOTIC FLAVORS...
101 FLAVORS
PEACH MELBA NUTTY FUDGE
WHIPPED PARISIAN PRALINES
PISTACHIO MOUSSE SUPREME
RAZZLE DAZZLE BANANA
...AND OUR OLD ICE CREAM PARLORS WERE LIMITED TO JUST THREE SIMPLE FLAVORS...
STRAWBERRY
CHOCOLATE
VANILLA
BUT THEY DID OFFER SOMETHING THAT IS NO LONGER AVAILABLE...
"...SODA JERKS THAT COULD ENTERTAIN US GIRLS TO NO END!"
5

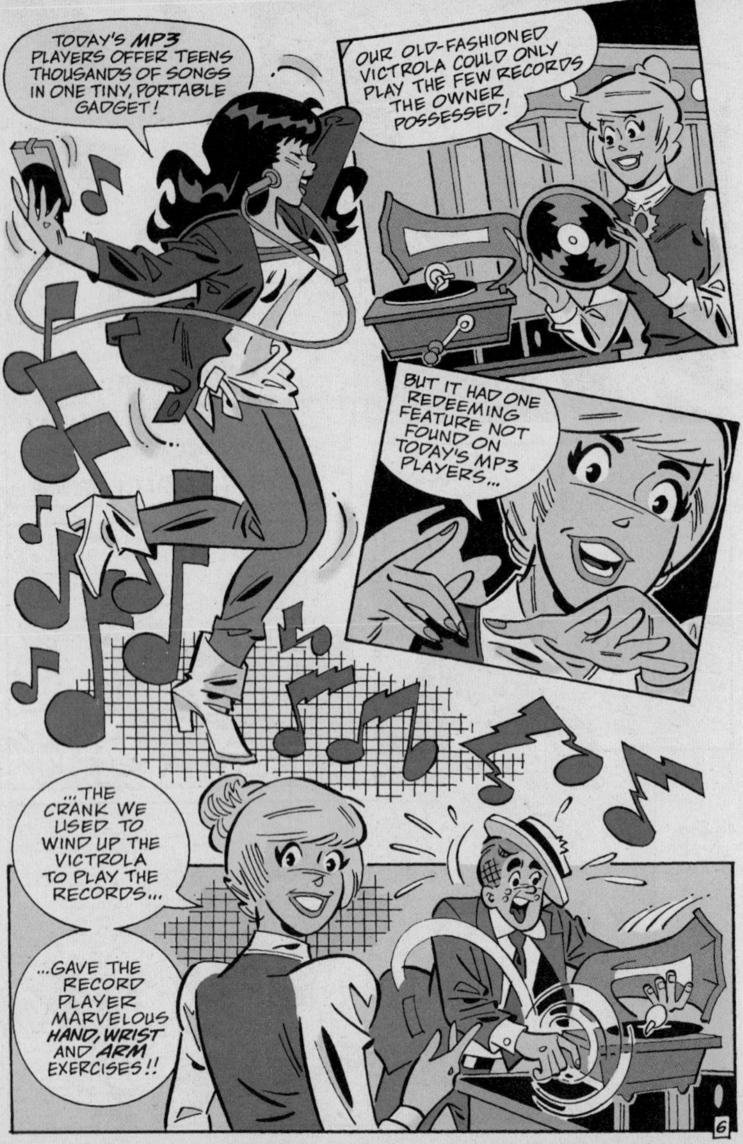
TODAY'S MP3 PLAYERS OFFER TEENS THOUSANDS OF SONGS IN ONE TINY, PORTABLE GADGET!
OUR OLD-FASHIONED VICTROLA COULD ONLY PLAY THE FEW RECORDS THE OWNER POSSESSED!
BUT IT HAD ONE REDEEMING FEATURE NOT FOUND ON TODAY'S MP3 PLAYERS...
...THE CRANK WE USED TO WIND UP THE VICTROLA TO PLAY THE RECORDS...
...GAVE THE RECORD PLAYER MARVELOUS HAND, WRIST AND ARM EXERCISES!!
6

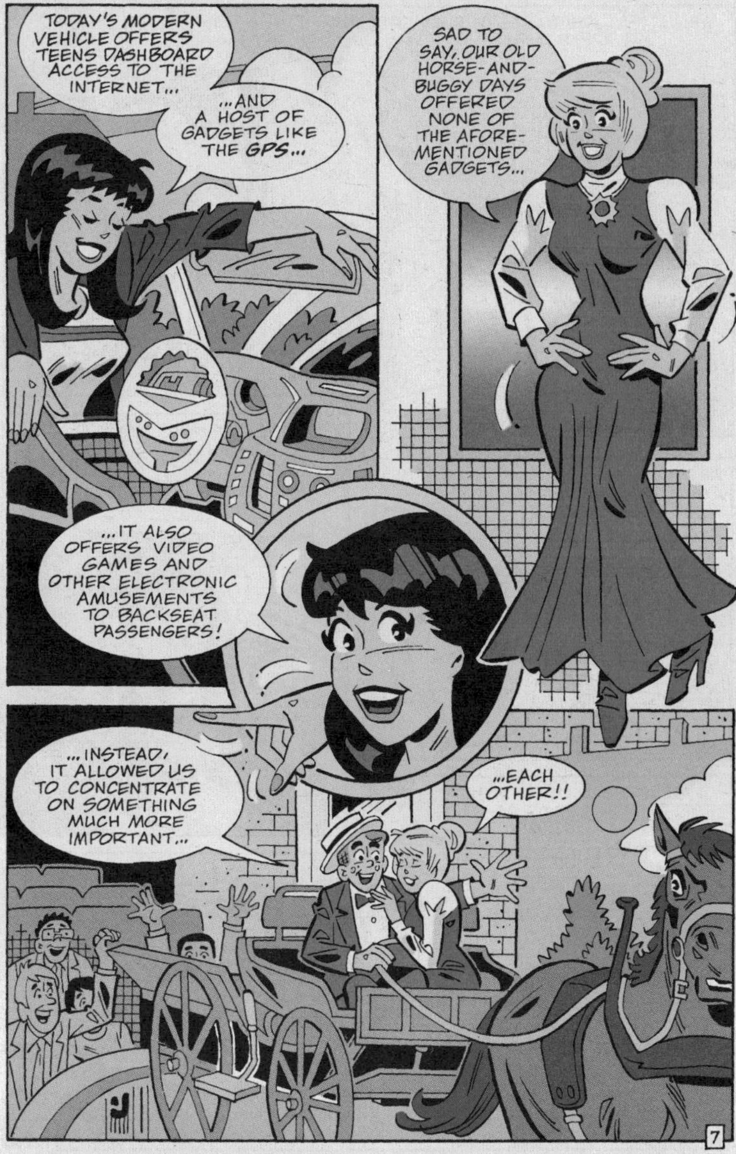
TODAY'S MODERN VEHICLE OFFERS TEENS DASHBOARD ACCESS TO THE INTERNET...
...AND A HOST OF GADGETS LIKE THE GPS...
SAD TO SAY, OUR OLD HORSE-AND-BUGGY DAYS OFFERED NONE OF THE AFORE-MENTIONED GADGETS...
...IT ALSO OFFERS VIDEO GAMES AND OTHER ELECTRONIC AMUSEMENTS TO BACKSEAT PASSENGERS!
...INSTEAD, IT ALLOWED US TO CONCENTRATE ON SOMETHING MUCH MORE IMPORTANT...
...EACH OTHER!!

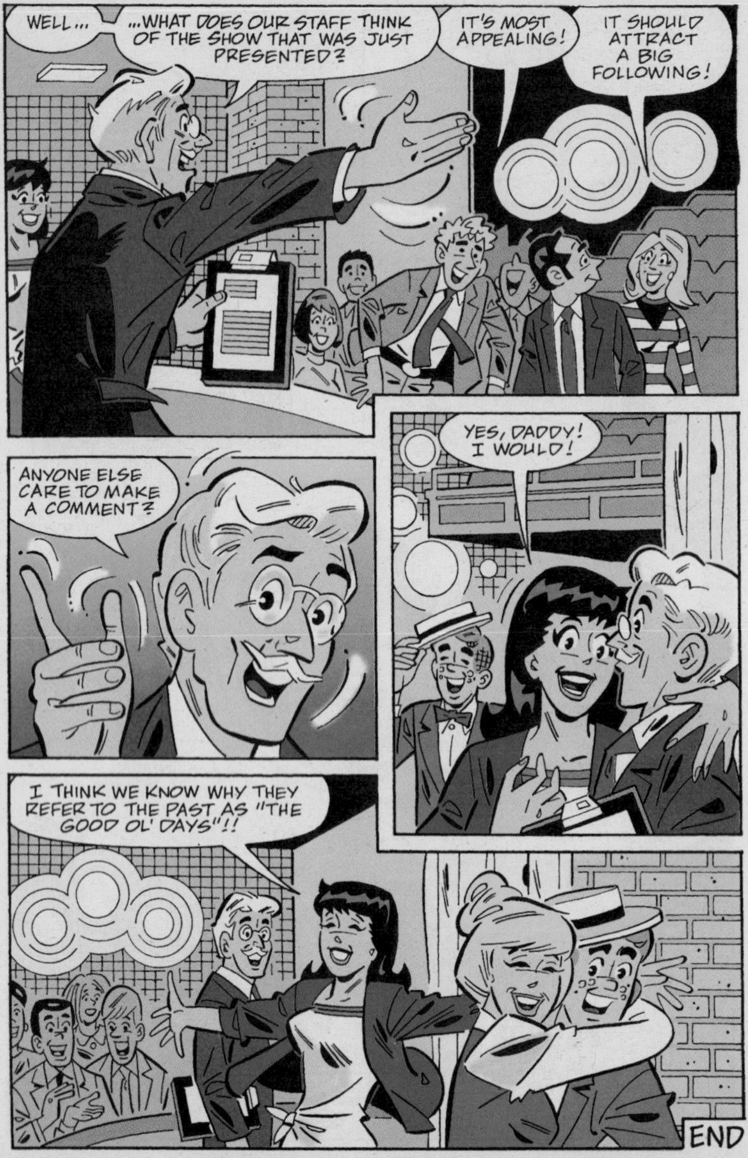
WELL...
...WHAT DOES OUR STAFF THINK OF THE SHOW THAT WAS JUST PRESENTED?
IT'S MOST APPEALING!
IT SHOULD ATTRACT A BIG FOLLOWING!
ANYONE ELSE CARE TO MAKE A COMMENT?
YES, DADDY! I WOULD!
I THINK WE KNOW WHY THEY REFER TO THE PAST AS "THE GOOD OL' DAYS"!!
END

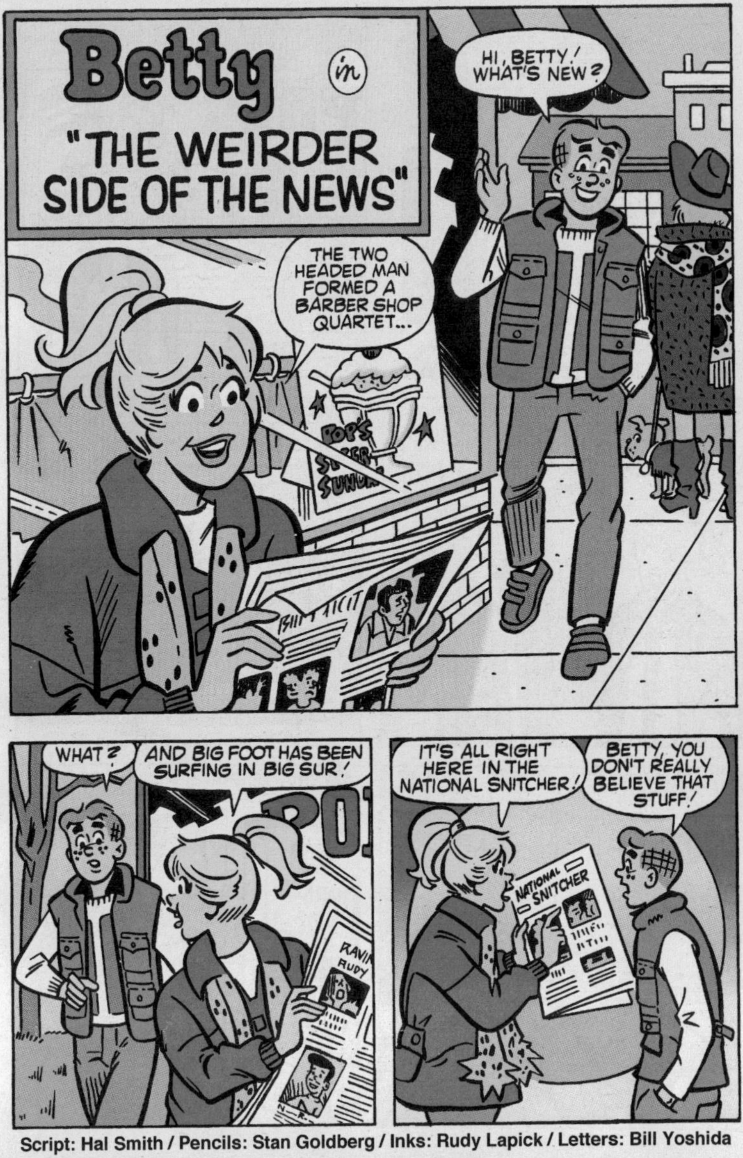
Betty in
"THE WEIRDER SIDE OF THE NEWS"
HI, BETTY! WHAT'S NEW?
THE TWO HEADED MAN FORMED A BARBER SHOP QUARTET...
WHAT?
AND BIG FOOT HAS BEEN SURFING IN BIG SUR!
IT'S ALL RIGHT HERE IN THE NATIONAL SNITCHER!
BETTY, YOU DON'T REALLY BELIEVE THAT STUFF!
NATIONAL SNITCHER

Script: Hal Smith / Pencils: Stan Goldberg / Inks: Rudy Lapick / Letters: Bill Yoshida

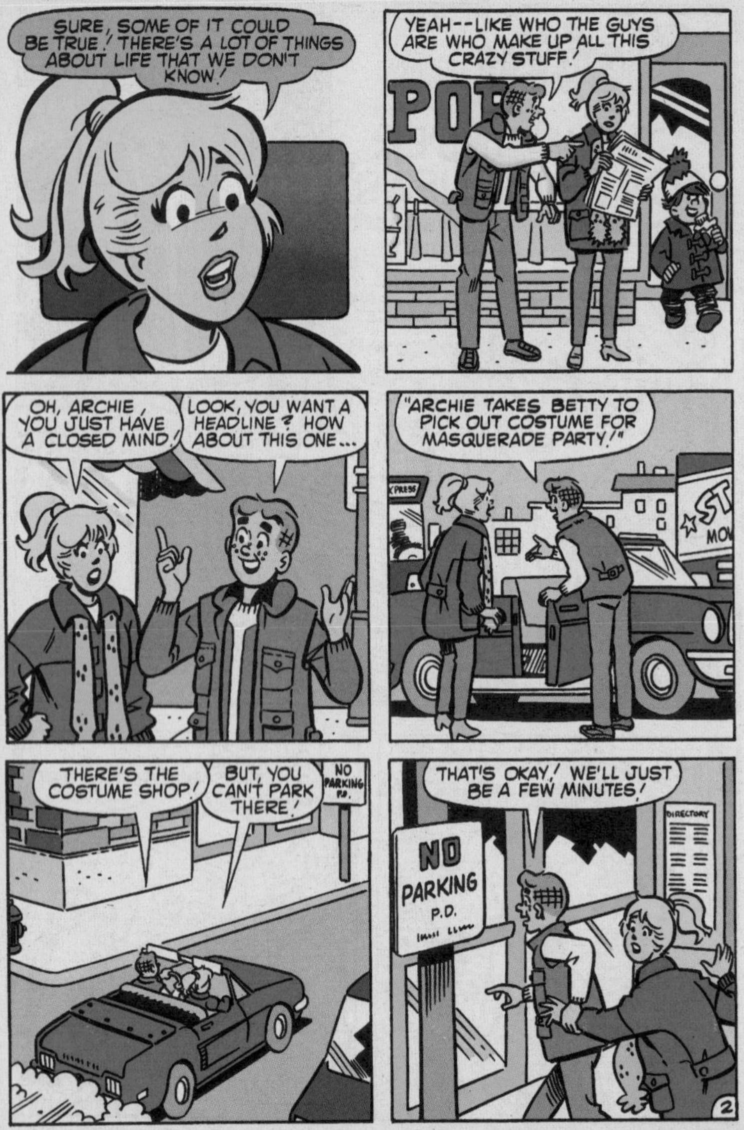
SURE, SOME OF IT COULD BE TRUE! THERE'S A LOT OF THINGS ABOUT LIFE THAT WE DON'T KNOW!
YEAH--LIKE WHO THE GUYS ARE WHO MAKE UP ALL THIS CRAZY STUFF!
POP
OH, ARCHIE, YOU JUST HAVE A CLOSED MIND!
LOOK, YOU WANT A HEADLINE? HOW ABOUT THIS ONE...
"ARCHIE TAKES BETTY TO PICK OUT COSTUME FOR MASQUERADE PARTY!"
XPRESS
THERE'S THE COSTUME SHOP!
BUT, YOU CAN'T PARK THERE!
NO PARKING P.D.
THAT'S OKAY! WE'LL JUST BE A FEW MINUTES!
NO PARKING P.D.
DIRECTORY
2

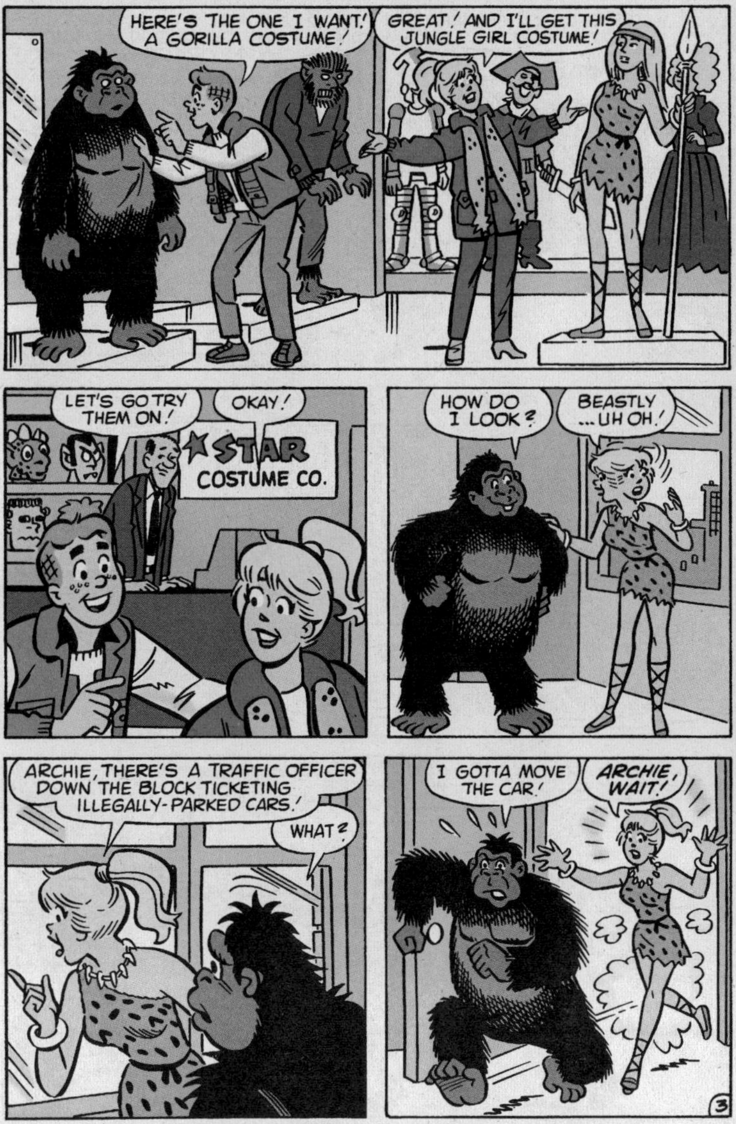
HERE'S THE ONE I WANT! A GORILLA COSTUME!
GREAT! AND I'LL GET THIS JUNGLE GIRL COSTUME!
LET'S GO TRY THEM ON!
OKAY!
STAR COSTUME CO.
HOW DO I LOOK?
BEASTLY ...UH OH!
ARCHIE, THERE'S A TRAFFIC OFFICER DOWN THE BLOCK TICKETING ILLEGALLY-PARKED CARS!
WHAT?
I GOTTA MOVE THE CAR!
ARCHIE, WAIT!
3

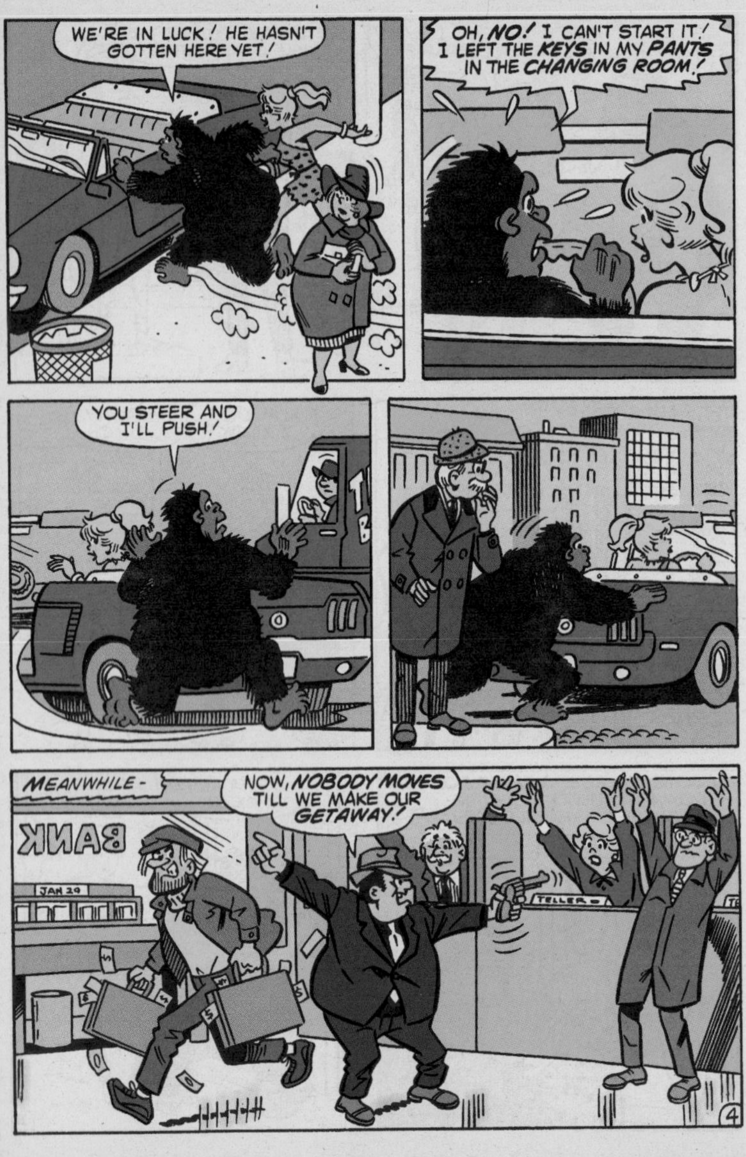
WE'RE IN LUCK! HE HASN'T GOTTEN HERE YET!
OH, NO! I CAN'T START IT! I LEFT THE KEYS IN MY PANTS IN THE CHANGING ROOM!
YOU STEER AND I'LL PUSH!
MEANWHILE -
BANK
JAN 29
NOW, NOBODY MOVES TILL WE MAKE OUR GETAWAY!
TELLER
4

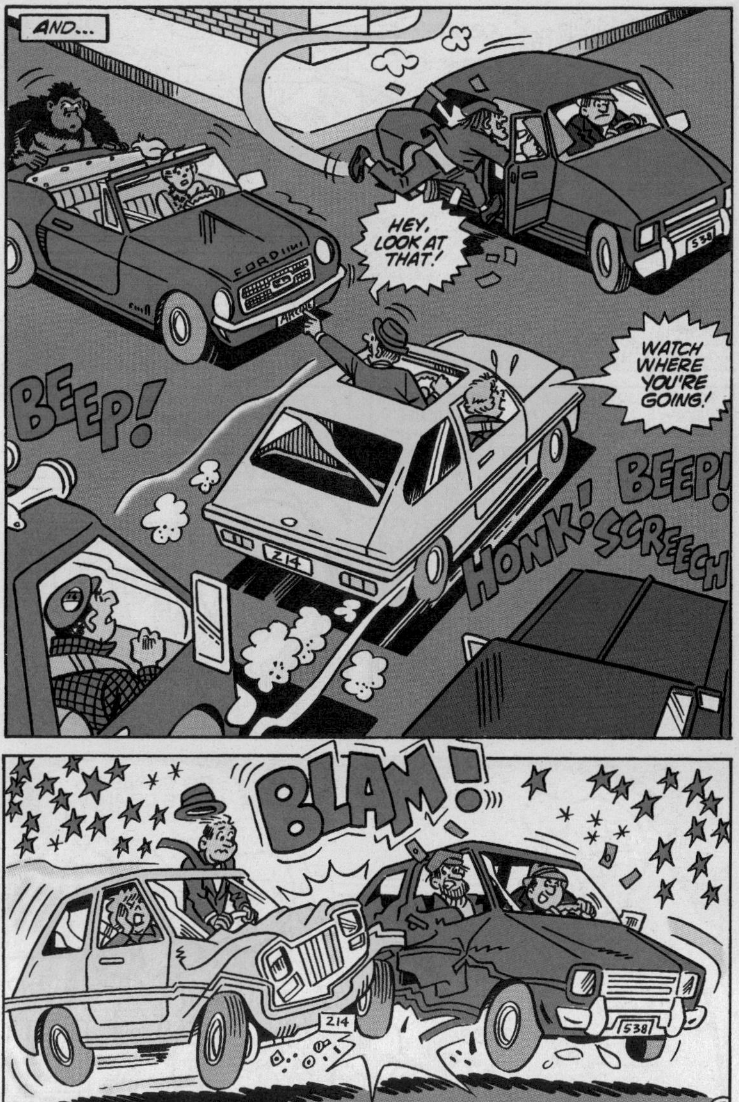
AND...
HEY, LOOK AT THAT!
538
WATCH WHERE YOU'RE GOING!
BEEP!
214
HONK!
BEEP!
SCREECH
BLAM!
214
538

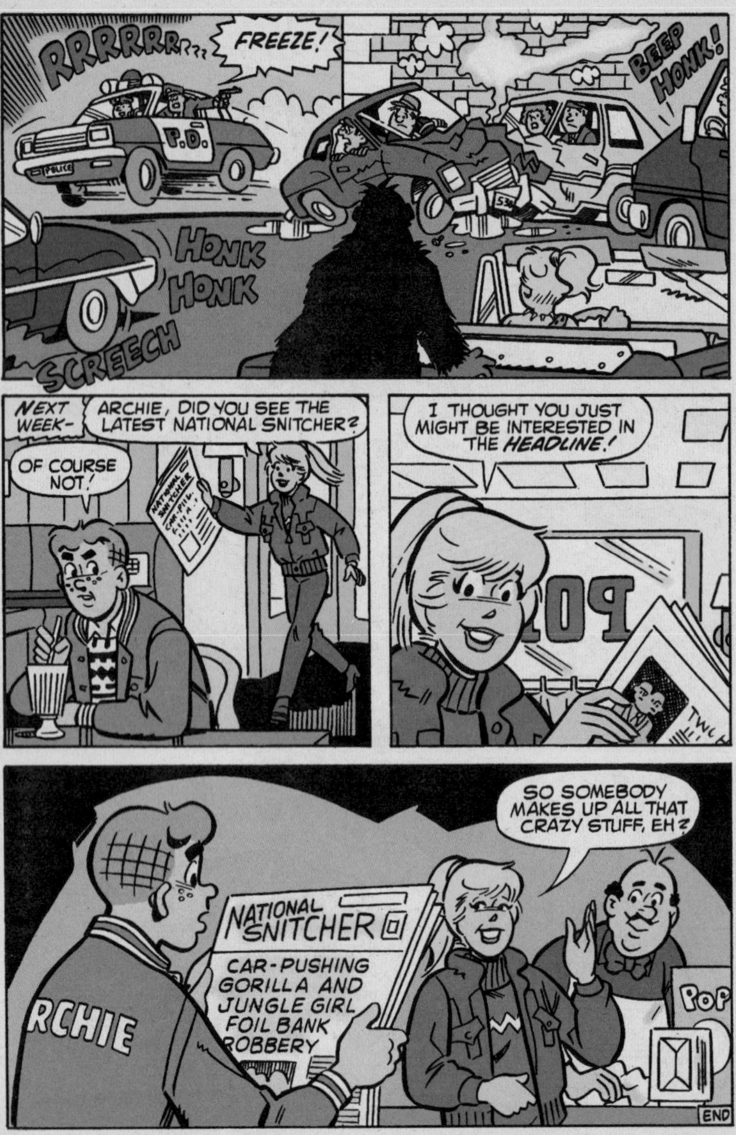
RRRRRRR???
FREEZE!
BEEP
HONK!
HONK
HONK
SCREECH
NEXT WEEK-
ARCHIE, DID YOU SEE THE LATEST NATIONAL SNITCHER?
OF COURSE NOT!
I THOUGHT YOU JUST MIGHT BE INTERESTED IN THE HEADLINE!
SO SOMEBODY MAKES UP ALL THAT CRAZY STUFF, EH?
NATIONAL SNITCHER
CAR-PUSHING GORILLA AND JUNGLE GIRL FOIL BANK ROBBERY
RCHIE
POP
END

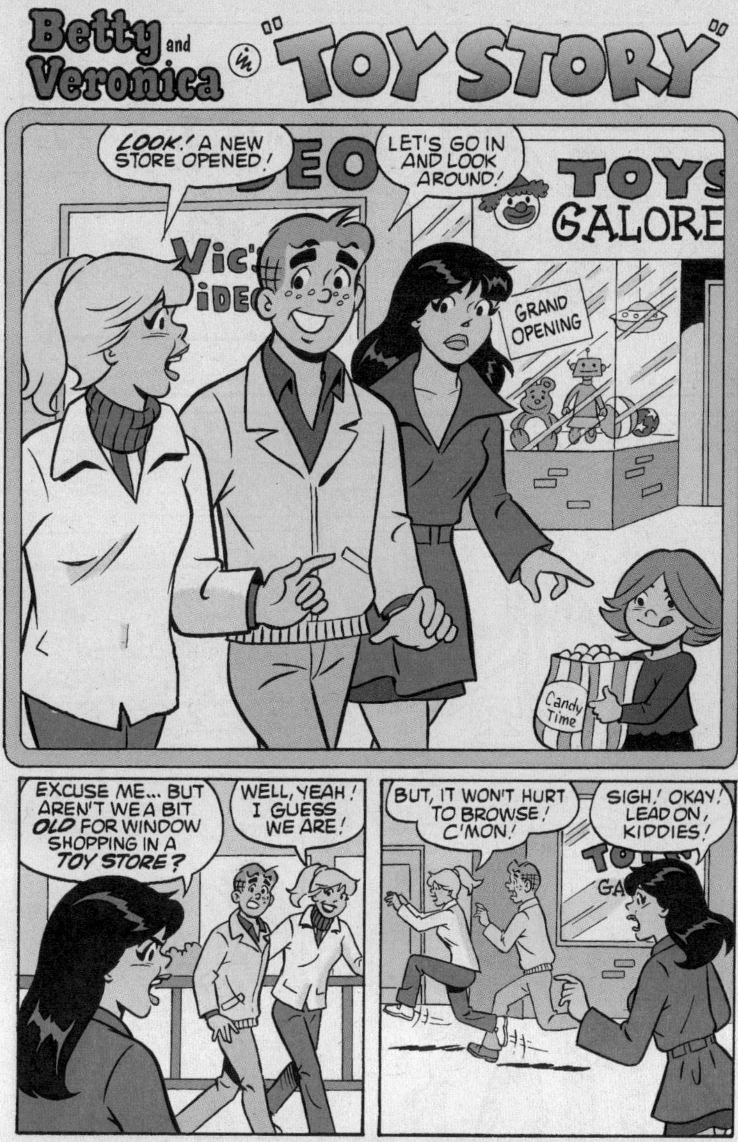
Betty and Veronica in "TOY STORY"
LOOK! A NEW STORE OPENED!
LET'S GO IN AND LOOK AROUND!
TOYS GALORE
Vic's Video
GRAND OPENING
Candy Time
EXCUSE ME... BUT AREN'T WE A BIT OLD FOR WINDOW SHOPPING IN A TOY STORE?
WELL, YEAH! I GUESS WE ARE!
BUT, IT WON'T HURT TO BROWSE! C'MON!
SIGH! OKAY! LEAD ON, KIDDIES!

Script: Mike Pellowski / Pencils: Dan Parent / Inks: Jon D'Agostino / Letters: Bill Yoshida

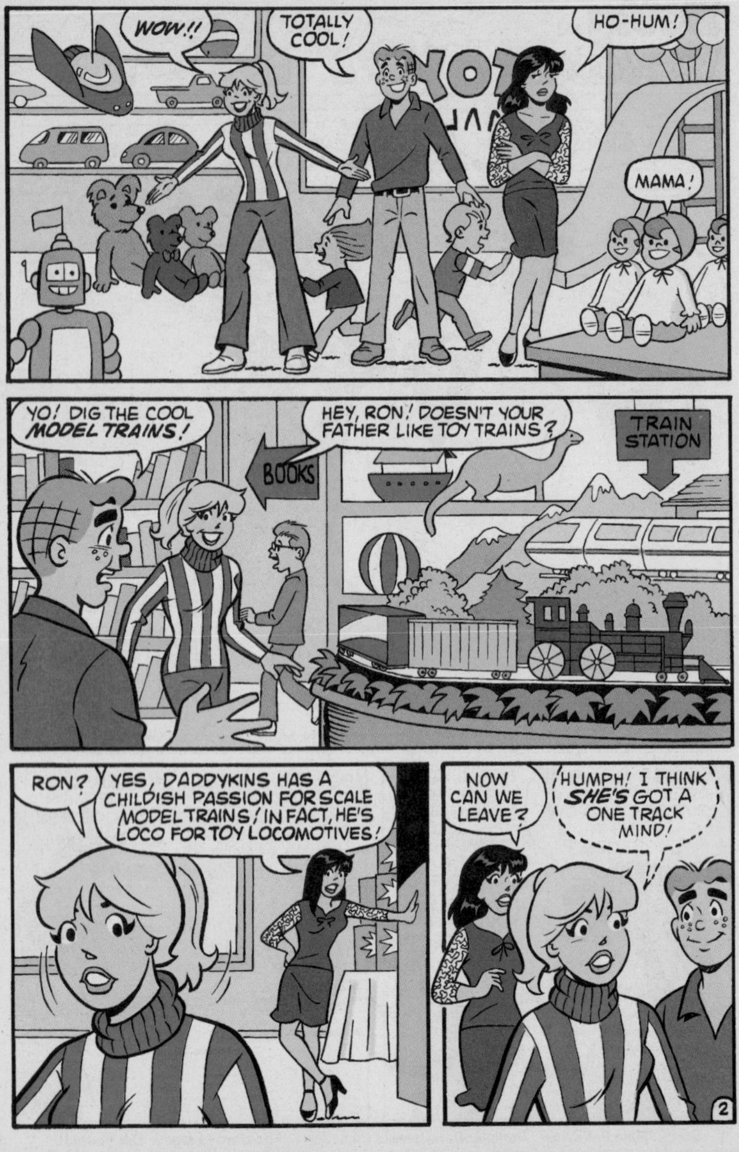
WOW!!
TOTALLY COOL!
HO-HUM!
TOY
MAMA!
YO! DIG THE COOL MODEL TRAINS!
HEY, RON! DOESN'T YOUR FATHER LIKE TOY TRAINS?
BOOKS
TRAIN STATION
RON?
YES, DADDYKINS HAS A CHILDISH PASSION FOR SCALE MODEL TRAINS! IN FACT, HE'S LOCO FOR TOY LOCOMOTIVES!
NOW CAN WE LEAVE?
HUMPH! I THINK SHE'S GOT A ONE TRACK MIND!
2

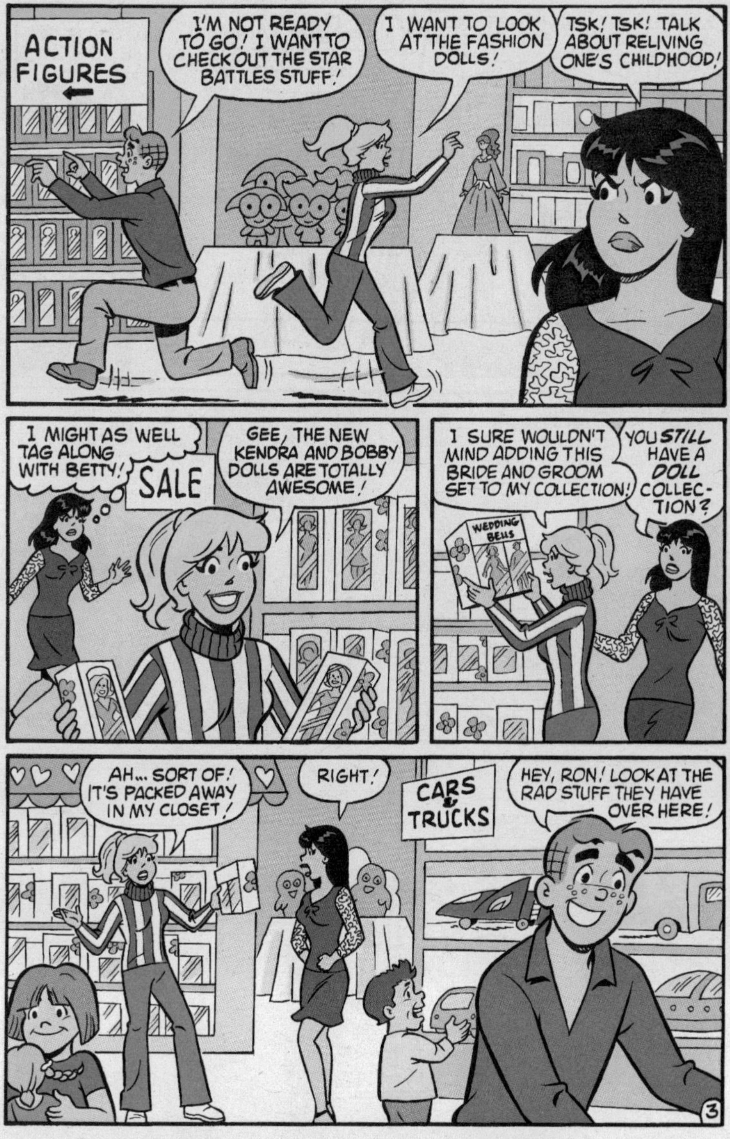
ACTION FIGURES
I'M NOT READY TO GO! I WANT TO CHECK OUT THE STAR BATTLES STUFF!
I WANT TO LOOK AT THE FASHION DOLLS!
TSK! TSK! TALK ABOUT RELIVING ONE'S CHILDHOOD!
I MIGHT AS WELL TAG ALONG WITH BETTY!
SALE
GEE, THE NEW KENDRA AND BOBBY DOLLS ARE TOTALLY AWESOME!
I SURE WOULDN'T MIND ADDING THIS BRIDE AND GROOM SET TO MY COLLECTION!
WEDDING BELLS
YOU STILL HAVE A DOLL COLLECTION?
AH... SORT OF! IT'S PACKED AWAY IN MY CLOSET!
RIGHT!
CARS & TRUCKS
HEY, RON! LOOK AT THE RAD STUFF THEY HAVE OVER HERE!
3

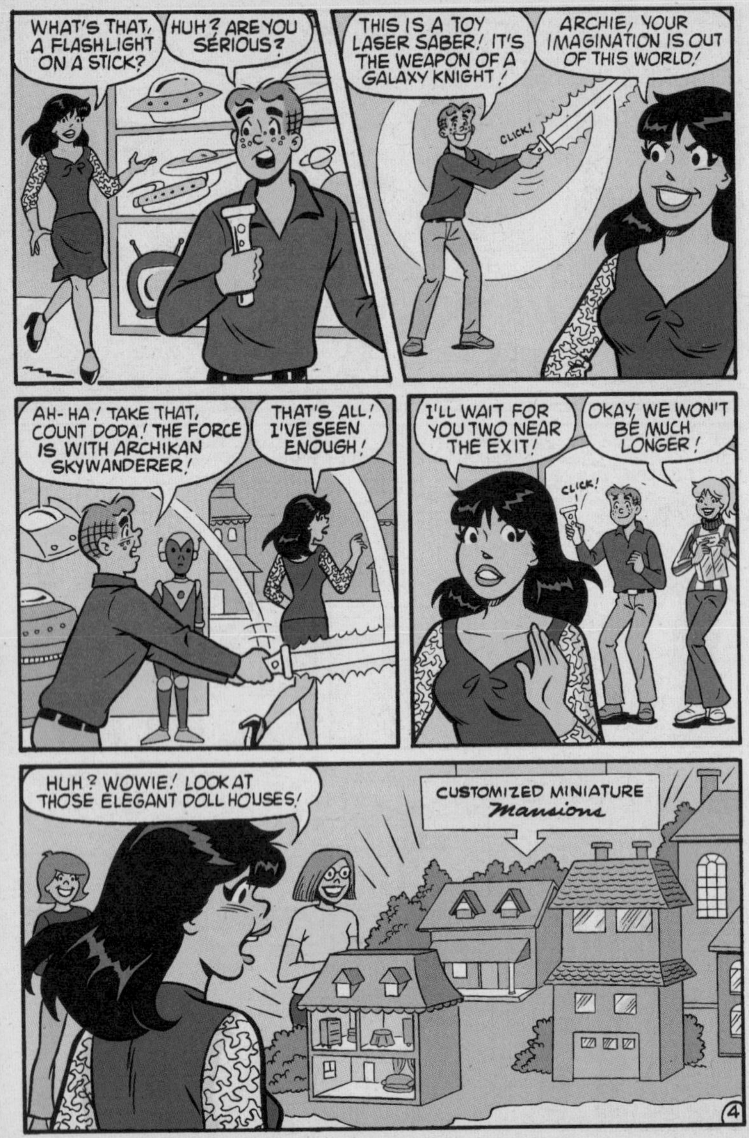
WHAT'S THAT, A FLASHLIGHT ON A STICK?
HUH? ARE YOU SERIOUS?
THIS IS A TOY LASER SABER! IT'S THE WEAPON OF A GALAXY KNIGHT!
CLICK!
ARCHIE, YOUR IMAGINATION IS OUT OF THIS WORLD!
AH-HA! TAKE THAT, COUNT DODA! THE FORCE IS WITH ARCHIKAN SKYWANDERER!
THAT'S ALL! I'VE SEEN ENOUGH!
I'LL WAIT FOR YOU TWO NEAR THE EXIT!
OKAY, WE WON'T BE MUCH LONGER!
CLICK!
HUH? WOWIE! LOOK AT THOSE ELEGANT DOLL HOUSES!
CUSTOMIZED MINIATURE Mansions
4

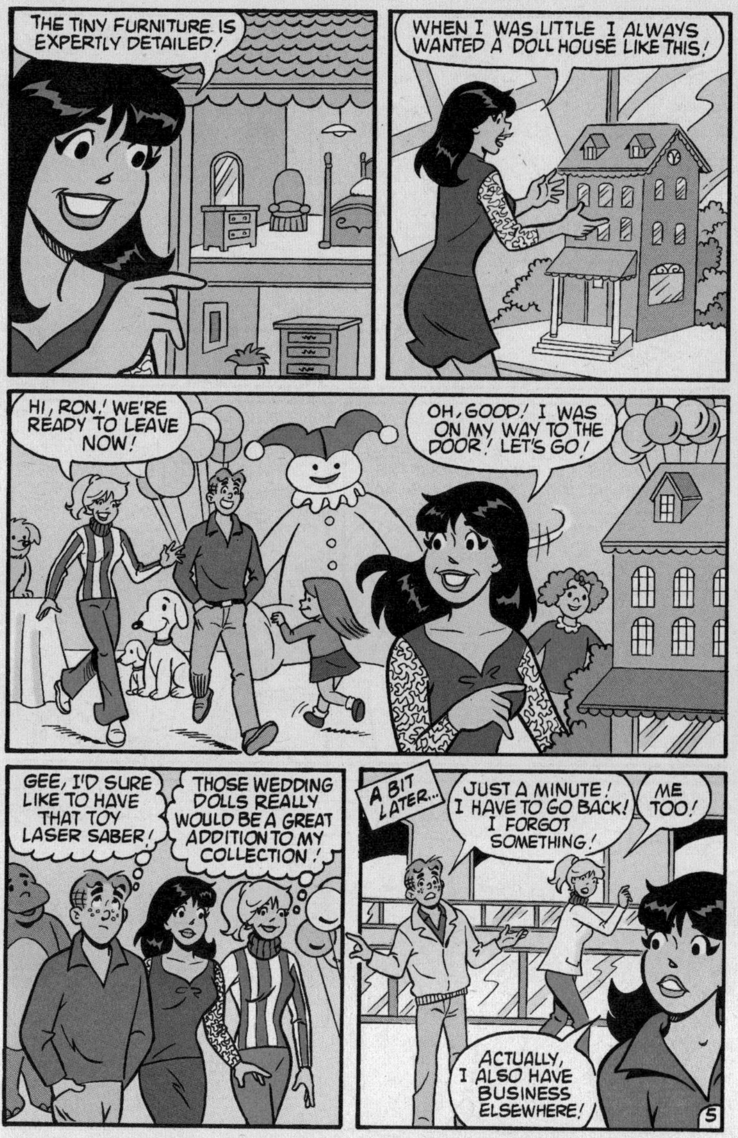
THE TINY FURNITURE IS EXPERTLY DETAILED!
WHEN I WAS LITTLE I ALWAYS WANTED A DOLL HOUSE LIKE THIS!
HI, RON! WE'RE READY TO LEAVE NOW!
OH, GOOD! I WAS ON MY WAY TO THE DOOR! LET'S GO!
GEE, I'D SURE LIKE TO HAVE THAT TOY LASER SABER!
THOSE WEDDING DOLLS REALLY WOULD BE A GREAT ADDITION TO MY COLLECTION!
A BIT LATER...
JUST A MINUTE! I HAVE TO GO BACK! I FORGOT SOMETHING!
ME TOO!
ACTUALLY, I ALSO HAVE BUSINESS ELSEWHERE!
5

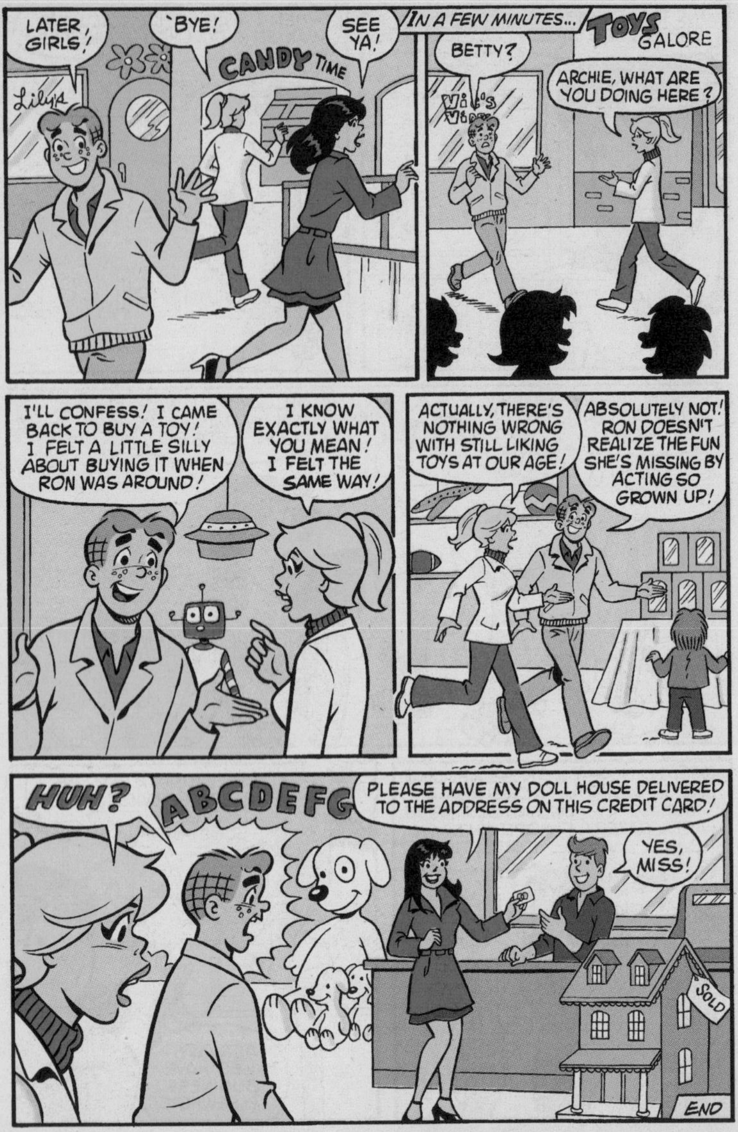
LATER, GIRLS!
`BYE!
SEE YA!
CANDY TIME
Lily's
IN A FEW MINUTES...
TOYS GALORE
BETTY?
ARCHIE, WHAT ARE YOU DOING HERE?
I'LL CONFESS! I CAME BACK TO BUY A TOY! I FELT A LITTLE SILLY ABOUT BUYING IT WHEN RON WAS AROUND!
I KNOW EXACTLY WHAT YOU MEAN! I FELT THE SAME WAY!
ACTUALLY, THERE'S NOTHING WRONG WITH STILL LIKING TOYS AT OUR AGE!
ABSOLUTELY NOT! RON DOESN'T REALIZE THE FUN SHE'S MISSING BY ACTING SO GROWN UP!
HUH?
ABCDEFG
PLEASE HAVE MY DOLL HOUSE DELIVERED TO THE ADDRESS ON THIS CREDIT CARD!
YES, MISS!
SOLD
END

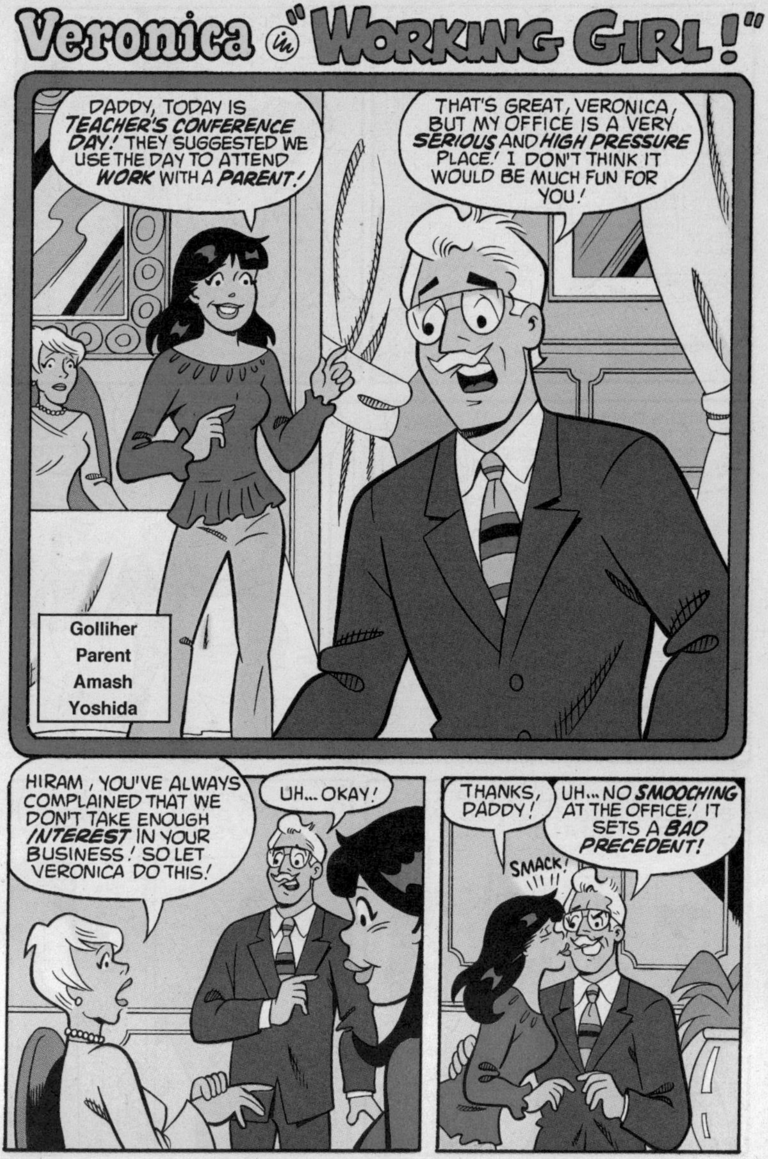
Veronica in "WORKING GIRL!"
DADDY, TODAY IS TEACHER'S CONFERENCE DAY! THEY SUGGESTED WE USE THE DAY TO ATTEND WORK WITH A PARENT!
THAT'S GREAT, VERONICA, BUT MY OFFICE IS A VERY SERIOUS AND HIGH PRESSURE PLACE! I DON'T THINK IT WOULD BE MUCH FUN FOR YOU!
Golliher
Parent
Amash
Yoshida
HIRAM, YOU'VE ALWAYS COMPLAINED THAT WE DON'T TAKE ENOUGH INTEREST IN YOUR BUSINESS! SO LET VERONICA DO THIS!
UH... OKAY!
THANKS, DADDY!
UH... NO SMOOCHING AT THE OFFICE! IT SETS A BAD PRECEDENT!
SMACK!

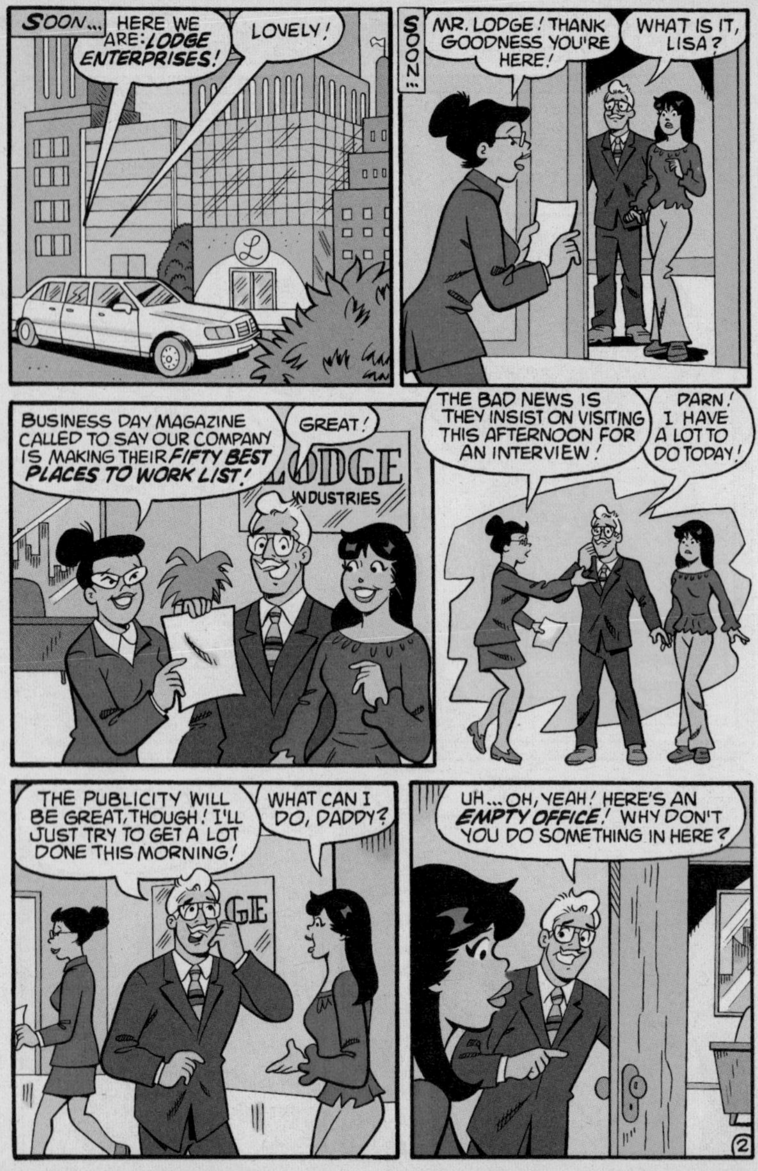
SOON...
HERE WE ARE: LODGE ENTERPRISES!
LOVELY!
SOON...
MR. LODGE! THANK GOODNESS YOU'RE HERE!
WHAT IS IT, LISA?
BUSINESS DAY MAGAZINE CALLED TO SAY OUR COMPANY IS MAKING THEIR FIFTY BEST PLACES TO WORK LIST!
GREAT!
LODGE INDUSTRIES
THE BAD NEWS IS THEY INSIST ON VISITING THIS AFTERNOON FOR AN INTERVIEW!
DARN! I HAVE A LOT TO DO TODAY!
THE PUBLICITY WILL BE GREAT, THOUGH! I'LL JUST TRY TO GET A LOT DONE THIS MORNING!
WHAT CAN I DO, DADDY?
UH...OH, YEAH! HERE'S AN EMPTY OFFICE! WHY DON'T YOU DO SOMETHING IN HERE?
2

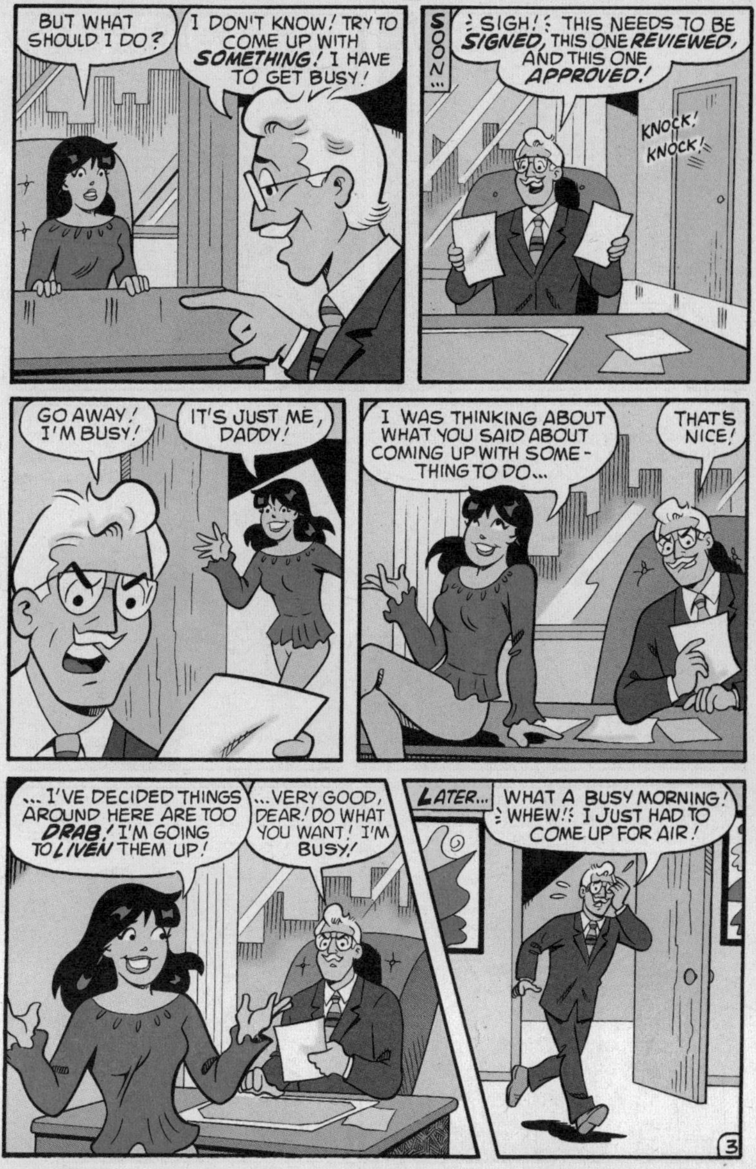

BUT WHAT SHOULD I DO?
I DON'T KNOW! TRY TO COME UP WITH SOMETHING! I HAVE TO GET BUSY!
SOON...
SIGH! THIS NEEDS TO BE SIGNED, THIS ONE REVIEWED, AND THIS ONE APPROVED!
KNOCK! KNOCK!
GO AWAY! I'M BUSY!
IT'S JUST ME, DADDY!
I WAS THINKING ABOUT WHAT YOU SAID ABOUT COMING UP WITH SOME-THING TO DO...
THAT'S NICE!
...I'VE DECIDED THINGS AROUND HERE ARE TOO DRAB! I'M GOING TO LIVEN THEM UP!
...VERY GOOD, DEAR! DO WHAT YOU WANT! I'M BUSY!
LATER...
WHAT A BUSY MORNING! WHEW! I JUST HAD TO COME UP FOR AIR!
3

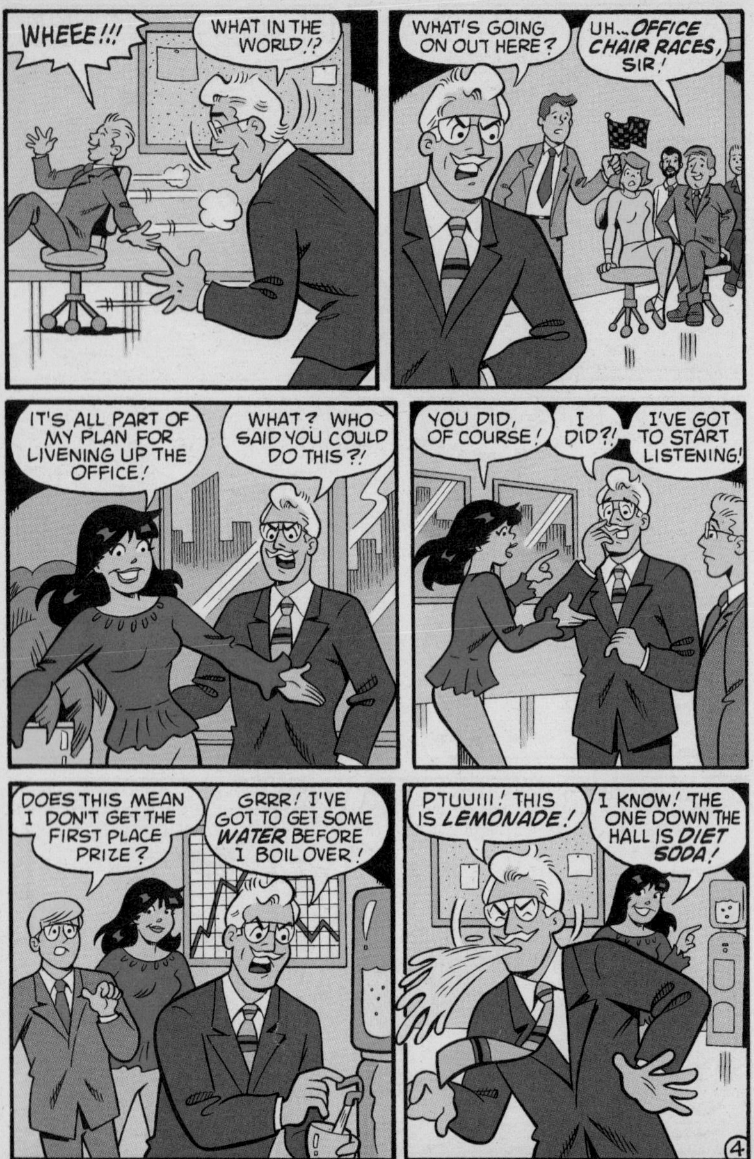
WHEEE!!!
WHAT IN THE WORLD!?
WHAT'S GOING ON OUT HERE?
UH...OFFICE CHAIR RACES, SIR!
IT'S ALL PART OF MY PLAN FOR LIVENING UP THE OFFICE!
WHAT? WHO SAID YOU COULD DO THIS?!
YOU DID, OF COURSE!
I DID?!
I'VE GOT TO START LISTENING!
DOES THIS MEAN I DON'T GET THE FIRST PLACE PRIZE?
GRRR! I'VE GOT TO GET SOME WATER BEFORE I BOIL OVER!
PTUUIII! THIS IS LEMONADE!
I KNOW! THE ONE DOWN THE HALL IS DIET SODA!
4

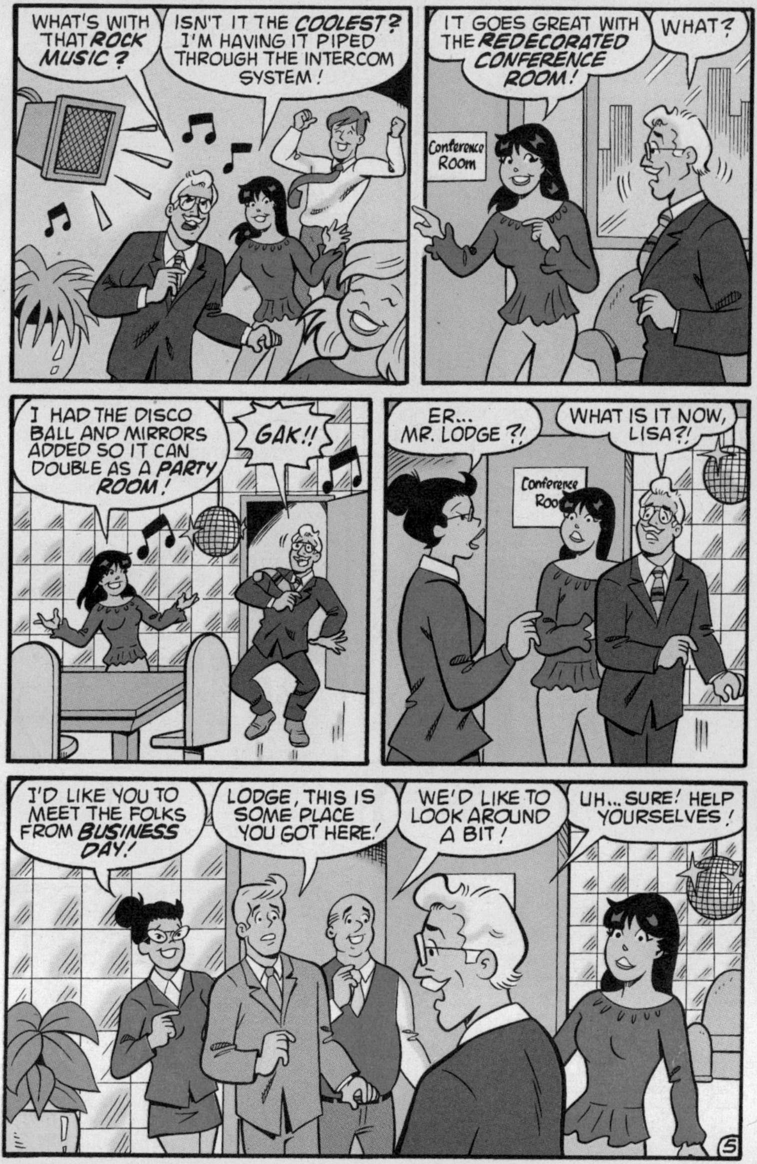
WHAT'S WITH THAT ROCK MUSIC?
ISN'T IT THE COOLEST? I'M HAVING IT PIPED THROUGH THE INTERCOM SYSTEM!
IT GOES GREAT WITH THE REDECORATED CONFERENCE ROOM!
WHAT?
Conference Room
I HAD THE DISCO BALL AND MIRRORS ADDED SO IT CAN DOUBLE AS A PARTY ROOM!
GAK!!
ER... MR. LODGE?!
WHAT IS IT NOW, LISA?!
I'D LIKE YOU TO MEET THE FOLKS FROM BUSINESS DAY!
LODGE, THIS IS SOME PLACE YOU GOT HERE!
WE'D LIKE TO LOOK AROUND A BIT!
UH... SURE! HELP YOURSELVES!
5

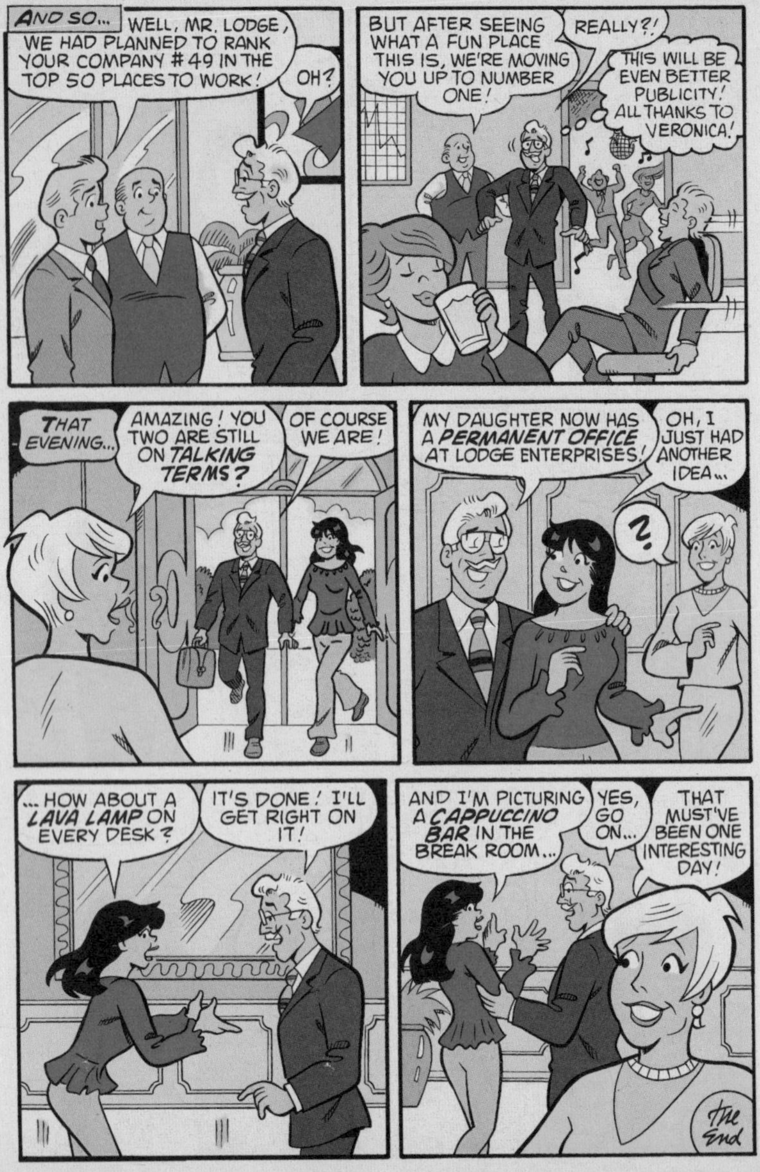
AND SO...
WELL, MR. LODGE, WE HAD PLANNED TO RANK YOUR COMPANY #49 IN THE TOP 50 PLACES TO WORK!
OH?
BUT AFTER SEEING WHAT A FUN PLACE THIS IS, WE'RE MOVING YOU UP TO NUMBER ONE!
REALLY?!
THIS WILL BE EVEN BETTER PUBLICITY! ALL THANKS TO VERONICA!
THAT EVENING...
AMAZING! YOU TWO ARE STILL ON TALKING TERMS?
OF COURSE WE ARE!
MY DAUGHTER NOW HAS A PERMANENT OFFICE AT LODGE ENTERPRISES!
OH, I JUST HAD ANOTHER IDEA...
?
... HOW ABOUT A LAVA LAMP ON EVERY DESK?
IT'S DONE! I'LL GET RIGHT ON IT!
AND I'M PICTURING A CAPPUCCINO BAR IN THE BREAK ROOM...
YES, GO ON...
THAT MUST'VE BEEN ONE INTERESTING DAY!
The End

A SURE THING

YES! IT'S A *SURE THING*!
I KNOW ONE PLACE WHERE YOU
CAN *ALWAYS FIND
MISTLETOE!*
JUST *CIRCLE* THE BOXES
CONTAINING THE LETTERS
M-I-S-T-L-E-T-O-E
IN THE UPPER CORNER FOR
THE ANSWER!

Veronica

A C	M I	B H	I N	C R
S T	D I	T H	L E	
G S	E D	H T	T I	
O C	N M	P A	E T	Q S
R I	M I	I O	U S	
S N	V W	W O	X N	
Y D	Z E	T A	A R	
B F	L R	C U	D L	
F D	G A	E Y	I S	

THE ANSWER

IN THE DICTIONARY

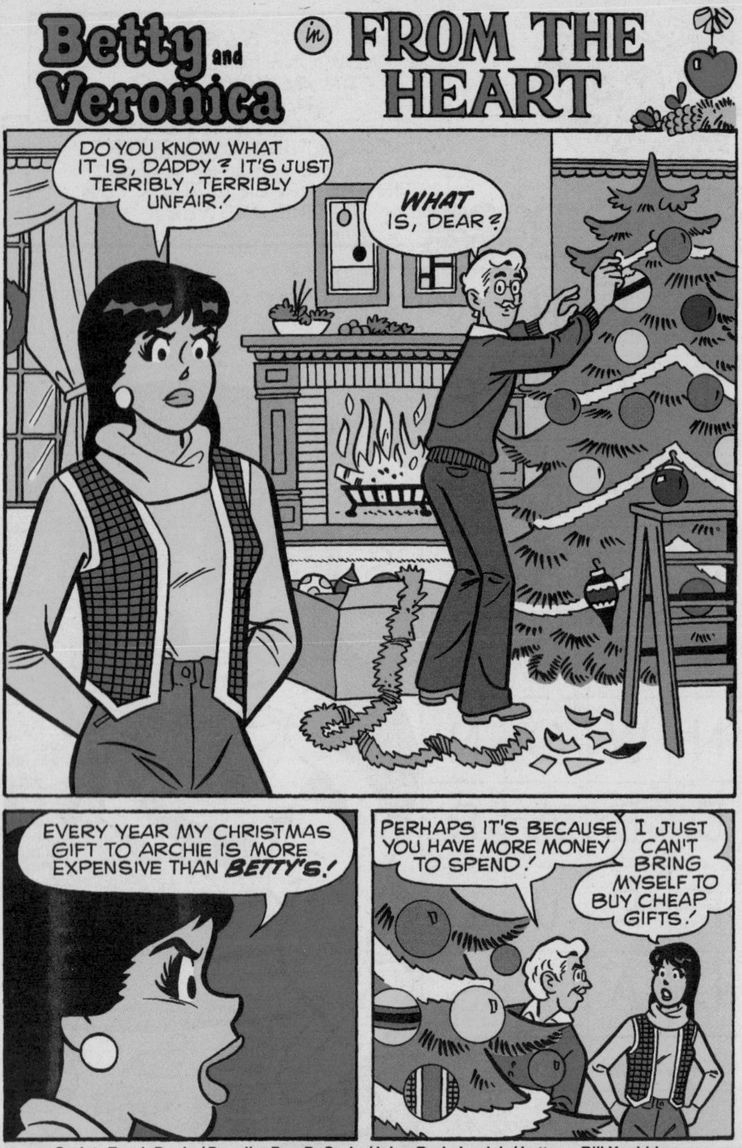
Betty and Veronica in FROM THE HEART
DO YOU KNOW WHAT IT IS, DADDY? IT'S JUST TERRIBLY, TERRIBLY UNFAIR!
WHAT IS, DEAR?
EVERY YEAR MY CHRISTMAS GIFT TO ARCHIE IS MORE EXPENSIVE THAN BETTY'S!
PERHAPS IT'S BECAUSE YOU HAVE MORE MONEY TO SPEND!
I JUST CAN'T BRING MYSELF TO BUY CHEAP GIFTS!

Script: Frank Doyle / Pencils: Dan DeCarlo / Inks: Rudy Lapick / Letters: Bill Yoshida

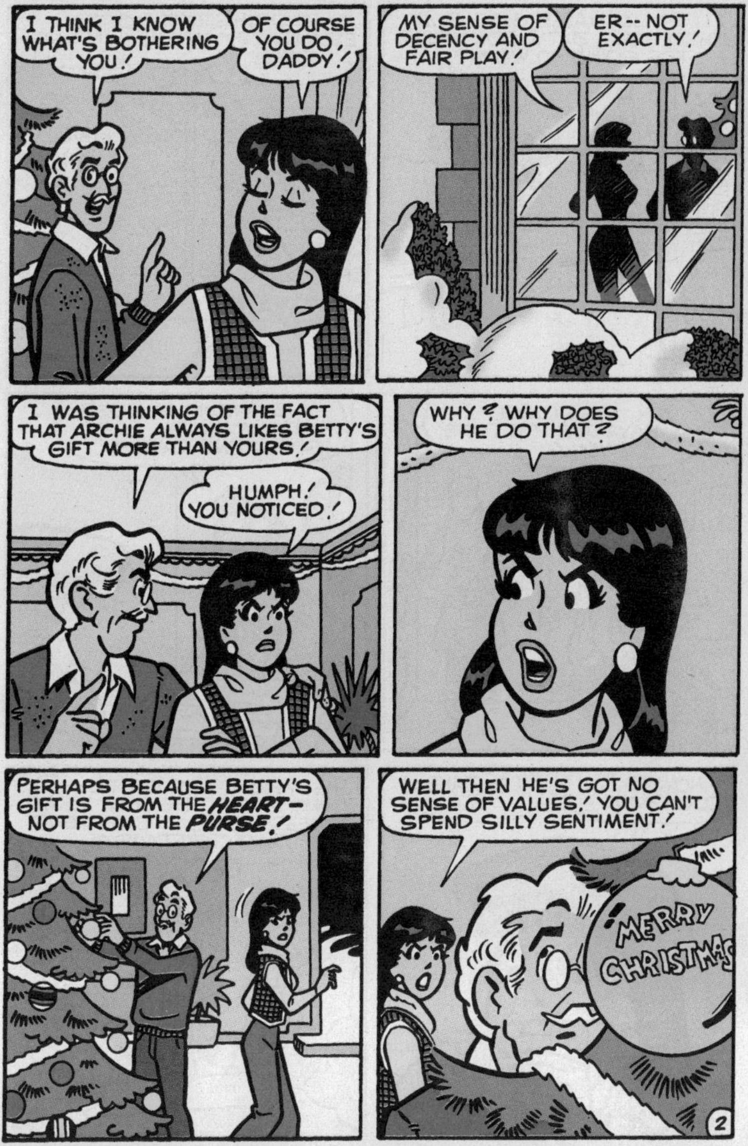
I THINK I KNOW WHAT'S BOTHERING YOU!
OF COURSE YOU DO, DADDY!
MY SENSE OF DECENCY AND FAIR PLAY!
ER -- NOT EXACTLY!
I WAS THINKING OF THE FACT THAT ARCHIE ALWAYS LIKES BETTY'S GIFT MORE THAN YOURS!
HUMPH! YOU NOTICED!
WHY? WHY DOES HE DO THAT?
PERHAPS BECAUSE BETTY'S GIFT IS FROM THE HEART- NOT FROM THE PURSE!
WELL THEN HE'S GOT NO SENSE OF VALUES! YOU CAN'T SPEND SILLY SENTIMENT!
MERRY CHRISTMAS
2

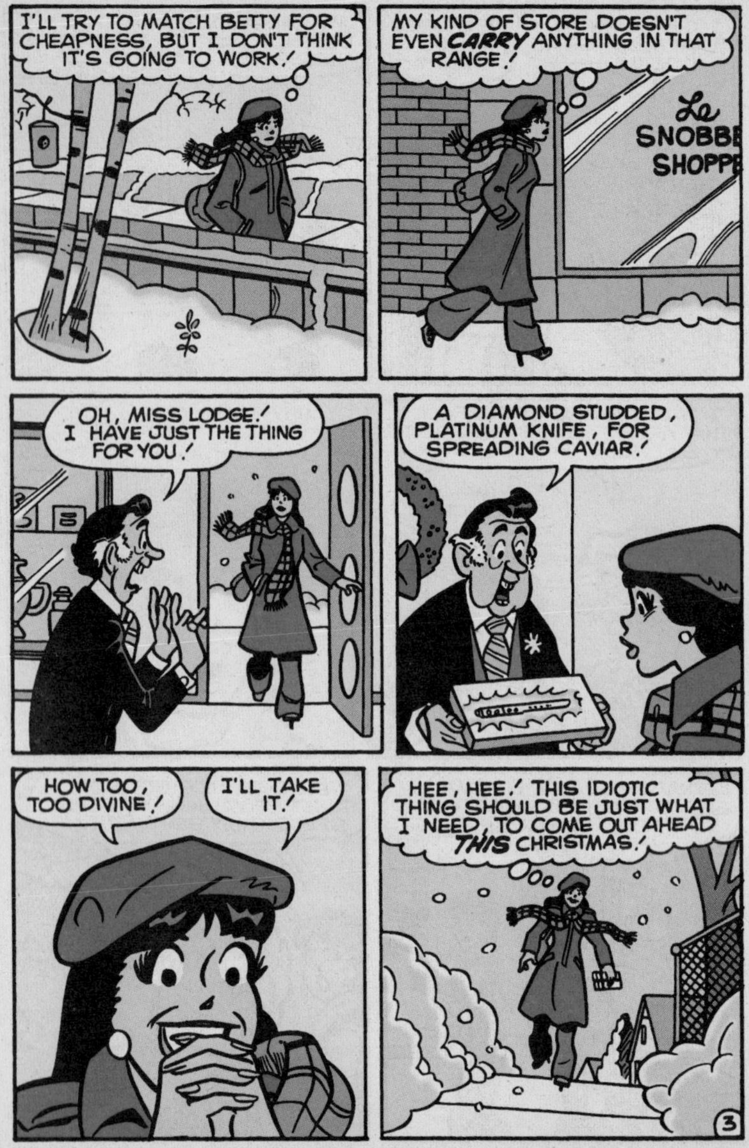
I'LL TRY TO MATCH BETTY FOR CHEAPNESS, BUT I DON'T THINK IT'S GOING TO WORK!
MY KIND OF STORE DOESN'T EVEN CARRY ANYTHING IN THAT RANGE!
Le SNOBBE SHOPPE
OH, MISS LODGE! I HAVE JUST THE THING FOR YOU!
A DIAMOND STUDDED, PLATINUM KNIFE, FOR SPREADING CAVIAR!
HOW TOO, TOO DIVINE!
I'LL TAKE IT!
HEE, HEE! THIS IDIOTIC THING SHOULD BE JUST WHAT I NEED, TO COME OUT AHEAD THIS CHRISTMAS!
3

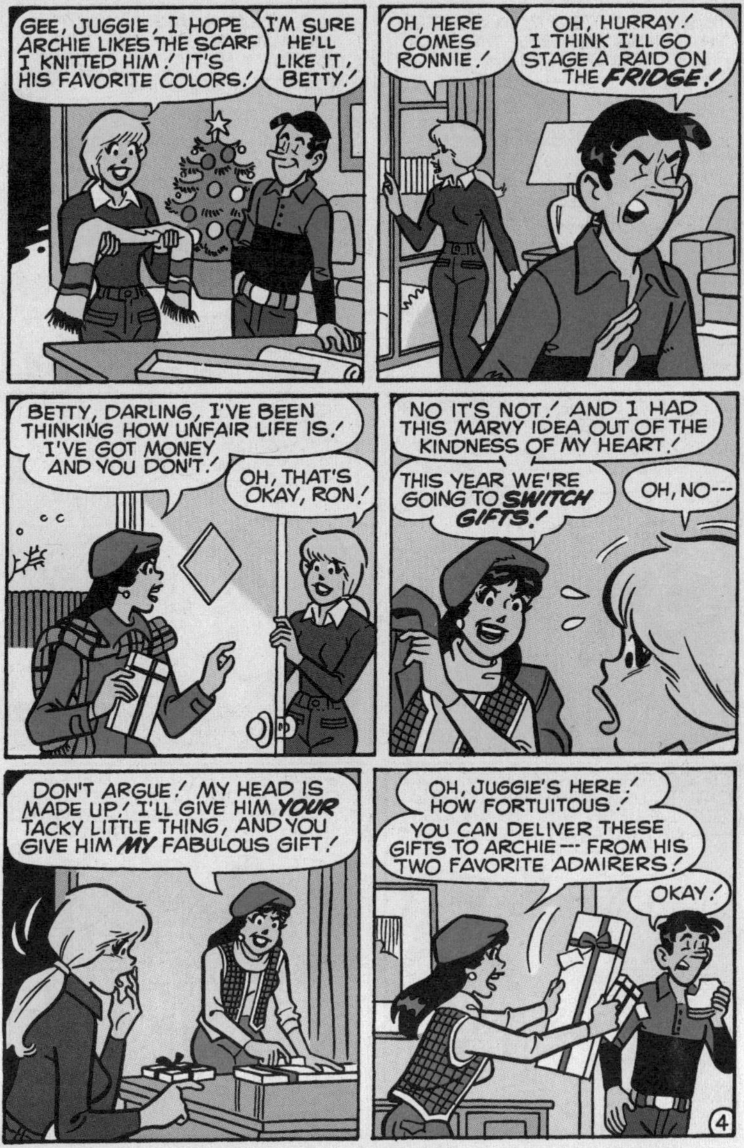

GEE, JUGGIE, I HOPE ARCHIE LIKES THE SCARF I KNITTED HIM! IT'S HIS FAVORITE COLORS!
I'M SURE HE'LL LIKE IT, BETTY!
OH, HERE COMES RONNIE!
OH, HURRAY! I THINK I'LL GO STAGE A RAID ON THE FRIDGE!
BETTY, DARLING, I'VE BEEN THINKING HOW UNFAIR LIFE IS! I'VE GOT MONEY AND YOU DON'T!
OH, THAT'S OKAY, RON!
NO IT'S NOT! AND I HAD THIS MARVY IDEA OUT OF THE KINDNESS OF MY HEART!
THIS YEAR WE'RE GOING TO SWITCH GIFTS!
OH, NO---
DON'T ARGUE! MY HEAD IS MADE UP! I'LL GIVE HIM YOUR TACKY LITTLE THING, AND YOU GIVE HIM MY FABULOUS GIFT!
OH, JUGGIE'S HERE! HOW FORTUITOUS!
YOU CAN DELIVER THESE GIFTS TO ARCHIE --- FROM HIS TWO FAVORITE ADMIRERS!
OKAY!
4

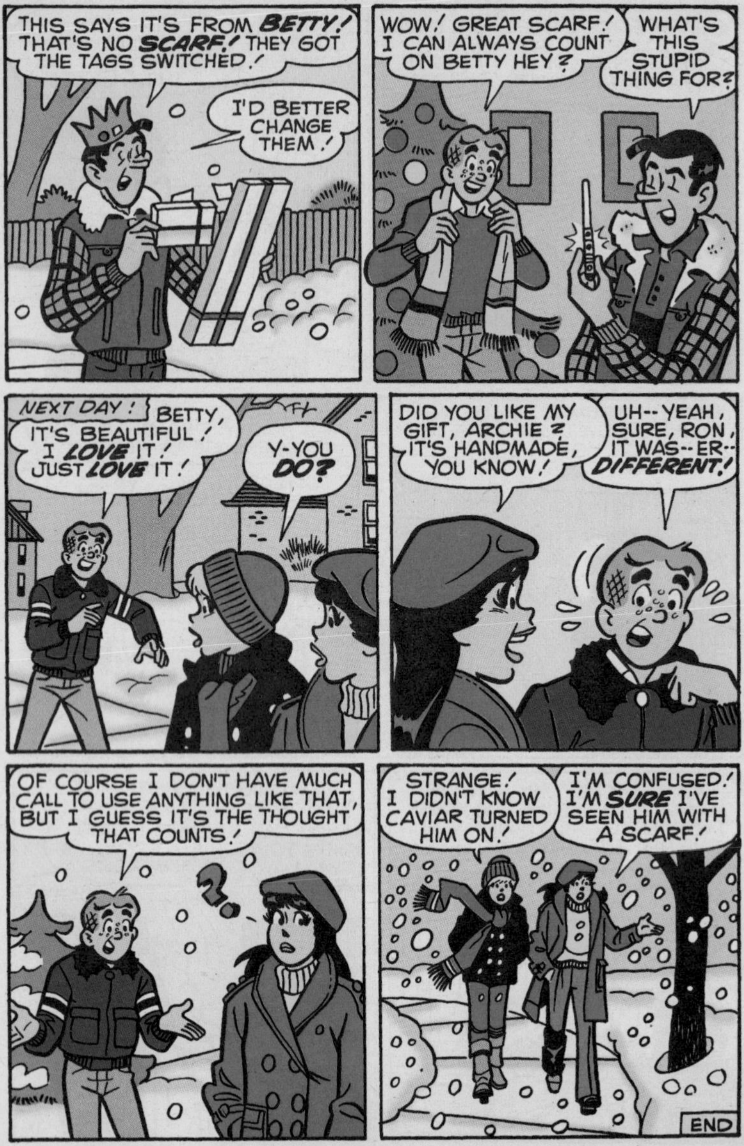
THIS SAYS IT'S FROM BETTY! THAT'S NO SCARF! THEY GOT THE TAGS SWITCHED!
I'D BETTER CHANGE THEM!
WOW! GREAT SCARF! I CAN ALWAYS COUNT ON BETTY HEY?
WHAT'S THIS STUPID THING FOR?
NEXT DAY!
BETTY, IT'S BEAUTIFUL! I LOVE IT! JUST LOVE IT!
Y-YOU DO?
DID YOU LIKE MY GIFT, ARCHIE? IT'S HANDMADE, YOU KNOW!
UH--YEAH, SURE, RON, IT WAS--ER--DIFFERENT!
OF COURSE I DON'T HAVE MUCH CALL TO USE ANYTHING LIKE THAT, BUT I GUESS IT'S THE THOUGHT THAT COUNTS!
STRANGE! I DIDN'T KNOW CAVIAR TURNED HIM ON!
I'M CONFUSED! I'M SURE I'VE SEEN HIM WITH A SCARF!
END

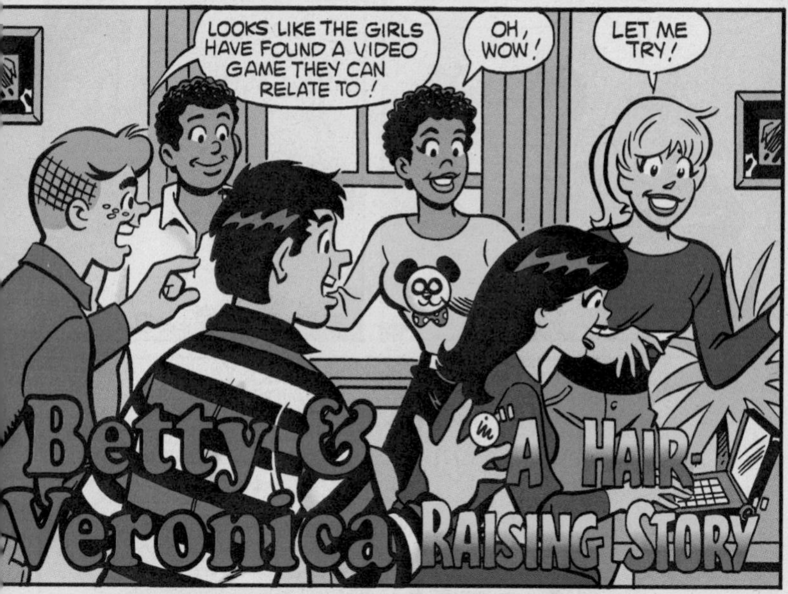
LOOKS LIKE THE GIRLS HAVE FOUND A VIDEO GAME THEY CAN RELATE TO!
OH, WOW!
LET ME TRY!
Betty & Veronica
in
A HAIR-RAISING STORY

SCRIPT: GEORGE GLADIR PENCILS: JEFF SHULTZ INKS: AL MILGROM
LETTERS: BILL YOSHIDA

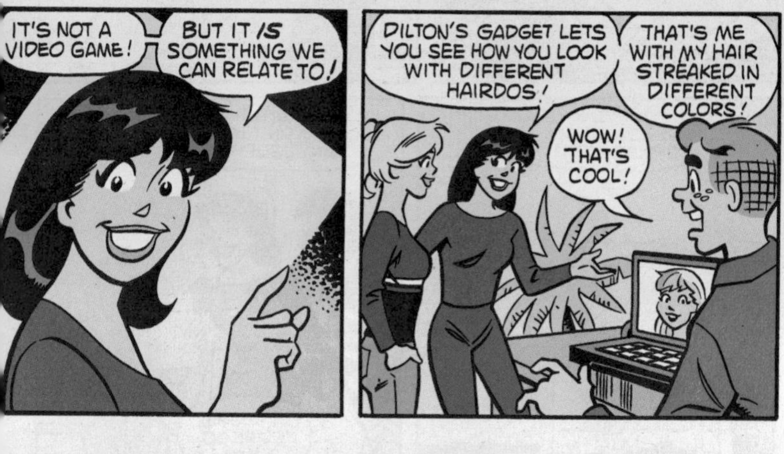
IT'S NOT A VIDEO GAME!
BUT IT *IS* SOMETHING WE CAN RELATE TO!
DILTON'S GADGET LETS YOU SEE HOW YOU LOOK WITH DIFFERENT HAIRDOS!
THAT'S ME WITH MY HAIR STREAKED IN DIFFERENT COLORS!
WOW! THAT'S COOL!

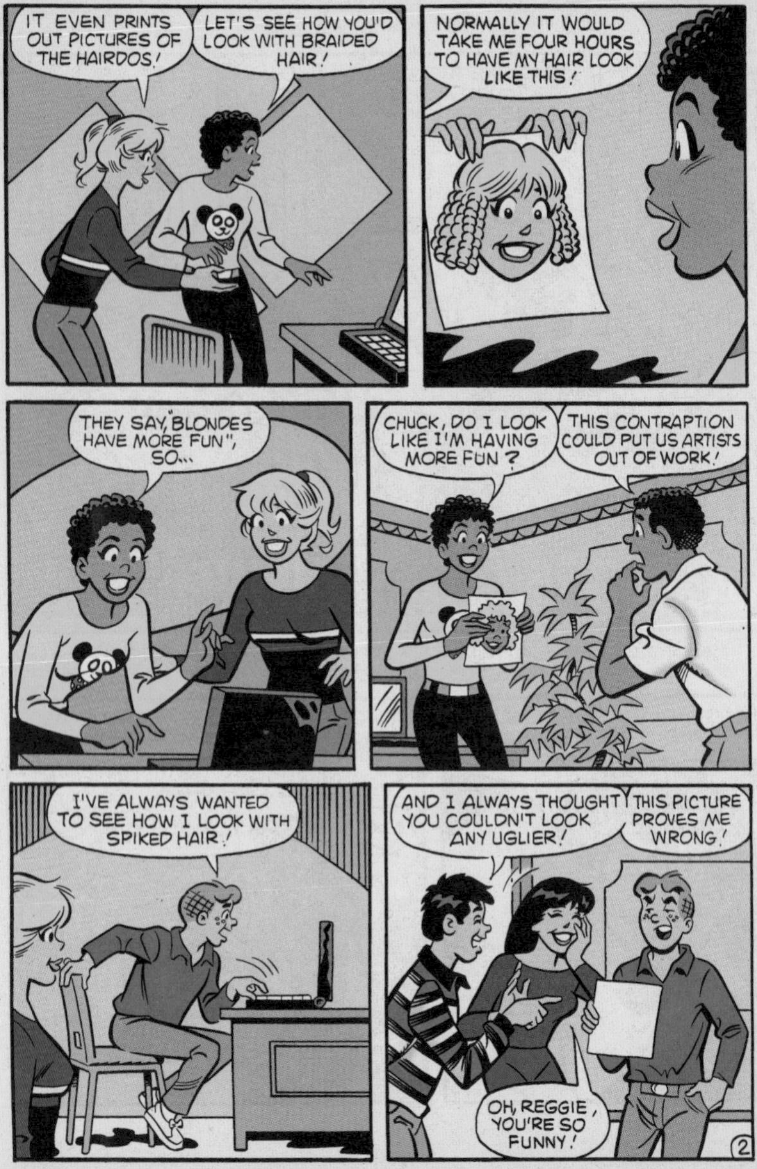
IT EVEN PRINTS OUT PICTURES OF THE HAIRDOS!
LET'S SEE HOW YOU'D LOOK WITH BRAIDED HAIR!
NORMALLY IT WOULD TAKE ME FOUR HOURS TO HAVE MY HAIR LOOK LIKE THIS!
THEY SAY,"BLONDES HAVE MORE FUN", SO...
CHUCK, DO I LOOK LIKE I'M HAVING MORE FUN?
THIS CONTRAPTION COULD PUT US ARTISTS OUT OF WORK!
I'VE ALWAYS WANTED TO SEE HOW I LOOK WITH SPIKED HAIR!
AND I ALWAYS THOUGHT YOU COULDN'T LOOK ANY UGLIER!
THIS PICTURE PROVES ME WRONG!
OH, REGGIE, YOU'RE SO FUNNY!
2

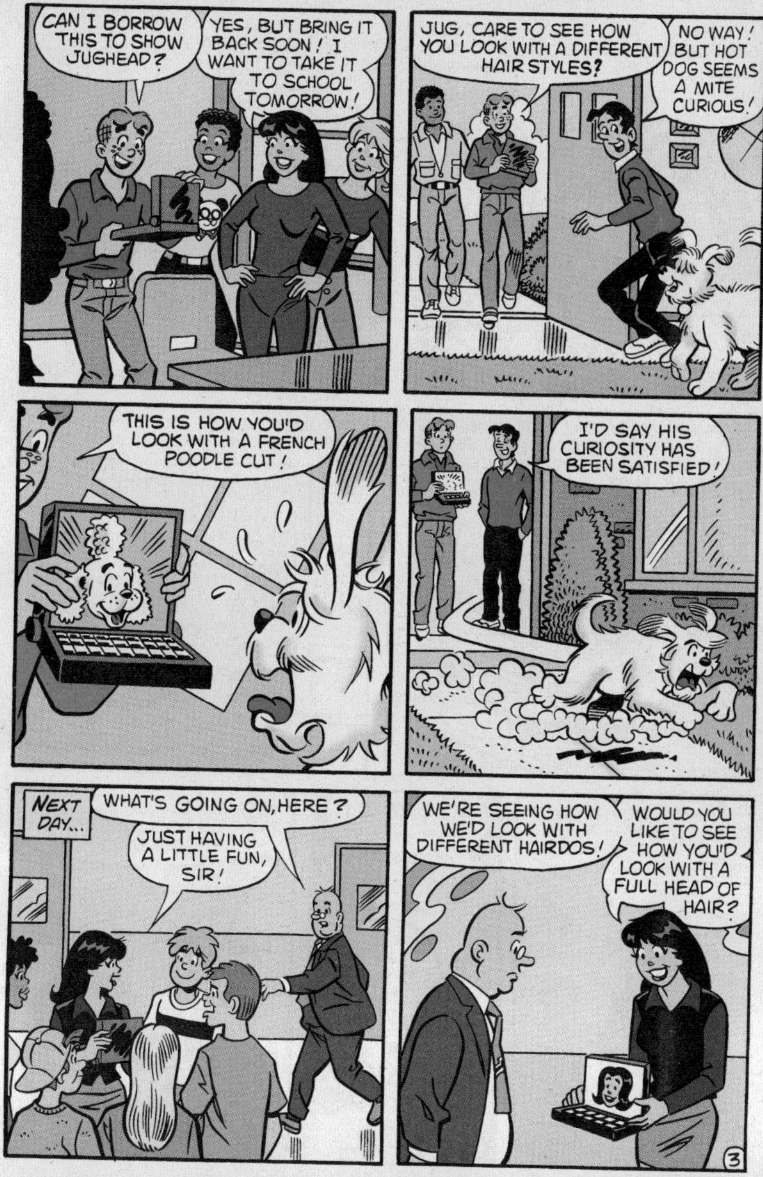
CAN I BORROW THIS TO SHOW JUGHEAD?
YES, BUT BRING IT BACK SOON! I WANT TO TAKE IT TO SCHOOL TOMORROW!
JUG, CARE TO SEE HOW YOU LOOK WITH A DIFFERENT HAIR STYLES?
NO WAY! BUT HOT DOG SEEMS A MITE CURIOUS!
THIS IS HOW YOU'D LOOK WITH A FRENCH POODLE CUT!
I'D SAY HIS CURIOSITY HAS BEEN SATISFIED!
NEXT DAY...
WHAT'S GOING ON, HERE?
JUST HAVING A LITTLE FUN, SIR!
WE'RE SEEING HOW WE'D LOOK WITH DIFFERENT HAIRDOS!
WOULD YOU LIKE TO SEE HOW YOU'D LOOK WITH A FULL HEAD OF HAIR?
3

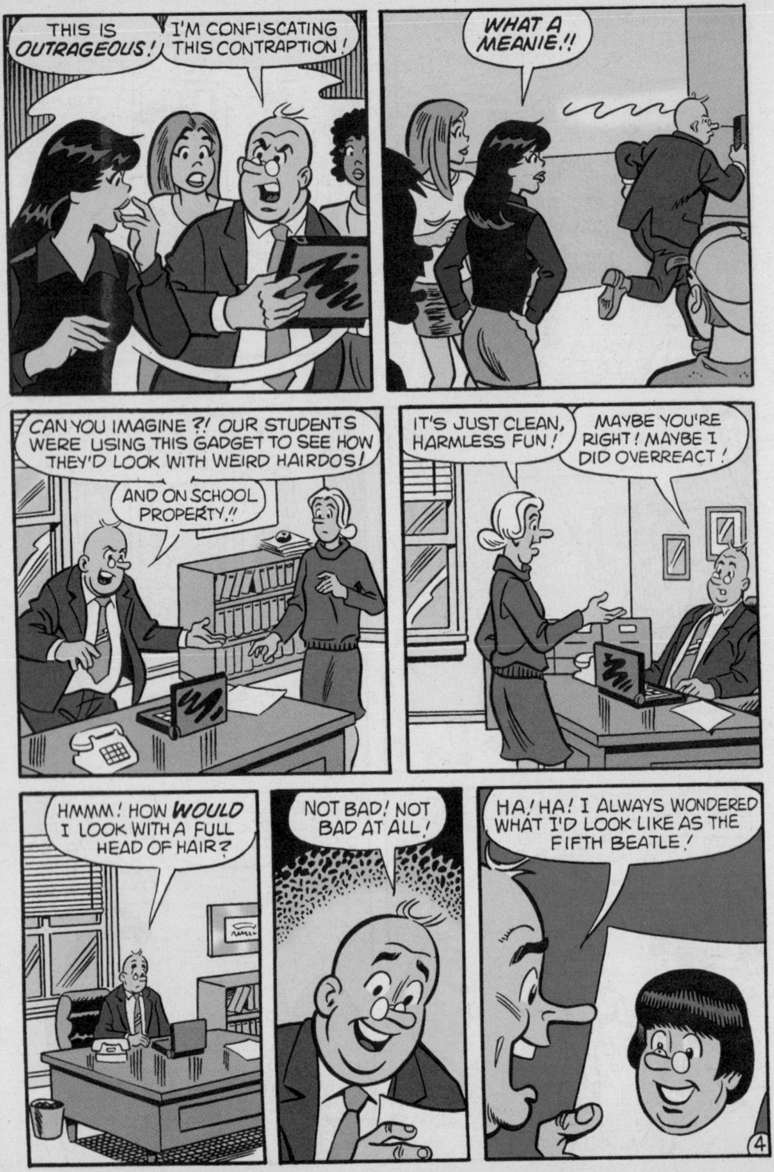
THIS IS OUTRAGEOUS!
I'M CONFISCATING THIS CONTRAPTION!
WHAT A MEANIE.!!
CAN YOU IMAGINE ?! OUR STUDENTS WERE USING THIS GADGET TO SEE HOW THEY'D LOOK WITH WEIRD HAIRDOS!
AND ON SCHOOL PROPERTY!!
IT'S JUST CLEAN, HARMLESS FUN!
MAYBE YOU'RE RIGHT! MAYBE I DID OVERREACT!
HMMM! HOW WOULD I LOOK WITH A FULL HEAD OF HAIR?
NOT BAD! NOT BAD AT ALL!
HA! HA! I ALWAYS WONDERED WHAT I'D LOOK LIKE AS THE FIFTH BEATLE!
4

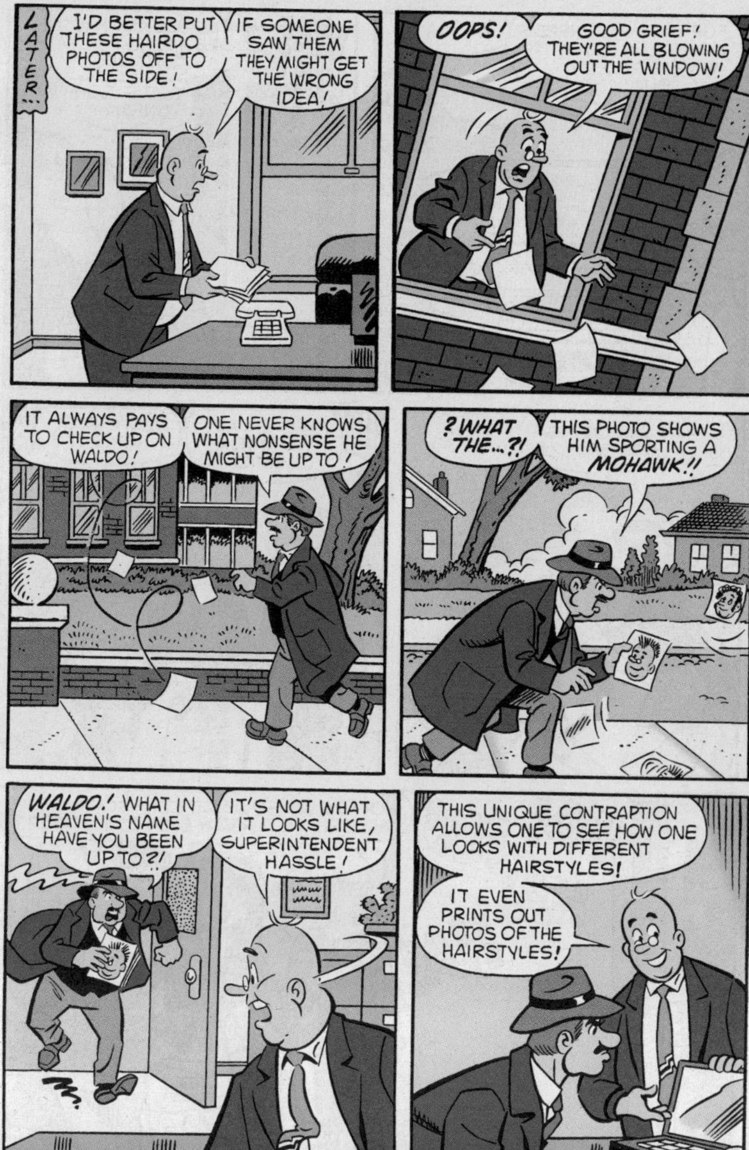
LATER..
I'D BETTER PUT THESE HAIRDO PHOTOS OFF TO THE SIDE!
IF SOMEONE SAW THEM THEY MIGHT GET THE WRONG IDEA!
OOPS!
GOOD GRIEF! THEY'RE ALL BLOWING OUT THE WINDOW!
IT ALWAYS PAYS TO CHECK UP ON WALDO!
ONE NEVER KNOWS WHAT NONSENSE HE MIGHT BE UP TO!
?WHAT THE...?!
THIS PHOTO SHOWS HIM SPORTING A MOHAWK!!
WALDO! WHAT IN HEAVEN'S NAME HAVE YOU BEEN UP TO?!
IT'S NOT WHAT IT LOOKS LIKE, SUPERINTENDENT HASSLE!
THIS UNIQUE CONTRAPTION ALLOWS ONE TO SEE HOW ONE LOOKS WITH DIFFERENT HAIRSTYLES!
IT EVEN PRINTS OUT PHOTOS OF THE HAIRSTYLES!
5

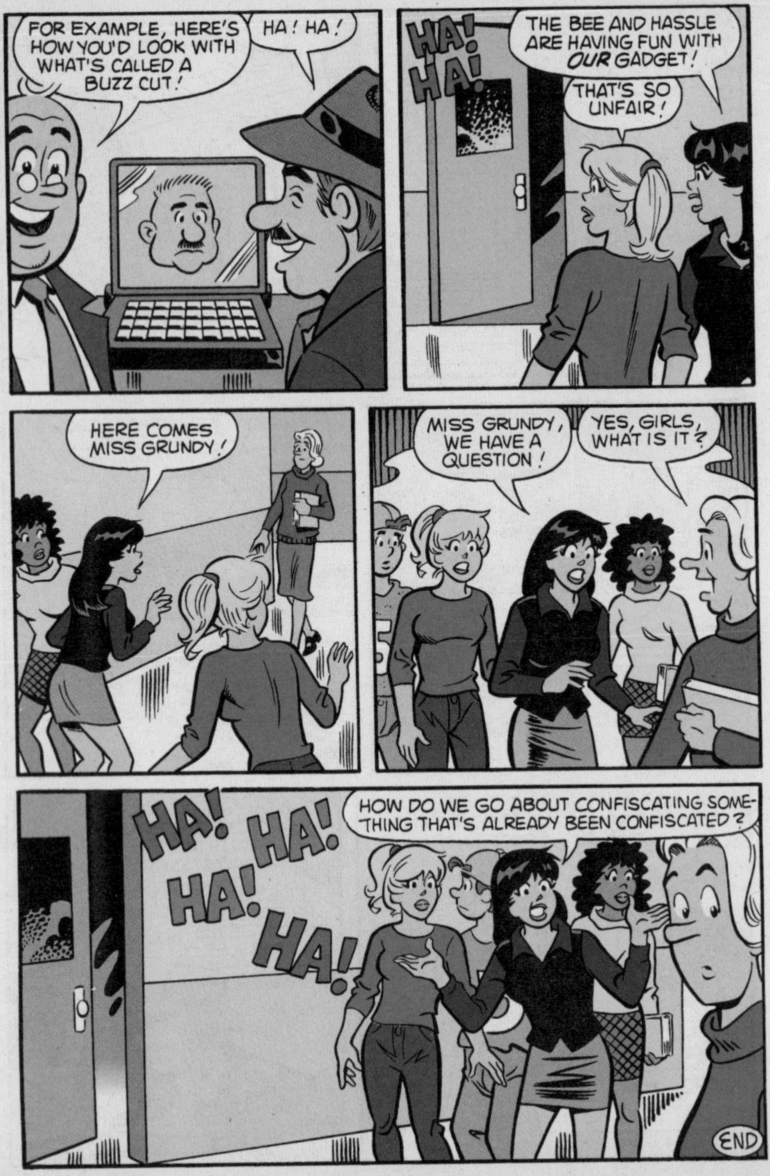

FOR EXAMPLE, HERE'S HOW YOU'D LOOK WITH WHAT'S CALLED A BUZZ CUT!
HA! HA!
HA! HA!
THE BEE AND HASSLE ARE HAVING FUN WITH OUR GADGET!
THAT'S SO UNFAIR!
HERE COMES MISS GRUNDY!
MISS GRUNDY, WE HAVE A QUESTION!
YES, GIRLS, WHAT IS IT?
HA! HA! HA! HA!
HOW DO WE GO ABOUT CONFISCATING SOMETHING THAT'S ALREADY BEEN CONFISCATED?
END

Betty in "Practice Makes Perfect"

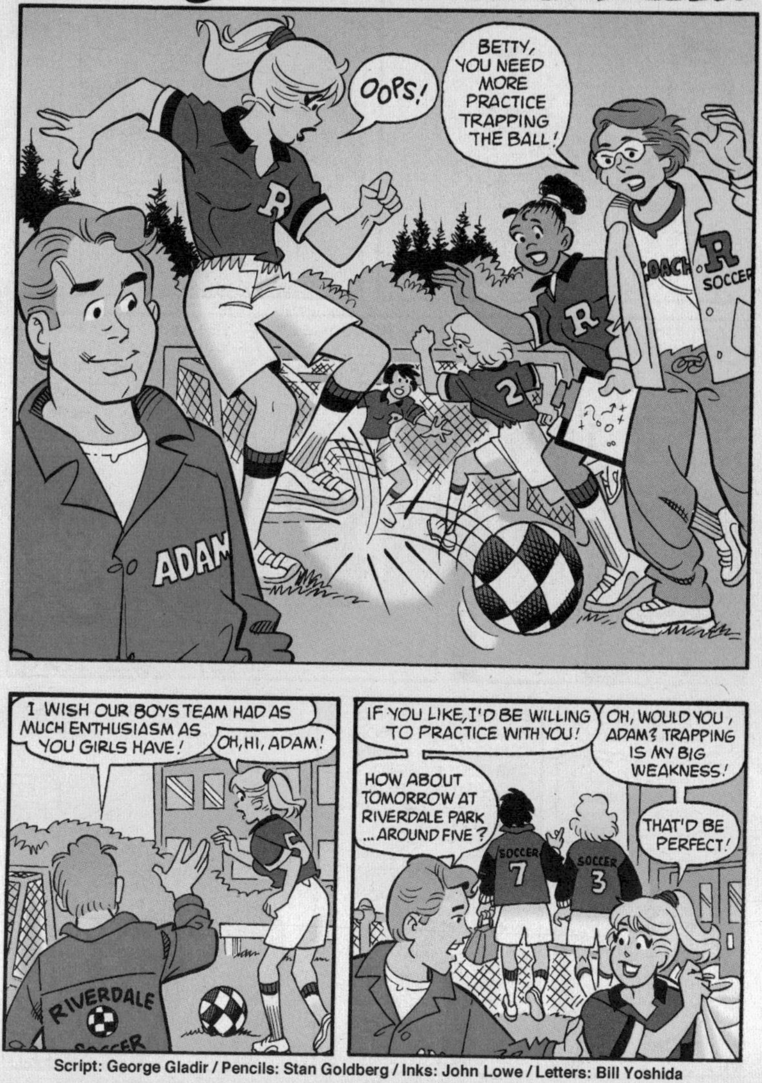
OOPS!
BETTY, YOU NEED MORE PRACTICE TRAPPING THE BALL!
ADAM
COACH
SOCCER
I WISH OUR BOYS TEAM HAD AS MUCH ENTHUSIASM AS YOU GIRLS HAVE!
OH, HI, ADAM!
RIVERDALE
IF YOU LIKE, I'D BE WILLING TO PRACTICE WITH YOU!
OH, WOULD YOU, ADAM? TRAPPING IS MY BIG WEAKNESS!
HOW ABOUT TOMORROW AT RIVERDALE PARK ...AROUND FIVE?
THAT'D BE PERFECT!
SOCCER 7
SOCCER 3

Script: George Gladir / Pencils: Stan Goldberg / Inks: John Lowe / Letters: Bill Yoshida

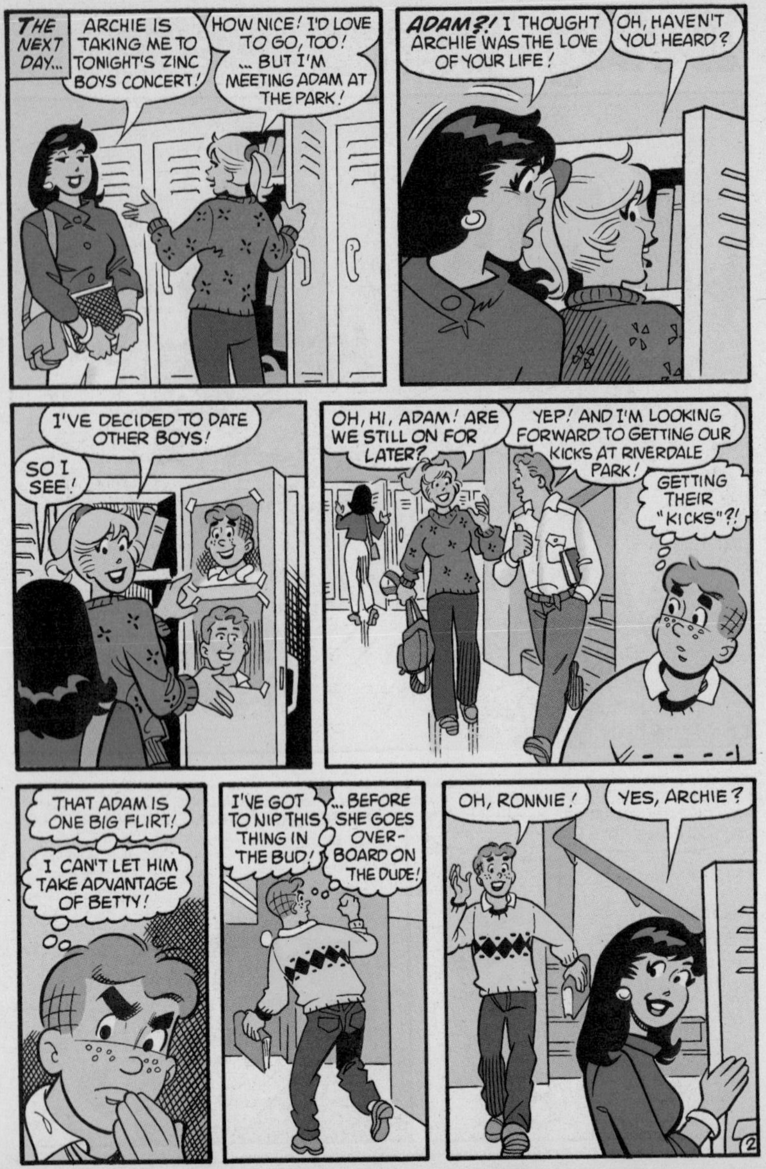
THE NEXT DAY...
ARCHIE IS TAKING ME TO TONIGHT'S ZINC BOYS CONCERT!
HOW NICE! I'D LOVE TO GO, TOO! ... BUT I'M MEETING ADAM AT THE PARK!
ADAM?! I THOUGHT ARCHIE WAS THE LOVE OF YOUR LIFE!
OH, HAVEN'T YOU HEARD?
I'VE DECIDED TO DATE OTHER BOYS!
SO I SEE!
OH, HI, ADAM! ARE WE STILL ON FOR LATER?
YEP! AND I'M LOOKING FORWARD TO GETTING OUR KICKS AT RIVERDALE PARK!
GETTING THEIR "KICKS"?!
THAT ADAM IS ONE BIG FLIRT!
I CAN'T LET HIM TAKE ADVANTAGE OF BETTY!
I'VE GOT TO NIP THIS THING IN THE BUD!
... BEFORE SHE GOES OVER-BOARD ON THE DUDE!
OH, RONNIE!
YES, ARCHIE?
2

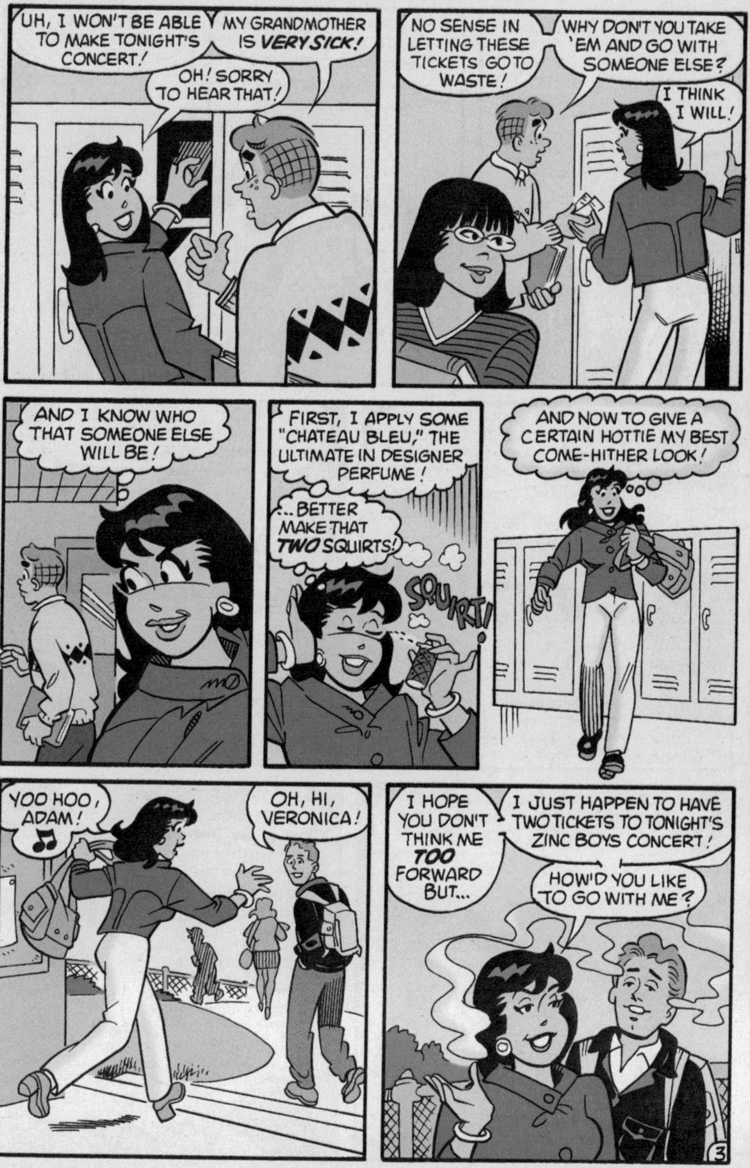
UH, I WON'T BE ABLE TO MAKE TONIGHT'S CONCERT!
MY GRANDMOTHER IS VERY SICK!
OH! SORRY TO HEAR THAT!
NO SENSE IN LETTING THESE TICKETS GO TO WASTE!
WHY DON'T YOU TAKE 'EM AND GO WITH SOMEONE ELSE?
I THINK I WILL!
AND I KNOW WHO THAT SOMEONE ELSE WILL BE!
FIRST, I APPLY SOME "CHATEAU BLEU," THE ULTIMATE IN DESIGNER PERFUME!
...BETTER MAKE THAT TWO SQUIRTS!
SQUIRT!
AND NOW TO GIVE A CERTAIN HOTTIE MY BEST COME-HITHER LOOK!
YOO HOO, ADAM!
OH, HI, VERONICA!
I HOPE YOU DON'T THINK ME TOO FORWARD BUT...
I JUST HAPPEN TO HAVE TWO TICKETS TO TONIGHT'S ZINC BOYS CONCERT!
HOW'D YOU LIKE TO GO WITH ME?
3

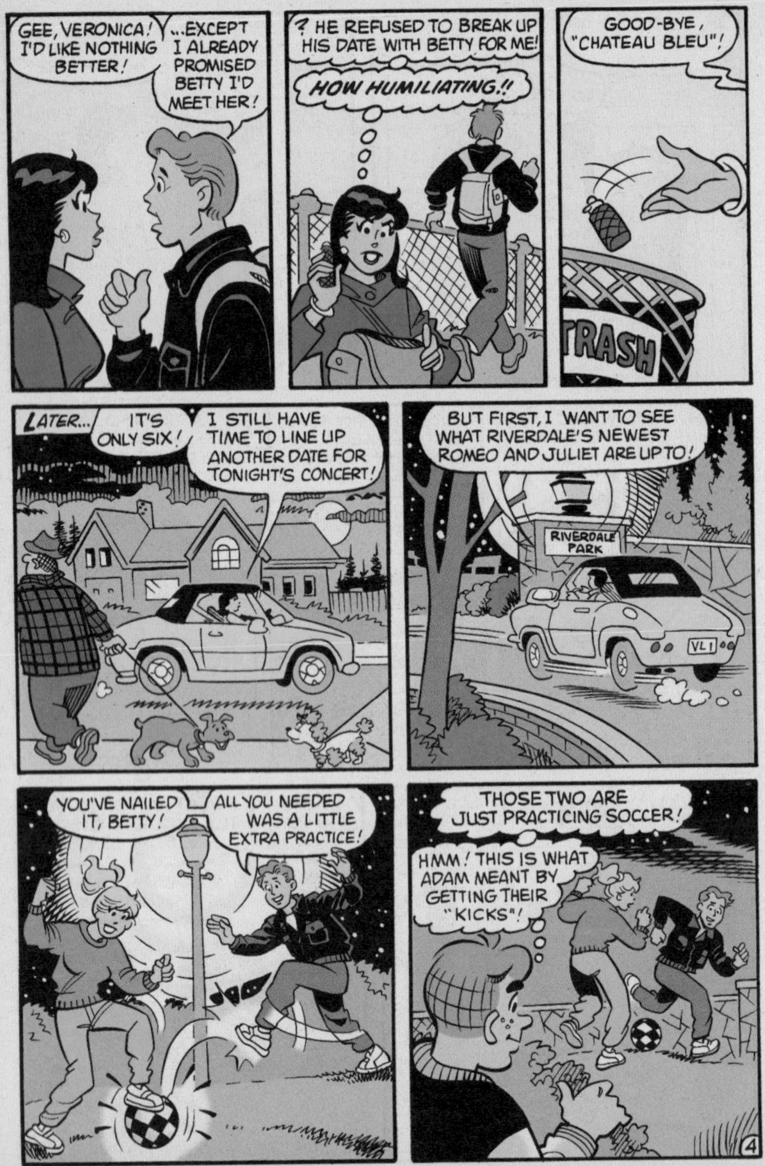
GEE, VERONICA! I'D LIKE NOTHING BETTER!
...EXCEPT I ALREADY PROMISED BETTY I'D MEET HER!
? HE REFUSED TO BREAK UP HIS DATE WITH BETTY FOR ME!
HOW HUMILIATING.!!
GOOD-BYE, "CHATEAU BLEU"!
TRASH
LATER...
IT'S ONLY SIX!
I STILL HAVE TIME TO LINE UP ANOTHER DATE FOR TONIGHT'S CONCERT!
BUT FIRST, I WANT TO SEE WHAT RIVERDALE'S NEWEST ROMEO AND JULIET ARE UP TO!
RIVERDALE PARK
VL 1
YOU'VE NAILED IT, BETTY!
ALL YOU NEEDED WAS A LITTLE EXTRA PRACTICE!
THOSE TWO ARE JUST PRACTICING SOCCER!
HMM! THIS IS WHAT ADAM MEANT BY GETTING THEIR "KICKS"!
4

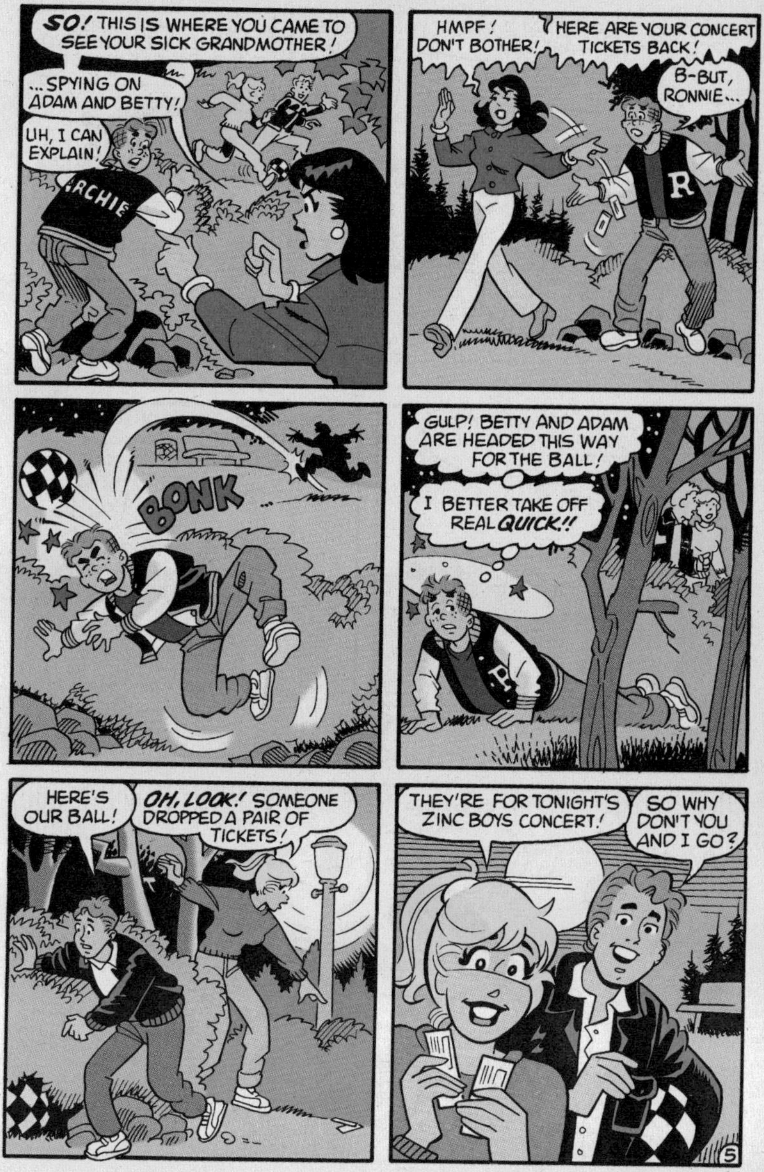
SO! THIS IS WHERE YOU CAME TO SEE YOUR SICK GRANDMOTHER!
...SPYING ON ADAM AND BETTY!
UH, I CAN EXPLAIN!
ARCHIE
HMPF! DON'T BOTHER!
HERE ARE YOUR CONCERT TICKETS BACK!
B-BUT, RONNIE...
R
BONK
GULP! BETTY AND ADAM ARE HEADED THIS WAY FOR THE BALL!
I BETTER TAKE OFF REAL QUICK!!
R
HERE'S OUR BALL!
OH, LOOK! SOMEONE DROPPED A PAIR OF TICKETS!
THEY'RE FOR TONIGHT'S ZINC BOYS CONCERT!
SO WHY DON'T YOU AND I GO?
5

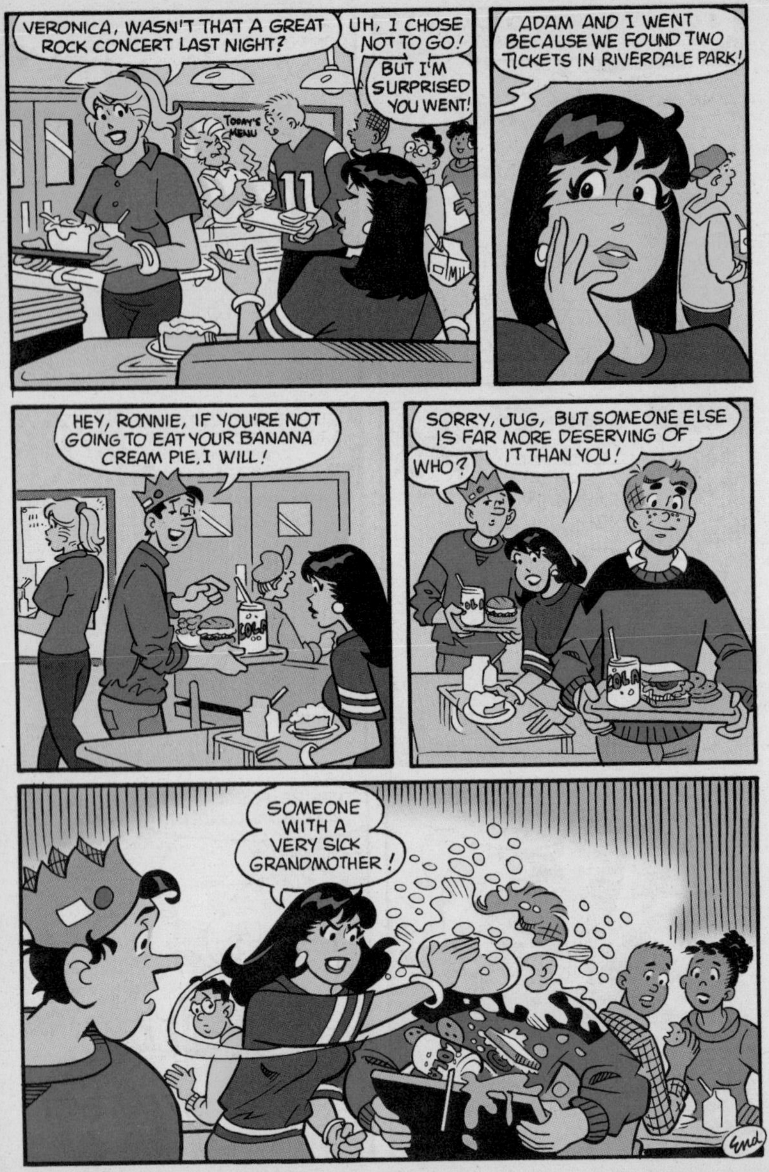
VERONICA, WASN'T THAT A GREAT ROCK CONCERT LAST NIGHT?
UH, I CHOSE NOT TO GO!
BUT I'M SURPRISED YOU WENT!
TODAY'S MENU
ADAM AND I WENT BECAUSE WE FOUND TWO TICKETS IN RIVERDALE PARK!
HEY, RONNIE, IF YOU'RE NOT GOING TO EAT YOUR BANANA CREAM PIE, I WILL!
SORRY, JUG, BUT SOMEONE ELSE IS FAR MORE DESERVING OF IT THAN YOU!
WHO?
SOMEONE WITH A VERY SICK GRANDMOTHER!
End

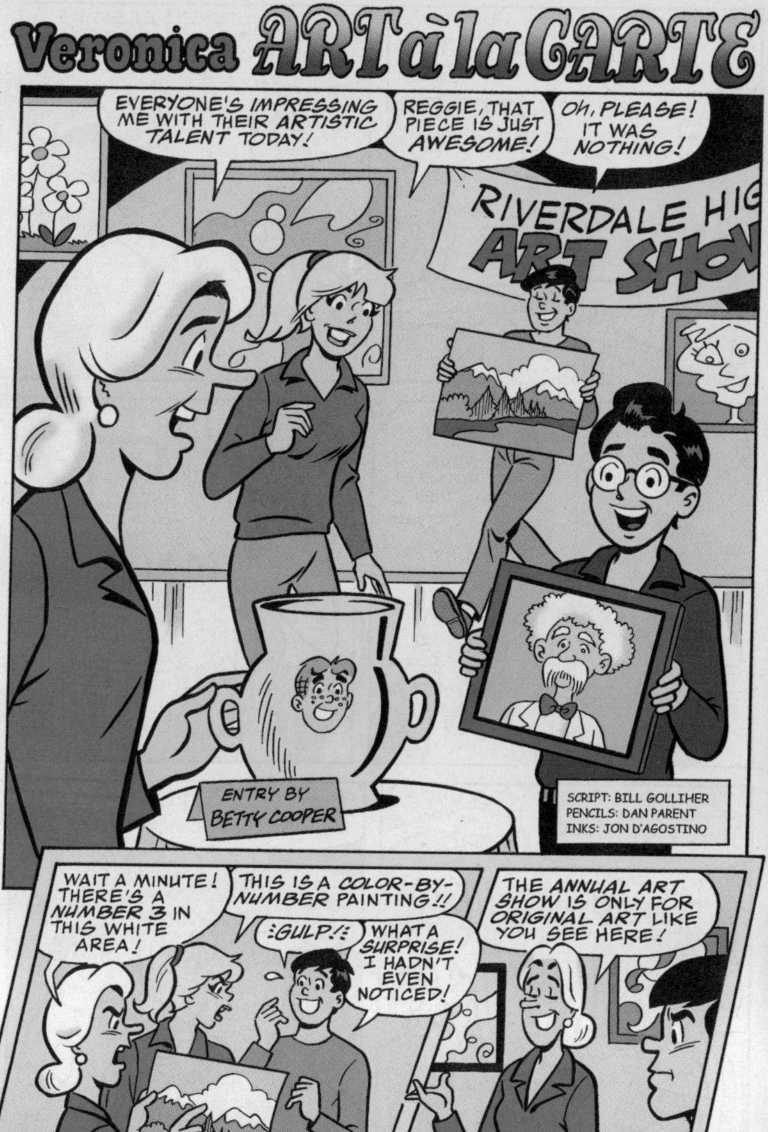
Veronica ART à la CARTE
EVERYONE'S IMPRESSING ME WITH THEIR ARTISTIC TALENT TODAY!
REGGIE, THAT PIECE IS JUST AWESOME!
OH, PLEASE! IT WAS NOTHING!
RIVERDALE HIG
ART SHOW
ENTRY BY BETTY COOPER
SCRIPT: BILL GOLLIHER
PENCILS: DAN PARENT
INKS: JON D'AGOSTINO
WAIT A MINUTE! THERE'S A NUMBER 3 IN THIS WHITE AREA!
THIS IS A COLOR-BY-NUMBER PAINTING!!
GULP!
WHAT A SURPRISE! I HADN'T EVEN NOTICED!
THE ANNUAL ART SHOW IS ONLY FOR ORIGINAL ART LIKE YOU SEE HERE!

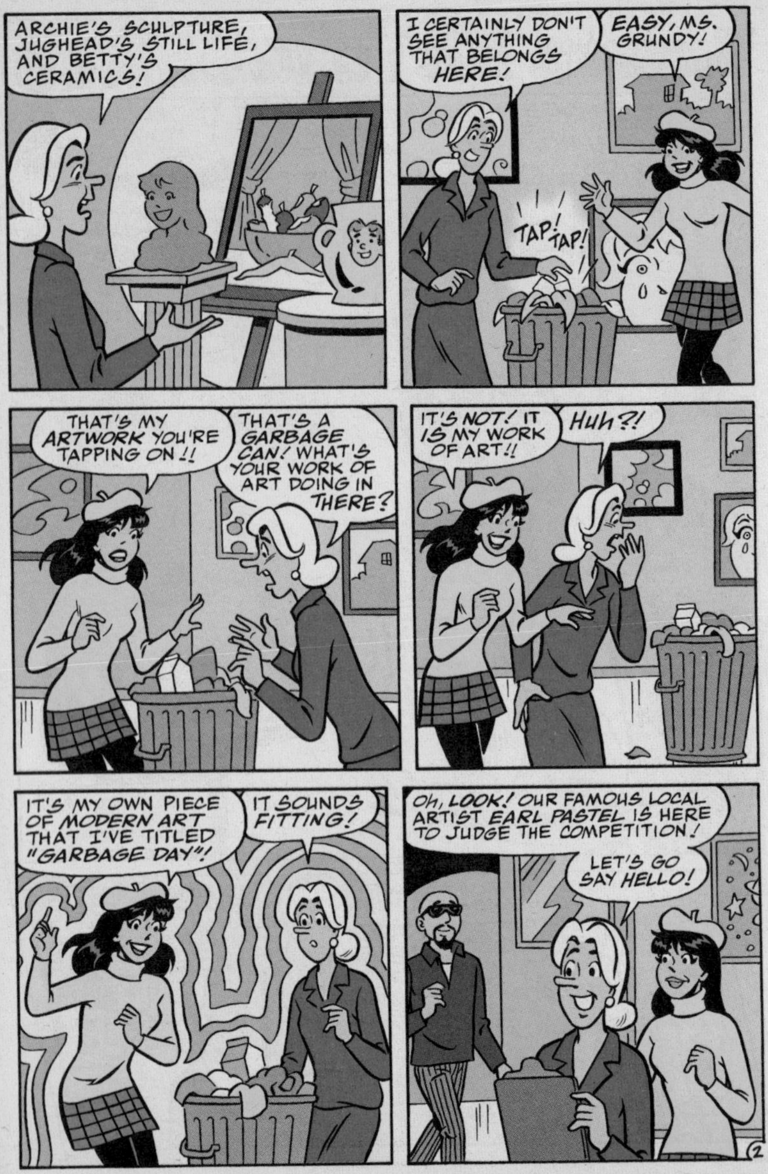
ARCHIE'S SCULPTURE, JUGHEAD'S STILL LIFE, AND BETTY'S CERAMICS!
I CERTAINLY DON'T SEE ANYTHING THAT BELONGS HERE!
EASY, MS. GRUNDY!
TAP! TAP!
THAT'S MY ARTWORK YOU'RE TAPPING ON!!
THAT'S A GARBAGE CAN! WHAT'S YOUR WORK OF ART DOING IN THERE?
IT'S NOT! IT IS MY WORK OF ART!!
Huh?!
IT'S MY OWN PIECE OF MODERN ART THAT I'VE TITLED "GARBAGE DAY"!
IT SOUNDS FITTING!
Oh, LOOK! OUR FAMOUS LOCAL ARTIST EARL PASTEL IS HERE TO JUDGE THE COMPETITION!
LET'S GO SAY HELLO!
2

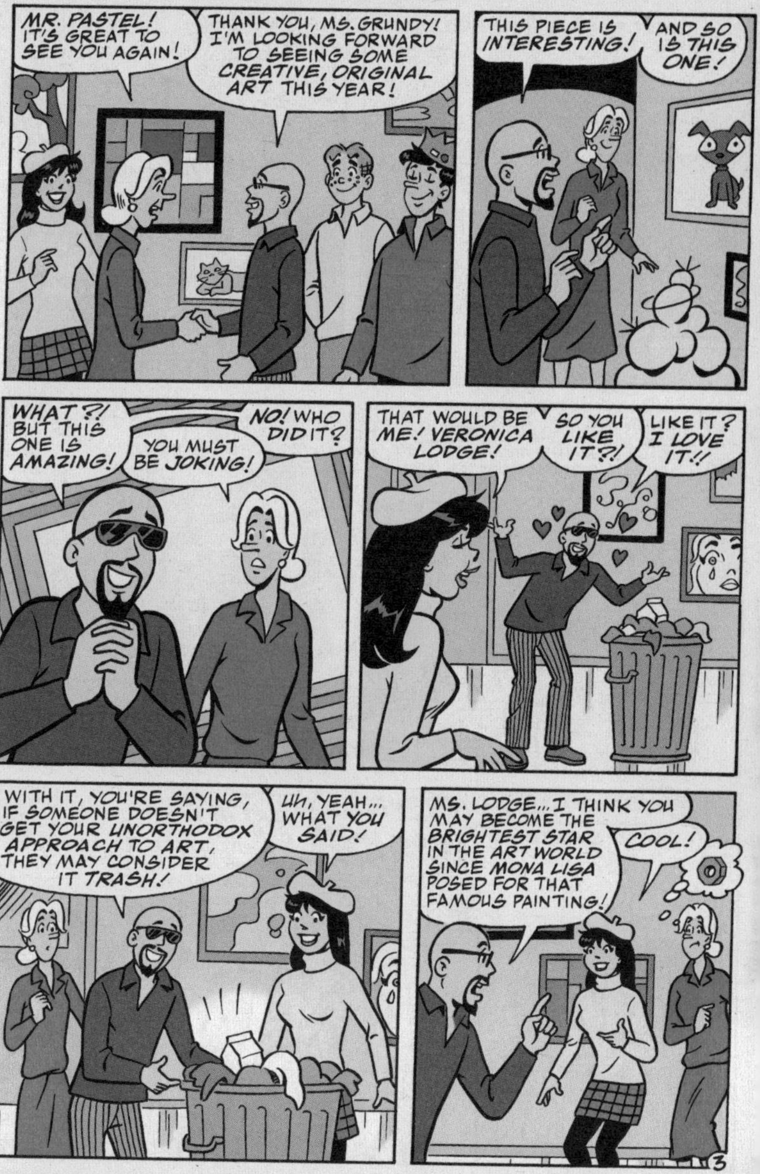
MR. PASTEL! IT'S GREAT TO SEE YOU AGAIN!
THANK YOU, MS. GRUNDY! I'M LOOKING FORWARD TO SEEING SOME CREATIVE, ORIGINAL ART THIS YEAR!
THIS PIECE IS INTERESTING!
AND SO IS THIS ONE!
WHAT?! BUT THIS ONE IS AMAZING!
YOU MUST BE JOKING!
NO! WHO DID IT?
THAT WOULD BE ME! VERONICA LODGE!
SO YOU LIKE IT?!
LIKE IT? I LOVE IT!!
WITH IT, YOU'RE SAYING, IF SOMEONE DOESN'T GET YOUR UNORTHODOX APPROACH TO ART, THEY MAY CONSIDER IT TRASH!
UH, YEAH... WHAT YOU SAID!
MS. LODGE... I THINK YOU MAY BECOME THE BRIGHTEST STAR IN THE ART WORLD SINCE MONA LISA POSED FOR THAT FAMOUS PAINTING!
COOL!
3

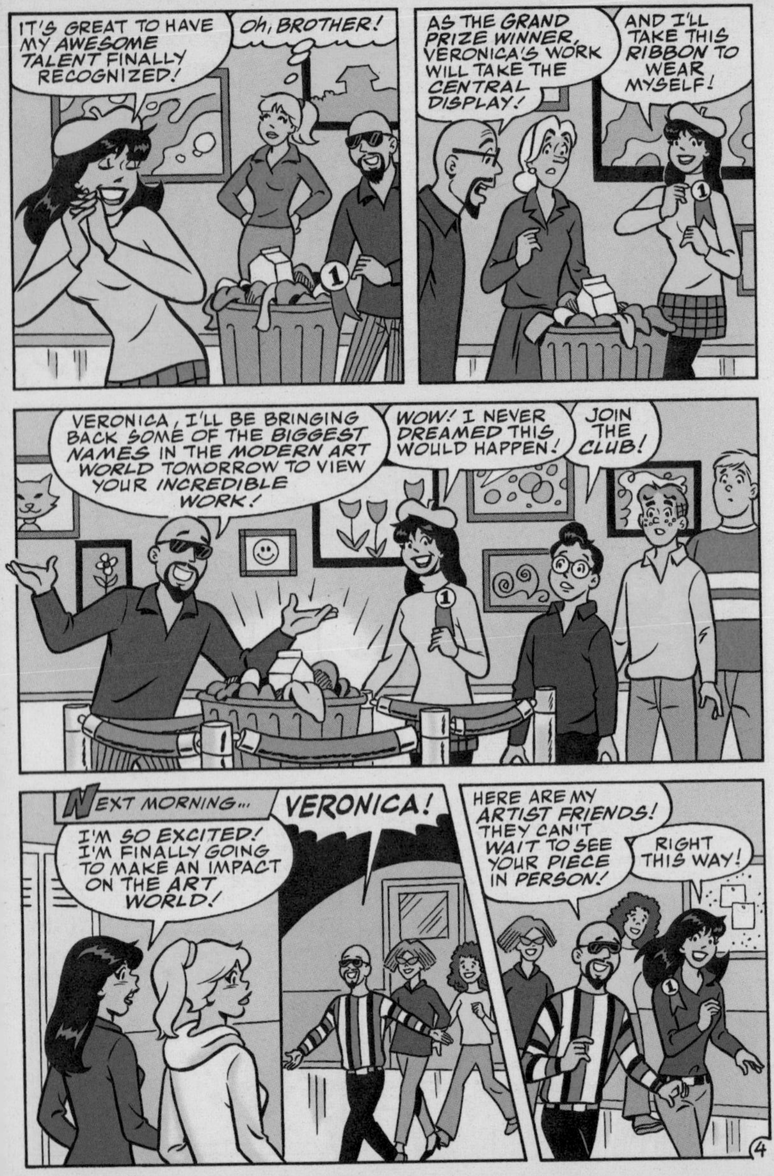

IT'S GREAT TO HAVE MY AWESOME TALENT FINALLY RECOGNIZED!
Oh, BROTHER!
AS THE GRAND PRIZE WINNER, VERONICA'S WORK WILL TAKE THE CENTRAL DISPLAY!
AND I'LL TAKE THIS RIBBON TO WEAR MYSELF!
VERONICA, I'LL BE BRINGING BACK SOME OF THE BIGGEST NAMES IN THE MODERN ART WORLD TOMORROW TO VIEW YOUR INCREDIBLE WORK!
WOW! I NEVER DREAMED THIS WOULD HAPPEN!
JOIN THE CLUB!
NEXT MORNING...
I'M SO EXCITED! I'M FINALLY GOING TO MAKE AN IMPACT ON THE ART WORLD!
VERONICA!
HERE ARE MY ARTIST FRIENDS! THEY CAN'T WAIT TO SEE YOUR PIECE IN PERSON!
RIGHT THIS WAY!
4

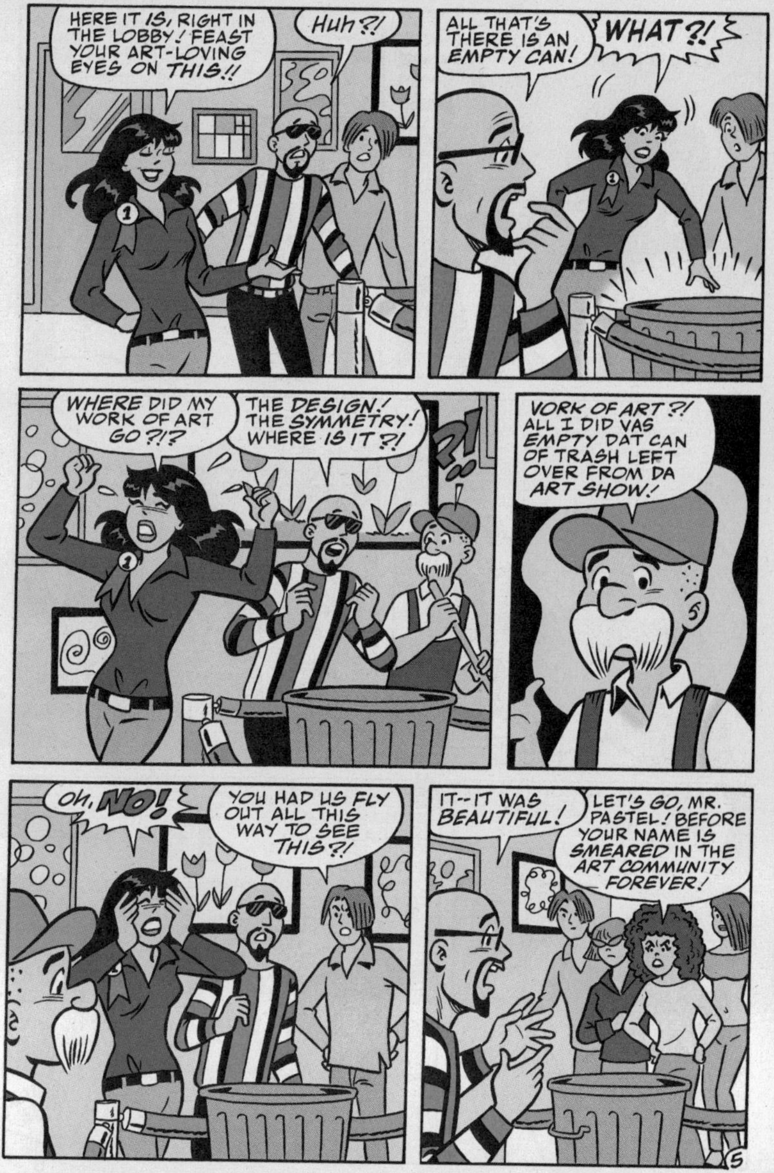
HERE IT IS, RIGHT IN THE LOBBY! FEAST YOUR ART-LOVING EYES ON THIS!!
Huh?!
ALL THAT'S THERE IS AN EMPTY CAN!
WHAT?!
WHERE DID MY WORK OF ART GO?!?
THE DESIGN! THE SYMMETRY! WHERE IS IT?!
?!
VORK OF ART?! ALL I DID VAS EMPTY DAT CAN OF TRASH LEFT OVER FROM DA ART SHOW!
Oh, NO!
YOU HAD US FLY OUT ALL THIS WAY TO SEE THIS?!
IT--IT WAS BEAUTIFUL!
LET'S GO, MR. PASTEL! BEFORE YOUR NAME IS SMEARED IN THE ART COMMUNITY FOREVER!

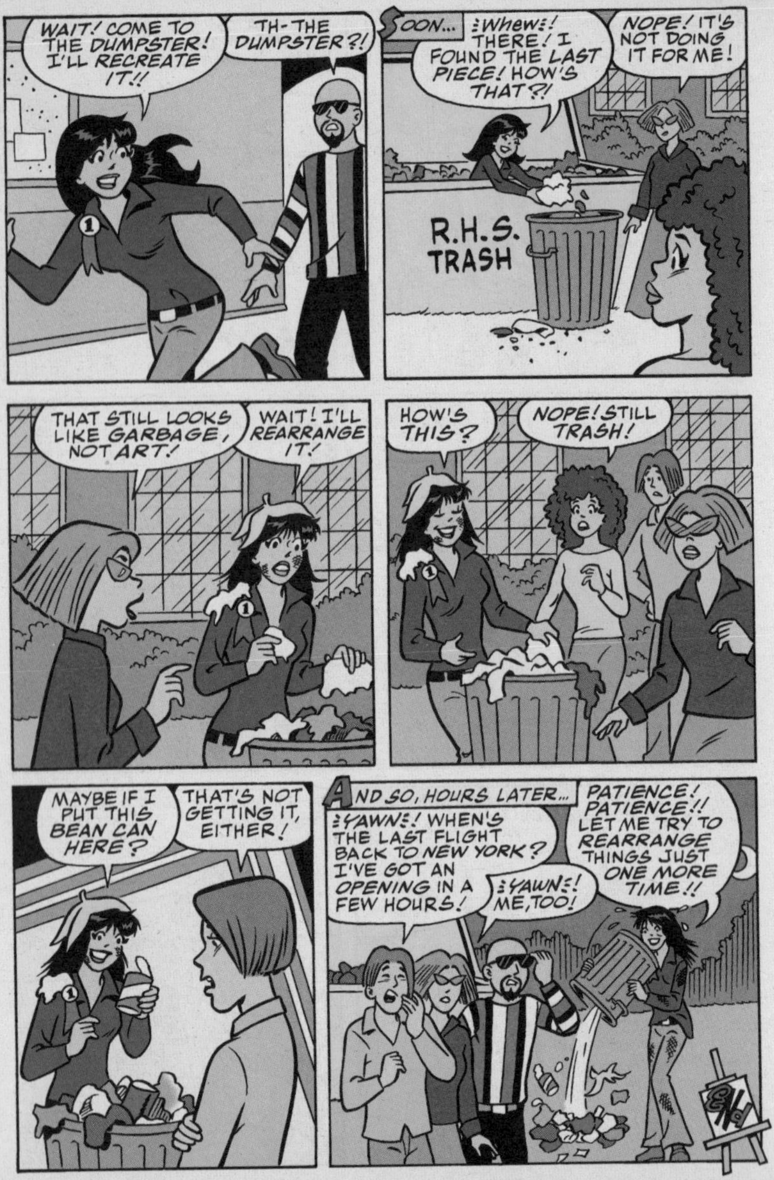
WAIT! COME TO THE DUMPSTER! I'LL RECREATE IT!!
TH-THE DUMPSTER?!
SOON...
:WHEW:! THERE! I FOUND THE LAST PIECE! HOW'S THAT?!
NOPE! IT'S NOT DOING IT FOR ME!
R.H.S. TRASH
THAT STILL LOOKS LIKE GARBAGE, NOT ART!
WAIT! I'LL REARRANGE IT!
HOW'S THIS?
NOPE! STILL TRASH!
MAYBE IF I PUT THIS BEAN CAN HERE?
THAT'S NOT GETTING IT, EITHER!
AND SO, HOURS LATER...
:YAWN:! WHEN'S THE LAST FLIGHT BACK TO NEW YORK? I'VE GOT AN OPENING IN A FEW HOURS!
:YAWN:! ME, TOO!
PATIENCE! PATIENCE!! LET ME TRY TO REARRANGE THINGS JUST ONE MORE TIME!!
END

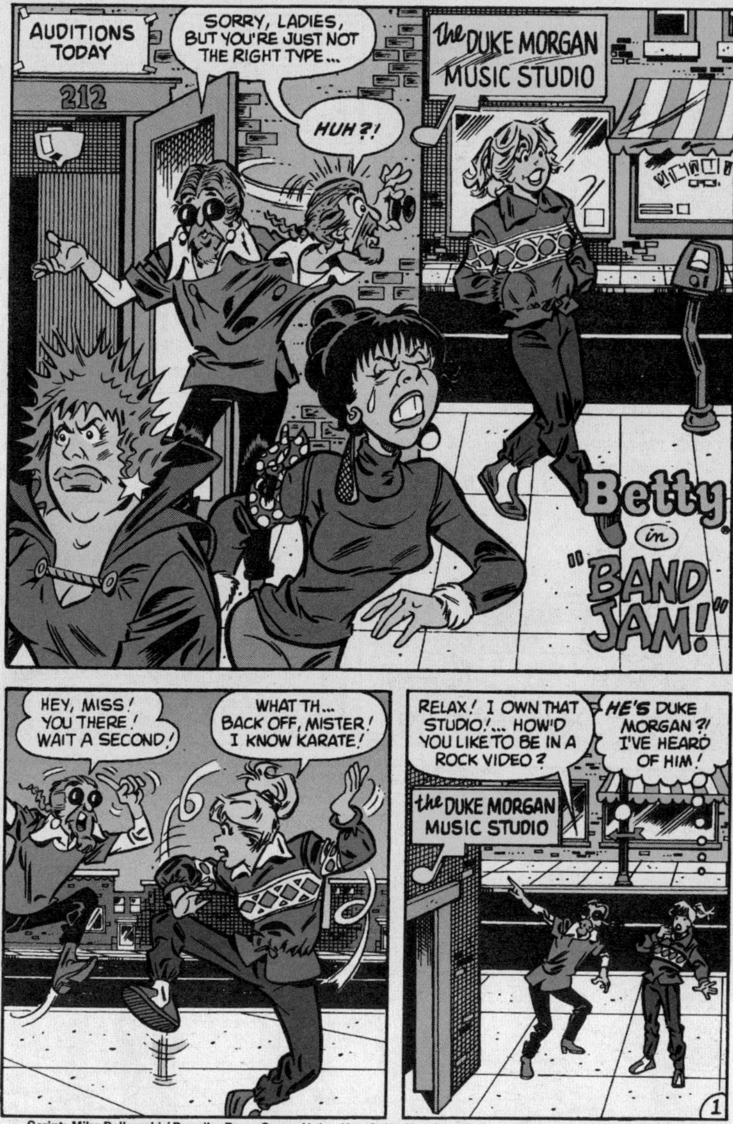
AUDITIONS TODAY
212
SORRY, LADIES, BUT YOU'RE JUST NOT THE RIGHT TYPE...
HUH ?!
the DUKE MORGAN MUSIC STUDIO
Betty in "BAND JAM!"
HEY, MISS! YOU THERE! WAIT A SECOND!
WHAT TH... BACK OFF, MISTER! I KNOW KARATE!
RELAX! I OWN THAT STUDIO!... HOW'D YOU LIKE TO BE IN A ROCK VIDEO ?
HE'S DUKE MORGAN ?! I'VE HEARD OF HIM!
the DUKE MORGAN MUSIC STUDIO
1

Script: Mike Pellowski / Pencils: Doug Crane / Inks: Ken Selig / Letters: Bill Yoshida / Colors: Barry Grossman

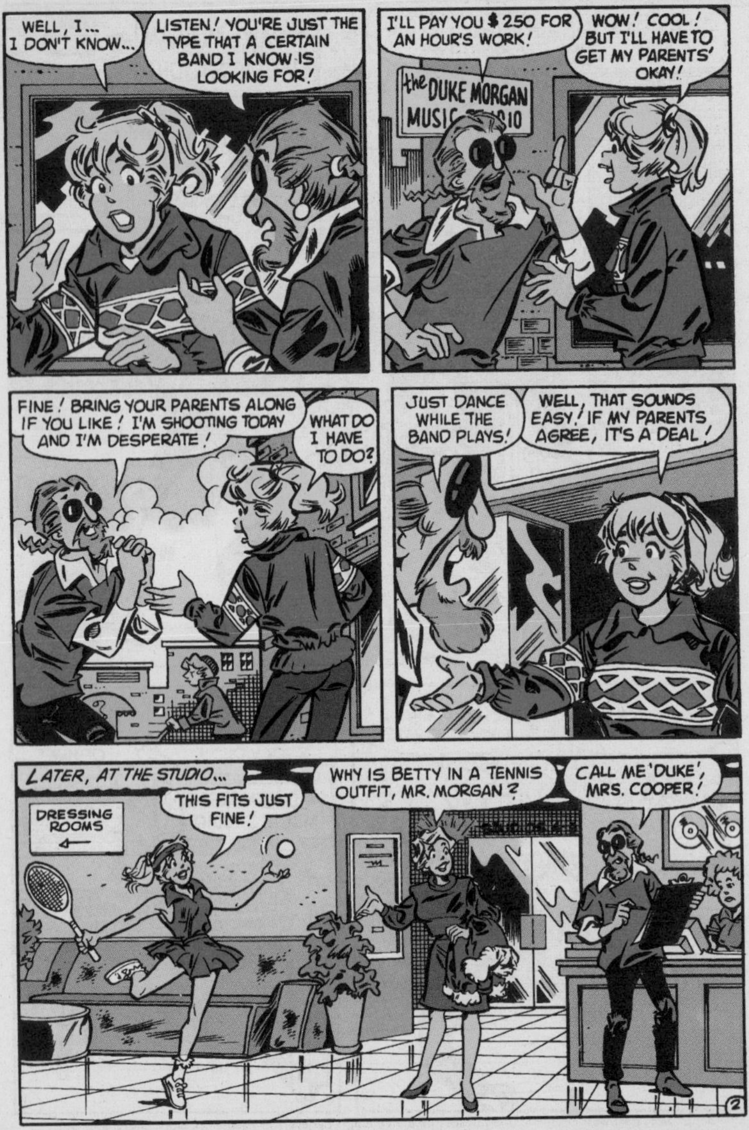
WELL, I... I DON'T KNOW...
LISTEN! YOU'RE JUST THE TYPE THAT A CERTAIN BAND I KNOW IS LOOKING FOR!
I'LL PAY YOU $250 FOR AN HOUR'S WORK!
WOW! COOL! BUT I'LL HAVE TO GET MY PARENTS' OKAY!
the DUKE MORGAN MUSIC
FINE! BRING YOUR PARENTS ALONG IF YOU LIKE! I'M SHOOTING TODAY AND I'M DESPERATE!
WHAT DO I HAVE TO DO?
JUST DANCE WHILE THE BAND PLAYS!
WELL, THAT SOUNDS EASY! IF MY PARENTS AGREE, IT'S A DEAL!
LATER, AT THE STUDIO...
DRESSING ROOMS
THIS FITS JUST FINE!
WHY IS BETTY IN A TENNIS OUTFIT, MR. MORGAN?
CALL ME 'DUKE', MRS. COOPER!
2

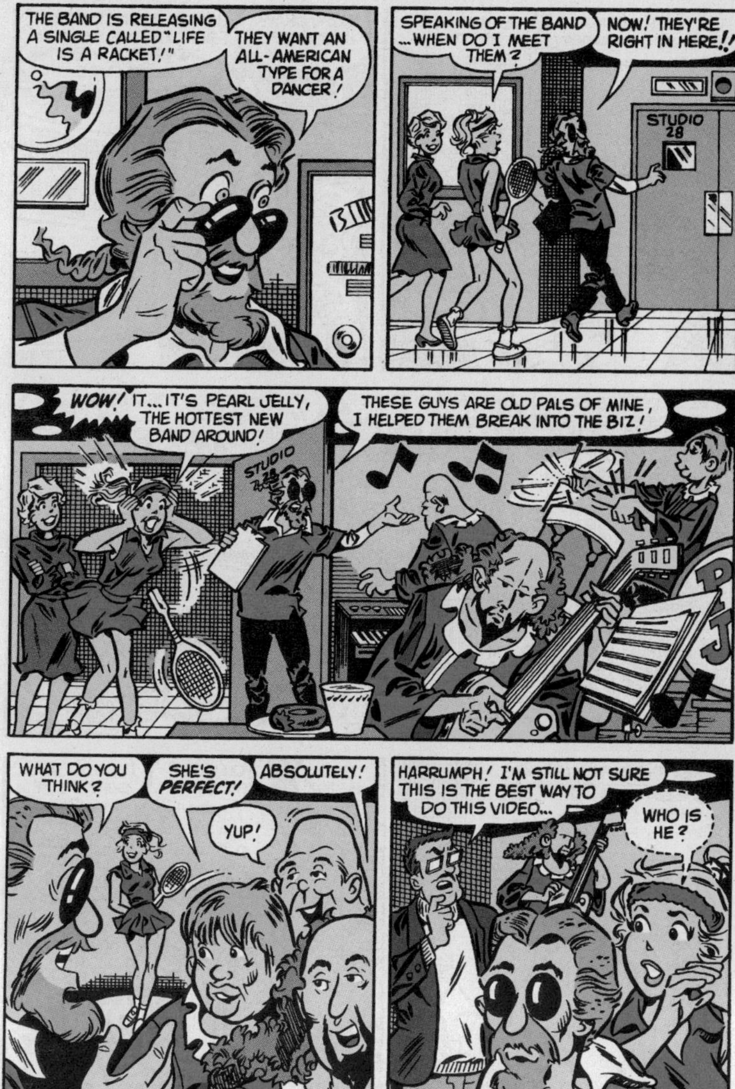
THE BAND IS RELEASING A SINGLE CALLED "LIFE IS A RACKET!"
THEY WANT AN ALL-AMERICAN TYPE FOR A DANCER!
SPEAKING OF THE BAND ...WHEN DO I MEET THEM?
NOW! THEY'RE RIGHT IN HERE!!
STUDIO 28
WOW! IT... IT'S PEARL JELLY, THE HOTTEST NEW BAND AROUND!
STUDIO 28
THESE GUYS ARE OLD PALS OF MINE, I HELPED THEM BREAK INTO THE BIZ!
PJ
WHAT DO YOU THINK?
SHE'S PERFECT!
ABSOLUTELY!
YUP!
HARRUMPH! I'M STILL NOT SURE THIS IS THE BEST WAY TO DO THIS VIDEO...
WHO IS HE?
3

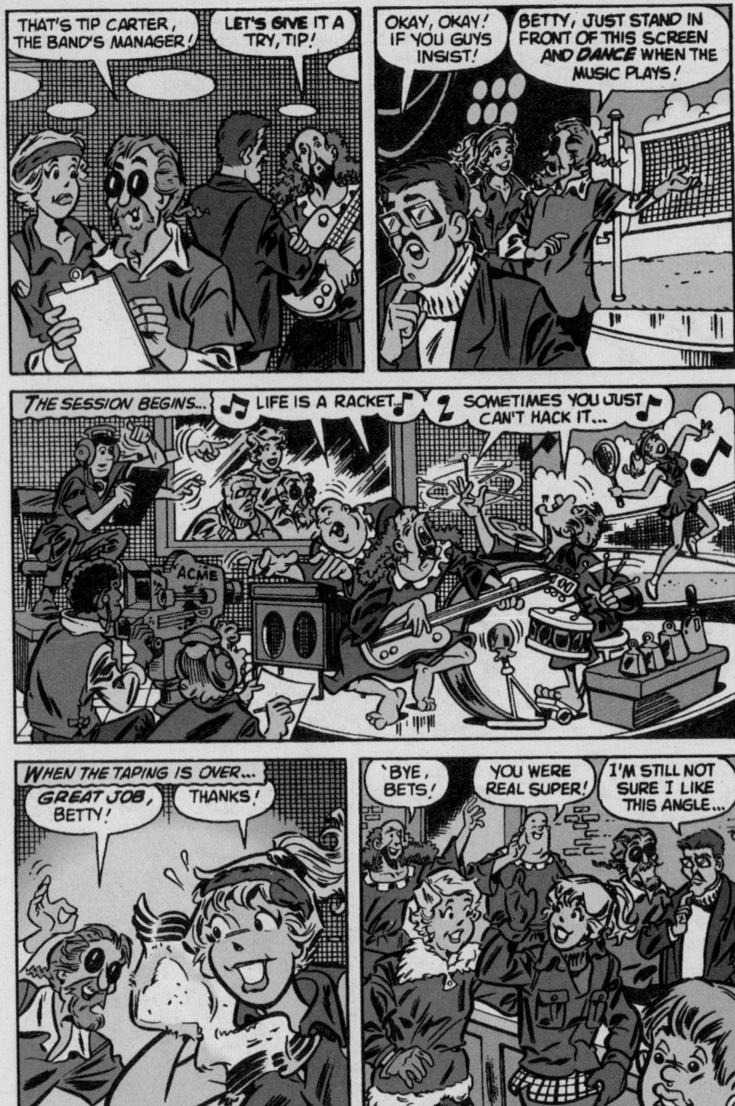
THAT'S TIP CARTER, THE BAND'S MANAGER!
LET'S GIVE IT A TRY, TIP!
OKAY, OKAY! IF YOU GUYS INSIST!
BETTY, JUST STAND IN FRONT OF THIS SCREEN AND DANCE WHEN THE MUSIC PLAYS!
THE SESSION BEGINS...
LIFE IS A RACKET...
SOMETIMES YOU JUST CAN'T HACK IT...
ACME
WHEN THE TAPING IS OVER...
GREAT JOB, BETTY!
THANKS!
`BYE, BETS!
YOU WERE REAL SUPER!
I'M STILL NOT SURE I LIKE THIS ANGLE...
4

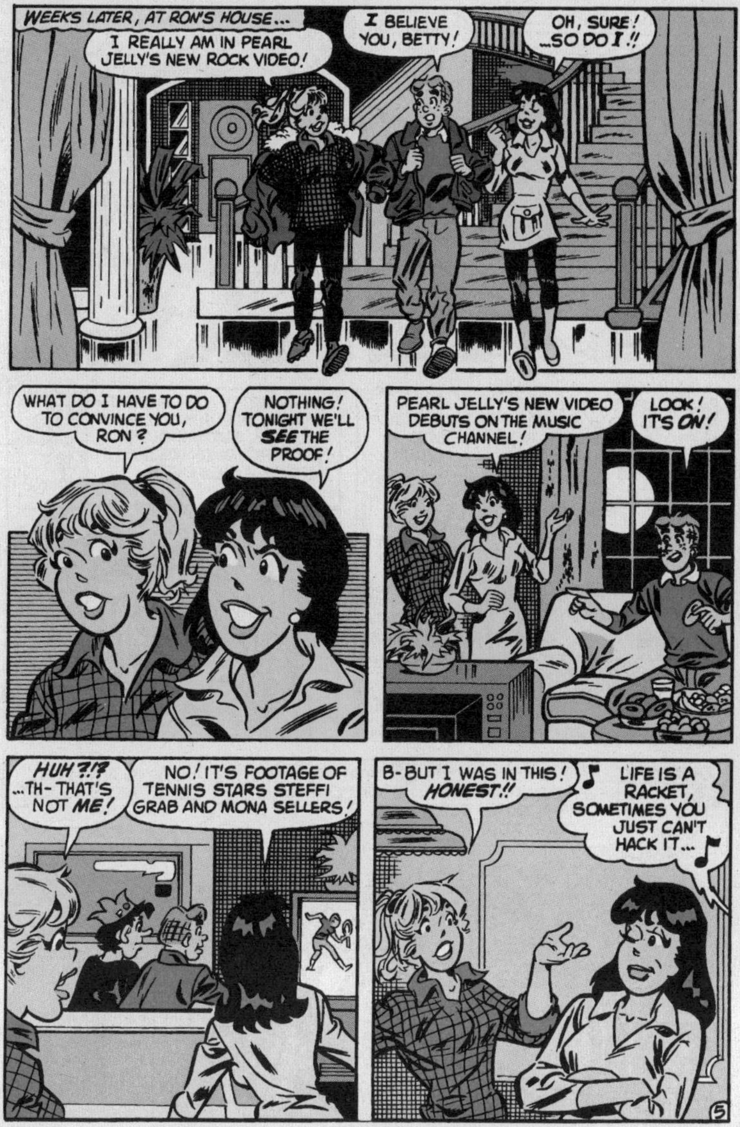
WEEKS LATER, AT RON'S HOUSE...
I REALLY AM IN PEARL JELLY'S NEW ROCK VIDEO!
I BELIEVE YOU, BETTY!
OH, SURE! ...SO DO I!!
WHAT DO I HAVE TO DO TO CONVINCE YOU, RON?
NOTHING! TONIGHT WE'LL SEE THE PROOF!
PEARL JELLY'S NEW VIDEO DEBUTS ON THE MUSIC CHANNEL!
LOOK! IT'S ON!
HUH?!? ...TH- THAT'S NOT ME!
NO! IT'S FOOTAGE OF TENNIS STARS STEFFI GRAB AND MONA SELLERS!
B- BUT I WAS IN THIS! HONEST!!
♪ LIFE IS A RACKET, SOMETIMES YOU JUST CAN'T HACK IT... ♪
5

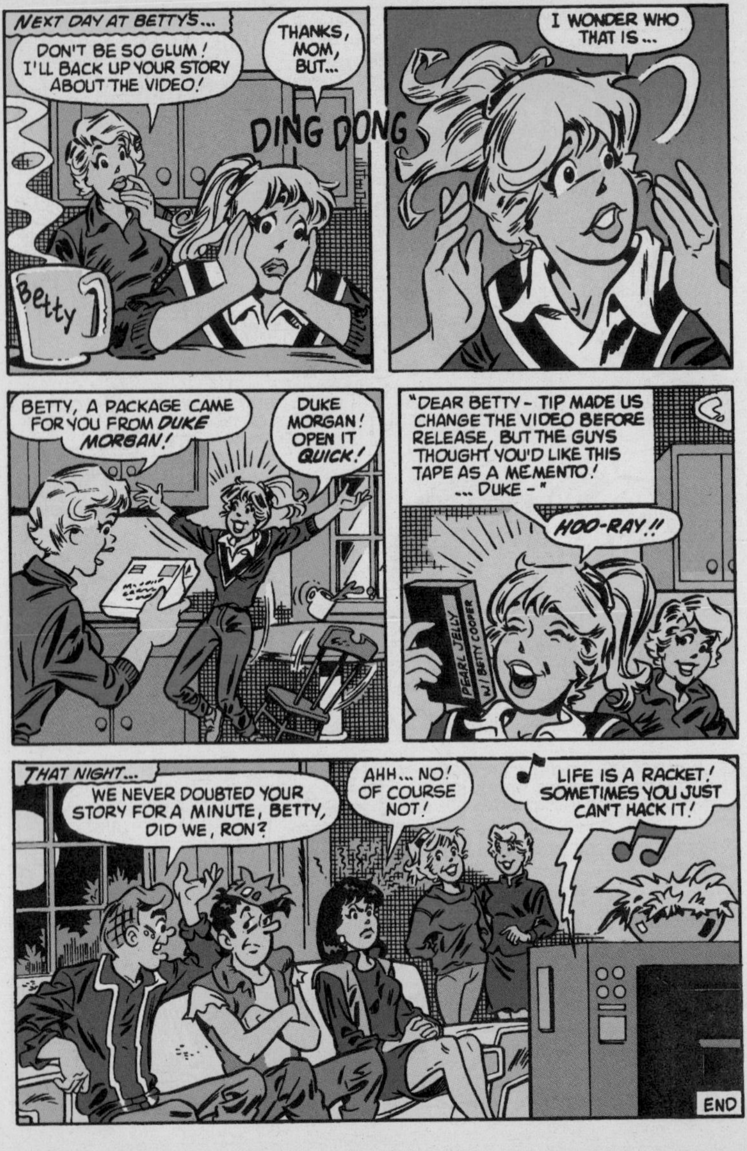
NEXT DAY AT BETTY'S...
DON'T BE SO GLUM! I'LL BACK UP YOUR STORY ABOUT THE VIDEO!
THANKS, MOM, BUT...
DING DONG
Betty
I WONDER WHO THAT IS...
BETTY, A PACKAGE CAME FOR YOU FROM DUKE MORGAN!
DUKE MORGAN! OPEN IT QUICK!
"DEAR BETTY - TIP MADE US CHANGE THE VIDEO BEFORE RELEASE, BUT THE GUYS THOUGHT YOU'D LIKE THIS TAPE AS A MEMENTO! ... DUKE -"
HOO-RAY!!
PEARL JELLY
W/ BETTY COOPER
THAT NIGHT...
WE NEVER DOUBTED YOUR STORY FOR A MINUTE, BETTY, DID WE, RON?
AHH... NO! OF COURSE NOT!
LIFE IS A RACKET! SOMETIMES YOU JUST CAN'T HACK IT!
END

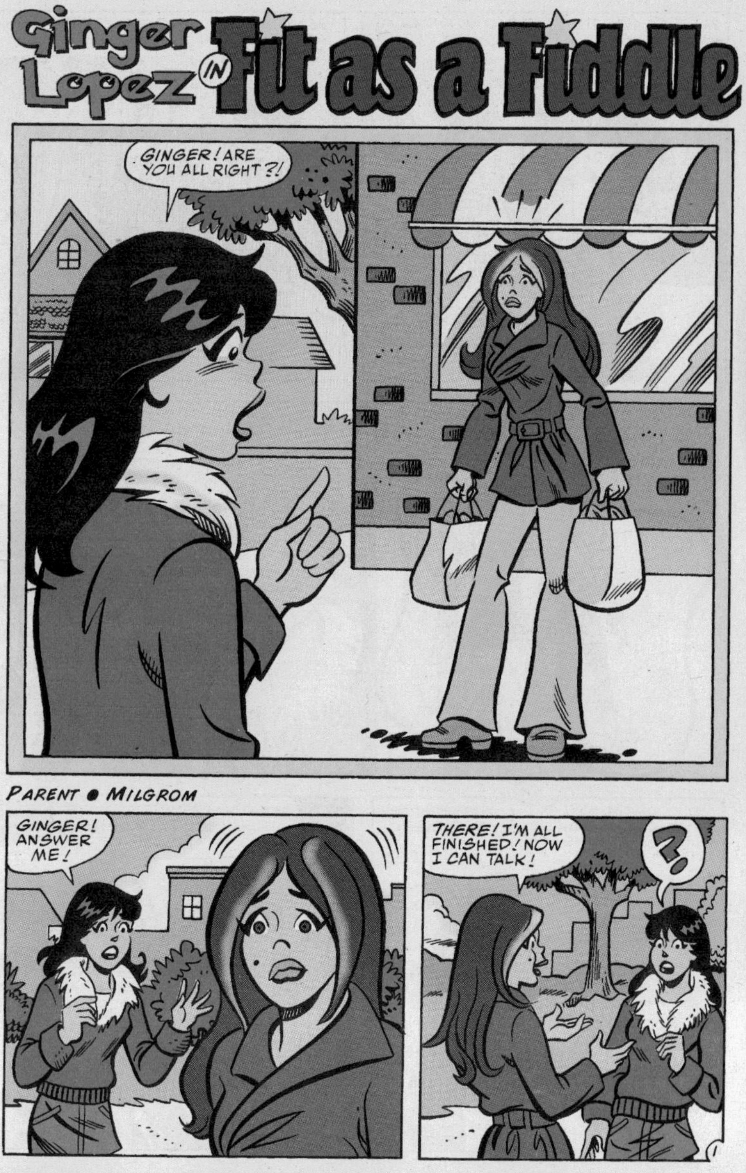
Ginger Lopez IN Fit as a Fiddle
GINGER! ARE YOU ALL RIGHT?!
PARENT ● MILGROM
GINGER! ANSWER ME!
THERE! I'M ALL FINISHED! NOW I CAN TALK!
?
1

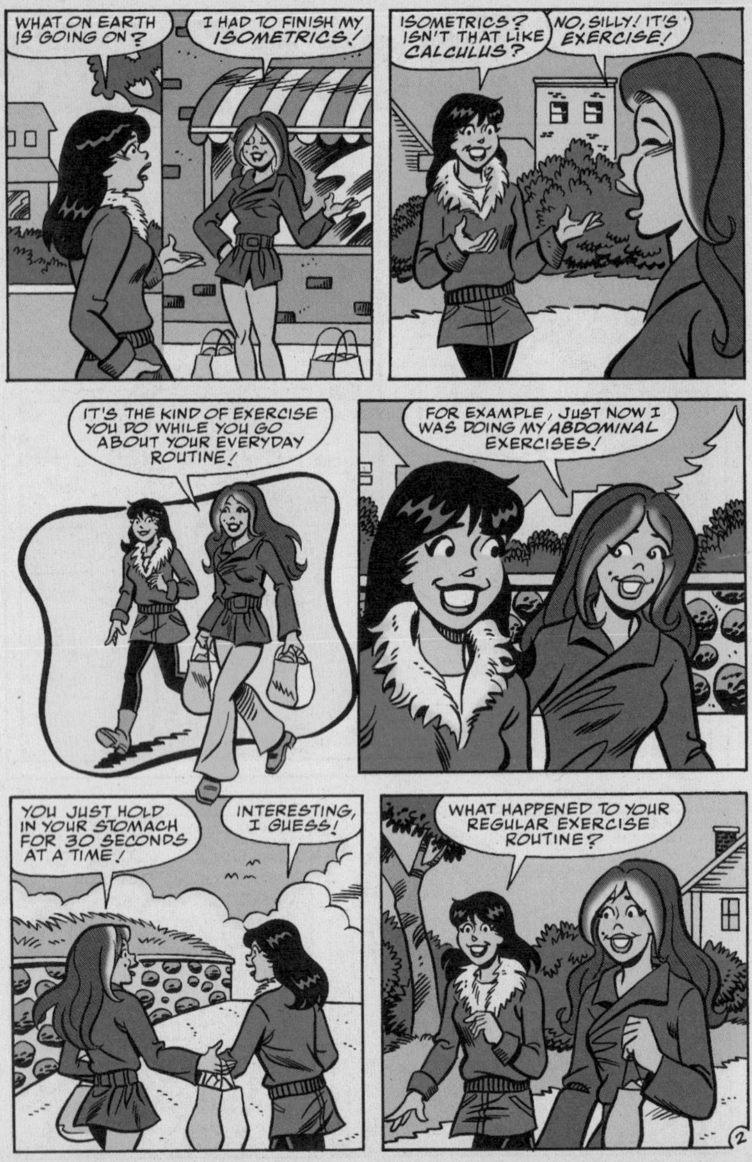
WHAT ON EARTH IS GOING ON?
I HAD TO FINISH MY ISOMETRICS!
ISOMETRICS? ISN'T THAT LIKE CALCULUS?
NO, SILLY! IT'S EXERCISE!
IT'S THE KIND OF EXERCISE YOU DO WHILE YOU GO ABOUT YOUR EVERYDAY ROUTINE!
FOR EXAMPLE, JUST NOW I WAS DOING MY ABDOMINAL EXERCISES!
YOU JUST HOLD IN YOUR STOMACH FOR 30 SECONDS AT A TIME!
INTERESTING, I GUESS!
WHAT HAPPENED TO YOUR REGULAR EXERCISE ROUTINE?
2

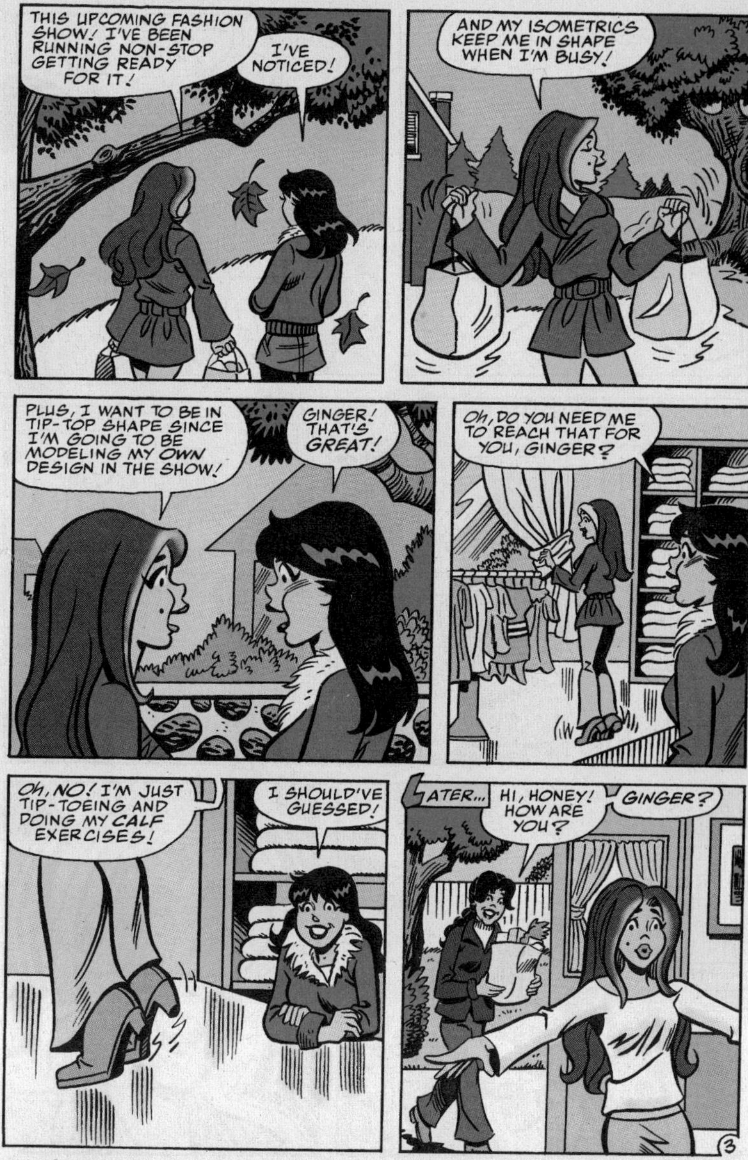
THIS UPCOMING FASHION SHOW! I'VE BEEN RUNNING NON-STOP GETTING READY FOR IT!
I'VE NOTICED!
AND MY ISOMETRICS KEEP ME IN SHAPE WHEN I'M BUSY!
PLUS, I WANT TO BE IN TIP-TOP SHAPE SINCE I'M GOING TO BE MODELING MY OWN DESIGN IN THE SHOW!
GINGER! THAT'S GREAT!
Oh, DO YOU NEED ME TO REACH THAT FOR YOU, GINGER?
Oh, NO! I'M JUST TIP-TOEING AND DOING MY CALF EXERCISES!
I SHOULD'VE GUESSED!
LATER...
HI, HONEY! HOW ARE YOU?
GINGER?
3

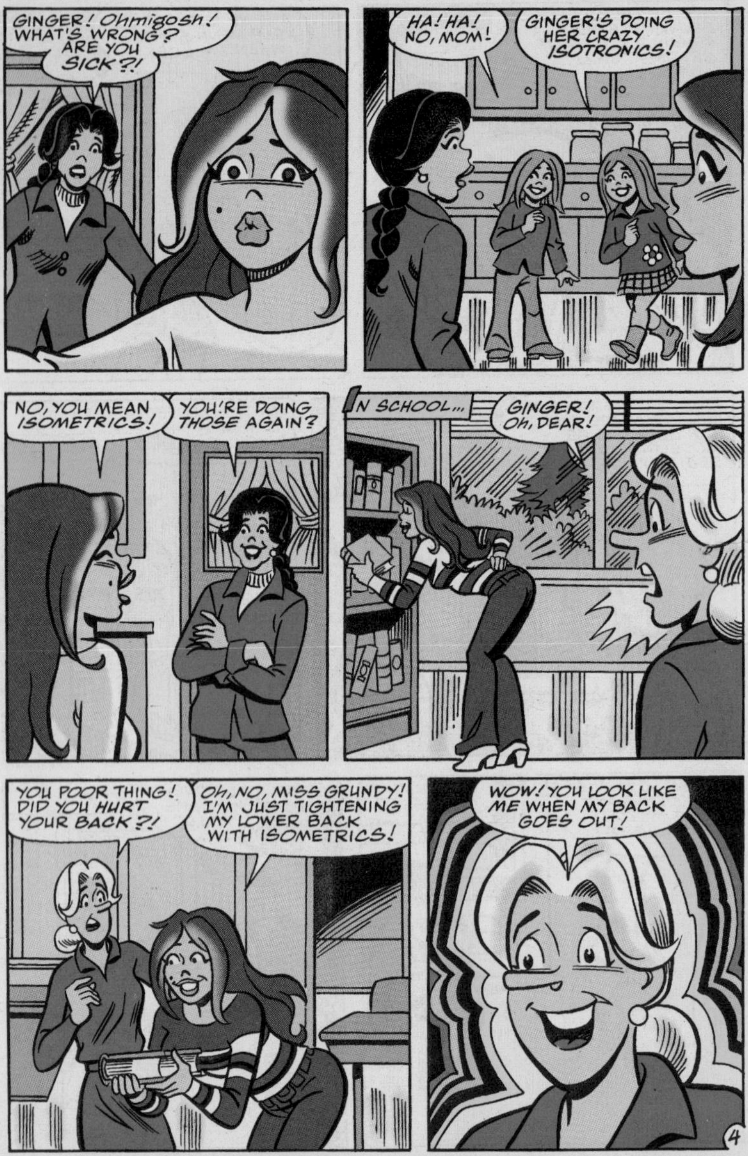

GINGER! Ohmigosh! WHAT'S WRONG? ARE YOU SICK?!
HA! HA! NO, MOM!
GINGER'S DOING HER CRAZY ISOTRONICS!
NO, YOU MEAN ISOMETRICS!
YOU'RE DOING THOSE AGAIN?
IN SCHOOL...
GINGER! Oh, DEAR!
YOU POOR THING! DID YOU HURT YOUR BACK?!
Oh, NO, MISS GRUNDY! I'M JUST TIGHTENING MY LOWER BACK WITH ISOMETRICS!
WOW! YOU LOOK LIKE ME WHEN MY BACK GOES OUT!

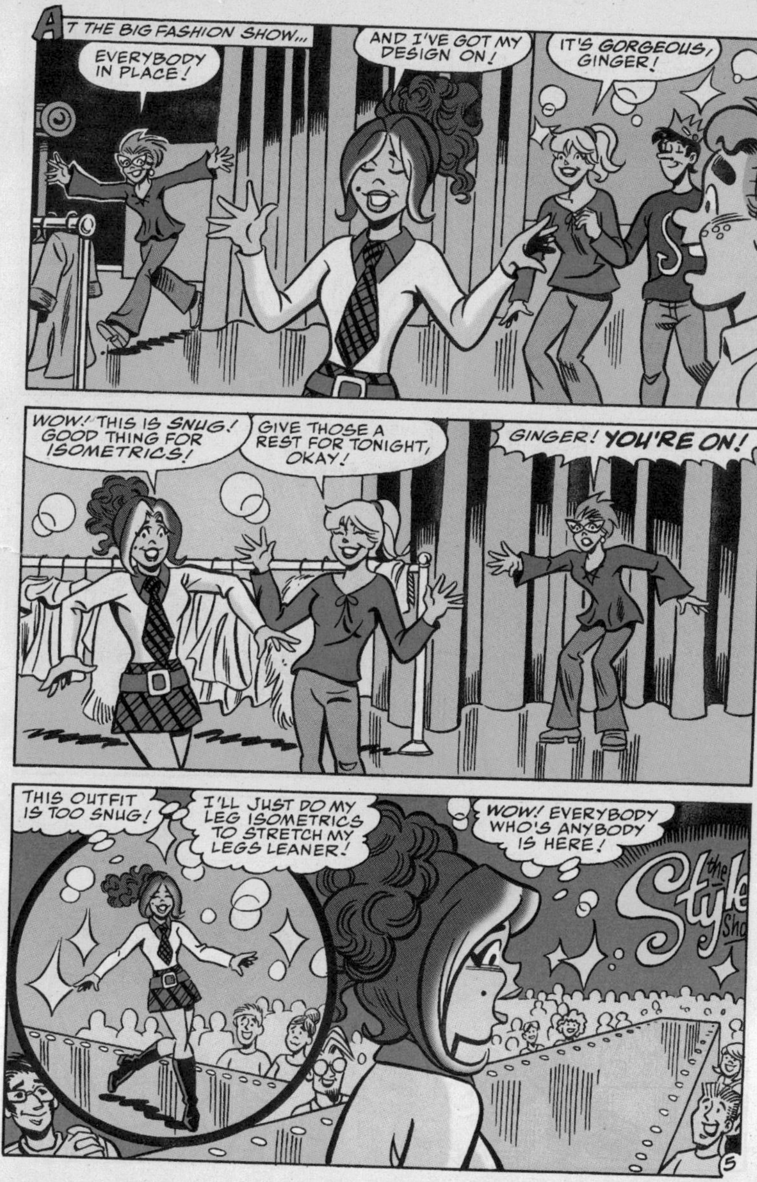
AT THE BIG FASHION SHOW...
EVERYBODY IN PLACE!
AND I'VE GOT MY DESIGN ON!
IT'S GORGEOUS, GINGER!
WOW! THIS IS SNUG! GOOD THING FOR ISOMETRICS!
GIVE THOSE A REST FOR TONIGHT, OKAY!
GINGER! YOU'RE ON!
THIS OUTFIT IS TOO SNUG!
I'LL JUST DO MY LEG ISOMETRICS TO STRETCH MY LEGS LEANER!
WOW! EVERYBODY WHO'S ANYBODY IS HERE!

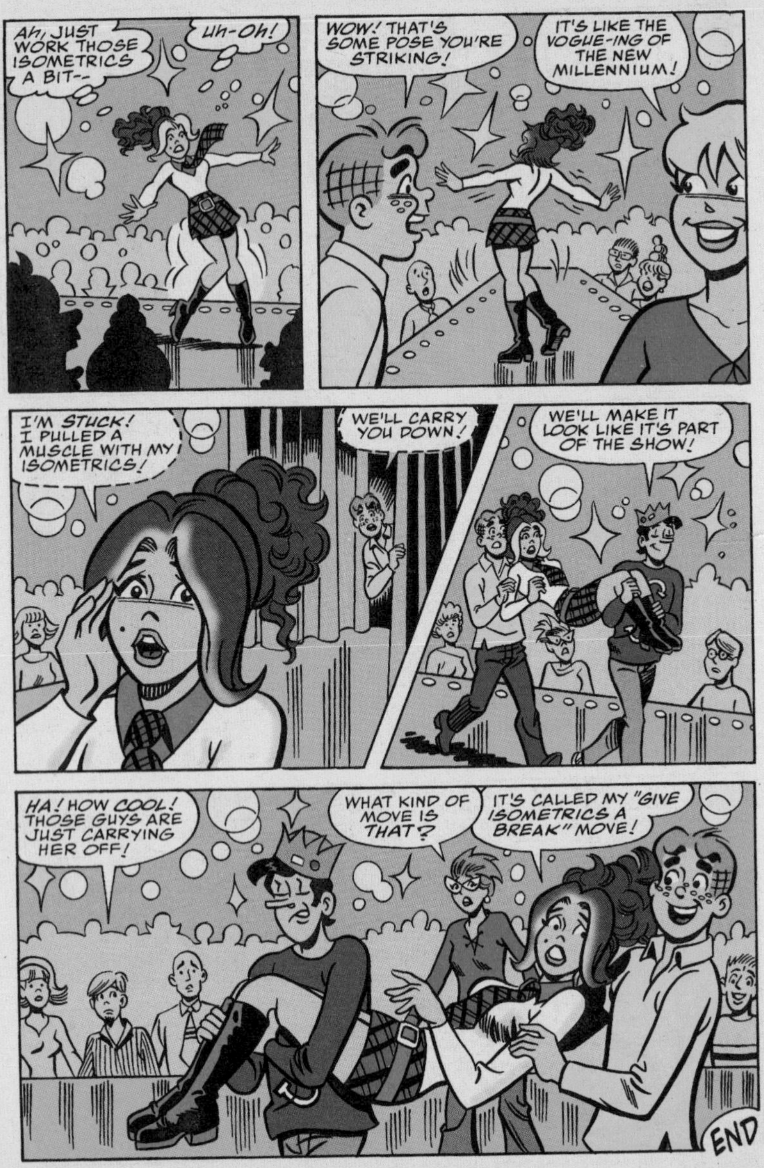
AH, JUST WORK THOSE ISOMETRICS A BIT--
UH-OH!
WOW! THAT'S SOME POSE YOU'RE STRIKING!
IT'S LIKE THE VOGUE-ING OF THE NEW MILLENNIUM!
I'M STUCK! I PULLED A MUSCLE WITH MY ISOMETRICS!
WE'LL CARRY YOU DOWN!
WE'LL MAKE IT LOOK LIKE IT'S PART OF THE SHOW!
HA! HOW COOL! THOSE GUYS ARE JUST CARRYING HER OFF!
WHAT KIND OF MOVE IS THAT?
IT'S CALLED MY "GIVE ISOMETRICS A BREAK" MOVE!
END

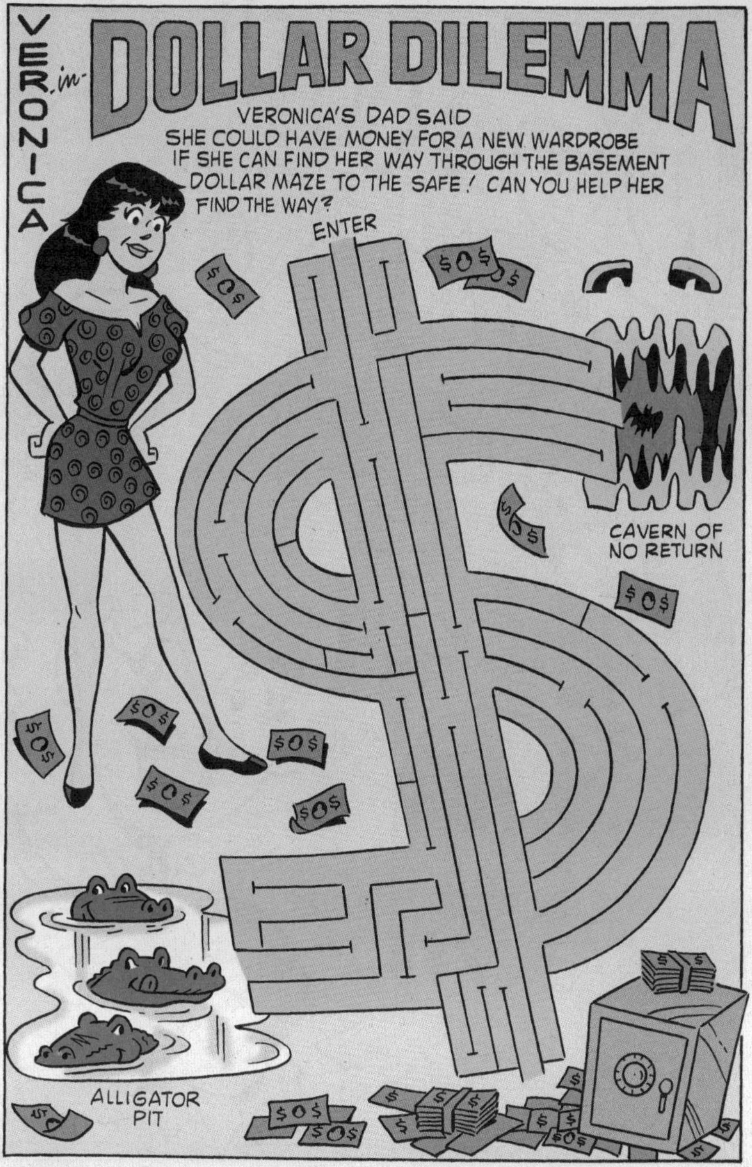
VERONICA -in- DOLLAR DILEMMA
VERONICA'S DAD SAID SHE COULD HAVE MONEY FOR A NEW WARDROBE IF SHE CAN FIND HER WAY THROUGH THE BASEMENT DOLLAR MAZE TO THE SAFE! CAN YOU HELP HER FIND THE WAY?
ENTER
CAVERN OF NO RETURN
ALLIGATOR PIT

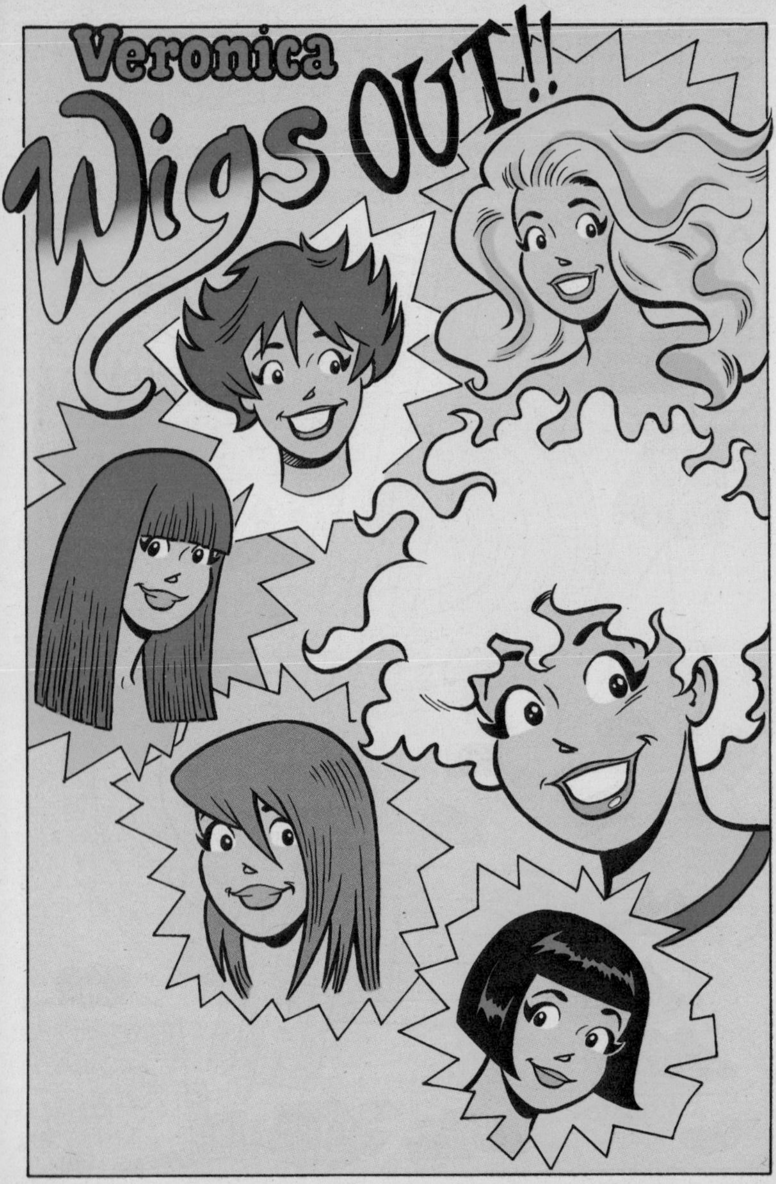
Veronica
Wigs OUT!!